Oliver Carey grew up in East Sussex, England. Reading and writing was a way for him to remember and embrace what was happening around him. He would walk with a dictaphone to describe something like a fragrance with eyes shut to learn how to feel his surroundings. *This Is It* is his first book to date, after writing many short pieces of work. A novel which has taken him on journeys over time to develop.

For the Carey and Delassise Family

Oliver Carey

THIS IS IT

AUSTIN MACAULEY PUBLISHERS™

LONDON ∗ CAMBRIDGE ∗ NEW YORK ∗ SHARJAH

A CIP catalogue record for this title is available from the British Library.

ISBN 9781398416987 (Paperback)
ISBN 9781398416994 (ePub e-book)

www.austinmacauley.com

First Published 2022
Austin Macauley Publishers Ltd®
1 Canada Square
Canary Wharf
London
E14 5AA

I am extremely grateful for my parents, Robert and Nicole, for always encouraging me to be who I wanted to be and not what people wanted me to be. My sister Céline, my brother Scott, for being well adjusted heads when I was losing my own. I cannot express my thanks to my family who tirelessly read early drafts, shared advice on the cover and supported me.

Is This It!

The Moment is Now. What was Eddy's now? Was it when Eddy's pen fell? Was it when he finished writing? Was it when he stopped thinking? Stopped liking? Loving?

The involuntarily taken, smoothly flowing, black ink-nib pen rolls off his exercise book. The slight bump of the black clip thuds like a jackhammer as it trips the short circular roll to the creased brink of the end. Across the thick, red paper-covered landscape hiding the paper, torn in places. Worn on the bind. Notes are scribbled in different colours. Passages scrawled like some poorly done, doodled graffiti. Some crossed out on the coffee-ringed cover with a forceful scratch that nearly drives through the jacket, showing glimpses of the blue-lined paper. Where he devises his thoughts. His simple, but unrealistic pipedreams.

The pen reaches the end with one last echoing thud. It falls. In slow motion. Days, rather than seconds, pass slower than weeks of yearning. The pen descends the short drop to the ominously varnished wooden-planked floor below. It takes just two tinny short bounces before the pen lays to rest. Then, the World. The scene. Eddy's scene. Eddy's entire world. It stops. At that precise moment. At the precise moment that the pen stops. Eddy stops. Was this, now, the moment?

Peculiarly enough, in his mind's eye, Eddy still plays the animated scene laid out before him. The many people scurrying like mice on a mission for cheese. Hurrying in all and every direction. Finding the scent, but not following it. It is no longer peak hour, but the station is seldom quiet. For this station, in the very centre of Sydney, is the heartbeat. The people the blood, the essential matter in all life. The trains are the venules that collect the blood from the capillaries, the platforms. The tracks are the veins that carry the blood into the city, giving it the life to beat, pulse, be alive.

With a choreographed dance-like precision, the crowds of individuals move around the platform dancefloor. To avoid every stranger, they stop, dodge and negotiate each other with preamps of clarity. With each and every step, they improvise an unrehearsed dance of irregular proportions. It is a great mystery how people do not bump into each other when they stop, turn and pivot on a five-cent piece. Thus, it does become a prime area for people-watching. Almost hypnotic. This dance. This monotonous, tedious and pedestrian exercise that a majority of these people do Monday to Friday, that does not seem to get tired. It has been an unwritten tradition for many years. At the same time, they are here. The safe money bet is waged that come this afternoon or late in the evening, they will be the same people, dressed in similar attire, at the same place, going towards the same direction.

These people are halted with the pen at precisely seven minutes past ten in the morning. The dark wood of the train platform is smudged in rainwater, carried from outside. This gives a brooding, slightly sinister darker hues that bleed into the clear pattern. Spreading its darkness. The droplets of rain are precariously close to disconnecting their tenuous connection to their host. Like frozen icicles their hanging on for a few more moments by the slightest thread of a silver-string rain drop from the hat, umbrella, nose, earlobe. Glittering as lingering in suspended time. Collecting rainbows and lights from the huge screens transmitting the train times.

The flashing lights are still transmitting the estimated times of arrival, but they do not move with the time as if a nervous twitch in the electronic muscles. This exact time is not a fire in which they burn, but a block of ice in which they stay frozen. The footsteps that echoed in an unmusical arrangement that were competing with the lazy voice of a single lady bellowing out of the talon are extinguished.

It is an eerie moment when so many people and unseen noises are silenced simultaneously. The motion is paused. Not even the slightest breeze is felt. As if watching a painting through a glass globe to this precise moment, the world has stopped turning. Gravity seems to have stopped as a coin is suspended in the air as it leaves the pocket of an older man retrieving his mobile. No noise. No sound. No beeps. Nothing but the flash of the red and golden light. Although, life still beats.

Eddy's thoughts pause with the light above his head shining only for him. An epiphany. An idea. A notion. He knows what he needs, nay must do. His deep, brown eyes look straight ahead, to where he is going to be. His focus is unfocused on his surroundings. His focus is focused on the eventual verdict, his end, climaxing final result.

Two months ago, he did not know what he knows now. Heck, six months ago, it seemed perfect. He did not see the future as he felt safe. He felt that everything was going well, so why look too far ahead and miss the moment you are in.

Today is the day that I officially come in. I will not introduce myself. Most books would take you to the beginning. I will tell you what happened, but over the course of telling you the beginning. The beginning of the end of a relationship that was built on fragile bricks, on a fragile foundation. That left a fragile heart. Shattered. Destroyed. Unfixable. I have been pivotal in Eddy's life. I have watched him live his life through various emotions. These have proved a gulf of knowledge for me. I have learnt so very much. The time is for Eddy to learn from me.

Six Months Ago...

Like a thread of cotton caught on the exposed rusty nails of the house of cards, their love story was beginning to unravel. The house of cards contained so much promise. So much joy. Alas, the house was collapsing slowly as the thin thread pulled the nails further and further out. Regrettably, eventually, it will be coming down around Eddy.

In the moonlit darkness, a soft beep comes from Eddy's mobile, followed by an immediate illumination. With the skill of a magician, it enters his hand with a slight, unseen flick of wrist. It is not a message he so badly craved. He discards his mobile on the small glass coffee table in disgust. It skips and bounces away as he goes back inside his own head.

The messages were becoming less frequent. Eddy was placing calls that were increasingly becoming missed. Worse still, not returned. The deafening silence vibrates within Eddy's as warring silences. Unbearable. Like the slow drips of a leaking tap that seems to echo louder and louder. When the drip turns to daggers, stabbing his head, causing unseen pain. It is in these moments of aggravating pain when his mind wonders. Racing around like a rat in a caged maze. Going out of control, in different directions. Arriving at different dead-ends every time. Each route a question, each question provides no answers. Just the ability to turn around to travel another route to ask yet another unanswerable question.

Ultimately, Eddy concludes that it is he who needs to change. He who has done wrong. He who has done something. He can't think where? Or what? Or when? But he is convinced that he has done it. He wrote the wrong, it is up to him to save his love story. He must write the right.

Eddy starts by repeating each and every conversation in his head that he had had with Beth-Annie. He re-reads messages left on his mobile. Notes, letters. He lives through the time together, living through his body language. Her body language at response to her questions that he gives. He is bordering frantic uncontrollable energy which will overflow as he sees nothing.

He slides doors to a different scenario. Reliving in the mind-maze as he stares at a projection film of each moment. A moment that has been. Has been gone to the archives of the past to never be coming back. No matter how hard Eddy wishes for a repeat of a precise moment, to change the outcome, it is impossible. The past is just that, completed. It has elapsed on time. No-one on this Earth can process the key to turn back time to one specific moment. Just for the future to be rewritten. The past is wistfully vanishing in the breeze of time to become just a vanished moment in yesterday.

He lets himself smile. A half smile that flashes across his face as quick as lightning, for people would blink faster. As a different action, word, sentence is imaginatively created from the past to flawlessly perfect the dreamtime picture. His mind races. his stomach is in knots trying to wring out the thirst, his hunger, his negatives. He lives another make-believe whim. He asks another question. His mind is exploding with telling a glorified story of 'what ifs', 'buts', 'maybes' to generate an edited magnificent fictional exploratory story of this love.

His face solemnly shows a glimpse of what he is hiding. What he is going through inside. His inner torment is shared with o-one. He deals with it each, and every passing second of every day.

This morning he went through his normal, morning routine in a walking daydream. He left his home, went to work without a single interaction. He did not check his phone at all rather than check that the yearning for message had come. In himself the lights were on, but no-one was behind the wheel. His vacant stare, hidden behind his inner torment that burns furiously as the devil stoked flames of hell.

Eddy's hands are masked in a beautiful velvety shine of deep red. The Ferrari shine flows over his knuckles, through his fingers like a caressing viscous untamed river. As fast as his years of experience would allow, he is skilfully flaunting the joints laid in silver metal shallow dishes. He chops, slices, cuts and rearranges the joint for different uses, different prices, different uses. His hands and brain work in a rehearsed play for which no thinking is required.

Eddy has been a butcher for most of his adult life. He knows meat, poultry and game as a surgeon would know the mechanics of a human body. For the soft drone of music in the background, the splatter, the razor-sharp precision cuts of the tears of fibres and muscle would only be heard above Eddy's own soft unnoticeable shallow, rheumatic breathing. He has a white apron, for which he uses for preparation before the doors of the shop open.

Considering the amount of meat that he has prepared thus far, his work station is still kept considerably clean. The signing, delivery of stock and the general lifting, pulling, pushing and tugging this white apron shows the smallest blemish of fresh claret. The ragged, threadbare white apron itself is not holding well to the tests of time. Yellow-stain spots from previous explorations in the adventures of meat are forever remained after more washes than Eddy has had hot dishes. This was one of his service aprons before.

He wipes his hands on a linen cloth that hangs over the apron strings as he walks into the cool room. The door easily slides on the runners as he puts little effort into opening. A soft bounce at the end announcing the end of the line as he pushes through the plastic ribbons of curtain and into the cold air inside. Everything is labelled with dates, products. Everything has a home.

This is for the raw meats, so poultry is spread out on one of the longer sides, the meat on the other and the smaller end of the backwall is reserved for game, special orders and promotion. He knows exactly what he is after as he stoops over-so slightly to pick up a metal tray containing a joint of glistening topside of beef. He returns to the red chopping board, places the meatal tray to the left as he is right-handed. From behind him, he collects a nest of white melamine containers of various shapes and spreads them out in front of him, behind his board.

He reaches to his right and picks up his favourite rosewood-handled Victorinox knife. He was given this in the early stages of his apprenticeship by a chef that taught him so much. Not just about the chef's life, but navy life. He was a navy chef born and trained but managed to leave to create a following as a respected chef in Sydney that owners and managers alike wanted him in their kitchen. Service staff would let him know if positions were available. He was loved in the kitchen, outside on the floor and for his life. A wicked sense of humour that bordered on the dark side of whether he should be able to get away with it, but after all it was a joke. Not seriously meant, but he was respectful enough to know his audience, thus not upsetting anyone.

It was he who told Eddy to focus on an area. Of course, he meant within the kitchen brigade, but Eddy was drawn to meat. Maybe he had underlining currents to a psychopathic tendency. This was by far the heathier option.

The blade of the boning knife had curved due to the amount of times it has run down a steel to sharpen. The wooden handle knows his hands as well as he knows it. The knife is an extension of his arm. If he ever lost this knife it would feel like a lost limb. The knife moves around the bloody palm, twirling like a cheerleader with his baton in celebration of the artwork he is creating before him. His fingers gently feel for bones as each cut is with the precision of a pit-crew of mechanics working on a Formula One Ferrari with pace, speed and perfection.

He has been at this shop down a lane off the main streets of Sydney for over six years. He knows his job well that it has become second nature to him. Many people in hospitality in particular, move often. However, he has frequent holidays, enjoys the customers, the staff and the owners so why would he change. Only for the money. It is not the best, but as he puts it—

you cannot beat enjoying work for enough money to live than to hate work to reluctantly enter the doors five days of the week to doom, gloom and pessimism.

To the right are silver bowls for different usages. As he cuts, weighs and positions the meat into the melamine trays for service, he uses the silver bowls to obtain the whole use out of the joint. The fat and sinew go into one of the silver bowls with a splish, splash and splat, to be rendered for cooking fat. Scraps that are too small go for minced products such a sausage rolls or burgers with larger offcuts diced for pies. Nothing goes to waste. All the bones and other wastage items go to a separate bowl to be sold to catering companies to use in their stocks. When he has enough wastage in the bowls, he decides what to make.

From experience, he knows the best sells. This is not to mean that he gets caught out every now and then. Being cloudy outside, not the greatest day in Sydney, he is opting for pies. Although it is coming into summer, so burgers and barbeques are on the agenda. Yet again, it is only Tuesday. He finally opts for the pies. He is still undecided on the flavours to incorporate. This, coincidentally, is the first time he has consciously used his brain since waking up today.

He glances at the old-looking dark-brown stained wooden clock that sits above the entrance as he places the last piece of meat in the desired tray. He carefully lifts his red chopping board, so the blood does not spill everywhere, to place into the sink behind him. With the slightest sidestep to his right he spins around fluently. With his right elbow he turns the dog lever of the silver tap with its shining blue crown to allow the water to pour into the small square-bottomed metal basin. Blood and soap squelches from his white calluses ridden hands on to the basin sides and the metal splashboard. When rinsed thoroughly, he turns the tap off.

He returns to his station. Glad-wraps each of the display containers as tight as a drum and places them in the cabinet ready for service. Just in front on the small ledge is the spikes of the meat and the price for which he places in order. This will be the first job of the next staff member, so he can see the cut and price before placing it in view of the customer. He wraps the silver bowls with a label ensuring date and product before sending them back home in the correct place in the cool room. He washes his station down for any blood. Sanitises it. Washes his board, knife and scales as he leaves them to airdry as he returns to his station and using a dry paper towel finishes the cleaning, so it is as he entered in the morning. Ready for use. He glances at the clock again. It is almost time. In half an hour, the shop will be open. In fifteen minutes, normally punctually on time without a second to spare, the next worker will enter.

He returns to the handwash sink. Using the red crown, he adjusts the water to a hypnotic whoosh of steaming hot water. Every day he always makes sure that he has time to meticulously wash his hands properly. Using his own hand-wash-kit he picks under his fingernails, in the carves and brushes his nails. Using his cleansed palm of his right hand he hovers under the soap dispenser that proceeds to place a perfectly measured amount of soap into the palm of his hand. He scrubs up to his elbows in a frenzy of soap suds, steamy hot water bellowing up. Scrubbing hard like a surgeon after a triple bypass operation he checks numerous times his hands and arms before for one last time returning to the hand soap dispenser. The pink liquid with a hint of lemon beckons as he lathers himself once again.

He wonders why the hand soap is only nighty-nine-point-nine percent focused on killing bacteria. Why not the full one hundred percent? Is it a legal obligation so as not to get sued on the off-chance someone would blame the soap for not cleaning their hands properly. That nought-point-one percent could be the defining moment in being sued or not. Or, is it that the point-one percent can go off on a mission to warn its mates of the impending danger that they are nearly extinct?

Bizarre thoughts often enter Eddy's mind. This is not an exception. He finishes washing his hands and turns off the faucet. He pulls a sheet of paper towel to wipe the splashboard, the taps and the sinks with its stubborn lingering remains of a few bubbles of soapsuds and meat to make the area as dry as it was on arrival. He discards that sheet and the folded remains to the bin as he reaches for another sheet to dry his hands and arms thoroughly.

A few short steps to his right, he discards the soggy paper into the bin with one hand as he reaches to his shelf with the other. His wallet and keys are to the right. His mobile is propped up in a manner that enables him to see the banners that spring through the screen with a soft beep, softer light. As he cannot always get to his mobile in times of service, he finds this is a way for him not to miss that important call. To the left are the folded, freshly washed and ironed service aprons. He discards his preparation one to the shelf below the pristine ones, jams it into a red and white stripped canvas bag to take away later at the end of his shift for washing.

During the passage of time in as a butcher, he has resorted to a three-striped blue tricolour apron for the customers' benefit. Also, so he does not keep getting mixed up with what he uses for preparation and service. No matter how long, hard or frequent he washes his preparation aprons, the stain of blood remains. Whether in colour, or the rich metallic iron smell of blood and raw meat. It is as if the meat wants to live on in clinging onto the last piece of fabric that he or she contacted with. Eddy goes into the cool room and brings out a joint of glistening topside of beef. He places this on the plastic red chopping board.

He places the new apron over his hand and ties the strings as he returns to the display counter to carefully remove the Gladwrap. Using a yellow-handled brush with plastic blue bristles, he delicately brushes each of the display meats with a swift, gentle stroke of vegetable oil to give the meat a fresh, inviting and appealing look.

He enjoys this time of the day. He is the only one at this early hour at Jones Family Butchers. Eddy likes it that way. He gets lost in his thoughts. As peculiar as they can be. He sometimes is accompanied by the low murmur of the radio. Other times the shop becomes his own disco emporium. Most days, the slight buzz of the various fridges and freezers. The hum of the lights. The clicks of the irregular defrosting cycles or the fans cooling cycles are the only sounds he hears. A rush of unwater water from the ice around the fans in the cool room and freezer are in time with a surge of power that turns the fans on and a knock at the door.

He hides his disappointment behind a grin as he reaches for his keys. Eddy's best time of the day has ended. He enjoys the lull. The time where he is busy enough to be alert in his surroundings. He has not had to engage with anyone with meaningless talk. As he walks around the counter, he puts his pretending happy face that everything is okay for himself, the customers and staff.

As if he has bene waiting around the corner for the correct time, at exactly six-forty-five, he knocks on the door in tune with the second-hand crossing over the middle twelve above him. The door is slightly ajar when Kai, pronounced Car, comes bouncing through. An interpolated jumble of questions and answers follows as he works through, not really listening. Just the mundane course of the everyday verbal dialogue that opens the communication. The 'G'days', 'How are yous?', 'What's happening?' and 'How has your morning been?', that are clipped short with even shorter answers, 'fine', 'good', 'no worries'.

The great thing about the morning spiel is that it does not really matter. They have a great code that they sit down, sometimes over a coffee, other times a beer to go through the plan of action for the next day. They clear down the operation, put things away and just before doing the mopping of the floors they stop. They have a single list in front of them split into tables, each with a heading. Another one for the ordering. The messages get checked on the phone and email. The invoices are written straight away. Eddy brings them over in tune with Kai bringing the coffee.

Some places have standing orders on specific days which make it easier, so these are done at this time for the next day. If the companies ring before five, before they shut, they get their orders on the first run, early before eight in the morning. Depending on the order Eddy sometimes stays late to prepare and pack them, other times he does it in the morning. These are written in the first column, under the simple headline, EARLY. As he goes through the invoice, he separately writes the orders.

He has a great understanding with the farmers that they order before six, they get their stock before six. As each invoice, with a duplicate, is placed in the manila folder, they are placed in order of route. Later when Kai goes, he will type out the route, cost, and signature column so this can get signed as well as the invoice. Each customer is a number; hence each prepared carton is marked clearly with that number. If there is more than one box, after the company is a number in brackets that signifies the number of cartons. Fool proof, well, most of the time.

Fortunately, Eddy can get a lot of these done during the day. He checks the messages on a lull and prepares what he can. Places them in the cool room ready to be packed, or sometimes he can pack them straight away. Kai is here for the second run. This is before twelve, midday. These are the ones placed after the cut off time. It tends to be shorter but still a hassle.

Eddy follows Kai as he scoops up the Manilla folder and the keys to go outside. Eddy stands on the concrete step to tell him it is packed in the order with the first at the front and so forth. Kai gives a peace sign through the white van window as he leaves a trail of dust in his wake from the carpark that is in dire need of resurfacing.

The second column is for Kai. Another is for third. This is a royal pain. It is basically that phone call after eight in the morning where a business has forgotten to order something, or that the functions and events team have dropped a bombshell of a surprise function. Although Kai will get back just after the shop opens, sometimes he has to go out again and complete these orders. The mornings are seldom busy with the exception of long weekends and holidays.

Eddy is alone again. The tornado that is Kai has swept through leaving a messy trail of wet boots through the shop. He sighs as he clears it up and prepares the shop fully for the day. It is a quiet day of orders. Although there is no quiet day normally, just a more manageable day.

Eddy has worked at Jones Family Butcher for a few years. The name is a bit of inside running joke. The signage is only thirty-three-point three percent true. The name. The owner, for whom they see more of a solar eclipse than they do of Sam Jonas. He is a great boss in the way he stays out of the way. He gets the figures daily, at the end of each shift. He comes in when everyone has gone to collect the cash from the mincer, bank it and leave a post-it with any questions or simply a smiley face. He is a man of few words. Nice enough.

Eddy or Kai send a text at the end of the day with takings, summary of service and issues. They get a reply of an emoji with some thumbs up or a thumb down. He anglicised his name to sound friendlier for the sign. He is one-hundred percent blue-collar Australian, but his parents were immigrants from Slovakia. His siblings do not work here. His name is not spelt or even pronounced correctly. The only part of the signage that is true is the trade—butchery.

He has a late order. Not a huge one so he moves to the walk-in fridge, nearly tripping on the flat red non-slip floor as his grey-scuffed white gumboots are slightly too big for him and make an annoying squeaky noise as they grip the floor. He slides the cold metal grey handle to the right. Piercing through the plastic flaps for which the thin mist of cold air escapes. The slight change in temperature shakes down the slight icicles of frozen water that have attached themselves onto Eddy's clean white butcher's jacket.

His look is more of a laboratory scientist than a butcher. An icicle hits his face, but he moves through without noticing. He bends down to pick up the heavy brown carton of short loin beef that he needs to break down into T-bones, porterhouse steaks and club steaks. This is for a local hotel that has a reputation for ordering late, then complaining that it is after lunchtime service. It is a fun game of calls, messages and emails that normally fall to the same deaf-heard response, for it seems to be a weekly treat.

The shop has specific health codes. One is the barcode from the meats. Eddy thinks that this breaks about five different contradictions of the act but follows them anyway. The barcode on each carton displays all the information for the Environmental Health Officers. The numbers tell the story of the breed of meat, farm, abattoir, date of slaughter, date of package and means of transport. He keeps each and every one in order of supplier and date for six months. Each day a new small castaway is placed in these for the end of the day labels and placed in an envelope to sit in the filing cabinet to go mouldy and smell of rotten flesh.

Eddy is once again working on auto-pilot. The shop goes through trends, needs and customer requirements but these do not faze him anymore. He predicts the changes. He has seen the cycles. He is Michel de Nostredame, Nostradamus of the Butchers' World. He is not an astrologer, a seer nor a prophet; he believes that history, as well as trends, just repeat themselves. Eddy rarely looks at what he is doing. When he does, he is not focusing on his own hands, the knife wielding in the air or the joint in front of him. He looks up as his hands continue their work.

He glances over the glass counter shelf of the top of the refrigerated display unit. Through the water-dripping windows of the Sydney rain that has decided to drizzle down. It drops in a frenzy over the Royal Blue signage of Jones Family Butcher and onto the very quiet street. The people he sees are head deep in their own collars or cowered under an umbrella. They are on their mission to get out of the rain, which he presumes will be work. It is still a little early for the streets to be busy, but being that a very popular coffee shop is next down he normally sees the lingering, loitering suits as they wait for their java.

Occasionally, a truck passes, cascading bright amber hues of lights fleetingly through the window. A van flashes past. The blinking red, amber and green lights play music for the falling rain in a dance party solely for them. They accompany with music that hits the metal corrugated roof of the bus shelter with the delicate touch of a meat tenderiser. The splash in the forming puddles are seen but not heard over this din. A faster, machine-gun burst of rain ratters the shop front windows, ousting the streams that were minding their own business. He sees but does not react. Again, his thoughts go into a wondering format.

Normally, his weekends would be spent with his partner. He would have been enjoying their time together, learning a little more about each other. Thus, falling for her a little bit more. He is wondering why it did not happen again last weekend. They did see each other through the week but those pockets of appearances were not enough for him or, well, previously, her. He predicts, Nostradamus-style, that it will happen again. Or not happen as the case will be.

He was ready for last weekend. But a cold, short, dismissive text message late last Thursday night deflated his heart as if a harpoon had penetrated it. The text simply said, 'it would not be ideal'. No pleasantries before or after. No kiss marks. No questions about his day. No stories about her day. He was very disappointed. Not just about the nature of the message. But the cold, abandoned action of it. That was the last message he received.

He carried on sending messages. He had given up on the calls as she did not pick up, never returned them. He religiously sent his morning text message when he went to make his morning cup of coffee at four in the morning, before his shower. Eddy continued to do this as if not preforming this task would accentuate his fear. It would be the nail to forever close the coffin of the relationship that was doomed to end. Endorse his thoughts, his feeling that it was over. Eddy wanted Beth-Annie to know that she was his first thought of the day. Eddy wanted Beth-Annie to know that she was close, no matter the reason. She was so close, but too far to touch. Emotionally, physically and, it would seem, electronically.

The funny thing. But not in a ha ha, roll around on the floor until his sides split funny. The thing was that one text message from her would give him respite from the emotions. The grief he was feeling. It had only been the Wednesday since they last spoke, saw each other but the very style of the abrupt message seemed out of the ordinary. He knew something was not quite up. Love is indeed a drug. Beth-Annie was his fix. He needed the high again. The brief reconnection wears off like the aftershave at the start of the day to barely leave a trace. The high, like the smell is instant. The low is the gradual search for reactions. The rain continues to fall. He did not know when he stopped working. The rain is the curtain where Eddy wants to isolate himself, further. He needs the addiction.

Beep beep.

From his mobile came the light, staccato, high-pitched ding of a message. The screen emits a soft light from his silver mobile. For where he was positioned, he could see perfectly his propped-up mobile. The noise brings his focus promptly back into the present. He snaps his neck around to see the location of the mobile. His heart is hopeful. He glances away from the splattering blood to the clean, area of an oasis. The name is there, followed by the first two lines of the message. His heart is heavy with glum pessimistic negatives from his optimistic positives. The message is not the desired person, or one. His phone reads, 'Paul O'Reilly: Running late, Bro…waiting for bus.'

For some reason that he did not understand, he was angry at Paul. That it was not Beth-Annie. He was back to work but had to move away from the meat as his smooth slices were becoming angered stabs, daggered motions like an American psycho.

Paul was not his bro. He was the more than capable apprentice. He was always late. Whatever the reason he coined it, more than twice. He was as inept in his time management as he was competent of being the best apprentice that had passed through any butcher's doors. He was not young. Eddy was starting to regain his calm. Paul was skilled with a hidden talent that was instinctive from a passion to do this job.

Eddy returned to his station after a short recess to pound a few irrational snake in the grass outraged sentences in his head filled with venom. The truth was he liked Paul. But in that instant, he had nothing but acrimony. That ebbed away as quickly as the fury flow of anger. Paul was English-born with an Irish mother. She had firmly embedded the Emerald Eire into his making. He was trustworthy. He was hard-working. He was unique in his appearance in the beauty in the eye of the beholder kinda way. He put on the Irish accent to meet women for nightly escapades. It worked so well.

Eddy had no fear that this was the true reason he was late. Eddy actually did mind being called 'bro' by someone that was not his bro, or even a relative. Someone with no relationship to him apart from four days of the week at work. This was not a battle deemed fighting. He brushed it off like the rain of the shoulder of a jacket. In turn he called him bro to soften the remark. It was his own private joke for himself as he was taking the piss out of him. He wished he could brush Beth-Annie off.

With the light quickly fading from his mobile, his heart continued to fade down to the depth of his torment. With his heart falling, his shoulder slumped over the joint of beef. His eyes glazed over at the job quite literally in his hands. The thing that caused that spark of rage was uncomplicated. If that message had been from Beth-Annie, he would have been given that addiction, that fix, the glimmer of energy as a sparkplug on the engine of his Ferrari blood-stained hands. He would have known that she was thinking of him. He would have felt self-worth.

I look on. I have the power. I hold an unseen smile to the future that is unfolding.

Eddy goes effortlessly through the motions of his day. With the opening of the back door, a soft, but heavy drone echoes to inform the front of the shop that someone has entered the rear. Kai has turned up earlier than normal after his deliveries, he must have had a good run. With parking in the city, any city, it is hard. The park rangers are quick as fire to give you a compliment with a parking fine in seconds.

Kai yells out through the open door, 'Morning Rob,' He is shouting something about the deliveries which is normally about one of the guys, as Eddy hears the softness of plastic boxes being stored with a soft thud on the tiled floor, hopefully correctly. He knows Eddy cannot hear him properly, but he continues shouting anyway. Then, a sudden stop in his monologue as Eddy hears a skid, followed by his roaring laugh which always seems too loud for his slender skinny figure as he nearly slips over the threshold, on the tiles, as he brings nature's worst elements inside.

Kai seems to just have that happy-go-lucky attitude to everything that makes him so loveable in and out of the workplace. It is a contagious trait that is infectiously pleasing. Eddy has heard many times that people are an asset to work with, but he strongly believes in Kai. At the end of the day, it requires no talent to be on time, have a great work ethic, energy, attitude and focus but he does these seamlessly. Amongst the laughter, he squeezes out 'nearly went arse up then' with another roaring laugh.

Yes, they had seen each other at the start of the day but the yell out was more to tell Eddy that he is the one at the backdoor. Before they went through the procedures of greeting, this time around, it was genuine. They both were listening this time as they asked the same questions as earlier. Together they hear each other, but Eddy, this time instead of a grumble, he shouts simple one-worded answers of being 'OK' towards the back, as Kai gets ready in the same white attire that Eddy wears.

Kai has the knack of laughing at himself, over nothing most of the time. Eddy hears a metal clothes hanger hit the floor, a giggle, as he washes his station down again, not for the last time today, but to be prepared for the customer portion of the day. He lets the air dry his clean sanitised work station. He dries his hand with a paper towel as he walks towards the back of the shop, towards the voice of Kai. Each step he adds the layer of make-up to put on a happy shiny veneer over his boiling conflicting commotions.

On approaching the threshold to the changing room, Eddy calls out 'Morning Kai. Raining out?' with a slight joke in his tone.

Kai looks back in dry working attire but sporting a soaking face, hair and a red, dripping nose of resilient rainwater. 'A few drops are in the air,' he retorts. 'I guess with that joke, we are ready for the day?' They continue their small talk and banter as they pass papers of specified deliveries, orders and standing orders to the relevant piles on the large marble thick desk which is as heavy as it is strong.

Then Paul announces his arrival by slipping on the same patch that Kai did. 'Maybe I should do something about that!' Kai suggests with no motion to actually do anything. Paul enters just in time, a few seconds before being officially late. He has the all-important coffee in brown paper mugs with 'Have a Coffee' printed in white scripture. The smell caresses Kai and Eddy with hooks pulling their eyes to focus on the cups with small steaming streams of water from the two tiny holes. Before looking up at Paul's face, they have their prize in their hand. Water is essential in the hospitality industry, mainly for this black gold beverage that warms, sooths and energises the body, mind and spirit.

'So, erm, Paul, did you have a brownie?' Kai asks in a stifled laugh, which he tries to conceal with his paper coffee cup. However, this does nothing to stop the flooding hysterics as he erupts with the slightest look at the face of Eddy who is about to burst. His cheeks are bulging, eyes squeezed shut, face trembling. He cannot hold it. They look at each other and the floodgates burst into roaring rivers of laughter.

Paul immediately places his coffee down and rushes to the small postcard-sized mirror over the makeshift shower and toilet. All around his face is chocolate war paint. He is a forty-something male. You would think that by now, he would have mastered the ability to eat. That simple process by taking the food from his hands to his mouth. They also have worked together for years. As an inside joke, they have the self-appointed nickname of being The Three Musketeers. It is a little nerdy, but just like them, they are inseparable friends with the similar motto of being there for each other.

Pommie Paul has been a bit more of a fly-in, fly-out worker in search for that greener grass. He never finds it so has inherited the nickname of Boomerang Paul as he always comes back. With this connection of mateship through working closely together, they have developed a working relationship that knows when it is time to play, time to work and time to leave the other person alone. Having said this, they are not emotional people. They are not people to talk about their feelings. They are interested in each other's lives, but they talk more about sport, stories from times gone-by and news rather than love. For this alone, was the basis for the perfect relationship for people that actually spend more time together, with each other than they do with their own family or loved ones.

Over the coffee break, Eddy told in the most blasé way that the good ship Beth-Annie was going through some stormy weather but did not elaborate on it. They did not ask. He respected them for that. Mates.

Although Eddy is sharing in Paul's embarrassment, the humour he is showing is his own mask. Which he placed on without being subconsciously aware as Kai came through the door. This is the mask until he closed the front door of his place. This mask is on for the rest of the day, firmly in place. As for Eddy, he is no oil painting himself. He is not ugly, but handsome.

Eddy, born Edvard Steven Quarrell, is in his late thirties and has strands of grey hair coming through his dark brown short-shaven hair, which his barber describes as feathered. Shining in the fluorescent light, a customer has told him that his grey hair would make him a handsome silver fox when he is older. That twenty-something customer made his day then, for when she enters the shop he thinks of that exchange. He often shares small snippets of another people's life and tries to remember them all. He often scribbles down notes like birthdays, events or other information to remind him when people return that he will engage them to address them about the event or occasion.

He strived to say that thing to make the customer feel special. He likes to make customers not only feel special, but he strongly believes that this makes them be special. Eddy is slightly gaunt in his facial expression due to not having a great night's sleep since, well, he cannot remember when. His eyes are retreating further back inside his skull. His lines under his eyes are getting darker with each passing day. His skinny face is drawn around his angular features with a stereotypical Parisian nose, for which he can thank his Romanian mother for. When he smiles, he radiates his perfectly formed white teeth with the slightest small chip on one of his front teeth if you look really hard. This was done while watching the racing cars, his first love, after food, before finding out what women were all about.

The young, naïve Eddy got too excited during one of the races and fell from his perched metal railing down onto the top of the barrier with his tooth jarring the top of the metal. His thin lips curl into a smile and his crow's nest in the corner of his eyes show that he has had a beautiful past of laughter and good times. His white pen that is clipped to his jacket has more meat on it than him. For he has not eating properly for a long time.

Since the inevitable started, he has dismissed food. Using the age-old proverb, an apple a day seems to be keeping the doctor away—he literally does just that. He exercises a lot, to the extreme, which would put the world's marines to task, to enable a good sleep. These exertions fail to get his desired reward. He is an intelligent person that thinks too much over things. He is constantly thinking of ways to make everyone around him better, with himself taking a backseat.

His left-hand man was Kai. Japanese-born, although he was bred in Australia. He came over when he was a baby in arms, still in nappies. He was brought up with the language, the traditions and cultures of Japan, nevertheless he was as Australian as a koala, as a cold beer. Although he was born Hinata—Kai states that means sunlight, warmth and a sunny place. For which Eddy could not agree with more. This was a name that could not have been more aptly suited. He grew up in Western Sydney near Penrith, the school guys thought was from Vietnam. This became a bit of a running joke, then the nickname Kai came in. It stuck. Nowadays, it would probably be deemed as racism but then it was, but not being in the society we are now in, when we must check everything we say so that we are not offending anyone, it was meant in jest. It still is meant in jest.

Kai had the greatest catchphrase that he always executed at the perfect time. For no matter what mood Eddy was in, it never failed to make him smile. They both would accompany this, more often than not, with a silent boyish giggle into their collars. Kai, using his perfect Japanese. Screwing his face up to highlight his already prominent Japanese features. He would stick his teeth out in the cartoon pose that he watched as a toddler growing up and he was ready.

Kai normally waited until Eddy was at his most stressed. His most busiest. When he was feeling the most pressure. When he was verging on the high-pitched urgency in his voice as he was asking for help. Kai would turn to him. Sensing that he was being watched Eddy would turn to Kai. Now, face-to-face in the close confides of the shop, barley any space between their noses Kai would say, 'easy-peasey Japan-nesy'. Priceless. Simply comedy.

They laughed. With each laugh the layers of pressure evaporated. They got back onto the horse and rode it home, through the busy period and to the end with that vigour of a second wind.

Now, for an outsider looking in, this may not seem funny, but the customers in the shop. They laughed and smiled with the playful act behind the counter that they were putting on in front, on their stage, to include them and spread a little happiness to them through the day. To mix things up, Kai sometimes did it with the most Bogan Australian brogue. In seeing this, Australian, with Japanese features, with a thick Australian accent saying this made them laugh. This morning, he needed this.

Seeing that Eddy was not himself Kai preformed it as he entered the shop to ask what was needed first. Eddy was thankful that he did not delve harder into the problem with Beth-Annie, but went with this mateship route. A time and a place, and all that. This was not the time. Later, it may be the place. Mutual respect in their environment, their own being, made their friendship as well as work ship unique, unsurpassed. It is the main reason they have worked together so long. It sure as hell was not the money!

Paul on the other hand was a typical pom. He was an Australian Citizen, lived in the country more than his native England but held the same accent, the same miserable expression and outlook that made him the ridicule of jokes. His father is Australian which brought them over here as a young family. He was a large bald man with a prominent beer belly that strained his white attire. He had grey, thick lensed glasses that balanced at the edge of his wrinkled nose with more hair coming out of his nostrils than his head. He was a gruffly spoken bloke's bloke that spoke his mind in every circumstance.

A case in point was when he was at his uncle's funeral and he turned to his auntie. His mourning, weeping widow to state openly in front of the congregation that 'at least you can spread out in the bed now!' He did not think he said anything wrong. He had no scruples. For that people loved him with the same intensity that others hated him. He had more jobs than anyone they knew. No doubt he would have done any job of the ones that came into the shop or brought up.

Maybe, and more precisely not for long, or for that matter done well, but somewhere he would have a pay check for it. When he was complaining more, they knew he would be leaving. The thing with him was he was a great butcher. So, with him he would leave with no notice. No problems about loyalty, about upsetting anyone or making anyone's jobs harder he would send a nonchalant, carefree text message to Eddy in the morning stating that he would not be coming in or he would just write 'I quit'. Every time they took him back. Each time it mystified them to why he insisted on coming back and being called the apprentice.

Paul, like most Englishmen, loved a drink. Loved gambling, particularly with losing at poker on a Thursday night. He loved women, and surprisingly, women loved him. He was nothing to look at. Did nothing to keep in shape, but he was a charmer. The rare days that it rained in Sydney for more than three or four, he complained. If it was too hot, he complained. Too cold, he complained. Eddy and Kai stopped finding logic in his illogical understandings, but he did make them laugh. He came out with the most random logic that defied reason but was just so Paul. They worked with everyone hard with ethics, passion and demonstrating a rich knowledge of their trade.

It is Wednesday where Eddy's day changes. He had finished work. He still had received not the smallest trace of information from Beth-Annie. For all he knew she could be in hospital. But, at the late time of night. The quietest, darkness of the night. When he should be sleeping. For, in a few hours, his early start will happen. He lies, imminent for the arrive of his alarm clock to vibrate into life with a loud dinging bell.

For the past few months, he has waited at night. His mind seems to become more active at this time. He cannot sleep with the voices in his head. He is beyond blue at these late stages of his own darkest hours. Eddy has not had a good sleep since, he can remember. He lies in wait for a message, for a call. But normally it is his alarm clock that shakes and stirs him to get ready for the day. Sure, in the wee small hours of the morning, he dozes.

But he drifts in and out of sleep like an unmastered ship. He is captain-less on the seven stages of his death-marked acceptance. He waits for his nautical north to call, to message, to let him know that he is being thought of. That Beth-Annie is thinking of him, as he thinks of her. Periodically it comes. Frequently it does not.

Eddy knows this is the end but by a cruel twist of a hand-operated drill that pierces, slowly, into his heart. He tortures himself worse than any Japanese prisoner of war camp officer could imagine. He does this in hope. Nothing more. The small glimmer of hope that all his wondering. All his overthinking. All his, for a better word, paranoia, is in vain. Nothing but a cruel joke.

Eddy once read 'A life without pain is not feeling truly alive'. He would love to meet that writer. Go up to him or her without saying a word and punch him or her, in his or her face. He would then ask the writer if that pain made him feel alive. I am sure that the response would be a contradiction to living. With the response to maim, twist and injure, possibly kill. All depending on the writer's specific mood that Eddy had caught the person in. Eddy's overthinking often took him down the rabbit hole to the pure absurd.

In trying to curb his reactions and restrain his actions, Eddy has gone to writing. On notes, coasters, receipts. He has written many scribblings and rambles for which make sense. Only to him. Many lands in the bin but some stay in a book for another time. If he has no paper, he makes notes on the phone. He speaks into his mobile, he saves the voice messages. These scribblings are notes to himself, for himself, for no one else. He edits them. He re-words them, formats, and rearranges them. He rarely looks back at them when he thinks they are complete. They never are.

Just like Admiral Lord Nelson in the Battle of Copenhagen in 1801 when he deliberately disobeyed the flag signal from the commander to stop attacking the enemy, thus holding the telescope to his blind eye in order not to see. Eddy opts to turn a blind eye to his amateur writings. Akin to his relationship. Unlike Lord Nelson he thinks he will not win this battle.

Eddy looks at the ceiling in the dark shadowy light of the early morning for which he has traced and retraced for countless early mornings. He lies awake just waiting for his alarm clock to go off. He thinks if Beth-Annie is sound asleep. The advent of the breakdown of this relationship that meant so much to Eddy was over before he knew. Was he that stupid to not see it happening around him?

With the sound of his alarm, he quickly rises. Eddy puts a mask up, a different face from the one he puts on as he crosses the threshold to his home and closes the door on another day. A mask he sports around the day, to hide behind. In life, as we all do. We do this in different circumstances.

Despite the fact that he wore a mask for many times through his life as a self-preservation survival instinct. Despite knowing he was doing this. Yet, for the first time he met Beth-Annie he did not put on a mask on. He was honest from the start. He was genuine. He did not want to hide behind a mask in front of her. Behind her. This, actually, scared the shit out of Eddy. For reasons that Eddy did not know, and honestly, he did not actually look for, he did not care that he was so open to her. He felt an instant connection. He felt that this person was his companion. His soulmate. His forever.

The farthest star known and seen in the galaxy is Icarus. The supergiant star lives over halfway across the observable universe. Despite this it still took an amazing nine billion years for its shining light to reach Earth. The star that is five billion light years from Earth is official named, MACS J1149+2223. For this reason, they used to have a quirky saying.

'How much do you love me?' Beth-Annie would ask.

Eddy would answer back, 'To Mach and back.'

The Romans believed that many years ago, people were born with four arms and four legs and during a war were split in half. People search for their connective spirit. Some find them. Some settle for the person they think is right. Eddy believes for the first time he has met his connective spirit. Eddy has found the person for people go through their eternity, entirely focused on finding that person. This was the main reason he did not want to give up without a fight. He did not choose, but felt it was his destiny to be together. She was not his to lose or let go.

While Eddy was in the shower, a message comes through. Eddy reads it while drying the water off his body: 'I can't see you this weekend'. Short and to the point, it was from Beth-Annie. Eddy did not respond. He was hurt. He was angry. Back to being hurt again. He thought so hard to why, that his hair actually felt like it had emotions. His hair felt like it was standing up and generating a nervous energy. Why was it that he wanted nothing more than to see her and she wanted nothing more than not to see him?

He threw the towel aside as he finished getting ready. He was a zombie that was dying inside.

From the beginning of his relationships, Eddy was not accustomed to being alone, without a partner. When a relationship ended, he often would jump back in, like a duck to water after a few months. He was not the notch on the bedpost kinda guy, but occasionally, when he needed to just have that feeling for a physical connection, he would indulge. Well, he was only human after all!

When that human contact was needed, he would go out and shark. Sharking was very much a term he and his mates used to describe going to a bar or club and looking for a one-night stand. They would circle the sea of people in the dancefloor and home in on the prey. They would be merciless in their lies until the shark had what he wanted, and then left. Blissfully uncaring about the stream of broken hearts that were left, discarded in the sand.

He did not like doing this. In all honesty, it did the opposite effect for what he was after, by making him feel worse. In the morning, his stomach churning with guilt and regret he would take those slow, deliberate movement to remove himself from her sleeping position. To carefully shuffle out of the side of the bed, trying to be as smooth as possible. Find his clothes in the darkness with the only hope of any light often coming from a digital readout of the time. Then counting his tip-toed steps before stepping across the threshold with his bundle of creased clothes cradled in his arms.

When clear, he would hastily throw his clothes on and leave. Being extra careful with the latch and the door to not generate the slightest of sounds. The bright sun would attack his eyes and he would squint at the knowledge that he had no idea where he was. He would guess a direction after no deliberation. He would then walk confidently, resisting the urge to flee, until he found some human life or a bus stop. Then he would ascertain whether he was in walking distance of his home or had to catch a cab, uber or bus.

Eddy's relationships had taught him many different things, so he thought. No matter the way in which he entered a relationship, the outcome was different, the income was so very different. Eddy would never understand the workings of a women's mind. He would never see the flawless logic of their actions. The same could be said for him. When he thought about it, he really did not understand himself, his reactions, his good ideas that were bad ideas seconds later. Most were based on pure emotion and contradicted any rational thought.

It is another silent night, at the end of the day. He did not respond to Beth-Annie. He wrote many times, but each message sounded either weak, strong. He could not find the right words. He convinced himself that they were no right words. He wanted to respond as she may take a non-response as being her way out. He starts to write a letter. Side-tracked, he gazes up. He looks up at the darkness but sees nothing as he reaches to see into the darkest places of his mind.

Eddy is staring up at a projection of her pervious relationships that went wrong and left him alone. He analysed them and thought if he had lost a love or let one go. Eddy was looking if his past could affect his future and save this relationship he was currently holding on to by the fingertips of his slipping grip. Staring down at being alone. Fighting to not only stare up but, climb up to the person he felt a pure connection to. He replayed his previous relationships to learn, see, find something that could give him optimism. An encouraging reassurance that he could save this.

Twenty-Four Years Ago
A Shark's Lust for a Mate

Sharks will be sharks, for even just one day. Boys will be boys, for their whole life. Everyone has heard the saying—boys will be boys. Everyone has wanted to believe that boys will be boys. Especially when trying to brush over something that has been done by his or her son, brother, husband. They will attempt to justify their actions in the use of that expression. Eddy is no exception. Although he has no husband. And yet he would feel slightly annoyed to find out that he did have one. He used this expression to justify his young misadventures.

He and his mates have found an unexplainable animalistic urge. Barely into their teens, it came to them unawares. One minute playing with their toy cars, the next, the seductive curves of womanhood. The sensation that came to them when seeing a female. The new curves that were developing. They were no longer just girls, they were objects of a yearning desire. The apple in the Garden of Eden that they could see, told not to touch, but like Adam and Eve—they touched. They took. They devoured.

They not only found the impulsion, the urge, but knew a way of directing it into something that felt right. That righteousness put smiles on their faces. That made them feel validated to be called a man. No longer a young boy, a teenager. Even if the truth is that they all are, fundamentally still both. The notion. Simply generated a feeling. The conception in believing that they were a MAN. This mere pretence was as foolish as it was considered to be, so very wise. Yet, the losing their innocence in a sexual action made them complete that stage. The first step from awkward adolescent, to be standing on the brink of maturity.

For Eddy, this act was satisfactorily fulfilled at the young age of fifteen. Then, he was the youngest of his group of mates. Some of his friends were sixteen years old already. They thought they had all the answers to life, Eddy thought they did. They were so assured, so confident. They were older. It was So, So easy. Fools. Looking back, Eddy knew exactly how little he actually knew then. How little he actually knows now. What can he learn from this? His mind cast back to see.

This was the beginning of an energetic newfound fragment of a strange path. Eddy walked as a new cub in an exotic stimulating forest. Bright eyes looking at everything around him. They had only just begun to discover this life. Moreover, this encounter of a newly found way of expressing an animal urge. In this, a clumsy act of sex had the hyena's laughing. Had the gorillas thumping their chest in machoistic support. Had the lions and cubs growing with pride. Had the birds singing for them. He had every right to be part of this jungle.

The funny thing that the animal urge had just opened was a whole new chapter, with many scenes and acts that were not even part of Act One. Those parts, that they would not see it coming until it came. This after all, was the painful passage of the formalities, the maturing rite. The direction that this new encounter has for them was not even the tip of the highest mountain. It is barely a lost snowflake on the top. The fools have no idea what this Pandora box would unleash on their souls. Eddy had no idea. Then it was for laughs. Now he saw what this new development of life would make. A vast string of complications, like a firework it would burst, explode with light to dark. Sex is complicated.

Eddy reminisces with a nostalgic smile of these easier times. Sure, for sure, he knows how foolish he was back then, but this was all part of growing up. And after all, boys will be boys, right? Right?

The Thursday night streets are like a concrete urban jungle. The whoops, shouts of alcohol adolescent fuelled adrenaline. The blue costumed police are on their patrol. They walk amongst the screams, laughs and abusive nature. Some directed at them. That is the reward they get for being a police officer. It is ridiculous really when you think of it. For protecting and serving the laws of the great southern land they get ridiculed for it. When you need them though, all that is forgotten as quick as the first shot, and you support them.

Eddy thinks back to when he first got his driving licence and getting pulled over for speeding by a policeman with the surname Rasher. You could not make it up? Seriously, PC Rasher. He thought it was hysterical. It was such a talking point for him to relay that story to everyone, anyone that would listen. He held on to that story for weeks. Who was he kidding? He still told the story to this very day, with a clarity like it happened yesterday. It was a favourite one of his, because it sounds like it should be made up, but it was, hand-across-his-heart-and-hope-to-die true. All the jobs in the world that would have suited him more, he chose to be a police constable. This could have been a slant on his dark sense of humour. As he appreciated, everyone has a sense of humour. Some have to share theirs, as some people are just not funny.

Back to the Sydney streets of the suburb of Redfern on this balmy Thursday night. At this time, the neighbourhood had a bad press. It was not that bad. It was just, like anywhere, depended on where you went; whom you mixed with, and with what was your reason for coming to this area. You do not walk into trouble intentionally, unless you are looking for it. On an unfortunate occasional you find yourself doing just that, well, you walk back out of it. It is a great place to go out. Mainly due to police respecting the area for the danger it possessed, so drinking underage was not a problem for Eddy, or his mates.

For the drinking establishments, age was nothing, the person was money. The law had no place here. This was a place to get train wrecked, written off and to get rooted. For the non-ANZAC's out there, rooted means having sex. Eddy's first touch of lust was his pure animalistic sexual urge with satisfaction. This was with a girl named…

Eddy was not proud. Okay, honestly, he was a little proud of not knowing her name. He knew it began with 'G', so for the purpose of his nostalgic trip, he is going to call her quite simply, G.

Back in the day, every Thursday and Saturday night, Eddy and his mates of fifteen years plus used to descend to this neighbourhood suburb to go to a club aptly called 'The Crypt'.

Eddy and his mates would get ready at their homes in casual attire and put enough cologne on to sink an armada of ships. The wave of the sweet, cheap aftershave would drift around them as they swaggered in a beeline route to the train station or bus stop. On route, meeting some mates at a set time on the corner of roads, or at their homes. The preferred mode of transport was the train, where they would jump on.

Mostly, they would try to skip the fare for the fifteen-minute journey stopping at every station to the top of South Sydney. Then they would walk down the small residential hill to the club. As they flooded out of the train carriages, they saw other people from school, from the week before and chatted, laughed. The simple life of school was epitomised in these moments. They had no worries, no stress and no plans other than what happened in that immediate night. What they wanted to happen in the night was the topic of discussion. Not what they wanted to be? To become? They then split into small groups and took it in turns to go down the backstreet.

This time, Eddy got the short straw and thus, went alone. He strolled with a confident strut down a dark narrow pathway. A small cracked red lit sign above the painted black metal door. Where the brick walls whispered. Where danger lurked behind every metal bin. In front of the grey rock-wedged open door, two large looming security guys would look at his fake identification card. Know it is a fake, but will deliberately deny recognising the forgery to allow him in. Not everyone made it in. They had to refuse some people, so they always met up at the same place to see who, if anyone did not get in. The unlucky ones would literally be left out in the cold.

Instantaneously, the threatening, stern grim-faced security guards parted, revealing the entrance. He was greeted with slippery beer-enhanced concrete red and black stairs down a narrow dark passage into the basement, the club. It could not be any more dangerous if it was designed by Al-Qaeda. The walls crumbling with plaster, paint under his trailing hands that gave him the impression of safety. Each gently, lingering rub of fingers exposed the fire hazard for which it was. It was for this opening introduction to the club below that his mates referred to it as the trenches.

After years of people touching, hence removing layers with their hands down the steps as they hope for any support, corrugated steel walls had been uncovered surrounded by the brickwork. The narrow steps could fit two people, just. But they had to be thin, slim and turn sideways to enable the passage of people ascending and descending. This was the only way out, the only way in. At the time, he does not think about the danger that he could be in by entering The Crypt. It could possibly be that he would be entering his very own crypt. If the slightest fire happened, it would spread. Alcohol lined everywhere, even the ceilings. Cloth on seats, clothes on humans and plasterboard partitions. It would go off quicker than the underage youngsters who spike with newfound liquor-enhanced confidence that all think they are bulletproof.

As he descends down into the dark pit, a thick layer of dark grey smoke fills the air, with all the smells and flavours as he gets deeper into the depths. He has barely made the last step when he is offered something stronger. A little something to help him on the way. Drugs available everywhere. It is offered so blasé and carefree as if the guy in the nice, new leather jacket was suggesting a charitable donation.

Nearly slipping on the final step onto the formally burgundy floor that has more scuff marks than an unkempt NBA basketball court, he is in The Crypt. Here, he would be trapped. If a fire was to strike, everyone—him included—would be lucky to survive, but you would make those last minutes drug-enhanced calamities to numb the forthcoming doom with splendid oblivion. The guy in the leather jacket would be his newfound best mate as he tried to take anything, everything to not feel any pain.

After barely navigating his way down the stairs, on the left you pay the gold coin to enter. A wrinkled twenty-something that was being propped up by the older till. A shell of a cigarette hanging from her thin, pale red lipstick lips that was nearly burnt to the butt. Ash scattered over the counter that was nothing more than a shelf. She took the money in a heavily bangled gold looped decorated wrist. Her severely punctured ears sparkled in the random lights that flashed in tune with the independent, underground music that was too cool for the Arias. She was skeletal thin. Looking older than she should have, her clothes wore her rather than she wore the rags that were covered in holes, no doubt smells. Every week, she was there. A chipped glass of ice and a brown liquor which got topped up by a bottle under her till. The only glass in the whole building. The rim stained with her lipstick.

Without looking, Eddy knew where his mates would be. Eddy would instantly be directed by an unseen thread to the meeting of his group beyond the veils of smokes, the sweat of dancers, the overexcited pushes or pulls. A slight detoured was made with getting a tinny as he fought through the hot testosterone imbalanced crowd. In front of a long wooden scratched, blemished grey bar full of young revellers celebrating their youth he shouted with a hand sign his order. A reach across the damp bar between the shoulders of others. Where the staff got the cheap cans of beer straight from large black plastic bins of icy water, wine from goon bags or tequila shots in a plastic thimble. The dripping tin in the bar hand. His free hand waiting for the cash. He let go when the money was in his hand. No words were exchanged, except his ordered drink.

He carried on weaving his way through the attire that was casual and bordering on anything but, being naked. That involved everyone's styles from the goths, the alternative indie crew and the townies. Townies was the slang word for people who dressed in immaculate designer labels. They were normally from the Eastern Suburbs, or the Northern Beaches and came from the richer families. They had so much product in their hair they would cause Greenpeace to come if they decided to take a swim in the harbour at the end of the night due to the resulting oil slick.

They would normally be found in the trendy, clean bars in the centre of the city. The laws were tougher there, so this was the only option. Yet, not everyone was discriminated in the balance of people here. No-one cared what you wore. If it was counterfeit, real or your own personal design. The purpose here, was to have fun and enjoy themselves. Through drink, drugs or both. Most of the people were younger than the actual drinking legal age and no-one objected.

After the end of the long bar navigating, the slick, now black shiny floor which led to a dancefloor he could go around or through. He chooses to go through as he could grope, fondle while being incognito. It was early in the night, so he had no problem trying not to bang his head as he bowed through the brick arched remains of the basement, that had and will see heads cracked on it tonight. The floor changed to a dirty, scratched and shoe printed red again. Painted with a smooth effect, where people 'mushed', jumped around and into people to the beat of the music. The dancefloor was on two levels separated by a single kamikaze step. Eddy had fallen down a few times. Everyone had. It was a rite of passage here to get pulled back up, then to continue dancing.

At the far end, a dark corner really was the disc jockey hidden except for his head. Bobbing behind the wall of the long bar wearing hat and sunnies. where no hat and sunnies were needed. His hands floating around spinning the reflective vinyl before placing it on the turntable. Opposite the disc jockey was another arch that led to a corner and the cloakroom. Eddy walked through. To the right was the smell of the male toilets, a strong as a wave of odorous sewage. A distinct mix of urine and faeces, of overpowering cheap aftershave and deodorant, of sickly smoke and young sweat.

Ahead of him was a surly lip-ringed, black lipstick-wearing goth where she guarded the cloakroom beyond. She took his lightweight beige coat and another single dollar was passed through. Eddy's coat got snatched and hung up, in return, he was given a raffle ticket with a number for him to retrieve the coat when he wanted to leave. A collection of red plastic, torn and scruffy seats to the left, that continued through another bricked arch with a small, cosy seating area. People pashed. People drank. People recovered. Further through another smaller bar opposite the ladies' toilets.

Eddy's mates always committed on the Ark as they called it as this is where the girls always entered and exited in twos. Two large black vibrating speakers acted as a border between the ladies' toilet and the other side of the dance floor. It was a hole, a cellar, their house, the Crypt. It was a place where they felt like Kings. Their Kingdom. It was here in between the female toilets and the speakers that they always met up. It was the quietest section. Here they discussed the plan of the night. Truthfully, it was the same every night, but felt good to share the first drink with some male bonding and jeering esteeming roars of encouragement.

Thursday was student night thus, it was the cheapest night to go. Everyone was here. This was great for Eddy and his mates. Due to still being in school, they only worked at the weekend and that was all the money that they had to spend. The work normally involved medial tasks like washing-up, food serving, cleaning, or anything else that involved minimal training or responsibility for the employer. If you entered the club before nine in the evening it was free, hence saving money and then they would get a stamp allowing them to come and go, in and out, as their pleased.

In addition, they would take the decision to walk the hour home as a group or alone straight down to the harbour to discuss the night. Then with the rising sun walk, the beachfront coastal walk. Truly, it was quicker than a cab. As queuing for the cabs was a joke and the cost involved, which at that stage in the evening, no morning, money had been spent on alcohol. Then they wanted to sober up a little before getting back to home and to the parents' house. Or if the sharking mission was a success, to be able to perform. These possible outcomes realistically never worked out as planned, but every week they thought it would. Idealistic teenage optimistic innocence, no, stupidity.

Being fifteen years old, they had no idea of the boundaries your body has on the limits of alcohol. Twenty-four years later, Eddy still feels that he has no idea. He continuously pushes his boundaries to the limit. Often, too often, too far.

One of his mates, Tommo, was involved loosely with a girl called Xena. They met every Thursday and pashed. It was a routine that they got used to. They teased Tommo about him not making a move. Not going past the first point. For not heading into boobtown to take things further, quicker. As if it was that easy. As discussed at Tommo's house, Eddy's role involved him being the wingman for the night. As tonight was going to be Tommo's night.

By this, Eddy had to distract the accompanying friend, who insists on hanging around like the bad smell from the urinals. This is where G comes in. He had no physical feelings for her. No interest in her appearance other than to play the part of a best mate. He started chatting her up in a nervous, induced way of not knowing how. Not knowing what to say. Where to put his arms. He used his arms like an Italian to explain what he was saying. Pausing on syllables in words that needed no accents and speaking in a musical way. Why? Eddy had no idea, but it was proving a nice icebreaker as it was making her laugh. Probably at him. But as he was laughing back, it did not seem to not bother any of them. Without realising, Tommo and Xena had moved away to the darkest of the dark corners. The next few hours of pashing had commenced.

Eddy glanced around to see his other mates at the bar. This was his moment to be the perfect wingman. He suggested getting some air outside, away from the noise. After getting the stamp for re-entry, they left The Crypt. They had walked down the long street to the harbour front. After the rejection from the first bar they got into the familiar Pig and Paradise. An establishment that was in need of some serious love. It was off the main, all singing and dancing bar joints with their overpriced cocktails, their fashionable, no doubt expensive clothes and their hip and cool demographic.

However, the Pig, well, it served a purpose. People came here. So was it really worth spending wasted money on it. The Pig had a reputation for trouble. But, with this trouble it encountered somewhat messy situations. The Pig was The Pig and exactly what it was, maybe, just maybe, by not scrubbing off the blood-stained door frame of the night before would take the gloss away from the pits, the place. This will seem immaterial come chucking out time as another richly coloured claret would reappear, that was a guarantee. It was full to the brim. After using their elbows to force their way to the bar, the tricky task of getting the drinks, un-spilled, back to a safe hole where they stood close enough to feel each other's breath on hot flushed cheeks. This process took a whole new skill.

While Eddy went to the bar, G had found a place to stand. Literally a pocket where they would form a close-knit circle, standing to shout over the heavy metal music that boomed out of the speakers. It was ironic that they went away to get away from the noise and the music was, if not louder it was definitely more aggressive here. The closeness of which they had to talk made the normal personal space dissipate. It was the good o'days. Eddy smiled to himself as he thought of this encounter. He knows now that this time was easier, he wishes he knew then. They laughed. They kissed. Eventually, it was time to get back to the club.

They moved and had enough drink in them to feel the effects without feeling drunk. They walked and talked, mainly about music. This was the universal topic that connected them all. Eddy took G, the small steps to the harbour. The nights air had a chill, then again with their beer jackets on they did not feel it that much. Under the old coat hanger, the Sydney Harbour Bridge on the green banks of grass another kiss started again. A kiss of more tongue that was needed. A saliva-induced smashing of lips that was very clumsy and awkwardly rushed. He fondled her breast with his free hand. He had never felt the unmoulded curves of a girl's breasts before. It aroused him.

She yanked his penis with a disregard that it was attached to him. He said nothing. He suppressed the pain. He came so quick and purposeful in her hand. She wiped it on the grass.

He was embarrassed, but wanted to elude that sensation so deluded in tricked gullibility that he would be ready later. Inside, he hoped that it would not be as quick. He hoped he would last a lot longer. He went down with his fingers under her large golden buckled belt that was an accessory to her plastic red skirt. 'Later,' she promised in a seductive tone in his ear.

Still, he was not sure it was lust, opportunity or his first real kiss but Eddy felt close to G. What was her name? He was having different feelings away from the urge.

They staggered, leaning on one another, arm-in-arm, sharing each other's warmth, eyes for each other as they sauntered on while scrapping their feet back to Redfern. On re-entering the club, Tommo and Xena were in what appeared to be the same game of tongue wrestling. He saw mates around and knew where they would be congregating. For this reason, he made his way away from the unison of Tommo-Xena and away from the normal assemble point to discuss the sharking plan.

Eddy and G got a drink. Once again, it proved to be Eddy's round. They moved around to the quieter part of the club near the ladies' toilets. Ladies being as loose a term as the male toilets being called Men's. With a flimsy red plastic cup of Budweiser beer, for which he thought showed his high level of sophistication. An imported beer rather than local beer. It was probably watered down for which they had no idea being naïve to this drinking, socialising and meeting world that they found themselves cast in. And a thimble of Tequila for G, a classy bird.

On handing over her drink, Eddy attached a clumsy miscue. Eddy leant in for a kiss to distract G from Xena, as he saw her looking around for her. This could not have been more embarrassing for him. As he missed her mouth and managed to nestle himself into the top of her white, bare exposed freckled shoulder. Behind him, he could hear Tommo in the mateship that surrounded them offering encouragement, by falling about in roaring laughing mauled by contemptuous jeers.

Eddy could imagine him pointing with the laugh and relaying the story to Xena. Who needs enemies when you have mates like these? To not look around. To regain his self-confident coolness. To avoid the laughter at him. Eddy went in again. Lifted, gently, G's chin. And this time got the smiling, open mouth of G and proceeded to throw his tongue down her throat, as if trying to sample her last meal. He was inexperienced in kissing; this inexperience led him to be too fast, too aggressive in his approach and too eager. G was the same. It was a flurry of tongue, lips, spittle and noise that could not be heard over the independent music that was way too loud to start a conversation, let alone keep one.

Eddy found himself with his back to the speaker that separated this small standing area to the death-trap of the dancefloor, rich with a silky screen of sweat and puddles of drink. The smell of cigarettes and smoke added a mystery to the enigmatic feel of lust that was flowing over him. His desire was getting aroused again. Behind G was another large, heavy tall black speaker pounding out the music and the ladies toilet was a door on the other side to that. They kissed, long, hard. Hands a frantic, wild caresses over her body. Eddy would have liked to think that it was passion. It was not. It was pure animalistic overexcited nervous desire. She did not know what to do. He did not have a clue. Therefore, with the reliable resource of films and movies that are always what happens in real-life, she reached.

Reached for his groin with her free hand and fumbled to undo the zip of his pale blue jeans. He did not need to do anything but pull her knickers down slightly as her skirt was little more than her brown, leather-imitation belt. Like a blind woodsman, he delved in and tried to find that hole that he had heard his mates talk about in the playgrounds and sporting fields from school. He found it and then did not know what to do.

With the moist feeling on his fingers, he was a little revolted. No-one had mentioned this? So, he just poked and jabbed at it like a kid with a stick. It was pathetic. Her hand joined his and helped. Eddy needed it, she yelled a supposed-to-be-whispered 'softer'. It was a high-pitched exhilarated squeal of eagerness.

She, on the other hand, was not taking her advice and yanked his penis for a second time, repeatedly as if she was driving without using the clutch. 'It is attached at the moment,' he yelled with bated breath, breathlessly explaining, 'and I would like it to stay that way'. G shouted in her ear a noise he had never heard before. She did not ease. If anything, she was now driving a rally car. She was yanking, tugging and pulling his penis around. She was helping a lot more in her department. She was getting more thrilled. She gripped harder. He was starting to beg her. Her body convulsed in sharp, jerking quivering motions. She released her grip to a soft, long-awaited cradling. His lust, her noise had formed an erection and they were ready to commit the sin. Right there in the club.

Then, out of nowhere. Out of the dark recess of their own space in between the two speakers, a large hairy knuckled hand grabbed Eddy by his grey T-shirted collar. A tight shaven-headed male barked spittle descended hostilities as he spun him around. Eddy's jeans dropped further down his pale legs. He held him by the arms of his large puffed black coat, no doubt to make him look more formidable than he already was, then yanks him off her. His Levi's fell to his brown shoes. He struggled to pull them up as he was being dragged along the greasy floor, through the pointing, mocking heckles and claps of his counterparts. He was bounced up the steps, left at the top in a crumbled heat surrounded by embarrassment. A little satisfaction.

He was thrown out, in the rain covered street in a heap. When did it start raining? His jeans still exposed the throbbing urge he wanted to be relieved off. A few seconds later, as he was trying to pin his penis under his belt to stop people seeing more of the obvious, G appeared. She was given the ceremony of actually dressing herself and being escorted vigilantly up the steps, with a little encouragement from security.

Into the street she saw Eddy. A privilege that was denied by him, she saw him as he was still getting dressed. She ran over and launched over him. They kissed. They headed to the grass park from the doors of the noise pumping club and the wish to continue where they were so rudely halted, took over again. It had never left. The rain was unnoticed, it had started to softly fall. They persisted. The mud of the damp ground. They did not care. After three attempts of trying to put a condom on in the nervous shake of his wet, sticky hands he managed it. The unknown way of putting them on was apparent. Which was the right way round?

In hindsight, he wished he had paid attention in sex education. Instead of blowing up the condoms and letting them go, to whizz around the classroom in hysterical abandonment. He wished he actually used the test tube put in front of him, to place at least one around it. It looked so simple. He was too cool to try. Being sure that it was not torn he went for it. They were jumping on each other, slipping in and out. It was very tight on Eddy and hurt him. By the look in her eyes, every now and again, he was sure that pain was in her eyes as well. This was not like the movies. They never really expressed the smell that came with intercourse.

In minutes, it was over. They had both let out they own juices in the heat of the summer rain, on the muddy grass. They were so in wrapped in each other that they did not even see if anyone was watching. If anyone was with them or close to them. As Eddy slid off G's sweaty body and rolled onto his back on to a wet puddle he breathed heavily. He pulled his jeans up that only managed to be around his ankles. His shirt, torn above his chest from either this act or the security guards' assault.

Like now, he was free from care. He breathed hard. He looked up along the stone wall and saw a smiling Tommo looking down. He gave the fist in the air, a 'respect' sign as he bumped his right chest once and then turned with a smile on his face.

That was Eddy's virginity taken. He did not know if it was G's or not and, in all honesty, he did not care. He got what he wanted so he could be a 'Man'; no, for this week, he was the MAN. Well, in the eyes of his schoolmates. He was the perfect wingman. He gave himself a pat on his back.

Although G left later that week. Her dad got a job on the mines. That summer her family and she left for Queensland. Even though G knew this, she did not expect what had happened to happen. It was the longest relationship that they both had. Nearly two whole weeks! Eddy moped and brooded about what could have happened. He never admitted to it to his mates, but he held a candle to her for a long, long time after. They did not stay in contact as the craving fizzed out like the summer sun in a hollow cold winters moon leaving only the solo aching howl of their pain.

It was a one-night stand that left him with an emptiness he could not understand. It was only over the course of a few subsequent weeks that he realised it was the loss of his virginity that left a hole in him. It was the loss of his first lust. Possibly, the loss of love. A love he told himself it was not.

Over the course of the week, he told, retold and embellished the story to be better each time around. He hid behind the comedy of his loss. The following Saturday night Tommo got his taken. It was only until Tommo could relay a similar story of a sexual encounter that Eddy became old news. His healing begun.

As for Tommo and Xena they stayed an item throughout the Summer, until the end of school. They were at two different schools, so it was easier for them both to act at school in a way that did not upset each other. As contrasting to the no-mask approach of being behind the closed doors of their parent's homes.

As for Eddy. He was still finding grass-stains in his privates three girlfriends later, but he was happy to have successfully taken that fear that all men have. Eddy often wondered why they chose the club to have sex in. Then the park? Was it the thought of getting caught? The adventure of the outdoors? Or the simple and true fact that they really had nowhere else to go. The desire of that physical craving. He lost his virginity. He was a man. He thought he was a man. He had sex with G, the girl whose name he would never know. She was, and always will be known as, G. His first. In more ways than one.

Twenty-One Years Ago
Second Love Around

Eddy's genuine, first emerging taste of true love had been with an Egyptian beauty. He was the one that destroyed this relationship. He did not know how to react to the sensations that were circling in him like leaves in a tornado. In his mind, he can remember the turn of events and the consequence that saw him sitting on the broken pavement. His back against the cold metal street lamp. The only light shining down reflecting of the parked cars in the darkness of the silent street. His white T-shirt with the familiar small blue Levi's emblem over his heart, the black trim around the bottom of the short sleeves and the V-neck collar. His tight Levi's black jeans were wrinkled at the back of knee, while being worn on the left thigh and both of the knees showing the white threads of cotton.

His dirty black and grey Adidas classic shoes that were so comfy. That even though they were destined for the bin many months ago, he still insisted on wearing them, as they formed around his feet, making them so damn comfortable. And at the end of the day, especially in The Crypt, for which he still visited, occasionally, at the tender age of eighteen, nothing stays unadulterated and so pure forever. The Crypt is still linked to have the essence of a single thought of going there, anything clean and innocent would be ruined in a few seconds of entering. That included the people. Their souls. The stages of growing up is to have your eyes open to see more than the front dust cover.

Drugs were worse there than before. The violence was getting out of control. He could have been oblivious to it before. Or, it may have been that his mate got bottled in an unprovoked attack late last year while outside that took his gullibility of the world. It is harsh, relentless. It is not only shiny lights and good times. It has a dark, sinister element. The simplicity in his view of the world was squashed into a tight ball and squeezed, so any remaining innocence was wrong dry. In that cascading sound of shattering green glass. The slow-motion hearing as a scream from Mark's depths of despair in himself that had never been shaken awake. The loose free fragments of glass, blood, beer and trust broken in unfixable shapes on the roadside, left the mark of fear.

The face of hatred from his attacker that fled, never to be found. He got the wrong person. He saw that as Mark's mates, including Eddy, got up as quick as a lightning bolt, filled with an electronic impulse to avenge with brutal, violent retaliation. Some pursued. Others helped the clumped body clutching his right eye that transcended agony. This act for which he can see clearly projected on his eyelids. The way Mark had to learn to see again after months, years of therapy. Still today, he gets headaches. His vision is still impaired.

Eddy came back, fruitless in his and Tommo's frustratingly pursuit as the attacker vanished under the curtains of cowardice. They breathlessly arrived with regretting shakes of their head. They returned to the scene without the anonymous assailant. Without a reason for why this feat was done, and with such brutality. They hear the screeching of the sirens in the background looming closer. See the shocked gaping expressions of the youngsters around. This act that lasted a few short seconds shattered his naïveté that everything smelt of roses and tasted of chocolate. Concisely he saw things differently to what they were and actually, what was going on around him. His naivety of the place had been embedded and the cynical aspect had flowed forth. He could not undo the scene he just seen.

Eddy dived into work after this experience. He submerged himself in learning a trade. Hiding under the waves of the heavy workload that he was generating. He kept his washing-up job on the Saturday and Sunday mornings as he followed a professional career in butchery. He worked four days, full-time hours at the Butchery in Ultimo with one day at Tafe College. He used the washing-up work as his spare cash. He needed this extra wage to buy essential things like bread and milk. The apprentice wage barely paid his rent. He was slightly better off than a chef's wage but still these were stained with nothing more than slave labour.

The owner, seeing Eddy's drive for food, recently gave him extra money as he did his normal tasks but evolved to include the heady heights of being the resident vegetable mechanic. He worked earlier to get these prepared for the chefs when they arrived later, but then they work later. Swings and roundabouts. He arrived at the same time as the owner. Firstly, unpacking the brand-new Audi filled with supplies from the market. Then he bashed a sack of potatoes. Peeling them, to people not accustomed to the catering trade speech within a commercial kitchen.

It is not just shouting and swearing in kitchens, work actually takes place. Then the peeling of carrots and preparing the other vegetables. Then the bonus of peeling and slicing copious amounts of onions. Peeling bulb, after bulb of garlic. So, the pink in the onions caused the tips of his fingers to be stained in a soft, unappealing grey in blotches. The smell of these particular vegetables made his hands smell no matter how many times he washed them. The chefs had appeared by now, so the washing-up was starting to build. He enjoyed being a vegetable mechanic early with the tunes of Triple J playing in the background. Being lost in his thoughts. Also, being out of the sink of hot water the whole day was a bonus.

This was starting to dry out his skin with the concentrated washing-up liquid. The powder designed to aid this was not being the kindness to his hands. Hence, his hands were looking remarkable older than the rest of his youthful body. But this way he got to wash the burnt pans, they were not the best chefs, as he washed his hands to reduce the smell of his hands. Later on, he would trim a lot of the joints of meats. It was here that he really excelled and loved this part. Getting a joint or cut of meat and changing the dimensions with each slice, cut and incision to change what the meat was going to be used for. It was here, years before, that he decided that butchery was going to be his profession. Even away from the apprentice job, he relished doing the meat here. Showing to the owners here what he had been learning. Practicing and applying his chosen trade.

Eddy met his first love, Mahina, at work. She did not work there, nor did she ever. Nevertheless, on that hot, sunny lunchtime that was where he first saw her, while he was the one that worked. The windows of the sink looked out to the patio area at the back of the bistro. Here, just south of the city in the up-and-coming hipster suburb of Sydney, Newtown he was washing-up. The potential of the suburb was just being tapped in, realised and released with a contagious net infecting everyone it reached with a cheerful vibe. The whole area was transforming into a positive new look with a vibrant electric energy.

Unlike the implementation that the city of Sydney applicated after World War Two, where they took the regrettable step to destroy older buildings. Seeing the crumbling of history forever depicted only in books brought a tear to the eyes of the old, as well as the patriotic, devoted younger generation. Each tear was a lost symbol of the nation. That unforgettable destruction of the older buildings to the ground. Where the history was trampled on by brand-new developing world of skyscrapers, step-by-colossal-step.

Fortunately, in Newtown, they were doing this undertaking differently. A lot differently. The old warehouses and factories were being converted, but with the exterior staying the same. The walk down the High Street did not lose that authentic unreplaceable charm. Here in Newtown, the history was left to be appreciated to generations to come, with the interior was where a world was removed. The modern positive direction inside was enhanced by keeping that authenticated charm outside. Yet still, with this realisation, came the opportunity for people to cash in. Unfortunately, this is where the source, that in all honesty the government should have denied, was inappropriately funded. Not many Australians were the source. It seemed to be coming from overseas.

The Australians, the residential natives, were living here. Where seeing the prices going up with the improving evolution. The people investing here were experiencing no change at all. They were deaf, dumb and blind to the crippling effect that they were having on the people that lived here for generations. They were in office blocks, miles away. Looking over different cities, most in different countries. From their screen they saw a procession of figures, maps and images of data in charts, statistics without even setting foot in the location they were exploiting. Not witnessing the communal decay in the preservation of the historical yesteryear.

Hence, the outcome was the prices of everything going up. To cause daylight robbery. To line the already gold-leafed pockets of the corporate trade with more money with not so much as little, but no care for the people that had lived and worked here all their lives. Each dollar bill was muffling the sounds of the screaming locals who creating their lives, brought more lives and enjoyed their surrounding home life. They were getting pushed out of their home, as the money was coming in. They were getting tightly squeezed out as easy as juice from an orange. Wrung out of them by the overseas landlords. They saw more money could be made, so they put the rent prices up. Thus, this made these average people unable to afford to stay. The ones that made the community suffered, they bled what happened in the community as a clear as tears to what it should be. A bonded community getting exploited now. A fragmented shattering to cause the bond to drift away on the same tears they cry as unable to save the true sense of a community neighbourhood. More money brought only less community. Money grew greed and isolation.

For Eddy, he had a true sense of Sydneysider pride. He not so much wore it, but it was entwined into the fabric of who he was. He never showed the fact that he loved that this bistro was run by locals. It was part of a small network that strived to save the community with action. Not the brandishing of large wooden signs, chants and protests. Warfare was fought with accomplishing a foothold in the market. Preserving their life in unwavering success. Being resolute by standing tall.

The name of the bistro was a play on Newton's theory of want goes up comes down it was called Newtown Thirty. The number was the age the owners, Mike and Loreena, when they opened the doors. It worked well. This was one of the first to step up from the café formula with not only continental influence but a healthy is great mission. The café-bistro offering was at a reasonable price.

However, he saw the exotic commodities of the food coming into the kitchen. Where the finished dish that subsequently left the kitchen, Eddy was in awe at such a transformation from the paddock to plate. The price was not justified. In the centre of the city, it would have been more. Not only was Newtown Thirty owned by locals, they helped the locals. They brought the produce from the surrounding farms, the markets. They believed in what they were selling as a complete assisting single extended family.

The small white-painted wooden cross glass windows that looked out to the courtyard looked out to an enjoyable scene. Yet with the painted white steel of the security cage on the outer surface were edged by a flurry of colourful pot plants flowering from the window sill. Consequently, on sunny days this precautionary measure in the uncomplicated design made Eddy feel like he was a trapped prisoner, rather than a paid employee.

It was one of these ill-fated dragging sunny days that another light came through. The sweet floral scent of the flowers was laced with a delicate stimulating perfume that enticed Eddy to lift his head from the plumes of steam and white rainbow trapped bubbles. There she was. His star-crossed lover. It was as if the light was perfectly placed to highlight her as the focal radiant brilliant rose amongst the peripheral prickly mediocre thorns.

She sat outside on the rustic community-made table oh so near to him. Looking directly through the window pane, but not seeing him. Smiling with her other friends without any burden on her delicate smooth naked shoulders. This connection through the glass was instant, for Eddy. He was magnifying her through the glass as his amplifying heart heightened its aching longing throbbing beat. He stopped in mid-wash, the hot water streaming down the plughole. Transfixed.

He paid no attention to the people she was with, he was spellbound under her magical lure. As if an invisible fish line had caught him and he was being attracted, reeled and drawn to her by an equally invisible convincing force. Her flawless mocha coloured smooth skin with no creases, wrinkle of stress or anxieties. He yearned to meet her. He hastily walked to the hand wash sink at the edge of the washing-up section and splashed some water on his face.

Looking up at the small postcard-sized mirror that gave the head chef, the owner, Mike, a glimpse into the preparation room. From where he stood working in the main kitchen, he could see without moving, that work was being done. Eddy was not happy with his reflection. He had needed a haircut but kept putting it off time, and time again. He roughly scuffed his hair with a little pool of water as if he could magically transform it into a better style. He pulled his eyes, cleaned his mouth out with the warm water, tidied the collar of his unkempt blue check shirt that had never seen an iron.

Looking away from the mirror, his attention turned to what he could amend, modify. He turned around to change his filthy light grey plastic apron to one of the untouchable crisp, white freshly laundered chefs 'only' apron. He quickly hosed down his apron and hung it outside so any question to why he had changed was simple, and although motived by deceit was actually the truth. A white lie if you will.

He decided to clear tables to distract Mike's objections as to why he had left his station. He never had done this before. Mike looked up from his latest creation. He was a nice guy but not a smiler, not a laughing person. A quiet, reserved intelligent person that only said what was necessary. This act actually gave him a wry smile. A smile that said; at last, the boy is finally using initiative. Mike did not see the motive. Then Eddy let his devotions known. It was only when Mike saw his glances up towards her table. The African beauty. This happened way, way, way too often.

Eddy was doing this in the hope that eye contact would be made. Mike was not a fool. He invented this deception of coincidence. Eddy continued to make an effort, alas in vain. For the hour in which they had their lunch and chatted, he could not engage her. Then they all had left. He was back in the kitchen. In that short passage of time to rush back his awaited vision was replaced. Flickering in the smooth warm breeze was a colourful array of notes under the peppermill. She was gone. An angel, in his eyes, had passed on. He had blown it. He was not going to get this chance again. He had never seen her before. He thought he would never see her again. Crestfallen.

He returned to the kitchen rueing his lost opportunity with a shuffle of feet on red tiles. So that he would not be noticed, he snapped out of it quickly. He returned to work. This last hour, he worked hard with an infuriated driving aggression of not being able to say what he was thinking. He thought of what should, could off happened if he had spoken. Furious with himself for not being able to do the simple thing of going over, with confidence and stating that he was Eddy and this was his number if she fancied getting together sometime. So simple. Yet. So incredibly hard. In contrast outside Mike strolled like a proud general at the freshly swept patio. No litter, no leaves, no trash. The courtyard had never looked so well-kept through service. Still no smile was perched on his lips.

Mike never engaged in mindless chat for he found it tedious. He did not mind it going on around him as long as the work was being done. What happened as Eddy was getting changed to leave surprised Eddy. He showed he was human. He was leaning over while doing his runners up.

'Eddy,' he smoothed his thick moustache with one hand as Eddy slowly lifted his head. He could see the coils in his mind processing the correct words. Eddy was genuinely worried that this was going to be bad news, that he was going to be let go. 'Eddy. Never think someone is out of your league. Why did you not say a single word to her? Even a polite comment about the weather, the food? Why not a single word?'

'How? But…' Eddy was a little gobsmacked. He thought he was being subtle.

'You see, in life if you want something, you have to go for it.' His questions remained hypothetical. 'You may get your fingers burnt, your heart broken, but my dear boy, but isn't it better to know. Than not?'

With that he firmly placed a hand on Eddy's knee as he pulled himself up and marched his way down the restaurant on a mission. Eddy cherished those simple metaphorical words. Effectively sincere. Be that as it may. It may too late now. Retrospection can be cruel.

That whole week he could not get this Egyptian goddess out of his thinking. Everything brought him back to her. That week was like a slow torturous death. He anticipated she would frequent the place again. But when? With whom?

He could not believe it. He had been waiting for the Saturday to come around. The slowest week he had experienced. Long-sufferingly in his silence so he could go back to Newtown Thirty. For Work and optimistic hope. He woke up with a start, late. He had barely got no sleep-in anticipation. And, he was late. He had forgotten to set the alarm clock on his mobile. How? He did not know. He had woken with the slam of a car door. So, the light shining through the window. Looked over at his mobile.

Something told him inside that he was tardy. He launched himself out of his self-made pit with barely eleven minutes to get showered, brush his teeth and get to the bus stop. That in itself was a seven-minute walk away. He rushed like a mad-man to get this bus as he knew, from a previous episode, that the next one was over thirty minutes away which would render him late for work. He threw on clothes and it was only after the rush of getting ready, dressed and the sprinting to the bus stop with the grainy taste of toothpaste still around his gums that he saw the bus, his bus come to a halt. He pumped his legs faster as he shouted and waved his hands in hopeful encouragement for the bus to stay. Anticipation that the female bus driver would linger a few seconds, so he could get on board. She did.

He leaped up the metal steps, expressing his gratitude through breathless puffs of air that stated that cardio was not his forte. Paid with coins before he sat on the closest blue, hideously designed, seating of the Sydney network bus system. Regaining his breath as he slumped forward. It was in this moment that he actually paid attention to his attire. Green shorts, red top and yellow runners. He looked like a rainbow had thrown up over him. He looked a right state.

If he saw this person that was looking back at him from the large reflective tinted front glass, he would not look again. As he would not be able not to erupt into uncontrollable wild roars of laughter. One last look, only to see that his eyes were not deceiving him. Why did he have these clothes in his wardrobe? Out of the blue he saw that he had just walked past a jumble sale of clothes destined for the bin and thought that would be the fashion of the day. It was God's cruel joke.

He arrived at work, precisely on time. He had an enthusiastic vigour in completing each task correctly with a newfound speed. He was going on with his duties without paying attention to the chatter around him. He was working efficiently to enable him to have time for a chat if she bestowed herself for a second time. He did not know what he would say. He had rehearsed lines in his head over the past week. These would not be used he feared. He felt he was going to lose his nerve. Lose his lines. He should just go for an honest approach. But, nothing. Work was over.

Each glance to the courtyard, down the restaurant, was a glance of anguish. His tormented hope had been cast out to a stormy sea to be left unanswered, lonely. The lost love, a mere raindrop in the ocean. She did not return to the scene of the crime when she plundered Eddy's heart. The day had gone quickly. He succeeded in his defeat. He would never have that chance of a lifetime ever, again.

Looking down at his feet as he scuffed his way to the bus stop after work, he played out the perfect scene of what could have happened for his own private movie theatre in his mind. The perfect words. The perfect smiles. The perfect world. His hands sunk deep into his green checked felt-like short pockets. Rueing his attire that he grabbed in haste that morning, he was looking forward to changing. Maybe throw this ensemble in the bin. He felt everyone was watching, pointing and laughing at him. They did not blink an eye. The people around him had their own agenda to worry about. They did not care.

He even rummaged through his locker after work with the hope of finishing something, anything. He had no choice but to wear the same hideous attire again. There he stood, at the bus stop in his embarrassing clown apparel, waiting for the bus. When shimmering into existence, the beautiful image of that girl from last week came walking down the road. Towards him like a mocking mirage. What were the odds?

He looked through the blue skies beyond above him to whisper under his breath, 'Are you bored up there?' This was a message to ask, 'why He would do that?' Now, when he was at a weakness ebb of self-confidence. Last week, he was too bashful. He was too shy to talk. This week, he was too self-conscious. Humiliated with his outfit. She stopped next to him. She looked so good, better in person than his mind. She queued up next to him. She smelt great. He was mortified beyond words. His face was flushing red to add to the colourful ensemble of what was already a discombobulate.

In the few seconds that it took for her to float like an angel to the bus stop, he was thrashing out the humiliation that rushed through him. He decided to beat it out of him in seconds. He then went for it. He took Mike's advice. He had nothing to lose. She stood next to him in a light cream and blue-flowered stencilled summer dress that was fashionably elegant.

He then took the bold step of asking about her meal the weekend before. It was all he could think of. It was out before he could wind it back in. Eddy, in his awkward stammering, had to explain what he was talking about. In his haste, he blurted out the question, with the inability to realise that she had no idea who he was. Then, with the quizzical look of confusion, he attempted to rephrase.

After a brief touch up of the question, he aided it with an explanation, he said he worked in the kitchen at Newtown Thirty. He could not help but notice her. He then regretted that, as it did make him sound like a stalker. He looked down at his feet as he hesitated to gain some form of composure. She gently laughed as his fumbling. His nervous actions. She softly lifted his face up to look at hers. Smiled. She was touched by how humble he was. Delighted by his confidence to engage in conversation with her, a stranger in the strange place.

In a posh upper-class British accent, she responded with a red-faced blush of her cheeks. When the bus came, there was an awkward moment. The instant that could change Eddy's life path. When he wondered whether to sit next to her, or not. He opted to cast a pair of dice down the felt carpet of the game of life. He gambled as she went first. She sat a few rows back, he sat next to her.

They were closer to each other on the thirty-five-minute journey to the centre of Sydney. He knew that the bus that they chose was not the express. Maybe He did have a plan despite everything that had gone wrong to this point. He knew that this one would stop at every stop, especially on a busy Saturday. People were everywhere. That was, of course, not his plan. However, he was going to use it to the full. To spend as much time in these opening exchanges to make a great impression. He had already made a bad start, so he could only go better from here forth. The bar was set pretty ow.

They chattered through the stops, the jerks, the slow, snail pace. As the end of the journey was drawing near Eddy could not believe it seemed so much faster. The normal pace seemed an eternity, but today it was over in a flash. Just before the end, he offered to be her personal Sydney guide. This was with only one clause, one condition. He insisted that they make a quick detour back to his place to change, a mere short few minutes away. She agreed with trepidation. They walked, talked back. While back at his place he took the bolder step to shower the putrid smell of the kitchen from him. This bizarre stench, a concoction of cooking food, preparation and hard work was on him. He immediately threw his clothes in the bin to get changed into a better subtle attire. The changing of clothes was the most important stipulation.

36

He could sense her nervous approach as she crossed the threshold into his apartment. She thought it was a pretence to get her back to his place. He was a gentleman though. This was the start of something for them both. Something that Eddy thought he had missed. Something she did know happened, had gone unnoticed. Now awakened. He wanted to go slow. Wanted to treat her and this fragile situation with a level respecting acquisition. This foundation was dry sand now and to build that castle they had to stabilise the foundation.

That first afternoon together was an enjoyable learning curve. The awkward clumsy initial stages dropped into insignificance alike to Eddy's awful clothes. He found a new confidence which put Mahina at ease. Simply uncomplicated. Easy.

Eddy saw Mahina for the intelligent person she was. An intelligence that she would become something, someone great and not just a footnote in history but a historical mark in the World. She was Egyptian with, what Eddy described to his mates as having a Queens English accent in a delicious milk chocolate exotic body. A posh, deliberate articulation where every syllable, letter was purposefully and importantly accounted for. Very much unlike the Australian brogue within him that shortened everything.

For example, the Irish Club in the city; quite simply, he shortened to the affectionate, Rish. In contrast to her precise diction, Eddy would shorten everything. Everything it would seem apart from Beth-Annie. She insisted on it not being shortened and he respected that. That is another story, and not this one, however. Eddy would glide over words and phrases, and his English, well, was not the greatest. He was, after all, Australian, and they use slang where appropriate.

That evening came around fast. They could not believe it was the end of the day. The hours had been seconds. As the sun was saying goodbye for the day and setting on their chance meeting, they went their separate ways. A tender dry kiss on warm cheeks. Just as Mahina slowly turned to glide away Eddy took his heart from out of his mouth and seized the day. He called out. She turned. Wow, what a smile. He leisurely jogged the few steps. He tried not to rush but he failed miserable and might as well ran the short steps for which his eagerness betrayed him. He asked her out, again.

She remarked, 'Next time, you will pay for nearly letting me go.' He glowed at the ease with which they teased each other. In a flurry of excitement, they arranged another time to meet up. Eddy had a double shift but planned to finish by 9 pm the next day. His mind was saying not to be too eager and leave it a few days. His mouth had different ideas. He asked her on a date the next day. She keenly accepted the invitation.

Hearing her swift willingness, she blushed, a glow of innocence spreading across her face, as fast as the smile replicated on each other's faces. He was so nervous when he asked. It did not show. They wanted it. They both enjoyed the day. Why would you want something that felt so good to end? When he walked away, he kept glancing back. She did the same. There eyes met many times. She played with her finger in her mouth as he could hear her giggle in the distance.

Unlike the arvo before, the Sunday went crawling, cruelly towards the end of the day. He finished early. Instead of the cheaper bus he took an Uber straight home. Minutes later he walked into The Oxford on, unsurprisingly, Oxford Street. He decided this location as it was close to where he lived so he could shower and change his attire. The whole day he was excited. He had a Cheshire cat smile like the cat that rolled his head off his shoulders in the cartoon adaption from Lewis Carroll's book, *Alice's Adventures in Wonderland and Through the Looking Glass.*

When his boss asked why he sported such a crazy grin, Eddy used one of the Cheshire cat's quotes: 'I'm not crazy. My reality is just different than yours'. This, for the first time since Eddy had worked there, had rendered the boss speechless. He had the most cheesiest popular love songs going through his head. He felt invincible. Like he was literally walking on air. Nothing could spoil this perfectly welcoming Friday feeling, on a savouring Sunday.

He walked into the Oxford and scanned the scene. Brown wooden tables and the lingering melodies of calming, relaxed music made the atmosphere perfect against the flicking of candles on each table. The soft glow of the candle lingers as the amber brushed Mahina's face as he spotted her, as she spotted him. Heartbeats skipped. He eagerly walked over around the tables, immediately cursing himself as in his head he spoke a mantra to 'Keep it cool. Keep it cool'. He leaned over, evading the naked flame to give Mahina a perfectly deliberate gentle kiss on her cheek before sitting opposite to her on the wooden seat.

As she spoke, he watched the candle linger on her perfect contours and over her smooth features. She could not have looked more perfect if she tried. The conversation was flowing. The right in the situation was just, so right. They ordered snacks to graze on from meats plates, olives and breads. They were not here for the food; they were here to learn about each other. They moved from the ambient eating area to the main bar as they were closing that section down.

The seats over in the bar section, as beautiful and elegant as they looked, really were not the most comfortable for extended seating. A barrier of a smoke-filled curtain separated the two areas and they sit next to an open fire. It was not cold, but the fire was purely ornamental and was projected onto the brick empty fireplace. They pay for the restaurant tab to order a couple of glasses of red wine for which they chink to. Eddy tried to act as though he knew what he was talking about when he ordered the Malbec from Mendoza. A universal toast to nothing in particular. Wordless nothings with the chime of the glass hitting the right note. They did this with every new drink. Just for no reason decided that they would Ching, Ching their larger than necessary wine goblets that resembled goldfish bowls.

Maybe the relaxing atmosphere helped them relax. Alternatively, maybe they just felt relaxed around each other. No mask. No deception. They had no faces to hide behind. They leant in to ask questions. To laugh, joke and tell stories that they have never voiced before, to mates, or family let alone a stranger. They had no personal space between them, it was mutually shared. Like the eating area this had a simple white candle that was halfway downs its wick, shedding its wax over the green glass of the wine-bottle holder and burning free and easy like the conversation.

A chime from a low-pitched bell announces that The Oxford will be closing soon. This was unexpected. Unexpected as it was 2 am and they had not felt the time go past. They wanted this moment to last. They left with drinks unfinished and went back to Eddy's place. The cold summer's air embraced them as the door swung open, a blasting chill from the sea. They strolled, he was linked in her arm, wrapped in his shoulder, one body, the short distance to his unit. They talked more, they learned more about each other. The fire of the candle never goes out within them. Burning on and on until sleep finally gets the better of them both. They fall asleep on the sofa, fully dressed together. In each other's arms. Feeling perfectly contented.

Nothing at that moment mattered to either of them more than each other. Eddy had never felt so relaxed with someone that he, in all honestly did not know at all yet. She seemed to have the power to open him up at her will. He was defenceless to act. Unwilling to hide anything she wanted to know about him. He opened the door for her and rolled out the red carpet for her to delve into his inner sanctuary and learn all his secrets, thoughts and ambitions.

Mahina was in Australia, but from England to Egypt. Her parents sent her to a private boarding school in England to get the very best education in the World. After years before she was even born, they both believed was the case in England. She would spend her British summers off at a destination in another part of the World to gain more experience of life. She only really went back to Dubai, for which her parents lived most of the time, to see her parents at what the British called half term. This normally fell for two weeks around Easter. And sometimes she would go back at the other half time, which was later on in the year.

For the most part though, any holiday, apart from the extended British summer holiday, she would spend with her family in England. She described her school as an old Abbey. A former monastery for monks. Surrounded by farmyards rolling with green lush grass, yellow noisy win-rustled straw. Where the white fluffy clouds of sheep frolicking, roamed in the meadows. The smell of freshly cut grass, flowers and trees blended with the sound of tractors, barks of darks and singing birds. The birds in the indigo sunsetting sky flew without a care, doing what Icarus could not. She described it as a picturesque postcard of how Australia see England from the television dramas, shows and the occasional movie that was not cockney, gangland related.

Most of the time, she would say, was for the more realistic rain, grey and coldness that she says happens from a single day to weeks at a time. Although the latter is not portrayed often on the screens, it is common knowledge that it does not happen from 'time to time', but all the time.

They became an item within the very first week. Contrary to what his mates thought, Eddy believed it was not too quick. It just felt so right. Although they did know it was a holiday romance for Mahina, they had confidence in a long-term relationship happening. Yet, the faith was built upon a flimsy paper house of cards. Thus, they did not want to talk about. If in speaking out loud their fears it would make the moment be too true, too hard to face. It was the unspoken white elephant in the room. It remained unexpressed.

Eddy excelled at showing off his town. He became a human guide to his own personal side of Sydney for Mahina. He took her to places that she had and would not see. His favourite places. His private places that took him back to his childhood. Places that shared a memory, a story for him to tell for the first time to someone else.

They were meandering hand-in-hand, around the curves of the stunning harbour on a tranquil evening in peaceful easy silence. A comfortable stillness in the air, around them, between them. As the waves crashed in gradual crescendos on the sand, this soft splash made them know they were not alone. By each dark blue wave making a different mark, a different hue in the yellow-golden grains of time. The few splashes of glowing white from the moon in the dark canvas spilled onto the marching dark army of the waves below. The lights from the street lamps cast colourful reflective shadows along the boardwalk arching over the sea.

Eddy and Mahina walked arm in arm. Eddy is being embraced by Mahina. With this embrace, they were in the masterpiece of their own design. A shiver from the coldness escapes him as it descends his spine. He suddenly had that anxious filling sensation of dread flowing through him. The very real thought of saying goodbye. Even though it was still weeks away, the months had now become a few weeks. The unseasonable warm night for April amongst the chilly breeze of knowing that the time together was coming close to an end was arriving. The cool gentle reminder was forced way down, but not fully supressed. He wanted to take this apprehension and every moment that surged, flooded his mind. It unsettled his steady love boat as a result of the smashed barrier. Fear was preceding their unstated pledge.

They paused. His world stopped turning. She looked out as she perched on the stone harbour wall. He looked at her. Her eyes were the scenery. As they gripped each other in an embrace looking into each other's eyes. Nothing was said, nothing was needed to say. A sparkle from the moon hit her eyes. She giggled as she saw him staring at here. They glided over to sit on the grass beside the boardwalk. They gazed deep into each other. The water-horses rolled gently over the sound within touching distance, but they were in their own personal piece of art, within this masterpiece. The sounds and dynamics of nature, the waves added texture. The sand, the moon, the stars, added the light and dark. The soul enriched couple made this a masterpiece. They connected on every level. Eddy was thinking Mahina was his masterpiece. A masterpiece that could end him in pieces by the end of this whirlwind winter romance.

Eddy was intrigued by all of her. He decided to cover his fears by means of essentially acknowledging them. He asked why the parents called her Mahina. It is not an English name nor is it an Egyptian name. She honestly only found out recently. She did not know but she had asked her parents a few days departing before this holiday. On the basis of what her parents answered she went a step further to completely research her name. She loved that she had a great answer to the reason of why the name existed. She clapped her hands quickly as she told him of her own research.

On hearing the source of the name, Eddy found it highly amusing that her parents chose Mahina. In his eyes, they went for the opposite. A name for a Hawaiian mythological name for a mocha-skinned, granted he would give them that, but for an Egyptian princess. For the Hawaiian myth, Mahina is a lunar deity. He was not alone in his association here.

As most people do, he associated the moon with being pale and whiter than white, like the colour of milk. He would laugh himself to sleep over the disassociation of the name to the image, to the Egyptian beauty. It gave him night giggles.

Another thing that fascinated him with amusement was when he was at school, he was sent around the Superior State of New South Wales with his family, his school. He was sent to the far reaches of crucial world historical significance towns such as Wagga Wagga, Dubbo, Forbes and Clyde River. She, on the other hand was sent to the big all singing and dancing cities of the United States of America, Asia, Canada and now Australia. It was only in him showing his town and his places that it dawned on him how lucky she was to see different cultures.

However, in truth, he would never change seeing his country more than other Australians. Her parents travelled a lot with work, so she was always kept busy. A suitcase, jetsetters lifestyle. They travel would sometimes cross paths with her holidays, so they could see each other, catch up. On route, in a complete out of direction route, her mother detoured for a few days on her way back to Dubai from Canada to see her daughter.

Mahina's mother worked for Coca-Cola, she travelled the world distributing and marketing the brand. Being 'across the pond' she decided it was close enough to spend a couple of days in Sydney. Her father was going to come, but at the last-minute work came up. This was a regular occurrence according to Mahina. Work dictating them. Her mother still came, but alone. Mahina had mentioned Eddy her friend that had become her tour guide, conveniently missing out the love connection aspect. Against his better judgement Mahina had coaxed him to be persuaded to meet her at the airport. She was staying close by, so she could be back at there, in what was now less than two days. Seemed hardly worth it but she had commitments elsewhere and as Mahina said on numerous occasions, work always came first.

On meeting them at the airport, Mahina's mother, Zara, was noticeably jubilant to see Mahina. She raced over at the sight of her. Yelling out, verging on screaming. Oblivious to the surrounding crowd, her light oversized handbag swung wildly on her right arm as she propelled herself towards Mahina. The closeness of the embrace was tight. It was a long time since they last saw each other, with the messages getting frequently more spaced out.

Mahina introduced Eddy while clutching his hand that said more than words. Zara was obviously annoyed by this boy. She did suspect a courtship yet tried to bury her qualms deep down. Mahina mentioned him far too often in all communications to be just, an ordinary friend. The intimate locking of their fingers around one another's hands restored her hunches to be accurately spot-on. She feigned interest with the weakest of artificial handshakes. She kept her hand close to her body, so he had to come forth. She put no effort into gripping that made Eddy feel he was shaking a wet fish.

She instantly forgot his name. She cared nothing for him. Eddy felt this aura of unacceptance, in conjunction with the glow of annoyance that he was even there. She focused on Mahina with given Eddy far too many sideways death stares as they weaved through the inhabitants of the airport to the taxi rank. For which Zara insisted on, to save time.

'No luggage!' Eddy enquired that came out more of an exclamation.

'I have everything I need on me. My luggage has been sent home already. Seriously. Why would I burden myself with my work here? Why would I need more than I need?' Zara spat out in quick bursts of sprayed irritation.

She was rude in her downtrodden retort for which she did not even give Eddy the courtesy of eye contact. Eddy took it as way of demoralising him over Mahina. He ignored the comments like the water of a ducks back to remain proud, tall to not resort to her level of foolishness. As they waited for a taxi, the small talk was cut short by Zara.

'I nearly forgot.' She rummaged inside her brown and gold handbag. 'For you.'

Out of her bag, she produced a stuffed Canadian tourist-ready moose in the red and white cliched maple leaf T-shirt. Her bright red nail polish brandished the teddy bear close in the face of Mahina who accepted the gift with a 'Thanks'. With the attempt of breaking the growing tension between her mum and Eddy, she remarked, 'It looks a bit like you, Eddy.'

Without thinking, Eddy replied, 'What? Horny?'

He immediately saw Zara's disapproval flood in a rising red mist through her face, reflected in his own. Whereas hers was anger, his was embarrassment. It was an unwise effort as de-icing the friction. In the split second of thinking and saying, he immediately wished it away. But it was too late. The words were out there. The implication was very much in the forefront.

By being in attendance, he was already not bestowing the greatest first impression. Conversing cemented that significantly. This was in jest. But particularly to a Muslim who believed in no sex before marriage. Especially to a Muslim's mother for whom he was practising sex before marriage to her very own daughter. Her mother did not see the intended joke at all. This was a colossal faux pas.

On hearing the words leave his mouth, she just turned on her heel in disgust, storming towards the closest taxi. In a trail of lightly laced green, blue and red scarf, she was through the automatic sliding doors, almost fleeing the situation. She pushed in front of a patiently waiting couple at the taxi rank, leaving a trailing cloud of fury. A soft but persistent poke on Eddy's shoulder from Mahina told him to behave. He was. His eyes pleaded. His arms opened his palms up innocently. It was a joke after all. Yes, a bad one, a rash one, but the nerves made him drop a horrendous clanger. They got into the ill-tempered space of the car. Eddy in the front seat. Mahina and Zara behind. He could almost feel the daggers in the back of his head as he stayed quiet for the short journey.

To say that day, that moment, was something that he hoped could be erased was a glaring understatement. He hoped that he would rebuild the moment, so he could patch up the calamity of errors that was dividing them apart. Click rewind. Have a restart. In all honesty he conceives that Zara had the preconception of Eddy before they had met. She had the prejudice that no one was good enough for her daughter, especially a paltry labourer from the backward country of Australia.

In the taxi, her mother made it abundantly clear that she wanted all her time by talking loud, brash and over-the-top. It was a ploy. Eddy was not nearly as stupid as he looked. She wanted Mahina to not be with Eddy. It was obvious. She wanted to force a wedge between them, alike the wedge the Eddy did at the first meeting. It would not work. Why would it?

Over the course of the next few long hours of the couple of days, he met up with Mahina in short stages. They sent messages and called, or rather, she called him back. They could not bear these few moments not together. She reluctantly told Eddy that she had lived a lie in front of her mother. She bashfully told Eddy that her mom thinks that it was all over between them. Just after the airport situation they had a row and it climaxed to her finishing it. This seemed to appease Zara, but infuriated Eddy.

Why should their blossoming love be a secret? She was not a Capulet, he was not a Montague. This was not a Shakespearean play. Yet, he did not voice his angst. No words needed to be said. She knew her behaviour was not appropriate. He knew why she felt she needed to do it. She felt guilt-ridden for lying to her mother, but more ridiculous and ashamed with the scenario that had put her in the position to have too. Eddy did not agree with this stance but lived the lie through her. Lived the lie for her.

Frequently, she sent cute messages of missing him, craving to see him more. He was her thirst that she could not quench. If it was not for affectionate electronic communication with each other over any, every one of the various and many mediums that they had access to the love would have wasted away logical explanation, reason. The foundation was only fresh, but remarkably strong enough so that this star-crossed act of dishonesty would have been harder to perform. This slow testing part of only a couple of days in the winter for him, the summer holiday for her, was the lengthiest challenge of their love for them both. If anything, it made the bond stronger.

At least Eddy had work to keep him occupied. He had his butchery training, had his neglected mates around him, nevertheless the downtime was a receding tide of longing. The late evenings. The early mornings. They were the slowest periods. The hardest. To pine for someone that you want and not have them close makes the heart ache that little bit more agonising. The only silver lining was that he did get up-to-date with his college work. Unhappily this was a mere consolation of something that not even resembled any form of comfort. This was the most apart that they had been since they met that fatefully exquisite afternoon. She had literally been staying with him at his apartment.

The day had come. The time was here. Mahina's mother's flight home was on time. Eddy was a nervous ball of energy as he watched the screens of the departing flights. He was already at the airport albeit the departure lounge, sulking in the shadows. They had planned this with precision timing so that they would not inevitably bump into each other. A flicker. 'Departed' flashed on the screen. Moments later, Mahina came rushing through the doors. Eddy burst up like a Jack-in-the-box, supporting a wide grin. An embrace.

With all good things, eventually, they do come to an end. Just like gravity, it is something that just cannot be avoided. So, it gets embraced welcomed. The good times are cherished. The great time that Eddy and Mahina was having was now staring into the face of the end. The end of the winters romance. This great time was always doomed to come to an end, in fact had started to unravel.

It was one of those days when the sun shines bright throughout the day, but now the wind blows cold. The summer in the light had turned to a darker shade of coldness. The imminent brewing, brooding tension was about to hit the pinnacle point of being burst and let free like Pandora's box on this relationship.

They descended the dark, filled streets with all the conversations echoing in their heads. All the moments and feelings. Each footstep jaunted another memory. They are on their last day. How had it come around so quick? They stopped every now and again and looked at each other in silence. So many words were racing around their heads. They wanted to talk. They each wanted to listen. Eddy thought about going to the UK. Eddy was thinking if he should. She had to go back.

Mahina had no options as to finish school. He wanted the ending to be right. Unfortunately, his words came out wrong. His actions came out misconstrued. He was ending a relationship he did not want to end, as he was too afraid to start a life on a whim. He was too afraid to restart. Instead of thinking about what could happen in a positive aspect, he thought of the negative. It consumed him.

So here he is. On the concrete of the pavement with his legs over the asphalt. His back against the cold grey, metal trunk of the street lamp. Mahina in front of him on the opposite side of the street, crying. Back to him. Shakes visibly seen as she tried to supress the uncontrollable, overwhelming sobs. It was their last night. Around him are faces and voices as they are not the only ones in this very busy street. He is slumped over. She is shocked. He feels to be the dark spot of mystery at the bottom of the well but is the misery. A joke had blossomed into an argument. The happy place had soon turned into dungeons and dragons and he is scared to do another thing. In case it is wrong.

He stays on the floor. He props the streetlamp up which needs no help. To be slumped over head in knees. He is worried that if he moves, says another word, or makes another gesture, the world in which they had lived in would collapse. This situation was as fragile as a house of cards. He does not want to generate a single tremor of air. Eddy looks down at his hands. He is stifling his cries of pain. If it was not for his red bloodshot eyes he would have succeeded. He turns his hands over in his own hands. He sees the smooth shaky hand of Mahina enter his vision.

He receives her hand and embraces it in his two. Goes to kiss the top of her hand but instead starts to cry. The tears could not be blocked. A thought entered his head as he felt her smooth, warm hands that tomorrow he could not. He would not be able. That thought alone opened the floodgates. She bends down to see his face. She smells amazing. With her free hand, she brings up his head. He is unashamed by his tears. He sees her wet eyes. She helps him up.

They walk back the way they came. They are both sorry. It was the frustration of the situation that caused the argument. They want to end the night happy. They tightly cuddle. They do not want to let go. Tears flow once again. They go back to Eddy's. They are happy. They are sad. As this is the ending of the relationship that was always based on goodbyes, but within the trodden ground of the sadness flowers the times remembered. The tear trodden ground of the finishing story. There was the blossoming of a stronger seed of friendship in the soil.

Although the destructive whirlwind romance had left a destruction within, which Eddy had never felt. He also felt that he could rebuild himself. He felt that he could love again. Although it would be different. It was not meant to be, in the sense of time. It was two people meeting together. Two people that were so right for each other but, quite simply had met at the wrong time. The heart broke smoothly, but not even. She wished him to go. He hoodwinks himself in thinking that the heart broke even. In his mind he knows she still had more of his than he had hers.

Reluctantly, this love ended and they parted company that next morning to never see each other ever again. The bus journey from central to the terminal was a flurry of excitement, although slightly awkward. No tears left to cry. They did not leave each other's side until they had to. Until it was time to say goodbye—one last time.

Fifteen Years Ago
The First Real One

The first time Eddy saw her, he was unequivocally captivated. He silently cursed himself. He was a sweaty mess with the combinations of the morning's workload evident on his uniform and face. She was fresh faced, on an induction. With all the alertness of trying to take every morsel of information in, with a hint of nervous worry apparently visible in her wide-opened eyes.

In a haze of colour, she entered the smelly, steamy atmosphere of the kitchen. Gas lights a blaze with flashes of orange and blue tinged light, the sizzling and boiling sounds coming from the vessels on the stove. The raucous loud yelling chatter stopped instantaneously. As she floated in as soft as a butterfly in the war-torn debris of the no-women's zone. The crackling tones of the radio barely audible over the dark, tightrope-bordering offensive conversation that was being drawn comically out within the working commotion. Gliding on a lingering wave of perfume, in a heart-stopping second in which Eddy literally felt his heart stop.

She was being escorted around the small, split-level narrow kitchen. The swish of the red swinging door with the bottom scurf mark of bare wood from repeatedly being kicked open, she awkwardly announced her entrance into the kitchen. She breezed through on a stimulating rousing aura heralding the fleeting winds of change. The magnetism fascination was instant. He nearly cut his finger off as his attention relinquished from the job, quite literally at hand to this eye-penetrating magnificence. She was nothing short of an enchanting colourful butterfly that mesmerised him. He did not even notice that he was surveying her sailing movement with appraising approval as she passed through from the restaurant, through the old barn and out to the top-level restaurant via the backdoor.

Eddy was in the United Kingdom, having arrived from Australia on a holiday visa to see the sights of Europe, but with the sole purpose of obtaining what he saw as vital working experience. Going backpacking was something that all his mates had done or were doing. It was something every Australian seemed to do, so he decided to embark on a trip of his own. His aim was not the clichéd theme of partying, frolicking off a year off but to learn. To be educated. When he first voiced the plan, so many mates were eager, interested to tag along.

When it came to the crunch though, people dropped down and out like flies. Instead of the simpler route of waiting for a travel pal, he elected to go alone. After all, it was so easy to never actually happen. For a week to become a year. To be forgotten completely with the hubbub of life, just getting, inconveniently, in the way.

He wanted to work straightaway. He applied for a job, many jobs, immediately while he was still shaking the long journey off his scatter-brain that was tired and weary. His sleep pattern still was not in place, even at this stage. He has been in this mysterious cold foreign country for just over a week. He got his break straightaway. Here he is known as FOBA, a slang term apparently for Fresh off the Boat Aussies. It still makes him laugh, not the slang, but the dictation in a proper, rich posh English accent.

All the jobs he applied for were on the way to the hostel in the backstreets of a shady alley in Westminster, away from the glitz, away from the magnificent buildings but concealed like an unwanted secret that wanted to be seen. He had touched down in the early morning; by the afternoon, he was having offers of trails, conversations on the telephone. It would seem that England was in need of cheap, hardworking labour that spoke English.

He applied for so many jobs that he found it hard to grasp who was talking from where. The first telephone call that he got a positive vibe from is the job he is in. He did not need to start work straightaway but since he had started earning, he had never been out of work, he had never had a regular stream of money coming in, so this scared him. Being in the situation to not be earning any. However, a base of English money would be nice to have before seeing what laid on the footstep on the mainland of Europe. Secretly, he wanted to start without delay, so he accepted the interview without a second to think.

Eddy started working at a beautiful old farmhouse that had been converted into a quirky, low wooden-beamed bar. The former barn amid the high pointed ceiling became the kitchen. The horses' stables became the wine storage with the top jagged tile-covered alcove the home for the cluttered relics of decorated past. The 'Smugglers' to the locals, officially called 'The Smugglers Tunnel' took its name from where it was rumoured a tunnel from the coast ended, to come up at the still operational fireplace to supply the traders in London with illegal merchandise.

Eddy had never heard of this exciting, interesting part of history before. He had never even heard of the small market town of Saxmundham, in which he found himself, with little to no more about the state or county, as they called them, of Suffolk. He stumbled on the valley, more than looking around rather than to stay and work there. He wanted to get out of London, that was for sure. He wanted to find a different Britain to the one that many of his friends went to see, coincidentally intentionally getting trapped in.

In his interview for the kitchen job, for which Eddy uses the word 'interview' loosely, it was an endorsement of his commitment to staying here to work for at least a few months, three being the minimum, he found himself at ease. He was giving a story of the history, with the town dating from 1086 as well as a history of the smugglers in the area. It was something out of a novel that got him enthralled. Something that he was reading more about as each spare minute came to pass.

Eddy had only started a few days earlier, after his successful trail period, then this fatal attraction. He found himself enjoying the early exchanges and learning the slight differences from pronunciation, to different names of certain foods such as zucchini being courgette and capsicums being peppers. His accent seemed to make the young child of one of the chef's blush and run away behind the checked trousers of Gary, her father when he spoke. Eddy playfully played along to put on a heavier thicker accent when she was around, incorporating more of the Aussie slang and sayings which made him sound more bogan, more prominent than his voice actually entailed.

It was an early morning rush when he first saw her. Not just service but the preparation needed for a Monday was all hands to the pump to get organised in four short hours that quickly disappeared out of the blue. He was still getting used to the pace, the home for things and general presentations when she disturbed his concentration. Her light ginger hair bounced off her white crisp blouse, which was the waitressing attire, down to a simple black pencil skirt cut just above the knee and awful blacker-than-black shoes. Her soft echo on the red tiles of her small black high-heeled shoes with barely a high heel to be given that name sounded clumsier due to these ridiculous working shoes. It should have been more like doorstop shoes, yet there were surprisingly quiet considering the grotesque, inelegant design.

She rushed around with Laura, the wife of Ken, the landlords of the Adnams Brewery owned pub, The Smugglers Tunnel. She held a confidence with an acute awareness of what was happening around her environment. She looked around as she entered and at the same moment, her grey eyes met Eddy's. 'That's our new chef FOBA' Laura casually introduced as she sped past on one of her routine busy missions. Laura was always moving, always doing something, never one to keep still for long, even at all. He hastily wiped his hands on a damp blue and white chuxs, which was called a J-cloth here. He rounded the bench as she stepped up into the next level of the kitchen and through where he was working. He offered his hand for the shaking.

'I'm no FOBA.' In his eagerness, he mixed up all his words. 'FOB, not name of me. My name is Eddy.' He blushed with his simple dialect; more awkwardness than he wanted to elude.

She took his hand and tightly but not firmly, gave a short shake and responded in an Emerald Irish soothing brogue, 'Saoirse. You're not from here, Eddy?' Being a newbie on the British soil, Eddy's accent was thick and heavy and clumsy when compared to this beautiful auburn enchantress' musical chimes. She had an enigmatic aura of a magical spider's web. He was the fly caught in her woven web of her seamless superb seduction. She had him under her spell. Within her trapped web.

Eddy never believed in love at first sight. Well, until this moment. He lingered his hand in hers for longer than a first encounter should take. She smiled, her grey eyes sparkled under the soft glow of the heat lamps reflecting off the stainless steel. The lamps were not the only electricity unseen at this time. The connection was made in real feel. Across the pass. He was sure that it had not been a one-way street. He was sure that she felt the connection. He decided to see. He pursued that likelihood, so he would never want to escape her web. To be together.

She was on his mind for the day. Eddy did not see her for the rest of the day. He enquired as subtle as a shark fin seen in the Bondi surf to Laura who told him she was working the bar today, the restaurant this evening. His heart sank, his only night off, out of the nights he worked why was this. The answer was obvious, Ken was working so could initiate the training. The silver lining is that he could work on his patter.

Gary and Eddy had just finished clearing up when his daughter came in fresh from school. In a drab grey and black compulsory uniform, she wore a dazzling smile. She stormed in from the back with glee before seeing Eddy. She stopped in her tracks. Her delighted smile turning to cautious uncertainty at the sight of this strange-sounding fellow. She giggled as she fled the longest way around the kitchen.

'Hi, Phoebs. What's the John Dory?' He had to lay it on thick, it was what she gleefully expected now.

Phoebe giggled as she scattered around to the familiar position behind Gary's long, thin legs hidden by the baggy MC Hammer blue-checked chef pants. 'I'm starving,' Eddy continued. 'I was in such a rush this morning I had a dingo's breakfast, then came to work.' He then went to the refrigerator to grab a prepared ham and cheese sandwich which he gave for a tentative Phoebe to nervously thrust out a hand to take swiftly with a mouse-quiet 'thank-you'.

He turned away as he finished his cliché monologue with 'Wrap your laughing gear around that'. She chuckled. She ate. The whole time not talking her eyes off Eddy from her post on the stainless-steel cutlery shelf. Of course, she was not scared of Eddy, but they had a playful banter that appeased Gary.

Unknown to Eddy, Saoirse was getting changed after her shift on the pale blue-worn carpet staircase that led to the landlord's accommodation. She smiled to herself at his friendly nature. Unknown to Eddy, he had a bunch of bonus points with just being himself. For being polite, funny and genuine. For acting the fool for Phoebe.

The landlords, Ken and Laura, insisted on wanted two days off together. Although one of these was doing office work, they needed to not be actively working. Eddy saw them every one of these days. They were fixing something, cleaning something or just tying up the ends of the week that was. Monday and Tuesday were the quieter days for service, thus ended up being the night that Eddy worked alone with a kitchen porter. However, this sometimes went wrong with every man and his dog entering the venue for food and beers.

Eddy relished the challenge. The normal calm nights that they were put on matched with the Gary the Head Chef, Alex the Restaurant Manager and Tintin the Bar Manager. With the hierarchy off it was a more relaxed atmosphere but they got the work done with cleaning duties. In any case the landlords were within hearing distance upstairs. They were fair, but strict. It was quiet most of the time that gave Eddy and Saoirse the perfect time to get to know each other, to flirt.

As luck would happen, it transpired that they lived in the same direction. At the end of the night, Eddy would wait in the bar while nursing a pint of the newfound, fond off Adman's Broadside warm ale until Saoirse finished. It was a strong drop of alcohol, so he sucked on it as he patiently waited. Everyone seemed to have been to Australia or knew someone. It was a constant stream of conversation that kept him not obscuring Saoirse's work. The conversation with the locals would normally go the same way. They would guess he was either a New Zealander or Australian. Then ask where he was from.

As he stated the city, followed by the town to the suburb, the local would get increasingly excited in tune with his voice that generated a higher pitch as he knew the place. It was hysterical for Eddy to see the reaction when they knew the suburb and a few landmarks around his home. He got to know the locals, make friends with the barflies, all-in-all with the single objective. He did this so he could walk back the twenty-five minutes together with Saoirse, down the hill towards the centre of town in the valley.

He wanted to get to know her better. He wanted to be sure that it was not all in Eddy's head. That there was in fact a connection. He did not push it. He actually was sacred to harm a friendship that was brewing. He was jubilantly happy inside to find out that they were on the same page. Unconsciously they accidently knocked each other's hands. The pause, the linger, the warmth was then held into each other's palm. They latched on. A beautiful moment of passion launching. His heart raced. His smile unconcealed, on show for all to see. She smiled as she looked into his eyes. They were happy.

It was a few short days into the opening exchanges when they shared their first kiss. On this particular occasion when a taxi would have been the better idea, but with a taxi is the shortness of the time together. In the pouring rain, where torrents ran down the sides of the road in an unspoken competitive race. The cold chill brought the redness out of their cheeks. The smell of leaves rustling in the trees and the combination of mud and grass under foot. They walked back in the moonlight, deprived of the elements of Mother Nature but with each other. The fluidity of the conversation did not stop over theses appalling walking conditions that they found themselves submerged in.

The weather in the UK was all that it promised to be, that it was becoming the unwanted norm. Windy, rainy and sunny in the same hour but never hot, always chilly or cold-er. Just four seasons in each day was the comically tragic standard. They united over stories. They shared dreams. They shared their past. They shared each other's warmth for warmth. But, when was the correct timing. When to go and take that leap, to have that first kiss. This was on his mind since he first saw her. When was the best moment? Is there ever a best moment? Could it actually be planned? They both were there for a short term, so was it wise to pursue what they felt? Would it inevitable end in heartache? Heartbreak? To leave a scar that never healed?

They stepped further into the horizontal windswept rain. The thought off taxi was not voiced. Puddles splashed under their feet. The coldness of the gale force wind went through to their core. They huddled closer. Head down against the onslaught of Mother Nature. Just as they were close to the haven of shelter, home, walking by a green, thick hedge row a growl ensued. A deep, menacing warning that made them both jump. They stopped at the same time, in a shallow puddle that lapped their shoes. In unison they jerked their heads around to where the noise emanated from. They heard a rustle fiercely.

Fast-moving, rapid, the huge muscular rolling shoulders of a black and white badger springing through the hedge with an almighty force. Racing between them before they had time to move. For such a large tank of an animal, it was fleetingly fast and away from them down the path in the direction of their origin, The Smugglers Tunnel. They both watched the badger splash its way into the rainy enshrouded night. Saoirse, dripping wet face, turned around and was close to Eddy's own face. He used the sleeves of his coat to dab softly the droplets. Who says chivalry is dead!

In all honesty, it was a futile exercise; nevertheless, the consideration was welcome. He did not have a thought as he chortled at his absurdity of smearing water around her face rather than away. Thenceforth instinct took over him. He gently stroked down to cradle her face under her porcelain chin. The rain unrelentless in its deluge. Eyes locked. He leant in for a kiss. He was too keen for this moment. With this, she was slightly off balance, unexpected was this sudden exchange, but wanted it. As when he went in to kiss her, she fell, slightly off balance, thus falling back into the hedge. It was deceptively weak as they plummeted inside to a green wall-like well of branches and leaves adorned with raindrops. He opened his eyes as she started to fall backwards.

He saw her bright grey eyes wide in shock as she had nothing but him to hold on to. He pulled her near, as she pulled him down. They fell in. Laughter erupted around the snapping of thin branches. They looked at each other again. On the dirty, damp muddy flowerbed. They moved in, as one. Her eyes and his closed once more. They continued at a slower, passionate pace. It was wonderful. It could not have been in a worse situation, but so perfect at the same time. At that moment, 'Nice night for it', came from behind Eddy as he saw the brown trench coat and bright white hair of the small, stocky 'H', a regular from the pub, moving at a fast pace down the hill and away from them.

They bashfully sniggered, shouted out a farewell as they got up. Clothes soiled in mud, grass stains. Eddy picked branches out of her hair. Saoirse fruitlessly brushed his muddy coat. They gave up. They continued their walk with a light step in each gait. He fumbled for her hand as they strolled the short final steps to shelter, and to his delight, she took it. It had officially begun. It was a connection. It was not in his head. It was a love starting. They swung they arms as they walked to parade that they were an item to no-one. No other person was so foolish to be out in this fierce storm.

At the end of the point, they were normal and had a long chat on a brick wall. The intersection where he would go one way, she would go the other. A short kiss happened. The rain was there but not there. The world invisible. They did not care for the wetness, the cold, the outside world. He wanted to walk her the short steps to her door, so he did just that. Maybe this being in England had rubbed off on him, as good manners are not as dead in Australia as people say. Or at least it is present in this Australian man.

She pulled her hand free and fished in her brown sopping doused wet leather coat and pulled out two single damp keys on a keyring with the real estate's tag keeping them together. He said 'goodnight' for which she gave the best response, 'it doesn't have to be.'

Eddy smiled, kissed her cheek as she turned to open the door. 'Coffee? Beer?' she smiled over her shoulder as she led the way through the freshly painted blue door, into a landing where one door led to a bottom unit and her second key opened the nicotine-stained cream door, that was once a white to be confronted by a set of narrow blue-worn carpet stairs to ascend upstairs.

She led him up the flight of stairs, gently pulling him up, closer into her domain, around the rickety banister officially into her unit. They had come up in the middle of a narrow and long split-level room. Very deceptive from the dark brick front as it was surprisingly bigger than he would have thought. Substantially bigger than his unit. The front room was assessed around a dark brown banister that made the landing. Through the first door, the small oddly-shaped room was equipped with a dirty red sofa and chair that were covered with brightly coloured mismatched cloths which Eddy assumed were hers.

She remarked, as if she needed to justify her chosen furniture, that this was a furnished unit and the furniture was not her choice. It was as if the landlord had gone to the local Salvo's or other charity shop to pick up what he needed without any care if they went together. The green worn thin-to-the-thread carpet, the red sofa, the painted white legged kitchen table – which was described as a working station by the lending agent – with the chipped Formica yellow plastic top over a corkboard interior made the mismatch of the living room.

The television perched on the low bookshelf was covered in a thin layer of dust as if it has never been turned on in the time that she had been living there. A stack of books leaned on the screen that confirmed that it was in fact superfluous to requirements. While he surveyed the room from the threshold, out of nowhere, a ginger cat with lighter strips matching

Saoirse's own hair came flying out from behind the narrow space between the cream wallpaper and the dirty-red sofa. It was a young kitten that was in the playful stage of life.

'That's, well, that was Vesuvius,' she shouted after the kitten as she jumped the two steps away from the front room and vanished like the smoke of the eruption in which she entered. The next room in the corner was a bathroom that looked out to the street. A simple, cramped shower and toilet did the job that this closet required. The pink and blue flowers on the tiles and the pink design of the sink, bath tub with a crudely placed shower attachment over the top as well as a mirrored cupboard that was too small to hold her products which were stacked and leaning around the sink.

Opposite the banister was the large square bedroom in which Vesuvius had made herself, nestling on the white, thick doona. The simple large wooden bed looked perfectly placed on the varnished wooden floorboards. This room seemed to have the mark of Saoirse. As Eddy went near to say a proper hello she lashed out with a small, but very sharp claw that penetrated the skin and left a few small droplets of blood on the top of the bed. He was embarrassed and said sorry as he made matters worse by rubbing the blood into the doona further with the sleeve of his soggy light grey jumper. Saoirse was relaxed about it. She unsuccessfully muffled a laugh with her hand as her free hand rested on his shoulder.

She reassured him it was not his thought, thus, not to worry. She gave a long-lasting peck on his cheek. Eddy understood why the flame-haired kitten had been named after a volcano, the worse European volcanic eruption in history. And the fury was instantaneous, especially when all he was doing was going to say 'G'day'.

At the very back of the unit was a kitchen. Saoirse walked out with Eddy licking his wounds. Promptly emerging from the bathroom with two red fluffy towels as she floated like a drenched angel up the three steps to the kitchen. Eddy followed, walking closely, slowly and tenderly connected behind. The wet-stains of their feet leaving a trail on the wooden floorboards. The yellow and white design of the compact kitchen with tiles of a yellow floral design that made him wonder if a five-year-old designed it at a school art class back in the nineteen-sixties. The whole unit was a mismatch of colours. If he thought the living room was bad with the mismatch of furniture, he had found a worthy opponent to fight for the unwanted title.

A ghastly affair for which if you actually bought it, designed it, you would require containment in a ward with padded cells for having this awful creative imagination. The amount of money to make you want to invite people around would take some doing for Eddy. It was hideous. However, beggars cannot be choosers for cheap rent in Saxmundham. She dried her hair in the soft light of the unshaded swinging lightbulb. The light reflected like glittery confetti in her hair. Even at her less than glamourous, she looked amazing. A true beaut.

Saoirse leant across the single white mug, the single white plate and pair of cutlery items to the cupboard on the draining board to pull open the cupboard, to pull out two mugs and a jar of Nescafé blend coffee. They were actually going to have coffee. Eddy was slightly crestfallen by the turn of events as he thought, innocently, that coffee was a code for something else—sex.

He noticed as he surveyed between chatter while the kettle boiled that not a lot else was in that cupboard. The fridge was covered with reminders, bills, last final demands, as well as a single postcard from Ireland. As she pulled the door open, the light filled the dark brown kitchen carpet, reflecting its light off the drab, featureless dirty white tiles. Inside was nothing but half an unpeeled onion, a couple of soft blackening carrots and an open jar of strawberry jam with a teaspoon rammed inside left as she brought the milk out. Her hip gently swaying to knock the door shut.

She smelled it before adding it to the steaming black mugs of darker coffee before her. Eddy did not take milk in his coffee but felt not to remark on it as she poured a splash in his. However, Saoirse, after adding it without thinking, recalled her error. She got the moment of remembering flickering in her head. She said she was sorry for adding the milk without looking up from the caramel colour that bled into the black within the cup before asking Eddy if he wanted a fresh one.

Eddy remarked about beer being offered. It was an intended joke, for which Saoirse looked towards Eddy with a stunned look before catching on and smiling back. A soft retort followed by Eddy that the beverage was not important, but the company, plus she had no alcohol apart from neat Bacardi in her cupboards. Coffee, milk and Bacardi is only the concoction at the end of a bender. Eddy felt that neat Bacardi was ideal but did not want to risk his luck any more at this time. Tonight, was not only the night he shared the kiss he had been thinking about. That was as perfect as he thought it would be, but had made it inside her home. It was the perfect storm outside to give the perfect scenario.

A leaning kiss inadvertently turned the light off. In the moonlit spill of the kitchen, through the ceiling windows, they talked. She told him that she was a natural blonde but did not want the stereotypical view of being a dumb blonde to come through, so she dyed her hair ginger. Although most people would go the other way, this suited her and added to the enchanting story of her Irish roots. It was funny to Eddy as he laughed a short, nervous laugh at the idea of being pigeonholed by the colour of her hair. Although he could completely understand why she would do it.

The postcard, bent at the edges, creased in the frame, magnetically placed on the fridge was sent by her friend back in Ireland. It was of her hometown.

'May I?' Eddy asked as he plucked the postcard up from beneath the magnet to look at the image. A grey stone building on a narrow stone-fringed road. The flowers had covered the stonework so one side of the building was a vibrant pink leathery skin of leaves, whereas the other half was a green and brown leaves with only the bottom window left uncovered. The white-washed frames of the windows and doors made this look a captivating place. 'Where is this?'

'Cúnga Fheichín.'

'Bless you,' Eddy joked flirtingly.

'Okay. Okay. Cong, Mayo to you, north of Galway.' Eddy feigned recognition without having a remote clue to the whereabouts. 'The Irish name means Saint Feichin's which narrows in reference to the converging rivers. The home of Sir William Wilde, the father of Oscar Wilde.' These points did nothing more to rekindle any light of a memory.

Saoirse took the postcard from Eddy. Lingered on the building while feeling the longing connection of sentiment to her hometown under the soft stroke of her fingertips. She evidently missed home, but not enough to go back, just yet. 'One day,' she answered to Eddy's questioning, 'but not today', with a smile.

She reattached the postcard back to the fridge with a different lettered magnet. Eddy sensed that there was more to this story but did not delve into it.

They talked to daylight. Moving from room to room. They spent the night together. They did not sleep together, but they slept in the same bed. She wanted companionship. She wanted friendship. She wanted tonight to be about true feelings, not the first interactions in her home to be about sex. Eddy was the first male that she had invited into her home. In actual fact the only person. He respected her provocative mission to not overstep the boundaries she had risen up. If the truth be told Eddy actually enjoyed feeling the warmth of Saoirse next to him. Her body warmth. Her smell. Her soft breathing through the night. He did spend a majority of the night trying not to get his pounding erection to stab her in the back like the end of a broom.

A kiss on the cheek by the warm sun coming through the large windows soothingly woke Eddy up. He glanced over the delicate white shoulder of the bare flesh of Saoirse, kissed gently as his eyes led to the red digital display encased in the plastic black box, '07:42'. 'Shit!' he brashly exclaimed as he got his stuff together hastily with the realisation that he was late for work.

Saoirse awoke with a start as he bounded from the bed, the worn springs gave enough restraint to domino to her in a wave, and then she mumbled what was going on as she rubbed her eyes open. Eddy just kept cursing under his breath, searching for his clothes and rushing to pull his blue jeans on. Turning in circles, trying to find his socks. Then stopping to stare at the noise of her unhelpful laughter. Looking towards Saoirse as she started roar with waves of laughter. Eddy standing crouched over, his jeans half on. 'What is so funny?' he demanded as he spotted his sock in the claws of the temperamental kitten. Then proceeded to gingerly edge towards her.

'It's Wednesday,' between smiling teeth, 'we are both not working today.'

His pupils sank inside as he was finding the part of his brain that showed him his personal calendar. Lightbulb. Then he sunk back into Saoirse's arms as her shoulders tremored a sniggering unmuted laugh. Half his pale blue quicksilver shirt on, the other travelling off his back, jeans unbuttoned and one sock on. He kissed her on the forehead. Laughed a little in recognition to just how stupid he must have looked. Then kissed down her pointed freckled nose and to her rose-red lips. It was delicate. Passionate.

'Come back,' she whispered as she opened the doona like a curtain. He crawled back under the doona while wrestling off his clothes. They giggled in each other's company. She poked fun at Eddy. They fell asleep again. In each other's arms. The morning spent in, out, back in bed.

That morning was so comfortable, so right. By the late afternoon they went for a late lunch by the sea at the small fishing village ironically called Sizewell. It was a short thirty-minute bus route away. Through meandering tight narrow laneways around the pockets of picturesque villages, patchwork farmlands while skirting narrow stone-built walls that crumbling in sections which made the wall somewhat pointless. Young sheep playfully filled the fields.

The spring feel of being warm enough for the Brits and cold enough for the Aussie was the only difference for Eddy. In spite of the beautiful British countryside which was still excitingly new to him, he had no eyes for the scenery, his masterpiece was next to him. They both were in a world of their own. He had eyes for Saoirse. She had eyes for him. They talked, laughed and embraced the charming scenic journey, which went by like seconds.

They find themselves leaving work for the day to stumble upon a pub called The Vulcan Arms. Oh, the irony, one pub for another. They look out, a stone throws away from the dark blue crashing waves of the sea before dipping their heads to enter under the stone archway to be inside. Eddy laughed at the name for which they both shared as a private joke as they nestled on the stools at the bar. To make matters sardonically worse, just like the one in which they both worked in, this had links to the smugglers trade for which the landlord felt the need to tell them in all its detail. The uptight Major-looking landlord disturbed their light-hearted conversation to abruptly tell them in a superior, condescending tone while he placed both the palms of his hands over the bar.

'Vulcan actually was the Roman God of blacksmiths and...' he stated matter-of-factly as he leaned in closer to them. His teeth tarnished with a nicotine-stained grit as he spoke through in obvious annoyance. 'And... And considering that you are standing in an old blacksmith's house, it has been the name here since 1844'.

Eddy and Saoirse looked at each other as the landlord uses his hands to push himself away after his brief altercating sermon. Before his back turns, still in the motion of pushing himself up from the bar and back to polishing the glasses, they laugh out loud. They had no intention of hiding the fact that they found his dementia nothing more than ridiculous. Through their giggles, they ordered a couple of drinks.

Sensing the steel-eyed focus of their landlord as he slammed them down in front of them, causing a slight spillage of the froth to hit the bar they pick-up their beers, to move to a table by the window away from earshot equipped with the food menu. The small alcove of the white wooden crossed windows around the curve of the booth was ideal for an intimate conversation. They decided what they wanted to eat. Eddy went up to order with the two empty glasses, as he got two more drinks as well.

In this brief transaction, he attempted an apology to the landlord if he caused offence; that was not his intention. This fell on deaf ears for which Eddy did not mind as nothing was going to ruin this day. They both went for the British classic of battered cod and chips with mushy peas. The landlord, still unsmiling, took the order as he watches Eddy return.

He has a stance and face of a Major from World War I. He would have looked completely at home in the green felt of the soldier's attire, standing in the trenches and barking out orders. After Eddy returned to collect the cutlery for the food, once again the landlord leaned over the bar and ruthlessly spoke a warning, 'Beware of the young lady dressed in black.'

Eddy must have looked baffled as his look was very true to how he was feeling.

'You did not like the history,' the landlord went on, stifling Eddy's interruptions of protest at his misunderstanding, 'so I will tell you that the place is haunted by a young lady dressed in black. She takes the forms in, also, other young ladies.'

The landlord glanced with a flick of his eyes in the direction of Saoirse staring out of the window, the sun beaming in a column of white light over the floor. Eddy started to protest his innocence again, stating that he was genuinely interested but the landlord had returned to the back of the bar. Polishing his glasses that did not need polishing. Uninterested in Eddy's efforts at resolution. He waved his arm in a show of indifference as he walked back to the booth. Looking towards the door like a guarding fierce dog rather than a welcoming landlord he glanced to the booth to see Eddy tell Saoirse the warning with a fleeting glimpse in his direction.

The awkward exchange was unwelcoming, but Eddy thought to argue the fact was going to make no difference as he had made the first impression and they was no changing. Eddy mentioned the strange warning. They laughed. They did not care. Nothing, but nothing was going to ruin this day. They first day on an open highway where nothing will stop them. They continued to explore each other's bodies and minds over the magnificent bar meal served by the unimpressive host.

Over the coming weeks they continued to learn more about each other with not a night spent apart. Either he stayed at hers or she stayed at his. They worked under the misunderstanding that their private life was just that. They tried to make it unclear that they were mates outside of work. However, it transpired that everyone around them knew. The owners, the co-workers were not daft. The town itself was small. It took only a local to see them in the town for the rumour to get back.

Australians did not stay here long. They continued the mysterious transparent veil of Eddy and Saoirse's relationship in the full knowledge of what was going on. It was only a when they were caught being a little too handy in the beer cellar that the veil was removed, as clean and swiftly as a magician removing the white tablecloth from a table setting. Everyone talked about it openly. Behind their backs.

Ken came down softly into the cellar to change a keg. For a rather large-set man he was surprisingly light-footed. He caught Eddy with one hand up her working white shirt and her hand down beneath the apron. Ken was shocked and mad at the same time but respectful enough to turn his back as they issued an embarrassed explanation that were all lies. He was a man of the world, not a young guppy.

Ken saw the funny side and made jokes, aimed at embarrassing them. They could be open at least. With all these laughs and stories, Saoirse was hiding one, a gigantic one. An undercurrent was definitely, however slowly, defiantly roaming under her soft-hearted light amusement amidst the connection of hearts.

Eddy thought about the next colossal titling of his own earthly world with this particular deep memory with affection, tinged with sadness. He could see her as clear as if it was a mere few minutes ago, standing, shuffling before him in his imagination. He could hear the words that left her quivering mouth so clearly. He could smell the mask of relief as she presented herself in the barest way imaginable. Fully clothes, but nakedly exposed. He felt her visible fear that she shared with him. Laying out her heart on the floor, unprotected, no longer in the shadows, but out in the open.

Eddy had realised certain aspects of her that she kept at arm's length. Why she wanted to keep them so concealed. So dark in the shadows of her mind. The rumbled down layers frightened Saoirse, that weighted expectancy of how Eddy would react. Would he flee? Would this be too much? With that one-sided conversation their bond grew with strength and resolve. Eddy sat down listening, his mouth opening every now and again to say something but then retracted living him breath open mouthed air.

After this revelation that left her naked, she was connected with Eddy as she had never been to anyone. She collapsed slowly into a heap on the floor as the exertions of the story had taken their toll. She was weak. Eddy went to her. Pulling a throw from the sofa he had been sitting on her covered her with it. She was not cold, but she was uncontrollably shaking. He cuddled her on the floor. She accepted his arms as she had hers wrapped around her jean-covered knees.

He softly kissed the hair on the top of her head. She cried. He had never heard anyone cry like this with such emotional fury, pain, torment in his young life and he would never want to hear this again. Everyone has a story, Eddy was no exception. Saoirse was no exception. Some are happy. Some are sad. Some tragic. Hers was a torrid repressing story of abuse. A mistreatment of sexual abuse for which the family were happy for it to be a little girls' overactive imagination in a web of deceit that made her feel, well, no words could describe that level of loneliness. To Eddy, it was pure cruelty.

The first time she spoke of the grave momentous part of her, Saoirse speedily sketched over the details like a skater over ice. She spoke about the events in a detached fashion. Almost as if it had happened to someone else. She used bullet points as transparent as pillared icicle harpoons that speared her heart open at the very scars that would never heal. Brimming with tears the ice-age memories melted before him in her eyes. A time forgotten was being thawed to live once again.

When it got too raw, too close to the mark, she would cut off. Instantly change the subject or move. She would hide behind a fake smile that give away more than the intended warmth of the smile was supposed to display. He went in for a reassuring hug. She moved away. She did not want to be touched. It was as if her expressing this brutal ferocious act was linking back to another Him. A touch by Eddy would have jarred like a touch by Him. She still, and always will regain the scars from the spurs of this horrific encounter. She will never forget. Always unsuccessfully try. Yet, never wanting to fully forget her past. As, at the end of the day it did make her stronger. No-one should have to go through what she endured, still endures. For her family did not believe it. Still do not believe her.

She went off to make tea. Eddy sat and waited. He was not sure what to do. Whether to follow or leave her. She was about to cry so he let her have those moments to herself. Saoirse was in the kitchen. She threw two teabags into two cups, leaned on the counter and wanted to scream. She turned around. It was time for her to lay her soul. For her the scars remain that in the physical action of sex can only be done in one position and this still causes a bit of pain. A bit of discomfort.

The position from behind with her bottom pointing skywards. This seems to be the smoothest way for Eddy's penis to pleasure Saoirse without the reminder of the past. Without the discomfort. It is a sad moment for her. She enjoys the pleasure of sex. She enjoys the physical expression but finds it hard to disconnect from the past. The pain brings back the past like a speeding freight-train to the impending collusion of two worlds colliding. Eddy found this odd, he knew that a story was manifesting itself in her soul, burning her core.

Just as Eddy was going to get up the door swung open. She stood before him. Pacing, fidgeting, worrying biting her nails, gnawing the skin on the bottom of her thumb. She was ready, but the words did not want to be released. Or, they did, but she was apprehensive. She had never told anyone. Why? Foolishly, she was embarrassed. As when she did, she was thought of as a liar.

Mortified to be in the position, in this position that she feels she needs to explain herself. She does not, Eddy offered words of discouragement for her not to continue, that she does not owe him an explanation, but she placed a hand up. Cut him off, looked away. 'Please…' she spoke in barely a whisper with a crack in her voice, 'please. I…need. I want you to know.' With a few deep breaths, she told her graphically layered horrific story.

'I was, it happened, it…' she did not know how to start. Eddy sat on the edge of the sofa, so wanting to put an arm around her but intrusively knowing discretion was the correct approach here, hence he stayed on the sofa and waited with implicated breath of what will transpire. She spoke after a few minutes of meditational breathing, 'When I was a young girl…'

For when she was younger, when innocence needed to be maintained, there are some people that selfishly think about themselves, their own wants and needs. This, this want goes far above anyone else want. Anyone else's desires. This person was a friend of the family. How often does Eddy read this in the newspapers? How often do we see this in the television? They have the trust; there, they are invited into the family circle, only to betray it. This person got away with it. Saoirse tried to tell her father, once. Her father dismissed it as a story, a barefaced lie. Dismissed it as a want for attention. A want to be with her workaholic father.

At the young age of seven years old, she was subjected to the family friend. Family fiend more like. It started as a small cupping of the bottom…however, Eddy is by no means saying that small is insignificant. Small is huge. People go through different things in different ways and people should not judge people for they reactions and the way they handle situations. However, this small start was an older man who should have known better than that, invading her personal space. For the sake of this passage, Eddy in his mind calls this family friend Bruce.

On this particular warm summer morning, Bruce and Saoirse were left alone on the family cream, leather soft couch. She sat there with her legs dangling off the edge, unable the reach the floor. A perfect picture of innocence while she stroked a small pink plastic brush through her doll's soft blonde hair in similar white summer dress to match the one she had on. 'Could I be this pretty?' the young Saoirse mused.

Bruce asked her doll's name, which he was told was 'Caoimhe'. He asked if he could help dress Caoimhe. He used the doll as a way of gaining, getting her trust. It worked. After a time, he was allowed to babysit Saoirse and Caoimhe. It was fun, they played. This playtime seemed innocent with Caoimhe and her other dolls, her plastic toy horses, her Wendy house outside that her father had built for her.

It started so very quiet. An eerie atmosphere was alive in the room, between them, with a painful opening of a wound stinging with the reminiscence of suffering anguish breeding innermost grief and affliction. Eddy struggled to hear her over her own breath, her heavy breathing that was masking her trembling, unsteady voice. Her power of speech lost beneath the layers of memories that buried this particular memory. Saoirse was barely audible over the thick silence within the room. Her hesitation. Her sombre pausing in the middle of sentences, ready but unprepared, wary to continue. The well-guarded words where ingrained into the pit of her stomach.

She struggled to search for those simple words to bring out. She then wanted, but, did not want to bring them to the light. Air them after so many torturous years would be reliving the agonising misery for a second time. That she had held the burden within her like a guilt-ridden hefty, thick chain that tried in vain to suffocate, to kill was an accolade of her strong formidable character. Yet the undesirable, and uninvited burden weighted her down. Hence, like a leaking tap, the dripping became more persistent. The water flows, but these were not waters to surf and play on. These would maim and destroy the incorruptibility virtue of what it means to be a child.

Eddy remembers the time, the point in the enlightened description that Saoirse erupted like a volcano with the seething sensations coming out like lava, the quiver in her voice like the earth shaking with the force and the pressure, with all the years of stress. The fury. She had mentioned little bits, and pieces, drop hints of what happened but changed the subject to something else when she was getting close to the nerve, the root of the problem.

On a completely unrelated windy night, where nothing out of the ordinary was happening. The branches of the leafless trees gently brushed the window pane. They listened to the soothing folk music of Nick Drake as they laid in the cool draught from the slightly loosened seal of the window. The mood shifted rapidly, the venomous ambiance tainted the well of comfortable silence. The screen of the pleasant evening when the outside world was less than pleasant seethed into the space they shared. There she revealed everything for the very first time. All out, open to Eddy's responsive empathies. The water, the rivers of distresses, the floods of troubled pain and sorrow. All the dark guts, with…no glory.

It was a late night at her unit. A late Tuesday night where they had finished for their own two days off. She laid in the dark after they had made love and they were both looking up to the ceiling. Naked, the sheen of sweat still lingering on their bodies. Their hands laid by their sides. The last track of the Pink Moon album finished. The silent hum of the low volumed speakers. A soft click as the power saving mode kicked in and the stereo turned itself off. It was silent, a comfortable calming silence.

Then it happened. And then it materialised. The one, the only experience that had caused her such torment. The hidden story that she laid down to rest, but not be forgotten. The awful story came out. She started to speak out. Towards the ceiling. To no-one in particular, but hoping that Eddy was hearing her words. Her words were almost unattached, sounding, once again like someone else was talking, that this thing happened to someone else. But no voice can make that sound of that inner ordeal.

'At first I thought it was a fun game. I didn't understand what was happening,' Saoirse began with trembling unease. Eddy gripped her hand ever so slightly to let her know that he was listening. She did not grip his hand back, although with her thumb she stroked his back. After a slight pause, after a tight squeeze of her eyes, she guardedly continued. She was cagily cautious as she gently pulled her hand away from Eddy's and placed it over her chest. Like she was in a coffin lying in wait, she positioned her hands over her chest, tightly, legs straight with her toes skywards under the doona.

'He was kneeling beside me. I…I could feel the warmth of his breath close to my neck. Then the game changed. I…I did not see it coming. I did not see it happen…ing. He moved around and, he, he, he pushed, HE PUSHED me. Hard, hard. Too hard. HARD. AGHHHHH. Onto the carpet. He, then, HE THEN lifted my, my, my dress up. This was not a game. Not a GAME I…I wanted to play. He lifted my, my dress high. I put my hands out to try…try and…' she paused.

She regained herself with some short, sharp breaths. 'I REALLY, I Really TRIED T…to stop him. He just waved them away. My pleas. My. He was strong. Me. Weak. I weak, I was weak. I tried. I really tried. I TRIED, AGHHHH. He pulled down my knickers. He leaned over me. He leaned over…me. His legs pinning mine down. My legs were. They were trapped. I started to silently cry. He shushed me. I couldn't get him off me. I screamed. And, and, he, HE…He HIT, he hit me. Later, he said to my father I fell. I fell. I FELL. ME. I FELL. AND, and, and he believed him.

'This crisp smacking sound please, it pleased him. He smiled through the single index finger as he shushed me…again. He shushed me. And, I…I did. I did. He pulled my legs, wide apart. I tried to get up. I TRIED. I really tried, but HE PUSHED ME A-Gain. He pushed me down. I yelled. I yelled out. No-one helped. I was…No-one helped me. Alone, I was so alone. Helpless. His large hand covered mine. My mouth. His DIRTY HAND COVERED MY, MINE, MY MOUTH. I…I could hardly.

'I couldn't breathe. I TRIED. His hand stayed there. With his free hand he undid his pants. Pulled out his…his, dick. I tried to move. I tried. TRIED I TRIED. His body was now squashing me, mine. It hurt. I was pinned to the carpet. Him on top. His body. Hurt.' She paused, not for the first time.

Eddy felt the mattress vibrate as her body shook. The only sound was her heavy breathing that silenced his shallow breaths. He tried to breath quiet. She continued with the slight quiver uncontrolled as it entered her voice. 'His body. His breath. His warmth. His stubble. HIS.

HIM ON ME.' She spoke in a breathless low voice, 'With a violent thrust he forced his. Him in. Him in me. He pushed his dick. His dick inside me. It hurt. It hurt so much. I screamed. It hurt. It, my voice, scream. It hurt, hurt. It was muffled. He shushed me again. He told me it was a game. A fun game. Fun? F-U-N, AGHHHH. I thumped his back. My small fists on his large back. I tried to move. I wanted to move. I couldn't move. I wanted to get up. To run. I could hardly breathe. My stomach hurt. Blood then flowed. It really hurt. Blood came from between my legs. The smell. The pain. The hurt. The…smell. Smudging the carpet. He pulled out. GRUNT-ed. He pushed his dick in his pants. He grabbed my knickers. He used MY knickers. MY KNICKERS, my knickers to clean the blood from the carpet. My knickers.

'I sobbed. I did not yell. I was hurt. Hurting. Hurt. I…I was in pain. I did not know what happened. I did not understand. I was only seven, seven and a half years old. He cleaned up the blood. With. My. Knickers. And then carried me upstairs. I was limp. Weak. Exhausted. He washed me. Put me to bed. I, weak, limp. Closed the door. Left the room. I never saw him again. Come back. How could he do this? How could he think of doing this? How could he think it would be OK? Was OK. I lay in bed, on my side, my thumb in my mouth and quietly cried.

'Tears of pain. Tears of not understanding. Tears of fear. I was so frightened. I did not know if he was going back, going to come back. I heard my parents coming back. I heard him laugh. My parents laugh. I felt so sick. How could he do this? It was not OK? I was not OK. I hurt. I heard him say to my father that I had fell over while running in the house. That I was ok but wanted to go to bed. That I had hurt myself? The next day I told my dad. He didn't believe me. He told me off. He actually shouted at me. Me. ME. ME! AGHHHH! ME…ME…Me…as…as…as if I made it…up. I never told anyone else. I. My father who was my hero told me off. I lost trust. My own father took my trust away, when…I tried to regain it.

'Later, I heard he was dead. He was dead. Died. I…I had to go to the funeral. I…wanted to make sure…make sure he was dead. Dead. He was not coming back. My father was there. He was sobbing at a lost friend. That was. Is. Is, was…is my closure. My father I love, but…I will NOT forgive him. That was when I decided to come to England. A new start. Away…a-way…'

Saoirse turned away from Eddy. She was the young version of herself. She felt like the youngster back then. She had finished her story. Eddy was sure that she was silently crying. He was sure her shoulders were shaking in the gloom of the bedroom laced with the torment of her story. Yet he heard nothing. Eddy turned to place his hand around hers. He did not know what to do. So, he gently stroked her back and laid parallel to hers with enough distance for their warmth to touch each other but no physical contact but his single hand on her naked shoulder.

Saoirse knew that this was not the way a person should react. She knew, but did not understand what had just happened. She was cast in her mind. She was the little girl again. She was impulsively crying as she rocked with her arms around her pink and white frilly dress with the spots of fresh blood above her thighs as she cradled her knees close to her chest. She impulsively cried. She knew something was not right. Something was not going to be the same again. That day when innocence was brutally taken away. That day never returned.

Eddy was amazed. He was in awe at Saoirse. How she dealt and is still dealing with the pain. To feel isolated, abandoned, as no one believed her. By looking at her now, you would not expect such a brutal, evil past that she had occurred. That continued to trouble her.

The next day, and the days that followed this topic was never brought up again. He did not want to push what happened. He felt privileged to have been the person for whom she confided to. He did not want her to talk of these things unless she wanted. Considering that she was not ready to express to any other person. That Eddy is still essentially a stranger it surprised her, as much as him to how graphic she got.

Her trust issues are easily shattered, so she does not give it away easily. She does not want to commit, and in her eyes be a burden on the other person. She does not know if the experience has affected her ability to have children in the future. As it has yet to come up in any of her relationships, she feels that it is not something that she is going to find out, until she has to. If she even wants kids at the risk that the same treatment could happen to them. She thinks about the scenarios often.

These hypotheses of maybes. Her things, her thoughts about what could have been and could become. The moment comes into her mind. As quick as they enter, she quickly distinguishes the thoughts to erase her broodings. She is not ashamed by her actions, but it is her way of coping. She has been doing in for so many years that it is a way of life, second nature. The only way she had managed to cope. She is strong. With Eddy, stronger.

The sun was casting small windows of light over the hideous tip-worthy carpet. Somewhere in the distance a truck honked its horn as it went passed the busy main road at the end of the street. All was good. This was a rare Sunday off that they shared. They were happily content in each other's company. The landlord, Ken, tried to initiate a Sunday off every month for all staff but seeing that they were a couple, it was a lot harder to accommodate. Hence, this Sunday was long removed, a long-time overdue weekend off.

They did nothing in the morning but spend the day as a couple, doing couple things. They went for coffee, read the newspaper, couple things. Nothing exciting but in its own special way exceptionally stimulating. The day had flown so as they let their very late lunch digest, they are in the front room relaxing, more. It was already late in the afternoon when Eddy looked over at Saoirse as she nursed a cup of tea in the palms of her hand. The day had raced too fast past but not escaped the moments.

He gazed at her. He tried to be blasé with this but ended up shifting his gaze from his book to her often. The sun positioned at the perfect point in the sky to shred its light over her porcelain cheekbones as it slowly signalled a final goodbye. He wondered what she was thinking. She was hypnotic in her scrutiny of the caramel brown of her tea swirling as she gently made a whirlpool using her teaspoon, let it rest to listen to the soft clink on clink as it moved clumsily around the cup. They had effortlessly got to the stage where they were comfortable in their silence. They did not have to fill the void with noise, activities or entertainment.

This, however, did not mean that Eddy did not think of what was going on inside her mind. Her mind was always working, always ticking and thinking. Ever now-and-again she should would blurt out with the most random, peculiar facts although not meant to be funny they made Eddy roar. Earlier this morning, before the sun had fully risen, they were walking about the golden leaves of the wooden small forest behind the town when she came out with a comment about ants. This still made him laugh when he thought about it.

'What if small people were inside the ants?' she contemplated out loud as she watched a trail train of ants shimmering quickly over a damp, brown large branch. 'What if we did not know, but ants were in fact tanks to a tiny, small, smaller than small person. A people army that lived in the soil, but it was not soil. The soil was homes, houses, a wee little village…' she went on with this casual wacky train of consideration as Eddy had nothing to say.

What could he say? He just had a stupid, dumbstruck expression of bafflement as he looked down at the ants. When she eventually looked at Eddy, when they both looked at each other's faces, he could not conceal it anymore, he roared. She playfully smacked his shoulder with 'stop it!' over again which seemed to heighten his expressed amusement into hysterical soft, probing teasing. She giggled as well. It was beautiful.

Back to reality, this sunny cool afternoon he was expecting something as bizarre to leave her pencil-thin pink lips. While wearing one of his cream deformed jumper with a crest with 'ESD' and 'Eastern Suburbs' etched in a blue emblem with red, white and blue stripes, under in which a red banner in white capitals was displayed in capitals 'R.U.F.C'. His old rugby top that he should, but never will throw out. A jumper that was far too big for her, in truth never fit him but drooped on his slender frame. But he smiled a smile that said more than many words could never express. For in his eyes, she could not have looked more casually glamorous.

The colours had been washed out as it hung on her. The original soft feel turned to a hard, brittle bristle of rough smooth linen like a soft dry sponge. Nevertheless, uncaring it draped down over her like a blanket, without the form it once had, past her naked knees that were folded over on the small single red felt seater. Apart from a pair of dark purple socks stretched high on her ankles, and a matching bra this was the only attire she had on. She was looking so calm reading her book. So, at peace. So, at ease.

One hand with her cup of tea, the other supporting her book in her hand with her thumb holding the pages down. It is a testament to her character that she has come out of the other end with such freedom, the ability to find such reconciliation. This is how she lived. Nothing got her down. Many people said that they lived their life as if it was the last, or the last day as if it was their last, but she actually did while shedding sensations of harmony and goodwill. She rarely said no to a question, she found the yes or accommodated a yes. She was always up for an adventure, a challenge. She had a zest for life.

Saoirse, her Gaelic name aptly means freedom. Eddy was thinking this as he nursed his own cup of tea, his own book opens on his lap when she looked up, away from the paper leaves fanning on her open book, towards him. He smiled, sensing her gazing in his direction. Looking up, he waited for her to say something.

'Do you want to go to Portugal?' she asked in a nonchalant offhand manner.

Eddy was not expecting that, so asked her to repeat the question with a tremulous half-laugh in his voice. 'What? Someday—'

'I leave tomorrow,' she interrupted him so flippantly, so blasé.

She had a chance to write about Portugal for a supplement in the Daily Mail newspaper within the travel magazine. It was a passion of hers to write. She wrote so well, mainly childlike stories that told a story within a story, a parable if you will. She had been spreading her resume around every conceivable media outlet that was online to get her own career moving. She did not want to be a server her career, she wanted to be a paid writer.

'What?' he breathed a smile through a frown as he perched on the edge of the sofa, his book falling to the carpet. Eddy could not leave. Especially tomorrow. He had a job. A career. He strongly regarded himself on being loyal. As a way of diffusing the situation, saving face and at the same time letting Saoirse know that he did want to go tomorrow, he mentioned that he would go in tomorrow and talk about the possibility of having some time off.

This must have happened at least a few days before. Eddy was slightly perplexed she did not forewarn him of this potential change in their immediate life. A life they were building, the foundation was not even set for a monumental change to occur. He was stunned, flabbergasted that she could be so cloak-and-dagger about this development that affected him, as much as her.

'What are you going to do? What about the Smugglers?' Eddy probed.

'Me. Nothing. I, well. Not going in. Not intending on going in. Going back.'

'What? What do you expect me to do?'

'The same. Simple,' she voiced with a shrug of the shoulders that said as much as her words. Nothing.

This simple question; do you want to go to Portugal? To a complex answer. This hotbed of a topic turned quickly into an argument of hostile antagonisms. The fight was as unsuspected in its critical advancement. As quick to fire, to engulf her flammable question for which the row fiercely burned from was dangerously getting rampantly out of control. It blew in with such immense force that Eddy did not even notice before it was too late that he was reacting by shouting aloud. Out very LOUD. An inferno of tension had entered the calm space.

'SIMPLE! SIMPLE?'

'You don't want to go?' Saoirse assumed by his lack of words.

'WHAT?' Eddy expressly shouted out with amazement in response to her statement. 'Seriously? WHAT!' He did not want an argument but found himself shouting in shock at her presumed scepticism.

'What! WHAT? Stop saying WHAT. Do it, then do it. WHAT IS STOPPING YOU? Really?' She walked towards Eddy as if offering a challenge. A single tear had starting to roam the creases of her pixie nose. Her red face to his white face.

'I…I…' he was stuttering, he did not know what to say.

'Come on,' Saoirse interrupted. 'What is IT?' Spittle surged through her gritted teeth. Each light blow felt like a cannonball of hatred on Eddy's face.

Silence. A long pause. A lull before another pending storm. A silence that felt like it was a second to Saoirse, rather than the minutes that Eddy felt.

'Look.' He struggled to find the words. 'I want…to be with…with you. I want to be with you.' Eddy attempted to distinguish the fiery scorching kindling of another short argument.

'Come,' she moved to the window. Looking out at nothing, her future.

Another silence followed. 'But…' Eddy hushed in an aspired breath.

'What?' Another interruption. Another silence. 'TELL ME,' she swiftly turned around and was pacing around the small room between the edge of the sofa and the solitary tall standing lamp next to the window frame. She was avoiding eye contact. Well, for the most part but to emphasis a point at each end of a sentence, she would turn, use her eyes to pierce through and into the soul of Eddy's like a blunt knife wound made with a spoon. The eyes spoke a questioning glare full of emotional hurtful questions unspoken. Eddy was silent apart from stumbling out one-worded responses like 'I…', 'but…' and the ridiculous 'calm down'. This was like prodding a wild rampant bear with a red-hot poker.

'What is stopping you?' Saoirse demanded an answer. She leant down in front of him. Placed her hands over his fastened fingers in the prayer position. Her voice still raised but softer, 'Tell me. What is stopping…you?' This question was the start of a raging torrent of questions. The official end of the lull.

'I want to be with you.

'I want you.

'I want you to come.

'I NEE…What is stopping you?

'WHAT?

'ME?

'If you want to go.

'Go!

'Walk out.

'Never come back.

'If you walk out, don't come back.

'Just don't…

'I don't want excuses.

'I don't want someone.

'Someone who doesn't want me.

'Doesn't want to be with me…so just leave.

'Now.

'NOW.

'If you don't want to go with me.

'LEAVE.

'NOW.'

Eddy was like a wounded animal. Weak, limp on the sofa. He had not been struck physically, but emotionally it was ruthlessly inhumane. The words where filled with such fury, a side he had never seen of her, that he did not know how to react. Each word of ferocity stabbed him like a psychotic killer wielding a small sharp dagger to repeatedly make a new wound. He was cowered on the edge of the sofa. She had slumped, exhaustingly on the peeled white ledge of the window, looking down. His eyes filling with an impending flood of tears. His hands were slumped on his knees.

He watched through the blur Saoirse suddenly push up, then start to move, fidget. Her tears streaming down her delicate cheeks. She was unfazed to hide her emotions. Her eyes were blood red, puffy, her cheeks burning on fire. She had been shouting with a vicious ferocity that Eddy had never heard from her. She was scared. He knew that this was a reaction to her being committed to Eddy. But, did she need to be so cruel. She had shown her so much of her world. He knew it was hard for her, he treasured this from her. More than she had ever shared with anyone. He felt as privileged that her long-awaited burden was shared. This scared her. It scared her. The whole vulnerability scared her. She had never felt so strong, but at the same time so weak to be dependent on someone.

Eddy's pride was wounded and he reaction was stupid responses. It was foolish that in the midst of this battle he was thinking of himself. He hated this thought that cropped into his head. His silence and stuttering answers gave nothing away. Gave her nothing to how he felt of her. This frustrated her, adding to the annoyance that Saoirse felt to why he could not just say yes, yes, he would go. He was having the same passages pass through his head like a stuck record. Although he was silent his mind was furiously noisy like a room full of typewriters that wrote the same thing over, and over again. The thoughts raced across his mind one after the other like a not-so-merry-go-round. He nervously picked at his nails.

He fidgeted as he watched her storming pace stirring the aura of the calm room within the brewed storm. Of course, he wanted to go. Yes, he wanted to go, but he wanted to be transparent with his bosses. He always had his word. When he had nothing growing up, he had his word. Yes, of course he wanted to be with her, but he did not want to let anyone down in the process. The last thought scared and surprised him; he loved her.

Yes, he loved her.

This admittance to himself surprised him. He had never truly loved anyone. Amongst the chaotic carnage that surrounded him. The assault of questionings in hurtful gunfire was violent in its honesty. The bruised battle of love was being played. Although they both did not realise it was happening, around them, within them. The fury was passion. The truth was he loved Saoirse. He was happy at the thought of the future, with her. He was unhappy that she might not be in it.

The argument fanned again. Going around in circles. The same questions, statements and acquisitions were being fired at Eddy. Back to the start. And, repeated in an unending merry-go-round. This went on before tiredness came in.

'You must have known this sooner. Why the FUCK? You have been secretive?'

BANG!

The force of the living room door slamming shut, buckling on its fragile hinges behind Saoirse. They never swore at each other. He was thinking it in the silence. Every thought came back to the first one. Then he released it. With all the thinking of those words he said them in the worse possible way. The door was still rattling when Eddy immediately took flight.

BANG!

The bedroom door slammed. He fiercely snatched open the door to see Saoirse bawling. One word. That was all it took. The passion in which she spoke it in a snarling affectionate way told him to back off. To give her space.

'Don't', so soft, so full of painful ordeals of anguish.

The noise of the argument was shut at this moment. He returned to the hallway, leaving the door open. A suffocating silence followed him in the narrow room. The friction from the noise and carnage was still present. Eddy found himself seating on the mix-matched sofa, for which he did not know how he got to the living room. The haphazard collection of colours and material of the sofa resembled his heart, mind, and instinct. Saoirse was on the comfortable bed which resembled his innermost feelings. Clarity. The one thing they both were doing was staring at the floor. Unblinking, very awake, unsleeping. Crying.

He thought of one simple question. 'What made him happy?' Followed by 'What did he want?' Then the all-important; 'What he could not be without at that moment?'

He had that love passage embedded in his mind. He loved Saoirse. Sometimes it is really just that simply. After all, it is called taking the leap. So, Eddy should jump. Really, what was stopping him? She asked it, Eddy thought of it. Eddy could not take it anymore. He wanted to go. He had no obligation to The Smugglers Tunnel. He wanted to see if this could actually go the distance. Hardly no time had passed, scanty a minute, but he did not want to be away from her, especially at this time.

Eddy felt weak at his knees as he rose up. He buckled as he crawled out the living room to the landing with his tale between his legs. He gently knocked on the open door. No answer. He was not surprised. She had made it abundantly clear that she wanted her own space, yet he was defying her. He slowly, slightly opened the ajar door further. He craned his head around leaving his body behind the door. The red glow from the alarm clock reflected her open eyes that stared through him.

He softly apologised and stated he did always want to go. He asked if he could come in. A grunt of indifference came from the bed. Nothing more, so he took it as a yes to enter. He gradually passed into the darkness letting the smooth, soft moonlight penetrate a shadow of him in the doorway. He felt like a schoolchild that had been summoned to the headmistresses' office. He perched at the edge of the bed, she moved herself away from him. Looking out with his arms resting on his knees. His head slung over. He could not look at her while she was so distressed.

He spoke in a deliberate whisper. He spoke about what he was feeling. This shocked Eddy. It must have shocked Saoirse. He was not a touchy-feely kind of person. He never talked about his feelings. As talking out about it would be a major flaw on his masculine persona. He spoke about what she made him feel like. What he wanted to do. Why he hesitated. Then he spoke the three words.

'I love you,' Eddy whispered. 'I never want you to feel that hurt again.'

Eddy got up to move. He said the words that he had never said, never said and meant to anyone before. He felt embarrassed and wanted to move away. A warm hand on his rising shoulder pulled him back to the bed. He did not turnaround. He felt her hot, tear moist cheek on the back of his shoulder. A tender peck of her lips. The tears that he was struggling to keep in his eyes since the start of the fight came out in an uncontrolled, red-hot intense flood. He gently collapsed on the edge of the bed. His back to hers.

He was, not for the first time, embarrassed. He had let his demeanour evaporate. For the first time since they had met, he felt he could say anything. He was not afraid of being honest. He was afraid of the vulnerability. He wanted nothing more than what he had at this moment. Together they had let their guard down. No secrets, just sincerity.

'So, you're coming?' She calmly searched for the answer she wanted to hear.

'Yes, but,' there was always a but, 'but, I can't leave tomorrow. I will go to work and leave the next day. I will meet you there. When is your flight?'

They discussed a lot of ways to meet sooner. Her flight was in the evening. He may be able to leave then. Leave together.

It was a while before they fell asleep. She had cradled her arm around his body in the foetus position for hours. They did not speak. No words were needed. After the tears had finally subsided, he felt he was composed enough to look at Saoirse. She smiled back at him. They shared a passionate moment. Although they did not make love that night they talked. They kissed. They explored they bodies, mind and just before they fell asleep in each other arms they spoke the words to one another with the breath of each word being felt on the skin. The eyes connected. The spirit, soul united. Heart beating as one.

'I love you.'

Eddy woke from his slumber, but felt like he had not slept a single wink. Saoirse stirred a murmured 'morning' that grunted out of her exhaled breath as he closed the bedroom door om his way to work. She was still holding a little vestigial resentment from last evening's row. This, of course, could be Eddy being a tinge paranoid. Maybe traced with the laced sensation of guilt for his part in yesterday's argument. Then again, she was more than likely vested with her undisturbed slumber and nothing more. He puffed his way up the hill that seemed steeper than the previous days. Sweat was beading down his brow on not a particular warm morning.

He was weighed down with the feel of apprehensively trepidation, bordering on fearful expectation of what was ahead of him. He did not know the reaction. Yet, there was a different unique feeling in his demeaner. He had never felt so clear headed in what he wanted in his life. The consequences of yesterday's laid bare honesty. The surprising fashion where the weakness was highlighted had given the day an aftermath of lightened energy in each, hard step. He had decided to arrive earlier into work by a full hour to discuss putting his verbal contract on hold. Ken knew straightaway that something was up. He did not move from behind the bar. His hands placed, looking down at a nervous, stuttering Eddy who stood on the other side.

Eddy glazed over the whole reason. He did not explain what had happened with Saoirse's job offer, but moreover that he had a chance to go on holiday with a cheap ticket. He asked for a holiday. Ken strode away from the bar, turning his back on Eddy. Eddy sat on the high stool. He asked again for a holiday of sorts, but knew he had not worked there long enough to warrant such a claim.

This lack of notice, where his mind saw Saoirse in his imagination already packing for the airport, was not taken lightly. He was told that he would not have to leave, as he would be sacked if he did not honour his verbal contract. Ken flew off the handle with his request. He pushed hard on the bar, leaned into it to tower over a shrinking Eddy.

He venomously shouted with enough spittle to make Eddy flinch at each small touching spit that hit him as soft as light rain, but stung like spitfire gunfire. On hearing the commotion from the kitchen came a loud snap. A bang followed from the swinging door from the kitchen when Laura blustered through. The door hinges protesting the force as it slammed on the wooden banister. She scurried around the banister, leaped down the three steps and behind the bar, demanding as she travelled what was happening towards Ken.

Ken turned and explained in blunt annoyance what Eddy was asking. Laura that told him to calm down with a rub of his strong shoulders as Eddy looked down at the wooden bar reflecting his drawn-out face as inside he reverted in the past to the feeling of a boy in trouble. Laura believed in spiritual lifeforms, where everything happens for a reason. She was a hippy at heart and never lost those Woodstock grassroots. She was murmuring to a furious Ken that was on the warpath to calm down, to look at her. He was on the offensive. He was ferocious, flailing his arms above his head as he spoke, well, yelled.

'This kind of negative energy was not beneficial...' she tried to coax Ken.

'But...he told me he will be here for the busy times.'

'...and,' Laura ignored his demonstrations to continue, 'you should not cut your nose off to spite your face.' A stern warning as she glared with swords into the heart of his eyes for him to cool down, to be wary of his audience. For a few uneasy seconds, an awkward silence filled the void between them and Eddy.

Eddy sat there like a guilty schoolboy, fidgeting as he ferried between picking the nails with his fingers, to his dry skin on his hands. He, himself was furious, extremely angry with this turn of events. The harsh way he was spoken too. They were not his parent, they had no right, he had never been spoken with that much malice. As the turbulence weighed heavier on the strained atmosphere around them, it filtered through to an uneasy stillness of agitated silence. He was unfocused to the hands before him, in his vision.

He was planning his escape today, in his split shift. He was as honest to Ken as he needed to be, without given an indication to the full reason. In being open and transparent he hoped to avoid this level of hostility, but it had not materialised the way he had hoped. In his mind it played out so much better, just like they did in the movies, a picture-perfect cherry-topped fairy tale of good luck pats on the back.

Laura turned away from Ken, so he could settle down his anger, so she could speak to Eddy. Ken quivered a white saucer in his hands behind her as he shuddered the half empty white coffee cup to his lips. Trembling waves of coffee spilled from the cup, missing the saucer to the floor. He turned away to the sprit shelf, not to have a stiffer drink but to compose himself, turning his back on Eddy and his wife.

'So, you want to leave tomorrow?' Laura soothingly confirmed.

'Tonight ideally,' with intent, Eddy defiantly answered. He looked Laura directly in her eyes. Ken slammed his saucer down. How it did not smash was a mystery.

'Get ready for service. We shall talk this afternoon. We will not resolve anything in this negative force.'

Laura, more than Ken, sensed his eminent departure. He was clearly angry. His body language gave everything away. The look of his direct confrontational stare said more than he wanted. With a sense of fear in being completely stranded, she opened an assuring hand to him as he made his way up the steps to the swinging door.

'Eddy,' Laura yelled out.

'Yep,' he spoke before turning.

'Thank you.' He was not sure why she said that. Neither was she. 'Please let's talk later. Don't react in anger. We can…something, can resolve this'.

He got changed. Ready for service in his whites, he put not only his uniform on but his professional mask to get the job done competently well. Laura brought him and Gary the customary coffee at elevenses with two chocolate biscuits each. It was as if nothing had changed. Nothing was spoken about. Although instead of the single biscuit, today they were two. It was uncharacteristically busy which made the morning go fast, which was good, with little time to cogitate over his future plans.

He momentarily forgot his dramas, joked with Gary as they danced the routine of service. In the clear up, when the last docket had been spiked, the debating thoughts came flooding in. In the attempt to thrash out a resolution, he bickered within himself. Eddy was so close to not even turning up after this morning shift, all that happened only a short few hours ago. He toyed with this idea repeatedly.

Yet, he could not do it. He could not even take a sick-day, even when he was feeling like death warmed up. He was annoying frustratedly loyal to the people he worked for, as well as with, due to the feeling of guilt to let anyone down. Let himself down. In all honesty, it was not a bad trait to have.

Eddy enjoyed playing his last act of entertaining Gary's daughter Phoebe, for which he was on the cusp of finding an upshot for what was the trio of dilemmas to satisfy everyone involved. He was changed and ready to leave, maybe not to come back. His whites stuffed without folding in crumpled heaps in the bottom of his backpack. Laura caught him for a chat just before he was due to leave. She called him, literally back from the white painted threshold of the old barn door. 'Let's go for that word now. Please,' she called out as she led the way for them to go around the back level of the restaurant.

With the only single light coming from the bottom level and the natural light coming from the large bay windows. In other circumstances, it would have been soothing. They sat down, tense, at a pre-set clear table in the darkest corner away from the view of any customers. Steaming coffee mugs of a cartoon-themed animals wisped heated smoke swirls into the air. No one could hear or see them from this level. On their day off, they calmly wanted to get to the bottom of the unexpectedly decision that had arrived on their doorstep unwanted this morning.

Laura played ambassador, representing them both. Once again, Eddy did not give anything away. Silently, he appreciated Laura taking her time on her valuable day off. He kept with his white lie to the start, but then it came out. Once he started explaining, he could not stop. He explained what was going on in all detail. No fluff, no lies. Eddy tried to speak without putting Saoirse in the frame, without even mentioning her name. He did not have to, as the unspoken name was assumed to be one of the causes. Although they knew they were an item, it was common that she was leaving. She had spoken about it at the start of her commencing work in the interview.

Apparently, she was applying for jobs before and during to get her start as a writer. This surprised Eddy. Why did she keep this insignificant magnifying gargantuan job element quiet but the titanic personal element open? Although she had not actually told them that she had essentially left yet, he did not mention this. After all, she was not getting fulltime hours and she did not intend to go back. She sensed, rightly, that this had everything to do with them as a couple. She was not a fool, nor did she suffer them lightly.

Eddy was on a different page to Saoirse. On one hand he wanted to go with his heart, on the other hand his brain. He wanted to use them, as a reference so did not want to burn any bridges of a country that he had just arrived in. Reluctantly they organised to work until the end of the pay week, as a mutual agreement. He did not mention if he was to be coming back for really, he did not know. The end of the brief, to the point conversation ended with a seated gentlemen's handshake.

Ken came up and between them they put him in the frame. He had calmed down. He apologised for his overreaction and his mannerism of vexations. But deep within, he actually respected Eddy's honesty. Although he did not mention this to him. Ken brought with him some notes. He gave him all the tools to help him with an olive branch, such as emails and contact details for them, or friends in Spain if he needed anything while away.

Clandestinely though, they hoped he would keep them in the loop. The last thing that was said was by Ken. Again, he apologised for his reaction. It did not need to be said for a second time, but Eddy was grateful for the way that he wore his heart on his sleeve and was man enough to acknowledge his pitfalls. He was pulled back from the precipice, his wings clipped.

In his normal quiet Monday evening shift, he managed to sort out his unit to be sub-let. His things to be in the same dusty red storage container on the outskirts of town as Saoirse. He did not have a lot but what he did have he practically planned to give away the larger items at a low cost. Finally, He got a flight to leave for Spain in four days' time. This was all done while working. He spoke to Saoirse before her flight. He tearfully said goodbye. He could feel the contemplation of what she was doing in her voice with a little excitement. She was looking forward to the new part of her life. With a few minor stumbling blocks, she was living her dream. He would be joining her soon.

In his whole entire young life, Eddy has not grafted so hard to win approval from his guilt-ridden inner torment. Those four days were self-demanding. He demanded the best of himself. As when all is said and done, he felt ashamed to go back on his word, his own unspoken loyal oath. He wanted to leave on the right notes, especially if this was to be him leaving for good. Also, maybe truthfully, he hoped that those days would go faster, the faster he worked, they did not. He worked so hard, putting in the hard yards, going above, going beyond that those working days flew by, the down time grinded to a shuddering halt. A snail pace.

It was his last shift, a blustery Thursday night. He had an enthusiasm for getting his work done. Everything he did, he did extremely well to finish in record time. Every part of the kitchen was spotless thus you could factually eat your dinner off. His fridges were one-hundred percent organised, labelled. A mise en place list left hanging from the ticket grabber. A soft shine under the glowing green fire exit sign made the benches sparkle as he switched the lights off in the kitchen for potentially his last time. Ken and Laura brought him a pint of the dark orange tanned liquid as he was getting changed. In the short time he had been there, he had become accustomed to this warm ale.

They reasserted the hope that he would come back, hence be welcomed back, and they thanked him for his time and all his hard work. Eddy drunk the pint quickly. He did not want to be there, he wanted to go back, to pack, to not be laced in a thin veil of guilt once again. He ran back, nearly vomiting with the washing-up bowl of the pint, swirling in the grips of a violent tempestuous ocean in his stomach. He showered, a warm soapy relaxing quick wash to clean off the Smugglers remorseful dirt. He climbed into bed so relaxed, but he could hardly sleep.

Eddy and Saoirse had only spoken by email with photographs attached and text messages. He was very excited, like a child on the eve before Christmas, with the prospect of seeing her soon, hearing her voice. He must have tossed and turned to check that all his alarms were set at least a dozen times. He rose ridiculously early, well before the required time to be at the airport. Alas, on Friday morning he was ready, waiting at the empty, hollowed sound departure gate hours earlier than was required. Late in the morning, he left Gatwick and flew into Valencia to meet Saoirse.

Valencia was a side plan of hers. A stepping stone of private self-sufficient tutelage before the paid work got started. The Daily Mail only paid her if they published an article, so she wanted to brush up on the many different writing techniques. She wanted to create her own crafting literary styles before she wrote the article that could be the springboard to propel her into a long lustrous career that could make her illustrious.

Being without Eddy for the first few days, although not planned, served as a blessing. She was free to pursue the marvellous city. She was free from the proverbial baggage with only her own luggage, her own weight of expectation weighing her down. She took pleasure in establishing a foundation of writing away from her familiar fiction. Surprisingly, she found it easy to develop her own personal style. Her own, j'ai ne sais quoi, for which she would be recognised for.

She was on her own to get in her own mind space. She terribly missed Eddy, yet, on the other hand, writing took her away from the heart-longing reality, even if she was writing about the thirst-quenching reality. She was pleased when Friday morning came. She had hardly no sleep as she imitated Eddy by checking her numerous alarms countless times through the hollow darkness of the warm, humid night.

A short flight could not have seemed to have taken longer. The end of his journey saw him flying closer and closer to the Lego yellow buildings sprawled out with dark yellows and greens of the countryside bleeding in and out to the light blue haze covered mountains in the distance. He was looking out of the plastic oval framed window as it bumped harshly on the runway tarmac, twice, but he was not focusing on the scenery. The bumps were a reminder that he was where he wanted to be. More specifically with whom he wanted to be with. He was thinking of his own masterpiece he yearned to see, now a few steps away.

Eddy arrived at the airport with his life in a small ASIC's carry-on black sports bag. Amongst the many people around the vicinity of Spain's third biggest city he perched, pivoted, spun, craned his head, sized himself tall on tiptoes to look over the colourful heads of hair, hats and heads. As if a glittering halo was placed above Saoirse head, he spotted her instantaneously in the crowd as she spotted him. They ran at each other. They could not, did not want to conceal they joy in seeing each other.

A sloppy saliva-fuelled noisy kiss ensued as he picked her up in his arms. Even though Eddy promised that he was coming, there was a small seed of doubt in her mind that he would not give up everything, for her. She, in that precise moment that was over too soon, had never felt so wanted, so valued, so loved. He was excited and optimistic as not only seeing her, but seeing a new city with her gave him a fresh enthusiastic energy. In the short time she had been there, she had already started to talk with a jargon of a tour guide.

As they boarded the bus to the centre she referred to Valencia being called the 'ugly sister' when compared to her other beautiful siblings of Madrid and Barcelona.

'I will devour your senses of what Valencia has to offer,' she kinkily teased.

'Devour-er?' he mimicked her smarmy voice with a bantering giggle.

She gripped his arm tightly as she smiled a laugh into his naked arm.

It was a warm humid day as they stepped out of the air-conditioned bus, but upon arriving in this emotionless, strange, unfamiliar city of Valencia, he felt lost. He could not believe that he had actually put all his feelings in this. He thought back to Mahina. What could have been? Then immediately back to Saoirse. What will be? He was jubilantly happy with the now. She was too. No need to look back.

They decided to get in reality lost. They turned their mobiles off. As they roamed unknown streets, alleys and parks in shared silence, nestled against each other's sides, the relationship created a beautiful bond. Feeling close. Nothing was needed to be said. They loved each other. It was that simple. An image of clear roads, highways of flat, never-ending journeys of futures to be made came into his head. And hers. All the things that could happen in his was now their future. These things that were not on the horizon yet.

This open road projected a blissful feeling that he was just so lucky to have found a love like this. That single image projected an excited sensation that implanted a motive, a purpose to why he was here. His being here. His leap of faith. He was thrilled, borderline euphoric to be captivated by the same intense emotions that ran through him. He wanted to shout out loud. Climb the tallest house, tower and yell over the red-tiled rooftops, above the city so everyone could hear his joy, to be touched by his joy. Shout proudly about his feelings for Saoirse. It was with him, no within him, that he had these triumphant moods that she made him experience. To be aware of these feelings that he did not know he possessed is all down to her, being her.

She was his purpose in life. His spine gave a racing tingle which shook down the vertebrae like a stick grazing the notes of a xylophone, the realisation that he was jumping with both feet into this relationship. Yet, it did not faze him. He welcomed the uncertainty like an old friend. His heart was open at the feet of Saoirse, for his desire for her. The hearts he had given in the past, to what he thought were loved ones were now not even close to the real thing. The fake loves were being trodden on the grounds below. As, his heart belonged, only to her.

Love had come out of nowhere. He did not come to Europe to find love. He did not go expecting that he actually would find someone that he wanted to share his life with. The comprehension in the understanding that he grasps hit him hard, but with a gentle caressing force of acceptance. It was a pleasant feeling. It seemed oh, oh, so right. They negotiated the uneven brick cobbled streets of the old town not knowing where to go. Knowing that she was feeling the same things. Knowing that he was going forward. Both were, to never look back. He wanted to make an honest woman of her. He wanted to marry her.

They were as lost as they could possibly get. They did not care. They were not terrified, they absorbed the architecture, the splendour. They had a lot to say but felt without the need of words that this was not the time. They walked in the sun through the cobblestoned old town. The winding streets that snaked around in seemingly no particular order. It was a haven for them to get vanished from everyone else in the world. Although the modern intrusion of signs, air-conditioned units and sounds of technology are everywhere, yet the old town itself is very well-maintained and preserved.

Every shop, every doorway, every brick is a new sight offered. What have these paved streets seen, heard, touched and absorbed into the fabrics of time. If they could speak would they divulge the blanket upon blanket of what they hide. Revealing different legends and chronicles with a few rumours thrown in of the feuds, scandals, friendships, reputes with passionate narrative melodies that have been played out here. The architecture is so different to what Eddy had seen before. Saoirse tells him it is a combination of Roman, Arabian and Moors with an outlining description of each. Her tour guide instinct to show off her knowledge was welcomed by him, she was embarrassed as she spoke, nevertheless did not stop.

The citrus smell of fresh juicy oranges caressed their skin making them taste, without anything coming to their lips the sweetness of the shiny orange orb. Around the squares are orange trees, in small gardens are an orchard of them with green lime-like balls yet to ripen up. Each tree is meticulously maintained, as are the worn brick streets. Café throw gently notes into the air on waves of invisible coffee and chocolate trails. People chatter, natter, laugh. The emotionless had become full of emotion.

Nestled between the bosoms of two quaint squares of the Plaza de la Virgen and Plaza de la Reina is the Gothic Cathedral of Our Lady. The sun was starting to fall. The casting of the shadows over the streets brought a cover of safety, which was bizarre considering that they did not know the place but felt welcomed into its chest and heart of the historic past. Saoirse grips Eddy's hand and pulls him towards the doors.

'You have to see this,' trails her sweet voice as Eddy is jerked towards the entrance. 'We will come back as here. Here is the true Holy Grail. Well, most people believe that chalice is anyway.' She idly points in the opposite direction to where they are going.

It is a hard climb up the two-hundred and seven stone steps spiralling around the highest tower, El Micalet. Here, he stands behind her as he strokes her shoulders. The sunset in all its magnificence makes a spectacular display of yellows, reds and golden glows that carefully caress the softest of strokes over the buildings as if individually tucking each one in for the night. In the different light the architecture shows a different character. She whispers as if in a theatre, so as not to disturb Mother Nature's actors preforming this feat of unique understanding.

She tells a tale about a Moor-fighting knight El Cid Campeator who was carried triumphantly through the streets below. She spoke with a fervour about him, despite only learning of him a day ago. The bells accompanied the colourful show as the golden hues give way to the deep pinks and blues as their echoed around the city. A soothing warm gentle wind slowly spun Saoirse around to Eddy. With a slight tilt of her head upwards, she tenderly kisses his orange-tainted lips. 'I am so glad to have found you.' She nestled in his chest as he brought her closer with his arms.

'I am… You are… I…damn it…' Eddy tried to respond with as much admiration. In his arms he could feel Saoirse laugh a silent laugh through her trembling shoulders as he stuttered the worse response, but still cute in her eyes.

Suddenly, they have been put under the spell of tiredness. As the sun set, the lights dimmed, their energy diminished. They walked back to the hotel. On the way they spoke about a restaurant around the corner that she had been to which was reasonable priced, authentic and that she really wanted to try the staple dish of the area, paella. Eddy wanted a shower, to wash the medieval dust of him with the lethargies which had suddenly overwhelmed him. As he leaned on the wall letting the warm water run down him, he was thinking that he really did not want to go out again.

He was hungry but wanted more than food could satisfy. As if reading his thoughts, the stained white curtain gently clinked aside, and they were a picture to rival the evening's sunset. Saoirse stood naked. She stepped into the bath, over the side and joined him in the bath-come-shower. The evening meal was not happening tonight, nor was any food. They craved each other. The touch. Later they enjoyed the soft murmurs of the noise of them nakedly sleeping. Basked in their reciprocal warmth.

A car horn alerted them both to the new day. The thin lace curtains from the open balcony lazily smoothed a rolling symphony to the sounds of the morning traffic, the voices of yelling people, the chirps of the birds. The smell of baking bread that drifted through accompanied by roasted coffee beans was all the encouragement they needed to get up.

Blue skies, warm temperatures and a light pleasant breeze. It seems that this is the perfect combination of never-failing weather. It is breakfast time, so Eddy is accustomed to starting his day with a black coffee. He does not know how people function without it to start. Yet, with today he was giving a glimpse into the minority of their world. For Saoirse insisted on them going to a bohemian, hip district by the name of Ruzafa. It was a short tip away which pleased him. Please her more as without coffee he could be detrimental for everyone, as he will become the incredible sulk. What did not please him. What was close for his metamorphosis to happen was the trouble she had on settling for a venue. They seemed to pass numerous cafés, all playing similar listening and talkable music, all similar.

Eventually, sensing his brooding mood approaching as fast as a locomotive, she picked up her game in her personal search. Around him people were enjoying brewed coffee, he went along then the remarkable happened, she chose one. She chose a small, quiet place on the corner of a side street neglected by the rays of the morning sun. An odd choice considering the others they past. The bright custard yellow painted walls did its best to reflect the light as they settled outside. In the framed column of the view of the main street, they noticed people pass in streams out of the corner of their eyes, but this was the catch up. Here was were the stories that had happened in not even a week were re-laid. She wanted a quiet place. She wanted to not just be with him but completely in the moment with him.

They surprised themselves that they had so much to talk about. He relayed the heated exchange of a belligerent Ken, while compared to a laidback Laura, a bad-cop-good-cop pantomime of what was him handing in his resignation. She insisted that he should have done what she did to avoid that unpleasant rigamarole. He was astonished to learn that she had rang from the airport. They never mentioned that to him, nor to the best of his knowledge anyone else. For a few seconds he was flabbergasted, too stunned to speak. She spoke that they were ok with it. That they expected it. What could they do really? She was at the airport ready to board.

He then touched on the potential hot potato of her always planning to leave, but did not tell him. She explained with no difficulty that this was a sensitive issue that she did not want to be laughed at. Not to be ridiculed. She explained that she had been applying for years, but had not gotten a slightest sniff at the budding ink still drying on her written pages. She did not want to be asked daily. She did not want to explain if nothing came. Her confidence had been knocked, that nothing had happened in so long that although she kept trying, she was losing her fight to continue.

Another two coffees each followed, and a croissant shared before they continued to stroll. Around the cafes, art galleries, bars, vintage shops selling clothes to records with the brilliance vitality of the street entertainers whether in their music, art or performances. The colourful street art on the walls displaying bohemian, free messages of equal rights, lesbian gay openness and freedom of speech. It was a festival of relaxation where nothing was done in a rush, no-one ill-tempered and no-one stressed. The colourful backdrop of the buildings, people with the warm temperatures made them slip effortlessly into this routine.

Absent-mindedly, they forgot about the sacred siesta. Luckily, they made it to a bakery to pick up a couple of sandwiches and some fresh fruit. They were hungry. A croissant all day, after no evening meal, was starting to rumble the need in their stomachs.

They stopped at a park on the outskirts of the rustically preserved walled old town in what was the moat of the medieval city. A band was playing gentle melodies from above, a place unseen but heard. Their sweet stringed music caressing the heated airwaves down from the elegant pearl white pavilion. People, families and couples were spawned out on rugs and enjoying a picnic, a bottle of wine and talking under the smooth acoustic music.

Love was in the air. Everywhere. Whether a love for their parents, their child, their lover, their dog, it was everywhere. Eddy spread out a tartan checked rug on a space under a tall, blossoming white flowering tree. This was hired from a grumpy moustached Spaniard at the entrance. He looked more like a stern bank manager that only said no to loans, than a welcome host to a cooling, but still warm pleasant evening.

Hand in hand, they shared meaningless gestures, jokes and stories. They touched, stroked and rubbed parts of their body with their hands, fingers, feet, knees at every opportunity a contact was made. He had decided to throw himself in. She had decided that night that she shared her innermost personal anguish and pain. Eddy was floating on air. Endlessly floating. Endlessly in love. She felt the same. She wanted the same.

The sky was a blue from a Walt Disney movie. As Saoirse rested her hand on Eddy's heaving chest, he looked up at the birds fleetingly shifting from his glaze he was thinking of only the moment he was in. His hands around the back of his head. So, relaxed. She was eager to tell him of what she learnt. She was falling in love with Spain. They laid in the dried-up former River Túria. After flooding for the umpteenth time in 1957, the city residents had enough. They redirected the river, hence stopping it flooding ever again.

Instead of becoming a road like in many other cities around the world, the city residents ensured it would be a public park. In hearing this, he was impressed by their foresight. They walk their picnics off as they are borderline close to falling asleep. Eddy returns the blanket as they stroll the length of the outstanding park. Under the many different bridges with different unique themes. Some were adorned with flowers. This made one in particular look like it was entirely made of pink and white flowers.

Another was sleek, elegant and modern. Another was an old stone bridge that seemed to be one of the original designs. So many people seemed to be using bicycles as a form of transportation. Hire ports were everywhere. Joggers of different shapes, ages ran at different paces, plans. All the bridges had a character, a charm and a description to express to each other which was a welcome distraction to the long walk. It was a lengthy walk of nearly ten kilometres when they were confronted by the futuristic City of Arts and Sciences. This should have been out of place but curiously enough fit right in. For all the history they had walked under and alongside, this was completely out of this world.

Out of the green strip of parkland, like the body of a large blue, grey and white literally shell suit-wearing robotic mouse this huge building blended from the ground, to the sky smoothly, effortlessly. A set of large and wide concrete stairs took them to the top of a view over the park with the pitched white zig-zag of a roof. Linking a silver bow in the sky equipped with sparkling, sun reflecting strands like a harp. They walked around the structures trying to make sense of it. Dubbed the 'White City', this was designed by Avant Garde architect Santiago Calatrava, used in many movies including George Clooney stared Tomorrowland. As Saoirse could not help but informing him.

Walking back a different route, the shops were starting to open again after the siesta. Eddy could not help thinking how this even started, for a whole nation to adopt. It seemed strange that a group of people were working, then to get onto the subject of going to bed, for it to actually become a thing!

The smell of chocolate caught Saoirse's nose like a couple of fish hooks that reeled in their bait. Inside the café was like stepping into her favourite grandmother's front room was the smell of freshly baked pastries, chocolate and coffee adorned with blue and white plates hanging on the walls. They ordered two different things that they had not tried before to share. The owner spoke a little English; them, they spoke no Spanish.

She had a heavily wrinkled face that moved with expression at every syllable around the dark circles of her wide brown doe-eyes that although tired where so full of life. She wore a large black dress with a floral pinnie covered in hand smears of chocolate and flour. She wiped her hands on the corner of her dress as she waved them away to sit. She came around the ceramic tiled blue counter with an agility of a mountain goat on ice to escort them to a table outside. She came over with two glasses of water with semi-circles of orange slices bobbing with the hollow ice cubes.

The hanging terracotta pot plants of fragrant pink flowers brought the buzz of excited insects to them, without them bothering Eddy or Saoirse. An elderly tweed suit-wearing elderly man with an unlit pipe hanging from his cleanshaven mouth dismounted an older grey and green paint-peeling bicycle. In the metal basket was a brown paper parcel held together by tweed the size of a book. He spoke to them in Spanish as he entered the shop with an acknowledging nod of his short-rimed blue felt cap. He looked like a fisherman, crossed with Van Gogh with a Victorian gentleman. From behind the wall, carrying out of the shop a cackle of erupting laughter came from the lady.

Moments later came the elderly man with his jacket removed revealing a brown waistcoat where a chain linked an unseen pocket watch holding a tray, with the unlit pipe still in his mouth. With all the pose and theatrics of a man showing off to a lucky lady he poured into a rounded white mug with a small round handle some very thick chocolate that steamed and smelt orgasmic.

'Chocolate con churros,' he said in a rough whisper of a voice as he placed seven curved ribbed thick rolls of pastry sparkling in cinnamon and sugar crystals in the evening light. In a tall, thick glass that rolled with condensation was a pale white liquid similar to the off-white colour of soy milk. 'Horchata,' he bellowed with gusto to finish his performance.

'What is this made from?' Eddy enquired in slow, pronounced dictation.

After a shout out to the lady and a short conversation in Spanish as the tray swayed with his animated speech, he responded with 'Grr-od tiger-knots.'

Saoirse looked at Eddy. 'What are ground tiger nuts?'

With shrug of his shoulder to Saoirse, and for some reason a hand-together prayer of thanks to the hosts. From behind Saoirse, the chubby grandmother host pointed at the two small rolls of flaky pastry that looked like a croissant gone wrong but covered up with icing sugar, 'Fartons.'

Eddy nearly reminisced the happy-go-lucky schoolboy with Spanish ladled fart in fartons with a childish snigger. They thanked their hosts again as they slowly sped away talking softly to them, but loudly to everyone within a twenty-kilometre radius. Making them both jump in mid-sentence, she came around the corner with a smaller glass of the horchata and a farton in her hand. Mimicking, then actually doing what she wanted was the customary thing to do. It was to dip the farton in the very sweet milky liquid.

She smiled as she dribbled a few streams of white liquid down her chin. She spoke with a rub of the tummy and did not leave until one of them did it. Saoirse did not want a soggy bit of pastry, so Eddy did it. She smiled with a single clap of her hands before picking her glass up and bobbing her way back to the unobserved counter. It was OK, not unpleasant, but he did not really comprehend any different from the way they were doing it. It was good. They could understand why such a sweet drink was done after a granny nap.

For the next few days, they gladly lived in each other's pockets as they explored Valencia. She wrote with a rejuvenated passion. She used a pencil to scribble notes when inspiration hit. She wrote on napkins, coasters, anything when she could not find her own notepad. She wrote while silently mouthing the words, with a smile, with serious contemplation. It was as if she was relishing, as if she was savouring and living each and every word that she spread in a flow of beautiful lead on paper.

Eddy found it was absolutely adorable to watch. To see an artist at work. Eddy worked, somewhat amateurish in comparison, on a journal of what he, they had seen together with childlike sketches, ticket stubs and a note of the photographs he had taken to be sorted out at a later date. He wanted his own memory to take back with him. They ate fantastic foods together. Foods that they never tried. Foods that smelled as good as they tasted. They connected strongly. Over coffee, chocolate, pastries, that craved traditionally authentic paella with no prawn or chorizo in sight but rabbit. They connected. Over everything.

It was a prize of epic proportions to get Saoirse to have an afternoon off. Eddy accomplished it. He insisted that she needed it, when in reality he needed it. He wanted to spend time with her. Hear her undisrupted laugh that was not preoccupied with work. Malvarosa was the first option, but after they hired a bike and cycled the short distance, they changed their mind. Even with the peak of summer not really in full swing, the wide golden sands of the city beach were awfully crowded. They got directions from a café to the coastline. They cycled around the marina. They saw locals, tourist, families and young people enjoying themselves. Some skated to the marina along the smooth cycle paths negotiating dog walkers and people in the pursuits of other exercise disciplines.

The salty fresh air brushed their faces, exposed skin. They absorbed the good vibes in sync as they weaved between the palm trees, the sunshine adding to the laidback atmosphere of a wonderful afternoon. They cycled around the marina once more before stopping for ice-cream. It was at a mobile stall of what seemed to be university students of a very few select flavours. She opted for a chocolate and mint in a wafer golden cone, he actually opted for the cliché orange ice-cream.

They sat on the lush, plastic touching rigid lime-green grass with the ice-cream melting quicker than they could slurp it down. They soon gave up until the end to lick up the spillages. They licked each other's sticky arms in the company of teenagers not too far removed to where they are now, enjoying a game of frisbee. The orange disc flying through the air with a smooth, soft whish to a crisp snatch of a catch. Each catch was applauded. Each drop was jokily booed and jeered in jest, to raucous ridicule. Without warning, Eddy got up. Walked up to one of the guys and before Saoirse could object, they were part of the game. It was fun, it was just what she did not know she needed. Just before the end of the afternoon was complete, they cycled back.

He showered first while Saoirse wrote a few things down. As he dried himself with the unflatteringly coloured small pink towel, she was in the grip of a writing frenzy. Possessed. He instinctively knew not to bother her. When sleep bestowed him. After they had not said a word since before his shower, he let sleep take him. She had not moved.

The soft clicking of the ivory keys from her slender small blue laptop that was only used for writing woke him. She had not moved. She was smiling. Happy. Her eyes wired open with bags big enough to hang all their luggage on. He slowly opened his eyes. He must have not moved as his last reminiscent image was her exactly where she sat. On the white plastic works chair. Perfectly straight back perched over the small wooden writing bureau. Notes and rags around her. Screwed up pieces, rags of paper erupting out of the beige wicker garbage bin. He watched an artist at work.

The gentle breeze moving the odd piece of paper. She flicked her right hand in the air as she placed a final full stop at the end of her final sentence. She leaned back in her chair on the back two legs. Hand stretched high above her head. She did not stop staring at the screen. She was reading her last paragraph. She rocked forward. In a few taps she changed something, rubbed her eyes and mouthed, 'done'. Her fingers rubbed from her eyes, over her face, through her hair while stretching her bowed arms and arching her back. She rose to see Eddy staring with an adoring smile at her. She floated like an angle towards him. Leaned in for a kiss.

'Done,' she confirmed. 'Shower. Coffee. Bed. In that order.'

Just before the second point of her simple plan, she emailed her work through to The Times with intrepid dread. She had set the bar high in her predicted outcome. She was absolutely pleased with her piece. She wrote three separate pieces involving history, culture and travel. She submitted the latter that was a combination of all, without the intensity of the previous articles. She loved the history so delved further into the background, researching and investigating to make sense of the invasions, withdrawals, conquests and surrenders. It purely fascinated her. Yet, she knew that this was for her eyes only and maybe one day she would publish a book of her own. Heck, she would settle for a blog of her own at this stage.

'Congratulations hon,' a coffee-tainted peck on the top of her head. 'Now. Bed.'

She did not sleep well. She got up so many times. Wandered over to her laptop. Clicked refresh. No new emails. She did this umpteen times before going back to the still freshly warmed mattress with its thin doona. This whole process was repeated innumerable times. Eddy had gone for a walk. Left her alone to sleep. He had no idea that she was putting herself through this cruel torture of mental affliction.

They went out for lunch. She was silent. Worried. She was preoccupied, her mind pensive to his words. He offered support, encouraging clichéd phrases, remarks and assurances that everything will be great. She was not listening. He knew. He did not stop. She moved the food around her plate. She had sat for a few minutes when she got up. Eddy grabbed her wrist. Motioned her to sit back down. They might have as well ran back to the guesthouse. She swayed her hips like a speed walker. Stretching her legs in front of his. He struggled to keep up.

On the refreshing click for mail was the message she wanted. The subject line was the same as hers. Nothing was giving away in the brief clipped start of the message: 'Saoirse. I have read your work…' She shook.

'I can't open it,' she paced from the sitting bright screen of the laptop to the bed.

'You have been waiting for it. Do you want me to—'

'NO. No. No…' Each no was getting more hushed. 'I will…do it.'

She did not sit down as she leaned over the screen. With a temporary halt. She then hesitated and clicked the mail open. Looked away briefly. Then she leaned in and scrutinised the message.

'YES. YES, yes, yes, yes. Read. Read it. Oh my God. I. I can't. YESSSSS.'

She jumped. She clapped her hands like one of those toy elephants with cymbals. She whooped. She smiled until her cheeks hurt. She read the email again in case she had read what she wanted, rather than what was written. She was in the state of shock. High on the wave of astonishing surprise to get this amazing, disbelieving response so quickly. She was euphoric in a real-life dream.

Eddy got pulled to the screen. He read it. He shared in her enraptured sensations. They howled in happiness. Jumped to rid some of the inherited energy. He was so pleased for her. They shared a moment. They went out to celebrate. Alcohol never tasted so good.

When Saoirse submitted her first work to the editor of The Times, she got nervous. She knew what she wrote was good, but was not sure if this is the style what they wanted. Seeds of doubts seemed to unfold into a vast rainforest within her mind. The responding email, in opposition, was a raving review. Although, the editor wanted another country, Portugal. Also, they did not particularly ask for the country of Spain, let alone the city of Valencia.

Though in spite of all that, he wrote about her smooth, easy-to-read writing flair. That she had an 'untapped talent'. She impressed them with the way her passion came out in her written words. That the descriptions bounced and jumped off the paper to create a wonderful landscape around, to enable her style to conjure up images in the readers mind. For what she was seeing, she wrote so the reader could be cast into the unknown or back to retrieve recollections but more importantly, wanting to go and see this enchanting place that she writes off. Just like Hemingway, she wrote about the taste of food, the air and all the senses to contribute to the laughing and smiling end that the reader made unconsciously.

The editor carried on in quickly typed brief sentences that she was 'gifted'. Ending with if she continued along the lines of this article, she could 'be on the books as a fulltime employer in no time at all'. In a separate email, she was immediately offered more paid assignments, once, of course, she had completed her Portuguese travel journalism. She was contagious with her fanatical energy that gave a drive, direction and vitality to her direction.

In an old laundry that reeked of the sweet, dusty smell of floral soap powder. The air thick with the stuffiness of damp, warmed fresh drying clean clothes. The rumbling noise accompanied by the rhematic beeps of the slowing end of their cycles. Like a heartbeat waiting to be silenced the beep goes on, untouched over the crackle of murmured conversations from the small portable paint-splattered grey radio from behind a secure locked caged. She could not help glancing at this gruesomely rusting caged radio thinking, 'as if anyone would steal that'.

She moved her glance to the open glass door kept ajar by a chain tautly straight. Glancing in hope to see Eddy. Eddy was not there, he had gone for a run in the morning rays of the sun. Now the grey cloud covered like a thick dense blanket. He posed her the half-hearted question if she wanted him to wait, but she insisted to have time spent catching up on her personal emails, all the while the washing got done. She actually missed him which came to her by the means of a pang in the deepest chamber of her heart.

Just as she finished rereading the heart lifting email over again, she was offered a different job offer. She was alerted to this new message from the editor. In the small dirty table of white and blue that resembled a coldly blue sky painted by George Seurat. The chalky remnants that covered the tabletop counter in soap powder with hints of pink from an unseen sunset she made room, her own personal work station for her laptop. The large window of the laundromat acted as a glasshouse to bring more heat in the already stuffy hot room. Casting small rainbows over the military lined washing and drying machines from the light drizzle of rain that was slowly falling.

She perched on the hard-wooden ledge to read the emails as their clothes bounced nosily in supressed thuds in the large beige tumble dryer to her right. She eagerly opened the unopened email envelope as it chimed and flashed in the right-hand corner of her screen. So eager in fact that she took three attempts to hit the fading envelope. Her trembling hands moved the sensitive touch of the pad away each time. After a few seconds with the page forming in small squares to fill the screen the message revealed itself. She was asked in no uncertain terms to write about Barcelona. Instead of going to Portugal, they insisted on her heading along the coast. They wanted to complete with another tabloid to debunk their reasons why not to go to Spain.

She glanced out of focus at the hard-falling rain. She was contemplating her thoughts. As she was feeling genuinely connected to Spain, she thought straightaway that this would be a no-brainer. Yet was she comfortable enough to alienate herself before she started on a very fragile tenuous subject that she had been tested with? She felt that she should write on the topic of the hotbed of this political avenue that she had been appointed. That was not the question. It was if she should.

She got told to read the forwarded part in the email. Pondering before returning to the screen to click on the attached link that took her to another page. Once it eventually opened in the painfully slow connection, an article came up from a newspaper in the United Kingdom that had stated in no sugar-coating claims that Spain was dangerous. The article was talking about rises in crime, rising unemployment that led to literal rises in street with marches and walks of protest and change and terrorist links from within the country as well as outside. It summarised that people should not go to Spain, particularly in the Basque region, and definitely not go out at nightfall. It was a fear piece of extreme proportions.

She went back to the email, the editor made it clear not to lie and write about the experiences in Barcelona, but they wanted it to be half political and half travel but all positive. She was urged to discredit the rumours that Barcelona was in turmoil and that foreigners would be risking with their own lives to travel there. To throw a negatable light on their competition while basking themselves in flooding heated beams of glorious. They also decided to publish her story, but wanted it quickly to be followed up with this contentious piece involving the different aspect of at least one more Spanish city.

With two steaming funnels of coffee coming from the blue paper cups as a sweaty, happy and drenched Eddy emerged out of the dark shadows with a high-pitched squeak, as his wet shoes pinched the plastic pale pink lino of the laundromat through the veil of the now pouring down rain. Saoirse did not see him enter. Heard him squeak and roared in laughter. She was more startled with the email with a flip of her mind seeing him to see that he was speaking. The thin, light grey laptop nearly bounced off the table as her knees struck the underneath as she jumped to say her hellos and sorry for laughing. When he laughed as he passed the coffee in front of her, she cuddled him. She did not care that he was wet, sweaty and cold. It was a welcome break from her concentrating and thoughtful mind.

She explained and showed Eddy the turn of events over the last few minutes. She was digesting the email while constructing a plan to write about this sensitive matter in the ways that would not upset anyone. She then turned to be a little frustrated. Honestly, she came aware that she was very annoyed by this inconvenient interruption to her strategic plotting in conspiring the correct information to defend Spain, Barcelona in particular but to maintain the safeguard for the humble tourist. It was going to be a knife-edged article. This hot potato could potentially make or break her.

Eddy sensed the frustration and perched far away. This made Saoirse guilty. She could not focus. She was irritated by Eddy's presence, yet, she went over to talk to him. She put her chaotic mind that was on a cusp of orderly to comfort a wounded Eddy. She felt guilty for her uncharacteristic temperament.

She spoke of the email. She spoke of the political, as well as the historical aspects of this very wealthy part of Spain. She first had to explain to Eddy some basics. The Catalonia region was in the north-east of Spain which had its own language, which some still speak, and its own culture. Eddy was enthralled by this. It is something that is not taught in Australia. Or, if it was, he had forgotten about it all together as this historic speech was all new to him.

She paced around as she spoke like a tutor in a private tuition. From 1714, when it was captured by Phillip V of Spain that was the pivotal moment in stepping forward to the resurgence of the modern state of Spain. Essentially though, Barcelona had never lost its vital, separate identity. Hence with this is the essence to spawn the desire of self-rule among the Catalans, for which they are known. This goes back centuries with each generation believing what their forefathers wanted.

In 1931, victory happened for a short time by the Catalan government. However, with the Spanish military dictator Francisco Franco, it was abolished in 1939. Under Franco's reign from 1939–75, he supressed the culture and the Catalan language by banning it in public places. But following the restoration of the democracy, Catalonia was declared an independent autonomous region within Spain, yet somewhat more as it does have a high level of self-rule, but these do not extend to issues such as tax control. The majority of the Catalan wants full independence.

Many within the Catalans strongly believe that the Catalonia economic success is significantly the tool that props up the rest of Spain. If this outcome was to come into acquiescence it would characterise the country's biggest political crisis since the Franco dictatorship. The smudge print on the economy would be huge. A country where Catalonia's economy is larger than that of Portugal. Not just impacting Catalonia, Spain, but the world.

She came down to sit next to Eddy. He stood there, taking it in. He could not help but think of coincidences with Australia becoming independent from the Commonwealth. He did not voice as much but compared it, so he could understand the complexity further. They sat in their own silence. The light metal tinkering of the finished tumble dryer as the components rested and the grating voice of the crackled radio was the only sound inside the laundromat.

Outside, a car splashed through a puddle as the rain started to slow, the grey blanket starting to reveal the blues beyond. They shivered. They still did not move. They absorbed the information. They absorbed the article, whether it should be written. The ideal against the idea. Eddy's intuition told him to not do anything as Saoirse's mind was again strategizing a plan to tackle this subject. Written by an outsider, it would not go down well in Catalonia, so she had to tread carefully, but at the same time purposeful.

She drew a notepad out of her brown leather laptop satchel the way a cowboy would draw a pistol and scribbled decisively with each letter making a shape on the next page. Eddy took this as a cue to gather their clothes. The warmth on his exposed skin to the sliding cooling temperature was welcoming. One thing left to do before heading into the unexpected downpour was to book the bus to leave as soon as possible. Tomorrow. Mind was made up.

The bus journey was a strange one. Eddy had slept well. Saoirse was wrestling with her turmoil of journalistic suicide. Only a few minutes prior, they had gotten ready in the normal way colourfully tinted with flirting, smiling, laughing and joking. But the tense aura of a fractious fragile balance where a single accent on, or not on, a word could generate an awkward escalation of issues.

It was true that Eddy was feeling a nervous uneasy apprehension about what to expect in Barcelona. He had read the article of fear from the editor. He had then spent the evening reading about the worse. The Australian warning that the government put on its website to warn people about traveling in this area. The recent protest of last weekend that was held to be a peaceful march. These had quickly escalated into riots, violence. Police used force. Force was confronted with force. Gas was used. Batons drawn. Rubber bullets sprayed. He was focused on this.

On the other hand, Saoirse was heavily focused on the article, on other things. Both different opinions were going on without the other person knowing what the other person was thinking. She was thinking about one very important thing in particular. The journey passed orange trees with the loveliness of the pretty Spanish countryside of golden oranges, yellows and greens. The bus held the tension. It was a delicate frail balance where no words were spoken. Where no touch was made. Where no precarious movements in anyway were made to risk the impending catastrophe. Eventually, Saoirse succumbed to sleep. She involuntary placed her nodding head onto the shoulder of Eddy, who welcomed this contact.

He gently woke her as they were on the outskirts of the city. The countryside had slowly blended to the grey urban matter of residential buildings. The tractors replaced by cars. The cows replaced by scooters. The dirty overalls replaced by suits, fashion. The flat barn warm homes to the tall cold climbing escalating steel, the growth of where to put all the growing populates. They get dropped off on the said outskirts of Barcelona. The ice-cold temperature rises as they set off. The smell of flumes hit them. It was the first time that they lingered a look at each other since Valencia.

They strolled sluggishly in the direction the young flippant driver points them to, the city centre. After negotiating where they had to go, their mobile directed them through a thin tree-lined strip takes them to a steel unwelcome metal door just off the Ramblas. In the brisk breeze they see a dirty metal white and red sign for a hostel swinging in its creaking hinges. Although the outside may differ, this is perfect for them. Saoirse expressed her desire to stay in a mixed dorm room to gain stories, local and the naïve tourist hot and cold spots. For some reason she was under the misconception that although she knew she could learn some more knowledge from their unlearned temporary friends, they were the ones that held the superior wisdom. Fool.

The narrow light pale stairs took them up to the very top of the ornate metal staircase with an echo of their footsteps resonating down the metal stairwell. A red cushioned door with a single buzzer to the left told them they had reached the place. A buzz, a soft click and the door started to open with a gently push they entered into a small cramped room where in front of them a single desk and chair makes up the reception. Dimly lit corridors like spread out wings spread out either side.

The guy is not the friendliest but with the sensitivity of a robot, he fakes a welcoming smile that flashes over his lips. A brief monotone matter-of-fact unemotional rehearsed speech follows. He is back to his robotic theme as he dictates the laundry and kitchen times, where the television room is and the dorm itself. A deposit for the single key to share passes hands. Instead of the 'enjoy your stay', he ended the interaction with 'bring your linen at checkout, ten in the morning.'

A short walk down the corridor where they cannot help but aid the paint being peeled off the walls as their bags rub along. With a slight jiggle, they turn the lock of their room. There is no-one in the cramped bunk-bed room with a mess of clothes sprawled all over the floor. Hanging from the metal runners, dirty smudge-stained towels hang around one of the bottom bunks to create a solitary space. Two bunk beds were along each wall. Only the top bunks were left. It was stuffy, putrid body odour reeking stink, unkempt and unwelcoming. Saoirse races to the barred window immediately like a prison to open it. She quickly finds out that they are crudely nailed shut.

Below her, in the dirty pothole-ridden side street are numerous overflowing large wheelie bins. Where a litter of skinny, unfed stray cats rummage on a burst, torn bag scattering the contents over the street, and large seagulls nosily pick at the peak of the black plastic shredded tat. They dump their own bags on the two empty beds to claim their space. Saoirse strokes with unspoken discontentment at the touch of the thinnest dark brown blanket and they both felt no need to state about the amusingly small nature of the single marshmallow-sized brown pillow.

They cannot stay here in the suffocating stench for long. They quickly check out the kitchen. Arrayed in bright red garish plastic chairs and tables in an unruly disorderly abandonment are many chairs around equally hideous red plastic tables. The kitchen had all what was needed. Signs for hygiene everywhere. Small though so they make a mental note to use it either early on or later to not be here on peak times. They go back out to the Ramblas, where they get offered to have their worn-out runners shined, for which they both found hilarious.

When the Romans invaded, this area was a plain, sandy and dry area they called Arenno. When the Moors came later, they translated the old Roman name to become Ramla, eventually becoming the Ramblas. The Ramblas is a road that follows the old wall of the small fortress defending town and is nowadays very much the heartline of the city.

It is late in the afternoon. The sun is a vibrant orange glowing sphere lowering in the sky, throwing golden coins of light that cascades treasured gifts onto every reflective surface. Even the postcards look magical in this light on their peeling white plastic stands. They stand at the bottom, looking out over the shimmering enigmatic mist of the sea. Port Vell a marina adds the sound of the clinging of roped ties and colourful sails onto the masts in the light bitterly cold gust of sea air. The port is being guarded by a statue of Christopher Columbus. When he was here, it would have looked so much different.

Here is a beautiful beige wooden boardwalk where people stroll and get their exercise. Restaurants look out which are busy even after lunch and not quite dinner time yet. A small crowd is gathered around a bare-chested trio of youths doing backflips and somersaults to music in golden tracksuit bottoms that compliment with winks to the lowering sun. Eddy felt a little embarrassed when he saw a small metal plaque stating: 'Las Ramblas—named after the sandbar and canals'.

He had somewhat naively thought that it was named Ramblers, as in walking, due to a profoundly pedestrianised street. In a point at the sign, he chuckled to himself before quickly deciding to share his revelation with no-one. Underneath the green canopy of the fringing trees are artists selling their creations. Around each flickering into light lamppost are a ring of vivid flowers which cast out their spread of glorious floral scent on the travelling surges of salt from the sea.

They have no map, no direction. They are happily strolling. The atmosphere from the bus journey laid to rest. They get pulled by an invisible force through beautiful side streets like Carrer del Bisble. They head to where something catches their attention. Disgruntled gargoyles in immortal poses of dark stone look down as if watching their every move on the tall light brown tall walls with high windows that cannot be seen into. Up the smooth paved hill through a magnificent archway with a platform on the top they stop to take photographs. They did decide that they would get lost in the sensation of being unsure, but Eddy started and then Saoirse joined in to the act with implicit acceptance.

The teardrop arch sheds its reflection on their faces which makes them squint in the setting sun as they walk underneath it. The street is quite silent, considering the amount of people is unnerving. Yet the slight sea mist holds a mysterious quality that is made more intense by a solo busker playing a violin in a small recess. He blends in well in his black sweater, black trousers and black scruffy shoes as he plays a haunting single-stringed melody that seemed to have been written for this precise moment.

They walked through the old gothic street accompanied by this perfect score. They held hands. This was the first proper contact that they had made since leaving Valencia. It was shockingly welcoming in Eddy's hand, but very surprisingly for her to finally show any emotion after her stream of rejections today. With the sun winking at them as it slowly bares it head down in a finally hurrah, he grips her hand tight. One thing that Eddy has been vocal about is the paramount length of the sunrises, but in particular the sunsets. The sunsets in Europe seems to take a lot longer than in Australia. They turn.

They look at each other. Not just into each other's eyes but through to their very soul. Eddy could feel a difference. Saoirse wanted to say something. She half smiled before looking down at her feet. He slowly lifted her head. She did not resist. He tenderly kissed her forehead. He felt her hand tighten around his. She cuddled him. He cuddled her. They strolled back to the heartline of Barcelona.

Saoirse was bent over, laughing uncontrollably. Falling about in fits of amusement. She had tears of happiness in her eyes. She could not stop. She was holding her ribs to stop them being ripped apart. Trying to stop the embracing pain. Tears of joy were streaming down her face. Roaring laughter. This made Eddy have hysterics, but he was trying to stem the flow.

He was repeating himself with short sentences of, 'That's enough', 'Okay, Okay', 'Are you done?', 'Come on', 'It is not that funny'.

They were back in the dusk light of the main street with the streetlamps making the trees and flowers glow. Eddy had just confessed to Saoirse what he had thought La Ramblas meant. Predictably, as he had thought, she found it hysterical that he could be so naïve. She kissed his cheek amongst the giggles to whisper, 'You are so adorable...so cute.'

Eddy could not entail if this was mocking or not. Although he was enormously partial to seeing her laugh like this. It seemed ages since he had heard these stomach-rumbling teasing from the depth of her soul. It warmed him more than the sun could ever do to hear her spirit so lively. Still dabbing her eyes from the tears. Still smiling so her cheeks and face ached. Still fighting back, the brink of her incontrollable snorts and crackles she breathed deeply. A vain attempt to oppress her emotions. She could not look at Eddy in the face.

She cast to her right. The moon was casting a ghostly silhouette over the bronze Christopher Columbus statue. People spilled out its cast iron Corinthian column after seeing the sun setting from the gallery within. Under this light accompaniment by the bustling restaurants filled with chatter, clinks of wine and the sounds of metal on crockery. They thought it was busy earlier, that seemed to be just the normal trade. Each place was full, bursting as much as Saoirse sides. With various acoustic soft melodies on the gently sea breeze the identical figures of the four continents around the base seem to be enhanced with a rich new dimension.

Again, Barcelona had delivered in giving the perfect score to a perfect moment. Slightly more lively music with occasional roars of approval between songs made them both join in with claps of their own. The sumptuously decorated allegorical statues of the figures of Spanish history tell the story of the Italian explorer. Where some historians claim that this was where he was born in Spain, rather than Genoa. They stop to look up at Columbus whose trailing right hand is said to point towards where he had just been when arriving here in October 1492 after discovering the Americas.

Actually, he points to the southeast, towards the city of Constantine in Algeria. Reluctant, and maybe a little ashamed to admit that they had him pointing in the wrong direction, the claim is that the true point is that he is pointing towards his home, the sea. Columbus thought he had travelled to India, which is why he called the native population 'Indios', the 'Indians'. So, in an ironic twist of fate, the sculpture has him putting in the wrong direction, for a person who went in the wrong direction and stumbled rather than explored a new world.

Saoirse tells Eddy that they are always talking about talking this down. She has finally managed to compose herself for the time being. Evidence supports that he discovered America but also was responsible for the Native Americans suffering through slavery, brutal pillaging and genocide. His left hand holds the charts close to his chest, his said hollow heart. Saoirse cranes her neck skyward. She cannot see his eyes but see the direction he faces. She wonders, almost speculating the moonshining reflecting her cold clear inner mood of wonder.

Wondering her own philosophical reasoning to what is at the end of her world. Wondering what is forward, towards the unknown, towards the future. She is wondering how to tell Eddy the future that she sees. It has played on her mind since the morning in Valencia and rather than being a flashing disregarding seed it is boring into her mind as actually being the righteous motive for both of them. The hand of Eddy brings her back down to reality. She mouths an intention to eat as she pulls her hand towards one of the busy portside restaurants. Throughout the light dinner she kept gazing towards the back of Columbus, wondering. Just wondering. The same thing. A different ending. Yet, she unfortunately can only see the same ending.

Across the polished beautiful mosaics of the floor surrounded by perfectly lit architecture they head back a little tipsy from the three last ones for the night. Close but not touching they stagger back. Back in the hostel, Saoirse's idea to get some stories bore an abundant of fruit. She only wished she was clear-headed to remember. She was writing them down on the sticky, crumbed table top in the television come dining room frantically hoping that she could read the scribbles in the light of day. Everyone was so friendly. Everyone wanted to be here to travel, to see the world that the atmosphere in the worst possible room was easily unobserved.

Eddy thought he knew many of the con tricks, yet one enticed him in. This involved the dropping of coins as they passed. Eddy harmlessly had never thought of this. But if you hear the tell-tale sound of metal coins hitting the pavement, you instinctively reach for your wallet. Just in case it is you that has dropped them and need to reassure yourself. This human nature response shows the robbers where you are keeping your cash, which in turn makes it easier for them to get the fruits they desire quickly without rummaging unnecessary pockets. So simple.

The other is a little craftier. The robbers would actually spit on your shoulder. Eddy must have given a baffled brow-wrinkled expression as his young storyteller laughed and offered an explanation. The mark, victim-to-be, would think he had just been pooed upon by a bird. The robber would come in very close to offer assistance. Close enough to get your camera, passport, money or jewellery. It turns out that they are a lot of scams. Of which Eddy knew...none.

Although Eddy was dubious when Saoirse wanted to stay in a hostel in what he read as being known as the European New York for petty crime for travellers. In reflection he must admit that he was actually becoming more worldly-wise and enjoying the generous vibe. Although they had separate beds, Eddy was comfortable in his higher bunk when Saoirse on the return from the bathroom joined him. It was surprising but absolutely not unwelcoming. She had been so distant. Her thoughts her own.

Any attempt that Eddy had to touch her affectionately was brushed aside. For her to be nestling close, her back thrusting into his stomach. She takes hold of his right arm, pulling it over her shoulder, wanting it to be draped over her body. Hands locked she held it close on the soft linen feeling her rhythm of her heart. She kissed the topside of his palm. 'Goodnight' she softly murmured. He pulled her near. Which was more an act of acceptance in his longing for her. This contact changed his view, as the frequent thoughts that were going through his head all day were verging on the doom and gloom. This simple act. The forceful human contact was all he needed to know that she did, in fact want him.

The grimy brown-stained rags which were a poor excuse for the curtains did nothing to stop the bright, sun from basking through the large floor to ceiling windows, but everything to contribute to the atrocious aroma. The rays casted the thick window bar shadows over the faces of Eddy and Saoirse as they stirred to be more like the first night in an incarceration cell, rather than a dorm room. The heavy smell from their arrival had not disappeared, but they had unfavourably seemed to have grown accustomed to it through the night.

Earlier, they were woken by a younger man with an inconsiderate abandonment. He came bursting through in the early hours of the morning. Flicking the light switches without a care in his, or anyone else's, world. Then rummaging into his bag under his dirty makeshift towel screen. The rustle of plastic, the swearing, the muttering and straining high-pitched creaking of the bed, for which he seemed oblivious to the other three people that were asleep. Generally, he was being an increasing pain, before one of the accompanied other beds shouted a snarled warning to decrease his infernal racket.

A wounded dog regarded the darkness where the voice derived from with a brief pause. Then quickly resumed with an ashamed reluctant to stop looking for his treasure. He sulked over to the door and turned the light off to a gritted-teeth 'thank you' from the same bed.

After a few long minutes, he retrieved his prize with flashes of his mobile light guiding him, before getting up to leave, slamming the door shut behind him. That could have been an accident. The return to turn the light on, to then slowly close the door was not, it was pure vindictiveness.

This morning, that same young youth was half in his bed, half out, sprawling his legs onto the floor. His multicoloured boxer shorts left nothing to the imagination as there were endeavouring to stay on the bed as his body slowly gliding out. Eddy went over and draped his white thin bedspread over his modesty. They could have easily been a noisy nuisance themselves, but when has revenge prevailed in solving anything?

Last night's voice from the darkness was nowhere to be seen, just a small hole in the mattress. After playing a good Samaritan for his daily allowance, he turned around into the embrace of Saoirse, in the middle of the dorm. A close cuddle. A purred 'Good morning' as she lifted herself on tiptoes to kiss him tenderly, affectionately and yearningly, wanting more than the touch of his body, his lips on hers.

She looked adorable in her pale-yellow crop top, hair a mess, no makeup, white panties and surrounded by the pure innocence of glowing as being touched for the first time by the morning sun. Today was her day. She had a content appreciation for art so wanted to take a day off from her writings. A day off with Eddy. A day together, to spend together, to love one another. With no rush. No tricks, just them.

They were ready quickly, at the train station before the heavy commuting activities of locals going to and fro work had really commenced. They were lucky in a game of chance to catch the train that disembarked in a few minutes to Figueres. A pleasant trip north with the soft thudding of the train's heartbeat the duration of the two hours trip. Smoothly bumping its way along the Catalonian countryside of browns, oranges and greens. Chatter happened in between the sightseeing but was more 'look at that', 'how stunning' or 'that looks the life to have'.

Saoirse had a limited grasp on Spanish from her days in Irish school but, knew enough to hear when it was time to get off. They were the only ones to disembark the train onto the concrete platform towards the simple, but elegant brick train station. They did not know the route to go. It was still early but the sleepy elderly lady behind the small porta hole-type round window pointed them up the road. She also followed this up with animated hands while saying something too fast for Saoirse to fully interpret. Though she read between the words to make a logical and confident appearance to be knowing where to go.

Eddy saw through her like glass, but mockingly followed her bold stride through the narrow, small houses that fringed the grey bumpy road. The pavement was virtually too small for a toddler, let alone an adult, so they walked up on the pitching part of the gutter. Each house was similar but attention-grabbing unique. A pitched roof, to a low flat roof decorated with patterned wood, ornate stone, to decorative sunbursts of living colour to the monotone black and greys. It was all in all like walking a filmset tour rather than a quaint village. The walk was long.

Eddy was doubting Saoirse understanding but then when he thought he would ask the next stranger he saw a blue metal sign pointing them in the direction that they were seeking. A smile spread over Saoirse's lips, as she too was sensing that she was going down the wrong path, but just like Columbus had found the destination when appearing to be on a different course, so did she. As of yet, the museum was not open for tourists. Eddy softly tugged Saoirse over to the empty café, that they had just passed by, with a single man reading a newspaper on the table outside.

He was in a heavy looking like a large olive with his dark green waistcoat with a perfectly ironed white shirt underneath that was rolled symmetrically up to his hairless elbows. From his grey bushy moustache, a shiny mahogany varnished pipe balanced effortlessly between his systematic grinding of his nicotine-stained teeth. The small peak from his brown cap hid his brow where shining small cycles of glasses rested on the tip of his large, red nose. His pronounced cheekbones had shown a lifetime of smiles, laughter but these days seemed a forgotten passed as his dark brown eyes are gaunt, staring down a bottomless well where the soul lurks, feigning any contact. Happily silent, untouched and unloved.

As they walked past him, he peered over the top of his newspaper by making a slight crease down from the top, as if suspiciously inspecting them on entry. His head did not move but he eyes followed them until there were inside. They noticed his scent of tobacco from his smouldering pipe combined badly with the reek of cheap, sharp vinegar-tainted cologne. He knew that they were tourists. That they were not from Spain without them saying anything.

Even without their camera in hand, their small backpack filled with a day of walking activities, he sensed the foreigner in them.

As they walked in with a telling glance to each other. A stare that spoke the words that they both wanted to say. But to make sure in a quick snap of the neck backwards towards the old man, they gave a unison agreement to his mistrustful concept of them. Once inside Eddy gave a proper look of the character of the place. For the first time, Eddy noticed him in a wheelchair. For some reason his bad thoughts were now clouded with a heavy sense of guilt. Although he was not mean, he did have mean thoughts.

In this association, he felt embarrassed for himself. Saoirse did not, or refused to notice as she walked up the single blue line step into the quaint, low-ceilinged café. To their right was a delicious array of velvet shined cakes and pastries on metal cooling racks on the large, block brown wooden counter. An old-style metal till with elongated number presses like metal fingers soared into the air. Each item they asked for the jack-in-the-box numbers bounced within the glass chamber on the top in perfectly elegant, black scripted font on single white squares. The smell of the freshly baked goods coming from the cluttering kitchen from along the door less thin wooden framed were enticing. They stopped in front to bend down to gorge their eyes at the magnificent display, to inhale the freshly baked goods. They noticed someone watching.

A person fleetingly looked around the corner, before they noticed them, they did. A ghost figure saw them watching, so fled with them seeing only the trailing cloth that hung from his, or her apron spring. The skinny young lady behind the counter was librarian in her appearance. Quiet, humble and friendly. She smiled a shy one, for which she was not sure if she should stare, wait or pretend to be busy.

As Saoirse gazed for breakfast, Eddy made small talk. He attempted a clumsy embarrassment of Spanish, for which she spoke in an American-influenced accent near perfect English back. Startled Eddy asked trying to speak in slower words to where she learnt English. She replied that every summer, for the past three years, her father has insisted on her travelling to Summer School in the states to learn. With that, she pointed towards the guy in the window. The penny dropped that this was her father, his shop. Eddy smiled through the lettering in the window as he watched them carefully. As if they were here to steal.

'Long Black?' Eddy asked with the expression of confusion spreading over the young lady's pale face. 'Sugar and milk-less coffee. Americano, that's it!' he tried again, 'and a cappuccino?' He asked the lady while facing down in the directing of Saoirse who was always changing her mind. She nodded. For which Eddy nodded to the host.

'Have you decided?' Eddy asked as he perched a hand on her shoulder which was returned with a soft touch by hers. She was crouched down, looking at the fantastic display.

'They all look wonderful. And the smell…' she sighed with a breathless strong desire. 'You decide…'

'But…what if I—'

'You won't.'

She raised to stand tall, with a seductive steaming hot wink as her hair flickered behind her. Her hips swayed as her red and blue summer dress clung around her to flatter her curves but also fell away in the right areas to entice, to tease the want to go underneath as she sambaed outside into the spring heat of the day. She perched on one of the select few flimsy looking metal blue and white seats outside under the small plain cream parasol. She put on her thick sunglasses as she watched the town starting to wake up. She acknowledged the old guy as he tapped the crest of his hat in acknowledgement. He still glared as Eddy came out with two brown paper bags of food to share with two white plates with a blue trim.

The librarian floated behind him with the coffees that smelt fantastic. She returned moment slater with an espresso for her dad. They spoke in whispers. When she went back inside, he smiled to them with a cheer's mimics with his coffee cup in mid-air. Up until this moment, he was glaring at them, making them feel uncomfortable. They were not encroaching his space, but he made them feel they were encroaching his peaceful recollective moments. This smile broke the barriers down. He went back to his newspaper, they went back to their chat.

'Xuxo,' explained Eddy, convinced that he has the pronunciation completely wrong. 'Here is a cream-stuffed croissant—'

'Sorry,' the host interrupts with a butter knife. 'I have story. Legend states that a troubadour was in love with the daughter, daughter of a baker. One night, he was close to be caught in her room, erm, by her father, yes. The Troubadour escaped. He jump, out of her bedroom window. He hid in the warehouse where they stored the flour sacks. While hiding, the flour entered his nose, yes, causing him to sneeze, yes, choo-chooooooooo! The baker, the father find him. HE want to kill HIM. The troubadour asked for forgiveness. That he would marry to protect her honour and teach him a cake recipe that would make him famous. This cake was named after the sound of his sneeze.' She swiftly floated bashfully away immediately after the last word. She returned inside like a solitary stationed meerkat behind the counter.

'The other is a lemon muffin type rectangular-thingamajig,' Eddy continues. 'She did say the name. Something like Sobais but I cannot remember. Told it is nice though.'

They take bites while sharing their breakfast. Both are extremely nice with the deep-fried croissant, the Xuxo not being nearly as greasily sweet that she was expecting. The story that equipped the pastry was nice, which they commented with crumbling flaky pastry laced remarks. Saoirse apologised as she scribbled down the story in her notepad for the article, yet to be written.

Eddy mumbled words to brush it off, that it was fine and completely understandable. He did not mind. It was her job and things like this interested him as a traveller so why not tell the readers. Within her notepad, she saw a caption that she had squared off in hard gorging black pen.

'This was his home,' she mentioned, adlibbing the written pages in her book. 'Salvador Dali actually decorated his home to become a museum when he died.'

Eddy thought about that simple sentence for a while. He could not imagine making a house, a home that would one day be decorated in a way to become a museum when he died. Making a testament, a tribute to himself. They finish and leave a few coins on the table as they wave through the glass and to the man who had taking the step of putting down his paper to gaze on his quaint little town. As they turn the corner, they are confronted by this bright flamingo pink fortress of a house.

Stuck in time, Eddy was rooted to his position. His head moved but his body, arms and legs stayed motionless. The rooftop glistened in the morning glow of the blood orange Spanish sun decorated with large eggs, golden nude statues, that hold an uncanny resemblance to the Oscar awards. Lean green towering trees surround the walls that play a melody of colour with the light swaying of the thin rope-like trunks of the trees. These serenade a smooth compliment rather than disharmonic a harsh vilify in contradiction of each other.

Eddy is awestruck. It is truly amazing. He could not believe he missed it earlier. How did he not see the spectacle? He was so hellbent on getting to the entrance that he was not appreciating all that was around him. When Saoirse suggested this trip, he was not fussed. He cared little for art, less for Dali. Of course, he could describe some of Dali artworks. After all he was a famous artist with rememberable masterpieces that are known by the most hatred art disparager as himself. From the towering elephants on stilts, the melting wax-like clocks and the face around household objects but to name one of these, or a single piece, he was drawing blanks. Maybe, just maybe, he was starting to appreciate art for what It was. To be solely appreciated.

Different masterpieces that can evoke an emotion, a time, a life or a death. Art is a beauty within the eye that looks at it. It should not need to be explained to understand. Sure, sometimes it helps, but like any other sense you know if you like something or dislike it. Thus, it is really as simple as that.

Saoirse leant into the daydreaming Eddy with a dry peck on the cheek. With his slight jolt of surprise, he turned still displaying his gawped expressionless face for her to use her catchphrase for him, 'You are so cute sometimes'. He blushed with an embarrassed smile as he looked down while shuffling his feet on the spot.

Without hesitation, she grabbed his wrist to pull him near. He was close to a smile of a maniac on her face that infected him to respond with the same dilated vision of glee, as they embraced. A soft but tightly clenched hug. A delightful embodiment of their love, the same personification that Dracula would express and feel at his most decadent lust for the taste of the warm pure virgin blood. This loving feel was flowing through him as hot as lava, as fierce as flames. Her love for art was permeating through him. For him to gain enjoyment for art, well it was still a new sensation for him. Be that as it may her affection was breed as well as growing inside of him. He did not resist, nor try, he did not ignore his hearts yearning and blossoming desire for art.

Feeling her heartbeat on his. Feeling his warmth on hers. Feeling indestructible, she tugged him more forcefully towards the entrance with his wrist he still was holding. The unexpected force made him stumble forward, towards the forming crowds, tripping on nothing but flat cream tiles. People are everywhere. Even at this early hour of the morning, people are here to try, to fail in their effort to beat the rush. Like moths to a flame. What sweet music they make.

Considering the queue that has formed, they do not queue for long at all. The cashiers are dab hands that flow the people through easily. It was surely not seemingly possible, but Saoirse has made it feasible as she sports a larger beaming grin as she stops in her slow-moving pigeon tracks to see the first piece that catches her eye. A large holographic painting dominated the first room. She was awestruck. As if they were at a library and honouring the unwritten code of silence she whispered into his ear, 'This showed just how ahead of the game he was'. It was true, he was a true pioneer in this particular art movement.

At first glance, it is a block painting of Abraham Lincoln. After being encouraged to read a brief script first by Saoirse. She was satisfied by him to be incited to look through the telescope locked in place aiming towards the image. He crouched down to peer through. Miraculously, the blocks transformed in front of his eyes to the muse of Dali's wife looking back towards him, naked, as naked as she was when she came into the world. He stared through the viewfinder into the telescope. Back to the painting. Back to the telescope. As if it was magic that he could work out, he did the same routine again.

Eddy was won over, he enthused, the glow within him that was raging to a bonfire to tell Saoirse. She was leaning over and was seeing the transformation herself for a second time. Evident by the revolution altered in his own eyes, he saw a reflection in hers. He still felt the need to voice it to her excitedly. From this simple moment, he knew he was going to enjoy this museum. Rather too hastily Eddy took a photograph, with flash. It was an innocent accident. Signs were everywhere stating yes to photograph, but a big red cross signifying no to flash. The look that ensued from the security guard was as if he had signed his name on a piece of art.

He acknowledged an apology for which he just scowled an unspoken two words back through mouthed grit, no flash. Watching him like a hawk, Eddy could feel the laser-eyes of the security guard every time he got his camera out. Eddy brushed it aside. He was absorbed by what he saw. Some of the art was the fantastic, down to the damn right exquisitely strange. He had an array of talent in using everything possible. He painted, sketched, sculptured or propositions his art. Along one curved wall was the pencil sketches that involved bestiality, this was not to Eddy's nor Saoirse's taste for which their hurried hastily past. The circular motion of the building makes you go up like you are in a large screw top, spiralling the five stories.

To their surprise, they actually spent many hours here. They backtrack copious amounts of time, to then retrace their steps forward and then back again before realising that time had elapsed. They leave happy in the grips of feverishly jubilant conversation of the images that they saw. This day had almost given them a skip in their step. It injected them with a newfound love of each other, a newfound love of life. Of what can be done.

They resorted to juvenile innocent tomfoolery to lark around as they made their way back to the train station. About halfway, in the most awkward position, Saoirse is lifted up by Eddy, planted on the bonnet of an old red car and pashed upon. She giggles. He turns her around, so she is upside down. He bends down to kiss her the wrong way up on her mouth. Saoirse grips his head tenderly but with enough force to say she wanted it, craved it and desired more.

That night was spent sleeping in each other's arms. In the morning they were in the same position, locked in a wonderful sensual arrangement. It was at this moment that Eddy rued Saoirse's decision to stay in a hostel. He wanted to have his wicked way with her. Last night with the sensation not having ebbed by the morning. With the last few days being hectic they decided to sleep in for a bit longer. At seven in the morning that intention went out of the proverbial closed window. They awoke around the same time. Without words they decided to explore, to not waste a single moment. They had a timeline for which determined how long they could stay here. In hindsight that was such a shame as the city promised so much, give so much and wanted so little in return.

A flirtatious touch here, a cheeky pout of kissy lips there. A feather soft stroke on each other's exposed naked body as they shacked the cobwebs of the sleep off their bodies. This made Eddy feel that they were falling in love all over again. Moreover, deeper in love. While Eddy showered in a few minutes, Saoirse had the day organised. He did not mind her taking the lead. She seemed to know a lot more about what was to see than he did and for that he was eternally thankful to not look like a complete idiot. He scanned her plan as she took her shower.

The warm smell of a summer night's rain filled their nostrils as they stepped out of the stuffy, body odour smelling hostel. A short clumsy metro ride that jerked them along the tracks carries them to Antoni Gaudi's most famous works, the Sagrada Familia. Rising out of the green cloud of trees are the wafer intricate eight pointed spires that pierce into the blue skies. The symbol, the picture of the high towering jagged spires, is everywhere. It seems to be the logo of the city.

Eddy had seen it but did not want to ask what it was. As to do so would be a weakness of his naïve uneducated mind to what was inside Europe. He had already made himself look a fool with the La Ramblas comment, he was not going to make that mistake again. Once bitten, twice shy. As they walked closer to the eight spires that are built so far, Saoirse informed him from her tour guidebook that she cradled in her hands in a slow saunter that 'eighteen monumental spires will reach the heights when the project is set to be finished in 2028, just over one-hundred years since the architect's death.'

She goes on while frequently looking up, 'Twelve of these will be dedicated to the twelve Apostles, which are placed on the three facades. Six dedicated to the four Evangelists, Virgin Mary and Jesus Christ. The completed spires are the four Apostles of the Nativity façade, and four Apostles of Passion façade. The tallest one will be the dedication to Jesus Christ and surmounted by a giant cross.' Finally, she pauses to place her book in her brown shoulder satchel to gaze at the beauty ahead of them.

Churches have the uncanny way of transporting Eddy through to a time of an impressionable younger self. A person full of questions, with most still unanswered. Being raised a not-very-strict Christian, he has flowed through a mixed bag of emotions to the if's of fundamentally, if he truly believes in what he was taught regarding religion, the right one, the meanings, the understandings. However, stepping into a church brings all the righteous attitudes of understanding the knowledgeable religion to not help, but to identify with this culture. In all religions, it is to help. It is to support. It is to be kind. It is to be at peace. He still gets confused with the phrase religious war, or fight for religion. He is a novice reader regarding religion but from all he has read, he plainly sees that no good comes at the end of fighting. Someone will always be the defeater, the loser.

As they walked closer, he put to side his conflicting contradictions on the merits of war as the image was beginning to get clearer. The edges and intricate designs cleaner. Getting more impressive, if that was even possible. Under the heavy weight of construction, it is still a masterpiece, albeit unfinished. Gaudi worked hard on this, leaving plans for the entire Basilica for the architects after his tragic death in 1926, since starting the project in 1883.

Antonio Gaudi passed away at the age of seventy-three. To think this was by old age would be something that Eddy was pardoned with by Saoirse. Very courteous of her, he thought as he recalled the information she had just read, 'In fact, he was struck by a tram while on his daily route to work. He was actually not recognised as the famous architect for a while, can you imagine that?' She goes on to tell him that this is not a cathedral, which Eddy is constantly calling it since arriving here, but a basilica. 'Basilica means a church that has been granted special status by the Pope.'

Eddy cannot help thinking that she was a little too smug in her tone for her own good when announcing this little gem of information. Although he kept that too himself as she was probably trying to gain a comical bite rather than being, well, just a plain bitch.

They walked around, looking, scrutinising at each side, each façade. Each one is designed to respect a different stage of Jesus' life. Birth, life, death and the resurrection. Gaudi purposefully designed it so the sun would light each side in order to tell the tale of Jesus. What a vision. The queue to enter was like a boa constructor tightening its coils around the living and growing building. They joined the back, the far far far back of the multicoloured fabric-toting queue. How could you come, take a photograph and leave without seeing inside?

They watch so many tour groups that come, get off the bus in a large pack to leave moments later after a flurry of flashing cameras, whirring noises and numerous different clicks. This was to them look going or stopping in an airport lounge for a connection and saying you had been to a place. The queue was magically deceptive as it was moving pretty fast and in no time, they were paying the reasonable entry fee to what was essentially a construction site, that goes towards the funding of the completion.

They crane their necks until sore and stiff. They gawp, gaze and gape. They turn in pigeon-steps slowly on the spot. Twirling to the music of human sound, reflecting the lights from the tall stacked columns of coloured stained glass. Saoirse pauses, waits for Eddy to catch up. Hand in hand, for which they did not even realised the soft hold had happened they gaze at the altar. They tilt their heads slightly to lift their gaze to skinny pale peach Christ with bent knees towards his bare ribs wearing a crown of thorns, hanging from the wooden cross above the altar.

Above is the golden lampshade like marque of the baldachin, the representation of the Eternal Father which together takes on the symbolic role of the Holy Spirit which completes the full representation of the Trinity; the Father, the Son and the Holy Spirit. The baldachin is heptagonal for the seven gifts of the Holy Spirit; wisdom, understanding, counsel, fortitude, knowledge, piety and fear of the Lord. Around the fringe grapes in three colours hang, the symbol of wine of the Eucharist in moulded glass. Above are shafts of wheat to symbolise the bread for the Eucharist in golden curved leans. They move closer, underneath and really arc their necks skywards. The ivory bone-like honeycomb, the spotlights that sparkle like stars, the tall pillars that lift the building to near endless reaches of human design. The extraordinary site epitomised by stain glass windows that spill light in amazing beams of technicolour over the unique interior.

With a robotic turn of their head on their shoulders to adjust in a slow smooth circle, they iron out the aching pleasure-seeking necks. On one of the thick grey pillars, Saoirse leans to bathe in the glory of this sight which they saw so many people move away from after their photographs outside. Eddy thinks she looks so beautiful. There are no thoughts going through her mind apart from what the eyes are seeing, registering and appreciating. She is, for the most part, completely at peace.

In the museum is the miniature completion of the Basilica. Underneath their echoing steps on the yellow marble floor, resting in the crypt is the body of Antonio Gaudi. During his tenure on the project he used to sleep on site, now he lies in eternal rest within his creation. Saoirse cannot help but half-smile at the thought that he will always be not just a part but the part of his creation. Never knowing him, or reading extensively about him she likes to think that he would have just loved that.

The standard admission price does not include the towers, as they see people turned away. Without knowing that they had purchased the higher priced tickets intentionally they are equally jubilant that they had purchased a separate ticket for the Nativity Façade. They remember the questions but do not fully understand so just said 'yes'. They apparently had a choice of two of the intricate towers to access and involuntarily went for the Nativity with its sea views over the Passion with its city views. The fluke in their resolving 'yes' haphazardly with incredible fortuity merits them with the tower that was built and completed by Gaudi himself while he was still alive. With a whoosh they are transported to the top by a shaking but smooth, swift elevation with no sweat. The views, the history, the intricate designs. Wow.

They spend a long time appreciating the interior to the exterior from this viewpoint, their stand in awe on the shoulders of brilliance. They literally could be here all day. The design with the detail, the amount of time it has taken, it is taking to build will make this masterpiece thus a major-piece de resistance. Alas, not just for Barcelona, but for Spain, heck for the whole entire World.

Time has come for them to reluctantly go down. They spiral on adventure-risking stairs that are completely safe, but have no rails, but they had been told are complete safe regardless of the many warning and obligational legal approval signs. It spirals down, deeper down. Halfway a bridge connects the two of the four towers. This balcony with unobstructed views without cranes, construction and scaffolding that has become the part of the citadels view since the very beginning are all unseen, consequently ignored, therefore enjoyed. It was a glorious sight like site for being in a picture frame, framed by intricate columns to look out at the city. The sight of a carved snake is slightly peculiar on a church considering the connotations to the Garden of Eden tale.

Eddy was going to comment on this to Saoirse, but she had already picked upon the relevance as she scribbled a simple note of the significant finding in her a tiny bruised and battered notepad with pieces of ragged torn paper nestled in the thin plastic coils. This relieved him as he knew the summary of the story but never felt the need to read the completed story so was embarrassed to show his unknowing naivety.

Five hundred and four steps later, they are coiled around the tight quarry-rough walls to the bottom. To their surprise, this was not physically tiring. They had breath to debate over the finishing design. If it should be done how Gaudi intended or filled with concrete to enable a shorter timeline to complete the, sorry, his work. They never agreed completely with pros and cons, yet they both concurred that it should be finished with the architect's plans, no matter the cost and time. Either way, just like Gaudi, the project manager, the foremen and labourers have a job for life.

They talked at length of what they had seen. Often crossing over the same sight with emphasis on their shared enthusiasm for the fiery passion that burns inside of them bursting out in high-pitched words of gusto in short, detached sentences and words.

While sipping an aromatic black coffee with the slightest hint of bitter chocolate on one of the many bird-poo splattered benches, Eddy looks at the black umbrellas, the reflecting trees in the sea-green pond with the splash of light of colour from the people's attire. The noise of laughing, birds and the wind rustling the leaves. And the frenetic scribbling of pen on paper as Saoirse scribbled many bullet points and notes on her notepad of a design for her eyes only. She always believed in writing first before using a computer.

He remembers her remarking that, 'This connects me with the work I am doing' with adorable insistence. On the other benches are people writing their own mementos whether that be a journal entry or a postcard. Others are on their belly flat on the ground to take a photograph, others on tip-toes. The cameras were out in force, and why should they not be, Eddy was no different.

He already had numerous photographs but found himself getting up and taking another one, followed by another. One through a park railing with the black metal as a frame. Others using a person with a camera taking a photograph within a photograph. An array of easels had different views of the Basilica. Some would concentrate on a particular part in decorative ornate detail. Some picked a feature. Others the whole thing. Different aspects of the ways to show the art in colour, pencil, crayon, paint or chalk.

It was a fleeting look over the shoulder that he worked around as Saoirse got more absorbed into her own art. He absorbed their admiration in enjoying their hobby to look at what each eye looks at. What comes out of the mind for which the hands dictate with one in particular not just thinking out of the box, but fleeing from it entirely. Every now and again Saoirse repeats a word, whisper-quiet in a mantra that increases in volume as if struggling with the spelling, or grasping for another meaning.

Like the artists in the background, her wrist is possessed by her art, the written word. This invisible force is trying to describe so much that she is flicking through the plastic ring-bind notepad in a constant stream of blue-lined paper with blue ink in the margins, on the lines. Just like Victor Hugo did to the Notre Dame, she wrote with an inspirational respecting approval at this large piece of art. Unlike Victor Hugo, she did not write to save the building from destruction, but to enable the funding for the construction. Imploring people to come not just to the site but inside.

A sip, followed by a large noisy gulp of the now cold coffee and she was done. She smiled as she giggled a sorry for her involutory throat sing. Her belongings are returned into the correct place in her satchel as she rose to her feet. This was her announcing that she was ready to go. The paper cups discarded in the nearby bin as they head back to the metro, hand in hand, happy. She is cheerful with a light skip in each step.

From a recommendation from a hostel guest, they got off at 'El Coll La Teixonera'. It must be the Spanish for the underworld. They are in the depth of the deepest metro station in Barcelona. Although this was what it seemed, but in reality, they are still above sea level. The smell was revolting, causing Saoirse to gag slightly. A combination of the what humans let come out of them in a potpourri of unpleasant, all-powerful stench. With the dire need to vacant this place with haste they find the exit. After a teleporting ride in an inclining escalator ramp surrounded by light beams on the celling, on the walls and the floor, it was like something out of Star Trek.

An eerie silence surrounded the space with just the soft rumble and whirling of the machinery. The shiny, light reflecting hall soon showed the promise of a small square of light at the top of the end getting increasingly bigger, stronger. Fresh air was a mere breath away. Then in the light they inhale and exhale deeply. Trying to get that putrid smell out of their nostrils. Then they look at their surroundings. They are in a rustic local intrusion as they are stared at through the cracks in nearby windows. People in cars slow down to peer at them. They are in the middle of the residential area of Barcelona where tourists would not be seen.

At this moment he wondered if their hostel dormmate was having a secret laugh at their expense. That he had made this mistake and wanted others to be the thrill of his private joke. Nevertheless, albeit contentedly, they are seeing something that otherwise they would not see. They had made it this far, so they decided to venture on with the instructions given by the, in light of the day, dubious person. As they move on the rough gravel road to where, as promised, the road splits into a trident for which they take the middle one, as instinct takes over as their treasure map dictator did not incorporate this surprise into his instructions.

Amazingly enough, when they were doubting the correct fork, completely mistrusting the instructions given, they see a golden broad cross on an orange sphere. Everything was taken back in an instance with the sight of their destination. In this small green park, benches sit on top small moulds that look over Barcelona. The only residents today are the native pigeons. Below is their purpose, their journey's end highlighted by the gateau-like Pavilion below the trees. They zig-zag down the brown pea-gravel path. Two open large green metal doors welcome them inside Park Güell.

The modern-day Hansel and Gretel have followed the breadcrumbs of tenuous directions to two gingerbread houses. Bordering the entrance, these two buildings are plucked from the pages of Gaudi's original fairy-tale book shrouded in his minds to be flaunted in construction like a child pop-up book. They are all the shades of brown that you would find in the best bakery, topped with the most elegant of glistening icing fondants and crystallised sugars. The curved windows framed in marshmallow cushions of blue and white tiles. The roof very Gaudi-esque.

Coloured tiles arranged in bold ways to hide the purpose, in this case they assume chimneys. One has a towering blue and white checked spire that seems to move like a flag with the intricate design to be caged in a black orange orb and the golden cross they saw just as they were having doubts about their X marking the spot. The other building is very similar, though more of a cottage look with three floors and an attic. The waved roof of glowing white with angelica and marzipan line the pastry colours of brown.

'How would it be to design something like this? To go back to childish innocence to create...well...this?' Saoirse ponders more to herself, but out loud.

'They are unique, that is for sure. Nothing like this in the world I think, although my experience is...' Eddy laughs at his own stupidity.

With a mutual giggle but ignoring him, she goes on, 'Gaudi is such a rarity. I remember studying him in an art class and wanting to come. Finally. So many people have brilliant ideas but to actually build them. Put them literally on the map is marvellous. From conception. From design. To creation. Wow.'

'It is an expensive form of art. Look at the Sag.' Eddy had instantly abbreviated the Sagrada Familia to Sag, even before they were inside. 'Still not finished.'

'Creativity is not funded the way war is as you can make more profit in war.'

'Bit melancholic, Saoirse.'

'Think of it. Armies are better funded than education, health with creativity. Creativity in the arts down at the very bottom, one step off the scrap heap. It's bullshit. Think about it. Greed feeds. Arts are dying.'

Eddy did. He thought about the truth that she laid out in front of him. He also did not react as her provocative, confrontational tone that was quite argumentative. To all appearances fishing for a debate. Normally he would bite, clamp down and be involved in these types of challenging discussions but, he was enjoying the day, to start a needless arguing debate where no one would win he did not want to have it at this moment. All he said was, 'It was awesome that someone backed him.'

Looking slightly Walt Disney in design is the pale rose-coloured smooth-hued building of the Gaudi Museum. Inside where the light enters by symmetrically placed green framed windows with a binding ring-effect border in each side in the terracotta colours. It is as if the windows are open books to the world to read, learn, enjoy. Shaped like a wedge of cheese with its nose cut off, the centre is a large bell tower of sorts. They are not sure if a bell actually resides inside adorned with a pointed black with yellow starred cone to a crowning cross. This was actually Gaudi's home for twenty years until his death. It was a design house, as this park was going to be sixty houses like this for an upper-class neighbourhood. Not a park at all.

'You know,' Saoirse's tone has changed to a softer, pleasant music that Eddy is accustomed to hearing form her.

'Go on?' his voice slid to the question.

'Gaudi did not create this one. It was by Francesca Berenguer. Do you want to go inside?'

'Let's see the park first.'

'When this house was put up for sale, no buyers came forward. Güell insisted on Gaudi living here.'

'Who was Güell? I thought it was the name of the burb.' He instantly felt stupid again.

'He was a businessman. Catalan, I think, Eusebi Güell. Anyway, Gaudi. So, he took out his savings and moved his family and his father inside.'

'So, for the wealthy. Sorry, the working man, I am glad this became a park.'

'Another interesting thing. Park, P-A-R-K as it was inspired by the English Parks not spelt like Spanish, P-A-R-Q-U-E or Catalan P-A-R-C.'

With that, as if looking for confirmation, he looks for a sign to the park to see the spelling. She sees this and is quietly offended. As if she would lie.

Miffed, unknowing trying not to show just how much this simple act offended her, they officially walk in. They turn isolating away from each other, away from the gingerbread houses to face the staircase that wrap around the fountains. The local stone steps integrate into the landscape as if they are meant to be here. It is like walking in a dreamscape where she cannot stay mad for long. Her upset mind was instantly evaporated into tranquillity. She is still not purely happy, but it has gone from boiling rage to simmering controllable fury.

The multicoloured oversized lizard sets on a bright green bush. The blue striped head is known locally as the dragon. Eddy is reminded from something from the Dreamtime. The dragon is not that fierce as its dribbling out water from its open gapped mouth. Under the shady pavilion, the sounds of a softly strummed guitar moves smoothly though the area as a perfect accompaniment to the tourists and locals that mingle around here. As they look up their see stone, mosaic art in the coves in the ceiling. The Doric columns add an impressive take on the area with many of them making this area larger, or at least seem larger.

The waving serpent bench snakes around the border with small bumps in its design so that when it rains the tiles make it dry quicker and raised so you do not get your bottom wet if not fully dried from a downpour. They sit in one of the colourful curves which are makeshift booths to converse privacy. Looking around the social aspect of this area is amazing. The strange knobbly columns that lean into the level like fossilised tree trunks support the square above in pale brown scaled waves. It is funny to observe people looking around, taking photographs.

Eddy people-watched, then got up. The rest was short. It was more so Saoirse could write a few notes and Eddy could do what he wanted so he took a few photographs. They walk up grey stone steps to the park's highest point. Here a large stone cross marks the spot offering fantastic views of Barcelona. From Gaudi's creation, with the mountains as a backdrop they look over the rooftop blanketed view. Many people are perched dangerous on top of the tiny hilltop. No-one seems too worried about the danger, they all are getting selfies to send home, to friends, to lovers.

They chose to forgo the museum as they hope to see more of Gaudi before the sunsets. Their decision was based on talking to a couple in pidgin English that had just come out and from the brief discussion. They looked at each other as their voice, tone and general excitement was not burning them with a desire to go in. Although this could have been lost in translation combined with the shock of having two complete strangers taking to them, they decisively made the decision to sacrifice furniture and objects for other Gaudi sights.

Back on the metro, which is literally just outside the park, Saoirse hoped to scribble more notes. But this was not the case as this seemed to be where children make a cacophony of noise as they are having fun. They gaze at their watches to see if school is finished, or think if it even could be school break, but they seem to be everywhere. Having burrowed in their quietness in the classroom for this very moment to unleash the noise like bubbles from a dislodged cork from the bottle of merriment champagne.

She glares, Eddy shrugs his shoulders as kids will be kids and innocence should be maintained. The conversation is muted. The ruckus from the children with squeals and giggles has made it hard to talk even if they wanted to, so they sit in silence. Eddy looks through his photographs. Saoirse motionless and tensed up like the locked coils of a spring. Within no time, well for Eddy anyway, they are back in the centre of Barcelona. She sits with her arms folded as the metro pulled to a juddering halt. The rage is still on the hot hob.

He has forgotten, he has no idea why she is so cold. He assumes it is from the noise of the metro preventing her from working. He is no fool, he can see something is, has been up. Since coming to Barcelona, she has been a real ray of sunshine followed around by a little black cloud over her head that is ready for an imminent thunderstorm.

A short walk over the uneasily uncomfortably quiet street which finds them at the front of another one of Gaudi's famous buildings, the Casa Batlló.

'Hola?' The youngish smartly dressed doorman welcomes them questionably with a wonky smile, trying to hide his chipped teeth, at the entrance. He has a deep frown on his brow, topped with the slight tilt of his head that makes his smile seem straight while looking confused. In his brain they could almost hear the whirling of metal coils gauging whether to address them in Catalan, Spanish or English.

'G'day', Eddy replies, instantaneously mortified with himself. He quickly combined with a smooth as a fingernail running down a chalkboard, he stutters, 'Hi…hi…hi!' immediately after. It seems that since Eddy has been out of Australia, he has used more phrases, expressions and words that are not normally in his vocabulary to emphasise his proud Australian roots.

The doorman aligned his head, to return a large tobacco-stained pale-yellow grin with, 'Please. Please come in?'

They had been awestruck while in a living dream absorbing the blue and green floral reflective glass shards of glass when the words of the doorman released them from their hypnotic state. They survey the exterior once more. The design travels up the light brown walls like ivy in bloom. The seven ivory coloured skeleton balconies are reminiscent to frogs' eyes sockets with trendy lined sunglasses on that peer back down to and over them. The bottom level is crowned with a bold curvy wave on thin matchstick pillars where immortal birds nest. They are nodding their heads in approval. They are travelling up and down the building. High above them, hidden by the silhouette of the setting sun is the knobbly wave of the roof. They enter another hypnotic gaze for which the suggestion by the doorman once again snaps them out of the gaze.

'If you come in now, the sunset is the best in the world.'

A bold claim to behold. Eddy thinks that in Australia, pretty tongue-in-cheek, a café in the far outback has the 'best coffee this side of Italy' as well as 'greater curries than India'. They step up through the threshold to pay the price for entry which is very steep but as they stepped into the interior, they were instantly convinced to pay the smiling, not very talkative cash teller.

They read a sign that informs them of when the creation came into existence. Named after Josep Batlló who commissioned Gaudí to build this magnificent mansion for his family home in 1906. The inspiration surely comes from the nearby Mediterranean Sea as straight lines are obsolete, not a thing that can be seen here. A brilliant, rather, funky video guide is placed in their hand on entry about the size of a small mobile phone. Each room gives an audio, as well as a visual of what it would have been like to be transported back into the times of the original Batlló residence.

The funny animation brings a smile to them both which further brings this virtual screen image to life in their minds. A brush of each other's arms made them look away from their screens, look down to the presence of the touch. A lingering shared lovingly gaze deep into one another's eyes was shared. This spectacular building was actually giving them genuine goose bumps. Either that, or the chill that has arrived with the setting sun was reaching their bones. A slightness of a stroke on the soft unfelt bumps and they enter the large main suite. They look at a room made up of three interconnecting rooms.

As they get closer to the large windows where the top border is a form of blue colours from the round circles at the top which are stained-glass. These bubbles of colourful glass spill colours over the varnished light-coloured floorboards in a chessboard chequered design. They go to the window. Look out to the bustling leafy lined street of the prestigious bourgeois homes of the Passeig de Gràcia. They turn back, look up.

The ceiling waves look like an upside-down creamy trampoline caught in a gently breeze that swirls like a soft cream whipped ice-cream towards the centre of the exquisite golden orb of light like a plug hole. All this caught in a suspended moment, yet Saoirse can imagine the ceiling being brought to life, moving, swirling, dancing above her. Golden thin petals circular the light glowing the cream-coloured ceiling. Nothing is left to chance by Gaudí. The doorway itself makes an entrance in itself. The door handles, the trim, the attention is very much in the detail. Each and every room has the same theme, where no straight lines are ever present.

A long walk up some steep oak steps embracing the splendid marvellous grand staircase the ascends them to the dusk of outside cityscape. When they viewed from the ground is was a mere crack in the unopened curtains to what would be unveiled on the roof. Mouths open as they gape at the roof before them, the magnificent use of space, a hidden oasis. They are confronted in a way that nearly sends them backwards by the wave of the silhouetted view from the street below known, aptly as the Dragon's Back.

The coloured, sparkling mosaic spine wraps around the border in glorious vibrancy that seems to slither as scales off a dragon with the knobs resembling shell-scared snails that have retreated inside their homes, their shells. Four chimneys are alternate stages are disguised into fairy tale-warped castles of, towers of mosaic exteriors. The interior impressive, the exterior extraordinary, the rooftop spectacular. Put the trifecta into the locations and combine it to the views from here the whole experience is breath-taking. A looming peek over the dragons back see the street in the distance. The sounds off the traffic are muffled.

Eddy attempts to completely mute them. He lets the cold wind slap his cheeks as he slowly, deliberately closes his eyes and spreads his hands that hang loosely from his body. He tilts his head skyward. Almost in a self-meditative state, he takes a few deep breaths as he tries to block out his thinking but, in his mind, he is walking in a dream. Not towards anything but impulsively, he wants to be within one to appreciate this day. When he thinks enlightenment is close, the snap of an article of clothes brings him faster than a cannonball back along the white corridor of nothingness.

A strong gust of wind that lifted the airdrying laundry up and just as quickly released it to produce a short, crack of a large whip. He opens his eyes to look around and it seems no one had noticed his self-induced daydream. He slowly walks around the rooftop terrace. Back in reality, that moment of pause seems to heighten his admiration of the shapes that cast interesting shadows bouncing off, reflecting and flickering with a mutual approval and acceptance. He is gaining great pleasure in this day. This is intensified when he sees that Saoirse cannot stop smiling, without asking he knows this is her kinda bliss. She is very content. She floats over to him with open arms for a tight cuddle. Her head on his slow beating chest.

They gaze for one last time with Eddy's one arm draped around Saoirse's shoulder which she grasps his hand strikingly in hers. They rotate on the spot like two hipsters on a wedding cake to see and breath everything in its entirety all, in. They make their way unwillingly out of the building, with invisible anchors from their senses eagerly wanting to stay. In unison they turn to say an unspoken look of a cruel goodbye. Identifying intuitionally with understanding their emotional farewell the doorman, with a newfound confidence wishes them goodnight while announcing a snippet of local knowledge.

'We call this Casa Dels Ossos,' he pauses to see if they understood. They have not so he translates the name for them, 'House of Bones.'

A beautiful smile that said more than words could but meant to say thank you.

Noisy clumps of flat-hitting shoes that were not made for running. Hard exhales of bated breath. A sheen of sweat on their foreheads. Bowed, double over as if they had just finished a marathon run rather than a short block. Red faced. Eyes wide. They have arrived. They have reached the final destination of the day. It was quite ironic that they did not want to rush, hence their mutual decision to choose four feasible sights to see in a day. Yet, they somehow found themselves in a mad chaotic frenzy. They made it the barely five-hundred metres down the road. Yes, seeing this young couple, you would think they had just run over Barcelona. Obviously, cardio was not a strong thing of theirs.

All of Antonio Gaudí designs are uniquely brilliant. Here, they struggled for breath after their pathetic excursions to get to the front door. They rose up with the feeling of nausea gone to turn around after regaining their breath to lose it again. The corner which holds the Casa

Milà is outstanding. Straightaway they could tell that it had the only-one-of-its-kind traits of Gaudí. He really is undoubtedly one of the greatest architects of all time.

They had gotten here later than planned. They did not want to waste seconds asking for the time of closure so spontaneously launched into a sprint as if they were bats racing out of hell. In spite of them belting down the road they did not really need to rush as much, as they instantly see the closing times stating that the building closes at eight-thirty in the evening. Being that the hand of their clock had just ticked over past seven, surely, they had enough time to explore.

What has become the norm is to stare, ogling over the exterior of the building. Eddy cannot help that the curvy, wavy façade looks like the Flintstone's dream palace. Moulded into the stone work are curved windows that embed themselves naturally. Black, elaborate cast iron railings of an unrecognisable design from this vantage point settles elegantly on some off the very few balconies. This corner property states an imposing image, an imposing stature that it is here, never to be moved, never to be replaced, as natural as sand on a beach it will never be surrendered to urban renewal. Urban renewal destroyed many buildings, historical, cultural or significant to many towns in the world in the pretence of progress and production. For Eddy to see it in Sydney, he regards, after learning it in his school, as a great loss rather than a great benefit.

'The Casa Milà is often referred to as the Stone Quarry,' Saoirse joins Eddy's private party not for the first time today to take him out of his trance.

'Should be Bedrock Quarry,' Eddy retorts.

On seeing Saoirse's blank expression, remembering that she was not in on the conversation in his mind, backtracks a stuttering explanation that made the joke an epic fail.

'If Gaudí was alive, I believe he would not take kindly to that ugly nickname.' Eddy tries to bring himself back from the shores of embarrassment.

'Maybe not but apt to the stone, yes. Maybe not the quarry. That seems to strongly underline everything the building is not. It is made of stone though. Anyway you, let's yabba dabba go.' With a wink, a poke in the ribs and a light snigger, she mocks him as she walks in.

'Come on!' he pleads behind, trying to supress laughter of his own.

It would seem in 1906, Gaudí was rather a very busy boy. In that year, Pere Milà and his wife Roser Segimon hired him to build their new property. The main floor was for their private residence with the rest of the building converted to rented apartments. Roser Segimon was said to have loved the finished project and lived here until her death in 1964. Similar to Casa Battló, a very technical savvy audio and video display was included in the ticket entry price.

No numbers were needed to press as motion sensors sensed where they were in the building. *Pretty cool*, Saoirse thought. From leaving the exterior of the pavement, they are instantly outside again. Eddy gasped out aloud as he looked up at the courtyard. Positioned perfectly in the effectively distorted figure of eight shape to spill natural light in the form of small mercury marbles from the shining clear bright moon onto the reflective windows in the well of the courtyard. They took it all in, bathing in the moonlight. This was so romantic, the well of windows being kissed seductively by the moon with them in the spotlight of the centred floor. Perfectly lined in a circular curve with tall, towering separate pillars of stone separating each column of windows.

They danced in a music-less twirl in the beams of the moon, in awe at the natural beauty. In their gradually growing spin, Saoirse pulls Eddy just in the nick of time to stop him knocking into a miniature model for the building to see exactly how it is made up. This stopped their momentum, so they used the opportunity to peer into the yellow wax-like dripping model as if it was a new species of an alien unfamiliar to them. In a way it was. They decided to go reverse from the top down. After a brief survey, they see the lift and they cross the courtyard to go smoothly up to the roof. The damp smell of leather enveloped their senses as they looked around the cushioned walls.

The door opens like the curtain of a theatre production to show the rooftop screaming out with Gaudí's personality individuality. His love for curves, waves, circles is so evident. The audio guide tells them he liked to replicate nature, for which he called organic art. In an art of confirming what was being heard they both needed to point out what the audio was telling them, adding a commentary of their own. Together they pointed out various pieces of art that represented organic such as fire, earth and wind. As they were doing it, they felt slightly strange, but they could not stop stating the obvious.

Eddy is on trigger-finger as he snaps constantly but still trying to absorb everything with his naked eye. He makes a silent prayer to the digital camera as if this was a traditional roll who would have surely run out in mere seconds into the start of the day. He points to a cracked cross on a plinth of crazy, cracked wings to represent Earth for which he mouths over the audio but does not actually speak out.

What may appear to be random sculptures that adorn the roof are in fact disguised stairways for roof access, disguised chimneys and ventilation towers. Gaudí did not waste an opportunity of dazzling creativity to go to waste. These essential, everyday things were transformed into an artistic merit to fit in with his scape. Saoirse then produced a delightful soft giggle as, for the first time today, she insisted on having a photograph taken of her next to a large flickering dreamy torso sculpture that made her look smaller than she was. She was normally camera shy. She shunned the opportunity to have a photograph taken. She would hide her face if a camera phone came out.

Yet she beamed her perfect smile as she posed in different formations as Eddy impersonated a fashion photography to her squeals and glees. The cluster of chimneys were transformed into separate pillars of ostrich necks with scarfs and pointed medieval helmets. The only opening was the owl-like eyes of the soulless empty eye sockets that appeared to not appear. They were described as being the 'Guardians of the Rooftop' on the audio feed.

'Trencadis technique,' Eddy whispers to Saoirse. 'That is the form of mosaic using broken tiles, stone, marble and glass.'

He almost repeated the audio word-for-word as he pointed to the trencadis mosaic on the arches and walls. These giants of Gaudí art made them forget the actually purpose of the sculptures as they saw them as art as they walked around the rooftop of Barcelona.

From this vantage point Saoirse points the recognisable spires of their first Gaudí sight of the early morning. The magnificent sight of Temple Expiatori de La Sagrada Familia with its many supporting characters in the towering cranes is still awe-inspiring.

'Can that only have been this morning?' Eddy mumbles to himself in recognition at Saoirse's sticking pointed finger.

Like ants following each other in single file is the slow-moving traffic from the busy streets below. People going home after their day at work. The other side shows the equally impressive as looking up of the curves of the courtyard. Just a few minutes earlier they were looking up. They stare longingly as they leave the rooftop to enter the attic. To welcome them is a strange upside-down display of small linked chains. This sight does not seem to fully register for a few short seconds as the linked chains hanging over the mirror is how he designed the attic.

'Wait,' Saoirse interjects with a rising epiphany. 'I remember this theory. Hey…I am surprising myself. Back then I never thought I would use what I learnt in math but her—'

'What?' Eddy released in an urgent questioning plea.

'If you wait for me to finish.' She stares, wanting him to bow his head in a form of puppy-dog apologies before she continues, 'As I was saying. In math, I learnt. What-do-you-know, I actually did! I learnt to find a shape that a flexible chain takes up under gravity happen when the two end points are fixed to make a shape. When the chain comes to rest, the chain rests all the tension is pointing along the interior, outwards. Always outside otherwise the chain would twist, bend, be….er….be not able to, well…rest? Yes, rest. Er…not at rest. Gravity here has solved the problem of forces which makes the chain bend. When turned upside down and made to support a building. The force is now turned into compression but still point on the interior of the chain. So, it is strong to support without needed any flying buttresses. This stops the building collapsing inwards.'

'What…where did all that come from?' Eddy did not understand what she just said. It was as if Saoirse was possessed by Einstein or Hawking. He was proud, he was astounded, he was spellbound by her mathematical conspiracy.

'Do you want to sound anymore surprised? Hey…I listened at school. I just didn't use it.'

'I get it; you are ahead of the audio. That is the only way, only answer to how—'

'Oi! Cheeky, you are so getting punished tonight!'

'Mmmm.'

As if in tune, the audio kicks in to dissolve the growing electric atmosphere in their flirting ways to tell them the arch's keep the attic space as light, and as open as possible. The tone frame work of the attic are highlighted by a golden soft light from below. The sexual verve dissipates into the tunes of the warm Spanish dusk.

The two-hundred and seventy catenary arches made of thin brick went as far as the eye could see. The shell of the attic was amazing. The contents seemed to be filled with Gaudí's entire body of work. They were all reflected on the stone floor in pale blues, golds and silvers. Arriving late had huge advantages as it was noticeably quiet. The reflections of his art were echoed in their silent approval. This turned into the best way to end to the day.

Unknown to them, the museum had more models of the building they were in, as well as the places they had been to: Park Güell, Casa Batlló, La Sagrada Familia and many more other buildings. In glass cabinets, on pedestals they stood proud in the attic. It was nice to see them as a giant looking down at his dwarfing creations. The hollow thud of their delicately placed footsteps reverberated around the space, resounding a resonate love to his dedication on letting us all be grateful for his vision in his art. Items of his designed furniture was also on display on a white shallow stage that seemed to glow on a blanket of creative emergence.

Down some stairs, they link glittering eyes delighted and fortunate in what they have seen. They enter into the apartment area which displays in a few rooms how they were decorated when first built. Classic white squares with black smaller squares fill the living room with effortlessly placed antique furniture. It is strange to see these older pieces of antiquity within such a cutting-edge appearing building. This highlights to Eddy that Gaudí was very much ahead of his time.

A peek through the tall narrow slits of windows allows enough light in to fill the high-ceilinged rooms. These were designed for middle-class families, but what they see is screaming high-class wealth. Sewing machines, ironing board with an iron and wooden handle and other everyday utensils. The pride in which Gaudí took in his work is so evident in that fact that nothing is left. No stone overturned. The handles, the knobs, the mouldings, the doors the smallest detail is, all, true art.

On entering the kitchen, in a return to his roots, Eddy peers into the large black iron stove with copper and brass handles. A portal in his mind takes him through to the how's he would use this, how he would cook and how he would deliver the food. Red, worn hexagonal tiled floor like a beehive must have seen some exciting meals come from this area. Wooden utensils are in enamel jugs. Saoirse drags him away from the dreams with the simple words that he was thinking.

'Can you just imagine living here. And having that roof a few steps away to enjoy? It would have been lush.'

'Would love to have found out.' The only words that he could squeeze out.

Eddy though could not argue with her phrase. Well, assuming that lush meant great. They had had a warning that the museum, as they called it, was shutting soon what seemed like a second ago. Now, thirty minutes after that first warning it was a reality. It was eight-thirty when they were virtually frogmarched off the premises. They left the large doors to the silent relief of the workers. They looked up at the series of waves.

It was a slow, swaying twenty-minute walk back to La Rambla, they decided to walk it with the hope that they would find somewhere to crave their hunger. It had been a long, great day but apart from a light breakfast nothing, but water and coffee had entered their rumbling stomach.

Invisible twirls of salty smoky meats direct their stroll, mute their animated speech and lead them with the crowds of people down a wide cobbled pedestrianised lane towards a large pink pastel painted building with tall thin narrow windows. The sweep of the lit strobing lights across the theatre-resembling building has golden letters that shine in the gently sweep above the large arched glass entrance with 'El Nacional'. This was all dramatic, but the effects were lost as Saoirse pulled Eddy down the large brick-covered dark lane towards the light but guided by her nose, her hunger towards the lights.

As they loomed forward, the building grows as if they were travelling down the rabbit hole while shrinking. People are dwarfed as they enter the grand large doors, they pursue the ant-like trail that opens out to a majestic food court. They smell the foods but are not sure how it all works. Do they walk to the spacious large bar in the centre of this large pavilion with glass panes in the dome shaped roof with wrought iron embellishments? Where bottles of coloured liquids swirl and clink to pour and serve the well-dressed people leaning against the clean metal and marble serving desk.

The moonlight shines through the skylights to glitter its shine over the metal to twinkle. They think they have found it out as various, different cuisine-based restaurants surround the bar in satellite form. They think that they know what to do but know they are unsure of how to go about choosing a restaurant, do they go down and seat or wait to be seated? After a while of being two spares at an uninvited wedding they apprehensively, deliberately step slowly down the few shallow steps to the tapas area to take a seat.

Recycled old car headlights with a new lease of life emit a soft glow of amber over the glossy flimsy pale-yellow menu in Spanish and English. Like flies in a spider's web it would appear that they have stumbled on a tourist trap. In spite of this they are happy perched on the tall wrought iron seats with dark brown leather cushioned and lean on the bar in the spider's liar. The nest of a vibrant lively atmosphere with a busy, but cosy ambience. They order a couple of beers. If they had them in their hands, they surely would have spilt them as a guy leans across to the bar tender while animatedly shouting to the server.

All wear stylish attire that screams the glamour and glitz from the jazz era of the roaring thirties. As he waits for his order Saoirse asks what to do. With a glint in his smile that on any other person would come across arrogant, yet on this handsome young guy transcended unpretentious natural tolerant to explain the means. He points to another associate with a vivid interesting assortment of foods on an oval shining tray. Eddy cannot hear what he says as he seems to whisper very closely into her ear, but he does not help notice the way she flicked her hair back as she tossed her head back and roared a wild cackle of laughter. A pang of jealousy entered his throat to restrict his voice to a touch of her exposed arm to demonstrate that she was his.

'Basically,' she yelled over the high-pitched squeal of cornets over a low plucked bass strolling rhythm, 'you put your hand up if interested in what they shout out. They come over. They drop off a dish of what he is carrying. Marks the card on the table and goes around the floor.'

'How do we know the price?' Eddy enquires.

'Er...' with a shrug of her shoulders, 'well, we don't. Fun! No?'

'HUEVOS ESTRELLADOS CON JAMÓM IBÉRICO', is musically sung out by the suit-wearing enthusiastic waiter.

Saoirse, Eddy as well, has no idea what the designer stubbled waiter shouted but she launches her arm straight as a die into the air. Eddy looks on astonished at her adventurous side coming out with a certain thrill at what she is demonstrating. She never ceases to amaze him. He smirks down in the light reflecting bar. He places one then with Eddy's tediously finger wave he alerts him to place another down. Out of the back of his ear, he produces a pencil and marks two lines in the corner of the beer lauded coaster. They dig into essentially fried eggs and ham. It was nice. Simple but effectively ample for a taste of what is going to happen in the ensuing evening. They glow in the basking radiance of the dining room with their nervous energy dispersed to be replaced with a relaxing influence.

They talk above the noise. They do not get lost in the atmosphere, but they do get lost in a personality of idem fervent admiration for the glorious day to explain why it is so bloody good to be, thus, to then feel truly alive. To outsiders they seem to be talking over each other, but they are so connected to the greatness of the day that they are in tune with each other to finish some sentences, to start others. The aroma of the dishes, the meat, the sizzling sounds of cooking, the vibrancy of the plates surrounded by the thirties and forties décor gets them so stress-free, so unperturbed by the ruffled vivacity that surrounds them.

They eat an array of different flavours. They eat more than they need. They drink more than they need. They laugh more than they have for ages. They have not felt this connected for ages. The ambiance, the company, the free moving conversation is relished as much as the savoured tapas. From here they stumble home, arm-locked in a beer-hazed drunk love back to their hostel to fall asleep drunk-locked in aching desire.

One more day awaits them. They started Barcelona in culture so that it seemed fitting that they would end in culture. They are in no particular rush as they rise with a heavy head. Groaning, head in vice, they awake, dusty. Creaking their neck, perching head in hands on the edge of the bed. So much pain. Gradually, slowly opening their heavy eyes, lift their weary head. Pain. Shuffle around to get ready. The water bounces off their bodies as they try to rinse away yesterday's misdemeanours. It does not do the trick. They could get public transport but choose to walk, to hopefully arrive at their destination with a clear head.

This long distance, to another of Spain's favourite sons, Picasso, should make them pure again. The walk seemed so easy. It was, it was so easy to get, lost. They had, and they did numerous times on many occasions although they did not care. They took in the surroundings as they sluggishly lose the manacles around their arms and legs that drag them down for which they leave the footsteps behind of their hangover. The narrow streets where scooters fly past, where helmet-less youths with a reckless disregard to anyone else walking the streets brush past them. They, as they do around them, do not care.

They embrace their culture. Everything that comes hand in hand with it all. The nice, but strange smells. The colourful fashion in the dark, graffiti shrewd shadows. The beauty of every smallest thing that they take for granted growing up, much the same as every child in their hometown. They see it afresh, new and gorgeous. The smell of coffee, pastries fills the air, masking the open, dented rubbish laden garbage cans. From the unseen cafés they are tempted to stop, search, seek and end their hunger. But, they are happily lost. If it was not for the large banners travelling down the stone walls on Montcada Street they would have walked past their objective. Although if they had not seen the banners, if they had not turned the corner the long line would surely have given the entrance away. They were in less pain. Their dust cleared so they could focus. The headache replaced with untroublesome nausea.

Five grand townhouses, which are all former palaces, house the Picasso Museum. The first courtyard is truly amazing, a rich delightful taste of what is going to be subjected to. They walk under a stone curtain arch to be immediately engulfed in architecture with a few different eras shown in the windows, doors and masonry. The stone gargoyles of animals and people look down as if looking through everyone with that cold-steeled eye glaze of being scrutinised. The grand staircase is amazing. This alone seems to elevate the already elevated expectations of what to expect.

A light sprinkle of rain had started to fall down before entering that was getting increasingly harsher. The shimmer on the stone courtyard, the figures in the decor looking fresh but sad accompanied by the glistening rain streaming down in silky glossy threads down their polished cheeks making they expressions glower harder. The passing of the grey cloud, that had approached without warning looked to be here to stay. Fortuitously decent timing on their part to be close to shelter. Even so, this unexpected downpour has done nothing to dampen their mood, they have not fled the courtyard, they continue to observe as they absorbed the visionally treat as their skin repelled the bullets of the larger raindrops.

They have accepted the rain with wide open welcoming arms. They acted like children, fresh, innocent and naïve as they frolicked in the forming puddles, streams to the realms of the enclosed walls. They are simply in love for life. Savouring everything with their eyes. Looking forward to the day ahead. They leap up, they bound up the steps, skipping two at a time in their pursuit to the top. Passing the huge dripping palm trees in comically small red terracotta pots that seem unstable in the design, but seemingly effective in the execution, they trickle splashes of water with them into the entrance.

Before they had left the hostel, they had asked the extremely helpful owner for directions. He must be asked the same questions daily, maybe even hourly, but every time they have asked a particular question, he has seamlessly remarked the answer with joy, without a hint of revulsion at repeating himself. The owner of the hostel had given them a warning for them not to expect too much of the Picasso Museum. He stated that some actually come back disappointed. They are not many masterpieces of his later work from the cubism period in which he is better known for. Used more akin to demonstrate, through his art as a way of learning his early stages, where his created originally ingenuities were being produced. More importantly his life that lead him on the path of his unique niche in the art world.

At the top of the stairs, just before entering officially, a brief introduction to how the museum was created was voiced over in a smooth, timbre male voice in Spanish. Mercifully for the non-Spanish understanding foreigners, on the walls are columns of other languages to give to them what was ever so sweetly told. It would seem, although Saoirse is reading between the lines as she speaks aloud to herself in a careless whisper, Picasso's friend and personal secretary Jaume Sabartés proposed the creation of a museum in 1960.

On 9 March 1963, under the name of the Sabartés Collection, the museum opened. Picasso strongly opposed the Franco regime that was currently controlling Spain. He swore that he would not set foot back in Spain during the Franco regime, 'but he was totally in agreement with the museum', hence, he was not around at the opening. At the beginning, Sabartés and Picasso donated the artwork to make the museum, although many have contributed since. This was the only museum opened during his lifetime and holds nearly four thousand pieces of art in the permanent collections.

Starting from the humble beginning of his life. Born to the son of a painter and art dealer Picasso entered the world in Malaga on 25 October 1881. His full name is a shock to them. No wonder he shortened it to the easy rememberable Pablo Picasso. It is an astonishing twenty-three words, comprising of one-hundred and twenty-two letters. The full name for Pablo Picasso, which would not fit on many banners let alone the ones outside, is a mouthful. Deep breath—Pablo Diego José Fransisco de Paula Juan Nepomuceno María de los Remedios Cipriano de la Santísima Trinidad Martyr Patricio Clito Ruiz y Picasso.

'Seriously?' Eddy remarks as Saoirse reads his full name in a playful whisper with a sharp jolting poke in her ribs. Eddy, who was far ahead of her and was happily reading about his childhood, read something that made him pretty sceptical.

'Pencil. Bloody pencil was his first word…Seriously?'

'Shhhhh,' Saoirse frustratingly whispers through gritted teeth, while rubbing her fresh bruised side.

The museum is in chronological order which is helpful for them. Another shock bestows them as it surprises them both that the first artwork is at the tender age of fourteen. Normally gifted creative artists had pieces in single figures like Johannes Chrysostomus Wolfgangus Theophilus Mozart whose first ever composition was a minuet at the age of five. The amazement, nevertheless, came from the realism. They expressed the same astonishing reactions to how a fourteen-year-old could produce such realistic, accurate and natural portraits. When Picasso was fourteen years of age, they moved to Barcelona where he attended the Fine Arts School in Llotja in the vicinity of Barcelona. Unsurprisingly, this time in the advanced classes for two years.

After reading the blur to the right of one of his more famous early paintings, 'Science and Charity', Eddy starts walking back and forth as if on an invisible treadmill. He looks an idiot. Saoirse comments on this solo dance he is making with a slight embarrassed giggle to be associated with him. It was only when he explained what he had just read that she started doing the same awkward movement. The blur stated that the doctor is modelled on his father, which he did often, with his mother featured in many other paintings too but not this one. This clever perspective trick is that when they walked back and forth, the bed would shrink and grow.

Although they were not sure if they were getting hoodwinked into thinking that this was working or just them being further away each time. This is a large classical painting which appears in its composition to all the players here having a purpose within the small narrow room. For some reason, Eddy brought this into his style of cooking where everything has a reason to be on the plate, whether texture or flavour but not just to be there because it would make the plate pretty.

At fourteen years of age, Picasso first came to Barcelona and continued to frequent the city often. He official moved to Paris when he was twenty-three but never losing touch with the city, he considered home. Barcelona was where it begun for him. He gained a reach education, a keen sense of creativity meeting bohemian artists in the El Quarte Gats Café to discuss and push what was deemed to be radical, experimental and initially unacceptable art. He felt that his hands were tied at the Art's College. He used a common theme through his art during this period of a landscape seen from a window, which was perceived to be his desire to escape.

From what Eddy knows of Picasso, it is strange for him to see these paintings of religion and social theme as the common distorted faces and straight angles come into his mind when he thinks of the artist. He is gaining an appreciation to learning about him as a person, as well as an artist. They are highlighted towards the 'Harlequin' painted in 1917. This pale blue and white portrait of the jester is fidgeting nervously around his stomach with his hands, this was the first donation by Picasso for this museum.

When Picasso moved to Paris, he lived in poverty. He was not rich like he was later but sacrificed everything for his art. This started the Blue Period of his artwork. This dominate colour reflected his mood that at the time was quite depressing, very dramatic and to Saoirse quite alone. Sculptures of Fernande Olivier, an artist model, seemed to have a huge impact in his life. In many writings next to his art, she is mentioned.

She was his first long-term girlfriend. His artwork changed over the seven years with the Blue Period behind him he encountered a world through rose-coloured glasses to step, literally, into his Rose Period. These were different, very sexual. When she moved in with Picasso in 1905 her modelling days were over for other artists as he prevented it. She continued to model for him. It is at this point that the museum continues with his life but limits the artwork, as in 1908 Pablo Picasso with George Braque invent Cubism. Unknown stories are revealed. After he was questioned as a suspect when the Mona Lisa was stolen, he moved to this, defining part of his livelihood.

In 1911, after Picasso had been unfaithful with Marcelle Humbert, better known as Eva Gouel, Fernande left him. Picasso was said to be devastated by her early death. As a homage, a tribute, he painted 'I love Eva' in many of his paintings around this time. However, he did manage to comfort himself with her illness to start a relationship with Gaby Lespinasse. This was a short fling as he moved to Rome to work with Ballet Russes. There, in 1917, he met Ballerina Olga Khokhlova, with whom he married in the Russian Orthodox Church in Paris in 1918. Here the life was described as a 'conflict'. For she was high society, he was more avant-garde in his pursuits. Yet, they did bear a son, Paulo, in 1921. The artwork of Picasso changed once again to contain a more mother and child theme.

In the year of 1929, it was the first recorded meeting between two very different creative Spanish thinkers in Salvador Dalí and Pablo Picasso. Years later, in 1963, thirty-four years after that converging of great minds, Dalí donates his illustrated book containing thirty

Picasso etchings that he did in 1931 to the museum. Without knowing, as yet have not seeing the drawings it is pretty evident to them that Dalí held this collection of sketches dear to his heart, for him to keep hold of them for so long. Through an open doorway these are on show in a predominantly large whitewashed room.

Eddy looks over Les Metamorphoses d'Ovide. These thirty drawings seem to be sketches of work that are unfinished. Some looking pale in comparison to the large thick golden frames that border them with a simple gold plaque with the title. Others stand in grid-like patterns on a pale blue wall. The Metamorphoses was a poem by Roman poet Publius Ovidius Naso in 44BC. They read a brief introduction to Ovid's Latin-written poem. Reread it. Looked at it again. Read every word. It might as well be written in Latin! It was squeezing the juice of sense out of a juiceless lemon but getting none. They still do not fully grasp the pretence of the classic poem.

They go with the opening line of the blur, as well as from the book itself to strive for comprehension: 'I intend to speak of forms changed into new entities.' Nope. No luck there. Of the fifteen books, the books intend a poem chronicle of history of the world from its creation to the death of Julius Caesar with a combination of mythological and historical events. They got that, but still could not build a bridge to the now. The confusion on their faces must have been plainly obvious for all to see. As a relatively young smartly dressed worker came over to ask if assistance was necessary. Without a word of encouragement have been said by them, she started to voice her opinion on the interpretation of the poem.

'Metamorphizes is a fifteen-book poem which incorporates classical Greek and Roman myths. Mix with history as well. Ovid begins with invoking the Gods. He, Ovid, implores them to inspire his work. Gods and stars fill the heavens. Fish fill the seas. Beasts fill the land. Birds fill the air. Man, create to rule the world. At the end, Ovid ends with a concussion, concl-conclusion that a message, delivered – everything changes.' She smiles to symbolise the end of her explanation. She broke it down in perfect English articulation with a few verbal exploitational-humps on the way.

'Thank you,' they speak in a unison of agreement which encounters them utterly fulfilled with the quick, precise clarification of her speech.

'That was pretty amazing?' Saoirse offers more with a tone of astonishment, than the want for a response.

Halfway around is a mini tribute to Ovid which gives credit for his work through others. The short piece considers William Shakespeare as having been considerably influenced by this poem on no less than two occasions. The first in his play, Romeo and Juliet from the fourth instalment about the story of Pyramus and Thisbe, but then again during a scene with a band of amateur actors in A Midsummer Night's Dream. Another by artist Auguste Rodin during his visionary stories of Antiquity many times, but definitely in Gates of Hell. Although the sketches seem to be rather rushed, they both feel the need to circulate twice.

To really absorb what they are seeing as not just pieces of art, but a personal appreciation for another piece of art in the want to display it again in a different art form. They do seem to be the only ones to value three heads coming together in this very room in Ovid, Dalí and Picasso to feel a similar mutual interest. A hushed silence comes over them. An almost relaxing invisible hand of serenity.

Here, Picasso's life enters an even more complex larger-than—his-own-life story affecting not just himself but everyone he is in contact with. A contagious infectious relationship full of twists and turns with each ending as thorny as the bloody embedded painful spikes of Christ's crown. Or, on another hand, an immense extravaganza that is seat-perchingly brilliant and interesting as the next ground-breaking blockbuster. Although this heavily depends on your point of view. During the tempestuous marriage to Olga, Picasso met the then seventeen-year-old Marie-Thérèse.

When a relationship is quoted as 'conflict', surely that is the first clue that it will never work. Eddy and Saoirse both seem to be thinking the same thing as they look at each other with raised eyebrows, as if to say 'I told you so'. The thing that Eddy could not understand was the close proximity of her living arrangement. Picasso wanted her close, so he bought a flat over the road from his marital home for them to reside. But still out of the view of Olga.

Still Eddy could not believe that anyone could be so foolishly bold. He was not sure whether to be respecting his brave daring nature or gobsmacked at his reckless idiotic ways. It was as if he was trying to get caught. An old phrase entered his mind to explain, but not fully clarify the motive.

'More front than Oxford Street or King's Cross back in Sydney!' he whispered quickly to Saoirse. Then sheepishly spent the next few minutes explaining his statement. 'Come on!' he continued. 'Really? Seriously? It was only when Marie became pregnant that Olga knew. AS...IF!'

'I can read!' Saoirse clenched the words through gritted teeth.

'I know. I bloody know that. I was more saying it to myself.'

'Then do just that...in your head, I mean.'

Unsure to where that outburst came from, he continued to read that they had a daughter, Maya, born on 5 October 1935. He read in his head this time. Shortly after this, Picasso and Olga separated, but they stayed married, so she would not be entitled to half his wealth. Eddy wanted to comment on this, but due to the last warning felt it would be better to let sleeping dogs lie. This period had a profound influence on Picasso. These were obviously stressful times for whom he stopped painting for a year to divert entirely to write poetry for the next few months. Olga died in 1955, still Picasso's wife but as that is all the museum says, Eddy comes to the presumption that no love was truly lost.

Marie had him all to his own. Yet, she was beginning to become jealous of Picasso's infidelities, who was now fifty-four. His newfound interest was for the twenty-nine-year-old Dora Maar. They met a year after Maya was born but seemed to be spending more time with each other, in Marie's eyes, over the succumbing years. Marie was said to be the influence of Picasso's Vollard Suite etchings that are on display around the walls of this pale boarded floor. Named after Ambroise Vollard the French art dealer who gave Picasso his first Paris exhibition in 1901.

Over one hundred etchings done in seven years which Saoirse smirks at Picasso himself represented as a minotaur. Picasso produced these for Vollard in exchange for some pictures. The footsteps echo around the cemetery silent room as if in bereavement of the loss. The numerous people that are enveloped in a cloak of interest for a man they did not know, could not help but make a slight sound with the softest plant of their feet. But, amongst the hollow coffin like echo they all felt that they did know more of him since going through his life from baby to boy, adolescent to man through love, art and tragedy.

The silence was exhilarating in its librarian essence with a blind eye to this morbid unseen discomfort. What annoyed Eddy was no photography was allowed. He hated this rule. He understood and respected it, but it still irked him considerably. Saoirse was stopping to take notes, on top of more notes. Many times, they changed tact like an amusing cat and mouse cartoon where often Eddy was ahead of Saoirse and had to wait or backtrack to eat up a bit of time for her to catch-up for the roles to be reversed. Eddy was reading everything, moving through the segment, period or painting in question and trying hard to absorb everything around him but constantly moving as fast as a snail. Maybe, just maybe, the camera rule in this instinct benefitted him.

The bereft rue was still present that a photograph would be a great memory to recall fully what he was captivated with. Saoirse was reading, perched in an awkward uncomfortable position, standing still. Struggling to scribble down yet another note, all the time wrestling with her belongings. He could not help but think Saoirse's method was either like a dog that had to sniff everything on a new walk or a vacuum cleaner that kept getting its cord caught around the edges of all the furniture. Each anecdote was not meant to be a compliment. He saw the silver-lining in that he read in great detail everything, sometimes more than once. Normally around the half-way mark he would start skating over pieces, or missing them completely, but he was learning a great deal of his life due to his annoying, but precious vacuum cleaner cord.

The effect of Dora Maar was unmistakable. She was the Yugoslavian photographer who documented his brilliant Guernica. The depiction of the German bombing on the Basque City of the same name during the Spanish Civil War. During this time Hitler declared Picasso's art as 'degenerate'. They were not the only people to portray a snorted scoff at this overreaction. According to these writings on his life on more than one occasion Picasso referred to Dora as her 'Private Muse'. It was never said but heavily implied that something happened between the two, especially as the next part of his life near enough stated that a romance of some kind happened. For Eddy it was thus unsurprisingly the inevitable did actually ultimately happened.

The then 62-year-old Picasso left Dora for a young art student, Françoise Gilot who was barely twenty-two years old. Out of all the women in his life, this one seemed his second most important. Together they had two children, Claude and Paloma. The latter named after the dove of peace that Picasso painted in support of the Peace Movement, post-World War Two. But Picasso being Picasso.

Saoirse sighed audibly as she read about his self-destructive, male, dick-obsessed ways. His love for women controlled his love for anyone. His selfish nature that he wanted to go fishing, all the time, in the sea endlessly, without letting his line go without new fish. When he should be content with the fish he had already caught. Hence, after Picasso's numerous discretions, Françoise left him in 1953.

To rewind back before this event, the then seventeen-year-old in 1945 interviewed Picasso for a school newspaper. Saoirse imagined this now. How Saoirse would have loved to have interviewed such a great individual when at school.

'Some people get all the luck,' Saoirse rued.

She thinks back to a piece of work she read after college. It was banned in her school, like so many other schools, but not due to the connection with John Lennon's assassination which is the common misconception. But banned for the profanity to what the lead character was actually saying. Of course, her minds glances at the sun-bleached red top with the white scribbled lines of the light paperback cover of the American classic, The Catcher in the Rye. The 1951 novel is a narrative of the young man Holden Caulfield who is undergoing treatment in a mental hospital. It connected then and now with the young adults of the world with the first account of the innermost troubles of growing up.

'…in America when a school student interviewed Jerome David Salinger,' she continues. Although Eddy smirks humbly at her mention of his full name. This simple trait brought Dermot Hanlon, an Irishman he worked with in Australia to the forefront of his mind. He insisted on calling people by their given name to the fullest, no abbreviations, no surnames or nicknames ever crossed his lips. This did unconsciously stick with him, without him knowing as he always greeted a person fully until the said person told him how he, or she, would like to be addressed. It was a split-second of focal relapse, but he homed in to hear her continue.

'…he was famous for not being, not wanting the fame that his incredible writings brought him. He died a recluse, even his wife and child left him towards the end. He died…'

'I'm sorry but how did you…you get to from Picasso to United States, from an artist to a writer? What is the title? What does it actually mean?' He used his hands to scale out the uneven balanced to emphasise his point.

'You should be, how could you? Sorry, tut. You should be sorry, sorry for interrupting me. ME! And with so many questions. Shame. On. You.' A slight tone of wicked child play pleasure with a wink confirmed she was mocking an unsure Eddy. 'Jerome, the man who turned his back on success, was starting to open his heart after allowing school child from the local school to enter his home to be taught. This befriending led to being betrayed. In 1953, he allowed one to interview him for what he was told was the school paper. He found out that she released the article in the local newspaper, The Claremont Daily Eagle. On those pages were printed that same interview as a feature on the editorial page. He felt betrayed, very upset, he built a tall fence around his property to keep out everyone. He consequently seldom spoke to the press, or nearly anyone else, ever again. He carried on writing, but for the love, not for publication.'

'Wow. Truly…wow. I never read that book but it that sounds like a bio I would like to read. And, the title? I don't understand the meaning.'

'Protecting the innocence. Especially of children. Holden believes that to be the catcher in the rye, is to stop them falling off the brink. It is to save children from losing their innocence.'

'Impressed.' Eddy nods in agreement as he waves his head towards her and back.

She turns in an air of wistful prospects that dreams can come true. She loves this almost impossible possibility to be one of them. This is a dream she has not lost. One day she will interview a major life changer, in her opinion. Afterall it is one of her aims, her dreams.

Alas, what happened later may not have been her purpose. She would not do it for a gain for herself in courting anyone. I am not writing that Picasso did, although the evidence is stacked against him. For in May 1951, Picasso started an affair with the now-older 24-year-old Genevieve Laporte for over two years. The young lady that interviewed him years before. This is mentioned here in the exhibition as his 'tender period'. They both mutter with half question, half exclamation on that part of the paragraph. Eddy and Saoirse looked at each other with no idea what that means. Tender? Although Saoirse recklessly abandoned her own rule to be able to talk. Eddy notices this but equally brushes it away in just as abandoned disregard thus not to cause an argument.

With a little more than a bit of uncertain scepticism from them both, it was written that Picasso was alone for nearly eight years until 1961. It was the year that a then 79-year-old met a 27-year-old in Jacqueline Roque. She, as a result, accordingly became his second wife. People first thought that she was after his money. Hence it was said that little time passed for people to see that she apparently made him happy, very happy.

During this period, he produced more art based on her than on any other of his previous relationship. His many conquests. That included over seven different portraits off her in a single year. Unofficially after twenty years together, Picasso died on 8 April 1973. She, for reasons unknown, prevented his children, Claude and Paloma, from attending his funereal. Eddy could not help but refer to the painting of peace, which was named after Paloma, and felt that this action was challenging war. Saoirse gave a shrug of the shoulders to his exclamation that basically said, 'grow up'.

As thorny, tricky and equally fascinating and intriguing life that was Picasso's sordid love affairs, Eddy found himself being dragged back through the years to Las Menians. Known by many titles but most commonly 'The Family of King Phillip IV' for which it would seem that Picasso was equally as obsessed with Diego Velázquez's 1656, 'Las Meninas' as he was to women. He painted over forty interpretations with them working amongst many of them that are on display here.

They are mesmerised by the paintings with some bold, some are colourful, some black and white, with all of them very large. Here, in this open-plan room, they look over the compositions of all the characters of Velázquez's work for which a small print in the description give an insight into Picasso's own interpretation. In the short time of five months Picasso produced all these pieces that are apparently amassed to forty-five different understanding different versions. Saoirse pointed to the note before the pieces of work for which Eddy mutually shared a respectful nod of approval. They liked what they read that Picasso donated all these works of art as a homage to his friend Jaume Sabartés in 1968, the year he died so Barcelona could see all this work in its entirety.

As Eddy spins to leave in one quick fluent motion, for the last time, he then abruptly stops. He focuses on a portrait of Jacqueline. He leans in close, as close as he can. He studies it. Looks into the black eyes. Three colours make up this striking Jacqueline with a flowery straw hat. He sees the gouged-out paint that the knife makes like the sea as Moses walks forth, he delicately scratches the shadows around the cheeks, the brow and the ears. Eddy thinks her pursed lips and eyes hide a pensive longing, maybe for Picasso as they truly were in eternal love for each other despite the age gap with their reciprocated love for art, ceramics seemed to fuse them closer together. There are many portraits of her in different methods of art.

All the heads are unmistakably hers by the happy often laughing photographs on the walls. All the breasts are perfectly pert and the eyes black. She is looking at them while they walk around in every room. She is watching while lying, sitting, standing and dreaming, thinking, playing. She is the last piece of art that Eddy looks at with intensity. Moving up to her floral straw hat and away. He pulls away, turns and flees in a rushed stride, suddenly foolishly worried that Saoirse would be wondering where he had gotten to.

He speeds back through the rooms that not only have artwork in his paintings on display but many lithographs, sketches, incisions, ceramics and other sculptures that testify just how much Picasso was a complete artist.

Again, he slows to a snail-paced slide through the room that he nearly missed. This last part of the museum holds a few pieces from his later years. He really painted like a child. There is a whimsical innocence in which he gripped a subject to create an imaginational piece. Bold colours and cheerful aspects shine through. The last room is of many photographs that adorn the walls in a graphic collection of the artists last years. In most he looks happy. Jacqueline is her yet again. His mind looks as if it is ticking, always active. He looks so content. He has lived a great life. That is not to say that he had troubles, hard times but at this stage of his life when he is knocking on heaven's door, he must be able to look over his shoulder to the past to only see the glories.

Like all things tourist-driven is the money. So, in all its glory, they have to go through the gift shop to exit. In the souvenir shop is his quote about Barcelona 'Here is where it all began…this is where I realised where I could get to.' He had a long career that ended in Cannes with his death in 1973. An incredible portal that has let time fly out of their hands as quickly as sand blown carelessly blown around in the wildest windstorm. Seconds have seemed to pass when an incredible three hours have seen them finally leaving the building.

They both double-check their watches in unconceivable implausible preposterous recognition that the time did not lie. It was mind-blowing with the warning before they went unwarranted. They both found it spellbinding, that saw them in an interesting time warp. Without knowing it they have teleported to find themselves on a rustic peeling white painted metal chair in a delightful cosy café on one of the medieval streets around the museum. Eddy just wants to talk. He wants to share his knowledge. He wants to share a conversing conversation of what she saw to his, if she agreed or disagreed. He just wanted to talk about the last few hours.

Nevertheless, Saoirse wanted to scribble notes down of the past few days. She wanted to feel that she could go back inside if she could not remember a piece of art that she wanted to explain. They headed on an unnavigated autopilot that steered them to the first café that was slightly off the tourist route which was decorated with its signage to the museum and the train station.

They ordered coffee and a cream cheese-filled croissant each. Saoirse threw her notepad on the table with a soft thud to announce as a jury would a moment of order. She wanted silence, so she could write. Eddy kept interrupting her, he wanted to talk. He was excited to have found this brand-new outlook on art. This disruption of her mind to paper was making her increasingly angry. The pen was scratching deeper into the paper, nearly piercing through but leaving ridges as she turned the page.

Eddy kept pausing, apologising. Then seconds later doing the same again. He just could not help himself. She slammed the table in frustration with the palm of her pen less hand. This unforeseen tremor vibrated the fragile table top making a glass of water spill over her notepad, which she threw her arm out to catch the glass on the second bounce, her arm reflexed quick to grab before the damage was unsalvable. Despite the luck, with was her own doing, this heightened her fury. She grabbed her bag, notepad, napkin and moved to another table. The furthest away from Eddy. Eddy left her alone. The waitress came over and was a little confused. She split up the order by taking coffee to each table with the food. She then waivered in the middle of the fairly quiet floor with the ticket in her hand.

After a brief hesitation she placed it under the blue and white small ashtray on Eddy's table. He sipped his coffee looking out. He nervously picked at his pastry with his index and thumb, placing small morsels into his dry mouth. He was hungry. His appetite had diminished as his own anger took over the fires inside, to the pit of his stomach. He watched the passing parade of locals. They all seemed to be frolicking, laughing and everyone seemed a happy couple.

Interrupting his own thoughts that were crashing waves of negativity one after another with the same question: Why the fuck was he with her? She came back in silence. Around the other side of the table so his view was obscured by her. Looking at him. Waiting for him to look at her face, her eyes. He started down at her midriff and up. Notepad in bag. Frown on face. Her mannerism was closed. Her arms folded, apart from a free hand that drank the now-cold coffee she had left behind in her solo pursuit of writings. She might have as well throw it back into the saucer as she picked the croissant up and walked towards the station. Was she waiting for him to apologise? Eddy paid the bill. He was not going to apologise. He found himself chasing after her. He reached for her hand, cold hand. She jerked her hand away as if his touch was an electric shock. What just happened?

But. Yet. He knew. After the dreams of Dalí. After the fantasy of Gaudí. After the childlike innocence of Picasso. After the wonderful fairy-tale came the traumatic nightmare in a raging tempest. The reality. Hammering hail stones of resentful anger. Javelin icicles of sharp-tongued words. Each letter embedding Eddy's heart. Each word a log of flaming sulphur burning his silky heartstrings away with the flakes of naïveté flying briskly away on the violent airs of what-ifs and maybe's. Leaving only the smouldering ash of a former relationship.

The journey back was cold. She was agitated. Her mannerism in the way she scraped the writing into her pad as if a chisel on stone was with an unwarranted residue anger. It was a warm day, outside, clean. The rain had stopped and left a shine making everything seem fresh, pristine. Eddy hated these uncomfortable silences. He had no idea what to say, do or how to react to these situations. He kept with her silence. Looked out the window. Watched the residential aspects of Spain pass by in a green, brown and blue blur with yellow and red flags dripping wet on the slow bus to the city centre. Halfway through the journey, she finally broke her silence.

'I can't work with you,' she breathed out. She did not look up. Her hair was down, covering her face. Shielding her vulnerability.

'Why?' Eddy was stunned. 'What?' His mouth was wide open, but no other words came out.

'I have work,' she said into her notepad, in a way of offering a reason.

'I can change. The café. That was a mistake…I know I can, change. I can.'

'It's not just that.' She paused, long and thoughtfully. 'Why? WHY is this so hard, to…say? AGH!' Another silence engulfed the space between them that was as uncomfortable as the conversation that was not happening. 'I have been given a lot of work. More than I thought. An opportunity to do what I would, want to inspire to do. What I want to do. Since a young girl. I cannot do it with a dead weight.'

'Dead weight? Dead fucking weight!' Eddy was offended. 'Can you not see that I want to be with you, and I will follow you. Support you.'

'I didn't mean dead weight. I…' Saoirse figuratively did not mean that. It hurt him. It hurt her. She wanted to retract that word. She could not put into words what she was trying to say. She was fumbling for the correct words to end something she did not want to really end.

'Come on. We can work it out,' Eddy interrupted, to the relief of Saoirse. 'I can go back to the UK and work. While you work. We can work.' Eddy was clutching at straws at this point. He could see the magnificent image he had, had now, had in the future quickly unravelling. Like a jumper caught on a nail as Saoirse ran away from him leaving the thread to where she is going, away from him. Never finding this love again. Only an end. Not a complete presence.

The silence returned. Both looking outside the window opposite each other. Eddy felt it right not to push anything at this moment. Saoirse was thinking. She had made her mind up. She wanted Eddy. Loved Eddy but this was just the wrong time. She kept telling herself this. She was trying to make herself believe in this.

After a shower. After a rather uncomfortable late afternoon filled with friction, stuttered conversations, Eddy wanted nothing more than wanting to talk. He did not want to leave anything unsaid. After the shell shocking bus ride, Eddy proposed an attempt to reconcile a broke relationship. That evening they got ready for a date, which Eddy hoped would not be their last. He wanted this. Not just the date but the reconstruction of the burning embers of the relationship to come forth like phoenix from the flames. He wanted to try and save what could be saved. He did not want to be just some story about eloping that he will talk about, that he will reminisce about in years to come. He wanted to be telling his children how he met their mother.

He choose a candle-lit restaurant overlooking the port as the rescue setting, scene and act. Christopher Columbus high on his towering pedestal looking towards the sea, listening to all but not staring into their personal lives. The tree lined avenue danced in the salty breeze casting shadows from the lamp lights. The sun retreating in a shimmering yellow and red carpet behind the smooth rippling sea. The colours, even the bold ones looked damp and muted in the luminescent shine. Music played from bars by unseen musicians. Laughter erupting in impromptu bursts like lava bubbling away in a smooth musical piece of great times where only memories would be made.

The surface of a scene where dreams were being made. It would have been perfect. It should have been perfect. It was not. In the distance a bird cooed to another bird. Somewhere between the entrée and the main, it came. Eddy was expecting it, yet he was not prepared for it. Like a road train going through a bale of hay the sticks of straw scatter to resemble nothing of the former shape. The long and the short of it was Saoirse wanted to concentrate on her writing. On her career. On her.

Eddy had given up everything. Planned to give up everything including his address, his home but she would not accommodate him in her life. The expected way this evening was going to pan out, still was surprising. He was crushed. No, he was being crushed. It hurt. He had nothing more to give but felt he was not being giving any reason to why he should give anymore.

In a flicker of the single tall ivory candlelight, Eddy's future came crashing down in the casting shadows from vehicles flashing their lights across the roundabout. She leaned across the delicately thin white silky-smooth tablecloth. Her face lit up from below her chin, under the flickering candlelight. Eddy could not help but think with a whimsical abandonment how gorgeous she was, she is. She leaned through the burning candle in the lime-green grass holder for his hands. He retracted his hands. Not off the table, but out of reach. He knew that at the slightest touch, the pain would forcefully travel through like volts of ruthless cruel energy to the heartless region of his chest. It would linger. She reached further. He leaned back in his chair. His hands gripping the edge of the table. His knuckles white.

She tried to explain, fully. Her hands opened with palms facing the starry night sky. Wanting his hands in hers. Offering up her explanation. He was drowned in the airs around him. He could not hear her words, did not care for her words. They gurgled out of her like a drain, unplugged, free. He was not listening. This whole scene was something that he envisioned so differently when he was getting ready. He thought that the perfect table, the perfect food, the perfect setting with the perfect love would give the perfect ending to their beginning.

He hoped. Hoped for the truth not to be true. Eddy placed a morsel of bread in his mouth, it tasted bland. He was distorted at this sudden turn of events, that he saw unfolding but was helpless to stop the pages being turned. Why these crocodile tears? Not even a tear of a clown? Saoirse was not crying. This infuriated Eddy. Why was she explaining the motives to something she clearly could not express? Eddy involuntary begun to weep. It was not a blood-screaming flood of tears, but, a single soft delicate teardrop that followed the contours of his face down to the tip of his nose. There it remained. There it hung on, like Eddy wanted to relationship too.

But someone else played the part, a vital part. In him, Saoirse. In the teardrop, gravity. It fell into the untouched bowl of linguini. His head in his hands, over the table, over the pasta. He felt it before he saw it fall, land, disappear. She gripped his wrists. Pulling them towards her. Urging him to look up, at her. Hands in hands across the table. What he did not want to do. His hands limp nestled in her, hers firm merged in his. Her mouth moving. He only heard static air. She was repeating herself. He wrestled his hands away from her. Sulked back in his chair while looking hard at her as she tripped over tongue-tied expressions.

He needed time away. He pushed his body up from the chair, receding away the table in a slow jerking motion. Saoirse rested her head on the table with a slight, soft thud which Eddy heard as his back was turned. She was aspirated. He walked away and left her slumped on the table. But, a vision of beauty, alone. He did not feel him move but he found himself glided over by a force stronger than he felt at the metal railing that looked out to port, over the road. It was a cool night. He was looking out to escape. He was looking out to an unknown future.

He felt nothing in his surroundings, only the hurt where his heart had just been burst into surreal shards of throbbing pain. Shards of the haybale like a voodoo doll embedding his bleeding heart. He felt uncomfortable. The food was bland. The sea air, just nothingness. He wondered if he would feel anything sensationally good again. He had offered up solutions. He had tried to fight a losing battle. Give, literally his all. He turned around, back into the dimly lit restaurant.

Saoirse looked up. Her hair hanging in thin strands in front of her vision. Looking at the motionless Eddy. He was gorgeous. In the moonlight, with the streetlight highlighting his eyes that glinted hope but glimmered despair. She was fighting the tears that wanted to fall. She did not want to be sitting there. She felt exposed in a white shinny dress on a busy street. Inside she was crying, she was very vulnerable. Eddy was the same level of distress. They put it on view in different executed observations.

He gripped the railing hard that the blood left his knuckles in the same colour as the pale moon. He was anchored to this as if letting go he would crumble into a heap on the sandy-covered floor. He leaned his back into it, slowly with his feet rooted on the stone. He wanted to scream out loud to the darkness above. He wanted time to pause, time to relax. At this point he could straightforwardly have said everything that was on his mind. That reaction could have been for the worse.

This would not help by any finale being changed for the better. This would not have changed this outcome. This would not have been remotely beneficial to them being them. Thus, it would have come across vindictive, hurtful and most likely uncalled for as unnecessary as the amount of wine that they were drinking now that food was not an option for them. He left the words, sentences echoing inside his mind.

Although some people have a fantasy and a dialogue in their hands with what she was going to say, what he was going to say. And it will all end with them walking away happily ever after into the sunset. This was life. This was no fairy-tale. Walt Disney did not write this, so it will not end that the beast will have the beauty. All he was thinking was why she could not try to make it work with him? Why she had easily thrown him aside when she was obviously thinking about something else, but, he felt she was not being completely honest with him. He did not want to talk these reactions, so that is when he pushed away from the railing. That is why he just had to walk away. Take a time out. Waving his fists at the sky.

After the seconds that turned like the ticking minute hand. When he had cooled and calmed his frenetically talking head down. When he had got his head and thoughts back to a controllable rate he returned. After a few long minutes he did, in fact, return. Back at the table he leaned in the chair. Looked at her. She leaned forward. They spoke, softly, honestly, openly. It was littered with awkward silences. They ordered more wine. For which they did not quench their thirst. Wine could not satisfy the wanted urge. They talked a little more. Talked about the relationship. Made empty promises that they would catch-up soon. When the pain had healed, the wound a scar. They would keep in touch. They headed back to the hostel. Went to their separate bunk beds for the first time. And, they, eventually fell asleep. They did decide to keep to their original plan in the morning.

Silent. Wide awake. Shattered. Wide alert. Still. All night.

Sober and upset, they rose. It was a brand-new day. A day where they were single, but still together. They got ready and headed to Madrid as originally planned. They were just about to leave when they shared a mutual morning kiss on the cheek. It was more of a force of habit to share a kiss, normally on the lips but this felt appropriate behaviour under last night's circumstances. Instantly after the delicate peck on the cheek materialised, they realised that they could, or they should not be doing this anymore. Yet, it was the second cheek kiss. That coming to this realisation they continued with a lingering kiss that shared the warmth, the promise and the respect that they shared for one another. It felt wrong, but oh-so right.

The silent stroll to the bus shelter was not awkward, as it will should be. They were both broken inside. The bus was nearly empty as they said goodbye to Barcelona, and the division of their hearts in the break-up. A few people congregated in the seats at the front. They decided to be alone at the back. Sitting on the long stretch of striped red and orange fabric they talked, cried, laughed. They picked up where they left off in the restaurant, but, this time with a river of fluidity. The conversation was not pre-thought out before they returned with an answer, a retort, a quip. It was not drip fed, stammered. It was as free as they were. Are now.

With this reckless abandonment, they covered everything that needed to be said, accompanied by somethings not needed to be said in the eight hours of travel. The somewhat lack of sleep that they both actually had somehow got their minds in a better clarity of focus. Questions were re-asked, properly, with no flourishing or carefully treading. They had time to think them through or not before responding. It was comfortable, well, as comfortable that it could actually be in terms of the situation anyway.

Eddy did not agree with the outcome, but saw her clear perspective for which she was in. yet, in his mind he was thinking that she was a little narrowminded in her outlook of this relationship. He had nothing to lose in voicing it. She had nothing to gain in answering. They wanted the same thing. Just not at the same time. Eddy could not help but feel a little incensed that his time was now. People often speak about a mutual break-up. Eddy had never thought about it, before now, as this moment in the orange trees of the remote Spanish countryside. But at this specific moment, he believes that there is not such a thing. It is her way of saving grace.

In Eddy's personal opinion, it was impossible, as always, and he strongly believed this. Always one heart will want it more than another heart, therefore will not ever break even. He hid his feelings well, but, inside it was burning away. He was drowning in the fire of a love that was wrong. A wrong time for her, the right time for him is now, but…mutual. He scoffed at this thought, never. They do not get to choose who they love, and who will love them back. They have to accept that. If the feeling is not shared, then nothing will come of it. Honesty, a little sleep, and nowhere to escape made this a clear slate as the bus stopped in the grimy station in urgent need of love of its own.

As luck would have it, purely by coincidence, the guesthouse that Saoirse had booked back in Valencia was so close to the bus stop. Before the bus journey, she was thinking to dump her bags, flee, she woke up wanting to be alone, to be surrounded by her thoughts, to see if she wanted to turn back time. However, for the conversation on the bus a level of respect had been discovered. They started this journey as lovers, lost their way in the middle to be here at the final destination friends.

Both of their minds were clean, clear from any dust, fragments of mistrust and a window of honesty was left for them to clearly see the pathway to the future. They did dump their bags, as Saoirse intended, but explored together. A new city, a new day, a new start. Together they made those intrepid steps into the unknown together. They actually did not want to be alone, figuratively speaking, just, yet.

They walked the streets without direction, without a map, without a defined purpose. As they strolled the foreign streets of Madrid, they basked in the fiery afternoon sun. They chatted responsively. During this amble the evitable happened. They split up. Officially. They had nothing else to say. Nothing else to regret. She wanted to move on, he struggled to accept that, but accepted that. No loose ends. It was the finale of a beautiful thing.

Two countries colliding to enrich each other's future to separate hence, become estranged. No promises to rekindled romances in any future date to be set. No promises to stay friends. It was better to end it cleanly now than to let the love that was already bleeding to breed into a loathing hate. A bitter hate that would obliterate all the good memories that they had made, together, as one. It was visibly painful for them both as tears uncovered, unashamed fell. Leaving small blotches of dark grey on the dusty light cobbled stone floor. Inside them, the fires of hell were tormenting them for which they could not conceal on the surface. They did not want to conceal. It was something that they both did not want to happen. He resisted the urge to question her decision.

Through blurred vision, they looked at each other. They held hands in front of them with a clear gap between. They smiled at each other. They decided to have a good time with it. To make the best of a bad situation. They wanted a good break-up, if there was such a thing. They wanted something that they would remember. Something that they would not look back with a hint, a trace of anger or disappointment, definitely no regret. She had work to do here so that made it easier for her to concentrate and be consumed, to distract her from the separation. But, they decided that this would be the last night for them.

They left the hostel in Barcelona as a couple held together by the split ends of a thin taut cotton thread. They arrived at the guesthouse in Madrid as individuals. They were getting changed into smart clothes to end the relationship over a proposed great evening of dinner, dance and drink when Eddy glanced over at Saoirse. The large three gatefold mirror on the dressing table showed her in every angle of her, the exquisite gorgeous female that she was. As smooth as James Bond, he slid over to take full advantage of what he could. Afterall, he had lost everything, so nothing could be lost. The likelihood that this would be the last time he would taste her.

He had already decided that drink was going to be the answer. He was going out to drink, to get car-wreaked. Therefore, although he might try to have a last moment of love, his performance would be pretty awful. For the amount of alcohol he was hoping to drink he was half expecting not to be able to raise a smile by the end of the night, let alone anything else. He seized her in this moment. He moved behind her naked body as she brushed her shower-wet hair. The smell of passionfruit from the shampoo combined heavenly with her intoxicating floral perfume that floated in the air around her steaming body. He whispered the clichéd sweet nothings into her ear. She giggled in her sweet voice. He would never forget her laugh. It will always be pure untouched music to his ears. He already missed that laugh.

He cupped her naked bottom so gently with his hands while nibbling her ear with his lips. He moved down to caress her neck. She leaned her head backwards, her hair cascading down, suspended in mid-air. She let out a soft, pleasurable moan. Her eyes shut. He released his grasp. In one quick, fluid motion, he spun her around. He brought her near. He embraced her strongly. He was in control. He kissed her fervently. The passion was strong. She was now kissing him over his body. Ripping his clothes off.

It was strange to think that they had broken up, officially only a few short hours ago. They kissed hard. Harder. With a combination of tenderness laced with fear and a single-minded indulgent enthusiasm to enjoy this for the moment it was. He wanted her to experience the sensation of him. Wanted her to feel him. To know what she would be missing. He wanted to give her to perfect sensation. To wish for a second, a better opportunity. He would give her a better experience.

From Eddy's early sex-making days, for what he would blame on playground stories which populated boys growing up, he was fearful of premature ejaculation. This is really what all younger males worry about. They are told 'not to shout the load too soon' and 'not to be the fastest at the race'. Comedies highlight this in pre-teen films which does not help the problem, but only intensify it. It is for this reason that he developed an art for holding on to the load. A slight twist to his hips or a move would give him longer staying power. However, he controlled it too much to the point that he rarely came.

Fearful of this getting worse in his late teens, he went to the doctor that sent him to a sex therapist, Dr Kleine. This was extraordinary due to his young age, but he felt he needed to seek help. After numerous sessions, Dr Kleine would comically refer to his condition as the Delivery Boy Effect, after ruling out stress, age, drugs and alcohol. Although Eddy saw this as a great way to treat his lovemaking as they would orgasm first and second before he eventually came, but it was a curse. He could never climax quickly. This caused many women to sometimes be sore, hence having to stop during the process and never have a repeat performance for a long time.

Most though felt it was them. They were to blame for not exciting him. If only Eddy had a dollar for every time, he had had that, THAT uneasy conversation. For this reason, when Saoirse told him her secret, days later he revealed his. Not as shattering or tragic as hers but she was the first he had had this edgy embarrassing conversation with. He mixed his lovemaking a lot to compensate his, well condition, for a better word. He performed oral sex to ease the pain. Due to Saoirse's past, she enjoyed this aspect of love making, this foreplay. It showed consideration and recognition to her previous suffering ordeal.

Dr Kleine would go on to describe his condition as, '…lovemaking involves pleasure in both ways of giving and taking,' in a deep German accent. 'You are paying too much focus on her. Not enough on you. This loses your erotic focus that has interfered with your ejaculation, your orgasm.' Then she gave advice, which did not work. All the money he pissed into small plastic jars, specimens in small petri dishes and red-faced sweating embarrassments from the moment he walked into the doctor's office to be a burning inferno on his cheeks when he entered hers, the sex therapist's office. She finished the four weeks of weekly hour-long sessions with, 'value your own pleasure. Your move, more, more than a delivery boy. You deserve erotic satisfaction. Ask for what you want to help the process. Do not be afraid to talk about it.'

He did for the first time with Saoirse and the benefits were amazing. They continued to rock. They continued to move. They balanced on the small, low white cushioned stool in front of the make-up dresser before being on the hard, rope-threaded floor with all the carefree actions of two people on the brink of Nirvana. In grips of their highest state of happiness. Both at peace. Eddy lips moved from Saoirse's ears and the nape of her neck. It was not a surprise where he was going to end up.

Nevertheless, he made it into an adventure. Knowing, but still not wanting to admit it until it was being at the end. He desired this moment to be perfect. He defiantly took his sweet time. He explored every inch to make sure every surface bore his lips, his time. He used his fingers like feathers, a soft touch barely touching her bare skin. His silky lips explored every contour of her beige pastel skin. A Napoli-tan had happened on her sleeves due to the different length shirts and vests she wore. He did not want to miss a single inch of her taste. He lingered over her breasts with lips, eyes and nose. Smelled her. Felt her. Using his teeth to tease and slightly gnaw at the nipples. She gave a quiver of excitement. Another silent moan unsuccessfully kept quiet.

Her back arched upwards, skywards. She was touching heaven. He was kissing her firm stomach. His hands gently stroking her hips. She could not take it. The quiver was becoming a tremor. Her body shook with excitement. She was making more noise. Moaning louder. Her body shaking more. Her head was flung backwards on the discarded bed cushions. Jarring backwards. Her body thrust forward. She pushed his head down. Gripped his hair. His tongue became the leading character.

She was beginning to involuntary jack-knife on the hard floor. She pulled his hair. She tugged his head. Moaned. Spoke to God. She groaned. Louder. A high-pitched yelp. Shook. She screamed. Louder. His mouth filling up. Her pleasure on, in his mouth. On his lips. She pulled his hair up. Kissed him. Hard on the lips. Her hand on his throbbing, pulsating penis. She had never felt so excited by his sexual prowess. He had never felt this hard. It was aching him. She took control. Pushed him around. Rode him. This was a first. She was dominant. She bit the corner of her quivering bottom lip. It was hurting her. A thin thread of blood trickled down.

'You OK?' a concerned Eddy in a breathless voice posed.

'I', she exhaled out through the pain, 'love', through the pleasure, 'you.'

He smiled foolishly.

Her hands griped his chest.

He penetrated harder.

Her nails pierced his skin.

Eddy saw the pain and as she bit harder on her lip, a thread of blood was slowly seeping to form a small river. Eddy spun her around. Entered her in the way she was the most comfortable. Her screams unsuccessfully muffled in the hand. Her free fist pounding the wall. 'Yes. YES...' They moved in a beautiful swaying action, as perfectly manufactured organism. An entity of perfection. It was thrilling. It was free. It was a climax of passionate urge of what they wanted, need to close this for good, or bad depending on your own point of view. He climaxed the quickest that he had ever done. He shook. Hard. Trembling with pleasure. He sweated. She sweated. They were hot. Hot for each other. It was amazing. They both screamed.

The world moved with them. The earth shook. She peeled himself off her. Laid next to her. Body so close. Breathing hard. They both were out of breath. Looking at the ceiling. Laughing. They turned to each other. They looked into each other's eyes. They tenderly kissed each other's lips. They loved each other. They spoke the words to each other. The cuddled. They hugged each other. They were going to miss each other. Already missing each other.

'No matter what, I will always love you,' Eddy declared deep into Saoirse's eyes.

'Oh. I love you, Ed. I will never forget you'

With that a fiercely passionate kiss on closed lips. Hands griped on each other's cheeks.

Before sleeping succumbed, Saoirse took Eddy's hand and they entered the shower together. They washed each other. They resisted the urge to go again. The pulsating animal instinct was raw and as untamed as wildlife itself. They had dinner to get to, a last date. Was it really that important? Dinner? They have been on so many, therefore would missing one single dinner for pleasure make a difference? Eddy whispered the thought, what if they missed their reservation. Would it matter? Saoirse seemed to think so. They got re-ready to go out. Grinning. Teasing. Laughing with soft touches here and there. With soft, tender pecks on the shoulder, cheek, head but never the lips.

This would be the last page of this chapter in their life. Eddy did despise her for her decision. He hated that the love of his life was going to be moving on, into the future, on her own, without him. But, at this moment he loved her. At this moment they continued to love one another. With all their heart, and all their body they think that they always will. They souls will remain connected. In the dark recess of his mind he knows that he would love her more, always.

However, this is not a moment for melancholy and infinite sadness. This was the moment to celebrate their swift love with the touch of his lips, hands and body. A celebration of the intensity that they feel for one another. They continued the evening. It was poignant that it was the heart-breaking finale of the love that they felt for each other. The break-up had started well.

The dinner was about asking those questions that they never asked, that may still burn inside them. Yet they had covered them all on the bus. It changed course to be about them. About what they wanted in the future. They talked about dreams, fantasy's and the past. Childhood dreams, what they wanted to be when growing up. It was so easy. So, assured, effortless and comfortable that whatever the topics, everything and anything was spoken about. What they wanted.

The food was nice, but instantly forgotten, this was the main feature of the evening. The wine drunk, but did not have, or seem to have any effect. They had eyes for one another, only. The moment was they moment. No-one else was in this moment. The people around were mere extras. They were the only two main characters. They were the only ones on this Earth.

They recklessly danced in one of the main plazas to the soft acoustic strumming's of a guitar coming out of an open window. A place unseen, but picture-perfect for a movie scene that moments like this happen rarely in the real world. They cared not who saw them, for they did not have a care for this world. It was about them only. They were drunk. The visual scene of a couple enjoying their evening was a mask to the two hearts breaking inside. Stories were shared. Stories were made, hidden in their hearts never to be shared again. More drinks had, more drugs taken. Then in the moonlight they kissed. In their mouth they transported half of a blue pill on their own tongue to have, a single half of a Viagra each.

Pinball fashion, rebounding from one narrow bricked wall to the other. Immersed in laughter. Giggling like schoolchildren that had no worries, stresses, concerns. They made their way back to their guesthouse. Banging on the walls, ricocheting up the stairs to the room. They laid in the pale pink bed they enjoyed they last night together. The passion that they had before continued where it left off, it never left. From the late evening, they continued until the early hours of the brand-new day. It was paradise. It was heavenly. It was, alas, the divine comedy of being the end.

Birds sang. The paper-thin lace curtains flapped in the delicate breeze. The sun stroked its warmth on their bodies. The creak of the floorboards, a slam of a car door and they were waking up. After a few short hours of sleep, they woke. They kissed each other good morning. This time on the lips. There was no awkwardness. They did not find this strange, oddly enough, but normal. They spoke without any tongue-tied discomfort. They walked around naked with nothing to hide. They got ready to start their future apart.

The first day, of their last day, together. It was only just past seven in the morning, Saoirse had a pounding headache, for which, although he did not say much, he knew Eddy had too. He had that fragile state when tying up his shoes of not getting up too quickly. They were both sweating from the humidity in the air, surely not the last two shots of whatever it was, a few short hours ago. She dragged herself up to see Eddy shake four brown pills of ibuprofen into his shaky hand. Taking the half bottle of beer, he swigged it down, before passing the bottle to her.

'Coffee?' she suggested through the course of the gulping of pills.

'One hundred percent,' he responded between gulps of the lukewarm fizzy-less beer.

They agreed that being in a relationship was hard, damn hard work. Not only mentally but physically and emotionally draining, yet intoxicatingly wonderful. They both struggle to brush the cobwebs from their dusty brains. The first few minutes of payment for last night's indiscretions was rich as they held each other motionless in the shower. The warm air rinsing the sweat off their bodies. No movement from them. They cried together. It is in this time that Saoirse asks why people do this. Why are people drawn to the craziness of a relationship? The abuse, the vulnerability.

Nevertheless.

She would not have it any other way. It is the simple act of these emotional hard times that tell people that they have invested in the relationship. To be open, is to be hurt. They swayed, embraced, to no music as the warm water trickled over them unsuccessfully hiding their tears.

They had breakfast together. They propped their head up with no attempt to hide the feeling of nauseous in their stomach or the water of the washing-up bowl in their head. More of a couple strong black short coffees, espressos. Then they were ready. After the Picasso museum in Barcelona, they wanted to see one particular piece for themselves. They wanted to see it together.

They got directions. Left they bags in the storage and made their way across the city to the location. Once inside they beelined slowly, to the collage. It was strange to have an image in your head of what something will be like to see it and be taken aback to just how large a painting can be, equally how powerful. People are spread out looking at the mural. The muted washed colours of greys and blacks with the light provide an intensity to each of the motifs.

The simple greyscale of colours are essential to deliver the message of extreme tragedy in the Basque town of Guernica, where the 1937 painting bears the same name. Motivated by news of the German aerial bombing he, Picasso used this as a demonstration, as a way of testimony to the Spanish Civil War, as a way of forewarning at what was going to come in World War Two. This huge painting, this huge poster is cruel and dramatic in its creative art. The Spanish government brought this but when the Second World War broke, he decided that it should remain in New York's Museum of Modern Art until the conflict ended. He then extended the loan until democracy had been restored, and Franco, the dictator removed. The work eventually returned to Madrid and Spain in 1981.

In silence, they looked. Eyes moving, rather than bodies. Heads swaying over the animals; the large bull, the wounded horse yelling skywards in pain and the bird. The graphic human of a dead, or dying lying soldier and a number of women. One holds a lamp in the darkness as a curtain descends over the cruel violation as she leans out of a window, another is crying out to the heavens as a horse burns behind her. Another rushes from the right with what appears to be a baby by her breast, looking towards the skies wondering what is happening amongst the noise, carnage.

Finally, the one that Eddy fixates on, a wailing mother holding her dead child in her lap. The eyes may be different, but they teem with sadness, helplessness. It is a sad scene to see. Wails. Screams. Death. Life being ended for what?

They discussed this painting amongst all the others they had seen in the museum. Then it was penultimate time for them to move. Eddy and Saoirse were back at the guesthouse the way they came to the museum. Eddy collected his bag. They walked in sombre silence. One last lengthy kiss. A warmth of a relationship that had struck aground too soon to sink into the depths of history. Saoirse needed to, but mainly wanted to stay. She continued her work. Her writing. Her apparent priority.

Eddy could not help feeling a little bitter, but could not disregard her honesty. This would be the last time that they saw each other. The last time they would ever see each other. As Eddy boarded the metal worn steps into the suffocating warmth of the stuffy bus, he looked back. Not with a look of regret, or a look of what might have been, but a look of love. A look of happy satisfaction for having met Saoirse. For sharing some time with her.

With the look of tears welling up in their eyes, the bitterness evaporated. He was boarding a bus to London, then to change his flight to go home, back to Australia. He had enough of travelling, even after this short time, and wanted nothing more than familiarity. His mates. Eddy picked a blue seat near the window closest to Saoirse.

She looked shell shocked as she stood not trying to hide her tears, her sobbing. She waved through the tinted glass. He saw the tears fall down Saoirse face, this made him brawl. He was trying to stop the dam from collapsing until out of sight. He waved. He mouthed 'I love you' through a smile, through lots of tears. She mouthed back, 'I love you' through flooding tears that she did not wipe away. She wanted nothing to distract her vision of him. Nothing to stop her taking these last seconds to say goodbye. For good. He watched her move into the distance from the window of the National Express white and blue bus. Move into the past. As the bus turned, she was out of vision, she disappeared. This was the last time Eddy saw her. Heard from her.

In the opposite direction, he saw a sightseeing bus come into the bus depot. The title was spawned out over the sides in the bright green and yellow graffiti style writing against the pillar-box red body: 'Dura Toda La Vida'. He smiled through the sadness at this statement. Maybe, just maybe, he will continue travelling. He read it out loud. Out to himself. To Saoirse that could never possibly hear. Into his hands that were limply hanging in front of him as he leaned, head resting on the back of the seat in front of him. He then translated it to English. As he and Saoirse had parted, going in different directions in life that slogan seemed so fitting. They had parted company for life.

'Dura Toda La Vida,' he whispered again. 'It will last for life.'

'I will always love you, Eddy. I will never forget you.' A lonely Saoirse mutters as she watches the bus move until out of sight. He will not, never, be out of mind. She cries.

Reflection of a Window Pain
Fifteen Seconds into the Present Day

Drops streamed down the window. Cascading in mis-directional movements of speed. An erupting beam across the cityscape brings day time to the shadows of the dark night. Eddy flickers into a clear focus as he is left looking at his reflection on the dark pane of glass glimpsing a glimmer of pain in his heart. He thought of the last two relationships. He did not know what brought him to this point of contemplation. He was looking outside at the fast-paced storm that approached like a stampede of dark buffalos over the horizon, that covered the morning sky to an evening dusk.

Soldiers on their backs throwing spears of bolting light night that flies to light up the sky, to almost as quickly get engulfed into the darkness to disappear. He got woken by the first crash followed by the missiles of hard rain that plummeted down. He wandered into the kitchen for a glass of water. Then he was drawn to the window, thinking about where he went wrong. If he went wrong, but of course, it was him.

He thought of G as a conquest. The real things were firstly Egyptian beauty, Mahina, and the Emerald perfection, Saoirse. The object of desire was love. On this revealing inner display, he knows that everyone has one, those first loves. Everyone remembers their firsts. He remembers his first kiss. His first feeling of lust. His first feeling of love. His first feeling that love was reciprocated. His first rush of pleasure that enters, runs and pulses through his body that the person that he thinks, though in this case thought, was the most important person in his entire world feels, felt the same way is precious.

Nothing, not one thing at all, comes close to that first. It is a pure innocent connection that the body has no idea what to do, react and the mind is, frankly of no help at all. The firsts do matter. But most of the time firsts are followed by seconds. The thing with firsts are they have to end. Things remain. In all those firsts, it shapes who he is, who everyone is, what he is to become. A first is a learning curve.

Here he is, sitting on the white-painted chipped window ledge looking out, but not past the cool window. His black and white stripped coffee mug precariously close to being spilt onto his bare, exposed hairless legs. He should be looking back on it as a rite of passage, a nostalgic entranceway that teleports him in his mind to a time where he was nothing. A time where he would be staring at the precipice of anything, towards anything he could be. It was part of growing up, but part of who he grew up to be.

He could feel the first time a hand, other than his mother's, enter into his. The warmth, the shock, the wonder of how firm, how soft, how, HOW to hold a hand? Such a simple thing. He overthought it, nearly missing the experience altogether. On both occasions he did not have the, right, words. He spoke to fast, going past his point as fast as another burst of light that highlights the contrasting shadows of his serious expression. It was not that he was limited by words. It was not that he was limited in his vocabulary. It was that he simply could not articulate the firsts that were inside him. His heart broke for the first time. A first time where he felt that pain again, but did not shed another tear for that first loss.

He reflected his reflection as he lifted his weary sentimental head up to see beyond the pain, the pane towards the future. He loved the first as well as the present, but still could not clearly see enough into the future. That, unfortunately was as murky as the menacing, brooding clouds that share only the flashes and booms of destruction as a crash of rain brings him back strikingly fast to the present, where first times are still yet to be done.

Smirking, he still believes what he did then. Mutual break-ups are not true, hearts do not break even. Never, ever. His first love, although gone, he still never declared that love did not exist because of the broken, lost first. He did find someone better to understand the way he feels. Someone after that.

He gets up and goes back to his bedroom. Flicking the lights off as he purposefully ambles off one wall to the other. He glides into his cooled bed. Under his black silk doona that touches his skin, which is more for comfort than the ability to feel sexy. Contrary to what one of his recent girlfriends thought anyway.

The morning was still early and he had at least an hour before he needed to get up for work. So, he tried to get some sleep tonight, this morning. It was a night filled with unruly thoughts of the times of his nurturing, development of adulthood.

Gazing in the darkness up at the ceiling but not seeing it. He is unfocused, distracted by many thoughts of that trip back to the UK. He thought about Saoirse. He would still take her back. Absurd right? After all this time. Nothing is ever truly dead as he looks at the situation in just the right light. A light flashes quickly, swiftly by a shuddering vibration of booming thunder. To what happened next is where his mind is at. His eyes grow like a theatre projection screen to the face of Saoirse smiling, to what transpired after that.

Fifteen Years Ago
Moving On Too Quick?

Eddy was back in England. Reminders everywhere of Saoirse, the unreciprocated love. As he leaned on the dark grey, damp lamppost, the pulsating sensations were making his stomach fill empty, his head pounding a mallet blowing rhythm with his strongly hard beating heart, amalgamating to his growing anxiety. The coldness of the steel post penetrated through his thin clothes. His attire was more suited to an Australian winter rather than an English autumn. He half laughed, half smiled, at that thought of that unreciprocated love, Saoirse. As her face flashed across the puddle in the leave-blocking drain in front of him, from the reflections speedily moving from the headlights of a turning car. Without sounding like a stuck record. He literally would have given his all…for her all.

He glanced at the sinister building on this dreary day. Even on this dire day her numbness of his feelings still lightened his soul with a spark that would never burn. On the façades of the shopfront on the way down he saw mementos of recollected times where they shared a coffee, a laugh, a browse. He saw the slogans and familiar logo of the brewery in which they met. They courted, subsequently fell in love. The watering hole that he peered at from over the river-skating road. Each breath of wind that whipped through the cracks in the thin tall brick buildings whispered her name. A single droplet of rain caressed the exposed skin of the nape of his neck sending shivers of what could have been. Eddy would have gone anywhere with her if it meant being with her.

The rain fell down harder, a deluge stirred by the heightening wind. As icy cold as the intensifying rain was, he tried to ignore it. England was drawing in the end of summer with transitional weather of one day hot, the next chilly, one day raining to the next windy. He had no idea if this was the norm here, yet was well assured it was not his norm. Today seemed to be a combination of all the seasons rolled into a soggy, soft menacing cardboard parcel wrapped in a bitterly inconsolable completed bow. The chilly wind had survived to a subtle gale. uniting with that bitterly cold rain it was yet a different season for the day.

Eddy peeled himself from the lamppost. He stood, slightly crouched over. He brought the collars of his thin brown felt jacket around his scarf. He huddled inside that warm haven with his red weather-exposed nose peeking out. He was just like the television's screens portrayal of a nineteen-twenties secret detective snooping in the back alleys. A light grey and white checked scarf protected his neck from the downpour dripping down from his drenched hair.

The long jacket which looked like it should not be waterproof, mercifully was as the rain dripped in a waterfall from the bottom soaking his blue jeans and white runners. That was in hindsight a bad idea to wear such light shoes on a day which will see them worn-out too soon. He looked like he had a shower, then got dressed without drying to then step back into the shower before going out. You would not see this look gracing the Milan catwalk anytime soon.

He was staring at his former place of work through the wet clumped strands of hair that glittered, mirroring the coloured lights around him. The rope-like hair did not obscure his vision. He was plucking at his heartstrings for the courage to walk in. Previously, once in France, then again when he was on the shores of England, he had sent an email with his intentions. Expressions of hope. Even with the perfect reply back, albeit short, he was still nervous. Counting down from three, one large breath out through noiseless whistle lips he crossed the road on a mission.

With his focus on the building, he nearly got hit by a passing cyclist, who swerved, swore loudly and carried on splashing tides of muddy water in his wake. He cursed his good luck as that would have been the perfect excuse to delay this meeting. He licked his lips, which tasted salty from the rain, or undetected sweat. He embraced himself. He was getting his appetite ready to eat humble pie.

After the long bus journey back from Spain, he had time to reflect. He resolved that he did not want to leave the United Kingdom just yet. He also was determined to see more of Europe, have more memories to take back with him. He did not want to go back to Australia just yet. Especially after telling everyone of his love for Saoirse. He did not want to explain the torrid ending of what a few days was only earlier, the ecliptic love. Being back and on his own, he had time to heal. Time to explain. Honestly, he wanted a little more time to forget.

It showed the character of the people that he had met in England. It was with his tail between his legs that he went back to, got offered and accepted to work back at The Smugglers Tunnel. There is a reassuring glue that powerfully binds the British and Australians which goes back to the convict heritage. Eddy splashes down the tremendously deafening sound of the wind and rain. Quickly along the quiet pedestrian free pavement to impulsively stumble into a similar type of bar.

He has a sudden irresistible urge to want to drink. It was not even past eleven in the morning. He steps down two stone steps. Knocking his head on the 'mind your head' sign with a soft unpainful thud by the stapled cushion. He bows, he has to. He bobs and weaves under the thick rustic wooden beams of the roof to the small bar warmed by the open fireplace. The smell of logs burning. The distant sound of The Ventures' *Walk Don't Run* song, released before he was born, playing from the small speakers could not be any more out of place.

The stale smell of smoke remains even when that was made illegal many years ago, combined with the damp wet weather and cheap perfume he gathers on the beautifully vanished sliced truck of the bar. He orders a pint as he removes his soaked attire to dry by the open fire. He tries to collect his thoughts. Not for the first time. This luxury was taken from him. Unpredictably, against his own thoughts, he does not mind this intrusion.

'Australian, right?' an elderly man lifts his gaunt head from his golden-brown ale, littered with tobacco stains, the result of rolling, badly, his own cigarettes, around his damp coaster and neat alternate towers of perfectly stacked coins. Eddy thinks that this must be the presence of the stale smoke he smells.

'Boom.' Eddy goes for a fist pump with which the toothless companion shuffles on his seat closer, but remaining out of his personal space.

'Welcome back.' He splutters a laugh. 'Don't get many convicts over here?'

'You know,' Eddy chuckles in response to his predictable, but very self-assured joke. 'Honestly. I'm getting to like you, Pomes. You Pome bastard.' Eddy has always had a knack of retorting to the jokes, genuine light-hearted insults about the history.

'What does that mean? Actually? Pomes? Anyway?'

'Prisoner of Mother England.'

'Really?' He hoots with a slap of his hand on the back of Eddy's shoulder. 'Fuck off! But that means you Aussies can spell!'

'Others say it is English slang, an abbreviation of pomegranate.'

'Slang?'

'Pomegranate, immigrant. You know, your Cock-knee rhythm slang.'

'Cock-knee!' He cackles as he swings his head back in borderline frantically hysterical uproarious screams of delight. 'Rhythm. I like it. Mush, listen here. Firstly, it is cockney rhyming slang. Secondly mush, you need to count the syllables properly for it to work. That's not even close. Piss off and nick something mush.'

'Another round please,' Eddy buys it and remarks, 'Going by your logic that my mum was a prostitute and my dad was a thief, at least we are egalitarian.'

'Throwing out the big words now...'

'Going to ignore that,' a wink before continuing, 'with that social base us Australians treat everyone the same. It is not a bad way to live.'

Eddy's newfound friend has to nod a form of agreement before they go on to the universal subject of sport. Then putting the world to rights with politics. Homelife. Lost loves. He leaves with more than his quick drink, a haze of thoughts and a drunken smile with slowly closing eyes.

Not just this old guy who talked to a stranger, but it showed the nice people he has met in the norther part of England, at The Smugglers from the landlords to the staff. They were sympathetic to his decline. They did not jeer him or ask too many personal questions. Eddy needed to remember this. He appreciated it. There was great in the world around him.

That start day came around quickly. He was literally back for a single day in Saxmundham to accustom himself. He found a small room, courtesy of chef Gary who knew a mate that had a room for rent. It was a breezy day when he showed up with Ken sliding a list of notes in his scribbling scrawl that looked like he was writing with a broken hand. Immediately, he felt reassured. He had no idea what he was going to do.

Due to his former job being taken quickly, he was not sure of his role. He helped everywhere. He worked the bar, restaurant, kitchen and as the cleaner. He got up at stupid o'clock to clean the beer lines. He was the handyman. It was so nice that they gave him hours. He worked hard, extremely hard. Mainly to block out the pain, yet this worked in his advantage as the landlords saw him working tirelessly and relished in his work ethic, which worked hugely for everyone's benefit.

In spite of everything though, he struggled. He struggled with the whole thing that was familiar. The name, the place, the people. The foundation commencement of that love that blossomed here into a true flower, to wilt, to die. Every week being in the old cold, worn down cellar. Being in that suffocatingly small space numerous times a day. The area in which they shared a passionate moment on the dirty cold, metal kegs before hearing the landlord come thumping down, sledgehammer quiet, stamping down the wooden steps that disturbed them before they got out of hand. It was heading that way. It escalated to a peck, a passionate kiss, a feel, a touch and a strong desire to rip each other's clothes off.

Eddy struggled with the kind-hearted, sympathetic hand of mateship by the regular customers asking about Saoirse and how she was. If she was keeping well. If, they kept in touch still. If they will try again. He could only state so many times that they fell in love at the wrong time. He did not even know what he meant by that. It was a copout. He wanted to evade any questions to escape the network of stammering answers. He would never heal. Not here at any rate.

With a layer of irony. With a twisted wit, in a funny way, that he had to go back to Ken, once again with his tail between his legs. He just could not do it. He could not look up at Ken as he spoke, barely audible in his embarrassment. His humiliation. He was taken aback by his understanding. He was fantastic. Eddy was genuinely dreading the conversation. He had had it in his mind for a few days. Then deciding yesterday to think of the dialogue all through the night, and the morning walk. After taking him back. Thenceforth, for not even a month back on the grind, having to explain that he would be leaving again, soon.

They had taken him back without a question. He was reminded once again that he was not alone, and people are generally not good, but great. Ken spoke like a father figure, he empathised in his predicament. Afterall he was young once, he had gone through this before. He only asked, with a firm insistence for four weeks' notice, which Eddy accepted without question. He took his hand inside of Ken's and wrapped them in a firm, quick show of relief. Clumsily stumbling out 'thank yous', 'I will repay you with work'.

This was Eddy's first introduction into a winter in Europe. Although, he was persistently told, it was autumn. To the point of it becoming annoying. He did not believe it truly could get any colder. It was September, the weather was cold. At around eight in the morning, with the temperature to match the time he was on his way to work. Hoodie over his head, hands stuffed as far as they could go in his heavy, woollen brown jacket.

Briskly walking up the street lined hill to where the Smugglers was. He had to purchase a whole new wardrobe of warmer clothes recently which made this passage better endured. Looking down at the ground while he breathed into a thick black and green scarf as he shuffled into work, understanding fully the phrase of being cold to the bone. In Sydney, it would be cold in winter, but not like this. The only thing shared at this time of the year was the rain.

Sydney would be going through its transitional period between the seasons, so rain was often accompanied by thunderstorms, but not with the cold, it would still be warm, to hot. The forks of lightning covering the sky was an awesome sight to behold. The thunderstorms he has seen here have been more cloud covered flashes. If being freezing cold and windy, if weather was in an Olympic event, Britain would surely take out the gold on this score. Today it was not raining, thankfully, but the dark and the cold was equally as uninviting. Once at work he warmed up quickly as he strove to work harder that warranted. With a childlike knowing of someone he had been doing, or had done the wrong thing, he wanted to replay Ken back with the only way he knew how, with himself. His work ethic.

He put in more hours than anyone. First to arrive, last to leave. It was getting depressing to be dark when he arrived, dark when he left, but the days were counting down. That night after cleaning the bar and finishing the last job of the night he turned the heating off. On the floor, he spotted the newspaper he chucked away earlier and inadvertently found the back of the bin rather than the large black plastic void for which was larger and, surely, easier to find. Well, you would think.

He saw, highlighted for his benefit, where he wanted to go. Like it was planned, and fate had thrown him a unique opportunity. Some unseen influence had made this piece of paper miss the bin, so he would find it, read it. With that the universal planets became aligned perfectly. He knew what he needed to do.

This was going to be a somewhat different scene to the autumn of Suffolk. The flurry of snowfall, the chill of the wind. This was Eddy's first winter in England and at the start, he enjoyed it. The cold, the snow—the first time he had seen it—the houses that seemed equipped to keep the heat in, the general ideology of the Dickens, Victorian Christmas feel that he had never had before. From the day-off perspective, it was glorious.

That paper made him move to another part of England. He was now living in a place in the South East of England called Lewes. For which he pronounced incorrectly as Lee-wees, as that is how it is spelt! When he mentioned to the owners of the Smugglers Tunnel that he was leaving for 'Leewees', they laughed at him. They did not even try to hide the amusement as they took in his mispronunciation.

He came here by chance. He came by her by chance. A chance advert in a local newspaper left by a customer where he worked. The green felt-tip pen had been ringed by the previous customer and as all the others were crossed out in a crudely hard, etched cross, this laid for all to be seen. He picked it up and threw it in the bin as he was clearing the table back at the Smugglers Tunnel. Later on, through his clear down he saw the paper again and the advert he read for the first time properly not just the mere headline; 'Help Wanted in Lewes'. It was for a seasonal live-in post in the Southeast, at a place he had never heard of before. The job was looking after the family's pets while they went away for an extended Christmas and New Year break.

Why not? To get paid to live in a house. This would make such a refreshingly great chance to the broom cupboard he had been living with fourteen other Australians since outstaying his welcome at his first port of call, courtesy of Gary.

Therefore, he rang up, went down, had another interview and found himself here at the end of October. They wanted him in place earlier to get a feel for him. Show him the places around and make a trust connection with. They were only a few years older in their 30s. Both worked in London and commuted. Although he worked for home nearly four days out of the five days in the working week. Furthermore, due to the work that they were involved in, it was not unusual for them to be working through the weekend in some capacity.

They both were accountants that met at school, went to the same college, same university and worked at the same firm. Now if Eddy had heard this without seeing the couple, he would think it was the dullest story of love told. It still would not be a blockbusting smash hit from Hollywood, but a nice tale, nevertheless. However, the connection they had was infectious. They were made for each other. It made Eddy sick. After coming here to hide. He did not want to have his nose pushed in with the reminder of the reason he was here.

As the advertisement stated and the subsequent telephone call had elaborated on, they decided to go away for the winter to get some winter sun in Mauritius. Not a bad life, for some. They had talked about it for years and finally were going to do it. It was so hard for them to get time off, especially at the same time, being in the same firm, but this time they managed to swing it. They had decided to leave in the first week of November and go away for December coming back to spend New Year's in London with friends and family and then getting back to Lewes the first week of January to start work on the second week.

It was planned to the precise and intimate detail with no stone unturned. He could not help that on the fridge there were no unnecessary magnets or pieces of paper struggling to stay attached. Simply a clear printed calendar of the month. On it marked in perfectly black inked block capitals was what was going on for each of them, top half for her and bottom half for him. If they were doing the same thing, it took the whole of the small square.

Eddy expected nothing less from a couple that spent their time putting figures in boxes, to get the desired bottom line, to have such an organised, regimented calendar. He could imagine the calendar on their phones being just as organised with alerts, reminders and different colour-codes for different events, schedules and appointments. On a separate piece of paper was the itinerary of their holiday with what they were doing, where, when and contact details. It was too organised for Eddy who had come to the United Kingdom on a whim. Had travelled on a whim. Who went away and did what he wanted, innocently on a whim.

He arrived off the train from London for the second time this month and walked down the slippery blue, metal wrought iron steps up and over the tracks and down onto the other side. Here it was late in the afternoon and the wind was fierce, particular above the tracks. He was fighting for breath as he crossed the bridge with the ranges of the South Downs for which he learnt, were referred to as the lungs of the south east of England in between the South East of England and London.

On the other side, Daniel picks him up in a black, shiny by the rain rather than the new-just-of-the-court-look BMW black convertible. The roof is very much up due to the apocalyptic weather. He tells Eddy about his adopted home. Being born in Brighton, he always wanted to live in Lewes. So close to London but far enough to be close to the coast and the many walks on offer. Close to the family that still live in Brighton without being in each other's business and affairs.

Daniel's wife, Kimberley, had not returned from work yet and Daniel stated that he was waiting for a call to pick her up, but being so close he was sure she would walk. As she said in the same recurrent sentence, 'I wake, I sit in the car to the station, sit in the train, sit at work, and repeat. I need some exercise during the day.'

For which he spoke in a slightly higher, imitating her voice, finishing with a laugh to himself. Eddy looked out to see the trees struggling to stay upright with the growing force of the wind. On top of that, the wind was carrying a large downfall of water. He turns the BMW expertly and glides down a narrow alley that he drives down effortlessly without stress.

Although Eddy watched, stressed. The walls passed close to the wing mirror on either side, as a cat rang like a shadow from between two green plastic bins and narrowly missing the tyres of the BMW. He was unfazed. He parks in a garage that is off the High Street, then a tiny passageway rings us to the beautiful and modern house nestled amongst the older buildings. 'This was an allotment' Daniel states as he leads the way and opens the door of the detached cedar house.

Daniel was apologising for being late at the railway station but after work in the city he raced back to get the car. He was not late, but he did not stop apologising anyway. Australians take the carefree piss out of the British politeness. It is famous, some would say infamous. Many memes are out explaining the nonsensically ludicrous over the top reactions to the smallest things to apologise for. As if Daniel is reading Eddy's mind, he tells a story while still apologising why he was late.

'Sorry. I wanted to pick you up by car. The weather. I did not know how much luggage you have. Turns out not a lot. But yeah, I was on the bus from the train station. I accidentally rang the bell for the wrong stop. I prayed that someone would get off when the bus stopped. No one did, and no one got on. So, I got off earlier, so I did not have to explain my mistake and walked, ran back to get the car keys. Sorry.'

Eddy listened with the feeling that he did not really need to apologise. Daniel had the features and dress of someone that had just came off the pages of a large department stores catalogue, or poster. He was strangely handsome, with a designer stubble with slight highlights of distinctive grey coming through. He was wearing a dark blue suit with a pale pink shirt and a silky white tie.

It does sound a mix-match of colours, but Daniel wore it like he owned it, looking impeccably elegant. He had a superman style hairstyle. His dark brown hair was lightly gelled with a slight quiff that bounced slightly with his head moments. The wind did not affect his smartness. The speckled strands of silver locks added a refined style of sophistication. His black pointed shoes were polished to a mirror glaze. He was the image of success. Down to the smaller touches of purposeful intent. His bulky gold watch on his right wrist with light blue hands and digital roman numerals that knowingly matched his piercing eyes was no coincidence.

He was not built like a bodybuilder, but his athletic toned and fit, powerful figure let Eddy know that he was no stranger to the gym. His handshake at the station was firm with a touch of obliquely confidence. Unlike some of the BMW drivers that are pricks in their personality and attitude, he was not. He had the attire, the looks, the style that stated that he would be and would not care but he carried the confidence. Carried the high-powered job, car and lifestyle with grace. He was an agreeable person. Eddy felt himself drawn to him like a magnet, which also made him slightly envious without the green-eye of jealousy. He smiled at himself when he thought that he probably had a big dick as well.

He introduces his home, as he grips the brass lion-sculptured door handle of the bright red door, swings it open motioning Eddy to go in first. The door opens to a brand-new kitchen to the right with an updated calendar on the fridge to what he saw the other day, a bathroom to the left. At the back is the master bedroom, which Eddy will not be staying in, is large. The French windows open to a quaint but ideal garden where two of the black Dobermans have as their domain. For which they have a safe haven within the kennels at the very bottom of the wet, rain-ridden garden. These are what he will be looking after.

On a day like this, he cannot blame Mother, Eubank and son, Tyson for taking refuge in their large kennels at the end of the quaint, cosy back garden. Kimberley and Daniel are big boxing fans. A change from Danny Green but he knew many mates in Australia that came to the United Kingdom to gain experience. Mainly due to Amateurs are paid here, and the fighting level is higher than that in Australia. Therefore, they would come to gain experience, knowledge and be paid, while holding down easy jobs such as shelf stacking, washing up or something that will get the money in, but give them the hours to train.

Once in a boxing studio, they will get events, fights. It does cost, but for them the cost is worth it. Boxers who want to get better come to Europe, whereas if you want to get better at kickboxing, you go to Thailand. Simple. This was the first meeting with Daniel after having the initial conversation with Kimberley. He hung up his damp clothes, took Eddy's and left the luggage on the tiled entry. They walked to the kitchen where Eddy was instructed to sit at the kitchen island while he placed a coffee pot on to chit-chat.

When Kimberley was young, she had an illness. An illness that does not affect her at all today, but due to complications it affects her today. This illness caused her to lose the ability to have children. Eddy did not ask what the illness was or the problem that ensued. After all, it was none of his business. The conversation was glanced over. It moved as quickly as a blur of a passing advertisement board on a bus. As Kimberly could not have kids, the Dobermans became her children. She cooed over them. Brought them gifts and read to them at night. They also had a fluffy white ball of fur called Calculus. It had to be something to do with numbers, Eddy thought.

She was docile and well behaved. Eddy, not being a huge fan of cats, thanked his lucky stars for her docile behaviour. The French windows pull to the living room come dining room. Above the living room is an attic for which they are thinking of converting into another bedroom as an investment opportunity for later selling, but used for a guest room for now. Up a staircase was his room. A window portrait to the 'famous' Lewes Castle shows the outside world.

He places his meagre but essential belongings on the pale beige rope carpet. He will unpack later. The shower is shared downstairs, but he is quickly shown the wardrobe, which has more blankets if it gets cold at night. Daniel was a tall man so had to slightly bow his head in this room, but this did not stop him explaining the room and gushing with a sort-of man crush his love for the castle beyond the window.

Just as Daniel finished his whirlwind tour, the sound of a key hitting the lock was heard from downstairs. They walked down as the door bellowed open accompanied by leaves on the coldness of the dark winters wind. At what Eddy considers, being a late finish Kimberley comes through the door in a thin layer of glistening rain that shines her angular features. Kimberley is a skinny, tall woman with angular features that resemble a Nordic lady with high cheekbones that angle towards her thick lips that are in an eternal pout. She does not seem to be wearing any make-up. Or, it got washed off in Mother's Nature's earth wash.

She is immaculately dressed in black suede sock-length booted high heels that are slightly blemished by the puddles on her short walk from the railway station. Black see-through tights exposing nothing more than her lower legs and the top of her knees where a pencil black skirt with thin vertical grey strips to a thin, black leather belt and a white blouse covered by a black and grey matching blazer. Her dark blonde hair done in a tight perfectly formed bun. On entry, she lets her hair cascade down loosely as she closes the door with one hand behind her. She pulls the thin invisible needle that was the key holding her long curvy locks in place. They bounced off her shoulders as she removed her blazer and muttered something about taking a 'proper' coat tomorrow.

The light from the coat hooks reflects in a transcending soft glow off the mirror, which cascades a radiant illumination, to frame dreamily this as a vision of true beauty. The moment was over too quick for Eddy as she turned around. Her bright red umbrella slid in the Grecian black and gold urn, placed outside the door before she gently closing it shut. She stripped off her gloves after hanging her blazer up and placing them in the inside pocket. As she took off her outside garments, she was organising them as she went. Folding and placing them in the exact place that they belonged. Placing her keys on the single hook that was exposed next to three other hooks with different keys seemingly colour coded. Flicking the light switch off to plunge the small hallway into darkness with only the light from the kitchen flowing in. She ever-so-slightly raised her voice to a hello.

Daniel responded from the kitchen enquiring if she wanted to eat first or shower. She mentioned 'eat' as she turned the corner and saw Eddy leaning over the open divide from the dining room into the open kitchen. Compared to the rest of the house the brand-new kitchen was the smallest room of the house. Eddy thought that this was as they considered it the lesser important room, but did not opposingly voice his criticism, which he believed would not come out as he intended of being positive and constructive. It was smaller, but had everything they needed. The whole kitchen was covered with the cream, café au lait colour doors, and drawers hiding the bin, oven, extractor fan, dishwasher and the crockery and cutlery.

Once again, everything had a home. Everything was placed in accordance to a methodical order. For example, the perfectly matched cups and mugs were placed near the hot water kettle and coffee pot which was hidden along with the cream toaster under a cupboard on the preparation table. The workspace was ample for a small family. Daniel was washing as he went so no mess was around. Eddy asked many times if he could help and he was motioned away with a wave of the hand, but encouraged him to talk from the island. The smell of freshly picked rosemary coming off the New Zealand lamb, which Eddy found out was cheaper than the British lamb; *bizarre*, he thought.

It was a Friday night. A busy night for Kimberley, who after enquiring how much time she had, changed her mind and opted for the shower first. She apologised in true British style, way too much as she sped away to shower, get dressed into fresh casual attire. The pale cedar varnished planks of wood cover every space of the floor with rugs placed in accordance to make the room cosy, or whatever level of perfection that was needed for them to feel relaxed. A large think rectangular wooden dining table stood in the middle at a slight angle to the white plastered and painted walls to make the room flow. Rather than seats, each side had the identical version of a bench with no head or tail chairs. An upright piano perfectly fit between the wall and the doorway to the living room.

Calculus lazily sat on the top with her white bushy tail hanging down and flicking every now-and-again. An acoustic Martin guitar was propped up next the piano. Eddy had enquired about the musical instruments to which he was told neither of them played. It was part of the homely interior design. This was the first thing, and he was betting the only thing, that he would see that would contradict the perfect arrangement of everything having a home, everything brought and used for a purpose. Nothing, absolutely nothing brought to keep up with anyone but themselves.

A single Matisse copy hangs on the other side of the doorway where a comfy looking single brown seat with the same straight angles of the dining table underneath. The French windows dominated the other two sides, that let so much natural light in it was a warming pleasure. Daniel had put the heating on and the rooms were cosy. Kimberley remarked on how hot it was, as she finally seemed relaxed. She motioned towards Daniel and placed a subtle but lingering kiss on his right cheek as she leaned in from behind. They had a little small talk about their days for which they would apparently speak later about. Kimberley remarks on Daniel's former dark ponytail with grey highlights running through it that had recently been cut into this new style. There was a fanciful flick of her wrist to where it would have been. This was to let Eddy know that this was from the days of their first meeting, as the only difference in his physical appearance is the grey highlights that are coming more frequent.

Daniel was strong and tall and next to Kimberley, they looked the perfect couple. So beautiful, well suited to each other and perfectly matched. Eddy was in a perfect home that screamed delicence and elegance next to a couple that complimented the home. Daniel was animated in his hands as if they were required to make his voice speak as Kimberley stretched behind to turn the computerised dial on the central heating down. Eddy liked this couple. She was very independent, organised and assured in herself. Daniel was ambitious, knew what he wanted and was going to get it, but they also shared a common love for life, laughter and each other. It was a chemistry that worked.

Eddy felt that they were contagious in their happiness. This positivity was infecting him. Daniel had been cooking a roast. The smell from the kitchen was salivating. He was no rookie to this. Daniel changed into attire that is more relaxing while Kimberley talked to Eddy about his day. He came back, Superman quick, wearing black jeans and a blue and white striped shirt with the top buttons off and Kimberley wearing blue jeans and a black shirted top with her wet hair stroking the shoulders of Daniel they could have come straight out of a Myers catalogue advertising the latest fashions.

They both wore limited jewellery. She had the smaller diamond stud earing when she worked in and still wore them with the thinnest silver necklace around her lightly dusted freckled neck. She wore a single horseshoe-style ring around her little right-hand finger. He wore a watch that did not look like much to Eddy's untrained eye, but he would imagine it was a costly affair to have on while cooking.

Eddy felt very uncomfortable. Here he stood in scruffy brown cheap runners with blue jeans, torn and ripped around the knees. A baggy brown jumper that he got from a charity shop that was slightly deformed to show his white T-shirt collar underneath. The openness of them was transparent as they did not judge him at all. He was not being stared at like an animal of revolution in a human zoo. He felt like an equal. It was a testament to them that they saw people for people. Not the status that they were, the material assets that they owned, or the power over people that they have.

Eddy thought that this was very Australian of them. They would have so much respect in their fields from everyone that they encountered. In and outside of work this would drive people around them on, rather than having a negative impact. Eddy could not help but feel slightly jealous by them. It was a passing emotion. Eddy always thought it was a wasted emotion, nevertheless he did feel the green-eye monster lurk its head every now-and-again. He was equally as quick to push it down again.

Eddy was shocked to find out that they were both married, as they wore no rings to signify it. They explained that they did not need a ring to tell them they were married. They were childhood friends. Thrust into each other's world by their respective families. They shared their first kiss together. Their first love together. Their first sexual encounter together. They have only ever had eyes for each other. They have never ventured away. Never felt that they were losing out with someone new.

They were very, very happy in the knowledge that they were committed in love, hate, friendship and war, to be with one another through it all. It was not a hard relationship where they constantly tried hard. It was not an easy relationship where there were always peaceful calm seas. They surprised each other often. They never saw the relationship as a guarantee. They loved each other. With this rare love they allowed them to express what they wanted. They kept each other happy.

They asked about Eddy's relationship for which he just gave a blasé response and asked about the dark, cloudy, warm drink that he had in his pint glass. Daniel continued to talk about the different ales, beers and lagers in England. He had a certain thirst on this topic and enjoyed telling someone that did not know the fundamentals on the breweries around Britain with the history. Daniel thrust another bottle of Harvey's into Eddy's hand as he relinquished the empty one into his glass.

'It's the spring water, you see,' Daniel gushed with expressive delight. His hands moving as much as his mouth. 'The spring water gets filtered through the chalk of the downs to the brewery', a slight drink-influenced mispronunciation.

'Really, darling?' Kimberley asked in a mock questioning tone. 'Do you think Australia does not have beer? Or breweries?'

'Of course, I don't. Nevertheless, the flavour? The tradition of generations? Not yet. Australia will never be able to resemble the superbly balanced hop enticed bitter of Harvey's. This is Sussex in a bottle.'

'What?' Kimberley laughs through a smile. 'How many have you had?'

'Dear Kimberley. My dearest. Harvey's Bitter was established in 1770. Australia was found in 1790. I bet Captain Cook had Harvey's on his voyage.' Daniel had the dates wrong. With his drink-influenced brain, he had mixed up the dates of Harvey's and Australia. Maybe to convince himself of his own personal argument. 'In fact...' hoisting his, while slightly spilling his glass into the air, 'Jesus was a brewer.'

This statement made Eddy choke on his mouthful of the pale bitter. He laughed out loud with a dribble as he wiped his mouth with his free hand. Kimberley laughed too, but with more elegance. Daniel laughed; his laugh was a slight sputtering low gruffing sound whereas Kimberley roared a musical chorus that was the hook for everyone to join in.

They discussed more. They touched most of the topics of the day. Personal and issues all touched on. It was a conversation as if they had been school mates and were meeting up again for the first time in a few years. It seemed so natural. They all did not have to get up early so enjoyed the freedom of recklessly that involved no time watching, checking. They seemed to enjoy having new company and someone out of the circle in which they interacted on a regular basis.

Over the roast New Zealand lamb cooked in rosemary butter, duck-fat roasted potatoes with scatterings of roasted turnip, swede and carrot with a mint sauce. 'This was traditional English cuisine,' Eddy was told. Well, apart from the lamb which they would have preferred to have gotten from Romney Marsh. Eddy remarked on how good it was. Something he genuinely believed in. The presentation and the cooking were perfect. Eddy thought that sorry was a verb for them.

It seemed to be used so often to Eddy, to each other, to nothing in particular. If Daniel bumped the table on the way up, he apologised. Eddy found it funny. He did not think it was the free-flowing bitters that were doing this, but a force of habit that he, that they could not break. The conversation was flowing faster than the bitter. It was faultless and covered so many topics but now had entered the religious aspect of England, football. Eddy slipped a few times but going back to soccer but with a look from Daniel, he corrected himself immediately—football.

He learnt that the local side of Lewes play at the Dripping Pan. He could not have heard that correctly, surely. When you go up to the top of a chalk hill, maybe tomorrow and look down. The pitch is the shape of a frying pan. Daniel was a true-blue supporter in the way of Chelsea. Kimberley had the same passion and followed Reading. As they played in different divisions, it had not yet caused a war within the walls of their perfect home. Eddy went for Leeds. Although did not share a tenth of the same passion as they did it was many due to the Australians that he followed Leeds United. Harry Kewell, and the formidable talented for which he felt the rest of the soccer, sorry, football world under-rated, was the impressive Mark Viduka. Later Michael Bridges coming over to play for Newcastle Jets made him follow that team back in Australia. He often asked himself why and got a lot of stick from the true sky-blue followers of his native Sydney FC.

With a grinding of the chair legs, Daniel rises to do the dishes. Eddy and Kimberley both rise to help. He waves them back down to sit, insisting that he will clean, no help needed. Despite the pleas from them both, he snarled at the slight offering of a hand. He playfully nibbled on Kimberley's hand as she passed an empty plate. He carried his voice over from the kitchen to join in the conversations that had now gone onto Eddy and his hometown of Sydney, with the emphasis of his childhood growing up.

It turned out that Eddy knew rather little about the origins of his family. He actually felt quite ashamed, tinged with guilt. His only saving grace was that he had heard of a place in Kent, called Sandwich. This name had come up before in family reunions. He only remembered that as being a food and found it a strange name without deriving a conclusion to consider it was the birthplace of the sandwich. It was only when Kimberley mentioned that the Earl of Sandwich wanted a snack to play cards, poker, with. He did not want to get his fingers dirty, eventually pausing the game, maybe stopping the game, hence the sandwich was born and named after the creator.

Feeling slightly stupid, Eddy felt the penny drop inside him with the significant splash of embarrassment. Kimberly sensed that she might have been a little precocious, so redeemed herself and Eddy by changing the subject to music. This brought up the piano and the guitar for the second time. Eddy dabbled at best, in music. They shared an overall interest for all types of music. Daniel came back in with more bottles of bitter. They retired to the living room with the dishes air-drying on the stainless-steel rack. Kimberley put on a vinyl record. They both shared a nostalgic value of records over compact discs.

From the perfectly placed speakers came the Rolling Stones album, *Let It Bleed*. The haunting riff of the start of Gimme Shelter with the enigmatic chorus notes by a female singer, the soft snare drum, then the bass notes of a piano come in followed by the unmistakable sound of Mick Jagger himself. It is a comfortable moment where they find seats and just listen to the opening minutes of the song before starting up a new conversation. Eddy being a third wheel gets great gratification to feeling the pleasure of being welcomed into their home, their life.

This was a slightly smaller area than the dining room but with it simple large black and white paintings of faces in charcoal and chalk around the centre of the plaster and painted white walls. The light yellow of sun kissed sand cloth of the four-piece suite of two single chairs and one long three-seater sofa that horseshoes a miniature table based on the one they had just had a rather late dinner. Each corner of the table is lined by the perfect position of the cork base coasters. On each corner, to the exact millimetre, they are placed to the point that Eddy needs confirmation to move one. This comes in the sliding of Kimberley who positions one closer to her.

These have a simple sunburst yellow design that matches the surrounding furniture. In the centre is a yellow bowl of many hues resembling that of the vase in the Sunflowers painting by Van Gogh. Inside are the rich colours of unblemished fresh fruit comprising of mandarins, bananas, red and green apples filling the bowl. A low dimmer light of the spotlights is low, casting a thin white light that casts thin shadows over the area. It was comfortable and soothing. In front was a large black television with no wires seen hanging at a slight angle on the wall. To the right, a fireplace with logs in a wicker basket ready to go with hanging small gold poke and shovel. The black iron fireplace is old and restored. Kimberley states it was her grandmother's.

When she moved to a home, they made sure that they took it out before it was sold. Eddy had never heard that expression before, so after probing found out it was a retirement village. Above this on a rescued piece of shipwrecked wood, she has memories that she did not want to let go off. Photographs of family members, relatives are placed with different mementoes like a ring, a medal. Kimberley glazed over them as stating she changed the photographs frequently. Due to running out of bottles of bitter, they had now all moved over to red wine.

'I got this for you,' Kimberley mentions as Daniel thrusts the bottle of wine showing the front label in front of Eddy's nose.

'Heathcote, ahh Victoria. The Mexican state.'

'It is said that an ancestor of the Tyrrell family fired an arrow that killed King William II. Wait, what Mexican?' Daniel scans the label in an attempted to show off.

'You don't need to boast, dear,' Kimberley smirks. 'But you do need to pour the Shiraz.'

'Mexican state?' Daniel asks once more.

'North of the North South Wales border. Stupid joke. But it works.'

This was more to Eddy's taste. He was not a big wine drinker, by any means, but found the Harvey's to be heavy and very hoppy in flavour. Frankly he was not used to this as a session beer. The red wine swirled a bright purple hue around the glass as he ineptly poured with an involuntary uncertainty in his own ability to stand straight. It was full-bodied, heavy but the grapes with their vibrant berry flavour with a hint of pepper made it very easy to drink, and, of course to enjoy.

Over dinner, Daniel and Kimberley competed in a conversation like it was rehearsed. Questions were sprayed like bullets from a machine gun. They told Eddy about the everything, which made their everything. Here, as the afternoon bleed effortlessly into the evening. With the white pale moon high in the sky spilling light through the window. The comfortable seats where Kimberley and Daniel shared the three-seater reclined. Barely any space between them. Kimberley's hand in the lap of Daniel stroking his groin. They not only seemed more relaxed, they were relaxed.

They were at ease from the start, but now seem much more comfortable. They are now talking about the town, with no less animated, but the barriers were coming down. The root of why they loved the town was clearer. The tide of alcohol ultimately burst the walls to make everything free. In due course of the waves of honestly no topic became off subject, nothing was caged in, no holds barred. Eddy felt like he was not doing too much of the talking, more answering questions and listening to their tales. He was told about fancy-free Brighton, 'a day-trip away' as a must see. The passion they had for one of the oldest castles in England was infectious. Built after the Norman Conquest of 1066 for which his bedroom window looks out to, Lewes Castle, has great views and 'brilliant, just brilliant'. 'It is a must', they both agree with a clink of their glasses. A glint of adoration in their eyes. A loving lean of bodies touching with a soft laugh.

Eddy has no idea of the time when he ascended the cedar wood stairs that curve to his room with all the grace of a fish out of water. The insert of the stairs acts as a bookcase on the bottom two shelves from reading to work material, framed photographs of family, friends and loved ones in the centre and more books finish the last two shelves. It is a fantastic idea. Eddy almost slipped on the curves of the steep smooth wood numerous times, but managed to catch himself most of the time from falling back. This was fortunate as the drop would have been back down to the floor, as no barriers would stop his descend.

Bizarrely, he was more worried about the noise, than of him injuring himself. He is up in the rafters. Knocking his head, he saw his goal, a low double bed. He continued to smack his head while stripping off his clothes on route. A small chest of draws, a double-doored mirrored wardrobe, a bedside table and a single chair all in the cedar furnishing the theme that runs through the house, swung around on a merry-go-round in front of his eyes, as the room started to spin as he laid on the soft, goose hair filled doona. Faster, faster but without the joyful squeals of weeeee. A white and yellow sunburst designed lamp is on the bedside table with a clock face in the old white dial style, surrounded with black Roman numerals and two large golden bells straddling the top. Shining, perfectly polished is a duo of golden ringers like golden mallets, posed, tight and ready to be unleashed to crack the bells.

Eddy tried to focus on the clockface to stop the world spinning. It did not work. A single semi-circular window lets natural light in. He crawls to the window, feels the coldness. He looks out towards the castle. It is lit in a magnificent golden shine of kissing light that brushes the castle tower to stand out like a beacon over the quiet, sleeping town of Lewes. He slumps back onto his new bed. He heard about hanging his leg out of the bed to feel the comfort of the hard floor. It was all lies. Above him is the black blind-covered skylight.

He focuses on the hanging swaying string from the skylight. This seems to work to slow down the horror-ride. He retires happy with the decision that he had made. Eddy must admit to feeling a lot of nervous energy after accepting the role, but now here, he sees the job. He was not worried for the reason that he cannot do it, but more if he was not in the correct headspace to do it.

The shrill. The peace-shattering squeal of ear-piercing noise. Eddy groaned, a reluctant want to get up. Until now an incandescent essentiality to get up from the place that he would want to be. The vibrating alarm bell not only seemed to penetrate louder with each golden hammer on the golden dome, but bored a large drilling hole with each throbbing ding. This discord seemed to echo within his head. He brushed in the air, flailed an arm. Probing and searching in the light of day. His eye still unopened. Floundering more frantically for the origin of that punishing sound. A clasp. He found it. Hand in a fist around the bells. He did not let go. Silence descended. He pulled his heavy free arm around. He fiddled for the small switch to go up or down. The button, a switch, something, just to turn the tormenting, anguishing ringing off. Ending this aged torture. The pounding of that infernal racket stayed in Eddy's head long after he turned off the source.

As he made his way up from the pillow, he was deliberately slow. As if his head had become a full washing up bowl for which a wave on any of the sides caused lightning strike of pain. He peeled his sweaty hair off the cotton pale peach sheet. His hair pulled away in tight, pinging releasing hooks of restraint. He was struggling not to spill the precarious content, as each wave was a shocking ripple of pain. He was as ungraceful as Bambi on ice, stumbling down the stairs in a fragile state as he was attempting to wake up. Making it, barely, without throwing up.

126

He stood in the too bright glow in the bathroom. His toiletries wrapped within a black and silver towel was dropped into the sink as he leaned over. Burping, holding his chest, holding in his alcohol threatening to leave from the same way as it entered. He leaned over, sweating. The mirror above him. He looks down. Breathes hard, meditate. He gradually peeps up, winching up his head by the rusty clogs of his neck. To meets the ghost of his former self. He tries to smile. He sees someone looking back at him who is as weary, exhausted and fit to drop back into bed as he thinks he feels. This is how he looks.

Turns the cold faucet, splashes cold water onto his face. Before recalling that his toiletries and towel are in the basin. He tries to care. Slowly turning the tap off. He looks towards the shower. Salvation, surely within that clear, glass cubicle. He can wash the hangover away. Well, he will try.

Although feeling tired, more than having that empty churning feeling in his stomach of nausea, these effects did tell him something. That he had a great night. It was just before eight in the morning as he shuffled back down the stairs, after getting dressed for the day. He had to admit the shower, the brushing of his teeth and that he was actually sick seemed to benefit him immensely. From the hallway, he heard Daniel and Kimberley talking. The familiar salivating smell of bread being toasted filled the air with the unmistakably lure, the heavenly aroma of coffee. He quickly composed himself on the last step, on the stairs looking, unfocused at the front door, before making his way, pretending to feel composed and confident into the kitchen.

He was surprised to see them both ready for the day. Suited and booted. Looking great. Without a glint in their eyes of a hangover, for which Eddy was feeling, unsuccessfully concealing. They were outside in the chilly air. On the wooden deck of the outside seating area, basking in the morning sun surrounded by puddles from what apparently was a nigh time rain. Both were stroking their dogs absentmindedly with one hand, a coffee in the other, animatingly talking feverishly. The dog's eyes were both locked on the toast in the centre of the table. Not noticing the affection. Yet, on feeling a different presence, they turn to see Eddy. They glowered directly at Eddy.

The dog's alertness made Daniel and Kimberley pause in midsentence, they turned, smiled, and beckoned him towards them, to the spare wicker seat. Eubank and Tyson stopped in their enjoyment of having their ears stroked to rise on an attacking pose on rigid legs. Eddy hesitated ever so slightly as he rounded the corner of the kitchen and out the elegant garage-type roller doors that made the living area expansive and become one passage on united interior splendour. Their ears picked up as he made his way forward. Vigilant. They did not bark but watched his every move. Aware. The pleasantries came out from Kimberley and Daniel as he poured a cup of black coffee from the percolator in the centre of the table into the clean cup to officially join them. This was his official meeting of the mother and son team to their acting-keeper. They were stunning with a majestic pose of authority. They did not leave their owners side but erected their stance in a convincing attitude of protection. The larger, in height, was the mother, Eubank, slightly slimmer and no less gorgeous. They both had the same light brown rust marking on the side of their nose, above their eyes, the inner tip of their ears, bottom of their legs and feet and just below their tail. Except, Eubank had a diamond mark just before her tail. Eddy motioned closer. Encouraging tones from Kimberley made him braver. A soft growl. A warning. He put a hand on the smaller one, Tyson's back. He did not flinch, Eubank did. His eyes watched with a warning to not hurt him or he would be hurt. The jet-black short coat was as smooth as silk with an equally resembling shine. He introduced himself fully as he crouched down to stroke them both. He was positioned between them so not to take precedence over one or the other.

Tyson licked his face with a cold, very moist wet tongue across his formally cleaned cheek. 'They like you,' Kimberley remarked. 'We are going to take them for a walk if you would like to join us.'

Eddy nodded, but they still let a slight growling tremor every now-and-again. As he swallowed a large gulp of black coffee, that seemed to struggle to make its way down, he got

127

up a little too fast and left his head behind. He composed himself once more. He wondered if dogs could actually sense honesty and trustfulness. It was apparent that they accepted this new arrival in Eddy as quick as a switch the growling stopped. Eddy sat down, nursed his coffee which each mouthful diluting his nausea, dissolving his headache, making him feel human once more.

This was the principal day. Like a curtain moving in the breeze, the conversation was a smooth process. Today was pointy day, the business day. The day where they talked of all his responsibilities, in true accountant fashion by holding everything accountable by placing everything in a box, they covered everything. Making sure that they have ticked every scenario, so they could have their perfect holiday with all their state of affairs in order.

Eddy listened to them without helping he was sure that they would, also, have their estates in order. There was one, for them significantly critical pebble that they turned, examined, explained and reiterated. They stressed to emphasise the looking after cherishing treatment of Eubank and Tyson. Their food, their two walks a day, one in the morning, one in the afternoon. Both the same duration, both at a brisk, fast pace. They must, must be exercised. They are not show and tell; Eddy needs to heed to their instructions.

Daniel accentuates that Kimberley loves them nearly as much as she loves him. They are very intelligent dogs that do not suffer fools lightly. With mentioning that Daniel firmly states that Eddy must be strong and confident with them but not too harsh and disrespectful. That will definitely end badly for all considered. Eubank and Tyson, the two Dobermans were very much the main priority of his job. They will take precedence over everything, absolutely everything else. The list of routes for walks, runs and what to take for the games is all in a bright blue lever-arched hard folder positioned on the shelf under the stairs. A food plan, times and meal plans. Sheets of what to do if they are ill, do not walk well, are cold. A list of what he can do and cannot do with them.

This folder was bulgingly thick with information. It was good that it was written down as the information was a lot to take in. After his brief, that was not brief, the connectional of material that did nothing to aid his aching aftermath of the night before it was now into the early part of the afternoon. It was finally time to take the latest newfound methods into practise. He was given the reins.

It was a warm in the sun, but chilly when the wind broke through the breeze break partitions as for the first time Eddy walked in a town, he had not heard off a few weeks prior. They were strong, but obedient, very strong. The tension in the red lead never waived, often taut as the curiously smelt, see everything like it was their first time walking this patch. Both, Kimberley and Daniel were constantly two steps behind Eddy, yet he blocked them out. This was unexpectedly therapeutic. It was in the basking sun that the enlightened moment warmed his cheeks to kiss him in realisation that this was, indeed, the perfect job to get over Saoirse. Tyson and Eubank knew the rules. However, some could be bent, but not, ever, strictly broken.

The afternoon turned into a highly windy night with cold vertical rain. As Kimberley glanced out of the window, through her own reflection and towards were her children rested she mentioned the one exception to them being allowed in the house. The only situation was in the event of a particularly cold or a highly stormy night. Then, only then they did not mind them coming in to the central-heated warmth of the indoors, but did not this to be a habit on their return. The whole procedure was a very strict agreement to preserve and serve. Back in Sydney, Eddy had looked after his mate's pets while they went on holiday, but this pressure that they put on him paled in significance. Nothing compared even closely to it. As Daniel mentioned, they were really treated like their babies.

A beautiful bottle of red wine swirled in their glasses as they sat digesting the fragrant Thai takeaway for dinner. The whole day had been dog-orientated, it was fitting for the evening to be in exactly the same theme.

'Dobermans are not normally pack animals,' Daniel voiced in a smooth tone between sips of wine.

'Yes,' Kimberley muses loudly into the conversation. 'Against my intentions, Daniel tried—'

'—in vain!'

'Yes, in vain to split these two up. It was not something Eubank or Tyson were going to let happen. Do you remember?'

'The noise,' he laughs. 'They went off. Barked loud enough to raise the dead. Then, back together…silent.'

'Together silence is golden'

They talk together finishing sentences for each other or restarting them to tell Eddy about their love for each other and their Dobermans that the behaviour was apparent from that moment. That these were going to be two-part deal, or no deal. Kimberley wanted this from the moment she saw them through the thick light grey barren caged bars of the rescue home. She had no problem with it. Daniel took a very little persuading.

By the time they had mulled it over the short strides back to the car, he was won over. They turned just as the alarm beeped twice off to turn it back on as they walked back into the rescue home to accept the terms of them becoming part of their lives, home and book of their life. But now, Daniel could not even believe that it was even a topic for discussion when he looks back on the doubts in his mind, the short sentences and them as a family now.

Just like the previous evening, over dinner Daniel had brought, much to Eddy's disappointment, more Harvey's bitter as they went through the rules once more with a cheat sheet. Here in the living room, another sheet was produced from the side table with a list of numbers and names of emergency contacts and of friends in the town. The whole manual was not just the one folder, but two. This one, a pale sky-blue folder, was the other bits of information. The entire package was an in-depth manifesto, a manual of anything and everything from Armageddon and the four horsemen of the apocalypse entering the homestead to natural disasters like earthquakes and eruption volcanoes. In Lewes, in Britain. Eddy cannot help but this is a real problem in England, especially in Sussex. One manual solely for the upkeep of the Dobermans, Tyson and Eubank. The other everything else. Both bulging. Both overloaded.

Contrasting to the morning before, he woke with a clear head. Yesterday he was given the rein of the Doberman, today he was handed the reins of the house. It was yet another strict affair. This very tidy, organised home had a home for everything.

Although he was accustomed to this, as he was a rather pretty organised individual person. This level of rigorousness was a completely new aspect of obsessive-compulsive disorder to what he was used too. By leafing through the pages of the other in-depth sky-blue manual it was either not their first rodeo, or they were thorough in their approach to making sure that every 'i' was dotted and every 't' was crossed, or they just hated not being in control of their life. It was a further week before they left. Eubank and Tyson accepted Eddy very well, which astonished Daniel and Kimberley.

Dobermans have a reputation of being unfriendly, mainly as they are a guarding breed and very possessive of their owners. Apparently, they take to strangers with a sceptic questioning demeanour for which they would sniff without getting too close to them. They would assess the person before making an educated conclusion whether the person can be trusted or not.

With Eddy, they jumped over and embraced his morning ritual of coffee on the decks while he gently stroked behind their ears. They accepted him. After two days, he felt that the week was more of a formality to see how he would cope. Formally, how the Dobermans would interact with him. He went on with his tasks as if they were not there. They left for work, doing more hours to tie up more of their own work demanding errands. Eddy went on with his job as if he was an old sailor returning to the seas. They only asked him to cook extra meals for them to take, thus, to heat up at work.

A question that he did without complaint, because at the end of the day, it is easier to cook for three than one. His cooking did not go unnoticed. They were privileged to have a keen, passionate chef in their kitchen who made cookies, pastries and made meals from their own garden and their own paddock. They had a daily budget for food which came out of their account into his. It was up to him what he did with it, but to have this on top of his salary was a remarkable bonus.

They got on very well as a perfectly formed trinity. Each day they learned more of each other. Considering that, they were strangers, the fluid conversations, exchanges and connections were tied strong and tight very quickly in becoming friends, rather than employer and employee.

Three days in, on Wednesday, Eddy was left completely to his own devices. They not only left merely for work, but they were remaining in London for an early Christmas dinner to thank their immediate staff before they left on annual leave. He heard the door latch return to its closed state, to convey them leaving, before leaping out of bed, to bound down stairs to place the percolator on. He grasped the warming yellow, thick mug of coffee. Sipping the coffee at the same time as looking out at the pending menacing clouds gathering over the tall pine tree forest beyond. The clouds look more darker with the luminous of the darkest green trees in the backdrop scene of the greying white smooth appearing chalk cliffs.

Despite this appearance of doom, he had a joy in his body that pulsed positively lively. Coffee drunk, rugged up, as he makes his way down the soggy grass where Tyson and Eubank bound out from their large wooden kennels happily scampering to see him. He attaches the leads for his first walk as a new trinity. He learns quickly that the weather turns. For sure, he saw the dark glimmer of the approaching clouds slowly moving towards him, but he did not foresee the escorting howling wind. Barely at the turnaround point his elation was being shaken quite literally to his chilling core as a torrent of bitterly cold rain volleyed down with vehement hostility.

Through this atrocious weather, Tyson and Eubank seemed happy enough, they were used to it. Eddy was cold to the bone while getting an ironic new appreciation for the heaving lungs of the south of England. He did it, washed the dogs before taking another shower to heat his body back up, changed his clothes and lit the fire rather than turning on the central heating. Warming himself while nursing a cup of steaming coffee, he wondered if this was the coldest he would feel, surely it would not get colder.

He still had the afternoon walk to go, he vowed to get some gumboots. A break in the weather and he ventures into town to get would he learnt, through the laughter and mocking of the comic genius of the female shop assistant. It would seem that gumboots are called wellington boots or wellies here. Donning his dark green new wellies, he ventures with the worse of the inclement conditions over as he feels he is wearing clown feet, but on observation many wear the same around him.

A new day where a new lesson was learnt. He looked forward to this day from the moment they announced that they were staying overnight. He took it as acceptance, a nice blow to his ego. He was relishing his chance to be on his own, without the uncomfortable white elephant in the room, sitting constantly on his shoulder wherever he went. Although he was not an introvert person by his own character, he savoured being alone. He thinks he is not alone that occasionally, from time to time, all people like the time inside themselves, withdrawn like a hermit in his shell. This was a different loneliness.

As the darkness came, ominous in its emotionlessness creeping of frosty wintriness. The evenings drawing of the darker, colder, silence of which he had never heard before fell, swiftly into the house, over the house. This was what he wanted. Although he felt a depressing solitude in the spooky, unnatural stillness. The peace he craved made him miss what he had. He missed the laughing household that was, only just a few hours ago filled, very close to bursting with amusement, affection, with love. The chats about everything, sometimes bordering on the inappropriate but not really overstepping the mark, but swaying on that knife edge. He needed to get some noise back into the house. He hastily sprang over to the record collection on the far wall to pick out the first record that he came to.

He slowly pulled out a random record around the middle. In his hand held by the tips of his fingers the suggestive innuendo of the close-up of jeans and belt around an obviously male crotch in black and white. He spun the square cover around to look through the track list. Back to the front, the red stamp of THE ROLLING STONES bordered in a red-outlined box. Below that in the same font and style at a different angle is the name of the 1971 album, STICKY FINGERS.

Carefully sliding the black vinyl out with the first usage of the now infamous tongue and lips logo of Rolling Stone Records. He places it gingerly in his finger tips for a while as if it was his prized possession, before carefully placing the record on the record player. Sets the turntable at the correct speed. Grasping the stylus with steady hands, with the frailest touch of a snowflake the needle stroked the black plastic. Through the speakers that static rumble of the amplified silence, then the beats of *Brown Sugar* starts the tirelessly magnificent album as he stands, head lifted looking at the black mesh of flat speakers where the sound originates in appreciation.

The music massages his soul. The music helped with the silence, but did not wholly fill the hole inside of him. But, music was the medicine. Mick Jagger screaming in perfect harmony with Charlie Watts, Keith Richards and the unmistakeable sound leads him back to the sofa. Eyes closed, cradling a goldfish bowl of a wine glass half full of red wine that he retrieved from their own possessional stash with the vow to buy and return. As the double, short staccato chords, then the moment of echoing ringing as if they were in the same acoustic holding room. Before the chords sequence really begins, he opens his eyes. This announces the third track, Wild Horses. The opening line makes him smile as he feels comfortable with the words resonating within him.

'Childhood living is easy to do…'

Perfectly potent to his current sensations. He knows the song but does not think he has truly listened to each and every word before. The last lines of the last verse could not be any more compelling in explaining his moment of this evening.

'Faith has been broken, tears must be cried

Let's do some living, after we die.'

He had made dinner after the evening. After buying the ingredients, toiling. After preparing and cooking, he scarcely ate more than two mouthfuls. Scraping the contents into a large takeaway container he turned off the record player, walked up the stairs, got ready for bed. That night he went to bed early. For the first time in a long, long time, he felt isolated. He felt the scar that was healing from his recent break-up reopening. He started cursing Saoirse. It was strange that he felt he had accepted the moment but found himself missing her with a new passion. He went to bed upset that he was feeling bad thoughts of a tragic, but beautiful love affair. He wanted to do some living, after that love died.

As the winter's sun kissed his face through the cross-glass window, he roused. Instantly, unreasonably, he felt in a better mood. He had no idea what had brought on last night's unsettling mood. Maybe the coldness. Being alone. Being tired. Maybe the music stirring the settled seabed of rested memories. Being alone for the first time since before Spain. Maybe he was feeling vulnerable with the weather. Maybe he just wanted someone to say, 'Suck it up, Princess'. Someone, a mate, to give him a hard, strong bear hug of encouragement around his shoulders with a vigorous short tremor. This early Thursday morning, he felt back to the older Eddy that he once knew. The happy-go-lucky Eddy. He was optimistic by nature.

As he sipped the first hot sip of his black coffee while Tyson and Eubank played around his feet, he thought about how stupid he had been the night before. The cold dark air that was drawn through the open patio doors, snaking, coiling around his bare feet, spiralling up his legs, over his body and into his lungs. He shivered ever so slightly through Daniel's big grey woollen jumper, for which he had borrowed earlier in the week.

The carefree and light-hearted Eddy had returned as his watchful guise followed in his shadow. He smiled to no-one, the streams of hot tendrilled curls of wisps enticing through his mind sending euphoric fireworks of optimism of the roasted coffee beans in liquid form.

Maybe to the arduousness of himself. He was, indeed, moving on. Last night was a relapse. An unexpected setback but he had bounced back through the turbulent night, conquered the tempestuous storm from within and was ready to move on, stand firm once more. He believed this, as much as he was saying it out loud with plumes of warm air from his body, connecting with the cold air, as if he was smoking the natural air around him.

'Strong. Desire. Want. Need,' he muttered.

'SUCK…IT THE FUCK UP!' he yelled towards the grey cloudy skies, startling the dogs. Followed by a resounding, deep rich laugh. A passage that startled him, made him laugh, made him believe.

The natural blissful ecstasy of joy. The very real impression of being excited in being alive. Feeling the senses. Feeling in splendored disarray as all became one. Feeling on cloud nine to be deliriously alive.

The end of the week flashed around. Before he knew it, it was Friday. Daniel had worked at home and made sure he was finished at five. Kimberley was working another late shift. She had done, was doing everything she could so the holiday was relaxing. The last week was a mad rush of chaotic ticking, flicking and cross-checking.

Kimberley was essentially the worrier of the relationship. Whereas Daniel gave a lot more trust in the people around him. Kimberley could not let it go, she felt that she could do it better and more methodically than her colleagues. This assured a larger workload and a double-edged sword of double the stress.

Alas, a miniscule of a degree of less stress, as she would had set the model foundations in place of her high-level of standards to make the work progress. To move like a well-oiled machine, combined with a sophisticated intensity of getting the targets in place before the deadlines. Daniel, on the other hand, was the risk taker. He who gave the apprenticeships added responsibilities to see if they could deliver. Of course, Kimberley's strategy was in the long-term better as it was more fluid, whereas Daniel would have to retrace steps and, in some instances, redo the whole spreadsheets to rectify other people's mistakes.

These days Eddy heard a few frustration stamps from his office in the private reaches of their home. When entering out of the office, he never showed any tension or stress. He was always welcoming and forthcoming in conversations and questions asked by Eddy. He left his work literally on the hideously bright pink doormat between his office door and his home.

At five-thirty, Daniel barked up the stairs, 'Pub in ten?' Eddy heard his footsteps lead away, then the burst of water from the showerhead, muffled singing. He guesses that was a demand, rather than a question to get ready to leave. Afterall, this was the first proper Friday for Eddy. Daniel wanted to take Eddy to his local pub, to visit the locals, to give him a place where he would feel at home, away from their home. On the brisk walk where the wind stopped any normal conversation, just shouted exchanges, Eddy counted six different pubs that they walked past to get to his local. It took fifteen minutes through the wind, their scarfs tailing behind them towards the Snowdrop Inn. Daniel shouted above the wind, while Eddy listened with his neck firmly tucked into the collar of his brown, woollen-lined coat.

'I have got to show you this pub,' Daniel bellowed above the cold gusts of wind.

'Why this one? Not that one?' Eddy responded by pointing out one warm-looking glowing pub, then another.

'The Snowdrop Inn. This pub. This pub was built on the site of Britain's worst avalanche, in, in, in 1836.'

This new news to Eddy did fill him with pending dread.

'I have got to show you this pub,' Daniel bellowed above the cold gusts of wind. 'This was built on the site of Britain's worst avalanche in 1836.' Eddy could not help but feel a little uncomfortable with hearing this again. Feeling unsettling with that last sentence.

'On Christmas Eve,' Daniel continued, oblivious to Eddy's unease at learning that they were going to the place that is, essentially, a graveyard, 'during a heavy snowfall and gale force winds, similar to now…' he laughed. Eddy was not amused. 'The blizzards of a Christmas night had built up a deep layer of snow on the edge of Cliffe Hill.'

Daniel pointed his black leather gloved hand upwards, above the pub in the distance that they were walking to. 'Now called Boulder Row where Snowdrop Inn is, was a row of seven workers cottages on South Street. These were poor houses. Some people noticed the impending danger, alerted the residents, and advised them to move. The residents refused, even when a large fall of snow from the clifftop fell onto a nearby timber yard destroying it and swept it, the whole bloody yard into the River Ouse. The following day in the morning, the huge weight of the snow fell swamping cottages on Boulder Row. The actual number was unknown, but newspaper reports fifteen people.

'The papers state the cottages were swept,' he coughed out as he exhaled a blast of cold air that carried the start of the raindrops, 'into the road. A mammoth rescue effort ensued. Lasting seven hours, I think, yes, I am sure, at least, if not more, and managed to save six or seven people. I can't quite remember, sorry. The victims were buried in unmarked communal graves at South Malling Parish Church.' He pointed to an area behind them. Eddy did not turn his head but focussed on the glowing warmth ahead.

'A fund was set up to provide financial aid to the survivors and bereaved families.' There's a beautiful chalk cliff wall behind the Snowdrop Inn which makes a picture perfect background that appears deceptive to the story he was just told. Although cold, that prospect of the avalanche happening tonight was about as likely as Lewes running out of Harvey's Bitter.'

They come to the pub where a painted picture of a huge snow drift with chimneys and roofs penetrating the cartoon type illustration with people running with shovels waist deep in the snow swinging with a cast iron spear. A banner in yellow underneath the painting, but painted on the black border at the bottom states that the pub was built in 1840. Above, in a red rectangle backdrop in capital lettering that reads, SNOWDROP INN, in a blue to white icicle-coloured effect. This playful cartoon scene did not soothe Eddy's anxiety, not even in the slightest.

They were finally here though, close to the warmth of the golden light of the windows casting welcoming hues. Outside, shivering in long-sleeve shirts were people smoking. Some actually sat on the damp wooden bench table ensemble with a pint, covered in a raincoat talking to another bloke as if it was summer rather than a cold winter. It was raining quite heavily at this point and even the rain splashing into the light brown ale of their pint glasses, did not stop or pause the conversation as they shared a joke. The Brits are mad, he thought as he followed Daniel through the black thick wooden door into the warmth.

A slight slip on entry on the rain-soaked timber floor, for which Eddy regained control very quickly, did not humiliate him, although made Daniel have hysterics to make the small table nearby turn in unison at his roar. Inside the Snowdrop Inn the somewhat gloomy exterior, not quite depressing but definitely bordering on the fact the inside is not cheerful by the décor but characterised by the people from many walks of life. A tradie talks to a suit. A student talks to a postie. An elderly person talks to a twenty-something.

The fire from the old fireplace spreads its warmth through the wooden building. Daniel takes his coat off and places it on the entrance hat stand, for which Eddy takes his cue from and precedes to do the same. From the wooden ceiling hang jugs, urns and baskets. Pub memorabilia and knickknacks are everywhere that could look cluttered, but Eddy must admit, although not his style, it is done very well and tasteful. On the walls are framed photographs of history and music. Ripped posters showing entertainers that preformed in Lewes, old advertisements, such as the Rolling Stones, are protected in glass wooden frames. Puppets gathering dust surveyed the Friday afternoon crowd that were having a drink and sharing jokes. The puppets would hear a lot from the people here before returning home for the night, as they stayed perched in a slump on a shelf above the bar.

A bruised, chipped and battered life-size yellow Labrador or a Golden Retriever model is near the bar. A box hangs around the dog's neck with a slit for coins—a charity box for the blind. Although Eddy thinks this was not the original concept as the Blind sign on the brown box seems very new compared to the surroundings it is on. Around the feet were black scuffed pups playing in an immortal scene.

The island bar is in the centre and it has a massive wooden cabin feel. The atmosphere is very convivial. People smile as they make their way to the bar. The mood is warm and friendly. This is combined with the fire burning from the fireplace next to the piano and the wave of conversation on the heat that was penetrating the chilly Daniel and the freezing Eddy as they entered the pub.

After the somewhat strange tale as they enter and hang, their coats on the brass hooks of the fake wooden coat stand, Daniel states that the pub is known for its beer. From the local brewery, Dark Star, Daniel ordered a pint of Original. He points to the white beer tap with the red lettering as a dark bitter with no head apart from the foam from the nozzle lands in front of him.

The ulterior motive soon became apparent. Daniel wanted an informal discussion in an informal setting. Purposefully he decided the pub as the perfect relaxed setting of people finishing their week. That cheerful dynamic atmosphere was perfect for asking how Eddy's first week had actually gone. Fundamentally if he would be able to do it without a safety net. He came out and announced his plan to Eddy. Eddy thought something was coming as he insisted on taking Tyson and Eubank for a walk on his own.

'Daniel?' came a voice from behind them, Daniel turned to see a man.

'Marcus! How the bloody hell are you?' Daniel erupts in smile and they shake hands enthusiastically followed by a thumping hug heightened by a slap of their free hands on each other's back.

The thin brown hair of a ponytailed Marcus points towards a vacant seat where food is left behind. Daniel mentions he will talk later but just needs a few minutes. He encourages Marcus to go back to his food.

'Are you eating?' Marcus insists as he pulls Daniel towards his table, his friends. 'Come and join? Who's this? Nice to meet you? Come. Sorry to interrupt. Come, please, and sit. We make room.' The questions and requests came quick and fast like a blizzard that Eddy had just walked through. Daniel had to politely interrupt, with more apologetic sorry's to Marcus, to get him to stop and explained that they needed to discuss a bit of business first and then would come over.

Marcus did not stop and was remarking on his rabbit that he had ordered and suggested it to them. He is flailing his arms, striking out his fingers as he points again towards the deserted wooden stool with half-eaten remains of a stew in a white bowl as he almost clotheslined an unsuspecting punter.

Eddy had not opted for the now-becoming-familiar, yet less enjoyable, Harvey's Best Bitter as his next drink. Although Eddy protested and urged Daniel to try something else, he mumbled 'maybe next time' but was beaten down and ended up ordering the same as Daniel—Harvey's.

They bustled their way through the busy traffic of the bar to a corner. Although no seats, they stood and perched their pints on a thin wooden bracket less ledge. The voices hummed and whirred as the evening grew. Eruptions of laughter came from different corners. Nothing but formalities were discussed. Daniel wanted to have confirmation form Eddy in his own words that he would not only look after their home, but also their children, Tyson and Eubank. Eddy was worried by the motive but soon felt at ease that Daniel just wanted to be one hundred percent sure. It was with a handshake at the conclusion, that they went to join Marcus. En route they stopped at the bar, Eddy ordered quickly, well tried.

'Two of these,' Daniel spoke with more of his hands than his words with a victory sign for two, with one hand as he tapped the top of the bright pink circular metal badge of Manchester Tart.

Eddy peered at the label. In the centre, a pencil drawing of a rabbit. Around his neck is a matching pink and black polka dot tied napkin as he holds a fork that is nearly as big as him. In the distances on a simply drawn table is a pie. In black, MANCHESTER TART arching inside a pink banner with crudely drawn coconuts. On seeing his interest, Daniel remarks, 'It is based on a dessert from the north.'

'A dessert?' Eddy needs to clarify that he heard it correctly.

'Yes mush. A custard and fruit tart with raspberries and coconut.'

'This is a beer, right?'

'Yes,' nodding as seeing his confusion as well as his expression. 'Raspberries and toasted coconuts are added into the process to replicate one of our favourites.'

Two orange-hued hazy pints are placed in front of Eddy, as Daniel leans through to pay, resisting the money of Eddy in his hand. A small white head with the tell-tale aroma of citrus with berry chimes. Eddy takes a sip before the change comes. It does have the subtle flavours of the raspberries and coconut, but is slightly overpowered by the breadish, herbal finish. A completely different beer to what he would go for, but he enjoyed this beer. It was not as intense as Harvey's and more of a session beer, by percentage nothing more, that he was used to back in Australia. Squeezing, twisting and wriggling through the dense crowd Marcus bowled through clearing the way in a chorus of sorry's. So British, so apologetic.

Marcus and Daniel embraced each other once again with the longing of friends that did not meet each other as often as they would have liked. Marcus introduced Eddy to everyone at the long wooden table littered by empty glasses and remnants of a hearty meal on the table, littered as if left for a smorgasbord for rats. Of all the people, Eddy's eyes lingered, to remember one name in particular. This was his first meeting of Sheralline.

Sheralline did not rise as she held out a delicate small hand without a single ring on her fingers, as Eddy shook everybody's hand around the table nearly knocking over a candle in a still-life of a wax-covered waterfall over the green glass bottle. Their eyes met. Eddy was captivated by her. Her eyes enchanted a mesmerising spell of lust. An instant connection. Eddy fought to break the bond as not wanting to be obviously in his immediate affection for her.

He noticed a small tattoo of a boxing kangaroo on the underside of her wrist. She saw him catch a glimpse of the tattoo, and instinctively pulled her sleeve down in a failed attempt to cover it. 'Life decisions, right?' Her voice was sultry, smooth. She looks down sheepishly.

'We are, all have those…' Eddy brazenly offers reassurance. He was about to continue when he gets motioned to be introduced to someone else.

A pause of conversation, he looks around the bar. As the crowd started to thin out, he saw the red bold painted with wooden black painted frames on the bar. The inserts were paintings. Of flowers, a spring day and warmer times. The bar was a mess of optics, bottles, pens and coasters but the three members of staff behind hardly spoke to one-another as they guided around seamlessly, from what looked a disordered clutter of an untidy state with the grace of ballerinas.

One short respite happened as a frenzy of cloths, sorting, young black-clad T-shirt wearing youngster came in, head down to change the slim-jims of empty bottles for clean, disinfectant pine-tinged fresh empty ones, dirty cloths removed, white bin-liners rustled, travelled out. As they left, another different demographic wave entered, merging into the retiring packs for the night. Out departed the suits, in came the smarter casual attire of younger people that were starting their night out, rather than finishing their working week.

'You out on the Razz? Eddy?' Marcus invites him, bringing him back from his daydream.

'Razz? Er…'

'Razzle? Tiles? You're not from 'ere, are ya? Are you out for the night? Clubbing? Pub until chucking out?'

'No Marcus,' he waves his head to indicate a firm no. 'A couple more then I am back. Going back with Dan-o. I need to learn the correct English I think!'

The conversation around the table had shifted to Bonfire night. It was obviously a great event with an electric energy travelling over the already animated strangers.

'You must go to the biggest celebration of the fifth of November in the world,' Marcus asserted with a firm resolute demand. Eddy had no doubt, having not really heard about it before, but seeing the transferring of energy he thinks he would be a fool not to go. 'The bonfire, the processions with each of the societies going different routes,' Marcus continued making it sound more like a cult rather than an event. He sustained, his already definite answer that he would go, yet continued to be remarked on the costumes, traditions, tableaux and set pieces to their own fire sites.

'What is it all about?' Eddy enquired.

Silence descended quickly over the table. Smack in a splashing pool of spilled beer came Daniel's empty pint glass on the wooden table, 'My round,' he called as he rose to his feet, trying to grab as many empty glasses as possible. As he bent down, he whispered to Eddy, 'You had to ask! You just had to…'

Eddy had no idea that he had asked the wrong question. Sheralline must have heard the story before as she quickly offered a hand to Daniel as she remarked, 'I will give you a hand.' It was just Marcus looking over the table with the well of eyes transfixed on Eddy. Marcus, with a wave of hands, leaned towards Eddy. He had waved them away, he will control this. It was a conversation solely for them. The other friends around the table had started separate small conversations but Eddy could tell that they had an ear prickled in their own dialog.

'Well,' Marcus intensely speaks in an authority tone of learning. 'Back in 1605, old Guido, or as you may have heard Guy Fawkes, did the Gunpowder Plot.' Eddy shock his head, no. He had no idea about Guido.

'What? Really? What do they teach you in the Queen's prison? I will come back to that. My mate Guido,' Marcus enlightened Eddy, his uneducated mate in the ritual. 'What you have not heard, well everything, but I will give you an insight into what is the greatest, what every young'un knows, even before they can talk. I am sure is, it is about the Seventeen Martyrs. Burnt at the stake they were. In fifteen-fifty something-or-something-or-another Queen Mary, or Bloody Mary killed over three-hundred people publicly. Hence the name. Bloody Mary. Burned to death they were. Why you laughing?'

Eddy sniggered at the burned to death remark as if they would just singe their hair or give them a nasty burn as a punishment. He looked down and waved his right hand on the table with the motion to continue.

'Where was I?' Marcus searched his thoughts. 'Yes, these people were burned to death'. Marcus paused slightly to look at Eddy for a flicker of mis-concentration before progressing once again. 'They refused to renounce their protestant beliefs. You see the last Tudor, Bloody Mary, used this act to restore the Catholic faith in the country. It actually didn't work. She stuffed these people in barrels to burn them. Seventeen in Lewes. Look it up Eddy. Fascinating bit of history. Look it up. Promise. You will bedazzle your mates back in Oz, you will, that you will.'

Eddy had heard of Tudor but was not sure what it meant but he really did not want to prolong this slow, enduring torture. This is not to say that he was not interested, but a Friday night surrounded by laughter was not the time in his view to have a history lesson. Especially a few sheets to the wind. He also wanted to engage Sheralline into a discussion to see if they can relate to anything at all in the hope to see each other again. Appearance alone, she was right up his view of the perfect women. Marcus was undeterred by Eddy's lack of engagement. Marcus carried on regardless.

Marcus started to sing in the hope that people around him would join in. They did not. He was undeterred and continued while he swung his pint glass from one side to the other. Got up. Bowing over Eddy as he sang, badly, loudly.

'Remember, remember the Fifth of November
Gunpowder Treason and Plot.
I see no reason why Gunpowder Treason
Should ever be forgot.

Guy Fawkes, Guy Fawkes 'twas his intent

To blow up King and Parliament
Three score barrels of powder below
Poor England to overthrow

A penny loaf to feed the Pope
A farthing of cheese to choke him
A pint of beer to rinse it down
A faggot of sticks to burn him.

Burn him in a tub of tar.
Burn him like a blazing star.
Burn his body from his head
Then we'll say Pope is dead

Hip Hip Hoorah!'

Eddy had turned into himself, a little ashamed to be sharing this table with a drunken guy that sang, literally, like no-one was listening. A strange song about the Pope dying. Eddy obviously did not understand the full meaning of the song. He was halfway through Marcus explanation of events. It all became clear Daniels comment when he left. He now understood Daniels excuse to leave. It was not lost on Eddy that Daniel, and Sheralline, had both not arrived back yet from the bar.

With his back to the bar, he is not sure if they had started to come back before the impromptu off-key song. Marcus loved this topic, that was clear for all to see, to hear. He was born and bred in Lewes, which was normally quiet apart from this Bonfire weekend. This is when people came from everywhere. He likened it to the Brazilian Mardi Gras, although Eddy could not see any similarities apart from the crowds of people that were expected. He glanced behind him, at the bar to see Daniel and Sheralline talking to another couple. Did he just refer to Daniel and Sheralline as a couple? *Lucky pome bastard*, Eddy thought.

'Now, my mate Guido.' Marcus was still talking. 'My mate Guy. He was the one to light the fuse. The leader was Eddy Catesby. A lot of people forget this, that crucial fact. All the fifteen conspirators were devout Roman Catholics. Guy was tortured on the racks that stretched his limbs for hours but did not say a word. Catesby confessed under the rack and with the other conspirators was tried for treason. In one stroke of a match, they wanted to wipe out the government.

'In the confusion, they would take over England for the Catholics. The plan was simple. They rented a cellar and used an extension to store barrels of gunpowder directly under the Palace of Westminster. No-one knows how the filth, sorry, police found him. Guy was caught red-handed moments before, BOOM!' He slapped the table with the palm of his hand with a moist squish of beer-soaked bread. 'They were given a gruesome death. Hanged. Drawn. Quartered.' He mimicked the act with his animated arms and hands. 'An act was passed that still stands today that forbids any Catholic subjects to have any successions to the throne.'

Finally, Marcus ended his educational lecture. And yes, it had felt like a lecture to Eddy. Marcus had now returned to the reason of Bonfire night in Lewes. Another person from the table had joined in to the events that was going to be happening soon.

'Lewes has freedom of speech. I have seen many effigies burnt and blown up. A fat cat on a crying pink piggy bank, Osama Bin Laden, Pope Paul the fifth or sixth I can't remember which, George Bush with Tony Blair's head on a dog's body on the lap of the former president and many more. This is done to highlight a problem around this time. A grievance that me and the other common people feel. It is not to get people hurt. Maybe there, their ego and pride.' He laughs to himself.

'Do we really want to go back to a place where we have no freedom of speech, no freedom of religion, no freedom of politics?' then Marcus leaned in across the table. His sleeves of his brown shirt resting in the spillage of drinks. He was as close to Eddy's face as he could be across the thankfully divided table.

'Don't. Don't,' he whispered through a slightly closed mouth. 'Don't go back to Oz crying if you don't like what you have seen. The effigy. Do not throw your toys out of the pram. It is about FREEdom of SPeech.' He emphasised the last three words as he pushed back into his red cushioned wooden stool. 'Where are those drinks?' scanning the bar and shouting to Daniel. 'Oh, mush. Oi, Daniel. Do we need to send the RNLI after you?'

Daniel and Sheralline returned in time to hear Eddy unthinkingly state of misperception about the effigies. 'So, you celebrate a terrorist?' Marcus' face dropped. Daniel laughed and smacked Eddy on the back as he defended him.

'He's only joking, fella. Pulling your chain, that's all. Calm down, mush,' he mocked a laugh for which Marcus dropped his defence, his straight as a broomstick rigid back relaxed. Daniel glanced a look at Eddy to plea him to shut up. This would open a barrel of worms which would never end. He clinked his glass to confirm what his eyes were telling him.

They changed the course of the interrogation to agree to meet up again for the Bonfire, next week. On the way back, Daniel said that they were going to have to do one more week of work so would be around here and London to tie up more ends as a contract was not signed. Their flight was for next week anyway, but were going to use the week to see their family as an early Christmas social gathering.

That last week went so fast for Eddy. He felt more relaxed in his role. He learnt a lot. He managed his work. He was left to his own devices. He cooked meals for Daniel and Kimberley when he cooked his own. With all his past trainings he placed any remains in takeaways and labelled them with a brief description of how to reheat the dish. They were getting excited for their holiday, but with a lot of added pressure and stress. Very thrilled to have trust in their new-found mate that was going to be staying in their home. Everyone was happy.

Eddy had managed to get some shifts at The Brewers Arms on High Street. A pub around the corner from where his 'main' job was. Daniel and Kimberley did not mind at all. They encouraged him to get some social outlet, as long as he kept to managing the house, walking the Dobermans, with the few shifts not turning into a fulltime position.

The building was something out of another century. The small brick bottom floor was supported by black-painted timber rafters and joists with a white paint, what Eddy could describe as a mesh of sorts. The landlords were Ricky and Lorraine that lived upstairs. They were getting old and past the conventional age of retirement, but did not want to give it up until they had to. The customers used to joke about them saying that this would be their last year, ten years ago.

Although they worked hard, they did not put in hours they once did or could. A cleaner comes in the morning. Then the staff arrive here, with them helping rather than actually working a full shift. It works and the customers like the fact that they can ask for the usual and get what they want. They remember birthdays, anniversaries, and little snippets of information and always remember to ask them, about them. It is really down to them that the staff enjoy working here, which Eddy is one.

Eddy had not heard a bad word against them. Why would he as they were a lovely couple with old-school values. Inside the red garish wooden bar, it is small in comparison with the rest of the open space, but like a dance to music the barman expertise his movements to twist, pour and serve while picking up change in a fluent and effortless motion. Arthur, the gangly insect-like barman has been here a while and has no ambition to move on.

The customers talk to him as he does his work perched on their green, worn but clean cushions of the high barstool. Behind them is a pool table where people enjoy a game as balls rattle in the pockets to cheers and jeers. Softly the jukebox plays whatever the last customer has wanted to hear, Freddie Mercury sings with Queen's I Want To Be Free. Unlike most bars, this is free, and they do it to keep people in. The seating areas in this section are blue cushions with a combination of round, rectangle tables and dotted high tables for standing around. The red, purple, blue and green worn fading carpet is hideous. Eddy wonders if it was laid when the bar was built.

The atmosphere is electric, most of the time, even when quiet. People come for the friendliness of the staff, the recognition rather than the décor of the historical themes that are splashed over the walls from a days-gone era in Lewes. It is open from ten in the morning, for which Eddy normally starts at nine-thirty to do the morning shift to finish at four-thirty in the afternoon on Monday, Wednesday and Friday. This way he could still walk Tyson and Eubank before and after.

Sometimes he is asked to work some evenings, and this was one of those, bonfire night. He expressed his interest in going to the Bonfire. In all they were magnificent. Lorraine took some persuading, but Ricky was amazing. He understood that this was probably the only time that he would see it in the United Kingdom. And to see it here was the 'place to see it' but did insist that he worked the Saturday morning. Eddy already had the spiel from Marcus; unfortunately, this did not stop Ricky from reiterating the facts with more information thrown in.

Eddy was not going to burst his excitement bubble and was fully engaged like an actor for which he had played once in a nativity adaption of the Birth of Jesus when he was seven years old. After the tale, he asked if he could leave earlier as he was due to be ready by four in the afternoon. So, with the handover he was wondering if Arthur could do him a favour and come in half-an-hour earlier. He could not believe the effortless of these three people helping him out.

The end of the week was around. The day of the Lewes Bonfire was here. As he ran out the door at seconds after four, he thought that he would repay them if they asked him to work more, longer or another day. He rushed home and tried in vain to get the stale smell of varnish, beer and over-greasy fried food that seemed to be the staple of the bar by showering. He was ready just in time as a knock came promptly, at not a second past four-thirty on the door. He opened the door and in came from the cold were a group of people. Where a smouldering fire was on its last legs, keeping the place warm.

Daniel had worked from home and was now getting ready himself after wanting to take Eubank and Tyson for one last walk before leaving. Kimberley was running late, as usual over these past few days. He had brought a few beers back from the pub and invited them in. They shook the cold off and entered the warm haven. So not to get the upholstery tarnished, they all stood around the dining table introducing themselves. Coats were left in piles on the chairs with the accessories such as scarfs, gloves, hats and beanies.

Marcus was first and played the host by telling Eddy each and every person with a rough description of what they do, throwing a joke here and there for his own amusement. The accents sounded so posh, but they were far removed from this pompous association. They did not look down at anyone. Trudie, Sam, Kevin, Hannah, Sheralline and Marcus's girlfriend, Samantha. Eddy found it odd that no names were shortened.

In Australia, the name would have been shortened or an 'o' would have been added to the end such as Trud, Sam, Kev-O, H and Sam. True to form, the Australian's name was shortened from Sheralline to Shez. Shez was as Australian as you get with a slight hint of Oriental features. Big brown go-to-bed eyes with dark olive skin. A pert tiny nose and smooth features that seemed to be cast from porcelain. An elegant black dress clung to her slender and small figure on thin legs that waltzed with her steps in delicate nude high heels.

Kimberley entered through a blaze of haste and urgency a few minutes later. She declared herself with arms open, shouting out a 'hello' as she kissed, cuddled and embraced their friends. She hurried through the crowd saying hello to everyone, leaving an intoxicating smell of fresh perfume behind her as she sped back into the bathroom to finish getting ready. Daniel had entered the room from the bedroom and was talking to everyone. He seemed to know all the people. He conducted himself with no edgy awkwardness. He seemed calm in this situation.

Eddy had finally spoken to Shez, glided over with the coolness of a bear directed to a pot of honey. He mentioned that he had noticed her last week, but did not have the opportunity to talk to her, properly. She smiled as she said that she had noticed him noticing her, and she had noticed him too. Eddy's cheeks erupted with a red glow. He felt like a schoolboy shuffling his feet, tongue-tied as if something had taken his voice and shy, fearful of rejection.

It is a little later than planned when they step out of the warmth, to be immediately greeted by the cold, crisp November air. The streets are busy, the roads have become converted for pedestrianised use. Police are scattered around, some on horseback and cars are being detoured to other places away from the growing crowds and the closed streets. Everyone is dressed in similar attire of warm coats, hats, scarves and gloves with only patches of people's faces being exposed. Marcus and Samantha lead the way through the crowds at a slow pace.

Due to being later than they wanted, they fortuitously managed to get a space close to the metal barrier with enough space for all. They dare not to move so they can see the procession of many colourful floats through the narrow streets of noisy, cheerful, music abundant Lewes. Different bonfire societies, for which Eddy learns through Marcus are seven, have different effigies through with different routes. Each society has their own motto, colours and a personal competition for the best effigy is an unwritten, unspoken rivalry between them all.

Eddy has no idea what he is seeing, but the costumes are unique and take some real thought, not to mention effort to make. Donation buckets are around the borders of the walk as they collect funds for next year. The clink of coins is hardly heard over the exuberant, cheerful crowd. Marcus is shouting over the hullabaloo but still is not heard. No doubt yelling facts, figures, dates and anything to show that he knows the relevance of everything here.

Eddy is shocked by the image of burning crosses that looked similar to how the Ku Klux Klan is portrayed on the media. Yet this is to do with the religious story that Marcus told him. The fire is intense from our vantage point and amidst the smoke he wonders how the bearers are not getting hot, burnt. Although this warmth was very much appreciated by all.

Although Marcus explained the effigies, he was still surprised to see a bare-chested Vladimir Putin, the Russian President, in a get-up attire like a GI-Joe action figure with Khaki green, brown and yellow camouflaged pants and a rifle straddling a bullet-hole ridden crashed Malaysia airlines plane on a rolling green base to resemble the crash-site ground. It is huge. He cannot help but snigger. Last week in the Snowdrop, when Marcus was explaining the effigies, he had no idea of the size in which they were going to be. Sam comments that he hoped it was going to be Kanye West burnt, as an effigy of course. Although the wink she made, made him mockingly speculate.

As one large united group, we follow the last float of the procession and go to the firework site. This is ticketed, for which Marcus has and is telling the young bright-red wearing volunteer who is in his party. Kevin is from Scottish and Eddy struggled back at the house to understand his thick accent and incorporating the noise now, the bang of the fireworks he is really struggling.

Eddy hears enough to hear that he 'gets sunburnt when watching fireworks'. Eddy laughs in recognition to his joke. The fireworks are spectacular. Nothing compared on the marvellous New Year's Eve Sydney Harbour lightshow, but a fair second. In every direction is another one. Against the chalk cliffs, they complement each other and feed off each other. Hisses, screeches and bangs fill the air with oohhss and ahhhhs from the crowd. The bonfire is immense. Lit in the centre of the field where they are quite far from, yet still feel the scorching hotness. The smoke is intense sometimes, which causes people to cough and splutter. The smell of burning wood is something that takes Eddy back to his childhood.

It is a flaming spectacular display. The black skies are brought to life under a kaleidoscope of colours. Without realising, Eddy has the greatest smile on his face. Shez remarks with an approving grin of her own in recognition. In the excitement, he went to shout into her ear. Unpredictably, they ended up locking lips as she turned when he went to speak. Remarkably, they both did not pull away. They re-established their lipping connection. Not to let go. They shared a kiss and everything around them went silent. Shez's cold nose pressed to his. It was only when Eddy was accidently knocked into that they stopped. Again, Eddy's cheeks went as red as his cold nose. They bashfully looked down. She felt for his hand. They gripped their gloved hands, locking their fingers together. A short kiss.

The burning of Vladimir was funny. It was more of an explosion. So funny to see, so loud to hear and people were laughing, cheering and applauding. The softest applause you would hear due to the gloved hands. They entered many pubs in a slow pub crawl. They apologetically fought with the crowds that aided them to get to the bar. It was part of the fun. Nothing was personal in their space.

It was late when they returned to Daniel and Kimberley's house for snacks and drinks. This was not planned, but after the busy schedule of everyone. It was past eleven, where had the time gone? The explosive affair had infected them all as they were in a place where nothing mattered apart from the people within these four walls. Eddy had a great chat with Shez as they rummaged through the cupboards in the kitchen and found some food to rustle up. In no time, they were chopping, slicing and cutting vegetables and a cooked untouched chicken that was going to be their tea early into a large pasta dish.

As an afterthought, Shez was making some garlic bread and a salad to accompany the unanticipated feast. Daniel was getting the fire started in the living room. Marcus was putting music on. Kimberley was raiding the drinks cupboard. Even at this time and impromptu event, Kimberley was sitting up a dry bar on the dining table with correct glasses and playing barman. Bottles of wine, spirits, with bottles and cans of beers set up on one side of the table. The other side had bowls, tongs, utensils for eating and paper napkins. It was a party.

It escalated so quick, from a nightcap to a party with food. This was one of the best nights Eddy had had. Was it always the way when an unplanned series of events turns out to be one of the best nights. One by one they started to move back to their homes. Kimberly and Daniel had gone to bed leaving Shez and Eddy talking. In front of the fire, they kissed passionately, this led to more. Under the soft glow of light from the fire. The moonlight spilling its white illuminating glow through the leafless trees and window. The warmth of the dark black coals. The smell of the burnt logs. The smell of the drink and food.

All this was a vivid memory of the past. It was very much in the present but forgotten as the soft, caressing fragrance of the perfume on Shez's smooth lightly bronzed neck. The whispered purr of her appreciation as her head is slowly tossed backwards. Her hands searching, exploring and moving between his layers of clothing to his bare skin beneath. His hands gently around the top of her neck along her slender jawline as if drinking from the pure Holy Grail, his lips kissed her neck. They continued into the now morning until sleep succumbed.

Eddy woke in front of the glowing shining ash and the smell of charcoal in the air. He searched with his eyes shut for Shez and felt nothing but emptiness. A light brown blanket was draped over him. He was alone. His first thought. Although, it was more of a hope. He thought that Shez was in the toilet. Then he felt a piece of paper along the crumbled ridges of the soft blanket. A note torn from the pad by the telephone and written in a dark claret red lipstick. It fell to the floor and he nearly knocked over his full glass of red wine beside the couch in his frenzied search for it as it sailed to the floor.

'Ed, had to go. Call me. XXX'

A short, precise note. Nothing more.

Eddy was wiping his eyes as the smell of coffee came to him. He quickly got his clothes from yesterday back on and stumbled into the kitchen feeling just like Daniel looked. They exchanged muffled greetings as Daniel poured the coffee for them both. A shake in his hands made him grip the counter as if it would stabilise him. In his pale blue untied dressing gown with white socks, jocks and T-shirt, he opened the door to the backyard. He moved out to close it behind him, the cold was uninviting. Daniel did not seem to mind as he sipped his steaming cup of coffee that whispered smoke up into the air and waited for the dogs to come.

They heard the door latch and were there quickly. Daniel stroked them. Eddy could see his lips move as he spoke to them as they energetically moved around him.

After a few minutes, he returned into the kitchen, sat opposite Eddy who had a metal washing-up bowl in his head and a sledgehammer striking it with a powerful resonance.

'Kimberley and I were talking.' As these words left Daniel's lips, Eddy's heart sank, were they going to fire him? Did they not approve of Shez? Did they know? Did they know she stayed? and they had sex on their sofa? Breaking one of the rules from the manual...no guests to stay. Eddy looked up, giving everything away in one look. 'Oh, don't worry, Eddy,' he croakily laughed with a clasp of his hand on Eddy's shoulder. 'We were talking that this would be our last weekend in Lewes.'

Relief spread over Eddy's face as Daniel spoke into his coffee mug. 'I know we talked about the end of the month, well, things change. We trust you...and feel you know what you are doing. A mature head on young shoulders. You don't need us hanging around. We trust you. Kimberly has been late to work so finishing later in the day to make up for the lost time. This is due to the trains. Mainly anyway. Not sure if you have been aware of that or not. She has been finishing on time this past week.

'Every day the train is delayed. It happens every year. It is annoying. Very frustrating. However, every cloud and that. She has been working on the stopped train. Everyday there has been a delay. We have decided to stay in London. We have friends that are welcoming us for four nights. Work and then go. Go on holiday. Today,' a smile at the last word at the anticipation of a break. 'So, we will still be close if you need us, but not here. I think yesterday was the last straw for her. The train. Late. AG-AIN. She...well she, well we, just doesn't need that.'

Eddy did not mind that they decided to leave early at all. He was settled. Although he kept thinking back to the first evening alone. This was quickly cancelled out by the note folded in his back pocket. He was not going to be alone. 'Are you wearing the same clothes as last night?' Daniel interrupted Eddy's thoughts.

He snapped back and said, 'I was going to clear my hangover by having a walk with Tyson and Eubank before I got ready.'

It was almost seamless. The sentence came from nowhere, but actually made sense. He glanced at the time on the oven, which read just past six in the morning. Still very early. He had no idea what time he went to sleep, but, can only assume that it was a few hours ago. Then his thoughts went back to the note. No number was on it. This was not the time to ask for it. How was he going to get it? With the thoughts running through his head, he managed to compose himself to ask Daniel, 'When are you going to leave?'

'Today. After lunch.'

'Today? That is...' looking at the clock, 'five or six hours away?'

'Yes. Is that a problem?'

'No. No. No. Just. Just surprised.'

'Kimberley has another pack for you with all the information you need. To be honest, probably more than you need. She is very efficient. Very proper. She is ready and packing the bags. We may be back if we forget something. I doubt she will. In the time being. The reins are yours.'

Daniel poured another cup of coffee for himself and one for Kimberley as Eddy put his black and red runners on. It was a calm day. The remnants of last night were in the streets as he walked Tyson and Eubank through the debris of empty paper cups, firework casings and some items of clothes scattered around. The streetlights shone from the pavement onto the road. No cars passed at this hour, but he still carried a sense of caution. His mind was very much elsewhere. He looked around the note again as if it was a treasure map, searching for the elusive contact detail. Just six digits that was what he was after for a landline, or eleven for a mobile. He might as well be cracking a safe from Fort Knox, as it was not anywhere on this parchment.

He returned to the house, still not sure what, or how to ask for the number. Her number. Daniel was bringing the most meagre amount of bags out of the bedroom. They were ready. When the hour came that they were leaving, they were so relaxed. Eddy was dreading this as he had in his mind a fluster. A hectic situation happening around him with a simple question, that could not be harder to ask.

Kimberley and Daniel were so calm, they were fantastic. They had decided only in the morning but, it must have been talked about before. It was precision in timing that they sat for their last meal for a while. A ham and cheese sourdough olive sandwich with a boiling hot bowl of pumpkin soup flavoured with caraway seeds. After giving the last manual over like a baton. It was a not so much a manual but an USB. 'These are some photographs from the past few weeks from my phone. Thought you might like them. You know what I mean. Something to show your family that you have made friends. Great friends.' A wink.

A nice touch, Eddy thought as he accepted the black and silver USB to look at later. The longest time with the goodbyes was spent with Kimberley saying goodbye to the dogs. To her children. This was where the tears started to brim at the bottom of her delicate eyes. A quiver in her voice was developing. Daniel expertly took over and continued the last of the speech that gave last minute instructions. Just as he was leaving, he pulled out a piece of paper with a friend of his on it.

'Oh. This friend of mine lives here, Marcus. You have met him. Last night. Remember. As I am aware, you don't know anyone. I thought. I would. I asked Marcus and Samantha if they, you know, wouldn't mind maybe going. Taking you out for a drink, meal. Erm, or something… with you. No pressure. I just. Well I, er, just thought. Er…well.'

At this point, Kimberley placed a tender hand on his shoulder to silence his stammering. Eddy received the number with 'I appreciate it. I will call him'.

With that, the goodbyes were concluded. A black cab came to the front to take them to the train station. They were off. Eddy was alone at the doorway. A smile on his lips. He glanced at Marcus's number. He beamed. He had a link to Shez. They had no idea just how precious that piece of paper was. To him, it was gold.

He picked up the leashes and braving the now heavy pouring rain, he went out to the backyard. Shoulder held back he embraced the elements and walked Eubank and Tyson away from the house in one direction as Kimberley and Daniel got driven, towards the train station, in the other direction. He had the number which could get him the number, the person he craved, Shez. He was high on life. His hangover was almost forgotten. Tiredness had taken over. He needed sleep.

It had been nearly two weeks since the passionate night with Shez. He had not mustered the courage to call Marcus asking for the number. Shez had not been in contact. It was getting very cold now. Day by day, seemed colder and colder. Being born and raised in Australia, Eddy heard so much about the snow. Off course skiing was very much happening in the Snowy Mountains, and around but he had never been. From snowball fights, that you see in the movies to the sledging down hills at breakneck speed, everyone is happy. People are moving around with smiles on their faces and arms balancing colourful boxes with radiant colourful ribbons and bows.

To the cold weather. This was an understatement, he has found out the cold was a tip of the iceberg. Literally. Eddy could wrap himself up to protect him from the cold with layers of thick wool jumpers, socks. So many layers of socks, and other items which make him look like the stay-puff marshmallow man. What people exclude to mention, is the wind. The wind that comes straight from the neither reaches of Jack Frost's underpants. Filled with a coldness for which Eddy now understands the expression, to be chilled to the bone, on a daily basis. The rain that is horizontal due to the wind through the chalk cliffs.

Accompanied by the lack of shelter on the hill, in which he is calling his adopted home, for the short period the wind did not stop at him but, carried on through him. The daily attack of the nice-sounding Mother Nature, for which he learns is evil and sinister in her approach, as in her retreat. He also now knows why Rudolph's nose was red. It was not to lead the sleigh. Oh, what a myth that was. It was due to being at the front. He was exposed to these glorious elements throughout the one day he worked in a year. He was cold. Freezing cold.

Eddy seemed to be constantly cold. Whenever he saw the pictures on cards, on the shop front windows, or on the adverts of Rudolph he had a connection of sadness, for his coldness. Even though most of time he was smiling, laughing and generally happy. Eddy's hands tingled, he does not seem to be able to grip anything with his hands as well as he used to. His light luggage load has tripled in size due to the increasingly layers and thick, heavy clothes that he needs to fascinate his body warmth in.

The black ice that is as dangerous as it sounds. Eddy could be happily, well, not happily, but walking to the shops when his feet are taken from him by this invisible sheet of invisible ice. For which his cold backside would fall on the icy, hard ground and he would swear, embarrassed with himself as he looks around to see if anyone else saw him fall. Then he would rub and sooth his new soreness. This was the reality of living in a cold, wet and very dark country.

The night time seemed to take forever to come down. From being light, it seemed to toy and gradually bring in the darkness until it was pitch dark. In Australia, it happens quickly, as if a curtain has fallen down over the light. The lies of the Australian winters' illusion of snow, sleighs, snowball fights that hid the secret of the cold, the illness and the darkness that comes with it. Ah, Charlies Dickens made such a faultlessly harmonising illusion. It was fiction after all!

Eddy found the bar job handy to meet people. To stem the flood of loneliness away. Eddy had found himself talking to the dogs as he walked with them. He understood Kimberley's bond with them now, more than ever. The bar also helped for other reasons. As he saved all that money and only used his 'house-job money'. One particular cold, windy and wet day where he walked the short distance to work, he might as well have been naked. It was so cold that he actually thought that the layers of clothes were actually doing nothing to stop the passage to his skin and being naked was an actually good reality. The cold must be affecting his mind.

He might have well have walked through a carwash as he was saturated, cold and feeling very sorry for himself. He entered the bar and bee lined straight to the metal radiator. Cuddled it like a long-lost friend. He almost burnt his cold cheek on the metal ridge in his haste to get warm. The landlord laughed as he remarked that 'it was only the start', with a customer adding, 'you wait until the real winter really arrives'. He was not convinced that he was pulling his chain, but then his co-workers told him similar fables.

True to their promises, it did get colder. It got wetter. It got worse. His days off were spent wrapped in a human roll, with his doona being the pastry as he struggled to get, and subsequently keep, warm. The fireplace was his warm friend. He exhausted the records in Daniel's collection. He played them most nights rather than turning the television on.

Finishing work. He was thinking of Shez. As if the moons were aligned. As if horoscopes did come true when they stated the hopelessness in relation to a hope of love. It had now been over two weeks since that exquisite night.

Since that wonderful night. On one of his, what was becoming frequent, visits to the ground. After slipping on black ice after finishing work, so close to home, salvation. He laid like a cockroach on his back. Not sure whether he was hurt on not. He felt in pain. In his vision of the brick buildings, the streetlamps and the stars in the sky, Shez appeared. She helped him up, giggling.

Although he was cursing the thin transparent ice. Although not needing a hero to help him up, or save him. He took her red-gloved delicate hand without looking at her face. He then saw her. Her eyes. Her cold red cheeks and nose. A coincidence. A chance meeting. Destiny? It was her radiant smile that warmed Eddy up to a temperature he had almost forgotten. It was the angelic shape of Shez.

He was mortified, as in comical detail she explained his feet had slipped. They talked in a disjointed awkward fashion. She apologised for not being in touch, and asked him why he had not been. He explained that a number would have helped. They laughed at the cross-wires and moved into a café doorway for shelter from the elements. He asked if she wanted to join him on the evening walk, but she was on her way somewhere. If it was an excuse, he could not blame her, it was not exactly a glorious evening. They arranged to meet up tomorrow, Saturday late afternoon at Daniels house after Eddy had finished work, and taken the Dobermans for their walk. He went against their wishes and picked up a few extra hours of bar work.

Shoulders hunched up, head bowed he thought of Shez, he thought of the winter illusion once more. He blames his school, childhood readings. Charles Dickens portrayed a dreamy white Christmas in England. He remembered reading of the snow-carpeted streets growing up. It sounded great, looking back just too good to be true.

His writings of the 'Christmas Carol' brought to him what Christmas should be like. A completely different version to his, sitting on a sandy yellow beach, scorching in the sizzling sun, with the colourful birds fleetingly overhead in a clear-cloudless blue sky. He thinks to the moment two years ago. In a nostalgic, wistful glimmer of what he was thinking when he was in that fantastic place down under. Drinking a beer from a plastic bottle, in budgie smugglers, while he went out in the surf with mates to decide to come to the United Kingdom.

The image to the reality were harsh, two very different things. To spend the first few months of the year essentially in a broom cupboard. Other weeks in a unit for which he could not swing his arms around, let alone a cat. Not that he would want to. In addition, to spend a majority of his time cold, freezing cold. It was beautiful though. He had to admit it. He does not regret. He sees it for what he has seen. He stopped into the library on his way. Using Daniels card, he beelined, sought Charlies Dickins under the Classic headlined mahogany bookcase. When he reread the works of Charles Dickens, the opening pages, he smiled as they took him back to Australia.

Back to a younger Eddy in grey school shorts and blue shirt with white buttons on the wooden pews of his school looking at the blackboard, to the winter wonderland of Christmas in his hands. Imagining the scene in his mind with, 'The Night Before Christmas', putting Santa Claus on a sleigh pulled by reindeer for the first time. From that, piece of work no-one has looked back. It was not that bad a memory.

Eddy read with a feverish zealous permanent grin on his face. Fire cracking smell of toasted bread. He read the novel. With that memory he wondered to bed. As he wrapped himself in a multi-layered colourful cocoon for the night. Eddy went to sleep with Dicken's dream inspired by 'A Christmas Carol'. The idea of family, charity, goodwill, peace and happiness that Dicken's, pretty much singlehandedly inspired to create the Victorian Christmas for which we are all familiar with now. Although Dickens did not invent it, he must take credit in bringing it to the people.

The chance meeting with Shez had lifted his Christmas spirit. He no longer zoned in on the cold, but the time of year. He was in these thoughts when the telephone rang. He glanced at the time. It was well after midnight. He dashed downstairs, tugging on his blue dressing gown he had borrowed from Daniel. Worried as the telephone never rang. What was the problem? He picked up the receiver to hear Marcus on the other line.

Over the telephone line, Marcus was an even more animated guy. He could hear in the tone why himself and Daniel would be mates. He was surrounded by a screen of relief. Marcus also slurred the occasional word that told him, that he had had a few. 'Get to the point', Eddy thought impatiently. The fire had burnt out, so the creeping cold was in the house. He could see Marcus in his mind using his free hand and waving it around, just like Daniel does. He was so excited. Saturday night he was going out with his girlfriend and her friend Shez, so he was invited along with 'one of your kind'. He wanted. He tried to interrupt to say he had plans, but Marcus was not stopping.

'Sheris-aline.' He slurred out. 'Shes is going. That pulled away. Came from…from Kangaroo Valley, liveshh here, got a transfer with work down…down here.' Marcus was hardly making sense. From Eddy's experience in London the natives, or locals as he learned they preferred to be called in earshot, liked to refer to the suburb of Earls Court as Kangaroo Valley. Mainly due to the community of Aussies and Kiwis that call it home. Like the British have taken over Bondi.

Mind wandered back to his first hostel in Kangaroo Valley. It was true, though. But he hated to admit it, even before coming, he was told to stay around there. Essentially as he will find vegemite and other things that would remind him of home, in a good way. It did not work there and made his mind up quickly, before he was tired of it, he had decided to integrate into the English scene with the pomes.

'Thanks, but I have plans,' Eddy interrupted, back to the monologue.

'No. Dear boy. Come out with us,' he insisted, ever persistent.

Marcus hung up over the remonstrations from Eddy. Foolishly, he still did not get a contact number for Shez. Was she coming with them? Had she made an excuse herself? His sleep was now interrupted by questions. No way of obtaining answers.

The day came around slowly. Each second watched. The night was restless he was tired, still sleepy. The day itself was slower. He gives up on sleep. He leaves his bed earlier than he wants. Lights the fire. Eddy does not help the situation by looking at the clock every second while awake. A watching kettle never boils. Saturday might as well be called snail-day. He takes the dogs for a walk as he tries to simplify his mind. He decides to let fate play out the day.

As he could call Marcus and cancel, but does not know what Shez is doing. He could end up on his own. He will see. After a promise of seeing someone that could mean a lot to him, this day could turn from a dreamlike fantasy into a cruel nightmare. Funny enough when he got back, he slept for a further couple of hours on the sofa with the Charles Dickens book falling to the floor. I naturally woke in a better sense of mind. It was not like he was leaving tomorrow? He had time to make this right?

Just before five in the afternoon, Shez knocked on the door. He tried in effective success to hide his relief that he saw her at the doorstep. He ushered her inside. Took her coat as they moved to the kitchen to offer a drink. He relayed the baffling conversation he had had with Marcus in the early hours of the day. She said Samantha had called her in the morning. She did not know what to say. She heard he was going, so decided to go with it.

The two unsolved conversations to two different people finally made sense. Marcus in his drunken state had concocted a night out. She said they would meet here, as it was a good central point. She arranged for seven, so they had time to spend some of the evening with each other. Eddy's heart skipped, literally. She wanted to spend time with him as much as he wanted to spend time with her.

It was a good idea. They shared a drink and the day was now going too fast. Snail-day of an ultra-marathon had turned into a ten-metre sprint. The couple of hours they spent together went so rapidly. In that time a romance had started in Eddy's mind, he hoped it was mutual. He felt he was getting the right signals.

Cursedly on cue. Right on schedule, the knock on the door that announced the disturbance of this passion burning came. Without introduction, without waiting for permission, in walked Marcus, followed by Samantha, who politely waiting for a 'come in'.

After finishing their drinks, they walked to the place where the originally meet. In this time Eddy finally got a taste for the local brew as they talked in the Snowdrop Inn. He still called Harvey's a modest ale that was not as good as the brew back home. This was more so as it got a rise out of people, especially Marcus and added to his comic value. He laughed during the course of his joke, but still liked the reactions he received.

Marcus could talk the ears off anyone. As Samantha saw an unmistakable spark between Eddy and Shez, she tried to steer Marcus to friends within the pub to give them space. Her efforts did not work. Marcus was unaware and quite ignorant of what was unfolding in front of his very eyes. He was good entertainment, so they did not really mind too much. Over the top and they both wondered how Samantha lived constantly with him. She was shy, timid and quiet, maybe because she could not get a word in. A real chalk and cheese couple, but with a genuine connection. The shared jokes, the look in their eyes, the slight stroke of a knee. Eddy did make sure he got Shez's contact details back at the house, early in the conversation so he had no excuse to call.

As they left, the temperatures had dipped noticeable. Eddy had noticed this particularly in the first week in Lewes since December had started. The nights got extremely frosty. Kimberley supplied additional blankets for Eddy in the airing cupboard, as well as his own in his room. They walked back towards Daniels house. Marcus was singing, badly and out of key, uncaring. He seemed to do this a lot after a few drinks. His Christmas Carol was somewhat not your traditional take, but made Eddy laugh. He had never heard this song before.

'It's Christmas Day in the workhouse
The snow is snowing fast
I don't want your Christmas pud,
So, stick it up your arse.'

Shez was nestled into his arms with her two hands at his elbow as he had them stuffed into his pocket. Samantha subtly steered Marcus away to walk a different route to leave Eddy and Shez alone. Steamed words of goodbye were sprays out. Hands firmly in their pockets. Yells were still being made from Marcus after they had turned to walk away. Eddy and Shez made their mark in the freshly-laid sheet of snow as they made a mark on each other.

Eddy threw his arm around her when they had turned the corner, bringing her closer to his body warmth. He lightly kissed the top of her head that was covered in a multi-coloured beanie with a sheen of snowflakes. They had a glorious night taking. Curled up on the sofa. In front of the fire. Déjà vu like, but this time kissing was the only fluid that was exchanged from body to body. They were learning about each other.

In the morning, fog and frost give an enigmatic feel to the small passageway that leads to the busy High Street. From struggling to stay on his feet to the salt and sand covered pavement of the busier areas. It is unusual apparently to get snow this early, but some parts of Scotland and northern England have experienced the first of what the experts on the television and radio are discussing is the first chilly wind blast of winter with warnings to brace yourself for a record-breaking winter in terms of coldness, rain fall and winds. Joy! Shez and Eddy walked Tyson and Eubank around Lewes feeling only the warmth of each other.

The following days, Shez had been around most days and if not seeing himself at his adopted home, she would head to the bar. They were getting on well. They had so much in common. Not just the Australian link, but their personalities were in sync.

On the second Saturday of December was a Christmas Fair in Lewes Town Hall. The snow was falling heavily this morning. Like an illustration from the Christmas chocolate box, he walks the snow-laden streets of Lewes. He feels like a penguin, wrapped up and waddling like one to the Lewes Corn Exchange as he makes purposeful, small steps towards his new girl. It had been short but felt right. They were open about the relationship. He was her boyfriend and she was his girlfriend.

At this point in time, nothing was burning like the winter's cold wind on his face. On the corner of the High Street is a busker sitting on a makeshift barrier from the white snow of a flat-packed brown cardboard box. He waits for Shez. He glances at the very talented busker that is sitting in the snow. Eddy wonders how he is not cold and how he can pluck away on the guitar when his own hands are freezing and not working properly.

In a jazz-cum-rock feel, he sings out Christmas carols while people throw change into his open guitar box in front of him. A kid was being pulled by his father on a red plastic sled up the short hill to his right. It did have a modern Dicken's feel to the scene. He peers at the castle with its dark grey background and leave-less trees with scatterings of settled snow like icing sugar dusted on an elaborate designed cake. The golden lights that shine on the walls give a glow and make the vision something out of the movies.

He heads there with Tyson and Eubank who are not straining so much at the leash but actually going reluctantly with the flow. Similar lights to the castle cascade up the walls of the sandstone building where once farmers and merchants traded cereals and grains. The two-story building is grand and imposing with a large white dial with black roman numerical digits above the entrance. The time is coming to eight in the evening. He walks up the doors. There is a slight queue on the grey steps. He sees inside and stalls with Victorian themes everywhere. The smell of roasting chestnuts infused with melted chocolate and a sweet-sickly smell of wine come drafting out into the cold streets. Eubank strains as Tyson tries to get a closer look.

The noise is gleeful with squealing children enjoying the spectacle display. Most of the stallholders have really excelled in their design. Some taking the occasion far too far, dressed in elaborate, well researched Victorian gear. Others just had Victorian hats trimmed with feathers, flowers, or ribbons. It was like a scene from Pride and Prejudice with a contemporary twist. One side was stepping out of time, where you walk the length of a wooden plank of wood and have returned to the correct present date.

One family even had their young child dressed in Victorian attire. She wore black shoes, black leggings, and a black coat with shining gold-coloured buckles. Around her neck was a sort-of triple layered cape where the gold-coloured buckles were a four-pointed gold star. Somewhat angular, and thick looking, made of what he would guess was a plaid wool. He gets to the top of the steps and is greeted by the elderly volunteer, in a bright green Victorian dress with white gloves and a green hat like a Leprechaun had thrown up on her.

In true British politeness, the woman told him in an apologetic friendly manner that no dogs were permitted inside. He apologises as he tries, strains and slowly manages to pull a reluctant Tyson back from the open doors. So, after queuing for a while in the cold, he bought two tickets. He was still waiting for Shez, so he returned to hear the busker belt out more tunes.

He was getting unbearably arctic, so he decided to turn around to go home, drop the dogs off and then come back. He pulled out his phone from his pocket as his teeth pulled off one of his woollen gloves, so he could write a message to Shez. She had beaten him to it. He had not heard it go off. The message read: 'Not my thing. Beer? Snowdrop? X'. Just as he finished the message, another came through, 'running late'. He responded with his plan and they just arranged to meet at the Snowdrop soon. Although dogs were allowed, he decided he was halfway back home, so he would drop the dogs off before returning the distance and walking the fifteen minutes to the pub.

As he walked to the Snowdrop, he could have sworn he saw Shez travelling in the opposite direction being driven by someone else. They arrived at very similar times with Eddy noticeably cold and Shez noticeably warm.

'Did you get a ride?' Eddy asked.

'Oh no.'

'But. But you're warm,' Eddy probed.

'I was just around the corner. A mate's unit. Talking. You know what us girls are like.'

It did not seem a valid excuse. Eddy was not entirely convinced. She turned, too swiftly, and walked towards the bar, ordered drinks before returning to face him with the offering of a clink of beer glasses. Although something felt strange, he wisely decided not to investigate further. He feared that any level of questioning could lead down a dangerous path. A path more slippery than the black ice outside, with the snowballs as interrogative becoming as hard as cannonballs. It would surely turn into a fight. A war where no-one wins. Only losers. He let it go.

For the first time, Eddy found himself really missing Australia for the first time. Christmas was a strange time for him. It was on this day that he woke with a cloud over him. He could not shake the grey, heavy pouring cloud away. Although nothing around him had the slightest resemblance of Christmas. He did not decorate the house. There were no decorations, no tree, no Christmas cards on display and no presents to open. He felt, he was right in his feeling that it was Christmas, but it did not feel like it. He even checked his phone for the date, to be sure that it was, in fact Christmas Day.

Before Daniel and Kimberley had left, they both offered to put a tree up with some glittering, sparkling decorations, Eddy is experiencing a little remorse at the refusal to decline that kind offer. It was now that Eddy knew. Without knowing the why.

He took Eubank and Tyson out, while losing himself, he just carried on, and on. The weather conditions did not penetrate into sensations on his skin, in his body. He had so many layers on that he struggled to move his legs. Many people were out and about. Everywhere was shut. He recognised some and nodded his head as they acknowledged him. The friendliness of the people was very strong.

Everyone, he could not believe that everyone, wished him a Merry Christmas with a cheerful smile. Apart from today, strangers in the south seemed to be colder, in the north, warmer. Ironic, really, as the temperature gets colder, until now, it was different, today was the coldest day, but the warmest connection to a stranger. One elderly lady walking her small ball of carpet even offered him a candy. Christmas really did bring out the best in all people.

After letting the dogs out in the backyard, he strolled around to the front. Fishing for his keys as he looked down at the stone crazy paving walkway, he looked up at the red front door. In the gentle chill of the snowflake-carrying breeze, a piece of paper rustled from under the brass horseshoe doorknocker. He tore it from the tapper to see a shopping receipt, in his haste he nearly ripped the note in two. The walk rejuvenated him with the affectionate glow of humans being human. He read it out loud without meaning to:

'Ed. Merry Christmas. Missed you but would like to see you, X'

At that point he heard her voice. He thought he imagined it.

'Ed.'

She had just literally placed the note there. Armed with a plastic bag, she expressed her desire to be asked into the warmth. They embraced, warmly, she did not really need to ask to be invited in, she was immediately welcomed in. Of course, she had met the two dogs before but sensing a different presence, they were at the patio glass door, watching. Glaring in a security pose of protection, a slow, low growl towards Shez. Sensing all was not well, Eddy slid out of the slimmest crack in the glass door to escort them to their domain at the bottom of the garden.

'Bizarre,' Eddy shivered through rattling teeth as Shez kissed his cold cheek. He sideway glanced back towards the dogs. It was a very strange reaction from them. 'Why the mistrust?' he mused before Shez broke his view with a warm hand to move his face to her lips.

There is a great myth of the three-month period in relationships. In fact, there are many myths. Such as the seven-year itch, allergies turn in a six-year cycle from which said allergen will either get worse or better, as well as many more. Is the three-month period a myth though? The three-month period is believed that the lovey dovey honeymoon is well and truly over after three months. The clear zinfandel pink fairy candy skies with white strokes of white fluffy puffs of clouds. The Disney fairy land vision of everything is perfect, everything happy.

With bright, bold and vibrant colours to assert, this feeling is starting to get replaced. The dark uninspiring clouds start rolling in with an impeding ferocious storm. It is within this raging factors that a relationship truly stands tall to the elements. Or, crumbles, falls apart to be no more, a footnote in history. Consequently, after three months, quite simply, the shit gets real. The flaws in the other person, for which they have been spending a long time in each and one other pockets, are getting noticeable.

In the beginning, they would happily wave them by without a need to address, like gently moving your hand to make a fly move, which has settled on a hand. This flaw, however, becomes more persistent and now is the mosquito that keeps them up in the dead of night. The mosquito is moving on, going on to the most personal parts of the body. In the inner parts of the ears. On the pupils of the eyes. On the moist lips. Annoying. The tiny fragile fracture of a flaw is becoming a canyon where a flood of negatively is being unleashed. A slight trickle is now rising inside. The pressure is growing.

That is just one aspect of the three-month period of breaking, or staying in a relationship. As a relationship consists of more than one, this may be easier for one than the other. The period has ended too soon and the innocence of what could have been is ending with more questions than answers. This was not three months in however, but barely five weeks. Surely the honeymoon cannot be coming to an end. Not yet. Surely?

Eddy hung his damp clothes in the bathroom. Meanwhile, Shez unloaded the plastic and paper disposable bags on the kitchen counter island. Out came a bottle of red wine, Victorian Shiraz, followed by a six-pack of the bright blue cans of Fosters. The shame of it. She winked at that display with a silly snigger. With a short hiss, she opened the ring pull by a lipstick matching bright pink nail. She slid to Eddy a can as he came in after drying his hair in the bathroom. She was nervous. Eddy sensed this, just like Tyson and Eubank had earlier.

'Seriously? Bloody Fosters, mate?'

'I want to take you to my home,' Shez wished out loud.

'Tonight?' Nearly drowning through a sip of beer.

'Tomorrow. Shit, I was not s'pose to say that. I want, I have a few items to cook. I want to cook for you. For once. I am going to shut up now...'

The evening was pleasant. They was something in the air. Something that was keeping Shez at an emotional distance. Eddy had never seen her so nervous. So agreeable to everything. She normally had a bit of fight in her conversation. Eddy could not put his finger on what was happening. What was the flaw that was going to get unleashed? Eddy did not want to know. He was happy in the ignorance. He continued the evening. They made love. They slept together. It was a lovely evening. What storm was coming? Gracelessly, uncomfortably disorienting.

The flaw that Eddy with was in his eyes...major. After a few weeks of getting to know Shez, he was finally given access to her inner sanctuary, her home. Eddy walked Tyson and Eubank alone on the insistence from Shez that she needed to make some calls. The truth was, as Eddy saw it, the Dobermans would react to her in an undesirable way. It would be destructive to a relationship that only a day ago was a lot more durable, but now stood on fragile ground. After the walk, he got ready.

Mistiming the stroll. It was closer than he had thought. A shorter ten-minute walk in the opposite direction to the Snowdrop and a building he would have passed many times with Tyson and Eubank. He had not noticed it then, but the street was familiar. Although the outside was nothing out of the ordinary, the inside was vast. She rented this for a pricy sum. She beckoned him through, into the double black door with silver trim. Indoors was a huge imposing hallway with art deco designs to the two lifts.

A key actually operated the lift, that was how old this building was. This key took them directly to the unit, into the unit. Eddy had only seen this kind of thing on television, in the movies. The lift opened to a fully furnished, immaculate place. These was all hers. Every piece his eyes beheld within the unit was hers, as she rented this as being unfurnished. It was funny to think that she paid for this with just an average administration job at a local car dealership. Beautiful things that were minimal in design, but her wardrobe. It had only dawned on him now, that each time he had seen Shez she had been wearing different attire. Different, elegant attire with those tell-tale notorious designer labels. The wardrobe was a room in itself, that she accidently left open. How did she afford all this?

It was within her inner sanctuary that she had expressed her secret. The storm. The secret was out like Pandora's box. The misery was transmitted into Eddy with a force that nearly knocked him off his feet. And not the pleasant kind! It penetrated through him, devastating him.

I took my teachings to how we became who we are to replicate what happened before, many years before. Brothers, Prometheus was assigned to create the race of man to form the human race with Epimetheus to populate the Earth with animals. However, Epimetheus went too fast, too quick and exhausted the supply of gifts that were allotted to them for the task. Prometheus was forced to steal fire to finish his task. This angered Zeus who created the first mortal women, formed by clay as a delivery of evil into the house of man. She was beautiful, and despite the warnings from Prometheus, Epimetheus received her.

Pandora was under Epimetheus' spell. In no time she was being married to Prometheus's foolish, younger brother, Epimetheus. They were given a wedding gift. More so, Pandora was given a jar as a wedding gift, but entrusted not to open it by the provider Zeus until he was in the house. So, when Pandora opened the jar, all the spirits inside escaped leaking misery with Elpis remained to comfort mankind. Elpis plays many parts in all our lives, as a spirit of hope. For I have given Eddy the false hope. The false hope that Shez was the one. The untruthful dishonest and deceitful expectation that Shez was sincere in her past. She lied, to gain Eddy. To enter his house. Inside him, to see the heart on his sleeve. Shez unleashed her personal box of misery upon Eddy.

Shez gripped Eddy's right hand in both of hers while leading him to the centre of the room, where a two-seater red and gold sofa aiming directly at the larger widescreen smart television. He was not really taking in what was around him. It was a blur of bling, ornaments and photograph frames. Stupid thoughts were going through his mind distorting his vision. What was this secret going to be? He gradually sat down. Perched uncomfortably anxious, back rigid straight, Eddy watched Shez pace close enough for her scent to leave seductive traces in the space between them. Her pale beige high-heeled shoes echoing on the hardwood in slow, focused repeated footsteps.

'Say it!' pleaded Eddy. Hoping for her to put him out of this misery.

'Look…' A pause. She turned on her heels, faced him. Tears forming in her eyes.

'What…What?' Gritting teeth without showing anger, showing infuriation. Clenching his jaw tight.

'How do I begin? How do I say? Say it? Grrrr. GRRR. Look…Eddy. My darling Ed. I am, was…I…an adult escort.'

Eddy flinched his hand as if a sharp electric shock had passed through him. He did not want her searching hand to touch him.

Shez revealed to Eddy that she had been an escort. Was an escort. Had been an escort. It was harder than she imagined to say. This was the first time that she had said it out loud to someone she genuinely cared for. She opened the tap of truthfulness and the fountain flourished all that needed to be explained. In full disclosure, she gave him scrupulousness honesty. She fully explained how the process worked. How she worked.

Basically, she would receive a message on her other phone, her exclusively for work mobile, which stated a client or potential client's name. other information would be revealed when she opened the message which would state the likes and dislikes of the said client. For instance, hair tied up, down, skirts or dresses. Then another line for the occasion, business event or casual affair with decree of dress code. If she would come to an agreement and accept, she would let the agency know. The agency then would send her more comprehensive specifics.

The agency would tie up the particulars, thus arranging everything. They would then pick her up at the precise time, drive her to the job. She normally dressed in similar attire, classical elegance, unless specified. In the past, she has been requested to wear a grey woollen miniskirt, black tank top and leather black jacket.

At the client's residence, she would go to the door, while the driver waited. Kiss the client on the cheek in arrival, as a seal of the contract commencing. Enter, have a quick summary of the rules that would have already been signed in the terms and conditions before this meeting. He would hand her a sealed blank envelope. Shez would excuse herself immediately and go to the bathroom. Count the money in the envelope, text the driver, which acts as a chaperone as well as security, that she has the correct money, also confirming that she was okay. The money would indicate the time. Most paid for five hours upfront. Accordingly. to the amount paid, in the message she would direct the payment, time to be finished and if any extras were agreed in the opening exchanges.

The information flowed very fast from Shez in a blasé fashion. Compared to Eddy, who was upright, tense. He sat uptight, unflinching in her gunshot barrel of straightforward bullets that breached his skin, gored his soul and bleed his trust. He sat there taking each blow, with all the sensations of heartache, emotionless. He was numb. Feeling out of sorts. She spoke like a flowing fountain, he took her information like a swirling drain. In seconds his world had crashed around him, imploding inside him. He had a sense of a tempest coming, however, no warning of its destruction. Unresponsive in his silence, but with so many questions. The deluge had opened wide, a tsunami had saturated him in a cruel, cutting way that he never experienced before, or ever wanted to ever, experience again.

Silence. The onslaught was brutal.

Ceasefire. So inhumane, yet honest.

Sincere. Eddy had to admit it was.

'I…' Shez was sobbing tears of forgiveness to what she had done. The knowing deceit. Struggled to compose herself for a full sentence. She was just blubbering out the words of a sentence.

Eddy placed his hand up. Waved her to shut up. She cried. On the floor in a praying, begging pose to the disconnected Eddy. She did not stop trying to talk.

'Sor…re…'

'How much an hour?' Eddy spoke for the first time. A sense of anger was clearly recognised in his unrecognisable tone. He was stunned by what he said. He could not understand. Of all the questions he had floating in his head, he spluttered that one out.

'Does… What? Does it matter?' Shez looked up as astonished at the question as he was. Although tried to guide it away in a nonchalant way. 'Come…on…Ed?'

'Yes.' He spoke through her, over her, to the wall.

'I was this, when, then…before I met you. Now, not n-n…now. It doesn't matter.'

'It does.'

'No.'

'Tell me then.' He turned. He was starting to show his emotions coming as a single tear escaped his bloodshot eyes. 'If it doesn't matter. Tell me.'

'Will it make you—'

'TELL ME!' His shout was earthshattering, yet did not release any anger.

'But—'

'Wait. It was you. You were in that car. That night going in the opposite direction to the…'

Her burst of wails of apologies said it all. 'One hundred and fifty pounds,' she relinquished.

'An HOUR!' Again, Eddy yelled, without meaning to.

Eddy strode to the other side of her lavish apartment with his back to the crumpled heap of Shez. He needed space. He needed to organise his thoughts, needed to calm down. His mind was acting irrational. So many poor reactions were consecutively running through his head at break neck speeds. He needed to calm down. He needed to. Quickly.

'Look…Ed. I have served, severed ties…stopped with this industry. Last night, the last time. Promise. I feel so much for you. Why, just why I had to say something. I don't want to hurt you.'

'Last night…' The words were choked into the back of Eddy's throat making him grind out the words in a rationed breathless discord. He got up to leave.

'Wait,' beseeched Shez. 'We cannot end it here. I mean. We need to talk. This can…not stop here.'

'I need to go. Sorry, not sorry, but…bye.' Eddy turned, marched towards the lift. Paused. Head bowed on the steel mirrored doors.

'Wait. PLLLEEEASE! I stopped for you. STOPPED. NO MORE. I am falling for you. Fall for you. I am loving you.'

Eddy paused, trying to muffle his sobs. Pinching the corner of his eyes with his right thumb and index finger like a tight pincher. He thought he had taken too many emotions for one day, he turned, ignoring eye contact with Shez. He returned to the scene of the violation, but did not sit. He stood, hearing her weeping, looking at the sofa. Feeling his own tears cling to his nose, before failing onto the wood leaving a blemish of darker stain. Smelling her perfume. She smelt so nice. Eddy considered what had just happened. He guiltily and sheepishly returned closer to the sofa, slowly. He then abruptly changed his course to a soft red chair as far away as possible, but remaining in the room. As Shez continued to explain everything in an irrepressible rant. Shez did not get up, as if she had melted herself into the floor. she was talking in short words. Not real sentences. Eddy listened. His gaze was fixed into nothingness.

'I arrived. Needed money. Fast.' She tried to make clear the motives to why she started, then fell deeper into the industry. 'It was. It is addictive. Try. Understand. People would throw money at me. I came from a small town. A town where people would shit on me, rather, than speak to me. I came here. They gave money. Spoke to…me. I was a Queen for a night. At a ball. A princess. As quick as that,' she clicked her fingers, 'I could easily be back, back down there. Back in the shit. A nothing. Then you. Then you came along. I never thought. I hoped. Of course, I hoped. Never thought. You existed. That someone like you was there. Came here. Someone that liked me for being me. Not for something for themselves. A trophy. On arm. You liked me. Actually, liked me. You still like me. Right? You made me believe in me. You still like me? Right?'

Eddy did not register. He sank into the chair like a rescue victim without the strength to rise, to react. Exhausted.

'I…' Shez continued, 'I am feeling you. For you. Something I never. I…Have…NEVER…felt this way'. Once again, she burst into cries of remorse. Cried out the tears that she was struggling to hold back. Tears that exploded out. She collapsed further into the floor. Her legs towards her strongly beating chest, in the foetus position. Still bubbling through tears. 'I am telling you. I want you. That is why. Please…please give me something. PLEASE. Talk to me. Please. It was the feeling of the power, not the money. The feeling that you have given me. That you give me, when I hear, see you. It's not important, the money…you. Are. You are.'

From the open kitchen, the tinged aroma of roasting lamb and rosemary was masked by the smell of burning smoke. They both detected the evening meal being ruined, but did not care. They had more pressing things to contend with.

Shez continued justifying that it was the money that kept her doing it. Until now, it was all that mattered. It all came down to the money. She genuinely said she did not enjoy it, but Eddy struggled to believe her. Shez was a spider and Eddy was the bug. He was in the web of fabrications that she had woven, bound by deceptions. They had talked about marriage. The possibility of kids. That was a good time to bring up her secret life.

The very real idea of them both returning to Australia as a couple, with a future. It was a bad idea, but in the short time Eddy had to admit that he had fallen for her. He had fallen for a lady of the night without knowing it. Shez had fallen for him. The chat went on into the early hours. It was mainly one-sided. Eddy asked a few questions but Shez was the main voice. They were reconnecting in a way that made Eddy, and Shez, feel that this flaw could actually be overcome.

Food did not happen. They left the burnt remains to soak. Eddy stayed as he had had enough for the day and could not take any more. He was weak, exhausted, drained. They slept in the same bed that night, but did not make love. Eddy resisted her advances of a cuddle. He slept far away from Shez, teetering on the edge, leaving a vast chasm in the centre of the king-sized black silk-lined bed.

Eddy woke first in the morning and left. He tiptoed out like a thief in the night. He did not leave a note. He went home, walked the dogs and thought. His mind had not stopped thinking. He did not get much sleep. With each passing minute, that he was not with Shez the more the flaw heightened. The mountain-making molehill that was a mere grain of sand is what he was constructing in his mind. It is pretty amazing how something so small can grow so fast. That, without the knowledge it is too big to shrink back down without having some kind of mind explosion.

Shez and Eddy spoke later that day, over the telephone. It was a tear-induced conversation that returned to the conversation of the night before. It was clear to think better being a small distance apart. Shez was in a fit of tears for days. She showed real remorse in deceiving him. She showed a real effort to change. She seemed sincere, but Eddy was left stupidity wondering if she would be the same girl that he had fallen in love with.

A week later, Daniel and Kimberley arrived back. Eddy and Shez had rebuilt a wooden bridge, which was based on concrete supports, and the shaky dry sand foundations which were as fragile as a bridge of cards. It did not happen overnight, trust was still flimsy. It was nearly a week before they shared a kiss again. It was a passionate kiss that gave all the reasons to why not to end it just yet.

Marcus was holding a New Year's Eve party. Everyone was invited to his home. They were getting ready when Shez's mobile beeped from her inside pocket. Another beep immediately after from her proper mobile on the table. Why did she have the exclusive one again? Shez was in the bathroom. She rushed out on the beeps of her mobiles.

'Why have you two phones again?' Eddy picked up the phone on the table out of the trailing grasp of Shez and read the message on the screen: 'Miss your hands, come soon.'

'What...Is...This?' Eddy accented each word as he pointed the message on the screen towards a furious Shez.

'You read my message?'

'Seriously? Is that the issue? Here? REALLY? You lied. AGAIN. HOW? It...Your other phone. What did? That is, your...work, no, your escort mobile! How could I be so bloody foolish?'

'I missed the money. I—'

'Missed the taste of this man's dick on your lips, you mean.' Eddy instantly regretted that. It was cruel. It was unnecessary. Eddy was not that person, but the anger in him seemed to be coming out in irrational spite filled sentences of unadulterated venom. He could not stop the verbal attack. He kept coming out with poor choices of sentences. Poor words that complied the vindictive, hurtful, and malicious condemnations. Eddy had pronounced her guilty without judge or jury. Each verbalisation was an exaggerated sarcasm.

Shez erupted into tears. She left Daniel and Kimberley's house with the doors open. Rumbling out in the unmelodiousness of stomps, wails, squeals and shame. Nothing weighed as heavy as the self-afflicted manacles of besmirched disgrace. The snow was falling hard, as her footsteps were left printed in the newly laid snow. This was a blizzard that had started with a single light snowflake. This was not unlike to the storm that had been brewing inside of him. Cool, relentless with an ending known. It cannot snow all the time. Like a ghost, she had vanished through the snow and out of his life. Not leaving a presence, but an impression inside him.

Shez ended it with the defamation that Eddy was too jealous. Although he felt that he could not be blamed for how he felt. Yes, it was jealousy, but was that the main fire? The main cause of the destructive fire that engulfed him, blanketing him in the smoke that suffocated his voice was down to her. Her secret. Her subsequent promise. Her shattering of trust. Her deceit. She had tried to unleash the ties by severing the industry, but the ties had not untied from her. She was in fact the spider caught in the web of the self-destructive industry. She could not let go of the wealth. Eddy the dying bug. Left to decay. He felt insulted. She tried to make herself feel better by assassinating his character in messages. She did not pick-up her mobile but attacked with numerous messages.

Eddy did not go out. He did not feel like celebrating. Daniel and Kimberley offered to stay in. He was thankful for that, but rejected their offer. As he heard the booms, squeals, pops and hisses. Saw the flashes and the odd colourful balls in the dark night sky that was on any other day a beautiful phantasmagoria. Tonight, it was an evil hallucinating nightmare. He was feeling horrendous. He wrote a letter.

Shez,

You ~~are~~ were my first love, after my break-up. Although my heart ~~will, is ached,~~ aching, my heart is constantly sore. My heartbeat suffocated with my emotions bubbling around with no logic or purpose. Each separate emotion are bouncing and crashing into one another you ~~arrived~~ came. Everyone told me in Lewes that they could see me falling for you. Your affectionate arty ways. Your devil-may-care attitude. Your passion for life. You were just what I was looking for when I was not searching for you. I wondered if I was not to ~~wonder if~~ good for you, that I would not do our time together just course (justice). I go back to that in a flash. I would pause, only to replay exactly the same thing again with no alterations but to live it fully.

It was your laugh. The way that you could light up a room. A knack that you would light the fuel for a party to start. Your laugh that brimmed with innocence. Your laugh sealed my fate. While I marvelled at the complete you, I saw the beautiful peculiarity of you. I knew, we knew deep, deep down that it was, and always would be a fling. I practised packing my life with you. Forever. I knew it would not last. How? I just knew, as I believe you did too.

Your last kiss.

Your last kiss was everything. It was quick, intense and romantic. A stolen love that was not mine to keep.

What you need, unfortunately it not me. But. I thank you. You taught me that my heart was never closed. You taught me to smile, to laugh, and to cry. That it was, alright to. To live in that moment. Whether it was happy or sad. Most of all thank-you for making me and believing ~~it me~~ in me. Reminding me that it is okay to feel utterly drunk in lust, love. In that you showed me that life always goes on, that I can fall in love with someone again, but ~~con~~ be in love with everything in this world again.

This is goodbye. Goodbye. Goodbye, my lover. Goodbye, my friend.

Sincerely Yours,
Ed X0-x0-x0

It is mystery. Love. The snow has been replaced by cold rain. Eddy is out walking, by himself, surrounded by many wearing the inappropriate attire at the early hours of a new year. He places the note under Shez's door. Lingers with a speculation of what was going on within these closed walls. He wants to leave. His job is complete.

Days later, he slowly staggers with a heavy backpack to the train station. The cold rain seems to be falling through his heart, the piercing wind driving daggers through his heart causing him to ache and crumble from inside into ruins. Before leaving, Kimberley had said her grandmother once said, 'Summer friends will melt away like summer snows, but winter friends are friends forever.'

Eddy was not sure if she was remarking on themselves or on the relationship of broken dreams. Was this sentence, this saying, designed to make him feel better? He had explained to them both what had happened. He did not need to but in doing so helped him to heal. He went in unusually exhaustive rationalisation, leaving nothing unturned and unscrutinised. Over the course of two alcohol-fuelled days, he described the turn of events that they had missed.

He was sitting on the empty bench on a busy Lewes Station. The birds were singing. It might have been pretty, but it was not for them that they are singing for. The winter was cold in many ways and not just the temperature, but Spring was approaching. In Australia, it was summer. At this moment he was sure he did deserve the heat. He was travelling to the airport.

The relationship had ended badly. The memories of the tortured love clouded the good ones made. The enjoyment and joy that was felt is forever hidden. Forever buried beneath the negatively of the emotional actions and reactions. Eddy thinks of Shez with an anger. With disgust. This is a real shame considering she was an object of his affection. On top of this, all he feels is a deep humiliation. It turns out that everyone knew what she did, apart from him. He was angry with himself, at himself, as he disregarded the gut instinct that he had at the start, during, and near the end. He boarded the train, to get a plane home.

Eddy left his travels.

Eddy left his broken heart in Europe.

A few days before, Shez was sitting on the same train station bench. Eddy's letter in her graceful hands. She read it for the umpteenth time unashamed of the free-rolling tears that flowed. Blotches on the paper, making the ink slightly run. She squeezed the corners in her hand. She tucked it into her bag, she will keep this letter. Keep the memories in her heart. Love him always. As the train pulled into the station, she got on board without looking back. That part behind her on the new path in her future. She left Lewes for a new destination. Like Eddy, never to return.

Present Day
Sentimentally Cynical

Crack. The thudding sound of a knife slamming off a knuckle. Eddy curses to himself at his clumsy rookie mistake. Foolishly, he knows his error straightaway. He knows that the skin side of the spatchcock should be touching the yellow plastic board. If not, the bone splinters. Like it has just done. Using his trusted Victorinox boning knife with the dark, rosewood handle, he investigates his damage within the tunnel-boned spatchcock. Cursing again, more at his wandering absentminded concentration. He looks down at the jigsaw puzzle of bone fragments that resemble his life. Something that no-one, not even himself, could ever reassemble seamlessly again. Would he want to?

'You all good, bro?' Paul questions, reacting to his swearing under his breath.

'Uh, yeah. Bloody fractured on me, didn't it?'

'On you?'

'Have I ever told you that I hate being called bro?'

'Daily. Never grows old.'

Paul was slicing near the back thinly tomorrows order of ham, as Jones Family Butchers had taken its mid-afternoon lull. Thick-lensed glasses perched precariously close to falling of the tip of his nose, if it was not for the greying wisps of wirily hairs.

Eddy's point of his knife carefully removed the splintered white bone as his mind disconnected from the movie reel of his past. He finished the last of the twenty-five on his mandate, vac packed them and placed them in the correct Warwick tubs for tomorrows deliveries. Thoroughly washing his station down in methodical preciseness, serving a single customer and drying his hands, he leans on the wall, thinking of the words he wanted to ask Paul.

'Yes?' Paul elongated his question without looking up, sensing his presence.

'Random question…of the day.' He clears his throat. 'Do you ever think about your exes?'

Paul looks up. Repositions his glasses to the centre of his nose to clearly see a bashful Eddy drying his knife in his hands. 'Coffee?'

'Yep. But would rather whistle and ride.'

A plume of cold steam, the tendrils of the clear plastic flaps resettling over the open door as he disappeared for a few seconds into the cool room. He returned with a carton of lamb saddles to prepare, specifically for a certain customer's requirement.

'Mate. You are not alone. Seriously mate, I do, but fondly.'

'Fondly? Huh,' he snorts.

'Look. I have no idea why after all these years of working together, of being mates, you decide to be poignant now. Look, over time, the sharp edges of those harsh memories soften. You remember it differently. I look back with fondness. You also remember it better than it actually was.'

'I assure you that I don't.'

'Wait. Look. Let me finish. I'm just saying that the pain dwindles, that's all.'

Within Eddy's conscious mind, his brain was fine tuning a neutral pathway of listening without acknowledging the happenings. Paul was triggering missiles, firing neurons while he was on that solitary path. But, all neurones are connected, so that when they fire together, they are wired together. This act forms stronger connections. He was listening, but daydreaming a complex interweave of stitching's together that merges into a rich, superficial tapestry of a life when he was happy, optimistic. A lie. Once he learnt these words of wisdom from Paul his brain would thereafter preform the recognition as an unconsciously mess of lies and truth.

'Look. I think of my exes, sure,' Paul stays on track. 'They actually make me feel better. Give me a boost. I look at my wife. Where I am. My past made me come to this destination. Lightens my mood, gives me self-esteem, gives me…identity. Just, maybe you should not fight off your past as much as you do.'

Paul pauses to serve a customer while Eddy thinks of what he has just said to him. His hands in the lamb, his mind in the faces of Shez, Saoirse, Mahina.

'Look. The first real love is a novelty. Everything is better when fresh. This burns itself out eventually. Come on? Would you really travel three buses, a walk in the rain to get to their house over an hour away? Don't answer, it is not needed. But, I thought not. What use is missing uses old selves, more than uses exes.'

'You? How old are you? You do not have the answers?'

'True bro. True. Why ask? I am in my forties. You, in your thirties. In our twenties we are still learning, heck mate, we are still learning now, I am. But. But in my twenties I didn't know. Did you? Who you were yet? I was horny, hormonal and very much on the game. First relationships are full of dramas. Come on mate, we think that is normal. Everything that we see, read, hear is a drama when love comes to it but now. My life is boring. I don't need the BS. Don't need it. Don't want it. Life is not like the movies. Live with it.'

Eddy was sentimentally cynical with more distrust in him the more he grew old. He found it increasingly harder to let go, to give out his trust. When he did with Beth-Annie he thought it would be the last time.

'Look Eddy. Think of your exes. Don't recant but remember the past. I implore use. It may not be with the ex that you long for. It may be remembering that person you were, a relationship into what a person made you, YOU, feel like, about yourself. Feeling valued. Feeling loved, by another…human being. This may actually increase your fulfilment, the quality of your current relationship with Beth. Think about it.'

He did. He thought. He delved into another relationship. Was Paul right that he could learn from it. That he should have that reckless abandonment to dive into the relationship headfirst.

'Use finished the saddles. Let's have that cup of coffee and get that taste of this openly feel mumble jumble crap out before it changes us. Changes our relationship. Ha ha.'

Eddy slaps a lingering firm holding hand on Paul's shoulder on the way to the blood-tainted plastic kettle. A thanks for the trusting honesty he gave in his answer. For his knowledge. A show of thanks. Nothing left to say. That was all that was left to be done.

'I will keep with the truth though…in my past, huh, memoirs,' he smiles for the first time today. 'Bro, yeah, I am trying it on Boomerang, your advice was good. But your grammar! How many times *use* is not *you*…'

Amusement fills their lungs as the five o'clock rush starts trickling in.

Twelve Years Ago
The Grass Seemed Greener

Dripping in incessant silvery bubbles from his forehead, the foamy soap suds fell into the white porcelain basin. Paul's wisdom soared into his awareness. He blindly cancelled the sound of the rushing water. His eyes closed. He leaned against the shower head. The water flowing over his head like a shiny waterfall of white clouds. The hot spray turning to warm, cold droplets.

Drops leave him as he saunters barely wearing a crisp pale blue towel, leaving a watery trail from the bathroom to the kitchen. He lethargically dried himself, badly. Eddy was not the typical all-night partying thirty-something in the heaving grips of a midlife crisis. Sure, he enjoyed a beer, but found out that a moment occasionally was better than always having a beer continually.

Hence, he developed, to a certain extent, into a little introvert. As the chilly air washed over his sodden skin he shivered. He bowed down, leaned in and picked a chilled silver and dark blue tinny of Young Henrys Newtowner. He brought a six pack about three weeks ago, five still remain. He wandered over to the large floor to ceiling clear glass door, that leads out to a concrete slab of a brown-desert appearance tiled balcony. As barren as the Sahara with no furniture. He looks out. Déjà vu from a few nights back, but this time he stands looking across the urban sprawl.

Nursing the tin by the top, flicking the ring pull with his index finger in a slow steady tinging rhythm. In the dark kitchen, mock black marble counter his dimly lit mobile is on charge. This is a good thing, as after a few drinks he can be a bit of a social path. The hypnotic ting from his nail on the tin accelerated with a considerable boost into his own virtual world, propelled by Pauls assisted words earlier in the day. He was not sure if he was imagining it, but the twinkling lights reflected in the silver of the condensed tin. He mulled over the words Paul had said since he spoke them, but now. Now, it was a driven force that carried him back to a different time. The time when he returned to Australia as a beaten, crushed twenty-three-year-old boy.

When he returned to Australia after the European romances, he disavowed himself by burying his head in the sand. He concealed his passions by drowning himself in work and alcohol. It is not something that the doctors, the physiatrists would recommend, but he believed intensely that this method worked for him. The act of keeping busy at work stopped his mind from wondering. The 'what could have been's? Work stopped him from retracing every aspect in the finest of detail. To analyse every side of the arguments that attributed to the end. Fundamentally, work stopped him from painfully scrutinising by peeling every single piece of tough, reality-heeding skin to examine how HE could change.

Eddy blamed himself. It was never something that the other person did, or done, did want or, at times done. The alcohol made him forget. The fizz, the burn at the back of his neck, the bitterness made him feel good. From past, detrimental experiences, he always drank in company. When he drunk alone, the monsters came out to play, in an undesirable, damaging way that was not constructive or, anyway helpful. It made him incredibly depressed. Hence, he secretly drunk on his own. But, when he was three sheets to the wind, on the plus-side, alcohol also made him fall to sleep easier. Not particularly well mind, but it made him hit the pillow, couch or floor and have a type of soporific sleep.

Both of the relationships in Europe took a while to die within him. Constantly, he kept drudging them up. Always going through them as if he could naïvely have changed the consequential outcome. A foolish endeavour. If there ever was one. It was in the past. Each thought came to him at separate times, about separate women, but particularly, Shez. Shez came up often. The slenderest thought of her, even a happy one, would catapult quickly into a hatred fiery ball which plummeted abruptly into the earth. The impact triggering a self-attacking, self-abusive anger.

He was extremely fragile. He hid it well, too well. People thought he was fine, okay, that he was entirely on a life buzz. He had turned into a functioning alcoholic. He craved a drink when he could not have one. Instead of a cup of coffee in the morning, he reached for a bottle of vodka. Eddy would never admit just how broken he was, to anyone. Let alone himself.

He laughed to himself when he thought that he had lost his own control on his life. He laughed hysterically with a single thought that he was on the edge. He uncontrollable frantically laughed vigorously at the thought that he would actually jump. Regrettably, more to the point, sadly, he did have these contemplated plans. If he did. If he really did. Jump, would anyone care? Would anyone notice? Taking the leap, or the jump made him giggle in reference to the expression of falling in love. Whereas coming out of love.

Losing a love literally made him really feel, really want to take the leap, the plunge, the jump. Leaping from a bridge, a building. Not like a Superhero. Not to come down softly, but as hard as his cold, frozen emotions to shatter like ice on the ground. This black comedy would in turn help him through the dark moments. Eventually he would see the comedy, within the tragedy to be able to move on. Conversely, work and alcohol would play in the aftermath of love.

So many relationships are about the learning. The education within the loving and the ending. Eddy believes, or believed a new relationship would help him. He messed about with any women that would give him, any time of the day. Anyone that would give him that moment of human affection. He was kidding himself to think that he was ready to disembark on a new relationship. He was, 'not over it', as a mate insisted that he was. The same mate told him to 'find a new bird', a fling rather than a relationship. This would be different. It would provide a contrast. A different incite. Eddy, however, wanted to work to exhaustion. Simply so he could sleep at night with alcohol, as his loving companion.

Months had passed. He was not drinking as much. He was trying to fix himself. A written warning, followed a verbal warning, that his work was suffering. The latest was a response to a complaint about his unusual volcanic temperament that was growing, forever brooding like lava to erupt suddenly, devastating everyone that was close.

Back in the present, the warm, slippery unopened tinny dropped to the floor, out of his grasp. 'Air. I need air,' he shocked himself with the vocalised expression. He threw on some black sports shorts and took the dusty, stone fire exit steps up the eight flights. Bounding skyward to the strictly out of bounds after midnight rooftop. It was only when he opened the door that he wondered if it was alarmed. It was a balmy humid night. He often came here to disconnect. This was the latest that he had been up here though. Over the dark blanket of the night the glowing yellow, orange and red hues scattered across the human mountains.

Above, the bright stars, dim, uneasy to see in the presence of the artificial hell below. He stood, belly on the rusty railing that had been painted a few times but now the owners had given up and left it to slowly peel back to the metal. A metal barrier, that resembled a dingo fence below, between the rail and the plummeting drop with the effectiveness of a cotton thread. The fence teased him, beckoned him, brought back those desperate suicidal tendencies. He focused on the drop. Then. Exhaling heavily, he looked up, between heaven and hell, once again. Towards the past.

It was unusual for a twenty-something to shun the nightlife, but he was trying particularly hard to go cold turkey and give up the beer altogether. He was rebuilding himself. Work was going better. He even got a favourable comment from his boss that his attitude was becoming the old Eddy. Platonic in his friendships. Celibate by choice. Nonlibidoist by design.

Then, then came a relationship when he least expected it. But then, are we ever expecting it? Then came Jennifer. An instant reaction materialised in his broken heart, fusing the wounds, fusing the fractured trust. Eddy literally felt a beat skip. The snapping of weighty chains containing his shattered romances. His heart did not fall apart, crash down, but floated. The chains dissolved to steam, he was getting hot. All the clichés were taking place. For which he never thought he would feel again, even at his young age. What could be said for this tall lady from Port Stephens, up the picturesque east coast of New South Wales. She looked like the stereotypical surf beauty portrayed in all the broadcasting advertisements.

Jennifer had shining, almost white unicorn-esque straight blonde hair, the colour of glittered sunshine on the bronzed sandy beaches. Cascading down like a silver waterfall down to the top of her perk, petite bottom. Which she got, with her figure, thanks to a vigorous combinations of workout regimes involving runs, yoga and stretches. Her sapphire light-blue eyes, mirroring the same reflection of the waters for which she would always call home. Although she had not lived there, since, leaving when she was a young teenager in pursuit of the ideal life. Like all youngsters, chasing the dollar. The slender curves of her tall, slim, toned athletic body swayed slightly like the tides of the Pacific Ocean when she moved.

She had a faithful, friendly smile on her face. It was a perfectly permanent feature which transmitted happiness and a zest for loving life. Quick to laugh, always. Sometimes at herself. Mainly due to all her beauty came a hidden cost, a burden. She was intelligent, but people did not see past her glossy cover. With that she performed the unconventional steps of trying to prove that she was bright and smart to strangers. To any person that did not know her.

For this reason, she over-contemplates by trying far too hard. She would purposefully use larger words that she did not need to do, to give the illusion of her intelligence. But in her haste, she came across dumber, witless. She either used the words out of context, or the completely wrong word altogether. Nervously giggling to her mix-up, enhanced her infectiousness of her character that surrounded her pure, butter-would-not-melt aura. Her carefree character would turn anyone's bad day into a great one. She just had the magnetic charm where people were drawn to her presence.

Eddy mentioned she did not need to prove herself to anyone, ever. He pointed out that the only person that she holds her in accountability was herself. Nevertheless, she still slipped upon many instances in endeavouring to justify her intelligence.

Jennifer worked as a Front Office Manager in the centre of Sydney at one of the busiest, largest hotels on Circular Quay. She loved her job. Yet, she found it increasingly difficult to do the one thing that she loved the most about her job. This was the interaction with the customers. Hearing their points of view, their day, their plans. She wanted to give them what they wanted. She fed off their passion for the adventures in a new city to where she lived, her accepted home.

She often found herself juggling the room rates, payroll, to keep the management at the very top happy, to the forecast, budgets and actual for which they wanted. She had to generate a constant stream by issuing spreadsheets of documents, figures, projections, reasoning to why figures were isolated since the last email. She always had to have a reason to argue, hence, to persuade the management above, that the path she was going was for progression. Specifically, when they, without warning, rang.

The soft ding of her computer, her mobile, might as well be a click of the fingers as they expected it within minutes of the question, or this was how Jennifer heard it as. This was not the nine to five job that, she wanted as a young girl growing up. It was not the job where she was going to help people. Is there actually such a thing anymore? Some days she reflected on the negatively in moments of weakness that fleeted into her mind, to be gone as quick like the voice in a wind. Still, she loved the job. She felt she was serving her staff's needs, her customers wants and requirements, making all the visitors get the very best from the city that she calls her second home.

Jenni grew up in the peaceful Hunter Region of Port Stephens, which to the locals is simply called Port. One of those places that only a local can abbreviate. When Eddy used the reduction, Port, Jenni would give a sideway frowned, glanced that warned; Don't You Dare. Same as taken the piss out of something about the area that you come from. If you are a local, you can do it, get away with it, but being an alien, the defensive walls comprehensively surrounded the area is a cemented fortress of protection for which they are proud of their home. The back of the local's hairs goes up in an attack manner. The spittle of honouring the area, is a vast tribute to the fantastic positives here. A place where, a few moments ago, they were slagging off.

The landscape is shaped over many years by human hands, but still has the scars of the natural vegetation in the rich, patched-worked bush land. Often, she would speak favourably of the encouraging hopeful features of growing up in such a friendly place that was by the coast, close to the city without being in it and close to the wineries. Abundant in its locally sourced foods from generations of merchants. She spoke of times when she would hike in the bush, feel exposed, naked and alone, but at the same time sheltered, protected and safe in the neighbourhood. She could not explain, Eddy understood that she had an affinity with the place.

Jenni left for Newcastle University, literally over the river as she put it. She did not need to move out but felt the independence was vitally essential for her to grow-up. She was top of her class; therefore, she obtained a scholarship into management, a huge leap across many stepping stones on the path to entering the world of hotels. This sent her to work for a few months here, a few months there.

Starting in the outreaches of the dusty red centre in the middle of Australia to learn different aspects. Then to be transferred to the contrasting heat and humidity of tropical north in Port Douglas. To the barren beauty of Western Australia with its privileged sunset magnificence of Broome. Ahead of finishing in the colder, winter temperatures of the snow-gladdened fields of Snowy Mountains in Victoria. Ultimately, finally ending in Sydney. Here is where she has been ever since. Perfectly located close to home when she needed to escape the hubbub of the relentlessly endless disquiets of city life.

Nowadays, it seemed that the only seen progress in the city were hotels and coffee shops, one or the other was always at every corner, or being built. Always going up, growing tall. That she was in one of them made her an unknowingly contributor to this growth. In addition to the over-complicated, inconveniently warranted continuous evolving construction to develop, or upgrading the transport networks. The city seemed in an unceasing everlasting building site. Despite all of this reorganising upheaval, she loved her job, and Sydney.

It was through a mate of Eddy's that they met. One of Eddy's catering mates from TAFE. He introduced them, one splendid late evening at the annual Late-Night Food Market in Sydney's Hyde Park. Although Eddy does hold a completely justified misconception that it was a match-making ensnarement of a wannabe cupid, in this case Tee's, arrowed noose. Eddy normally steered clear of these markets, with this one altogether number one of his imaginary lists. Principally, it was a taste thing, rather than the cost. To buy the exorbitant cost of a meal, that was pretty average and ordinary. When he easily could just walk a few metres down the road and get something authentic, tasty, and warmer in Thai, Korean or Chinatown.

He was one-hundred percent certain that it would be wonderful, although, he conceded the presentation would be woeful. These mediocre products, again he was sure, would have been batch-made and placed in warming trays or boxes to be re-acted in a steaming wok for the customer's peace of mind. He was convinced that if it was not for the carnival noise, everyone would hear the tell-tale high-pitched ding of a microwave. The reheated, portion-controlled to the gram dish, next to be placed in a sizzling wok. Just so, it seemed fresher than it actually was by the sound, fire, smell and chefs' showmanship overreactions and theatrical performances.

Besides the expected, Eddy agreed to meet Tee here. Through the packed shrove of people, mainly tourists, and the aid of their mobile phones they found each other. However, if the truth be told, you could not really miss Tee. Tee's name was actually Anthony, but since, well, the age that he cannot really remember everyone called him Tee. It came from his father who wanted to call him Wally Lewis, the King of Rugby League, but lost that battle to his wife.

As a form of protest, he nicknamed him Tiger, for his beloved West Sydney Tigers. From the early stages of school, in true blue Australian custom Tigers mates shortened his nickname to Tee. Hence it became, as it was, always will be, his unofficial name. Tee was a larger man. With all the colourful lights around, not quite a vast glow as the New Year's celebrations but enough to shed a light on his Vegas-like flamboyant white, blue and orange floral water coloured short-sleeved shirt.

People would not call him fat, but really, he was. He parted the crowd like Moses as he waddled over, phone held high on spotting Eddy over the grass eating area. He was one of the few from his TAFE mates that stayed in the trade. He did not just taste the food that he cooked, he had mouthfuls of it before it left the kitchen for, 'he needed to see that it tasted right'.

Despite having the equivalent of at least, a meal at work, Tee would retire home for the night and cook another larger than necessary feast, before going to bed. He wondered why he was putting on weight.

One afternoon, this came up and Eddy, who can be a blunt and to-the-point person, stated, with no sugar-coating, that he cannot be surprised that he keeps putting on weight. Eddy was very impatient if he has to explain himself constantly that sees him not shy, or backwards in going forwards with his views.

'Tee…' Eddy exhaled out with a sigh, clearly exasperated, with a strong tone of being sick and tired of explaining the same thing. Like a stuck record, he had told, retold, told again this information before. He had, but he continued anyway to repeat the same threadbare dialogue once again. 'Tee. Tee, Tee, Tee. It is simple. You will keep getting fatter if you put more calories than you burn. FACT. No bull. Mate. One, You do no exercise. None. You even Uber it to the train station. Two, Your portions are huge. For a dinosaur. Huge. Let alone a human. Essentially, a land-dwelling mammal. Less is more, remember that from TAFE.'

Yes, it was deemed harsh. Eddy wanted it to hit home but knew, in his heart, that it would not. He was just trying to make Tee understand. They had been mates long enough to appreciate truth. Real friends stab them in the front. His daggered attack was aimed to be beneficial. For this growing weight issue was not making him happier. The more he ate, the more he hated himself. Eddy tried to get him to take control of his diet. This night, was not the time, nor place, to bring this issue up.

He saw Tee go to one shack of food, then another, like a pinball, as if it was his last meal for a while. Like a child in a toyshop he was bright-eyed, taken in by the smells, sounds and colours. As he sat on the red plastic chair that looked child-sized under his large frame. The legs seemed to creak and bow slightly under his weight that made the chair look even smaller than it actually was. He planted the food around him in the white-squeaky polyphone bowls.

Satellites of fried, deep-fried and shallow fried unhealthy badness. In-between mouthfuls of mashed noodles, vegetables they shared a joke. Eddy had just a plastic cup of lemon tea, because quite honestly, he was not hunger. He was also hiding the fact that he was a little drunk. He had had a bad day, negative thoughts created a thunderstorm in his mind. This caused him to crave, want, desire. The pressure proved too much. He violated his promise. To fall off the wagon. He hated himself for it.

He was in a persona of being perfectly well and in control of his life. He had finished a shift at work, drunk, showered while drinking and came straight out, drink encased crudely in a brown paper bag. Even though, he admits to Tee, the smell of the food enveloping his senses did make him feel the hunger, he did not crave it.

Then Jenni walked past. Tee stood up sharply, nearly knocking his food out of his own hand and relinquishing a spattering of chewed up morsels of food—'Jenni!' Tee reached out a bare, chubby pale white arm as he shouted, waving. 'JENNI!' with a showering multicoloured display of partially chewed food flying out of his mouth, jumping out of his bowl on his lap. Splattering onto the unsuspecting victims around him in an unwelcome turned-on sprinkler.

'JENNI!' he shouted once more.

She spun to look around. The wind catching her red dress as she twirled, resembling a catwalk queen. She smiled, raced towards Tee with a smile as wide as her open arms. A strongly gripping hug and smooching kiss on Tee's unshaven baby-faced smooth cheek. Tee did not seem, or did not care to hear the murmurs of discontent with the unwanted food shower from the people sitting nearby, below his projectile food-shot.

'You lost weight!' Jenni exclaimed through a delighted scream. She held her arms up wide, parallel across Tee. 'I swear, Tee, I can almost put my arms around you now!' This was a regular joke that they shared.

'Getting there', Tee unflinchingly lied through his probing finger, as it dug around in his mouth for a morsel of food embedded between his teeth.

'Sit. Here. This is Eddy.' Tee gestured the very same food-free arm to point him out and his empty seat.

Eddy got up to shake her hand. He turned into a baffling assortment of muddled up words. Even more ridiculous was the added bonus of moving his head in an equally perplexing way that made him look like a parrot, trying to act like a human. The flummoxing open-mouth, coupled with an astounded glaze by Jenni just happened to nail in the last embarrassing shame coffin he had placed on himself. An eternal split second passed before Jenni laughed at his horrific first impression with, 'Do you want to try that again?'

Eddy nodded, really appreciating her sweetness. His heart skipped a beat. He sat back down. This time he got up smoothly, which was the original intent compared to the thing, he would just call it a thing, that he did a split-moment ago. This time he lightly held her hand and kissed her on her cheek with the relaxed welcome of, 'Hi. I'm Eddy. How's it g'ing?' For sure, it was generic, but he felt more at ease. Perhaps it was her smile, accompanied with her eyes that lingered with his. Their eyes seemed to travel an invisible sparkle, an instant connection.

'Tee!' she exclaimed. 'How ya going? I haven't seen you for time.'

'Busy. You know me. A social event here. Meeting with mates there. One gala closes, and another ball opens. It is tough at the top. Someone has gotta do it. It might as well be me. Ha Ha.'

'Really?' she laughed a sweet, easy on the ear pleasant-sounding giggle.

'Yeah mate. Would I lie to you? Have I ever?'

Jenni's red dress wrapped around her curves without clinging, with enough exposed flesh to see her olive-beige tanned legs to her white Havana thongs. Her shoulders were exposed in a horizontal line by the strapless dress. Delicately thin looped golden earrings danced with the lights around the festival. She was captivating. Eddy tried not to stare at her like a Hollywood starlet from the silver screen but could not stop. Her laugh and smile danced with her eyes. She was nothing but exquisite. She was his dream girl. Heck, everyone's dream girl.

Although Eddy was the third-wheel in this conversation, he enjoyed hearing the stories coming up and out. It was nice to be the audience as he watched, listened. Trying in a poor attempt not to stare too much. He successfully failed this bid.

'So, tell me about you.' All of a sudden, Jenni brought Eddy into the conversation. A little earlier than he saw coming, but just when he placed a gulp of tea into his mouth.

'Nothing to tell really. Born here, the North Shore...'

'Where?'

'Narrabeen.'

'I'm from Newcastle, well, Port Stephens. I say Newcastle, force of habit. It is easier. We. My family used to holiday there. And Collaroy. Love the place. Great memories. The lake...'

'Awesome, my old stamping ground. Many summers nights camping.' He was not interested in speaking about him, but wanted to learn about her. 'What brings you here tonight?' he changes the tide of the conversation.

'Meeting mates. They bailed. So…finished work and thought I might as well have a look. I was just on my way home when…' she aimed a grin at Tee. At which point she threw a cloaking arm around him. 'This guy is great. Don't see him often enough. Why is that?'

They talked as close friends. They included Eddy, so he was not excluded in silence and he, in turn, was enjoying the amusing banter that proceeded. This was the start for Eddy and Jenni. A sparking ignition of a flame was lit. It was a slightly awkward in place for Eddy, when it did go silent, or when Tee left for the call of nature, but at the same time totally awe-inspiring. They shared many things in common. It was the normal meeting conversation of home, live, work and hobbies together with growing escalations. This was the start of something special.

Laughs were shared between the three. Then the evening ended. Yet again Eddy did not exchange numbers. He was making a bad habit of this. Awkwardness came over him. His timid blushing of asking for those magical ten, contactable digits caused him not too. For some ridiculous reason, that he could not explain, he did not want to make his feelings clear in front of Tee. Tee would not have judged him, but he was more than a little worried about the possible condemned rejection. It was only a number though, not a ring, a marriage proposal.

Over the next two days, his working life suffered. Eddy could not shake her spellbinding vision, her sweet voice, her smell of her coconut soap-scented skin out of his head. He worked on autopilot, silent to the streaming ways of the busy, rushing operations around him.

Out of the blue, on the third day, Eddy was doing his shopping at the local Coles supermarket when he coincidentally bumped into Jenni. His diet was not the best outside of work, but the moons and planets must have been in perfect alignment as good luck would have it, he had a basket teeming with fresh fruit, vegetables and a single piece of fresh swordfish. Normally, it was tinned fish, beans and dehydrated noodles and the other bad health choices of quick to cook junk foods.

She was in a rather unflattering grey work ensemble of black flat shoes, knee-length skirt, white blouse and grey blazer. As uncomplimentary to her as it was, she wore it well, despite looking like she was dressed as a negative newsprint. He wore a pair of pale blue, black and white boarders with a faded, creased-up blue singlet. As he just finished work and was getting some things before going home. Times like this he wished he carried an emergency canister of deodorant on his possession.

She did not mind that he smelled of raw meat and iron-strong induced blood. That his hair was unkempt, in need of a neatening trim. She carried a ready-made chicken pesto sandwich, a single red Gala apple and a small plastic container of cut honeydew melon. A clumsy greeting. Although they did both seem genuinely pleased in bumping into each other. They talked over their groceries as if they both wanted to meet again. They both had not worked out the best way of getting the contact details. Someone had to take a chance.

She mentioned a film that she wanted to see. A chance. Eddy suggested going together, as it was one that he was keen to see. Although he did not want to say it, he did not want to be Norman No Mates in the cinema once again. To be spending time with this beauty was a bonus. His fear of being alone, inheritably resounded a feeling that he did not want encouraged. Being alone amongst a crowd of people with other people sentenced, this doomed feeling of isolation. He suggested a textbook first date of drinks, movie and meal. The movie made the dining conversation something that they could talk about. An ice-breaker.

Eddy had felt an instant connection with Jenni the moment he saw her. He started to feel a stronger bond to her. Eddy was falling quicker than he had ever done for anyone. He did not know her, but he was falling for her. Wanted to know her. They arranged to go out that very evening. It was early in the afternoon. Eddy finished his shop, she went back to work for the last few hours. Time for a drink was practically impossible, so they decided to meet on George Street, outside the cinema in the space of four hours' time.

Eddy might as well have bathed in his cologne as he carried it like an unwelcome, welcoming friend. He was like a woman, as he tried on, discarded, retried numerous ensembles. He elected on smartly casual. He left his unit wearing relaxed comfortable brown suede shoes, light blue jeans and a dark green and brown V-necked T-shirt. He waited in the humid air and shuffled his feet together as he glanced up and down the road. He was nervous. He had not made the greatest first impression, but she wanted to see her again.

Was this a date, he wondered, or just a one-off arrangement of coincidence? A twist of fate? He did not care for the answer, as he was going to make this twisted fortune, work in his favour. A white taxicab pulled up outside, in front of Eddy. The door opened and Jenni appeared. Wearing casual black high-heeled ankle boots, dark blue jeans and a yellow smiling face white singlet. Both relieved at seeing that each other went for seamlessly casual, both had not gone over-the-top. She touched Eddy's bare arm, kissed his aftershave-sprayed cheek.

'Sorry I'm late. Hi.'

'You're not. Previews have not even started.'

They walked into the sparsely populated red carpeted entrance of the cinema towards the booking office. She was quick with the money, but Eddy was quicker.

'I appreciate the reach, but this is my shout.'

The theatre was pretty full, as expected for a new release. They walked up and down a couple of aisles before finding two of the worn red heavily stained seats together.

He watched the movie, but every now-and-again he did re-enter the world of fantasy and wondered if he was dreaming. Was this evening actually happening? The rustle of a crisp packet, the silent talking and giggling, the occasional shhh. The warmth of the too hot darkened room, that had increasingly become hotter with the body heat. His rising body heats. Normally cinemas are too cold, they must have been a problem.

When the movie finally started, Eddy could not see many spare seats in the theatre. This was a rarity. Most people did not go out anymore, they waited for Netflix, the DVD or the Internet in one form or another, to supply them the escape from their own reality that they could experience in their own pleasure and comfort of their home. The movie was over before it began. Indisputably captivating from beginning, to the credit-rolling end.

They were both pleasantly delighted with their shared choice of movie. The movie was a drama with enough comedy to keep it happy when it was getting a little too depressing. Not the conventional choice for a first date. A touching story of a child with cancer. Her younger sister born to be the donor of the first child. The youngest ended up taking her parents to court over the treatment of her body. It was tear jerking in places. Fortunately, it was dark as Eddy, who was not an emotional person, did feel it tug on his heartstrings. It definitely tugged at Jenni's who sobbed, silently.

She was so cute as she dabbed her eyes. He watched the flicker, the noise and the sound of the moving screen with a corner of his eye looking at Jenni. At the end he sat good-naturedly. He was giving her a moment to compose herself. Jenni was not shy of her emotions and turned towards Eddy. Red-eyed, but smiling. His mind was not fully acknowledging the moment that was happening right in front of his very eyes. She had noticed him being a gentleman.

As the credits rolled, she dabbed her drying eyes, trying not to smudge her make-up. He patiently waited as the lights glowed on, the patrons moved towards the red curtained doors leaving empty drink containers, crisp packets and a scattering of crumbs over the thin red carpet. He still was not fully grasping the concept that she had in her mind. She turned. She was radiant. She briefly deliberated about her next move. Deliberation over. She went in for a kiss.

With the credits finishing in a fast white-worded document of copyright, came Eddy's rise back to the present. The lights fully came on in a flash of eye-squinting blindness. The crunch of a miss-eaten overly sugary snack under their feet as they moved on the red carpet up the small steps to the exit. Murmurings about the film inserted with a nervous slash of a scalped knife over the moody, dramatic stringed arrangement of the arrival of the plastic bag dragging cleaners in tune, to get ready for the next performance. Rumbling short murmurs of conversations travelled in hushed tones.

As if embarrassed by talking after such a long pause of silence. However, out of the red, velvet heavy curtains and into the light of the foyer came the crescendo of questions, answers and remarks about the film. The burst of noise from the cinema speakers around the movie hall advertised the next 'big hit', the adverts enticing the next movie to go and see with a flash of colour, lights and noise made Eddy hastily exit the cinema altogether. It was not a phobia, as he just wanted to be out. In barely two hours of the movie, he had experienced a different form of emotion to what the movie was conjuring. He was trying hard to understand if this was actual true affection, or aversion, that he was feeling.

He had been scarcely out of a relationship in terms of his detachment, acceptance. Was Eddy ready to re-enter the world again? Or was he scared of being alone so much that he saw this, this potential for love, and seized on it like he was catching a beautiful delicate butterfly to ruthlessly squash the question. He had to quickly put his emotions aside. He had to get his rational presence back. Jenni had returned from the bathroom where she had been reapplying her make-up.

The movie was good and gave them a great deal of conversation as they walked to a bar. Any bar, it did not matter. They equally shared the desire to not want this evening to end, just yet. Another short, tender kiss in the light drizzle of raindrops as they uncomplainingly waited for the red standing man to turn a green walking man.

They had walked across the glossy puddle settled, freshly rain brushed black road into the closest open premises to escape the cold and the howling bitter chill of the wind. Jenni pushed to the front of the crowded bar. She insisted on paying this time. She was now conveniently in front of him. Eddy could not help but stare. She had a fantastic figure. He welcomed the cold nights' air in comparison to the hot box they had both endured. He welcomed the gentleness of the kiss. The moment which had ended too soon to principled chronological his emotions.

His state of mind was just that, in a state. He gingerly touched the side of her waist. Was it his imagination or did she want it. Did she move into his hand, towards his groin. She gracefully spun with a dancer's poise, intimate enough to taste Eddy's cologne. Clutching the bottles of beer, a smile on her face. A face that was in friendly competition with her body. She unintentionally cast aside the line of which his mind was racing on. That smile. The cling of the bottle necks. The following kiss as she pressed past towards the wooden post, calmed him. Relaxed and excited him. He was ready. Ready to move on.

Eddy excused himself to go to the toilet, murmuring, with a taste of her ear, that he would go to the bar on his return. On arriving back, she had disobeyed his request. Been to the bar, refreshed their empty bottles, and commandeered a relinquished table. He did not mind that last addition. Two fresh water-dripping beers sat on the varnished table, soaking the cardboard coaster. He shook his head in a defeated, mocking show at the sight of the beers. He did not argue, but toasted her.

They slowly drank that beer, and the others that followed. They stroked, touched, caressed each other's hands. They leaned into the table towards one another, hands always close to the centre. They rubbed each other's legs under the table. They craved the touch of each other. They talked with a smooth fluent pleasure, as if the connection of desiring souls was taking place. It was not a fantasy. It was not a dream. It was happening. It was just like the movies, at long last.

They got a cab back to Eddy's place, barely keeping their hands off one another. Mysteriously, in the undisclosed unit, they contained themselves to be familiar free in banter. Yet in the bar, seemingly restraining the yearning to tear each other's clothes off. Eddy circled the kitchen. Made two hot chocolates in a mismatch of dissimilar mugs. His whole place was built for one, nothing matched. Only in this moment did he realise this was his existence. But he could change all that, the choice was very much, in his own hands. At this moment. In this moment.

He surprised himself that he made the hot chocolate. Let alone offered the question from his wind-dried chapped lips. Over a rather unusually plume of dense steam, from a brown terracotta mug of the hot milky chocolate he handed over to Jenni. They talked on his black and grey sofa. She had her legs folded up underneath her, after slipping off her shoes on entry, for them to find their own space on the floor. Fortunately, Eddy had actually zoned in enough to pick-up and put down the questions that she voiced, remarking appropriately. She enthralled him.

Everything she was saying was making him more enchanted. The movie that they had just seen together, would go into his archives of, err…I think we saw it. It was hardly going to be a classic, in his mind. In Eddy's mind, the movie was already forgotten. A new movie was being made.

Twisting her hair, spellbinding hypnotic in her finger tips, smokily captivating Eddy's glaze. As her head rested on the back of the sofa, she chattered. She watched him sip from his black and white striped mug. Through the vapour she spoke about her years of growing up in Port Stephens. He let her speak, with reminisces of grins, laughs, gleams in her eyes at an unworldly youthful incorruptibility. Of a whole new world, yet, to be discovered.

This relaxed Eddy, made her seem vulnerable. Accessible. She was thought-provoking. With revealing her inner sanatorium, Jenni felt more relaxed. She felt so much better for someone to listen to her story. It seemed to Eddy that no-one actually, listened to her before. Sure, she had mates, but from her time in Sydney, it seemed to Eddy that no-one thought to care about her life before she arrived.

Perfectly posed, it was indisputably a date. This time was no longer in the world of make believe, as essentially it was a date. Sitting on the fabric with its upholstered buttons. The soft touching of their knocking knees. The lingering touches. The expressive signs of something developing was evident. That genuine sensation, the feeling of a soft touch untouched by his.

Her body was caressing thoughtlessly, but at first sight, effortless, uncomplicated. Longing at first sight. A short, jokingly smack across the shoulder. It was happening. The soft, slow and tender kisses between the mouthfuls of conversation and hot chocolate going cold was heating their affections. Love had crashed through the stronghold of his heart with little resistance. He let her in. He was happy for her to play the notes of his life with soft poignant delicate fingertips on his heartstrings.

Over the course of a few weeks, they developed a stronger bond. They were not falling for each other but, had actually fell for one another. There was one obstacle that was nothing more than a blade of grass to brush over in Eddy's mind, but not in Jenni's. In Jenni's it was a bale of hay. She often brought her age up. Too often for Eddy, who kept putting to rest the accusations that the age was an obstacle.

It was only eleven years. It was nothing. He did not see her age as a concern. He was also getting increasingly frustrated that she seemed to see it more than himself. They got on well. Why would age have to play a part in that? If you judge a book by the age what are you really looking for? Age and love have no boundaries. It is a feel that you have to go with. A gut feeling. To cut off the presence of love by a mere figure is, to Eddy, absurd. Meaningless. Farcical.

Then, of course, was the other man, the older man, the father figure that was a part of Jenni's life. Whether Eddy wanted him in it or not, was apparently irrelevant. Colin was the mate that she loved like a brother, who Jenni did not want out of her life. He had been there for her when her childhood sweetheart, for whom she felt she was destined to be with her entire life, had broken her heart. Shattered her heart into pieces. This episode took years for her to rebuild. As a consequence, her heart was now ridden with thin, fractured scars until now, still, very fragile. They had been together since the age of seven years old. Grown up next door with an indestructible bond as mates. Boyfriend and girlfriend by the age of thirteen. Lovers at fifteen. To subsequently be together for nineteen years from that day. Staying together through the distances involved in her career. That day then, when she did not see the end. The ex had seen the end. The ending, happening.

Eddy had never known this boyfriend's name. She spoke of him in the past tense, without a name, just a casual him, the ex or the former was always implied. Colin was a mate of them both. They also grew up together. He heard the story and disregarded The Ex as a former friend. He stood by Jenni. Giving her the support that she needed to rebuild herself, and her life as a single lady. He was kind, friendly and always concerned with moments in her life.

Jenni never told Eddy what happened. One day, watching the strong waves hit the brown cliffs of Maroubra, Colin told him. As they walked to the shore to grab a coffee after watching the cricket at the local oval, he insisted that he should stop asking. He did not appreciate in the slightest the condescending way that he played the protection card. Why did Eddy seem to pick these girls with extra, unresolved baggage? He got sucked in to think that Colin, was actually going to tell him her secret story.

Back at Eddy's unit, which they might as well shared, Colin's tough talk made him want to ask. He poured two glasses of deep ruby red wine. He passed one to Jenni as he moved towards the two, brand new to them, tweed chairs that dominated the outside area, with the opened bottle of wine. She recently wanted to add more than one of everything. She wanted enough for them both. The day that had scratched, horrid memory scars covered into Jenni's heart, like the roots of a tree, unseen, however there if you dig hard enough, were starting to be blown, glimpsed, exposed.

It was if she sensed he was going to ask as she started the conversation, 'So, I hear Colin said something to you.'

'Er, yeah but. Hey, I can fight my own battles. I get it you have secrets. Honestly, no idea where it came from. I was looking out for whales. Not sure, unless, I don't care why. I care about you.'

'It is time you knew…' she grasped his hand, swallowed a large mouthful of wine, filled her glass up and spoke emotionally, with a loving timbre respecting what they had then. What she has now. 'Don't judge. I have never told anyone.'

With the echoing of her words, she spoke frivolously, dismissing the true effect that it has on her in a candied jokily declaration.

That day. That gut-wrenching day. Jenni had been planning that day for months. The perfect moment. That imperfect moment. Finishing at work, on The Ex's birthday, purposefully, especially early to surprise him. What she was not ready for though was the sight she saw. On entering her home, that sight caused a bigger surprise for her, than she could ever think was by any means possible. That day. That damn day. She rushed home.

Through the dry summer heat in the rare light Sydney traffic. The blue skies turned to grey. A stillness in the air. The warm smell of a lawn being freshly cut. Then a light downpour pounds her face from her open window in soft suffocating, sleepy slaps. She quickly put her window up. The world was being cleansed. She was feeling so jubilant. She could not help but smile, beamingly to everything. She was appreciating all was around her. Nothing, but nothing could derail her positive train of thoughts. With the rain brought traffic. She was still unmoved by this negative impact on her buoyant feeling of floating on air. Longer than it should have taken, she crawled up to the east coastline of Coogee, outside their modest home. But their home nevertheless.

She knew he was at work. He was a carpenter. She was going to prepare a love-filled, wonderful dinner in their brand-new home, barely a month old. Decorate the bedroom and the dining room to make his birthday, something to remember. That, it was. It was a surprise. Not in the way that Jenni anticipated. She rushed in not worrying about any noise she made. On entry, she placed her overloading brown paper box and grey plastic bags to the side of the hallway to run upstairs to the bedroom. She wanted to change into comfortable clothes before beginning. Something she did not mind getting ruined. She heard a padding of tiny footsteps. A soft thud from the other side of the threshold that made her abruptly stop. *Burglars*, that was her first thought, so she shouted out, 'Who's there?'

Silence.

What should she do?

She shouted out again. Waited, while scanning the area for a weapon of some description. As she was about to grab the lamp off the side board, she heard her husband call back, 'Me...Darling. I'll be out...in a minute'

Eddy did not realise she was married. But this story was not about him.

'Ah. Oh,' Jenni exhaled with apparent relief. 'What are you doing here?' she placed her hand on the painted wooden doorknob and turned it. She had a smile on her lips that quickly disappeared. As the gateway opened, a view she wished was not true was unveiled. She opened the gateway to her personal hell. She had no anger within her. Just shock. Just betrayal. Just...pain. So much pain. An invisible, serrated knife had impaled her heart. An intense scorching pain deep within.

Directly in front of her. On their new bed with ruffled, used black silk sheets was a chaotic panicking scene. On the floor were discarded items of clothes. Littered out, in what only could be described as a call of passion. The Ex was leaning towards the door in a pose to keep the door from opening, that was too late. A hand in still-motion reaching for the white door. His naked body leaning towards, trying to get there before she did. The face of a boy being caught in the midst of an act. An action which was not either truthful or acceptable. Hastily doing up the buttons to blue jeans was Patrick over the other side of the bedroom, the other side of the bed.

Pat was a long-term friend of both. Pat knew everything about both their lives. Almost everything, not that Jenni was going to surprise her husband on his birthday. She was the one that ended with an immense surprise on his birthday. She was to learn in the harshest of ways that her ex and their male mate were lovers. To be cheated on was bad. To be cheated on by a mate seemed worse. A lot worse. Did the gender matter? To Jenni it did. It made that knife that impaled her heart dig in further. What did he have that she didn't? What could he give that she couldn't?

No words could be expressed by Jenni. She sank to her knees. A supressed blood-curdling scream filled with pain. Pure stinging pain coming from all reaches within her. Tears, incontrollable, heated and intense streamed down her face. Mascara ran down her cheeks. Fingers gripping by her sides into clenched balls. Fists thumping the floor. She raised her head. To the ceiling. She screamed. An excruciating, heart-breaking scream. Her neck tense. Veins in her neck pumped up. Eyes squeezed tight. Trying to stop the tears. Overpowering tears continued to flow. Shoulders jerking. Uncontrollable spasms of grief.

The Ex placed an arm around her, to comfort her. This was not welcome. Unappreciated. She pushed him away. Forcefully. She shouted out unrecognisable words. A warning. Eyes on eyes. She was hurt. He was wounded. She was distraught. He was barely injured.

Jenni choked back the fury that was building inside her to inadvertently shout out in a scream. 'WHY?' followed quickly by 'HOW?' The love had well and truly been obliterated, never to be replaced. As she quickly rose to her feet, she stumbled. Her legs would not hold her grief. She leaned forwards. Stumbled towards The Ex. He caught her from falling. She slapped his chest. She would have rather fallen then be touched by him. Slapping his bare chest while shouting out the same single-word questions, as fast as a machine gun fire. The Ex tried in vain to hold her wrists. To stop the confrontational attack. Fruitless.

Pat scanned the floor under his bare feet, not sure what to do. He was cornered. Anger was making her stronger. A combination of weakness, fatigue and the overall toll of the ordeal was leaving her arms fraying. Succumbing to soft brushes on his chest, barely moving the hairs. The Ex instantly went to grab her wrists. She pushed him away. Shouted a warning. At the wall. Like a ravished animal. Teeth exposed like a rabid animal. Foaming loathing. Speaking revulsion. Venting an extreme repugnance.

'Why?' Again, she asked before screaming the elongated word again for the umpteenth time. 'WWWWWWWWWWHHHYYYY?'

'I-I-I...' The Ex stammered, 'love...'

'Please,' Jenni interrupted, 'just don't, don't.'

'I do. I…'

'Sure. SURE?'

At this moment, Pat made the foolish act of trying to intervene. Jenni's anger was directed firmly at him. The strength had returned in a second wind of fury. 'Why are you still here?' she pointed towards the empty wide-open door with her fiery gaze fixed on a naked Pat, over the crumpled sheets she asked. 'Get THE FUCK OUT.' Thankfully, Pat left rapidly. He did not need a second invitation. He did not even pause his fleeing momentum to put on his shirt as he bolted, escaped. Happy to leave. He scooped it up as he ran out of the door muttering an apologetic sorry. A sorry that fell on Jenni's deaf ears. She was not interested in the tedious insignificant sorry.

'How?' she almost pleaded as she focused back on the ex. 'You mongrel.' Jenni continued her tirade. 'You useless piece of shit. You. Seriously? What the fuck? What the ACTUAL FUCK?'

'It happened,' stuttered the ex. 'It just happened. I never. I would never have, want, to hurt you.'

'Are you fucking serious right now?' In the last few exchanges, Jenni had cursed more than she had done since her birth. 'Get out. Leave. Fucking GO. LEAVE. LEEAAAVE!'

He tried to reason with her. This was an unproductive exercise. The grief-stricken damage had been done, the destruction was never going to be rebuilt. There was to be no happily-ever-after. The fairy-tale had quickly turned into a nightmare. In her head was a whirlwind of emotions, thoughts. Her mind just could not cope with what was swirling around. She could not think clear. She was in a vomit-inducing vortex. She did not want to speak to him. She did not want to hear him. She did not want to see him. Feel him, smell him.

With the sound of the front door closing behind the Ex, she collapsed in the bedroom once more. Into a pile of tears, anger, screams, hurting. Not knowing what to do. The whirlwind in her head was increasing with lightning strikes of pain. Her stomach was a tornado. Turning around rapidly moving empty emotions. She coughed. She threw up. She did not care that she was making a mess. She just let the dry retch happen as she laid there. Make-up mixed with the orange, grey watery spew on the timber floor. Her heart draining of love. Even her hair felt like it was standing on prickly end, trying to escape the voluminous uncontainable sensations.

The intensive unmanageable turmoil left her weak. She laid in a heap on the floor for a long time. What does she do now? Obviously, leave him. Divorce him. All the fun and games that come with that subject matter. However, what to do at this time? She cried. She could not understand what happened. She had been smashed into the blind spot at a crossroads in all four directions. Weak. She did not deserve this.

In the days that followed, she still could not understand what happened. On that day, as her heart bled out, bled out all the love it held. Drained hollow, leaving meaningless pieces of the fragmented fundamentals of a former relationship. That can, would never be rebuilt. If, a big if. If it was, it would never be as strong as it could be, ever again. Her life crumbled. She wept every night. Cried every day. In the weeks that followed she wondered if she would ever feel like the sprightly, younger Jenni ever again. She had given him her best years. What was going to become of her now? Tossed away on the garbage heap of yesterdays, old news.

Signal Colin. Colin had helped her come out of the cataclysmic explosion of her life as she knew it. Drawn her out. Made sure she did not refuse life.

Jenni's flashback of frankness brought her back to the present. Her mind, in which she was explaining the worst day of her life became clear. The dark clouds had vanished to leave the blue skies and golden sun of the present sunset. Of Eddy. Uninterruptedly reassuring her with doleful eyes. Condolence deliberate, slow strokes of comforting fingers on her holding hands in commiseration to the way The Ex had made her feel.

The one-sided conversation came about like an attacking plane out of the blue skies, unexpectedly in the content, without warning, showering machine gun fire of a tragic story.

Explaining the aftermath impact which Jenni held. Jenni had been thinking about telling Eddy the full story for a while, before. She wanted nothing more than to explain her story. The reasons for having her immense barrier around her castle, combined with a shark-infested moat. Enter at your own risk. She wanted to outline why Colin was so important to her life. To explain to why she was protective of her feelings for him. Nothing was mentioned furthermore. The subject laid to rest. They finished that bottle, then another and talked about their days.

The next day, they drove to the north shore. They just wanted to be in unfamiliar settings. They had a delicious, albeit not quite value for money breakfast at a beachfront café. They laughed and talked, then went for a beach walk towards the ferry station. Then Jenni sat down, all of a sudden, on the beach, midstride. She looked out where the surfers frolicked. Her mind transported her back to that day in the past. Many, years, before. Her worst day. She shivered. She pulled her bare knees involuntarily up to her pale blue T-shirt covered chest. For the first time since sitting down, she turned to Eddy, not the crashing waves and spoke to him.

'I will never forget that moment. The memory will last. As fresh. As raw. As very real. As painful as the day it happened. I thought we were happy. The man I wanted to have children with. The man that talked about having a family together. The man I wanted to grow old with. Heck, I had started to grow old with.'

'You're not—' Eddy thoughtlessly tried to reassure her.

'I wondered who knew,' she continued, oblivious to Eddy's interruption. 'At the time, my sisterhood of mates said that they didn't know. That, though. I felt that they did. I thought, still think that they lied. To protect. Some protection. My mates were supposed to have my back. Huh, my husband was. I was so, embarrassed. I couldn't, I didn't trust anyone. How could I again? Colin helped me open up. Eventually mates started to say that they suspected something, or they had heard a rumour, they didn't know for sure. Every single one mentioned the same fucked up excuse, for why they didn't tell me. For why they didn't choose to tell me. They said, that they didn't want to hurt me. Well, I hurt more than they would ever know for not knowing.'

They sat on the fine sands of Manly Beach. As Jenni opened her sealed treasure chest of impenetrable guarded soul and grief-stricken memories, he listened. Eddy, somewhat selfishly wondered what he would have done. To have the ability to end a marriage on hearsay is a major undertaking. For which you have to be one-hundred percent sure. You need to have all your facts correct. If he were her mate at this time, he would love to say that he would have told her, let her know. However, without being in their shoes, he truthfully really did not know what he would have done.

Were her mates worried that in telling her the rumours, would their inadvertently destroy their friendship. In hindsight it did. So what the matter? Jealousy is a funny thing. It can turn its green head in a multitude of faces. Would she blame them for constructing lies to gain her husband, lover, mate. Would she, like we all would, not want to hear it. Would she be like us all. Be thinking that, you are kidding yourself if you do not believe this, be in denial. For better or worse, right? For richer or poorer, right? In sickness? In health? Till death tear us apart, right? To be lawful?

Eddy listened and let her vent and express her harbouring emotions. This moment was very much in the eye of the storm. He did not want to disturb her thoughts into words and intrude into her all-consuming, circling memories.

'I was betrayed by my lover. By my mates. With that, my trust was destroyed. My confidence destroyed. Should I have noticed the infidelity? The betrayal, affair, the deceit that was happening under my nose? In my own house? Our bed? What signs did I miss? Why didn't I see it coming? Nights wasted crying over him.' A pause, reflecting through the looking glass. 'Every cloud and all that. The experience did make me found out…more about myself. I was once an attractive woman. In my twenties, I could have had any man. I rejected everything around me. For my love. Life. Our life. Together. That I had a life. A life that was jealously viewed by others. It…was perfect. In my thirties, I was alone. I was less marketable. A term they use…as they say at work.

'Ha! I am less attractive. Older. I had achieved a great job, home, but…there was something I could not change. I could not turn the hands of time. Could not reverse, redo, rewrite. I was not young anymore. I spent my twenties becoming independent as a couple. That does not even make sense? I…I was striving for a better salary. Getting the promotions. The pay rises that came with it, with a great man by my side. I was indestructible. I was a fool. Foolish,' she whispered the last word under her breath.

A sigh, before resuming. 'Then. In my thirties, I found I was unhappy. I achieved independence. Actual proper independence. On my own. Down to me. No-one else. I was successful in my job. I threw myself in. I was looking for a man in a dating scene that had changed. A man that was independent. Had a good job and knew what they wanted. The men that had done this, are looking at the younger age to make them feel powerful. It was all in reverse. Topsy-turvy. After a few years, I stepped into the dating scene. Confused. These things I did for myself. My money. My promotions. My house. My…divorce. Well, I did that all without my man, men. I didn't need one.

'Now, my, I have finished with my single-minded focus. I want to settle down. The men I shunned are off the market. I feel. Felt…that I would choose a man for the sake of having a man. To go to parties with. People seemed to expect that you are part of a couple at my age. You know, a plus one. My expectations are high. My dating pool is small. I had a great man that approached me in my mid-twenties. He was going to change certain aspects of his lifestyle to fit in with me. To be with me. He saw me, as a person that was…something I wanted to be. Anyway, I turned him down. Harshly. With no reason. Not even a proper conversation. I unforgivingly cut him off. Like unwanted rubbish. He was perfect. Was perfect. He was handsome but didn't meet my standards. Then. He was a little older. Only nine years. Nothing. Now. I had my ex. I did not need anyone else.

'Anyway. I am not a unique book. Everyone has a story. It is time to leave the past in the past. Time to leave the skeletons in the closet. I don't need to wear those skeletons on me and out with me. That's past. It has…for sure, shaped me. It has not. It will not, shape my future. My present…now. It will not define me. I am a lot more open. I talk more. Much more than I did in my twenties. I talk openly. I am honest with how I feel. This scares me. This scares some people. I'm not perfect. I am not seeking Mr Perfect. I am seeking someone I can be honest with. Someone I can tell everything to. I want to have fun with that person. I think I have found my Mr Perfect.'

Her hand reached out. Eddy launched his in her palm in anticipation. Then covered her hand by wrapping his around while sliding over the sand, closer to her curving, arch back. She slowly lifted her face, her eyes closed. Her nose nestled into his neck, prodding up, before pecking a compressing lingering kiss on his cheek. They cuddled. Arms over shoulder. In silence. Eddy had nothing to say. He did not want to say anything. He did not want to ruin this moment. His heart was beating fast. He was so happy for her to say those words. Her head rested, nestled into his shoulder. He kissed her head through her hair. Gripped her closer. She wrapped her other arm around him. Linking her hands around his body. Not letting go. He leaned in. He loved her.

Eddy was thinking of what had just been said. Age, once again came up. Although the roles had been reversed, in the male and female ages. She was older. Was she a little scared that he wanted a newer model, so to speak. Eddy was wondering why he was thinking about this. She had just said she wanted him. Age, as aforementioned, held no boundaries. Then, to confirm the age difference he was thinking about, a dog raced past into the surf to retrieve a tennis ball.

'Get out, Lola. You know you're not allowed in there.' The shout came from Colin. The wanted mate by Jenni. The unwanted mate by Eddy. Colin disturbed this moment. Could he not see it was a moment to leave? Perhaps he did, and this was part of his strategy. A fantasy that Colin held that they were meant to be together, not this new man on the scene. Not Eddy, but him. He was just happening to walk his brown whippet, Lola. Named to stand for, Laugh Out Loud Always, as he felt his whippets face was like a constant laughing pose. He had decided to let Lola off her leash.

All dogs must be kept on a lead in this area and he let her go. Eddy could be paranoid. But this was feasible to disturb a perfect moment. If it was strategy. Well, mission accomplished. Eddy and Jenni got up. Colin ran over and apologised as he saw the red puffy eyes of Jenni. His jubilation of seeing Jenni was instantly changed to concern. She waved away the concern and cuddled Eddy once again. The three of them talked while Lola ran around sniffing them, trailing behind with her lead back on. *Convenient!* Eddy thought. He said nothing of what he was feeling towards Colin. She had just explained that he was important to her. A mate, nothing more.

The association of Colin seemed to contradict Jenni's perception on age. Colin was fifty-eight years old. Although Jenni said, which Eddy trusted, that nothing had happened, he still harboured doubts. She was a different person around Colin. She seemed to regress into an inner child. Her voice would heighten slightly. She would develop a skip in her step. She was unconsciously excited by Colin. They had gone through a lot. Eddy was looking into this far too much, but he just could not help in feeling suspicious about Colin. He was jealous of him. Although stating nothing had happened, Eddy saw these signs as if Jenni hoped that something would happen. Colin worked as a cellarman at the pub next door to her work. He had the tradie, gift of the gab.

Not in the mood to argue, Eddy resisted the urges to insist on going to another place to have a drink. Barely past midday, Jenni wanted a quick wine to take the edge of the unlocking of her chest. As Colin lived on top of the bar, it would be perfect as they could give him and Lola a lift as well.

They walked in the small bar below to where Colin lived, The Local. Immediately when walking in you journey down a small narrow corridor the to the left for the entrance door, as if going down the side gate of a house. Colin continue walking to his unit, yet not taking the hint. He stated smugly that he would put Lola some food out, then come and join them. As mentioned, Eddy did not want to argue, he could vision this coming a mile off. The long, dimly lit bar was, as the name suggested, a local bar. People worked past it as no sign was at the front, but a small hanging awning has The Local, that is it.

Regulars liked it as you can hide in the shadows along one side of the high cushioned booths, and have private conversations below the windows. The soft natural light that emitted the slender slivers of prismed rainbows, where no-one can look in and see you. Or, you could sit at the bar in the L-shaped other side where people could peer in and see you perched on the high-stool like a bar fly. It was a very busy broad walked tourist sector, with nothing on the cracks of the window. So, unless people were particularly persistent, they would have to stoop, refocus and get very close to the glass window pane, cup their hands to see clearly if anyone was in. No-one did.

Colin felt the need to involve Eddy into his life. He did not always work here. He operated, successfully, his own business in the pub trade, decided to take a step back. He sold his mini cellar-keeping empire a few years ago. In truth, he could retire and live on the money he had earnt. He successfully failed in that option. He could talk his way out of a round room without doors.

A charm that would literally make women swoon and men hold a disgruntled grunge of awe, with a touch of respect. It was not his appearance. He was not in the Hollywood idols category of attractive older actors such as Richard Gere, but he was ruggedly handsome. His unshaven growth around his face, his unruly grey hair that would glide into his eyes, and his crooked smile with his missing tooth capped with a gold filling. He style would have made a great pirate. His personality was a rock star. His dress was a resurgence of an aspiring younger self. The afternoon was uncomfortable.

By the end of the week, they had formed a great union. On Friday, Eddy was on his way to see Jenni after his work, when his mobile went to alert him of a message. A simple, but nice not overcomplicated message from Jenni said she was going to be busy seeing mates, but would see him back at home later. Annoyed but not anticipating no consequences, he called his long-suffering mate Davo. A life-long mate from school; although they did not see each other often, they remained the bestest of friends.

Davo was with Steve, another school-mate, and literally around the corner catching up. Although the place could not have been worse, he thought while there he could persuade them to move on. Eddy nervously crept into The Local, where Davo and Steve vigorous in the throes of conversation loudly called him over to the booth where a clean, undrunk schooner of golden liquid sat. He quickly scrutinised. No Colin, phew, maybe he could relax.

Davo worked in finance with Westpac Banking for which the financial district was close by. Whereas Steve was a magnificent useful jack of all trades. Anything involving drills, mechanics, carpentry, renovating, plumbing he could do it, he was a master at all. He happened to be working at a construction site close by. He chose this as it was literally where he could park his Ute to pick-up the next day without a ticket.

Fun times, he missed these mates and catching up after so long was like nothing had changed. They literally could pick-up where they left off and resume at the full stop. It was here that the ill-fated turn of events unfolded.

Out of the corner of his eye, Eddy spotted her first, then him. Jenni came into the bar, arms locked around Colin's arms. The green-eyed monster of jealousy reared its sinister head. She still not had clocked him as she perched on the far corner of the main bar. Looking unpretentiously cute, more on her tip-toes then the leaning tall bar stool on its two front, skinny legs. On her right, Colin leaned further forward to order the drinks, saw Eddy, said nothing. His mood heightened with this show of nonchalance.

Eddy tried not to let it change his evening. This proved futile in approach. He spoke too loudly to compensate. Roared with laughter, waved his arms and hands around animatedly. Even though he did not speak to his mates, they knew of his time in Europe, and of Jenni. They had only met her once, they approved. He did not need them, or anyone for that matter to approve, but, it was noted in his archives. He looked up, Colin gave a sly smile.

Eddy wanted to knock that smile off his smarmy face. He withdrew himself from the conversation. He kept an eye on them in an unbroken gaze. Seething, growing more incensed. The flames of rage that were boiling his blood, were brought to a gentle simmer as Jenni did seem to be holding Colin, correctly in his view, at arm's length, as they talked. Colin, obviously, still had not mentioned he had seen Eddy, as no look was exchanged. It was as if he was playing a cruel, unjustified prank on him. Thus far she did not fix a determined gaze at Colin. Her touch, non-existent.

It was after a few minutes that Eddy's fury was starting to boil over. He needed to calm down, to get some perspective. Eddy had been holding, the barely touched schooner of Fat Yak in the air when he placed it coolly down. He took a quick glance to Jenni as he slammed his hands on the round, black table that sent a vibration to stop Davo and Steve's drunken witticism. Announcing to them that he was leaving, going around the corner to The Wellington. He marched through the door. It was then that Jenni saw him. He carried on a soulless mission out to the always busy streets of Sydney.

He had not seen her notice him. He was hurt. He could not believe that she did not even acknowledge him. Hypocrisy in his approach. She did not give him any time of the day. He strode up the street as Jenni belatedly followed. She shouted. He was lost in his own fire-burning thoughts. Losing him at Nurse's Walk. She returned back to the bar, flustered. Trying to get it out of his mates who were getting their coats. They were patriotically loyal to Eddy. He was annoyed beyond words to why she lied. Why did he not say she was seeing Colin? Why lie, unless you have something to lie about, or something you are ashamed about.

Within minutes of him ordering a drink. Eddy got back up to finish the round, just as his mates strode past the stained-glass window. Truth be told, he actually heard their boisterous banter before seeing their silhouettes. They joked, but in true mateship they were genuinely, obviously concerned for him. Asking if he was ok. Eddy was worried. Once again, he blamed himself. He was disturbed that his suspicious, jealous actions that took control of him, actually affected his future, his relationship with Jenni.

'Did I make a scene?' Eddy sulked with an uneasy probing question. As they took a seat at the small round table, with their drinks in the very quiet, almost deserted bar.

'No. But Jenni was just getting up when you walked off. We think to say hello, but you just carried on walking away from her, well out. She chased you. Came back. Asked. Then Colin asked something. They argued. They seemed to be upset. I think. I think that you are right. They are seeing each other. Well. Jenni is seeing both of you.' They both competed in the passages of news.

'Knew it. I fucking knew it. I should have made a scene.'

'No. Look Ed. Chill. It is out in the open. Jenni has to decide. That was clear mate. Colin, basically walked off. He gave her the ultimatum. He knows now what you suspected. See what she wants. She was on her own as we left. It may not be. It, she may not be cheating. Not in the conventional sense.'

'Conventional?'

Eddy was seeing his mates in the shoes of Jenni's. Trying to make sense of this riddled cryptic, nonsensical drivel that they drunkenly, inundated him with. Surely, she would not cheat on him. Not after what she had been through. Surely not. Was he in denial? Especially recently. Especially. Eddy's mood was not lifted by his mate's rally of support. Eddy did not stay out long. He went first, it is pretty amazing how someone can sober up when they have had a shock. They offered to come, he waved them off. Goodbyes made, they went their own ways that evening.

Eddy strolled the streets in thoughts of wondering whether to call or text Jenni. Checking his phone numerous times, hoping. Hoping that a text came through from Jenni, that would elevate his mood. He did not know what it would say. He imagined a line, a word and many other things many times without actually coming to a conclusion, just a blankness, to what would come through that would make him happy. He got home. She was not there. Where was she? He tried to go to sleep.

Later on, while he was up staring at the darkness. He had not made it to bed, did not even try. He was inactive in his grotesquely collapsing state on the sofa. Head resting on the back cushion. Neck bent at an angle, back contorted like an accordion, legs splayed-out clumsily. He was as uncomfortable as he looked. He was still in motion. His mind active in movement. Over-thinking when the soft light of his mobile lit up with a name flashing on the screen for four seconds, Jenni. It was Jenni. Relieved. He opened it to the message.

'We need to talk. Can I see you tomorrow?' The mandatory 'x' was not at the end.

'Come home. Where are you staying? X', Eddy was as quick with his response. The short passage of time that encircled around him like a frosty cloak of undesirable time. Procrastination was nothing more than a thief of time. Yet, he should have been the first too reach out. The first to speak out. He hoped she was crashing at her mum's, a mate's, anywhere but Colin's.

'I'm safe. Goodnight.'

Quick in the answer pleased him, thawing out the coat on his back. Sending shivers of the unknown down his spine in tingling chimes of the sound of change. With whom the bell tolls, time always, always marches on. The past in its wake. The future in its slumber. Untrodden to awaken to a path undiscovered, masked in mystery.

No kiss symbol made him worry. He was afraid. A stream of short, regular messages followed. Where Jenni maintained that she was ok, but did not say where she was staying. Where they both did not apologise. Where they both did not acknowledge the scared, incontrovertible sentence that wanted to be conveyed. Over a rapid connection they concluded that she would be around in the morning, seven. Tilting his head to the top of the mobile, he saw the time. It was already morning, seven was barely four hours away. Safe in the knowledge of her well-being he succumbed to the weariness of his tired mind.

That night, well, morning was the longest transit from rise to sleep and return. He had the answer. He knew it. Why delay the inevitable? The unescapable pull of fate was happening in front of Eddy, but he could not impede what was to be the unavoidable. Bringing the end of a love that could have been more. The wind was blowing the chapter shut, the more he struggled, the move the wind blew. He was not hungry, but had an emptiness inside. He could not drink, but was thirsty for the appraisal. He was warm, but coldness occupied him.

Since six in the morning, he had been ready. Watching every passing car, dog being walked, bird soaring, doors being slammed shut, hearing engines being started as he anticipated Jenni's arrival. Glued, as the rays of the sun shone through, removing shadows, he watched from the small top floor window unit that viewed out, over the street, the entrance. Towards the train and bus station where she would have walked and the only parking for non-permit holders with the street reserved for residents.

Ghosting a trace of a recognisable figure tops the small crest. A deranged figure staggered into view just before seven. He inspected it closely. A brief study saw that it was Jenni. Wearing loose fitting, dreary grey slacks she was looking at her shuffling feet as she slowly unwillingly moved forward, like a person going to the hangman's noose. The weight was visible on her shoulders. Heaving undetectable links of guilt, remorse, regret. The anguish scarred in wrinkled lines across her formally-soft face. Vague expressing. She scarcely held herself pulling her legs under the strained intensely cumbersome manacles of emotions, of questions, of wonderment. Wrestling with the indiscernible non-existent chains. Generally doubting what to do, or merely wondering how to say something that was making her head heavy, her heart empty, her soul cold.

The front porch hid the door itself. Jenni must have been plucking the confidence of her discouraging sensations. She was shaking with dauntless fear. Seconds hung in the air. Eddy knew it was coming, but the low drone of the buzzer still made him jump. Without saying a word Eddy buzzed her in. His front door was already ajar. He heard the ugly metal fire door shut, followed by the echo of steps in the tinny lobby as he went to the kitchen. Jenni shouted a timid hello as Eddy finished making two cups of black coffee in her disgustingly mustard yellow mugs.

He waited on the kitchen side of the island as he placed another cup opposite. He saw she had taken her runners off as she tip-toed silently into the open space. They hugged. An awkward hug which was all arms and face, their bodies positioned in an archway. This was the first time that he looked into her eyes. Immediately he saw the water brimming on the edge of her eye lids, tears ready to fall. Eddy knew. He felt the lever pull as he hung above an empty chasm. He knew his fate. Their fate.

Jenni did not sit down. Purposefully pacing slowly in the small area between kitchen and living, death and life. Giving fleeting glances towards Eddy, rarely giving eye contact as she explained herself. Well, tried to. It was obvious to him that she had been struggling to think of the way to explain, but in her execution came the words and sentences in an avalanche of disjointed meanings. Continuously, layering excuse, after feeble excuse, in no sensible order. Clumsily laid on top of one another in fragile disarray. Eddy saw. He knew what she was saying.

Jenni loved them both, but had chosen Colin, the older man. Again, Eddy was confused with the chasm of age. A subject in which she would pick up and put down. Maybe she was trying to put Eddy off. Shake him off her invigorating scent. By making allowances for, to why they should not be an item. She was steering the way free for her and Colin. She stated that she was just about to say hello to him in the bar last night when he stormed out. Did it matter now? She kept repeating herself in-between the layers of an 'Almost Love'.

Eddy was hurt that she had chosen Colin over him. What did he have that he did not? What could he give that he could not? She had come so far in Eddy. Being the first person that she had told of the break-up, for which was not part of the unforgettable episode that she tried to bury from many years ago. Did she feel love for Colin, or dependence? Love? Jenni said that she was not in a relationship with Colin. Eddy felt in a different way.

This relationship triangle, where Eddy was at the bottom point and the flat, equal sides above him were of Colin and Jenni. On the same level, on the same page. Colin was there for Jenni with the cape of goodwill when Jenni's World collapsed. With a force inside that Mother Nature could not even muster in all her fury. Maybe, Eddy thought as Jenni continued to ramble, it was partial due to the fact that Colin's marriage collapsed around him. With that, they shared their journey on mutual ground. They understood where each person was coming from. It was this good intention of a helping reassuring companion that a relationship could materialise from. Eventually blossom.

Colin being twenty-four years Jenni's senior did not cause the same level of conflict that Eddy's and Jenni's eleven-year age gap experienced. A strong current of jealously burned a green fire within Eddy. Why was Colin still holding the cape of goodwill after all these years unless… It all became clear. He was waiting for this moment. It was under Eddy's nose that they seemingly got together. It was ironic that his presence actually made their connection stronger. Colin was always around. Not always present, but in some form he was nearby.

Colin was safe. A safe bet. Colin was a homebody that was going nowhere fast. This burning resentful flames within Eddy was always going to be there. He was infuriated by the seldom-voiced blazes but sometimes his actions, his body language spoke in violence that he tried in vain to silence. He could not stop becoming a hellish inferno.

Jenni left. There was no hug. No last kiss. Eddy stood in the same spot that he had when she arrived. Coffees cold, untouched. He was confused if Colin and Jenni were a couple. It was very much immaterial now. He let her walk out of the door. He did nothing to keep Jenni loving him and tried everything to gain the love. The truth was the she wanted the friendship of Colin, not Eddy. Eddy wondered after she left if he should have fought. Fought harder. Was he a fool to not fight for her? To shout out to her, that he was the better catch. The better man. The better choice.

But like a wounded animal, Eddy let her go. Without a sound, not even a mere whimper. Not even a measly whisper. A whimsical ideal of enigmatic proportions followed. The hope more the realism that she would walk back in, floated into his head, like a dream. Thus, to instantly dissipate in the lingering smell of her perfume. A giggled ideologic formication at the absurdly high levels of preposterous proportions. Say, she had made the wrong choice. That she wanted him as much as he wanted her.

He did not lose his mind when he let her walk out of the door, as he did not mind. He lost his mind, when he let her go. He replayed the scene and Eddy saw what he could have said, should off said and would have said now. Now, as often as it is. It is too little too late. His mind was lost without a thought. After everything that had happened. The vast story that she had talked about. Although she says, she said, she did not cheat on Eddy. She felt more for Colin. Abandoned at the moment, now, that he needed a thought, he had lost his voice. No hesitation that she could leave. He gave up the 'almost love' without a fight.

The high-pitched double beep of his mobile retracts him swiftly from the past. Beth-Annie. He speedily scanned it, then rang her. He knew should have her mobile on her as she just sent the message. It went to voicemail. He was not surprised but rejected.

Everyone has stories. Different people have the ability to evoke different stories out of people. Some people share, some people share without sharing who they are. Beth-Annie choose strange times to share. She gave it out on small breadcrumbs, a trail to her haven. Eddy guesses it is a combination of factors that make people share. A code that is different for everyone, that does not need all the factors. But, age, respectfulness, rivalry, the want, the will play their part. The number one, above everything else in his point of view, is the reason.

Reasons to let people in to see someone's weaknesses. To let the drawbridge down, to allow someone to cross into a person's fortress should be simple. It is far from it. It is not easy to let someone in. When you do. When that someone hurts the someone that they had let in. It hurts so much more. So, they not only draw the bridge up, they build a stronger wall, place electrifying sharks with lasers on their heads as an additional defence. A hidden key to the lock that is concealed with a special person to unlock each dead bolt, padlock and chained latch.

This was not a sharing message. More a message to say she needed time, more time, she was going away with her family to a Pacific Island. She gave no other details. Eddy was on the verge of acting irrationally. On impulse. He respected her message with a simple message to enjoy herself. He threw the mobile away, far down the countertop table. The trouble with acting spontaneously is that foolish passages in text messages can be misconstrued in unfounded ridiculous voices. Thus, he put his mobile out of harms reach. He did not want to ruin something that was built, but crumbling around him. The one-sided communication where the strings are pulled by Beth-Annie was driving him mad. He could not contain his thoughts.

Time for work.

Ten Years Ago
Commitment

It took two years for him to rebuild himself. The cracks on his character and ego had to be strengthened before he could paint over them. He shunned physical contact. This time, he did not go down the path of drinks or drugs, but work and exercise.

After all these years, Eddy had returned to the adrenalin rush of a kitchen. He wanted a change from the butcher's shop. He had been trained as a butcher, he loved it. This forever remained as his first passion and something that he will return to. The desire would be more important than money, it outweighed all the pros. However, returning to cooking within a brigade of chefs, cooking to order was a task that he found extremely hard to resist. It gave him more hours, tough long hours, which he craved. He had done it in the past, but fleeted in and out of the kitchen battlefield.

Ironically, the hours were his undoing. He always wanted to regain his touch and familiarity in the kitchen. The order, the fast pace, the passion of the hot plate, the fury of the servers at the battle of the pass against the fury of the chefs. It was intense, it was hot, it was exciting. Eddy felt a healthy surge of adrenalin with each service. He felt great to look back at the end. When a hectic service had finished. The last plate of food having left the kitchen. The serene calming breeze of composure would welcomingly return to the minds, eyes and hearts of the staff that had been working on pure passion with a strong hint of caffeine.

The chefs would take a deserved breather with a plastic bottle of cool water, which would immediately drip in condensation as it came from the cold walk-in fridge, into the humid heat of the kitchen equipment, the pass, that is simply called the line. Some would hold it to their brow to cool them down. Sweat cascading and shimmering on their face and neck. The redness in their cheeks and face. Eyes still wide open, laced with weary exhaustion. Chef whites dotted with colours. Fresh burns on the hands, that they were only discovering now. Small cuts around their fingers. Fingernails covered in food debris that stained their fingers with sight and smell.

The satisfaction that in the hectic two hours, everything went well. The happiness that everyone was satisfied with their choice, their food. The chaotic speed, heat and noise had ended. The clean-up, clear down, ordering and day would be ended in an hour. Kitchen staff would spread out, to regroup in barely seven hours' time. Where the Groundhog Day would repeat. Slightly different but with the same ending. The hours of preparation would be for the final push. To do it all over again in the morning with fresh produce.

It was a fantastic rewarding passion of creating something out of nothing. Being proud of what he was sending to the customers that he really enjoyed the kitchen. Each time he goes back, he wonders why he leaves. It is an unexplainable rush. He feels personally disappointed when a compliant comes in. These are rare but do happen. He feels guilty that he had upset someone's experience. Maybe they were here for business, a birthday, an anniversary, a first date and he had just ruined the occasion by overcooking a dish.

For example, a couple of days ago he and his team served a fish dish. The skin on Red Emperor Snapper was cooked but the weight he presented on the skin was rushed. The Snapper fillet rested on a fragrant and light saffron and pumpkin risotto drizzled with a light lime and coconut dressing on a soft herb salad. He was rushing. Eddy does not use that as an excuse but a mere fact. He did not give the proper time to evenly press the skin to make it equally crispy. He had all the tools. Everything. He had great chefs at his disposal. He had great working equipment. Phenomenal produce.

All the preparation of the dish was done. He had messed it up on the final hurdle. The cooking. At the time, he rectified the mistake to make the customers happy, but at the end, he would pick the bones out of it. After doing eighty top-end fine dining meals well, this single one, well, it was to make the others irrelevant. He learned from it and would not do the same mistake again. He should never have done the mistake to start with. No food should ever leave the kitchen that is below the high standard that he prides in himself on.

In this battlefield of hospitality, where some things were not always hospitable, was where a rebirth of love blossomed out of the flames. In the fire, the heat and the passion of doing something well came a seed of fancy that went unnoticed for a long, long time. Eddy had shared a laugh with the manager of Empire, the place he worked. She had an unapproachable aura about her that resembled an ice queen, for which other employers nicknamed her the Ice Bitch. This rare laugh that bellowed from her was completely out of character, but he did not expect any other moments that she would let her guard down.

He definitely did not see her as anything more than his boss. He did not see her as a potential mate and did not realise he was actually flirting with her. Actually, courting her. Maybe it was because he used words like 'potential mate' and 'courting'. He did not think that an independent and strong driven lady would think anything more than him. In Eddy's eyes, he thought she was just a human being with a number on the weekly payroll. This came to a different conclusion one evening.

Over a glass, maybe one too many glasses of deep red, full-bodied Malbec, his preferred choice; they shared a long drawn-out kiss. They were alone. They were finishing off their own jobs. Eddy doing the ordering and checking the ticket machine. Checking the stocks. Checking, that everything was clean, organised and ready for the next day. She was counting the tills, checking everything was away, locked, clean and also ready for the next day. All the staff had gone, they were alone. She was starting a day off tomorrow so was scribbling down a handover for Jake, her assistant manager. She had sent an elaborate email but always liked a handwritten note to give him the most important job that needed to be done first.

They sat at the end of the long metal bar. Away from the peering view of the city in the shadows, they themselves sat in the shadows of the restaurant. Seating in the dark corner of the waiting-to-be-seated area. He had set aside his mobile down after placing the last order on his notepad of notes, scribbles and ideas. Normally, he would sit here alone. In silence, going through the day, rechecking and thinking if he had forgotten anything for the next day. On this occasion, the manager sat down next to him with an empty wine glass. From the open bottle, she poured him a glass of the deep cherry-red wine. No one could see them in the gloom, unless they got close to the window and cupped their hands. They could see the odd lights of a car, a bus pass. Lights and shadows would dance off the cream painted walls. They talked about service. It was all so innocent.

Her parents named her Carroll, from the popular penname of the author Lewis Carroll who wrote the classic *Alice's Adventures in Wonderland*. Her mother was an English teacher who loved reading all types of books. Her father, a math teacher who shared a passion for numbers. Who loved equations and algebra with the same level of desire that her wife had for the written word.

Hence, Carroll got Euclid as her middle name. A Greek mathematician from the 4th century known as the Father of Geometry. Her parents taught at the same school where they met, fell in love and married. Eddy overheard her friends call her Caz or Cazzie depending on the levels of alcohol consumed, with the emphasis on the 'ie' that tailed off like a woman being pushed off a bungee ledge, without the cord. Eddy called her Boss. After all, that was who she was to him. Well, until this moment, after this everything changed. This momentary lapse in order. A lapse in the hierarchy that existed between a head chef and a general manager.

Now, he was ready to listen. In order for self-advancement, he must open his ears to hear the tantalising breeze of affection. To listen to the want comes first. Louder, the sound of love draws closer to Eddy, like a harness of horses looming closer. Increasing in sound and feeling that a stampede is imminent. Despite the fact that Eddy is scared to open fully again. The unrestrictive ties that bind a love are not something that can be tied down. Non-seductive as the will is. The will itself is just a frail borderline to waver towards empathy, towards hostility. To put behind, free himself of broken dreams, to forsake the past hurt for good.

If there, in reality, was such a thing to believe in. Caz was not Eddy's normal type. She was slightly taller than him, only by a few centimetres, but in high heels this was more apparent than he really liked. Not that he felt intimidated, on the contrary it was her. She felt invigorated by the difference which made her a little too self-assured, for which he found particularly unappealing. She had a straight, little chubby figure from eating on the run, drinking every night and generally having a poor diet due to the demands of running a busy restaurant in the city.

She was always immaculately dressed. Smelled remarkable, not too overpowering. Spoke to everyone with a strong, powerful authority voice that was polite, genteel enough to command respect. Likewise, with this level of respect she in turn received the best work out of all employees. She was a firm, but fair boss. Basically, if you worked hard you were rewarded. If you were lazy, you were shown the same door that you walked in through. She was born intelligent and well educated. She was known as being as cold as ice, hence her nickname, Ice Bitch.

Outside of work, her dominating presence came down and she was relaxed and not as highly strung. This was never seen by the staff. Her personal life was just that, hers. She elected to live in this misleading world.

Amazingly enough, in her work persona she was organised, in her personal she was worlds apart. To Eddy's frustration, she seemed to make the smallest problem an ordeal outside of work. Instead of rationalising to methodically streamline a problem, she seemed to go around the house before finding the front door. Not always, but often the case outside of work. In work, nothing more than a gun. She would shoot the problem down effectively neutralising any challenging threat.

Another thing that frustrated Eddy was when she would say to friends and family how hard a task was. It would be highlighted to draw attention to the laborious chore. As if she was justifying the trials that her job faced, for which she wrongly assumed the staff had no idea that she dealt with these problems, on a daily, every single second of the day, basis. For which they thought her job was 'easy', just one of the remarks she heard alone when people thought she could not hear. Something that could have been as 'easy' as asking for an additional day off.

The staff did not realise that the assigned staff were for a reason, to bring a balance to the day, the roles that they can or cannot do, the roster coaster, to be beneficial to events, owners and staff. Everyone has his, or her cross to bear. Sure, Eddy was no different. He too was not flawless. Yet he did not sweat over these little 'easy' flaws, he would purely brush them off and accommodate.

Carroll had been alone for a long time. So, obsessed in driving her career that she forgot, that she needed someone out of her work. She did not know just how much she needed the feel of compassion before Eddy came along. She dived headfirst into work, hardly ever coming up for air. She lived, she breathed work. Without consciously knowing, she actually was swimming head down, without taking the time to look up from the waves of paperwork, graphs and spreadsheets to what was the devilish other side of her demanding role. Another side, outside of work. For what the people were coming to Barfinda for. Fun. Laughter. Happiness. To live life. She had lost that insight before Eddy. It was perhaps for this reason that the kiss started a relationship faster than an unforeseen bushfire. She forgot, deferentially, to love.

They moved on with the relationship faster than an Olympic sprinter. Through the stages she marched, through them as she had with work, impetuous and headstrong. The normal things that everyone goes through with a conversation, they did without a pause for breath. She treated the relationship a lot like her job. All passion but sometimes a little too controlled. She went in impulsively, strong, clear and focused on getting to the final chapter. What that final chapter actually was, Eddy did not know. He actually believes that Caz could not even tell him, even with a gun pressing hard against her head.

Within two months, they had moved in together. She lived down the road from work, which when Eddy found out did not entirely surprise him. 'The closer the better,' she retorted at his flirtatious comment. The easier to prop up the working weight on her shoulders if she wanted time off and needed to go running, walking, some fresh air…to get out. He sub-leased his unit for the last few weeks of its tenure to move in sooner.

A short five-minute walk down the road was all it took to get from their place to the place they worked. Conveniently, the unit was located opposite his favourite watering hole. This was how he knew about the vacancy. The relationship felt right. Although the workforce condoned it.

During the tourist period of January, Barfinda closed its doors. There main trade was the corporate business, around in the office blocks that towered above the small, cosy beautifully decorated restaurant. It was more an eating and drinking establishment for the suits, rather than the camera totting, selfie stick-brandishing travellers. The cliental that would not be back to work until the middle of January. It was also much more profitable to give people a three-week holiday here than try to accommodate another two-week period during the year.

This actually was a huge draw for many employees as they were also closed Christmas Day, and for most kitchen staff they did not work on the evening of Christmas Eve, so could go away to see family and friends. It worked out so well. Therefore, after New Year's Eve and into New Year's Day, Barfinda closed until the twentieth of January. It was perfect.

So, Eddy and Caz decided to go away. They spent Christmas with the family and felt the New Year was going to be the perfect start. They decided to go to The Gambia in the west of Africa. Mainly because airlines were doing cheap deals. And also, they wanted to go somewhere different. Somewhere, just away from it all. Honestly, it was somewhere that Eddy wanted to go, rather than Caz. He had always been fascinated by Africa and wanted to see and always wanted to explore the country.

They decided a bit close to the button to finalise that the trip was happening. They got the vaccinations, tickets, and information within that week. Even with the busy period at work and this being decided a mere month before travelling, they managed to fit it all in. It was Caz, who thought that it could not happen. This was the first time that Eddy had experienced the negative side of Caz. Frustrating was not the word. It was definitely not a turn on. Therefore, he did all the arrangements. He took it in his stride. Got it done. Ticked all the boxes by taking the weighty burden off her.

So, on the second of January, they arrived at the airport, boarded and started the long flight to West Africa. A tiny country that Caz had never heard of. The whole way it seemed she moaned, no, she did moan that Bali would have been cheaper, shorter, would have been better. Eddy was determined to make her enjoy this. Concealing his plan that hopefully this trip would make such an impact that he could do his dream holiday of an African safari travelling from the south to the north, one day.

On arriving in West Africa, they felt so drowsy, so tired. They crossed an invisible threshold from the cool, air-controlled cabin of the plane to the dusty heat of the orange sand of Africa. On disembarking the plane by the thin, child-sized metal stairs, the warm, humid heat grabbed them and dragged them down. They were feebly ushered alone by smiling light grey wearing airport staff like cattle to do the formalities that they really did not want to do while they had been couped up in the metal capsule. Wanting nothing more than to shake-off the itchy feet.

Although tired, they were not ready for sleep, they just wanted to get out and explore. The formalities were very quick and painless. The security was effortless, which was great as they did not really want to argue with a machine gun toting official. That, like the other Gambians, had a permanent smile on their face. This visual picture was as disturbing as it was encouraging. Encouraging that they take security seriously but, disturbing as the accompanying huge teeth-baring grin. Was this meant to be welcoming or, did the guards enjoy the power that they had at the insignificant twitch of his index finger being bloody significant. Once again, they did not want to question their own questions. Yep, the holiday started well.

A mere fifteen minutes' drive from the capital Banjul, they were at Kololi Beach and their hotel. They got off the air-conditioned minibus into a strong peanut smell of poor visibility. The temperature was stuffy, uncomfortable. Standing still they sweated, waiting to be given the keys to their room. Later, by the helpfulness of a young-looking cleaner, they found out that the fine sand that was shielding their views was down to a sandstorm in the Sahara Desert that had spread over Senegal into Gambia. As cool as this was, this momentarily upset the balance of the air quality.

This did not spoil Eddy and Cazzie's first taste of Africa, literally, as they breathed in the sandy, warm grains of the desert. They unpacked and made themselves a hotel room home, away from home. They showered and chilled by the pool while Eddy enthusiastically read up on the history, culture and origins of the smallest country in Africa from his smallest travel book. Swinging in the shade between two large elephant-skinned tree trucks, Caz lay, rocking into sleep on the rope hammock.

Her closed eyes shielded by dark sunglasses, wearing a thin excuse for a red bikini. Fabric of which was no larger than a T-bag, with slender taut strings precariously keeping them from revealing her modesty. She was ragdoll relaxed, as she swayed so gently. The sun was giving her rays of sunshine, but she was the main body that was radiating an intense penetrating feel of heat within Eddy. He kept looking up while stating a fact, but words melted off his tongue with the captivating sight of Caz. That bikini was made to measure. It was a lazy afternoon that if his life paused here, he would not complain.

Later in the evening, they had a traditional recommended dish in the local restaurant. The name alone interested Eddy; Caz, on the other hand, was dubious.

'I'm sorry, what?' Eddy exclaimed as much as he questioned the server's recommendation.

'Chewi Kong,' the repeated response from the smiling server who tapped at the menu with a bony twig-like finger.

'Sounds like a cross between Star Wars and King Kong. Let's have it.'

'It's a popular Gambia dish. Fish of cat.'

'Sold!' Eddy put his hand up to stop a further upsell and ordered 'one to share with rice please'.

Caz just stared at him. Not so much a stare, but a scathing glare. 'That better be fish,' she snarled, 'cat-fish. And nice.'

Eddy waved off her warning to stretch in his straw-coloured wicker chair. Scanning around as he leaned back to people watch over the muffled chatter, clinking of metal on china, glass on glass, and scrapings of spiny shiny metal legs on the large pale brown tiles inside the nest of close-confined tables. He was in a perfect position looking out from the edges. It was pretty dark in the low-hanging covered restaurant with small candles struggling to stay ignited in the soft breeze. They wanted outside, and so did everyone else, so all the tables were taken.

They sat partially inside on the border of the two, the best they could get at this greatest operating period. Her disapproving scowl with the flickering of the candlelight made the snarl more animated and real. Reminiscent to when an evil Disney character comes on the screen, just without the brooding music. The open-air part of the restaurant was scattered with white tables and chairs with simple wooden ornaments that held all the candles. The bar, an island in the centre was busy with an assortment of red pandas nestled on the bar stools. The sunburnt faces with the sunglass wearing eye patches were amusing.

Many servers came along with pieces of paper to leave with loaded large black trays with an array of colours in the assortment of glasses and bottles. All dressed in elegant formal \ wear of black polished shoes that returned the coloured lights, black perfectly ironed trousers, pale green impeccably ironed short-sleeved shirts and a black waistcoat of 'KBB', the unfortunate acronym for Kololi Beach Bar.

The warm salty breeze was pleasant through from the nearby ocean that danced with the linen awning. The air quality had improved a little. With the sunset came the noise of the surrounding wildlife. As the light descended the high-pitched rhythms were ear-piercingly loud. They did not understand at first why the glass in their hotel room was so thick, now it was obvious.

Back at the table, gracefully planted in the centre was a black and brown patterned bowl of Chewi Kong, garnished with green and an assortment of nuts to break up the dark brown sauce tinged with a red hue coating the large chucks of fish flesh. The steam produced a beautiful exotic smell of nuts, herbs and many spices. An even larger bowl of heaped white rice was put next to them that could feed twenty, let alone two. Caz had not relaxed a little as Eddy pleaded with her to try the unknown.

If she did, thus disliked it, they would order something else. He was very much the adventurous eater. The differences that two people receive in the same environment or setting can be so diverse. Eddy thought of the saying, *Beauty is in the eye of the beholder*, this was so true. Where Eddy appreciated the sounds of the penetrating wildlife and the unknown paper rustling leaves of the shadows in the tall green trees. Where Eddy found the feel of the humidity and heat nothing to worried about. Where Eddy relished in the smell of the peanuts and log-burning smoke. Where Eddy found these exotic and exciting.

54*Caz saw contrasting. Caz found them upsetting and completely out of the realms of which she could control. Eddy did take a little bit of a guilty pleasure in feeling her discomfort. Although she was taller at this point, he felt he was the dominating victor towering above her. Both out of their comfort zone. One thriving, other failing.

A dripping small spoon of the smallest found piece of fish hung in the air as she wordlessly dared herself to place it in her mouth. As her mouth opened, her eyes squeezed shut. Immediately to open with a relishing chew and smooth swallow. Success. Caz liked it, she found it tasty. In anticipation Eddy spooned some rice on her plate, letting her to do her own Chewi Kong. Eddy liked it, although was expecting something different, a curry-type thing, he concluded in his head. This did not dampen his pleasure of the grainy sauce and the butter melting fish. It was a delicious form of a fish stew, heavy on the garlic and the tomatoes with cabbage, herbs and light aromatic spices with a smoky flavour. An identifying produce, many chucks of something like potato but, a little too bitter for potato. Eddy had to know. In a spoon he displayed the rustically diced chuck to ask a server who replied, 'cassava' in a trailing voice, before he quickly ran off on his heels without stopping his stride, without waiting for another part of the question. Leaving Caz and Eddy in bewildering silence.

After retiring early to bed they consequently woke earlier, to some extent due to the difference in time zone as well. Caz was not sure about stepping out into the brave new world, but Eddy was only too eager. He yearned to discover. They agreed to stay in close proximately to the resort. They learned, well Eddy learned in being too quizzical for his own good that peanuts were the main trade, for which this solely was what The Gambian economy was heavily reliant on. They did trade in other goods such as oils, palm wood and hides. Caz raised suspicious glances that were left unexpressed so not to cause unsolicited effects, of the hides not only done humanely, but also legally. They wandered the area down from the resort which was called The Strip. In the light of day, they could see that the noise of squeals, rustling of trees and light-hearted vocal mischievousness came from the surrounding Bijilo Forest. Today, it was pretty quiet in daylight, under the cover of darkness they must feel protected as the noise ascends as they breed a new confidence for the monkeys to be heard.

Down the strip, everyone is trying to sell something. They wonder, like in Australia that some 'authentic' Aboriginal art is not what it says it is, that it is the same here. A lone man sketches in the shade as he kneels over a small piece of paper in the raptures of creativity for which a modest crowd has gathered. On string and clothe pegs his magnificence is displayed above his bowing frenzied form. He is truly a talent. From what they can see no-one buys anything, but seeing him passionately strike with a combination of chalk, charcoal, his fingers and thumbs to produce the greatness of what he sees around him in the hectic strip, someone surely will. From dusty baskets local try to sell what they have grown. Sweetness fills the air as the bellowing sun can be seen today with the sandstorm having passed. The time flew.

Back at the hotel before nightfall they did not hear the insects and the monkeys until they opened the front door. Caz instantaneously jumps back in as she yelps, to uncontrollably giggle, clutching her stomach as one scuttles along the railing outside the door, up above so quickly, so fast, a blur unexpected that left the nail din of the tiled roof above, as it would seem a troop escaped their unthreatening threat. They ate in the restaurant hotel as they had made an unknown promise to one of the many resort's workforce. As they left the resort as planned to go to another restaurant, they had seen today, the same worker remembered.

As they went to walk out, he appeared in different attire. Gone were the cleaning clothes of the gardener, arrived were the smart elegance of a ceremoniously designed uniform in the form of The Gambian's culture to announce, 'best table, tis waiting as promised'. How could they resist that smile, that virtue from such a young man. Immediately, they changed plans, there would be other nights.

They decided to sit at the ship-shaped bar first while they looked at the menu. Part of the plan that if they were not interested, they hoped that they could casually glide out undetected. The bar was not particularly busy, yet their order, which was the same, seemed to take a while to show up. Caz had noticed that her wristwatch was not changed so glanced at the porthole wall clock to change it to GMT. Their conversation was fluent, relaxed as the two cocktails got placed in front of them with elaborate decorations of fruit, tiny umbrellas and colour.

The large bartender laughed lethargically as he noticed Caz's delicate fingers turn the tiny silver dial backwards to the time. He even spoke slowly in a low timbre as he remarked, 'GMT hey…Gambian Maybe Time.' Now they got it. As he turned as fast as the Titanic to serve another customer, they thought quickly that indeed everything did seem to be done at a leisurely pace. With the recommendation of the barman they ordered the food to have where they sat.

Eddy could see a strong contested conversation between the young man that brought them in, and the rotund older looking barman as he carried their order to the kitchen. He mentioned it to Caz who leaned around the column of the worlds every spirit bottle on the mirrored ship hull created pyramid to the wooden naval artefacts at the top out of arms reach. She denounced him for ordering here as she returned out of sight of the dispute. Anger entered her voice with the strong possibility that she was correct that they probably worked on commission. From the animated annoyance in the smaller man, the indifference of the barman.

He should be frustrated that it had been stolen from under his nose. He was offended by her accusation that he intended to do this. After all she was sitting next to him when they asked for advice and ordered. All the while, she had said nothing. After a brief debate themselves about was Eddy in the wrong, really? Did Caz do anything to stop the outcome? No, the answer to both, no. Eddy promised he would tip him as they walked out.

After a now expected really long duration, the food was plonked down on the bar by the skinny man. *Bang goes his tip!* Eddy thought to himself. Droplets splattered over the folded white napkins from the mess in the bowl, narrowly missing their clothes. The smell was very peanut-influenced. Unfortunately, not Eddy's favourite. He was not allergic or anything to peanuts, in fact he quite liked the taste, but hated the texture, detested the smell.

In the pristine white bowl with tide marks around the side was a muddy brown thin liquid with red oil pockets. Brown-green vegetables stuck out, maybe trying to escape. It took a while for the ripples of the circulating tide to slow down in the oval bowl. They looked sceptically at the presentation, which was very ordinary.

'Domoda,' the barman drooled. ''Tis the best food 'ere in The Gambia.'

'What is it?' Eddy was taken aback by his trembling, nervous voice.

'Fish of cat, peanut. Stew.'

His voice had a thin whistle to each s due to a missing tooth in the centre of his mouth. He continued to polish what seemed to be the same glass that he was doing when they walked in. In the centre was a perfectly compact, classic nineteen-seventies style rice timbale. It was packed so heavily that Eddy stabbed it to break it up, only to retrieve the whole timbale on the end of his prongs like rice impaled ice-lolly, rice cream.

They both played with their food with their spoons before trying any. Abundant chunks of fish cut by a blind woodsman made him wonder the price difference from here, compared with outside when it does look very similar to the night before. Eddy smiled at the anticipation as he was the first to go.

Caz turned her nose up, screwed her face up at the pending revolution that she was sure she was going to savour when her tastebuds kicked in. Crimson grease shone the empty spoon when Eddy removed it his pursed lips. Caz turned her nose up at the thought. Eddy tried another mouthful of the greasy sauce with a larger chunk of catfish.

'Delicious,' he proclaimed with a smile that spread around his face in surprise.

'Reckon?' Caz gravely asked with suspicion.

'Too right. Remember, I can't stand peanuts. The smell leaves a lot to be desired but flavour…mwah. Remember the plane. Holy shit, Caz. When they brought those bags of peanuts. The cabin. Shit, it was my nightmare,' Eddy said around another mouthful as he ladled the stew into his smeared not-so-clean bowl in front of him. 'Give it a burl,' he enthused.

To Cazzie's astonishment, she was shocked to discover that this unpleasant and poorly presented dish was actually brilliant. She enthused Eddy to find out what was in it, so they could replicate it back in Sydney. He asked for a recipe but got a list of ingredients that he had no idea what they were. Maybe they were called something else here. Maybe they were throwing him off the scent. Maybe they wanted it to stay in Gambia.

Nevertheless, it was terrific, they could not stop eating the Domoda. They finished the meal that was for one person, but they shared it and they were stuffed full. After a long day of discovery walking, it was perfect. A successful encounter in the taste of Africa so far as they were ready for bed. To the sounds of the African forest, the crash of the Atlantic Ocean, the squeaking bugs and the high-pitched noise of mosquitos they fell asleep, like darlings in each other's embrace.

Caz still did not feel comfortable in leaving the hotel on the second day. Eddy could not believe it but did not want to press the issue. She had foolishly read the tourist advisory sites which stated the doom and gloom. Then taking them entirely to heed. This negativity was the second time Eddy had seen it from Caz. Once again it was not an arousing moment. Although on this occasion Eddy had a new sense of why she was so negative. He attributed it for her being cautions, hence he did not force the issue when she voiced the thought.

On the plane, she gave a revelation which made Eddy understand. Like looking at a dusty mirror where you can make out the face, but it is distorted. To wipe it clean and suddenly everything becomes clear. The wiping of the dusty mirror was her revealing the face, her secret. Amazingly enough, it was her first time out of Australia. Eddy thought everyone had ventured out of the country, as he, and everyone he knew, was so well travelled. Still, at the age of twenty-nine, this was Caz's first time out of Australia.

Hence, due to this, Eddy left Caz to laze around the resort as he went out on his own to explore. He held a guilty secret of his own close to his chest, that he actually preferred this. He could be as reckless as he wanted and not have to worry about anyone else but himself. He abandoned all caution when he was alone. He would walk down dark alleys. He would talk to people on the street, off the street. He would take food from strangers and try it. He would smell the new exotic aromas of a new continent. He would live life.

He exited by the rear of the hotel along the wooden boardwalk towards the strong, forceful ocean. Today the visibility was so much better, back to normal. Last night's wind had blown all the last grains of sand out of the air. From the back door onto the beach a beggar or bumster, as they are called here was the first person he sees. A bumster is a person who realises the freshness of you, sees you have just arrived. He asks you all the questions under the African sun to obtain a level of trust. Where are you staying? Do you want skins (drugs)? Basically, he just wants your money. By whatever means.

Basically, he is a male prostitute, come tour guide, come rogue. They are not threatening, rude or aggressive. They are, however, very persistent. Being Australian, it is hard to see the true beggars from the professionals. So, to see these genuine beggars and the hospitality behind it, Eddy finds it very unique. He is not a fool though. He will not be sucked in. He will not needlessly part with his hard-earned money. After five minutes where the first bumster tries to sell everything from the sand to the sky, he leaves as he sees another potential victim, someone that might actually give him money. Cue another bumster.

This cycle continues the whole stretch of the golden shores. Eddy does not need a big neon sign with an aura proclaiming that he has just arrived. He is noticeable fresh on holiday as he is taking photographs of everything. His eyes are looking everywhere. One of the bumsters catches him off guard. Eddy is not rude, he will talk to them all. This one asks more personal questions. It is here that he sees a different layer of Gambia that is right under his nose. For this bumster asks if he has a girlfriend that he would like to sell. So blasé, so offhand.

While waiting for a response, he breaks it down in a stage production of what essentially is sex tourism. This insight made him really look around him. Eddy intensified his observation. Around him he sees older white pasty women, with wrinkling rolls of fat overhanging tight shorts and skirts with tops that are supporting with grimacing straps, straining the buttons and seam stretching connections the unhealthy lifestyle that has caught up with them at a rhino's pace. The person locked next to them are very different. On their pale, flappy arms, that is illuminated by their white denture cleaned false teeth, is a young, athletic shirtless Gambian boy, barely in his twenties smiling. Peering into his eyes, Eddy sees his soul of sadness. His skinny legs are supported by designer black Armani casual shoes and a pair of long beige Armani denim shorts, which, Eddy is presuming, are the real deal.

After the speech by the bumster, who had become nothing more than white noise, he sees that the old white women have come here for love. The young Gambians, on the other hand, are looking for money. They will marry into money to get it. A prostitute, no other word for it. That signals that not only sex really does sell. But it is accelerating with a pace faster than a young Gambian who has sniffed out, like a trained bloodhound an old, divorced or widowed woman getting off a flight from outside Africa and is wanting to mislead her into thinking his love is for her. Not her money.

Eddy returns to the beach scene. He has continued to leave footprints in the sand behind him as the bumster explained, as he really saw. He is again polite with his brush off, but queries how much would be in it for him. What followed was a gobbledygook attempt at duping him. He laughed as he walked off none the wiser. But with no intention of carrying out the façade.

Eddy launches himself into discovering the new sights, smells and tastes of Africa. He has walked to the city of Banjul. The beach is behind him, the sun casting reaching shadows towards his new destination, beyond the undulating sand dunes he scurries like an insect up, down and over. The small riverbank is left behind with its large and small boats bobbing on the light winking waves, the clinking of the metal poles that hold the sails ripple in the gentle warm breeze, that compete with the energetic frenzy of the scavenging birds.

Walking up the final steep sandy bank of loose grains he stops to look back, lets himself slowly slide back down. This feels like he is going the wrong way on an escalator with the pull of the sand bringing him down to nearly where he started. In due course he swaps one picturesque scene for an equally good one. This one is so different. The noise intensifies as he gets closer.

Nature is submerged into human hullabaloo. People are friendly bantering over a stall. The smell of fish. The smell of dust. The colours. Eddy's senses are bombarded as he gets on the merry-go-round which is the Royal Albert Market. He walks the confusing narrow, cramped labyrinth of passageways between ramshackle, rickety stalls with rusty poles that slide on the grains of dust, heavy-looking colourful tarpaulin that lean into each other keep them anchored on hope and a pray.

He is cautious as the Jenga-cum-domino multihued arrangement is teetering on the strong possibility of an imminent collapse. No-one seems worried at the impending doom. No-one but him. People shout out as he slowly passes, he jumps in surprise. They are talking to mates, or colleagues over at the other stall, sharing a laugh, a joke, a story. Mateship is on display here with the general necessity to survive, combined with the fact that they grew up here, like their father before, they great grandfather before him.

Generations as deep as the roots of the tallest tree that are embedded in an undeclared, but endeared level of mutual respect, tradition, bound in an unbreakable circle of trust and companionship. Eddy loves it. He sees it in their faces. The sensitive touch that they give each other on a conclusion of a story. The sharing of prized merchandise to one another. This is human kind.

Observing what he is seeing, he aims to absorb everything around him in an inhaling deep breath of the feel. To inhale the rich smells as he closes his eyes in the middle of the rushing stream of people. Oblivious to the world he is in, in the attempt to connect to it fully. Taking the small nudges, knocks and apologises he remains rooted to the spot, swaying with the accidental connections. He slowly opens his eyes. Happy. People must think his cheese has slid of his cracker. A glitter of water in his eyes. He brings his camera up. Pauses, midway. He puts his camera down to see through the eyes of his inner child. No camera could captivate what is really on show.

Eddy finds it astonishing that he appreciates the offering that they are taking for granted. As being established by their culture, for which he is unreasonably on the brink of tears. A feeling rushes over him that nearly causes him to lose control. A wave of warmth, of feeling connected to this magnificent harmonic pandemonium. He finds the unity so delightful. He slowly exhales through a pin hole of pursed dry lips. 'Incredible,' he softly gushes involuntarily out of his mind into the thick, soup-like dusty air of The real Gambia.

After a few wrong turns to a destination uncharted, Eddy notices the logic in the disarray of stalls, passageways, the disarray. It is apparent that the stalls are split into three sections. Eddy had started in the chef's dream. The fresh produce on display is a salivating treat for all senses. Fruit and veg, fish and meat and new commodities that he has not seen before. On a wooden board that is resting on the legs of a young man is a goat, that is getting crudely butchered, for a better word.

With each hack, the board alarmingly moves. Undeterred, he hacks again. Eddy thinks this is an accident waiting to happen, could it be any more dangerous. As the thought dashed through his alarming mind, a spurt of blood swells, pulsates out in a throbbing arc. Fortunately, from the goat rather than the young man. The machete-esque knife hack seems to have caught a blood vessel, instead of cutting through the bone, the knife had bruised and subsequently burst the pocket causing the gory fountain to display. Blood drops off the board onto his bare legs and he does not flinch, the glimmer of the blood-stained steel is high in the air to be launched back down onto the goat. The market is not for the squeamish. Thankfully, Caz is not here.

He walks back and forth from one stall, like a young boy trying to buy condoms but does not want to ask the obvious. Eventually, he plucks up the courage to ask what the strange looking things are. He starts with the dried flowers on a food stall. 'Err…excuse me. Er…what are these, are for?' he frustratingly stumbles out his rehearsed question. He is told after the old lady pushes herself up with the help off her knees to rock forward to see what he is pointing at. She smiles, explains. The colourful hibiscus flowers are used to make wonjo juice.

Eddy is none the wiser but will look it up at a later date. He did not want to ask any more questions as the aging lady said it with such a confident manner that everyone knew what it was, or everyone should know what it was. For him to own up to his naivety, would make him look a fool. More fool him. As who is more foolish? The one who asks when in doubt or, the one that does nothing?

On a ramshackle wooden structure that resemble scaffold-like tables are at the fringes of the market, where urban gravel meets natural sandy grains. Perfectly lined up fish that is smoking in the sun spreading steaming streaks of aroma. Vegetables, meat and fruit are generating so many people but, surprisingly not many flies, they are focused on the offcuts, spoilage at the edges of the sand.

Coming up from the sandy beach is a steady flow of fishermen leaving a trail like turtles coming to lay eggs. Freshly caught vigorous fish that is still clinging to life, even though they are circling the drain, they flip and flop in the blue plastic buckets dragging behind them with hardly no water but a strong will to survive. Greeting them at the top are the rewards for their endeavours, food. Roasted peanuts are being placed into plastic bags, that steam a sweet-smelling haze in the opening. Readymade food to buy is prepared over charcoal and wood fires. It is amazing and something that Eddy will passionately express when he sees Caz later.

The description will include everything down to the shrill high-pitched clucking of the skinny chickens in the tiny wire cages ready to be sold, to the dirty dusty jars of mysteriously variegated juices. The main stallholders are jolly women in colourful loose-fitting fabric with matching hats. They are smiling, helpful and trying to sell. Although they do not get up from their small wooden flimsy stool that barely holds one cheek, let alone their entire body. However, the stool does the job that it has been doing for generations. Eddy turns the corner and comes out of the Chef's Dream, plummeting deeply down into the Tourist Nightmare.

On the stalls are tacky, tourist souvenirs at exuberant prices. Clothes are hanging, barely moving with the packed state of the hangers. The white freshness of tourists are everywhere. The red pandas of too much sun the day before are walking bundles of money to the lurking smiling traders. The money that flows from their hands to the now considerable beaming Gambians are a testament that tourists are idiots. Buying a 'unique' piece of a wooden carved figure. This 'unique', this 'one of a kind' carving just happens to be one of thousands made the same, by the same factory, to similar markets across the African continent.

This has, and will never be Eddy's picture-perfect attraction. He retreats from these sections as fast as the emerging unbalanced scooter heading his way. On his departure, he pulls his blue thong-wearing foot away just in time, as it would have been crushed by the oncoming threat. His reflexive withdrawal of his white sock-tanned foot nearly knocked him off balance by the three boys that whizzed past on the red blur of a scooter.

The noisy piercing shrilling moan from the engine on balding tyres somehow, not only negotiates the limited passage space for the thin tyres, but also the intermingling head space for the hanging items on sale as they race through effortlessly without hitting anyone, or anything, leaving a trail of dust in their wake. That thin swirl is the only indication that they had just past.

Back in the chaotic and busy dream, he walks around a different route and ends up at the last section, a dollar store if you will. Here are the plastic buckets, bottles, gourds, and tins that are old and new and used for the produce market. Fake clothes and shoes for the people that want to look like a million bucks, without having a million bucks. He smirks at the clothes stall with second-hand bras as he speculates if there is a second-hand pants one, though he did not look. He walks again through the magical fresh produce section and gets lost in his hunger to create a new menu. Hoping to source these ingredients with this enchanting inspiration when he returns to Sydney with these motivating burning desire to design something different. He gets lost in the grocery maze and does not care.

190

When he comes out for air, he realises he has no idea where he is. He asks for directions from a young man, who asks for money. Unsurprisingly, he is going to give money to him so he can get back to the resort. What startles him is the guy who laughs out loud with a smack on his shoulder, a wave away of the notes that enter Eddy's hands. A cruel joke as that the man does not want money, he just toys with him.

Eddy chuckles at this new development that not everything is about money, smacks his new-found friend's shoulder and walks in the direction that he points towards. He follows for a few metres, saying that he knows a man that can drive him. Eddy was wrong, so far wrong. Here came the sell that he expected. He offered to walk with Eddy as it is getting dark, to be his bodyguard. He is a young boy of seven, maybe six and has arms that will break in a strong breeze.

Undeterred, he tries a pitch for everything. He will do anything it will seem. Eddy is polite, this falls on deaf ears, so he then, just falls into silence. Ignoring his unwelcoming walking companion, who eventually sees that nothing is going to be coming out of his pockets. He walks back to the wall in which Eddy found him, lazily trailing a stick in the dust.

Eddy has strolled and taken photographs while embracing his solitude. It is not quite dark but late afternoon, when he arrived through the glass front doors of the resort to be shaken by the artic breeze that bellows out. He heads straight to the outside pool area as he makes the presumption that is where she would be. She was not there. He was unconcerned by this development. Scanning the area, he lingered on the bar. He should be the chivalrous boyfriend and go to the room to see if she is there. The temptation is too much. He orders a cold beer as he doubts his decision. But, where else would she be? This self-asking question caused a negative spiral that rose in him. Spurred on by anger that was pushing the negativity up, heightening his irritating itch of wrath.

Eddy was frustrated that Caz was missing so much of today, the trip. Initially, he relished being alone, but that disappeared as he saw many awe-inspiring sights that he wished he could have shared with her. Essentially, she was doing what she could do back in Australia. This was her first trip outside, and she stayed cooped up in the resort. This baffled Eddy.

The first sip of the ice-cold beer, the smile from the petite bar-lady that could hardly see over the bar let alone grab one of the bottles off the hull, he was vacant, submerging his thoughts. He was telling himself to toughen up, that everyone has a choice, their own free will. At the end of the day on the plane she explained her motives and also, more importantly, it was Caz's life. Watching the sun dance in the reflection of the large centred turquoise pool he saw a sparkle of pink and tan shimmer across. He rose his head as the negative, pessimistic thoughts instantly evaporated. Caz was here in the pool.

His pensive frown turning into a lucid-living dream. His heart galloped as he gulped a large mouthful of beer. He smiled, he did the most liberated unorthodox wave with limp wrists that he was straight away embarrassed by doing. Her face preformed a winning, endearing smile over the gently ripples of water. Everyone noticed her exceptional exquisiteness. It was plain for Eddy to see why. They can watch, stare, ogle from their poolside blue and white heavily cushioned wooden loungers but he was the only one that will take her to a hotel room, a bed.

Sporting a micro pink bikini that did made the women jealous and the men swoon, she dived elegantly in. Barely a splash as she gracefully entered. Swam underwater in a clear shimmering curtain of water. Eddy was enticed, beer forgotten. He moved towards the edge of the pool. Although as aforementioned, she was not Eddy's normal type, this does not take anything away that Caz is drop-dead gorgeous. Eddy came to the edge of the pool as she launched herself out. The waters grudgingly leaving her as she shined in the basking sun to throw her arms around him. He cared not that she was wet and embraced her in his arms.

'I missed you,' she whispered alluringly in a hushed smooth tone as she nibbled his earlobe.

'Tomorrow. To…morr…row,' he was like a schoolboy again, stuttering and nervous. 'Tomorrow we will be together.'

'Yes,' she gushed.

'You…You're so, so very beautiful.'

He knows that he is a lucky man. He had plucked a blue complimentary towel up as he walked towards the edge but had dropped it in his rhapsody. He slowly knelt down close to her body, featherlike stroking her skin to the towel without taken his eyes of her curves. He draped it around her body. *I need a drink*, he thinks as he is ready to explode below, he needs time to recharge.

With two glasses of vodka and lime, minus the ice-cubes, they head to her book on the far-edge of the pool. Her suggestion as she read to avoid the ice cubes in drinks. At this moment, she could have anything she wanted. She is still dripping in water as she dries herself. She is a true image of a pure beauty. Her long brown hair clings enviously to her large chest as she shakes the last of the drips off and flings her hair over her head in a whip of sexual arousal. If she was trying to look sexy, she well and truly accomplished it.

He watched her while mumbling about his day in a futile exercise in trying to deny the throbbing in his shorts. Yet, he could not. She could not only equal the stimulating sex appeal of the big screen sirens but surpass. Ursula Andress from the 1962 James Bond film *Dr No* has nothing, then later Halle Berry in a similar scene when she portrayed Giacinta 'Jinx' Johnson in the 2002 James Bond film *Die Another Day* were not even a close second and third. Eddy gets up and aids her, she does not need help but wants to feel her touch, her body warmth.

Caz acknowledged that she knew this with a sly smile. She welcomed it, smoothly thrusting herself towards his hands. She obviously wanted it too. She giggled, teased. They both flirted as the day was forgotten with this erotic stirring display that they did as if no-one was watching. So. Why was he so angry before?

The afternoon was lazily spent back and forth from their room to the pool bar. Always together, stuck like stamp to a letter. Giggling, in the glossy, easy going untroubled ease. They were looking deeply into each other's eyes, the slightest of contact with the pulsating electric marvel of two souls connecting. Cuddling like love-struck teenagers. The red orb of the sun is warm and hot, but not scorching. They did not notice. For them both, work is hectic. It seems that life just gets in the way.

Many people are back in Sydney, here in Banjul, even in this hotel. They are rediscovering each other just as Eddy and Caz were. This was perfect. A way to unwind. To learn new things. Somethings that get misplaced in the chaotic work, rest, sleep life-cycle for which they both are very much part off. Work becomes an existence, with play a second-hand emotion.

Come evening, they head to the in-house restaurant. Once again, they see the same server come running from behind the bar. On Caz's insistence, yesterday Eddy did find the young man to thank him. They left in his labour-ravished tough hands what they felt was a modest tip. Which they found out was a great deal. This was even more surprising to the young Gambian server as from previous experience, Australians do not normally tip.

He announces, enthusiastically bellows out the evening's specials with all the gusto of a car salesman. As enticing and tempting that they sounded, Caz wanted to be out of the resort. They let him down easy by saying that they were going to go for a walk. Undeterred, he waves his hand in a welcoming gesture as he motions them towards the entrance of the restaurant. He entices, he tempts to stay with everything in his arsenal but when someone's mind is made up; to change it takes a special gift of the gab. Unfortunately, on this occasion, he is not up to that level of persuasion. They take their newfound reigniting of entrancingly enchanted love for each other outside the walls of the resort. The first time for Caz.

The lights, minimalistic folly is left behind them in a swoosh of the glass sliding automatic doors. Out on the dusty Strip neon lights, music of a street party is applauding Caz on her first footsteps into a strange new world. Grasping her hand Eddy knows this is a giant leap for her so he simply ventures across the road to a busy restaurant. Eddy has ensured her that she will be safe in his arms. They are easily influenced by the music of the African drum, for which Eddy dances to as he walks over to Caz's embarrassment. The loud music comes from just four players in thick, heavy brown and beige suits. They must be hot as they energetically play, dance and sing.

One on a series of different size and shape drums which he plays with every part of his hands in a blur of precision. Another on a string instrument, which is a guitar but not a guitar, who also is harmonising with a trumpet player that makes the instrument sing, echoing a young Louis Armstrong. The singer plays to the crowd, he meanders around the candle-lit white linen tables as if he owns the place.

The singer is a fantastic showman. He coaxes in a gentle probe to persuade the hesitant tourists to dance, sing and join in. He has a magnificent soulful voice with a timber that contradicts his youthful appearance. They get escorted to a table as water is poured. Menus handed which are at once discarded for the moment as they hold hands in the centre of the table as if they had just met, no words spoken, no words needed.

The server was very insistent. Friendly and courteous yet obviously trying to work the tables to get more tips. After the third time, it was deemed by Eddy that they should order. He beckoned the man over, when he saw a slight limp in his gait. As a chef he thought in the service point of view to not have the soup. On his arrival, he seemed happier, if that was at all possible to give his trained speech.

He informs them perfectly floating his gaze in an imaginative game of tennis between Caz and Eddy, that as a collaboration the main chefs go down to the market together. Get the best ingredients, then decide the menu to cook. For this reason, he forewarns that some dishes are currently limited, with others completely run out. He apologises in true British-style. Being well over-the-top with a hint of being melodramatic. It has been a long time since they gave The Gambia the independence, yet some roots remain.

On the flipside, the server concludes that all the food is guaranteed to be 'one-hundred and one percent fresh', 'unique today' and 'especially for 'hem''. For Eddy, this was the icing on the cake. The day was perfect. It could not get any better if he designed it to its fullest. He ordered the set-menu with a nod of agreement from Caz which was the fresh produce. Fortunately, everything that they selected in the offering was still available.

Respectfully tardy, the entrée arrives on a black terracotta plate. A fresh, crisp salad that holds its own for how fresh the leaves are with a julienne of assorted vegetables topped with a small whole smoked fish. They both were curious to what the fish was. Eddy had seen many fish on wooden racks drying under the sun like a giant's staircase with a carpet of fish patterns. It smelt great then and he wanted to taste it. He asks, to get told Bonga.

He looks at Caz in a told-you-so manner as if verifying that he heard the name correctly earlier in the day. They laugh and share a stupid private joke involving hash-ups of the name such as Bonkers Bonga Fish. He is really enjoying himself. She is too. They are so happy. She laughs, as he is zealous to the point of fervently describing the market in the city. This was a side of Eddy that Caz had not seen for long, too long this passion has been missing. He was inspired again. He had found his heart for cooking and embraced its outpouring of why he started cooking in the first place. His heart has a voice again. His hands his tools.

He dances a bit more as he has all this energy that he does not know what to do with it, or how to release it. Cazzie's laughter adds melody to the music, to his dancing. He had not heard her laugh as much as she was doing now, while being away from work. He did not see just how much the pressures of work was burying her from being her. From being the person, he had falling in love with. Having said this Caz has more self-respect, thus does not partake in the dancing. Perhaps seeing Eddy embarrass himself was just enough embarrassment for her to take.

The vibrant main course arrives in colour and aroma. Even before tasting the dish this combination made the meal lovely. They choose the same dish as yesterday to compare. Today was fish dish on the menu as everything seemed to have a version of it. Domoda was a more golden colour of the setting of the sun with the peanuts a little more coarser. Larger pieces of white tender meaty fish were bound with the peanut sauce where red capsicums, zucchini, okra and a spinach-type vegetable laid. The fish melted in their mouth as the peanut sauce savoured around their tastebuds.

This perfectly collaborated dish was slightly better than the resorts offering as it had not as many peanuts which, for Eddy whom did not relish the texture or smell, felt blessed. Caz teases him that maybe his perception, in her eyes absurd averseness to peanuts, has finally changed. The rice shattered like glass with the slightest knock of his fork. Proving to Eddy that the most basic cooking techniques can be overlooked to destroy a dish. Nothing here was at fault.

Caz remarked that it was the best Satay that she had tasted for which Eddy held his tongue between his teeth. It was better to have blood in his mouth than the ground. It was a completely different type of sauce in Eddy's opinion that he chose not to share at this moment, even if he did take it as a personal attack on the chefs in the kitchen's behalf. Within seconds, the wave of the unspoken chef's protection act had left his boiling veins and the entertaining endorphins had returned in abundance. Caz saved the conflict by announcing louder than she wanted to how scrumptious this was between each mouthful. The teasing colours, smells and taste wanted you to take another spoon full before you had finished chewing the last, let alone started to swallow.

The atmosphere in the restaurant was incredibly animated by the smiling staff, band, dancers and the people at the tables. It was not even subdued when all of a sudden, the whole area was plunged into the deepest darkness. The lights went off with the music as if a black canvas had just been laid over Kololi Beach. The music carried on, but no speakers made the sound a little tinny. The candles came out in a rehearsed synchronised staff routine of displaying, lighting and illuminating the room within seconds.

The whole restaurant is told individually by their servers that the country experiences random electric and water failures for which they do have a generator, but may take a few minutes to kick in. True to form, as the server finishes explaining what was happening, the clunking sound from above and behind the scenes followed by the flickering of the lights coming on around the room and on the display refrigerators, followed by the clicking sound of the machinery shuttering into life again. Not sure if this was the generator or the actual power grid but really, did it matter?

With the settling of the meal still resting on their stomach, the dessert came out. The mere sight of the heaped, tall layered martini glasses filled Caz and Eddy with a bloating feeling of dread. 'Chakery,' the server smiled as he gently placed the glass down as if it was made of snowflakes. They stuck their spoon into the white creamy couscous porridge textured dessert with various colours of fruit comprising the layers.

It was refrigerator cold and bland but with the sweetness from the fresh fruit a refreshingly light complement to the meal, suited perfectly as the ending. Rather tart more than overly sweet, this was the fitting end. They amazed themselves that they both finished the very substantial meal completely. It was a wonder how much they ate, but they sipped the wine as they gazed into each other's eyes while talking, not even contemplating moving. A final glass of wine over the free-flowing conversation was the perfect end to a perfect meal on a perfect day. If they could suspend this day and repeat it would be lush, yet, life does not work that way. They waddled back to the hotel over the road to finalise the perfect conclusion of the day.

The next morning in the shower, still in the exhilarating embrace of basking in yesterday's pristine day. Just as Caz was finishing putting the shampoo through her long hair, the water stopped. Followed immediately by the electricity. She stood there in the pitch dark with the sound of dripping water. Afraid to open her eyes as the soap was running down her face. Getting cold, she could hear the loud erupting laughter of an unsympathetic Eddy from the doorway of the bedroom to the bathroom.

'You are not helping!' Caz yells from her unhappy wet cubicle.

'I'm not trying,' Eddy replied through unmasked laughter.

'Helping or hurting?'

Eddy just laughed more. Then with a clink of the metal pipes, the water came through. Caz yelped as the water was stone cold. Eddy laughed even more. In no time, the water was heated and Caz had finished. She smacked a still softly giggling Eddy as she exited the bathroom for Eddy to go in next while remarking, 'Can't wait for it to happen to you!' She was annoyed that Eddy's shower was uninterrupted as she dried herself hoping, wishing and praying for a stop. Welcome to The Gambia.

They took breakfast by the pool. They were both dressed, ready for the day. Sipping a black rich coffee for which he cradled into his hands as he gazed into the orange fiery ball as it slowly, lazily made its way skyward to observe everything with its basking warmth. He had just finished trying to persuade Caz to leave with him. She was so eager yesterday, so ready. Yet, she was going to stray the strip on her own later in the morning. He was annoyed that he was going to share, what he knew was going to be another great experience, on his own. He finished his coffee and pecked her lingeringly on the cheek. For a split second, he was convinced that she would change her mind. She did not.

He left through the doors of the resort and instead of turning left down the strip, he turned right towards the unknown. One minute he was walking on tarmac, to dirt, to stone, to sand, to dusty uneven trails. Eddy relished in these new surroundings, seeing the stark differences between living and life. The social structure was different. Everyone was smiling. Poverty was here, like everywhere in the world, but everyone worked hard with a grin to build themselves or other people out of it. The poverty was shared, what one person had more off was shared with another. Poverty was right in Eddy's face, but no-one seemed to starve. No-one seemed poor. Everyone was supporting each other ready to lend a hand, a corn, a lift.

'Crime, low. No crime here.' A beaming bumster tells him.

Eddy had come to label all strangers her as bumsters. This guy was different, he did not try to sell anything, he pointed things out such as the fruit in the tree.

'Do you all speak English?' Eddy contemplated loudly without meaning.

'Yes.' Eddy's embarrassment at the crassness of his tactless question was brushed aside by his recently acquired walking tour guide. 'Yes, English is spoke but us. We speak Mandinka and Wolof though when with parents. Funny story. Here only one set of traffic lights. Drink.' He passed him an ice-cold dripping water bottle from a roadside seller as he passed the money over without hesitation. 'One set for The Gambia of traffic lights—'

'CAZ,' Eddy yelled, interrupting the bumster. 'Sorry,' he implored, 'my girlfriend.'

Caz turned in a swirl of white, which in hindsight was not the best for the dusty road. The connection was instantaneous, an electric spark pulled them together in a rush, as she flew to him, he flew to her. They embraced closely as if they had not seen each other for days rather than a few hours. It was not even midday. He passed the water bottle over to Caz to sip as he gave a very brief introduction to the bumster before saying his goodbyes. Hand in hand they walked back to the resort with Eddy enthused by her confidence. He honestly did not believe that she would venture out the doors, especially on her own, but, here she was.

'Remarkably enough, when The Gambia got independence from Great Britain in 1965, they tore all the traffic lights down, but one. Only one set is in all of the country,' he giggled, replaying the information to Caz that he had just learnt.

'Wine? Let's have a glass of wine.'

She ordered with more of an order to Eddy to have one than a question. They did not sit down, but stood as Eddy continued to infuse his new-found knowledge onto Caz. 'Tearing them all down? Imagine? Well, someone must have had this great idea. Great, great as in great fuck up. Ha Ha.'

They strolled to the end, the beach side of the resort. Where a wooden door told them no glasses beyond this point, this was public property so leave valuables in your safe, was another sign. A stern looking security guard stood with a large machine gun, shades and blue-grey uniform. He was hands-down the most miserable Gambian they had seen. In the open, unshaded gateway wearing the trousers and shirt in the shade of a grey nurse shark with a shine coming from the sweat he could not hold on this scorching hot day he stood, ready. On a table of sorts, they left they empty glasses as he opened the door for Caz. It might have been the wardrobe to Narnia as she stood rooted in her space. Unsure whether to continue.

'It is only out to Kololi Beach,' Eddy softly coaxed her to moving.

She walked onto the sand from the paving stones and let the fine sand pour over her sandals onto her toes. She gingerly stepped on the hot sand like a cat on a hot tin roof. The sun had warmed the grains to boiling point. Together they waded into the Atlantic Ocean to cool themselves. They paddled in, splashing warm waves of the ocean. The Atlantic had reclaimed a lot of the coastline by huge erosion. Squinting down to the ends of the beach The Gambia is trying to reclaim their shores back by a fleet of operating diggers, trucks in sparkling yellow shining lights of orange twinkles that the sun has shed from its body.

They could be walking happily, knee deep, to suddenly step down into a hole, submerged and fighting to get back. Falling many feet below, where the beach ledge is still being claimed. Fighting up from the waves before flinging his body out into the air, in the hope that he was still in The Gambia and not in Brazil in nothing but his Speedos. Even this skirting danger was invigorating. They frolicked in the strong waters. Even in the waves with Caz, a bumster, on hearing their jovial squeals, comes splashing in juggling an array of ice, water, ice-pops to authentic Rolex watches, buy one get one free no less, in his arms.

This did not aid Caz's uneasy feeling of the place outside of the dungeon concrete safe-haven of the resort. Eddy ignored the intrusion but watched the bumsters hands around Caz. Just one touch and a shattering of abuse would be volleyed at his undesirable contact and bothersome intrusion. He did not push for long as he saw no opportunities with Eddy glaring a non-vocal warning. They stayed out for the day between the beach and the waves. No-one bothered them as if the original bumster had been prewarned of Eddy's hostility.

Another morning, this Friday, Eddy wanted to go the long way up the coast. He had planned it over dinner the night before, Caz was not interested. He wanted to start before the vengeful heat of the sun was at its peak. He left the sleeping angel of Caz, who stirred a mumbled goodbye between a clenched smiles and closed eyelids. The moon was still leaving as he waked knee-deep along the coast towards Bakau, a fair distance away. The coastline is stunning. It is unspoilt, no one wants to build here with the risk of the ocean taking it away, thus the odd colourful tin scattering of small, rustic huts with fisherman or traders inside are isolated under the tall trees.

As he gets closer the ocean is left for the welcoming shelter of the fringe lining tall, bushy green vegetation of the sand-hugging trees with huge leaves casting a welcoming shadow over him, protecting him from the blazing heat. Rustles of squawking bird life as in front of him the yelling off fishermen's cambering into paint-peeling long boats in a mass parade of the fisherman out to sea compete in the best noise. He takes photographs from his secret location, unseen, to get the most natural of shots.

Behind his back. Through the lush, deep unkempt flora is another aspect of Gambian life. A few steps away is the bustling, noisy, pollutant environment of Bakau. One side are the fisherman in organised, routine and high-levels of trusting teamwork to bring the fish, from the sea to the shore, to be smoked or to be sold. The other, the fend for yourself city of the self-regarding commotion of the hustle and bustle that is a city. On comparison they all served a purpose, but the fisherman seemed to enjoy their work as they played, laughed and bantered with friendly exchanges.

Eddy reluctantly left this paradise of the beach to the hell of the city. He shuffled through a cramped craft market that was directly in front of the beach. The heat outside was hot, the heat with everyone in one place in these close quarters was smelly as well as unpleasantly uncomfortable. On hearing swearing he snapped his head around to where the disturbance was coming from. He saw the vibrating red tonsils of a man screaming. To dart his vision down to the arm he was holding with his other hand. An arm with blood running down his left hand in a steady flow.

As he struggled with his right, trying to remove a splinter from one of his own carvings. The splinter is almost the size of a large kebab skewer, almost a bloody javelin. Another man goes to his aid. They talk frantically. They struggle to pull the wooden javelin out of his wrist. It was very gruesome. Very alarming but people flocked to him with water, towels and general aid. He got it ripped out with a last grimace from the puller and the victim. Thrust his hand out, grabbed and poured water from a rather dirty, dusty plastic green bottle. He thanked his fellow traders. He then took his shirt off by one hand, wrapped it around his left hand. Tied a piece of string around it and returned to work.

In Australia, he had seen people signed off work for less. He actually started singing to himself as he worked with no less speed or fluency. Eddy was the only one watching. People offered assistance, but he waved them away with a smile. He was fine. He definitely seemed fine. He was oblivious of how that spear a few millimetres to the other side would have been his undoing, he would have bled out. Blissfully unaware that he just cheated his own death.

The smell of rich iron from the blood and dust is strong but does not mask the incredible compelling intense stench of raw sewage wafting its disgusting odour. He darts out of the market and down a short-looking small alley. The traders, the homes tip all their rubbish out of the doors into the alley that Eddy is negotiating himself around as he does not know what they entail. As Eddy reached the end of the alley, he was thankful that the putrid smell was replaced by the rushing of the salt air and the light of the sun bouncing on the ocean waves once more. At sunset, these disgusting unpleasant reeking piles would be set alight in a controlled river fire of waste.

Eddy breathed in the fresh air in a succession of deep, meaningful breathes to cleanse his nostrils. He then did not know where to go. He looked left and right, right and left. 'Nothing ventured,' he mumbled under his breath. To his right are layers of five steps of five metres by a good metre of bamboo designed scaffolding with layers of filleted bonga fish and butterfish drying out in the sun getting ready to be sold. This is what he saw the other day, to subsequently eat that very evening. Thus, with a better knowledge he could understand what he was seeing.

Eddy had reached the main fishing port. People were busy fixing nets, running down to sea with blue plastic buckets to pick up fish from the boats. People on the fringe of the beach and the ocean sorted the fish out into separate buckets was a speed that was mesmerising to watch. And of course, other people were fishing from the beach. Everyone had a purpose, a job to do, a direction to what had to be done. Others filleted and cleaned the fishes with a skill that would make a samurai warrior blush at his inadequate techniques with a blade. He sat under one of the large, looming green trees and watched in mesmerising awe. He was not bothered by anyone.

He took in the colourful scene. The smells of the fire smoking some of the fish mixed with the salt in the air. The smiles and laughter from the fisherman. He desired Caz could see this. It would be something that he would explain later, but very hard to put words into the picture he was seeing. He wanted her here. She was missing out on a great treat, Eddy thought. He was in awe at the hard work for little personal gain.

That evening over a tasty steaming bowl of hot mess, he tried in vain to explain the true beauty of his day into words. Attempted to paint a picture of what he saw into her mind. He felt he was not winning but then it happened. Finally, Caz said the words that Eddy had longed to hear. She said, 'I want to come.' Nothing had sounded so horny to him. At long last Caz wanted to leave the safety net of the resort.

Yet, there was a clause. She would only venture if it was a paid excursion. The candle shook, frighteningly close to toppling. The wine glasses catapulted pearls of red droplets high into the air as Eddy knocked the table in his haste. Like a jack-in-the-box he was immediately up and running Usain Bolt style towards the reception, he surely would have struggled to catch Eddy with this opportunity in his grasp. The red droplets had not even rested when the ghost of Eddy had left in a cologne dust cloud.

Caz let out a giggle as she leaned back with her rescued glass as the ornaments settled once more. With a Cheshire cat grin, he returns waving a fan of confirmation papers and the pamphlet of what they were doing. Caz leaned forward and gulped as he sat down opposite, excited.

'Do you want to know?' Eddy spat out between his chewed bread.

'Er...' Caz looks into her glass of wine as if a fortune teller looking for the future. 'Um. I'm nervous.'

'No need.' Eddy could not conceal his excitement. He leaned over, grabbed her hands, looked into her eyes. 'I cannot tell you how much I am looking forward to spending the whole day with you. So, do you wanna know?'

Caz had not taken a sip of her wine. She looked out to the exotic unknown. The enigmatic paradise for which he dived in and she will also go headfirst in tomorrow. An apprehensive Caz downed the half glass of wine, strode off to the room. Eddy paid the check and wondered if he had pushed too hard. He watched her leave from two steps behind. Her long pale-yellow dress clinging to her graceful legs as she graced over the road to the resort. He saw her looking down, then she seemed to embrace it. Acceptance shun on her as she stopped in the lights of the reception. She turned, grimaced provocatively. She did cheeky so well and motioned him forward with a jerk of her head. He was way too eager as he bounded over. Cuddled.

'I can't believe you talked me into this. But. Well...you have.' She gulped, she nibbled the corner of her thumbnail as she twisted out the reluctant words that finished the long, pausing sentence. 'Surprise...me tomorrow.'

Eddy was not sure if Caz was joshing with playful ridicule, but enjoyed fooling around with her in this form of banter, kidding and jest. He decided to take a joyful tact against her outrageous accusation that he forced her to do this.

That night, Eddy hardly slept. He could not believe that they were going to spend the day together. He wanted this from the very first moment the smoke trail bump of the aeroplane tyres hit the African continent. He laid as rigid as a steel board waiting for the alarm to chime. The shrilling noise came from Eddy's side of the bed. Even though he was waiting for it, the loud din made him jump. These chimes were not the only alarm bells that was shaking through her head, penetrating her core, shaking her confiding bravado.

Eddy was the complete opposite. He leapt out of bed with the gusto of a child on his birthday. Caz lay there with the springs of the mattress settling from Eddy's explosive exit, dismayed at what a few glasses of red wine had made her do. She no longer blamed Eddy.

He was Superman-quick in his readiness. An animated leap, faster than a speeding bullet in his step, as he bound out of the bathroom followed by the steaming heat clouds. In the time he spent in there, Caz had composed herself with an echoing mantra to 'relax, enjoy, embrace'. She cheekily slapped his bare bottom, a tag, baton exchange on her way to the bathroom. She wanted to give a performance of conviction so not to overshadow Eddy's high-spirited energy.

She had decided to embrace the feeling of dread, behind a façade of comforting composure. Door creakingly shutting, the latch of the lock clicking. She exhaled a deep breath. She did not even realise she was holding her breath. Leaning over the hideously pale pink porcelain basin, with her weight on her shoulders being transferred she unfocused downwards. A burden shared. She looked up, focusing on her reflection in the oval mirror. She was brimming with tears. Her mental strain was presenting through a physical manifestation. She could do it here. She could let out her reserved fears, but when she left, she needed to leave these insecurities on the bathmat. She brushed her teeth as the salty taste of tears were overpowering the spearmint.

Then it happened, a resignment. A feeling of fulfilment that she could triumph over her fears. As water sprinkled down her body it rinsed her uncertainty. She was going to be with Eddy. Afterall it was a tour, it must be safe. The water did not cancel out the noise rumbling inside her, but soothed over the hard rock of doubts. They had breakfast together, in nervous silence but expectancy of a different day to be had. Caz had hardly nothing to eat but shakenly finished her coffee. Eddy ate her share. Today, for the first time, they left as a couple, together.

Waiting outside the hotel in the unrelenting heat for their chariot. They hear before they see it, being the appropriate word. Rumbling in a dusty plume of sand and filth. A white dazzling smile was seen riding a frail, rusty motorbike. Although Caz looked scared, she got on with no helmet, following the lead of the driver. Truth be said, a little wheedling by the sweet-talking Eddy. Behind her, he got on, gripping her tight with a reassuring whisper of support. He wanted to be the cushion, for if she did fall off—of course, he kept that thought to himself—he would take the impact.

If the bike was struggling with the weight, it could not be heard over the high-pitched grinding of the oil-thirsty cogs of the machine. The motorbike danced along the uneven road as Eddy felt Caz's hands grip his thighs in a merciless squeeze. She was getting worried. The leaning of the corner made her hair drag lines in the dirt track. It was a good job he was behind, as he grimaced and yelped at her blood-constricting grasp. Her yelps were not to be heard over the struggling motorbike, the rush of warm air and the cries of startled pedestrians.

For what seemed longer than it should have been, they ultimately arrived, safely, in one shaken piece, at a quiet port where only a few boats could be seen. Caz bounced off the bike as if it held an electric shot. She was glad to be off the hot radiator, the death-wielding contraption. She mumbled a stern warning to Eddy along the lines that she will not be going back to the hotel on 'that death trap' through gritted teeth.

Eddy took the approach of just nodding and saying nothing. He heeded the caution. She was in pain, waiting for the blood to flow through her legs, rubbing her thighs. Caz rushed behind the motorbike, into the dry straw-like grass. She thought her coffee was going to make a second appearance as she leaned over the straw-like tall grasses at the edge of the gravel, dusty road. She wrenched. Nothing.

Eddy placed a hand on her shoulder, she jerked it away. Moved around. The big-dipper smiling motorbike-driving-maniac pointed them to a boat. They got pushed towards a dilapidated boat that was on its last sea legs. It was not the boat seen on the pamphlet. If Caz's eyes could paint a thousand words, it was all expressed to Eddy with not just: 'I'm going to kill you' eyes, but: 'I will make you pay with unsympathetic and unforgiven torture' eyes. The excursion that Eddy had booked was no secret anymore. 'ROOTS' was plastered over the small, for a better description, boat.

This tour, according to the pamphlet, promised to be informative. The Roots tour was made famous by the American author Alex Haley. In his book he highlighted the slave trade in the most horrific ordeal. Within the detail he was finding his own personal roots. This was to be, also upsetting. They were young when he made his journey to discover his origin so do not remember the impact this book had when first released. As with many African Americans, he was a product of the slave trade. Not directly, but indirectly. To make his journey distinctively trickier, was the very real fact that the moment that slaves set foot on American soil, they were given European names. The task was arduous as they did it to break any link with their homeland. Alex Haley was very fortunate indeed that he came from a line of proud Mandinka warriors. His ancestor refused to abandon his name, Kunta Kinte. This made the link easier to find, but make no mistake, no less hard. No less gruelling.

She darted another glare back as she walked the wooden, punctured gangplank of missing planks up to the panic-stricken boat. Once again, Eddy ignored the unspoken threat. He looked out at the rippling waters, listened to the birds and felt the breeze on his sweaty back. Onboard they were met by a small group of about twenty tourists, it would appear that they were waiting for them. They looked unamused.

It transpired that the tourists were mainly from the UK, but some from America and New Zealand as well. They apologised for nothing more but to get the unwanted gaze off them. This small group with an unknown reason to why they were the last on board. Alas they were not late, but felt they should say something as they swayed onboard. Eddy mumbled, 'Always one in a crowd, or in this case, two.' This did not get a laugh, did not get the desired effect of breaking the ice which he sought. The small group was perfectly sized as they could introduce themselves easily. Nearly remembering everyone's name.

With an unravelling of rope, a few short yells, the clunk of the gangplank being left behind on the smallest scruffy pier in the world. The crew rushed around ready to depart. A hesitant squeal of noise as the boat set forth from the pier in a grinding screech. The white, rusty stained small former fishing boat left Banjul and headed up the river to the ancient trading station of Albreda. Going slower than a snail as it fought with the flowing river they chugged along. They sat on long pews that were not originally designed.

Each pew held crudely together by thick rope, bent nails and a wobble with each ripple. There was nearly as many staff as there were tourists. They were friendly, helpful and gave more explanations to the wildlife in the air, on the river banks, in the river, about their country. The knowledge was amazing. The fervour to show off what, in this case, they had escaped. As they got closer to Albreda, they explained what made Albreda so important.

A dusty town where some got off, but many stayed on as it was all seen by the boat. This was a routine stop for bottled water. The only chance for a while to get some last-minute supplies.

Forever vigilant, Caz scans and observes, as incessantly outgoing Eddy glides from one person to another, making friends. She is intelligent. Calculating to conclude that there are four main people as part of the tour guides, that are helping out amongst the crew. They was San, the main tour guide, and an assistance of sorts in Shola holding the paperwork in a cluttered pile of printed type and eligible ink-scrawled comments. He was joined by a video man, a cameraman that was taking photographs and films of everything, no doubt to earn a few bucks later. Lastly was the guy, sitting with shades on, cigarette in hand and looking out to nothing in particular. The relaxed, large chubby driver of the bus when on land.

The sun was beating down. The onlooking bus driver was undisturbed by the strong winds every now and again that brought with it grains of sand and dust that made everyone else on the boat blink, squint and deter their gaze. Then a second higher wave. Unlike the first, which was a warning. This subsequent wave gave them all a rather cold and unpleasant sprinkling of water. Caz retreated, rushing with the others to the inner sanctuary of the cabin.

After two hours sailing up the Gambia River, Caz was being introduced by Eddy to everyone. It was as if it was his own, private boat tour for mingling party where he wanted everyone to have fun. The wideness of the river was outstanding. Caz had to remind herself that this was actually a river, and not the wide open out reaches of the ocean. San tells them in a loud, booming voice from his slender frame to check for personal possessions as they were nearly at their first destination, Juffure.

On entry towards the land, the evident port. The boat slowed down further. A nervous tension on the boat spread through them all literally, establishing a feat of approaching disaster. The boat twisted through the wreckage of eroding ships and rusting boats. Nothing inspires confidence, or encouragement than being on a boat afloat, surrounded by the horrific sunken finales of worse case scenarios.

Amongst the tragedy, Caz watches Eddy make a joke. A dad jesting pun involving the Titanic. He looks so happy, in his element. She observes Eddy as he does not see what she does. The person that Eddy feels of himself is only in existence with himself. He is meeting all these people for the first time. All have made an instant description of him in their heads. This happens every day, in eye contact, a touch, a voice. Due to this, they are many versions of Eddy in the world. Caz looks at Eddy laughing out loud while swinging his head back in rapturous ecstasy. She loves the description, the version of Eddy that she has, yet his version of himself will differ. She cannot find the point of her rambling mind. Only that she truly loves him for being him.

A bump, a rock of the boat shocks her back to realism. The vulnerable looking pier seems unlikely to take many more knocks. The crew factually jumps into action. Ropes are thrown over to the wooden pier with a soggy thud. Crew jump over to gather their toss. They all pull, tighten, tie and draw together the boat next to the pier to moor it safely. It was well rehearsed and precise. The staff helped the group with a gentle hand as they stepped from the swaying boat to the disturbingly rickety pier. The pier squeaks in resistance.

To add to the dangerous predicament of the instability of the frail, unkempt construction was the group of bumsters that herded forth, towards the fresh dollar signs of tourists. The flocking group conversed loudly with their heavy footing, shouting. If the group were feeling nervous, they hid it well. The young bumsters were selling sweets for them to give it to the local children.

'It is not as if they are animals in the zoo. What is that all about?' Caz remarked under the cover of hand to Eddy.

They moved in a single cell of colourful people as San tried to gather them under the shade of a large tree to start the tour, officially.

'Three nautical miles across the River Gambia is James Island. O'er there.' He points over their heads. 'Any slave that swam the distance. That got there. Touched the flagpole on Albreda was guaranteed freedom. But, sadly, no-one is known to have made it, ever. Albreda was, is, the neighbouring village of Juffure.'

Most are listening to San, most are looking at the large statue. A huge black statue with white borders depicts a bold, powerful body. The arms are upright towards the skies with palms towards the heavens in defiance. From the wrists are cuffs that dangle broken chains in a victorious pose. The head is a globe of the Earth and the only colour within the statue. On the triangle white plinth rising from the earth is the promised black written statement, 'NEVER AGAIN'. This speaks volumes.

To the right is an arch, which is poor in comparison to this statue that gets Eddy excited about what he is going to learn. He is a self-confessed travel nerd. He enjoys learning about a place. Whether in his homeland of Australia or overseas. Rather than just getting a photograph or selfie of him being somewhere he spends time in a place, speaks to locals and gets to know the history, culture and stories that layer, shape and mould the people and the community. He yearns to learn.

A dusty, sandy, bumpy track leads them from Albreda to Juffure village. As they walk the bumsters moult like feathers one by one. As they slowly stroll San explains the Maduka village. They see the picturesque straw huts with their pointed roofs of the tiny village that peak over the wooden branched fence.

'It was here in 1767, at the age of seventeen where Kunta Kinte, Haley's ancestor was taken. Was snatched from his family. Stolen from his life, as he knew it, to become a slave.' That last word lingered in his mouth. Leaving a bitter taste that years could not eradicate.

On his heels he turns, they follow like obedient sheep. San seems to be dabbing at his eyes from the figure of his back. Silence follows over them, creeping across the group, in mutual understanding of how raw the truth is on a connective level, but not a personal level. It would seem that time is not a healer. San beelines through the operating village to see the King of the village. Who, it transpires, is in fact a woman, but still called a King, rather than a Queen.

They are dumbfounded by their jubilation in seeing the King. She does not share the same feelings. She glares through a heavy head. In vibrant green attire with shades of different greens make the dress shimmer, shine. She sits on the wooden steps of her home, her castle in the shade. She is surrounded by women, to use a better word, servants, but they know that is a glorified word for slaves. She has an aura of a strict headmistress. She is unsmiling, unfriendly and her wrinkled face does not look strict or wise, but just mean and bitter. Frail. Fragile.

'Who wants da photo with a real King?' San gushes. 'A small fee, ya will get certificate. Presented by da King herself. Who's in?'

All but two put their hands in their pockets for the money, Caz and Eddy. They stand back. They look on at, what is in their eyes, a ridiculous scam. San joins them to coax them into this once-in-a-lifetime opportunity. They think the same but have not actually voiced their thoughts.

'Where,' Eddy pauses. He does not want to offend.

'Where does this money go?' Caz finishes the question for him.

'Where do you think?' San answers with a frown, no eye contact.

Eddy and Caz both look around, over the poverty-stricken village. They look at San. No words are spoken. He nods. More profoundly than the holy trinity, they are connected. He whispers shortly and abruptly into the ears of Eddy, so loud as Caz can hear but no-one else.

'Lines the King's pocket, no-one else, never shared.'

At that moment, his fire of excitement ebbs with the devastating validation of his worse fears. Slavery is not dead, it is hidden. It is looked over, ignored. San puts his arm around his shoulders as if reading his disputing mind.

'Look,' he whispers, pulling him close. San is tall so he leans to whisper to him as Eddy comes up to his bony shoulder. 'This is Africa. We do this to walk through. Da only way to the other side. Here we see two sides of Africa. Everywhere in the world da is this. Learn about Kinte. Be committed to learn. This is not about this moment, it is the moments you will learn. What had come from 'ere. We are happy. Poor, but happy. We are all trying to earn a dollar. Are you so much different? Now forget this. This, er, conversation.'

Eddy appreciates his fatherly gesture. Yet this is the first time he has seen a negative impact of tourism. He is still dedicated to learn, but is very sad that this is the downside of tourism. Would Alex Haley turn in his grave if he knew his tour was not benefitting his ancestors but making the situation worse? It seems that the tourist money sticks to the wrong hands. Eddy and Caz shift awkwardly in the stifling heat while getting harassed constantly by the children.

With open eyes, Eddy sees the stage that is the village. The thespians run into position. As they walk around the village the children dance, elderly women weave in the sheltered doorways. Both cease when they have all walked past. But the persistent, incessant begging from the children, which borders on outright aggression continues, this will never stop. The voice for Eddy is no-longer voicing like a stuck record 'No', this has been exchanged with silence. The image of the statue at the start flashes in a reoccurring film reel of mockery.

San introduces them to a traditional looking hut of the Museum of Slavery. This is where the passion for education resumes. He removes a notepad from Caz's bag and takes notes, they both take photographs. No-one was spared in becoming a slave. Children, men and women were all made into slaves. Each one cost 4,000 Cowra shells. Essentially, they were kidnapped, taken from their homes, their families to be sold around the world. To Caz, Eddy asks a rhetorical question.

'What people decide to do this?'

This opens a vault of questions in his mind that pour forth as if the door was keeping them enclosed like a dam. This wave of questions after another wave of questions turns into an inner tirade.

'What people have this idea?

'What people decide that this would be okay?

'Would they like it if it happened to them?

'But. They think it is alright for them to do?

'And. And…people agree.

'People actually follow it through. People actually agree. It becomes an actual trade. What the actual fuck?

'These people are human, right?

'Part of the human race?

'I see no race, just regression rather than progression!

'Part of humankind?

'I see no kind humans here. I read no humanity.

'Don't let me start on civilisation. I see nothing civil.

'If this is how the sophistication of evolution is a development, huh.

'Huh, it is nothing more but a regression of evolution.

'No progress.'

Caz says nothing as Eddy trails off in a repetition to his ramblings. She hears Eddy as white noise. Not because he is not making valid points, but she is reading everything. She is looking at the implements in the glass cabinets to retain slaves. From chains, locks, manacles to items that look torturous. Caz is seeing everything. She is learning everything new. She had no idea. She did not know this had happened in the way that it did. Caz had heard about slavery. Let's face it you would have to be living under Uluru, not down under, but out of the world not to have heard of this. But it was still a shocking slap in the face that it went on in this fashion. That it was accepted. That it became the norm.

Eddy walked with Caz and looked at the same things. He sensed that a lot of the group where here as a tick off the 'must do in The Gambia' checklist. Some took photographs and were finished quickly and going through the racks of postcards, keyrings, trinkets in the souvenir shop. The others used it to get away from the heat and a rest spite from the tenacious bumsters. They seemed not to care. San had done this tour many times and saw them paying particular close attention. He came over and pointed out things that were not explained. He gave them his knowledge. At the end they both walked through the mandatory shop at the end without a care for the glittering tasteless merchandise. They paid no interest to the T-shirts, bracelets…whatsoever.

Outside, ignoring the children, they focused on a painting depicting the slave trade as progression. Men, women and children in a line with thick heavy chains around their necks, together. It was here in the light of the impression of greed that funded this trade that Caz spoke for the first time since entering. She spoke about her feelings of what happened and how interesting she found it. Also, that they were taken into the country with open arms. The Gambian people may see them as money, but also, they have no bitterness. They respect them, as they, the whites, did not do to them over two-hundred years ago. Yes, it was a long time ago but the monstrosity of what had been done, could not be forgotten over time. Forgiven, yes, yet, never forgotten.

They returned to the boat. Everyone was taking photographs and laughing. Eddy and Caz walked in a numbed silence. As the groups back turned towards the boat. The thespians, the children, women and men placed down their props and pulled out a mobile phone. Eddy senses that it is not all forced poverty. The glossy veneer may be a travesty. In the middle of the Gambian River the boat takes a short, choppy ride over to the small eroding St James Island. This is where the ruins of the fort are located.

It was even harder to disembark this boat to the rocky, crumbling stone bank. San narrates the whole time. Originally, when slavery was at its peak, the island was six times the size in which they now stood on. Eddy tries to imagine the thousand, upon thousands, of slaves that passed through here to destinations unknown. Ripped away from the fabric of their family. From the thread of lines that was their history, culture and society as they knew it.

San tells them that the guards on the island were cruel. They played a game where they would throw food into a pen and watch them fight for it. The guards treated them like animals, not people. The slaves would get food and water once a day for two weeks. The motive was to be weakened physically, and mentally for the transatlantic voyage by ships. This was so that they did not cause trouble during the sail. Some would make it across, some never did. Locked in tiny cells on the ship and made to work, back to the dungeon, sorry cells, to sleep and eat.

The skeletal baobab trees rustled an enigmatic, mysterious soundtrack as they were escorted around the island. Eddy pointed out the baobab trees with excitement to promise to show Caz a flowering one bearing fruit before they leave. They walk as close to San as possible to regain, to retain all his brilliant information.

To have the museum first was a great idea to fully understand the footsteps in which they were walking. Some points inside the museum were brought up by Caz as they passed certain things, or San mentioned something about what she had just read. Caz was a lot better at retaining information than Eddy. Eddy would remember snippets. He would use all the information he had to write a detailed account of the day, for himself. No-one else.

Backing away from the awful stories, recounting a world that only a few years ago was ruled by cruelty. The stories on this small island, brutal. Such a beautiful name, St James Island, filled with a thorny secret as prickly and twisted as the depths of a dark undergrowth, showing only the red garden of roses. Back on the main land their walk through the embracing villages. These are the real stories of Gambian life. This shows to them the great for which The Gambia in Africa is renowned for.

These children do not sell them anything. They want to speak to them. To see this generation embracing the white tour group when, no uncertainty they had family members, ancestors that passed through this path to never be seen again. They were accommodating, friendly, eager to tell their story but did not hold a fist in rage. Yes, they had glimmers of sadness, but, no ability for hatred. The white men that caused this inhumane trade are actually embraced in The Gambia's chest in a heart-warming hug. This is humankind.

Mixed emotions are stirring around the bodies of Eddy and Caz. They are sad, although happy. The happiness comes from the manner in which the Gambian people have responded to such brutality. The dark history the runs like a dirty sewer under the beautiful cosmetic country. They load onto the boat slowly, pausing to turn to capture some last photographs.

Once onboard, San informs them that the scenic journey upstream is going to be faster this time around. In the bruised and battered boat, they head speedily back to Banjul accompanied by at least a dozen dolphins. This gets rid of the sadness, elevating their mood as they playfully dive up and down with the wake of the boat. Outrageously startling, at this speed a bumster tries his luck. In what can only be described as a newer looking boat they pull up aside as one drives, the other offers a bounty of drinks to sell. They skip in-between the dolphins, the wake to present a strange landscape. As quickly as they try, they fail in their attempt, but points for making an effort, for trying.

This day trip had found the hidden confidence that Caz had packed in Australia and never taken out. She had discovered that not was all bad out of the resort. She had done the rather stupid thing of taking for face value the travel advisory before coming out, literally and figuratively. They always stated the worse of news. This generated a somewhat, not overly reactive irrational fear of the mysterious unknown country. She had already made her mind up on the adversity that spurned the crime rate. If she had read about Australia in another country's point of view, she just may have read the same threatening forewarnings laced with dreading unsafe.

Yet that fear that a few words generated were hard to dislodge from the back of her mind. Now, she could see that it was all unfounded, for which she would have to be damn unlucky to be part of it. At the end of the day if you are looking for trouble you will find it. If you find it, stumble on it, you have the choice to walk away from it. Simple, but sometimes, bad luck does happen. It could happen on holiday. On the other hand, it could happen in your country, or your hometown.

For this reason, she does not want to advertise anything that could be taken. She heeds with caution and wears no jewellery or expensive attire which she takes the advice from Eddy before leaving Australia. However, the niggle remained.

They are starting to slow down as the straight shoreline comes into view. Swiftly followed by the features that make the landscape look like the crooked teeth. Not even close enough to see, Caz apprehensively spots the waving white-shirted man that escorted them here, behind him, he leans on the tin-bucket of the same motorbike. She pulls at Eddy's sleeve with a grimace, 'Not again! They must be another way Ed?' she pleads. Eddy wraps his arm around her with a sneer. This superman protective thing that he has going on is really giving him a kick. She continues to protest. He continued to ignore.

Amidst the protesting, Caz in the end complied to straddle the appallingly excuse for transport. Eddy sat behind while teasingly tickling her with a kiss on her brushed freshly sunburnt neck. This was to relax her, at the same time a gesture to show her that he was proud of her. This time the streets were busier, the tilts, curves, rounds and sharp braking of the motorbike were intensified. She gripped Eddy's thigh for dear life while removing the life out of his leg. His screams were distorted by the loud engine, the squeals of passing locals that shout a warning that goes unheeded.

They shower, change and Caz immediately orchestrates the determination to want to go out. Eddy did not need his arm twisted behind his back to accept this. They took the long walk to Bakau. They talked about the tour, the whole journey to this point. Before they had realised, they were in the energetic Bakau, after strolling for two hours.

Eddy leads the way subtly, as he heads into a district that he has not been. A dusty old town. Here, modern ways and traditional methods mix in their surroundings. Large in stature, skinny in mass are cows that pull patch-up carts full of hay, food and electronic boxes. A scooter whizzes by at a terrifying pace half-buried in the sand. Huts line in no particular order with peelings of whitewash plaster surrounding the base, television antennas sprouting out of the bamboo and straw roofs. Children play soccer, adorned in counterfeit replicas of the world's renown soccer teams. Old men crouched over, weighed down by hardship, examining an antiquated board game, share a laugh, a joke. Old women chatter into mobile phones.

The one thing that has not changed. The one thing that has lasted the tests, trials, and tribulations of time and modern corruption. That layers stronger with every generation. The single thing that unites all of The Gambia, in different villages is the community. The hero of the worlds, the kinship of a community. It is an unspoken, unseen, unheard entity. It is only felt. A spirit. A positive. A law that applies to all in this country, the entire world. Here, in the oldest part of the town of Bakau, this community is called Kachikally.

Eddy negotiates the camera while trying to imprint images to memory. He got a recommendation on one of his ambles alone. It was at this juncture with Caz by her side that he wanted to see this new site, which he had insistently been told to see by the young, wannabe-tour guide a few days ago.

They reached the fringes of Bakau before spotting a sign crudely hammered into a telegraph pole. Eddy did not say as much, but Caz was an intelligent woman. She could see that he was naïvely following the dirty, mustard yellow pointed signs that lead the way to the Crocodile Pool. Although she was uncertain to what would be encountered once they had gotten there.

Eddy was not entirely sure. This trusting following of signs on the back of a simple recommendation could have destroyed their innocence. Another sign said that the sacred crocodiles at the Crocodile Pool are free to see. Where they being incredibly gullible? They both thought but did not voice, as their aimlessly walked through the narrow alleys, sandy streets, grubby excuses for sidewalks onwards. After a short zig-zag walk, behind the main route that made them think that they were actually walking in circles rather to the destination, they came to what they were looking for.

Just when they were doubting the dubious steering of the signage, they turned a corner to be confronted by a vast colourful wall with an unguarded open door for the entrance. Proudly stated in bold lettering, the wall informs them that there are over one-hundred and forty crocodiles inside. They peak around the wall, they look at each other inquisitorially. Questions if this close proximity can hold, never mind the other question of could the open enclosure withstand safely, that amount of crocodiles.

In trepidation, they slowly edge towards the entrance. The path without warning narrows, bordered by large, green towering bushy trees that hid the scorching rays of the sun. They jump at the crack of a twig to their right. In the undergrowth they see the accused, an agile brown and white monkey. Above a loud abrupt squawk from a colourful bird to a flock of the same. A buzz in the ear from an insistent pestering large flying insect tenacious in its pursuit to bite them. A hasty mischief of rats that crosses behind their path.

Caz holds tight to Eddy's arm. Eddy acts, ineffectively underwhelming in his futile efforts to keep up the charade of being her Superman. He walks, back-straight with a strut, inside he is as fragile as jelly. She feels his heart beat faster with each rustle, noise, sound. Even not close to him she has known him long enough to see through his pretence like glass to his real frame of mind. In this case his jitteriness. Each noise on, around the narrow path made them think a crocodile was approaching, even absurdly, a branch being relieved of its weight in the green natural canopy directly above. Then the trees opened up like a curtain in front of them to reveal the main attraction.

A murky pool of still water. Covered in pads like lettuce leaves that have been strewn across the muddy brown waters. Inside may be a crocodile, concealed, more than likely more than one will lurk. In plain site are many that lie on the small risen banks, very still, waiting, anticipating, ready to attack. Not one, not a single crocodile is caged. They could even walk out the entrance if they wanted too. The writing on the wall was true. You can actually stroke them. They are so close. They watch numerous people stroke them like a friendly purring, predictable cat. Oblivious that they are a wild, alert, extremely unpredictable predator that has survived with the dinosaurs. Eddy watches astounded. His mouth agape, eyes wider. He cannot believe what he is witnessing.

Then the shy, the frightened girl that came to The Gambia boldly strode over to the nearest, bloody large crocodile, went behind its gigantic head to stroke the prehistoric animal around his scaly neck. He was admiring her self-assurance coolness that had transpired in a few, seemingly short hours. As if the crocodile was just like an adorable puppy, she rubbed softly the reptile's neck. She really was coming out of her vulnerable shell.

Observing in a silent tribute, Eddy sat with his wits about him on a tree stump, watching this Disney-esque scene of people stroking and walking around the crocodiles as if they were harmless black ants, without a worry, without a single care. He was gobsmacked by this lack of respect for this prehistoric killing predator that has survived that time until now, for the very reason that they found shelter, most importantly, food and drink. They are hunting machines, they are not the hunted.

A sign in front of the pool that bubbles a life unseen, states that these crocodiles have never hurt anyone. Eddy finds this very, very, hard to believe in. Caz returns with a smile. Mouthing with glee, asking if he had taken a photograph. He nods, she claps her hand like a jubilant seal. They stay for a while watching them do nothing, or move very slowly, as they were being watched slyly themselves. It was a stare game in which Eddy was not going to stay playing. To see if he would become the victorious winner. He knew that answer. After all, this is the last remaining dinosaur for a specific reason. Reasons that does not need any explanations. Caz does not want to leave just yet. She is relishing this once in a lifetime opportunity. She returns to another crocodile, whereas Eddy returns to the tree stump.

On his route, he slowly, cautiously walks behind a slow-moving crocodile with a tale that is a strong and lethal as a razor blade. Out of his eyesight a middle-aged woman takes and shakes his hands. He was expecting a sales pitch, she is firm with her shake. When she says nothing, turns with a spring in her step, she vanishes as quickly as she appears leaving no explanation, leaving a baffled Eddy tremendously confused.

'She will do that the day long,' came a voice next to him. 'Lamin,' a hand was extended for Eddy to shake.

'Eddy...Ed, no, erm, Eddy,' he stammered while accepting his welcome and shaking his hand.

'The trustworthy.'

'What?' he mumbles, confused.

'My name...means trustworthy.' Sensing the awkward situation, he continues as he points out the stumbling back of the woman moving with pigeon steps, aided by a cane amongst the crowd of colourful dressed women. Eddy wonders how he managed to find her as Lamin spoke over his thoughts.

'She wants child. The women here are special. They trained by ancestors. The trained women help women. Family chain of Bojang clan, the trained women are. They are blessed in helping women that cannot have child to have child. Of them own. After they must shake hand with anyone in Bakau. They choose you, not from ere. Lucky-er.'

'Ah.' Eddy surveys the scene of people praying, and people being blessed.

'Sacred pool. This heals.' Lamin fans his arms across the pool as if a magical sorcery exposing the illusion. 'It been here for five-hundred years. More, many more. Shown by Mandinka Bojang. Ruler's daughter named Kachikally. Name means pick it up and put it down after legend.'

Eddy waited for more of a description, but he smiled a toothless crooked grin as he walked away leaving Eddy with a mix of feeling educated on the area and about the view he was beholding, but still with a sense of bewilderment. The truth was Lamin left with more questions than answers in the short exchange that they had just had.

He cannot leave without partaking in the risky exercise. So, with the crocodile still, he navigated his movements around the pool he bends down, ready to leap as quick as a jack in the box back if needed. He strokes the formidable tail of the motionless crocodile. The skin is so thick, he wonders if the crocodile actually feels anything at all. He rises as Caz offers her hand, one quick selfie together and they walk out amazed at the enigmatic perplexity of the view.

From a previous walk Eddy shows off what he learnt, what he attempted to explain. Pointing out the kirinting huts near the loud animalistic forest with its very own roaring heartbeat. He explains in a style of knowledge when he has only taken this information at being factual. The kirinting huts are traditional and normally where the poorer Africans live, although as they both find out, only poor in a monetary sense. Not in appreciation of community, family or friend's impression. The whitewash that covers the mud made plaster hides the bamboo weaving of the walls. Some parts are exposed, to Eddy's delight. Now he can really explain with visual examples his knowledge that he has enquired over the short days that he had been roaming, exploring alone.

He is not done yet. He retakes her hand, guiding her through the makeshift stalls of the local market. Rubbish wraps around their feet in the slight breeze as they are surrounded, submerged by a kaleidoscope of different colours, shapes and smells. A feast for their senses. Piled high on unstable looking wooden shelves and tables are habanero chilli peppers, guavas, bananas, okra and other fruit and veg that could give way at any moment, to become a rainbow cascading waterfall. The combination of raw, stinky sewage, the sea air, the fruit makes a sweet, sickly and strong aroma that entices. Bringing forth, what seems like thousands of flies.

This area is teeming with them, they constantly have to swot them away from their faces, invading their eyes, nose and nostrils. Blood mixes with the dark yellow dust on the floor that drips off the circular handmade cutting board that was a trunk of a tree. Covered in deep gashes on the board, filled with remnants of meats in the gouged out crevices, the swishing strike of a gleaming shine of silver through the air. Kissed by the sun. Effortlessly passing through the splinted white bone and deep burgundy flesh of the leg of the goat, that makes a new laceration in the already dog-eared chopping board.

He loosens the blade with a wiggle as he moves the leg and sets aim to go in again. He has a splattered with red blood dots on his thin, plastic green apron, on his face, coating his hands. Like fresh rivers of blood, the viscous liquid of slow-moving claret runs off the edges of the board cradled in his bare legs, to his naked feet with sand on his soles, he does not notice, or, does not care to notice. The ground around him is where flies attack, the rich iron smell suffocates the sewage.

Looking more like a bloodthirsty surgeon than a professional butcher. He has a glint in his eyes with each merciless clout of a moist suction sound. He is not alone as the next few stalls here are decorated with joints of beef and lamb. With the stall owners and their families preparing the various joints of meat in the same deliberate act of debauchery, chatting to one another while doing so.

As they draw closer to the sea, the smell of rich iron starts to clear, they leave bloody thong-prints in the dust, as they carry sand beneath their soles. Enveloping them is the much more pleasant aroma. The smell of fish and seafood carrying a rich salty air falls on their lips. Getting more intense and welcoming with each step in the soft light brown sand. Beautiful translucent blue shrimps are for sale, Eddy cannot help by thinking if there was a barbeque back at the resort to cook some off. He cannot recall, so leaves them on the stall. He drools saliva at the missed opportunity as they drip fresh sea water in slow soundless pearls.

In huge contrast, an old guy fixes his bike barely millimetres away. He is covered in grease and oil from head to toe, with a dirty towel that is blacker and browner than the original, formally cream, colour would let you believe is impossible to return. He wears the oil like war paint. With that, he gets increasingly angry at the bike. He starts looking more like a futile warrior. Giving it a pathetic kick that accomplishes nothing. He strides away and then back muttering something under his breath, towards the bike. His chain has snapped, not meekly come off. It is going to be along walk back from the market for him and his broken bike. Yet, he is not alone.

As Eddy witnessed before, as Caz sees for the first time, in true community fashion people with plastic bags of groceries, fish and meat leave their possessions to help. Their bags lie around them like wounded soldiers in the dust, as they help a fellow comrade. Caz is amazed at the scene. She now understands the passion which Eddy would explain each day when he got back to the resort. It was not just the sights, but the people that had affected him so strongly.

This sight came tinged with a sadness. She was a little sad with only seeing this now. She feels that she has missed out on his experiences and adventures that he had had on his own. With a mechanism that MacGyver would be happy with their patchwork on the bike so he can get home at least. The anger dissipates to leave merriment, applause of thanks.

Eddy consciously wanted to walk back along the beach. He wanted to show Caz the wooden scaffold of shelves with Bonga and Butterfish being produced. The fishing, the filleting, the cleaning, and the final process, the smoking. He steers her to this course without her knowledge. She is in as much awe as Eddy was the first time, he saw this spectacle. Eddy is still in awe, if the truth were told. An unexpected gust of wind swirls up a mixture of sand, dust and smoke which causes Caz to cough as it enters her lungs.

She sputters a barrel of laughs through the curtain of black smoke as she runs down the wooden scaffold towards Eddy, back on the beach who had recorded the whole thing on his camera. She remarks on the taste being not unpleasant. She launches into Eddy's arms. He was not expecting it as his weight shifts, he topples over. They land on the soft sand. Caz's torso squashing Eddy's nose. She glides down with a smile that he missed. A cuddle rather than a kiss as they were both is rapturous screams of hilarity.

They either are more recognisable as not being a fresh tourist or just being recognised in general as they are not getting pestered by bumsters anymore. Maybe they are not as white as before. Looking at each other, rather than the sights around them. The locals just shout out a 'hello', with a smile, accompanied by a wave. They are slowly ambling back to the resort along the sandy beach. The sun dropping it jewels into the sapphire-emerald white foamed curls of the tide. They walk hand in hand talking about the day that was.

It is hard to imagine that this was the first day that Caz had been outside the walls of the resort for an extended period. She beams. Her eyes sparkle. Her poise restored. This is a perfect scene of a couple walking a tropical African paradise in the throes of love. The sun has turned orange, setting down in the navy-blue sky. The emerald crashing waves caress their feet, dragging the grains of golden sand back. Trying to stay on land with a pulling draw. The colours around them change. The rustling wildlife in the undergrowth. The twanging of the branches in the trees start to come alive. The smells of burning logs cooking, no doubt delicious, appealing dinners. The spilling of diamonds and pearls from the sun onto the waves, change the cloud-splattered skies to a ruby red, slowly and purposeful as if the sky is burning on fire.

The day is ending. Before they know it, they are back in Kololi and outside the beach access to the resort. They are not ready to go in. They do not want this day to end just yet. Closely, they sit on the hot grains of golden sand. They snuggle each other's neck as the sunset departs the skies, signalling the end of the wonderful picture-perfect day. The breeze caresses them, trying to squeeze them apart from their heart beating great rapture within their united bliss.

They kiss. In the gloom, in the darkness. The only luminosity in the slither of the silver moon. It does not matter for the craters in the shades of the moon, as it shines the brightest light in the darkest of nights. The sound of the colliding waves is heard but not seen or felt. The noisy wildlife in the trees above them. The smell of the cooking food with a hint of burning logs. The smell of the sea. The feel of the sand in their legs. The feel of each other's warmth of their skin. The taste of their salty lips as a combination of sea breeze, sweat, excitement. The taste of one another.

Stumbling through the low branches, the uneven brick path the unruly roots of the tree, they negotiate their way in the pitch dark to the rear of the resort. Through the loud, creaking restraints of the light door hanging loosely on their rusty sea salt ravaged hinges. The security guard lurks. Says nothing, beams shiny whites.

They navigate the brick path to the floodlit path on the other side. Drunk on love, they stagger to the poolside bar. Laughing on lust as they have just met. They order a couple of beers. The bartender tries to engage and interact with them, but they are only interested in the world that they have made for themselves. Apart from ordering the beers, Eddy only notices him when he places the open, foaming brown, cold glass bottles of the local beer which thuds on the bar. Caz distracts her attention from Eddy to pick up the Julbrew. Scans the bottle, for which she succumbs after many thoughts is a sacred crocodile on the label. They are talking animatingly with huge smiles, scrutinising and pouring over the glorious day.

This was the first day that Caz had actually been further than the strip outside the resort. With that adventure she had learnt a lot, grown a lot. She saw what Eddy was so enthused about at the end of each day. He saw the carnival of life. She prisoned herself inside the tomb of demise. Eddy took some persuading but finally she left, with him, she was so much happier to have taken that leap into the mysterious unknown. She seems different. From a nearby tree, a black small monkey with distinguishing grey highlights scurries down to join them. Observes them with twitching features for a while as in turn they watch the curious monkey before it retreats, back to the dark camouflaged canopy of the overhead leaves of the trees.

Returning, the monkey scrabbling down a different tree, from behind them which makes them snap their necks around. Fleeting in a fluffy ball of a black smear is a miniature friend. There are playing but instantly pause. Their heads tilt. They stare nervously at Eddy and Caz. They do not get closer but scrutinise them as if they had never seen people before. Innocence is not lost on the smaller, younger one as it rises on its hindquarters, edges towards them to softly scratch Eddy's arm. Not to draw blood but leave a white tally mark. Eddy remains taut.

Out of the darkness the noise erupts into a sea of monkeys that covers them and their surroundings. Some big, some small, some dark brown, light brown, some curiously looking on, but most are inquisitively probing their exposed skin. In all honesty, they have no idea how to react. They all are amazed at them. Caz and Eddy look on equally amazed. A shake of hands here, a soft pat there. The tide retreats, as quickly as the advance. No monkeys left, no evidence that they were even there. Leaving the lovestruck couple in the light of the moon, in the shadows of the fringing forest, the neon of the bar backlight causing them to glow in a soft pink hue, in the spectral vivid, gentle glow. The day ends.

The curtain lets enough of the sunrays of their last full day. Always passionate about ingredients, food and everything cooking, Eddy had his spirit watered and flowered a new zealous desire. He is keen to show Caz a flowering Baobab tree, as promised. He investigates via the reception who arranges them to take a drive, a short distance that seemed like a long haul.

Dancing on the rocky excuse for road on the back of a noisy lawnmower of a motorcycle. Caz holding on for dear life, cursing Eddy's decision to see something that she really did not give two hoots about. Jumping across the yellow pothole non-existent road for which the bike moaned, protested and groaned its way across the rustic African landscape. His passion was not bordering on being nerdy, she can agree that ship had well and truly sailed. Yet she could envision his beaming smile as the high-pitched jarring sound starts slowing, starts reducing the earache.

They are slowing down in the direction of the single blossoming tree looming closer in the hazy materiality. This tree could be imagined, rather than actually being real. A tree that would not be out of place if designed for the set of Lord of The Rings, Star Wars or any other fantasy or science fiction movie. It is steadily becoming a huge tree, with a huge bulb as the truck and thick, gnarly branches with clumps of leaves at the top like a bad trip to the barber. Fads involving superfoods have risen out of the ashes, given some poorer countries some much needed economy.

The flipside is the dangerous greed that sweeps this money into the lap of the rich, concealed and not to the farmers that work the land. Some of these superfoods have gathered pace and sped around the world, others have done their journey around the world only to deflate, to disappear. This is one that is starting to rise, as yet in the editing room to either be renowned for, or left discarded on the cutting room floor. At the present moment in time this is up there with kale and goji berry. The very young skinny boy, that has driven them out leaps out of his saddle to instantly turn into the guide.

'Symbol!' he shouts in gleeful exclamation as he jumps off the bike and points to the ugly tree. 'Strong. Enduring. Long life. This old, maybe one thousand years. Old, very old.'

'What is it?' Caz whispers, confused, into Eddy's ear. The vibration has rattled out the name out of her memory.

'Baobab tree,' he states with the added information, 'also known as monkey tree or upside-down tree.'

'Oh,' Caz sighed, but still no wiser. She tried to feign interest, but it did not work.

'It gets ground into a fine white powder and used in jam, juices, porridge.'

'Protected,' the young Gambian boy voices. He speaks in pidgin English with one-worded sentences. 'Its spirit protects us all. Gives food, shelter.'

'I thought I told you back in Sydney,' Eddy continues his conversation with Caz. 'It's rich in antioxidant, potassium. And. And. It provides six times more Vitamin C than oranges…and…double the amount of calcium than milk. That is only the fruit.' A smile spread across his face as his voice gets higher with his growing excitement. 'The seeds are packed full of protein. The leaves are potassium, iron, magnesium and more. Simply ticks all the boxes of a super-duper food.'

'Did you just say super-duper? You dork. Why have I not seen it?'

'Well…there is the snag,' he continues, ignoring her banter. 'It is not grown agriculturally. It is only harvested locally for as much fruit as the community needs to maintain the trees national productive cycle. Remarkable. It would need to be planted as a crop. It would take the land of the community. The community would lose their tree. Their source of food. The work would be good, but could you see the investors paying for their hard work? I can't.

'It will happen, as money wins. But the cost would be huge for Gambia. The Gambian people would be sheltered from the world. People would not know the effects. Would people care? Do people care about palm sugar? That deforestation that takes soccer pitches a day. Homes of the orangutans. All they would hear is the good it is doing for them, themselves. A selfish notion, but a calamitous true one'. Eddy turns to the tree in awe, as if in silent respectful admiration. 'It would be great to harvest this for the world. To then give the Gambian people fairness back. In work, export and they own tree. Still, in spite of that good news, when the investors see dollar signs, they only want to see more dollar signs after that. True. Fair dinkum. Sad.'

'Thank you, Miss Australia,' Caz mocks Eddy's speech. 'So. Can we use it in the restaurant?'

'Not yet, but it will happen. Trust me.'

Caz cannot believe she has wasted the morning to see an ugly tree in the middle of an acrid desert. All the things that they could have done on their last day. Eddy was focused on showing Caz this beauty, whereas she saw a monstrosity.

Still fuming, Caz masquerades her anger with her sunnies. Thankfully, the late morning perked up with a walk around town, a stop for lunch without a baobab insight. Great food, drink over conversation. They revisited places and finished the evening with a night on the tiles, clubbing.

Caz was dressed in a short red skirt and white crop top with high heels. Simple, elegant and immaculate. She was beautiful. She did not need high heels, but they did emphasise her stunning newly tanned long legs. Eddy in brown suede shoes, brown shorts and a blue and white light unbuttoned shirt that revealed a dazzling white V-neck T-shirt. He wore it well.

They went to a barn of sorts. A hot, humid warehouse with high ceiling and a wooden swaying set of stairs to a bar of sorts. Above, in the rafters was a steel, wooden mess of colourful graffiti supporting the two-storey building in The Strip. Surely the metal was too heavy, with the added load of people could not be safe. They moved in anyway in reckless abandonment of a life they are enjoying. The smell of stale alcohol, cigarette and marijuana smoke was heavy in the sticky clammy air.

The loud music that cracked over the airwaves was a combination of Western, local, dance and reggae. Every track was a feel-good song, not a tragic love affair but a love starting, that amazing magical place of time. This fantastic DJ helped the atmosphere stay vibrant, absorbing positive energies. They danced dirty. In the sweltering heat, they slipped and slid their hands over one another. The sweat cascaded off their bodies, mixed with the spillage from the bottled beers. They through caution to the wind. They danced like no one was watching. They were safe in the knowledge that they would never see any of these people again.

With that, the confidence they exuded was at an all-time high. Sexual tension was expressed in the aura around them. They embraced the freedom like a young driver learning to ride, never looking back but forward. Accelerating faster, gripping the seats in speed-rushing celebration of life. This was the restart of a love that was struggling in the wind of change and now a fire beacon of defiance, strength and unity. Eddy and Carroll, were back again, were an item once again. They Were One, Together. The holiday worked in bringing them back from the precipice.

Through the dusty glaze of a hangover they packed their bags for the end of the holiday. In an hour they are getting picked up to get to the airport to start their long plane journey back home. Caz looks out of the window, she feels as if she should have been more adventurous. However, she did embrace the last few days. Together, as a couple, they were closer than they have ever been. They enjoyed their time in The Gambia not to say the pace of life can be frustratingly relaxed sometime. Which is an understatement. It is slow which leads to the time zone being GMT, Gambian Maybe Time.

It was in this moment of euphoria that after breakfast of this last day that things started to unravel. They had packed, got ready for a mid-morning departure. Caz's mood was different. She seemed mad, but Eddy could not work out why. She was brooding under her skin. Blood boiling, ears steaming. They shared a great ten days away. They got to know a lot more of one another. They were setting the foundations for a true love story.

Eddy was not sure when this mood had started. It was with her when she woke up. As she stared broodingly out of the window. During breakfast.

Then, during the ride to the airport where she leaned looking out of the window, never at Eddy. The wait in the departure lounge, she feigned eye contact. Now on the departing and airborne, she still had not said a single word since breakfast. He shared a joke on the plane with another couple from Australia when he went to the toilet. As he rose out of his seat after the tell-tale ding of allowing people to move around the cabin, he stated, 'I would not press that if I was you', as he passed by Caz and pressed the call button above her head.

He and the other Australian couple found it funny, Caz did not. Not even remotely. Surely that could not have been the pivotal moment that changed the view that she saw him in. Alternatively, was it that he spent time exploring rather than being couped up in the swimming pool, gym and spa complex that was the resort? Maybe she did not like his sense of adventure? Maybe she did not like his sense of fun, games, humour. At the end of the day, those past few days were the longest time that they had spent together, sincerely the entire time in their pockets.

Sure, they lived together, but it was more of a story of ships passing either in the day, or the night than living with one another. Did Caz feel trapped, but decided not to voice it? Was Eddy overthinking it? That art of creating large problems from small problems that do not even exist, was in fact, very real. Was she just tired and sad that she was leaving when she just started to enjoy herself?

On the return home the gloomy, dark storm over her head did not pass. Even after some time back in the familiar routine of life in Sydney. She was noticeable different from when they were together. When she was at work or, when with mates. This mood was not a passing storm. It had made menacing roots that extended contagious negativity into their connecting lives. Causing arguments. Shouting matches. And, that was the communication that they had!

What is more, they were starting to be plain ignoring each other. Consciously, trying not to see or spend time with just themselves. This deliberate act of avoidance was impossible. Making it unbearable, intolerable. Having to consider they worked together. Eddy was a head of his department and she was the head of him. They also lived together. Moreover, it was unmanageable for them to live a happy coexistence.

Within a few weeks after, what he thought was a lovely rejuvenation away, life at home was irredeemable. It was clear that he actually wanted it more. Was it the commitment that he craved or the touch, these were questions he did not know the answer to. He had tried everything. The flowers he had sent. The plans he had changed so he could talk to her. The space that he had given her. Outside of work, that's unavoidable, but he tried. The things that he did, that he knew that she enjoyed, and many other things, he considered them all to get her to be the old Caz that he remembered. He decided to take the initiative.

Seeming to be incurable, he decided to move out, for a break. Inappropriately, his mates, who warned him about starting a relationship with someone through circumstance. All they offered him was a shoulder of an armchair to sleep on. Even though the makeshift bed was uncomfortable at best, it was better than the cold shoulder. The unhealthy atmosphere that was detrimental in maintaining a broken relationship. What he felt, what he told his mates were two, very different things.

He informed his mates that working and living together may be a little too much for her to handle. While not completely untrue, she was getting a raw deal from the other members of staff with references of presidential, favourable exceptions to the rostered arrangements. This was quite absurd in their rational operational functioning in their workplace. Considering Caz did the front of house and Eddy did the back of house roster. This was always the case, which had never changed. It was him that decided to move out. The inevitable horizontal gravity with what moves in, would eventually move out had happened. Was happening.

Dominoes continued to fall. One too many awkward moments at work, he tip-toed over the wobbling slab. Eddy took the decision to leave work. Caz did not want him to work his full notice, but she needed him. This hurt more than he wanted to let on. He made a few calls. He successfully negotiated a return to his old job at the butchery.

Over a month in which he had returned as an all-embracing couple, the dominoes had fallen, one by one. He had moved out of HIS home. He had moved out of HIS job. A job he adored and flourished at. HE had made sacrifices. Relinquished events, mates and HIS life. When she was sitting pretty on the throne HE had built. HIS life crumbled around. Hers was unmoving, safe, secure.

Eddy's four-week notice was cut short to a couple of days. As soon as the job vacancy went on the advertising forums, the phone rang off the hook. Caz hired one quickly, too quickly. It was in haste. Obviously, too obviously he wanted him out of her life. A knee-jerk reaction to get rid of the sight of him, to cut loose any ties. Transparently obvious Caz assured Eddy that it was the case to merge the changes to the new season, hence the new menu seamlessly. Eddy was completely unconvinced. Frankly, he did not believe her, at all. He paid him off, in cash, to get him out of another part of her life. That was blatantly clear. The last exchanges at work was an argument that escalated from this fact. He got four weeks' severance pay. He did not let anyone know that he was starting his new, but old, job the next day. This day was his last day as he planned, organised a quick get together with his former colleagues, kitchen staff to drink at the local bar.

The scene was set for saying his goodbyes at the Gladstone. A pub opposite Barfinda. The laugh was stuck as the reason became apparent, clear, focused and made crystal clear. The reason she wanted him out of his life so quickly. The reason that she gave no answers. The reason for explaining her mood. And, to think, for the past long torturous weeks Eddy had been blaming herself. It had to be something that he had done. He did. It turned out to be Kevin. Kev. The cause of the platonic shift that jilted him out of favour. The platonic shift that shock his world. The amicable break in the relationship that shattered the surface, penetrated deep within the fibres that connected the love strings of the bridges that brought two people together, was down to Kev. Solely down to Kev. Not Eddy. Not him, as he himself had thought.

He should have felt relieved. He felt ashamed. This is how the truth, like a flower blossomed from the lies that spread like ivy into a tangling, suffocating mess that left ruins of hurt, distrust and pain.

Who was Kev? Kev was the kitchen slut. A dirty alcoholic of a chef that felt he was the best. A reincarnation of the key attributes that made Gordon Ramsey a phenomenal chef. The extraordinary visionary that made Helston Blumenthal a revelation. The resounding attention to detail that make the Roux bothers conquer, succeed and deliver in the raging, cut-throat seas of the catering profession. Kev was that disillusioned. Kev was not, or was never going to be within a mile of these geniuses. Heck, he was not going to be within a world of them.

Everyone outside of his bubble believed that he had huge levels of grandeur. To even breathe his inabilities in the same breath was comical. His bubble consisted of him, himself, and, well that was it. Even his mates could see that he was not as great as he felt he was. There was no distributing that he great waste of talent. Without a doubt he had the makings.

As an apprentice, he had the opportunity to be a great chef, but drink always came first. A slippery slope that he fell, headfirst down…and out. The saddest thing is that he believed the hype without chasing to achieve the dream. He was a lost talent drowning in his own fantasy stream of positive feedback, pouring with alcoholic rains. He was ok, at best. On his worse, useless, incompetent. Nothing more than a cockroach crawling on his back to be trodden by the steel-capped kitchen shoe.

So…back to who Kev really is. Kev worked day shifts at Barfinda, but also moonlighted around the city in various places in the evenings. He worked hard. He needed to pay for his addiction. He was a slightly chubby bloke, but only around his midriff towards his dirty brown neck. Here is where the years of alcohol were beginning to take their toll. He seemed to always wear the same clothes. He stunk. A combination of body odour, stale tobacco and alcohol.

When he came into the changing room at the end of a shift, Eddy and his crew would step up their conversation and get out quickly before he took his shoes off. He had the worse smelling feet that you would ever have the misfortune to smell. Death warmed up, mixed with a hint of aged parmesan and maggot infested carcasses left in the sun. Somehow, though, he always found it into Barfinda for last call. Even more baffling, with a different girl in hand. No one had any idea how he did it.

Eddy was chatting to Kev and Davo by the bar in the Gladstone. It was an unusually busy Thursday afternoon. The acoustic guitar singer was all but defeated by the chatter. The workers were having a drink before going home alone, to loved ones or families. They were having a drink before going their separate career ways for the day. Eddy will wake tomorrow in at a different hour to get to a different working location. Davo back home, Kev to another job just around the corner.

Eddy bought the first round of Coopers Pale Ale schooners which hit the spot. Eddy choose to finish on a Thursday. For which he told everyone. The truth was, as Friday was the busiest day at the butchers, and he could get right in the swing of it straight away. He needed to work, stay active. Hence to do the orders and have a quiet weekend, looking for a new place.

They were here later than planned after an uncommonly busier service than the regular Thursday. They planned to be here by four in the afternoon. It was now their first drink at six in the evening. Many of the front and back of house crew of the Barfinda either had gone back to work or were hastily saying goodbye as they ran for their bus or train home. Some of Eddy's mates had long gone home. Under the family spell, for which they secretly loved being part off. It was only the three workers left from different jobs. Three friends that were connected in different ways.

Eddy was Kev's mentor at Tafe and taught him through his first years as an apprentice. They loosely kept in touch and often would share a story and a joke over a beer. Davo was at Eddy's first job. Although he was training to be a paramedic then. To cover the rent, he worked as a pot-wash in the kitchen to earn some extra money, as well as being his true best mate. Somehow, from these humble beginnings, he managed to go from being a paramedic, to be a successful banker in the city's newest high-rise building.

Back then, no one could have seen his meteoritic rise to his office standing, literally, on the shoulders of giants. Nevertheless, they shared interests. They went to watch sport at the local. They shared meals with respective partners. They had that bromance that you read about, hear about, and often see. An unspoken love for each other. That they would have each other's' back. This bromance was where they did not see each other for days, weeks and months but when they did, it was like they chatted yesterday. Where they talked like old women over a picket-lined white fence.

After the first round of drinks, Kev announced his leaving to go to work. He mentioned this at the start. Davo and Eddy wished him a great shift while mocking him with a cheer of full schooners while they continued drinking, chatting and laughing.

Davo's partner Sara-Jayne came in for a quick drink on her way home. She did not stay for long. She knew that a quick drink with these two was never going to happen. Nights written by them always rocketed to be a mess like the remains from a firework exploding. SJ made no excuses to leave. She always felt slightly intimidated being the third-wheel of their matiness. Not saying that they made her feel uncomfortable, but especially after a few drinks she had started behind the eight ball. Being a school night, she was not even going to attempt to catch-up.

Later on, the pub had thinned out. The acoustic guitar had baled. They had not moved far at all from the bar in which they started. Same spot, same beers. It was here that they had decided to go somewhere else, to where people would be. Davo led the way. He was first out of the corner doorway, only to suddenly stop at the stone steps to turn back in. He motioned to get another drink, then bellowed, 'fuck it'. It was supposed to be more of a mutter to himself, but ended in being towards Eddy. They walked out.

Eddy was a little dumbfounded and confused by his hesitation and made a slight unfunny joke to mask it. Then he saw. He saw the reason why. All the whys. Why Davo was acting strange. Why his relationship knocked over one by one in quickly succession. The haze of confusion rapidly evaporated before his eyes. Davo paused, as he was going to protect him. Then, decided in the same instance that Eddy had to see what was really going on. More importantly, to see with his own eyes what was going on.

Opposite, outside work, on the other side of the road stood Caz and Kev. Kev was weighed down by a few dark grey bags full of groceries from Woolworths. Caz, the princess, talking on her mobile phone, checking out her reflection in the restaurants window. The lying

214

scumbag Kev grabbed Caz's hand, the cheating bitch accepted it. Anger erupted inside of Eddy. They were walking close. Obviously, to the same destination. In the same direction. To the same place. It did not take a mathematician to work out what was going on. It did not take a scientist to see the chemistry that they evidently had. It did not take Sherlock Holmes to solve this mystery.

Impulsive action took over Eddy. He promptly marched over. Ancient wild primitive actions took over his reactions. He did not even look across the road as he ran across. He was strongly focused on getting answers, and answers he would get. He was staring steely-eyed towards Kev. The look in Kev's eyes said it all. Kev staggered a little. Wanting to run, was rooted in his spot. The true thought of actually sprinting away was racing through his head, to leave Caz. She did not even enter his mind as being protective or chivalrous. Thanks to Davo, Eddy had caught them.

What?' Kev spluttered out. 'You're still here. Still drinking?'

'Just as well. Eh!' Eddy spat out in fury. 'How long has this been going on?' Eddy scanned a terrified Kev, followed by a sheepish, shielding gaze from Caz. Caz looked equally terrified in her facial expression but with a trace of relief.

'I'll call you back.' She finished her phone call with abruptness.

As she apologised with mumbled meanings of how she did not want Eddy to find out like this. That it just happened. That it only happened recently. Eddy saw holes in that story like the Swiss cheese that was now on the pavement floor of the dropped plastic grocery bag. She went to speak, nothing came out. Eddy pushed Kev in the chest. He dropped the remaining bag and hit the glass shop front window of David Jones hard, with a satisfying noise that penetrated from his head.

'I didn't mean to cheat…on you…mate,' Kev spluttered out from uncontrollable sobs of tears. This clearly was not a masculine moment for him.

'What do you mean? Mate? Cheat? You? MATE. Bullshit mate. It was her. My girlfriend.'

Eddy's face was so close to Kev's that the raging temper made him spit out 'cheat', leaving his saliva only one place to rest.

'It happened when you got back,' Kev divulged the information faster than a dropping penny. In Eddy's mind, the penny dropped further into making sense.

'From holiday?' Eddy enquired. 'When? When we were still together!'

'No.' He looked down at the ground as he nursed the back of his head. 'From your parents.'

'Christmas? You fucking what? At bloody Christmas? Merry fucking Christmas then. Arsehole,' at this moment he was so close. He could see the lines in Kev's brown iris. He could feel his fear. His heart racing. Eddy had never felt this surge of anger before. He retracted his body just enough to clench tightly his right fist to throw a punch with all the fury in his soul, with all the hurt and betrayal in his heart. It was lucky, for Kev, that Davo intervened.

Davo, ninja-quick, held Eddy's right hand that was white with tightness in the backswing of a punch in mid-air. This was to stop the follow through. Davo was a small, but strong guy, built like a rhino, but had trouble holding Eddy's skinnier arm back. That gave enough time and space for Kev to slide away from the window. To hide. Yes, he did, he actually hid behind the screeching noise that Caz was making trying to get Eddy to stop. It this does not speak volumes of the type of character he is, nothing does.

The type of coward that he was, he is, nothing will change that character flaw. Caz was screaming sorry. Screaming out. Asking Eddy to stop. Asking Eddy to understand. Caz had never seen Eddy so full of wrath. Eddy had never felt so angry. He was not hearing. His mind was blocked to the outside world. The red mist had come down faster than the final curtain. He did not care to hear her. Look at her, or even attempt to understand her view. For him there was not one view that could make him feel differently. No view would take away this hurt, as she had taken and burnt away his trust.

Davo's arm was shaking. He was still holding Eddy's superhuman arm strength that possessed him. He pushed and pulled him away, forcing him aside. Reluctantly Eddy moved away under his shove. Davo shouted words to Caz and Kev that they should go through gritted teeth, as he wrestled to move Eddy away from the confrontation.

Then Eddy, with another wave of strength, turned around. Resisting Davo's attempts to hold him back. Eddy ran back up to Kev's wet sobbing face.

'I bought you a beer,' he roared. It was as if it was not the relationship that hurt him the most. The fact that he had bought him a beer. As a mate not knowing the evil thing he had done, was doing, no doubt continued to do and, was going to continue to do. For he had dealt with the relationship ending. He did not like the outcome but was learning to move on. It was the hurt of the friendship, the mateship that he could not understand at that moment. Would never understand, ever.

The unspoken code amongst mates. You never root another mate's girlfriend unless. UNLESS. Moreover, this was a big, important consideration. Unless you have spoken to the mate beforehand. The violations that he had broken in the mate's code were a fate worse than death. This break of the code was a tough pill to swallow. Eddy was not a violent man but, on this occasion, he wanted nothing more than to see Kev's blood. Blood streaming down his face like the tears he shows, cascading over the grey pavement. He wanted to hurt him outside as bad as he was hurting inside.

At that moment, he wanted to transcend in penetrating his pain. He wanted to see the pain that he was feeling. He wanted him to smell the burning, the destruction of the bridges of friendship that Kev had destroyed. Forever. Davo again pulled him away as he made a movement to make these thoughts a reality.

Davo shouldered Eddy to shuffle and escort him back into the Gladstone. He was steaming. His drunkenness evaporated into soberness. Davo ordered a drink, a shot. Davo had to persuade the landlord who had heard, before seeing the events through the window. Eddy wept. He was ashamed of it. He was surprised by it. He did not weep for a relationship ending. He wept for the humiliation. The shame of what had been done to him. The shame of lovers that could not be trusted. The shame of mates that could not be trusted. That was the hurt. A mate that could not be trusted.

The shot was taken. It calmed him down. Eddy thanks Davo. Behind them the last punter left with a slam of the door. The landlord, who knew them both very well gave them each a departing shot on the house. He shut the front door, locked it, turned the lights down. He got the bottle of bourbon from behind the bar and put it in the centre of the triangle they made. They talked, drunk until the earlier hours.

The door slammed shut as hard as that relationship ended. He regretted not punching him.

Later, through the weeks that passed, Eddy saw him a few times since that intense, vivid encounter. Each time, Kev crossed the road or walked in a different direction rather than having to face him. Kev was petrified of Eddy. Rightly so, as when Eddy saw him, the anger rose like a volcano that needed to erupt and spill the blood like lava everywhere to release the coiled tension inside of him.

The amicably ending of the relationship had finished in an intense wrath of passionate ferocity. That friendship had ended in a wave of violent vehemence. A bridge burnt. A river widened. Never to be crossed. A mateship incinerated, reduced to ashes, destroyed.

Back to the Present
Two Polar Opposite Loves

I did not involve Laverna in this plot, yet Kev did. Unknowingly, his trail of being a cheat had led her into this. To hide his crimes of deception, he had called in Laverna to help. The Goddess remains on earth in the company of thieves and cheats, living in the shadows.

I am talking to her body. Through her neck comes the soothing, enticing chimes of a voice that tickles the curiosity to get people to be mischievous. Her extremely beautiful head is down on earth. She sometimes appears to me this way or just head, rarely together. It is a way she deceits people, by swearing on her unseen body, or unseen head as payment for her deeds.

Laverna was given the title of the Goddess of Dishonest and Disreputable people by Jupiter. She relished it. She acted crafty in her act. She loved the ending of this story by watching in the reflective shop windows her destructive, damaging composition.

Eddy thinks on. That was the end of that story. No turning the pages back. But, for some reason until this arvo he finds that he is thinking of it again. The first time since that awful end of summer. Admittingly he did not find Caz attractive from the beginning. From the offset of that glass of wine, that first kiss the balance tilted. He fell for her overtime.

The horrid break-up told him that it was not a strong relationship and pretty much doomed to fail. The mateship though, that hurt. Hurt more that the pain of love could ever have done.

He never saw Kev again. He moved to a different part of Sydney. Out of choice as he wanted to be within walking distance of the butchers. Caz, he heard ended having a kid with Kev. He did not know more, wanted to know less and cared for even less.

This was one relationship that, although it took time, he did not stand a chance with. He did not blame himself, anymore. Looking at the way he dealt with it, he really should not have got involved in the first place. That was something he learnt for this relationship. He wanted someone. At this point he did not care who. He yearned for a companion, more than he desired a true love.

Jenni was a different story. He still loved her. Still thought of her. Still would take her back...

Eddy was travelling on the rainswept bus from work. In his mind, he sees Jenni as clear as day. The rain stops, starts, the wipers are rushing in the large window in the front battling against the divulge of the quick turnaround of a beaut of a day to a thunderstorm. A wave from the deep puddle misses a walking couple by a few inches. In his mind, a wave takes over his emotions. He wonders what, if anything, he has learnt from Jenni. On reflection. On board he cries. He has his sunnies on. His skin is wet from rain. He conceals it well. His embarrassment is hidden under the veil of the deluge that is outside but being brought in. He missed Jenni. He had the ashes and dust feeling all over again. He never wondered what could have been until this moment.

Eddy learnt that time is a factor. That timing is everything. Her right time may be now, in the present. His was then. You cannot trick people into loving anyone.

Seven Years Ago
The Rebound?

It was more the love than of Jenni that he thought of. He actually craved her touch. Caz was a distraction, not a love, a lust at best. In the three years after these doomed relationships Eddy took some time out of dating. That was not to say he was single. That was not to say he was alone. He just seemed to skip that part of the relationship stage altogether. To be together for a few minutes, not to stay even a night. Never to share anything more than sweat and saliva. He cared not to learn about someone.

That crucial part of being there, getting to know someone. The part of being genuinely interested in another person's day. This disregarded emotion was skipped completely, to just go straight to the sleeping with. To wait for her to be asleep before doing the Harold Bolt. He was quite promiscuous. He enjoyed the lack of commitment, but, he was never that guy. Never had been. Never wanted to be. It did not seem right that he was doing it. He knew deep down why he was, but he really did not want to admit to anybody, let alone admit it to himself. Himself the accurate core.

Truthfully, he was not ready to commit. He was fearful. Mixed up. He did not want to be hurt again. Eddy, well, he was scared, petrified in fact. More to the point he did not want to feel excruciating throbs of pulsating unhappiness, resembling loss, ever again. He did not want to hurt females in his fun. While he found what he was looking for. For that, he could not even answer that question himself to why he was doing exactly that. Eddy, was playing the field, hence keeping himself safe from harm. This unknowingly made Eddy more horrified.

Do not get him wrong, he did enjoy the sex. Let's face it, who doesn't. However, the feeling of having someone to talk to. The feeling of finishing work, to go back and tell all to someone is something that cannot be beaten. Sure, mates were good at that, but a mate is a mate, and somethings are left away from mates. Eddy was a typical male in that connotation. The word and feelings of love did not come into the conversation between mates, unless you wanted to be ridiculed and torn strips off over the drinks at the bar. In jest, but knocking the inner steel caged fortress of his sanatorium in his deepest part of his very soul.

Immoral as his actions were. Honourably he stood by that with relationships, he enjoyed the build-up of getting to know the layers of someone. He enjoyed the connection of being in a relationship and connecting them with their friends, work colleagues, acquaintances, families, as well as enemies.

It happened. Quickly. Lightning had struck again. Eddy noticed what he was unknowingly looking for. He noticed her first. It was lust at first sight. He knew her. He had met her before when working at Jones Butchers, but this time she was different. She held an aura of confidence that was seductively attractive. It, of course, helped that she was in fact, incredibly attractive. Eddy developed a desire to ask her out, but he lacked the confidence in himself. He did not want to make the working relationship suffer for his desire.

Around her, Eddy was clumsy, tongue-tied and generally embarrassed, borderline mortified with his behaviour every time they would talk. He would overanalyse the meetings, or the way he dribbled black coffee down his chin. He had no idea if she had a partner, boyfriend, husband, or, wife. He hoped with each meeting that she would portray a little piece of her personal life. Then he would know if he had a chance. Instead, he held a schoolboy-esque candle to the hope of a development.

She was a representative of the main slaughterhouse in Sydney. He found it odd that such a radiant, striking Italian woman could be representing such a death marked passage of life for animals. It started as flirting. Harmless flirting at work with no attempt to take it further.

Then it happened one Saturday afternoon. On this fateful day, Eddy was taking one of his jaunts out to another suburb within Sydney to find his way in Leichardt. He was not at work. He would do this occasionally, on his day off. He would get on a bus, or walk to stumble on a café that he could sit, relax and catch up on news away from work, his homely environment. On this particular jaunt, he came off the main road and sees a delightful whitewashed brick café with what appeared to be driftwood doors as the walls. Thick rigging rope around the border with deep blue paint to fill in the spaces. In a nautical theme, that was done well, as to appear light-hearted.

Giving the perception of space and light in a confined room was a stroke of genius. At the same time, the café felt cosy and discreet. A mix of music was subtle as the undercurrent of a calm sea. He ordered his coffee to Billy Joel's magnificent Piano Man and preceded to sit down to a hip-hop track, of some description, with a smooth beat and a guitar loop from the Beatles, While My Guitar Gently Weeps. He ordered a long black to nurse the hangover from that good ol' quick drink the night before.

As it was. As it always will be. One drink with Davo never happened.

Eddy had the Sydney Morning Herald spread out in front of him. His brain just did not want to register. The creased edges of the thin paper sheets laid out on the brown, thick table. His head bowed over, he slumped over the print as he read each headline, some of the paragraphs of the report, story or fabrication without registering any of it. It was something to give his mind a focus to stop the nauseous tremors from inflicting vomit. He was feeling better after the long walk here. Nevertheless, he was not denying any attempt that he felt normal, that he felt energised, that he was not hungover.

He had the attention span of a Duracell bunny with obsessive-compulsive disorder. The way he skipped around the newspaper in front of him proved this. The coffee and the ambience relaxed him, working their magic. He was sipping his black elixir from a thick blue mug, while surveying his surroundings in a silent appreciation, when he saw her. Through the window like an image from the silver screen. In different attire to what he was used to seeing her in.

The shimmering candle of lust had turned to a fiery, towering uncontrollable inferno of love. She was a breath of fresh air in his lungs. He breathed in at the sight of her. His eyes opened wide so not to miss a single part of her form. He felt hot under his loose-fitting attire. She floated inside. She did not notice that she was being appreciated.

For what she would later describe as being fate, for what he described as a mere coincidence, Mara leaned on the counter as she ordered. She had tight black workout yoga pants, which accentuated her curvy legs and tight bum. A loose-fitting grey tank top clung around her midriff that was splotched with sweat stains. Her long black enthralled rustically tied up hair, sticky with sweat on the nape of her glistening olive tanned neck. She lingered the waft of the smell of rubber mats. Her large dark brown eyes sheltered behind her small round glasses with the fragile-looking silver frame. She looked as if she had just stepped out of the gym. She was slightly flushed. To Eddy she looked amazing, so incredibly sexy.

On seeing Eddy, her face turned another, darker shade of red. She was embarrassed that he had seen her in this relaxed state. She only came in for a takeaway. She wanted to get in, get out with a coffee in hand. With her self-respecting dignity intact. He motioned her to sit down. She rummaged around her hand for an excuse. Coming up only with air, she gingerly tiptoed over. She apologised for her appearance as she shuffled her feet. She was embarrassed for her attire, as she looked down at her pink and red runners. Tapping them to take her anywhere, maybe to the magical land of Oz. Apologising for her smell. There was not one, but freshly grinded coffee beans, bacon, eggs and toast. She would have apologised for everything, for which the gentleman, that is Eddy, dismissed and said the right things, that made her school-like giggle into her chest. Blushing as she could not give him eye contact, but thankful for his reaction. Reluctantly, she sat. She wanted to, but not like this. She wanted to be in control of her appearance. Yet.

This was the beginning. A spark was ignited by Eddy's inferno, or at least he believed that subconsciously. She somehow felt more comfortable. She sipped her takeaway coffee. Licked her lips. They talked, exchanged numbers. Instead of a work mobile, Eddy actually got her personal mobile. Indeed, it was the start.

Eddy called Mara soon after this chance meeting. He could not help it. The morning into the afternoon. Tick Tock. TICK and a TOCK. His mind raced. He paced faster. His body, his soul, active. The time slogged. The spark of time laid dormant. Quiet. Asleep. Unmoving forward. It may have appeared to be desperate, as he twirled the mobile in his hand. Lingered over the numbers. Her name appearing ready to be called.

That evening, Eddy made the call. He was a man of action. If he wanted something, he, well, went for it. The same could be said for the if, if he did not want something. He would either pursue or walk away. For instance, if he was at a party, if he was involved in a circle of conversation which moves to something that he really does not care about, he will just, move away. He will venture to a find a conversation that interests him without any guilt, remorse or regret. It took him all day to get to this point, but he got there.

After numerous night calls, until they fell asleep. Copious cup of steaming coffee, that was cold by the time they finished it. Masses of messages throughout the day. The first thought, her, him. The first message to her, him. After all this, the officiality of it all was sealed on a blustery chilly morning. They started dating in the winter of that year.

With the distinctive racket of grinding metal on metal and stone being forcefully removed against its wishes as an accompaniment to the growing city, he waited for his bus. Over the bin in shabby florescent yellow vest with dirty dust and paint-covered desert boots, jeans and T-shirts ridden with holes are a group of tradies smoking over a metal bin. As if it was a burning fire to keep warm, where as the only controlled fire was the perfectly cylinder white hand-rolled cigarette tilting from their parched lips. In the midst of nervous conversation, they bring to chapped lips to ignite the orange fires at the end to leave a dark plume of smoke.

The smell does not annoy Eddy as much as the smoke. With the tradies assembling around a cauldron of smoke arises, thick and suffocating. He edges out of the line of the wind carrying toxic cloud, yet it is futile. Thankfully turning under the railway arch he sees the yellow neon numbers of the bus he waits for. Flags it down more feverishly than required. Clambers on board and releases a breath. A large exhale escapes him with him only realising at the moment of warm clean haven air inside the Sydney bus that he had been holding his breath.

It was a short fortyish-minute bus ride from each other's unit. The past few times he had made this trip, he had seen the prompt manner in which they delve for their yearning accessory. The mobile phone, if not in their hand already comes out like a magician revealing his final magic trick. Now and again he admires the person that had brought a book. But most surrender to the need of mindless, soulless and wordless connection in a world of noise getting muffed shut but their electronic hand-held box. The lights illumine in hues of yellow shadowing their faces, bent over in gormless expressiveness. Around them the world passes them, literally by. He is too excited to concentrate.

His phone is firmly in his pocket, silent like a sleeping mouse in his burrow. Between the people on the bus, the passing streets of Sydney and the road ahead he connects to his moving surroundings. In his own revolving cityscape, the corporate gives' way to residential. Kids playing in the park, mothers pushing prams, people jogging, in a few short years to succumb to the people on this bus. Trapped outside, but very much inside their personal mobiles. Ironically that have made them immobile.

The bond between Eddy and Mara was instant, before they started dating. She waited for him at the bus shelter. A light flurry of soft rain had started to descend. She wanted to take him to breakfast as a new joint she had been recommended. They embraced like long-lost lovers, a short intimate kiss. A lingering look in their eyes could see the gusting sails of possibility.

This was not the rebound that his mates insisted it was. He knew it. This felt, well, unlike anything that he had felt before. Eddy had left a tip-toed soundless trail of shattered uninhabited promises in the early break of the morning light of many a bedrooms. All of these bedrooms where a single female slept in ruffled disarray of doona and sheets could be accounted for his, rebound. For he could not be more strongly adamantly resolute that what he and Mara had was not a rebound, for this, felt so right. For him it was a different experience of love.

They did have what was deemed as a perfect situation. During the weekdays, they toiled relentlessly. They sent messages at the start of their days, on their way to work and then got on with their day. It was rare that they messaged each other through the day. This was more seldom than an actual telephone call, the latter never happened. For the time in work was just that. After work a message was sent. Their jobs were not the office nine to five so the reply from another person would come when they had finished.

Then the phone calls began. Sometimes while running, while at the gym, cooking dinner. These could last for ten minutes. Or, they could last for two hours. They literally lived for the weekend. As soon as Eddy finished on a Friday, his tools washed, wrapped away. The lights off, the door shut and locked. He raced back to his unit, showered and picked up the pre-packed sports holdall and took the short, brisk walk to the bus stop. He then made the fortyish-minute journey to Mara's place.

He intended, and tended to, finish first on a Friday so he would arrive at Mara's unit just after five in the afternoon. Perfect timing for her to come in, make small talk as she undressed to redress for the gym. She would go off and do her evening course of a rotation of an aerobic forty-five-minute extreme workout one week, intense biking spin class the next. He would have his exercise in the morning. So, while she was doing hers, he would cook a meal. This was, a simple Friday ritual that worked, and worked well, very well. It made her happy, to do her thing. Him being in her life did not disturb her habitual catch-up with mates, a heavy sweaty workout that set-up her weekend to live against the sword. He was happy, cooking for her.

Then with the timing it was perfect. That when she got back beaming and sweaty, showered, dressed into relaxing attire the meal was close to being finished. They chatted, ate and enjoyed each other's company. It was effortless. It was how it should be. Soft touches. Playful banter. An electric charge of being transparent, honest and open in their progressive bond.

Sometimes the meal took second place. The sight of her, the sight of him. They would sometimes make passionate love, sometimes not waiting for her to take a shower as an urge came over him, or her. Them. In seconds they were infused together.

When the lights turned off at the end of the night, Eddy could still see, a light of love shining, like an electric sensation between and around them that soothed them. The slightest gap separates them as they lie next to each other. The body warmth is unquestionable in the closeness that they both feel for each other. This could be one of his favourite moments. The comfortable relaxation of blissful enlightenment.

He would love waking up to see her face. See her resting with a permanent half-smile on her lush lips. Her chest gently heaving as she softly breathed. The subtle smell of her perfume combined with the floral scent of her sheets. He loved watching the sunlight kiss her cheeks in the morning. Then he would peck her on the cheek or lips, or both. They would cuddle and the day would already be great.

The year had flown past. Of course, they had their arguments but that shows how passionate they were invested in the relationship. That showed that they cared. Career driven as they both were, they decided to plan a longer-than-usual time away. They decided on four-weeks through some of Europe, as opposed to their normal week in Australia littered with interruptions. They had the character to work, a strong ethic to want to do well by the people they worked with and for. Flogging themselves without time-off, only taking their rostered days off for which, unfortunately their phones kept them always connected. A monotonous repetitive weekly cycle that needed to be smashed, broken.

Eddy talked often about his time in the UK and wanted to show Mara where he worked. Not in Lewes though, as he had a sneaky suspicion that Shez was still there. He never knew what happened with her. This was the first time in a long time that the figure of her loomed out of his subconscious. She was a beautiful lady. Nevertheless, he did not want to bump into her again. Monetarily, Shez was onto a good thing. Morally, Shez was going straight to hell. Without passing Go. Namely for the lies she told to herself, to everyone.

Eddy wanted to show her, rather show-off Saxmundham. The beauty of Suffolk. For sure they would have to touch on London. A trip to Europe always must integrate a little London. This is just one of those maiden thirsts for Australians travelling in Europe. Seeing the sights of the capital that have been portrayed in every form of media interpretation. Walking over one of the many bridges that cross olde Father Thames. To see where the Queen lives.

After a collection of notes from these two ships that pass through each other's working lives, they manage to organise the cusp of an itinerary. The first week in the UK, then travelling through France, stopping at places en route. The second week in Italy, with the last week to be played by ear. But for cost, they had to make it back to the UK for their flight home.

Mara was born in Australia. The first of her mother's generation. She yearned to know the country her mother spoke of. The country that her grandparents came over from with her young mother for a better life. The town her grandparents spoke of with a strong, firm pride of exhilaration. When they spoke, their eyes transported to a younger them, when they wore younger couples' clothes, with a reminiscence twinkle of a magnificent recollection bordered by their wrinkled bordered, contented eyes. Although she felt that she had been, she had never actually seen Italy. She desired the same bond.

Therefore, she organised this trip as a stepping stone to get her Italian nationality, citizenship. In one fell swoop to see where her grandparents were born, lived and married. The place they turned their back on as a young family, recently married adults with a baby in arms for the promised land of plenty, Australia. After the war, times were tough. When their parents passed it was time for them to create their own life. They chose this path with, even now, no regrets.

As they organised this trip. As they started to finalise plans, such as time off, booking flights, places, looking at sights to see they were getting focused in the pursuit for happiness. The fevered upbeat open-minded energy was being broadened. The excitement between them grew, as they in turn grew closer. It was going to be great. It already was great.

Hindsight is a fantastic thing. Eddy looks back at these memories and seems to see, with the aid of THAT fantastic hindsight, that he was the springboard that propelled her to find her heritage. The aid for her to embrace where she came from culturally. To start learning her grandmother's and mother's village tongue properly. She had learnt the true Italian of the country, not the village slang, abbreviations.

Mara would feel left out at parties when the family got together to talk about this and that, of the village, in their native tongue, with references to a place she had seen but did not feel. She felt like an outsider, adopted. Eddy was the means of access to a completely new world, but the key to her inner world. In hindsight, once again, he was just a foothold for her. He is not being cynical at this revelation but actually proving a fact. That fact he did not see when planning the trip. A fact he regrettably will ultimately see.

After many weeks of planning, getting more excited at the pending holiday. They had the sketched remnants of a schedule. Then the rumbling in the distance started to draw closer, louder. The dark clouds of doom. The last of the calculator digits displays the earthshattering blow. It took a while for the truth of what they were seeing to flow in with realisation. It was apparent that they did not have the funds to be self-supportive for the duration of their trip. How was this possible? Simply they loved life. They lived life. They did not save, until it was too late. This was disappointing, but not a deal-breaker. This new revelation meant that plans needed to be changed to accommodate these glowing neon figures.

Watching Mara not cope well in a ball of sobbing mess. The sheets of planning, the conversations disappearing beyond a waterfall veil of tears. Eddy took the initiative. He proactively sat on the sofa and emailed The Smugglers Tunnel. He may have seemed that he was not comforting Mara when in fact he was striving for a solution. A to the point, direct email thumped out on the pale white keys with purpose. An electric message of hope. On the off chance that the landlords, Laura and Ken, were not only still there, but more importantly, had work.

He was lucky in his timing, as no sooner that the email got sent, he moved the device aside to offer consolation. Thinking of the bordering on encouragement that he could voice that all was not lost a soft beep resounded. Stopping him in his tracks. In the bottom corner of the screen he saw a reply. Missing at the first attempt to open it he landed to get the answer. In response a relevant email. To his surprise, they were still there. But, they had no work. He did not have any options. She had no options. Sleep came over them when Mara's tears had steamed to annoyance.

The following morning, the mood was no different. She was still crushed mentally which gave her the appearance that the world was placed firmly on her shoulders. He got up and lifted his mobile to see a string of emails. Like a beacon in the sea of electronic waste he saw hope. As he read the email the floods of disappointment started to ebb. On the horizon were crystal clear formations of possibilities. The true, real fact that this dream trip for Mara will come into precision attainment.

Laura had emailed back a recommendation from a place, just down in the centre of Suffolk at Bury St Edmunds. A job that was his if he wanted but he needed to work set dates and duration. He did not care. This trip was more for Mara than himself. Eddy cast his mind back to know the place as a visitor, but nothing more. Certainly not well enough to be able to explain it fully to Mara.

'MARA,' Eddy shouted from the kitchen table to the bedroom. 'QUICK'. She raced over, fearing something had happened. In splattered spray of toothpaste foam she looked concerned while brandishing her toothbrush like a sword in defence. Concern turned to confusion as she watched Eddy nonchalantly sip his black coffee.

'What? You OK? What's—'

'Pack your bags. It's on.'

'No.'

'Yes.'

She screamed as she rushed Eddy with the grip of a python suffocation the fear, trying to keep from her dreams to once again blow away, escape her grasp. His coffee spilt over the table, fortunately away from his mobile. She squealed with delight at Eddy. Smearing toothpaste over his shoulder. The minty flesh covering his cheeks, his lips. The holiday was back on the tracks in the sky to Europe. She could not let go. She started to sob. This time in celebration. In rejoice.

Over the course of the planning week, Mara took the reins of the sights, the touristy things. Eddy sorted out the finance. Ken gave the contact details for Graham at the Red Lion. Who was looking for urgent help in the kitchen, as well as someone to fill in the bar, organise and clean? The regular staff couple that worked were taking holidays, with the replacement pulling the pin. Eddy would have to work two people's jobs. After numerous emails and conversations, they had finally committed to a date. Finally, they had a leaving date, after weeks of planning, it was set in stone.

He learnt a little of the connection with Graham and Ken through the various emails. Eddy found out that Ken went to the same school, although not great mates, they did have the occasional beer and chat. When they got into the pub game, they reconnected and forged a rich friendship based on beer. Those ridiculous customers that make the days either fun filled, short, or long.

Ken, the landlord of The Smugglers Tunnel, had gone out on a limb to vouch for Eddy. He spoke highly of him as being a perfect short-term candidate. Rather than hiring someone for a few weeks, train them and the overall hassle that comes with a newbie. Eddy required limited training and was hardworking, reliable and would not let him, or Ken for that matter, down.

When they arrived, they firstly beelined to Ken and Laura who had a spare room for them for a couple of nights to get over the long flight. They were so helpful and recommended the cathedral at Bury St Edmunds in emails, telephone calls. He remembered why he had next to no recognition of going back to Bury St Edmunds again. The problem was he compared it to Saxmundham, which, honestly, was not a fair comparison.

It was the tale-end of the summer in the UK when they would arrive and was a little cooler but would not be unpleasant.

It was predicted that the pub was going to be quiet. After the school holidays in the UK, everywhere was quieter, apparently. Graham was reluctant, or more correctly, he did not want to pay someone for a short period of time. Then to have nothing for them to do for the period between September and November. Other though it started to pick up momentum for the festivities he did not have enough for three people to do. He would have to try to find a job for them when the couple returned within the small bar. This situation with Eddy was perfect. It was a lucky break for them both. In the emails that followed before leaving, the holidaymakers, that were going away were mentioned as a couple, as if they were joined at the hip, with no names to go on, so he also referred to them as, simply, the couple.

Regrettably, he was required to work a month. Due to Eddy's self-appointed honour system, he respected their wishes to fulfil his promise to Mara. This would perfectly tie in with the couples being away. The agreement was met. Both with applause and jeering. It was averse to by Eddy's job. Negotiations were made that the hours he did not have he would be in negative owing, rather than having time off without pay. This was part of his financial calculations, he needed the money. They agreed but he would have to work off the hours when fit, overtime or additional days.

Mara was so much easier. She had been at the company for a number of years, not really had a proper holiday just the odd day off here and there. This pleased her employers as the hours were becoming larger than warranted and getting out of hand. Mara was not happy that Eddy was going to be working for four weeks only leaving them two weeks touring. She had the freedom to do her own thing. He was being chivalrous, a knight in shining chef whites.

Then came the clutcher of a deal, the ripper—Graham threw in accommodation. It was the last email. Graham was evasive to offer the option, as although his pub, they had made a home above it in the landlord's former residence. He had a few ideas, whether it was a short-term room at a family members home or his own home. He did not want to promise anything. They would be staying at the couple's live-in residence above The Red Lion. Bonus. No hotel bills.

With this added money in their kitty, they decided to travel the mere two-hour train ride away on his days off to do the obligatory sightseeing. Furthermore, they would sightsee the area. There was so much to do.

Eddy was hell-bent on taking Mara to Saxmundham. Predominately to thank Ken, which they had to do. Secondarily to show Mara the place that he holds in the greatest times of his fondest memories. He never mentioned Saoirse in depth, but she is aware of the connection. Not the full story, but spoken in ways of a fling, rather than a love lost.

It was all planned. After the first week, Mara would travel to Italy for a week, then travel back, to help as well in the pub on a casual rate. After saving a few pounds, they would squander the saved money to have a great couple of last weeks around Europe. Ideally, Eddy would have loved to be with Mara as she made a connection to her heritage, but that was not something that could be arranged in this trip.

They talked about it down the line when they came back. They had not even gone yet but they were talking about the future. That would go together someday, maybe to get married in that same church that her grandparents did. The future was so theirs. They talked about many aspects of what the future would hold. Their perfect two-up and two-down house, with cars and a great healthy, fit, and social lifestyle. Children never came up for long in the conversations. Something that they did not see as being pressing, or important, to discuss at this stage. But it was something that was on the cards in the future. One more thing before they went. They organised an agent to holiday-share their unit, so they were at least not losing out on the rent for the six weeks while they were away.

With all the organising. Making sure, everything worked and worked well the time was on them. Before they knew it, they were double-checking their lists and making sure everything was correct. That they had the proper visas. Unfortunately, Eddy could not get one to work, so he instructed Graham, who was okay with it for such a short term, to be cash in hand. If any questions were asked, he was going to say free board for a little work.

They were packing their suitcases one last time. The night before, when the true feeling that the planning was actually becoming an action, hit. They were so excited that this week, then, this day, had finally arrived. In the middle of July, they left the cold Sydney winter for the summer of the UK.

In true UK fashion, they arrived in London, touching down at Heathrow Airport. The English summer. They were welcomed by pounding heavy rain, greeted by strong bitterly cold wind and embraced by colder temperatures than they left the winter's sun of Sydney for.

'Could you imagine Noah coming here?' Eddy joked as he struggled with her overpacked, bursting at the zip, bags.

'What are you talking about?' a weary Mara irritably queried unenthusiastically.

'If he came here before building his ark? Shouting that they would be forty-something-or-other days and nights of rain. Probably shouting over the wind and THE rain.'

'What?' she asked, rubbing her eyes, barely interested, wondering what he was talking about.

'Come on.' Eddy was thrilled to be on holiday. More thrilled to be back in the UK to show off his knowledge. 'Moses, well, he would get laughed at. Forty days of rain? They are probably on FIFTY or something, at the moment.'

He giggled to himself as he stared at the rain from the large floor to ceiling window. Mara just stared at the back of his head, unimpressed with being spoken to for what was an awful joke. Outside, the wind blew the large, fast raindrops nearly horizontal. In layers, they seem to lash the runway like a huge carwash recklessly making their way across. Through the wet-lashed window, dripping with rain from the overflowing gutter above, Eddy felt a great feeling of returning. A feeling that he was once again ready in his heart to explore, learn and enjoy himself. Although grey, cold, wet and miserable looking outside, he smiled as if he was the prodigal son retuning home. He felt hot, dry and delighted to have returned.

The custom officer was a lot friendlier than Eddy had ever encountered. He absolutely had his milo for breakfast. He took his and Mara's passports in hand. He mused aloud, 'Australians hey? Welcome back! Returning to the scene of the crime'.

He followed this by asking a few routine questions such as what are they here for? You know you cannot work on this visa to Eddy. Mara could, so this caused him to probe a little bit more. Have you been here before? Which Eddy found odd as just answering that he had worked here in the UK before, hence the non-working, but tourist visa. Eddy answered resisting any condescending tone. Satisfied with the answers that they gave. Without looking up, he opened the passports and gave two loud quick thuds. Harder than necessary, he stamped the open pages of their passports on the plastic desk, before smiling and wishing them a great holiday.

She collected his light sports bag of luggage, he got lumbered with her heavy bag with wheels that hardly spun. He dragged, she skipped to the train station to get the train north. They easily found a seat on the blue, uncomfortable, hideously designed chairs. Placed their bags on the steel rack above and settled. Before the train had pulled away, Mara was asleep. An amazing feat considering the chairs were more fittingly designed for torture. Yet, she did not sleep much at all, if any, on the plane. Hence why on the platform, when exhausted she did fall asleep that she got woken by Eddy. Eddy wondered if this was wise, but after insisting that she stay awake as they waited on the platform, it was a mistake he had done. He felt she could learn from the mistake he made, on her own.

When he first arrived. He slept on arrival, at the platform to miss copious amounts of trains heading to the city to walk shivering, cold and hungry. He decided to stay awake this time. As for sleeping on the plane, nor did Eddy get much. It was very turbulent, but he had an ability of working on little sleep. He was also a kid in a candy store. He was so excited to be back. It was not to say he was not tired, but his body, mind and soul had gotten used to working on little sleep, on little food as the endorphins kicked in to mask the truth.

On arrival into the countryside. The view was non-existent as the rain created a shimmering silver beaded veil. So, he put his head down to read his book. Looking up at each station to try and read the platform signs occasionally.

Glistening in black bold paint, the white as clear as a cloud, the border of a sea-green blue shows that they have arrived. Bury St Edmunds is proclaimed. The metal decorative poles are painted in the same blue as the border. From the old brick railway station with exterior modern touches that were distinctively out of place he woke Mara up. Almost carrying her, her luggage, his bags they got a shiny black taxi to the Red Lion. Evidence of rain reflects the head lights of the late morning's dark day.

The pub was slightly off the main road, in a potholed scattered Church Street. It they knew where it was, they would have walked it as it was that close. Yet, to live is to learn. This was the sort of place a tourist would miss altogether, so it was no wander that Eddy had no recognition of the place. The backstreet was nestled in the shadows of what was a thief's dream. Now lavish accommodation to the masses. They seemed to backtrack a little, which gave the impression that the taxi driver was a little apprehensive to the exact location.

As the taxi got closer, the clouds emptied their load. Eddy could see the glistening picture of a red lion on its hind legs. A simple angular burgundy red cartoon of an angry lion's face breathing out red fire in a side profile, boldly executed on a black crest. A sign that was creaking in its holdings, in the strong wind and lashing down rain that had abruptly begun. A sign that looked even angrier as it fought to stay in its brackets. Dripping in torrents of raindrops.

The Victorian brick pub was a shade of yellow and the oldest building in the backstreet. The buildings around had grown around it. The old warehouses had been made into apartments above shops that backed from the main street. They also were dropped off the other way around, so the front was the main street, and, here Eddy and Mara arrived at the back with bins out, plastic milk crates and flat-packed cardboard, soggy wet exposed and drooping out of the overflowing large plastic bin. It seemed odd, like one of the bars in Sydney that was trying to be trendy and not have a sign, name or entrance for people to know it was there.

Later, they would see that there was another entrance at the front, but this former main entrance was the one the taxi had used. That the regulars used. They got out, they ran around the back to collect their bags while the taxi driver looked on from the dry and warm driver's seat. The boot was drawn shut. As soon as the click of the lock sounded, the taxi had driven off. Obviously, the moody driver was on a promise! They walked up the three steep stone steps into the bar.

It was just before midday and Graham came running out from behind the bar and embraced them like long-lost friends. He was expecting them anytime now so knew the drowned rats in front of him with sodden luggage would be the Australian couple. The welcome was amazing. He snatched the small suitcase off Mara and walked at pace, as if it contained feathers. Surely, he could see Eddy was struggling with Mara's luggage. As he went, he apologised for not picking them up. Apologised for not giving them a proper welcome. Apologised for the weather. Graham kept apologising as he spoke. He made it known that the bar was unintended. He needed to be quick, he would make up for his brisk manner. He apologised again.

They walked behind the bar, through a painted brown swing door with paint on the bottom right that was showing layers of older paint. This was the point people kicked to gain access when hands were full. They immediately turned up some steep narrow stairs with white paint peeling from the walls and up in a tight U-turn and they were at their new, temporary home. They were in the managers flat of the couple that was shared with Graham. He pointed out doors as he gave them a hurried tour.

He mentioned his room-cum-office at the top of the stairs. as they hurried along, past a small kitchen, bathroom and down a couple of stairs was a large living room that moonlighted as a dining room. This looked out onto the rain-saturated main street. His no-nonsense whirlwind was over, and he apologised, again, as he vanished back downstairs imploring them to shower. Bellowing out expressions behind him for them to make themselves comfortable, to come down for something to eat when ready, and to chat. With a diminuendo of apologising sorries, he descended the steps and back out, with a swish of a door stroking the carpet, to the bar.

As much as they wanted to just have a day in, they could not upset their host. This want was emphasised, especially after they showered and changed clothes. They really wanted to snuggle on the sofa and listen to the rain lashing at the window. Reluctantly, very, very reluctantly, they walked downstairs like hard-done-by teenagers. At the bottom of the stairs was the bar's kitchen to the left.

A loud commotion of pots, chatter, laughs and blurs of stained whites floated the narrow passage. Straight ahead of them were steps that led to the basement. The door would not open fully with the steps positioned to gain access to the cellar. It was like walking in the trenches. Dust of plaster exposing pipes and steel sheets running near the ceiling. The brickwork exposed in places with peeling white paint and plaster and brick crumbling like sand, exposing the skeleton of stone. The dusty stale house smell in the air.

The poorly lit stairwell had a hand-rail that was not worth having. Hanging by screws that could not take much, if any, weight. If they were dressed in Second World War attire with a picture next to this backdrop, it would be like extras on a wartime movie set. They composed themselves in mind. They placed a smile on their dial. They inhaled a breath and exhaled slowly.

They walked thought the burgundy red swing doors, which were newly painted, ironically, to Mara, on the wrong side. They were back into the restaurant for which they skipped the three steps down into. They must have taken a wrong turn somewhere as they were sure that they entered by the back of the bar. Yet they motioned towards the island bar from the lush red, blue and gold flowered carpet designed to separate the main eating area, and the wooden, worn vanished planks of the bar. It does not sound like it would work together but it merged and blended very well.

Graham was chatting animatedly to an elderly man that was sitting with his flat cap on, golden wooden cane resting on the ledge of the wooden bar, no teeth but an award-winning smile, nevertheless. They were gripping each other by the one hand on each other's shoulder, Graham standing on one side over the jump, bridging over to the elderly man seating on a high stool at the bar. They arrived in time to share the aftermath of a loud joke. His free hand wrinkled in a fist that pounded the bar approvingly, his left colourfully rich veined hand nearly knocked over his half pint of Guinness as he swung it around, and his breathless laugh barely audible over the slight low pop music.

Graham looked around and saw them. He was still laughing, and his face was beaming from the joke he was having. He was over in a couple of steps.

'See where H is sitting?' Graham pointed the elderly guy out. 'Well, H loves a drink. We recently changed the door handles. Under the bar is one of the door handles placed vertically. If he feels he is going to fall, he has something to grip on to.' He roars a loud laugh.

They both inspect underneath to see the door handle. They see the polished sparkle of a brass handle and smile towards each other at the British quirkiness. Graham goes over to a small dark brown, almost black side board. Menus clasped in a quick-reflexed motion as he walked hand outstretched to handshake his newly arrived employees. He apologised again. A theme was setting in. His favourite word, it seems, was sorry.

He said for them to order anything. Told them the specials and said a guy will relieve him for the afternoon at three. In this period, for which he normally does the books, orderings, and odd jobs before starting again at five, he was saving for them. To give an introduction to the job, the work, the place and their home.

For this period was the quietest time of the day he would work on the administration and financial side which the evening workers got ready for the five o'clock rush. He normally did it at this time aiming to finish each day a little early. He seldom did. This was his choice, as he normally had a drink with a punter or caught up on work that he did not get done. He was always working. Always living through the pub. The pub lived through him. He lived the pub.

They studied their new temporary work place from this stage-like restaurant that looked over the low-lying ceiling bar. The bar was an island where you could see every corner. A low island in the middle allowed enough passage to see the other side between the various spirits in hanging round gourds in colourful optics. It was well designed and one of the sides was identically matched to the other. Dominating the bar were two giant shining steel vessels, where two beers for the pub were brewed. This has been a talking point for over one-hundred and seventy years and never changed.

The authentic brewing of the local brew, not the vessels which were shining bright and very new looking. Either that, or the maintenance, the tender loving care of the vessels would be the masterpiece to envy any knight in shining armour. One of the large gleaming polished steel vessels held the never-changing beer of the Red Lion Best Bitter. The other was a seasonal brew. The chalk written blackboard that was hanging on a rustic broken, on purpose, sign from the vessel was perfect for the establishment. It was elegant, it was homely.

The description stating the contents was a hoppy, citrus and refreshing ale and called the Gentle Dragon. Eddy had noticed a trend lately and was happy that this said exactly what it wanted and nothing more. Before leaving for Australia he was in his local grocer when he was looking at some Spanish Ibores Paprika Cheese. He smiled and took a photograph when reading the description:

'This cheese evokes a set of sensations
linked to a land of beautiful landscapes with mountains and scrubland,
dotted with rock roses, heather, thyme and lavender fields.'

'IT WAS A CHEESE!' Eddy shouted in his head at the time. 'Not a blur for a fantasy novel set in the lochs and valleys of Scotland.'

Eddy, as did Mara, felt that food and wine were becoming over descriptive. Mara had to do it for work and could completely understand that clients wanted the origins, type, marbling and maturing days. However, she could not understand that some clients wanted to know what the cow's parents were, if the second, twice, removed cousin was married to a nice cow, or a frenemy. What their hobbies were or what they did for a living. Of course, she was overreacting and dramatizing what people were asking for, but sometimes it did feel like their wanted everything down to the poor deceased animals' dental records.

Back to the Gentle Dragon. This will be sampled later, Eddy thought as he surveyed more of the surroundings. Overall, the décor and the furnishing were easy on the eye and uncluttered. On the rich, lightly earthed coloured walls were old advertisements of beers, ales and other various pub merchandise. The wooden tables were shiny with varnish and complemented the room and the wooden floors. It was relaxing with an unpretentious feel that was equally as humble and down-to-earth as the landlord. His character open for all to see, he was bountiful and, in the bar, and restaurant it seemed to open up in a welcoming open arm greeting that encouraged people into his home.

The menu offered the promise of local produce. Beautifully displayed on a black slate board that was in a chalk font, not one of those messy over scripted typefaces that seems as if each letter needed a looping inflatable to float off the pages. This was clear and precise. It was easy to read, read very well, simply, it sounded great. Honest, respectively priced wholesome food. They did not need the menus they were given.

As Eddy and Mara read through the offerings their mouth watered. It was teasing them like sirens playing with their indecision over what to choose, enticing them on their ships to the rocks, to different dishes, different textures, and taste. They were so torn to what to go for. Which siren was going to get their attention? They both ordered different salads, as they wanted something filling but not heavy.

As they were looking around again, the food came out. A speedy service. The server was very friendly, young and a little nervous. Eddy tried to tell her everything was fine as she visibly trembled the large white bowls with a Royal blue trim in her tiny, long fingered hands. Carefully as carrying eggs, she placed the salads in front of them both. Graham would later explain it was her first day that would justify the nerves. Eddy went for the classic Tuna Niçoise.

Being a butcher, he actually liked fish when he cooked at home or ordered out. Both looked colourful, vibrant. The tuna was an actual thick steak seared. For the price, Eddy was expecting a thin collection of slithers, but was not complaining by any means. It was seared to have a crust on the outside and medium rare inside, perfect to not make the delicate fish dry. Mara seemed to have the green-eyed monster of envy in her eyes as she examined Eddy's meal being presented in front of him.

Mara had a warm potato, broccolini, quinoa and mushroom salad in chimichurri dressing with sous-vide slices of beef brisket. This also did look great and the smells that came from the combination of chilli, fresh herbs and beef brisket was salivating. A side portion of crusty olive sourdough bread was placed in the centre, for tearing is sharing. They talked as they ate this marvellous food. It was nice to see something that could be potentially done badly, done bloody well. After they finished, they bantered in a playful manner bordering on flirtatious intentions.

Just after three, Graham bounced over with an abundance of energy that had not wavered since they first saw him. Where did he get it all? If only he could bottle it and sell it, he would make a killing in profit. To think that his energy was still with him after a busy service from where Eddy and Mara sat. After the people from the surrounding building had emerged from the floodgate doors, like a suited, booted, white collar-wearing army onto the wooden floor of the pub and descended onto the island like a wave lapping onto the bar to order.

Food coming in on handwritten paper dockets, food flying out of the kitchen on crockery by the fleeting, efficient soldiers. Empty plates going back by the same smiling troops, happily content with full bellies of food and drink. Graham pouring drinks with a long-term employee Stefano with no conversation. A mutual silent understanding of what was going on. What they had to do. Minds calculating, remembering money, orders, change, who was next and who was after that person. No one waited long. It was a production that a director would have been proud to release.

The eye of the storm was when they were eating, drinking and talking. It was a calm where the empties were cleaned. The clean-up started. The single drops of spillage were mopped up. The next storm was calmer. The next wave was a ripple as people finished at different times. Some had another drink before returning to work. Most just had the one drink, meal and left.

After all this, Graham sat down with them. Eddy and Mara felt guilty to be sat watching the finishing scene wind-up, without getting up to help and feeling more of a hindrance. Graham brushed their worries aside. Graham smiled, he was proud of that service and it showed in his eye contact. Here he sat, not really, if ever, relaxed. Here he explained what his

229

rough hours were. What he expected off Eddy. His work ethic, and that he did not expect Eddy to match it, but to get close by at least seventy percent. Hours that he expected Eddy to do, later what Mara to do and, maybe the most important, the pay. Many of these things had been covered, but it was nice to go over the proceedings again. To have them confirmed and clear.

Although Eddy was not expected to start until the day after tomorrow, Graham wondered if he would like to see the brewing procedure. He explained that he was due to change the guest ale and he would be getting up unusually early to load the malt, prepare the wort and add the hops. Eddy was excited by this.

'What's wart?' Eddy timidly enquired.

'Wort,' Graham corrected but not in a condescending manner. 'Well dear boy. Wort is the mashy produce that are the sugars. These are essential, absolutely e-ssen-tial in the fermenting yeast to produce the alcohol. I will show you tomorrow. Explain all. Sorry.' He rose as he spread his arms. 'Tomorrow, I will show YOU the magical wonders of brewing beers. But…if you would excuse me. Sorry.'

Graham turned in a smooth pirouette as he glided down the small steps to return to his comfortable place, on stage, behind the bar. He quickly smiled as he relieved the waiters, some to go home, some to go on a break. He ushered the new waitress over to consul below par performance that everything would be better. That he did not believe in first impressions and wanted her back tomorrow.

Graham was a stone looking man. He was not friendly to look at but when he spoke it was a masquerade to the big friendly giant brooding underneath. It did take people to realise his jokily jovial manner, as he did have a very dry sense of humour. He wore a smile, but it did not fit his face. It seemed fake. The creases around his eyes did not move with his smile. No sparkle travelled to his eyes, rather a missile of fireworks lit up his irises comparable to a bomb raid on a small town. His eyes looked fierce principally carried by stout dark panda bags. It was as if someone was holding a smile over his lips, rather than him willingly smiling.

Later through their relationship, Eddy would learn that there was nothing fake about him. He was as honest as Ken. Also, as trustworthy and genuine. Graham had a captain attitude, with his straight back posture at all times. His small perfectly trimmed moustache, would adorn a man shouting commands in the trenches. Round glasses that bordered his deep brown eyes, wrapped in circles of wisdom. His hair was feather-dusted with white that blended into the white temples of his forever clean-shaven cheeks, shades of former lives. This baffled them even more, he was immaculately groomed, dressed, yet had some gnarly attributes. Examining in probing inquisitiveness his mad-scientist scruffy eyebrows. He was impeccably dapper, all the time.

Today he wore a white shirt, separated by red tie with smart black trousers and shiny shoes. He looked a professional with a proud, pronounced attitude and demanded respect for himself and everyone around him. He liked people, but did not socialise outside the pub. He was open seven days a week, from ten in the morning until late at night. He would clean the pub in the mornings. Organise the ales and beers. Stock the fridges. He was kind-hearted but, did not suffer fools.

For the troublemakers, he was subtle in his malicious approach to get them to leave, and the severity of his harmful intent was determined on if he wanted them back or not. Forever, to the point of bordering on annoying, he was happy-go-lucky and optimistic that tried to find the good in everyone. The saying, a leopard does not change its spots, was something he did not believe, as he wanted everyone to have a great chance to change. He saw it as a personal challenge.

He hired former convicts, hence the Australians. He was a hard worker that was meticulous and fastidious that some staff members found picky, fussy. He wanted the best in his appearance, thus in everyone else's. In a nutshell, he was a proud man. He was generous and magnanimous to everyone that came through the doors regardless of absolutely anything.

They were treated as friends, until they broke his trust. A trust that he gave very easily, but to get it back you would have more chance getting blood out of a stone.

Graham mentioned on several occasions, amid the sequence of frequent sorries, that he was recently divorced. Graham mentions recently, well, even more accurately it was five years ago to the week. He just never really moved on. He still counted the days that it ended, or was he counting the days since her return? It was never going to happen. She cheated on him with a punter. He never wanted to be hurt again; a feeling Eddy could relate too. That isolated unforgettable love burnt Graham's soul. A scorching burn that he had never healed from.

Some might say that only his soulmate could inflict such a ruthless scar that just forever weeps with pain, suffering. Love and Hate. Nothing, not anything can heal. Time was not a healer. No time. Not another love. No space. No hate. Nowadays, alcohol was his companion. To the point that he was a clandestine functional alcoholic to others, a bordering alcoholic to himself. A belief that he believed he could cast those reins aside at any time. Maybe he could, but then again, he never would. It was a loyal old friend, forever dependant, trustworthy. Trust-worthy. As the alcohol never affected his work, it was swept under the carpet to be ignored.

This blasé reaction amazed Eddy and Mara. They found out that he never let alcohol disturbed his working ethic first hand. Even as most days he never actually made it to bed. Perched on the edge of the solitary single red chair in the living room. Softly playing music whisper-quiet from the speakers he would stare into space. A time unspoken, for him only. Nursing a bottle of Bacardi, or bottle of beer, a liquor to drink the pain away. A short-term self-help remedy, which became long-term.

Alcohol feeds the brain at this time. When the monsters come out to play. He would never take her back. He would never forget her, but he will also never forgive her. He has only one photograph left of her. A creased, worn, scruffy photograph that he keeps in his wallet. A photograph he retrieves every night to drink with. It is only of her. A smiling memory of a time that everything was perfect in the World. A photograph from a party. She is mirroring a cheers pose with a half full glass of white wine lofted in the air as she wears an ivory short strapless dress.

Graham cannot remember where it was taken, but it was a joyous occasion, possibly a wedding. They had many good times. Just one bad time. That was the only one his heart could take. This was the time, before sleep succumbs that he would, if truth be told, take her back.

The alarm went off at the ungodly hour of three in the morning. Eddy was awake. His body clock was nowhere near in tune to the new time zone. Mara on the other hand was sleeping like an Italian princess. She was woken with a start by the low drone of the alarm. By the time Eddy had done his teeth and returned, she was back pushing out the Z's. From the open threshold. With the light cascading in from the hallway sending a soft orange glow gently stroking over her porcelain smooth cheeks. He thought just how lucky he was. Furthermore, she was so kissable he watched her for a few seconds, he could absolutely nestle back in. Thinking. Slowly turning away at the temptation. Floating down the hall. Thinking how happy he was.

Eddy sneaked into the living room expecting to have to wake-up Graham. He had gotten up in the night to see where the low music was coming from to see him, mouth agape, in an alcohol induced stupor. Saliva foaming out of the corners to drool slowly forth. Disgruntled wheeziness akin to horse-like neighs escapes of air, to vibrate as the air was retracted back in. However now the scene was different.

When he timidly appeared into the living room. The curtains were open to the darkness outside. He could hear the wind rushing up the street in all the nocks and crannies. The mysterious time of the silent night is when the chaotic winds has its time to take control of the streets, like a cranky ghost trying to find his body. The wind made noises around the metal bins, the empty glass bottles, the hanging creaking signs. But, no Graham. He shivered slightly with the chill in the air. Eddy reminded himself that it was summer. He needed to, as

231

it was cold, he was cold. He also needed to remind himself that he was not a stranger to a British summer as he has experienced this before. It should not be a surprise to him. Yet, it was.

He sneaked downstairs feeling like a cat-burglar rounding the kitchen into the bar. There was Graham, awake, smiling. Holding two blue-rimmed white mugs of steaming liquid. He heard the slight creak of the door and the brush of the bottom on the carpet. He knew this building like a friend, no, a brother. He lived and breathed this pub. He knew its creaks, its secrets. So, when hearing the heaving pressure on the antique floorboards beneath the carpet, he was walking towards Eddy before he had fully seen Graham looking totally wide-awake.

'Good morning, dear boy,' he boldly stated, not attempting to soften his voice. He placed the cups on opposite sides of the table that they shared yesterday. It was mere fluke, it happened to be the closest.

'Er...good morning,' Eddy whispered uneasily with a slight look towards the ceilings in anticipation of a creak of the floorboards.

'Don't worry,' sensing his thoughts. 'I have soundproofed the floors upstairs as this can get very loud sometimes, bloody loud. And also, I could, HA, can, I get very loud. Coffee? Milk? Sugar?'

'Please mate. Love a long, a, erm...a black coffee.'

Graham forced the cup into his hand. 'Same. Let's get going, boy.'

He was up and moving. They had barely sat down.

Graham was dressed in jeans and brown shirt. He walked with a spring in his step. He genuinely, really enjoyed what he was doing. He smiled and enthused confidence in what he was doing that was contagious to everyone around. Graham led the way. He used boy as a note of affection, term of friendliness, not a patronising timbre was sensed, or meant. It would have annoyed Eddy most of the time, yet by Graham, it was returned with the manner it was given, cherished and respected.

Back the way Eddy had just come, Graham escorted Eddy through, for the first time, into the cellar. Dipping, as the 'mind your head' sign denoted, Graham whispered as he bowed his head to enter down the single tiny brick step. The door narrows in its gap as it sings a slight heaving squeak on its hinges to avoid the pipes and step. The first small room was where the beers in metals kegs and ales in firkins were kept. The grey, stone floor well used, worn glistening like a midnight sky.

He knew the system well, as having worked in The Smugglers Tunnel. He cast an eye over the network of clear pipes filled with liquid hues of orange and black. It was slightly different, but the principal was the same. All were in different angles with different pumps, at different levels coming out of them. For reasons that Eddy did not know, this intricate image was something he missed. In the far corner, almost hidden in the shadows was another door. More of a door to a secret garden behind a hedge of kegs, firkins and barrels.

The dirty-looking, but worn white door was hanging from the stone and brick wall with dents and scars of time. Hidden by the mysterious corners of the recess where spiders scurry, cobwebs sway in the controlled temperatures chilling fans. Reaching the doorway, Graham opens to a drift of stale yeast. Stepping over the small narrow step, through the threshold, the stairs were even older than the building itself. Like a wooden assemble in an old merchant ship galley they were narrow, steep, rigidity, rickety and extremely wonky. It was an immediate announcement to descend further down.

Descending the short flight of stairs down, he reaches an uneven concrete floor that slopes to the centre where an orange terracotta cracked, open drain in the floor makes him stumble towards it. He tries to disguise his stumble as he leans towards it as he ducks his head from the cobwebs, dirt and stages of development. It is a lab for which dust will always penetrate. A space which could be found in books of serial killers, murderous crime novels.

They set foot into the cool, dry and elaborate area. Cosy for two people, crowded for more. The shine of the equipment, the cleanliness, and the organised manner scream out the character of Graham. He likes his life in order, his workplace clean and tidy and his appearance inside and out, just, faultless.

The creaking of the unsettled floorboards, the dripping of water, the musty smell of yeast, beer and ales. Amongst the difference in the two different rooms Graham clears his voice. Its reverberations bounce delicately around the basement. The single bulb swings from the rafters as the light strokes Grahams aged wrinkles. His tones mimic the sombre room under the basement as the betraying metal clung, compression springs of a garbage trucks draws closer.

He subconsciously starts preforming his lecture. He is clear, precise, strong and flawless in his explanation as he talks about the quantities of ingredients for the batch that is going to be next. The garbage trucks moves over. A brief silence rests above the street before the shrill of noise appears with a whistle of the wind shaking the padlocked fastened trapdoor. Eddy listens attentively. Graham gives so much information from the quantities of ingredients, the temperature, the duration of brewing which form the key attributes in making a specific style of beer, that Eddy not only wants to be respectful but also to absorb the knowledge of his know-how.

Graham points to one of the corners, puts his hand in to a wooden crate that Eddy did not notice was open and shows him the barley husks. Opening his hands in the strobing light so Eddy could see clearly away from the shadows. He tilts his head forward for which he peers as if he is showing Eddy his readings in the husks.

'These barley husks are what is going to make the malt.'

Graham motions Eddy to follow his hand as he points to a metal vessel. Inside are barley husks immersed in water that are just starting to sprout.

'This is when it germinates. Here it is taking place.' He continues, 'You see, then, they are dried in the kiln. This kiln.' He pats the curve of kiln as if an adorable puppy, a soft half-hollow thud lowly tolls out. 'This beautiful kiln determines so much by the simplest act, the act of temperature. If I, sorry, we. If we want a pale malt, we use a lower temperature for pilsners. Or. If, I, sorry, we roast the malt at a higher temperature, we then get stouts. Between these two vast extremes of a few degrees, we, we can go in-between. We have the boundaries. But, the field in between is ours. Let's play.' He smiles. In this pale light, he almost looks like a maniac. Similar to the glint of a mad scientist ready to place the electricity, the power of making a dead thing alive, so alive!

Eddy asks a few questions about this vast amount of knowledge that's being rained down. He is genuinely interested. One day, Eddy would like his own bar. He wants to fully grasp the method being explained, on the pretence of using the process one day in the future. Graham is explaining the way very well. Through his vast experience, the knowledge gets absorbed. This makes him really understand his wisdom. His effortlessly way of patiently divulging the development from ingredients to liquid. Eddy finds it easy to be taught these foreign, unknown jargon, methods and equipment for which is observes anew.

'Yes. Yes. Yes,' Graham applauds his capturing of comprehension in short happy bursts of excitement. He almost squeals with each word as Eddy's thirst for knowledge inspires him to continue to tell his life's passion.

'Befalling. Sorry, I…I mean being the summer. We are going for a lighter but slightly above the pilsner. Over Christmas, I am busy, sorry, we are. I have been known to buy this product in, the premade malts. It is something I do not like to do. But, means make it a must. Sometimes, sorry, you have to bring your horse to work, yet never make it a habit. The summer I have time. Maybe as it is warmer down here and even chilly, the winter chill makes this seem even more colder.'

Eddy was still processing the statement about a horse. He only assumes that it means do not become a cowboy. Eventually he came to the conclusion that Graham meant that you can cut corners, sometimes, but it is not, or should ever be common practise.

Graham continues with the obligatory, 'Sorry.' Followed by a raspy cough, which the back of his hand shields any germs present. 'My cellarman is away. Donnie organises this whole area. Sorry if it is a mess. I try not to. Donnie would just kill me.'

Eddy considers his environment as he views that everything seems tidy, clean and not messy in the slightest. Graham continues to speak as he sees not a single thing out of place, not even close to being untidy.

'Donnie is fantastic.' He muses to the hair-brushing floorboards above. 'Donnie is a great bloke. He organises the whole keg room, the wine, the cellar, does the ordering. Donnie has this passion for work ethic. He shares my passion for this trade. The passion that the ale is a living thing that should be treated correctly. Treated with respect. It is still living. Donnie used to work at Cannon Street Brewery where he went from boy to man. He did enjoy his time there but felt he was restricted in his creatively. Here, he has a little more experimental license to use his artistic license.

'Donnie is a great guy. A miserable, grumpy fuck sometimes. But, let's be honest, everyone has their cross to bear. One thing. The most import thing. He is great at this job, his job. He is Donnie. He is a great guy, most of the time.' He winks. 'As you can see. Around you. Everything is methodical. We walk around the room as the process goes around. This is not an accident. This has Donnie's stamp all over it. This is his intention.'

After the acknowledgement of an accolade to Donnie. Graham shows, like a model displaying a prize on an eighty's television show, the mill.

'Here the mill cracks open the barley kernels. Inside here are steel rollers. We are after, we want to take the starch, the starches inside. The starches convert to sugar. That then convert, eventually, to, alcohol. This broken kernel is called grist. Any questions?'

Eddy nodded to say no and mumbled for him to continue. Eddy was fascinated that not only he knew so much but, also the manner in which he was explaining it was actually staying in. He was grasping Grahams expertise. Eddy understood this like a new-born duckling going to water for the first time. It had been years since he had been into a cellar of this design. With the times, back at the Smugglers Tunnel were coming to him in different visions of appreciation. As clear as the day that had still not broken. This day. Today.

'Well, moving on to the mash tun then.' Graham points. 'The grist goes into here, where hot water is added to get, a, erm, porridge? A gruel-type, sloppy sand-like consistency. The promoter is the hot water. In, an hour, give-or-take, the hot water acts as a catalyst to convert the starches to sugars. Then we have the wart, as you say.' He light-heartedly nudges Eddy in his ribs with his bony elbow in jest.

'Wort. Wort. Wort,' Eddy silently repeats like a mantra with a smile to understand his joke, and to play along to Graham's witticism.

'The wort,' Graham displays a copper urn that sparkles as if it has golden rings running around the cylinder. 'For a crisp dry beer, the temperature for a higher fermentation is 62.7°C. For a sweeter and richer beer, the temperature is 68.3°C. Once the wort...' he slightly pauses to see Eddy smirk. 'Once the wort is achieved, the temperature is jacked up to 76.7°C to end the conversion of starch to sugars. Sorry, for the precise temperature but it has to be, sorry. The wort is easier to separate at this stage. Behind you, Eddy, is the lauter tin. In layman terms, a big sieve. This process separates the barley kernels from the liquid that will become the beer. At this stage, some, just some mind, some of the wort is added. This stage is, which, is called the recirculation stage. Also, additional water is added. This is called the sparging.'

It was at this moment that Eddy was getting lost. He got the figures, saw the process but the names of the processes gave him nothing to associate with. This made it harder for him to remember. So as Graham spoke, he spoke in his head an echo of the name, the process, as if logging it down on the paper bark of his mind.

'The sparging stage is to get sugar out of the mash. The temperature of the water again is the key. Too cool, it will not achieve anything. No sugars will be extracted. However, sorry...' For once, this sorry was acceptable. This was warranted as he accidentally stepped on Eddy's foot.

'Too hot.' Graham waves his bony finger for emphasis. 'Too hot and the wort becomes bitter. Sometimes you see a wort receiver. That holds the wort until it is ready to use. Due to the nature of the business here, we do not do this process and go straight to the brew kettle.

234

Here Donnie would check that the sugar concentration is at the desired level. Measured by a percentage of the sugar by weight. In the trade this is professionally known as the original gravity of the wort.

'The wort is boiled in the kettle with the hops. The boiling sterilises the wort. It also makes sure that the yeast is the only microorganism in the wort. Also, it extracts the bitterness from the hops, flavouring the beer. Also, sorry yes another, also, sorry, also, lastly it coagulates malt proteins so that they can be skimmed out along with the hops. After the first round, a second round of hops can be added for aroma. That last process takes about two hours. Donnie has to be careful as a little too long, and the wort will be bitter. Funny though, it is called a bitter wort. Publican humour, I guess. It *is* called that though!

'This vessel acts as a whirlpool that draws the solid matter to the centre and, the wort can be drained from the edges. The wort is cooled to the correct temperature fast. To above 12°C, it then goes to the fermentation tank where the yeast is added. This is where oxygen is added. This helps the yeast split into multiple cells. The yeast consumes the glucose, maltose and maltotriose. I will get you to say that after a few pints. The reaction of the yeast causes the temperature to rise. Donnie pays close attention to this. He takes cooling measures if needed.

'The wort is now called beer. Its official. The filtering begins. This is an expertise, that the right amount is allowed through. To…to give the colour, aroma and flavour of the beer the style that I, and, that Donnie wants. The lower temperatures, near freezing, take little time for the beer to become an ale. This bright beer tank conditions this process. Donnie leaves a small amount of yeast and sugar in the final product to allow a natural fermentation that produces a carbonation in the barrel in the bar. This means we can call them real ales.'

'How long does this take?' Eddy finally finds his voice after a long silence.

'Good question, boy. About four weeks for a dark ale. The summer one we are brewing takes one to two weeks. At the bar, we use a pump. Donnie is back today so today is the best time to show you. In fact, he should be here soon.' He glances at his old, plastic wristwatch that has seen better days. 'Let's go back upstairs. Let's meet the cantankerous old bugger.'

They walk back as Graham's voice carries like steam from a train as he continues his lecture. As he leaves the cellar, his tone changes to his normal gentle voice. Maybe it was the acoustics in the narrow cramped room that changed his intonation. It is amazing to think that all of that happens under the floorboards of a quaint, old pub. Graham explains that his side of the road is the only side with a basement.

During the monk days, a passage went from the Abbey to the Armoury underground. These are partitioned for the businesses above now. He has been here for over twenty years and has no desire to leave. He loves his locals. His locals that he is yet to meet. His suppliers and his relationships that he has developed over time. The town. He purely breathes it. Adores his life that he has made.

The twinkle in the creased corners of Graham's eye. The painful contours of his face as it grudgingly rises to form a genuine grin, despite the fact that he looks slightly sinister. The thirst of each syllable that he draws in, as he simultaneously releases the words of a sentence in his admiration, his adulation that he holds for Bury St Edmunds.

Graham just finishes making a cup of coffee when Donnie walks in. He curses his timing as he returns to the coffee machine to make one for Donnie. Eddy was not sure what he was expecting, but on seeing Donnie he did expect this vision that emerged from the rain. Donnie shakes his umbrella half inside, half outside to get rid of the excess. Drops it into a brass hollow tube by the door, takes off his large heavy coat, hangs in on the coat hook above his resting, dripping umbrella and turns around. He barely casts a presence in the open bar with his frail-looking physique. Then he smiles, this immediately radiates an affectionate aura.

Here was an elderly man, albeit the posture of a former muscular young man. Skinny, now, in a long white lab coat with a little glimpse of a blue shirt with matching blue tie at the collar. His glasses hang, but rest on his chest by black lanyards as he smiles at Graham who murmurs a hello over the frothing of his milk. Donnie knew he hated making coffee for anyone but himself. Donnie went over, arm outstretched. He introduces himself to Eddy, who rises from his chair to take the startlingly strong grasp of his handshake.

Eddy explains that Graham had just finished showing him his handiwork in the brewing process. This wins Donnie over straight away. Donnie's eyes light up as he plays with his glasses in his vein-covered scrawny fingers that could tell more than a story or two. He asks questions as he muses over Eddy's answers. He nibbles on one of the arms of his glasses as he thoughtfully explains a process in all its necessities.

Eddy feels a little awkward as rather than a get-to-know, this seems more of an interrogation. Light-hearted by nature, but an interrogation nevertheless. Graham comes to the bar where they stand, without leaving his comfortable place behind the bar to chat more about brewing, over coffee. His intrusion has not come a moment too soon. Eddy silently wished that he would change the subject. It was not happening anytime soon. He wanted to share the spotlight.

'I have been in the pub game for years,' Donnie enthusiastically answers Eddy's question to why he still works past retirement. Eddy is thankful that he does not take any offence to his speculated query. He lets his bated breath out as Donnie continues. 'The public houses are the homes for people away from homes. The places for talking. To argue, huh. Places to meet. No-one can deny the sense of belonging a pub brings to someone. To everyone. You can share a drink called loneliness, but isn't is better than drinking alone. It has to be a comfort zone. A comfortable place for people to feel comfortable. This is why I work here. People, myself included, can come here and shut off to the outside world, and…relax. I can escape in here. On my own, surrounded by people. With mates. With workers. Some people have a church, a religion. I have a beer, my pub.'

Graham reels him in as if he was a dog on a leash. Not taken the pull of the reins lightly, thrashing out in many ways to keep his voice alive. Sniffing over Eddy with interesting antidotes, talking about himself. Graham again heels Donnie away, towards him. He laughs out loud, he mentions that there will be time for the Spanish inquisition later. They share this secret joke over their own brews, as they discuss the own ales, brewing below them.

Donnie and Graham fervently discuss ales. Graham bounces ideas off Donnie as he explains a few problems that had arisen last week. Donnie listens to his remedy, explains possible scenarios that could have contributed to the cause without appearing condescending. Eddy watches as there is not a single student on view, just two masters that are forever learning. He listens without talking. To Eddy it is like a secret code language that only publicans and brewers understand. A secret society that you have to be a covert member of.

'Before I go, work to do,' Donnie states as he turns to Eddy, bringing him back into the conversation, reality. 'A little story for you.' He softly nudges Eddy's elbow. 'This is true. Did not happen here, but close, close by. After one busy Saturday night the police, as they do, were waiting in the carpark of the…erm, a pub. For the sake of argument, we will call it, the…the, er, King's Head. As it was chucking out time, punters were rolling out. One guy appeared worse. This guy in particular got to his car.

'He dropped his keys. Nearly fell over when attempting to swoop down to pick them up. Only to drop them again. Went to the back door. Went to get in. Realised that it was not the driver's side. Went to the front door. Dropped his keys again. Opened the driver's door. After finally finding the key hole for the ignition he turns the key to start the motor. All this time people were flooding out from the King's Head. Getting into their cars, driving off.

'The police waited. Watching. They could not do anything until the engine had started. They swooped. The carpark was empty. He jerked a reverse, with high screeching revs. The policeman smiled at each other. The lights flashed blue. The jam sandwich, err police car, rolled by the drunk driver. He stopped. Rolled his window down, as the police did the same. They instructed, they shouted for him to turn his engine off. To get out of the car.

'The drunk complied. The police went around and asked the normal questions. His name, address, how many drinks? He was not slurring, he did not slur his speech. He responded none to any drinks. The police were not smiling anymore. There were confused. They had watched him drunkenly try, try to succeed to get into his car. Letting him know he was risking losing his license they brought out the breathalyser. He showed no alcohol reading, at ALL. The police asked again. How and the why? The drunk, as calmly as you like. Standing without swaying. Not a slur. He soberly stated to the police, with a wink, a smile, I am the designated drunk driver!'

Donnie laughs out as he shuffles off down to his own laboratory, hoping that Graham had not upset his own particular balance too much. Outside, Eddy and Graham gaze as the sun struggles to come through the foggy grey whispers of mist. It is seven in the morning. Eddy has something on his mind. He decides to bite the bullet and ask Graham just how Donnie does the cellar work at his advanced age. He lifts, moves and works in the cramp conditions daily.

Graham smirks as he reassures him that he is stronger than he looks. That he is a machine. A gun. In a nutshell he works smart, not hard. He is here for every delivery. He asks the drays to place them where, or at least, close to where he wants the delivery for maximum benefit. His son, Jake, is in the business. Jake comes in once a week, at Donnie's discretion, to be the most useful. Eventually Jake will take over. Donnie is grooming him for his role before Christmas. Jake has giving notice, for which he is working through. Also, he needs to relocate his family from Leeds. Not only for a new family home, but a place of work for her and a school for his child, Jon, to get established. It is not going as easily as they have planned, but they have six months to get to this point. The trouble is the trek down for only one day a week. It is not far, but far enough to make every Thursday, the main day he seems to be doing, a very, very long day.

With a guilty pang of realisation, Eddy suddenly remembers that he is not alone. He has been listening to their stories. Listening about Donnie's personal life to remember that upstairs, Mara was sleeping. Was she standing on the threshold, nervously wondering whether to come down, enter? Eddy clumsily plants his coffee cup in the saucer with an unnecessary clink, spill. His turn to apologies as he reaches for a cloth that in a swift action Graham has and is mopping the small puddle of black gold. He voices his concerns about Mara.

Graham stands in the aftershock of Eddy's dust for where he was sitting just a few seconds ago contemplating, not in a demeaning way, how cute young love is, how adorable, sweet he is. His voice is echoing out the swinging door leaving in its wake a trail of confusion. Graham stares out the window momentarily. A little dumbfounded by his thought. He sees he gaunt reflection staring back. Maybe his cold heart is not the blackhole that he accepted, that he believed it was. He smiles and clears the three cups. Now, Graham is left on his familiar own.

As the dust settles with the waves of the mist clearing to shutter-like forms of sunrays. Seconds ago, three people were sharing a joke. He stares down at the black sheen of Eddy's half empty gleam in the blue cup. He understands Eddy's sudden, poorly explained abrupt flee. Three generations in a room; Donnie widowed, Graham, divorced/separated and Eddy's path unwritten. Graham likes this boy, he likes this couple.

Eddy leaps and bounds Superman-quick, as agile as a ballerina up the steep, narrow stairs. To his surprise, Mara has not only gotten up, but was ready and dressed for the day. Eddy was half hoping that she would be still asleep so the guilt he feels would disparate. Mara turns her head in a vision of beauty, lost in paradise. She was writing in her travel book. Not much written but a few single, incoherent words. What caught his attention more than her was that this was a leaving present from her mother. On the flight, she vowed to write in it every day.

To give the present as a gift to her mother when she returned to Australia. A gift returned with memories of things shared with a mother that was a real friend as well. She knows these clichés are used, but, in this instance. It was true. Eddy saw this first-hand. He could not see any differences in the interaction surrounded with her mates, as she did with her mother. The openness, the honesty, the beautifully brutal truth that made their relationship a lot more than purely mother and daughter.

Mara smiled at Eddy. She stood, as Eddy came to plant a morning kiss on him. They looked vacuously out of the window. Her body was there in the living room. But, her mind was thousands of miles away. Crossing continents, oceans, seas and countries to Australia. By the connection of her mind, she feels that she is standing in her childhood home. In her bedroom, as an eight-year-old child. She is dressed in her favourite dress. Looking, feeling like a princess. Her pink, frilly light dress wrapped around her legs as a breeze plays with the lace. She slowly twists, turns in a swaying full-length mirror that was creaking on a worn, tired hinge. In the background. Her mother is crying tears of joy. She perches on the edge of her daughter's bed. Slightly out of sight of the reflection that Mara joyously sees herself in. Through her mother's hands the edges of a gleaming dazzling smile is unmistakable. Diamonds glitter in Mara's eyes.

She turns, swiftly, towards her mother. Her mother pulls her hands from cradling her mouth, to stand, to hug her daughter. Keeping back the tears. Embracing Mara with love, intensely to concrete they abiding bond. With a passion that is unrivalled. A durable undeclared pledge that only a parent would really, fully understand. Mara is dressed up for her first, ever dance. A school dance for which she has been looking forward to for weeks. The first time she has been to a party with school friends, and that not a birthday party with a select few. She is feeling cute and adorable. Her mum sees her as she will always see her, as a princess. Mara feels like a princess.

Her mum, her mum is so proud. This is a moment she shows it. One time of a few that it is shown, always felt. Mara is stuck in a loop, in this scene. She is relaying that moment. Back to the mirror to turn and see her mother one more time, to repeat. Why that moment is anyone's guess. Mara thinks it is the first moment that she feels like she is beautiful. Feeling like she has finally made the first, teeny-tiny steps to come from a girl. To start blossoming into a woman.

Back to the present. Her body stands still, as fragile as a porcelain statue. Her mind poignant, stirring around the moment miles in the past. Sitting on the soft couch, it was only a few minutes before Eddy arrived inside that she had walked into the front room with her mother's gift. Oddly enough, this was the first time that she had opened the deep burgundy leather-bound book properly. In her right hand, she grasped a photograph of her family, her relatively large family. A snapshot in time taken before Eddy had got together with her by a few short days. It was a vision from a birthday of a relative back in Balmain.

It was seldom that the whole family could gather on a specific day, but the stars and planets aligned to create this perfect family portrait. The whole day was a happy memory. A day that was too short with laughs, tears and smiles. Staring back at her were numerous grins of many people staring back towards the camera, hence her. A slight tear of joy was starting to form in her eye. This was the only sign of recognition that she was here, in the present.

Eddy unintentionally broke her spellbinding trance. He would have rather her come out of the trance herself. He could see that she saw something away that was making her happy. He placed a hand on her shoulder. His hand was not cold but might well have been made of ice as she shuddered as his touch. For hidden in the gift of the book was this photograph. As she opened it for the first time, like the first leaf in autumn, this photograph fluttered to the floor as the pages spread open. She had mentioned that she liked that photograph that took pride of place at her parents' home in the family room. She did not know that this cherished photograph would be here.

She spun slowly around to face Eddy. She showed him the photograph, but did not let him feel the matt finish. She pulled away as he launched forward to go to grab it. It was at this moment that she focused on the back. She saw the note, for the first time. Teasing with a handwritten cursive on the back revealed:

Stay safe, love mammina xxx

Flickering in the light cool breeze from the draught of the window the photograph almost waved to her, from a far. She felt her heart dance. She cried tears of happiness to be involved in such a loving family in the embrace of her man. Her tears plummeted to the timber floor as Eddy kissed her forehead, stroked her shoulders. She had only been a way a few hours into her first day, but she cried missing of a missed home. She explained the vision of her dressing up for her first dance as an eight-year-old to Eddy in glorious detail. Mara explains that she does not know why that particular image had come to her first after so many that could have been placed before it. Including this photograph that brought the vision. Surely this party, a conversation, a joke or something someone else had said would have been the natural thought process to react to. Nonetheless she is wearing a beautiful dress with her mum applying, at her insistence, too much make-up, rose cheeks with shimmers of glitter. Smiling. Happy. Beautiful.

As quick as she teleported to this time, in the same lightning quick pace she was back. Eddy had taken the step by opting to lean into Mara, let her cry those soft tears in silence as she spoke of that time. She flinched occasionally as if the tears had hit electricity. She is in England. To her, a different world. She moves the photograph up behind Eddy's back so she can see it over the hillscape of his shoulder. He breaks his silence by asking about the dance itself. It was an affectionate cuddle. A nice moment. A few steps further they walk to the larger of the two windows. The one that spans the Main Street.

Eddy softly cuddles Mara from behind, one arm around her chest. The other around her waist in a resolute show of protection. Below them, people are huddled over protecting themselves from the wind and the rain. Mostly black or brown umbrella tops are struggling to stay in their designed shape. Mara grips Eddy's arm around her chest hard. A Thank-you. They turn to face. Her eyes blotchy in red, but so very glad. A slight peak on the lips, another. They cuddle close and tight, leaving no space in each other's personal space. This feels lovingly comfortable. They look into each other's eyes. A great moment.

After a splash of water on her face, Eddy invites Mara downstairs for a nice cup of coffee. Hand in hand they stumble down the stairs not wanting to let go, even though this would not only have been safer, but easier. They have a quick meet and greet with the early starters, the kitchen brigade, as they walk out. Stepping into the cloudy, warm rain-soaked summer's day with a faint outline of a rainbow hovering in the sky. They head forth to explore their home for the next month. Splashing in the shallow puddles likes kids in play they talk more about her family.

This was the most open that she been about her Italian roots, where she came from, her family emerged to Australia from. Where some of the members have gone, if they had gone back, the jobs that they chose. It was a miserable cold, drizzling day of frequent showers but, a fantastic day. This was day one, only the first day, but Eddy sensed the homesickness that she was already feeling. It was natural, he told himself. People react differently to being put into situations that are not familiar to them. Mara just needed more time than most. This was the first day. She would adjust. It was not a permanent stay after all. It was not forever, but a few weeks. In total only six weeks, forty-three days.

That was the only time that she would not physically see her family. They spoke over coffee as the rain became heavier and lashed the large window pane obscuring the view. The coffee was not as good as Australian standards, but nice enough. In an attempt to steer the conversation away they talked that Australians often commented that the coffee was not as good as back at home when they holidayed. This could be in striking places such as New York, London, Berlin as if they had forgotten that they had come to a different place for a holiday. Not the coffee. They laugh at that private joke. A joke that could not be explained in all its comedy glory to get the fullest of their humour.

They were having such a great day that Eddy did not feel a single tremor, warning to the impending storm that was brewing. Little did Eddy know then that this was going to be the only great day of the week. Mara, he felt, knew it was a charade. Mara was feeling out of the ordinary. She could not put, place a finger on it. The reason to why she was feeling so disconnected, with, herself. They were connected, but something, something in the air was unsettling the sensitive balance within her.

It was not the first week that they had envisioned. This great start was on a thin pane of ice. This great start got quickly harpooned through as it shattered so terrifying fiercely. So sudden in its approached that it all changed in a blink of an eye. When back in Australia, they only saw the positives. They did not even think of the negatives, or even the possibility of negatives. Why would they? They had the perfect life in Australia. They were getting on so well, so seamlessly that other couples would actually look at them through hazy green eyes with a level of discontent.

To be absolutely honest though, they did not notice the stares, the glares from anyone else. It was as if they lived in their own seamless bubble. As they never noticed what was happening around them, when the blow came from within them the shock left them in a shell of disbelief, rich with veins of sceptical doubt that this was really, truly happening to them. Seriously Barbie and Ken would have looked at them with envy.

A tremor would have been a warning. The steel hard, the jolting-cold realisation was a surprise. There life was not all vanilla skies, fairy-tale lands of princesses, princes, wizards and sorcerers in big castles of any towers conducting potions and brewing remedies. It was as dark, gloomy, cold, stormy and dense as the swamplands ravished in a never-ending battle of trolls, ogres and goblins. The fairy-tale had turned into dungeons and dragons. The path had changed to the yellow brick road with the lions, tigers and bears persistently looming, waiting and ready to attack from the darkest shadows, to come out at too regular occasions.

I have not been present for a while. I wanted to see how this panned out. It was tedious. I asked Echidna to send one of her offspring. She responded with sending someone else's. Echidna, with the bottom half of a deadly snake, top half of a beautiful women, but do not be mistaken. She is all monster. She is all pure evil. She had turned her hair on her head with as many species of hissing snakes to give me what I yearned for.

The snake as hair would be a trait that she would pass onto her daughters, the Gorgons of Medusa and Chimera. She is deemed to be the Mother of Monsters. She inherited this nickname by me as she gave birth to the most fearsome and dangerous creatures that visibly roamed the Earth, roam the underworld. They now even guard the gates of the underworld itself. Rather than going herself, as I would have liked, she sent her offspring. She sent the Algae.

Algae was the character of all the spirits of pain and suffering for the body and mind. They brought the uncontrollable tears and weeping fits that was becoming a daily occurrence for Mara. Not wanting to take a back seat. After pleading with me, Oizys went into the world unvisited in a long time. The Oizys brought misery and sadness into Mara's life. With the help of Oizys, Algae was accomplishing my request. They did what was instructed. They were upsetting the perfect balance of a perfect relationship. I led the excuse that I wanted to see how Eddy coped. If, for that matter, he coped at all.

I was interested to see how Eddy would respond to the distress that Mara was causing without logical explanations to why. Why she was hurting the man she loved. The Algae was not letting the positive feelings in. When they came knocking, they got pushed far, far away. She did not go an hour without feeling negative. Even in her sleep, she cried.

Mara struggled to adapt to being away from her family. The howling negative wind was relentless. The destructive gust was constant. The constant demands were straining them. They both wanted to hold on, but the conditions were making the grasping purely by their fingernails. Pulling the seams of their love apart, where, no seams existed before. They could not stand on the rocking, rolling platform of their ship.

Every little relapse in the storm was a tease. They were knocked over by an unexpected large wave that would knock them off balance, back on their arse. To struggle to get up. Each blow, seemed worse. It was a case of ships that pass in the night for their relationship to not cause an argument. They were fighting to be on the same ship, trying to meet together in the calm. A pipedream in reality when they could not even stand on their own two feet. The planets were not aligned with the stars to make the passage smooth sailing.

240

When they did have time together, they had walks that turned to arguments, that turned to tempestuous volleys of cruelty. Until both would pull apart, into pieces to leave. Storming off in different directions. Literally as well as figuratively. Eddy hated with a passion to have his dirty laundry aired out in the street. This did not help the situation. It would seem that Mara did this to antagonise Eddy. Mara was making his blood boil. She was fishing for an argument in the smooth seas.

It was always agreed that they would work hard. Eddy was working hard. Harder than he had ever done. Harder at work, in love. Mara was not working at all. If she worked, she would preoccupy her mind and not feel as homesick. The amount of money that he shared with her. He worked his tale off in the UK to pay for the rent, bills and general living while she did not a piece of work, not even around the small cramped living area. He did it all and then, Then was expected to pay even more when he had that rare day off. He did this as he felt that this was going somewhere, so, he did not mind. He did not see it as a money lost. It was to make her happy. It seldom did.

For now, he sees it as money wasted. He actually supported her pursuit. It turned out that Eddy actually was not only supporting her but was actually saving for her too. Eddy paid the flights, extra clothes, accommodation and mobile bills to enable her to get to her goal. Eddy unconsciously did this as he genuinely believed in them. Believed that this was the future that was yet to be written, but was going to involve them both walking together on the route. The same route. Growing up together. Growing older together. Living to the invariable dying together.

The arguments were fear. That was what Eddy had in his mind. The only conclusion he could find. The arguments were being scared. That was what Eddy believed in his heart. She was not a bad person. The arguments were anxiety. That was what Eddy transpired to be true. Eddy felt no reason. No reason at all to be apprehensive in trepidation to dread that this was wasting his young years. She was homesick. She never denied this. Mara missed her life that she had made. Mara was taking her insecurities out on the person that was closest to her. The one person she loved with all her heart. Mara could not stop hurting him even though this was the last thing that she wanted.

Was she just homesick?

Eddy seemed to think that she was, as she had told him it was. It was that simple. Eddy thought that the familiarities of knowing the place to get her coffee, calling mates were a circumstance in which she did not predict when she boarded the aeroplane from Sydney. Missing the simplest thing like, buying the irresistible, crunchy chocolate biscuit snack of Tim Tams. Chocolate that tasted like Australian chocolate. With a coffee that tasted like Australian barista-made coffee. As the days got closer to Mara's planned leave for Italy, she was getting closer to Eddy affectionally, but physically, she was getting further, further away. The longest days of the longest week was coming to a bittersweet end.

One day, with Mara in the shower, he leafed through the pages of her travel diary. He needed to know if something was wrong. He needed to know before she went away. He wanted a reason to why she was treating him so badly. He knew this act was wrong. He was once told that you are not born a thief, but you are made one by temptation. Opportunity. He applied that to this moment. He convinced himself, but not entirely. He did not read a word of it. He placed it down and walked away. As if the Gods were smiling on him for once.

For at that precise moment that he walked away from the bedside table. Leaving the fruit of temptation where she left it on the bed stand, the shower door opened and Mara ran out naked to get a shampoo she forgot to take with her. Eddy liked what he saw. Mara did a cute little shuffle just before she closed the bedroom door. Eddy took this as an invitation. He unbuttoned his shirt as he left the bedroom. he opened the bathroom door and slid into the warm steam-covered room. This was their last evening for a while.

Mara was dressed and ready early. Her demeaner had changed completely towards Eddy. She did not say anything, but her non-verbal attributes were affectionate. She was unconsciously gripping the small trinkets, the camera that he had given her. She would touch, stroke or linger a fingernail on Eddy's arm as she leisurely got ready. She did not want to take a whole lot of her luggage with her, so she burrowed Eddy's lighter sports bag.

Eddy did not need to ask hard to get last night off or today off work. He asked Donnie if he would not mind giving them a lift to the train station. Thankfully, being the friendly, charitable person that Donnie was, he not only offered, he insisted on driving her the two hours to London Heathrow. In Australia, this is not a great distance, but in the UK, it seems that the traffic, the weather and the general roads are just not equipped for long journeys.

Thus, this was a huge favour with Eddy appreciating the magnitude of it, rather than Mara who in pure Australian fashion thought it was, 'just down the road'. She was not arrogant in her thoughts. This, though all being said and done, Eddy declined respectfully as he wanted to talk to Mara. Mara also wanted to share the time with Eddy. To use an understatement, the past week had not gone to plan. They did not want one life of the two lives to separate on a jagged knife's edge. They shared a steaming pot of coffee watching the rain through the window in silence. It was pouring, torrential borderline biblical. The rain was accompanied by such a cold breeze. So much to say, nothing to say. A honk of the car horn, Donnie below in the carpark.

Yes, it was a short journey, but in this weather a walk to the other side of the road was a long way. Eddy ran with Mara's luggage over the packed car park to the ornate steel awning cover of the station. Mara close behind in a newly purchased bright red trench coat tied tightly around her small waist as she negotiated the puddles in her black high heels. She looked elegant. Eddy looked more casual than casual. She wanted to arrive in Italian style to her family that she had never met.

They waved to Donnie and collected the train tickets. They had timed it perfectly. The train was waiting at the platform as they made their way across the steel bridge and down over to the other side. They held hands on the short walk with Eddy trying not to appear as if he was struggling with saying goodbye, as he adored her touch. He heaved the surprisingly heavy, ram packed sports bag with his free arm. It felt nice, the holding hands, not the unintentional workout.

The train journey was an assembly of tears of joy and, tears of pain. Hearts mending. Love regrowing. Minds activating. Souls connecting. Bridges rebuilding. Eyes open. Ears listening. Mouths tasting. Body aching. Stomach churning. Teeth biting. Mara and Eddy mutually reciprocating with body, soul, and heart.

What, at the start of the journey, was a breaking unison heart. By the end, that same heart was fusing together. Eddy believed, believed with all his heart that the love was going to grow again. Using the cliché, they both believed that distance would make the heart grow fonder. The storm had passed.

By the time they arrived, their eyes were dry, their mind was clear and both were in better spirits. The authentic smile was back on their faces. The spark was back in their eyes. Even the smell of putrid sewage from a burst water pipe on the side of the road, at the entrance of the airport did not dampen the rebuilding of their fractured relationship.

As they waited for the boarding, they shared an intimate chat over a coffee. It was not lost that they had met over coffee. That they sorted problems out over coffee. That they made plans over coffee. Hence why not honestly be brutal in not just putting a Band-Aid over the problems, but reconstruct with reinforced cement. Over a coffee.

It was a long wait that went by so fast, too fast. The call for the flight to Bari, Southern Italy echoed in Eddy's head like an unpleasant shrilling morning alarm. At this stage, it was unwelcoming. Eddy wished he could pause this part of his life and continue the talk. However, this is not the movies. The call does not come at the perfect moment. Tears were shared, once again, each painful droplet was laced with anguish. As they cuddled out their goodbyes, they whispered emotional support. Their gripped each other, as if their lives depended on them feeling the intensity of their love. She walked through the automatic glass doors.

Looking back at the shell that was Eddy, she lingered. Eddy hoped that she would return. Prayed she would. She was at the cusp of a new journey. She was on the precipice looking

242

over the abyss. In front of her was her beloved, behind her was the unknown family that could open up a different World to her. To answer the unanswered. She was balancing on the tightrope between the two. She smiled with tears streaming down her cheeks. She waved, slowly, with purpose. She blew a slow kiss to Eddy, turned slowly. Made one last seductive look as the frosted glass door slid shut.

It was all in slow motion to Eddy. The second hands were ticking in minute time. Each strike was an echo. Vibrating in the emptying body that was draining. Eddy could not put a finger on what was leaving him. He was not sure if he had let the woman, he loved go, or, if the woman he loved, had just left. Either way it was sure that he did not sacrifice a big enough fight for her to stay. He let her go like the sand being spilt through his hands in a gale force wind. He was losing himself as she walked away. He could hear her footsteps over the commotion. Eddy could not help the feeling that this could be the last time he would say goodbye to her. He wondered if he would ever see her to say hello ever again. After the week that was. The train journey that gave so much more than a finishing single destination. The positive that was felt a few minutes ago. Now. Was. Gone. Empty. Hollow.

The difference that the same train journey can have on Eddy was contradictory. He was surrounded by noise inside and out of the rocking speeding carriage. He vaguely stared out of the window. The rain lashing the window. The wind alarmingly bending over the trees, but the strong resistance of them make them stay rooted to the ground. The noise on the fast-moving carriage was mute. His body, numb.

The cold that was drafting through from an unseen open window further down the carriage failed to make Eddy shiver. He was as sad as the weather. He knew he would see Mara in a weeks' time but, could not help feeling completely alone. His reflection was what he was unconsciously staring through as his glaze was focused on nothing in particular. His thoughts were of what would happen now? Was he truly alone? For the first time in a long time he was scared of the unknowing.

The pavement that led from the station had turned to tar. His legs felt heavy. He struggled to place one foot ahead of the other. The weight of the world was on his shoulders, like Atlas. Unlike Atlas who was given the task on the western edge of the Earth, Gaia, to hold aloft the heavens. A punishment bequeathed by Zeus, to keep them apart. So they could not resume the original hold to leading the Titans into battle against the Olympic Gods for control of the heavens.

Eddy was not being punished, but felt he was being chastened by chains, drawn down. His mind was a river of thick mud that unclear, as it was unkind. The rain was ineffective in causing him to think about anything else. As he approached the door, Donnie exited. Eddy quickly put on a masquerade, a handshake, a smile. Unfortunately, there was no tradesman's entrance where he could be incognito.

'You two,' Donnie conjected. 'That was just like your first days. I see all, say fuck all, but I see all. I do not need to be Sherlock bleeding Holmes to work out something was wrong. But today. You, well, both, yes BOTH of you were back. I could see the love.'

Eddy could not speak. He thanked him with a soft pat on the arm, letting his hand linger for a few seconds too long. He valued his gesture, but, he did not feel better.

'Look.' Donnie paused. He could see that he did not feel right in himself. He paused to attain the correct words. Sighed before continuing, 'This week will pass. The time will pass and, and the feelings will, I assure you, they will subside. No-one said love was not a flat sea. With fresh wind in your brief farewell, your sails will be set afresh.'

Once again, no words could be formed. Eddy was catching the tears at the back of his throat. He patted Donnie on the arm, let it linger with a short, tight clench. He mouthed the words that did not come out, 'Thank you.' He was so happy that the bar was full of suits, tradies, students. He beelined through without seeing anyone. He waved to Graham, the staff but thanked his lucky stars that he could pass through uninterrupted. He went directly to his, their room and, basically, did not do a lot. Stared at the plain painted yellow-stained walls with a projection of his mind playing in his eyes.

That night, Mara did not call as promised. A simple text message was sent to say that she had arrived in one piece: 'Arrived. Good Flight. X'

Eddy did not respond straightaway. He had been waiting since late morning for the call, and all he got was this short generic message. Better than nothing, he kept telling himself, but he felt she should have called, at the very least done better. Eddy held unrealistic expectations sometimes to other people's plight. He generally fears relationships. Not because of the intimacy, or the touch, but for immediate resolve in solutions. If he has a fight with a love, he wants an answer immediately to where or what they have to do to fix the premise of the argument. If not, he overthinks. His mind constantly works, heaven forbid to shut down.

If he does not get an answer, his mind will throw up numerous scenarios to create different outcomes to what his next move should be. It is a flaw. A flaw that Mara had seen. She accepts his flaw, yet she behaves in this way. She understood when he explained that even though years had passed and he was happy in himself, sometimes his mind would trick him into thinking that he could do better, should do better, or is better. Thus, tricking him into thinking that he was not happy in, or with himself. He puts it down to caring too much. Mara puts that down to bullshit.

He did overthink things. He had a habit of making something larger than it should be. Hence, he waited before responding. A few minutes turned into hours. His response was equally as brief. Not to be vindictive, but in his mind aloof.

'That's great. X'

Simple. Maybe too simple. Although to get to that text he wrote it, re-wrote it, deleted and then changed it altogether to come up with that. Not quite Shakespeare. He felt obliged to put an obligatory 'X'. He once got told not to follow his first instinct if he was upset, or angry. For him overthinking was a fire that he thought he was in control off but never was. It certainly destroyed the path for which he wanted to walk on. It had burnt him in the past. It had made him look back on the ashes with a regret that something could not grow back.

This overthink caused him to have one of the worse night's sleep. He blamed his hectic mind, but it could have been not having someone next to him.

Finally, late on the next day, in the afternoon between shifts she called. Eddy was pleasantly surprised, he had been expecting a text. It took a couple of rings to register as he composed himself with deep breaths so not to seem too eager. He had sent a morning text and got nothing. The morning was spent with him looking back through the message. Was it read in the same way as he wrote it to be read?

On the third ring, he answered. She was very chipper on the clear other end of the call. His overthinking mind dissolved into relief. Was it the fear that something had happened, yet another scenario that he played out in his mind? He did not want to dampen her enthusiasm with his unnecessary worries, his own dramas. Honestly, he was relieved to hear her voice. A little belated, but to hear singing in her voice ironed out his wrinkles of stressing. He held the receiver as she lushed over Bari, the port city on the Adriatic Sea.

The embracement of the warmer temperatures tinged with a sea salt smell that came off the sea to touch her lips. Her enigmatic explanation that she struggled with in putting into words the maze of rolling, narrow streets with laundry flapping in the wind above her head. The brushing of the sun rays casting flickering's of shadows resembling ghosts and spirits swimming overhead in the skies. The day spent on the crumbling stone walls basking in the sun, sheltering in the heat. The unique to her, and Eddy, that the professional food vendors on the street sold orecchiette that was not only cheap but tasted great, and filling.

It would have been amazing, she gushed with cooing admiration, in any restaurant in Australia. And here, were she was, it was street food. Mara painted a scene of children barely older than kids on scooters. Fashions of the most colourful attire. The smells of cured meats, fresh fish, pasta. She mentioned it was if she stepped into the past, to how her past generation would have seen it is how she is seeing it today.

In the suburb of Bitonto, just half an hour on foot from Bari was were her family lived. Some of the family lived her. They had taken her in with warm open-arms. She lived with

244

them and enjoyed the family meals, gatherings, and different cultures of family life. She had to remind herself that it had not even been two complete days yet. Mara felt so, at home, so, comfortable. Happy. Today she walked through olive groves that gave the nickname to Bitonto, being the City of Olives. It was as if she returned home, although never been here.

Her first European holiday out of Australia and she felt that she was at home. What was that all about? She continued to brag to Eddy. She enthused him, her plan. Over the next coming days, she was being escorted to all the places that she wanted to see. The church were her grandparents got married, their former home, to meet more of the family.

It was in these exchanges over the following few days that she was getting her old self back. Spirit she felt was lost had returned quickly. The Algae had left. The Oizys had left too. Their relationship sabotaging job done. The week for Mara went by so fast. Over the last days of the week, Mara kept in touch with Eddy and they did speak daily.

The last night of her time in Italy, the week's end, was a strange telephone call. It was almost disconnected by emotion. Mara was torn. Eddy reassured her silence as best he could, but to no avail. It was friendly. With Eddy trying to sound dismissive and not excited about seeing her when he was. Mara was talking about what she would do in the morning before her flight. Something to take a great memory back with her. Something that a photograph just could not capture or perfectly master. This was to be their last telephone call. The next time they talked, Eddy would be greeting Mara at the airport. The next time they would be talking would be face-to-face.

Eddy was thrilled that Mara was coming back today. He had hardly slept at all. This time, thankfully, not by overthinking unconstructiveness, but by pure euphoria. In his restless state he had scrubbed the room clean. Done all the washing and the ironing. He had scrubbed the bathroom so vigorously that he proclaimed to Graham that, 'you could eat your dinner off that seat.' He had been shopping to buy all the ingredients for her favourite meal of Baked Ziti. Traditionally more of an American-Italian dish, but once coming across it by way of Eddy, she had adopted it as her new favourite. Eddy had bumped into it accidentally.

He had gone to see a childhood mate that had migrate to Los Angeles. On his first night, they had gone out for a meal, around the corner from his home in the suburb of Los Feliz. There in a quaint cosy restaurant called, Little Dom's, lit by candlelight's he saw this previously unaccustomed dish. A dish made from ziti macaroni for which he scoured the supermarkets in Bury St Edmunds, until eventually finding it in a specialised delicatessen. The one he had back then was done with zucchini in a tomato, cheese and capsicum sauce. He had adapted his own version, and was happy with the end result. Although not a patch on the original that had wowed him all those years ago, great enough.

Donnie, this time, did not take no for an answer. He persisted in an adamant, non-negotiation manner that he would drive Eddy to the airport. Even though this time she would arriving at Gatwick, which was actually further around the south side of London.

The late morning telephone call was unexpected by Mara, but Eddy before answering it assumed it was to reconfirm the arrival time. It was not. It was an order, a demand, rather than a plea or question that she would remain in Italy for a further week. She was getting to know her extended family. She wanted that to continue. She was getting to know Italian life. She wanted nothing more than that to continue.

Eddy was disappointed but tried not to show it. He failed successfully. His toned changed. His words empty. Mara sensed his disappointment but decided not to voice it. She went on about the reasons why. The rationalities for it to make sense. Mara explained that Eddy could continue working, and work hard without feeling guilty to be buried under work. She was looking for excuses for why. She was extending a well-rehearsed script of bullet points.

Eddy heard but was not listening. Mara was saying that Eddy could do the hours, get paid for the hours, pay minimum rent and board, be self-supportive. She was not paying rent and enjoying her time. She was not working, or looking for work. Although she was still taking out money of their joint banking account. Eddy's work. Eddy's, how she elegantly put it, hard work.

That week turned into another, until the final fourth. Mara was taking money at a weekly basis from Eddy. He started putting less into the joint bank account, not putting in all his earnings that he started to do. She was taking more, more and more. He decided to travel to Bari, and they could go on a travelling trip from there. A slight change of plans, but they mentioned going to Croatia and travelling from there down to Greece.

Mara spoke about finding the house that her grandparents lived. Even knocking on the door and asking to go inside. This did not go as well, but it did show the newfound confidence that was surging through her. The church that they got married in. Seeing them together. Eddy telephoned her to tell her of his plans. Mara seemed excited to have Eddy to come. Although the money saved was not as high as Mara did keep taking like it was her own personal banking account. The weeks that he was paying for her to enjoy her time.

Then the last day it happened, the brewing storm. This was not the storm that he was looking forward to, by the same token it was not a storm he was expecting. She called from Italy. A telephone call from her extended families house. An unknown number flashed on Eddy's mobile as just that, 'Unknown'. Due to this, he was not going to answer it. He had a firm rule about not answering unknown numbers, but sometimes he broke his own rule to answer them. This was one of those times. She was almost surprised that he answered. Mara was hoping that it would go to voicebank. Stuttering by being caught off guard she got to the point quickly. She wanted to go alone. She did not want to split up, but needed space to gather her thoughts.

After weeks that turned into a month apart, she wanted space! flashed in lightning quick anger across Eddy's mind. His thought nearly betrayed him as he was so close to being vocal with his irritation.

It was and felt like a kick in Eddy's guts. As a last attempt, he grasped at straws. He offered her hand in marriage. As the proposal was leaving Eddy's mouth, he visioned getting married at the same church as Mara's grandparents. However, that vision was shattered in the next split second. Marriage declined. She did not need to think about it. It was something that she knew she did not want, so she answered instinctively followed by a sorry. She answered honestly. Sure, Eddy liked her a lot. Seriously, he was not ready for marriage.

If he was openly truthful with himself, he did not really know why that question slipped out. Mara liked him a lot. She obviously in the same way was not prepared to take the steps down the aisle to wed either. Maybe one day she would feel more. It was not quite that deep love, but close. In a poor attempt to understand the whys, it was just not there, after two years of spending time together. It was such a shame that the feeling she felt was not stronger. The feeling he felt was not reciprocated by her. Was it love? Or a fabrication? It was an awful telephone call before he went downstairs to work. She actually said that she was hoping that he was already working. Talk about premeditated.

The last day at work was just to be the morning. Then he was travelling down to the airport and to see his beloved, Mara. A day of so much joyous promise was the worse day. He asked Graham to stay on for a while. He found it hard to explain but Graham had the answer. He wanted him to stay, even with the couple coming back his work was valuable. Although he would have to find his own place, for which he would help.

That last day he was dropping things. He was being told things, then asking the same question again. He was clumsy. He was not Eddy. His mind was scattering. All his thoughts were acting like a pinball bouncing around fast, hectic and unpredictable inside his head. He was so happy when the hour came that he could finish. He had a plan at this point. He even worked through his break to get an early mark so he could put his plan into action. Graham forgave his unpredictable unstable work to let him leave even earlier.

The shortest shift, but the hardest, longest shift that he had ever put in had finally finished. On finishing work he raced into town. He had been thinking of certain things to tick off his head list. He walked into the banking smell of stuffy carpets and disinfectant to arrive in the remarkably quiet Lloyds Bank.

At this time of the day, it was always busy. Eddy went straight to the counter to change the banking conditions, that mercifully was all in his name to get the money he was working for, to make it solely his own. The money placed here for emergencies, so she could access it easily in Europe. The money that was not hers for the taking, but the money she was using like her own private trust fund.

He found no money. He was surprised. He did not know why. That was the reason why his actions today were so preoccupied. He knew that this is what he was expecting to be see. Yet, be that as it may, he was still rendered speechless. He should have prepared himself better to see the printed statement laid in three creased, clean and crisp folded paper, columns of the debits. The last one late last night. He could only see zeros, but not in the good way. The bottom line read £0.01. Numb emotionless fury followed.

He took the paper. Clasped the evidence of betray in his fist and rammed it deep into his pocket. He exited into the gloomy afternoon. School children were happy, laughing as they were finished for the day. Taking over the streets like busy swarms of ants. He accidently knocked into one of them as he, at a snail's pace trudged down the three sandstone steps into the pavement, into the young kid. He could not speak. He felt the contact. Yet, just carried on dragging his shuffling feet. He was in shellshock. Autopilot took over as he staggered, drunk in treachery. Wrath was raging, brooding through his body. Disloyalty had a face.

The iceberg of love was melting. Rapidly. The love was placed by a furnace, before it happened, it had melted leaving a hollow, nausea churn within his stomach. This was global warning placed on fast forward. The global warning that his mates warned him about. Treachery. The frosty ice was not cooling his temperament. His mind was filled with fiery rage. His thoughts, fireballs of fury. The spark that was a candle of love, gone, extinguishing by the flames of hatred. Like watching an admired hero in his eyes, to turn around and be the despicable evil mastermind.

The hero that Eddy had placed on a pedestal was Mara. She was strong, independent, a personal Jesus that was suddenly shown in a different light. A dark light of a weak, dependant, personal shadows that nestled out-of-bounds to lunge to the fore. The respect for her completely extinct with the click of the computer that printed the statement. The incensed indignant furious passion distinguished the spark, to the point that not even smoke remained. He was empty inside. No spark. No fire.

Fury raged inside but without substance, presence. He was a fragile shadow of his former assertive self as he made the last steps to the bar. He cursed that no tradesman's entrance assisted him, for he did not want anyone to see this bruised lapse in himself. His trust abolished. The wall of trust, love, for the sake of argument we will call it love. The support and faith had been destroyed to the point of being eliminated by a wrecking ball. Not many blows, but a single blow had completely obliterated the wall of their fortress that they had built together, he had built for her.

Mara was at the controls of the crane. He saw her smiling in his mind's eye, smiling, laughing. Mara was the cause of his emptiness. Inside of him, she had ripped out, squeezed and then proceeded to jam her sanctimonious attitude of being holier than him. She was a snake in the grass, that carried a dagger to compound the misery when his back was turned. Eddy felt betrayed. Cheated. Robbed. Taken his heart, his money, his soul. He was Adam, she was the snake. He got victimised, she got protected.

'BITCH!' he shouted in the middle of the High Street. Again, shouting up to the heavens, 'GRR...BITCH!' before slumping to his knees. The cold, dirty puddle that he found himself in, was used. He was like a child have a tantrum as he futilely splashed in the shallow puddle with fists towards the ground. Hitting his reflection for his stupidity. Again, he was taken for a ride. Again, he was left exposed.

Eddy had a tough choice to make. Not for the first time, Eddy did not want to return to Australia yet. He felt embarrassed. He did not want to answer the copious amount of questions and feel even worse about the situation than he did already.

In the perfect moment, when no-one was around, he leaned on Donnie's wisdom, his experience to listen. To give words of advice as soon as he felt fit that he was asking, and not just using him to vent too. He spoke to Donnie at length about the scenario.

One morning, Donnie spoke the words that Eddy was hoping would come from his mouth.

'I would like you to stay. It has been easier on me life. My boy has not had to commute from Leeds. Concentrating on his family. It would be a blessing for me, and Graham. You are a good worker. A rare breed. A good 'un.'

Over the morning preparation in the beer cellar, before the cockerel had sounded, he still seethed. The anger was still as very fresh as the first blow of the unstinted amounts of dagger thrusting punctures. Yet, he felt wanted.

Today, he managed to speak frankly, taking the anger out of his voice. He spoke to Donnie, and to Graham, over a steaming black coffee in front of the pub on a bitterly cold morning. No one dared to be out in this wretched weather. He was a shattered shell, slowly being replenished of hope in the world. Thanks to these old souls. He agreed to work the full month as promised. On top of that, when he was supposed to be enjoying his hard-earned money with the love of his life, he agreed to be working that period as well.

Therefore, he worked another fortnight, hard. He took every single hour he could, so he went to bed exhausted. He kept busy. He kept preoccupied when not at work by running. A new passion for him. He regained a fitness that he had not had since his school days. He was fixing his fault lines from earthquake Mara, slowly. On his own, he thought, overthought. The reality is that Graham was helping him. Donnie was helping him. Without Eddy knowing, they were the open ears listening.

The open mind to his questions, which they did not answer for him, but let him figure out the cryptic reasons without finding a rational to why he was treated the way he was. They were the arms that gave him that reassuring pat on the shoulder. That slap across the face, figuratively speaking. They were the eyes that were watching him work as if he was a madman possessed. Run hard, happy, as if he was being chased by a zombie apocalypse. Breaking down the barriers. They were the support for his broken shell to not shatter into pieces but fuse back together. To rebuild from the ashes. Eddy appreciated the help. However, he did think he was doing it alone.

He got taken to the airport for his flight back to Australia by both Donnie and Graham. A short time working together, but they had a unique bond, a mateship. He could talk honestly about Mara with no more tears to cry. It was then that he realised the immense help that Donnie and Graham had on his state of mind. He felt stronger, that he could answer those questions. He felt he was leaving a family behind. He felt better to have at least a little money that will be a bond, if nothing else. In that final three weeks, every time he thought of Mara, he mentally beat it out of him. Resisting that strong urge to use media to connect her.

The flight back to Australia however was a different situation. This unforeseen circumstance was the first time he had sat down for a long length of time in the past weeks. His mind wandered to Italy. His mind thought of Mara. Where she was? Whom she was with? How she was? Was she happy? Was she sad? He did not know. How would he? How could he? He decided not to search her through the numerous sources available in the good-old age of everything being online. That indispensable evil. He successfully cut her loose. Although she, in reality, did it first.

Now, in the solitude of the aeroplane cabin he wanted nothing more than to see her happy. With. Or. Without him. For a reason that made no sense to him, all he wanted was Mara to be happy. After the weeks of undulating fury directed at Mara, he only wanted that one thing. Her happiness. Bizarre as that was.

Although he did not travel physically, Eddy felt that he had travelled in himself. He returned to work, in Australia as planned. He had been in contact back in the UK to state that he would be back on the Saturday morning, he would let them know that he had arrived on Australian soil. He really wanted to start straightaway, on the Monday. After a back-and-forth game of emails asking him to reconsider, they reluctantly accepted his insistence of his start date.

True as he is. True to his ever-reliable word. He was there. In the dark. In the early hours of a windy, chilly Monday morning. He was, if nothing else, dependable. Just like before he had left, he was the first one at work. As if he had never been away. He merged straight back into the workforce of Jones Street Butchers. In true mateship, his workmates took the piss out of him. They ridiculed him. It was light-hearted, but it did hurt Eddy, even though he was a man. He did not let it show. He laughed it off like water of a ducks back, with their, seemingly continuous stream of ribbing.

As it always seems to occur. Just when Eddy was getting back into his routine. Two weeks into being back in Australia, at work. One busy Thursday his mobile went off, ringing in his pocket. He did not hear the chimes over the din of everyone ordering at the same time, the noise of knives, the high-pitch scratch of the slicer as it scraped the meat into slices, ring of the bell on the door. He did feel his mobile vibrate. Not once, but twice in his right hand black trouser pocket. He could not answer it. His hands were covered in sticky blood. Then, the shop telephone went off as the vibration stopped. It was chaotic in the shop. Filled with people.

It was the lunchtime rush, but the busiest that it had been for months. It was a week before Christmas all over again, but in winter. The shop telephone rang off the hook once again. Barely heard over the customers raining orders down at them all. Another vibration emulating from Eddy's pocket. He started to get the sense that something was wrong. He made his apologies as he left the trenches in the midst of battle. They all looked his way. They assumed it was Mara. He knew it was a concern. He had his mobile in his wiped, barely clean hands before he had fully left the line. In his hands he saw four missed calls. He redialled the number. Instantly, his brother answered.

'Hel—' his bro was interrupted by Eddy.

'Bro. What's up? Bloody busy 'ere, mate.'

'I've been trying to—'

'What's up?'

'Er…it's Dad…'

What's up?' Eddy had a feeling of the answer. He needed the confirmation.

'Dad's. Well, Dad's…' he stuttered. The last word holding back at his throat as if launching it out would make the reality too real.

'What?'

'Died,' he sobbed in uncontrollable howls of anguish. 'Dad's…Die…D.'

Eddy opened his mouth to speak, but only wheezing air came out. He was breathlessly answering as he dropped his mobile from his ear to the side of his body.

'Eddy. EDDY. It's Doreen.' On hearing a different voice, he snapped sharply his arm to bring the mobile back to his ear to hear his aunt, his dad's sister speak. He stuck a finger in his other ear to try and muffle out the raucous roar from the shop. She spoke in monotone connection, with less voice, added breath, that was as alien to her, as much as him. 'Your dad died in a crash. Driving from The Entrance. On his way to Taree.' She gives the details as deliberate bullet points, as if speaking fluently would be too hard to elegantly compose herself. 'To see mates. He got hit.'

'Eddy, it's Joe again. Take Two!' Eddy's bro was back on the line with a little humour, at the most inappropriate time, but used as a sword to protect himself. His voice cracking as he spoke softly. He paused to compose himself to restart again, to try again. 'He did not feel a thing. Apparently. He got, was hit, by…by a road train. A ROAD TRAIN. All he's been through, stopped…by a bloody ROAD train. It didn't stop. Took him…out. Took his car.

Him. Hit his side, when it did not stop. At a crossroads. He. Instant.' Joe ended the conversation with a fit of tears that was brimming throughout the brief exchange. He then blood-curdled the words that he never wanted to speak. 'Our dad's died!'

Silence on the line. Everything around him was in silence. A selfish thought entered Eddy's mind as he could not answer. Did not know the words to use. Did not know, the right words to use. *What would he do without his advice?* echoed in his mind, as family member followed by family member came on the mobile one by one, with different words and sentences but the same sentiments.

Eddy had his head in a vacuum. He could hear the muffled incoherent sounds of voices. Eddy was besieged with the dreadful news. He had never felt pain like this in his whole life. He was distraught. He had no tears. As if a ghost had rugby tackled him, he sunk. He collapsed. He suddenly fell. He tried to use a shelving unit to brace him, to stop him from tumbling. Alas, he was down. On the floor. A broken heap.

The shopfront was oblivious to the hell that he was going through a few, meagre metres away. No-one heard the clutter of empty containers that fell with his flailing arm. Eddy was in shock. He shook. He trembled. Hands over eyes. His whole body convulsed as he started to cry. His tears turned to an uncontrollable sob. He muffled a wail. Muffled a bellow of hurt. A roar of pain from deep, down, within. Etched on his concealed face. Drawing lines of his pain. His hands could not conceal. He stifled his resentment. The hatred of the unknown person that took his hero away. His dad…away.

What would he do without him in his life?

Eddy had questions that started to form. Foaming wildly to resemble a bubbling geyser. His mind was a melting pot that was ready to boil over. He also realised that his thoughts were selfish. He kept asking how it affected him. Not about his family. Not about his younger bro. Not about his father's mates. He kept repeating questions to how it affected him. That was his concern. He should have felt guilty for the selfishness, but he could not stop the road his mind was racing down.

What would he do without his smile that spoke more than any word?

Eddy was devastated. Like Bambi on ice he struggled to get up. He was on the floor for what seemed like an eternity. However, in all reality, it was only a few seconds. The longest seconds of his life.

Mitchio saw him. He came running around to see where the bloody hell he had gotten too. Then he saw him. His feelings changed. He did not know what the story was, he knew that something had happened. Something was not even close to being the right form of right. He came over with a hand of comfort. Eddy pushed him away. Mitchio was not taking any action for a no. He went in. He helped him up. Took him, nearly dragging him outside. Sitting on the sides of the blue plastic milk crates he placed a hand on his shoulder, for support. A simple gesture to let him know he was not alone. Eddy sat, shaking tears out.

Mitchio looking awkward, not sure what to really do, wanting to comfort Eddy. To find out what happened. He stepped back in. He told them that something was up. He returned with a bottle of cold water. He motioned it under Eddy, getting splashes of tears. He gripped it. Looked up. Nodded.

Against all the wishes of his employer, his workers, he took one day off. The funeral. That was it. He wanted to work. Keep busy so he would not think too hard about the loss in his life. Just like his mother's death he would learn to live with the pain. He dove in with a reckless leap to get over the latest obstacle in his personal book of life. Eddy lost his mother at an early age for him, an early age for her.

When he said he got over it. The truth was, he truthfully never really begun to get over it, but he did learn to live with the painful hollow she had left. He had to. He had to be strong for his younger brother. His father. He would still have a part of his mother. Now a part of his father inside of him. They both live on through him, and his brother. He picked up his sense of humour from his family.

The way he walked was similar to his father. The volcanic explosions of passion. The way they yelled at the television when they watched their beloved Eels lose yet another rugby league game. He grieved at home. When alone. For work was for burying the unhappiness within his aching heart. For running was a way of running out the pain. A heart that was throbbing for desire in his want to spend just one last day with his father.

A couple of weeks had past. Just two. The pain was still very raw. As raw as a recent fresh knife wound, but he was coping.

One busy Friday. He finished later than planned. In all honesty, he was not rushing to get out. He did a heavy detailed clean, alone. This was the last day of the week. In himself he knew that the next two days were going to be dragging longer, as if the hands of the clock were fighting against the anchor keeping them from progressing. He had been working seven days, his boss finally laid down the law to give him his rostered day's off. Away from work, his mind was too clear to overthink.

He went for a short run after his cleaning to expend any excess energy. Treading his tired feet around the harbour without earphones, as the sunset soothed the Sydney landmarks a last stroke of warmth before saying goodnight. He basked in the rays, momentarily forgetting his traumas. He weaved around the revellers making their way out after work. He finished with a sprint, as fast as his legs could carry him, up that last steep hill.

Back at work, a new dawn occurred inside him, he had to say hello to two days on his own. He sweated as he picked his bag up. He was not sure if it was the intense workout or fear. Light out he closed, locked the door to travel home. He was still perspiring, breathing heavily, verging on a panic attack. For once he was thankful for the traffic, so he could relax himself rather than pulling over.

He had returned home for a few short minutes. He had showered quickly. Strange as he was really looking forward to taking the smell of raw flesh from his skin, his hair. Yet the moment the warm water descended on his body he found the noise of the pellets hitting the tiled floor hypnotically depressing. The sound of the water was similar to an ensemble of grieving widowers, which was not the desired effect of a relaxing cleanse that he was after.

When showered, he was barely dry when he thought he heard something, maybe the door. Or just an excuse to get out of the shower. His towel hanging around his hips, he strode over to his shut door while rubbing his hair dry with a small blue towel. Grabbing the door knob, he opened it briskly, to gaze upon, no-one. Nothing. He poked his head over the threshold, glanced up and down the hall. Nothing. Just a corridor of closed doors. He retreated to the living room, collapsed in a heap, his towel barely hanging on him. He was chilling on his soft brown leather sofa. If anyone looked upon him, they would believe he was relaxing, acutely unaware of the thunder raging inside his soul.

His feet swung over the edge of the armrest. He leaned, he stretched over to pick up his current book. He started escaping into the world of real true crime life story of the murders in the White City, Chicago, during the World Fair Expo. Reading his new book. Something that he chose, as it could not be more different to his current plight. With the wide balcony doors open letting a soft, warm breeze roam freely in his small, some would say cosy apartment. But, his apartment.

It was his Friday night. He had hit the drink hard over the various bars since being back. Since a double blow of losses. This was the first night that he was not going to have a few stubbies, not going to have a single drop of alcohol. His previous healthy routine was coming habitual once again. He was aiming to go to bed at a reasonable hour. To wake refreshed and have a clear day off, instead of a hazy, hangover-ridden struggle of a workday, to then do it all over again. To disturb his thoughts that were focused on his book, a knock at the door echoed through the silence. This time he was sure that he was not hearing things. He impatiently looked towards the closed pale-yellow door. He was not expecting anyone. He did not want to be disturbed. He bordered over the line of answering or ignoring the knock, but curiosity got the better of him in a few short seconds.

Dramatically he rose up, letting the seldom calm of a night in dissipate in tiny pieces of what was seconds before. He threw on a singlet and some shorts from the clothes horse. He stormed towards the door, trying and failing to shake off the annoyance, to piece back the tranquillity with each pounding step. He gripped the door, pulled the door wide open with an abrupt jerk.

Dumbfounded.

Hit with a four-by-four, he was stunned by what was waiting on the other side of the threshold. His eyes stretched wide. His mouth opened just as wide, possibly wider, smacking the floor. His eyes grew wider than saucers. He could not believe who was standing in front of him.

In front of him was a vision of a forgotten beauty. A nervous looking, fidgety, dark blue high-heel shuffling woman, with a stuffed bag of a matching unfamiliar blue suitcase bursting at the zips. A female stood before him in a smart bright red raincoat. It was Mara. He could not speak. Her eyes looked up, nervously, her head rising in fearful condemnation towards the judge of her jury. Her eyes reaching up, towards his shocked glaze.

She mouthed a wordless 'hi'. She was gorgeous, Eddy forgot just how striking she looked. A mischievous sprite in angelic disguise. She always had been eye-catchingly stunning. She appeared to be the old Mara that was confident, independent, brimming with flirty banter and gift-wrapped in a lovely attractive package. He opened the door as wide as it would go. Without words, she accepted the invitation.

She stepped over from the outside, to be inside, figuratively factually. He moved to one side to let her breeze in. With her radiant aura she unintentionally trailed an enveloping smell of intoxicating flowers radiating from her perfume. Right then he was a fly caught in her web. He gripped the suitcase that she left in the corridor. Without thinking, he pulled it in, underestimating the weight and staggered into the legs of Mara. He tried to recompose himself as he pulled the suitcase into the unit. Into their apartment. Their unit.

In a split second, it was no longer his, but theirs. Eddy had already fallen for her again, instantly annoyed with himself. What was she doing back? Eddy did not consider the option that she would come into his place for which she spent so much time in. He had forgotten that she had a key. He felt thankful and comforted that she did not let herself in. He took something away from that. An affirmation, a nod that she respected him enough to appreciate his boundaries. They walked in silence to the kitchen.

He made her a cup of coffee in silence. He grabbed a stubbie of Stone and Wood for himself. His good plans gone by the waste side by a single knock at the door. They proceeded to the sofa. Mara on one side, Eddy the other. A clear gap in-between. Silence. It loitered like a deliberate past catching up with the present. She picked up the resting book that Eddy was reading. If she actually read the blur, this was up for debate.

Eddy thought that she just was not registering the writings in her hand. That she was using it as a prop to find the right words. In this situation one word, an accent on a syllable, a question rather than an exclamation could break this fragile line for which they each were holding. Who was going to break the silence? Who was going to risk the all for something? Or, the all for nothing?

'So...' Eddy attempted awkwardly.

'Yes?' Mara quickly interrupted without her gaze leaving the printed pages clasped in her hand. It was in a way a question, but not. Happy that he had broken the silence. Even though it was just a single word, drowning in the ocean like a single drop of water. That single word meant so much. He was searching for more drops, to form the waves of a sentence.

Mara, for the first time, looked up across the chasm of regret towards Eddy. Eddy looked back. The arm reach between, was still too close for comfort. He could not sink any further away from the back of the sofa. He tried again. Tried for a sentence.

'You're...well, so...you're back!'

'Err...apparently. Will sorry? Will sorry help?'

'What do you think? Seriously? What do you really think?' Machine gun fast. Fury laden bullets. Eddy was off and firing. He wanted answers. He wanted her back. The human mind is a mess when more than the single person is involved. 'I am. was…am…so….so…disappointed in you. What you did. What you. Who you. What you. How could YOU? Argh!' Frustration was growing that he could not put into words. A well-rehearsed conversation in his mind over the past few weeks had come out into an incoherent inarticulate mess of staccato yelled exclamations, cries of pain. Once hidden, now displayed.

'I'm…am…' Tears were falling through her hands as they shielded her eyes. Her face. 'Ed. I am so…sorry'. The book had fallen from her as the composure she had entered with crumbled into pieces. Her words were barely audible over the irrepressible sobs that overpowered her carefully controlled poise.

Eddy wanted to reassure her. For a reason that was not the least bit rational, he crossed the chasm of regret. He threw his arm around her like a cloak of forgiveness, sewed together by tolerance. She pulled in close to his chest. Arms around his waist. The heat from her face was felt through his red singlet onto his chest. The tears erupting as uncontainable as lava, hot, forceful. She cried hysterically. Her shoulders shook as she repeatedly tried to speak. Noises came out of her mouth, but were unrecognisable as being English. She tightly. held him close. She held him near. Comforted in his arms of supported reassurance.

Eddy was not sure what was happening. He had an arsenal of questions but no weapons for the trigger to fire them. He wanted the answers but dared not to speak them. The bullets to strike home to give out the truth he desired, craved…needed. Was he in need of extra comfort since his dad passed that Mara came back at the right time? Eddy's most vulnerable. His impermeable wall was weak, susceptible and the slightest toothpick could make the fracture-thin cracks expose him for Eddy. He started to think about telling her it be alright.

The open beer rested, undrunk on the table. Eddy was thinking; 'What was he doing?' He was staring at the beer, an excuse to leave this embrace. Secretly though, he missed her touch. Then he started telling her, without a proven perception that he was going to speak that she will be alright. To, it is alright. Disappointment rose around his body, but he could not stop the emphasising fortification claims of his actions. Hands in the air. He was surrendering. His good and bad on his shoulder both turned and vanished. Hands washed and for once the two sides of rationality actually agreed with each other. It was left for Eddy to be the force that was fighting the tide, efficaciously.

'Tell me everything,' Eddy pleaded in a soft yearning. His voice muffled slightly by his lips nestling in Mara's hair.

Mara talked through Italy and what she did. It was a stop, start heart-to-heart. Eye contact was rare. They did not stop hugging. She said she pushed him away as she wanted to stay in Italy. She wanted to start a new life, without him. She did it for him. She loved him, but wanted something more. She feared the love that Eddy was showing her. She got her Italian passport and wanted to be Italian. An Italian, proper. She said she was confused. How many times has Eddy heard that line? He let it go. He did not say anything, just listened to her.

She was in lust with the perfect picture of life that was offered by the Italian-dream, but missed Australia. Missed Eddy. She wanted him after a few days. Craved for him after a week. Ached for him. She was too ashamed to call him. To explain what her confusion made her do. Her panic of what she thought was going to be the right passage. She was wrong. She was sorry. Two sentences that kept returning to her story. She sounded genuine.

Eddy's supressed feelings for Mara returned, bubbled back to the surface. He felt the loss of love return. Frankly, it had probably never left. After convincing himself that it was not love but a mere infatuation, he was now turning a full circle back to love. He talked. Eddy tiptoed over everything, his bullets made of feathers as they tickled the surface. Talking on shards of broken glass below his feet as he probed delicately for answers. He successfully tiptoed the broken glass. Any move, particular a wrong move lead to pain. A scar was open, but at the same time healing. They talked. They had cleared the disordered acrimonious closure.

They felt that they be free in there uncomfortable, excruciating sore discussion. It was a very emotional chatter over beer, spirits and, eventually they got drunk together. When the mixers run out for the vodka, which was all that was left, they mixed it with chocolate milk. It tasted great at that time, but would they honestly have it again, in a bar. The chocolate mix was a mistake. The jury was still out on the return of the relationship.

They had drunken, make-up sex. It lasted all night. It was passionate. It was angry. It was happy. It was a pure display of alcohol-fuelled, monster-playing, anarchy-driven emotion. They slept together. Eddy got up to leave for the sofa, but got pulled back under the doona. Mara smiling. They fell asleep looking into the eyes of love returned. Mara had returned. Eddy had taken her back. They were back together. All forgiven. All forgotten.

Mara's unexpected return to Eddy in Australia caused Eddy to ask questions outside the world of them. Eddy's quickness in forgiving her, asked unwelcomed questions within himself. And, Eddy against his better judgement beat himself up for taking her back with open arms. Against his mates advise. His mate's bafflement was brutal. They could not understand to why, he would even consider going back out with Mara. Especially after what she did, so brutally. What she took.

Taking everything into consideration, Eddy chose. He went with his heart over his mind. He went back to her. His mates thought he was foolish. Thought he was being a fucking idiot. They resumed the relationship, but something had changed. Something was to Eddy unrepairable, but something had changed in her too. Mara felt a stronger love. She was trying desperately hard to make it all right once again.

Eddy was struggling with her trust. He would not even leave his wallet around in their unit, just in case she would help herself. It was absurd really to think that he trusted her with his heart, but, not his material things such as money. Was this a fragile foundation of a relationship built on sand? An impending rainstorm brewing close, that the atmosphere was vibrating it to change over his own skin.

However, despite the common cause, everyone carries a war within him or her. Eddy may even be the catalyst. Mara may have been the spark. There was no point, in pointing the finger. The blame game rarely solves any situation. At the end of the day, the blame game rarely makes that person feel good. In the short term it may just as well help, but, again...what's the point? The war of love and hate will collide and continue to rage until they find their soulmates. That very person will quell the flames of hate and heat the flames of love.

Were Mara and Eddy soulmates? Eddy did not want to miss the opportune prospect if this was the case. Mara wanted to board the boat, as she believed he was. They had traced the scars. Picked them open to let them re-heal. Scars of their life together. It has reminded them of the good times. Times where they fought for something. They had fought again. They did believe in them, in their love.

As he held a paper cup of now cold coffee, Eddy glanced over at the sailing boats one Tuesday afternoon. He had bought it a while ago, but had not taken a sip. He was transfixed at the hypnotic nature of the sailing boats. Many variations of masts, sails of different colours, holding shades of beautified enrichment in the afternoon sun. He had finished work on this gorgeous sunny day with a chilly breeze that he did not feel. He worked-out before going for a walk. A feeble attempt to clear his mind.

He found himself in a secluded cove within the Sydney harbour. A crumbling grass covered wall is what he leans on, with his elbows in a triangle to the coffee cup at the point grasped in both of his interlocking hands. A short step away is a many-times painted green wooden bench which is slowly rotting in the salty air. He spots it, after such a long time of trance-like surveying. He proceeds to move towards it in an unenthusiastic walk, and slowly places himself on the planks of wood, that bowed with a resisting creak under his light frame. He leans forward with his elbows resting on his knees, his head sunk down towards his chest. His head hangs, as if around his neck is a heavy medallion filled with all his worries and anxieties.

In the lidless cup, his reflection shines in the still dark brown water, tilted on the straw-like wiry grass. The fast-moving water splashes on the stonewall in a rhythmical serene sound. Dogs are being walked, some are having colourful or worn tennis balls thrown for them to collect, to bring back, to repeat. The barks and the howls are all muffled above the soft cashing of the waves on stone. He looks up for the slightest moment and allows himself the slightest smile before bowing back down. Looking, but not seeing the dusty brown dirt with grass around, but losing a battle against the feet that will, and do destroy the lawn.

He wonders of the many different stories that each foot would have walked to have put themselves down on this exact spot. Each ripple of water is highlighted by the gold deposits of the setting sun. In the distance is the building scapes…yet so near. The clink of string sways in the chilly breeze, clipping the masts in an irregular rhythm. The birds sing to each other. A dog skids to a halt as a tennis ball plunges into an area of muddy grass. Eddy leans back and opens the front pocket of his black and blue Billabong shirt and removes his black shiny mobile phone. He toys with it in his hands for a while. He seems to be slightly shaking. He carefully types in a message. He holds it in his hands, unsure of his next move.

After a brief hesitation with despair etched in his face, he turns the mobile off and returns it to his pocket. He flings off his shoes, casts them off. They fly a short distance in the air as if he is casting away some metal ankle cuffs. He stretches out his limbs. Closes his eyes and listens to nature, undisturbed from human interference. He shakes himself with a frustration as he gets up and throws the full cup of coffee in the bin. He goes back to his unit. His aim for feeling relaxed enough to release his mind from his decision, yet to be really made, has not worked.

Eddy showers as if he has not showered for weeks. He scrubs and allows the hot water to sort out what he is feeling. What he wants to do. What he feels is right to do. He lazily dries himself as he catches a glimpse in the steamed-up mirror and swore he saw his father looking back where his face should have been. He was leaning over the white basin, his arms straight and locked out, his head bowed down. He glimpsed his father. *No! No, it was not possible*, he thought. He looked down before slowly glimpsing back, peeking under his eyebrows. His father was still there.

His father died. He loved him so much. He loved him too, although he never said it, he was sure. He needed his advice now more than ever. His imagination was running riot. He knew it was not real, but he felt his father's observation.

'What should I do?' Eddy asked. Asked out loud, feeling slightly foolish to be talking to his own reflection, that was mirroring his departed father's worn, tired and wise face. To his surprise his father's voice answered. The mirror portrait with the beads of condensation gently rolling down the screen did not move. However, his father's voice was clear. Unmistakable. The visual mirror image of his father rather than a projection was a strange moment. He was so absorbed in this strange moment that he heard, but did not listen to his father's voice. Eddy repeated the question.

'What should I do?' this time with a tormented anger that cracked at the end to an exhale of teeth-gritted breath.

'Son,' his father's voice repeated without the slightest tremor of annoyance, 'it is up to you. However. Would you. Would YOU like to be with someone that may, sometime, one day, could, have the capability of someday loving you? Someday be all that you think them to be?'

Eddy looked down, away from his father, down in the basin, at the slight drip that escaped his forehead and down the sink, 'I guess not', he concedes quietly in a sound that was barely a whisper. He confesses not to his father but down, down into the curve of the white ceramic sink too ashamed to look up. To look into his father's kind, warm eyes and the gaze of them, gazing at him.

'Well son,' with a sympathetic tone, a pause. 'Do you really need to answer the question of an answer you already know? Are you looking for reassurance? A hope that I agree with your thoughts. That you are doing the wrong thing to feel that you are doing the right thing.

The WRONG thing, is that the RIGHT thing? I know that answer. Son, you know that answer. Yes son, so do you. Stop tormenting yourself with this and be at peace.'

Eddy turned on the hot faucet with one fluid twist of his right wrist. Water gushed down, roaring with power, steaming with heat. He splashed his face, hoping that the hotness would sting his face to strike some realism back in him. The water would wash away his thoughts of what he should do for him, what he should not do for them. The steam plumed from the sink, misting the mirror. He was shaking his head to his father's honestly. Shaking his head from side to side to rattle the truth away.

He knew that his father was right. He knew what he must do. He snatched up the grey hand towel in his left hand and without thinking wiped the mirror in fury. Instantly regretting this action, as the grey cloth moved the mist away and revealed his own face staring back at him. His father disappeared. His father had vanished. Of course, that was if he had been in the bathroom with him at all. Or, just a deception of the shadows and light, his mind playing a cruel trick. His imagination running amuck. He missed him. Although at this point where he wanted his advice. He realised that he really missed him a lot more that he had initially thought.

Eddy wondered if he had been daydreaming. He was feeling that this was his own conscious opinion talking to him. He finished getting ready for bed, as he wept openly, unashamed. As he settled, his phone rang from the charger on the beige shelf, vibrating in the front hallway. He was going to ignore the chimes. He knew who it was before he made the short few steps over to look at the screen. Correctly predicting the name, it was Mara.

He picked his phone up and retrieved the unsent message. He sent it. It was a message to meet up tomorrow evening. As this evening fell on a work night, Mara was instantly suspicious. Mara was doing business calls in Wagga Wagga. She rang again. Eddy wanted to answer, at the same time, he did not. On the third ring he did. He never wanted to be one of those people that just went quiet when the going gets tough.

On the other line, Mara sounded confused. Eddy said he wanted to see her face to face. He wanted to ask questions. He did not want to do it over the phone. Mara decided at the end of the telephone call to go to Eddy as soon as she could. She spent that evening renegotiating her work calls so that they were all packed into the morning. Thus, consequently freeing her afternoon so she could travel back, the long monotonous drive to Sydney as soon as she finished.

Let's face it, she was not going to sleep well with that unanswered motive of an unscheduled meeting imminent. Especially with Eddy's statement; 'I don't want to do it over the phone…' she apprehensively recalls him verbalising. Moreover, meetings are not what lovers had. They had dates. They had get-togethers. They had rendezvous. They had courtship. They did not have meetings.

That journey home to Sydney seemed slow. Mara kept glancing at the speedometer sure that it would read a slower reading to the speeding she was doing. She was racing the time, the clock, Eddy finishing work to be at home in the swift motion of him arriving back. All this came around at a slow, snail pace for Mara. She had a feeling of how the evening was going to pan out. She hoped she was wrong. She prayed she was wrong. She drove through the city, as she deemed it quicker against the peak hour traffic. It actually turned out to be the correct move. She was at Eddy's in no time. She parked up. Fluttering in the gently breeze was a yellow post-it on the cream door of their unit.

She read it: 'At the cove'. She paused. For a split second, she was rooted to the spot. Plucking out the courage in her soul, she then walked the short distance to a sandy, dirty looking part of the harbour, which was the result of all the salt and silt from the water flow. Eddy was there striding from one point to another on the green, straw-like grass. She watched him for a minute. He was looking down at his shuffling feet. Mara greeted Eddy with an unexpected awkwardness. He spoke too quickly. Her voice cracked into highs that she had not spoken since her schooldays.

He spoke in the dry, wordless, unattractive clichés of how he feels so much of her, but not enough of her. He had worked the lines of this conversation for days. Not one of the perfect mind-worked lines came out correctly. He wondered that taken a few schooners of Dutch courage was wise. He blamed the alcohol for the disjoined words, the jumbled sentences, the incorrect tones. He made a second attempt. In all honesty, he probably did not need to. The message was very much understood the first time around. This assertion was in fact not needed, as halfway through a sudden glow of pain erupted from the right side of his cheek as her palm connected, oh-so-perfectly.

So perfect, that with the crisp flesh-smacking-flesh clap, it was so clear that she understood his meaning. So loud that people whom were minding they own business stopped to stare, to make it their business. Birds flew from the treetops in panic, as if the slap was a pending attack. Some of these people felt the need to enter this personal scene that they were having. Some laughed. Some looked in as much shock as Eddy. Others cheered. Others applauded her actions.

Straight away he sensed than seeing her turn and flee, with tears pouring from her eyes, her hand over her mouth trying to muffle the sobs, hearing without necessary seeing the slap around his face, they created a bond with the unknown beautiful brown hair girl in the red coat that was fleeing away. In the eyes of the observers, the victim was not Eddy. In their eyes, he was reaping what he sowed, even if they had no idea what was going on. And they didn't. The one that got hit deserved to be hit.

Eddy was the creator of his own treatment. He did deserve the inherited reaction, yet he was not the creator of this whole situation. He did not want to, or, felt the need to explain to strangers what had just materialised. What had happened for him to feel the way he did. However, he did want to explain fully to Mara. He called out. His left hand held in the direction that she had fled, his right hand massaged his very sore cheek that was burning on imaginary fire. He ran after her. He was stopped by a stranger. This disruption was something he did not appreciate in the slightest. He pushed him aside. The stranger's judgemental eyes, which were the judge and jury, and now the executioner kept blocking his move.

'Let her move on,' the stranger said.

Eddy scoffed and again pushed him away to continue his pursuit of Mara. All for no accord as he turns the corner in time to see Mara drive away. The smoke bellowing from the exhaust of her small Toyota Swift. The bulldust from the dusty grey road. He wondered if she saw him in the rear-view mirror. Running up to explain. Running up in anger. Running up in sadness. Or running up in regret.

Eddy returned to the cove. Noticeably oblivious of the voices that circulated about the scene that had just unfolded. He descended the last of the small, broken concrete steps on to a carpet of fresh cut grass. He felt numb, apart from his burning cheek. The slight breeze gave the slightest taste of salt, the taste of the sea. The taste of a relationship gone sour. He closed his eyes. On his eyelids, he played what just happened. He started to cry.

He did not shield his eyes. He did not hide his irregular rhythmic chant of his breath trying to keep up with his flooding emotions. He was in all purposes inside his own dark room. His own dark cell. He felt so isolated. If what he had just done was right, why does he feel so bad? The breeze whispered to him. Without realising, he had sunk to his knees. He had his legs drawn up to his chest. His arms tightly wrapped around them, with his hands in a vice-like grip on each of his elbows. His face buried in his knees.

He was rocking like a war-torn, damaged soldier. He had blown his world apart with his own personal grenade. He had caused the destruction. He was left in his own aftermath of his own battlefield. In his dark shell. In his dark cell. He was isolated. He was in a tight human ball in his own dark, endless, no future room. Alone.

Emotions hit him so suddenly. The realisation of what he had just done took seconds. It hit him so hard like a shot from a cannon. Hard. It hit him hard in a merciless body blow. But, he did not move from the impact. He did not flitch. He did not react. He felt each and every blow. He felt he deserved to feel the blow. He was scared. Alone. Isolated. Alone.

Eddy wondered if he had just had a mind explosion. A moment where he lost his mind. A distant memory that happened a few seconds ago. He hoped it was a dream where he did not do the thinkable, but did the unthinkable and strived to save the relationship from his own rejection. He had a beautiful lady. He, had, Mara. He had loved Mara. Mara loved him. She did everything to keep Eddy in love with her. Well apart from the thing he craved to have with her, he wanted to put a ring on her.

Over the course of the next few days, Eddy tried to call, text, but got nothing. He did not know what he had, until it was gone. Until he let love go. At one point in our lives is that point where love is not shared. Where a heart is not even. Not beating in unison. At this point to save further hurt Eddy felt the need to let Mara go. He was fed up of living a lie. That lie that he sees so many people live each and every day. It is never easy to do. To take that decision. Eddy knew this.

This is not the first time he has done this. It is never easy. The heart is never broken even, as one part does want it more, fact. FACT! This is why Eddy does not believe in the cliché of *mutual break-up*. One person will hurt more than the other, regardless of the circumstances, they will. One person.

In this case, it was Mara. She did not see it coming until that message on Tuesday. It was a surprise to her. Eddy wished she would respond, so he could explain. Eddy believed that although Mara's heart was broken, it would be fixed, eventually. She would find someone better than him. Someone that loved her equally.

Over the course of a few weeks.

Methodically, one box a week.

She sent his stuff in small ashes of charred remains.

Hell hath no fury as a woman scorned.

At the Cove

Eddy is back at the cove. He is seeing the place many years ago, when he lived just a stone's throw away. Where he had a life with the aforementioned Mara. The cove itself has not changed. The houses are bigger, looming over him. They shard, long dark shadows of shade greater than him, blocking out the sunlight for which the trees need for growth. It is said that the world is growing around this hidden oasis, but nothing seems to be stopping them. The edges of the bushes are brown with lack of sun. The vegetation is slowly dying, slowly moving further from a habitat to being displaced. Shrinking to be dwindling, less significant, to become smaller. Trying to thrive, but fading to disappear. Progress for mankind, regress for nature.

Eddy should be saddened by this more. He is, inside, but his mind is unfocused on the present. He kicks the newly cut grass from under his feet as he shuffles around the small green area. Thinking of Mara for the first time in years. After that meeting, at this precise spot, he never heard from her again. He tried to contact her, but each call was rejected, each motion to connect was unsuccessful. She slammed the door on him just as he did to their relationship. He watches the grass move from beneath his feet as he thinks of the why. He was worried that she would be deceitful again. That was the bottom line. He did not trust her.

The big answer is that the psychologists could very well be correct. They claim to have known for years that people make self-destructive sabotaging decisions when under pressure. Like a deer caught in the headlights, his mind sees what is happening, but has the inability to react. Being stuck, paralysed, the brain stops running in surges with what it should say, but for some reason reacts differently.

Taking a last-ditch response in an attempt to survive a relationship from the most primitive beginnings, to do nothing. It is strange to think that the nothing, in a reaction, is actually the emotionally suicidal path on the way to relationship annihilation. Is this what Eddy has always done.

The thing was he was willing to try, yet he could not get the idea out of his head that she would neglect him and deviously destroy him again.

Her lies bred a fear within Eddy, born from her betraying disappointments. He never reconciled the experience. He was stung. He was hurt. He was humiliated.

A mate of his once said to him that nostalgia gets in the way of the future. Eddy never used to look back too often, he was not the one too. Yet since the brittle shaking foundation of his relationship with Beth-Annie. He finds himself not only looking at the tattered remains of his romance, like a cryptic Japanese puzzle box where he hunts to discover the commands for the map to find out his perfect solution. Also, he finds himself looking back constantly, like it has become habitually. Ingrained in the back of his head, all these experiences, which whether he needs them or not, are suddenly coming to the forefront.

He is dissecting them, searching for that piece of information that tells him what he needs to do to make his present one different. The way time flows suggest that the present just might not exist. He rummages into the pages of the past that could make the ending different. Before he knew it, his mind went back once more. Apart from his first, this must be one of the most important loves of his young life. This one was like a love affirmation. Love was out there. Up till now, he did not go searching, it fell into his lap.

Four Years Ago
Meeting an Askew Love

Eddy is now in his thirties, early thirties, barely even over the sunset years of his diminished twenties. Well, that is what he tells himself to make him believe that his age has stalled. That he is the modern-day Peter Pan. His mind may be young but, he is covered with the deep-ridden scars of his life. His appearance is precarious. Wrinkles line his face, appearing overnight for when he fell asleep with smooth, youthful skin. He aches in places he did not before. He used to jump out of bed. He still does, but instead of an eager clap of the hands to get his day started, Eddy wakes with a leap, followed by a groan, tenderly rubbing the small of his back. A trudging bare-fleeted shuffle to salvation, the idle coffee machine. His precious excelsior to kick start his day.

He is thinking back to when he turned thirty, as if it was yesterday. He thinks back to his twenties, his lost, misplaced youth. The memories are so clear in his mind, as if they were only yesterday. The lines around his eyes tell him the truth. He is thinking back at how incredibly stupid he was, well, he still is. Nothing has changed. Through his teenage years he thinks he knows it all. In his twenties he thinks he has everything mastered. In his thirties he thinks he has it all worked out. The soul-crushing reality is he has not. Eddy is no different to anyone else. Eddy finds out, just like everyone else. Anyone that has had, or has been in a relationship. He continues to find out the same way. The hard way. To live is to learn, in life, he never stops learning. Never stop repeating the heart, headstrong reactions to how he feels.

Can it be only Eddy? Surely, he is not the sole contributor to destroy everything he cares about. He does understand. He states it as a self-mantra of debauchery in a mock gesture at himself to be in self-control. Each person has different needs. Each person has different wants. Each person that he has had the pleasure to have met is different. Each person is a different character. A different ambition. Each person has an idealistic view of the person that they want. The person that they want to essentially be with. Then, when they find that person. They realise that they do not want that ideal person after all.

They do not stop the search though. They keep searching for that ideal person, the holy grail, their soulmate. For the most, they will stay alone. The truth. Their truth for them is no-one will reach their expectation that they have placed on a pedestal, a table that Alice in the Looking Glass is struggling to reach. For on top is the key. The key is a way for her to enter the garden. She needs this key. It is a desire for her.

Eddy needs the companionship of another voice. He desires the want to find a special someone. Alice struggles to reach the table as she has shrunk herself. Straining, jumping and trying to reach the prize, a prized possession. Eddy is also trying to reach for the prize of giving his heart to someone filled with his trust, love. Alice jumps up, stretches to reach something, like Eddy that is simply out of reach, unobtainable. Frustrations grow, as helplessness fills the head with negativity.

Eddy's disappointments spread as large vulnerability. This fans the engulfing fire in his brain, with the smoke leaving a thick soot of insignificance. A lost feeling that he is going through the motions of work, sleep, wake, repeat. A feeling that gets too much and suffocates him sometimes. He, tends to have more than his fair share of quiet days. Mates call this his moody days. Eddy learns, he does not. Eddy must realise that he will never find his ideal person. Eddy must accept this reality. This is not to say that anyone will do. He has to accept that the ideal person is the person that he feels right with. A person to share with.

A person to share the quiet times, strolling around David Jones bedding department on a boring, tedious Saturday arvo when the sun is hot and beckoning people to the sandy beaches. Eddy will be happy in these moments, as well as the bad moments. As these bad moments are always for the shared mutual love, that show they care about each other. A person to share the great times of laughing until your sides split. A conversation that he would, could like or dislike, but listens and hears, nevertheless. It is in his thirties that he starts to question this idealistic vision of the perfect soulmate is out in the world or only in his imagination. Eddy is now in his thirties, wondering where he went wrong in his romanticised life decisions.

Eddy would never admit to anyone else, let alone himself that deep down, he is a romantic at heart. He does not need a prized possession by his side to be valued. To fit into what society deems appropriate. He does not need someone to take to parties, engagements, office mixes, to stop him standing near the door slowly edging his way out so no one sees him leave, not that anyone would notice. He does not need someone for that. He needs someone for him. Him, alone. His needs run deeper.

He wants someone to connect with mentally, as well as physically. To have as much fun picking brains about the topics of the day, as to talking about silly things. Discussing the world's politics, country economies, while putting it all right over a cup of morning coffee. To be there for someone in her moment of need. For someone to be there for his. To share a comfortable silence with. To listen to his monotonous, rather boring daily routine. To not judge him for stupid remarks made, that were either taken out of contexts. Remarks he had made while he was just having an unthinking, impulsive chuck away comment. He wanted the fairy-tale love. That was it. Yet, that IT seems a mirage as he stares out of the window, down at the footpath, the people.

The older he gets, he felt that IT was slipping away. Faster than the copious different leaflets on a blustery morning on the harbour lost out of the grip of the businessman rushing to his next meeting due to being late, well he was going to be later now.

When he was young, he had the pick of anyone. He was selective in his approach. Cautious and calculated. Now with the pool, more of a puddle, he sees that he was foolish. That is not to say that he should have settled on the first, or the last, but more, that he should have been more open to the idea of opening his love up to be accepted. It was not too late. On the other hand, was he searching in the wrong places? The internet highway has many avenues, paths, which can get him what he may want from a casual hook-up, a date for a night or, sex to a promised insinuation of more. It seems that it cannot find the thing he wants in real life, or on the internet.

Eddy wanted the movie ending. The happy ending. The make-believe tale. He wanted to meet someone out in the street. Not on a computer, whether that be a laptop, mobile or iPad. He wanted to feel a connection, with someone that wanted the same. Not a connection through a connection.

This is what most people want, he guesses. That is why so many people go on Tinder, Hookup, Casual, eHarmony and the like. Why are so many people searching for that unrealistic reality? Some find it, of course. Some are lucky enough to have found their love. Some are pushed, into it. Some learned to live, in a love. Some do it for the children. Some are too blind to see. Some are too lost to be found. Eddy was all the above, minus the children. He had done all these. Then just when he had resigned his love life to a footnote in history, it materialised.

He fell in love. Mind first, over some innocent messages. Then physical. They just seemed to work well together. To use a cliché, they just clicked with a magical chemistry of attraction. They met in a coffee shop. They would go in at roughly the same time through the week, before they both started work. One day she missed the mutual rendezvous of a nod of the head, with a mirrored smile. As he waited for his coffee, he took the bold, unlike-Eddy step to break the chasm of ice.

He mentioned that he had noticed that she was not there yesterday. She was flattered that he had noticed. She was happy that he had noticed her, as she had noticed him. Each meeting thus after, the banter grew more friendly, natural and flirtatious. Their conversations grew in a way that they were getting to know one another. To the point he dived in, he asked her out through a sip of coffee. She did not hesitate. She actually blurted out 'about time'.

A fire was started. A flicker of potential love. A true prospective of correlation was rousing. Stimulating and accelerating each other's heartbeat when they spoke, listened, saw, thought, felt each other. It was an intensifying love that was almost at that stage. When all was lost, he was finally found.

That Askew Love

'Spasiba.'

An ethereal soft, calm voice in the still of the night. Eddy was not sure if he had heard this or imagined it. A single word, spoken with a nervous tremble.

'Spasiba.'

A fractured word definitely escaped her unmoving body. But for the silent breathing and slight movement of the doona on her chest. A soft barely audible whisper in the small bedroom, that meant the world. If Eddy, had not just heard the recounting of her tempestuous voyage from home he would have been pushing out the zzz's himself. Maybe as restless as she was doing right now. She opened up her treasure chest of memories that was locked up tighter than Fort Knox. The memories of her escaping, being pushed from her former home. A country that was down on its knees, praying to get answers. Receiving none in response. No helping hand to help them back up. A lone country left to fend for itself. A country that single-handedly survive against the odds.

Eddy lay on his back. The slight cool breeze stroked him on his exposed bare arms. The light of a lone streetlight reflecting a golden hue on the cream walls could do nothing to pierce the pitch of obscurity. Eddy had been staring skyward into the darkness as he laid on his back for some time. It had been a while as his mind ticked. He thought Sofija was asleep. Maybe she was. She thanked him in her native tongue.

A dialogue that she rarely, if ever, spoke. She had no hint of an accent of her former past. She was essentially an Australian. No-one would think or sense any other cultures that were prominent to her, being her. When she opened her memory chest an accent arose as the lid opened further up. If Eddy was not awake, he would have missed her voice. He would have missed a memory of his own to put in his own personal treasure chest. He thinks that 'thank you' was directed at him.

Eddy would never forget Lia. Although her name was Sofija Liama, she chose to use an abbreviated form of her middle name, which was her mother's name. Liama meant lucky in Latvian. Often it got mispronounced to Lea and spelt the same way with many people jumping to the wrong assumption that it was short for Leanne. She never put people right. It did not bother her. Her name, however, was plated with gold amber.

Lia had a personality to match her name. She was extremely happy-go-lucky. She was a magnet for which people were attracted to her positive attributes, her smile, and her infectious laugh. However, all this disappeared instantly in the conversation that they had just shared. Well, Lia spoke, Eddy listened. She shared. She spoke of her growing up as if in a third person. She was disconnected and unemotional.

Although not all doom and gloom. Her voice was disconnected as she travels in her mind, to the far reaches of the darkest corners of her memories. Once there she reminisces the time. Here lies the battered, wooden, worn chest of a series of locked memories of her childhood. The submerged innocence that was not maintained.

Lia was a beautiful brunette, with her unofficial first name coming into association once again. Lia, the Latvian Goddess of Fate and the Goddess of fortune. She seemed to live her life as if she had lived before. She appreciated every single moment. Learned from every experience. Loved every scene. Sometimes the latter coming with the ability of hindsight. Lia had one green eye. This she proudly states was her mother's. The other eye was dark blue; equally as proudly, she states this was her father's.

That day before the restless sleep started like any other…

They woke up on a day off together. A rare day-off together. They did not rush to move. They cuddled each other beneath the warmth of the doona. They effortlessly got ready. Rubbed their eyes with the light being brighter than the darkness outside. They left the apartment and went for a run together. Finished at the familiar coffee shop where they had started a slate to pay every Friday after work. They talked. Did the mediocre, mundane things that had to be done, such as the washing, ironing, shopping. It was a cool sunny day with a bone-chilling breeze. A typical day where summer was leaving Sydney and winter had one foot in the space left behind. Impulsive, but not unusual for them. They decided to have lunch in the small park near where they lived.

On the patchy grass worn park that was water-starved due to a longer dry spell from summer, Eddy spread out a red and blue tartan-style rug. Meanwhile, Lia opened her protected mystery bag that she had lovingly prepared. With a flourish, she retrieved each item and spread them out with delight. Revealed on the rug was corned beef, cornichon and Dijon mustard olive sourdough rolls that she had made while Eddy had showered the morning running excursions away. An exotic bowl of diced, fresh tropical fruit and the crisp edges of the morning's newspaper. The colourful squared design, that their folded legs rested on were a heavy contrast to the yellow, straw grass area of what normally is lush green carpet grass.

Around them, the Saturday morning dog walkers compete on the narrow path with runners in a silent courtesy dance of manners. Although not quite lunchtime, they were both so hungry so what was going to be the difference of now or later. They had been going together for a few months and enjoyed these moments where not one of them had to rush off somewhere, that somewhere being, normally work.

Lia touched on Latvia occasionally, with Eddy only discovering that she was born, to be moved away early in her childhood only, a few weeks ago. It was a reluctant move, Eddy sensed, from her beloved home. More it seemed heart retching to be pulled from the arms of her country, furthermore, to be yanked, and at the same time pushed from the cradling arms of her dearly loved Mother. Barely to know the world outside, other than the capital of Latvia, Riga. It was frightening to leave, to be taken from a place that was all she knew. To be placed in a new town that she had never heard off, in a country that she never been told off. She was, rightly, so scared.

Lia had actually lived in Australia longer than her native Latvia. She did not know that when she said a tearful goodbye through disconsolate eyes of sadness that she would never see her Mother again. To hear her voice, they spoke every week. It was a ritual that was never broken, just the once. A ritual that it was the same time, same day, same personal place that would never be broken. Without fail it had happened. Then one day it did not. She called. No answer. She knew. Something was wrong. She cried. She heard officially a week later by the most impersonal letter that she had ever read. A letter from the government authorities stating that she had died and left nothing.

How dare they?

She had left her!

Her mother had left her behind…again. Lia missed her so much. She would occasionally stare into space and think of her face. She would be in so much pain that no-one could possibly understand, let alone cure. Then again, Lia would not want her to be cured, as she felt this pain a blessing that she was missing her. She would never stop missing her. Lia would never learn to live without her fully. When she died, to use a cliché, a part of her died.

Due to her childhood, Lia struggled with connection. This was a shocking discovery for Eddy. For Lia was such a friendly, talkative and social person. It was a genuine surprise to Eddy that she did not have a broader spectrum of friends. Out of the blue skies above them dotted with the white flight of the noisy squawking white, yellow-crested cockatoos they looked upwards, on their backs. Lia talked, she was explaining over the delicious rolls which scattered their crumbs over the blanket.

Birds were waiting in trees, seemingly listening to the story. In reality, they were after the food. Some bolder ones came closer to the ground. An ugly white ibis strutted his stuff as he nonchalantly walked past, with his sideways glance looking at his prize, to quickly walk off in another direction away, to resume the charade just as quickly. If Walt Disney ever included an ibis in his films, it would have to be portrayed as the most wickedly evil character, they just have that look about them.

Lia gave great consideration to who she would class as a mate. A greater consideration to a friend. She consciously limited them as she knew that the chosen few would be there for her. In this, she did not and would not expect anything in return. She wanted to know that she had a safety net if she needed to use it. She talked about her Mother. Then silence.

'We need a holiday!' Lia pronounced unexpectedly to shatter that long silence.

'Yes. We spoke about this but never decided where.' Eddy tried to be calm.

'My old home.'

'Latvia?'

'Why not?'

'Well. Err. How about China?'

'Wh—' Lia went to interrupt but was cut short by Eddy.

'I would like to do the Tran-Siberian. Why not start in China. Go through Mongolia and Russia to Estonia then down to Latvia and finish there?'

Lia thought about it. Said nothing.

'Or…' Eddy attempted a clause in his last suggestions, 'in reverse.' He failed.

'Russia?' Lia posed. 'Well. It would give me an opportunity to brush up on my Russian.'

Sensing that a yes was close, Eddy could not contain a smile from beaming.

'Yes. Okay. Yes. We need to do some planning but…yes.'

From that initial conversation. Once they had decided to go. The hard work started. It was decided to travel through Russia on the Tran Siberian Railway first, the wheels were in motion. They got excited. With every moment they had they were thinking, reading and learning about the nearly ten-thousand kilometre of track. The hardest was the itinerary.

Being the world's largest country, where would they stop, explore. What would be the better places to see without following the tourist routes? From the far east station at Vladivostok to the west in Moscow, the continuous train journey would take seven days, a week to cross the nation. Coming from Australia, they were well aware of living in a large country. But to go from Sydney to Perth is half the distance, less than half the time. That shows the size of this untrodden, unfamiliar landscape for them.

They learnt that stops in the smaller towns normally took two to five minutes, whereas in the larger cities it could take thirty to forty-five minutes. There was the option of a bus, which was cheaper, but the train is an icon in itself. This suggestion by Lia was quickly, swiftly waved off the table by Eddy. He was hearing none of that bus idea.

Also, he used as a way of settling that argument from prospering, 'we would have more comfort space for luggage and, AND a bed to lie down in. A toilet with boiling water for free.' He giggled at his own mistake before backtracking. 'Well, you understand the toilet and the hot water is not the same. You know…not in the same, erm…Moving on. Also, also on the train is a food carriage.'

He was sold on the idea. It was sold in his mind. What caught Eddy unaware was that the tickets were booked out for over a month. Currently, forty-six days were booked out online. So, they booked it quickly for that date. It was pleasantly easy. Only requiring the full names, username, date of birth, password and the question and answer to a secret question. With that, Eddy hit the print button. From the other side of the room the printer whizzed into life, buzzed and churned out two E-tickets. It was with the picking up of the crisp white paper that it was officially going to happen. They were going. Still not an itinerary made, but that was just nit-picking.

One thing Eddy really wanted to see was the Terracotta warriors. So, while he was online, he booked the flights from Sydney to Beijing, Beijing to Xi'an and back with a tour guide to meet at the airport. He did this on the presumption that Lia would not mind a slight detour in the journey. After all when was he ever going to go back to China? He sent a simple text to Lia.

'Get ready, we leave in T-minus forty-six days. Flying out from Sydney.'

Instantaneously, a message vibrated on his resting mobile, an emoji, '☺ X'. Although he had neglected to mention his detour, he felt that it would be a very pleasant surprise. Eddy told himself that she would rather it come face-to-face rather than a cold, electronic message. He almost believed in that logic himself.

There was no stopping them. They had calculated enough hours saved from work, so decided that would be the time. The cusp of a plan was starting to be established. Not a lot of time to iron out the details but Eddy was on top of the visas, being the most important part. Three weeks to travel from China to Latvia with a full five days in and around Riga. It was too easy. Easy to plan. The guidelines came together effortlessly. No problems with visas, just the getting the passports back, to go back and forth to the various embassies. No problems with tickets. It was uncomplicated, some would say natural. They were to leave six weeks from now.

The time was going fast. Every second away from work they worked together, alone but putting everything together so one person could pick it up after another. It was astounding how in tune they both were. It was so, very easy. They did it all together, without stress, with no worries.

May in China

It was a colder day than the average May in Sydney, as they excitedly boarded the flight to China. The wind coming through the exposed, narrow gap in the metal ramp that joined the airport, Australia, to the plane, the destination, made Lia shiver. It was with a nervous step that the coldness hit as Lia made the step onto the aeroplane, towards her seat. It was finally going to be the first step to where she belonged. A country that she yearned to go back to. The place where she was born. Home.

She fiddled at the cold-gushing air from the grey plastic vents. Turning it off, moving the socket towards Eddy. Eddy who was settled and gently holding Lia's hand. Trying to relax her with touch alone. She talked animatedly about this trip, edged with intrepid courage but as the day dawned, she was silent. She was noticeably nervous. Lia was, not for the first time, scared. She had thought of this moment. She had dreamed of this. Doing this trip back home. Now, it was a reality. It really was now. It was so very daunting.

The connection of the three different planes, were without any delays, so they landed on time in Xi'an, China. Being in China, Eddy was not going to pass up an opportunity to go here. A place, as a major civilisation capital, that shared equal fame with Athens in Greece, Cairo in Egypt, Rome in Italy. For him, it was just a distant dream. He honestly did not think that he was going to genuinely see them. However, since those early days surrounded by wooden desks, the smell of chalk, lead from the pencils and the shrill being dampened to a soft murmur as Miss Wookie described this place.

Miss Wookie, the history teacher with a greying, split haired beehive that she had, no doubt since the swinging sixties. A small stature of a delicate body. A perpetual beaming grin on her creased story-travelled face. Her arms ridden with veins running along her bony fingers as she pointed to the large map of the world. Out of her delicate chest was a booming, empowering voice. Small in stature, but large in personality. She was one of those teachers that left an optimistic impression on Eddy's life. For she not only spoke, skilfully taught these classes of young impressionable minds, but engaged their receptive minds on the cusp of potential to be whatever they wanted, dreamed.

Her perfectly erect beehive of a wig never moved in the wind or with her own head movements as she peered forever watching like a lioness over her cubs in a maternal, protective manner. Eddy never heard her raise her voice. She had an uncanny way of telling a pupil off without shouting, but making them understand their fault without belittling them. For this approach, she had the respect of all the pupils, her peers and most importantly the support of the parents. This, of course, did not stop the innocent from testing the parameters every now and again; after all, kids will be kids. Innocence needs to be maintained.

Eddy thought she was old then. She shuffled with low sole-worn shoes from behind her large block of a light wooden desk, to the blackboard behind. Stretching to write the odd words down from the books that was open on the ink slotted, sanded down thin lid of the desk by each of the pupils. They looked at the colourful illustrated pictures next to the text as their thin, smooth fingers stroked the sentences as Miss Wookie softly lectured the class in her raspy voice. Eddy was not a history geek by any means, but from these humble beginnings, he did find cultures, history with the rise and falls of empires, interesting.

He enjoys learning with an unquenchable thirst for knowledge. If he visits a place, he likes to throw himself in. He loves to learn what was done in the past as well as the present. See, do, eat and experience what the locals do, as well as the tourists. This journey, with its timeframe may be harder, but he did have a few ducks in a row that he hoped to at least see with his own eyes. He hoped that he could feel enough to experience the essence of a different life.

He wondered why people would live in certain places, environments that can be extremely hostile and to why they insist in staying there. The history that brought them there and why they stayed. Facts fire his interest. Hence this is why Lia had nicknamed him Travel Geek, rather, she says, My Travel Geek. She often gets entrapped in his stories from Europe. His energy portrays into his telling which keeps her from interrupting. So, since a young 'un in schools, this was one of his bucket list places. He smiles as they land with a wink in Lia's direction, who returns the smile with a kiss on his warm, flushed cheek.

They disembark the aeroplane with their light luggage to the exit and the baggage carousel. The electric doors swoosh open. Immediately they see their names, 'Mr Eddy' and 'Mrs Lia' on a white, shiny cardboard sign in blue marker. Nestled at the feet of a young petit Chinese lady, who looks up occasionally from her mobile phone. A nod of agreement with a smile as they head towards the sign, the elegantly dressed stranger. In a swift, flowing motion she picks the white board up. Hugs it under her arm as she thrusts a small, pale hand forward, slightly hidden by her large sleeve of her woollen long coat to shake both of their hands. She states in perfect Americanised English, 'Mr Eddy, Mrs Lia, Welcome. Please, I am Jessica. Let's get your bags.'

She swivels like a fashion model on a catwalk. Her nude-coloured low heels squeak as she struts with the tails of her coat bellowing behind her. Eddy and Lia briskly follow her light blue jeans, shining in the bright reflective sterile white, clean floor of the soft, glowing modern airport lights. It is busy, but spookily quiet. Like the start of a horror movie. Echoing footsteps are all that is heard. Her light brown hair shines behind as it flows, bounces with her walking rhythm. Eddy and Lia have been sitting for the most part of a day, so are slightly awkward, legs are stiff as they eventually catchup with the fast-stepping Jessica. It must look like an Asian beauty being followed by two hunchback, dishevelled beasts.

As they wait for their luggage, uneasy small talk is exchanged, the type of chatter from people that are not acquainted with each other's lives. As always, the safe topic comes up, the weather. Mercifully this torture ends quickly, as an orange siren signals a warning drone as the conveyor belt whirls into life. The wait for luggage is not long. Jessica exclaims surprise in the small size and the light nature of their bags. Without even reaching for a level of assistance to help with their luggage, Jessica turns again and walks out into Xi'an, towards the waiting black car.

A thin layer of mist shrouds the busy city as they negotiate the heavy, noisy traffic to the hotel. Outside they stop and she orders, rather than asks them if they can be ready in twenty minutes. On first impressions Jessica comes across as high maintenance, she is beautiful which they both note that she has become accustomed for people to do as she asks, without question. It is still early in the morning with Eddy happy to keep moving, thus keeping awake. So, they do not object to her demands. They are looking forward to the Terracotta Museum.

They effortlessly check in with the aid of Jessica. They are in their room freshening up with a hot, steamy shower in no time. Eddy is positive, after all this was his preference. They head down a few seconds after the time with Jessica posed on the edge of a lightly coloured beige leather single armchair in the foyer, with her legs crossed, back and arms straight with her hands overlapped on her knee. She springs to get to her feet with the sight of the refreshed, changed Eddy and Lia. Eddy insists for her to drop the Mrs and Mr from their name, as they head back to the black car.

Inside, the tour officially starts. Jessica cranes her neck from the front seat as she yells over the horns and beeps, but with the same delicate ease. She tells them all about the city, which has been her home since her family brought her a house so she could go to university here. She states that this is apparently the norm. She edges about China overall, but really focuses in the Shaa-Xi province.

'Just like bamboo,' she tells them from the front seat. 'Inside you empty. You learn. Bamboo is sign of, for modesty. You learn. But you still never fill bamboo!'

Although Eddy and Lia are tired, they are absorbed with the information that Jessica is flowing with a passion. There first misconceptions are removed as she seems to relax into her role. In the distance, on the wide highway, the Tang-Dynasty pavilion looms closer. Inside here is the largest collection in Asia of historic and cultural artefacts. All the houses that they pass seem nice, spacious. Jessica states that it is expensive to live her but, 'money is never a problem'. They do not quite understand that comment. So, ignoring it completely they ask about the forthcoming pavilion on the horizon, that is the Shaanxi Provincial Museum.

They get dropped off at the entrance. On the breeze, a farmyard smell carries manure with no livestock to be seen. The car immediately moves away from the kerb as the latch connects to signify the doors are shut to park. A chill greets them to envelops them from behind. A large grey stone lion greets them. Protected by a small chain fence behind the magnificent loin is a large landscape of the yellow river basin. Standing out in three-dimensional impression, Jessica proudly states that this is the only one carved by an Empress. They enter inside the impressive museum. Jessica promises them in a short, well-rehearsed speech that the museum will take them on a vision journey through the earliest known civilisation, to the introduction of religion, Buddhism. It is well arranged, with great descriptions in English, as well as Chinese, but she also states that she will escort them around.

As like outside, a huge artwork painting draws them in. A large delicate silk painting of Qin Shi Huangdi shows him wearing a pearl veil, and shoes that are turned up like a pantomime character. The shoes are a sign of rank, the more of an upturned point the more important the wearer is. The pearl veil was not a fashion statement. It seems that legend states he had very poor skin. Thus, to hide this from the court, to avert the gossip of his people so they would not fear it being contagious, that could lead to them being unconfident in his leadership, he wore this elaborate veil.

Holding pride of place on a large plinth and under very thick glass is a small bronze tiger shaped tally, inscribed with gold Chinese scripture. Looking more exquisite due to the crisp, white linen soft bed it lays on, with a light casting directly down showing the slightest hint of a shadow. The tally was split in half. Qin Shi Huangdi had one half, he gave the other half to his general, this would entitle him to fifty soldiers. The aim by Qin Shi Huangdi was to limit the number of soldiers, so his general could not organise a rebellion. Only during a war was he entitled to have the other half of the tally, to make a whole army. A simple, but very effective system that worked, worked very well.

Eddy is absorbing the new information that Jessica pours out, like a sponge. Lia is interested, but the travelling is starting to take its toll as she starts to drag her shoulders that are starting to slump. Eddy points to get Lia to look up, as Jessica explains a number board that was found in the foundation of the city walls. Jessica was not only a tour guide that knew the facts and information, she was also a great storyteller.

The legend, according to Jessica, was the common folk were uneducated and could not understand how the small bronze square of the thick board of numbers could equal one-hundred and eleven in each row. They thought it was magic, so buried it in the foundations of the wall for good luck. Eddy could not help whispering a joke to Lia that this was an ancient Sudoku. They were as frustrating in years gone to try and solve, as they are today! Jessica speeds to another artefact.

Unlike some museums, this was not overloading. Of course, it may be the way in which Jessica relays the information. Jessica lets them roam at their own pace after she had shown, in her opinion, the museums highlights. Now-and-again she stopped them. She pointed to explain the must see piece of history that they nearly walked past, as she paced behind them. Struggling to not keep interrupting their time. Lia and Eddy both leave with an awe, a respect of the smallest item to the grandest. The paintings and sculptures. Each one was different. Beautiful. Story-telling evoking.

The museum walked through the years. Archaeologists believe that as a civilisation grew it understood better how to evolve in themselves. How to use their own fingers, their own thumbs for tasks. Make tools to better suit their means. Eddy thinks back to his niece and looks in his mind's eye. He sees her struggling to eat, learning, but gripping the cutlery in a primitive manner to get the food from the bowl, to her mouth by a pink plastic fork. He understands this and puts it in a principle he understands. They did spend a good few hours here. They could easily have spent more.

Eddy and Lia have been in transit for two days, they are very tired, exhausted. The second and third winds had vanished like the effortless motion of time. Their shoulders are slumming down, giving them the impression that their whole posture was in danger of collapse like a flimsy building in a shantytown. Heads nodding, in a jerking push back, as they wrestle with the looming slumber which will render them surely dead to the world rushing around them. Jessica drops them off at the hotel. The whole way back, she had been pushing them to go to a restaurant together. Eddy was not in the mood to argue, but he was resolute in his no's. The verbally spoken clear word of his educated self became more of a primitive grunt from a caveman as the journey continued. They are worn out. They want a bed. But most importantly, they want their own time.

They both must have eventually succumbed to the dragging chains of sleep as they were woken by the soft words of Jessica to inform them that they were 'home'. An odd choice of a word, but they guess correctly for the next few days anyway.

They rain down thank yous outside the hotel. They watch the car merge effortlessly like a zip into the smoked-filled, horn-blaring traffic to get lost in the sea of metal. They cuddle each other, more for support under their own weight. They watch the winking of the revolving glass door swish in front of them. Impulsively they stop, as they take a stubborn step towards the turning automatic glass doors. A slow lethargic turnaround. They unhurriedly walk through the silent, quiet streets of Xi'an in a sluggish, weary tread.

A backstreet just a few short steps makes them feel that they had stepped through a portal. The comparison from the other street are complete polar opposites. The only sound is from the passing lonely scooter with its short, high-pitched beep as it negotiates the holes in the street, and them. Behind them the muffled chorus of the traffic is fading with each step they take away. The lights of the edge of the road, shine beams up into the green bushy trees to illuminate them brighter than normal. The street lights twinkle like stars. Red blinks in the night sky from the taller buildings.

They huddle together, not because it is cold, but to lean on, to prop each other up. They languorously talk about the museum with an interest but a mumble, rather than an engaging conversation. They start to wilt further under the tiredness that they are showing, blistering quick. Lia's head rest on Eddy's shoulder. They are tired, too tired to eat.

They are not sure why they are fighting their bodies. They turn once again to head back to the hotel. The short walk seems uphill, in thigh-high snow, towards a gale-force headwind. Tomorrow is the reason they have really come. They see a sign for ten Yuan, or a couple of dollars, a set evening menu. They decide to venture inside as they feel that they should eat something. They walk inside. Instantly with a striking smile, they get greeted, escorted to the light twined wicker chairs on opposing sides of a pale-yellow wooden table.

Gracefully decorated with thoughtfully placed ornaments, a bonsai tree in a shallow grey, clay rectangle pot and bamboo place mats. They have not even rested their feet for a few seconds when green tea is poured into an egg cup sized, blue and white china glass, in the middle. They look up to see it is by the same blue, silk-dressed attired smiley petite waitress. She places the huge, heavy-looking blue teapot in the middle of the small table gently between the two cups. She runs through, in confident but broken English, the menu. Without knowing what they are going to eat for the set menu, they order with a little apprehension of her suggestions. She bows in recognition with a smooth turn. She seems to gracefully float away on a carpet of air.

Instantaneously, a tasse comes out with a clear soup, the consistency of egg white. One sip and they recognise the taste of chicken in a mutual mouthed, wow, of amazement. It was good, very good. This, they think is the delicacy that Jessica mentioned in the car. Within the strange viscous consistency is a brunoise of egg white and pork. They mumble, slump over with basic table manners going out of the window as they are struggled to stay upright, with the burden of exhaustion.

With the last mouthful just hitting their tongue, a chicken is place in front of them. At the same time, the soup crockery is removed in a magician swift, fluid motion. They are obviously going for volume. The smell of soy, herbs and garlic floats into the air from the steaming hot food under them. The mould of rice that is placed in the middle cascades like a landfall when Eddy cracks the top with the white porcelain spoon. He gives a heaped spoon onto Lia's plate, cascading some grains over the immaculately varnished tabletop as he stretches across.

Lia cuts into the chicken, a smooth pool of clear liquid, chicken juices escape towards the rice. She moves a piece to a mouth when an elderly server accidently knocks her elbow. Smiles, nods, prays with apologies as another dish is placed to her left. Eddy smiles, the chicken is fantastic. A subtle taste of a sweet, salty and spicy escapes by releases of refined fireworks within his mouth. The display is simple with nothing outstanding; however, the marinade and general cooking process is an art that belongs in the museum that they have seen, just that afternoon.

Without a word, Lia takes the initiative to open the scorching hot cooper pot. In a large pluming cloud of steam escapes the salivating mouth-watering smells of shallot, sesame, chilli and vegetables. As the white-handled steel fork, she twirls like pasta a ball of thick bright yellow noodles entwined with shredded cabbage, coated in sauce and slops it over to Eddy. He scrapes it off the two prongs as she goes for one for herself. Eddy says nothing after his taste, as he watches Lia. Then sees her eyes grow wider, he smiles, giggles as Lia reaches across and smacks, playfully his resting arm. It was hot, wave after wave. Another wave getting more hotter, intensively dancing heat on their lips, tongue, throat.

It was funny from Eddy's perceptive. They giggle. They are full. But more was to come. To finish, a crumbling corn-coloured poppyseed and orange bread is placed. They place more crumbs with the scattering grains of rice, splatters of sauce and other pieces of food that have been spilt over the previously clean table. Empty sauce laced dishes are scattered across the table with food still inside. Eddy wonders if they reuse the food for the next people. It tasted great, at a great price and finished the great first day of the adventure for them perfectly.

Strands of noodles are resting from Lia's sleeve, unnoticed until Eddy pulled them like loose strains of thread from a jumper. The price was for one and they were so happy they shared it, as it was so filling. They struggle against the reins of sleep, very full, feeling like it would be easier to roll back to the hotel. They arrive in the early evening. The task of staying awake as long as they could to get into the time zone sooner was accomplished. They take their close off quicker than they have moved in the past few hours. They slump into bed, into each other's arms and sleep, profoundly undisturbed and peaceful.

After a good sleep to end all good sleeps, they both wake up groggy with a noticeably thickhead. It is within these moments, the moments like this, that they realise that too much of a good thing, turns into an actually bad thing. A warm, steamy shower shakes the last restraints of slumber away, effectually. Finally refreshed, ready for what the world will throw at them.

They leave early to walk to the Big Wild Goose Pagoda. They passed this yesterday on their hazy tired evening stroll, so they knew that it was not far. They could not really appreciate it for what it was then. Yesterday Jessica gave them an option to get picked up at the hotel or, at the Pagoda. They chose the Pagoda as they would be in a car the whole day, thus not be able to get a lot of exercise.

A walk through the brightly blue, red and gold decorated eaves of the tiled entrance of the Da Cien Temple they crane their necks in all directions, in respected amazement. In the centre of the huge, flat grey courtyard is the enormous, magnificent towering brown and grey pagoda. On the right-hand side is a drum tower. This is designed to let the monks know when to go to bed. Opposite, on the left, is a bell tower which lets the monks know when to get up, this is a common theme in Buddhist temples. They walk between these modest brick structures, past an ornate black incense burner. They stare up at the many layers that make the pagoda skywards towards the heavens, rooted in their stance.

'Hierarch Xuan Zang travelled to India through deserts, along the Silk Road,' Jessica explains. She made them both jump in her stealth like sneaking from behind them. They were both planning to head out again to meet her, but curiosity took over them to have a sticky-beak. They turn to see the nature of the voice. Jessica looks radiant in the morning sun as the ray's peak around the corner to stroke a glitter of flashing, blinking lights that illuminate her small studded diamond earrings from the large open doors. A simple, warm green woollen jumper nearly disguised by the same long brown coat with jeans and black boats. She had continued to speak as they mumbled good mornings. She has already told them it was built in 652AD during the Emperor Gaozong reign in the Tang Dynasty.

'So,' she continued, 'Xuan Zang, from the cradle of Buddhism, endured seventeen years as he walked over one-hundred countries collecting Buddha figures, over six-hundred kinds of Sutras and several Buddhist w-relics. With the Emperor's permission, he was granted permission to build this pagoda to store his treasures. With the Royals' support, he asked fifty hierarchs into this very temple to translate the ancient Indian language of Sanskrit in the sutras into Chinese. Over one-thousand volumes are here. He wrote many books. One the 'Pilgrimage to the West' was one of his most famous.'

Jessica points at the tourist stores of tarpaulin blanketed open stores. Crudely supported by metal rods, anchored down by ugly rugged stones. In every single one Eddy and Lia see the books. Jessica continues to tell them about the religion of Buddhism, why it was called the Wild Goose Pagoda and many facts of significance. It is all very interesting, but Eddy is itching for the Terracotta warriors. With this in the back of his mind, he is only half listening.

Finally, for Eddy, the slow walk around the temple draws to an end and they are heading towards the same black car. They get in. Halfway along the long road they stop. They look confused, then see that they are at a Jade museum. Eddy refuses to go, initially. He is not happy to have a sales pitch to him. Lia goes in to use the toilet as a stubborn Eddy reluctantly follows in to gaze with mock interest.

Back on the road, Eddy asks many questions for which Jessica answers. She was a little miffed with his attitude in the Jade Museum. Eddy assumes that she would get commission from a sale, maybe a little feign interest inside would have helped. But, she got past that slight speedbump quickly and they were back talking again. He could understand that she wanted a bonus, and why not, yet Eddy wanted to see the sight he had paid for, without rushing due to time. Thus, he did not appreciate this waste of time. If anything, he depreciated it.

Jessica continues to talk. Instead of giving the mass recollections of history she starts to give information about the culture. Eddy is very surprised to learn that the one child rule is still in place. For reasons unknown he assumed that it had been abolished. The repercussions of this seem extreme. Eddy embraces this new knowledge. He leans forward, the seatbelt straining as he grips the head rest as a pillar of support to anchor him, so he does not spring back into his back seat. People can actually lose, or be fired from their job, legally, for having more than one child.

By law, one of the questions that must be asked by employers is how many children that they have. Although it works differently. For example, if someone in your family cannot have children but, this segment of Jessica's talk was lost in translation. Even after Eddy asked her to repeat it fully, he still did not fully understand the, in his eyes, ridiculous rules. Eddy rolled his eyes towards the patiently listening Lia. He believes it would be the same if he tried to explain Australian Football Rules. For barely nine Yuan, you can get married in five minutes.

Going back to the children, Jessica explains how the shift of preference has flipped. In days-gone couples wanted a boy. Mainly due to a boy will turn into a man. Once married, he will stay at home with the family and his wife, thus looking after the parents in old age. However, nowadays, the boy tends to get his own apartment, hence the, 'want for a boy', has become a, 'want for a girl'. The girl will live with the boy at the apartment. She will get half his wealth, thus helping to support the family. How Eddy is not thinking that Jessica is a gold digger, but rather thinking she is a Jade digger, but...

The countryside of carpeted rolling hills with many topped by overlooking places of worship, temples and shrines. The monks wanted to build on high ground to be closer to the immortals that are always above them. The monks obviously do not only want to exercise their minds, but also their bodies.

They have not been driving for an hour, when they slowly pull over to a small quaint wooden two-story building advertising, ten yuan for a set lunch. Jessica tells them it is good and so much cheaper and closer to the Terracotta Army. They walk in and get seated quickly. The mandatory green tea is poured unto a white egg-cup sized china cup, the comical huge light blue teapot is placed next to the cup on Lia's left. Lia has been pretty quiet this morning. Smiling and taking on all the information that Eddy and Jessica have been conversing with.

While they talk, Lia grips Eddy's hand under the white lace tablecloth, Jessica orders. Within minutes a clear chicken soup comes over with fine brunoise of egg white and pork swimming in the steaming tasse. A chicken dish comes with carrot, cucumber that is laced with soy sauce, garlic. A mould of rice comes out. They are halfway through when a chicken with carrot, cucumber set on a bed of steamed rice appears by a flick of the wrist to Lia's right.

To Eddy's right comes a black serving pot with noodles, spring onion, shavings of beef and chilli. The sauce wraps around the thin, string noodles like a thick soup. The beef dish was hot in spice with the flavours laying in magnificently within their palette. The julienne ribbons of cabbage within the noodles had a flavour in which Eddy could not grasp. It was Moorish. Just like their evening meal, a dry orange and poppyseed place was placed on a blue rimmed white oval. They look over their brown wooden table at the array of different dishes, which has splattered remains of the meal on the white lace tablecloth. It was so cheap. It was a shame that all the food could not be eaten.

They are full. They try not to fall asleep with the final minutes of their journey. Looming in the distance is the site. They pay the entrance fee with an additional five Yuan for an electric car. This was Jessica's suggestion, as the pits are far apart and this will allow them more time to see, rather than walk. Jessica takes them through the souvenir shop for which Eddy thinks *here we go again*. Eddy is ashamed that he jumped to the wrong conclusion.

Here, Jessica points out, the chance to meet the one and only farmer that discovered the terracotta warriors when he was digging a well. For a ridiculous fee of two-hundred yuan, you can not only get his book signed by him, but for the same money again you can get a photograph with him. Eddy sees it but still can see the wow factor in paying the exuberant cost evaporated faster than ice in boiling water. However, Jessica really guides them to a theatre. The farmer is just a sideshow. In there is all the information needed as they watch a fifteen-minute film, or rather documentary explaining what they know about the warriors, including the discovery on 29 March 1974.

Lia thinks the film is very educational, but really not having a real incentive to come here she is suddenly intrigued to what she will see. She is now looking forward to seeing the Terracotta warriors. Eddy laughs at her comment, as now she is here, she really does not have much of a choice. The auditorium is a circular presentation where the film goes on around, coming from different views which keeps them focused.

They scoot on their white golf caddy car to the first pit with a high-pitched whirling annoying squeal. They park with the other white mini-army of caddies to walk into, what looks like an airport hangar from the outside. They go from the bright light, to the dark, dimly lit area. Wow, they are instantly in awe. Here in the large, vast space of two merging aircraft hangers. In an area that is all covered to span over two football pitches is a silent army below.

They slowly scan the sight slightly below them, mouth open, aghast. Below them the silent army is one direction look on. This sight really takes their breath, well and truly away. Here they look down at one of the most significant discoveries on Earth in recent years. They are standing in the presence of a creation, an army built over two-thousand, two-hundred years ago, and, only discovered over forty years ago. Just an electric buzz of excitement was running through Eddy. Without knowing it he was fidgety inside, but so very still outside. They both stood speechless. Goosebumps escape up Eddy's arm. Eddy still cannot believe that he is here, amongst a pit, a space, a place that contains one of the most significant discoveries on Earth in recent years. A huge tick off his want-to-visit sights.

A remarkable extraordinary army built in 221BC in a battle formation in eleven columns, comprising of different ranked warriors of officers and soldiers each holding spears and swords. Some of the pits are left covered in the same dirt that they were found. This, Jessica explains, is due to the oxygen. Elements in the air change the colours, so when the terracotta army is exposed the coloured features disappear in three days.

Scientists are baffled to the reason why, but are working on a technology to preserve them fully. Until that day, these warriors, this branch of the army is going to be preserved, remaining for the time being, unseen. This also gives a unique opportunity to see the wooden beams that imprint the carpet used to house the army. Due to the weight, over the passage of time, the wooden beams became warped. These are imposed in the soil as well.

They walk into the centre of the second pit for which the experts think is a battle room. At this crossroads, they have a choice whether to walk right or left. Jessica notions them towards the left, the quieter side.at the moment. Close enough, but still a stretch too far are the warriors behind a small chain linked metal fence. A skinny guy is holding imaginary reins from his baggy sleeves of a horse-drawn chariot.

'That is you,' Jessica states with a giggle.

Eddy remains speechless. No words can describe the feeling of seeing this with his own eyes. Having seen the sights on so many forms of media, nothing comes close to seeing it with his own naked eye. This happens so often. They hear, see something, but when people see a promised land with their own eyes, the perception that they have formed. The exquisite vision in their imagination, is sometimes vastly different from the actually real thing. Eddy takes his memories back for an example.

Without hesitation, the Mona Lisa comes to Eddy forefront. Eddy thought it was going to be a big portrait, he did not expect many people to be crowding around a glorified postcard in the Louvre. This was a disappointment for sure. This one was so different. He was awe-inspired. This went beyond his expectations.

Jessica escorts them through to another room, another pit. Pit three is what they believe to be a planning room. These figures are in different stances. No general is present. Casting Eddy's memory back to yesterday, he can see the rank from their footwear. This was told in the documentary. Glass cases protect many warriors in various poses, from fighting, archers or stances ready to fight. Here they walk around the glass cabinets. Up close the magnificent detail is amazing. They look, really look at the remarkable specific, precise detail. The tread in the bottom of the shoes, the lines on the palms, the wrinkles.

Each one seems to be different from the face, hands, creases and the uniforms. This is magnificent artistic merit. By the positioning of the sitting archer, they believe that to generate a machine-gun effect the standing archer can hold three arrows at the same time. While fanning up-and-down with a sitting archer in front they can continuously fire at their enemies. Photographs are adorned on the walls of the army when originally discovered. Each one shows what the glass cases terracotta warriors looked like, with the comprehensive paint clearly visible. The Royal blue, red and detail explains fully why they are trying to protect the remaining unseen army.

Brushing past a red velvet curtain, they enter. Through to a very dark room named the Chariot Room, draped in black curtains, black as the night sky. It takes a while for their eyes to adjust to the gloom. For some reason, everyone whispers as if they're all in a tomb. Even more astonishing is that Eddy and Lia do the same. A dimly lit light shines down to reveal the secrets. These chariots and riders are slightly smaller, but have a significance as they are made of the expensive material of bronze. So, unlike the chariots of wood in the second pit, these remain completely intact.

Two chariots are on display, one being open, the other closed. When the Emperor left his residence, as procedure, another eight chariots left with him. Each one going in different directions. Even the driver did not even know if he was holding the Emperor as a passenger until he was away from the residence, and only then the destination was given. The bronze umbrella that supports the driver has numerous uses. It can be tilted to cast shade on the passenger, hand-held to shade the face of the Emperor and, importantly, it can be used as a weapon.

The glaring brilliant lights from the Chariot Room make them squint. Directly outside the room on a table is a replica, surrounded by numerous people. They wrestle their way to the front. The replica umbrella shows that with a stroke upwards of a button the top comes loose to expose a small dagger. Small, but lethal, which can be used as a dagger or a javelin, come spear. It is also bronze. Although they do not play with the real one, Jessica ensures that this is a perfectly made replica with the original still in working order. Jessica keeps mentioning that it is a dagger but in other countries, including Australia, this blade, is simply called a sword.

Reluctantly, they have to leave. The time spent has been a full afternoon, the museum is closing. Eddy is pulled by Lia, like a schoolchild that wants to go back into the funfair. He smiles but wants to go around again. Wants another go on the roller-coaster ending. That, he wants to immediately go on again. He feels like he has fulfilled a childhood fantasy. Although Lia may not admit it to Eddy, she is glad that she came. She would have gone on the ride again. It was exceptional to see such an array of warriors in a large place, in a mountain no less.

Jessica tells them that they think there are two more moulds in the vicinity. A grand plan is to link them all as one huge open-air museum. The Emperor was said to have prepared for his death by building a replica of his kingdom underground, talking seven-hundred and twenty-thousand people to build it over thirty-seven years.

'That's a long time to think about dying!' Lia breathes to Eddy, who softly giggles in replication. She was right.

The Terracotta Army was placed here to defend his underground kingdom from attack. Eddy would like to come back in a decade, or two, to see if this dream was coming through to premonition. As the trio walks out the hangers, they are confronted back into basking sunshine. This causes him to squint and sneeze. Instead of blessing him, Jessica says, 'One sneeze means someone is thinking of you. Two sneezes is someone talking about you.'

'What about three?' Eddy plays along.

'Three sneezes. You have cold,' she giggles as she steps forward, leaving him behind. He looks at her shuffling shoulders as one arm hails the driver. He can see her right hand sheltering her mouth muffling her giggles. Eddy cannot help thinking that this is her Chinese hospitality shining through.

The whole journey back sees Eddy grinning looking like a village idiot. Lia is smiling too. She is genuinely surprised at what she had seen. Although she was a little miffed to be taking this, for what in her mind was a huge detour, she is now happy. She will go as far as stating that she is on the borderline of being privileged, to have been dragged along. They never thought it would be like this. Thinking about it, they were not sure what they were really going to see, but stating it was a great experience does not do the experience justice. Jessica gives them a refresher on the auditorium film with the first Emperor of the Qin Dynasty, Qin Shi Huangi making the estimated eight-thousand warriors.

Being at the kerb of the hotel, they are still smiling. That is the end of the day, and the tour. With the descending sun, the whispering lace clouds drifting over the pale cream moon. The temperatures cool to a warm, comfortable, pleasant ambient feel. Jessica will see them one more time, tomorrow, to take them to the airport. They get dropped off at the hotel with a vocal list of recommended places to eat. A quick detour to chuck their day bags in and they are off again.

Walking the city, taking in the sights. The unfamiliar sound of bagpipes draws them like the Pied Piper drawing the children. Wandering around the ancient city wall, busy with traffic going in all different directions. Children precariously cling to sides of rickety bicycles, as vehicles move precariously close. A scooter passes them on one side, flanked by a fast moving red and black bus dangerously close on the other side. They wobble by the backdraft, but do not look fazed. This is Asia after all. A place where Eddy once was told on a holiday to Vietnam that, 'life is cheap'.

Until that day many years ago, he never really understood what the elderly man at that coffee shop in the middle of Hanoi meant. They, Eddy and two mates, had just witnessed a scooter getting taken out by an unstopping car, going by the noise. The squealing of steel, the crushing of bones, the thud on the tarmac, the rider was not getting up on his own accord. Eddy was in a state of frenzy. He was trying to get people to help. In any case, over the road, barely a few metres away was a hospital. Then, still, he could not understand why no-one stopped. No-one helped.

The elderly man in the coffee shop next to him lowered, just enough, his paper to peek over the top before asking Eddy to calm down. He was more irate. Why was no-one ministering first aid? It was the uncomplicated way he mentioned that statement. So effortlessly he shrugged his shoulders and breathed through the smoke from his cigarette, 'Life is cheap'. Then went back to his seemingly more important newspaper.

Fortunately, history was not repeating. The tall grey, rough brick walls lead them to the sound, ironically coming from within the magnificent three-tiered bell tower on the Wild Goose Pagoda compound. On the lower two levels, and the steps leading to the entrance, was a collection of black clocked bagpipe players. With black felt hats that resembled witches' hats, a burgundy shirt underneath the black cloak they gently play. As Lia spots drummers in the towers, she points them to Eddy. They perform three songs that they heard before marching in a silent rhythm back down. A lady mentions they are a group from Spain. Eddy could not help voicing.

'So. Let me get this straight.' He digests the reason. 'On an ancient wall in the west of China, is a Spanish band, playing Scottish bagpipes, to Australian tourists…amongst others. Is this a normal thing here?'

'Shhhhhhhh,' Lia whispers as the players walk by in a perfect single-file march beside them.

They ask directions to take a snippet of Jessica's advice and go to have a dim sum dinner at De Fa Chang, 'the place to go for proper dumplings', that she had insisted to try on more than one occasion today. It is close by. Right on cue, before seating down properly, green tea is being poured in front of their eyes. On bamboo steaming baskets are an array of different colours, different size dumplings. Each one is explained. Here are some that contains nuts, fruits, meat, vegetables and tofu, with fourteen altogether. Sided with salted fried nuts and crispy anchovies. The waitress mimics to them to mix the soy, vinegar and chilli together for the dip, in a precisely perfected charade.

A small pot in the style and shape of an incense burner, with a small but sufficient flame underneath, was placed next to Lia. Small pearl-sized dumplings with, what they are told, is a pork filling are added to the broth. They are told to ladle a spoonful into their white, pristine cups. As the ladle splashes the liquid with the pearl dumplings into the white bowls, they get told by the male server in a perfectly ironed white shirt. He states that the number of pearl dumplings tells a different story, even if they get none. The clear chicken broth with vegetables gets poured into Eddy's cup with three small pearl dumplings.

'Ahh, no worry about money,' he tells Eddy.

'Ahhh…Luck.' As Lia gets five dumplings. 'You get good luck.'

He bows as he moves backwards away from the table, close to knocking into a passing waitress on her own hidden agenda. In all honesty, the server could have made it up on the spot. They were not to know. But this did generate a conversation between them.

They finish with a small glass of rice wine served hot, very strong tasting and very nice. Over the course of the dumpling feast, they talk about many conversations. Smoking is still very part of the background scene in China. It is a little shocking to them, considering that it is long gone passing abnormal ritual in Australia. When they left the hotel this morning, a man was smoking in the lift. The host is smoking over the podium, while greeting and talking guest names. The smell filters into the eating area with no-one talking any care. It is purely a trivial issue in this world.

The dining room is full to bursting. They have got so many tables inside that Eddy and Lia feel close to being in the lap of the person next to them. The low brown, heavy ceilings and dim lighting do not help them in the feeling of an uncomfortable claustrophobia. They eat quickly. They walk the city. One last evening stroll around. In the surprisingly silent darkness. For a bustling city, as soon as the moon hits the sky, the traffic winds down to a slow, infrequent trickle. The numbed noise of the birds returns. The occasional bark of a distant dog. The sound of food being cooked. The smell of many flavours and spices fill the air with the accompaniment of crackling of woks, pans and the scraping of utensils. Laughing from raucous students in small, tiny groups shriek in a private joke, on their way back to their student homes.

Jessica is extremely prompt to pick them up. As if she wants to get rid of them. They thank her for her hospitality, with animated actions still flying high on seeing the Terracotta Warriors, but she was more interested in their late-night meal.

They board the flight. They sit. They wait. Not understanding what is going on, they disembark the plane that only moments ago they boarded. Still not sure what was happening. Back in the airport lounge, they ask the service desk. They are sure that it was slightly lost in translation, but on hearing the words, 'the plane would not have made it'. That humble declaration did not aspire confidence, but they were, bizarrely. They were told to wait for the next announcement, or as the customer service agent elegantly put it, 'they hope to be ready to be flying to Beijing that very evening.'

It was a long, tedious wait in the airport. Time that could have been spent better. They could have been looking at the sights of Xi'an. However, Lia did not want to miss the flight so saw this as a risk. Eddy took the opportunity to catch up on sorting his photographs from his digital camera and adding writing to his personal notes. Lia was right, he was a travel geek.

Finally, it is late in the afternoon when they are invited to board their flight. They feel like they have wasted a day. The only silver lining is that Eddy has completed his writings with photographs to match. After a rather turbulent plane journey it was early evening when they eventually arrive into Beijing airport. From the bumpy landing, to get to the hotel, it takes only one hour and fifteen minutes that involved a train, the metro and a very short walk.

All things considered, this aspect of the journey was very quick. One thing that they both noticed from the landing was the high level of police. Even out of the airport they were constantly around. This made them feel very safe. But. At the same time a little cautious, as to why it should be place on such high vigilance. On the metro itself, all their bags were checked as in an airport security. This confused them, as they were leaving and expected it to be done the other way.

However, this was not an isolated event it happened at all metro stations that they went on. Later, they would find out, this procedure is also the custom at tourist sites, protected sites and general high human traffic areas. At each school gate they passed, a guard was present, this was both sad as well as reassuring.

After a long, unproductive day around the airport, they both needed to shower the restless aura off them. It is at that moment that they look at each other. An unspoken awareness, that they both realised. They are in Beijing's, China's capital. They dress to go out, to explore. They wander down dark, brooding alleys, the type of places that tour guides advise against.

Here is the underlining scene of real life in a Chinese city. Here is where people are spitting without watching where their large mouthful of saliva ends up. Where people do not acknowledge them in, for which they are, being stared at from the crevices within the shady corners. Here they find themselves in an area for which tourists should not be in. A patchy stubbled, pudgy chef is smoking in dirty, stained brown and yellow whites while scrubbing a large pot with soapy water. He sits on a blue milk crate, but stops mid-suds to stare at them both suspiciously.

Within a few short seconds of conversation, they realise he does not speak a word of English. Or he is playing arrogant. Hence, using the universal language of hand talk, involving smiling, pointing and general hand waving, they manage to get a bowl of steamed rice to share from the said chef. Whom of which has a glint in her toothless smile that looks sinister in the dimly lit corridor as he peels potato's with a small rusty knife. He motions them to sit, with a wave of said knife. They do as instructed, and sit on the wood boarded steps with wooden chopsticks.

Another older chef, looking vacantly gaunt and tired, comes out with two bowls which he spills a little, as he walks with a slight limp-hop like a pirate with a wooden leg would. He smiles, an evil crooked one, that glints the pale brown eyes from the resting rusty, sharp knives holstered under his apron strings, as he pushes the blue porcelain bowl of mystery food under their noses. The smell is salivating as it plumes in thick, fragrant smoke. What looks like pork ribs in a sticky sweet and sour sauce tastes just amazing.

They both make a mutual umming sound with their first mouthful. A look of approval. Speeding on rusting bicycles that streak and moan under the strain, child pass. They crane their rubber necks at them as their pass. They do look out-of-place; they do not fit into this scene at all. The moon is shining, the temperature is still quite hot which leaves a layer of smog above the city that is starting to nestle down for the night. They finish eating while washing the meal down with a cool bottle of beer called 'snow', for which they chink as a thank-you to the chef. Lia cannot help thinking that as a young child, in the snow in Latvia, she was told not to eat yellow snow. And here she was, drinking it.

They embrace the backstreet of China around them. Children playing at a safe distance from the unfamiliar aliens. Another group of child pass on their old, rusty bicycles. After paying the bargain price of next to nothing, they stroll, a little bloated, back the way their came. The Forbidden City gates are graced with lights. Through the mist, the enigmatic smog that is swirling around the gates, they pause. This shimmering effect makes the gates look more majestic, much more awe inspiring.

The next morning, they rise by the same motion as the sun, slowly. They are staying near Tiananmen Square. It is barely past five in the morning, the sun has been in the sky for an hour. It has tried and failed to burn the pollution away. The rays of heat have started to carefully bleed into the city, as if the clouds are sifting the sunrays through in neat little tubular rays. They go for a run. This is a start of a routine to stay healthy. Before they left, they had started each day with a short run. They wanted to keep this going. They will be eating different foods and travelling a lot. They want to stay within the level of fitness that they have been accustomed to back in Sydney.

They ran a calm eighteen kilometres, with the time going so quickly. They were pointing out sights to each other as each lap opened their sense to something new, something missed on the first, then seen on the second and something else seen on the third time around the vast square. This was a great way to start the day. They head back after the final lap to get ready with a light breakfast at the hotel.

They have three full days in and around Beijing so go to the sites that are on the list of must dos that they complied late last night. They have a bucket list of things to see, so they start and head down the road to the Temple of Heaven. A huge two-hundred and sixty-seven hectare park which is completely walled in. Immediately Eddy learns a lesson. Just because something looks close on the map, that they got from reception, it does not mean it actually is. Eddy strongly underestimated the distance. With the short walk turning into a lot longer than they both thought.

Although they did take the opportunity to take a lot of photographs for which they would have missed on public transport. Once they got to the gates, they already had decided to take the metro back. Strange to think that they have not even entered, yet they were thinking about leaving already.

They mistakenly buy a ticket which allowed access to most of the sights, rather than all the sites for which they believed and understood, as it turned out, wrongly, that they did. To live is to learn. And they learned.

A striking, elaborate white stage in Ming architecture which was used to preform solemn rites by the Son of Heaven, to pray for a good harvest confronts them. This is a perfect place to visit. There is enough shelter from the sun, whether it is in its long beautiful corridors with the blue and green eaves on red small pillars, the many leafy lime green trees, or the many intricate arches. Each are refreshingly lower in temperature, when compared to the suffocating Beijing humidity. They subtlety latch onto a tour group, a smooth as a fish joining a school. They do not even feign a safe distance, they get in close enough to listen to the English-speaking enlightening guide.

Many people are dancing and, or, singing with a hat or a tin in front of them encouraging money but giving no direct, confrontational hassle, for which they appreciate hugely. The tours follow a strict pattern, for which Lia and Eddy observe, flawlessly drift between them all, so they are not too obvious. The rose garden envelops Lia and entices her to the fragrant waves that are harmonic, with the relaxing music that is gently piped through. All aspects of the tranquil garden cannot help them to be feel happy.

Lia pulls Eddy's sleeves, but he is standing, rooted to the spot, looking up at the magnificent Heaven Hall of Prayer for Good Harvest. The smell of the roses is a forgotten subtext. It is something that also stops Lia in her momentum to the Rose Garden. They stand, they look at the three separate tiers that are defined by white marble clouds, phoenix and dragon. The craftsmanship is outstanding. The red base with glossy glazed blue tiled roof in three-tiered shines in the sunlight. The people at the base look inferior to the huge hall.

They slowly walk up in silence. Ants crawling up an iced cake. Not even their own footsteps are heard on the smooth, worn wide steps. The interior cascades soft lights over the colourful painted wooden chamber. Amazingly enough they learn that the seemingly small wooden pillars that support the ceiling, are assisted with no help, they are completely without any other fixings like nails or cement. On reading that they are amazed. Still motionless. They gawp.

A sealed off red door with a light blue tiled roof stands close by. A sign in English states that this is called the Seventy-year-old Door. Built in 1779, when Emperor Qianlong was seventy years old. He was starting to feel weak at this point in his life, his health was failing.

The Ministry of Rituals suggested opening this door to the Imperial Hall of Heaven so the distance to walk was shorter. The Emperor accepted, but, with a decree stating; 'From now on, only he among my offspring can enter or exit by this door who has reached the age of seventy'. Hence the name, however later emperors never reached this advanced age, thus Qianlong was the only person to have ever used this door, and who will ever use this closed door.

Eddy glances back at the blue tiles that roof the Heaven Hall of Prayer of Good Harvest. The contrast against the pale blue clear skies are outstanding. The large grey courtyard is sparse with tourists. The exquisite craftsmanship of the dragons, from the surrounding walls, that look towards the hall are perfectly crafted. In the shade of the other buildings, people stand or crouch under to take photographs. Before they had known it, they had nearly spent an entire day here. Although not wasted at all.

They have a self-made list to see today, so on a completely different contrast they head to the metro. Heading to the former Olympic village from 2008. A modern architecture gem was the Olympic National Stadium, or to give the unofficial name, yet the more familiar, the Bird Nest Stadium. To see it, it will give you the answer to the name, as it looks like a huge steel nest, gleaming in the sun, being in China it shares a rather apt name. This is off no coincidence. To reflect the bird nests architecture, many of the stairs are in a similar style as do the surrounding small path lights that flank the pathway.

The huge spotlights around the deserted Olympic Village remind Lia of H. G. Wells imagination. They resemble something from War of the Worlds. The steel webs, the steel orbs, the alien science fiction feel are incorporated around them. The site is pretty much empty, but for the huge presence of security. It is said to become a shopping mall very soon, as only Jackie Chan has sold out the event since the grand and glorious 2008 Olympics that wowed the world's audience.

The aquatic arena in the pattern, shape and style of an ice cube will become public baths. They have been numerous ballets preformed here, such as Swan Lake but it is a beautiful neglected site overall. Eddy finds it interesting. Lia is not as absorbed.

They pass a bridge to get a better look over the village. From the Chinese Ethnic Culture Park of ramshackle rooftops of tiles, that are barely staying on and appear to be many grey post-its stuck in no particular order on a small grey brick house, with wooden rectangle windows and wooden bars, like an old prison cell. It is chalk and cheese, from old to new, modern then to modern now.

From here, for Eddy and Lia, it goes a little downhill. Somehow, they get lost. Well and truly. No-one they encounter speaks English. They do not even know the basics of Chinese to get out of this predicament. When Eddy thinks, or thought he had the universal and global hand signals down to a five-star rating, he is hit with blows to the head from an imaginary steel bar that give him a halo of shining rotating stars. Eddy is so wrong, so very wrong. After two hours of Lia moaning, and for them getting lost and deeper further into the never-ending backstreets of Beijing he admits defeat.

Although he tries to soften the blow to Lia. He fruitlessly states by going this lost route, some of the sights will be sights that no other tourist would have seen. He, of course fails. She is far from being amused. Eddy hails a cab. Lia is happy. Using the recommendation of not only having the hotel card, but having the Chinese written on the other side, they hand it over to the driver.

He grunts as the card get handed back to them in the back seat, without a smile, with no hospitality. They are an amazing one hour and fifteen minutes away in a car. The traffic was not that bad, so the walk would have been longer, much longer. Obviously, of course, if they were going in the right direction. But, going by the white and green cabdriver's U-turn, they would have more likely ended up closer to Xi'an.

On the journey, Lia insists on seeing a sight while in China, at this stage Eddy was in no position to argue. Nevertheless, when she voices it, he is also keen. So, they head back to book the trip on the last day. The day has flown past. Tonight, they indulge in Peking Duck.

Somewhat cliché, but it surely has to be done. They go to a restaurant that the concierge at the hotel states is where the locals go. The ducks are roasted directly over flames stoked by fruit-tree wood. The smell is beautiful as they get close. No smoke is seen, but the aroma layers in perfect deposits on the warmed breeze. The cooking of the duck is done by weight, on large S-shaped butcher hooks.

They ask many questions. The perfectly English-speaking host makes sure the questions are answered by a specifically selected black and red suited server. In American-accented English, he states that they get one-hundred and twenty sliced out of an average duck, with every piece having a whisper of crispy skin on it. The server is impressively knowledgeable. He is an older gentleman with an effortless poise, sophistication of a person who knows his job, knows his job very well.

They are given paper-thin pancakes, julienne of shallots, fresh hoisin sauce from a polished, vanished shiny wooden trolley that the server wheels over straight out of the kitchen. Another server in a starched, bright white jacket brings the duck. His perfectly ironed blue pants with a clear smile on his lips and a twinkle in his dark brown eyes reflects on the blade of the shining sharp, long curved knife. The duck shines dark red. As the knife rests, dissects the skin, it crisps. What a sound to behold.

As he carves, a crack of the crispy skin keeps filling the vacant air between them. He presents the slices on their white plates. The originally server in his shining black and red suit translates his question: 'Is that enough?' They nod eagerly. They want to be left to devour what they smelt and are now seeing. He bows, smiles, before moving to another table. The smell is salivating and has them drooling.

The dining room is a large red carpeted space, with plenty of room between the tables for the trolleys to effortless glaze, glade around as if the servers are also on ice skates. The flames from the burner in front of them, dance flickers of pleasure on their faces. The candles twinkle the dark greens and reds that make up the painted walls. It was slightly chilly in there, with the aircon pumping high, compared with outside, but nothing that their jumpers could not protect them from.

They looked at the other guests in the room. Not one local, it would appear the concierge got a good commission from here. Although they both agree that it was quite expensive, they would pay it again to have this level of great food and atmosphere. It was bloody awesome.

In China, the culture is one thing, but within lies another culture that is different. The aforementioned smoking. The constant pushing and shoving. The relentless spitting, and the throat-gurgling vile sound which seems to be a necessity to produce. Then, in complete contrast, the admiring pride of the history. The beauty on every single thing, within every single thing. The strong, smell of the colourful flowers, the vibrant green-leafed rustling leaves in the thin trees. The smell, the aroma, the sound of cooking is around each and every corner. Musical, hypnotic sounds that are being transporting from the slightest crack in a closed, wooden door.

The amazing colours and craftwork in the smallest toothpick, to the largest, grandest temple is simply awe-inspiring. The local language, the native tongue which sounds almost angry, even volatile at times, but delicately written as a superb art. The many tastes, with, what really surprises Eddy is that tofu can actually taste good.

As they walk, hand in hand, back to the hotel, cotton-like seeds float from vibrant pink petals around them in the light breeze. Portraying a magical, mysterious ambience like feel to give a vision, which has just been plucked from a winter's scene in a Dickens novel, although in the humid heat of Beijing. At this time of night, it is thirty degrees, but they could almost teleport to a cold winter's scene, with the cottonseeds being the soft cascading fall of snowflakes.

An overwhelming day, which could render the most stable to lose his or her mind. They both agreed that it was stunning. They are truly happy. They walk pass the low-lying grey houses of Diamen Daija with people and bicycles negotiating the smooth walkway. They remember seeing an English sign for a rooftop bar. As Lia mentions it, she points as she instantaneously sees it. No words needed; she is going. They walk in and up. On the flimsy wooden balcony on the rooftop is a small bench with a thin red rectangle cushion. She sits down, while Eddy struggles to order.

Eventually, he points with a smile, gets given and brings over the beers. Sometimes, when people have walked miles, nothing is more pleasing than the sight and taste of a great ice-cold amber nectar. They sip the snow, as they survey the busy Hutong below. The temperature does not move with the setting of the sun. The golden glow of lights starts to flicker on, around the sprawling city like Christmas lights, as they laugh and share stories never told, never shared.

Another long, slow run starts the Groundhog-heated new, but same day. But as they run, if anything, the smog is worse today. They head back to the world's largest urban square. At forty thousand metres square, paved with specially treated granite slate tiles they stroll, inside of run across, around. Eddy is told by Lia, as she reads a sign, to try and imagine ninety football pitches side by side so that over one million people can be seen at any one time. They stand at one end, without seeing the end, not due to the smog, but the effectiveness of the vast area for which they stand on. This is a focal point of various political, religious and social scenes.

Here was the scene of the infamous Tank Man Incident in 1989, during the student uprising. The photograph that was seen around the world. A photograph that was amazing as well as heart-breaking at the same time. A bitter, and sweet, display of courage. Incredibly, very unbelievably, most Chinese people do not know the story behind this photograph, of this brave man. With, for which Eddy finds even more incredible is that many younger Chinese people are not even aware of the protests, or, this is what they say anyway.

The story that the west got told was that Chinese troops stormed through Tiananmen Square, killing and arresting thousands of pro-democracy protesters. Mostly young students gathered here to protest. They called for the resignation of Chinese Communist Party leaders. A day after the massacre, on the fourth June, an unknown man was photographed in front of a column of tanks, stopping them from progressing forward. Martial law ensued for the following months.

Eddy learns from Lia that the Chinese government downplay the significance, even today, labelling the protestors as 'counterrevolutionaries', also minimising the extent of the military actions. Public commemoration is banned, officially. Officially banned.

From behind them, they leave the Qianmen, Front gate, on the far south of Tiananmen Square. It is ridiculously impressive. A huge brick wall for which a red, tower tops it, like a cherry on top of a cake. It is impressive. They walk through the centre; the studded large red doors open wide. Arrow Gate is bordered by the cave-like shape with white zig zag steps, that lead to the top of another impressive tower. These two towers are the remains of the original impressive gates, that was the ancient wall of Beijing.

Leaving the watchful gaze of Mao Zedong, they continue strolling up. Passing large monuments to the Peoples Heroes, which stand in front of the less intimidating block that is the Great Hall of the People, National People's Congress, or as the rest of the World would call it, Parliament House. From here, is the huge portrait of Chairman Mao. It is watching over the whole, large area. Magnificent lights are at the same, precise interval with balls of perfectly, soft light. Cameras are everywhere. Each pillar has numerous cameras like an ugly Turner Prize entry. As well as the heavy police presence, they feel continuously watched.

Below Chairman Mao are sixteen- to twenty-two-year-old soldiers going through their fitness routines. Wearing black shoes, that shine in the sunlight, dark green creaseless pants, light green short-sleeved shirts with red lapels, and the same short, neat, trimmed haircut, they are choreographed strictly. Mirrored by the instructor, in similar attire but with different gold badges on his lapels, he mimics them. Chairman Mao mausoleum is closed, so people are not around the main square.

They go to buy tickets in tight, sardine crammed queues. In queues for anything, people tend to invade Lia's personal space. She stands close, but behind Eddy, with the guy behind her so close that he is almost pressing against her. She finds this uncomfortable to say the least. However, it seems to be the deal in China. She feels weird and changes places with Eddy. With the feeling not going away, she decides to leave the queue completely. She takes up residency away from the long lines.

School children, like a flock of pigeons over a single white breadcrumb gather around Lia. They try to practise their English on Lia. She is violated by so many selfies, questions thrown at her, as piercingly as spears. She is trying to be polite, but is gingerly trying to wave them away. She wants to be in her space. The reason why she left the queue to begin with. Eddy comes, not a moment too soon, with the tickets.

'Bloody hell, Lia. Why do you have all these people hustling over you like a seagull over a chip?'

She waves her head and giggles. His analogies never cease to amaze her. She is relieved just how quick the long queue had ended with him getting the tickets. Eddy bows down to be at the same height as the children. He clichés as he puts on a true-blue Australian accent to the most prominent as he sings *Waltzing Matilda* in a hushed, but animated tone with lively hand signals. They giggle behind closed hands. Lia looks down at Eddy and smiles. He is so good with children. She actually can see him and her together for the long haul. She is falling more in love with him, just when she thought that she could not fall anymore, she was so wrong. He was so the Mr Right.

Crossing a magnificent series of marble bridges, which involves showing their purchased ticket numerous times to the point that they stop putting it back in their pockets. These interruptions fails to take the polished gloss off the iridescent shiny finish that reflects, flickering rainbows that warmly embraces them. The young militant faces of the smartly attired armed forces show serious weighted, heavy lines of worries. The expectation to ensure that this sight is avidly protected make them look at everyone as if they are convicted criminals before, even committing the crime.

Staring to see what everyone is carrying, watching what everyone is doing, looking beyond their evidently innocent eyes. Vigilant security checks are expected, whirls of cameras unseen, but they are under no illusion that they have entered into a world within a goldfish bowl.

Thoughts enter slowly for Eddy. But crawl silently like a spider creeping in and building a web in inconspicuous restraint. The thoughts enter as a person sleeps to awake, to a vision, an intricate web of beauty. A thought that spirals into a rational process of what really do they expect to see here? What are they looking at? Beauty, yes, but Eddy has not a single clue what this City is. He tries to hide his embarrassment with an off the cuff comment.

'Err...erm. So. This is where all the people are hiding. Eh!'

Lia is not stupid. She senses his awkward, uncomfortable nature. She does not heighten it, she nurtures it. She explains with deferential consideration where they are. They are in the mysterious, unknown entity of The Forbidden City. A City that has had a turbulent past. Once again, Lia's research comes into play. Eddy rues the decision not to read up on more of the sights before coming on this journey. He should have had swotted like Lia. Lia has read a lot. It was apparent. Also, with the history, the good, with a little bad and at least, a lot of the ugly. She has read a lot of negative publications on the Forbidden Palace being in disrepair.

For over five-hundred years it served as an Imperial Palace. Built in 1420, taking only fourteen years to build, by over two-hundred thousand workers. This Palace had been the home for twenty-four Emperors of the Ming and Qing Dynasties. It is an amazing seven-hundred and twenty-thousand square metre palace. That holds an awe-inspiring nine-thousand, nine-hundred and ninety-nine and a half rooms, inside the handmade city of over eight hundred buildings. No place could have more rooms than heaven, which has ten-thousand. The Forbidden Palace was out of bounds to the public, and here they were just about to walk inside, and through it.

Now known as the Palace Museum in China, it was only open at the beginning of the twentieth century. Eddy should feel privileged, as Lia is showing all over her face just how honoured she feels. Eddy feels confused, unsure and worried that he will miss out on the experience all together due to his innocent stupidity, in the purest form of naïveté.

The first tragedy to bestow the Forbidden City occurred with the Japanese invasion during World War II. The Japanese stole some of the treasures inside. After the war, some, but not all, were returned. Some, others say most, were taken to Taiwan where they are…no-one really knows. Or, no one really owns up to it. The second tragedy happened when the People's Republic of China was established. With a little history repeating, some more of the treasures were taken.

Passing under the large wooden gate, they are thrust into a huge square of rough cobblestone pavements, that is capped by the dominating Hall of Supreme Harmony. Like crossing a portal from the new world, to the old, with only the people staying within the modern theme they have teleported back in time.

In the robust attempt to regain his own crown. The self-title, which she proclaimed him as, that he accepted. The Travel Geek, Eddy, without Lia's prior notice, paid for a tour guide. They met in the corner that was the quietist from the gathering crowd. After the polite commencements were made, he nearly gives the word-perfect, identical introduction that Lia had already aired.

'Please ask,' Kevin implores. 'Please turn your watches back one hour, six-hundred years. We will begin.'

This brings a chorus of laughter from the crowd. Lia is taking photographs, she turns to not understand the joke, as she had not heard it. As the tour guide, Kevin, finally starts to stroll over the cobbled stones with his following flock, Eddy relays the joke to Lia's amusement. Eddy is thinking back to the crouched-over elderly lady, with a low-grunted creak in her breathless words at the ticket counter. She had strongly recommended a tour guide so they could see places, be educated, to be told what they are looking at. Otherwise they could be wandering lost, around temples, halls, houses and rooms with no idea what the significance of them is.

Kevin stops and speaks about one of the glorious temples. They are standing in front of a sign that has an English translation, as well as Chinese, obviously. Kevin is blatantly reading from it. Eddy hides his concerns that he could have been duped from Lia, as he sees that all the places, all the stops have a similar unconcealed topic.

The largest, the most important Hall is the Supreme Harmony. This is the first of three major halls within the Forbidden City. At a very relaxed pace, Kevin guides us, as part of the group of twenty tourists towards the Hall, supporting a bright yellow flag high in the air. They rise the marble steps up the three-tiered base, following the waving, tailing flag like a happy golden retriever's tail. The chained off centre of the middle is a dragon engraved in the marble. Kevin tells us that a dragon was a symbol of strength. It has always represented the Emperor. This one is said to be carved from a single piece of marble.

They stop, looking at the intricate marble dragon. Only the emperor was allowed to be carried over this dragon, via a cradle, where his servants used the stairs on either side. The beautiful red glazed tiles of the four-hipped double roof, with the corners of the eaves showing ten animals looms closer, as they soar higher. The roof guardians, that adorn the peaks of the tiled roof, show the importance of a building. A human figure riding a phoenix leads a number of mythical animals, with the Imperial dragon at the end of the line. The more guardians, the more important the building. Eddy looks at Lia. Beaming, who is rubber-necking to look up at all aspects of the Hall. She is upbeat in her pleasurable aura. She notices him looking at her. Giggles coyly, as she bashfully looks away as she nibbles her finger, in a cheeky show of embarrassment.

At the very top, none of the hall can be entered. But the doorways are locked by gates. Leaving only a few open, with a thick roped velvet cord, to be able to view what is inside. The middle doorway is the best view. Not by coincidence, but by the hordes of people surrounding this small, opening segment you can see why. Eddy and Lia use their elbows to push their way forward, to the front. The view is limited. Cameras, phones, selfie sticks, videorecorders, all are held, aloft in the air, trying to capture a good picture, to become a great photograph. The floor is paved in clay golden brick, with a red, dragon carpet leading up to a modest stage.

No treasures are inside apart from a few vases, but the ceiling is crafted in intricate detail. Large decorative bronze vessels are in each corner. Lion moulded masks grip the large, thick heavy carrying rings of the vessels that flank the hall. Many more just like these, scatter around the Forbidden City. Although Lia very much doubts that anyone can lift these heavy pots, even she mocks, Eddy, being her Superman. These were used to extinguish fires in days gone by. During the colder months a small fire was placed underneath, so the water stayed liquid, thus did not freeze. For a peculiar reason, these cisterns fascinate Lia.

This hall definitely does set the bar high for the precedent that needs to follow. For the extreme demonstrations of art, skill, craftsmanship and attention to detail that the first hall displays, means that the palace has to delivery this high standard, throughout.

Kevin gives details of the numerous wooden buildings. Which they also learn is the world's largest collection of wooden structures. They are both rouses and enthralled by the information, surrounding the sights. The tiniest, little attention to detail gives the largest impact. The hue, or different colours on the pure artistic craftmanship grips their visionally fleeting eyes that cannot keep their attention on one treat. A treat thrown to them, as a 'well-done you noticed' invisible indulgence that satisfy their senses.

Fine cracks have appeared over time. In this, the cracks are vibrant testaments to the rock-scurrying pioneering imagination of these artists who have made something that can be preserved, can be standing, still, after so much time. With the unknowing harsh weather elements combined with human interference as well as, good old Mother Nature playing her part in trying to test the structures, literally to breaking point, with her earthshattering quakes.

Lia and Eddy stop at most of the signs as Kevin talks them through, as slow as he strolls so they are not rushed, they have time to appreciate, time to capture an image, time to see. They can, cat and mouse, with the group to hang back a while, to catch-up, or to go ahead without the feeling that they have missed something. Passing many additional parts of the City which involve a cost Kevin stops outside one. He strongly recommends going to this one for an extra ten Yuan, the Treasure Gallery.

Obviously, as the name suggests pretty blatantly is where the treasures hide. After the two human tragedies that affected the City, this is where the stolen artefacts were returned to, to be safe, back at home within this very large palace. Eddy and Lia look at one another. They observe the majority of the small group enter. They outspokenly agree with a mutual word to follow the flock like lemmings to the edge of the cliff, they are the last to enter. Surrounded by the wooden walls are clinical glass protective counters, blocks and cabinets which look out-of-place to display the defended treasures. Yet, the glass is plain and simple against the complex background, that highlight each piece with a soft glow the sophisticated, elaborate detail in each historical object.

It is easy to see why many get too close. A smudge of a sweaty forehead imprint, or the many greasy fingerprints for which people have literally loomed in closer until being abruptly stopped. Although rather off-putting with one of the larger glass cabinets holding the ceremonial headdresses, seals, large and ornate Jade carvings and weapons, they look past the murky human-tainted veil to the clear beauty. The descriptions are very vague. It would be like saying this palace is a little big, where a more descriptive narrative would be appreciated. Kevin, is outside, so Lia takes a mental log to ask after this worthwhile diversion. She points to a large, heavy looking sword. A wooden handle is printed with entwined strings to make a quite gorgeous, exquisite design embedded with tiny, sparkling stones.

The sword itself is hidden within an imprinted flower design of brown leather, with a gold-plated centre scale design. Next to this is the frustratingly simple description, 'Magic Sword. Qing Dynasty 1644–1911', nothing more, nothing less. They both debate the magic as being the sword, the use or the story. They flip-flop between them all. Although, this is highly hypothetical as they have no idea, but amusing, nevertheless. They wonder if they should add this to the growing list to ask to Kevin when they leave. But like the other numerous questions, this thought has gone by the rivers of time.

They see one of the phoenixes and guardians from the roof top eaves up close. Wow. In a single act they conversation pauses. Even the tread on the guardian's feet is included, even though from the ground you would not have the slightest glimpse of it. The consequence is getting the minor detail absolutely right must have so important to the craftsman. Eddy things back to Italy, whereas the sculptures are completely finished, even an unseen back, nothing is left unfinished. Two different cultures, the same work ethic in the artist.

Being the last to enter, they are the last to exit. They arrive back in time to hear the beginnings of another of the stories of the palace that the signs do not tell. Kevin relays one of the most suspicious circumstances that he taints, without a hint of what he thinks. Not a single blemishing stain on his voice gives his view away, whether he thinks it is true, if it is all lies, fact, or just fiction. The story involves the last Empress Cixi.

Kevin guides us away from the direct sunlight when he sees the remainder of his group return. Under the large, old tree with the green enveloping shading branches he begins. He points to a door, he tells us that the represented dragon within the design, is the portrayed lady, Empress Cixi, the 'dragon'. Eddy scoffs a private joke under his breath as this is the affectionate nickname that he has already given to his beloved older sister since he learnt the word as a toddler.

Without noticing Eddy's hand-wrapping muffled schoolyard giggle, Kevin continues. He states with an air of indifference authority that very much gives nothing away, firmly sitting on the figuratively bench. He quivers slightly that the events arouse suspicion for the Emperor. After all, he was all powerful. He had so many vast enemies. Thus, no proof ever came that she was responsible for what happened.

The former concubine, Empress Cixi, led the court from behind her five-year-old son, Tongzhi, when the Emperor Xianfeng died. However, when her son reached nineteen, the age that he could take over by himself, he mysteriously died. This left Cixi's three-year-old nephew, Guangxu, to became Emperor. This in turn made her a Regent again. She stayed on in this puppet state-of-power until her death in 1908. Nevertheless, she was not the only concubine that the Emperor had, had. He, as well as the Emperors before him, often had one for each day of the week, sometimes several thousand. They are not sure why he ended with that part of the story, other than to explain that she could have been the good apple of a bad bunch. He leaves them, and the group wanting more of this story. Alas, he has moved on, tying the hesitant group to drop that subject to view something else.

The Forbidden City is big, really big. Some many buildings, houses, temples, pavilions and other wooden structures. This causes them to start to get wooden-palace fatigue. It is unfortunate, as the beauty is starting to get lost in a wash of waves that make each unique building start to look the same. It was at this correct moment that Kevin, for which is was obviously not his first rodeo, directs them to the Imperial Garden. A more than welcoming break for everyone involved in the tour group. The cobbled stones seamlessly merge, without any feel underfoot, to the tiled floor. The impressively small size of the painted pebbles, that make up the mosaic design, shows a different aspect of talent in the ability of the artists.

Each square, with individually painted pebbles pave their way into the waves of blossoming pink cherry blossoms. The cascading pink petals radiate a fairyland of fantasy in the rich company of fragrant, soft agreeable perfumes, which causes them to breath in, slowly but heavily, to lightly close their eyes, to feel perfectly peaceful, relaxed. As if they are in a dreamscape, they float. A serene hush has descended over the group, and for the first-time even Kevin is quiet. Since his opening introduction, his verbal constant informative diarrhoea has ceased.

The smooth sound of running water from the decorative rock formations in the gardens. The birds, singing above them hidden in the trees, the slight rustle of the leaves in the light, warm breeze and the panpipe whistle of the bamboo mute the echoing footsteps. The at ease nature of the stroll in the valuing shade from the beating rays of the sun, is sheltered by the very shady knotted cypress trees. Within this oasis are four, colourful impressive pavilions which symbolise the four seasons. Yes, they are wooden, but a different environment does give them a different form of context for Lia and Eddy.

Kevin finds his voice. It has been a while for him, so a slight crack starts his lecture, and this feels like a confusing lecture. Kevin tells them of the parks and gardens. Tells them without, for the first time, not clearly informing them. Eddy is confused, so is Lia. They are not sure of the difference between the bases of the legends, or on the life forces or if a combination of both are present. Lia shh's him. She can tell he is on the verge of asking a question. Up until this point, no-one has spoken out loud in the group form. All have chosen to ask the questions when they are in-between sites.

'What are the life forces?' Eddy shouts out aloud. The first person to ask a question in front of the group was sledgehammer loud. He was intending it to be a silent whisper, but loud enough to express; he failed. All eyes turn to spotlight him.

'Life forces are the sun,' Kevin seems pleased that the group has found its voice. He clears his throat as he continues his answer, 'Life forces are the sun, the nocturnal bright, the—'

'What?' Eddy interrupts first, then raises his hand as if back in school, 'What is the nocturnal bright?'

'Moon, the moon,' he states as if everyone should know this. The annoying tone for which he fails to conceal as he had been interrupted is only in those three words. Instantly he returns to his almost, musical connotation. Before continuing his answer, he clears his voice again.

'So,' a cheeky wink. 'From the beginning.' Another cheeky wink, this time a little awkward. 'Life forces are the sun, the noc—the moon, heaven or earth, clouds, rain, wind or thunder or some other.'

Eddy has found his platform. He wants to ask another question. He prods, in a pleading manner for Lia to ask. She is either looking at her feet, or, has found a more meaningful vision in the coloured paved tiles under her feet. Eddy has to admit defeat. He wanted to ask about the legends. He still did not fully understand.

'Each building, park or pavilion in Chinese culture has a different supposition, an even bigger meaning,' Lia whispers.

'Even. Even with not always knowing what it is?' Eddy implores in his tone, his soft jabbing for her to ask the question.

'Yes. Sometimes. Unfortunately, yes, sometimes things are not always knowing what it is.'

Surprisingly, they exit the garden to find out that they are only in the middle of the Forbidden City. Palace fatigue sets in once again as Kevin guides them through the last sectors of the Forbidden City. It is well worth the money as Kevin takes them into corners that they would have missed. Tells them stories, which they would not have heard. Gives them jokes, to make them feel comfortable. Offers all the information to make Eddy put back on his title with pride.

They are near the door to the exit. Keven shakes each person by the hand with the charisma of a wet fish. His hand is limp in theirs as they shake a one-handed shake, with him warmly cupping his free hand over. He bows to the whole group many times as if waving goodbye with his head.

After being bumster-free for the last few hours in the City, they are thrust back into that world. There are lurking like vultures on the brick wall. As they leave, they swoop down hoping for the slightest morsel of a prize for their persistence.

On Kevin's suggestion, the group negotiate the busy major road as he instructed. To go over the connecting bridge with the golden, red shimmering carp that swim in schools below, glittering in the sunlight. Behind them they glance back for a photograph opportunity for a selfie with the colourful painted wooden structures, yellow glazed tiles and the green and white marble at the back of them. Above this perfect scene is the not-so-perfect grey sky of smog. The smoke-stained buildings and the wake of bumsters holding, aloft colourful T-shirts, knick-knacks and other various merchandise that are oblivious to the pending photograph that they are attempting to take.

Persistent in their striving, like an explosion in a paint factory that is bellowing towards them in a relentless wave they flap, flutter and gesticulate that they want to buy. They use trickery, asking if they want to go for 'coffee' or a 'gallery'. With an unpleasant shrieking constant chatter, like the annoying evening and morning call of their homeland cockatoos, they too become a shrilling sound of nuisance. In fairness Kevin did warn them before venturing outside to be wary of this con.

Kevin stated, more than once, that the offer of 'coffee', or a 'gallery' was a way of luring them away to take their money either by guilt, or of more confronting manners. As he had advised they ignore the hostile soundtrack to continue their stroll. Albeit the bordering, hysterical unyielding waves did not disappear entirely, the kettle of vultures were scattering to their resting place to form a committee. They talk about the Forbidden City as a distraction. They shared the amazement that a palace of that size can be so vast, smack bang in the centre of the capital of China, Beijing.

Some of the group have not been as forceful. Yet, with Kevin's recommendation, they slowly walk up a tall, steep hilltop trail within Jingshan Park. The green and gold sparkling glazing tiles from the pavilions, set on brick pedestals get closer as they emerge through the green leafed trees and colourful scented flowers. They gather, with a small cluster of cameras, selfie sticks smiling tourists with the spectacular uninterrupted panoramic view of the Forbidden City and its surrounding moat and wall.

Eddy cuddles Lia from behind, nestling a small, dry cracked-lip kiss on her neck. The golden orange roof tops are glittering. The green leaf from the trees are a blossoming vibrant in comparison. It is as attractive as a Christmas tree to a child. They are standing on a self-made hill that, according to Kevin, actually came from the excavated earth to make the moat that surrounds the large, vast City below. This was a private park, a playground to the Ming and Qing Dynasty Emperors for nearly five-hundred years. Just imagine that this space was part of the Forbidden City. It is five Yuan each to enter, with the views well worth the entry alone. They can see the money being spent on the upkeep.

Since entering the park, not a trace of litter can be seen anywhere. So many silent gardeners are tending to the flowers, gently manicuring the trees, hedges and the various gardens with honour and passion. For a local, it is free. They take full advantage of this. Some are the pests, like the bumsters. Others, by using the peaceful oasis to relax, while other do the blissful, slow movements of the medicating exercise of Tai-Chi with a peculiar large roar of a word every now and again. The first time this happened, it made them both jump.

The second time around they thought they would be prepared for it, they were not. As they weave through many people around, their eyes are focused permanently on the views. The numerous gardens, the shimmering metallic egg-shaped oval of the National Arts Centre that seems to penetrate a smooth blue hue, and the peaceful city that is being tucked in to sleep under a grey hazy blanket of pollution.

The day has turned even hotter. The shining of the bright sun is playing havoc, reflecting with the smog, that causes all the photographs being produced with a somewhat grainy appearance. Lia disappointingly looks, flicks and scans her photographs, brooding a silent wish that it was a little clearer. Eddy drapes his arm over her shoulder to console her, in silence. Enveloping her with his arms of a cape. The soft, spoken words whispered into her ear for at least they have the clear memories. That it could have been worse, such as wind, pressing cold and freezing rain. He is not sure if his effective efforts where appreciated, but she nestles into his chest as if to be pleased by his understanding.

She stops suddenly as if frozen. She storms in a rush, to sit on a small red plastic chair outside a rustic, looking shack, that once resembled a café. She points to a Jiaozi, on another table as Eddy comes to sit opposite her. The three locals on the next table are eating. Eddy goes along with it, not sure what to expect, why they stopped. Lia orders with a point at the local's food. She is not sure what it is either but wants to try. Eddy has missed this adventurous side of her. Within minutes, two small meat-filled dumplings in a shape of a shoe comes on a decorative blue and white plate. A plate that goes completely against the grain of the appearance. Although small, it was extremely filling.

Eddy has to smile surprised, as a term of agreement in a great choice of a snack venue. These were amazingly beautiful. They get warm water, not for the first time. After asking the concierge in the hotel why this was, they are informed that this is for hygienic reasons, hence the water is boiled to purify it first. The other reason is a cultural one, that apparently warm water is better for digestion. Either reason, they sip a little, but prefer their shop-bought bottled water.

They had heard about the cultural blanket, that was so different from anywhere in the world, that they aim to see the pedestrianised street with their own eyes. Yet, this evening was not the planned evening. They stumble, accidently on the street, Wangfujing Dàjiē. They knew it was convenient in the location of the city centre. They were heading to the early evening Donghuamen Night Market, but Lia decided that as it was early, they would wander the streets. For arriving too early it would not be open, hence they arrived here at the glittering stalls holding foods of the exotic, the wilder side of the food menu.

They traverse from one side to the other without knowing where they were, before realising that this was the unique street of Chinese delicacies that they heard about on various documentaries, various travel guides and various friends that have been here. Somewhat apprehensive, they see the unconventional, instead of conventional, but as they stroll, they are gaining confidence to actually try, for experience. Wangfujing Dàjiē, translates as Well of Princely Palaces, that dates back to the fifteenth century when it was the sight of Royal Palaces. The locals state that they were fittingly destroyed to make way for the Palaces of the People.

Hustling around the crowded street. The soft red lights cast to reflect down from the vibrant red paper lanterns that travel down one line, down a row of low-lying wooden shacks. That touch almost, bleeding, merging into one another, like the scales of a snake. The other side are more permanent brick buildings of light grey bricks in a row with red small canopies of hipped roofs at irregular lengths. This side is tasteless merchandise of trinkets, toys, accessories. They edge, sway and lean towards the wooden wheeled shacks for the real experiences.

Swaying lanterns overhead, shine hues over the swirls of steam from the quaking, rapidly boiling pots of a damp stench under the blue, orange large flames. The disagreeing aroma collides with the unappetising meat, fish, vegetables and sewage that paints a picture that is not an ideal setting for food. Yet, it seems to bother no-one, anyone or any person, animal, that has been drawn and attracted here for distinctive, uncommon reasons that are purely theirs to know. The locals stick-out with the tourists that stick out more amongst the maddening, organised crowd.

Like dark, gnarly flowers from a horror script are the crisp thin wooden skewers capturing the barbecued, fried centipedes, scorpions and seahorses in a frozen dance. Lia freaks out as one offers a 'hi' in a wiggle of one of its legs. Then the other three legs join in. All of the squirming black bodied, yellow legged scorpions that penetrate skyward like a strangely bizarre bouquet of exotic insects that gesture in the cool breeze, join in. Pointing upwards on the outer bouquet are the five-points of the soft orange starfishes. Pierced into the tummy are tiny golden seahorses. Below the 'soil', in the bowls are various grey, brown and black bugs of variety. Snakes frantically crawl over one another as if the more traditional noodles had spawned into life.

Eddy dives in and orders a piece of snake. His confidence slightly falters when it is time for him to actually eat it. He slowly brings it to his lips, pausingly opens his mouth, reluctantly and closes his eyes as he bites down. His eyes open wide and he chews faster. Through his mouthful of snake, he spits out.

'Wow! This is actually really good. Really tender. Really beautiful. Let's play.'

Here they let their inhibitions take a backseat as they challenge each other to taste things. With a twinkle in his eye, Eddy sets up a game of Russian Roulette involving food. They dare each other to try something as they walk the red lantern cobblestoned road. They choose the stands that are having the most people hence the better turnover of food in their opinion.

'Your turn.' Eddy winks as he points towards a centipede on a larger than necessary skewer. Bantering is encouraged. English is limited so a calculator works as the voice for all three of them. The storekeeper punches a figure and displays it to them. They return the calculator facing the storekeeper with a different figure. This method was new and unique to them, but funny and comical at the same time. After this back-and-forth game over a few cents, they buy a skewer with two wiggling centipedes. The vendor takes the squirming, protesting skewer and submerges the insect into the yellow bubbling, smoking frying oil that stands under the larger than required blue gas flame. He hands them over without letting go until the money is in his black soot-covered palm.

'Three…Two…One.'

Eddy counts down as they both insert a centipede into their mouth. This was initially beautiful, then a wave, like a relentless flood of tangy bitterness in the aftertaste that fills their mouth. This makes them pat their sticking out tongue, in the feeble attempt to clean the taste away. It was truly disgusting.

'Next,' Lia turns, she points and pays for a few crickets.

Again, they countdown and throw them like popcorn to the back of their mouth. With the bitterness of the centipede still residually coating their mouths, they do not know what it really tastes like.

'Better?' in an unsure question was Lia's response.

Sure, it was. These had a very mushy taste encased over a crunchy shell with a similar taste to sunflower seeds.

'Let's go for something bigger?' Eddy raises the stakes. 'One starfish please.'

A golden hard starfish comes over. With a scene to resemble *Lady and the Tramp* in a different dimension, they go to a different leg and bite down at the same time. The crunch is raw. The crunch is crisp. The outside shell was very hard to penetrate with a very rich fish flavour, this should not have been unsurprisingly, but hey, it was to them.

Lastly, they have to try the scorpions. This may be their only chance. The squirming scorpions enter the boiling oil. Instantly, the futile resistance was over as they materialise in scorched still portraits. The shopkeeper drags it through a cumin-type spice before handing it to Lia, while Eddy paid. Crisp and very sweet, delicately balanced with a bitter, salty aftertaste. In a word, they were delicious. They were surprisingly delicious. The spices complemented the scorpion perfectly. Eddy suggests to Lia that he should put it on a menu back in Sydney. By his tone, she cannot be one-hundred percent sure if he was joking, but she laughed it off anyway.

Chicken skewers are on the next shack with a variety of dumplings. The scruffy, holey fabric of the formally white T-shirt wearing vendor points and grunts to them in order of the steamed dumplings, 'Chicken', 'Pork' and to the golden-brown fried dumpling 'meat'. This, if it was a play, the vendor did well as Eddy was intrigued. He bought and bit into the flaking crispy skin of the warm dumpling with the spoonful of red, sticky chilli sauce dripping over his unshaven chin given the perfect amount of heat to the rather plain meat inside, which he thinks is beef. Maybe he misheard his grunt.

He passes the other half to Lia to sample. She is as unimpressed as he was. Neon-coloured drinks with a cream-coloured yoghurt served in brown ceramic clear jars, topped with a drum-tightness of paper kept in place by an elastic band. A couple of unconnected tourists buy a jar for which they are given a rather grubby bright yellow straw, they hand over the money and the vendor states in an abrupt tone.

'You. Bring JAARR BACK,' as he turns and speaks in his native tongue, to the locals standing far too close behind them.

The state of the straw. The dusty jar made them make their decision not to gamble on their stomachs surviving this treatment, especially with their day planned tomorrow.

A youthful, baby-faced woman powders what appears to be a handful of shiny hair extensions. He finds out it is named 'horse's tail'. A delicacy that used to be reserved solely for emperors. A royal dessert. They decided to do this one together. They each placed a piece in their mouth. The stringy, chewy sweet took a while to chew. As they chewed, more the hair-like texture formed into a glob of caramel. They look at each other confused. Confused to what was happening in their mouths. It could not be explained. It could not be replicated. More chewing ensued, without the bubbles.

The last sight that they see makes Lia sad. She had heard of it, read about it in various guidebooks but chose to ignore it. Chose to think that it was not true. The truth is it was. They are near the end. Looking at a shack selling tiny fish, turtles and lizards in sealed bubbles of plastic filled with water with green ties as keychains. These animals are very much alive. The oxygen in the water however will only last a few days so they will die a painful, unnecessary death. The bugs, meats seemed okay to eat, but when alive and inhumanly dying in plain sight, it is a tougher pill to swallow.

Next to this, the final shake is the very adventurous shack. They both are genuinely full. They are exhausted. It has been a hot, long, fantastic day. They are wondering if they should go for the large spiders, tarantulas, lizards and turtles that are in neat skewer rolls on yellow plastic trays. They have been here for over an hour going up and down. They exit the way they came under the golden yellow archway that is not the sign for McDonalds. The inhumanely strong stench, like an unwashed fish market in the hot sun, through this whole time did not get easier to manage, or, ignored.

They slowly stroll, carrying heavy shuffling exhausted bodies on fatigued legs in the warm temperatures, with a bitterly cold breeze. They chatter, as they pick the morsels of food out of their teeth. Gossiping about the wonderful, tiring day with weary smiles, fatigued laughs, as they head back to their hotel. They walk by the lit-up Tiananmen Square with the stares of the security that is ever-present, always watching. On the white door of the idling police car, with the dark blue middle strip is a crest bordered by white. The dark blue crest with a white laurel at the bottom, up the sides.

A large gold plain stair is at the top of the crest with four smaller stars in an upward arch underneath. Between the white laurel and the gold stars, just below the centre is the plain simple yellow design with black outlines that simply depict the Great Wall of China. The sight that they will see tomorrow. As if a sign, symbolises a sign, this is their last sight behind the camera lens before retiring into the hotel bed, to a comatose restless undisrupted sleep.

They wake so fresh with a perfect run around Tiananmen Square that dreamily starts the ideal, wonderful day. Eddy has a slight tickle in his throat. At first, he thinks that he is coming down with an illness. Then it dawns on him. It is the pollution. The run for a healthy start, actually turned into breathing more of the harmful fumes in. That is why he was coughing every morning, like he had smoked a carton of smokes the night before. It was uncomfortable. He was now happy for two reasons. Although he liked this city, he was happy to be leaving the polluted city behind for the day, that was proving to be quite toxic for him. This in turn, was a sight that Lia really wanted to see, and her happiness made him happy. A cliché but true. Or, was it that she being happy, made it easier for him to enjoy a moment. No.

The other reason that he was happy, was to be going into the countryside of China. After Xi'an, that was his choice, one of the most fitting sights to see. This was her choice, the Great Wall of China. They thought about taken a bus, but so many people, although said it was far cheaper, also said it was far more of an ordeal.

Thus, they go for a tour group. After a mini tour of the hotels in Beijing it is only one hour and thirty-minute ride to the Mutianyu segment of the Great Wall of China. They did have a choice of the closer Badaling segment, but it is said to be tourist heavy, thus Lia conceded that it would be bumster heavy.

The peaceful, relaxing journey involves a pre-recorded audio of facts about the wall. It is pretty interesting but with no animation, it had the dreadful allure, the presence of a monotone lecture at school during a sunny, hot summers day that bask the welcoming want to go outside, but the feel of prisoners unescapable.

The small white minibus leaves them at the bottom of a gravel park surrounded by lush pine trees that emit a fresh fragrance. They leave with the audio continuing without adequately coming to the conclusion, not quite set to the time and distance of the journey accurately.

Above them, unseen birds sing, rustle about the golden leafed canopy from their hiding places as they footsteps crush a crisp, quick squash on the grey irregular pebbles. The carpark is half full, which Lia finds reassuring that she has chosen the right part of the wall. They were at a higher chance of seeing wolves from this vantage point as they see the signs of promise for the Great Wall but do not see any remnants. They are in a forest carpark. The long and winding path takes them to the base which opens up in a golden arch of falling leaves.

The myth that it is seen from space is actually untrue, which disappointed Lia in ways that she just could not explain to why. The driver points up an opening in the trees. The opening is dark, shady. The sheltering tall pine trees hide the rays of the scorching hot sun which is a pleasant cooling feeling as the walk is steep, slippery underfoot in places and treacherous, not for the weak-willed. Then, the opening. The wall. The Great Wall. Lia looks at the opening steps that lead onto the Ancient sight. They seem to enter through a crumbling section of the wall, rather than an official entrance. A peak under their eyebrows, a shrug of the shoulders, they scale the large boulders, rocks and dust. They carefully rise above the loose rubble.

In amazement, they behold one of the wonders of the world. Snaking around as far as they can see over the green hills and mountains, glimpse over the valleys and gorges. The wall disappears every now and again to coil, rise up, to resembling the arching slither of an enormous serpent to fade away and rise to grow in another part of the whole bending, twisting, meandering northern frontier of the Ancient Chinese Empire. They can imagine the wall living and patrolling the border as if an incarnate entity.

At over six-thousand, seven-hundred kilometres in length, the whole construction of the Great Wall was built by hand. Manmade labour including soldiers, criminals and workers built the wall in seven-hundred and seventy BC. At the time it was the first such wall to prevent the invasion from the other states, being built to protect the Chu State. However, after the unification of China, the wall, under the orders of Emperor Qin Shihuang in two-hundred and one BC, used the wall to reconnect, connect and extend to form a completely defensive military wall to be over, a gargantuan twenty-one thousand kilometres in its entire length. Built larger to defend against the nomadic tribes of the Mongols, Turic and Xiongnu, from modern day Mongolia and Manchuria.

It was mentioned on the minibus that at its peak, over one million soldiers defended their country. They have hours of free time to enjoy the wall. They are in no rush, so choose a direction and hike to scramble like ants over the ancient marvellous, hand-literally-made magnificence.

The first foot on the grey, worn, smooth large stone gives Lia an electric jolt of satisfaction. Lia strains to think of words that have not been said. That have already been said about this sight she beholds. An immeasurable feast for her eyes. What words could accurately express the words that the eyes struggle to adjust too. All the photographs, pictures that they see give an idea of what to expect, however the reality is far different. Truly overwhelming. A huge tick on her personal bucket list.

The air is filled with a breeze of caressing pine touched by a sweet ripening peached perfume. An air that even tastes of fresh, pure, clean air. They are part of a mutual appreciation, a processional human rollercoaster with other tourists, locals alike, as they descend, ascend to various tower points, some steeper than most. The taste of salt, from each bead of sweat. The liquid combinations of the exertion of the steepness and the temperatures trickles into their opened mouths. As their gape openly at the sight, as well as letting more oxygen into their bodies. The sound of undisturbed silence, well apart from the heavy breathing is, in its way, breathless. It is something else. Something, that they could not expect to be, so internally moving. A goose bumped prickle along their skin, to create external water to build in their eyes, but not heavy enough to fall. It is truly amazing for them to be here; they both hold hands in a tight grasp to show their gratitude.

A mixture of steps, slopes of smooth and rough tiles. The deep, noisy breathing of the surrounding tourists that have spent too much time on the couches as they lessen to turnback. They walk on further. They hike, committed to see as much as they can in the timeframe that they have been given. They take many photographs. This is a once-in-a-lifetime thing for them, so they indulge with all their senses, and burrow images as mementoes. Some of the steps are so steep, others small, some large with barely space for their toes. Beautifully unique. The steeper it gets, the less crowded it becomes. The golden silence. The utopian appreciation. The purist form of awe. They are them, and no-one else.

They are cuddling on a crumbling tower, viewing over the shoulders of the other, the expanse of Chinese countryside. Looking over at the brown-grey wall that negotiates the endless, spectacular stretches of greenery. They are alone. They look around to where they have been. Where they cannot go, due to time. They are smiling. Breathless. Happy. Tinged with disappointment that the journey has ended, and they have to turn back. More photographs. More memories are made.

They are the last to arrive back at the white minibus. The small collection of people inside are not smiling. They seem upset to be waiting for them. Instead of happy to have seen something vast and significant. They nervously bow their head to enter under the door, then bow further to apologise at the same time as mumbling an unfeeling, unsympathetic sorry. They believe they have nothing to be sorry about. They arrived back on time, okay a little late, but really? They all should be sharing photographs that they took, talking animatedly about where they have just been, what they have felt. They are mute. As if they are coming back from a funeral.

The door squeak to a loud slam. The engine, on the second attempt, cranks into life. The driver punches a few buttons on his dashboard to commence a new audio over the old engines rumbling roars. This time a soothing female voice tells a story from the wall called *Meng Jiangnu's Bitter Weeping*. Loud enough to hear as everyone is hushed.

Meng Jiangnu's Bitter Weeping is an apparent true story about an old man named Meng, who lived in the south with his wife. One spring, Meng grew a seed in his yard. It grew bit by bit, with its vines climbing over the walls into his neighbours, Jiang's yard. Just like Meng, he also had no children. As if this own plant was a shared child, they both grew fond of it. Watered it. With both men tenderly taking care of the plant it continued to grow. In autumn, it gave a bottle gourd. Jiang plucked it. The two men shared it; hence they went to cut it in half.

To their surprise, when they cut the gourd in half, a pretty young lovely girl was lying inside. They both felt happy to have a child. Together, they brought the child up. Using their own names, they named the child Meng Jiangnu, to mean Meng and Jiang's daughter.

As time passed, the girl grew into a very smart woman. She took care of the old men. One day she saw a young man in the garden and called out. The young man came out of the bushes. At this time, Emperor Qin Shihuang started building the wall. Emperor Qin Shihuang announced to 'catch' as many men as possible to build the wall. He protested that he was in the bushes hiding from the officials. The man, Fan Qiliang, was an intelligent man. Meng offered his house for him to hide. The old men saw a suitor for their daughter in the handsome, well-mannered man. They decided to wed the young couple, which they accepted joyfully.

However, three days after they married, the officials broke in, took Fan away to help build the wall. This was hard on Meng Jiangnu. She missed her husband. She cried every day. She sewed clothes for Fan. Then, she decided to go and search for him. Saying goodbye to her parents, she started the journey over mountains, through rivers. Slipping and falling on her dangerous journey, but each time lifting herself up until eventually she arrived. She arrived at the foot of the Great Wall. Yet. Yet, she was too late. The news came that Fan had died of exhaustion and was buried in the Great Wall. She cried, wept. Her heart wailed. She collapsed onto the ground.

Suddenly, with an earth breaking noise, a four-hundred-kilometre-long section of the wall collapsed over her own bitter, heart-aching wail. The workers, the supervisors were astonished. Emperor Qin Shihuang, on seeing what happened, was outraged. He was ready to punish Meng Jiangnu. However, coming closer, he saw her, he was attracted by her beauty.

Instantly changing his mind in killing her, to marrying her. She agreed, with three terms. The first, to find the body of her beloved Fan. The second, to hold a state funeral for him. The third, the last, was for the Emperor Qin Shihuang to wear black, in mourning for Fan and to attend the funeral in person. The Emperor thought about it, before agreeing. She was ready to go to the palace, to become the Empress. When the guards stopped watching, she suddenly turned around. She jumped into the nearby Bohai Sea.

This time the audio track lasted the entire journey perfectly for all. They arrive back with the story ending. Lia and Eddy looked at one another. What was the story about? What was the moral? Was it to show the cruel conditions of literally slave labour? The power of the common person? The wisdom of the Chinese culture? That hard work ethic of the Chinese to work until they drop? Lia looked but could not see the reason. Eddy half-heartedly looked but decided that he would not worry about it as a moral, but just a nice story with a rather huge, unmistakable anti-climax. He joked about Humpty Dumpty, with his own twisted witticism about the resemblance of a wall, a fall and a moral that was equally mystical. Lia laughed out of sympathise cuteness for what Eddy was struggling to make into a comical story of his own.

They arrive back to their hotel with a sticky layer of stale, dried sweat cracked only by their teeth baring smiles. The white residue of salt like clown make-up that has run in the heat borders their cheekbones and temples. They immediately ask the concierge if they have a recommendation for the late afternoon. She, without a second thought states 'Summer Palace', as she firmly draws over a small colourful map and slides it across. Eddy places it in his pocket without looking, as they race upstairs to basin wash, before returning faster than Superman changing in the nearest telephone box. Time is of the essence. As they were about to leave, the concierge interrupted their brisk pace to suggest:

'Beihai Park. May be better. Less time before shut. Better for you. Closer…Two…Too.'

She slips over a piece of torn yellow paper and points towards the subway. It is only when they start walking that they look down at the piece of yellow, now creased paper to notice that the good information, the great intentions are revealed. Yet unreadable, she accidentally wrote in her haste, in her own native language. Completely indecipherable to them both.

With that, they shrugged they shoulders and continue their walk, on the presumption that they will be able to decipher, to them, symbols which were an unearthly code once at the subway. They look at the large map, for which they find easily by the biggest dot where they are. Lia uses the map, while Eddy looks for the letters on the paper to see if he can find the correct stop. He might as well be looking for the golden egg at the top of a beanstalk, a broken tulip in seventeenth century Amsterdam, a needle in a haystack. Lia, on the other hand, finds the stop that they want on the map. She is chuffed as she struts off with an air of righteousness towards the ticket booth.

With no words, the lady through the plastic clear screen nods, points as Lia does the same. Everything is done in a mime. Lia is trusting the information, while Eddy is on his own mission impossible. Lia pays. The lady writes on the map that they got from the concierge that she slid under the small opening for cash. She writes in clear, precise handwriting of art, the platform. Then points to the sign behind Lia. She turns, recognises what she is pointing at and returns a recognition nod.

The young beautiful Chinese ticket vendor then writes the train number and points again. She had even drawn a sketch of a train with a block to where the number would be. Lia giggles thankfully as she turns to retrieve Eddy who missed the whole charade of exchanges. She tugs at him with the tickets as she leads him as instructed. For a reason she does not know, she found herself waving back at the vendor. The vendor uneasily raises her hand without a wave back. This works out very well. Seamlessly easy.

They leave the smelly, darkness of the subway to the blaring bright, brilliant lights. At the exit, soaring above like nuisance vultures around fresh meat, are bumsters. They had not seen any today. They had forgotten about these enraging pests. They did not pause for a split second. They were fortuitous in their exit as they find themselves confronted with the main entrance. A sign in red bold capitals, for the foreigner in English, lets them know that they are at 'Beihai Park. The World's oldest Imperial Gardens'.

After paying with a small fee, a large thirty-six metre white Dagoba dominates the park. They stroll over the beautiful small bridges, over slow moving or calm waters reflecting the colours of the temples, pavilions. The many walkways through the lakes, manicured gardens where the elite in Chinese society stood, strolled, discussed numerous important and flippant issues for which they were doing the same many, many years in the future. Sometimes they have to take their cameras from their eyes. See the surroundings around them, just as they did at the Great Wall. At the Forbidden Palace. Over the Terracotta Army. Sometimes, well, always, they have to stop in their tracks to remember where they are, where they are standing, who had stood there before, who has yet to stand there. It is a privilege to be in places where some people do not even know that they exist. Who have no desire to see. Who know not what they are missing.

In a designated café, within one of the pavilions that takes nothing away from the past they stop. For the first time for the day. It is their last day after all. They order a tea. They get given a small beige wooden tray with a delicate teapot that is thin and tall in the corner. Also gracing the light tray are two small cups without handles. They sit, legs folded on the red panelled wooden seats that border the pavilion, half looking out, half at one another.

A slight tilt of their head and they are looking out, basking in the sun shine, sipping the green shaded, sweet tea looking over the pagodas, temples that are the landscape with the sculptures, artistic merits and where an Emperor would be alone, minus off course his servants and concubines. Here the scene is changed to that of tourists.

Returning the tray, they continue to appreciate the gardens and every intricate detail that they offer. They pass a marvellous colourful, dimensional wall topped with a green hipped roof with orange highlights, called the Nine Dragon Screen. Unsurprisingly, nine coiling dragons in various poses against a textured sky-blue background over rolling green grass in waves make the scene. Bordered by shiny orange, and green designed glazed tiles. Eddy laughs with a nudge and a nod of the head towards the marble sign etched with information.

'It is about 25.52 metres long, 9.96 metres high and 1.60 metres thick,' he reads. 'Very precise for an estimated about!' he concludes.

Being over two hundred years old, the same marble sign tells them that the nine main dragons are nine of six-hundred and thirty-five dragons in all. They did not count them. What cannot speak surely cannot lie, after all this passage is set in stone, not ink.

Through shading arches, around some more temples, negotiating the small pockets of groups on the Jade Islet surrounded by vibrant green pine trees they make the short walk up to the white Dagoba. Originally built for the Dalia Lama in 1651. The remains of Buddhist monks, as well as other artefacts, are inside the smooth-looking white walls. The view is amazing.

Looking over the blue ripples towards the five dragon pavilions that blink the green glazed roof with orange hipped edges supported by prominent red, cylinder pillars with the dazzling white walled border where the sea falls is said to be shaped, based on a dragon entering into the sea. Eddy and Lia were not sure if they saw it only, because their overactive imagination was willing them to see it or if it was, in fact, actually seen for almost reality. A sense that is not unalike when you look at clouds in the sky. When someone points out a form, the mind sees what your imagination wants you to see.

Lia breaks this silence with the surprising proclamation that it is eight in the evening, still daylight. They have seen a lot, but still have a lot to do. Tomorrow they are leaving. They are not ready. They are hungry. Surprisingly though, not tired. But what a great day. A great time in China.

By means of a deep unwavering drone from the alarm clock, in the silent dark is how the immunity of sleep is shattered. The unwelcoming, hostile noise brings an alert, frantic urgent rush. Sometimes a good idea in the dark of night, manifests into a bad idea in the light of day. Late last night, they took the seemingly correct decision, which now proves to be the foolish decision, to rather than pack when they arrived back last night, to pack in the morning. With the shrill of the alarm, Lia jumps into the shower, while Eddy starts to pack. Then they reverse their roles in a move that running relay teams' opponents would envy.

Eddy jumps into the hot running water of the shower which Lia had left on. As he lathers himself, Lia shouts or rather squeals complaints to Eddy through the glass, plastic clear shower door as he had packed the clothes she wanted to wear. Then she could not find her brush. Another chorus of frustrated noise emulates from the bedroom as she shouts for her make-up. As if it will be retrieved for her by a magical dog.

He showers, towel-dries his hair as he wonders why he even bothered, with the remains of unrinsed soapsuds sliding down his body, he is unfazed by the commotion. If he had done nothing, she would have grumbled. He did something, she grumbled. He was in a no-win situation. He was finishing getting ready, safe in the knowledge that his stuff was packed. His clothes folded on the black leather office chair he will slip into once exiting the bathroom. He was content to leave her packing. He was in the doghouse already, so thought he would just continue to get his own self ready.

Back in the cross-fire of the bedroom, as he was getting dressed, he asked Lia if she needed help and got the predicted answer. So, he leaned in for the morning kiss, for which she turned the other cheek as he turned to walk out with his bag. He had time to go down to the dining room for breakfast. He should have felt guilty, but he tried to help, asked her if she needed help and got rejected so he went down to have the complimentary breakfast and still make the train even if that did mean Lia was left rushing. He was not leaving without a strong black coffee, that was for certain. He followed that down with a couple of slices of toast with a very sweet orange jam.

Shortly after he finished his toast, Lia came down. He was ignored as she shovelled a dry, toasted muesli of nuts and raisins resembling something that got swept from the sidewalk this morning. She had not sat down. Between mouthfuls, she demonstrated his unhelpfulness. Eddy did not argue. He knew her frustrations of not being organised was being transmitted by angry acquisitions that were downright wrong. Sometimes in the heat of battle, you have to take the brunt of forceful wrongs. The person directing the wrongs knows it is not the other persons fault, but sometimes to find someone to blame, helps. He has been accustomed to this treatment before so just bears her frustrations, safe in the knowledge that the guilt will be played back to him later today in a positive, sorry, apologetic manner.

The comically short walk involved a content coffee-filled stomach of Eddy, with the somewhat opposite of Lia. Who did not have time, even though Eddy would have waited the few minutes for her to have one. He, maybe, no, he, definitely should not have told her to stop being so stubborn. He was still firmly at blame's door. He shrugged it off, as her having nervous energy. Like water off a duck's back, her words did not stick, not personally, instantly forgettable. This is not to say he did not care, well, he didn't. She was trying to walk fast but the rollers on her small suitcase were protesting the speed. Catching on each tiny join of the cement floor. Enabling him to catch-up without having to lengthen his stride. He did care, but not for her childish tantrums.

It was six in the morning when they saw the brightly lit corner clock towers of the front facade. The yellow roof twinkles, the black clock face and white numerals illuminated, over the three low green and yellow arches was the red Chinese words on unseen black spikes, with the English underneath stating; Beijing Railway Station. They walk under the red cloth canopy entrance, over the red carpet into the station, as if on award night at some glitzy event. This seemed to calm her down a little. The being on time helped, the being with Eddy helped. That she would never admit to anyone, not even herself, but inside she did know the truth. Although she was calm, she was still not in full forgiving mood, but leaned into Eddy's chest as they walked the red carpet.

With the printed vouchers they went towards the metal, grated ticket counter to swap it for the proper real, slim postcard sized tickets. They are ready to go. Excited. The wave of energy over them has soothed and caressed Lia's worries away. Lugging their light, but a little bulky bags they realise a hopefully rectifiable mistake. They did not click the box in which they get clean sheets. They, without more ado, put right the misinterpreted mix-up. They hand over one-hundred and thirty-three roubles, for the clean sheets. They receive a plastic bag containing two clean folded white sheets, a pillowcase and a soft, but small flannel-sized towel.

They are advised to go up to the second floor to wait. The empty room, like a prison cell. In the centre a single metal seated bench stood, barely enough for a dozen people to sit uncomfortably on. Safe to say it was full like an untinned can of sardines. They stood in the corner. Looking at the flickering, static, snowfield screens. Hoping that it would change the instruction with each page. A few minutes later, at just before quarter to seven, they saw the change on the digital screen, followed by a loud muffed radio-interfered call out. It was time to board.

Looking down at their tickets they make their way. They shuffle along the busy, narrow platform to search out their correct sleeping carriage. What looks like newly painted shiny green carriages with a rich golden yellow trim above and below the windows look so clean. On each side of the carriage is a large crest of red and gold. The gold-coloured three-dimensional borders, the familiar four small stars and large stars on the police car door. However, the golden embossed building which appears to be the Forbidden City replaces the Great Wall. It was looking so posh for them. Gloriously far from their semi-bogan roots.

As they saw, what was going to be their carriage, they were unwelcomed by a male guard. His greeting left a lot to be desired. He opened his palm to receive the papers without a word, eye contact or any other of the basic welcoming codes that are unspoken in adulthood, but hammered in you as a child. He was obnoxious in his manner, just damn right rude. The male train guard again thrust his hand forward, with a little upward wave of his fingers. The attendant wore white pristine gloves, as he took, rather snatched their tickets, then their passports and flicks the pages to check for correct visas, that their photographed inside the passport matched them standing in front. His green cap, with a grey trim, shields his eyes as he looks down.

They cannot see any features move on his face. There is a morning chill in the air, for which he has not noticed a bit in his short-sleeved crease free dark blue shirt with a thin black tie. With no words, just a slight bow of the head and a guiding white hand up the steps, he passes over their documents. Shows them again when they do not move, with an impatient flap of his arm where to go.

They squeeze along the platform. Passed people tearfully saying goodbyes. On board they knock their bags clumsily up the steel steps, through the green, narrow doors. Shuffling along the tightest of hallways their bags shush as they stroke the narrow fragile walls to find their cabin. Inside, the bronze numbered two leads them into the third-class compartments. They are the last to enter. Hence, the bottom bunks are taken by Jade, a Canadian, and Oleg, a Russian going home to Moscow. Oleg sees that Eddy and Lia are a couple, so he quickly gets up. Smiles as he gathers his belongings in a disorderly pile, throws them on the top bunk above Jade, where a sleeve of a beige jumper hands down like a ticking tock.

He vacates his bed to go on the top, so they have a bunk bed to share. That was nice of him, as the mutual appreciation is delivered with a bowing nod of their head. Both of the bottom bench seats lift up to become a place underneath for their bags to be stored. They take a few things out, such as their vital travel documents, a book, paper and pen before pulling the top down to create a bench seat. The tobacco-coloured soft material walls, two soft blue and green bunk beds and cream plastic small shelves and the smallest table, the size of a bedside table for all four of them to share make up the extremely cosy enclosed space. On the soft, small marshmallow pillow is a clear plastic bag, with a neatly folded light brown blanket. They rip it open, to jointly attempt to make a suitable bed on the top bunk. Then the bottom. It is lastly that they offer introductions of their names to the other inhabitants of the compartment.

This is their first part of the real journey towards their destination—Lia's home. This first part will be about thirty hours from the capital of China to the capital of Mongolia, Ulaanbaatar. Each carriage is patrolled by an attendant who is in charge of the general cleaning and protection of them and the contents, inside the carriage. She, well, she is huge in size. Huge in life, someone that you would not like to mess with. Not because she looked strong, but more that she looked like she would not take any trouble. She had a stern, resting bitch-face. The attendant was such a romantic word for a security guard. They thought the guy looking at the steps was the attendant, but it turned out he was just checking the tickets, she is the one in charge, called the provodnitsa.

Dressed in black flat sturdy shoes with brown tights until her loose blue skirt starts just below her knee. In the same dark blue is the blazer, with a winged name tag on her right breast over a white shirt supporting a light blue tied, linen scarf. Her blonde hair is tied back into a short ponytail. Her face has the bare minimal make-up. She came through into the cabin with an aura of authority, rechecking the documents, the tickets corresponded with where they were. She left with a smile. A grimace, more than a smile, that really did not suit her. She actually turned upwards into a sinister, evil, mischievous grin, brimming with sinister motives.

Each cabin can be locked from the inside. Also, for added security, if everyone wanted to leave the cabin, she would lock it. To only reopen it with a proof, such as a ticket. As the train starts its forward momentum, they introduce themselves properly and make awkward small talk about themselves.

At the end of each carriage near the provodnitsa compartment, is a water boiler, the samovar, standing proud and tall in its glittering metal, with a gauge on it to see the temperature before you fill up your cup. Lia goes by the old name of samovar. A name she had forgotten but comes running to the front of her mind. Oleg, a traditionalist, interjects that, that thing in the corner, that metal keg is not a samovar. He is very passionate as he describes the samovar being heated by firewood, and for tea. This is nothing in comparison.

On learning the new word, she bows her head, curves her lips downwards in an 'oops!' gesture to Eddy, who giggles beside her. It will remain the samovar to them. On each end is a toilet and shower, well, if you bring your own attachments anyway. The one thing they forgot with their checklist was a showerhead. Although it is only now that Lia alerts Eddy that the provodnitsa still has their tickets.

He heads down to her cabin. Gingerly knocks on the door and enquires. In a stern way, the way that a headmistress would tell a child off, she abruptly lets him know that she will keep it for the duration of the trip to Irkutsk. With a broken English threat, sincerely: 'I will throw you off when we come to the stop.' Confused, worried and wondering if she would genuinely chuck them off. She could, if she really wanted. Factually and metaphorically.

From the uncomfortable silence comes a voice from the top bunk.

'Why do you travel?' Oleg asks as he leans over the edge looking down like an inquisitive sloth.

This question has been asked to Eddy many times. This is the first time it has been proposed to Lia. In different locations this question has been asked by different people. Eddy still does not know. Eddy answers a different answer every single time.

This time he goes with, 'the thrill of seeing a postcard come to life'.

Lia looks at Eddy, bewildered. 'Where did that come from?'

'Honestly. No idea. I have so many different answers. I am looking forward to this land crossing. To see the differences, unpeel themselves.' He also was protecting Lia by answering for them both. 'It is about the journey…but for us,' he was addressing Oleg now, 'the destination.'

The provodnitsa interrupts with an insistent loud knock where she walks in uninvited, to give out tickets for the dining car. It has a time printed clearly for dinner.

Lia and Eddy were surprised as they were not in first or even second class but third class of the carriage. Over the speakers, Oleg tells them that the dining room has just opened. Lia has not let on that she can speak and understand Russian. She felt that it was not the time. So, they gather a few personal possessions to make their way down to the dining carriage.

Delightfully decked out in blue. It has four spaces to each table that is in a pale blue leather-bound booth on each side of the aisle. At the end is a small bar. They decide to share a table with their newfound bunk-mates. Oleg has warned them not to expect great food. Over the speakers is a mix of curious music that has yet to make it to the Aria Chart lists. The menu is vast, huge and endless. They order. Time after time they get told 'Sorry', or to be more precise, 'Sorry, Nyet'. They come to the conclusion that they will ask what they have, rather than go through the menu, which is sounding like a record, stuck on repeat. Oleg takes charge, orders. They are given rice, celery and two pork meatballs. Filling and good, considering the level of expectation was so very low. With the meal, Eddy orders a beer, which he promptly pours over himself, the adjacent window with a light shower of splashes going in the direction to go over Jade and Oleg. A cacophony of the sorriest, jittering apologises fell in clonking disharmony. Eddy offers them his serviette. Well, that broke the ice at least. Even if the unpleasant stares below their eyebrows, as their eyes look up from their soup spoons full of dripping red borsch, tell him otherwise.

Within an hour, the concrete busy, city life was forgotten. The grey drabness was replaced by roaming mountain ranges with small, glistering green shimmering lakes that mirrored perfectly the bushy green trees, the grasses. The perfect paradise of tranquillity. In the forefront was a reflection of cold white, fluffy clouds in the light blue skies staring back from within the clear lake.

On the banks, people were sporadically scattered in silence either sitting or standing looking at this lake. Or that what it seemed at first sight. As they looked closer, they could see fisherman with the tiniest rods on unseen silvers of shiny string, hoping for a bite. Sharing a giggle an elderly couple of men share a smile, a joke over the thin perfect string that dangles in front of them into the water. It does not seem to be about the fishing par say, but more the contemplation of a perfect silence in a rushing world.

This beautiful changing scenery was absorbed by Eddy who watched the motion from the clear, large smoothed cornered train window. He was excited and never bored watching the rising, jagged, razor-sharp mountains that dropped dramatically to form a near perfect flat lines, that separated into grids of farmland crops, paddy fields. Where horses pulled agricultural machinery with the guidance of a farmer, women with wicker baskets bent over in colourful garments tending to plants, vegetable or some unrecognisable foodstuffs from the fast-moving, blurring train windows. Isolated houses of brown tiled roofs and lighter brown bricked walls blend into the greenery.

Lia, on the other side of the bench which will be her bed, had fallen asleep before the train had really left the centre of Beijing. They stopped ever so briefly at a few Chinese towns before coming to Earlian, a Gobi Desert town, the border town of China and Mongolia, at a little past eight-thirty in the evening.

The train slowed to a roll, as an announcement came over the loudspeakers which seemed to be outside, as well as inside the carriage. Eddy strains to listen and feels he can understand, yet Oleg talks over the announcement, infuriating Eddy at the time, but in hindsight was probably for the best. He really did not understand a word. A stirring Lia had lifted her head and rubbed her eyes. Eddy thought she looked lovely, always had, always will. A deranged, waking sleeping beauty. The movies could never capture the true unique essence of seeing a loved one in a natural, glorious state that grabs eye contact with a silent, mutual connection of happiness. A sensation that feels not only the heart, but the whole body of everyone in the same room.

Oleg, in a matter-of-factionary speech that they must stay here and are forbidden to leave the cabin, even to go to the bathroom. Lia was slightly agitated by this as the first thing you normally do when you wake up has been taken from her. Fortunately, it was early into her sleep before she was gently aroused by the slow-moving momentum, followed by the loud speakers. The toilet has no tank. The waste deposits straight onto the tracks that rush by in a blur, hence, understandable the town does not want to see a steaming pile of pooh left behind after they have pulled away from the station. This was the same for the whole journey. They both figure out, and completely understand very quickly. The provodnitsa shuts these toilets down before the announcement, so Lia's rush was cut very shut, to the point her fragrance was still lingering in the spot that she vacated seconds before. She deemed it worth a try.

The normal formalities are processed by the three Chinese custom inspectors that are wearing the same attire as the male at the start of their journey in Beijing. The already crowded carriage was made very cosy as they checked their passports, visa, departure forms and insurance forms as the provodnitsa handed over their tickets to prove everything married together. It was a quick, fluent exchange that proved no problems.

For some reason though, Lia and Eddy both tensed up as if they did something wrong. Illogical thoughts raced through their heads wondering if they had the correct paperwork. After they had checked it numerous times before leaving. Double-checked it again on the plane. Then the customs guy scrutinised it all over again in Beijing. It was highly irrational, but all the same, they were nervously waiting for the outcome. As expected, tick, an approved pass.

At that juncture came a bizarre exchange. The Chinese officers had left. The Russian attendant returns and tells Oleg, in Russian, to store these small bags of 'tea' under their benches. He refuses and instructs them to do the same. A heated, hushed argument ensues with Lia hearing, understanding every word but staying mute. Eddy confused watching the dialect while moving his head to the provodnitsa, back to Oleg in a verbal tennis game. The provodnitsa pushes Lia who involuntarily breaks her vow of silence to join into the long, argument with the Australian coming into the ensuing conflict.

Lia's single Russian word stopped them arguing for the slimmest flicker of a microsecond before she rallied more to try to get them to stop. To get the provodnitsa to take no for an answer and in turn trying to ignore Oleg in his persistent questioning on how she knows Russian. After a few tense minutes, the word 'no' is finally accepted and the provodnitsa leaves the cabin with her two grey, duffle bags of 'tea'.

Literally minutes later, a new trio of Chinese guards burst into their compartment. These looked a lot more official. Dressed in perfectly creased dark green shirts, black pants with a golden trim down the sides and black shiny smart decorative, less sturdy shoes. A darker green blazer with an official looking badge on the left breast and an identity clip-on badge on their right breast. With the mentality of a man on a mission, he instructs them to get up and wait outside. He does this by pulling the arms of Oleg down from his bunk, Eddy into the narrow space outside for which a forever silent Jade and Lia follow suit.

They watch on through the crack between a guard, more like a soldier, and the curtain into their sleeping compartment. They look on the top bunks, quickly brushing their black leather-gloved hands over and under. They look under the thin mattresses. Then under the bench seat for which the provodnitsa moments earlier wanted to store her belongings, her 'tea'. Then a quick brush around and they were instructed back in. The door latches shut with a slight click.

In unison, a mutually collective silent phew fills the cabin with the tension evaporating of a close escape. Had they just been potentially set-up to take someone else's fall? The door opens again. Another guard motions them all to stand up. From behind him a weedy man made to look even smaller in a large white baggy lab coat, that was at least two sizes too big for him, emerges from his shadows. In his right arm he brandishes a magic wand like a sorcerer, however this was no trick.

His close to exploding vein-filled hand grips a white infra-red thermometer fiercely, as he uses his other hand to grip the back of each of their heads. He then shines this contraption onto each of their foreheads. Yep, foreheads. He leaves in a trail of his white cloak, leaving the room last. Leaving the four of them to look at each other, confused, extremely mystified. Oleg states a quite simple, but shared opinion of everyone when he remarked, 'Well. That's different.'

Slowly, but defiantly, the train rolls backwards. Grudgingly, digging its wheels in the high-pitched resisting squeak. As this was not for what they were designed for. They do as instructed by the driver, squealing back towards China. In the cabin the kangaroo momentum makes the four of them be forced to sit down. This sight role reversal confuses Eddy and Lia who look at each other bewildered. A heavy jerk stops them looking at each other, as they grip the bedsheets so as not to fall off the edge. A shunt, a thrust, they roll forward on a different track as if the driver has been replaced by a learner. The disconnected roll rattles them into a large steel hanger.

Light wooden timber arched roofs, like a cathedral, are supported by thick iron girders of a worksite and the ancient decorative old, sandstone walls of an old-fashioned piece of history. The train shakes as it moves along. They glance out as the platform staff seemingly salute the train as it slowly passes into the open shed. Red hydraulic lifts line the track where trees, fences and benches were the previous setting. Against the walls are row upon row of wheels, bogies, being lined up in neat columns. Huge old-fashioned horned speakers blaring out classical music vibrates and protest with the louder than necessary volume of the music. The loud and very poor sound quality music is finished with a short break of canned applause. This is strange.

An instruction is spoken over the speakers in the carriage but cannot compete with the racket from the speakers. They look at each other, not sure what is going on. The music rises. The violins squeal like nails on a blackboard over what should be melodic, pleasant music if played a few decibels lower. Hence the speakers could contain them instead of the cracking statically recitation of the onslaught of injustice.

The platform staff are nowhere to be seen as they are replaced with light blue overall wearing workers with a yellow strip, thick around their chest like a pulled-up cumber band. These Lego-dressed men in their dirty, smudged yellow hardhats with bright, easily noticeable pink, soft earplugs watch them pass by until they stop. They silently gather around each of the red hydraulic jacks on each side and adjust the figures and push them closer to the carriages. A final jolt as the train jerks forward a fraction of an inch. This happens a lot, over the next few hours. Lia goes to take a photograph of the proceedings around them.

'NNNOOOO!' Oleg screams. 'No PICTURE. No Allowed.'

Lia shrugged his protests off as she takes photograph after photograph. Oleg continues to insist as he heard it in the announcement. Lia calms him down as other train passengers are doing exactly the same in the narrow corridor, not making it subtle, whereas she, Lia pointed out, has not left the cabin and is not jostling with others to take the perfect photograph.

Then the bizarre happens. Another out of the ordinary, peculiar moment in this short passage of time occurs. Lia places the camera down with wide-eyed stares. Gripping the free hand of Eddy, hard. The red hydraulic lifts elevate the carriages into the air about two metres. So slowly, but not smoothly. Whistles, horns, voices and shouts, all add to the din from outside. Flashing emergency yellow lights with red warning sirens turn around casting lights and shadows over the shed reflecting in the surrounding metals. Flashlights from the workers underneath the carriage are all that is seen, but only by the sweep of the spotlights.

Lia slowly releases her tight grasp on Eddy's top of hand as it dawns on her. She remembers reading about this, paying little attention to it, if any, but the subconscious remembers all. Eddy and Lia are glued to the window as they watch the slightly wider Chinese bogies, which were previously unfastened and left on the tracks below them.

'Bogies,' she remarks.

'What to the WHAT?' Eddy asks, bewildered.

'The wheels. The wheels that the train runs on are called bogies. That's it. How was I so stupid? The bogies change. I can't believe I forgot.'

'If you would like to share, now would be good!'

'Honey.' A little patronising, but Eddy let it slide. 'With a fear of invasion, the Chinese and Russian gauges are different. If they were invaded, they could not use their train system.'

'Are you serious? That is really their main concern? If invaded, the train network would not be high on the list. Maybe, just maybe, I think it would be the fact that they GOT invaded!'

Ignoring his startling admission, Lia scans the view outside, a gigantic mechanically working shed. Overhead a gantry, a crane whirls and whizzes above them. It moves backwards and forwards like a panic-stricken fly that a child has pulled its wings off. Expectantly, like a bird of prey the crane watches, waiting, judging for its precise moment. Attacks, its chains clatter as the hook crashes down to abruptly stop, wave, hover over a single carriage. Many men in bright fluorescing yellow vests, donning bug-like plastic googles and white, dark smudged blemished hardhats camber on top to grab the swinging hook. Clip it to the clutching loop, shouts out. He almost slides down the side of the carriage as behind him it rises into the air.

Their carriage shakes. A thud, a clunk, a final jolting stop, and as if they had almost forgotten that they were slowly rising, they have finished rising. The unconcerned mechanistic earthquake is over. Oleg was making his way down when the sudden judder caused him to slip, ungracefully fall from the middle rung. Lia, concerned, helped him up. In contrast, Eddy could not help as he erupted into crying roars of laughter. He was not improving his previous first impression of the beer spilling saga.

The choking smell of dense coal smoke enters the cabin. Oleg returns to what he was planning to do, he closes the window. He dares not to return just yet to his bunk but positions himself in the narrow space between the two bottom beds. He glances at Eddy who is still rocking with sniggers, avoiding any eye contact in the feeble attempt to compose himself.

The crane buzzes down to pick up the Chinese bogies, which are manually pushed from under to the opening. These are lifted, placed by the side of the wall at the edge of the tidy, but no-where-near to being clean workshop. The crane then comes back with the closer, narrower bogies. These are manually placed under the carriage with a lone, thick, wooden handled metal hammer, stopping them from continuing to roll away. It seems not the most ideal way, but if it is not broke, don't fix it. Loud, unseen bangs, thumps, shouts, and then the disco lights return. The borderline, bogies dancing Emporium with the canary yellow workers bopping around. The Lego men move away with frustrating, tense shouting.

This brings a sense of fear into the cabin. Dread tells them that something was going wrong, when absolutely nothing was going to happen, nothing went wrong. This truly was the most bizarre, never seen stage production of a day in the life, on the quiet border town of China and Mongolia, which Eddy and Lia have or will ever see. This pretty essential procedure takes a long, a very long time. Each carriage gets lifted one by one, which explains the long duration. But they cannot move.

Apparently, according to Oleg, they had a choice at the platform. Why he divulges this information now is beyond them both. The touch of a proper, clean toilet that does not leave you in parts of the countryside would have been nice. Accepting. It definitely was not a Formula One Grand Prix pit stop, as this was a noisy affair of lights, music, sound and burning smells of coal, and greasy dirty mechanical oil. They, nevertheless, found it fascinating to watch.

Over four hours later, within the shed, and a long time from the first border documentation check, they are finally moving forward. After that episode, which they never expected, thus if Lia remembered her research, they would have had an inkling. Never have they ever gone through and, they strongly doubt, if they would have to endure again.

Mongolia

They are now officially in another country. It was a new day, it was three-thirty in the morning when they rolled into a new country, the country of Mongolia. Nothing was seen in the shadows through the windows. No lights, only dark shapes of natural surroundings were made. They rolled into their beds, fully dressed, tired and ready to sleep with the smooth, steady beat of the train lulling them to slumber town.

For what seems like a long sleep, where they were dead to the rushing world beyond the window pane, they wake. It is light outside, yet only a few hours since they fell into bed. Outside are a herd of brown, two-humped camels dotted within the white thin flock of sheep. The dramatic change of scenery from the green, vibrant, living countryside to a barren, lifeless looking vast land. A dramatically change like chalk to cheese, night to day, male to female. Although the last would cause a few debates. As the age-old unresolved conflict of men being from Mars and women from Venus. Sometimes, Lia thinks that there is truth in that cliché. This would explain Eddy's strange tendencies to say the wrong thing at the wrong time to catastrophic consequences. For which eventually they both, or one, decides it is time to make peace.

Lia is indifferent to the real-life movie going on through the window screen, but Eddy cannot tear himself away from the flat, dusty infinite space, where they are a mere dot on a squirming line dissecting the country. This is the Gobi Desert. A world renown immense, dry region known for sand dunes, mountains and rare animals. The unexplored, waiting to be explored. The undiscovered, remaining undiscovered. To Eddy, it resembles a scene from Lord of the Rings when they are in the evil parts of the Kingdom, enigmatic and mysterious. Where the dark corners would hide more than just secrets. Where the light flats would give the answers to the unanswerable questions to the world. Like solving the enigma to where Genghis Khan is actually buried. Letting the world know where the treasures are hidden.

How could an Empire be so vast. How an Empire could have affected the whole human race to the point, that it is estimated that one in three people have an ancestor that is related to Genghis Khan. Eddy looks on, ignoring Lia's teasing solo comical routine. She is restless in her sleep. She snuggles into her thin blanket, moves her feet as if running. Eddy stares back through the reflective window. Looking back at Eddy is the unparalleled architecture of the Gobi Desert. Silently screaming a vast extreme noise of just how Mother Nature can give another side of beauty, in the confrontation of a limitless nothingness of the continuous sea of greying-brown sands, dirt.

Lia dozes, angelically awake. Blindly grabs for her travel book. She does not lift her head up, to peak at what has got Eddy so captivatingly mesmerised. She resorts to reading about Mongolia, rather than seeing it for her own eyes. She shares a little of newfound knowledge. Something that Eddy actually finds interesting. He actually peels his face away, to look towards Lia. He shrugs a humming approval together with a nod of his head.

'The desert, Gobi Desert spread over China and Mongolia. Surrounded by grassland. Erm, la la la. Oh, surrounded by the Altai Mountains which is a place that touches four Asian countries: China and Mongolia, obviously, and Kazakhstan. Oooo I would LOVE, love, love to go there. And, where was I…Russia. Of course.'

'Kazakhstan? What?' Eddy's focus is interrupted by Lia, who in turns interrupts his questions.

'Yes, Kazakhstan. Moving on. It covers 1.3million square kilometres. I can't picture that, but it sounds big. Really big.'

'Bloody oath, but is that Kazakhstan or the Gobi?' he pauses, as he cheekily winks at Lia. 'Kidding, Lia.'

'Gobi means Waterless Place.'

They stare out at the Waterless Place of the dry Gobi Desert that jaggers, troughs to peak brokenly up to the light blue skies, in silence, that is mutually returned.

They stop at their first station in Mongolia, Choyr, for just short of an hour. Eddy is up and out like a jack in the box to set foot for the first time on Mongolian soil. In shorts and T-shirts, open thongs he jumps out onto the ugly concrete platform. Naïvely he lunges, the coldness hits him hard, instantly. The empty paved platform is as cold in sight, as the feel of the temperatures. In substantial contrast from the warmth body of the carriage cabin.

Apart from a slight jolt, he is unfazed though. He is excited, giggling like a lunatic on a day out from the asylum. Finally, he has gone outside for the first time in hours. A single small white-washed building in large red lettering, between the Roman columns in a block cubism style states, Choyr. Displayed on a light green steel roof the name sits proud. The light blue and white decorative façade is a cross between Iran and Indians influences, very strange, and not fitting at all. He is close to running as he crosses the threshold.

Jiggling in his pocket, he has taken with him their last bits of Chinese currency in the hope to spend it. He has success, as he uses it to buy instant coffee, noodles and with his last pieces of shrapnel, a piece of bread. He is slightly unsure how long he has been, so he races back to the train. He, it seems is the only one to take advantage of the nicer toilets, get rid of the unusable money from this point forward and, to get out of the claustrophobic environment that they find themselves in.

Oleg babbles greatly. The only noise that is coming from their cabin is the incessant prattles of Oleg. Some people share, some do not, and then they are some, that over share. Oleg was one of these, that gives his all, and more. In the short space, in the short period, they feel that they know more about him, then they do themselves. Although Eddy does wish that he would shut up, part of him is glad. For Lia has been disconnected since Beijing. As Oleg continued to constantly speak, Eddy persistently thought. He could not grasp the concept to why she was so…detached. She had got more evasive since speaking Russian. As if that sole point actually drilled home the reality of what was coming sooner, than soon.

Lia was fearing the next stage of her journey. She no longer saw it as their journey, their trip. She saw it as her journey, her trip. Her, own personal journey. It was absolutely irrational. Lia, obviously did not divulge this information to Eddy. In her head it was sensible. Yet, saying her thoughts out loud, she feared that it would sound selfish. It was, of course as they had embarked on this journey together, but for two different reasons. She was starting to fear returning home. She yearned for it, so very much. But now with each passing minute of each day, it was getting closer. She was fearing it a little more, as the days got less.

He remains stretched out, there, alone, thinking, looking out of the window. An idea blossoms. He will let him know that he is there for her. With that single, presumption, in a solitary split-second Eddy chooses. An answer, a welcoming warming hug. He turns from the bottom bunk, as he leaps up the steel steps to surprise her. His elevation in his mood is plummeting as if he was soaring. Doubting if this was such a great idea. A different answer. He is promptly shot out of the sky. Lia is crying silent tears into her pillow, on his bunk. Her shuffling, jolting shoulders give her away as he peers over. When he, earlier, had returned from the toilet, she had taken his bunk. He had left her in it for the past few hours. Now was the time to reclaim. Two birds with a single stone.

He does not quite know what to do, so he strokes her back. She spasms like his touch was electrocuted shocks. She pushes his hand abruptly away, with a strong violent force. He tries again. Once again, he fails. He feels rejected. Eddy deals with this in an unforgivable way but ignoring her was inexcusable. So, third time's a charm. He positions himself next to her. Leaving a clear gap for her to breathe, for her to feel comfortable. He turns, picks up her travel book, to act nonchalant, while looking at the pages, pretending to read.

His head was having a conversation. With another two people in the cabin, it was hard to act as if it was just the two of them. His reaction then, would have been to continue on the venture on the course of action as the first, the second attempt, the third, until she reacted, or did not, as the case would be. However, they are not alone, so he has to ignore her. The

303

relentless persistence would have caused a row. This turns out to be a strange convulsion that begins a silent argument, where he is not sure what he had done wrong. She unleashes her tears. Each drop, a silent triumph to her failing to express herself adequately. Eddy with a smooth touch, tenderly, barely contacting Lia. He makes the smallest pat on her cold shoulder as he turns away. Returns down the rungs, without his bounty. A mission unaccomplished. He lies, staring through the steel shelf, the mattress to where she lies.

It was time for bed again. Well not really, but there is only so much window staring, card playing and book reading that can be done in a healthy stint. This awkward relationship. This undesirable speed hump, made the next leg a fidgety, tension driven wheel turning journey. Eddy could hear Lia tossing and turning in the squeaking of the loose springs. Lia could hear Eddy doing the same in the rocking of the bunk, that was not just the graceful pounding rhythm of the train.

Lia was starting to worry due to the impending date coming quicker. After all the planning, that end day was coming quicker than a steam train. Eddy, on the other hand, he was trying to formulate a plan to raise Lia's spirits. He was baffled to what he had done, if he had actually done something wrong, but, his mind was a cluster of if's, but's, maybe's. All of which that came up, with a tangent of inconclusive results.

From the resounding stillness, they all overheard from outside an intensifying crescendo of grunts. Altogether they rush to the window to see what the commotion was all about. There arrived just in time as racing through their vision they see a lone horseback rider with a long pole yelling. Heads pressed onto the cold glass they squint the length of the window to see a dust-cascading hurrying herd of brown camels. The smartly dressed rider with a green velvet flat cap-type attire, thrusts a thin, long blunted stick and prods them. The morning sun looked warm but, going by the layers of clothes, the knitted gloves and the thick green hat it was a mere façade.

From between the carriage windows, Eddy and the lone rider had the briefest interaction of a spine-chillingly, direct eye contact. He looked over his herd after the briefest of seconds whereas Eddy started to panic. Eyes locked. He found himself irrationally frightened. It was truly absurd. The lone rider shepherded them over the hill and out of view. They have no idea what it was about. It was perfect, though, for moving the awkwardness of the cabin into the simplicity of life going on around them.

Eddy had just inadvertently found Lia's smile. He not only felt fear, but looked terrified of the unwarranted threat from the ominous stranger. Lia giggled without any up-roaring sound. This break made her relax a little. It derailed Eddy's panic train to the ridiculous talk about the long border crossing, seemingly a long time ago. Also bringing back the unanswered questions about the unexpressed tea-gate saga.

The provodnitsa has been very sheepish indeed since the loud session with the 'tea'. Friendly but keeping them at arm's length. Lia opens the hypothesis that she may have scared her by the way she spoke in Russian. Up until that moment, she may have thought she was a dumb tourist. Eddy lets her believe that one.

Once again, Eddy was surveying and searching the charming charismatic scene beyond his own personal window of pain. The fast moving, momentum passing landscape was hypnotic in the comfortable, calm peacefulness. It was repetitive, it soothed him. Almost tantric meditation that clear his mind of the difficult emotions he is encountering in their relationship.

Unlike his fellow cabinmates, this did not grow old for his eyes. Small towns with half a dozen gers as a settlement came out of nowhere, to disappear as quickly in a blink of an eye. A place where people are just like them. Going about their tasks, their chores, their life. In the far distance, barely a hazy sight of the blurred lines of wind farms that spoil the view but give essential energy to keep the natural environment, liveable. On another track, beyond the cabin and viewed from the narrow passageway was a seemingly endless train. Carriage after carriage of black coal, loaded beyond capacity going in the opposite direction slowly, just kept on going.

Suddenly, the landscaped changed again. From the dark shades of browns and oranges to gorgeous green steppe, rolling green lush hills. More signs of life in the herds of livestock grazing on the lonely turfs of sprouting green grass, emerge from nowhere. The stunning visual silence of the Gobi Desert. The unique way that the empty land sings in the blowing of the soothing wind is left behind. Isolated gers supported by a lone horse, sometimes two, are spread out on the slopes, but become few and far between. The train was experiencing more hills. It has seemed to slow down a little.

With each curve on the track, that encircles the base of the growing hills that go around them in large scenic sweeping arcs make for excellent photographs. Even Lia has become intrigued by the view. They take photographs with the hidden smiles that have been deserting them for most of this journey. For them to be seen doing the thing that they were told as a youngster not to do, stick their head out of the window to get as much of a curve of the train, with the exquisite backdrop in the single frame. This was better to get a photograph than the less-than-clear carriage windows, but they still were very cautious.

They felt the sense of looming near to a city was happening. The landscapes were changing. The noticeable increase in traffic. A settlement of gers surrounded by a brown, twig, fence blurs passed the windows, these will be the last gers for a while. Grey featureless concrete block buildings are rising up with colourful roofs of red, green, blue and yellow. A weak effort to prettify the deteriorated dreadful unattractiveness. The beauty was being replaced by the beast.

At twenty minutes past one in the afternoon, they arrive in Ulaanbaatar, the capital of Mongolia. In the winter months, the coldest capital on the world. They tediously, slowly pull into the covered train station. Nothing more than a glorified shed, yet, it is modest and organised.

The platform is so very busy. They had plenty of time to check that they had everything, to double and triple check. They step down to weave through the crowds like a fine thread, while trying not to hit too many people with their trailing bags. People are talking, laughing, embracing, crying. The squeals of joy. The smell of nostril-widening grease, cigarette fumes. The obvious chill in the air causes Lia to bring her collar up. The smoke and dust from the train. They see the exit, as going the other way would be the end of the platform. They proceed to head towards what deems to be the logical route. They have to push their way through, as no-one moves out of the way. Eddy leads the way, and just like a supportive boyfriend, every now and again, he looks back to see if Lia was still close behind. Honestly though, they are not sure where to really go, it is more of a hunch. They need to leave the platform.

They come to an opening. Lia dumps her bags at Eddy's feet to take charge. She leaves him there, without a word. He is unamused, mystified. Lia is off to find a cab. Leaving Eddy to watch her disperse into the throngs of people, to vanish in the constant flowing flood of human pandemonium. Moments, only a couple of minutes later, she returns from the other side to where she vanished, like a buoyant buoy. Waving both her hands and arms in an animated gesticulation for him to go to her, to follow her. He has all of the luggage. He throws the straps about his person. Feeling like an average mule, he huffs and puffs as he negotiates everyone, everything, to get to the other side. Into the large beautiful tall ceilinged grand entrance of the train station, which he barely notices under the strain.

She sprints like a mouse, scurrying away, clambering the steps, not wanting to get caught by the cat. Outside, in the grey gloomy, overcast day she waits. Leaning into a small, dust-covered silver car like a lace blanket, with no signage she speaks to a stranger. Turns, see a sweaty Eddy, she beckons him forth. The lack of signage, for Eddy, makes him sceptical. After whispered, concerned words into Lia's ear, for which she just brushes them aside. Lia just sharply insists that all was alright. Without assistance, he huffed to make a point, as he put their bags in the open boot. Feeling very ill at ease.

He makes his way to the open door, where Lia is perched forward talking to the driver in Russian. He barely has enough room for him to squeeze in without the door touching the other blockading cars. It is tight as he squeezes in. He is narked that she knows what is going on but seemingly keeps him in the dark.

Although this was not her contention, it infuriated him, nevertheless. He slammed the door. His anger taking over him for an instance, for which he automatically apologises. The railway carpark was a disorganised mess of a jigsaw puzzle, that a child had gotten annoyed with and thrown it high, into the air for the pieces to be a disorderly chaotic mess. Cars, minicars, bikes were in no particular order, squeezed into every angle that could be imagined. How did they get so closed in? The manoeuvring of the vehicles around them, going back and forth, made it clear to why many are missing, or have broken lights, bumps and countless scratches.

Reversing and accelerating forward, bit-by-bit with mere centimetres to spare, they edge around. They finally make it out of this logistic puzzle. They had just noticed the frantic, fraying arms of the policeman issuing disrespected orders. Eddy watches him as he thinks, *bless him, he tries!*

The policeman on duty is shouting, waving, making movements with his baton. Cheeks turning red in small balloons of exasperations as he blows, hard, manically into his whistle to get the cars out onto the street. Finally, it was their turn. The cab driver, who Lia ridiculously introduces as Captain Nemo, uses the policeman, random strangers, outside help and other people in other cars to get out of this disarrayed jumble. Lia had now repositioned herself at the front. Scrambling over the front seat to peer out, pointing spaces the size of keyholes to unlock their metal prison. Trying to help as well. A tense Eddy was waiting for the scraping of metal on metal that, fortunately never materialised. After some nervous minutes, they finally find it out on to the streets, this is when the carpark jumble is explained a little.

Traffic is as disorderly as the carpark. Block cars are facing in all different directions. They pretty much go in any route that they want to go, to get to where they want to go. Road markings are nothing more than pretty decorations. Pedestrians take their chance in a game of a Mongolian-style of Russian Roulette as the purpose human crossings, do not necessarily mean that the traffic will stop for them. The traffic lights are just appealing colours, with no bearing on stop or go. In all purposes it is like a fairground ride of colours, noise and speed.

Captain Nemo is not afraid to use his horn, he uses it even when he does not need to. The window is down, he pumps his fist in the open air as he shouts at another driver. Road rage is the norm; no-one seems to get hurt, but it is very intimidating for Eddy in the backseat staring through his fingers, as it is for Lia, who seems, on the contrary, invigorated by the passion.

Entering the chaotic scene, a middle-aged lady tries her luck in crossing the road.

'She'll bloody need it!' Eddy believes as he watches the potentially, unpreventable accident transpire. This shows the respect that the drivers have for no-one. Someone's mother, daughter, is obviously struggling to hobble with her bent cane across the road, as the cars are so close that the dust from the cars leaves an imprinting smear on her trailing, colourful woollen jacket. Stranded, she is left in no-man's land, in the heart of the fast pulsing traffic, rushing past in both directions. Of course, she gets beeped at to move, but really has nowhere to move to. It is farcical. Eddy cannot bear to watch as they, indeed, blur past. He hopes she makes it. No crash, terrible scream happens within earshot, so he assumes Lady Luck smiled on her, today.

Eddy taps Lia on the shoulder to ask Captain Nemo if this is peak hour. She does and he laughs with an explanation.

'Well,' Lia relays back to Eddy, without turning around, captured, intently on the real-life movie in front of her very eyes. 'This is always peak hour. A constant jam.'

'Get out, here!' Captain Nemo points, as he yells at Lia in Russian.

'What?' She shockingly demonstrates as her hands, arms and body gesticulates in broken contemporary dance movements devoid of music.

'Hotel is there, two hundred metres away. We not going to get closer. Pay. Pay!' His tone sounds agitated as if he has just heard the warning to leave the city of impending doom.

Despite this, he has the uncanny ability to not come across rude. Yet, his tone is rushed, impatient. The facial expression of Lia, combined with her waving hands of a distressed drowning victim. She does not understand him. She is seemingly, adamantly refusing to listen to his instruction. Eddy knows that something has happened, but is perplexed as to what. She quickly explains as she opens the door in a mix of Russian and English. She heads around to the boot with the pose of frustrated steps.

Eddy follows her lead; he understands enough that this journey is over. She instructs him to take the bags as Captain Nemo throws them, nearly onto his feet. She pays. With the dropping of the notes on his rough and dry, callus ridden palms she clicks. The lightbulb gets turned on to what he was saying. She understands the full meaning to his instruction inside the cab. She smiles, apologises. Gives an impromptu hug that she, as well as he, was not expecting. His tone changes. His smile is hidden behind a thick, black curl of immaculately kept glistening twirling styled moustache. He points, they walk the few metres to the hotel. She copiously apologises again to convey her guilt before she turns away.

'Prostite. Izinite. Prostite pozhaluysta'.

It is a lucky coincidence that they do not have to cross the road, which relieves Eddy. She seemed annoyed, but in true Lia fashion, that changed in an instance. The flushing bright rose blush in her embarrassed cheeks was not fading fast.

Effortlessly, they arrive at the door of hotel. 'It is so much easier when two take the luggage,' Eddy attempts to break the ice with a joke. A joke that falls on selective deaf ears. They check in with Lia doing all the talking. Lia is getting more confident in her Russian speaking, this makes Eddy happy. Before they arrived, they were not sure what to expect, but with a relieved phew, it turns out that most of Mongolia also speak Russian. So, it should not cause too much of a problem for which at the planning stages of the journey thought could be a stumbling block of sorts.

They want nothing more than to have a shower after the last day sweating on the train, but they also do not want to miss a thing. If they shower, another part of the day will be gone, lost. It would have been nice, easier, but not helped that a shower will then turn into a relax, a meal and subsequently a lie in a proper soft, motionless bed to sleep. They did not even want to fully check out their room. When they went up, they opened the door to chucked in their bags onto the bouncing bed. Quickly visit the toilet and they were off again. No bite of temptation was going to happen.

At the reception, Lia got instructions for Sükhbaatar Square. They decided to cross the wide road, not so much of decision, but a means that they had to do. Lia is nervous. Eddy, due to his time in Asia has some experience in this unruly patchwork of colourful blurs of painted metal. He takes Lia's hand, fiercely. Together slowly they walk out, remaining forever vigilant to their changing surroundings, but also continuing to walk forward. The trick is that the drivers in the cars do not want to hit people. So, as long as they carry on walking forward, the cars will, surely, miss them, like being a pebble island in a violent flowing stream. A car narrowly missed them by a few centimetres as Eddy dodged his hips out of the way.

Seemingly unflustered, he carried on gripping Lia closer. Inside his ribcage, his racing heart however told the definite truth. They were only halfway. Behind them, the screeching crunch of metal on metal. A wind mirror is thrown into the air, as light as a plastic bag, torn off as they turn around with hunched shoulders expecting impact, to see the aftermath of a close collision. The shouts, the horns, the skid marks for a few seconds in slow motion, then to nothing. Just the cars driving off missing a few cosmetic pieces. No insurance papers, details passed just a volley of swears and hand gesticulations. Their heart rate is high. Their feel stressed. They have to keep moving, as the cars around them do selectively oblivious to what the surroundings are unfolding.

Finally, they are safely over the road, onto the cracked slabs of pavement tiles. Eddy resists the appeal to kiss the dusty, downright filthy grey floor. In unison they relax. They can now walk the rest of the day stress-free.

Standing in the impressive main square of the city, named after the hero of the revolution, Damdin Sukhbaatar, they chuckle breathless stutters of relief. Sukhbaatar declared Mongolia's first independence from the Chinese in July 1921. He is surrounded by a large black heavy chain-rail fence. Shiny yellow upright-sitting dragons, cradling the chains in their mouths to protect the grey step-layered plinth are forever vigilant on each corner. On a large brown boulder, with a depiction of the restart of the Mongolian Republic is a creamy-brown charging horse. His right leg in the air, ready to start a celebrated parade.

On the decorated horseback is the namesake of the square, the revolutionary leader. He who established the Mongolians People Republic in 1921. His pose seems to be offering his hand in a wave to the people below him. His hat has a slight tower in the middle. They remark on the significance without knowing the answer. Sükh means axe, Baatar means hero. The people below are not gathering support for him, but a small handful of tourists, taking photographs. Close by are bicycles for hire, families meeting up, friends chatting. No-one but the tourists are actually taking any notice of this huge significant icon. They look around it as they circle navigate the large statue. Below the charge of the horse is a tombstone-type inscription, for which they are not sure what it signifies, other than a monumental tribute.

Around the square, like a wall, are several large buildings that peer down, as if looking down an open well. Although the statue is deemed to dominate the area, this is purely due to location, not its size. The large green pastel buildings with darker green roof are the stock exchange, museums, town hall and the main theatre. In the modern looking block building, with large clear blue-glass windows is the Government building of Parliament house. A modest light police blue material belt on blue metal poles politely cordons off the area. The hero of the Revolution looks towards this large building, respecting the out-of-bounds tape.

Many small steps lead up towards the entrance. Guards looking like toy soldiers in a dark green cloth uniform protect the unknown contents. To the centre of the entrance in a gigantic, dark alcove. Inside is a rather chubby Genghis Khan, cast in bronze. He sits on a large decorative throne, glittering in the small rays of sunshine that penetrate the gloomy skies. His legs wide open with a robe protecting his modesty. The robe, belt and attire depict a heavy metal cloth. It is made of bronze, but the layers of thick material that would be traditional give the appearance of looking heavier. He looks on with a smugness, long hair perfectly cut, flawless skin. Each, thick arm rest cradles his large boulder, muscular arms to his curling chubby fingers around the edges.

This square holds many stories. On this same, very square was the foundations that built this city. Some of the soaring block grey buildings that surround the area like decaying birch trees, nearly seventy years after they were quickly erected, protests took place. These led to the fall of Communism in 1990. As the name, Ulaanbaatar is a Soviet name from the communist era meaning, Red Hero, a large majority of people want to change the name of the capital. The public census is to an ancient Mongolian one. This, according to Lia's research will happen one day, sooner rather than later. But until then, the residents will have to wait and live with that constant reminder of the former Soviet life that they had endured.

Around the square are young girls wearing what looks like French maid outfits. Entirely out of place. Balancing with light tapping as they delicately shuffle around each other, complete with dark patterned stockings and black stiletto shoes. They are shaky, bambi-esque in there higher than high heels with twig-thin legs that could snap in a light breeze. Finished the somewhat erotic attire, are gleaming white, perfectly creaseless ironed aprons. This gets Eddy's attention. As confusion, for each girl is pure jailbait. Confused, he does not understand what is going on.

On a windy, chilly day are young girls in French maid outfits looking at Genghis Kahn, while getting their photographs taken by smartly suited young men. Lia is as confused as Eddy. She asks a passing elderly lady what is going on. They talk animated in Russian, well, to Eddy's untrained ear anyway. With a slight disjointed conversation by Lia's rusty, pigeon pronunciation. Along with the fact that the elderly lady is speaking a slightly different dialect, they conclude the conversation. Lia giggles as she finally turns to Eddy.

'They, they're school children.' She shrugs her shoulders. 'Apparently!'

'No! No way!' Eddy exclaims, aghast.

'That is the uniform. The white shows that they are not at school today. The white apron. Today, it is a public holiday. If they were at school, the colour of the aprons would be red.' She tries to compose herself throughout the explanation. Eddy's astonished etched facial expression and his mouth wide open in evident, but understandable shock at this revelation, does not help her situation. She barely controls herself to share the unoffered information from the elderly lady.

'She also told me that no taxis are in Mongolia. So you just put your hand up and someone will give you a lift, for a small fee of your choice…normally. See! See! You see Eddy! That is what I told you on the way to the hotel. Captain Nemo was correct. And to think. To think that YOU, you, doubted me…Tsk.'

Unable to conceal his outward showing fixed all over his face, Eddy unpeels his eyes to move from his rooted position. The assistance of a sharp tug of his sleeve from Lia sways him towards the edge of the square, the roadside. Taking the advice of the elderly lady they try to see if her tip deems to be successful. It works. For less than a dollar they get driven back to their hotel. Or so they thought. Or Eddy thought anyway. Lia was talking to the driver. Where they should have zigged, they zagged. Eddy can tell that they are not going the right way, that this was not the way they came. He fidgets in the backseat.

Lia turns behind, sensing his nervous energy and just smiles. Sharing no hint of what is going on. Without Eddy's knowledge, she had decided to go on the driver's recommendation. Rumour from the driver has it that this is a must-see site. Lia had, in a split second. A motive that was completely out of character for her. She had been persuaded, to successively agree with the driver. She had arranged that they get taken to the site, to view a sight he spoke high off. The largest and most important monastery in Mongolia.

It is a short drive to Gandantegchinlen Khiid, for which Lia relays to Eddy that the taxi driver, and she uses that term loosely, has told her that it means the Great Place of Complete Joy. She follows with a disjointed translation of the history. The large 1838 monastery, is the most important within the Mongolian culture, as eighty percent believe in Mahayana Buddhism. Outside the wooden gates, the driver insists on waiting until their have finished viewing the site. They both try to get him to leave. They do not want to feel rushed. They do not know how long they will take. Money is a concern, so they do not want to be charged for his waiting.

This proves to be a fruitless argument. They turn defeated. They leave him by his battered fiat. He leans on the dark red bonnet, scratched as if a steel wool rather than a sponge has been used to buffer it. He looks down at the driver's door, for which they did not see before. This has obviously been rebuilt as the two tonal colours of red do not match. He withdraws a thin, long white stick. Lights it with a flick of a grey lighter with a large flickering flame and continues to puff on a cigarette. With each inhale, he exhales into the sky. He looks into the skies as he blows plumes of smoke up and smiles. He is a happy young man.

Eddy and Lia enter the temple, they glance back at the driver who seems wistfully content surrounded by his smoke. A silent beggar sits on her haunches, next to her is a cane resting on her grimy blue blanket where her body and legs are wrapped in an uncomfortable rigid ball. She is positioned to observe everyone, with a cold steel eyed, defiant stare. Her cream, beaten white hat and white-clothed mouth guard shows enough of her alert wide eyes, that she sees entirety who comes, who goes. Vigilantly watching. They feel uncomfortable by her persona. Without intending to, they leave a slightly wider breadth to avoid being inexcusably grabbed.

They feel her intensively but, without seeming to, quicken their stride towards the wooden entrance. The focus of that sight is a colourful painted affair of flowers, rings, surrounding the timber with nothing left plain. It is a beautiful, elaborate and elegant entrance that gives them the perfect excuse to keep staring at. With a soft smooth smell of fragrant incense delicately caressing their noses, they breathe in the crisp chilly air. Underfoot, the gravel changes to small cobbled grounds, worn smooth by time. In the distant monks can be heard chanting in unison. All the soft, complete words make the sound outside of the temple become a pacifying hum, but precisely in time. Soothing.

Just before they cross the threshold, a monk greets them. Realising very quickly that Eddy would not be the perfect choice to converse with, he speaks to Lia, who translates for Eddy. The jovial monk, bordered by sad eyes, tells them to be respectful. It is not quite an order, or a warning, but with enough sternness in the expression to adhere to his commands. Obviously, even to Eddy who cannot fathom where the dialogue has turned, he senses sadness. The monk evades deep eye contact. He has a crack in his voice, a scar which no time will heal. He pats his eyes from tears that have been shed, a freshness that can continue to fall. The memory, as raw as it was when it happened.

Eddy stood listening. Not understanding anything, but patiently waiting for an explanation. Lia, with a tremor in her voice, repeats. The sadness of the story has been infectious in her translation. She explains that this was a place of horrific destruction and slaughter during the Soviet times. He explained what happened, what is happening, as they walk towards a colourful red prayer wheel, in a pale sun-bleached red timber framed green, yellow and blue painted wall-less shelter. The story and the surroundings do not match. Lia pauses every now-and-again to repeat the occurrence. The haunting circumstances to Eddy. He is picking up all that she puts down but is disjointed in her clarifications.

The entrance acts as a curtain to present the main temple. The faint chanting of the monks gets louder as they walk closer to the origin, the main green hipped roof temple. The monk shadows them with his informative speech. The soft touch of the bell starts to ring. Unseen cymbals crash in a dull clink, as if metal garbage lids have been quickly placed together. Around me snuff is being sniffed. An elderly lady that looks the same to the one outside pushes some money notes into the hands of a monk who gives blessings in exchange. They watch the monk's mouth moves as his arms wave around her. She bows her head. Her eyes smile, sparkle.

As they draw inside the temple, the chanting sound begins to be a loud whisper. The monk instructs them to be respectful, to not take any photographs. To Lia's untrained eye, it looks very Chinese in the influence, just like a building in the Forbidden City. The green hipped roof with the creatures on the eaves, the golden yellow crown of a small pagoda type crowning feat. The pale, but vibrant red wooden pillars for the green, painted colourful eaves. Inside monks, forcefully whisper, prayer. Icons are adorned with money notes stuffed into the crack's, the crannies, the feet.

A collection of many, different buildings are within the complex, each with different story, a different tale to be told. A simple symbol of support is placed outside one of the temples. The slight metre tall statue tells the story of an elephant that could not reach the apples on the tree. He asks a rabbit to help, so the rabbit gets on his back but still cannot reach. They ask a monkey who does the same and still the trio cannot reach. A dove finishes the symbolic statue by being on the monkeys back and reaches the apple. By standing on each other's shoulders they get to reach the apples, then handing them down, one by one, so each essential link in the chain can have a rewarding apple. In Australia they call this mateship. It is a rich word that describes the cultural uniqueness of Australian life.

For being an important monastery, it is not that busy. Sure, people are around, but the sound of the monks, the occasional birds whistling in the now blue skies, the sound of the murmuring blessings. These are the only sounds. The only evidence of life.

They have taken their time looking at each of the different buildings. Listening to the monk's tales. At the exit, the taxi driver is still there, smoking what seems like a never-ending, smouldering cigarette. He comes over with the cigarette hanging limply from his mouth, a smile on his lips and a hand waving them forward. Apparently, he has had an idea. He tells Lia, who feigns interest. She explains to Eddy who cannot understand why she is pretending to be interested to go. Evidently, the driver takes no to mean, well, yes. They are being driven to the only surviving palace in Mongolia, the Winter Palace of the Bogd Khann. Lia is

310

unimpressed. Arms folded ready to unleash a mini tantrum. Tiredness is starting to change her mood, as well as being hungry. Cranky when without food, she has the sinister bite of a gremlin.

They are dropped off outside a brown area. Straw squares of dry grass make up a drab quilt. 'This can't be the place,' Eddy thinks as he surveys the barren, derelict space. Then around the corner they peer, towards the wild pointing instruction of the driver. Vast, thick red pillars of timber like nervous walking legs support green Chinese hipped roofs, as if they are in a still picture of a march. Wooden soldiers protecting the entrance but in a patrolling moment frozen in time.

Behind this impressive gate that mimics the colours and the Chinese influences seen at the monastery, is the entrance. The centre of the entrance is a three-tier roof flanked by a two-tiered roof that towers above the small red, timber wooden wall that surrounds the enclosure. They pay the fee before setting foot inside. Within, the grass has been watered slightly, it now holds flickers of green. It is not the most manicured, but it is a light straw feel of a dusting of green.

The main house looks like an afterthought. The curved green building, a wooden corrugated pattern with yellow rims has been erected in the middle. Beautiful nevertheless, although it does not quite fit the surroundings. Yet, this structure housed the eighth living Buddha, and, the last King, Jebtzun Damba Hutagt VIII. Here is where he lived here for twenty-five years.

Eyes wide, Lia is not feigning interest anymore, she is genuinely happy to be here. For sure she is tired, almost certainly hungry but the realisation has hit, she may not, if ever come here again. Frustratingly enough, once again, no photographs are permitted inside. Looking more like an antique shop, which has been added to over, and over, again but has not had too much sold to declutter the stock. Each ornament has a sign, a tag and label describing what is being exhibited. It is too much. It becomes too much of a blur. Too much of a hectic explosion of unsystematic artefacts, jumbled together in no logical order, to make sense. They see it for the beauty that it is, without trying to piece together the disorganised chaos, to make a well thought out structural process.

Standing out is a single colour photograph in a simple, gold rimmed frame. This shows the Emperor. This is the only photograph that they see. According to legend, a picture is believed to shorten a life by one year, hence every photograph, where here there is only a few, he is not smiling.

Eddy leans in and whispers to Lia, 'If you were going to have a photo taken at the cost of a year. Why? I mean, make it a good one. You know! A big beaming smile. Be happy. Rather than looking. Looking, well, frankly, irritable. Make it…dammmn good-looking. This. Well, he is miserable, probably because of what it cost, but smile. Smile a big smile. Not. Not, this miserable, unapproachable, inhospitable face like a smacked arse.'

Lia giggles and tries to retain the laughter inside her from pouring out. They walk out in muted conversation, with the shaking of shoulders from laughter within. Back in the straw-grass square they speak the same mutual idealist notion of what should be represented inside. They do not argue that it was nice to see such a great piece of history, but the arrangement was pretty amateurish.

On their approach back around the corner, they half hoped that the driver was not there. Although they did not know where they were, how they would get back, they wanted to cut these ties loose. For which they were getting more of that unpleasant feeling, as if they were puppets being directed by him, in his own personal puppetry. Behind them, the halted gate that had come to a standstill in chasing them off the former King's residence, they optimistically held their breath. Their heart, as well as their chin, drops, hits the bottom.

The cheery cab driver throws half his cigarette to the side as he exhales a thick grey cloud through a shouted Russian hello, 'PRIVET!', to reveal an open passenger side door as the smoke clears. They trundle grudgingly to the enthusiastically positive driver. They both board into the backseats and shuffle together into the centre, as the creaking door slams shut, they hold each other.

In true salesman style, he plays his temptation persuasive card. He tries. He attempts. He gives so many reasons why they should go to this sight, to that sight, to see as much as they can. He is unrelenting in his pursuit. However, Eddy and Lia want to go back to the hotel. They have not started driving when their protests are eventually heard. Silence that no noise could cut was inside the cab. Around them, the outside world continued to honk and swear. They were dropped off back at the hotel, albeit one last throw of the dice, his business card. Somewhat creased, to some extent tarnished, but legible, well, to Lia all the same. They pay the ridiculously cheap charge and leave him at the kerb while he not so much asks, but yells to them to call him if they need anything.

After being cooped in a carriage for over thirty hours, they want to shower the filth off. However, time's a-changing. They get into the foyer and talk to the concierge. She takes no time in considering as she quickly recommends a good walk. He did eagerly propose, which she insisted they should leave now. Thus, to get there and back before nightfall. They look at each other. They take a split-second, a moment to think it through, mutually in seconds they turn back to the entrance, the exit. They are on their way.

To get to the base alone was a longer than anticipated walk, but they found many topics to talk about, and the silences. When there was silence that reared their agreeable head, they found them to be soothing, comfortable, lovingly natural. They thought this was going to be the hard part, the distance. However, as they got closer to the peak of the steep incline, bear in mind that they were not halfway up yet, it was as if they were on a treadmill, going nowhere fast. Their head pushing with force down, pressing into their collars. Jumpers brought up tight, shielding their mouths. Eyes squinting against the compelling splinters of dust piercing through the air. The wind was getting replaced by a borderline hurricane. Slowly, but surely, they got to the peak. All the time thinking if it was going to be worth it. Amazingly enough, the tempest diminished to a low, but very cold wind as they reached the plateau.

At the peak, they are in the presence of a towering monument for which their use as protection. A feeble attempt to restore the warmth. They shout above the howl of the wind, as it moves around like supernatural movements that show their tight passages, but not for whom is making the voluminous advances. They cannot hear each other but they understand why the concierge mentioned that it will be hard. Somewhere that was lost in translation, for what they thought. This was not due to the distance, or the steepness, but it was difficult due to the wind.

Literally standing boot high, they look up, squinting under the sun, which is warm, but the wind takes away any pleasurable basking temperature to a nose-running cool chill. On the fifteenth anniversary of the Communist Revolution is a huge grey stone towering memorial. This honours the Soviet and Mongolian soldiers who died in World War Two, in the fight against Japan and Nazi Germany. The main statue is a block Soviet Soldier carrying a flag which waves behind him joining a huge stone ring. The soldier looks into the distance, looking stern, strict and focused. His left arm straight by his side gripping a rifle, his right straight in the air holding the flagpole for the blowing flag behind. The large ring hovers in the air, with the statue masking as a supporting column. Medals and badges are on the outside. Whereas in the middle, circulating around the inside of the ring, is a colourful mosaic composition illustrating friendship and accomplishments between the two countries.

They walk around the soldier's feet, struggle up the small flight of stone steps into, to found themselves inside of the ring, to glance around. A Russian astronaut in an orange attired spacesuit looks towards the centre. Equipped with a white helmet with the lettering CCCP in his right hand, as he holds hands with a lady in a white long-sleeved dress. Where a young boy in front of her holds a white dove. So many depictions of agriculture, space missions, various industries. Pivotally, historically, displayed is the putting down of the Nazi flag, below the raising of the red Soviet flag with the golden sickle and hammer. In the centre is an eternal flame that is winning the fight to stay alight in the bellowing wind. Flickering in a deep bowl that surely must be powered by gas to keep it alight.

The chilly top of the rather small hill, armed with the steep ascent of Kosciusko, shows the sprawling low-lying concrete capital below. Uglier in the manmade design that spreads out similar to an unwanted virus. The saving grace are the magnificent grey hills, scattering with magical green fairy dust as the backdrop to urban progress, which to Lia looks like urban decay of, what is, a stunning countryside. As they look over, they do exactly what everyone else does, they look for their hotel. Trying to find a landmark of only being here a few short hours is the first task.

This proves a little harder, but they eventually find their starting point, Sukhbaatar Square. From here they trace, with their eyes, a walk that should be where the hotel is. Yet, a large blue shining modern shell of a building is in the way. They denounce that the hotel is behind the blue orb. This was going to be the tallest building in Mongolia. However, the best laid plans, became a flaw. This is when they realised halfway through the construction, that it was leaning, essentially falling. After much talks and discussions. Throwing and weighing up many options and solutions. There was only one choice left on the table. The only thing to do was to bring it down, bit-by-bit, to start again, to reconstruct it properly. A disaster, but it could have been so much worse.

The chill has turned into an even stronger, briskly cold relentless streaming gust of blustery wind. The gathering for warmth did not work as the wind seems to be coming from all, and every direction. Quickly, they snap a few photographs before heading back down the rubbish torn hill. This blot on the landscape, they did not notice on the way up. They head back down to the city, which, unfortunately cannot, thus far, be described as beautiful. They find it easier to look as their descend.

The old Soviet Union lingers with evident appeal, lingering in the city with its architectural block buildings built fast, cheaply and dam right hideous. The old, very old in some cases, Russian cars blow out dirty looking, smelling smoke that you expect more from a wood fire chimney, rather than a small fuel powered exhaust. The drab apartments pierce the beautiful clear blue skies to penetrate the whispers of grey-tinged clouds. That blatantly potently illustrate the unattractiveness of the boring, chunk of grey stone buildings.

The destruction, the systematic obliteration of cultures and religions unrecognised by the growing armies in World War Two in the form of monasteries, palaces, temples and other holy institutions make the concrete urban spread with the word jungle, never being more aptly used as a description for a city. They erased the beauty and replaced it with this, parking lot.

As they walk back through the capital, they murmur that it is not what they expected. They mutually agreed that they did not know what they expected, but they thought it would be more colourful, more, much more pretty. The city does have a fascinating blend of lacklustre communist with brilliant Asian architect. However, the Stalin architecture crumbles in faded grandeur as the history is remembered, but left to fall from the unremarkable greatness, with shiny modern buildings being erected. Slowly the city is growing up, rising from the communist era's ashes.

To conclude the busy day, they go into the hotel to ultimately relax, to freshen up. Eddy tries not to fall asleep as he lies in the heated hotel room in a woolly white hotel dressing gown. He has showered, shaved and was having a well-earned break. Lia bursts into the room, she mischievously looks at Eddy as she seductively casts off her blue coat. Recklessly kicks off her dirty white runners, a twinkle in her steely focused eyes fixed firmly on Eddy's. Peels off her tight blue jeans, her loose woollen red top, she lazily throws down, unto the lush floral carpet, as she, all the time, motions towards where Eddy lies. She winks.

She launches at him like a beautiful naked bird with just her pale blue lingerie in flight. She gracefully lands onto the space in the bed next to Eddy. He bounces as the springs compress and release around him like a waterbed. A flashback to good times, carefree times, as a very young child on a bouncy castle. She is visually excited as she tears the timetable out of Eddy's hands. Leafs through the timetable for their next destination of Russia, a new country, a country closer to her destination. Her home. Eddy was thinking one thing was going to happen; unfortunately, the opposite occurs. Nothing sexual.

'What's going on?' Eddy smoothly ponders to Lia.

She smirks. Her voice peaks slightly in a higher octave with an animated musical aspect as she tells Eddy of her plan tomorrow.

'Well, we are—' then she changes her mind. 'Nothing.' She leaps out and slowly takes her bra off. Wiggles her knickers off and makes her way into the bathroom.

'Get ready; we are going to the State Theatre tonight,' she yells as the door slams shut behind her. The sound of the rushing water from the shower. Her singing.

'Was that an order?' Eddy asks, more to himself. He lays there for a while. Confused. He then proceeds to do as she instructed.

As Lia gets ready, she explains that she has also arranged an evening at a Mongolian Cultural Show for, which she waves the tickets under his nose. She still does not let on tomorrow's plan. Eddy muses once more to himself, about it being a ploy by the concierge to gain commission, a tourist trap no less. He hoped it was wrong, but they will see in the next hour. An experience anyway he deduces.

Under the angelic male intonation from the huge, gorilla-sized mammoth of a gruff-looking man on the front desk, they started walking. His soft, gentle demeanour was a surprise to them, so much so that they did not fully follow his loose direction as he answered their question. The distance was short, thankfully. They were at the theatre instantaneously. Eddy shows off his chivalrous side by opening the heavy oak door for Lia to gracefully glide through. The heat of the theatre is suffocating, it knocks them back as if they were punched. A warm slap in the face literally takes their breath away.

After a few precious seconds, they recompose themselves. Present their tickets, to get ushered silently into a cosy room as they wrestle to take off their coats, to acclimatise fully in this uncomfortable parching high temperature. Inside the velvet-lined doorway that leads into the cosy chamber, a thick, heavy red carpet with a colourful green, gold, cream and red symmetrical circular emblem dominates the centre with a cream border of the carpet. This plays as the stage.

Frosted windows with green Chinese-influenced geometric green borders are blackened out. Softly swaying, as softly as the same cloth lantern bands of light blue, red, yellow and dark blue that hang from the cream and red ceiling, softly brushing the air leaving space to the stage for the performers. The room is stuffy and hot. They are motioned to sit on the small red cushion with gold tassels looking towards a white cloth screen with the same green borders as the frosted windows, flanked by red cloth drapes with golden Chinese symbols and dragons. Beside us is a huge colourful green thick drum hanging by red string in a red frame with a large brass horn cradling in the middle. The stage is set.

They could set their own watches by the precise time a group of eight musicians appeared upon the carpet, the floor stage. With the main middle-aged man dressed in silky blue attire, weighed down by numerous gold bands as belts and a black brimmed hat with a conical cylindric blue top he swept over the modest crowd with his small, piercing black eyes. He was confidently prominent in his open stance, that was a full step in front of the assembly.

All the females have the same blue silky coloured gown with a black robe over their shoulders and split in the centre with silver trims. They wear a silver crown that towers up into a round cylinder similar to a perfectly formed meringue-topped pie, which then hangs down like silvering twinkling hair. Forming small beads that droop down to below their shoulders, they all look elegant. They are beautiful in facial features with tiny, small waists but akin to ice queens or princess with this elaborate frosty glimmering headwear. The assortment of instruments are different to what Eddy had seen.

At the end of the first opening piece, they are absorbed by the sounds. Fortunately, an English translator, from the side of the stage, explains the traditional music, followed by the musical instruments as they are introduced to the crowd of mostly tourists as a performer plucks, blows or strikes softly, as the description is presented. Unique sounds, costumes, each as magnificent as the last, makes them think that the concierge may not have been after a quick buck after all.

A man on the far right plays a horsehead. A square-shaped guitar with a long neck played like a cello, with a bow brushing over the two strings, this is called a marin whoor. The translator proudly states that this has been around since Genghis Khan. Eddy cannot help thinking that it did not catch on with the rest of the world though. The sound is a vibrating soundbox of a quivering note that shivers its way to them. Slowly pacing with the traditional music, they form into exceptional music from what seemed like irregular chimes at the start.

From one side, in elaborately dressed vibrant red with symmetrical burgundy flowers. Mirroring thick golden bands of the first man on his gown a youthfully, thick, top-heavy male enters the stage on pencil-thin legs. Wearing a thick heavy gold waistcoat that gets done on one side and a black hat he has his arms folded in front of him, as if cradling his barrel chest, with blue frilly wristbands, which seem a little out of place, a little modern with his prior time-honoured attire. From the other side a women smoothly paces towards the man, as if floating gracefully on air. She is dressed very similar in a bright red silky own with burgundy flowers a black hat. She also has blue wristbands that support her hands like warmers as she has them in the same position as her counterpart. They both stop, just before they meet in the centre. They pivot sharply, they both point steadfast towards the audience. Dramatically placing their hands back inside their sleeves. They both open their mouths.

'What?' Eddy cannot help asking out loud. 'What is THIS, er, sound?'

The sound was strange, unearthly. The translator tells them that this is Khoomi, Mongolian throat singing that is apparently famous, world famous. Obviously, it has not hit the shores of Australia. The sound that they produce is a strange mix of two different sounds at the same time. One sound is a low pitch guttery growl, as if a bear is being strangled that then joins in to the other. The other is a high pitch, melodious whistle, but seems to be coming from the chest rather than the lips. It is spookily pretty, certainly it is the only noise of its kind.

When they had finished, the translator talks more about Khoomi, with only four universities studying it. It is a very difficult technique to learn. So hard that many people do not make the grade. She says more facts, but they are both absorbed in this new sound from a human body, and the new sounds from the instruments with a combination of different notes, music that drowns out her useful knowledge.

The rotund man is left on the stage alone. He closes his eyes, creases his brow as he performs a magnificent solo. The strange buzzing sound that oscillates and vibrates over the sweet fragrant incense burning smells in the air to the small, intimate crowd. It is impressive as if he has swallowed a mandolin. The crowd enwrapped, even if he does look slightly constipated as he performs his five-something minute solo.

Back on the stage, accompanied by the male musician he plays the marin whoor with a very serious look on his face, as two dances in white silky baggy robes with a floral black and red tunic performs around them. On the heads of the dancers are a light blue skull cap, where a china bowl-like a rice bowl is stuck on. In her hands are a white rice bowl in which she uses as she gracefully sails over the red-carpet seas on the waves of the singer. She is strikingly beautiful with smooth skin as smooth as the bowls. A touch as gracefully effortlessly silky as porcelain. Yet, she looks as if she was doing the dishes before bursting into a ballet-esque dance.

A very young lady, whom appears to be barely sixteen, dressed in a skin-tight white body suit with purple highlights, as if she was an Olympian athlete, rolls, literally rolls in. She bends her body in ways that makes the whole audience in unison grimace. This freakishly impossible act should surely hurt. Still the smile on her face states it is pleasurable, devoid, free of the slightest hint of any pain. With the suppleness of a rubber band she uses poles to balance, to twist, turn and construct her body in inhumane ways that bones should prevent. This girl was amazing.

Eddy and Lia were, not for the first time this evening, transfixed as she went through her routine breathlessly with her body contorting into such extraordinary complex positions. Cirque du Soleil has nothing on her. All the surrounding noises could be heard from outside, but in this room, the trapped breath of everyone inside rendered the room as silent as the cloud-like girl that preformed before them.

The performance finishes with all the performers in intricate, more detailed dresses in gold and silver returning to the stage. The attire is completed, they would not say complimented, with a colourful rainbow throwing up over them as they cover their heads with huge animal masks that cover the head like a huge cumbersome helmet, with comical tongues sticking out. They cannot see the eye holes in the ceramic, very heavy looking masks. Their small human hands look wacky in comparison as they hold lamps with maybe a genie inside, as they move, float over the carpet.

Although this was a tourist trap. Eddy had to fully admit to Lia that it was not the waste of money he thought it was. The feast of hearing the music, watching them play, the dancing, the incredible contortionist, the traditions, it was a great hour that flew past fast. The detailed intricate dresses, uniforms, music floating like a butterfly with the colours stinging like a powerful heart stopping punch.

Eddy is starving. He is literally ready to eat a horse's head, but not a marin whoor. To his mocking surprise, this is a common meat.

'When in Rome...' Eddy muses as they find a restaurant around the corner from their hotel and on their way back. It is busy so they use it as a good sign to enter. Nothing elaborate here. The walls are plainly painted, poorly brown with paintbrush streaks in nonsensical wavy lines. The table is chipboard covered in a brown cloth, white paper napkins and cutlery in a clay pot. They are not fussy. They give Lia Cyrillic menus as she addressed them on entry in Russian.

'Horse it is,' Lia mocks as she goes for a chicken salad. Eddy suggests they share. Lia was not convinced, until Eddy in the end convinced her. It was not quite an arm twist but a substantial resistance.

The thinly sliced horse meat comes out on a black iron sizzling dish supported on a wooden board. A thick, gloopy brown gravy covers the meat. The steam from the black tray and the bubbling sides did not stop the server from stating the obvious; that it was hot. The smell was meaty, no surprise there. Lia's salad produced a slight chuckle from Eddy. Literally what it said on the tin, fried chicken on a bed of dressed lettuce leaves. She got what was written. Eddy's dish was getting larger. A side of vegetables dripping in water, a salad and some very crispy deep-fried potatoes liberally covered in dill, wholly served in a ramshackle of crockery. The meal could have served three or four. It was huge. They shared their meal.

'Not bad,' Eddy acknowledges as he tries horse for the first time. 'Stronger flavour than beef with a, a slight spice, a pepper? Maybe to it...erm...but, not bad!'

They discussed the performance. They laughed, clinked their glasses of water and tried to finish their banquet. Making it through two thirds there were tired. They needed sleep. They returned. Not even going through the formalities of brushing their teeth they collapsed into their tightly made bed. Holding hands. Asleep instantly.

BEEP BEEP BEEP.

The telephone piercingly rings an odd tone through the pale light as it vibrates, literally ready to ring itself off the brown wooden bedside table. Lia jumps up to answer her prearranged wakeup call while Eddy peels himself from the ceiling. Eddy has no idea what Lia has signed him up for as they hastily pack. They get ready to depart to the square where the local bus will take them to the secret destination to Eddy, but not for Lia of Terelj National Park. Although he was relieved to be spending a day out of the unsightly capital, into the Mongolian countryside. He thinks it is a day trip, Lia has other ideas. Yet, another great surprise for which he takes as her mood is enlightened today.

By the means of the agitating aid of Lia's feverish harassing hands to rush Eddy along, to the point of getting on his nerves, they nearly sprint out of the hotel glass doors without settling their account. Consequently, arriving early, before the scheduled time. As they turn the corner, they see, what they presume is the bus for their journey, is already there. They think quickly, maybe they got the time wrong, or the concierge did, were they going to miss it? So, in seeing the rusty bus, they rush over to the other side of the large square, cumbering with all their luggage as if the flat paving stones had turned to an uneven mountain trail path.

It was so impromptu, therefore, the straps were not in the correct position to run. So, they bounced on their collarbones, rubbed their backs and bounced around, defying gravity for seconds at a time, to come down in a bruising brutal touch of soreness.

In what can be described as a metal cage on wheels, they try to carefully place their bags inside, the driver has other ideas as he breathlessly shoves them into place. Lia examines, having a quick inspection around the minibus, as their luggage gets heaved and rammed shut by the metal cage door. Once it was dazzling white, now it had every shade of torment-afflicted colours in the form of dinks, scratches and dents from several crashes, near misses. This does not inspire confidence.

Peeking into the open passenger's slide-door, into the interior of the tired tinned minibus, was like looking into a can of sardines. Compressed faces peered back, holding onto each other and possessions for dear life. It was cramped with a rich smell of oil, grease, petrol and sweat. They wrestle, nudge and wriggle into a space. The screech and scrape of metal slides the passenger door shut. As haunting as a coffin lid closing down, forever. The squeak of the driver's doors slams shut, which vibrates the whole minibus, the door itself nearly bouncing back out of its loose latch. Lia sees him tie a piece of knotted grey rope around the handle to the steering wheel. She was not reassured by this action.

After a few stuttering, hesitating to move tries, the engine splutters into a remnant of life with a huge bellow of thick black smoke. Undeterred, he presses the accelerator down, removes the choke as the car coughs like an old man at the end of his days. He crunches the minibus into gear, not before lighting a thin cigarette. Exhaling the fumes through corrupted lungs, he moves forward, without looking into his cracked, redundant mirrors. They rickety shake with equally protesting noise from the worn-out minibus into the traffic.

When in motion, they glide distressingly unsteady on the smooth road. Cutting traffic off, weaving in a slow but purposeful style as if he or the minibus was on its own personal death wish. They tried to look back, hoping that the luggage would remain on the top of the roof, but more so their luggage at the back, all that they own, would be at the final destination.

Settling into the jerking pattern of the journey they thanked that they were not carsick, they prayed that they would remain in one piece, they hoped for a safe voyage. Barely fifty kilometres out of the city the smooth tarmac is forgotten. The road changes to gravel. This abrupt goodbye to paved road was welcomed with Lia smashing her head on the roof of the minicab. If the smooth road was rough, a name for this in the canned minibus—was a word that had not originated yet.

Photographs out of the window were a joke, never going to happen. They shook, danced and vibrated their way on the two-hour drive through glorious landscapes. Through forest and mountains and out of the valley where Ulaanbaatar rests to the real Mongolian experience, that was not just getting there. Ahead is a dirt road, road is very much the only thing you would call it, but even that is stretching the truth.

Dotting the undying landscape are yaks, horses, goats and cows. The jagged mountains, green lush trees, everlasting splendour. This is what they were expecting. Of the whole population of Mongolia, over half live in the capital, Ulaanbaatar. The rest live the traditional, nomadic lifestyle in the countryside.

They arrive. Finally. Like being back from sea their legs are a little weak as they adjust to the normal gravity. The fresh smell of a mint like aroma greets them as the door grinds open and they pour out like a tin of live sardines fresh to water.

Lia races to the visitor's centre, popping out like a cork. While Eddy stands outside wondering where she is going. She darts through into, what he presumes is the warmth leaving him shivering in the cold. He gathers their luggage that has been hurled onto the grey sandy earth before him. Dusting down the bags, half angry, half annoyed. Before preceding to follow to the building where she went. At the midway point, she erupts out in smiles, waving a large map. Eddy was so perplexed and flummoxed as to where he was, what was happening. He was led to believe that they were going to go back to the hotel tonight. Foolishly, irrationally, the penny only just dropped that they had paid in full, at the hotel.

'What's going on—' Eddy demonstrates as he drops the bags down.

'You need to calm down,' interrupts Lia.

'What? ME? Didn't we? Lia, please,' he begs, 'what is going on?'

Once again Lia ignores him as she reveals the second part of her surprise. The first being the traditional cultural show last night. This surprise involves that she had booked an allocated ger for a couple of nights to experience the nomadic life.

'A what? Grrrr. A GGGrrrr. What the heck is a Grrrr?' exclaims Eddy.

'Ger,' Lia giggles at his mispronunciation.

'Okay. To be pedantic, a Ger. What is it? What is a Ger?'

'You'll see.'

'Are you kidding me right now? Hey, where you taking…me?'

The wind whistles across the countryside and stings the exposed cold noses, but Eddy does not fully notice. Annoyed as he is, he watches Lia tantalise, tease and torment him as she sways her body like only a woman can. This does in fact calm his mood down, but he is still so confused to what is going on. She slowly winks, taunts him with an innocent charm over her shoulder, polished up in a smouldering seductive look. Even in her long, rather unflattering brown coat, trailing dark green scarf, her body moves in a way the leads Eddy, like a ship by her siren.

He hurries over for the short walk around the corner, behind the brown, grey rocky hill. There she heads towards a round tent covered in colourful canvas and cloth, supported by a wooden top with a metal chimney sprouting out of the softly peaked centre. Soft plumes of grey smoke spirals upwards. In sprinklings up the hill are various white, thick heavy-laden cloth tents like candy on a summitting cake. She looks down at the map in her red, cold dry hands and then up. Motioning up, she moves towards one of the tents on the hillside via a twisting manicured brown soil path.

'This, my love, is a ger.' Lia displays with hands raising as if a gift on the Price is Right outside, as Eddy carries the luggage like a mule.

She patiently waits for him. A quick photograph to show his struggle up the hill. Not concealing her delight, not even trying to. She was actually physically quivering, beside herself with exhilarating excitement. Still smiling. Eddy hates her in that very moment, proving that he can never stay mad at her for long.

Together, they open the small golden-yellow door with a colourful red frame, a large blue flower and other smaller painted flowers before they climb up the three wooden green steps. Each step produces a gentle echo. They feel like hobbits entering a house in Hobbiton. It is wide but small. It is remarkable to see the size of the inside, compared to the depiction that the outside would suggest. In the centre is a black, iron log burner for which the red metal chimney comes from. The log fire inside is full of life. Next to, precariously close to the licking naked flames is a blue metal bin full of small cut logs.

The warmth inside is cosy, a little stuffy. A concrete floor is met by a row that has the same panelled design of the door bordering the floor to the ceiling. A light blue, with lighter blue flowers goes around the sides with a header of a gold framed dark blue panel of silk. The canvas roof is supported by orange beams with patterned bands around the middle. This traditional ger is used by the nomadic lives of the Mongolians. The Mongolian land is owned by the crown, thus locals, travellers can spend the night, or they can live wherever they want.

One single family owns this tent, which runs the small area of gers. They use the visitor's cabin as an office but leave on the top of the hill. The small log fireplace successfully keeps the ger very welcoming, while leaving the cold outside. The curved walls have four largeish beds that makes Eddy wonder if they are going to be sharing with anyone. The heavy wooden orange beds are high off the ground with forest decoration and a white blanket on the top of a thick grey bedding sheet. Each bed has a small orange cupboard. In the centre is a small lace covered tablecloth with a glass ashtray and four yellow wooden, varnished stools.

Lia looks around their new accommodation as Eddy cuddles her waist from behind, to reach over her shoulder with his lips to softly peck her neck. Lia leans backwards into the kiss as a magnificent surprise. She moans in appreciation. Eddy pulls the scarf down further. She giggles. Eddy whispers sweet nothings. Lia stops Eddy with a breathless whispered promise, 'later'.

They put their luggage on two of the beds next to each other, to claim them, before walking out to survey their new land. This is Mongolia, the real Mongolia. The wind has picked up and snaps, rustles together the colourful prayer flags on strong, bending in the wind thin poles that are outside each of the gers. Of the few gers that dot the landscape high on the hillside is the larger main family ger. This is long, rather than round, but in the same style. Two thin lines of smoke rises from the two chimney sprouts from either side of the long, elongated ger. This is where the meals are served so they head up for some lunch. This is included in the price.

A young woman with intensely dark brown eyes that almost hide the pupils completely greets them. High, prominent cheekbones with small triangle lips which express happiness. Her thin body is tightly wrapped in a lighter green dress than Lia's scarf. She greets them in timid English, and direct them to a wooden pew to sit on one end of a long wooden table. Once they have settled, she nods acknowledgement before floating away.

Shortly, she stealthily comes back with two steaming hot bowls of light brown lamb stew, with dumplings in a thick brown sauce. The steam condenses on their face as they both go in to sniff the dish. They try it, gingerly. Although quite doughy it is very nice. The same magnificently striking young woman brings some boiling hot tea in a blue pot to pour into the resting brown clay cups. They eat, they enjoy and then they are warm, ready. Lia gushes over what they are doing, while Eddy feigns interest. As she has made her mind up, Eddy has learnt not to try and change the plans that have already been made. After all, it, this is a surprise. They, rather Lia decides to go for a walk after lunch. They wrap up before leaving the aromatic combination of wood burning and lamb stew to enter the cooling, windy elements.

Although this seems unwise after being for the first time in days not only clean, but warm. They have spent a lot of time in confined spaces, literally living in each other's pockets. After enduring that unplannable obstacle, they are still talking to one another. They hike, they talk, they laugh, they embrace. It was a relief for Lia. They had passed the first test.

Since leaving Australia, this is the most relaxed that she has been. They passed the same wildlife that they passed in the bus. Yet, in this countryside here but seeing the animals, walking next to the woolly, thick black hair yaks with curved grey horns, larger nostrils. This close proximity sees them a lot more forcible then they looked a few minutes ago from the, somewhat safety, of the death-warranted minibus.

They talk about the gers being better for families. No television would surely encourage open conversation. They have found this as they are not glued to their mobile phones, iPads or computers for which they purposely left back in Australia. They are better. They feel healthier that they are talking constantly, even when in silence they are reading each other. In the ger the family would be forced to communicate, it is not as if you can avoid seeing each other. It is not as if, if you get into an argument and storm off you cannot slam doors on your escape. You cannot hide in a room without corners.

The straw-brown grass protests slightly as it snaps, crisply under their feet. The coldness, for them, is either getting warmer, or there are getting used to the conditions. The pine perfume is a refreshing change to the musty train carriage, polluted Ulaanbaatar and the wood smouldering tainted ger. They are being consumed by nature. There loving it. The endless magnificent landscape. They ramble through the fantasy like scenery of enchanted, forbidden forests. If in that instance, that specific minute, a unicorn erupted from the undergrowth, hurried passed them, so quick to immediately fade to bush, that enactment would not have surprised them for a second. It would have perfectly fit into the view.

This was what they expected for Mongolia. Uncontrolled, unspoiled nature with gushing rivers, leading to the roar of unkempt natural power in the small waterfalls. It is the smooth, soft artisan cheese to the white, dusty chalk of Ulaanbaatar. It is magnificence munificent, all philanthropical for the whole world. Small gers dot the scape with camels, sometimes horses tied up next to them, chewing the cud barely noticing them walk by, uncaring. This area is known for its steppe, vast swathe of high-altitude wilderness highlighted with an enigmatic ambience of pure innocence with the undercurrent of raw, layers of stories that are forever, untold. Unknown. Forgotten by those outside but remembered every day in their culture.

The Mongol culture was founded by Genghis Khan in 1206 and ruled much of Asia at its peak. An area that covered everything between the Pacific Ocean and the Caspian Sea. The rocky out drop, the rolling of the green, the desert, the most sparsely populated country in the world at three million, where three-quarters live in the capital. Young children here have a remarkable, for both of them, envious innocence of simple dreams. To support, build and provide.

At this stage they are chasing goats and sheep, while the vultures circulate overhead in silence. Silent. The shadows of the evil that is broodingly around, weaves over the pale grass from above. But goes largely unnoticed by these children playing their foolish, but very jubilant imaginary games. Innocence is being watched by the malevolence guillotine, ready to execute the preserved.

Unexpectantly they come to a simple dark green painted frame arch with a yellow top, crowned with a blue and gold flowered design in a peacock-feather-esque design. Beyond a wooden panelled bridge, in the close distance climbing up by scaling steps, up the grey rocky, flawlessly framed environment, is a white temple. They stop in their stride. Think. Wonder. What's inside that gem? Curiosity takes over as they venture onwards.

The mountains suddenly fragment to a chasm. Bottomless, fog showing the tops of trees. That is all. No bottom can be seen. Further on, a few short footsteps, a wooden bridge, a loose ramshackle, a precarious decrepit bridge. The first step by Lia, onto the thin, fractured floor-planked bridge, begins the bridge in a swaying movement, like a pendulum. She grips the worn, thick dirty rope, hard. Gripping hard to life. Petrified. Unsure. The second step made by her, the first by Eddy.

They both are now stepping forward, on the bridge together. Behind, close behind. In support. In unison. If one goes, they both go. A gust of wind. A sway. Holding both sides they hold, tight. Another gust of chilly air. Tighter. White-knuckled. Terrified to continue, to go back. Safe and still. Frightening the bridge swings harsher, like a scene from an action movie. Stubbornly they move onward. The rope gives way to a wooden railing, to one side, the left. Like a fence. Designed to keep people in, but not the elements out. A safety barrier, that is not the definition of what it is supposed to be.

Lia instantly reaches for it out of habit. Her feet do not move. She reaches hard. The barrier gives way, falls, below, to make the safety barrier no bloody use. The momentum of the lost barrier nearly makes Lia slip off the edge. She moves down to her knees, wrapping the rope around her hands, wrists, arms, as breathless words mumble a mixture of other words that are not fit for children's ears. Eddy shuffles behind her. Whispers a hope, a plea. Pleading to turn back. She just concentrates on her breathing. Ignores his sound. Loud, but controlled by her heart more than ever.

Once her heart stops beating faster than designed. Not once, but twice her heart, and his, nearly bounces out of her chest. Loud enough to hear amidst the howls of the wind. They heart relaxes, just enough to move on. She does not get up from her knees. She decides to crawl the rest of the way. As Eddy offers the encouragement of a cruel child, that sees the benefits of teasing as a form of fourplay. In doing this, he tries in vain to hide his own fear. She does not look down, but straight to where she what's to go.

Tough love does not work. It does not even remotely work. She yells a few things as he teases, such as, 'So chivalry is dead?' He is not sure if it's a playful game or not. So, he does the thing that probably will be his end—he continues. Slowly they rock, sway, crawl over to the safety of the other, maybe the same mountain. A nervous, treacherous air dance, to the other side. Eddy reaches the end first and turns with a sinister look. Lia points straight-armed towards Eddy, close enough to brush. With a snarl through gritted teeth, she warns, 'DON'T…YOU…BLOODY…DARE.'

Eddy wisely did not risk, even the attempt, to create a little dark humour in this terrifying situation. Even though it was a joke, he knew that this life choice was not worth the repercussions. A couple of long, for Lia, hard seconds later, the self-proclaimed torment was done. She was over. Relieved. She still did not remember Eddy passing her. Alas, she did not care. She had made it over. The bottled-up terror turned quickly to release all the pent-up exhilaration in an erupting, refining geyser of relief.

She rises to her feet, strides steadfast towards Eddy, who opens his arms for an expectant hug. She shocks him by slapping him around the face. Harder than she intended. However, she did not relinquish her authority. She stayed in control. Before his face had returned to the centre, she warned him. By gripping his cheeks, firmly, together in the claw-like pinches of her thumb and index finger.

'Never, ever, be that cruel again.'

Followed by a lighter slap with her free hand across the other cheek as she releases him. Tail between his legs like a dog he whimpers, like a ghost unheard. Like a schoolboy that had done wrong he looks down at his feet, shuffles them in the dark brown sandy earth. Saying nothing. The warning been heeded. He soothes his raw bruised cheek, his ego. He follows her.

Lia stops to stare uphill at her, their prize. High up the steps is the Gunjiin Sün. From this distance, for which they still have to negotiate the many steps, the Manchurian influenced temple shines out on the wispy silver threaded clouds, like a mirage, on a pedestal. Outlined below by a lush, flowing border of the green forest trees nestled in the hundreds of different shades of the mountains rocky grey, the white temple, shines like a beacon. If anything, the smell of the fragrant pine is being gracefully caressed by the breeze, seemingly exquisitely more intense. Seems to shimmer, strikingly in the air with the pleasant feel of magical freshness that hangs delightfully around.

According to the primitive map that was given to Lia when she checked in at the tourist office, it states simply that this is the 'only one left in Mongolia'. Leaving no indication for what the 'one' is in reference to. She states the fact to Eddy, all forgiven, all forgotten. They speculate as they tread the dusty brown track that leads to the start of the stairs.

They walk the bordered white painted framed brick, stone steps in exactly nine flights of thirteen, to the top. It is a breathless undertaking for which they glance to look back every now-and-again to see how far they have gone, then to see what is yet to be done.

Tired, with a fresh pain in shooting at the top of their thighs. Pearls of sweat roll down their foreheads despite the coldness in the air. The sticky, clammy, uncomfortable sensation under their armpits. That transcends cold shivers that run down the inside of their chest, skirting their ribcage, to brings them back as they catch their breath. They appreciate where they have come. The glistening black banister around the temple have small wooden crowns of a silver Buddha in the centre facing the same direction. Each one as if made yesterday, still perfectly intact.

Above them, the colourful, brightly eaves of green, red, blue and gold, complimented by the blue skies as they look newly vibrant. The wind is chilly, silently evident. The wooden eaves, that panel the roof space where previously they had not noticed, suddenly become clear. Inside are portrayed, rather strange motifs. Both are unsure if, or either, they depict torture, punishment or bestiality. Tilting his head to one side, as if to figure it out. He momentarily enters a trancelike daydream, for which his head is quite literally in the clouds.

Scaring Eddy's body to the high heavens, nearly jumping so high as to bump his head on the paintings, a monk appears from the corner, from nowhere. Bringing his focus back as if he has fell from the heavens his heart raced a sprint. Returning to its marathon he smiles at his awkward noise which escaped his body. A noise he had never made before, or ever will again. To his side the monk removes his dark red hood to reveal a shiny, small pinhead of a face. Broadly smiling with broken black teeth, he pulls Eddy from the eaves he was looking at. He drags him, with a sharp tug towards other paintings. knocking him off balance. He points out the other paintings.

He speaks in a musical language for which Eddy gives Lia a look for which she shrugs an I-don't-understand-either. He uses his head to point, to gesture towards a grey painted dog biting a man's testicles off. He points with thin, frail hands that do not see to be the same as his youthful face. Both his hands gesticulate, as the baggy loose sleeves dance in time. He explains what they are seeing. Eddy shoots a look at Lia that she returns, a bewildered, unsure and damn right confused look of her own. They do not remotely understand.

The monk eventually sees this. He ponders with his fingers stroking the thinnest grey whiskers under his chin. He tries to explain again, with more hand signs, more head pointing, and arm waving, slowing his speech down. All this, to no avail. All of the time gripping, almost pinching Eddy's elbow gaining intensity. Finally, he releases Eddy's elbow, to search for Lia's arm behind him. He inadvertently gropes where the sun does not shine. Eddy see the unintended motion to quickly intervene, he is one hundred percent sure that he would have touched her if he was not quick to act.

Lia gives the panic sign with her eyes that not so much shouts but rants, raves and screams out that she is leaving. She abruptly turns. It may have been an accident, but she was creeped out by his demeanour. The unsettling way he appeared. The familiar way he latched onto Eddy. The bizarre odd behaviour, as they were in a foreign land, but his actions seemed more foreign than a native local.

She briskly makes her way down the steps to the bottom. Almost fleeing. Eddy follows suit with a shake of the hand from the monk, whom of which reluctantly lets him go. Eddy defends the monk, genuinely thinking he did not mean to grope. Lia was not hearing. Or not choosing to listen, either way they were at the bottom of the flight of steps before they knew it. It's funny what anger shields away.

A path starts from the overgrown straw-like grass. Not so much of a path, but more of a passage made by animals, they blindingly follow, giving into another dramatically exquisite scene. A step-stopping outstandingly different landscape for Eddy, as Lia stomps a trail, blazing like an elephant with the impact of an ant, in a huff. Eddy notices she has hastily moved forward, he clumsily follows by tripping over the un-trippable hazards. Purposefully, moving in the opposite direction of the treacherous, precarious bridge. She leads, he pursues.

She still did not say anything with the steam still bellowing from her wide nostrils as she pauses, looks behind, ahead. Eddy gasps as he catches up. Unexpressed, they voicelessly mutually decide to climb the land around the valley. It looked like it would be hard, but not too bad. Instantly this was going to be harder than it looked. The gravel, the small stones beneath each footstep, gave way constantly under them. As a result, they would sometimes take one step forward, to find themselves sliding two steps further back. The rocks were not stable to hold on for support, this did not stop them trying in an act of human behaviour.

However, most of the time they would find themselves coming away from the mountain with the shrub, rock or thin, gnarly grubby root in their tightly held grasp. To stumble, nearly fall with their unwanted prize of the former terrain held high in the air, aloft, as if they were holding a championship winning trophy. The dead roots of trees crumbled in their hands, scattered over the hillside also offered no brace, nor support. The chill in the rustling air carried them to a new settling place.

Nonetheless, they continued to go forwards, upwards, round and down. Afraid to stop for too long as momentum would then vanish, which would leave the seeds of doubt left to blossom. The moss underfoot, proved to be slippery as ice the higher they climbed. They are amazed that anything could grow on so little earth, a mere dusting. At the halfway point, they were going to get to the other peak, before the descent down. Although they both feared getting lost, they did not share their thoughts. They continued on the untrodden path of discovery.

Lia arrives first and stands tall. With a successful sense of achievement, she proudly surveys her well-earned prize. Shortly behind, Eddy scans the vast magnificence. He walks behind Lia, ever so tenderly cuddles her waist. They both set eyes on their reward. A landscape out of a movie set. Enigmatic and unreal. Layered mystical mist act as a halo to the smaller mountains. The whispers of which, weaves in and out of the valley. Jagged grey sharp rocks make a barren, dusty landscape with areas of green forest trees that descend into the distance, purely marvellously exceptional.

Birds hover, soar and chirp overhead. Colours of fairyland proportions blend effortlessness into the natural art that a drama, mythological and fantasy scape, could all play a role here in their imagination. Here is this true Mongolian beauty that they were expecting. Nature is at its very best. Nature is touched, graced by the sun rays above that spotlight through the light grey clouds. No light is bad light with these surroundings. The cuddle. The affection felt. They appreciate. They shiver in the silence. They smile, humble at the great scenic pleasure before them, around them.

Sadly, the cold defeats them. The shivering becomes more apparent to a tremor when they decide to keep moving on. But down. Slowly, carefully they skid a few times. Stop, take a photograph in an ineffective endeavour to capture the scene in a still, futile photograph. Alas they arrive in one piece back at the bottom with a mind full of memories, a camera full of photographs.

When they got back to camp, about five hours after they had set off, a group of people had gathered in the adjacent field. From where they were, they could not see clearly. With inquisitiveness triumphant they venture down to the paddock to take a sticky beak. Eddy helped Lia over the small log constructed fence. Now they could see what all the hubbub was about.

A relaxed tanned Mongolian stands in silence. He softly instructs and moves the hands of Lia, navigating the large wooden bow. He then goes behind and gently pushes her back to an arch that resembles the bow as if a shadow. He nudges her feet more apart with a probing kick of his own. He then gets very close to her ear as he places a thin, light pale arrow in her bow and positions his arms around her. Eddy cannot help but feel a pang of jealousy. Such a wasted emotion. Lia lets go, with a slight twang as the released tension of the string returns to its comfortable place. The arrow soars through the air towards the animal hide, that is the target supported in a wooden frame of sticks. The arrow falls agonisingly short.

Nevertheless, she feels jubilant that the arrow has flown. She beams as she turns towards Eddy at her own accomplishment. It was Eddy's turn. His attempt was useless, worse than worse. The arrow fell a few centimetres away from his own foot. The less said about the feeble effort the better. They spent the afternoon here in a disorganised system of taking turns. Lia got better. She was excellent, a natural. She giggled with glee as she got close to the target on every attempt. Archery was hard on the arms and wrist, but Lia made it look so easy. A contrast to Eddy. He, well, made it look as hard as it seemed, as it is. It was as fun to do as it was to watch.

Eddy talked about giving this a go back in Australia, making it a hobby. This made Lia chuckle as she has heard his aims, heard his ideal hobbies and his plans in the past. Apart from his exercising and keeping his body, mind and soul fit, he has rarely followed through into fruition the other whims he has expressed.

Darkness decided that they were going to end the, nothing short of remarkable, day. In the centre of the campsite a shower cubicle that smells of yak poo, with a trickle of a leaking tap, rather than a shower. They try their best to cleanse themselves. The muddy ground instead of a concrete slab gets worse with water which really makes it hard to wash, stay clean and get back to the ger, with the intention of being exactly what was intended, to be clean. The water was a slow drip, a warm trickle but not the warmest, but warmer than outside. They are quick due to combination of not-quite-hitting-the-mark factors.

They do return to the ger feeling better, cleaner but not one hundred percent refreshed. They are a little fast, they are scantily covered when they opened the door of the ger, get dragged in by the glorious fingers of warmth that grabs them back into the soft comfort like a caring, maternal embrace. On the two empty beds are too new acquisitions. They are not too sure who was more surprised, them or, Eddy and Lia. An awkward stumbling short sentenced greeting ensued. After a while a calm settled, and they were more comfortable. Lia and Eddy were dressed more appropriately.

Introductions done and dusted; awkwardness left behind; they all relaxed. Nathan and Kim, also from Australia, from the far Tropical north of Queensland in Mackay, had unpacked the essentials as they spoke of their travels. Like them, they were also travelling the railway but were going in the opposite direction. Hence hints, tips and ideas were shared. This was the first interaction with Australians for a long, long time or so it seemed, so they jumped on it. They laughed over the mutual distaste of the urban concrete jungle that is the capital.

Together, they strolled up to the top of the hill for an evening meal. It was warmer in there, a little too hot. They decided to sit together, to forge a common bond. Nathan and Eddy tried the local beer that was on offer. They seemed to bond quicker than their female companions. The beer on offer was a choice of a 3.3% or 8.1% long neck which did not even cost more than the two-dollar price tag. They drunk to that. The stronger was called Jalam, for which they opted for. Eddy had this delicious sheep stew with rice and a dark green vegetable broth. Lia had a flat fried pancake stuffed with unrecognisable heavily spiced meat that was covered in a yellow sauce and tasted different, but still divine. They shared each other's, with Lia asking the host what hers was called—'Khuushuur'. Then, pointing to Eddy's, 'Stoew'. Eddy was convinced he was trying to say stew. They laugh.

Over the modest, satisfying dinner, they share tales of home, travels and personal stories. It is funny how people open up with strangers when they travel. They have a connection in being Australian, which seems to be the strong basis for a great night. Towards the end, they look around for the first time, outside their bubble to see that they were keeping the family awake. Everyone else had left to their own gers.

The family, host, owner of the campsite came over and sat down with them. Her English was non-existent, but she was followed by her husband who spoke a little Russian for which Lia was the translator for the group. He had a chubby face, that was fringed by a brown fur hat that gleamed resembling the shimmering of the moon. Unannounced he got up mid-sentence.

Moments later, he came back with a delicacy. He slammed six small patterned mix-matched, assortment of odd-shaped glasses in front of each of the occupants on the table. Out of a dimpled glass carafe, he poured a creamy, off-white thick liquid in each of the glasses before taking his seat. In unison, they asked Lia what it was. She said to toast, to drink it first so not to offend, then she will ask.

He shouted as he raised the glass into the air. They mimicked him and then drunk. The warm sour cream sensation hit the back of their throats. Following by a sparkling edge that trickled down their throats, leaving a thin, but not thin enough layer tantalising their mouths. The revulsions of squeezed, contorted facial expression. The slight cough. The gasp for clean air. They all seem to be trying not to bring it back up, but all fist-pumping under the table unvoiced encouragements, as they all try to force the swallow. They all did not want to offend anyone. The look on everyone's faces shows different looks of distaste. Some commented that it was really salty, others said sour. They all agreed it was not very nice at all. Pretty disgusting.

'Arak,' Lia loosely translates, not entirely sure of the pronunciation. He continues to explain as she continues to translate. 'They leave the yak's milk, sometimes horse milk, camel milk, in the sun. On this very roof. In the sun from the start of the day until the end. They skim it. Refrigerate it. This is two percent alcohol. This is horse.' She peers back into the cream remnants that coats the glass. '…apparently? Taste a bit…mmm…No. Not for me!'

It was at that moment that Eddy surveys the room, taking his mind off his agitated stomach that was threatening to disburden its contents. In the corner are two children, one was a boy no older than two, one was a girl not older than six. The six-year-old stands naked, using her two hands to clinch the dirty, dented metal cup, without a handle. She guzzles the boozy milk hurriedly, while some escapes to dribble down her chin. The metal tin cup looks so large in her tiny hands.

The boy plays with a rusty car that from this distance Eddy thinks is made of lead. He says nothing, then changes his mind to murmur a concern to Lia who shrugs. Reluctantly they have their glass refilled. They do not want to offend. They do it. Mentally holding their noses. This time though it is harder as they know what they are going to be tasting. The unexpected is expected. This is the roadie. One more revolting shot before saying goodnight.

In the darkest time of the night, Lia wakes with a shiver. She is cold within, as well as without. They slept in separate beds to be respectful to their roommates. This shiver prompts her to go to the fire, check that a log is smouldering, check the heat. It is an ember but emitting enough warmth to heat the small enclosed room with the help of the body warmth. Eddy senses her near, he whispers through the darkness, 'Are you OK?'

Lia is startled by his voice. In the soft golden flickering hue that bounces of the fabric walls, she snaps her neck around. Eddy lifts his doona as a welcoming door for her to enter. Lia crawls inside. Eddy is a furnace that grabs Lia like a ravaging animal. He apologises for his roughness but the moment that he opened his warm bed the cold entered, and he wanted it shut as quickly as possible. Eddy had no need to apologise as Lia actually enjoyed the maternal instinct that was somewhat ruined by his solidity, his voiced, 'sorry'. It is a squeeze on the small bed, but with Lia being the little spoon facing the furnace she feels protected in Eddy's arms. Lia quickly falls asleep in the safety of Eddy's clutches.

Lia wakes to the rustle of plastic as Nathan rummages in his backpack. It is one of those things, when people try to be quiet, they often end up making more noise. He places his left hand in the air as a form of apologising, for which was accepted with a lethargic nod. Lia gingerly peels Eddy's arms off from her chest in the attempt to not wake him. This proved unsuccessful as she did the opposite effect. Eddy stirs with a moan, smiles at the sight of Lia and embraces her, pulling her back under the doona.

Lia smiles back with a soft kiss as she cranes her neck, yet prises away at the same time deeply leaning into his bare chest. Eddy reluctantly lets Lia leave his floundering arms in the sea of multi-coloured blankets. The contrast from the bed to the outside proves a very obvious chill. Eddy watches for a moment before getting out of the snug haven himself.

They get ready, step outside to a light, barely drizzling of rain and a very chilly breeze. The bleating of goats and sheep, the squawking of bird's overhead, in the leafless trees seem to warm them as if they are one with nature. However, in unison they zip up their coats in a quick snap, snuggle their chins into their collars to walk once again up the hill to the main tent. The feeling of not only being in the countryside but being surrounded by nature immediately does what no pill, no treatment, no placebo can ever do. They feel alive.

Yet, Lia is feeling down today. Maybe it was the lack of sleep before falling in Eddy's arms. Maybe it was just her feeling pretty ordinary. Maybe she was just being human and having an off day. But she feels like walking again. She does not want to waste a moment of being here, in the present.

They plan a different hiking route over breakfast, well Lia does. She tries to occupy her mind. The family hosts bring a very milky tea looking as cheerful as ever, followed by an even more milky porridge with a puddle of a berry jam in the centre. They hope this is not horse again. This warmness of the soup-like oats is perfect to warmth them on a particular cold day. The taste was not without its charm, but lacked the sweetness that they are used to, with sour undertones. They ask if they can purchase a couple of rolls and some bottled water to take on a hike. They receive something of a mystery bag in two separate grey canvas bags which they are asked to return with the rubbish at the end. They resist the urge to take a peek. It will be a surprise for them.

They have it firmly etched into their mind to hike a lot over the days that they were off the train. It could have been being couped up in a railway carriage that, for them was unnatural, back home, in Sydney, they were always outside. Within a few short days the prospect of more confinement was on the not-so-distant horizon. This imminent offering made them enjoy the splendour of the outside world even more visibly. Too not take as much advantage to what they feel and see, but relish and enjoy all. The nature here was exotic in an unconventional way that was peaceful, calming.

They walked, talked. Passed herds of camels that blocked their path. Their sideway glance told them that they had noticed them, but a smugness from the herd was etched over their face, on the demeanour. So, they do not react a bit as they have to move around them with only their wide, pong-pong sized eyes tracing their every movement. This is repeated often. They were on their turf so did not mind this slight detour.

They leisurely, unconsciously beat a little bit of the sprouting emerald pearled treasure, the radiant ceaselessly surviving grass underfoot on the otherwise barren, brown terrain. To their left, an unconventional row of animal skeletons line some of the path. With an intertwined boundary of abundant different sized skulls on unbalanced spaces, that act as a border, also a deterrent at the same time. Each end of the rustic area is cornered by a large wooden, thick branch that has the largest of the horns placed upright towards the sky. A final warning of a no-go zone. No-one was around.

The enigmatic wonderment of what laid beyond, played imagination reels in their mind. They resisted the compulsion to crossover. The colours that praised the countryside were as soft as the silence. No persons anywhere. If the birds did not sing. If the wind did not rustle as it softy stroked to caress, to play the tunes in the trees or, if there was not the distant bleat, a murmuring moan from a concealed animal. If natural melodies were not surrounding them, they would feel as if they were the last beings on an inhospitable earth.

They could not help but keep stopping, more than a few times to take photographs, to embrace the impressive location that offered so much, but wanted nothing in return. Not noticing the hunger, that crept up on them. It was well past two in the afternoon when they finally opened their mystery bags with a rumble from Eddy's stomach.

They had the same. Yet Eddy decided to display his on the grey canvas bag. Carefully positioned was a heavy-crusted sandwich of a white strong-smelling cheese, soggy lettuce leaves doused in a tomato salsa, of sorts, a large bottle of water-to share, a large saucer-sized biscuit and a bun that looked sweet. With looks to be deceiving the bun was far from sweet. Nestled in the centre was a sour filling that they both could not pick. Either by taste or out of their mouth. Lia left hers, but Eddy, after taking a photograph of his lunch, devoured the lot. Even the sour-sweet bun.

It was here on the crisp, light green grass under a tree that had seen so many sights in its time. Them for the first time today. Resting after the hike, allowing the food to digest, it was at this moment. The sun in the blue skies transmitting no warmth but purely, just for show. Eddy with his back against the tree. Lia inside his legs. Her head resting on his chest. The only sound was their breathing. They felt relaxed but Lia wanted to share something. This was the moment. She picked at his right arm hair as she started to speak.

'I'm scared,' she confessed. 'I am scared of going back home.'

'Why?' Eddy thought about being silent but decided she needed some soft prompting. 'You're, but, you're going home.'

'Former home. My FORMER home.' The last word breaking into a breathless hope. 'What if I am not welcomed by my family? What if? If THEY see me as a Judas? A girl that left when the going got tough. A-A—'

'Lia. You spoke to them!'

'Yes, but that. That was at home…' she trailed off as the following words became incoherent.

326

'You're going home,' Eddy kissed the top of her head. 'Home.'

'My family…I'm scared that they will not accept me. I—'

'Lia. Stop it.' Eddy turned around to face Lia. Her back positioned awkwardly against the tree as he straddled her legs. He looked deep into her eyes, his head resting on her forehead. 'Listen. Lia. You have Absolutely, NOTHING, nothing,' with a grit in his timbre from the back of his clenched teeth. To immediately tone it down to follow his reassurance with a softer voice. 'Nothing. Lia. You have nothing to prove to them, just yourself. Nothing. You do that, you prove every day. I mean, you only need to answer to yourself. For me you prove it every day. If they are your family. If they love you. They will see that in the first glance. The family bond is a bond that cannot be broken. A bond that cannot be…' Eddy overstretched himself. He did not know any words that could finish that sentence.

'I know. But…but what if?'

'Do you remember the first email you sent? I do. It was a quick response by your father. He wants to see you. He wants to show off his daughter. He is proud of what you have done, doing and well, do. Lia…you have nothing to be scared of.'

'Maybe not.' Lia smiled, as a single tear escaped her eye. She felt by just having this small conversation it had made a huge difference to the way she felt. An almighty, bothersome affliction was lifted.

'Absolutely not. You have nothing to worry about. I will be with you every step of the way. I will not leave your side. I am…' He smirked with a wink. 'I am your knight in shining chef whites, remember. Remember?'

Lia laughed as she pulled him close. A kiss on his forehead. 'You idiot.'

She turned around to be lying on top of him. They embraced, kissed and explored with their hands each other's bodies in the open countryside of Mongolia. It was an impulsive way to act. They wanted to make love there, and then. They had to imagine carthorses pulling them apart to stop. They were on the edge, ready to dive into love. They had nothing to rush back for. They jumped. Eddy pulled a bright red and yellow blanket out of his contrasting backpack to the dark earth colours of brown and green. Eddy laid it over Lia letting it find its own way, over the shape of her body. Their hands caressed each other's bodies. They kissed, stroked and spoke beautiful nothings.

Eddy's hand started to undo her black pants just enough to get his hand down. Lia did not protest. Eddy pulled out all his resources to relieve her stresses. They pleasured each other. They are subtle, so smooth. They do not care as their moans, groans, screams of delight are echoed around the valley. An impulsive action ends swiftly, tenderly, but loudly. They lay. They drift into a light sleep. Wrapped in the blanket, semi naked. Sharing the body heat in the cold countryside.

After a few minutes, the warmth of their bodies proves not enough. They moan awake as the cold air torments them, gets them to rise. They redress. Do up the unbuttoned buttons. They pack up their spread, their rubbish. Arm around shoulders, linked in body, mind and heart, they continue their hike. Free hand grasping to the other free hand. It did not seem possible, but they were actually falling more in love with each other. Before this journey started, they loved each other. However, as the time went by, by each passing second. Somehow, they are falling deeper, further in love with each other.

With the noise-breaking crow of the rooster, the next day arrived. The break of dawn came with the break of the blissful touch that surrounds them. A soft strum of fingers on the heartstrings, the sensation of a touching feeling that Midas would put down as being unrealistic. It is the end of this countryside marvel.

They drive in a lefthanded, Mongolian local bus from the ger camp back to Ulaanbaatar train station. The black, dark smoke plumes out of the minibus that has seen much better days. It only took a few minutes when the trek is brought to an abrupt stop. They were halted by a herd of yaks that blocked the path. Trees and undergrowth enclosed them. They could not go around. Eddy was relieved as he felt that this minibus would not cope with cross-country. He had huge doubts if the minibus would even finish this journey on the attempt of tarmac.

The driver jumps out. He surveys the scene, pauses, in a shrug of the shoulders he resigns defeat. An elderly man gracelessly slides out. The large set of a man, who they thought was a regular passenger, pulls out a dented brown metal tin and opens it on the bonnet. The lid comes off and the dark brown snuff threatens to spill out. He uses the lid and sniffs a nice small ball full of tobacco. The driver turns, takes up the invitation. One by one everyone gets the message without having to be told that they will be going nowhere until the yaks decide to move. Eddy and Lia are the last to get out. The elderly man has been sharing his snuff, he offers it to them. Eddy tries it.

He is in the middle of nowhere, with three formidable black long-haired yaks with large curved horns in the middle of the road, snorting some snuff from a random stranger with no words but an appreciative nod of their heads. Temptation took over. After a short while Lia tries some for herself, for the first time. Straightaway she knows that it is not her thing, not her thing at all. She sniffed the elderly lady smelling perfume that was beside her. Exhaling but trying to draw in the lady's strong scent of mothballs. Instantly trying in vain to reject the snuff from her nostrils.

The wrinkled face of the elderly man beamed a smile from under her dark grey felt hat. Bushy, wiry eyebrows sprout slivers of grey that hide his eyes. His wrinkled face comes across as friendly, like a gently giant. He mutters something with a pat on her head. Like she was a stray dog. Eddy smirked at the look she shot at him. He either ignored it, or blatantly did not recognise his insult. He returned the closed tin into his dark material thin, green jacket with badges on the lapels that make no sense to her. Immodestly, he struts to relieve himself by the side of the road without a single care in the world.

Eventually, the yaks move, they clamber their way into the rusty minibus. The hard dancing road made them hop, bounce and sway as their danced their way back to Ulaanbaatar. The windows were drawn so the noisy engine of the minibus with no suspension was accompanied by the silent tune of the countryside, the loud neigh of small shiny horses, the bleating of the goats and sheep, where mouths moved but no sound ensued. All suffocated by the noise of the polluted, road-illegal minibus.

Suddenly, the clear countryside is a forgotten vision, as they are back with the intense, chaotic traffic, the green trees have turned to grey concrete. The pungent air of fresh livestock, goodness is replaced by the gritty feel at the back of the throat of pollution, the slimy grease over their skin. After much persuasion, Eddy got Lia to ask why the cars are not all right-hand drive. She came back with the somewhat confusing translated answer that made no sense, 'the cheaper the better'.

As remembered, the muddled-up train station carpark is a mess. They are dropped off on the side of the road. No warning, just a jerk of the brakes. A rock of the heads swung forward, then snapped back. They weave through the cars bumper to bumper with their luggage. Towards the light beige and light grey block building with the red lettering of Ulaanbaatar. No cars are moving, just honking. They walk up the steps. They need to buy the tickets for the next stage of their trip.

Lia buys the tickets while protecting the luggage; Eddy goes to buy some food for the train. A lesson learnt on the previous journey. As hot water is provided, he has a good idea of what to buy. He comes back with a large cardboard box of items lost inside. Coffee granules, bottled water, ready noodles, a loaf of sliced semi-rye bread, golden honey, sunflower seeds, oranges and apples which slip and slide clumsily within the considerable room inside the box as he briskly hurries back.

In Mongolia, Genghis Khan is known as Chinggis Khaan. Eddy relays, with numerous quips, that everything is Chinggis. You can buy Chinggis shampoo, rolls, wines, beer and the list emphatically goes on, and on in the same rhythm as their steps to the platform. As they wait at the platform, they both look back in their minds, at what will be the last steps in Mongolia. The broken pavements that they each had a turn of tripping over was not going to be missed. The morning runs were made more of a steeple chase as they step-watched a route around the vicinity of their hotel. The countryside was a make-believe haven of beauty.

The Mongolian history is fascinating for which they make an empty promise to read more into it when they get back to Sydney. It is the same promise they had made to Nathan and Jade, back at the ger camp, to stay in touch, to meet up again. The reality is that this will rarely happen.

As they board the sparkling clean dark green brooding carriage Eddy has all the luggage and struggles, whereas Lia effortlessly takes the groceries. To the left the carriage assistant, the provodnitsa, carefully places paintings inside. She looks suspicious as her eyes flick around the platform. The grey cloth that conceals them falls over one and reveals the painting that she is smuggling on board. These have been seen on the corners of tourist sights to sell to the dumb, foolish tourists that think it is one of a kind, original, unique.

No doubt she was going to try and earn a few bucks on the train trip herself. They wave the grey concrete crumbling new city of Ulaanbaatar farewell as they embark. The white carriage number in a steel three-dimensional signage in the middle shows the elegance. On top is a gold ring and a blue background, a golden flying horse is in the centre flying over a grey vase top motif. Purely well-designed, stylish engineering impressiveness. It looks solid, it looks safe.

Within minutes of finding their cabin, getting in and not even unpacking the essentials. Without even, warming the seats of their new bunk. The first word is offered with a wave of a dusty unclear liquid in a frosted glass bottle. With a small delicate stemmed shot glass in the other hand, designed with glass-cut floral tulips he thrusts it forward. He frowns with a rasp, husky voice, 'Vodka'. They guess this will pass for hello.

As it was not even passing the hour of midday, they politely declined. The two claimed bunks get up to introduce themselves. Oleg and Vladimir are the Russian cabinmates that are similar in appearance. Their cheekbones are pronounced, their eyes intense, the shaven receding hair with them not taking no for an answer. They really do not take no for an answer. They are relentless. To the point of being rude. They decline as they sort themselves out. Just before one in the afternoon, oh so very slowly, the train pulls away for the twenty-six hour journey from Mongolia to Russia.

After the first passage of the train route being called the Trans-Mongolian, now it is time for the Trans-Siberian train. The next stop will be Irkutsk. The skeleton thin, tall leafless bare birch trees whizz by as the train picks up pace immediately after leaving the concrete sprawl. Lovely green undulating countryside dotted with animals and the occasionally gers is much more auspiciously agreeable to the eye.

The cabins are wider, a little more comfortable, bunks are longer. Clink, clack, clink clack the rhythm of the train becomes a familiar heartbeat over the next few hours that lulls and sooths them into relaxation. They numbingly rattle towards the border. The journey was not wasted. Lia relayed her book with a passionate energy. Her mood was different. She was upbeat.

'Tsar Alexander III wanted to unite Russia,' she spoke softly to Eddy as they laid on the bunk in each other's arms, the book, with numerous creased corners, colourful highlighted segments and words, scribbles in the margins was brandished, outstretched in front. Eddy peered over Lia's shoulder, soothing her hair.

'He was fully committed to the huge Russian continent to be assessable.' She recited from the book in the style of holding a lecture, in a lively narrative. 'He ordered work on the railway. This, the Trans-Siberian commenced in 1891. Not only for people, but for reaching the mineral-rich land in the hard-to-reach areas. Also not forgetting the convicts, the prisoners of war, the political prisoners to be sent away. Also, another add on, to enable the quick, swift movement of the troops to the Amur region which was under constant pressure from invasion from China. The story says that the first commission, announced that his proposal would bankrupt the country. With this news Tsar Alexander III sacked them. The newer, newly formed one, commission, concluded conveniently that it could, would be done.'

They are surrounded by Russians; this is not a tourist train. They are sharing the four-bunk bed in second class. Outside, brightly coloured roofed wooden houses have white spouts of smoke bellowing out. They are in isolated locations. However, they look cosy, comfortable.

In a quick, few hours they get to the border of Mongolia just before midnight, shrouded in darkness. A Mongolian featured man enters the cabin. He smells of fish paste, grease of mechanical engines covered by a sweet, sickly smell of moisturising cream, or soap. In seeing the obvious foreigners, he forces them to store a couple of packages under their bunk. They refuse with the Russian guys not saying a word but pushing them out of the cabin to the Mongolian man's protests. The 'tea' debacle comes to the forefront of their mind. In the narrow passage outside Eddy sees if they are leaving. They are bothering another cabin. Above them a ceiling panel comes, marginally down to reveal a few packages stuffed, carelessly inside. The taller of the men promptly raises his hand to slam the concealment inside the roof.

'PASSPORT!'

From a cabin or two down the carriage comes a deep male voice followed by a short thump on the door. Soon it was their turn. The soft thud. Oleg opens it to two large, stern, serious uniformed dressed men that fill the cabin as they peer in with their hands outstretched. They all pass their passports over. The soldiers peruse them for a few minutes looking up at their faces, down at the passport. They are tossed back in any direction. They leave as the cabinmates swap around the passports to their correct owners.

As always, the customs is a little painless mission of prolonged waiting, but nothing to stress out over. At the end of the day they have done nothing or have not carried anything that was wrong, illegal or not theirs. Pitch black muscular dogs sniff and search each cabin. They checked their bags quickly but seemed to be taking twice as long with our Russian cabinmates. Eddy takes it in his stride and remarks, 'that the land crossing heightens the overall travelling experience'.

However, these words come back to bite him on more than one occasion after the two and half hours on the border. What he thought was an Ernest Hemmingway remark was starting to stretch rather thin. Also, his bladder was bursting. As they locked the doors of the toilets just before coming into the platform and still had not opened them. Finally, with his ears starting to smoke like papa's pipe they are in motion, on their way, carriage by carriage into Russia.

The Russian lady fills the air over the loudspeakers. Lia picks up that a food carriage has been added to the long train. But most importantly she motions the toilet is unlocked. Eddy races down and joins the queue that has formed so fast, it would seem that he is not the only one that was in need to use the facilities.

Relieved he is back. They kiss and get comfortable again laying close to each other on the narrow bed with Lia reading the history of the train. From Eddy's view he watches the darkness outside bobbing up and down. The odd lights that shine through at irregular moments. The carriage is hot, stuffy as they sweat their way over the Russian continent. The cold air outside is apparent as a slight chill goes through the cabin offering momentary release as a window is slid open a fraction from the corridor by another passenger. But then as quickly as this reprieve, one of their Russian companions in the carriage gets up to close it again. Then they recommence their sweating. To try and sleep better, Eddy suggests a beer called Menbhuk from the dining carriage. They set off, down the silent carriage, apart from the clink, clank rhythm of the train tracks.

They open up the food carriage to see a surprisingly, large number of passengers already have descended there. With the décor that they would imagine not unlike the Orient Express they get shown to a free table. Blue cloth covered large semi-ovals open into the middle of the carriage. On each of the tables is a large white doily lace circle for a setting for four. The seats are pews with leather panelled cushions on the grey metal frames. The shiny yellow lino floor is in comparison to the faded curtains that hang down from the sides of the large curved rectangular windows to the middle, tied to let the darkness in.

They sit and order a couple of beers. These are cold. Perfectly doing the intended job by cooling them down straight away. Lia asks Svetlana, the server, what the packages was about. She mentions for which Lia translates that it is not unusual for Mongolian traders to try and smuggle goods across the border, to sell at a higher price in Russia. And then to go back the other way with different merchandise. They tend to go for tourist as they are easy prey.

Oleg, their cabinmate, joins them involuntary. Literally plonking himself down as if it was his own house next to Lia, almost on her lap. A little too close for Eddy's liking, alas he said nothing as Lia's eyes said that she felt the same. Their own private conversation without delay coming to an unwarranted end. In the pale glowing light that descends from the art deco furnished side lamps, Oleg's bony features are striking. A straight sullen expression that he immediately opens his thick, red heavy leather book as he sips his own beer that he had got before interrupting them. He writes. He has not spoken apart from the single word, 'vodka'. He has only either read, slept, drank his vodka since they have seen him.

Vladimir had introduced them both. For the first time, Lia notices that he is a military man by his uniform. Realisation creeps in as she registers that they are wearing the same jacket. Both are very silent and barely talk to themselves, who she sees are the same rank, so must know each other, let alone anyone or somebody else on this trip. They feel tired, so head back towards the cabin to try and sleep again. This time, the beer works as they both fall asleep very quickly.

Russia

The sun shines through the smeared dirty windows, caused by the dust outside, to stir them awake. They, or rather Lia hears the call for their impending station. They get ready somewhat slowly. They are yawning. They are very tired, although they did have an otherwise restless sleep their body clock is all out of time.

By the time they arrive in Irkutsk, they are ready to disembark. Lia's hair looked like the hair-designer from the Exorcist had had a go, a little straw like and very greasy. They have not showered properly since the Ulaanbaatar hotel, so they fear they smell a little of yak, camel, and general body odour. Obviously, Eddy sees the mess before him, but love is blind, and all he sees is her beauty. Eddy told her she looked fantastic, even as he did, he brushed his hand through her greasy hair like he was handling cold, oily spaghetti.

The deliberate relaxed entry to the station makes them feel as if they have landed in a real-life movie with its rich, impressive scenery that transforms to a strong, fortress-built train station. They stiffly step out of the cabin, onto the station and immediately find a bus stop. They take the advice of one of the other military guys in another cabin with whom Lia spoke to on one of her walks to loosen up. He recommended to take the bus to Listvyanka, the nearest village to Lake Baikal.

As if the bus had read the script, in the midst of Lia only just starting to decipher the timetable, around the corner came the light red and white bus. A brief pause half in the bus and half out sees Lia ask a few questions before she commits fully to boarding. Eddy flops on the light red two berth cushioned seats on the smart, modern bus with Lia snuggling in comfortably next to him. They store their luggage between their feet, as the bus is pretty empty, they nudge it further away. They have not even left the bus stop when they both fall asleep, without warning.

It was a longer than expected bus ride taking just over one and a half hours. Obviously, they did not notice a thing as they were asleep. They were woken by the booming voice of the driver when they arrived. They were startled and got their bags together, while yawning. They were still tired and yearned for a clean long, hot shower and a proper bed. Lia had arranged a homestay in a house back in Australia, so they were greeted by the host, Tanya.

In the freezing cold dribbling of rain, she stood. Wrapped up in many colourful blankets with her curved back stooped forward her whole face creased and wrinkled as she smiled a toothless grin. She instantly came to them with such a ferocious welcoming expression as if there were long-lost family, rather than strangers. She has walked the short, steep gravelled walk up the hill away from the lake many times. It shows. As agile as a mountain goat she seems to float effortlessly up, whereas the younger, fitter duo huff and puff their way into the drab council estate compound of grey buildings, ugly block features in such a beautiful setting.

Inside the block of apartments, the grey corridors emit no light and make it dark, unwelcoming and, when it seemed impossible, even uglier. They rise a few floors, walk down far, to the end door. Tanya is embracing the company and talking constantly to Lia. She fishes for a large metal key and opens the chipped, dented green metal door to a unit inside that is very clean, immaculately presented and cosy. The hard, thick metal door with a velvet red cushioned in the interior, like a smoker's jacket, closes with a soft thud.

Inside is a distant cry from the grey corridors, lightness stealing dark walls of the soul-destroying outer shell where cockroaches scrawled in the shadows. It is like they have fallen into the rabbit hole into another world. Tanya is quick to explain that next door is where she lives with her husband. The odd smell of stewed vegetables fills the rooms as she shows off her place. She is obviously proud of the small, cosy living quarters.

She lightly, but forcefully grips Lia's left arm as she shows off the modest rooms as if she had come to inspect it, to make an offer on the place to buy. She points with a trembling defiant finger, family portrait gatherings on the tables, sideboards and decorating the peeling dark forest green wallpapered walls. Swiftly, with a proud tone, a glint of achievement and honour to them, she gives a brief description of them all as Eddy wanders off to inspect the sleeping area.

A short few waded steps she points to a small door. That they walked by thinking it was a cleaning cupboard. Yet, this leads to the bathroom. They peak inside the flimsy wooden door to a light, pastel green small basin with two small smudged grey taps to the right. The same ghastly design forms the toilet on the left. Against the wall is a smaller than small bathtub for which Lia and Eddy would have to curl their knees up to fit. Overhead, a swinging piece of string operates the lightbulb with the thinnest of clicks.

Opposite is their living room-cum-bedroom. A slightly bigger room, where the bed is to the right, flush against the walls covered in so many different coloured blankets like a rainbow had just thrown up all over the cream doona. Mismatched wooden glass display cabinets show more photographs and memorabilia of their roles as the devoting mother and father to what appears to be three children who have left the coop to fly their own lives. This is the only time they see the husband, the father. He is the still sombre looking elderly man whose mouth is hid behind a bushy white Santa Claus-inspired beard.

Most of the photographs show him sporting a brown tweed cap, with all having a pipe hanging from his concealed lips. In the centre, a small table occupies the space which is covered in magazines strewn open, papers in nonsensical logical flimsy piles and an assortment of pens scattered in different points of rest. She asks Lia not to touch as they are sorting something out. She leaves it at that, and they respect the untidy organisation pattern of her personal privacy. Back into the hallway, they enter the adjacent kitchen to the front door with its many coats hanging like they are waiting for the gallows, hung by the tops of their hoods.

Into the kitchen where the worn faded blue carpet gives way to a beige nicotine-stained coloured plastic lino, worn to the wooden floor in places. Here they find the origin of the smell. Under a small white laced cloth are warm crumbling pastries of mini cabbage pies called pirozhki. She ushers then to sit with a wave of her frail, determined arms. They do as instructed, they crouch on the light wooden stools that are too small for regular adults, around a cramped yellow laminate countertop that has hinges on it to tell a story of it being wall side for most of its life to give more space, but on the other hand to give the extra shelf or table if needed.

She stoops further underneath to check that the flimsy piece of wood is strong enough to keep it upright. With a feel of her hand she is satisfied. She places the cabbage pies near the centre. With a magical flick of the wrists she removes the lace cloth in a single motion. She turns to retrieve a dark brown wooden chopping board from the small metal drainage area by the small, obviously custom made to fit, sink. In the kitchen everything is a turn away. It is very small, like a small boat's galley. Add into this mix the addition of three adults, the space is almost suffocating. She turns with a small beige-stained chopping board, a cheap serrated blacked chipped plastic handled knife. In front of Eddy she places them gently, urging him to cut, as she places the freshly baked rye bread on the board with a soft crisp, a jar of sweet, juicy dark red cherry jam with a metal knife protruding from the top.

Tanya has joined them. Nestled in to cut a small slither of bread for herself. Eddy had cut a couple of poorly cut doorstep-thick sliced of warm bread. Lia had started to spread thick layers of cherry jam on her own as Eddy takes a bite out of the corner of his. His eyes speak the words that scream, delicious. Tanya's bum has barely settled when the shrieking whistle of the metal kettle makes Lia jump. Tanya shuffles over and pours the tea into a prepared pot. She inadvertently spills a bit over herself in her haste, for which she recoils but battles back just as quick, too ashamed to admit she may have hurt herself. She is nervous in her attempts to leave a great impression. She has already accomplished this great single feat by standing in the cold rain for them.

Nevertheless, she inhibits concerns. This is portrayed in her demeanour. Her shaky hands are a rash tremble. Her mistimed actions. Her small errors that she would normally not let happen were, in fact, happening. She was fidgety. Her eyes only giving the slight contact with Lia or Eddy before fleeting off to the stove, the ceiling, the floor, anywhere but those eyes. She was posed on the edge of her seat, ready to pounce, like a lioness awaiting her prey.

Lia's Russian helped her be more easy-going. She soothed the creases of worry to help calm her down to an extent. However, the truth of her nervous manner slowly became apparent. She revealed with a strong of repeating 'sorry's'. Spitting out mumbled apologies, after apologies. She slowly, drip fed to them that regrettably, due to the extreme cold, then the contrasting heats, the pipes had cracked, resulting in no hot water. They were disappointed. But, due to Tanya's relief at this cataleptic end of the world, her tremor was a normal slight shake. Her weak smile returned that placed so many folds and wrinkles in her face that each line etched a different story. Eddy's and Lia's bitter disappointment, frustration was concealed from Tanya.

After the ger camp, the sweltering carriage, the general time lapse that seemed an epoch away since their last shower, they were convinced they smelled of yaks poo, mixed with a blend of body order and sweat with a tangy aroma of fart, for their greatest accomplishment, they covered their momentary set back with relative ease. Tanya, not sensing their brief pause was slightly upbeat with a never-fear type attitude as she was up again.

Flinging open the low cupboard to reveal an assortment of mismatched saucepans to ensure that the gas stove would give all the hot water their desired. They overdo the dramatically, over enthusiastic appreciation here, for which Tanya noticed with a squint of her eyes. She was no fool, but went along with the charade to broadly grin, nod as it made her feel so much better. They have finished their huge snack. Ready for bed, but wanting more, to out to explore.

They stand to get ready. A prompt for Tanya to leave them be, so they can go out to explore. Tanya stands with them. She softly, firmly grabs Eddy. Not letting him go.

'Do you know,' Lia translates without thinking. Tanya speaks with Eddy, who looks uninterested about the story of Lake Baikal.

'She is an ancestor of the indigenous group, Buryats. Act surprised, Eddy.' Lia was getting frustrated with Eddy's lack of respect. 'For Christ's sake. An earthquake nearly destroyed the world. Here an earth…the earth cracked; a crack opened. Earth shook. Trees shake. Lava came and caused fire. Eddy, PLEASE, act interested, move your face. People fled, scared, could not escape the fire. They begged the Gods to stop. The earth, the…it do, didn't stop. Death was coming. People screamed. Panic. They shouted Bai Gal. It means Fire Stop. The earthquake stopped. The fire stopped, erm, burnt out. The crack was filled with the tears of the Buryats. Eddy, please, Do SOMEthing. Laugh in atonement. Astoundment even. Not for me, for Tanya's benefit.'

Eddy tries to feign interest. He established for her this is not where his future would lie. For this was far from being an Oscar nominating, let alone an Oscar award winning performance. He self-interestedly turns to walk out. Lia takes Tanya's hand like a relative. She polishes off the icy-cold rudeness that for this scene, showed Eddy in a bad light, to prove to him that she was in fact the better half. She honestly thanks her for her food, hospitality with direct, pure eye contact. Tanya was defiantly in need of some companionship as she boosts her family's achievements. To venture out would be a great excuse. It turned out to be their excuse.

Decisively, she leaves. Lia slaps Eddy hard on the back of his shoulder. Although they were both so tired and the bed that is the table for their bags looks so inviting, they decide to leave straightaway.

Not sure where to start, they stumble down towards the lake. They take an educated guess that this would be the best place to start. Also Eddy recalls seeing an 'i', which he assumes was for information. At the bottom was The Lake Baikal Museum. In a modern, but wooden style building to fit into the surrounds they enter. Fortunately, a tour had just started for which they latch on to. Their lack of sleep proves to make it difficult to stay focused. Lia cannot even be bothered to concentrate her hatred on being angry at Eddy anymore. Barely seconds in, they cannot even remember the name of the tour guide as Lia rests her head on Eddy's shoulder mussing over being tired, exhausted and generally sleepy as they lethargically follow.

Many facts are reeled off machine gun style, fast and on point. They pick up a few things, such as there are on the shores of the deepest lake in the entire world. Soon, sadly the tour guide notes, it will become the fifth ocean, although they did not hear how soon is now. The two plates are still moving and splitting the continent apart. This will eventually burst the banks of the lake forever. Even though the facts, information is so very interesting the delivery is not. It is awful. She talks in a monotone voice that carry's all the appeal of a high school teacher lecturing the daily lives of a garden snail.

It was the new animal, that they had not heard before that happened to get their attention back on track. This being a black-eyed nerpa, a freshwater seal. Apparently one of the world's only freshwater seals. Behind her is a picture of one of the said species with black greasy skin, bright adorable eyes, looking straight at them. To the right in a large dark blue tank which is in dire need of a clean, shows the swift moment of one fleeting past in a shadowed form. Inside, they are told that the very large tank holds two rescued seals. As they dash past their view, Eddy thinks they are like swimming, ballooned zeppelins.

'The nerpa,' she says, what is her name? She continues to lecture the very small contingent. 'There. See it?' Her voice did not even rise the slightest bit. 'The nerpa can maintain without water for seventy-two minutes...' Here is where she made it interesting, but in the same monotone factual deliverance, '...to find that information, many seals died.'

Lia's head snaps up from the resting position on Eddy's shoulder, to look around for the...what. To confirm what she thought she heard was correct. Eddy was surprised, but Lia's meerkat craning of her neck made it even more humouring, even more though, considering he actually thought she was asleep. However, they look at each other. They cannot help but roar with laughter.

In their heads, they're picturing, concocting the same image. The image of a nerpa's head being plunged into water, firmly submerged underneath. The timer ticking, the water thrashing. The timer held in the hand of a long white-coated scientist, tocking over to seventy-three minutes. To pick the nerpa's limp, lifeless body out of the water and proclaiming that this one had died, to try again. Stating out loud that this time they will do seventy-two minutes to see what happens. Ready, let's go. Splash.

Loudly, they pathetically fail to smother the hysterics that they could not hold in. Every time they took deep breaths to compose themselves, they looked at each other, the amusement began again.

As always, like every single museum that people go to in the world, the end is a mandatory walk through the souvenir shop. Here you can buy unfiltered Lake Baikal drinking water. Eddy cannot help himself.

'Are you kidding me right now? I mean, well, yeah, I actually mean. Really? We are standing practically in it, at the edge, why, why the living fudge do we not get it yourself…for FREEE!'

They leave the smothering warmth of the museum with an unwelcoming nippy breeze, holding a slightly prickly edge in the air as their nose and ears feel the worse of the temperatures first. They walk hand in hand around the Lake. They were thinking the chill would alert their minds, but the last few days have started, scrap that, have taken their toll, there are exhausted. Falling petals descending from the trees in the light breeze add to the magical, dreamy essence of a real time fairyland. Lia lathers her lips in strawberry Chapstick. Eddy asks for some. She leans in. They kiss. What anger?

On their way back, they stumble onto a market. Lia has had enough, whereas Eddy takes the approach of we-are-here, just-do-it. Eddy has a second wind. He storms around the place like the wind that has started to whistle through the shoreland village. He has a beer. Lia wants bed. A sleep. The simplest of pleasures. The smell from an open fire transcending with sweet smelling smoke blooms from a stall. Although the smoke is thick, it does not sting their eyes.

Eddy pushes Lia into speaking Russian to get information. She lazily translates. Her mind is fuzzy, dusty. The tiredness is starting to have an effect on her speech as she slurs as if she is drunk. It is still not second nature for her to speak Russian. Even though she was brought up speaking it, it has been a long, long time where she has spoken it for such an extended period. She still finds herself translating from Russian to Russian, to Australian and then back to Russian as that is exactly what she has been doing for the past few years. For her it takes a lot of concentration, of intense focus.

'Omul,' she wearily states.

'Omul!' Eddy proclaims. 'Omul sounds like Elmo's cousin,' with a scoff.

'Are you going to listen or not?' Lia snaps.

'Listen…' he pauses, thinking whether to play that game of poke the bear. He, wisely, thinks better and keeps his mouth shut.

'A warm smoky trout texture that is a white flesh. A delicacy.'

'Why didn't you say? Let's try some.'

Lia is too tired to argue. She does not even ask Eddy but orders a bit, to taste. It is very smoky, very delicate, very nice. Warm, crusty bread was served poking out of the paper bag for which they spread it on. Local beer, local food, could life get any better. They are shivering, uncaring on an orange wooden bench with black iron frames looking out to the lake that goes on, and on. Lia recites a story as they huddled up together.

Legend has it that submerging yourself into the lake can give you ten years of youth back. Eddy looks at Lia as if she has just challenged him. He bolts out of the bench and towards the shores. Lia follows like an argumentative teenager. The freshwater lake is so clear. So, inviting. Crystal clear and blue like a Disney movie. They feel as if they are looking out to sea, rather than looking at a lake.

Impulsively, Eddy undresses. The temperature has not been getting warmer. He took a split second to decide that the time is now. He will test the theory out. He is down to his white elastic dark blue bond underwear when he descends the stone steps. The last one makes his mind up. If he had the slightest piece of doubt, that last step took it away. He slipped. In a feeble attempt to adjust himself back to being upright he falls in. Fully submerged. The coldness shocks his body. He breathes in underwater, to not being able to breathe in as the cold has literally taken his breath away. His headaches. His muscle twitches. He climbs out as quick as he can. He moves like a lightning bolt.

Dancing to no music as if no-one is watching. Lia laughs. People are watching. They're laughing at his dance, they had heard the splash. Eddy looks like he has ants attacking him, with him trying to rub them off his arms and legs. Lia sees his panic-stricken face. Lia laughs more. She just cannot control the impulsive nature of his heroic stance a few seconds ago, to weak pretence, now. If it was nothing, it was comical, to Lia. After composing herself just enough, she flings her arms around an almost naked, shivering, pasty white Australian that is dripping wet in cold, bloody freezing waters. She rubs his exposed arms to get blood circulating. All the while laughing. He is trembling uncontrollably as he tries, fails miserably. Lia helps. Still laughing.

Back at the apartment, Tanya looks at Eddy, then at Lia. Scrupulously, she asks the question. Lia, who had only just composed herself on the walk up the hill, loses it again. She bursts into laughter as she explains to Tanya the turn of events that has led to Eddy looking like he had entered, to only re-enter a carwash.

Tanya fleetingly retreats to grab a pale blue towel, to throw it over Eddy's shoulders. She turns to the laughing Lia to lead her back into the kitchen. Eddy slides off to get dressed into warm, not damp clothes. In the kitchen Tanya has been cooking since they left. The smell is enticing. She has truly outdone herself. Eddy enters as she is carefully ladling into brown bowls, a caramelised smell of a rich dark mahogany brown soup. He is still not warm, to see the steam rise from the bowl lifts Eddy's spirits up.

Tanya gestures him to sit, Lia translates with a whisper as soft as the rising steam—shallot soup. The liquor was amazing. Just what the doctor ordered for Eddy. Inside were relatively small pork dumplings called pelmeni. These are delicate. Eddy cannot help but wonder how her shaking hands managed something so fragile. The whole dish was divine. Both, Eddy and Lia complemented the brilliance of such a simple dish done incredibly well. The dish that must have been passed down in the family, for no recipe book could teach, explain or reproduce this without prior knowledge. This was enough, however being the perfect host Tanya brings out more.

Through the whole process Tanya does not stop talking. A constant stream of animated stories for which Lia has given up translating. They do not want to be rude, but they really want to be left alone. Tanya bows down to the oven and brings out sliced pork cooked in an egg and milk mix, layered on a bed of steamy hot rice. Tanya was, is, so eager to please. She spoke intensely with Lia giving simple one-word answers. Whereas Eddy felt like he was four again.

He felt like he was around his mate's house in Redfern. He was feeling very, very uncomfortable as if he could not say anything in the presence of his mate's mother. He felt nervous. Tanya was prepared though for Lia. Like a sister that she never had. This time she had folders overflowing with pictures and paper cut-outs. She had albums of photographs to share with Lia. As uncomfortable as Eddy felt at this moment, he could have departed. Yet being in a couple was supporting one another without the other needing to ask. As he sat there, timid and shy, little did he know that tomorrow morning, a mere few short hours away he would be making this situation even worse.

The next day seemed to come around quickly. The sound of a lone garbage truck reversing woke Eddy up. Lia did not stir. She was dead to the world. He wiped his eyes. Glanced at Lia, his sleeping beauty. He preceded to the kitchen. Turning on the gas, filling water up in the pots and pans. Putting them on the naked blue flame. He headed to the bathroom to brush his teeth as the pots full of water heated up. It is chilly.

He looks up at the mirror. The bags under his eyelids are hanging to the point that a panda would be proud of the dark patches under them. He retrieves the hot water, one after the other. He pours the hot water into the smallish bath in the bathroom, before refilling the pots, returning them on the stove, to heat for Lia. Forever the gentleman. He uses a nearby plastic jug from the kitchen to do the best that he can do. A sponge, soap and he is doing the job adequately. Then a putrid smell enters the bathroom, which evokes suspicion.

Ohhhh, breakfast does not smell good, Eddy thinks to himself as he finishes the washing process. He steps up, over and out in a swift moment to draw the same pale blue towel as yesterday. It is cold in the apartment. He dries himself quickly with the glorified flannel that he was given. The blue piece of cloth was small enough to leave nothing to the imagination. In the need to warm himself fully he swings the door open. Thick, black smoke enters the bathroom. He chokes downward as his eyes glance leftward. Out of the corner of his eye he sees the kitchen. He sees the stove. The flames. Panic sets in.

He runs over to the stove. The towel falling to the floor. Trailing in his wake. He instantly sees his mistake. He has turned on the wrong hob. The wrong gas. He is not heating water. Somehow the magazine on the counter had blown onto the naked flame. Not needing a second invitation, that is all the fuel that was needed for a fire. He reaches to the towel around him. Grips nothing. The towel was not there. He looks. He sees. He grabs the damp towel and places it over the flame, while turning the hob off.

Job done. He turns to the window. Still in panic. Still in control. Still on adrenaline. Nailed. It is actually nailed shut. In a series of many windows, the smallest is the only one that can be opened. It is better than nothing. He needs to get the smell out. Tidy the ashes. Destroy the singed towel.

So, at this stage, Eddy is still dripping wet. Eddy is naked. Running naked, which is worse. Eddy is in a stranger's apartment. In a foreign land. Praying that Tanya would not arrive just yet, or, anytime soon. He is cold. His head is spinning and thinking.

'What is the Russian for sorry, I burnt your unit down?

'Shall I wake Lia?

'FUCK!'

In the next room, metres away, Lia is unfazed, oblivious to what is going on. On hearing the commotion. The slapping of wet bare feet on kitchen tiles. The swears under Eddy's breath. She murmurs between closed eyes if everything was OK. If Eddy needed help. Eddy responds quickly and defiantly to go back to sleep, with the lie that he has everything under control. His nerves betray him as he tries to calmly shouts that there is nothing to see here.

Aforementioned, it was a very cold morning. In his frantic panic, Eddy finds another window. With hope, a prayer and a God he does not believe in, maybe, just maybe, he can get away with this. This new window is even smaller than the first. The size of a postcard, but he is ridiculously optimistic. Lia stirs, not believing Eddy's answer. She opens her eyes to see Eddy do a naked jig. In a speed that only an agitated frenzy could accomplish, he has finished cleaning the mess, tidying the kitchen, when he hears the all too familiar noise of a key entering a lock. He cannot, for the life of him, smell anything but burning paper. He asks Lia if the smell still remains in the unit, or in his nostrils. But on hearing the noise he sprints. He is still naked. In a fluent motion. He enters the bedroom. He dives under the blanket covered bed. To leap up again to dress.

Lia is laughing. She is in hysterics. Not helping at all. Tanya enters. She senses something is not completely correct. She is no fool. Lia collects herself enough to address the problem to Tanya. Eddy is embarrassed. Too embarrassed, very humiliated. He does not want to leave the make-shift bedroom. He is, officially, four again. The problem is resolved. Tanya laughs it off as no damage has really been done.

Lia re-enters the bedroom to see Eddy shuffle from one foot to another. Looking down. Distraught. Lia helps, well not really, but she laughs at his boyhood appearance. He is so disappointed at himself, but quietly pleased, a little relieved, with a hint of happiness, that all those pointless fire training meetings, conferences, had actually sunk in. For the first time they had actually come into use. With the coaxing of Lia Eddy returns to the kitchen. He struggles for eye contact. Tanya is fantastic. She reassures Eddy with no speech, but a resting, loving tender hand on her right shoulder that it is ok. He looks up. He sees a worn, wrinkled smile of affection. All is forgiven. No harm was done. Well, only to Eddy's pride.

Tanya goes about her plan. She cooks stacks of blini with cherry jam. More beautiful cabbage pies. It takes no time for them to pack, as Tanya insists on walking them back to the bus station. She pushes into the palm of their hands, without taking no for an answer, she thrusts some cabbage pies for them to take. They wave goodbye to Irkutsk, to Tanya.

The myth, the stereotype that Russian people are as cold as the landscape has been forever squashed by this simple, alluring interaction with Tanya. The weather on the other hand was as unpredictable as general human behaviour.

Irkutsk welcomes them in an enveloping of grey haze, strong pelts of wind forced rain. They planned to walk around the Paris of the East, as it is known, but this dreadful weather is not the most inviting for that kind of activity. However, with the stopping of the bus, the rain stops, the wind is still relentless, and the grey clouds are reflected in the drab buildings of the bus depot.

'When will we come back?' Lia remarks with a shrug of her shoulders. As if she had just read Eddy's mind.

Very uninspiring, dirty garbage blows over the wet-sodden tarmac. The sewage smell flows unpleasantly around the excuse for a bus station. In the corner is a small shack. Inside, a small lightbulb that barely illuminates any brightness swings in the dark gloom, a single high-pitched buzz from a fly for company. Lia hesitantly strolls over, as Eddy retrieves their bags. This seems to be a common occurrence. Eddy gets the bags as Lia walks to get tickets, or do anything but help with the bags. Heavy loaded he shuffles to the shack. He waits outside looking at the same building in the postcards, books and chocolate boxes, over and over again. Lia giggles as she sees him staring into space.

'What are you laughing at?' Eddy asks irritably.

'The coldness of that lady. She looks so welcoming, but looks are definitely deceiving. Ah... you are looking at the Lace House, she did seem to strongly recommend seeing that.'

The map that she opens out has a thick felt tip shaky line of red. This is a walking trail, although she states, without reason, not to keep to it. They have time, they share their luggage and take the red felt-tip route, as uninstructed. The lightness of the world outside of the tourist office dungeon is so much better. Looking at the brooding thick, dark clouds they stick to the advice to stay close to the city centre, as not only are they lugging their bags, the promise of more rain is not so much an assumption, but a presumption.

The buildings are stunning, beautiful and unique. The city is always revolving. Always growing. Some have lived through the hard times. Some have been destroyed, then rebuilt the same, or better. Some are just beginning. Frequently placed black cast iron benches tell of the recent celebration of the birth of the city. The wooden and stone architecture shows a city of many influences. They look at the water-droplet marked map, around the sights that surround them, the sites of things that have been, that are coming.

A short tram ride on the shaky deserted tin can takes them near to the banks of the calm ripples of the wide Angara River. The deepest river in Siberia, opposite is the Irkutsk River, a lot smaller, but gave birth to the name of the city. This seems to be the perfect place to walk back in the direction of the bus station. The promenade is a red brick wide walkway where skaters speed pass, expertly missing the lone dog walker who is looking as cold as the chilly blast of the sub-freezing air feels.

In the darkness of what should be the daylight, the Siberian Baroque movement is hard to miss. As if designed by Walt Disney, it could grace any palace in a fairy tale dream that Disney imagined and then created on the silver screen. The wall is a background of whitewash, decorated in complex full body icons of saints in picturesque frames. The sparkling golden onion domes are held aloft by salmon pink, white and green towers. The belltower, in all its fifteen-metre glory and splendour, tries to piece the grey clouds above to the blue beyond, but to no avail. In complimentary assistance are the red, orange and green colourful highlights that attract them like a magpie to treasures.

The Bogoyavlensky Cathedral is the largest, most valuable in Siberia. Originally made of wood, but destroyed, rebuilt in stone. To be better, more expansive, more expensive. Once it was used as a bakery, during the Soviet times, as well as a soldier's dormitory. Now used for its intended use, it is eerily quiet. They hear the splash of the small puddles made by their feet, but the sound seems to be menacing looming. If this was a horror movie there would be attack in the upcoming moments as the screaking high-pitched violin comes more intense, louder and sharper.

The salmon-red brick exterior, with many elements is mirrored inside with magnificently preserved iconostasis that present a festival of colour with no surface space left for any more detail. Open-mouthed, they nearly trip over their own tongue as they slowly glide forward, as if an invisible rope is controlling their actions.

Just like Listvyanka, the wooden houses are well preserved. Police light-blue shutters on dark green houses contrast respectfully against the shadowy greys of the deep, heavy clouds. They gaze and scan the streets, as they attempt to absorb themselves in the exquisiteness beauty against the dreary backdrop. The smell of freshly cut grass seems to heighten the pine, cedar and larch tree houses with a different, somehow more real feel. Attractively carved framed rectangle window. Ornate shutters. Colourful homes. Wooden lacing. Some are up for sale, with ugly canvas banners shrewd across the eaves.

The city had just celebrated its three-hundred and fiftieth birthday, with cast iron benches with '350' in the spectacular artwork that gleams from the recent rain. In the floor is a green line, for which is a 'walking trail'. They are travelling it, backwards, but look at the map that follows the red tip felt squiggle, near enough the same route. Why did she not say this in the tourist dungeon office.

Behind the Cathedral is the large, impressive Eternal Flame Memorial, dedicated to the Siberian soldiers that died in battles against the Nazi's during World War II. The eternal flame was lit from the same flickering flames which are alight at the Tomb of the Unknown Soldier at the Kremlin in Moscow, after arriving by a much-rejoiced torch relay. The memorial commemorates the two-hundred and thousand men that left to go to the front to fight. Of them, fifty thousand never returned home.

Three white, slender rectangles tell the death-marked story. The central one is supported by a medal as a header in black, below in the same black are thirty-seven names, neatly carved. These are the names of the seventy locals that received the title of the Hero of the Soviet Union. The Russian flag wrestles with the invisible wind on the top with another one. This has the pale blue narrower stripes on the sides with a white band dissecting the middle.

In this is a bright green laurel, where a black ferocious animal of mythical proportions holds a dead blood-red object in its mouth. The animal with its bushy tail like a fox, webbed back feet like a duck, whiskers like a cat is, apparently, said to depict a black tiger, and in its mouth, a sable. Eddy does not fully believe Lia's explanation so grabs the book and reads the small column about the flag of Irkutsk. He looks at the printed words, back at the fluttering flag, and down again. What cannot speak, cannot surely lie, but the artistic merit has a little to be said. Lia says nothing, her eyes say everything.

Opposite is a shiny polished slab of granite that flickers the eternal flame in its surface as it stays lit in the wind emitting from the central star in the middle. A stern, looking guard supports a rifle with a strong poker face. He has a felt grey cap and a heavy grey long coat. It is cold but he is not showing anything. In an open plan of steps and displays the area ends fragrant perfume caresses of flowers from the many bouquets, wreaths and tributes that are left around the memorial in a neat, organised manner. The colours break up the smooth deep red granite of the area. Pine trees rustle as they walk up the green hedge flanked steps. The area is vast. The air cuts through them with the penetration of small, effective daggers. Their footsteps make monosyllabic, hollow noises that the wind immediately takes away.

Looking over the vast open space, they head back down the steep, concrete grey slabbing steps to the banks of the Angara River. A graffiti writer has written on the wide promenade, a tribute for a very simple message to, what they assume, is a now happily, wed couple. The curvy white letters simply read: 'I Love You Ewa'.

For a good twenty minutes they walk, leaning onto each other, taking in the attractiveness of the wet-covered sheen as their luggage follows behind them making fresh track marks. They stop, stare at the blue onion-topped, golden star dotted tops of the white elegant towers, with dark lime green tiled glazed roofs of the three-hundred-year-old Znamensky Monastery, the Church of the Holy Sign Painter. It is a hidden gem that they were not told to visit. They appreciate from afar as they try to cross the hot wheel frenzy of small cars that think they are Formula One racers.

It is seemingly impossible to cross. They want to cross the thundering racetrack of a road that seems to encourage cars to wind up around the ridiculously immense roundabout before letting go, close to flying off. They are very patient and dare not risk a potential fatality. Finally, safe and sound, on the other side they enter. Lia stops Eddy with a tight grasp on his wrist. She had read the sign which states no speaking in loud voices, no photographs, no hands in pockets, discussions to be short and necessary and to not walk around unnecessarily. She relays this with a warning tone, rather than a mocking manner.

They are confronted by such a beautiful hall basking in yellow hues. It is deceptively smaller than it looks, but the intrinsic detail of the paintings, icons, quite, literally take their breaths away. It is a struggle to resist the temptation to talk about what they are seeing. Portraying all the exquisite skill of a magnificently iced wedding cake the exterior is showcased by wonderful murals. Dark wooden vaulted ceilings reached by towering iconostasis and a gold sarcophagus that is rumoured to hold the relics of Siberian missionary St Inokent. In a light thin wooden frame is a painting of St Inokent, or Innocent, or to Eddy and the rest of the world, John.

He was born here then became the first archbishop of Irkutsk, the Enlightener of the Aleuts, the Apostle to the Americas as well as also known as St Innocent of Alaska. His long-elongated fingers dangle green beads in his left hand and a red cross in his right. Covered in a light red cloak over his brown robe with red lapels with a golden outline of a cross on each side of his chest, highlighted by a bold cream aura behind, that shines resolutely like a full moon. A square-topped burgundy cap covers his head and flaps to his shoulders. His manicured beard wisps with grey in the light brown, his eyes look tired with a slight tear welling up in the corners. Behind him in the golden yellow background are Chinese symbols and the rays of the sun kissing him from the left corner. This is obviously one of the main icons to be prayed to with the flowers, coins and trinkets that scatter in front of him.

Outside, they still have not let their voices be heard. Through the ravaging green grass around the monastery is a who's who of celebrity Russians. The nautical themed white tomb with sea ropes, anchors, hourglass and the maritime themes around the plinth, is of the explorer who claimed Alaska for Russia. Grigory Shelekhov died nine years after leading an expedition to Russian America to find the first permanent Russian settlement in North America in 1786. He is portrayed within a rope frame as a black silhouette, within an obelisk crowned with a bright gold cross that glows in the damp residue of the showers.

In contrast to that glory is a modest, humble white headstone belonging to Decemberist wife, Ekaterina Trubetskaya. This is where Eddy is confused, so Lia introduces him, for the first time, to The Decembrists. All this time Eddy naively thought it was just a name of a band. Lia seems to have unlocked a fountain of knowledge that she did not know, forgot or chose to forget, yet, she obtained it all.

'The Decemberists were a Russian class, kinda upper-class revolutionaries,' Lia announces with the same pace as they walk. 'Exiled to, erm, here I think in 1820s. Yes, 1825, I am pretty sure. A group of army officers occupied St Petersburg in a rather poorly attempt of a coup against Tsar Nicolas I. The Tsar responded by killing sixty. Most of the leaders were then caught and executed. The rest sent here, in, I think, or around here, anyway in exile that is sure…for sure, I am, yes. I am sure.'

Eddy understands, but feels he needs to do a little research of his own. Time is flying faster than the wind that seems to be picking up with the forecast of rain to start pouring again soon. They decided that they have to move on, quicker. The brooding clouds are moving faster in the skies above.

As they leave the grounds, basically outside the Znamensky Monastery, very near the entrance, is the White Russian commander Admiral Kolchak, looking down from a ridiculously high, block cement decorated plinth with soldiers depicted, looking at each other in different attire within. They saw it as they were entering but did not pay any attention to it. As they are walking past it is time to pay notice to the magnificent statue. At their feet is a large green wreath with red and white blossoming flowers with no aroma on a light brown, raked bed of soil. Above them is the looming Admiral in a black iron overcoat.

Lia reads from her book that this was controversially erected in 2004, which explains the newer look when compared to others that they have walked around. Although she does not state the why or how it was controversial, she does proceed to state that the plinth is so large to deflect die-hard communists from vandalising it. Kolchak seems to be walking forward in thick leather jackets and a large coat that hangs from his broad shoulders. He looks strict, in a foul temper. It is said, on the night of the sixth of February 1920, the Supreme Leader and Commander-in-chief of All Russian Land and Sea Forces, Alexander Kolchak, was shot dead, executed by Bolsheviks on this very spot.

He was the leader of the White Movement, the White Army that fought the Communist Bolsheviks, the Red Army. That would explain his dour looking mood. Bizarrely enough a cross indicates the spot. This symbol, like a target from a gun, this was not the time for jokes but Eddy, well, being Eddy, could not help himself. In this risk, the joke was perceived pretty well by Lia who muffled a laugh, when she did not want to laugh.

Each and every corner of this purely delightful city has an interesting piece of architecture. They have quickened their pace now as time is approaching to leave. However, they cannot help but keep stopping to admire another gem. They pass a dominating Moorish-style brown-red building with beige frames above the windows. It is huge and takes an entire corner of a block. Eddy is tugged by Lia before finding out what it is. He has a fascination for buildings. He looks for pieces of interest in the simplest building. Looks them up and down like a beautiful woman that has captivated his senses leaving him to go into overload at the unique little finishing touches, the ode, the things that an artist leaves behind in a bitter twist, a polite twist of a knife, a love gone bad, a love that is forbidden. He searches. He is not given that privilege as, and he has to admit begrudgingly, that he has not the time today. As he is being, rightly pulled, tugged. He attempts to persuade them to stay one day. Would it hurt, really?

He pulled out every excuse in his favour. Verbalising the sights to be seen, the sights to be cherished, that the luggage is getting heavier, so much more to experience here, but these all fall-on deaf ears. Lia has a schedule. She has a motive. She wants to be at home on the date that she said she would be. She has a deadline.

The mature lady, who may have been younger than her gaunt, pale zombie-featureless appearance would portray, back in the dungeon. Chained for eternity at her minuscule desk at the dimly lit tourist office, where rats rule the bus depot floors and unseen spiders in streams of silver webs rule the roost. Her voice quivers timbres of aged chords as she profoundly insisted that they go and see the Lace House, the House of the Shastin, which is also known as the House of Europe for its many names that she throws at Lia in a verbal volley of fired reasons to go, to just go.

The elderly lady kept using a plural form, as assuming that a lady, this lady standing alone in front of her, Lia, would not be travelling alone. By the end, her voice was almost a shrilling plea. She remembers her forcing the nib of the demonstrating pen to blunting point, on the exact spot on the map, labelled Shastin House. To further prove a point, as she repeats the instruction, the pen nestled in like a dagger marking the aforementioned treasure. She looks at the pinprick of a hole that her force had caused. To then, ever so slightly turn her head, Lia in her minds-eye visualises her gestation of her flabby free arm as she demonstrated the abundance of merchandise around the small, cosy shack.

The Lace House is portrayed in everything from snow globes, postcards, books to paintings, brochures and pamphlets. It is a richly carved wooden house with timbers eaves in a baroque style. She has to admit it does look gingerbread sweet in its elegance.

But at this point. At this precise moment, Lia is reluctant to go. She is cold, physically shaking, her hands grasping together through the woollen pockets to grip as if retaining as much of the warmth contained within her grasp as possible. She is tired of heaving her luggage around the cobbled to gravel to paved streets of the city, possibly due to her not being used to it. She does not have the same eagerness as Eddy, but he twists her arm, somewhat easily when he insists that she would probably regret not making the effort. Dragging the heavy casket of clothes, they bump along in the direction of the spoken treasure.

Arriving moments later, this was not an ebb and flow affair. Rather a stop, start, retrack, turn and eventually stumble on this magnificent building. Reminiscent of a gliding plane to seemingly spiral around to eventually corkscrew to the point in the map. It is stunning. Instantly worth it. Awestricken. They gawk. The clump of the plastic handle from Lia's luggage hits the road as she did not even notice her hand letting it go. They deliberately glance, unhurriedly over the cream panelled windows with shutters. Lia was stubborn in her response. She could not help but think it was like the numerous other wooden houses she had seen on the powerwalk throughout the entire city.

Although Eddy was amazed that a house of merchants, the Shastins, was built in 1907 and was still standing tall, he was not startled that the beauty would be protected. In a town built as a jail-fortress, high on the banks of the river, this gingerbread house with its sleeping wizard capped conical roof was well merit of their visit. He thinks that Lia is being stalwart in her pig-headedness. Wisely, he only thinks this, he does not hedge his bets in stating his own personal opinion.

Lia's heels were digging in. Her wheels of her bags dragging along in conceptually quick setting cement. Yet Eddy insists that this is the correct route to the train station. She is not swallowing his story by portraying her expressions of distrust in manifesting heavy-footed stamps from each of her feet, that create small splashing brown, grainy upsurges in the struggling to dry puddles. All the same, he storms in his pursuit, leaving behind the sulking temptress that grudgingly follows his lead. He manages to offer them a different view of the Angara River, trickling waters as grey as the skies cascading its shiny droplets.

Reflecting in a lighter shade of grey is a statue of the only Tsar ever to visit Siberia. On a rain-glistening red plinth with the two-headed eagle in metal holding a readable scroll with its talons, the Tsar Alexander III looks on. This is also the only statue that remained from the pre-revolutionary times in Irkutsk. They are looking up to the creator, the trailblazer for the train that they are travelling, the Great Trans-Siberian Railway built on the people's money. The scroll is the Royal edict for the construction of the said railway. In laurels on the other sides are portraits of people who explored and developed Siberia.

The Tsar looks on proud. His right arm by his side and his left is in the position of trying to feel for something that he has lost and cannot remember what. Or he was once holding a very thin baton or, an invisible piece of string for an imaginary balloon. Eddy would like to stay longer, but the evident signs that they are tourists, foreigners, have brought the beggars and entertainers around them like the squawking two-headed eagle that is looking at them, following them, ready to pounce. Lia conceals her surprise with the broadest of smiles that she has not had on her face for a while. It was now Eddy's time to sulk, just a little bit.

On the first pedestrianised street in Russia, Ul Uritskogo is the shopping area with familiar brands within the shells of former great buildings which may be why it is dubbed the Paris of Siberia. Within the familiar, are private, glitzy boutiques, international brands and undiscovered fashionable diamonds within the sparkling gems. Europe has unquestionably arrived here in Asia. Eddy has taken far too many photographs of buildings but still continues to snap more. It is a very walkable city which is lucky for Eddy who has had the sole responsibility of being the porter, the guide and the shoulder for Lia's crocodile tears.

Without warning, the heavens open. The sky amazingly was getting darker, it was similar to a light night-time when they sensed the pending rain that was lurking. In a remarkable win, it seemed to happen at the end of their walk. They got a little wet, well a little is to say Lake Baikal is a mere puddle, they were beyond dry, saturated. They spot transportation which Lia quickly translates as the route to the railway station. In a hurried spray of water kicking from her fiercely turning small bag wheels, the trailing tails of her coat and muttered words she was off, for Eddy to become the pursuer.

They board from the rounded smooth cobbled stones onto the plastic, slippery grey trolley bus. Their shoes squeaking on the plastic floor. They plonk themselves on the soft seats, Eddy composed, while Lia more exasperated. They look at one another in the eyes, at their wet hair. Lia gently slaps Eddy around the face, to immediately bring it back to kiss his lips while laughing. Muttering an angry, 'Gee, you, you…' Her finger prodding sharply into his chest like a woodpecker as she finishes her sentence through clenched teeth. 'You are such a shit…sometimes. A shit.' Another slap around the cheek as she turns to accidentally slap him with her matted, drenched hair as she gazes out of the city through the pearl veils of her graffiti strewed window. The tinny sound of a rattling bean can is heard from the white top, with its red bottom stripe which was getting a good clean in this downpour. A jolt with the slight electric buzz, screech and sway of the single carriage that waddled them around, over the bridge, up and down streets towards the railway station.

Eddy's view of the front was a distant haze of a road being there within the briefless reveals of the single sweeping windscreen wiper. As they exit, Lia pays. Eddy clumsily tries to rush in nervous imbalances with the bags toppling, causing many apology's as their wet bags tumble on the dry trousers of the passengers trying to get off. Outside the cream grand wide railway station transcends an imposing welcome. The railway station looks more like a palace with its pale green highlights around the vast long rectangle windows with curved tops.

Even in this non-existent light of the day, the darkness has confused the iron street posts with three lanterns which have flickered on, to go off again, to light up again in hesitant indecisiveness. In the rain Eddy readjusts his hands on the luggage, before feeling comfortable once again to proceed.

They walk into the vast hall. They almost feel guilty as if they should be taking their shoes off to enter, let alone bring in the wet to dirty up the inside. The doors are giant, fit for immortals rather than mortals. Immediately they look for a screen, something with information. Behind them is a black electric screen hanging tall and proud, directly above them. Lia turns around after Eddy located the desired information which was illegible for him. She tilts her head heavenward to scan the red lights of words and then moves to a ticket window. Uncertain of the correct pronunciation, she nervously asks for the ticket. In silence with a nod of the head, the sour-faced older-than-time man presses a few buttons on his keyboard.

After letting her change pour into the turntable tray, a high-pitched fleeting hum starts and ends with a ticket coming out of the side of a black metal box to her left. He motions her along without glancing up to give any sign of her face. She places the tickets into another window that looks more like a highly designed old bank teller than a ticket booth. The frail hands pick up the papers on the other side of the brass bars behind the glass, rips them apart. She peers at them over halfmoon glasses, through a magnified circular clearing in the glass.

From behind the frosted glass, the lady does not look up as she stamps a pink imprint over both of the tickets that is unclear, smudged, illegible, before sliding them under the glass back to them. Lia retrieves the thin, fragile feeling white paper ticket, the size of a small postcard which has all the information in Cyrillic but in the centre is a small table that gives numbers. She thanks the lady, predictably gets no recognition back. Both of the workers here seem to be not enjoying their job, and not even try to pass any façade to prove otherwise. Lia looks and points at a platform sign to their right, with the time of departure, carriage and seat on the ticket. They have time to get some supplies. Why were they both whispering, as if feeling that they should be respectfully quiet.

343

Lia stands waiting with the luggage as she looks around at the grand hall, as Eddy at long last has the handled grip of any luggage taking off him. It was not so much offered as in taken for granted as he bombs away, weaving like a bee amongst an array of colourful flowers dripping in the morning dew in search for the guidebook-mentioned market.

He cannot believe what he has come across. The market is not the standard railway store. It is an animated mosaic of colours, aromas, scents and savours with an assortment of varieties. Everything from alcohol to water, fresh to frozen, baked to roasted, cleaning to be cleaned. He gets the essentials, plus the paramount, the all-important—vodka.

'Vodka is cheaper than water!' he yells to Lia to justify the three bottles of vodka that he has clinking in his brown paper bag, waving around like a born-again child with a bag full of sweets. Lia just smiles back. No words were needed. After all, this subsequent portion of the journey has been dubbed the vodka train, so why not embrace it rather than fight it.

They wait. Lia patiently leans against the redwood like pink champagne marble column. Eddy paces like an expectant father. The large black and white suspended clock face ticks on, and past the departure time. Still no train. Well past the time now. Still no train. Eddy's tapping right foot echoes rapidly in the platform shelter as if taunting him. They are agitated, Eddy seems to be broaching this more than Lia by catechising her, with a tinge of aggression, to go and ask what is going on. They are worried. Worried that they have missed it. They look around at the small pockets of people on other platforms.

Finally, Lia admits defeat to Eddy's beseeching moans, she decides to go to find out some answers. She rapidly jumps up like a jack in the box. Turns in the same swift movement. Is off. Without a word. The seconds tick, echoed creaks of time that increasingly sound like a hammer blow on solid steel. Eddy is waiting. The time seems fast, but goes slow. Eddy stares back and forth from the clock, to the vacated empty space where Lia had disappeared.

Then she arrives back. Like a mirage, she is shimmering along the platform, gracefully rolling. Slowly strolling, without a worry. Laughing, without a sound. Shaking her head, without a question. Talking to herself, without a care. Eddy stands up. Tapping his foot. A frown etched over his brow. An impatient fraying off his arms outstretched with palms upturned in an expression of 'what's going on?' He was restive. She struggles to speak with the grin high in her cheekbones.

'You would not guess what?' Lia nonchalantly asks with a blasé flick of her wrist.

'What?' an impatient Eddy retorts. 'What?

'Well. Funny thing…'

'Out with it.' Eddy's frustration is rising. Lia is still giggling her way through the story to where the train is.

'Well. That time on the ticket. The time of departure—'

'Please. Please tell me that you read it right. That the date is right. Its RIGHT?'

'He whom has little faith, young Eddy. Yes. I am great. I read it right.' She self-mocks herself. 'One tiny. One little, small, minuscule thing.'

'You're starting to piss me off, Lia. Re-ally piss me off.'

'Well…' Lia was the cat, Eddy the ball of yarn.

'PLEASE!' failing in his attempt to not snap.

'OK. OK. OK. The time is not in Irkutsk. The time is in Moscow time. Apparently, I have been told. All the times that the timetables, tickets and the like will be, from this point forward, Moscow time. The time is in Moscow. Hence, we…'

'Bullshit! Really? What is the time difference?'

'Let me finish. Hence, we are five hours early.'

'We still have another four and change hours to wait?'

She bursts into a fit of laughter. Eddy fails to see the humour.

'But, but you looked at the timetable when we came in?' Eddy implored, not quite believing Lia's explanation, even if it was the truth.

'I missed it.' Still laughing, not trying to control herself. 'Let's go. Have a meal, something to eat. Come on you. Grab the gear. Come on.'

With the measured inward bounding of the smooth countryside mirrored green train to the platform, Eddy lets out a deep exhaled breath of relief. Lia nudges Eddy light-heartedly in the ribs, looks up, winks with a gleaming flicker of mischievous intent and smirks. Inside, she has not stopped sniggering.

The train eventually pauses with an intense short shrilling squeak that makes them jolt alongside the train. The train itself is noticeably different, it appears larger, the impression of being taller, more sophisticated. The interior mimics the exterior. It seems to have more space in the cabin, all the while with a very similar layout. They have not properly settled when they hear the checking of correct tickets cascading closer from cabin to cabin. The clump of thick heavy steps on the thinly carpeted floor, the crisp click of a hole puncher and a few mumbles of exchange.

The carriage attendant, a Russian immigration officer equipped with bedazzled acrylic nails asks for their passport and papers without crossing the thin line into the cabin. As she flicks through their passport and tickets like she was a casino showgirl counting off peoples hard-earned cash dreams, she asks for their destination. She is in charge, known as the provodnitsa. The heavy uncomfortable looking gleaming black shoes with the slightest of heels seem a size to big in her small feet.

She wears a blue uniform of a short skirt and blazer, with a white shirt that barely hold in her Las Vegas stripper-sized breasts. A thin blue ribbon ties a hairdo that would not seem to be out of place at a drag queen convention. She is a built unit, not fat, not muscular, but radiating undeniable affirming authorisation in her assertiveness and pose. She tells them that the timetable is in Moscow time and not local time. 'Where was she five hours ago?' Eddy states under his breath in slight intimidation of her.

She does give some other information in a not so much broken, but shattered English, which is great to know. Such as some of the names are different when compared to the timetable and to the station. The provodnitsa states that she will let them know when they are at Yekaterinburg, the first city in Asian Russia, their next destination. She mentions that the station is called Sverdlovsk, which was the name of the city between 1924 and 1991.

They have time to become peaceful in their space and organise their meagre possessions as the train squeals, yet another shrill before gradually building up momentum to leave the station. On leaving Irkutsk, they skirt Lake Baikal. Eddy looks longingly out of the window rethinking that he could have been there for a little longer with a choice, in prison, possibly without a choice, if he had in actual fact burnt down a KGB's mother's house.

The sunlight is leaving the sky, spilling sparkling diamonds on the rippling freshwater lake the churns beneath. This was mentioned in Lia's book as the hardest construction of the railway for the convicts using picks and shovels, but what a view. They use a spectacular route of tunnels, bridges as they curve in the vicinity the largest freshwater lake in the world. This turns out to be the fabled vodka portion of the train. The aptly, somewhat unexpectant, but appropriately named Vodka Train. The Russians in their cabin insist on sharing their food as they encourage them to play chess, or cards.

It starts so innocently with monosyllabic conversations by Eddy with the help of Lia to translate. The rough appearance of them. The scruffy clothes and the general voices of them both that resemble a frog having a bad cold, could have made this a daunting, nerve-wrecking affair if he was solo. Yet in the contentment of each other they took solace. The evening came around soon. They had gotten settled, had a rough snack made by cutting the bread and cheese, by means of using Eddy's small bloodred handled Swiss army knife to make a poor imitation of a sandwich. The sun disappeared past the leafless trees. Like an umbrella stand from the bag of Mary Poppins, the vodka transcendentally appeared from the dirty dark grey duffle bag.

The Russians are one side of the lower bunk, Eddy and Lia are on the other. They teach them the traditional proper way of drinking vodka. Sniffing a cucumber, taking a neat healthy sized shot of vodka, then biting a small piece of the said pickled cucumber. Lia asked, but got no logical reason to why this was done. When the cucumber stock was depleted, this vegetable

345

changed to a smoked cheese in a stringy form that resembled entwined rope, but tasted bloody good, or was that just the vodka talking and tasting.

The single bottle of vodka had turned into three, with this one coming to the end, just as the night was starting. Eddy felt relieved that the last drops were being shaken out equally into their glasses, the night was, thankfully, coming to the end. He was legitimately very tired, ready for bed. However, just when the last drops descended into small drips, with all the will that the eyes of Oleg, the cabinmate, could muster by the Russians using all their hope, the last of the vodka plunged into Eddy's half empty plastic cup with a single, thudding splatter.

He turned as he spoke to Alexii. His eyes widened as if he had indeed forgotten. Out of his equally smudged stained bag which resembled a giraffe's neck, he fished his hand inside the half-unzipped bag to bring out a dirty, dusty fingerprint-marked clear thick liquid, which could only be one thing—more vodka. It opened up with a slight fizz as Oleg fished though his other dark khaki green cargo bag for some dark, dry rye crackers. Lia translates for Eddy who they were. They were friends from school who were travelling back after a week away. Obviously, their holiday was not over yet.

'Moonshine!' she exclaims, pointing to the dusty syrup like liquid pouring into their plastic cups with gusto, as Eddy visibly shows his dispiritedness. 'Or,' she roars with her head tilting back and the fillings of their fellow adopted compatriots laughing a remark that Oleg had spoken. 'Sorries, my love. They, they, they call itz, the, simply, thee teeth drier.'

As Eddy took the shot, he did not want to be rude, they diluted each one with more water dripping from the edge of the cup than inside, he found out immediately why. The moonshine touched the back of his throat, through clenched teeth and lips that are open he breathed in sharply. This was strong. Even mixed with water, it was very, very strong.

The moonshine seemed to penetrate the back of his throat and go straight through his skull, avoiding his bloodstream to penetrate fully his brain functioning abilities. Vodka has a great knack of creeping up on people, especially this "moonshine". The dry crackers were supposed to lighten the effects of alcohol. This was a myth. They were fine. They felt ok. They were fucked. They were not. They were rooted. Unconditionally, unequivocally drunk.

Giggling like children. Talking louder. Shouting out. Laughing raucously. Getting rowdily with every sip, not even a full shot. They enjoyed themselves. They experienced a different part of themselves. They found it very hard to get them to understand that they did not want any more drink. The Russians did not like to be refused an offering of drink. They tried to get onto their side of the carriage. Onto their bed. They tried to push themselves to accommodate themselves, which Eddy resisted, sat firm. Not very Australian.

Eddy's patience was tested. His patience was pushed to breaking point. He pushed Oleg back, who stumbled without control into Alexii who in turn powerless to control his own movement, let alone being struck to move another way, hit his head, fortunately sweetly, on the metal frame of the bunk bed. This got the attention Eddy was after that they were not welcome over in their personal space. They were all incredibly drunk. With vigorous coaxing, shepherding, they went to their side of the carriage. After a few heated demonstrations and protests by Eddy, they stayed put, whereas Lia had slumped into a ball on the unmade bed, ready to sleep. Eddy and Lia curled around each other.

They got woken up a number of times by bangs on the paper-thin walls of the cabin to be told to shut up as they were snoring louder than the wheels of the carriage, which was a magnificent accomplishment.

Amazingly enough, they both wake clear-headed. Tired. So very, ridiculously fatigued, but hangover free. The wide-eyed expression of astonishment as they focus on each other needs no words. They do, however, have a slight memory lapse of what was said, done and acted out over the course of the evening. Taking it in turns they wash as best they can in the small stainless-steel round basin in the toilets, in the attempt to carry away the effects of any unremembered embarrassments from that night, last night's self-indulgent debauchery, down the darkness of the plughole onto the fleetingly whooshing of the railway tracks.

Lia looks up from the faucet, hands resting on the curved cold sides of the basin to see the drooping face of sleepiness. No soap and water was going to take the appearance away, only the feel. Well, that was temporary. The moment she steps back into the cabin, sleep flits in, dragging with it an unknown invisible heavy cloak of enervation that swallows up any uplifting feel that she managed to muster in the bathroom.

Immediately, she takes action to move, to insist that they get something in their stomachs. They walk the walk of shame to the dining cart making apologies as they pass each cabin along their carriage. As a scrunching sloth like towering crawl, they make their way along, pinballing from side to side in the narrow corridor of each carriages through the Alice in Wonderland assortment of seemingly many doors at each end. For what seems a ceaseless, unavoidable torment of fragrant, mouth-watering aromas that originate from the dining cart, they eventually open yet another door to arrive at the journey's purpose.

They see a free table from the door and proceed to slump on the chairs as if they had just ran a marathon. An obviously drunk waitress comes over that was swaying, not due to the motion, but due to her own personal moonshine. She was so funny. She was like a little ball of nervous energy, rebounding from one table to the other without stopping until she felt the table with a clumsy bump of her nude-coloured tights. She would be covered in bruises by the end of this train ride, with no recollection to why. Drinks were knocked over; sorriest apologies were made, fruitlessly, as she returned with new drinks that spilled their way up the narrow aisle.

Lia grabbed her and ordered what a couple opposite where having as the smell drifted over invitingly. She brought over two deep bowls of Solyanka. As she placed them down many mini ripples in the bowl lapped the sides but did not splash over. Lia spoke to her after she had placed the bowls down, they laughed. Eddy actually found himself laughing about nothing he knew to jump on the band wagon. They looked at him, and laughed more. Was it about him? He was too tired to be paranoid so brushed it off as quickly as it rose inside of him.

Solyanka was a thick soup with mushrooms, cabbage, cucumbers, spices, capers, tomatoes, lemon juice, mushrooms and something else that Eddy could not pick out. He was familiar with the taste, but his brain could not pigeonhole the flavour. This bowl of heavenly goodness was, to them, simply called the Saviour. Eddy took a spoonful of the sour soup, but not in an unpleasant way, the spice seemed to balance it out, perfectly. He was surprised at the glorious pleasant sour that settled on his stomach.

Going by the silent facial expressions in Lia's eyes, Eddy could tell that she felt the same. With unnecessary uncommunicativeness they slurped, hunched over their own bowls. The bellowing cloud, upon cloud of steam filling their senses. The clinking of their spoons trying to drag up every last morsel of flavour from the empty bowl. They returned, hand in hand to their cabin to read, sleep and relax through the rather uneventful next forty-eight hours with a warm, full belly of bliss.

Halfway through the sleep, in the middle of the second morning, Eddy wakes with a pounding headache where he is the mortar, the train, the pestle. The noise of the rattling, swaying train was not that intense, but it might as well be a builder's drill to remove slabs of concrete. Each irregular conk, each rhythmic clank, each recurrent clap of the train was a cymbal, a crash of cymbals being thrown down a flight of stairs, right next to Eddy's ears. His washing up bowl in his mind was constantly at tipping point with each sound broadcasting tremors that were close to tipping that fine balance from manageable to unmanageable.

'Urghh…'

Eddy stirs in the thin blanket covers of the ruffled sheets, with Lia murmuring a noise of discontent as the ripples of the bed rock gently, but feel as if she is at the mercy of the raging seven seas. Okay, now the delayed, dreaded hangover had well-and-truly kicked in. They both daren't move.

The Australian side of him wanted to have a smoothie, go for a run. The European side seemed confused as to why to run? Were they being chased? The Australian side wanted to run away from the torment, leaving the hangover behind in sweat on the tarmac. The European side wanted him to embrace the hangover like an old friend with a heavy iron cloak of regret.

He propped himself up, barely enough to peer over Lia's strands of matted hairs greasy in sweat. He squinted to stare outside at the blue skies with the industrial smoke-scape on one side, aimlessly destroying the beauty from grotesque steel, red briskness disarray. A slow, nervous turn to the other side, the opposite window. Frankenstein's brute was reflected into a contrasting scene of rolling hills with isolated wooden huts with wisps of smoke from the short, wide chimney pots. Stooped over were ladies, in their rowed vegetable patched gardens tending, with devotion to the gardens, their fruits, their vegetables, their food.

Local kids gathered worryingly close to the worn banks, close enough to touch the passing carriages. They waved, played and screamed as the train bent at large angles swimming through the hills like a graceful fish tail meandering around sea stones. Then back into the sunlight blocked, unproductive desolate forest at the heart of its own mystical phaenomenon.

Every couple of hours or so, the jerking stops where Eddy's mind nearly tipped the balance from comfortable to a God-rush to the toilet, a window, anywhere but inside the cabin. The stop of the rattle, the constant sway made the vice tighten around his head, to wish he wished that the train would start once again as before slowly and smooth. There was something therapeutic to the trains motions that the station stops prevented his natural healing. Each time, at every stop a knock on the windows by raising veiny hands like a scene from zombies coming up from the cemetery graves.

Faces below of crinkling, leering optimism of a sale bordered by colourful scarfs covering their hair. The windows were preyed upon by ladies upon ladies with homegrown or cooked things to sell in wicker baskets. Everything from smoked dark brown fish fillets to cabbage or potato cakes were being held aloft on the wrinkling pastel white forearms of numerous eager elderly ladies that wanted nothing more than coins for their hard labour.

Each stop brought a different array. Presented in the same way to be brought up to each window. All the time, smiling ladies would look up as they peered down. They did not speak but smiled a crooked broken teethed smile, covered in different colourful patterned headscarves with clear plastic bags or brown paper displaying their offerings of sale in the forms of colour. Blini, fruit, vegetables, snacks, drinks, cigarettes, you name it they had, or, could get it. Alas, no hangover cure.

The pine fragrant green pyramids had given way to bushy, wide fir trees that flaunt the picture-perfect Christmas tree getting ready for its decoration. In the soft pouring of the light rain, the blurry drizzle of the window screen made the natural artist's impression of a vibrant country life appealing. The pale yellow, almost green striped scenery with white beautiful building comes gradually into view. They have arrived.

The provodnitsa emerges out of her cabin clutching papers and stamps. With as much finesse as a juggling zebra she drops a few, as they glide to the floor, she grasps tightly the remaining pile. Swiftly scooping the fallen ones up, returning them with the others as one. A quick composure sequence ensued; straightening her uniform, standing firm then marching down her, no mistakenly it was hers, her corridor. Her black and white acrylic nails scratch their cabin window as she knocks steadfastly in passing. She calls out the stop from the opposing side of her carriage in a disassociated, ear-penetrating screech that would make wildlife scatter in impending fear. She struts back the way she had just come.

'Vasha OSTANOVKA,' she bellows as she swings their door wide open. Lingering with her face looming inside the cabin, a sinister look of I-know-what-you-did-that-night-and-you-don't-even-remember. A look that is thankful for getting rid of these pesky foreigners, even though the last two days they have been as quiet as church mice. Before all this, they had woken, washed with the liberation that their persecuting chains from their self-inflicted hangovers had finally been unlocked to disappeared. They feel tired but thankfully feel human again.

Ready for the day, they gather their luggage and leave the train. Feeling the tiny daggers of the stabbing eyes of the provodnitsa, they disembark in Yekaterinburg. A brisk chill whistles through the platform. The city named after Yekaterina, the wife of Tsar Peter the Great, Empress Catherine I. Secretly, Lia had been looking forward to this halfway point of the long train journey. She closes her eyes, tilts her head skywards. She bathes briefly in the city's glow.

The rain was starting to lash down in snowy heavy spears. That, with the heat of the departed carriage, the metamorphosis from warm to cold, they shielded their coats around them like a protective cocoon. Outside their haven, the cold winds blew ferociously into their exposed faces, which made them shiver, wildly uncontrollably. They pulled up the collars of their jackets over their mouths without a word. Failing to keep at bay the penetrating arctic gust, they shuddered. One hand plunged deeply into their pockets, the other clutching their luggage.

Under their contrite breath, they silently mumbled a few cursing words. Rueing the packing day of not purchasing, the heavily debated gloves which took centre stage over the open bags for, on the face of it, meaningless brushed away suggestions. Darting like the wind, weaving through the crowded platform the Russian cabinmates scurry away head down, back crouched, a brief recognition with their eyes, a nod of heads for goodbye, which was returned. Akin to magicians they vanished through the exiting grey-moving curtain. Never to be seen again. The pouring rain of the capital of the Urals, the birthplace of Boris Yeltsin, the smell of damp clothes and engine fuel greeted them with obstructed arms. They were in need of a warm hug, not this reception.

'Welcome to Wet-aterinburg,' Eddy chattered out mockingly, as he led the way, scurrying like the Russians for shelter out of the weather conditions.

It's hard to imagine that this first impression of a beautiful city through the veil of fine misty waters and cool temperatures is as a contrast compared to what they would have been introduced to a few years ago. During the Soviet times, this was an industrial city of smog, factory fumes and a different veil they see today. Lia had already seen the beauty, even beyond her own closed eyes, she had felt its allure.

Lia has had a few bad days, which Eddy put down to the hangover. Every now-and-again she lapsed into a depressive state. A state where she gets scared about the impending destination, home. Home. Why was she so worried? Why did she get these chills of nervous terror about going home? It was, after all, simply her, home. It should be her comfortable place, not her place of trepidation, which is causing her mind to worry. Many chats have elapsed over the past hours. For which, on hindsight, seem to be a temporary worked, mere band aid rather than a secure bandage. A plaster rather than a stitch. The flow of worries still, will ebb and flow. The grey nature of the day was not having a great uplifting effect. Eddy had not noticed her mood change from the elevating, initial step on to the platform. That joyful feeling has now been wiped out, fell away like the drips of rain from her face.

So…without looking back, doing as the Australian coat of arms instructs, he progresses forward, marching through the packed crowds of the close to overflowing platform. Eddy seizes the initiative by taking charge. He knows where to go as he had worked out the route on the train just for this precise moment. He plunges forwards, glancing back to see Lia's figure following, but not her clearly anxious, tormented face. He is in and out of the station building as quick as a blinking flutter of her tear-brimmed frightened eye.

Out in the open, open to the elements, away from the throngs of people, he waits for Lia. He catches sight of her emerging through. She feigns a smile to proceed in the direction of him. Then, as she is as close as necessary, he clutches her floundering hand that was on its way to shed a tear away with a flick of her index finger. Dragging Lia with him, he races across the pedestrian crossing that has just turned green. Unaware of her inner plight. They go opposite to the loud neon shining bleak sign of their booked hotel. It is too early to check in, but he does not want to. He wants to embrace the day, the cold, wet miserable day.

349

Looking out of the large floor to ceiling windows Lia stares at her own ghostly apparition, which speaks to her in mirrored words in the glass. Beyond this haunting window-pane was the weather reproducing her mood. An ordinary second felt strangely peculiar as she is pulled back to reality by the repeating question from the concierge desk.

A modern city, where the old is treasured. The rain is polishing the buildings, putting a shine on them to gleam, sparkle like a crown of jewels. Lia has found her unfeigned grin as she accepts the city, she is enchanted, the city had enraptured her with a sorcerous magic with a hypnotic click of her fingers.

They hold hands while walking, caring not for the rain. They head down Lenina Street. On the corner is a magnificent statement, a beautiful green, red and white building, a large mansion no less. Eddy snatches his hand back to take the first of a vast quantity of photographs. This merchant house could have been plucked from Florence in Italy, to be placed here. Picture perfect with its pastel colours, architecture. Lia looks over from the bottom up, at the pastel paintings, the pillars, the alcoves, cylindric balcony, all the way to the top pale blue dome.

Through Eddy's camera lens, she looked so small against this colossal background. She barely reaches close to the protective black ornate iron fence that stretches around this colossal building. The steps are popular with the locals skateboarding gang that surf, more than roll in the deep puddles from the rain. The sound of scuffing wooden boards on the tarmac, the soft splashes of water and the squeals of laughter from the kids. One kneels in the water, hand sturdy, right-angled-steady, holding a small camera. A permanent smile etched over his face as he looks on the small screen as the skateboarders take it in turns to go towards him to launch off the steps, without fear. A magnificence self-confidence in their ability to land safely.

The former owner of this building, Sevastyanov Manor, was a successful businessman that made his money through the gold rush. Many believe that this was a show of power, a mine-is-bigger-than-yours look towards Moscow and St Petersburg as his counterparts. Legend states that Sevastyanov wanted permission from the Tsar to cover the top with gold. This was not acceptable, not given. The main reason was that only churches in Russia were permitted to be golden, to allow the God to notice them. For this act of blasphemy, for even asking this absurd request he was ordered to go to church everyday wearing heavy iron-cast boots. Lia reads this to Eddy who scoffs the unbelievable plausible possibility that this was really true.

'Come on...true?' he jeers.

Later, this also served as one of the Presidents of Russia, Medvedev's summer residence until 2010. Lia reads another fact. This stops Eddy from laughing to contemplate for a moment. He digests the information that he finds amazing. It is amazing to think that someone had this beautiful building built, but for that person to not actually live here, was nothing short of preposterous. He rented it out. He did not even spend one single night in his remarkable accomplishment.

They retreat from the alluring scrutinising house, that hypnotises them to marvelling gawp, look intently, to cravingly desire. 'One day,' Lia dreams, 'one day.' A few steps down is the sour-faced bronze sculpture of the two founders of the city, Vasil Nikitich Tatishchev and Vilian De Gennin. Their immortalised stance could be made more accountable due to the weather, at last the rain had finally stopped and had cleaned them to a glistening shimmering glowing growl.

Sandwiched between them they hold the Tsar decree. They face, looking over with open, but unsculptured eyes at Plontinka. This is the conserved historic heart of where the city blossomed. The smooth-running lapping waters of the River Iset and the Weir, a low dam built to regulate its flow at the heart, the pulse. A recently wed couple braves the weather for the common Russian ritual that has generated, has spread across the world to lock a padlock onto a bridge. The beginning of the city is the clicking lock of their hearts, the birth of their new chapter, two books merged as one, a new novel.

This cluster of colours, sizes and collage of padlocks shows a lot of happy couples. The tradition that the bride and groom together lock the padlock on the bridge. Then turn and chuck over their shoulder the key that plunges into the river with a soft plop, before sealing their love with a kiss as the keys sinks into the brown waters, lost forever. The only way that their love will break is if someone opens the padlock with this exact key.

The city pond is on one side. A seemingly vast green park that surrounds the River. With the rays of the sun does not come the warmth, but, clusters of people have come out from nowhere since the rain has stopped to say hello to the world. It is as if they immediately expect this to be taken away, so to relish in the weather before the predicted cold and rain returns, they flock. Clusters of different demographics of people of different ages do different things. Some play in the company of others, some paint in their own solo meditation. Some lie without a worry on the wet grass, some chat as friends, some read on their own. It is their own park, a local park, a park to do what they want.

With a scary look of big brother is the beholding face of Lenin. It is in the five-storeyed granite and stucco façade of the city hall, watching. Across the road is a bigger commanding statue of Lenin, or to give his full name, Vladimir Ilyich Ulyanov. They both found it quite surprising that he was left unmarked, free of graffiti or some other form of vandalism.

Before their left the hotel, Eddy asked Lia to ask for a recommended place to eat. He was starting to get tired so persuaded Lia to ask for directions to that recommendation from the receptionist. He had recommended them to a self-service restaurant that locals use, simply known as the canteen. Built in a former KGB hotel where babushkas still service all the rooms. Lia reiterated for the first time this information the receptionist had mentioned to Eddy as they walked to the restaurant. On hearing this revelation, Eddy could not help wondering out aloud to no-one in particular: 'If only the walls could talk. What would they say?'

They sat down with their food in the midst of Eddy talking more about the if's, what's and maybe's that had occurred here inside the building of the restaurant that they are now in. Overhearing their conversation, they are told by a regular customer in slightly American-sounding broken English that if they would look down on this building, it is shaped in the hammer and sickle, the symbol of the communist movement.

Nodding a thanks for the intrusion, but also the body language that should have given all the clues of not wanting to engage in a full-bloodied conversation, they turn their backs on their unwanted dinner guest. Their neighbour did not seem to take this strong hint. They start their chatting once again between themselves as he taps Lia on the shoulder to give them both a history. A history that for him may have seemed brief, but to Eddy and Lia, it was far too long.

'...of the hammer being a symbol for the industrial working class,' he spoke with borderline intensity. Leaning into their personal space with unwarranted anger. '...whereas the sickle was for the agriculture workers. Together. To-GETHERR they showed unity.' He pounds the table, making the cutlery jump, rattle, the crockery bounce, clatter.

They half listen, half terrified, mostly dumbfounded by his invasion. They sipped their purchased borsch that tremors silent ripples. This pleasant taste blocks out his verbal tyrant. The burgundy red beet liquid in a tomato sauce is filling on this cold, wet day. Hearty with the many different vegetables was warming their bodies, with the heat of the canteen drying their clothes. Combinations of the rich smell and abundant taste of their meal muted the words of their neighbour with every spoonful swallowed.

Lia opts to stir in the sour double cream, Smetana, while Eddy goes for the little-dash-will-do approach. Eddy is really enjoying the food, not the undeclared shared company. This was not appreciated. He tugs a piece of his crusty white roll as it cascades a shower of pale-yellow crumbs into his red liquid. As he pulls another piece at it, he imagines pulling their unwelcome visitors head off as more crumbs enter his blood red soup. Throughout the whole meal the stranger did not budge and edged closer and closer until, in the end they had no choice, their left. In still damp clothes, ironically so not to appear rude, they ventured back into the elements.

The sun had predictably gone astray. Light grey clouds have rolled in starved of the promise of more rain this time. They stroll, using their tongue to pick out the morsels of the scrumptious meal that coat their teeth which, in turn softly slaps, caressingly seductively remnants that remain. The soup coats their mouth bringing the fond memories to their tastebuds, making them salivate, to enjoy once more. Slowly moving around the canal, they pass several interesting pieces of art as the wind blows aromas of burning logs, for which they suspect is from several fireplaces keeping home's cosy. Where families snuggle together basking in the warmth as a dog lounges savouring the glow of the flickering flames.

An artwork catches their eye of a bear following a giant stone keyboard, possibly showing the past life amid the now-present modern technology privileged driven world. Some artworks on display are just bizarre. Others unexplainable. A Beatle's corner with a colourful mural, messages written on the wall was being marvel at as a single raindrop lands on Lia's head causing her to look heavenward. Black as coal clouds had gathered without them noticing. As they both stare the rain falls with an unrelenting force. They scatter to a shelter, almost slipping on the marble-like tiles that decorate the walkway. They miserably look up, only daytime darkness is what they view, not a single glimmer of a possibility that the sun will return. They are defeated, sulking in the shadows of the large tree as the large drops of rain turns swiftly to biblical rain.

They know roughly how to get back. They dart in, out and towards shelter to weave an unconventional route back to the hotel. The tacky neon hotel light now looks tasteful and inviting as they turn a corner to see the flashing red lights reflecting off the rain-soaked streets. They walk into the foyer like they had taken a side trip through the canal itself, safe to say that their plan to stay dry had failed. They quickly check in. Leaving a trail of moisture on the tiled beige floors, they head to their room. Immediately, they shower together.

On the thick-laden blankets of the bed, on the pristine white fluffy humongous bathrobes they lay like two polar bears on holiday. They flick through brochures, flyers and internet sites on their mobile phones to plan a dry, or a wet day for tomorrow, over on the bedside table a cup of steaming hot room-made coffee waifs it's magical calming aroma. Like most people they have a certain place that they must go and see. A reason that most come here. Just before they go to sleep. Just before sleep succumbs. Cradling each other lovingly in each other's protective arms they decide, or more promise, that rain or shine they will be going for a run, regardless, tomorrow morning, before they start their day.

Through the night, they are irregularly woken by the strength of the rain. The wind smashing against the window throughout the night trying to get inside with the pent-up fury of teenage angst. That were let go by their paternal cloud to be unleashed below in anger, mis directional rage. Outside sounds violently terrifying.

They wake. They get ready. They have not plucked the courage to open the thick, heavy drapes so not to be put off by their pledge last night. They are ready. Their shoes are tied. At the very last minute, second, they sharply pull open the dark grey curtains. They are surprised. No puddles. No dripping waters from the signs. No evidence whatsoever of the plague of last night. No sign whatsoever of yesterday's triumph storm of the end of days. In the nervous pull of the curtains they see a complete contrast of the day before. It could not be any more of a contrast. They feel great. They are relieved, happy and ready. They had had an imperfect night's sleep in a very comfortable tall, soft, larger than large bed. They contentedly abide by last night's promise.

After their glorious romantic run, if there is ever such a thing, they are refreshed. They are now finishing their breakfast before heading out. Things here change quickly. In this different light of the day the city is even more beautiful. The sun does not just shine on the buildings it caresses them, strokes them, invigorates them to a magnificent symphony both from nature and the human race. Just like an unappreciated maestro below in the pit the sun gets no credit, while the band gets the plaudits and feels the glow from the applause. Here the buildings shine, they complement each other, were as the sun just highlights them perfectly. They are walking around like tourists do. Eyes looking upwards, at the sights. Seriously if a mugger wanted to see who the easy target was, they would stick out like a sore thumb, the obviously easy choice.

In the delight of refreshed vigour, they have a skip in their step as they head in the direction of the war monument. Here the sun shines in all, but for a few light tarnished white clouds, corners of its clear skies. Here, the weather is warm.

At the war monument, they witness one of the most moving pieces of art with such a powerful direct message. Goosebumps escape up their arms. Their spines tingle. Here they pore over a soldier. A soldier that looks defeated. He is deflated. Etched marks over his face showing for all to see, the lines of stressful struggle. Struggling to understand why. Why has all this pain begun. Why it begun. Why his life was taken away, ripped from inside with no external scars. All these lives taken away. These lives continuously being taken away. Against any logical explanation. It is madness. This is all shown in every crease on his face. Beautifully tragic. His eyes are on the brink of tears that he may never show. Not because he is stoic.

Not because he is an unfeeling person, but because he does not know how. For years he has bottled all of the hurt. For years the emotions inside have been shielded unnoticed, that now he does not know how to let them go. He is visibly tired, worn down. His posture is in a fallen, seating position. His gun points towards the sky. His arm rest on one of his knees, trying to use it to pry himself back up. His other hand grips his skyward gun. He resembles a soldier that is fading from the person he was at the start of the war. He is gaunt. He is struggling to go on. He cannot go on. Resigned.

He is that tired, the soldier is too tired to continue physically, mentally. A soldier that is fed up with it all. The insanity. This war of physical illness breeds psychological mental illness. He is despondent. Tired of fighting, killing…living.

Around him are different curved columns with different dates from the Afghanistan War, 1979–89, with names of soldiers laid to rest. Just so many names. These columns are to resemble a hull of a plane in a skeleton form. This sober monument that they were sombre, solemn walking around was called the Black Tulip. The name of the plane that brought back the bodies from the Afghanistan War. As they move effortlessly floating around the impressing, impacting monument, Lia pauses at each of the plaques, but she stops in her tracks as she notices all the plaques but this one in particular.

A simple plaque acknowledges losses in the cold war years. A war that is part of her life. Lia involuntarily starts to well up in her eyes. Waters starts to form. She fills quickly with emotions. Choking back the impending onslaught of abandonment sobbing. Although the Black Tulip did not affect her in any way, she is connected with the plight of the sad soldier. She looks into his cold bronze metal eyes. Struggling to control her impetuous connected sensations. She knows on a different level that the war has torn this soldier's family apart, like a different war has torn hers. Why the soldier had to come, why he had to leave.

Lia could not escape the emotional feelings that bubbled inside her in an escalating eruption. She boils over with an unconscious, oblivious wail. Eddy is startled by her reaction from the opposite side of the monument. He races over to her. He reassures her with a comforting cuddle that brought her close in the protection of his warm chest. That moment. It was that moment. That sense of another touch of human warmth, the sound and feel of his heart beating. That single point seemed to softly tap the button to release her emotions. She tries to hold them in but for that loving feel of Eddy's firm protection. Her strength is weakened. Releasing the bound-up pressure, she sobs, suffering cries. Loudly. Very loudly.

For what was only a few seconds. For what feels, felt like minutes she is suddenly exhausted. Lia has no more tears to shed. Eddy continues to hold her as her body shakes, attempting to squeeze out more tears. She actually feels better for letting her feelings go. Her feelings be expressed. Eddy is none the wiser to what actually brought these on, as she was coming out of the black hole, he felt that he would let sleeping dogs lie. A moment, momentarily paused in time. He wonders whether to ask. Silent.

They continue to stroll. Many questions flood through Eddy's mind but he keeps them there. They limply hold hands, but Lia also says no words. Eddy is expressionless, unsmiling. Whereas Lia is smiling with puffy bloodshot eyes. She swaggers, as if nothing has happened. She is different. Eddy is perplexed by the whole event. It seems the further she was getting away from Australia the more complex she was becoming. The distance between Lia and Eddy was also growing. The closer to her Motherland, the greater was her fear. She was losing herself more in the sea of emotions, drowning in the waters. Unknowingly, she was pushing Eddy away. Innocently losing Eddy's love. Yet, at this point, although they knew something was happening. They suffered the cracks forming, they chose to ignore them. Not speak of them, to wipe over them.

As they cross the vast continent, the changes are becoming more apparent. Europe is officially here, as children wear designer jeans, fashion-conscious complimentary garments and are making an effort to be more sophisticated. The warmth that they both benefited from seeing with the close-knit rural family was lost in the tangling pandemonium of urban growth. Their phones were their family. Starbucks and McDonald's, cafés and ice-cream parlours were their homes. Youngster sipping lattes over laptops, discussing the latest perfumes, shoes and designer labels. A new city. New continent. New era.

They move across the modern city in a deliberate, planned route devised by Lia late last night. It was not intentional, but they pass magnificent examples of architecture. Glass walled skyscrapers that shine like strong beacons of power, mirrored-steel reflective buildings that shield what they hide but not letting anything that is thrown at them penetrate. Ornate stone façades of government buildings and, not lastly, the magnificent craftsmanship of the uniquely, exquisite wooden houses with features including beautifully carved windows and eaves. All the buildings are exhibitionism bragging rights of the architects, as well as the city planners.

In no time, they arrive at a city park, they decide to detour and venture through its leafy canopy. With the carnival of activity in the noise from different demographics of people Lia's mood peaks faster than a space launching rocket. Eddy has suffered, really suffered through this trip. He has been there constantly for Lia, but who has been there for him? He has been a support, a confident, a friend, a lover. He does this, for his love that he feels for Lia.

Lia appreciates all that he is. Lia understands, without able to control the reasons for her actions. She reacts with Eddy taking the blows. Eddy lets the blows hit him. Rather than deflecting the issues off him like bullets off Superman's chest, he absorbs them, trying, although sometimes failing, to filter out the emotional effecting toxic venom that some of the points glisten with. Lia tries to stop. She truly tries.

She knows she is being cruel and remorseless, for a better word, a bitch. In spite of this, she was on this journey within a journey, were her emotions were coming out in peaks and troughs, irrational explosions of fury, tears, anger, joy. She was not handling the situation well. She would never admit this completely to anyone. Yet, she opened up to Eddy. She talked about the anxiety to Eddy. Eddy held her close. Every second that they were spending together, they were connecting deeper, but drifting apart. They huddle together as they slowly stroll around the deep blue lake, sheltered by green tall trees.

Immediately on entry, they slow to absorb the split second that the loud bustling city morphs into a peaceful calming retreat. The park opens up for them to behold. To their right, on the short-cut, uneven lime green grass, students lay down studying with open books spread out, pens twirling in hand, but the laughter, the skimpy revealing attire, the general tomfoolery suggest that not a lot of studying is really going on. On the loose small light pink gravel that snakes a path into the yonder, an older generation with paintbrushes frantically grazes canvases held on shaky easels. On the duck frolicking lake sits a rotunda, by means of a toothpick-thin wooden pale blue bridge is the empowered focus.

More students sprawl behind on the opposing bank, seeming to magically have a more modest appearance. As they saunter around the lake, they look at one of the paintings being created. To gaze over the shoulders of this oblivious painter is to spy a picture, within a picture that is realistically accurate. She is portraying a gift, a natural talent, as well as a hobby. The polished clean white rotunda, that has a flat roof rather than a dome shelters a small group of people fishing along its curved banister, yet a combination of diverging aged generations, these seem to be fundamentally male dominated.

The sun rays fade in and out straining through the fleeting clouds. When out, the heat is strong, but when the wisps of the white clouds block the sun, the temperature drops rapidly accompanied by a rather chilly breeze that lifts the hairs off their arms. They take their jumper on and off more times than a Las Vegas stripper. The smell of flowers in bloom and forest pine trees is displaced by a sweet pastry that fills the air from a nearby bakery. Lips licked as they close their eyes, for the first time today this salivating smell made them think of food.

However, they continue to stroll, ignoring the attractive temptation. They go through the forest-filled oasis of Pioneers Park, for which they are not the only ones enjoying the space, to carry on in the direction of the Holy Ascension Cathedral.

The stone temple base is speared heavenward by a towering temple. Inside is quite plain, no pews, no roof paintings, no stained glass, no furniture. Only a large wooden structure, akin to a movie set backdrop, adorned by paintings at the altar with a huge chandelier. To set the mood, a choir sings an instrumental tune as a scattering handful of people pray on their knees. Considering so many churches were destroyed during the Soviets regime, this was left off the list to be destroyed. Over forty churches were destroyed during the Soviet era. Here, it was within these light blue external walls, below the shining domes, it is said to have been the praying place for the Russian Tsar Nicolas Romanov and his family.

Eddy was a little naïve when it came to his knowledge about Russian history, but this journey was enlightening him. Even before the journey he plunged into any literature available at their local library to acquire information. He was embracing the education that Lia was sharing. Here, right on this spot was one of the tragic events in Russian history, the death of the last Russian Emperor Nicolas II. On one stormy evening in Sydney, Lia made the begrudgingly Eddy watch Rasputin as part of their, more aptly Eddy's, research on their trip. Surprisingly, to Eddy's amazement, he ended up enjoying the movie. Which in turn made him want to go back to the library later that week to borrow the biography of Grigoriy Rasputin. To subsequently enjoy that as well.

Here in the surroundings, Lia refreshed hers, as well as Eddy's, memory, as they sat on the dark-stained wooden bench about the circumstances before, and on that fateful night. Whereas conspiracy theories in the bubbling pot continue to boil and spit out different circumstances, reasons and philosophies to the real events that happened on that evening, to why. Some are very far-fetched. Some are very, considerable to be creditably true. For the first time on this journey, she speaks with a passion about something other than how she is feeling. She recites the story so clearly on that fateful night, on 16 July 1918, in the basement of the merchant's house. Where this church has been raised.

On that night, Tsar Nicolas II, Tsarina Alexandra Feodoroyna, Grande Duchesses Olga, Tatiana, Maria, Anastasia and Tsarevich Alexei Nikolaevich of Russia were murdered. It was heavily rumoured that Anastasia escaped and survived. The white Byzantine Church built on the blood of the murder is a memorial, although it is known as the murder, it would surely be more apt to be known as an assassination.

Lia says that the locals simply call this era, 'an embarrassment in Russian history'. This church was built in 2003, eighty-five years after the execution. They are standing in front in awe at the truly magnificent church. In silence they take in the impressive three throne, five cupola church with gold domes and white walls.

The sun had come out in full fury to showcase the sparkling gold crosses on each golden dome. Symmetrical with four smaller towers on each side around the larger, taller tower in the middle. A half dome tower is on each wall that supports another cross. The white daisy covered grass with buttercups lead up to the simple elegant church. Infront a black memorial statue is a memorial to Tsar Nicolas II and his family. They are portrayed around a cross, seemingly coming up from the stairs.

Lia comments that this is maybe to symbolise the basement in which they met their gruesome end. A simple, white marble monument and cross stands with a plaque that briefly describes an account of the execution on that momentous night. Behind is a smaller structure, the St Elizaveta Chapel, a slightly modest, but no less spectacular church that is made, apparently, entirely out of wood. This is to honour a nun and relative who were murdered not long after the Tsar, his family, his servants and friends. The relative was at the worse ending to a life, if that was even possible, she was thrown down a mineshaft, poisoned with gas, then buried...alive.

Eddy is listening with his ears, even so, his mind strays, he wants to get hold of a still memory with his other senses for them to reminisce in another time. He raises his camera to take a memory, a quick photograph. Lia reaches out to gently pull the lens down with her left hand. Eddy turns with a heavy-set scowl. Lia points silently towards a perfectly placed standing moveable sign that has the universal depiction of 'no photography', followed by the most popular widespread languages. He is literally standing on top of it.

Once again, Eddy was disappointed that he could not take photographs inside. Adoring the felt covered stands, photographs were everywhere, said to be done by a keen photographer whom at the time was not aware of the historical relevance that his timely photographs would reveal. The date was even more significant, 1909, as these are the only evidence of what was around here. Scattered over displays, held crudely in place by drawing pins are the various stages of what was here, once upon a time, until now.

Scanning the two stories that make up the interior of the church, the timber rafter networking of beams and joists modelling the shell up high are kept alive with statues, icons and burning candles that animate the sculptures frozen in time. Around them people float in silence. As if floating in the aftermath of a nightmare. Footsteps echo, bouncing off the walls. It has a library feel where people respect that quietness is the unwritten rule out of respect for others, but here it is out of respect for the dead.

In a separate exhibition, through an open door to the left, is a replica of the basement with descriptions of the events. In a barely audible whisper, Lia retells her story that she heard of the events. Eddy heard these in Sydney, but to be here, in the presence, in the, in that place of history that is forever stained on the history books, of not just Russia but of the world, it seemed a lot more prominent, important and reverberated to reaffirm in his heart. It gave a renowned notorious importance. On the threshold of that open room, they peak inside as Lia divulges the event.

'On the night of 16 July, Tsar Nicolas Alexandra, their five children, four servants were ordered to dress. Get dressed. Ordered to go down, to the basement, in a servant's house. This was the house that stood here, for which they were imprisoned. Arranged in two rows for a photograph they were told. Designed to stop the rumours of their escape, a story they were advised. That there were positioned in the basement, below our feet, you would presume that alarm bells were ringing.

Then...suddenly. It was a despicable moment. Out of the blue, when they stormed in, armed men burst in and shot. They shot fast, quick, killing the imperial family where they stood. To be sure. They then proceeded to stab them. With the smoke of their guns still exhaling, the trailing's of death. Reportingly stabbed them. You know to just make one hundred percent sure that there were all dead!'

'Why did they die again?' Eddy whispered into Lia's ear.

'The Romanovs had given Lenin a problem. A MAJOR one. Nicolas were mates now.' Lia attempted to inject a dark side of humour in this grisly tale. 'Nicolas was the ruler, the Tsar. The White Army wanted to restore him to the throne. Lenin did not want to risk them escaping. The Bolsheviks ultimately took the decision to kill them. In fact. rumoured. Well whirl pooled, escalated, plausible was. Well, the, that famous rumour was the escape of Anastacia, the daughter. The other which again was, is, who do you really believe? The other was that the Whites actually killed them, thus, to put out stories, to fuel propaganda that is just how cruel, mercenary the Red Army could be, or were.'

'Really? Do you, do you actually believe that?'

'No. Not really, but…an interesting theory nevertheless.'

'As for the Mad Monk. Rasputin?'

'Ah, Rasputin. He was the holy monk that Nicolas's wife, Alexandra was spellbound by. She believed that he saved their haemophiliac son Alexey from bleeding to death. The thought amongst the crowds where he was the true ruler, and, the Tsar was a puppet, a puppet master for him. There was truth, some truth in this, under the advice Nicolas took personal control over the army after Rasputin's advice. Not sure how many advice words I could put into that sentence! In the end he was stabbed, but lived. Poisoned, but, and lived. Shot, and lived. Drowned in icy-cold water, and lived. Finally, he was shot in the head, and died. Although the verdict stated drowning'

Eddy lets a laugh out, which is quickly forced back into his throat as people stare at him scornfully.

'A further, another myth echoed around,' Lia continued after nudging Eddy to remember his place. 'Rasputin predicted that if he died, then the Tsar would die. This myth was true, or was it a prediction, or a noticeable speculated estimation.'

At that moment, they were shooed by an elderly lady whom of which barges them out of the way, when they had left enough space for the largest man to walk through. They stare back, as if they are offended. She shoos them, at the same time shushing them. Afterall they are discussing in a hushed whispering tone history that is very relevant to the site, the place that they are in, and not talking about last night's drunken exploits. They continue to talk about what happened, ignoring the lady's rude obnoxious requests. They talk more about the myths, the legends, the stories that surrounded the events at the time and after. Although Lia has a lot more knowledge on this affair, it safe to say that Eddy did have a little input into this conversation.

As with most things that draw tourists are the people who are attracted to money, who always avert their dubious methods by stating that they have to earn a living. It has to be done, but seems wrong to see the array of carnival colourful stalls that have been constructed to sell numerous souvenirs of the city, more to the point to cash in, to get money from the tragedy. They restart their conversation as they walk amongst these stalls, ignoring the pleas and selling techniques. Behind them is the events former stage, skirted by the vultures that pick the bones off the tourists for monetary gain with each passing tentatively preyed upon target.

They pass a wooden striped black and white marker with a flat top that shows the exact distance to their next destination, Moscow, as they go towards the Iset River. A couple of tourists ignore the small droplets of rain to frolic. With a Canadian flag on his camera bag he crouches down to take photographs of a young woman in a long brown and light peach flowing dress. She poses with laughter, smiles as she swings around a lamppost like Gene Kelly in *Singing in the Rain*, while splashing in the freshly-made puddles.

Lia pauses to smell a vibrant purple belled flower; Eddy offers his camera. He knows the drill. He knows that she loves flowers. She will take photographs of them all day but not before deeply scrutinising them as if reading each line, each hue, each petal, each pollen strand. She then delicately sniffs in the aroma in the lightest of grasps with her fingers, eyes closed appreciatively. Lastly, she ends the performance with a single photograph.

They grab a coffee, just like the kids of Yekaterinburg seem to be doing. They look over the greasy green plastic table into each other's eyes, surrounded by the smell of roasted coffee beans, the noise of the soft thud from the handles of used coffee being empty, the grinding of the coffee beans, the chatter, the laughter, the clink of china cups on saucers, the beeps and tings of mobile phones. All this is a veil of distorted distraction that they do not notice.

They are deep into the tunnel vision of each other as if blinkers are around them, earplugs link their ears to connect them only to hear each other. They never cease to amaze themselves, to surprise themselves that they can still hold a conversation, so intense, and together that they can actually learn something different, or expand on an educational asset, to be, feel completely comfortable to teach, to educate and to not be intimidated by each other's abilities.

357

For this reason, they stop here for a longer time than predicted, far longer than expected. They have no grasp on time. It was suddenly eluding them, unseen like the wind. They loved this feeling of not feeling that they had to be somewhere. It had been a great day full of knowledge, education, ups and downs and a lot of walking. It was nice to put all these sights together, over a bitter brew of black liquid gold. The draught of the coffee on this damp day warms them up, but their love for today, is the only warmth that they truthfully need.

Before they know it, they awaken to their last day in Yekaterinburg.

'Good things seem to not last long,' Eddy sighs with pessimistic weariness.

Lia does not answer, but her silence states that she tends to agree with his brooding statement. To follow the trend of the other days, and Eddy's existing mood, the weather starts overcast and gloomy. Yet Eddy's mood will transpire into his happy-go-lucky personality soon enough. Will it, or will it not rain, that is the question. They do not know the answer, but will not let it spoil their planned day. After their mandatory run, they go out to explore. They take in the magnificent city, which is growing more beautiful each passing minute, like a blossoming colourful flower that envelopes the fragrant aromas of hidden gems, treasures and jewels of the city.

Eddy had thought that nothing could move him. Being here was a privilege. Two decades of travelling had opened his minds to new cultures, architectural prowess, communities and an array of surprising tastes, smells, colours, experiences. Eddy, in his innocent gullibility thought a city could not move him. He was wrong. This disillusioned spell he was under was not, so much as fractured, but smashed into hundreds and thousands of tiny pieces. He was no longer closed off as he absorbed these positive vibes from this city. This will bode him well for the future. He smiles to himself, being touched by unseen welcoming glows from the unrevealed imprint.

Later that warmer morning, the weather had developed with a bit of a nippy breeze to make them pull on their jumpers yet again. Once again, this proved that the weather here is as unsure as the clashing inharmonious flows of cultures. They have found themselves stepping on the geometric grey and red brick floor of the wide pedestrian Vaynera Street. Old-style architectural buildings loom down on them. So many benches being unused in rows with flower beds in between like a steeple chase to the human hordes that pinball around the shops that flank the edges.

Quirky statues with shiny golden parts showing the place where people have rubbed their hands upon. Such as a statue of a chubby man walking, with a bright shiny hand handling a cane and a bright shiny button nose. This would have worked perfectly for a Boris Yeltsin statue. The benches and other random structures, sculptures such as a cyclist and a banker, compete with fountains to fill the cluttered space where people weave. Lia voices her surprise that not one busker is present. Not one beggar. Not one street performer. She wonders if it is illegal, or if the freedom to perform was illegal.

A short walk takes them in the direction of the Stalin Town Hall. Shadowy looking over the shrouded brick laid car park known as 1905 Square. Named after a conflicting year in October between Russian radical monarchists Chernosotentsy, local Cossacks and revolutionaries during a demonstration. This demonstration quickly turned to tragedy, with many civilian deaths.

A few years ago, during the reconstruction of this square, dead bodies and various artefacts were found under the hand-laid bricks. No-one knows whose, or whom they belonged to. The Town Hall, a five-story peach and grey striped structure is supported by large, tree truck thick pillars that support a central clock tower. On the crest of the tower is a communalist star flying high in stunning, noticeable gold, surrounded by a clear laurel, both of which sparkling in the sun shine their reflection over the city, like a cherry on a cream cake it is obviously designed to show a penetrating symbol of bold, gallant support.

It was built by German prisoners of war, thus with it, carries the efficiency and pride of German skilled efficient work, yet, in Stalin's strong image. The statues on the corners of the building are of workers and peasants, said to symbolise the power of the common people.

Over the entrance are soldiers, that seemingly prop up the clock tower by their shoulders, this is in a show of strength and obvious support in the then current regime.

Looking at the city hall, in a pose exhibiting pride displayed on an elevated towering plinth is Vladimir Ilyich Ulyanov, known better by his alias, Lenin. Eddy and Lia mimic the pose in a form of comical spontaneous impulse. He, Lenin, looks before him, with his chin slightly raised, right hand gestured out as if speaking to an imaginary band of obedient followers.

In this reality, there are no supporters hanging on believing in his every single word, rather here are the tourists that are surrounding his base, who snap photographs on their phones and cameras. Others, sit like flowers around the small step at the bottom of his plinth. His left hand grips the lapels on his long iron coat in a powerful, formidable stance of authorisation. In this setting, to be honest, there is not a lot going on. His intimidating pose is from an era gone, but due to this and other statues, not forgotten.

Though in the centre of 1905, is a huge wooden barrel where many people are captivated by. Like them, they are drawn away from Lenin towards this attraction. As they get closer, they navigate the barrel to see the signage on a rustic, aged-looking wooden sign for a Russian drink made from bread called Kvass. It is barely midday but has to be tried right there, right then.

Eddy, with Lia doing the ordering, shares a small measure of a very dark-coloured liquid, which is nearly as strong in the murky depth to the yeasty flavour. It makes him 'oh' and 'ah' as he takes a large mouthful and passes it to Lia to take off his hands, to try and swallow an element of pleasure in the unique odd taste. With a jerk of her arm, Eddy swiftly pulls Lia's arm to direct her into a café at the square of 1905 to take the taste out of their mouths. It was not to his liking, unpredictably nevertheless, Lia seemed to like it.

She resists his jerk, pulls back as she polished off the remaining glass effortlessly. They ponder the Romanov myth, Lia over a Kvass for herself, and Eddy with a reliant strong black coffee, before reciting the afternoon activities and remarking on the beautiful city for which they will be unfortunately leaving tomorrow morning, tinged with an air of sadness.

A tipsy Lia, a clearheaded Eddy from here grab the local bus to take the thirty-minute journey to the railway station. They aimed to travel back to their hotel, they wanted to see just how far it was from their accommodation, what bus to take in the morning. On their return to the hotel, they have a little time to play with. Rather than a morning rush, they decide to do a little food shopping for the journey.

'You have gotta love the Russians!' Eddy remarks with childish glee as he shouts down the crowded supermarket aisle, bellowing towards Lia.

'What have you found?' A forbearing resignation in Lia's voice is evident. She does not look up from the vodka bottle that she turns in her palm, wondering if the temptation is worth going down that route once again.

Eddy holds aloft a collection of disposable cups and glasses for the train. 'Well. Look. This. Look.' He waves the cellophane-covered kit. 'This. Look! This has two plates, two cups, two knives, two forks, two spoons and two shot glasses.'

'You're joking!' Lia's attention is drawn and she giggles with a wave of her head.

'No, fair dinkum. Look.' Finally, he rushes closer, rather than continuing the conversation for the whole store to listen. 'Two fifty mil shot glasses. Probably for vodka no less. I really don't bloody believe it!'

'Well. Why not?' Lia places the small bottle of vodka into Eddy's free hand. Decision made. The shot glass combination and the vodka bought, with a little bit of food, more snacks. They walk the short journey back to do another chore that they have been avoiding, their clothes washing.

They go to bed early for an early start. They are going to pack in the morning as well which seems odd, but they want to get to bed and wait for their clothes to dry fully. Also, they feel that the packing will wake them up, or, more to the point Lia feels this anyway.

The sun had not yet penetrated the thin veil of a clean, but dirty looking sad excuse which passed for a curtain in their hotel room. They both stir, lazily awake. Glance at the flashing red lights that emits the time in a glowing shower of a soft red wine spill over the white silk bedlinen. Panic.

They both get up as quick as a jack-in-the-box as they see that they are late. No alarm, they are behind schedule. Blankets float to find a resting place, as they clumsily, with the grace of a brutally beaten boxer slither out, hop, skip, bounce, hustle and bustle to be prepared to leave. The amount of speed that they use to get ready could have broken records. When they rush to start the beginning of the end to pack. Eddy finishes, checks the room. Lia set off to check out downstairs as Eddy follows, predictable with the luggage.

They storm down with no aggression but faces of pure, raging frustration at the alarm call not being heard. They race to get to the train station, all the time intently staring to observe the clock in the tower that is looming closer in front of them, but still in the distance. The clock they see is just too close for comfort to the time of departure. They drag their luggage over the tiny cracks in the pavement that ricochet, barely staying on their small wheeled tracks. They run alongside the black iron railing gates that blur as if it magically distorts into a fuzzy black wall made of Velcro. They run around the corner, through the gates, under the arch. The bold black, cast-iron arch is adorned with a Europe-Asia continental border which tells them that they are saying goodbye, officially to Asia. The scent of that new continent, scarcely a few turning carriage rolls, circulating away. Europe is their next destination. This will be close to the end of their epic journey across Russia. If they make this train, today, they will be in Europe within an hour.

Close, too close but they make it. They hurdle the ticket booth; by the skin of their luggage cases, they make it in time. Weaving along the platform, they dodge around babushkas trying to earn a buck by selling everything and anything from large toy teddy bears to smokes. The food is pretty good though, so they do stop fleetingly to buy the reminisced cabbage pies. This was a food that Lia had expressed adoration for, to the point that she had actually developed a yearning desire on behalf of her memories.

At the same time, this babushka must have seen her coming as she ended up leaving with pickled raspberries, but fortunately, not the home-smoked fish, bread, boiled eggs, boiled potatoes flavoured heavily with the aroma of dill, pancakes filled with, what looks like goat's cheese, as well as, she reveals bottles of vodka or beer. Eddy found the pickled raspberries too tart, quite frankly, just damn disgusting.

Moscow station looms without an ounce of written English. This is surprising for Eddy as being in the cusp of Europe. Grudgingly he has to lean on Lia again. It is a day, twenty-four hours for which the journey ends. The early morning day starts with a light film of grey with a threatening of rain, but bleeds into a beautiful sunny day. They had slept, but are so lethargic. Their wearily lift their heads up to see the sign of their destination.

Without hesitation, they beeline towards the main attraction. If truth be told, they literally run to the red square. Surging with excitement like children searching for eggs on an Easter Egg Hunt, they bypass other sights through the city. An injection of energy breathes in that has dispelled the exhaustion from the train journey. This is one of the sites that people read, hear and see a lot off, but today they are not looking through the eyes of someone else, but with their own two eyes. Gleefully, Lia squeals as the square enlarges in front of them.

Ahead of them is the entrance, the urban obstacle course is ending. People are scattered over the grey cobbled floor like ants compared to the dominating buildings conceived in vibrant multi-coloured wrapped Easter eggs.

Out of breath they pant, leaning over with hands resting on their knees. For a couple of people that do cardio regularly, the adrenalin made them sprint. It was as if the Red Square was going to close, move or vanish from existence imminently. Just in front of the entrance is the Iberian Chapel, which houses the Iberian virgin. The legend states that the virgin has a wound on its face because the virgin brought one of the wars of iconoclasm to a short, abrupt end when blood flowed from the icon. Sheltered in a small leaf-green chapel with golden highlights of three-dimensional statues, oval windows and golden stars in the light blue dome roof. On the top is a golden angel holding a cross. They stop heavy breathing with a sip of water from Eddy's backpack to admire the chapel. A small film of sweat covers their brow as they slowly trudge forward, absorbing as much as they humanly can, to be able to preserve this in the room of their minds to retract perfectly as great times, if they were going through future bad times.

The all-imposing entrance. Comprised of dark red bricks, yellow and white highlights around the black cross-crossed windows. The thick pillars of the two main spiring towers are topped with green glazed and golden glazed curved tiles that make the supporting spine towards the two-headed eagles. This is the Triumphal Gate, also known as the Resurrection Gate. The latter is more in reference to the Icon of Christ's Resurrection above the gate. Yet, as sacred sites were systematically being progressively destroyed by the former Soviet Government these gates and chapels were not excluded, were not the exception to that rule.

So, what Eddy and Lia walk towards, take photographs of and look, striving to see, remember and reveal every detail is an exceptional replica that was built and blessed in 1996. The only side open is the arched right-hand of the black arched gate. Invitingly they float with the other people like a basin of water that has had its plug removed to be empty as they drain to flow down and through into the Red Square.

Immediately, the grey, drab stones give way to a more delicately formed pavement of stones. The surprisingly misinformation that Eddy assumed that the square was named after the Red Army, could not be further from the truth. Lia states from her guidebook some interesting facts. As it happens, the truth is: 'Red' translates to 'beautiful'. The word is so apt, nothing more, nothing less; they both concur that it is so beautiful.

To their right is the reconstruction of the Kazan Cathedral. The original was shamelessly destroyed by Joseph Stalin in 1936 so military parades could be held in Red Square. The Russian restorer Peter Baranovsky supervised the complete reconstruction of the church to its original design in 1993, after the fall of the Soviet Union. Although, he actually did try to save it from the original destruction in the first place. Thankfully, he did save another church in the Red Square, Saint Basil's Cathedral.

Surprisingly beautiful, Kazan Cathedral's pastel peachy-red and light colours, coupled with its police-blue outlines in the gloom seem to almost penetrate a glowing aura on this drab day. Initially built to commemorate the expulsion of Polish invaders in 1612 at the end of the Time of Troubles. At that time, Prince Dmitry Pozharsky attributed his success to the divine help of the icon, Theotokos of Kazan, to whom he prayed to every night. Erected skyward in layers building an alcove, they gradually raise their heads up. Up towards a barbican pyramid till the cylinder tower of the central white one with red highlights is topped with a shining, golden peakless cap.

Kazan Cathedral was considered to be the most important church in Moscow, so it was fitting that this was the first church to be completely rebuilt. Despite the fact that is was utterly blasphemous that it was torn down to rubble in the first place. Everything but the Kazan Virgin was meticulously restored by photographic evidence, detailed measurements and original blueprints. Although the original icon is in a safe place in Yelokhovo Cathedral.

Along the fringe, which spreads the entire east side of the square, is the GUM department store. The Russian peoples, and the world-renowned famous shopping mall, the Harrold's of Russia. The expanse is as notorious as the expensive store itself. Stalin closed it, then reopened it in 1953. As they slowly walk in the shadows of the building, famous photographs projected onto Eddy's mind as still pictures of the same image, but different views; Soviets queuing for food. One image stalls, pauses, at the back of his staring dead ahead eyes. He intently remembers it, focuses into the face, the hand, the tiptoes. That famous photograph of a young girl trying to reach for the last loaf of bread in an otherwise bare, endless shelfing rack.

In contrast, Lia has moved on. She is distracted to the characters around the square as many people are dressed as Stalin offering photo opportunity to every camera-toting tourist.

They try to accost Lia for a photograph, that rapidly returns Eddy back to reality. That arm of a stranger, flicking out to grab Lia as she twirls around as graceful as a ballet dancer doing pirouettes that stops her in mid-flight. She was so unaware, the look of her sleeve screwing up under his grasp, the leering beckoning that pulls her with certainty. Eddy races into action. Eddy acts as a protector, he positions himself to come between them, to light-heartedly shove him in the chest, gently in a calm, but reaffirmation show that he, they are not interested.

Opposite the mall again, before the dark red of the Kremlin wall is the brick, Aztec style pyramid red mausoleum of Vladimir Ilych Lenin. There disheartened that this is disappointingly closed today. It is even closed off to get even near to the exterior.

'Man walks up to the Kremlin,' Eddy starts a joke to lighten their mood. He whispers into Lia's ear as she furiously clicks, snaps photographs.

'Knock. Knock. Is Len in?' Eddy giggles amid Lia's confusion in not quite understanding, but reassures him with a soft, almost patronising there-there-type giggle.

Before them, inside the squashed red brick mausoleum is arguably one of the most famous mummies in the world. Aptly in a pyramid, is the mummy of Lenin which has not aged a single day since being placed here. He knew his end was near, when the leader of the Bolshevik Revolution died on 24 January 1924. Thus, in his will, he stated that he wanted to be laid to rest in the ground.

Little did he know that he was going to be embalmed above the ground. In fact, little did anyone know. The story that Lia reads to Eddy is that while the government planned to bury him, the local Russian people pleaded that the body would be preserved for future generations. A lady appreciating respectfully from the steel fence barrier senses their pining, as they do, she leans over, chin resting on cold bar.

'Looking more like wax fruit than a person,' she states. She does not give any eye contact. She stares forward. She does not recognise if she is talking to herself, or anyone else. Her English is strong, doused in a thick accent. She goes on, '...the warmly lit room with reflective temperature appears to make an illusion to appear more lifelike. You get only, allocated strictly, only five minutes with no talking, or photographs allowed.'

This was really starting to irk Eddy, the no photograph rule that seemed to be brandished everywhere like the no smoking signs, or the Wi-Fi symbols. Shivering a little in the chill outside Eddy tries another joke as they walk past racks of overloading souvenirs. He has just remembered it after seeing an array of the painted Russian wooden dolls that adorn each and every one of these tourist merchandise overflowing stalls.

'Look at those dolls.' He points with a nod of his head. 'They're so full of themselves.'

Once again, he laughs; she does not.

They have arrived just as some of the areas are being cordoned off in the Red Square. This makes great, greeting clear views for photographs with no-one getting in the viewfinder. Lia asks a Russian what is going on. He does not know. So, she asks another. It seems no-one knows. Later she finds out over dinner. By asking a waitress that tells them that it is for Russian Day, ironically most local Russians here did not know, so at that moment, they still do not know the entailment. If fireworks, festivals, music or any special events are taking place around.

It is still overcast with a slight nippy breeze. Eddy's brown suede coat is zipped up with the wool exterior keeping him warm. Heading the impressive square, the true throne at the end of the jewel encrusted hall for this fascinating space that enthrals in enchanting attraction is the fairyland dreamlike cathedral. Supporting ice-cream cones of assorted colours that is the sight of the saved St Basil's Cathedral that renders them speechless. The presence of the clouds that cast shadows that lack sunlight does nothing to distinguish the bright, vivid colours, the onion domes of magical whimsical dreams. No media publication has been able to transmit the bold colours that Dalí would have been proud to have dreamed up, that Willy Wonka would have been proud to build.

They are drawn towards it, trapped in the colourful invisible magnetic attraction, like kids to candy, eyes wide, slavering craving desire. They get closer, their smiles widen, their mouths slowly open, there are awe-inspired the dazzling display before them. They cannot help by feeling stirred inside. Moved inside. As they draw closer, the vision seems to edge away, the cathedral is like a mirage. To see the blue and white whipped cream straight-piped onion domes. The golden and red bobbled bauble. The red and green striped spiked dome. The horizontal *Where's Wally* red and white striped dome.

The gold, red and green feathered onion domes, twisting around the towering red, green and white centred spire with yellow emphasising lines, each dome topped with a cross. All unique. All visually photogenic high points. All, just either show the architect as a pioneer, or, a visionary, a creative thinker. He managed to include as many different things in one building as possible. Either way it works. No words are needed as they twinkle a smile, they both agree it works really well. Good job. A legendary story is shared on the grey steps as Lia relays from the guidebook.

'Built over the grave of Holy Fool Vasily, Basil the Blessed in 1561 by Ivan the Terrible.'

'There's a considerable contrasting difference of emotions in Ivan and Basil there,' Eddy offers his opinion, which was not reciprocated.

'Shhhhh.' Lia motions with a stern shake of his finger. 'Ivan built it to celebrate his capture of Kazan. In true terrible fashion.' Lia lectures without realising her monotone. 'The legend goes that, no way! The legend says that to stop the architect Postnik Yakovlev from ever producing anything so magnificent, he had the architect's eyes removed, he only bloody blinding, blinded him. Rumours spiral that Stalin did the same with his architect, architects.'

The upcoming celebrations have caused this landmark to be closed as well. Although they could not hide how strongly frustrated they were by yet another disruption to their must-see itinerary, their moods did not deflate. They slowly circulate the Cathedral by absorbing the details. Looking up and down at the splendour. Reading the plaques under all of the statues. Lying down, pivoting to get as many angles as possible from their camera for the perfect shoot. The age of the digital film is fantastic for this.

Although Eddy does miss the camera film, as he thinks you really take your time to make a photograph count. He feels that people would take more consideration, more eyesight, insight into what they were seeing, more open for smaller details to include, rather than snapping many photographs in quick succession. Also, the anticipation. The fun of waiting for the developing of the photographs. Going to a store with a small brown tape in a black plastic roll, to return a day or two later with an envelope of photographs. Then looking through each one of the photographs carefully, with a smile on his lips, a firework display in his heart. Each single captured shoot evokes a different emotion, memorial, story.

Having said this, Eddy embraces the digital film with gusto. Here he can take numerous photographs and edit them on the train, bus, bench. He can see them before leaving a sight to see if it is the photograph he wanted. If a man's head has not accidently got in the way. A shake of a wrist causing a drunken blurred captured photograph when he is a sober as a judge. That, is another expression which makes him smirk. They take it in turn to either take a photograph, or montage of shots as the other one reads about the sights around them in Red Square.

They interrupt numerous random strangers to take photographs of them both, rather than an awkward selfie. He thinks back to photographs as a memory. With film, every photograph told a story that was good enough for films. Nowadays, when everything is so easy to photograph people have screenshots, photos of their breakfast, juice, shoes they were thinking of buying, basically it is as boring with a pointless featureless story filled with pages of blandness. He is making his photographs count. Although there will be many, especially after this trip, he will only let people see the ones that he thinks will matter. Will matter to them both.

They walk back, but this time through the glass roofed, crystal-palace decor of the GUM shopping mall, a very fancy department store, supported by cream pillars. They suspect this would be the perception as if they were royalty. In the centre is a very grand fountain accompanied to classical music that scream out elegance. This, they both conclude, was not always the case from their history days. Inside trees enhance the grandest of effects. Each twig hides a tale, each leaf a legend, each flower a finale. The smell of the flowers cast down on ripples from the bakery entwined with coffee. They float through from one end to the other, a silent as graceful ghosts.

Opposite, over the red square with its red wall, is the close but so far Kremlin. They will go to this but not today. Looking at the massive buildings from the other side, they head out, to depart the square. Eddy glances over his shoulder back to the splendid colours, shapes and patterns of the glorious Saint Basil's Cathedral. It truly is a breath of admiration. At the end, they walk back through the entrance that was the Resurrection Gates into Manege Square. Across the grey square, small puddles strew from an ignored short downpour, with manicured strips of rectangle green grass dripping silver beads of water, they take stock of what they have seen.

In the grey reflections of the water are the surrounding red brick and yellow painted buildings. In front of the red imposing State Museums is a focus point, a large red marble plinth of Marshal Georgy Zhukov on a horse that has stopped in its tracks and been immortalised. His hand seems to be gesturing to calm down the imaginary crowd as he sternly, impatiently looks on. The most decorated general in the history of Russia and the Soviet Union is known as the Supreme Soviet. His horses' hooves trample a Nazi Flag in a strong resemblance to St George slaying the dragon.

Underneath him, his horse and the square is four stories deep of department stores. As if a turn of coincidence Eddy who thought of St George sees the large glass cupolas that offers the only natural light to the department stores below. Each one is topped with the said saint, which Lia tells him is the patron Saint of Moscow.

Downstairs, following the embracing aromas, they grab a pelmeni in the clinically brightly lit food court as a takeaway. This was more to fill a hole rather than a gastronomically treat but it turned out to be very pleasing. Rain starts to spit down as they walk through Aleksandrovsky Park, along the shining red tomb of the unknown soldier with golden words reflecting on the blood red surface. A large flower bed has a vibrant red star surrounded by a light grey blossoming ring with white and green flowers.

They finish walking the most famous street in Moscow, Ulitsa Arbat, as the rain stops. Although it started like all the photographs that they saw when they did their research, they took it all with a pinch of salt, the reality was actually close to what they saw. The magnificence of a nice old pedestrianised street with street painters, buskers and other street performers on one side.

Unfortunately, it soon turned into a rather tacky tourist trap of many shops selling the same tacky merchandise at expensive prices. People seem to be gleefully looking, rummaging through the bright coloured T-shirts with printed words emblazoned, *I Love Russia* or *From Russia With Love*. Such a shame to have this blot on the streetscape, a true blemish around the architecture delights sheltered on the sides of the street. It is disgracefully dishonourably, but unsurprisingly predictable.

The rain starts again, this time it is coming down faster. It is a day for disappointments, but also a day to rise above the misfortune. Once again, this latest turn of events does not get their spirits down. Lia has a treat for Eddy. She encourages for them to take the metro back. He is dubious, why is she so determined for this willingness. He is curious to all the whys that were bouncing around his head like a multiplying bean in a spray can. The rain is pelting down and getting everyone soaked in seconds, this proves to be the perfect antidote to her eagerness. They see the nearest metro and head to it. Eddy likes to walk a city, to explore, so the reluctant necessity for the underground trip infuriates him.

The escalator down was long. A journey in itself. Eddy looks at his feet moving on the rolling steel stairs. Over a hundred metres down they are slowly descending into a small rectangle of light. At one-point Eddy turned to not see the top, just a closing window of bleakness, to turn once again and not see the bottom. People seemed oblivious as they read their newspaper that was folding over, wet and crinkled at the edges. Drips from their hats, hair and clothes. Closer they arrive to the bottom the hum of orchestral music is heard. From muffled, barely audible, to gently becoming louder. No smell, just dampness from the other passengers on the downward gradient.

Eventually at the bottom, they are surrounded by a feeling of being in a palace. A museum. Lia's enthusiastic reason to take the metro has opened up in front of Eddy's eyes, in the form of enlightenment. The crystal chandeliers that shine a soft glow from the cut glass, stroking over the fascinating murals. The fine architecture of sheer brilliance. These were the most majestic. The most impressive station that he had ever seen. A highlight. A tourist destination in its own right. They buy a ludicrously cheap ticket which not only surprised Eddy but what really astonished him was how quiet it was. Not many people seemed to be using the metro. They jump from one station to another.

Marble walls, mosaics, bas-reliefs, marble floors, walls, from one unique underground palace to another. The impressive luxurious feel with the intricate mouldings, beautiful paintings. The smell of the underground, merged with the ozone from the rain, the damp from their clothes, from others, and the metallic fuel from the trains. To add to the grand affair is the regal classical music that gets piped in. They start to feel underdressed.

Unbelievably farfetched, considering that this is a public place, a metro, a means, a station to get from one place to the another. They are underdressed for this ballroom, this unseen classical orchestra. The presence of art, designs, sculptures. Each station has a different theme, a celebration. Whether it is the workers, military, farmers or some significant date in history. It seems odd to station-surf, but so great that the rest of the afternoon rushes past as they rush to one station to another. Unconcerned they are by the rain, the traffic, the tumultuous hubbub happens many metres above. These were used as bomb shelters during World War Two, although without the ensemble of a string section, but terrifying crashes, clatters. To the aftermath of screams cut short just before the spine-chilling black silence.

Just as the metro blew them away, they took what seemed to be a four-minute journey back up another escalator to the surface. To see, be confronted by the insane traffic once again that they had all but forgotten about. The cars inch along over six, sometimes eight lane highways. There is no such thing as rush hour, more like rush hours, that quite literally drag. They went down and it was peak hour. After a long, long time underground they have come back to the surface. It seems the same cars, are in the same position, honking the same longingly pressed horns with the same frustrating fury.

Eddy is baffled to why they do not use the beautiful metro stations below them. It is of no wonder that Moscow's traffic has been rated the worst in the world. Since the fall of the Soviet Union the explosion of car ownership has gone out of control, amidst the convenient luxury beneath them all. Was it the freedom returned that they thought they had lost?

They stop near their hotel and have a light evening meal. Well that was the idea, but it was a rather filling golden clear broth of odd shaped bright yellow noodles with mushrooms and chicken called a Lapsha. It was not as enjoyable as the cheaper pelmeni from the food court, but filled a hole. They both agreed that they would not be ordering this, any time soon.

Lia wants to go on the church route called the Golden Ring, however time, on this occasion is not going to make this feasible. Secretly, Eddy is relieved. He did not think of churches when they decided to go to Russia. They are everywhere. Considering religion was banned during the Soviet years. Some religious sites were destroyed. Some, since have been rebuilt. All the remaining original ones are as beautiful as when built. Some saved as used for other uses. Some used as warehouses. Some as factories. In the infamously famous Kremlin, it has four palaces and four cathedrals.

This is where they head to in the early hours of the morning, the Kremlin, Russian for citadel. The grey clouds are a thin veil for which it is an enigma if they will carry rain or sunshine. As for now a brooding evil, a somewhat sinister feel of impending doom. Although we are told he is not here today, the Kremlin is the residence of the President of the Russian Federation. They decide to get an English-speaking tour guide for what was recommended, three and a half hours. Then use the free time to walk around the site, maybe even returning to some of the tour spots.

After a ridiculously, although completely understandable strict security regime. Which thankfully, relieved them both, by stopping short of a gloved hand where the sun does not shine, they were through the arch into the Kremlin.

On the other side, struck by awe, they pass many uniformed guards, Nataylia welcomes them. She is a thin, tall woman with a short bob top of brown hair, smart clothes and an irresistible compelling smile in the shape of the Nike logo, a tick. She seemed to welcome them like a long-lost friend. She was contagious in her energetic will to show them around her passion.

In very, very specific details she describes in near perfect English, with an American twang, over the small group that she was escorting a little about her, a history professor born and bred here in Moscow. She precedes to introduce the history in front of Trinity Gate Tower. The red brick entrance with small windows. A blue-face clock tops the centre of the tallest tower in the Kremlin. This, there told, was where Napoleon's troops firstly entered, to then flee the Kremlin. Nataylia seems to not notice the rain that has started to slowly fall as she waves her hand in animated styles, with a crooked smile on her lips as she hides a relishing enjoyment as she explains the early life of the Kremlin.

Starting its life as a firebreak after the Mongolian domination which housed a city within its' walls in 1150. Eddy stares around and tries to imagine this. A city confined within these claustrophobic red brick walls. It is hard for him to imagine this considering it is big for a palace but, still too small for a city. They walk up a grey, wide cobbled stone ramp bordered by red waving pillars to the uppermost gate with the tops of the green-light wind blowing the leaves of the trees below.

Nataylia continues to speak as she slowly gracefully walks like a competing horse up the ramp. Guards are everywhere. Watching from every angle. Ready to shout, blow a whistle, bark instructions if anyone strays away from the path that is for the tourists. Even the guard boxes are completely clear, transparent window places except the two headed eagle on the side of the roof looking out, watching everyone as well as the guards in the box.

'Ivan the Great did the most drastic changes between 1475–1516. He brought Italian architects in to build the walls.' She scans, softly with her hands, over the said walls, '…that you see today.'

They look at the curves and the number of cathedrals inside in a red whirlpool. She mentions that the Kremlin, in which they have officially entered, these fortified walls have been the home for Ivan the Great, Ivan the Terrible, Lenin, Stalin, Mikhail Grobachev and Boris Yeltsin to name just a few that have made a mark in the pages of Russian and world history.

The dark mustard yellow walls, divided by white highlighted alcoves and window frames is the large Presidential home, also for the Presidential offices. Armed security guards are watching from every single corner. Black iron metal gates with the tiniest door are guarded before, after, in person and by technology. Soldiers constantly patrol the area. This is to protect and serve, but if they did not know any better, they would think it was more to keep the President in, by evidence of the heavy security, making it seem more like a prison, rather than a home.

The white Patriarch's Palace, which forms part of The Church of the Twelve Apostles is one of the oldest in Moscow, built in 1640. Four tall grey brick supporting columns with five cupolas that are above white pillars on the roof. To Lia this has a rather smooth lacklustre appearance, whereas the high tiered wooden porch is in Eddy's eyes somewhat beautiful. Each of the sparkling golden orbs carry a cross on all of the twelve gold plated domes, that represent the twelve apostles. After walking under a large, intimidating arch, standing in what Nataylia describes as Cathedral square, she points and voices so many facts that they can hardly take them all in.

As if the heavens have listened to their silent prayers for it to stop raining, the rain stops with the grey quickly given way to a light blue sky and white whimsical wisps of white clouds. The Assumption Cathedral is one, if not the most important church in Russia. In this light it almost hovers on the haze that the sun has produced from the wet, cold ground. Inside these large walls, is where the Russian Emperors and Tsars were crowned, where the patriarchs are buried. The magnificent entrance is a large mosaic of colour, shaded by the welcoming sun. That with the steps gives an intimidating presence. Their footsteps softly echo as they walk forward, with eyes looking everywhere else.

Back in the basking glory, they stop in the presence of a gigantic decorated forty-tonne cannon, that never fired a single shot. The large balls under its tube are hollow, and, comically do not fit the barrel inside. The symbolic cast friezes around the carriage has a lion and flowers. Whereas the barrel has vegetation arrangements, memorial inscriptions and an equestrian frieze of Tsar Feodor Loannovich.

'That was the Tsar Canon. Now, follow to the Tsar Bell.' She sways sophisticatedly over to a large bell on a block plinth of bricks, that never swayed. Bas-reliefs of Tsar Alexey Mikhailovich and Empress Ioannovna are magnificently displayed on here with floral ornaments and images of saints, angels, rulers, Jesus Christ, Virgin Mary, and an inscription telling the story of the bell. Nataylia continues reeling off facts, figures and tells the story of the failed lifting attempt of the bell from the casting mould.

'Huge she said!' Eddy exclaims to Lia. 'A bit of an understatement! Don't you think?'

'Two hundred and two tons that stands six metres high and seven metres across,' Nataliya continues. 'The largest bell in the world. A bell that did not serve its purpose. It has never chimed. Never ever chimed. During the cooling process, a large eleven-ton chunk of the bell cracked off.'

It was here that she floated around to reveal the crack, the piece resting on the block plinth. It looks thick, heavy and not going anywhere soon. The space is shielded by a black mesh. Lia presumes so that no-one walks inside.

'See.' Eddy starts winking to a slight joke in a hushed tone. 'I told you bigger was not necessarily better.' He sniggers as Lia nudges him in the ribs with a sigh of resentment as she cannot help by giggling at his joke.

The bell is in the presence of the white Ivan the Great Bell Tower. Its mirror reflecting gold-adorned domes that stands at eighty-one metres, was the tallest building in Russia for nearly four-hundred years when built in 1532. Inside the tower are twenty-one bells within the tallest building in the Kremlin. They wanted to climb to the top but got told that they did not have time on the tour.

The dominating square of cathedrals, hence the name, Nataliya gives them time to wander. They enter them all. The grand portraits, the dazzling sarcophagus and other various icons, portraits decorate the grandeur of the interior of all. They are amazed at the feast before their eyes, with a chunk of appreciation for the craftsmanship and just a touch of wonderment. Without realising they have overstepped their allotted time. They return to the group as Nataylia is in the throes of talking about the Saint of Moscow, Saint George.

'St George in Russia has a slightly different story. For here, he spoke to the dragon and tamed her. He then rode her back rather than slaying her.'

Someone in the group asks about the name of the city. She is slightly stumbled by her well-rehearsed script to answer.

'The name Moscow is a little mystery.' She points over the red Italian style Kremlin wall, across the Moscow River towards the British embassy. 'This area was swampy. Many believe that Moscow came from the old Russian word meaning, swampy. Here, where we stand, at The Kremlin, that means fortress, well, Kremlin was known as Pine Tree Hill.'

'Not really an inspired name, on both answers but an answer, nevertheless,' Lia whispers in Eddy's ear.

High above the Armoury is a maintenance man on a ladder inside a metal cradle repairing one of the large five-pointed burgundy Kremlin stars with golden veins. Nataylia enthusiastically points aloft, above the red brick tower and the green glazed dark tiles to the man in grey overalls.

'Take a picture,' she somewhat orders us all in the group to do.

Maybe it was the Russian accent, Eddy could not help but laugh, doing nothing to conceal his roar, all the while Lia sank into embarrassing silence as she rolled her shoulders over, brushed her hair and used her hand to conceal her blushing red face. Then a shaking camera shot as her shoulders tried to conceal the giggles that were trembling up inside her ready to erupt into laughter. This was thanks to Eddy who had the serious case of the giggles that he could not, or would not control. This is where the digital camera comes to providence as it took nearly eight photographs to get one that was not a shaking, distorting mess.

'You, YOU can really see how big the stars are, really are with a male next to them,' Nataylia goes on, unperturbed. 'Stalin, I mean. Originally, these were huge two-headed golden eagles, but Stalin had these removed, to, remove all relics of the tsarist regime. These shining large stars took their place. Each star is four metre by four metre and each one weighing a ton. Each one is covered with ruby glass. Always lit. Even in the day. They are the guiding light for Russia. The five points have meanings. Many ones. The main one is to symbolise each of the continents which are non-communist. Eurasia is classed as one. The other main meaning, you see there were two, was that these are the five fingers of the workers that will lead Russia to communism.'

The large green flat-roofed yellow and white big-top walls of the large Kremlin Armory has a fast moving queue for which they head to the back. As they hug the walls in the queue, they notice that they are on a slight slope as the wall gets taller to accommodate the downhill trend. They are like ants around an elegant wedding cake. As they swiftly make their way to the front, Nataylia bellows to them that they have an allocated time so, they must go in, soon. She silently, deliberately quieter, in a calculated tone, mentions that no photographs are permitted inside.

'What?' An astounded Eddy demonstrates to Lia. 'Again! This is. This is really...really pissing me off.'

Lia nods in agreement, with a little sense of being condescending that was not lost on Eddy. They get given an audio guide which is included in the price. They go through yet another security inspection to step into the first room. Religious iconography with delicate, intricate gold thread, encrusted with jewels beams invisible rays to attract them in. An arched cream ceiling with red borders and piping's that lead to large chandeliers is nearly lost to the artefacts on display.

The deep red walls reflect in the tall glass cabinets of the next room with dim lights cascading down on the numerous rifles, duelling pistols, swords and armour. Each room is different, unique that keeps the focus concentrated and enjoyable for them both. This is not only the oldest museum, they learn as they listen to their computer guide, but it was purposefully built for this collection.

Like a light switch had just been flicked on in their mind, they enter yet another room on the numerous floored museum to be surrounded by glass cases with Fabergé Eggs, ten to be exact. Instantly, it dawns on them that this is what the other English-speaking tourists were going on about on the train. They both had overheard the same conversation of people travelling from Moscow in the opposite direction when another couple asked them if they had seen the eggs.

Eddy and Lia were flummoxed by the conversation and nodded in a confused agreement with a mystified look etched over their faces. For which, the other four tourists did not pick up on. Some of the Fabergé eggs where on loan, with one in particular being described on the audio. Each one is unique. Each one has a relevant secret inside for the intended recipient. Some of these golden, turquoise and red eggs took two years to build. They seem to be drawn like a magnet to the golden egg.

This one is the size of an ostrich with elegant gold leading from the turquoise top into the two-headed eagle. Lia softly bumps her head on the glass as she leans in a little too close.

Lastly are five carriages, and one dynamic miniature egg in a rotating clock-like mechanism that shimmers in gold, which they are told is said to be still working. They wondered what the message inside would have, or, does actually read.

Some many historic artefacts are on display that they are ruing the rule to not allow photographs. Carriages for snow, carriages for road, with costumes from the driver, different armour, abundant sparkles of jewels, glittering silverware, twinkling goldware, grand thrones are all around the white walled, olive-green window frames and the wooden small stage for which they stand upon. Another floor has other notable items such as the original boots that were worn by Peter the Great.

'A huge mass of history under one roof, eh! Eh?' Eddy probes.

'Oh, yes…yes.'

After leaving the armoury, they do not deliberate in shelling out additional money for the entry fee to head into the Kremlin Diamond Fund. Being run by a different organisation, these tickets can only be brought once inside. Again, no photography. And just when they thought the security could not get tighter, they were confronted with a stricter code. Phones, bags, keys all have to be handed in. Then just as they enter the, what seems like a bank vault the beep from the metal detector sounds.

Lia's pen lodged into her guidebook had to be handed in as well. Into the darkened rooms of the Diamond Fund they plunge as their eyes swiftly adjust. A soft, amber light caresses the jewels reflecting off in equally calming twinkles. The sparkling wealth is glittering, sparkling and is impossible to try and hide in the gloom. The first display glass shows uncut diamonds grouped in size and colour, and arranged in tubes about the size of toilet rolls, with easily thirty plus diamonds in each tube.

The next room, the diamonds get even bigger. The wow factor of the first room comes out again, conceding that it was never really lost. This time however, Lia exclaims it out loud with even more gusto that she foresaw with a loud gasp. The water-clear diamonds here are accompanied by the blood red rubies, the evergreen Disney painting coloured emeralds and the deep blue sapphires. Showcased here is the focal point. Here is the climax, the world's largest diamond. It is huge.

Smack, bang in the middle of the room, is a large glass cabinet. Inside on the glass transparent shelf are gold nuggets found in the mines of Siberia. Most are larger than Eddy's clenched fist. Three Russian stamped gold bars are on display to the left. Looking deep into all the cabinets are lasers, beams and sensors. The sound of whirling cameras does not distract but give a gentle reminder that they are not alone. The gems look not only heavy, but almost unreal, as if they are going to be fake cardboard mock-ups for films to fantastically display replicas of what they really are. This cannot be tried or tested due to the security, nor would they. But having been left off the hook back in Baikal, Eddy was not going to test his 'fake' theory out.

Just as they were leaving the sparkling world of make-believe showcasing what they can never afford with the intricate, delicate and elaborate jewellery, Lia notices something and pulls Eddy over. A sign, she translates for him, is a massive Orlov Diamond encrusted on a handle of a pole.

'Gift by Count Grigory Orlov to Catherine the Great, eighteenth century,' she translates for Eddy. Then Lia remembered something she had read on the train. It flooded out of her as the gates gave way.

'I, erm, yes…it was a present, no, originally it was from India. Said to have been stolen from a Hindu statue in 17 something-or-other maybe, yes, maybe 50, without doubt 1750. By a deserter from the French army.'

As Eddy listened to Lia with his fist clenched, comparing the near perfect size of his fist with the diamond through the glass before him. Equally amazed by the jewels as he was amazed by Lia. She had the ability to remember things. She would read, see, feel or hear and be able to resight the information at another time that was relevant. He loved this about her. This total recall. He also detested this about her.

For, you see, she would remember the slightest throwaway comment, figure it out. To bring it back when she needed it, like a weapon. Just like an ace up her sleeve it would get produced to win an argument, settle a debate or just prove once again that Eddy's memory was far, far more inferior than hers. He agreed with her, but, would never admit it to her. Yet. He did love her, a lot, though.

Even though the tour and the museum were very expensive, it was something that they happily parted their cash with. They would not refrain from doing it again. A fitting end to an awesome tour in an impressive place fronted by a brilliant tour guide. Although not from and not in a very tipping country they would not have felt right not to give Nataylia a few bills and a shake of the hand while thanking and nodding their smiling bobbing heads. As Eddy walked away, he wondered how gay he looked in gripping her hand, one on the other and embracing them firmly but softly.

It is getting dark, grey clouds have returned to the skies. For some reason, Lia is insistent on seeing the Peter the Great Monument. A short metro journey for which Lia made Eddy do, for his opinion to see some more of the magnificent metros rather than walking. They promptly get to the river side. Then after a short, cosy walk they loom closer to their destination. It is hard to miss this colossal sculpture rising from the river. As they come closer to see it, the truth emerges on Lia's focused determination to see this sight that is completely against her recent wants to see, such as the more churches.

'This…' She points across the ripple of the grey marching armies with a slight breeze coming across. Fountains at the monument's feet give the impression that it is literally rising from the river's bed itself. They can see by other people that they can walk up to it, but Lia seems happier to see it from this vantagepoint on the other side of the riverbank. Fixed flags come from the hulls of the boats that protrude outwards and around the shipwrecked column. At the very top is another ship for which Peter the Great hangs onto the nets holding a golden scroll before him as the ship looks forward.

'This was Christopher Columbus. A gift to America. They did not want it, so they sent it back.' She sneers. 'A little rude, I think, but, but they made good of an awkward situation and changed the head, thus turning it into a statue of Peter the Great. It is not particularly liked. If it is the location, or if it is the statue per say, is unsure, but, someone. You would not believe it. I am not sure that I actually do. But someone, actually tried to bomb it. Too funny A!'

'What? Get the—'

'I read it,' Lia interrupted the upcoming blaspheme. 'Hence, well, it has gotta be true, A?'

'Seriously? Someone tried to bomb it?'

'Yep. Gotta believe it.'

The soft rush of the imitating fountains of waves in the river going forward in the direction of Christopher, sorry Peter, is facing to make it look as if the boat is in fact, in motion. The three sails above his head on the mast are in the state of blowing in the wind. It is a huge monument.

They conclude their large, event-filled historical-rich day to stride over the nearby bridge into a sculpture park to get the last remaining hours of daylight. This will soon be an arts museum, so they feel privileged to be walking around the green unkept grass, dotted with white daisies and blemishes of red roses that highlight the green, and compliment the tranquillity. The sculptures in here are all saved from places around Moscow. There is a Lenin statue with its nose cut off, no doubt to not spite his own face. Some bizarre statues, wielding and sculptures like a wall full of screaming heads kept together by black metal rods and barbed wires.

All have Russian Cyrillic with Eddy feeling somewhat wrong by asking what each one said. Granted, she would not have minded a little, Eddy did not want her to feel like a record playing dictating machine translating for him. So many Lenin's. A small grey head looking down with a cloak of white marble like he is neck deep in snow, ice or struck by the Marshmallow Stay Puff man from the Ghostbusters movie. The statues, sculptures and art caused a healthy, enthusiastic exchange of views concerning the meanings, and idea provoking agendas behind and between them as they strolled hand in hand through the park, to eventually end up back to the hotel under the cover of white darkness.

Eddy decided to go for a run around the former impressive Olympic city of 1980 which shows a neglected look, as Lia writes her diary. This is a shame considering the size of the stadium. The large floodlit bicycle paths highlight the cracks in the structures as well as the intended gravel path. Behind the hotel he bumps into Lia as she stumbles from one stall to the other in a souvenir den of many ways to haggle, get bargains, like a Fabergé egg for your friend, work colleague or lover. Providentially, Eddy arrives back in time to stop her making that foolish purchase.

This leaves them with just enough time to pack, check out and get ready to board the nine in the evening train for the last overnight trip to Saint Petersburg. Their last stop in Russia, their last stop on the Trans-Siberian Train Journey. One step closer to their real destination. One step closer to Lia's motherland. Lia's home.

Lia decided to pack a plastic bottle for which she has stabbed several holes in. She is taking heed from an Argentinean traveller who offered the tip that for a shower this is the method. She insists on taking some rope tied to the back of, say the door, or using one hand to hold, and the other to lathe, the water filled bottom would act as a shower head. She insists on giving it a try. Eddy mocks her. Insisting in rib-tickling tease that she will never do it. That it will never work.

After finding the toilets on the past journeys to be covered in, not the most modelled welcoming convenience, he thinks that she will not go through with it in the next morning. Lia is gaining momentum in her resilient mind in this harmless relentless joke. She is really becoming more determined to go through with the shower theory, to, at least, give it a try. On trying to stuff the plastic bottle in her bag she lifts out the forgotten bottle of vodka, along with the disposable cutlery set with the shot glass that were brought back at the previous train station. She holds them aloft to Eddy who looks at the white ticking wall clock to contemplate the correct answer.

'Let's get on the train first, A?' He begrudgery concedes.

The last train journey is set to take place shortly, with this brings excitement that they have not felt since the beginning of the trip. This time Lia remembers the correct time. Moscow time. She looks up at the wall clock. She shouts to Eddy a mess of words which he deciphers to make sense into. He concludes that they need to get their arse into gear to make the train. In eight short hours, in comparison to the last train trips, they will be in Saint Petersburg. But, they have to make the train first. They run. After all their planning to not rush, they have to rush. Their bags trailing behind their backs. The wheels hit more air as they bounce over the pavement. They arrived. They get the ticket easily.

They end up running for no reason as, with no explanation, their scheduled train is delayed. They stay around the train station waiting and waiting. Books come out to play. Temptation fuels the brain as vodka joins the party. The vodka top clinks open with an effortless unscrewing motion by Eddy. The cellophane snaps by Lia's long fingernails, as she pierces the tight wrapping so the shot glasses can be removed. They fill them to the brim. Smirk as they cheer with a soft thud, a non-existent clink of the plastic shot glass and take one gulp, swallow, followed by a shake of the head, an appreciated unison 'ahhh' amusingly towards each other. Again, the ritual is repeated. Breathing the alcoholic fumes over each other, they kiss.

The train finally rolls in. Considering the day was not that tiring, really. Sure, they walked a great deal, but they eventually got on the train. On the same bunk. Fully dressed. In each other's arms. They fall asleep instantaneously. The wheels are not even in motion as they slump into a slumber land. This may be the vodka and no food taking control, or its toll.

Travelling through the night the journey is slept quickly away and they arrive just before seven the following morning. They share a mutual annoyance for wasting time at the station while waiting for a train to arrive that was later, so much later than scheduled. They share a slight drilling headache. But, this is all shaken away as Eddy sees his own motherlands language. Finally, Eddy can take an element of control in the trip, as they come off the train and he sees signs written in English.

As the crow flies, they have travelled six-thousand and sixty-four kilometres, the even more unbelievable distance of nine-thousand, six-hundred and seventy-two kilometres by train, literally half the world.

This journey across Russia has been with great ups, and vast downs, great mountains of rolling humour, great valleys of rifting depression for them both. Stories with strangers, strangers with stories, stranger stories. Strangers that will remain strangers, which they will never hear, see, speak to ever again. It has been an epic journey, in all meanings of the word. Lia has brushed up on her Russian, which was her intention, and feels a lot more confident in conversing.

As they stroll through the station, trying to find the correct way, they encounter the usual shops. There are shops selling alcohol, food, souvenirs, reading material and guns. Yes, Eddy had to double take himself. He actually stopped walking to be rooted in mid-gait to reread the sign, to look into the clear shop display to see rifles and handguns through the glass window, solid grey railing bars on the other side like the weapons were prisoners. Not sure why you would need this at a train station, but they manage to stroll on with a cloud of wonder, a silver lining of amazement and their heads swimming in bafflement.

Just off the main drag. Just down from the train station is the road in which Lia had booked the hotel. The main drag of Nevskiy Prospekt is lined with the elite shopping names housed in the architectural buildings of elegance dating from 1753, each one with a story of its own. Each one a soundless trumpet fanfare to announce European fashions, cultures and customs have arrived. This is the best-known street in all of Russia. Running from the train station down to the Admiralty, thus the river is the main vein of the city.

They go to check in, to get told the same and unsurprising old-story that the room is not ready. The concierge is terrific though, the best one so far. She stores their bags while telling them that there is a free walking tour that will give them a great insight into 'his beautiful home'. There is evidence of a recent downpour, but the sun is shining with the rays adding an extra shine to the rain-washed architecture. Each building is like different cakes of different flavours in a giants bakery.

The receptionist intervenes to brush over the concierge in a teasing way to pass them a map. He glanced at his huge silver watch that adorned his smooth hairless wrist before snatching the map back with a smile, a gentle lingering tap of the hand. Not at them, but back at the receptionist. The sexual chemistry between these two males was evident, but very much concealed. He breathlessly tells them to hurry, rush, sprint to the meeting point that he boldly rings many times in red ball point pen. 'A tour is to start here,' he stabs the red pen in the sketchy circle.

He literally ushers them out of the automatic revolving doors and points in the direction of where to go, what to look for and how they can catch up if the tour has started. They walk fast. Caught up in the moment of their excitement to turn around a corner to see a young male that looked rather thin, as the bright white deformed T-shirt with the black capital letters was made to look bigger than it was. The spot that they were told to be, to see the T-shirt stating in bold letters that stand out: FREE TOUR.

They must stick out like a sore thumb as they arrive for the male guide to instantly spot them. He who introduces himself as Mikhail clocks them with a hand motion to 'come closer'. He greets the small cluster of people independently with a well-rehearsed overview of who he is, what they will see and what to do if they want to leave. He steps through the gathering crowd to introduce himself personally to every single person individually with a shake of the hand. His command of the English language is brilliant. He encourages them to circle around him as he starts a short history of Russia, and the city. He has a passionate delivery of information, facts and interesting stories about the churches, former churches, warehouses, statues, bridges and theatres. Most things are learnt for the first time for Lia. Everything is learnt for the first time for Eddy.

'During the Soviet times...' Mikhail informs them all with, not for the first time, an American twang in his voice. 'It was illegal to be unemployed for longer than six months. Soviet actually means council. The churches were used as warehouses. This is, in turn saved them from being destroyed like many, others across the country, which were demolished. The Church of Spilled Blood, for example, was used as a potato warehouse. This saved it.'

They quick-footedly follow behind him, as his long strides guide them towards the small low-lying, Lion Bridge casting its reflection into the Griboedova. The larger iron lions support gaudy gold wings. Each possesses a white orb of an unlit light on each side. The lions seem to be leaning back to hold the cables of the bridge in their mouths to keep the crossing from collapsing. The concentration of keeping the bridge, a bridge, keeps them for doing what Lia and Eddy, and for that matter the rest of the group are doing.

They look down the canals of St Petersburg, seeing their reflection. admiring the beauty, the mirroring architecture on the ripples, the classy extravagance with a mutual sharing mouth, agape. This let the salty air enter their bodies, it cleansed their soul. The first sight of St Petersburg has set the bar extremely high to follow, the expectation is high. The Lion Bridge is the earliest suspension bridge, dating back from 1825. Perfectly poised from this vantage point to make a terrific clarified route to frame the golden onion domes of the Church on Spilled Blood.

Once over the canal, Mikhail takes them to beneath the dark shadows of the ninety-six Corinthian column arc of the enormously imposing, Cathedral of Our Lady Kazan. They pass a familiar sight, being their hotel in the middle of the Nevsky Prospekt, where a slight click from Mikhail's pen occurs on his notepad to present the Kazansky Cathedral. This is teeming with tourists like bees over honeycombs. The nearby fountains have children frolicking, splashing around as they scream with glee with their parents looking on, nervously perched on the edge of thick wooden benches, ready to pounce with maternal protective wings if danger lurks, veers its head, begins to reveal itself.

The sound of the water is accompanied by a young lady brilliantly strumming a worn guitar as she sooths the ragged ages with her choirlike sirens. Observing the length and breadth of the scene is a statue, or more accurately, a colossal monument to the Commander in Chief of the Russian Army during the Patriotic War of 1812. It is said that just before departing to the front, Duke Mikhail Illarionovich Kutuzov prayed for the salvation of Russia in front of Our Lady of Kazan icon, which is held inside the then recently completed cathedral. He would be honoured that he is buried here. The war gave victory for the Russians. After of which, the stolen keys of the French fortresses were hung inside the Cathedral. Showcasing the bounty of war.

Mikhail takes their eyes on a journey up the granite brown stone of the Kazansky Cathedral that forms a Latin cross, crowned with a green dome topped with a large golden cross. Forwards they head towards the steps, they cannot help but feel intimidated by the large pillars, the columned arches crowned with engraved attics. They step inside to encircled fifty-six pink granite columns, with golden capitals. The grey and pink marble floor looks like a Vanilla sky. They float on the dreamscape where the winds of Mikhail's lecture are lost into muffled white noise. It was only when his voice pitched higher, in evident noticeable excitement.

Considering he sees this sight every day, it is a wonder to him, as well as the group to how it can still generate exhilaration. His high voice brings their heads up from floating on the tiles to the left of the sanctuary doors, he points to the crowds. Beyond of which the wonder-working icon is beheld.

'Fascinating,' Mikhail begins in a hushed tone. 'See. Look. Don't touch. Touch with your eyes. This is full of mystery. The icon first appeared in the sixteenth century, when Ivan the Terrible, Tsar, conquered Kazan. Later, in 1579, a fire broke out that destroyed the city's churches, cathedrals, and abbeys. At its height it destroyed half the Kazan Kremlin. It was rediscovered by a ten-year-old girl, Matron, who dreamed of the Virgin Mary who told her where it can, find. The young girl, with her mother find the icon and sent it the, to the Cathedral of, of the Annunciation.

'During this journey, two blind persons, Losif and Nikit, were cured. On the eighth of July, the day that the icons appearance, is a national holiday, held annually in Kazan, and then all over Russia. Several replicas were made from the icon, somewhere declared a working wonder. Ironically Our Lady of Kazan had been the protector of the Romanovs family. Are we aware of the Romanovs?'

A hushed silence descends over the group, as no-one wants to either admit that they know. You would have to be born under a rock to not be aware of the Russian pivotal tragic moment in history. If someone says yes, this could lead to more questions. These questions could follow, leading to them to being naïve, to feel stupid, to feel uneducated in the ways they have been educated rather than the ways the locals have been. Without being consciously aware they nod their heads for yes. Thankfully, deprived of any descriptions or questions. Without much of a pause, he continues.

'It was during the time of Peter 1 that the icon was moved and made a home here. No photographs inside, Martin, please. MAR-tin.' His voice is stern as he hesitantly places his hand softly over the lens.

As they exit from the candlelit, dim-lighted sombre cathedral they bow their eyes away from the bright sunlight that makes them squint their eyes. Iridescent wishy-washy rainbows dance past they eyes as they quickly readjust from the duskiness.

Slightly out of place but, oddly, at the same time in the right place is the Dom Knigi Bookstore dubbed 'The House of Books' by the locals. First and foremost, due to being very well stocked. In a former warehouse, former headquarters is the strikingly and graceful building with enough elegance to fit seamlessly into any city in the world. The spectacular six-story former Singer House built in 1914 is a tribute to the original, unique one based in New York, in the exact same Art Nouveau style, with the same j'ai ne sais qui. However, this is not so much based on the building, but a carbon copy, except for one distinguishing feature. The tower on the corner is smaller. Mikhail's hands thrust into the air with that revelation, he spins on his heels and is off down the street devoid of looking back, hoping that the group is following closely behind.

They walk around the pink gravel path with a small, humble arch of a fountain to get a better view. Negotiating the circular path around the fountain accompanied by the rippling, splashing droplets below and yellow flowers on the perfectly rowed out bed, they are halted. The chic of the flower display adds to the stylish, sophisticated landscape that they find themselves surrounded by within the scene. People read papers on the bright, smoothly painted glossy white bench, that blend into the picture perfect view effortlessly, flawlessly.

Mikhail stops to proclaim the best view of the Singer House. He is right, from this view they can see the intricate details. The supporting glass globe has the angels arching its back, as another stops it from toppling over. The tower has a clear covered glass dome, surrounded by angels and topped with more angels that survey, down at the main road of Russia. A road that leads to the furthest reaches of an eastern city in Asian Russia, if it was followed back the way Eddy and Mia had just come from.

'The tower is smaller…' Mikhail finally brings to light the ambiguous justification, but not without a little more teasing. 'Why?' No answer is given. 'Due to the…drumroll…the law of the city dictates that nothing can be built above St Peter's Cathedral.'

For some reason, they find themselves taking so many photographs of this building. They use the park's flowers as a frame, with the droplets of water stuck in a still-time. Mikhail, nevertheless, wants to keep the tour moving, so, they are hurrying fast on the slippery path to catch up to the group before their cross the unruly road.

Matching the blue sections in the field of the white cloud, freely scattered in the midst of the dark blue canvas, are the domes of the enormous white pillared, naval Trinity Church.

'Inside, over three thousand can watch a service,' Mikhail lectures as they draw closer and closer, competing over the traffic. 'Again, no photographs inside. That goes for all of us, Martin.'

Small, sneaking steps lead inside, away from the commotion. Still shouting the first words until he realises that it is noticeably calmer indoors. Like a state secret he whispers, that they have five minutes. On hearing this as they scan around, they move around quickly. They have the privilege of being able to come back if needed as they are in the city for a while, this is not a fly-in fly-out weekend trip away. Lining the walls are memorial plaques to regiments, similar styles but different sizes. Resembling impeccably printed tombstones on flawlessly polished stone, are the names and dates of officers killed and in what battle.

Above, hanging still, starved of a breeze are trophy's, in the form of flutter-less flags. Others have wooden or metal keys. Both are from forts of the opposition, during various campaigns to show their death was not in vain. Not even fully around they glance to see the time. They have no choice but to skim past the remaining unseen, to hurry back out onto the steps. Like crossing a threshold from paradise to hell, noiseless to noise, scented to stinking. They immediately target Mikhail. Right away, on detecting him they dash over and see, the rest of the group waiting, in the shadow of one of the great, magnificent columns. The groups scowl, but Mikhail beams over the sea of impatience. His happiness is contagious and turns the tide into reflecting faces of joy. Once everyone has ensembled he continues his tour.

'After a year of occupation by the Turkish in Bulgaria, the Russians had enough. WE...' He states proudly, patriotically, while thumping his chest, his heart. 'We liberated them in 1878.'

It is hard to believe that the Russo-Turkish War Column standing in front, almost takes the shine off of the church. The focus of the group has been drawn from the church to Mikhail's gesture. Their eyes scan the thin column, made of one-hundred and forty trophy cannon barrels, that were brought back from the naming war. Aloft, on the top of the eight-metre column is a winged figure looking down. He, is the figure of victory, Nike. In his right hand, he holds an oak leaf wreath, and a palm branch in his left. Eddy comments to himself on the idea of using the cannons for the monument. He sees it as a stroke of genius that fits the memorial perfectly, a light of inspiration.

In a slight contrast to the Naval Church, they get guided to a Military Church, St Nicholas. The golden baroque spires, winking domes glitter, sparkle and gleam with flashes from the arresting large sun. Overlooking the Kryukov Canal, that triumphs St Nicholas's Church is a thin commanding steep, sharp bell tower. Amongst the green trees of the path that leads to the entrance they tread with a cushioned supple crush of the gravel. The smell of industrial smoke invades the drawing attraction to make an attempt to mar the appearance.

They look to the source; the bland uninspired residential and commercial buildings are very much unbefitting of the location. Yet, inside, shielding the peripheral environment, the light blue and white painted exterior are in perfect contrast to the clean brilliant white and bright Walt Disney treasures which are more related to a Princess Palace. Magnificent columns that support the colourful domes tower above them as their heads tilt backwards in wonder. Wooden iconostasis in golden frames line the wall with decorated scenes of the Russian Navy. Afore them the pews have a small collection of worshippers dispersed in isolated spots in silent prayer, more than the previous church but still, it is not many.

The green and white icing of pure elegance blossoms from around the corner. Lia smirks in recognition, as she instantly knows that this stylishness building is the world famous Mariinskiy Theatre. The place where many Russian dancers yearn to dance on the stage, a stage where they all dream to one day perform. Then they know they have created precise beauty. It is the dream of many ballet dancer to perform here where the audience sees the peak of their private iceberg but not the hard work, commitment, sacrifices and sweat and tears that has brought them to the deserved fruits of their labour.

To grace the stage is the highest honour. To feel the love of the audience is the highest accolade. To feel validated for what they have tried, perfected, toiled and worked towards is the highest reward. This was not for Eddy, however, Lia expressed numerous times with sledgehammer-subtle hints that she really wanted to go, so he bit the bullet. He decided to go and buy tickets for the next performance. He thought he was acting chivalrous as he strides to the ticket entrance, ignoring Mikhail's address.

Lia pulls him closer, speaks softly into his ear with a knowingly, cheeky close-mouthed chortle. She divulges that, this was already done, by her before leaving Sydney. She chuckles further at her harmless deception. She cheekily winks, she kisses a surprised Eddy on the cheek. He shakes his head in realisation that he has just been hoodwinked. And how? They had not listened to a single thing that Mikhail had said at this point of the tour, but follow him, giggling like naughty children at the back of the pack to the following stop.

Mikhail stops abruptly in the middle of St Isaac Square with the groups open-mouthed in awe as they all look up, catching flies, at the imposingly magnificent brooding grey St Isaac of Dalmatia. He grabs their attention, snaps his fingers to break them out of their trance to explain the art of the building itself, all the while the group are now busy. They listen, however they are involved in taking numerous photographs from different views.

'Named St Isaac due to Peter the Great shared the same birthdate,' Mikhail speaks, undeterred by the distracted tour group. Lia and Eddy are the only ones listening, they feel they owe it to him for their mischievous behaviour on the last stop. While not taking a single photograph, but acknowledging the sight ahead, looking up at the huge cathedral with respect. Mikhail continues to list facts, figures and interesting notes about the cathedral. It is no surprise that it is one of the biggest in the world, as they look up, they can see it—it is vast.

'Although saying one of the biggest is like saying one of the best, that best. What is that about. That ONE could be number in one-thousand, in the thousands,' Eddy disputes loud enough for Lia, fortuitously no-one else.

Mikhail turns and walks off. They stare in a daze, thus, in a short scurry they follow him to the last sight of the tour. Then Eddy realises that they have not taken a photograph. Simultaneously so does Lia. As she has the camera she turns, her impulsiveness rules her reactions to right the wrong. She rushes back to take a burst of snapshots from different angles. She returns insisting that they return later, that none of them will be any good.

Maybe saving the best for last. The end of Nevesky Prosket, on the river. They have nearly completed a dented circle to arrive at The Palace Square. The imperial grandeur of sights which holds the Hermitage and Alexanders Column. They walk around one of the graceful curved wings with a mustard yellow large arch in the centre and another symmetrical arch running the other way like a laurel headdress. Each has copper motifs. Above the arch, on the roof is a sculpture of victory riding a chariot looking towards the Winters Palace, the Hermitage. Framed through the arch, is the large column and the green and white palace behind. It looks nothing short of magnificent, a showpiece that focuses all their attention towards it.

They move as if in slow, cinematic motion, under the imposing stone wall they float into the publicly enclosed square. Craning their heads like a curious cat to see under the arch. To uninterruptedly twist their heads around, to look back at the yellow and white three-story arch possessing many windows. All the time, while continuing to effortlessly drift backwards, to not bump into the overcrowded public space. They are not able to take their eyes of the mesmerising charming allure.

Mikhail gathers his flock, bringing them near as they are all on the brink of wondering off into the abundant amass of people. In due course, around the base of the main soaring column, Mikhail familiarises them with the arresting, commanding location. From this point, directly under the gaze of the sun, they cannot look up as the rays blinds them as if teasing them for what they want to see, but slyly screens it with a wavering glittering swelling of various winks.

He delivers a small conclusion to the tour. A gradual building of applause occurs to appreciate the brilliant result of a remarkably informative rich walking tour. Eddy cannot believe it. He looks at his watch, to gain confirmation, he looks for a second time. Has three hours gone past already. Really? He looks at Lia and mouths a soundless, 'wow'. She returns the sentiment. They are equally amazed that the time has disappeared, the end is now. Time is not so much a fire in which they burn, but an inferno in which time incinerates to cinders.

Individually, the group split, one-by-one they proceed to go up, to say thank-you, to say goodbye. After giving Mikhail a shake of the hand and a tip, they go to get lost in the square. Each bill was heavily concealed in the clasp of the handshake. As Eddy looked on, he could not work out what people were leaving, giving. So, they were not sure what would be good, bad or just a plain insult. While many of the group raced towards the authentic imperial-style Hermitage, it is as if they are racing each other to get to the back of the meandering multi-coloured queue.

But, on the other hand, Eddy and Lia patiently wait until they are the last ones left. Lia rolls a couple of bills in her fist with the hope that they have managed the borderline accepted value. Eddy does not plan to distract, but it transpires as a great diversion as Mikhail thrusts the bills deep into his pocket with the rest of the money, he wants to hear Mikhail's advice. He desires to go to the top of Isaacs Cathedral, to see the promised perfect panoramic view that he spoke about.

Be that as it may, he did not have his bearings, he, no they, were a little lost. He gives directions as Lia rolls her eyes. She knows exactly what he is after, it is his drug. Eddy can never explain to people, but for a reason he cannot explain fully to himself, intuitively Lia understands. He just likes to be up high. Looking over the top of the cities, countryside, landscapes on the shoulder of man's creations, natures creations. To be able to see as far as he can see, as the eye can see. His Shangri-La, his medicine.

The sky is an electric blue as he, with Lia lagging behind, heads back to the cathedral before it closes for the day. She wants to take photographs of the sun setting around the Square. Taking the directions that Mikhail faultlessly described, he ignores her deep heel dragging. The voltage is moving through their shared hands, it runs the current through their body. He is the positive that wants to go, she is the negative that wants to stay. They have three days here. In the conclusion before Mikhail finished his tour, loiters around for a tip which he knows that people will give him, he ends the worse ending for any holidaymakers to hear. He lets them all know that on average it rains once every three days in Saint Petersburg. Not the best way, the greatest sentence to leave them with, more a brooding cluster explosion in their heads. But fair to have that knowledge they have no hard feelings about, but unenthusiastically mutually agree that this could be one of the better days.

They are back quicker than they anticipated and go directly inside the cathedral. Lia is not fussed about going up. Eddy, well that is the reason he is here. He turns after paying to walk up the nausea inducing stone spiral narrow staircase. Rhythmically, one step after the other, higher up he treads climbing the two-hundred and eleven steps inside the tower of St Isaacs Cathedral to the top. Meanwhile, Lia decides to wait down at the bottom. The cathedral was built in 1858.

During the Soviet times, it was a museum of Atheism. Although officially, it still is a museum. The top of the domes are surrounded by angels, with one carrying a ladder. The roof has angels supporting gas lights, torches. Eddy embraces the fantastic view of a multicoloured fuzzy carpet of different coloured, material rising and falling roofs. He can see so far, as far as he can see, the buildings do not stop.

The buildings put on an orchestra performance of winks, blinks in the summer sun, as he slowly walks around the summit. A cool breeze does not chill his relaxing mood, does not sooth his feeling of bliss, does not sway his electric current of a thrill of being here. The last place on the train journey. The last destination. He searches for the train station. The faded golden dome, an almost dirty copper look compliments in the skies, compliments the buildings around, compliments the sights of the sites around.

On one corner, he looks at the Church of Spilled Blood that dominates the skyline like an ice-cream cone topped with the sweet, sugary delights that make children squeal with glee. On the other is the vast Hermitage. Every landmark in which they have walked today Eddy can see. He can sketch with his eye the line that they made to the point that he is. The Hermitage is impressive from any view but, from, this view it is absolutely remarkably extraordinary. He cannot wait to go inside to see the treasures within the jewellery box.

The day is late, so they are going to have to wait until tomorrow. Eddy looks down at the Hermitage with Mikhail's echoing voice that he was only mentioning a few minutes ago, 'if you look at each item in the Hermitage for seven seconds it would take you more than three years to view them all. Inside over 2.8million works of art are in the five buildings.' He shivers, not with the chill, but with the eagerness of witnessing those pieces of art very soon.

Although not as impressive outside as many of the cathedrals, this is the most impressive inside of all the visited cathedrals so far. The colours that are inside the cathedral are magnificent paintings on the walls, the columns, the ceilings. The light blues, the saints sitting on thrones, the faces in beaded circular frames, the smell of the incense sticks, all are focused with the smoke of the incense, the candles from brightly lit delightful, crystal chandeliers hanging from the high ceilings.

She walks in a turning waltzing, gracefully spiral with her head looking up, her mouth appreciatingly open, eyes wide. The paintings, mosaics and delicate priceless stones are extravagant, however the weight of all these treasures did not come into account when planning the building, hence, it is slowly, starting to sink. She envelopes the riddle in her mind, wrapped in a mystery, the Russian craftsmanship just keeps on astounding her.

Lia looks up to where Eddy is. Although she squinted, she could not see him. She sees the red granite columns that support the dome. The angels that are looking down at her as if protecting the city like guardians, well from this angle, the angels are more like cherubs. The guardian cherubs are protectively scanning over the Russian people. Lia is fidgety. She paces around the bottom, then cannot take it any longer. She wonders what she is missing out on. She tears herself away to get a ticket to climb, to meet Eddy. All the time hoping that Eddy is not on his way down. She has a romantic notion for which she wants to complete in her mind.

She comes from behind. A fast embrace. He jumps. He did not expect her. She laughs as he gets higher than he intended and turns. They hug at the top. Looking over the magnificent view of Saint Petersburg. They share a tender kiss under the setting sun. A picture perfect romantic memory. Lia sees the malachite and lapis lazuli columns that decorate the cathedral are even more impressive up close and she is feeling blessed that she made the decision to follow Eddy. As they walk down, they share another kiss. They attempt to go down hand in hand but that quickly, and clearly, does not work. Back on the ground the amazing flower rosette budding of the intricate carved square roof is an art of its own.

The huge oak and bronze doors show scenes from the lives of Saints and of Christ, with one of the smallest keyholes Eddy has ever seen on something so vast. It is comically outlandish. This is really a testament to then, and today's computer-generated architects for which they should be taking notes, picking up a pencil rather than an electric pen. To feel the paper rather than the warmth of a computer screen.

Hand in hand, they head back to the Hermitage in a hugging ambling embrace for reciprocated affectionate support, also for added warmth as it has turned a little colder since a light dusk had entered for the attire that they are wearing. They, or, more to the point Lia must see what time the museum opens as this is something that she really wants to see, something she does not want to miss. Even more so following Mikhail's tribute and how colossal she saw the building was from the bird's eye view. Eddy's suggestion of looking at the internet was not good enough apparently! Something to unquestionably lock in for tomorrow.

Outside in traditional attire are many impersonators. Too many that they have to compete in a jostle, grab, pull and tug of passing tourists. So many times, to be frustratingly rude, as they walk, they feel the claws thrusting out to grab them for a photograph like caged prisoners grasping for freedom, for which they had no doubt they will charge them an exuberant fee for the displeasure. They are categorically not interested. With Olympic agility they avoid the unasked for advances with hip sways, body curves and strong resilience. They gaze around to see no-one from the tour around the square is seen. They must have scattered like the pigeons that move as they approach the ticket office.

Around the entrance are three enormously fine-looking, handsome Cinderella style carriages. The mirroring black polished finish seems to reflect back in naturalistic choruses, at the same time absorbing everything around. The gold rims, two-headed eagles on the door, the white curtain tied perfectly symmetrical inside, the red velvet cushioned seats, all the sophisticated finishes gently scream stylishness. The red tail-coated driver somewhat spoils this perfect step-back-in-time illusion somewhat by sharing a smoke with another driver. The glossy, combed, healthy, unicorn-white powerful horse with flared long-haired feet would be graceful to watch parading the carriage or in mid-flight.

They are peaceful looking, with a calming demeanour and a slight turn in the nose that states that they know that they are beautiful, better looking than other horses. Perched on the cobbled-stone floor which blends effortlessly with the palace as the background evokes that this image would have looked exactly like this years ago, when this was the normal form of transport.

Lia, in her red imitation leather raincoat, walks into view as she negotiates the slight ruts of the floor in her nude, slightly raised high heels. She is a princess. She is a queen in Eddy's eyes. Eddy takes an immense sense of pleasure in the knowledge that this sexual being, who naturally combines glamour, elegance and style, is his for the taking. Even in tracksuit and fleece, she easily has the same effect. As he watches her charmingly move with poise, Eddy smiles to himself with this personal thought. He knows he has punched above his weight.

She twirls to point up to something on the roof. This motion pulls Eddy out of his trance. The roof is teeming with sculptures on a green and white exterior that is garnished with gold paint around the window, on the emblems. He does not hear what Lia says, but moves close and pecks a soft kiss on her cheek with a look in his eyes, for which Lia enquires, 'Is everything alright?'

He barely audibly breathes out, 'Perfect...' with another kiss, 'one-hundred percent...perfect.'

In the centre of Palace Square is Alexander's Column. Dedicated to Tsar Alexander I in tribute to his role in the triumph over Napoleon. The same creators as the ones that designed St Isaac's Cathedral. The grey podium on the column reads 'To Alexander I from a grateful Russia', with the inscriptions of the battle. Alexander I ruled Russia between 1801 and 1825, during the Napoleonic Wars. The soaring red column that is sparkling as if on fire in the golden setting sun is the largest free-standing monument in the World, ingenuously balanced by a six-hundred tonne ball.

A testament to engineering in a terrific piece of architecture. They look up at the column, the focal point of the square. Squinting their eyes, they look up at the bronze angle. Holding a large cross with his free hand over the top and throwing it high, skyward as if calling for a triumphant cheer. The face that cannot be clearly seen is said to have been modelled on Alexander I.

Overhearing these various facts from a collection of tourists that are on a walking tour that they fortunately stumble upon. They circumnavigate the column, the group, to try, obviously fail to seem nonchalant in the shadows of the looming pillar so they could come to know more about the centrepiece. Eddy reacts, he cannot help it. He loudly exclaims and questions with a 'Really!' followed by a 'True?', which makes him bashfully turn and sulk away as the group's eyes follow his retreat. His covered face matches the column as Lia giggles in his footsteps. Being the unhelpful accomplice to his stealing of knowledge crime.

They dawdle around taking in the details that surround them. The column seems to be polished by the last beams of the sunlight as dusk comes in, this is pretty much how dark it will get for this time of year. Around the square are preparations for the White Light Festival. Temporary plastic marques are being constructed that snap a rustling break in the wind. These structures are erected in the way of the architecture giving brief, unfortunate eyesores in front of the elegant palace.

With the setting sun, a nippy breeze enters the square. It is funny that the local Russians are still in T-shirts, unaltered by the biting soft wind, whereas they are cambering for their warm clothes in the bottom of their day packs. They hastily pullover their rainproof, windproof jackets that are creased in bold red pulsating veins, going as far up as the zip allows. With matching dark green, his and her scarfs tightly coiled around their necks, their chin nestling into their collars, they resemble gift wrap Christmas presents.

It has been a full day from the train station to them back in a full circle near where the day started. It was here that they finally acknowledge that they are starving. The whole day without anything to eat. It took the waif of a sweet, aniseed fragrant to attract Lia to a sign near their hotel. Before going in, as they both feared that once in, they would never come out.

'Borsch?' she asks with her body moving towards, tugging at Eddy arm in the direction of the green painted wooden door, her mind already decided that this will be happening. They take the two crumbling stone steps and enter inside. Into an age where time had appropriately forgot. The low beams on the ceilings made them both duck and bow as they are greeted by a petit young lady with worn red leather menus in her hand. Lia converses, in response to the question about the magnificent salivating smell, she orders two as they weave around the small low-lying tables.

The hostess cradles the menu with her arms as she graciously leads to a small brown study tabletop made of planks of wood. With a slow-moving hand, she steers them down to a very hard pew that stretches the back wall, the type you get in old churches. They sit looking at the far window that is draped in white lace to allow only the shadowing images of the shoes, high-heels and occasional dog to go past. They had not realised that they had stepped down from the pavement until now.

The flickering candlelight is the only form of light in the centre of each of the tables that generates a calm quality. They are surrounded by the working class in construction gear, next to the suits of office workers, all dripping the red, velvet borsch from their spoons as they wordlessly crouch over a blue and white bowl. They feel instantly relaxed as they remove their outdoor clothes in the stuffy warmth of the cosy dining room. Irregularly placed around the whitewashed walls, which highlight the wooden beams, are simple frames of photographed buildings from around Moscow in fading black and white. A simple decor without pretention and an incredible character of its own which tells them something of the owners. Something that brings all walks of life in from the cold with a protective affectionately maternal cloak to make them feel untroubled and at peace.

Life's problems behind the door. Here is to be in timeless bliss. Everything is clean. Everything fits in with the old-fashioned wooden furniture in the cosy room. It is warm, welcoming. The staff are busy, but all smiling with genuine motives, no artificial phoniness. The tables are filling up with people joining their table without a word, a sociable nod of understanding. I guess this is the norm in Moscow. Eddy has come across this once in Germany, but this is something that he just cannot get used to. It feels like there are invading his personal space.

The smell of borsch mixed with burning wood fills the low-lying room. The crack of the fire plays perfectly with the soft string instruments that is loud enough to hear, but not loud enough to drown out the soft-rumbling discussions taking place inside the room. The same hostess brings water in a vase-like carafe with a basket of bread for them and their recent guest. Eddy starts to calm down his beating heart of anxiety. Lia transmits his feelings by soothing them with the touch of her hand on his hand, the eye contact that speaks more than words could convey.

'For the table,' the hostess announces in Russian to Lia.

She giggles, which Eddy pries but gets nothing. He starts to wonder if that is really what she said. He probes but does not get far before the silky burgundy soup arrives in the deep bowls that are different from everyone else's. They tap the necks of their spoons as a cheers, before diving in. The ripples of the spoon entering the aniseed aromatic puddle shimmers like a shaking silk flag. Spoon in one hand, bread in the other. They mutually groan in pleasure. The carraway-laced borsch with hints of dill is nothing short of spectacular. It is not too filling, but has the desired effects of being enough to fuel and warm their cold bodies.

A conversation gets split to the other couple. Lia gets some information which makes her get up to leave. Eddy is bewildered. He knows that the short conversation did not upset her, but the long silence continued to ebb and flow his confusion. The confusion was gradually turning into concerning sentiments.

A short stroll and they are back at the hotel to finish the checking in process. They almost forgot that this was not actually completed. Before heading upstairs, via the lift, to shower and then they are off again. This time for the night cruise. It was only in the refuge of the room that Lia revealed what the other couple had strongly recommended.

Every summer a strange phenomenon to Eddy and Lia, that is considered to be the norm for the locals occurs. During June and July, the city does not get dark, even during the poorly named night, it is actually much lighter. This brings the purpose of this cruise in particular. As they are helped onboard by the impeccable dressed cabin crew onto a small single floored boat. Rope-tied plastic chairs looking out in the direction of movement with the captain high in his green and white enlarged cupboard with windows behind. They are ushered to one of the red plastic beach chairs.

An announcement bellows out that food and drink can be bought and is available on the vessel. The small boat fills the twenty-something seats in no time. With a vibrating roar, the engine bursts into life and they push away from the bank. The Veva Embarkment shows the sights that they had seen. Nevertheless, this iconic view seems to run through St Petersburg.

Over the low humming vibration of the engine a pre-recorded commentary starts that gives a clear, informative facts educating them as they take numerous photographs. The banks are lined with people hoisting up their camera phones on long poles taking birds eye selfies amongst the jubilant crowds and over at the scene. Ships past with colourful sails with lights shine on different shades. The boat purrs slowly negotiating the canals, other boats. An aura unfolds to drape over the shoulders of Lia and Eddy of romantic sensations.

The story over the sea waves from the audio script is back further than before. Back before the city was nothing but a vista of inhospitality uninhabitable terrain. It is hard to believe that St Petersburg was a grim, murky cheerless swampland, before Tsar Peter I, known as Peter the Great had a vision. A vision he made reality. The commentary states that he was inspired by Amsterdam. He went there to learn about shipbuilding. On seeing the canal laced city he returned. Using the streams as canals, the ambitious young ruler wanted to create his own great city. That he did.

Ironically, and not planned in the slightest, his plan to not close off the streams and leave them flowing actually saved the city. If he had filled them, like what happened in other cities, he would have left the valuable asset with the city unable to drain itself from the swampy land, leading to the constant threat of floods, unstable precarious land, which would make the city a laughing stock for other countries, not to mention domestically, a comical heart of his Kingdom. However, the natural streams remained. Amusingly this is now talked off as a great strategic decision, rather than pure dumb luck. Forty-two islands comprise St Petersburg.

Lia huddles into Eddy as they cruise slowly, purring down the Winter Canal. Eddy sums up the commentary to Lia to be sure that he understands the quick history that was announced.

'So. Is this right? Peter.'

'Friends now?' Lia interrupted. 'You and Peter, no longer Peter the Great?'

'As I was saying. Trying to say. Will say. So, erm for you…Peter the Great. Happy? Well, Peter returned to Russia, became Tsar, defeated the Swedes, retook the eastern Baltic, built this city on the River Neva. Basically, following Amsterdam's blueprint.'

'Yep. Pretty neat huh! Or, when I was growing up, as they used to say the Venice of the North. I guess it is still said.'

Under the three bridges attractively illuminated by small beacons of lights, it did not look real, like a cinematic glorious accomplishment to what could be conveyed on the silver screen. The balls of light bounce, to strangely compel a glittering-like silky shine reflecting the rooms from a pearl necklace over the narrow waters. Each one connects the buildings to each other, to unite the city in a radiant an enchanting forceful charm like sowed threads on an elegant ballroom dress.

The bridge acts as a perfect frame for the fiery sky display of Jupiter oranges bleeding into the yellows, dark blues and reds of the white nights that inspire painters to pick up their tools, lovers to announce their love, musicians to compose, and everyone else to feel lucky that they can witness such feats of nature.

Eddy tries in vain to softly soothe a description of Saint Petersburg by resembling the architecture to Vienna in Austria, obviously the canals of Amsterdam in the Netherlands and lastly the graceful bridges of the aforementioned Venice in Italy. He simply loses the battle and takes defeat on the chin. As he concludes that it is a stunning city with combinations of other cities to create a unique one of all the best features. She contagiously giggles like a schoolchild as she nestles, deeply into his chest. Feeling his heartbeat she feels protected, wanted.

The buildings reflect, rebound the lights of the sky, the other buildings, the bridges to generate a great soothing hue. They embrace, resting in their protesting plastic chairs. With the gentle rocking of the boat there are in a real life floating, rocking gentle dream surrounded in a well of endless beauty.

Just before midnight, a loud sucking pop, followed instantly by a loud crescendo of cheers, claps. Another extracting explosion followed quickly by others. Champagne corks fly through the air in powerful arch's, the cheers continue. Champagne fizzes over the edges of the glasses, foam spills everywhere, no-one cares. Bridges open to allow boats through.

It's like New Year's Eve. A celebration. A squeal of a thin white scribble of smoke followed by a loud snap, a blossom of colours that dissolves into the sky. Many sounds of whizzes, high-pitched squeaks, bangs, pops and cracks filled the air followed by a kaleidoscope of colours from different directions in the light skies. The wall of smiling, laughing faces gravitate to the colours on display like moths to a flame. A thin layer of smoke rests over the canals with a hint of burnt paper ash. It's like a twenty-four-hour party of white light, no night. It is getting close to one in the morning, if it was not for Lia's watch they would easily, be forgiven to assume it was hitting dusk, barely seven in the evening.

This is the darkest that it will get. This is when it will start lighting up again. It was not dark, at, all. The romantic feel in the air, the lively joyous occasion that anything is possible and the friendly mateship atmosphere vibrates with a positive electric charge of energy that is as contagious as a smile. As they leisurely float past, they see people hugging, jumping, screaming. These are grown men and women, not children.

In this scene, they are the civilised ones that are focused on the firework display. Adults are leaping into each other's arms. There is nothing contrived, there is nothing orchestrated about these beautiful affections. This was a passion of instinctive unrefined exhilaration. This is when they can believe, everyone believes that humans are kind. Humans are compelling. Humans are good.

For Eddy and Lia, being here is a privilege. It was a mere fluke that they arrive at the White Night Festival. It was affecting them optimistically, boiling in them a surge of togetherness. A healthy bond amongst strangers.

They re-enter through the oil painting of life where they are surrounded by the lights, colours, history as they face, without a tear into life's canvas of Saint Peters and Pauls Fortress. They are now on the River Bolshava Nev which flows just seventy-four kilometres to the Gulf of Finland.

As they leave the bridges, they salute in a display as they rise and lower to everyone that is watching the scene unfold, continuously unfold. The banks are fuller. Even at this time of night, it is light, it was just like in the middle of the day. The cruise is a magnificent way to past, two hours of unequivocal pleasure. The time flies as fast as the fireworks entering the skies. Reluctantly they peel themselves off the plastic chair to the starting point, back on land, on the banks with the other strangers. People were dancing all over the place, in the street, not to quote a Bruce Springsteen song. Smooth, instrumental high-beat jazz music was being played.

They share a dance, against what they normally do. They dance by the banks, in the troves of the stream of people. They look deeply into each other's eyes, pause, take in the moment, kiss, tenderly, lovingly. They huddle close to each other in the chilly air, embracing, sharing a precise moment which was written in their hearts, instilled as a personal memory that would never be shared. They feel tired, then again, energetic. They feel that they should go back to the hotel, as to make the most of the next day. To feel refreshed. Against the infectious carnival they do go back, unenthusiastically in a subdued manner to go to sleep.

The next morning, they wake early, before their pre-set alarm. They are still tired. They cannot shake the coils of sleep away. Yet, they are on a mission. They feel great considering that they just really should head back to bed after being asleep for barely four hours. They take a planned walk, for which they schemed over the borsch earlier last evening. Lia wants to see places from her nostalgic school days. She yearns to resolve some unfinished lost memories in her mind. To put a real-life place in a picture, a presence to the recollections described in the worn, page falling cotton-sewed textbooks of her youth. The plan to arise early was thus to be unrushed, relaxed and to accomplish seeing everything. The earlier start meant that they could at least have a proper coffee and a bit of breakfast.

They walk through a busy scene of laughter and talking as St Petersburg, it seems, does not go to sleep. It is very much awake now as they left it earlier this morning. Eddy is not convinced if the city really does sleep, striving to take that title away from New York City. To tick another city's feature off the growing list. Unknowingly observed by them, today is a Russian holiday, as well as their own White Light Festival. Eddy feels that this is not a coincidence. Lia, also thinks not.

The street signs are fitting in well with the city, easy to follow and on the eye. Eddy can actually feel as if he is taking control with a map in hand, the English signposts. For the first time in too long, he feels not one hundred percent reliant on Lia's Russian tongue to get by. But, unfortunately for Eddy this was quickly stricken from the records as they do not speak English, or choose not to. He is hungry for knowledge, but Lia wants to continue. She resumes control. She gets his pining for information.

They come to the picturesque Moyka Canal were a yellow building overlooks the rippling tremors of the water. This is where Yusupov Palace is, a museum in which they were hoping to see. They are very disappointed to find out that it is closed. The skies are a clear light blue which seem to make the yellow glow. The small green leaved trees lean as if parting a clear view to the Palace. Round cobbled stones of pastel colours surround a misshapen short crew cut of green lawn, that acts as a roundabout with a border of round light-coloured stones in a beaded necklace.

The simple bright mustard yellow, white framed windows, tall Corinthian pillars and wreaths around the overhanging tier gives the impression of being larger than it is. The Palace softly seduces a radiant calming effect of seductive exquisiteness. They are the only ones here. It was not just the museum that they hoped to see. It was more to go inside and be in the site of the holy man, Grigoriy Rasputin's, demise. They were hoping to get some more insight into the murder by Prince Felix Yusupov, however the amazingly carved wooden doors of the entrance are very much firmly shut. Although they got a win with the White Light Festival, this is the perils of travelling in a place for a short time. They win some, lose some. Cities hold various avenues of recommendations. This city is not different. So many things to see. So little time. Time for the next stop.

They inadvertently stroll some of the route from yesterday. Stumbling on a large shiny bronze statue of Peter the Great balancing on horseback, as the horse rears her front legs while her back legs tread on the snake of treason. Mounted on a huge slab of granite that looks to weigh in excess of a ton. For which Lia informs, from her guidebook, that it actually weights in excess of one thousand, six-hundred and twenty-five tonnes.

'So. Just a little bit heavier than I thought,' Eddy admits without holding back his sarcastic tendency. On the pink granite, a bronze inscription reads in Latin and Russian: 'To Peter I from Catherine II'.

Glorified in Decembrist Square opposite St Isaacs Cathedral, which they are surprised that they did not see it yesterday. Purple and white, red and white, yellow and white blossoming flowers surround the square setting off fragrant perfume scents. It is warm, but not Australia warm. However, with little daylight, and a dreadful long cold winter the opportunity to get the sun is not, is never lost. People are sunbathing on the manicured lawn. They appreciate the sun. They do not take it for granted. They will take in every ray of the Russian warming sun.

Once again, they are here, at the bottom of Nevsky Prospect. On the riverside, they walk hand in cold hand across the Palace Square towards the impossible to describe building of beautify elegance and power, but not being over the top in the design. A collection of courts, places and rooms. The rambling Baroque complex, the state residence, the home to the Hermitage Museum. Of course, they are back to this main focus point of today, getting here early to avoid the crowds. Thus, the Hermitage, however is, it will seem, always busy. The huge yellow arch borders the pastel green and white Hermitage, that is broken only by the column, now the marques are in the process of being taken back down.

On the ticket bought by Lia yesterday, they printed an allocated time to arrive. As they queued to be let inside, Lia reads that in the peak of summer over ten-thousand people a day pass through these very doors that they were finally walking through now. The other queue for a ticket states on a sign that two hours is the guesstimate queuing time, whereas they are quickly streamlined through in a matter of minutes. For a second, Lia's heart rockets into her mouth as she thinks she may have forgotten the tickets back at the hotel. However, with a huge sense of relief shared by them both, she fishes them out of her jumbled mess from inside her brown handbag of chaotic organised clutter, to see the rather precise black printed exact time of '11.22 am'.

They are early, very early. The time is ten in the morning. The lady sees no problems in letting them walk in though. They cannot hide their excitement, they are ecstatic. They thank her in their voice, their eyes, for which she rewards them by shedding out a tip, for them to start at the top and work their way down. This is to avoid the wait, go against the flow and see clearer the pieces of art.

The third floor is Eddy's preferred magical floor that he spoke about after seeing the museum's layout. Here are the many masters. Here is Eddy's personal favourite, Henri Matisse. Eddy shows a childlike excitement as he oozes enthusiasm of Matisse's use of limited colours, which he states are bold to heighten and dramatize his paintings magnificently. Lia laughs, as he is no critic. Eddy ignores her to commemorate his solo speech.

'For me. Simple is effective. Simple. Is. Effective. He, Matisse, is the master of the, this art,' Eddy acclaims.

'Why? Why Matisse? Why do you like him so much? I mean, over the others?' Lia, stops her mocking to be serious.

'I. Well, I guess, since school, really. I studied him at school. Grew to appreciate it all. Copied some from books. Simple.'

He smiles like a child who sees Santa across a busy shopping mall, focused on the goal, not the distractions. He looks at the bold colours. The kneeling salmon peach figures of musicians and singers on green grass and blue sky in 'Musique' draws him in to linger in front, smiling foolishly like a joker. The fruit, flower with his own painting of the 'Danse', within this painting. He is a child again. Feeling the surge of exhilaration. When he sees the 'Conversation', he is awestruck. The male in blue and white pyjamas talking to a seated lady in a black robe. Simple but so, very effective. Lia enjoys watching Eddy's facial twitches in his expressions more than the paintings themselves.

This most exquisite art gallery is strongly intimidating. The dawn of the gallery arrived in 1765, when Catherine the Great brought a collection of over two-hundred paintings from a merchant. During her reign, she collected over four thousand, some as gifts, some were brought. Eddy leads, dancing from one piece of art to the other. The awe-inspiring collection housed in impressive, as well as evidently costly and luxurious ballrooms, and throne rooms complement one another.

Lia is trailing behind as Eddy often thinks he is talking to her when he is two steps forward talking to thin air. The many types of art he views from Prehistoric, classical, oriental, Russian – of course, Italian, Spanish, Flemish, Danish, German, French, English and the nineteenth to twentieth century of European painters and paintings to find the one painting that he knows is here, somewhere. Eddy has always wanted to see the Red Room, or to give its proper title, 'The Desser: Harmony in Red'.

Eddy is squashed like a fly, disappointment etched over his face, for where the painting should have been hanging was a white, postcard size sign simply stating in Russian and English, 'currently on loan at an expo in Amsterdam'. It might as well have been a pop out punching fist that hit him hard in the guts. This does temporary dampen his elevated great mood. He regains it just as quick as it ebbs to look around, open-eyed, he is a kid in a candy store, looking but not touching the visual treats trying to pick one to have, if he could. He could never choose just one. Eddy beams a contagious Cheshire cat grin that affects Lia who is loudly laughing at nothing in particular. Maybe it is the delightful facial expressions that he is making. Maybe it is purely his happiness that is making her delirious.

In front of Eddy are huge panels. These behold the magnificent artworks of 'Musque' and 'Danse'. Lia likes the others as they walk back through and spend a little more time at Monet, Friendship, as well as others by Picasso, Pissarro and Cézanne, to name, but a few. Without them intentionally being aware, the third floor has accumulated a huge portion of their time. For Eddy it was justified. He, of course is no artist, but like most people, he appreciates what he sees. He gets a thrill of excitement when seeing real art with his own eyes, and not through the eyes of another person's lens.

Eddy finds that it is amazing to find that some of the sizes are bigger than he imagined, some are smaller. He does not knowingly realise when he sees something in a book, magazine or postcard that a size consciously rises in his head. He does not realise that he is doing it. He rarely, if ever, has actually imagined the right, exact size. He recalls the Mona Lisa in Paris, he expected that painting to be a lot bigger than it actually was. Picassos' famous 'blue' period is here, that compliments Matisse, or the other way around. Peeling away Eddy from the third floor was like taking the glue off a stamp, but Lia managed it.

Lavish decor of gold gild, canvases of master after master, intricately carved wooden doors. They zig-zag down the extravagant stairway to the second floor, bouncing from one side to the other to see unrestrained luxurious detailed features. At the far end they linger at a magnificent sledge that portrays St George slaying the infamous dragon. He is in a magnificent action pose with muscles tense. The coiling, squirming defeated dragon holds the carriage that he slays in.

On the second floor the Winter Palace is just what Lia expected from a palace. Room by room is a different experience which is no better, or worse, than another, but are individually unique and beautiful. Each different style is reflected in the name. Russian mosaic, inland floors and art.

Lia pauses in the Malachite room, with over two tonnes of ornamental stone, polished green malachite columns, vases, parquet flooring, gilded ceiling, doors and brilliantly polished golden brass bird claw handles holding a red cutglass opulent stone.

Just off this room is the dining room. Here holds a great historical event. Here is the significant event in 1917 where the revolution began. The Bolsheviks interrupted a meeting of government officials to declare an overthrow of the Tsar and his government. The grand clock on the marble mantelpiece indicated the time on which this happened. An inscription describes the day in detail on a wooden easel.

Eddy eavesdrops on a tour group to gain information, for which he duly whispers into the ear of Lia. The mirrors in certain rooms are placed extra high as it was forbidden to look at yourself, hence too high to view.

The tour heads into the imposing Raphael Loggia corridor, for which stealth like Eddy, with Lia in tow, follows the group. They are surrounded by an impressive and unique copy of the gallery in the Vatican. The only exception is that the floor of the Vatican is made of marble, here it is made of wood. This is due to the coldness of the winters. The surrounding murals catch the bible stories as well as the bonds between nature and animals. In one of the mirrors Eddy notices what looks like a bullet hole. After much time asking and getting nowhere, he still does not know if he imagines it, if there was really a story or if his overactive mind was starting to formulate a wannabe, make-believe story.

The only Michelangelo sculpture in Russia, the unfinished crouching boy is seen by them. It is here. This, although unfinished, shows how he sculptured his art, always from the back and then working forward. In this piece of art, the chisel marks on the arms and the perfectly sculptured back are evident. At the time Catherine the Great bid the equivalent of twenty united State dollars for this masterpiece. Now, priceless.

In the next room is a painting by Michelangelo Merisi fro, 1595, called 'The Lute Player'. The description that is elaborately described gives a tragic underlining story. This is the only picture painted by the master himself in the Hermitage. The still-life is read to symbolise the five senses. The violins broken strings and the tattered music book is said to symbolise the frailty of human life. The music transcript, 'you know that I love you' seems to send a hidden message. Lia and Eddy discuss like experts to what they thought was a typical genre. A typical scene, for which they then read the explanation. What they thought they saw is described differently. They see a whole different scene now, that they originally saw on the canvas. Lia and Eddy come to the same cliché understanding, to not judge a book by its cover.

Due to overindulging on the other two floors, the first floor proves to be a rush. The words of Mikhail also confirm to be trustworthy, when he explained his account of time to art equation. Aptly in a dark corner is a mummified Egyptian that takes centre stage as one of Eddy and Lia's highlights. Along with the brilliant statue of Jupiter. Impressive as it is, it was brought to this resting place while the hall was being built, so it cannot be moved. They think this was planned.

Made in AD 362 at three and a half metres high and an unimaginable sixteen tonnes, it really is as impressive as it sounds. Overshadowed by the golden cloth, spectre and raven which are painted plaster added in the nineteenth century. This is only temporary, quickly put in the shade to the colossal majestic splendour of Jupiter. Standing in front of a green marble background makes it more formidable. As people stand in front for a photograph, they look so small, they only barely come to the top of his ginormous feet.

After the big names on varied sizes of different canvases, they are in Ancient Greece. Tombs, bas-reliefs and painted ceramics. They walk through history starting from the Ancient Room from the late days of the Empire. Weapons and armour are on display from the Arabi, Ottoman Empire, North Africa and Iran. Some of these were gifts, some were the spoils, the trophies of war.

The Hermitage itself regularly rivals previous art displays that they have both seen around the world. The Pavilion Hall with its mosaic floor, headed by a huge twenty-three diamond sparkling gems that decorate a gilded peacock clock encased in a dome glass case. All the images flick through their mind in a projection show that you would not want to miss.

The day has gone so fast, but what came next was astounding. They got told that the Hermitage is closing early for which they both look at each other in amazement. No reason was not given. but they had spent a good few hours inside, so it was time to see what the outside world was offering at the moment. They muttered to themselves how lucky it was that they arrived, then to be let in early.

Outside, it was slowly raining, but warm. For the first time, they notice granite statues of Athantes outside the Hermitage representing artists, scientists and philosophes. They discuss that not only the art on the Hermitage, but the classy design shows the life of Russian royalty. Which included a footstool said to be used by Peter the Great. They shelter out of the rain as they plan a route. The rain does not bother them.

They stroll across the Dvortsoyy Bridge where two large terracotta red pillars come into view. This is an evident tourist route. Along the edge, on shaky unsteady tables are rows after rows of Matryoshka, the nesting Russian wooden dome doll that conceals a smaller doll inside, being sold by pushy Russian ladies. They focus on the pillars. These red pillars are closer and are, in fact, Rostral columns were originally used to guide ships through the busy port. They hug the riverbank until they come to their destination of Peter and Pauls Fortress. It was spitting rain the whole way but not enough to get wet or deterred. Having arrived at their objective, the sun is back out. Sunbathers line the beach before the fortress, taking advantage once again of the sunshine, however so fleeting that it could be gone in a minute.

In 1703, Peter and Pauls Fortress was built by Peter the Great to mark the founding of the city. Not only did hundreds of forced labourers die in the construction, but it was mainly used to guard and torture political prisoners, such as Peter's own son, Aleksey. Eddy was a little unsure to why Lia was so insistent on coming here.

Lia took the lead, she beeline to the Chapel. The golden needle from the bell tower pierces the sky, shining like a beacon on the shoulders of a curved dark yellowish-brown waving tiered levels like the framing of a grunge rocker from the eighties. Not alike to that look, which was firmly not seen nowadays, this was the ending chapter for Lia to tell the story of the Romanovs. The reason she wanted to come became apparent. This Chapel of St Catherine Martyr is the resting place of the Romanov family. Many Tsars rest here. They look upon the pastel high alter like an oil painting decked with gold like Christmas decoration.

The light cascades down from the windows of the bell tower, caressing, stroking the highlights of the gold frame. In a separate open room with marble patterned floor, soft red, wooden walls and a low cream ceiling is solely designated to the Romanov family and their servants. In the centre is a hexagon red and white cubed pillar, crowned with a painting of the Tsars done, resembling saint-like poses. On the walls are white Carrara marble sarcophagi with gold inscriptions of each of the members. The bright light from the imitation candle chandelier that traces a soft lingering stroke of light that glimmers, hangs and remembers the Romanovs.

Back in the glittering sun they squint their eyes in unison to glance once again at the highest point within the site. Lia makes out an angel, just before the cross, which is in fact a weathervane. Eddy strains to see anything but a rainbowed blur. Lia passes his camera so he can zoom in. It is as if the angel is climbing up the golden spire. They are in the shadows of the deep red buildings around the Trubetskoy Bastion.

The first political prisoner that was detained here was none other than Peter the Great's son, Tsarevich Aleksey, for treason. He managed to escape, to get as far as abroad, only to be lured back with the promise of a full pardon. This, was a false gesture, for which he was beaten and tortured to death. They step into what is now a museum. Fully with English descriptions to explain what happened here. The shiny beige floor is the first of the sixty-nine cells that they walk through.

The thinly pink and white striped wallpaper, a window high, out of reach, with two iron frames and bars with a metal net. A small iron bed with a thin white mattress, green blanket sits alongside one side of the sparsely decorated cell. Next to a wooden table with a narrow drawer, a gaslight. Near the cell door is a tin gash bucket, a small sink. Each cell is restored to the original. They walk around the cells, the date line to see the evolution of each cell that changes with time. The cells grow to be better, although they cannot really get any worse. Better, though consists of a spring bed, then a doona. Each cell shares a darkness, a small and unlit living area. The punishment cells are the same but far, far, far smaller.

Prisoners would be locked up in here for up to forty-eight hours at a time. Once every two weeks, the prisoners are taken out to the exercise yard for delousing. Inside, talking was forbidden, prisoners were not allowed to communicate. Thus, the prisoners found a way around this, they used the prisoner's alphabet. This form of Morse-code allowed them to 'speak' by tapping the floors, walls or the side of their bed leg. They shivered in the cells, it was colder inside than outside, and this was in the summer!

Independently, on the green fringes of the light beige gravel walkway is a comically malformed sculpture of Peter the Great done by Mikhail Shemyakin. Being born in 1943, he would obviously have had no idea of what he really looked like first-hand. For this sculpture he used a posthumous mask for, well, the head, a wax figure by Marolommeo Rastrelli for the body. The result is a peanut sized head on the top of a rather large mountain of a bronze body on a throne encased in a bulky, unfitting coat with skinny C3-PO legs. He looks serious, skeleton fingers fold over, gripping the arms of his throne. The commissioning agent must have spat his dummy out when he saw this travesty. They gawk, laugh and point at the freakishly ugly statue.

The secret passage in front of Petrovskye Gate has a guy down on one knee, looking up with a sense of trepidation. Infront of him pointing towards a lady, whom of which has clasped hands in front of her mouth, looking down at them. Between them is a glittering heart outline with the name, 'ZENA' in the centre made of the change of roubles. He is proposing. She has not given him an answer yet, but a small crowd has stopped to see what she will say. He is mumbling things to her, oblivious to the gathering strangers.

Lia looks at Eddy, who averts his gaze anywhere but her eyes. A cold breeze fills the air which is surprising as it has been quite warm in the sunlight. She says yes. Without warning, the hushed crowd erupts in celebrational applause, shrieks of delight. They embarrassingly wave a hand in responsive thanks. He launches into her arms who grips them around as they slop a clumsy kiss, bodies hugged so close to each other, gripping lovingly.

The orange, brown and grey small brick corridor of the secret passage is colder when they step away from the public display of affection. This was used for the extreme guards, so that the other guards would not see them. Now lit by floor lighting and electric, but in the walls, on one side, before electric is evidence of fire burning with black soot marks at regular intervals along the wall. It is a mystery to what actually happened here, but to have a secret passageway suggests that the goings-on were concealed for a reason.

They step under the grand brick arch that commands respect, under and through Petrovskye Gate, the grandest of them all. The huge archway has the Romanov double headed eagle above, an emblem of St George and the dragon adorned on the chest. The large, dark brown bas-relief is of Peter the Great's Russian victory over Charles XII of Sweden. At the very top, a figure is depicted to be falling. Represented is the winged sorcerer, Simon Magus, whom of which is being thrown, or cast, by St Peter. At the bottom are several figures pointing and seemingly cheering at his plight.

Lia seems happy that she had seen the resting place for the Romanov's. They have been around the fortress, gotten more from here, more sights then they thought was actually here. Heading off the island via the wooden bridge takes them away from the fortress. The island for which the fortress is built was called, and may still be called, Hare Island. Halfway over the arched bridge they look back with a sense of longing. They notice the shape of the island is all supported by dark, green stained planks of wood that are bound like barrels by iron cuffs.

At this point, out a little in the slowly rippling gentle waves of the water is a grey stone hare looking back at them from a tall wooden pillar. Below the hare, roughly the same size is a small pillar. They would have missed, they nearly did, as they were too busy talking about the guys proposal and what would have happened if she had said no. Surely that would have made a more appealing cruel show for the neutrals. However, the crowds that were over one side of the wooden barrister of the bridge catch their attention. They peer over. The people in the crowds are trying to cast a coin to make it stop, to stay on the plinth of which the hare proudly stands.

As they look closely over, they see some shiny coins on the three pale pine looking wooden stages and a few at the hare's feet. To cast a coin, for it to stay on the plinth is said to be good luck, hence the hare catching it. They join in. Lia wants to be the first to cast a coin. She hesitates, so they decide to go together, to try their combined luck. They cast their coins after the countdown from three, but instead of hearing the echo rumbling of the coins resting on the wood, they hear the familiar plop, the splash of the water. The coin descending into the slowly murky water below.

One more glance back sees the deep red border of the fortress rising from the sea, with a narrow strip of yellow sand already teeming with bathers in the chilly summer sun. Above the walls, the deep green trees line around in perfect symmetrical length up to the spearing golden bell tower that rises like a golden pin. An admirable indication to prominently let everyone know with a loud deafening defining scream that she is here. The snap of the camera does not do the image justice. A few more shots to try are taken.

Rather than the rumble of a coin settling on the wooden plinth, another rumble broadcasts loudly from Eddy's stomach. He is suddenly starvingly hungry. Lia is too. The sea salt of the air produces thirst to accompany the hunger. In the park, directly over, after they set foot off the wooden bridge, Lia sees a sign for a cafe and insists that they have an easy snack to eat as they go, to have a better meal later.

Following the dark blue signs, it is in a very short while that they stand outside, looking at a small café, literally embedded inside a small hill. The brown metal chairs are scattered in what appears to be in no particular order on the woodchip floor, nestling around small identically styled, simple foldable tables. Cramped inside are a few more of the same tables with funky James Brown music blaring from inside the hobbit hole. Inside, the faint scent of earth mingles with the overpowering roasted coffee, they order their coffee as they look for something to eat.

No food is cooked as the coffee machine itself, with the methodical order of beans, grinder to cup, takes the whole side of the back jagged rockery-type wall. Next to the metal cash box is the only available food. Encased in a glass cupboard are a few crispy golden pastries, shining iced cakes and sandwiches that all look freshly made, without an indication of where. Lia is insistent to grab and go. Eddy wants to sit. After a brief altercation, Lia agrees with Eddy. He finally won by stating that after the morning and afternoon that they have had, they need time to store, remember, absorb and appreciate all of the treasures they have seen.

Lia is in charge. She was fidgeting the whole, no more than barely a few minutes, that they were supposedly meant to be resting. As the last drop of the quite magnificent coffee had left his cup, hit Eddy's lips, she is making the charge, faster than a speeding bee away from a swat she is out of the hole-in-the-hill. She is on her mission to get to the next sight, Eddy has no choice but to pursue in a chase after her, yelling thanks to the startled young couple behind the coffee machine. The last morsels of the flaked cinnamon-spiced pastries have not even entered their stomach as she has made her, subsequently his exodus as well.

Eddy has not even gotten his bag properly on his back before she is increasingly becoming more distant through the park. He needs to sprint, then skip the last few steps to be in the same, rheumatic pace as her. He mumbles a term of bitter resentment in the urgent, unannounced rush. Lia hears but wisely chooses not to listen. Eddy did not mean it, but he needs to vent his state of mind, for what he deems to be, unacceptable off-guard method. He felt better in saying it, although a little guilty. He catches a glimpse of her attempting not to smile. In that facial recognition, his guilt ebbs away.

The silence that overcomes them is however short-lived with the view of a quaint wooden low-lying bungalow surrounded by a green metal fence topped with golden arrows. This stops her in her tracks. A panting Eddy enjoys the respite.

'This is the original home of Peter the Great,' Lia bellows with arms spread wide. So wide they nearly smack a kneeling Eddy, who bends forward with his hands on his knees, firmly in the face.

It is closed, heavily protected. Despite the numerous cameras that adorn each corner like it was a bank, the view is not obscured. Lia leafs through the pages of her guidebook as she was sure the hours stated it was open today. Eddy views to bungalow, he sees the area being a sense of protective pride, rather than protection from vandalism. He twirls to behold the scene around the whole area that he has raced to.

Over the wide river, he sees a sight that they nearly missed, the Church of Spilled Blood. He tugs at Lia's clothing to bring her head up from the book. The candyland sweetshop of clean lines of the blue and white onion top beckons them to come and seek. The guidebook is forgotten. Afterall, as if seeing the opening times in print, this will not be a magical vortex to open the doors for them to cross the historical threshold.

Over yet another bridge, Trinity Bridge, into the Field of Mars. Spiky lampposts with thin blood red glass skirt the path and the outskirts of the field. The perfectly symmetrical park has a larger square in the middle where an eternal flame burns. Firstly fired in 1957 in memory of all victims of St Petersburg, of all wars, and revolutions. People are enjoying the weather, but keeping that area out-of-bounds as a form of unwritten respect. They are ragged up with the bitter chill. Nonchalantly, the locals are in shorts, t-shirts, skimpy tops exposing more skin than necessary by taking in various forms of free time and leisure. On route through this decorated path where flowers graze on the manicured lawns, they are on a fresh mission.

They twist, turn and scramble over from the park, in the most direct route as they think is possible to get to the whimsical fairy tale, Church of Spilled Blood, concocted by a dreamtime fabulous visionary. Journeying over the bridges, narrow streets and skirting the many people spread everywhere, no doubt to join in the White Night Festival celebrations. Officially, the church is called the Resurrection Church of Our Saviour. This riot of colour is as explosive as the history. The beautiful church is built on the exact spot where, on the first March 1881 Tsar Alexander II was assassinated.

Eddy gazes over the intricate detail, he thinks that you could look at this church every day and see something that you have not seen before. An amazing collection of different types of art using different materials. Lia and Eddy light-heartedly disagree to what is more beautiful. Lia goes for the Church in Moscow, St Basils, whereas Eddy thinks this one wins, hands down. The light makes a difference, but here the weather is quickly having a change of heart. The clouds are returning in a light grey blanket covering over the blue.

Eddy rounds the corner to get a better, a different view. Here he comes face to face with this beautiful sight of the church that still, ceaselessly succeeds to take the wind out of his lungs to leave him breathless. Lia sees him dumbfounded, looking as if someone has just turned him off. With this unattractive pose she tells him to straighten up, shut his open gawking mouth and 'chill'. The marvellous church is amazingly unique.

Anticipation heightens as they enter inside. The interior was a little underwhelming, well, considering the breath-taking appearance outside. They could not believe that they nearly left St Petersburg without seeing it up close. They saw it on the river cruise and swore that they would come back but nearly, clearly forgot.

On every, single angle talented painters, artists are trying to immortalise the church in paint, charcoal and other drawing materials for mementos for the tourists that are here, like bees around honey, to take home with them. Nervously they peak occasionally, looking at the skies, predicting, assuming, having a premonition that it will rain soon. They pre-empt the possibility by closing some of their arrangements of paintbrushes, pencils, chalk, mirrors, photographs, sketches and other collections of work in progress, as well as other materials by placing them in their boxes, bags, cases and in quick reach to run for cover quickly, fleetingly and safe in the knowledge that nothing will be forgotten. At the same time planning to finish their main piece that they are working on. It is plain to see that they are used to the temperamental elements of Mother Nature in her house.

'Where would you start?' Eddy asks more to himself than to Lia.

'Start with what?' Lia asks ambiguously in return.

'Oh, nothing. I, well, more to myself. How? Where would you…I mean. If you were going to build this. Where would you…I mean, a blank canvas to…this. Where would you get the inspiration? The craftsmanship? You may doodle something like this but, how can you put it into. Put the wheels in motion to create this!' He portrays his perplexity by thrashing his animatronic arms, wildly waving his hands to gesticulate in the direction of the church in front of them. 'Where would you start to build this, this? This masterpiece?'

Lia thinks Eddy could not be any God damn cuter at that precise moment. His staccato lightning bolts of innocent thoughts that come out in these suffocated gibbering sounds, comparable to that as if he is a raving madman.

She sees the time and panic. They rush to the metro, the quickest route to get back to the hotel. As they ascend the dimly lit underground, the night is still bright as they come out of the dazzling brightly lit daylight dusk. They rush to get ready for Lia's own personal treat in which he drags Eddy too.

In their most elegant wear that they find in the crumpled mass at the base of their bags. They forget that they have these wears that there are travelling with. They hastily iron them. They brush down the sleeves as they enter the commanding Mariinskiy Theatre. It is strange to feel uncomfortable in what is comfortable back in Sydney, but as they have been wearing baggy, unflattering, heavy garments this comfortable, feels uncomfortable.

The smartly dressed attendant in precise attention to detail is faultlessly composed. He speaks with Russian, then English in a slight American-ism. His polite words are a little less flawlessly. He obviously is translating each of the words in ordered word of each sentence. He tells them politely, 'to not to take any clothes with them', by that the concierge meant additional coats, bags, they assumed. Although the translation made them stifle an ill-composed giggle.

As he pulls the door open to invite them in with a slight, gracious bow of his head, the sensational bubble of importance is burst a touch. They realise the importance of being on time. Paramount importance comes to awareness why it was so very worthy of the rush. She, without a sound remembers to have read some great advice to arrive early due to the strict security. Strict was an understatement. It was like they entered an airport, or a government building, rather than a musical performance. Was the Prime Minister here? The stringent nature of the security was not completely unfounded. It is an institution. A prime target for terrorists.

Once inside, they get ushered to their seats. They stop in their tracks. So, this is what it feels like to escorted inside an elegant wedding cake. The walls had three tiers of balconies, draped in cloth, a sieved amber golden hue cascades like a translucent waterfall. Ahead of them is the stage, sheathed in a heavy, embroiled curtain of blue drapes. They sit on the hard velvet fold-down seats that resemble thrones. Mouth-opened wide, catching the soft flowered smells, an amalgamation of subtle perfumes, aftershaves. Hearing the soft strings of classical music which heightens their anticipation, bizarrely the mood also relaxes them.

Eddy, for the first time, is actually starting to look forward to the show. They both look around once more. So picture perfect, the room, stunning, is filled with people filtering in to their own seats, in these impeccable surroundings. The magnificent huge golden diamond dripping chandeliers reflecting rainbows over the audience members that are all dressed up to their nines, unintentionally making Eddy and Lia feel underdressed in the overwhelming environment. An intoxicating smell of his aftershave bounces with her perfume, merging with the floral arrangement to blend and complement each other; he kisses her bare shoulder. Whispers into her tiny ear, sparkling with the diamond-crowned earring, to honestly state the truth, 'You look beautiful.'

She feels embarrassed, blinks, then again takes the compliment. Softly brushing her ear with her delicate fingers, rubbing her shoulder in the attempt to hide her beaming rosy cheeks.

The soft strings of an orchestral ensemble hidden before the stage continue to play, as they settle on their cushioned seats.

In his hand is the perforated ticket stub. He reads 'Le Parc' as he fidgets with the paper in his two hands. All Eddy knows about Le Parc is that it is a ballet of three acts. Fading interest, Eddy angles appoint of conversation in a hushed tone. To try and act interested, at least for Lia's sake, who had spoken about this moment numerous times through the past two days.

'What is the place, sorry play about?'

'The ballet. The ballet...' She gushes. 'This ballet is performed alongside, partnered seamlessly with Mozart's music. A loving, mysterious choreography where the dancers speak the words.'

'Huh! Huh?'

'Reality to dreams. Three acts are three times of the day. The lust, the chase, the love. Amazingly. It will grip you. It is so impressive.'

None the wiser by her explanation. He suspected that Lia was not sure, that she did not know, really know, what the ballet was about. For sure she knew the concept. He did not want to highlight Lia's holes in the plot, thus embarrassing her. This would have, no doubt, come out in fury, hence he went along with the vague description she gave.

Gradually, without any warning bells, the lights dim, a hush disperses over the crowd. Enthusiastic rapturous applause ripples loudly as the curtain rises and smoothly parts way. Thespians and artists prance onto the stage, the performance starts.

It is a long one hour and forty-minute performance, without an interval; Eddy would never get the time back. He admitted that it was beautiful. It was nice. He admitted though, to not have a clue about what was going on. This was after the first act. He decided to just go with it. Despite the fact that the storyline was ripped beyond recognition he absorbed the performance. He aimed to enjoy the show for what it was. Great music, great performances, great tight preparation that resulted in it all done bloody well. He stood up at the end to applause with the entire audience.

As did Lia, who was crying soft, silent tears of happiness. It was moving. He really enjoyed it, he was as staggered as Lia would be if he shared his thoughts. Shamefully enough, he was hoping to gain some credit for this act of chivalrous display. For he pulled Lia near, kissed the top of her head and thanked her for the experience that she had shared with him. Although the wrong word, in Eddy's mind, that was what he saw it as, a thank-you.

An open restaurant over the road. The only light that spills onto the dark pavement of the otherwise quiet street is where Eddy pulls Lia to. They cannot stop smiling, their cheekbones are starting to ache, they do not care. He is hungry, getting quite hangry, but then again hiding these sensations behind a smile. Menu items in the quaint garish bright red decorated narrow room dazzle them. For what they thought were uncomfortable seats in the theatre would have been instantly snatched back in place of these, plastic shiny stretched unpadded cushions on white metal chairs.

The decor was quite hideous, with more of a diner feel than a restaurant. Trying to imitate America, but doing an absolutely awful interpretation. The menu states Georgian-influenced Russian food, for which they both had no idea what that was supposed to mean. The menu was thrown at them by the angry waitress, whom they assume was hoping to close up soon. They did not feel guilty as they were not the only ones that be bequeathed the theatre for this eating place. They peel open the menu with a sucking side of unclean pages. However, they are hungry, they are going to eat here, eat here against their better judgement. They see the menu items illustrated with photographs next to each description.

He remembers this being a red light when in catering college to be one of the rules. He thinks back to his tutor Ron Lee. His robust frame of a stereotyped French-look off a wannabe aspiring Frenchman, born-Australian. A thin handlebar moustache that twirled perfectly at the sides. His want to always speak French whenever possible. Eddy can see him now, as if he was in Russia with them. He would jollily waddle around the tight corners of the training college kitchen proclaiming the do's and don'ts of menu design. One of which he sees here. Eddy can feel his authority, his thunderous voice booming out from the small head with receding thin hair on the round impeccably ironed chef white, button-straining jacket. He can imagine his speech.

'Any restaurant with photographs by the menus are trying to hoodwink you. They are not to be trusted. They are plastic, and the food will not look like the professionally photographed. Yee-haw.'

His voice would powerfully resonate around the captivated young chefs as he got the warranting respect he deserved. Despite the red light, the décor, the rude waitress they decide to whether the forthcoming storm. In the back of their mind there are hoping that food poisoning will not arise later tonight. Eddy gulps, he chooses first with the waitress that has come back in double quick time to hurry them. Lia orders and suggests a spare plate so they can share. The waitress, whom could not be any ruder rolls her heavily made-up eyes. They order a beer each. This is plonks on the table, foaming slightly over and she tuts as she mops up her spilt mess.

'Rasputin,' Lia states. Flabbergasting Eddy, whom thought that they were going to discuss the play, the ballet that they had just witnessed; alas, Lia has other ideas. 'I want to talk to you, what I learnt over the last few days while still in Russia.'

Slightly interrupted by the waitress in record-breaking time as she delivers the food in a welcoming act. Well, as welcoming as an unwanted guest who had called in to say hello. She puts the two dishes in the centre, a clean plate in front of each of them, without a word but a false smile between pursed lips. She turns to the kitchen via a swinging saloon type door where they hear the loud clean-up music and laughter echoing out.

Khinkali is slopped on to their plates by Lia in a less than elegant style. The steam is hot, almost microwaveable hot. On the plumes is a sweet, sour aroma. Five savoury crudely assembled dumplings swimming in a bright red hot and spicy sticky sauce gloop on the blue and white plates making their own pattern. The other centrepiece is Khatchapuri. A pastry dough that Eddy breaks with his fork to halve, avoiding the dripping spills from Lia's ladle, to release the oozing cheese that bellows out like lava, and no doubt by the churning clouds of steam, just as hot.

'Rasputin was a peasant, mystic. He. The. Well…Rasputin was a peasant that held an aura. Powerful aura over the ruler of Russia. His death on the seventeen of December 1916 is dramatic, a mystery. Really, it could NOT have been written.'

'This is not quite the dinner convo, A?' He toys with the idea to say that he has heard this speech before, as he plays with his spoon letting the reflecting red liquid talk to the candle flames, but he wisely decides to let her run through her rehearsed repertoire once again.

'Nonsense.' She continues, glaring over the table, the dancing shadows making light of her steel-eyed stare. 'Rasputin was lured to Yusupov's Palace, the pink one, you know the one we saw earlier, for a party. He like, liked a drink. He liked women. They, there he was poisoned. That was not enough. He lived. He was then shot by Prince Felix. Left for die, dead. When he returned Rasputin was not dead, but alive. He lived. A struggle happened. Rasputin disappeared to the courtyard. Fled. Shot. He was shot three times. Lived. Battered. Brutally. Battered. Lived. Dumped in the river. Three days later he was found. Dead. Finally, dead. A corpse, clinging to the supports of the bridge. Apparently, it is said, it is believed by some, not by all, but…apparently, he died from water in his lungs. Drowning.'

'Come on! Really? After all that, he died, was killed by the river?' Eddy remarkably played the role of astonished listener that he perfectly consummated.

'An enigma.' She did not register his condescending manner.

'Bull.'

'So what did you think of the ballet?'

That was a vastly different direction of conversation by Lia. She had told her story that she wanted to share. Then they spoke of the ballet. The stodgy, filling, flavoursome food that reminded them both of home cooking, rather than expected restaurant standards. They did not want to upset the waitress any further. So, instead of partaking in a drink their they head back for their hotel.

En route, they found a bar to drink vodka, talk about the day that was. A lot to talk about. Even as they have spent so much time together, they still have more to talk about. They have more stories to tell. Little things open the closed stores of chapters that spring open for them to voice. It could have been the alcohol loosening the lips. In the warm room that was comfortably welcoming they talked about the trains since China getting better, as they got closer to Saint Petersburg. The service being smarter, both in attire and service. They will not forget the experience thus far. For which they will no doubt bore anyone who wants to listen.

They leave the bar a little tipsy. Eddy opens the door for Lia, then follows. He walks out into the cold breeze, a young guy, literally with his head in the clouds nearly knocking him off his unsteady feet. The guy was head down on his phone. Head in the clouds has a whole different meaning today, as he was looking down with his head in the I-cloud. On hearing that they were English speaking in there rushed apologies. Out of the shadows an unshaven Russia friend of the young guy whom was not spotted before speaks in many layers of a thick, gruff accent.

'Religion,' he commences through a throaty, husky cough.

Lia was a little unnerved by the way he presented himself and immediately thought the worse. The stranger leaned in close, the smell of cigarettes was powerful on his breath. She clung to Eddy for protection, slightly hiding behind his swaying shoulder.

'Religion was the drug of the masses many, many years ago. Vodka was the drug of choice in the Soviet days. Today, it seems, the internet is the drug of the masses.'

He gulps down the last of the sticky clear liquid from his bottle. Licks his lips, wipes the dribble from his chin and moves to put it in the bin. He misses. The bottle falls in a twinkling baton of mirroring streetlights to smash on the ground beside the plastic wheelie bin. He stumbles on, unaware of what he had just done. They look at each other. Absorb the words. Decide to have one more drink. They enter back in the bar for a roadie. The waitress is not impressed.

Crossing into the Baltic
One Small Trip for Them, One Giant Trip for Lia

It is late in the day when they arrive in Tallinn, the capital of Estonia. In the Baltic State, they are now close to the destination. They are recommended a hostel on one of the journeys for which they cannot remember who, or which segment. A worn scrap of blue lined paper has an address in the old town. They make their way there by train, then bus. On the outskirts of the old town they get directed by the bus driver to walk slightly up hill towards Nunne Street. To stay on that narrow road and according to the bus driver, they 'cannot miss it'.

The hostel is not well seen. In fact, they walk past it four times before seeing the tiny wooden sign, with the sway in the breeze of the paint dripping black rustic sign of 'hostel'. Apprehensively they grip the cold metal doorknob, with a tight pull they enter. Directly in front of them is a narrow flight of stairs. No other options so they climb. Only a few short, very steep steps take them up quickly, vertically, to a bench that acts as the reception. The warmth is as welcoming as the temperature.

From behind the desk, the floor opens up and seems to form over the shops below. The long planks of the wooden floor dips, rises, steps and flows into different rooms. It is very nice, comfortable and embracing, the whole vibe is sociable with a smell of a park after a heavy shower. The New Zealand owners are new and so very helpful. The novelty of owning their first business is fresh, as evident as living in a foreign country which works well in getting Eddy and Lia in the most perfect mood to discover. They are accommodation and get them into a shared three-bed room, for which they are the only two.

A brief discussion with other travellers on what to do, to see and where to head out to over a cup of homemade pumpkin soup. As they are nattering, they decide there is no time like the present. It is eight in the evening, the sun is still high in the sky, although it is colder than St Petersburg with a bitter breeze which cuts through the old town narrow cobbled streets and through, rather than pass them. They ramble the old town in search of a beer. They had learnt from a traveller of a free tour tomorrow and stumble on the meeting place a mere stones-throw from the hostel.

They take some interesting night photographs. Below, via some steep stone steps they find a small bar in the basement of the old town hall. Inside in the gracious warmth they have stepped back in time. Immediately to their left is the narrow bar, where a barmaid in traditional attire, black dress, white apron, black and white headdress takes an order and guides them to sit at the only spare seats at a shared thick, planked heavy table. Fake furs adorn the walls, stone from the walls bleeds into the low arched ceiling where strings of garlic, onion hang, near the kitchen of wood being the theme, the fire stove of logs where the cook smokes and cooks beside in soot-covered white shirt and apron. Copper pots gleam in the flickering fire. Clay vessels of jugs and bowls hang on slender hooks for the soups, drinks, stews.

In the background, a silent violin plays a folk sounding song under the rumbling hubbub of happiness from the punters. On route to the table, Lia asks for something to eat and two beers. She turns, points at a pie; they nod their head in agreement. They do not speak Estonian, she does not speak Australian, hence the hand signals, smiles, nods and body language provide the wondrous trick to what words cannot.

Around them Eddy cannot help but see the other sharing language that does not need to be translated. In the sweet wood burning smell of the room, where cooked meats fill the air, laughter is encountered. You can speak any language and understand laughter. Eddy discusses with Lia that this is the only feeling that words do not need to describe, or that everyone from any walk of life can understand without explanation…happiness. He evidently is playing the wrong game. She offers love. The first that springs to her mind. Then anger. Hatred. For which he states is the same. It turns to be an interesting conversation from nothing.

A sweet dark beer comes in front of them frothy and enticing in yellow-brown clay pots with a shiny darker-brown polished rim. Then using the same style in plates are two pies with the pastry peeling, flaking off as it rests. The smooth pastry is resemblance to pain du chocolat, soft and too good, much too good to be good for them. Eddy gets his notepad out to scribble notes. He has not written since the trains in Russia. The train from Russia was spent talking, sleeping, relaxing, editing photographs. Lia closes the book for him. She smiles, a smile that says 'don't', 'please', 'let's spend this night together' and 'let's just talk shit together'.

Candlelight flickers like a movie star onto Lia's porcelain skin that is polished perfectly, laughter, smiling lines around the eyes which portray sexiness, good times, great memories. The unsanded rough table is wonky but does not spill the all-important beer. They feel cosy. Relaxed and happy. The forkful bite of the pie tells them it is chunky pieces of pork in a rich dark gravy. Also, that it is very, very hot.

It burns Eddy's tongue; he douses that fire out with a gulp of beer. It is bloody marvellous. They mumble pleasurable delight. In the far corner logs burn in an open fire. A rough piece of cloth acts as a napkin to wipe the meat gravy from their chins. Lia leans in and softly, with a pure seductress edge she licks a stray line of gravy from Eddy's unshaven stubbled chin. Her lips travelling in soft brushing kisses towards his mouth where a peck on the lips leaves him wanting more.

It is a great night not to feel guilty as they drink more than they should do of the honey-sweet beer. Talk about everything apart from their travels or where they are going. Rubbish, trash talk that makes them laugh, smile, comically throw references around. They banter. They talk at length about never getting the banya that they had talked about doing when planning the trip in Australia. Russia, that is the only talk of the trip so far that they touch upon.

They head back, unaware of the cold as the alcohol fuels their heart with warmness. Slightly lost but eventually they find the hostel again. They stumble, fall up the stairs and into roll the room. They fall into the one of the single beds together, slightly tipsy, falling more in love, in each other's arms, bodies entwined, their feet overhanging the bed, they soundlessly sleep.

The morning starts lethargically. Lia idly passes Eddy his blue jeans from yesterday by uninvitingly emptying his pocket of Kroon over the floor that turn, spiral and spill everywhere but the place they first made contact on. That delicate cluttering tinny sound was like a crash of cymbals falling down a flight of stairs.

'Do you remember what the local said last night?' Lia probes as she fixes her hair in the rusty-spotted mirror.

'Did we speak to a local?' Eddy asks a question with a question as he rummages around the dusty floor for his scattered distributed money. At the same time trying to find his thoughts, his memories from last night.

'Yes, silly. Don't you remember. Were you that drunk?' she jokes while nursing her own tender head. 'He said the name, the name of the capital comes from a Danish word with Taani meaning Danish, Linn meaning city. So, we are in Estonia, in the capital, that is called Danish City. Funny huh? Well, it was bloody funny last night.'

'I guess…' Then the lightbulb turns on in his mind. 'Yes. Yes I remember. I do. On the way out. Yes. Wait a minute. He also said that the independence was achieved through a singing revolution. Is that right? I did not believe it then but…did I dream that? Bizarre dream though.'

'Let me see.' Lia turns to her guidebook on the crumpled sheets of their bed. 'Yes. Why, yes. Actually, it is true. I, yes, I will admit that I thought I misheard from his accent as well, but yes, a true…truth.'

A little bit grainy in their minds, they are determined to not waste one single day. As they rush, just before noon to the meeting point a single bean is thrashing around their minds. With each knock against their skull the noise vibrates louder with an echoing sonic pain. They set out for the free student-based information tour that they got told to go to, with recommended enthusiasm by the other travellers.

Turning the corner, they see the cluster of people. The young lady in a green lined scarf, bright green thick tweed jacket, a red and green knitted beanie, tight black toothpick leggings from small childlike black tiny boots. Her impish nature is reminiscent of a miniature, female sized leprechaun. She introduces herself around the encircling collection of various languages speaking from many different characters. A green pocket rocket, who is extremely excited, who is full of energy for which that energy may in fact, they assume to be alcohol-based. She looks up to everyone as she theatrically bows in a curtsy to everyone. The group get involved to cheer and applause. Eddy and Lia try to compose themselves enough to restrain over rapturous fits of laughter at her jerky bouncy behaviour.

Unsurprisingly, the tour takes in all the main sights. She musically enlightens the miserable history. She makes it sound like Estonia was a walking mat for raw deals littered in times gone by to the present, from occupation, domination, invasion and at long last resurrection, as a solitary independent country to grew uniquely supreme. This tour serves as the essential bonus of allowing them to get their bearings very easily. In the two and a half hours the route in the direction, as it does a child that is learning to write a figure of eight, to a wobbly loop back to where they started roughly.

After the brief introduction, they start in the presence of the majestic Niguliste Kirke, St Nicolas' Church. The grey looming clouds circulate speedily above the dark grey steeple with gold at the tip that is trying to sparkle in the darkness. The cream tower nearly blends into the skies effortlessly as if painted by one of the masters. The red small tiled roof of the long church body is in two tiers, small narrow windows at the top and then they triple the size to the base. The top tier is like a mini version of the bottom. The whole church seems to have been built in stages. Around the foot of the slope, surrounded by exposed foundations of the church, is the remains of the original church that stood here until the Soviet bombings of Tallinn on the ninth March 1944. A quick photograph and they are off again, running after the diminishing green dust of the tour guide.

A slender strip of perfectly clipped, lime-green lawn is a modest park they stroll past as Varvaara points out large, oversized deckchairs.

'These,' she waves her hand as she walks with an air of authority, 'are expensive deckchairs, on an even more expensive landscaped garden.'

'But, sorry, but it is just, erm…grass?' A high-pitched voice laced in nerves from the crowd in a thick unrecognisable accent squeaks her question out.

'Yep.' She quickly agrees with a dramatic point of her finger towards the voice. 'Now, once again, my name, Varvaara, is pronounced Va-Va-Ar-Va, means stranger. By the end of this tour, we will not be. We be friends.'

Very clichéd, they think she meant it to be. At the top is a wide, tall glass Independence Cross sitting in Freedom Square. Around the square are glass windows in the floor that show old foundations that are protected. This area was going to be a shopping mall but when they found these foundations, they decided not to destroy the history. Around the cross is a protective guard rail.

Varvaara says that they, the Estonian government built this out of re-enforced glass which can survive a nuclear explosion, this made the cross a very, very expensive project to build. At the time that they are looking up at it the cross is not even a year old. The protective guard rail was added last week. For that weekend the city was even more windy than today, in those high winds a piece of the top fell off. The protective rail was put up then. So, this is a cross that is supposed to survive nuclear explosions, but cannot even survive high winds from nature!

'Kirk in de Kioke, Estonian for Peep in the Kitchen,' Varvaara announces, blasé. She has already moved on to the next stop.

'What?' Eddy brings his viewfinder down to instantaneously snap his head to Lia. 'Did she just say cock in coke?'

'What? Seriously?' Lia bursts out in laughter. Trying to stifle her pending giggling as Varvaara gives a bemused look. They both miss out for what she was describing as she gives an explanation of a wonderful thin brick tower with tiny windows, topped with a bright red coned roof where the tall green leafed trees try to reach.

'This is one of nineteen towers which have survived. They used to be sixty-six. They protected the city. This one is, in particular is specifically exceptional. It has nine different cannon balls in it. Still standing. Held its own. Each cannon ball is from a different war. From each cannonball you can tell the different wars and the years by the cannonballs. The Kirke de Kioke.' She turns towards Lia. She keeps the laugh within her as the warning glare tried to pierce her resolve. She holds her own, staying in common with the tower. They also thought they had missed the explanation, but she continues. 'This is underground tunnels. Only you can see three-hundred and eighty metres. See it later, in own time. Come.'

Someone needs to tell her that we are humans, not dogs, Eddy thinks to himself.

Varvaara leads them around the corner to the square Virgin tower around the city walls with a red tiled pointed roof. Slits of narrow windows in different positions around each face. The name came around when women where put inside and held until they got their virginity back. Eddy and Lia share a bewildered look not entirely sure how that would work, positively sure that it would not work. It was preposterous to think that could even be successful in producing that deed.

They come to a beautiful rocky courtyard space. Named Danish square with gnarly trees blossoming with skinny branches full of busy green leaves rustling in the strong wind. A small rock is pointed out below the grey stone wall by Varvaara as she describes how the oldest flag, that is still used to this date, originated.

'On an eve of a battle, the King was standing here, Danish Square, looking, asking, hoping for inspiration and God's help. He pleaded for a sign that the Almighty was listening. A torn, tatted piece of cloth fell from the sky, landed on this rock.' Once again, she points to a rock where the red brick cobbed pathway has merged around, like a river. 'Cloth fell there, right there. The King took it as a sign. From that day forward, that torn piece of fabric became the original design for the flag of Denmark. Beware. Here. This is also the most haunted place in all of the land of Estonia. Here you can hear. See. An invisible piano player from the Virgin Tower. Here you can handshake skeletons. See ghosts.'

A tremble shivers down their spines as they warily look around their scene. Eddy notices that Lia is not taking photographs. In fact, she is barely listening. Whereas Eddy is absorbed in the cartoon beauty of Tallinn, she is not fully escaping her suffering mind. Eddy tries to bring her back. Although she is walking, no pilot is behind her eyes.

In one of the narrow-cobbed line lanes, with black lights on black metal brackets from the rough, worn aged walls they walk under a small arch and up some narrow, small stone steps. Above the arch is a faded worn sad looking stone carving of Jesus with a child, or Jesus is the child, he is not really sure so attempts to make a joke about it with Lia. She smirks a quick, blink-and-you-would-have-missed-it smugly wink, then back to her fazed, unfocused haunted look to nothing in particular. Lost in her world. He takes his camera from around her neck. She holds no resistance.

A rusting long boot is known as long leg, the name of the cobbed street in the beautiful old town up the narrow hillside. They slowly rise with the pain in their thighs apparent with the steepness of the street. Up to the familiar Russian influenced landmark known as Lossi

Plats, Castle Square. This is where Alexander Mevski Cathedral stands. Dark grey onion domes aloft the red, peach and white cathedral with mosaic saintly pictures. Flanked by the long yellow Estonian Government building with no visible guards, Varvaara pauses.

'Here is a public toilet.' Varvaara points out an arched green marble, tin structure which is a tin toilet with a brass handle and coin-operated lock. 'This cost the government 2.3million Kroon to build. Known to locals as the cheapest hotel in Tallinn.'

'I've come to a conclusion,' Eddy makes another attempt to engage Lia. 'I think that the Estonian government have just too much money. They seem to have this knack of paying, getting, spending money on ridiculous exuberant priced things.'

Nothing.

She gives him nothing in recognition.

They hug the pink Town Hall to a tower with the Estonia blue, black and white striped flag blowing in the cold wind. 'That tower is said to be the birthplace of Tallinn. This is where the Danish knights of the Sword built a fortress in 1912. The tower is all that remains. Always the country's flag blows on top.'

From here Eddy glances over the red-roofed tile towers, the steeples, spires the charming old town, yes even the pink Parliament and Town Hall building sees the view plucked out of a cartoon comic book. They walk down the steep, old, worn stairs along the walls of what is of old local shops. A tailor, a veg shop, nothing but locals inside talking over an assortment of apples, not the garish tourist shops selling tacky merchandise.

Eddy hoped this would not change and the traditional would stay within the city walls. This is a pleasant change to what they see in old towns now. The narrow-cobbled streets with high walls do not allow much sunlight in on this grey day but offer a charming characteristic. They walk uncrowded narrow streets as if teleported back into the pages of the historical medieval days. The bumpy stone-faced curved wall with a comically small postcard-sized window is the oldest church in Estonia.

A Ukrainian Church with a huge, dark brown wooden door with long, black hinges is shut. Sometimes you can get in, so Varvaara knocks on the door, a muffled thud is all that is heard. No-one comes. The door remains shut. She explains that if they were to go in, they would have no choice but to walk over a grave, a tomb of Otto Johan Thuve. His last wish was to have his grave placed precisely across the threshold. He wanted his humiliation of being trampled over and over by footsteps every day so he should, would be redeemed for his cavalier lifestyle, for which he was renowned for. Others say, that in his death he still wanted to look up the skirts of women.

They come to a building which was once upon a time, how all good stories start, the tallest building in the world, Olaf Church. The main tower looks similar to Nicolas Church but with tall arched long, narrow windows and identical smaller windows at the top. The roof itself is a point with each corner a smaller replica. A lightning bolt caused a fire that reduced it to the present height, which could explain the simple nature of the spires design. Eddy likes to hear that a law is still in place that nothing can be built taller than this spire. Everywhere he has gone he has seen the ancient, older buildings and monuments being placed in the shadows, surrounded by larger white elephants, all in the name of progress.

They stop for a brief minute outside a nice, but rather ordinary grey building. The bottom windows, for which would have been the basement, have been bricked shut. Whereas the first-floor arched windows have an orange bas-relief of two separate designs at regular intervals under each window along the wall. The second floor seem to have been built on top as the brick walls give way to a smooth plaster finish, a lot more windows and a more intricate designed bas-relief in a similar style, finished with a brightly, newer orange glow.

'This is a scary house,' Varvaara announces in a hush toned.

The group looks at what could be government offices, or just ordinary offices for that matter. She then slams her palm at one of the bricked up windows. 'These were bricked up to hide the screams of victims. Prisoners. Being tortured to get information. This, my friends,

THIS, this is the KGB building. The main security of the Soviet Union. Powerful police force.'

'Who had more grasses than a lawn,' Eddy adds.

'This building struck fear into the public. The memorial plaque up there. See it, everyone? It reads…' She recites a passage that is well-rehearsed, monotonous and precise. 'This building housed the headquarters of the organ of repression of the Soviet occupational power. Here began the road to suffering for thousands of Estonians. Come, come.' Once more she beckons them like a dog, which Eddy is starting to get really irked over.

'This courtyard really worked one day.' She softly rapped a knock on the dark wooden planked door. 'When the guards were on day off, they went for hunt. Good hunt as they shot and brought a deer back here. In the closed off courtyard. Hearing the screams from the basement. They prepared their hunt for food. Being fresh the blood rushed out. The blood came under these gates here and went down the street. Blood river came from here. This caused panic. This spread around the city. People walking by saw the blood river. They spread words of human torture of the worse. What really was going on behind these doors. That is why we, Estonians, are by nature a quiet race. Friendly.' She glints a smile. 'But quiet. Especially when it comes to personal life. You will find the same along the Iron curtains. We lives, lived in fear for a long time. Me, I am another age, I am student happy, friendly, talkative. I am open.'

Along the other side of the road is the most colourful wooden door on a grey stone, castle like building. Shining in intricate carved wooden decorated painted gold flowers, with red diagonal stripes on each door pointing down towards the hinges in a dark, but brightly finished glossy green paintwork. The middle has a brown pillar design to the arch of intricate golden dragon heads, that look out. Fruit, flowers, a sword are depicted surrounded by a red circular frame. In which is a profile shot of a coloured man with black knotted hair and a gold head band, seemingly blowing in the wind. Only the red uniform of his shoulders is seen. The whole door looks like an upside-down crest, apart from the top arch above the double-doors.

'The Tallinn Brotherhood of Black Heads festival hall. Above is the coat of arms of the brotherhood with the picture of St Mauritius. In the wall is the portraits of landlords King Sigismund III and Queen Anna and other coat of arms. Colourful.'

Varvaara gives no more information. Eddy snatches Lia's guidebook from her open red and brown leather bag to quickly flick through and find out. Simply a little was said about it being the medieval guild made up of young, single merchants and foreigners.

Twisting cobblestone lanes where iron lamps hand from character driven stone walls leads them to Town Hall Square. Varvaara points high at a curved stone pastel pink building with marsh green highlights. It takes a while for the whole, small group to see what she is referring to as one of the chimney tops is a smiling man looking down, peering through spectacles.

'This old man's bust, he used to live here. A monument to a great man who was born, lived and died here. He was known as the man who looked through his window, down at the Estonian people, to gain inspiration to change the Estonian way in the World. Well…' she snorts. 'This is what the Great man told his wife. The truth is. Opposite, the truth is opposite.' Everyone turns around to see another beautiful building. 'That, over the street, is the changing room for a dance studio. He would watch. Sit and watch.'

'So,' Eddy adds purposefully loud enough for the group to hear. 'So. The Great actually stands for Great Pervert.' He receives a chorus of laughs for his intervention.

'The Town Hall has been here since the eleventh century, with the square next to it. On the corner, is the beloved apothecary. This pharmacy shop has been established here since opened, opening in 1422.'

They are encouraged to put their toes into the centre of a manhole. Then they are encouraged to look up for which Varvaara states you can see the five most famous spires in Tallinn. One of the roofs having a section cut out for this very purpose. To see.

This is where they were on their first night, last night. The gothic structure of the Town Hall looks as magnificent in the daytime as the night. Just as Varvaara ends the tour she proudly tells them that this is the only one surviving in Northern Europe. They give a few coins of change to her open palm. Hoping that it is just enough to not be construed as an insult. Old Thomas looks down from the Gothic building. The weathervane tops the 1404 Town Hall with an iron portrait of Vana Toomas, old Thomas, a guardsman in the sixteenth century and still, very much loved. So much so that in death he was immortalised here to become one of the symbols of Tallinn.

The names of the lanes, passageways are enchanting in themselves. Holding, within, a naïve innocence of a more trusting time. Eddy ponders if that is indeed the truth. He hears. He reads. He feels that a few years ago was a better time. Terrorism was not as spread, however he has a different spin. Eddy believes, strongly, that it has always been there. It has not gotten worse, or, for that matter, better. The simple fact is the world is getting smaller. He could not fart in the North Pole without a tribesman in Timbuktu knowing. Technology has made everything accessible. Everything seen that previously was not, well, in the global sense of the word anyway.

An eight-week voyage from the UK to Australia used to be taken only by boat, now it is hours by plane. A telephone call can be made on the way to the gym, work and be as clear as if you are speaking across a table to someone miles and miles away. Even video calls are undisrupted, undistorted, clear as a bell as if you are watching it live, in a stadium. Eddy believes that it is in your face every split second. Literally in the palm of the hand. If you want to find a story, a fact, a knowledge, a person, you can do so easily without looking particularly hard. All the information is literally always inside the pocket. If not, the fingers stroking the silky-smooth screen of their mobile phones for all the desired information, or people sending it to you or on a feed through someone else interested in a topic.

Eddy cannot truly get away from it, even if he wanted to. That is essentially the modern world. A modern world that will keep on changing faster than you can even read this sentence, but, it, will not go back. They have to be the fastest, not necessarily the best. In this scenario being quick is the alpha. A stroke. A flick of the finger. A two-pronged engagement or diminishment. The younger you have this at the end of your digits, the quicker your innocence will be taken from you. Alas, this is the modern state-of-the-art world everyone is born into.

The lane of Saia Käik got Eddy on this train of thought. Why is it that if people walk alone, a monologue races through their mind. Or, you have that moment when you have an argument with someone next to you when that person has no idea of what is occurring. Although Lia is next to Eddy, she is floating unaware of the fairy-tale land she is walking through. Shame. He tries to convince himself that it is the hangover, he knows the truth. In tiny small italic capital lettering is the English Translation of Saia Käik, White Bread Passage. This was the diving board to his thoughts about the modern world being too small. The airwaves that he plunges through are the simulated thoughts to not only reassure his correct way of thinking, but, added the fuel to the fire. To give him the comforting encouraging heat that he is in fact proven correct.

After hearing about Olaf Church and being able to reach the top, Eddy could not resist the opportunity to go. This time Lia is not consulted but dragged through the long, narrow steep two-hundred and thirty-five steps up to the top. At the top. When they are looking over the old town towards the new town, they can see why the KGB used this as one of their spying houses, one of their transmitting houses and spy from the one-hundred and twenty-four metre pinnacle of the city. They wipe the sweat that beads down their brow as they partake in the beautiful view.

Red-tiled roofs of different shapes and shades. Spires pierce the light grey veiled skies. Narrow winding passageways coil the old town like seas of squirming snakes. Character house, the old man with his spectacles, for which there are now looking down at him, even more after learning the real truth. Over the walls, skirting over green parkland and trees to the sea, towards Finland. Over the walls on the other side towards the blocks of offices, the far cry from the beauty of the old town.

The empty courtyard encased in the large claw-type KGB that offered so much rumoured-driven lies to encourage fear. The ragged lined walls are incredibly impressive. The towers striking up. Eddy tries to imagine the scene back in the day. He finds it impossible. The metal horn of the spire above Eddy twists sightly, the vane moving in the cool breeze. It is cold, but he stays to take photograph after photograph.

'It, is, stunning.' Lia's words shock Eddy from his goofy expression as he looks over the city thinking of what he had learnt.

'Welcome back.' As soon as these words left Eddy's lips, he regretted his honesty.

'I am scared,' Lia talks as Eddy listens but does not hear. He has heard it all before. This rant that she speaks of. This same he has heard many times on this trip. She talks in circles. Never reaching her point. This was why she was quiet. Eddy knew this. Instead of talking the normal tact of pursuing an answer, he decided that she was not going to ruin his day, not today.

Relationships change quickly like the wind. All relationships go through hard times. This what makes a relationship. Coming through the other end happy, together. Not letting these moments tear down the fabrics of what makes them complete. It is in the centre of the war that defines a relationship. Some come through, others end. They were not going to let this end them. So, Eddy patiently listens. He turns his back to the city moving below like an army of ants over a delicious red icing gateau. Lia looks out, unfocused as her lips move. Eddy nods. Unflinching. When he feels she has finished he goes in to cuddle her softly, announcing without words that he is there for her, he will protect her.

The sun shimmers away under the dark lace veil of the evening's clouds. Below them the lights twinkle around, blinking fiercely before staying lit from the metal wall brackets in the perfectly placed ornate iron baskets. Showering golden cascading buttery hues over the characteristic old town features. Each touch contains a stroke of strangeness that invigorates pure, unpremeditated strangeness. Nothing short of enigmatically fantastical gorgeousness. They stand above the shoulders of Tallinn. Silently they reflect on nothing in particular, but absorb the now, recognisable sights. In the distance a baby cries. The mouth-watering aromas of delicious home cooking carries on the cold wafts to linger a delightful imaginary taste from their nose. They shiver.

The scent tickles their throat, bringing up the sensation that all of a sudden, they are both feeling famished. Their stomach rumbles a soft tremor. They walk down from the top of the church. They go in search of a traditional Estonian meal. They try to recall Varvaara's suggestions that she pointed out as they paced the old town, however, they draw a blank. They cuddle, they stroll the route in anticipation that something will remind them. They get drawn to a crowd of people laughing, drinking. The clink of glass on glass. The smell of a group of smokers.

A wooden sign hangs from black brackets, swinging in the breeze. They both try to pronounce the name, one-hundred percent sure that it is mispronounced. Behind the frosted-glass windows are silhouettes of good times taking place with sociable cheers of joy. The smell of burning logs escapes the large open doors as a guy with a cigarette hanging from his pressed lips, scurries towards the other smokers seemingly looking back to regret his decision not to put on a coat, or jacket. The warmth from inside strokes them, lures them to cross the threshold like fingers grabbing them softly with the friendly welcoming warmth. They walk in and order a similar beer to what they had last night. They get a shaving foam frothy light-coloured amber honey beer that is refreshing, crisp, cool and slightly sweet. Leaving them both with a foam moustache.

Around them, they look for a place to rest their aching feet. They scan, there is nowhere to sit. So, they stand around a tall barrel made up to be a table that has enough space for them, sharing the space with other locals. They chatter about the tour. Although Eddy felt that Lia was very much not in the present, she had picked up a surprisingly amount of information

402

about the tour. They could not believe that they walked the whole way around, in just the old town leaving still a lot more left to see.

Effectively warmed up, they decide to walk further in search of food, with a seat. The breathtakingly quaint appealing cobblestoned strewn tapestry of the old town seems to generate a greater picturesque gorgeousness. Against the backdrop of the dimming dusk light, highlighted by the golden lights spilling glitter throughout the close, narrow streets, they feel like imposters. The silent void of traffic, just human voices, single birds singing. They have never felt so alone surrounded by so many. Meals being cooked from the resident's unseen waifs along the corridors of the city, for which their nose follows. The towers and the city walls are lit with a soft glow. The spires are illuminated with small purposeful decorative lights.

It is a pleasant romantic stroll as they embrace to find a typical Estonians fayre meal, but are left with the influences of many different countries due to the changes in history. They find a place in a basement. They dip their heads from hitting the dark brown thick wooden beams as the elderly waitress with a white lace apron ushers them to a large heavy planked table with simple clay side plates, shining metal knives and forks and a thick heavy white serviette folded simply in three. It is a long bench for which they share with others. They guess this is the Estonian way.

On sensing their language, she has transferred them to a younger waitress whom brings a couple of English menus with her, maybe an increase in the price. They will never know. After a scan of the Estonian name, then the English words underneath, he orders the beef stew. Lia cannot decide quick enough so panics, she orders the same. Eddy cannot help it, he shows more than a little disappointment in tutting noises, that she had not tried something different. They get a rustic cut of Leib, a black, heavy bread which is 'sacred' with the dish that they ordered.

The waitress lingers in the busy restaurant to explain a few traditions. She is riddled with pure innocence over her smooth skin. Happily, she explains when the French say Bon Appétit, instead in Estonia they say Jä tku Leiba. This translates 'may your bread last'. They think back to the Asian countries which hold rice in their food-religious grace. Each country has an importance which becomes a tradition.

In no time, a steaming brown clay bowl of chunky pieces of butter-melting cuts of beef swim in a dark brown jus with carrots and potatoes topped with ribbons of pickled cucumbers and juniper berries. The smell that envelopes their senses entices them to take the spoon and forage forth. The drips of the spoon fall without a sound back where they came from as they eat without words. The warmth of their bellies from the chill outside. The sour pickle, the tart berries, the tender melt-in-the-mouth beef, the slightly bitter jus and the sweetness from the carrots just keeps giving Moorish bursts of flavoursome goodness. The bread is the perfect wiper to make sure the plates are as clean, well, as stopping short of licking each last crumb and every last trace of sauce. This was in a nutshell out of this world. Perfect ending.

Eddy comes back from the toilet not being able to contain his snigger. This has pricked Lia's curiosity who starts giggling as she queries his unnatural behaviour.

'I just walked in on the ladies by mistake. The scream one of them gave. We must pay. We must leave. Now. Come on. Now.' He remains standing, edging towards the exit.

'But I need to…go. Before we, er…go.'

'Fine. I'll pay and wait outside. For your information, the triangles are not the best signs for the toilet. The triangle pointing up is the women. Not the one pointing down. Triangle pointing up, remember. Got it?'

Eddy pays and walks out letting the cold breeze shake of his embarrassment. The streets are deserted. A haze is hovering over the smooth stones. The reflecting light from the small streetlamps give a glimpse on the unchanged essence of just how the time once was.

Back at the hostel, they effortlessly fall into bed. It is a strange sleep for them both. Eddy had the feeling of Christmas when he was young. He anticipated the arrival of jolly old Saint Nick with the presents. He tossed, turned with an energy that was nervous for Lia, but excited for her connecting together her past once again. Lia was exhausted, totally exhausted. She was everything, a cauldron of emotions that were boiling, bubbling to the rim without streaming over in cascading waterfalls of rants, anger, tears. She was tossing a lot. She got no sleep.

The morning came slower than an unhurried schoolboy to class. The alarm told them to rise. Although they were both awake, so more a prompt with the shrill, shrieking tone of Lia's travel clock they sit upright. Around her head like vultures that circle over a moving pack of meats, each one an emotion. Not knowing which meal to go for, which emotion to surrender. To feed upon, to feel, to feel better, to be nourished. To befall with a little more sensation of soothing transpiring. He cannot be her hero when he knows that she does not want to be saved. She needs to learn this lesson for herself. She needs to answer her own questions.

Today. For, today. Today was the day. Lia had waited years, months, days and now it will be a few hours. This needed not to be noted, no carnival, precession needed to hold the traffic in the street to announce this. Lia knew today was the day. She was fidgety. She was on edge. The friction in the air was dense, the atmosphere fragile, posed on a precipice that could change the whole day. This was the crossroads. This was the moment where the right path could, be the wrong path. She was obviously trying to act cool, in control.

She failed miserably in getting her body from screaming out, her mind from acting out. Whether it be the spilling of the morning coffee, the dropping of her passport, the blunt and staccato syllables that she answered Eddy's innocent questions with. She was not scared. In polite terms, she was petrified. In layman terms, Lia was freaking the fuck out. Lia wanted to go. More than anything. More than anything she wanted to do this. She had always wanted to do this for as long as she remembers, but, a small piece of her wanted to delay, stop, pause, stay.

However, as agreed today was the day. They got ready, going through their routine on a knifes edge to leave the hostel. They needed to get a ticket to ride. They went to the bus company. For someone that wanted to go. Afterall this was the essence of this trip in the first place, she was digging her heels in. Eddy was dragging her, but, she wanted to go. Her feet felt like her shoes were made of cement dipped in wet tar.

Lia commented on wanting to spend more time in Tallinn. Maybe spend the day out of the city. She continued to look around. She commented on everything. She was giving Eddy an unsought DVD commentary extra for free as she got ready. The suspected weather brimmed with grey, heavy clouds. The forecasted rain for yesterday never happened but they would not bet against the odds of it happening today. Rain will be falling soon. Looking out it is like it is night-time, rather than early morning daytime. Lia was striving to change her mindset but continued to comment on everything, anything in a mono form of verbal diarrhoea. Again, she mentioned the distrusting weather.

When Estonia gained Independence in August 1991, they strove to remove the symbols of that era, they wanted to keep those pages in the history books firmly shut, only to open them when they wanted, rather than having a constant reminder. Although Lia looks above and sees what the locals call Stalin House, as she looked up rather than forward. They had gotten so used to seeing Soviet buildings that to not see the Stalin architecture was starting to feel strangely odd. Most cities got given a colossal, wedding-cake of a building.

Nevertheless, Tallinn got a much, much smaller corner building built in the same style, but nowhere near as fanfare. Nothing special about the house, so to speak but represented the design well. The Stalin Star, high on an obelisk spire on top of a pillared tower on the roof. This was not like a normal communist era building, as it had many windows. A border of stone, carved a tinsel-like displays showed a circular motif for which they could not accurately see from where they stood on the pavement. For Eddy, the star was nostalgic, history affirming.

For Lia it was scary, a symbol of what drove a wedge between her, the reason she had to split from her family. It does seem that a mansion was built on top of a four-story office building with a greengrocers below.

404

The Soviet Occupation of Estonia was in 1940–1 and again in 1944–91. After World War II the heavy bombing was so destructive that it left many empty lots in the city. Most of the buildings around their walk to the bus station are new, from the 1950s. During the latter period, plans were for the old town to be torn down. To be rebuilt in the Stalinist style. However, fortunately, the Soviet Union was starting to run out of money, so the plans were shelved. Never to be plucked down, read again, redistributed for production. This is the only prominent building that they see, the rest of the Soviet Union are hidden within the buildings. Hidden as stories, legends, as the past, history.

This new town is so much different. Almost cold in appearance. Identical office blocks line the street with vehicles going where they like. They miss the cobblestones. It is poles apart in character, as if they had stepped across an epoch. Around the main street they encounter a pothole ridden, puddle dotted obstacle course which leads to a green metal rusted shed. Blue and white smart coaches shine in the dark, dingy dirty area. No-one is around, but a dim light from the corner of one of the sheds casts a spotlight to where the office surely should be.

They walk towards it, negotiating the holes while carrying their luggage. There luggage has changed a lot. The smart wheeled bags have been replaced by easy lightweight carrying black sports bags. During the train journey they quickly found out that they were carrying a lot of unnecessary stuff, so slowly they been lightening their load as they went.

Lia walks up to the dirty smears of the glass window to barely see a lit cigarette dangling from the worn wrinkled red lips of a chubby elderly lady with frizzy dark red hair, grey glassed eyes and thick eye make-up trying to conceal the wrinkles. It unsuccessfully does not. In the gloom of the broom cupboard, every now-and-again the burning bright red orb is seen as she takes a deep drag off her cigarette. She struggles to look up when Lia enters the shed, falsifying any form of interest. Lia speaks in Russian, but she understands, fortunately. There seem to be a little pleading in her voice. Some protesting in the elderly lady's. Eddy can sense it is not going entirely to plan. Hand in the front of her mouth she rushes to Eddy.

'Tomorrow!' Lia shortly tensely states as she spins away on the verge of tears.

'No worries.'

'IT IS!' she screams, cutting him off. These simple two words slash the banks of water to a torrent of tears that surge forth. She does not care that she has sunk into the muddy coach park. On her knees. Inconsolable. What comes next is a blubber of drivelling nonsense as Eddy consoles her.

'So, we are to go tomorrow, then.' He pats, strokes her back while lifting her head and wiping her tears. 'It will, WILL, be alright. What time?'

No answer. So, he continues by reaching for her hand, where she grips their shared cash. She passes it easily like a baton for him to buy the tickets. Eddy kisses her forehead as he rises, turns to the ticket office. He goes to buy the two tickets with the universal language of sign. He will rescue her.

She has recomposed herself when Eddy comes back moments later. In an attempt to take the edge out of the situation, he jokes, 'Be careful what you wish for. You got an extra day. Let's leave the city. Go somewhere else.'

She smiles and turns her back to the ticket office. Her eyes red, puffy as she looks at Eddy, mouths a thank-you while snatching the money change back. She goes back in, talks to the lady. In no time she comes back with another ticket. Takes their luggage and passes it through a hatch under the rotting wooden shelve to the right of the ticket shed. The elderly lady snatches it through the gap, like an ibis snatching a morsel of food. They have only the clothes on their back until tomorrow.

'Let's go.'

Lia takes Eddy's hand. Turns the corner and they board the dirty small burgundy bus, with a grimy cream roof. Lia shows the ticket with a small chat to the sombre toothpick chewing bus driver in his clashing bright yellow and green uniform, like a sixties holiday camp entertainer, he is like a camp pirate.

Lia is not herself. Eddy has no idea where they are going. She explains what happened in the shed, with only one trip every other day to Riga. She had psyched herself up to leave. She was ready. She will have to mentally prepare herself tomorrow, again, for which, she is not sure if she can. So many questions spin around Eddy's head. They will get their luggage back, as she revealed it was only a daytrip.

The bus moves slowly out of the city, slipping out of the muddy gravel bus depot. Stopping, skidding way too often. This does not inspire confidence in the bus, or the driver. They jerk their way to a small highway where the scene of green is pleasing to the eye. Once on the smooth asphalt the bus smoothly, but still slowly makes its way forward. Trees fringe the whole highway on either side. After Lia explained her mini breakdown, she turned to Eddy, keeping the tears at bay to ask, 'Aren't you going to ask where we are going?'

'No. Was, but no. Thought it would be a surprise. This is your day. AS YOU planned. It will remain your day. And tomorrow. And the next.'

She nestled into his arms with her head on her chest, while gripping the same arm with both her arms and hands. She was struggling not to cry, so said nothing. She could not even look at Eddy, as if that simple act of seeing his sympathised, meaningful face would be, just, too much. He felt her shoulders shake. She felt his heartbeat. He said nothing. The rest of the journey was in silence. Until the bus driver squawked, loudly only a short twenty minutes later that they had arrived over a static tormented radio line.

Lia grabbed her belongings, her day bag. Motioned for Eddy to get off. They have circulated around to the shores of Kopli Bay. So close, over the shallow blue ripples is the familiar spires of Tallinn old town covered in grey, as if a watermark floated on green clouds from the waters due to the bushy green trees. An island in the green sky.

On shore, a pristine metal sign states, 'Rocca al Mare'. Italian for Rock by the Sea, named after a manor, built by local baron Arthur Girard de Soucaulos who lived here. In the eighty hectares surrounded by dense, fragrant forest to the shores of the sea is a recreation of how traditional Estonians lived only one-hundred years ago. Over eighty different buildings and thirteen farms ranging from the eighteenth century to the twentieth are brought back to life. Impersonators, actors, thespians walk around doing imaginary chores with real instruments in traditional attire around the various sets to give them a glimpse of days gone by.

Small villages with schools, taverns, houses, chapels and windmills but not the short metal ones that they are used to. Here the criss-cross wooden sails spin high and gracefully stroke the grass before soaring back into the air to complete a circle. The wooden planked tower with a small peaked roof is assessable from the back by some stairs with a newer yellow wood balustrade. Inside is the weights, ropes and turning mechanism that enable the wind to grind the corn, maize for the bread.

'Swing,' an elderly lady remarks. Covered in a ragged blanket of red, black, white and lace with a white banding ribbon. She peers from her sowing, over her halfmoon glasses that delicately balance on the edge of her button nose. Her body is still stooped over. Another actor is bent over in brown pants, braces and white grubby shirt in a vegetable patch. On hearing them speak, she correctly speaks English. 'Go…' She continues with a waving arm motion towards the swing, 'go and play.'

In a reaction with a return to innocence, where anything was impossible, where life was so much simpler, Eddy chivalrously takes Lia's hand. He nods a reassuring head as he starts to drag her towards the swing. She takes a seat on the brown plank of cut wood with dark cream rope in her hands. Eddy pushes her back. He quickly gains momentum for her, as the swing creaks with appreciative glee. Lia forgets her problems from the morning. Eddy carries on gently pushing her. She forgets her inhibitions. Her cares are released in the air behind her as she soars in a giggling arc towards the grey skies with a freedom as free as an uncaged bird.

She lets out a childlike squeal of delight. Free. Innocence retained. Worries evaporated. Eddy laughs. Eddy feels the connection. Feels the wonderful moment. Smells the fresh soil being turned. The wood burning from a nearby fire. Hears the birds in the trees above leaving their roost in alarm as she continues to squeal, before jumping off, just like she did when she was young. She stumbles. Falls. Eddy races to her as the concern spreads across her face. She turns. Explodes into a fit of laughter. Lies on her back. Looking up at the grey skies full of silver linings as the rain starts to fall. Her clean clothes are filthy. They giggle.

'Swing.' They did not even notice the lady waddle over.

She makes them jump, back straight to look up to where the voice had come from. The simple word had shattered their fragile childhood memory.

'Swing,' she continues, 'swing is what Estonia…People. They learn swing, before walk.'

She slowly waddles back, like a decorative penguin back up the two wooden steps to her wooden rocking chair on the porch of their make-believe home. There she picks up her needles and wool to continue sewing. As the male in the garden toils the brown earth.

Eddy and Lia look into each other's eyes before the giggles take over them again as they express amusement in what that moment had delivered.

The yellow-pebbled gravel stones lead them to different places, and they look, read some of the descriptions, stare into each other's eyes to carry on to the next building, or sight. Nothing will come between them. They simply have no idea of a lot of the buildings they see, they take photographs of a memory of the slightest information of what occurred here in the Rock. They do agree it is pretty though.

In the tavern where the dominating feature is the large peaked roof, they bow their heads to enter were traditional music is played. People dance in folkloric slow expressions which would be better if one of the dancers showed enjoyment and not a sullen, sucking a lemon expression of depression. The simple beef stew with bread is nice. The company is greater. This break from the norm. The overcast, spitting rain day. This day. This day turned out to be, was successful after all.

With the return to Tallinn city centre came Lia's return to reality. In the same medieval bar where they spent that first night, which seemed a life before, they return to as they enjoyed the ambiance to a great extent, wholly enough. Snacking on cauliflower patties. A rustic circle of mashed browned cauliflower, ham and breadcrumbs with a dreadful smell like a rotten gym sock left in the bag, forgotten for a week. In colossal contrast with this vastly different, differing taste that was wonderful.

Lia visibly shook. It was not cold. If anything, uncomfortable hot in this claustrophobic atmosphere. The warmth of the open fire with the low ceilings made it so. She had an agonising flare, after flare of disturbing eruptions of thoughts in her mind. She was suddenly confronted with the want to cry. To burst into tears. Eddy immediately sensed this. He soothed her. Spoke to her. Calmed her down from the sheer drop. Did not patronise her. He simply reminded her of the truths.

Her family wanted her.

Her family wanted her home.

She wanted to see them.

She wanted to see her home.

They wanted to see her again.

They wanted her home.

Over a tume, dark beer she relaxed while sipping the sweet bitter beer, the death-masked cauliflower from hell with a heavenly taste. They spoke. Well, Eddy spoke. He went back to the bar and ordered something else from the counter, a carrot and apple pie with another round of tume. The sweetness of the crumbling pie. The golden sparks from the fire animating the exaggerated hand, hair and head movements in long, brooding shadows across the walls. The moods were lifted to happier levels. Maybe the alcohol helped.

'Let's get out of here,' Eddy announced as he pulled himself up, scrapping the chair along the stone floor as it moved backwards behind him. 'Come.' Eddy called.

With a gesture of his right hand imploring Lia to place hers in his. Lia accepts the invitation. Placing her hand in his, she raised up. They have not removed their coats, despite the warmth. With Eddy's free hand he finds the money to pay for the food and drinks which he places on the wooden counter table, under the crumbed scattered clay grey plate of the remains of their unorthodox evening meal. Scrumptious though.

Eddy had wanted to go into a drinking house he saw since the walking tour. They walk a short distance to Hell Hunt, meaning, Gentle Wolf. He had been heavily influenced by the strange cartoon-esque logo. A naked lady, cuddling or gripping on as if her life depended on it, to the back of a running lone wolf. They walk into the wide, low heavy glass double doors. The extremely chilly, cold, windy street that wanders swiftly around the corners, nicks and crannies of the old town like noisy ghosts, are left behind as the double doors shut behind them, slowly with a soft, latching thud. The warmth grapples them in.

The dark orange walls are adorned with fake animal heads that do not stop at the ceiling, but continue to travel up over the ceiling like ivy. They unintendedly order a dark beer that is super strong. They drunkenly get merry. They continue to snack, rather than eat a meal. Pickled cucumbers is recommended by the bartender with sour cream. He also recommends the small rustic patties of potato, cabbage and carrot. This simple food is done very well. Easy to eat, gorgeous to taste, better to consume.

The old town of Tallinn is surreal at closing time. They stumble the worn cobblestones. The streetlights in the old-style but electric, guide them back to the hostel as they cast lights over the stone walls through the thin intermitting veils of mist. The smell of burning logs is trapped in their nostrils, on their clothes. Morsels of food is left in their teeth for which their tongues try to dislodge as they speak in nonsensical chatter. The burp brings back the taste of the beer. Eddy drunkenly talks Tallinn up, trying to sound worldly and wise, but probably comes across pompous and dumb.

'Tallinn, my dear Lia. It offers, offers a vast menu for which the most demanding conni-sir of travelling taste will leave please,' Eddy slurs, Lia laughs. 'The, this old town is the entree. The plate of the hiss-tory, life, the live, life and old. Just in a red tiled cattleman, castle-like thingamajig of wall. That is the main. The gastronomical treat. The return within the delights. Dee-lites of the, town, old town is the dessert of the old town.'

They stumble. They somehow, against all the odds make it up the narrow stairs of the hostel while falling up, a lot. Why is it when people try to be quiet, they tend to make the most noise. They giggle shushes that are in their head quiet, but in reality, loud. They smash into their had-been-but no-more vacant room. There, on the edge of the only other bed, is a glum-faced Italian.

'Have fun?' he solemnly enquired with a meaningful expression.

'Yesh,' giggled Lia and Eddy.

'Six month I been here,' he tells his story like he had just been asked. 'No Italy food. Place no good.'

'Mate. You're in Estonia, mate,' Eddy exclaimed matter-of-factly. 'What do you expect? Do they serve Estonian food in Italy?'

'The weather,' the Italian's moans continue. Either he is not listening to Eddy, or not caring. 'The weather, cold. Rain. Look. Now. It Summer. Should be sun. Hot.'

'Goodnight mate,' Eddy firmly dismisses his negativity quickly so not to affect his or Lia's mood.

Eddy strips. Losing his balance, knocking into the stationary furniture, falling to the ground with an almighty thud. He laughs his way back up to try again. Lia, who is equally as drunk, effortlessly removes her jeans, sweater to reveal delicate cream panties, no bra. Their worn clothes are left in piles on the floor as if they hated them. Forcefully Eddy throws of his blue and white striped T-shirt as if it had just offended him and left it, there in the middle of the room. He crawls under the doona, naked, exposing everything to the Italian, who acts as if he has little interest, but just cannot help having a sneaky peep. He embraces Lia. They kiss. They are cold. They shove at one another to sleep in each other's arms. Lying in a very awkward, uncomfortable position. Shivering until they fall asleep.

A shrill high-pitched alarm from the Italians mobile drills into their heads. The Italian grumbles a moan as he picks it up, stares at it for a while, turns it off and turns over, back to the wall. He quickly starts letting out the zz's in soft heavy breaths. They are fortunate that the Italian had set an alarm, as they had not. They look at the time. They decide to get ready.

The second morning where they have woken with a hangover. They grab something to eat by way of the free breakfast the hostel holds with toast and jam. The easy, everyday routine was challenging. They struggle through the easy formalities of getting ready, packing their meagre day bag, for which they left the others at the bus depot. Even the simple act of walking is hard. By the time the dry toast hits their stomach. The shower head drips to a close. The clean smell of their fresher clothes settles on their skin. The idle chatter of the communal, but very feral kitchen, they are back to feeling eighty percent of being human, human beings.

Destination Day

Today is the real today. It is the brisk early morning wind in the light rain for which they board the local bus to their destination. Passing, stopping at quaint villages, scenic magnificent picturesque towns, lush countryside's teeming with life and colour, working fields and fond memories they leave Estonia.

Scattered rustic buildings range to unspoilt pine tree farm cabins to monstrous ugly grey block buildings. This four-hour journey goes fast, smoothly. Lia feels great. Well, minus the hangover. She has no perception of worry. She may have finally excepted it. Eddy slept most of the way, but with a nudge sharply in his ribs he is welcomed back as they enter Riga, the Latvian capital, Lia's hometown. Her childhood memories. Through the dusty windows she peers at the city like a child peering through a candy store. The bus slows as it enters the city.

The bus slows, turns a corner and enters the black, looming thick iron gates of the bus depot. The black smooth tarmac changes to uneven golden, wet, soggy gravel. Through the dirty windows the wheels kick up plumes of grey water as they splosh, splash their way into the correct, somewhat invisible bay. A nervous skidding halts, eventually, the bus. The water settles into other puddles.

The windscreen wipers clears the front window. Through the front window, Lia's head snaps in the direction of beaming faces. To loud cheers. Five people are staring into the tunnel of walled faces, scanning, searching for the photograph she had sent of her now, not the child that left. Whooping. Excitedly pointing. They have spotted her. They run to the side of the window where she is. Softly bang on the side. She uses her sleeve to wipe a line in the window to clear the condensation. She cries, tears of joy, a beaming grin of jubilant triumph. Through the window the five faces look up. They peer in close. They touch hands with the glass window being a barrier. They do not care it is raining. They barely even notice it. They have noticed something for which they have searched for many years. Wondered if they would see again. When they would see again. Today is that day. Lia blushes. They all have tears welling up in their eyes. Lia's hand does not want to let the glass go.

Eddy escorts Lia through the commotion of the bus of people struggling with heavy bags from the overhead shelves, that really should have gone underneath. Having almost four hours to sort herself out, Lia is a figure of frustration as she taps her foot quickly on the metal silver floor. Timidly she asks to pass. She gets nowhere with that attitude as the requests go unheard. These are long, tedious seconds. They slow seconds test the thin fabric of nerves for which Lia's patience precariously hangs, though posed to snap.

Shuffling along the narrow passage they are finally at the door. Her foot is not on the ground as her family grabs her. Pulls her into a loving embracing cuddle. A love which is unconditional. A love that has not been felt for a long, long time. She feels the love. Loves the feel of this love. Eddy awkwardly stands aside. He feels like a spare plus one at a wedding. He makes himself useful by gathering their belongings from the kerb beside the bus.

He stands patiently as she talks in Russian with a higher pitch than normal with the level of excitement close to hitting the ear-piercing stage only useful for dogs' ears. Eddy stands aside, shuffling his feet from side to side. He feels as if he is back at school, at his first school dance. Seeing the girl he wants with her friends and too nervous to go and chat. He zones out. Stares at the scene unfolding in front of his eyes, but does not register what is being said.

Lia's warmth of her hand on his wrist brings him back to the present moment. She introduces Eddy to her family, in Russian, of course. He feigns understanding to their machine-gun explosive questions, maybe questions, maybe statements. Either way they kiss him on the cheek, they smile, they embrace him as one of the family, they make him feel welcome. Lia commentates the moment in Russian to Eddy. He turns, blank-faced. Eddy's English breaks her Russian speech as a shattering of lightbulbs overhead makes her realise that he has not understood the past few minutes of her correspondences, greetings, introductions and explanations.

A shuffling, stunting short walk that seems to take longer than the bus ride for Eddy as they jostle for Lia's attention. They arrive at the door of a quaint brown and red brick house. The top of the tiled roof is crumbling in places, but holds a childlike charm as if it is a well-used dolls house. A bright red door with scratch marks near the bottom, a small peephole in the middle, and a narrow darker red frame shows the entrance.

Cramped between larger houses flanking either side is the squashed family home. They walk across the threshold inside, and are immediately confronted by a small flight of narrow, almost vertical varnished worn beige stairs. Eddy, with great effort squeezes the bags upstairs without knocking any of the family black and white photographs from off the peeling cream paint walls to the bare brick stairwell. The ordeal of the steps abruptly comes to an end and they are into the living room.

Surprisingly wide. Eddy is astounded. It seems the entrance is literally a façade. The house is designed like a capital 'T'. The living space spreads over the two flanking buildings for which are the local grocers on one side and the local butchers on the other. Convenient. Being a butcher himself he clocked the exceptional window display of the butchers with meats hanging on silver sharp hooks, nearly bumping into the family as they abruptly stop at the door. The words of expressions come to mind, numerous pieces written by Charles Dickens come up in his mind's eye. He will go and have a proper look at some point to release his own daydreams.

Back in the living area a hideously lime green coloured square, hard cubed looking three-seater sofa dominates the back wall with a white coffee table on the rug covered wooden planked varnished floor. A modest small television hides in the corner with wires trailing like multicoloured snakes to the other side of the room under the cover of the tapestry of rugs. No paintings are on the cream, floral decorated wallpaper. Hanging proudly and setting the scene perfectly are more photographs of family members in portraits, celebrational events and good times.

Lia's grandmother proudly beams a toothless grin as she struggles to rise. She points a skeleton thin, veiny finger to a threadlike, smiling young girl looking gleefully at a rugged teddy bear with a crudely sown back on right ear in her arms wearing a black and white long horizontal striped dress. It is an old, creased at the corner black and white photograph. Lia. It is Lia. The teddy bear was her childhood toy, a rabbit called Emer. A name from a book her mother used to read to her. Behind her, in a thick, fur-lined coat with huge flared bottoms down to the older lady's knees and huge round buttons are her mother's hands on her shoulders. She seems to be roaring with laughter. Lia seems to be smiling with happiness.

'Emer? Emer!' Lia gushes to herself. Then she strokes the glass screen of the framed photograph of the face of her mother. 'Mamma.' Then the nursing torn ear and missing black eye of Emer. 'How did I forget?' She talks about Emer. 'My adored childhood toy. Why did I not take Emer with me?' More to herself she asks the unanswerable questions.

She cuddles her grandmother who looks up to her and states in Russian, 'You could be your mother standing there. Just as beautiful. So pretty.'

They cry in each other's arms, unashamed. Affectionately they get pushed, shoved to the green stained sofa where steaming cabbage rolls are brought out on blue china plates with a matching set of teapots and cups and placed on the coffee table. One of the family members pours and hands out the tea. Eddy stands in the corner sipping his tea while observing the family members sitting around Lia on her emerald throne, some on chairs, others at her feet looking up at her in awe. While firing questions.

Eddy thinks he is out of place as the Queen has returned. The family listen to her answers as if giving a speech. They are absorbed at what she has done. What she is doing. Where she is going. The lady she has blossomed into. Either side the grandparents hold her hand. Proud. Affectionately. Eddy feels like an imposter in a very intimate moment. He blends into the background. Not much effort is required as he is barely noticeable anyway. Every now-and-again, Lia mouths a 'sorry' in his direction, and he slowly waves his hand horizontally while shaking his head, mouthing 'it's OK' and whispering, 'I love you'. He feels awkward, but touched and privileged to be sharing this very intimate moment with the lady he finds irresistible.

When Lia prises herself away from her attentive family to spend a few minutes with Eddy, she cannot stop beaming. It is now late in the afternoon, but early in the evening. They leave to go for a walk. The sun is shining straight at them through the roads, reflecting off the windows as they squint their way through the unfamiliar but clicking moments of recognisable familiar points to Lia.

On the outskirts of the Vecrīga, the old town, they barely look at the rich collection of Art Nouveau architect. Next to them is the slow ripple of the canal. Lia is still glowing, blissfully floating on a cloud of exhilaration. Her reservations and fears dissolve away in seconds. She is left with an aura of confidence that has been missing since the start of her journey. Animated she explains the stories from her family that were shared over tea.

Each building that Eddy looked upon as Lia pulled her hands to swing to and fro at the same time gushing another story, followed by another, his mind wandered. Of course, he was listening. However, he could not help but think that each different building would have a collection of tales within its different characteristic walls.

On Meistaru Street, he looks upon a house with two towers, each tower has a rather unusual sculpture of a cat. Portrayed in a rather unique position of thrusting its bottom up into the air, both are pointing in the same direction.

'Wait. I remember. This building. The, the story.' Lia stops her one-way oration. Her mind travels back. 'I think I remember,' then it comes. She signs, 'I do remember.' She points at the cats, gasps. 'The Cat House. Oh my God. I can't believe it. I. I remember. My, my, my mother, she. My mother told me.' She started but pressed her hands over her mouth as she started to weep. 'My mother told me. She told me a story…the owner, the household owner had a membership rejected by a guild, a guild of some description. He then placed these cats on top, his house as, as an up yours, an insult.' She giggles, all the while weeping between a teeth-baring grin.

Eddy scoffed at the childlike pettiness of how adults can act. The boy grows into a man, but never stops truly being a child. He cuddles the exuberantly weeping Lia. This is the most silent she has been since arriving in Riga. Birds sing in the trees, cars pass, people shuffle by, laughter is heard, the smell of meals being cooked. It was the world around them that move, carried on, while they stood still in thankfulness. He knows she has been putting herself through hell, yet now he can see her touching heaven.

They are surrounded by crowds, a popular hangout for the Latvian people, Liv Square. When Lia was a girl, buildings, people's homes stood here. After World War II the last of the destroyed buildings were removed, never rebuilt, and now Liv Square stands in its place. Strange to be called Liv, when so much was destroyed. However, the life does continue. They are surrounded by cafés, bars, shops, local and family activities.

Eddy plants himself at a free outside table in the setting sun while Lia goes in to order a couple of beers. On hearing their conversation in English, an elderly man turns around. In broken English, he leans closer into Eddy's comfort, personal space zone to give his advice, 'Watch people,' and gives a cheeky smile.

His younger companion, who Eddy assumes is his son, finishes for him, 'The parade of blond women in miniskirts and high heels is a must for any red-blooded male over the age of twelve.' They turn back around to leave him resounding, to a certain degree bafflingly to their superfluous advice.

Lia comes out, not a moment too soon clutching the frothy, dripping beers in elegant glass goblets. A huge smile spread across her face. She places the beers on the wooden table and seductively licks her fingers from the spillage before leaning across with a delicate kissing whisper, 'Thank you'. She then sits down opposite. The soft breeze strokes her hair as the sun shines to accent her silky facial curves adding a radiant glow. She grasps Eddy's hands.

'You have been amazing,' Lia speaks softly across the table retaining eye contact.

Eddy was about to speak a mimic of the sentiments to Lia but was quickly interrupted before he could even start. She looked away, to continue her own personal tribute to him, for him.

'I mean', she briefly looks away again, as if hoping the breeze would give her the words she was struggling to find. As if speaking out loud, would shatter the magical chemistry that the essential foundations of fairy tales are built upon. 'I, really. I truly. I...love you. I mean. I don't, I really mean it, that...let me start again. I DO Love You. Home life had its...' She giggles as she pauses to find the right word. 'Home life has had its. Erm. Challenges. We not only rise above, but, we smashed through each one. The journey. This journey. Well, I have been a bitch.'

With that revelation, it was Eddy's turn to burst into laughter. He was not expecting that to come out of her mouth. Again, he opened up to speak. Again, he was shot down by Lia who started speaking again, ignoring his ill-timed guiltless insolence.

'I have. You know it. You won't say it 'cause you good, you're a good person. You laugh, but know it. If you are honest, you would call me a bitch, as I have been a bitch. I bet you wondered what you were doing with me. On an amazing trip. Through beautiful places. Meeting wonderful people with, literally, a weight...a ball on chain in me, a bitch pulling you down. You haven't grumbled. You are a good person. You have been...you are...you have been amazing. I. Love. You.'

'I do. I love you too.' Eddy finally gets a word in.

They lean into the centre of the table, allowing their lips to meet. Their hands clasp around one another's faces in a close embrace. They are precariously close to knocking the beers over as the table shifts, tilts and rocks under the weight of their elbows. They continue to kiss. Their knees touching under the table. The hands stroking each other's cheeks. A short kiss that was resoundingly deep, it spoke a million devoted words.

In unison, they whispered together as their lips parted company. 'I love you.' Resisting the urge to go back for seconds, they nestled into their chairs, clinked their drinks, held hands, said nothing more. Nothing more was needed to be said.

They walked back a different route. It was funny that although Lia was ever so young when she left the country, the roadmap in her head got unintentionally opened. She did not even recognise it was shut. She instinctively knew where to go. Everything felt so familiar. Permanently mapped in her mind. They pass a colossal Dome Cathedral for which they were mere mice scurrying along its side in its presence and back at her family home.

They did not even knock when the door opened to warmth in more than one way. The smell of home cooking wafted down and hugged them. Lia's aunt took them up, or to be more accurate, yanked them up. At the table, where a table was not their before they had left. It dominated the living area, covered in a pure white tablecloth like a delicate snowflake. In a festival of food in a carnival of colours. They take they assigned seats prompted by hand signals next to each other. The grip each other's hands under the table. Their knees touch. New family members and friends had joined into this momentous occasion.

Lia talks. Eddy nods politely. He takes small morsels of food, sips the red wine, feels like a born-again child, feeling as insignificant as a transparent ghost. Lia turns to Eddy's ear, leans in and with a hushed voice tells, rather than asks Eddy that the family will be taking them on a walking tour of Riga after breakfast tomorrow. Solemnly he nods in a lack lustred agreement.

The morning breaks to a smash, cluttering of pans from the kitchen. They have slept on the sofa. Although very religious, they had no pre-illusions that they were not cohabiting together. So, decided to turn the other cheek in this instance. Eddy glances at Lia's clock. It is early, too early. He leans over and embraces a wide-awake Lia who takes his arm and pulls it tightly around her.

'We must get ready,' she insists in a harsh, hushed tone.

'Really? Now?' Eddy protests. 'But—'

'No, we are up.'

With that last word, Lia, with the illusion of a magician, is up, relinquishing the doona off Eddy as he groans his unhappiness at this turn of events. She is up, pulling at Eddy's arms in a gleeful happiness like a young child pulling the legs off a daddy long legs. His head burrows into the pillow. She is victorious. He punches the pillow and springs off the bed. Grabs Lia on the way to the bathroom in an embracing tickle.

If the dinner arrangement was defined as generous magnificent grandeur, this breakfast would be vast majestic stateliness. The Queen was truly home. A presenting feast was spread out for her fanfare, a celebration that she had returned. Cabbage dumplings steaming on blue round plates, potato dumplings, boiled eggs in a woven entwined basket, streaky crispy bacon, grilled tomato's with fresh herbs, roasted mushrooms dripping in oil, breads of different shapes and flavours, pastries that would be better suited in a bakery, but made here in this very apartment, copious amounts of fruit. The succulent delightful aromas. The table is full of colour, made from euphoric kind-hearted adoration. This would be a buffet worthy of an eight-star hotel.

The small red leather-bound cushioned is arranged in the same dome seated layout as yesterday. The only difference is, it is pushed as far towards the wall as the wall will let it. This sees them seated with the luxury of space with the family insisting that they relax, wait to be called to be seated, as they fuss from the kitchen to the table, and back. The chime of the doorbell, the unanswered door is swung wide as footsteps ascend up the stairs in echoing frenzy into the living room. More family, friends, arrive right on time cradling more food of their own in bags, terrines and pots. More people than yesterday have joined the festivity of the prodigal daughter's homecoming.

Just as Lia takes her seat, from behind her a booming familiar deep voice penetrates her mind. It cannot be! The vocal sound steals her ability to speak. Resonating in her head like a slow-motion second. Causing her eyes to become as wide as the large empty main-sized plates in front of her, she looks forward, focusing on nothing. A little dustier than she remembers. Nevertheless, the voice still remains unmistakable. She swivels around sharply. The chair leans alarmingly close to knocking the table as she erupts from her seat. Leaps, bounds towards the core of the voice.

This happens in an instance for Eddy who turns around, just early enough to see Lia throw her arms around a bearded fellow as they tightly grasp each other. Eddy can see her shoulders shake. She is sobbing into the bearded guys shoulder. Silently muffled in his thick cotton jacket. She shakes more, badly, involuntary sobs of happiness. He is a stoic man, evidently proud by his stance, but tears are beginning to spring up, ready to flow. He reels them in from the brink.

'Pa-pa! Is it real-ally you?' She is breaking her speech, in the midst of cries of gladness.

Ahh, now Eddy makes sense of the scene. This small, but shoulder-broad elderly man with white highlights in the sides of his bushy brown beard was the father. Eyes holding the badge of regret. Holding onto what eyes should never witness. His arms are padded by a large brown thick jacket with shovel-like rough hands that have laboured for a hard life. One hand gripping the back of Lia's head nearly conceals it within his palm. Blue baggy jeans down to large nubuck brown working boots. In his other hand, that grips around Lia's shuddering back he holds an unlit mahogany varnish-stained pipe that is clasped, tightly in his thick wrinkled fingers.

His blue, worn, shabby beret is on the verge of slipping off to reveal a good head of bushy silver-grey hair. Perched on the edge of his nose are round reading glasses, where in the background the dark blue eyes surface shields of saltwater that glosses over his vision that leaves him without any focus. He will not let, not one of the brimming tears fall.

'Sofija.' He speaks in Russian. 'I have missed you. Missed you so, so very much.'

Eddy has nervously risen from his chair to be introduced to Gustav. Slowly, while lifting his chair so the legs do not scrape. Carefully gentle, to not make a screeching moment-breaking noise, he edges closer. She pulls away from the embrace but does not let go, as if the act will make him disappear out of her life once again. Eddy's hand looks so small in his thick hand to loosely shake his vice grip as he cannot compete with the surprisingly superhuman strength.

Eddy speaks in English, a formal greeting. Without letting Eddy's hand go, it was not as if he had a choice. He turns to speak back to Lia with an animated, lively statement. Eddy stares at Lia. Pleading, asking why, what was said with his eyes. Gustav releases his grip on Eddy's. They sit down once again for breakfast. Lia pats the tears from her eyes with the sleeve of her jumper. She covers up her lips to reveal the small conversation.

'He is not happy. You are my lover,' she murmurs. 'You are not only a foreigner. But a foreigner that doesn't speak Russian.'

Eddy immediately wants to protest the first impression. He goes to speak up to defend himself, but Lia pats his knee in a vice-like clutch under the table.

'He won't understand. Relax. Cool. Down. Chill,' she implores in an undertone.

In a childlike way, she continues to pat his knee in a patronising, it-will-be-alright kind of way, to insist adult-like, that this is not the time, or furthermore this is not the place.

Eddy's appetite has gone. He sips on the black coffee supported in his two hands. Regarding the scene all the way through the smoke bellowing up, reminiscent of the fury from his ears. He is fuming at the judgement, without the knowledge of knowing him. Thoughts race across his mind with negativity spiking and forming fork lightning, Lia senses the storm. Surely, she must realise the soft stroking, the patting on his knees is doing nothing more than heightening his fury. No matter how thoughtful the intentions are. Or the intended loving reassuring gesture is meant to be enticing, the opposite is happening.

After breakfast was cleared, the living room restored, while the rest of the family were getting ready. Outside they steal a moment which Lia orchestrates, to share a moment alone. Eddy was ready to voice the unspoken thoughts that had been building. Lia, in an attempt to defuse the situation launches herself at him as he opens his mouth to speak, or shout, who knew? As she invokes a passionate kiss intermittingly, with her reportingly saying sorry, over and over again. She felt he knew what he was going to say. She did not need to hear it. She did not what the day that she finally met her father, after so many years to be tarnished with an argument.

Although she was having questions of her own such as, 'Where was papa yesterday?', she submerged them. She wanted to focus on Eddy. She wanted to reassure him that no matter what anyone said, she was his. Forever and ever.

Refreshed, ready for the family tour her father insists on taking them. He wanted it to be just Lia, alone. She wanted Eddy there, Gustav acknowledged without resisting. It seemed in the few minutes later, outside, the whole family had transpired to come as well. To the benefited resolution for them to have this walk, while also making up for lost time.

The residential and quiet streets from the family home takes them back, a different route through back alleys, lanes, to the Riga Cathedral. As Lia and Gustav race in front, leading the vast crowd they talk. Lia is lively, many expressions gush over the steady, proud steps of her father's face. Eddy looks around in the warmth of the morning sun at the unusual, to him, architecture. The blue skies show the top of the cathedral over the rooftops. The spire has a golden sparkling small cockerel on the needle thin top. An Art Nouveau style grey roof has gold Roman numeral on a black clock face on each of the four curved sides bordered by a green mini balcony.

The red and orange brick cubed tower is Romantique. They turn the corner to the early Gothic hall of the cathedral. On a whole, the entire building catches so many architectural features with the Baroque influence also seen. This is the largest Medieval church in the Baltic States. Lia translates her father's words to Eddy, as they all gaze at the impressive large brick and stone building with magnificent stained-glass windows. This once housed one of the largest pipe organs in the world, with nearly seven thousand pipes and one hundred and twenty-four registers.

Eddy is left smelling the fresh, clean air with a hint of the salty ocean scent before he realises that Lia has been led away by her father. They are over the other side of the cathedral. A short walk sees them at Liv Square. In the light of day, the smell of beer is replaced by the roasting fumes of coffee. Large cream alcohol emblazoned square parasols cast shadows of shade over an array of yellow straw and brown wooden tables and chairs. Like the farmland fields they passed on the bus coming in, each business that looks out on the square, has a different strip of tables and chairs in their own style, and a different alcoholic slogan.

Surrounded by colourful floral laurels, aromatic bouquets and single flowers neatly arranged in, almost polite rows, at the base of the Freedom Monument makes them linger for just a single second. The entire area they serenely stroll is a large park with some small slow-flowing streams, bright vibrant flower gardens are manicured and very well-kept. Birds fly above, a waddling train of ducklings led by a mother strut pass directly towards one of the dirtier looking streams. They are plenty of benches to rest, that are being utilised which offers perfect views of the old and new town from this meeting place of unwinding locals.

An imposingly commanding enormous sculpture is noticeably loved and taken care of by the immaculate preservation to the presence of security, cameras and reserved respect. The guards in smart black uniform with shiny black boots, lapels as blue as the sky, gold buttons like the sun stand at the bottom. They look so small around the plinth of deep-red stone. On the corners are different figures of different wars. Above them are many standing figures covering the obelisks base of white stone with clear, unsculptured eyes looking out around every corner of Latvia.

The tall white stone bleeds out and up to a smooth green statue of Liberty called Milda. Immortalised in a tight flowing dress with a thin gold belt. She holds aloft a triangle of three gold stars that represent the three historic regions; Kurzeme, Latgale and Vidzeme. During Soviet Times laying flowers at the base of this sculpture was a crime. This held the rather stiff recourse of being deported to Siberia. Today they seem to be making up for lost time. The symbol of Latvian national pride. Gustav adds that it always was, but now it can be openly referred to it as such.

He seems reluctant to head into the old town, reeling off excuses, like it is only for tourists and locals would not be seen down there. Lia pleaded by pulling, tugging at her father's arm as if she was a young girl once again. With Lia persuading heavily, it was clear that she could not let her little girls wishes be screwed in a rustic ball and cast away onto a pile of trash. They enter the old town via a small bridge which the cobblestone ground starts and runs through, given the authentic look that it has been untouched since being built. Young women are walking like Bambi on ice as they pass them in high heels for which this terrain is not the best for this showy parade. Very bumpy, uneven and not catwalk ready. The intended elegance has been replaced with clumsy, jerking, as if drunk walking. It seems the only cars allowed to venture here are either residents or the very occasional police car.

The old town, Vecrīga, is a wonderful wander for Lia. Eddy seems to be the third wheel as he stops to take a photograph before running to catch them both up. The rest of the family have headed back to the home. The Eddy procession of photo, catch-up, walk goes on before they leave the older architecture and authentically dazzling brilliance, to the rich collect of equally lovely, Art Nouveau buildings surrounding the newer part of town. The slow-moving, calm canals conjure lazy days spent in Eddy's youth around Sydney Harbour's parks. These have helped dub Riga as the Paris of the East. Each building has a character, a story hidden and untold.

The Rātslaukums Square, Town Hall square, is very new as it was built in 1999, but very old looking as they built it how it was prior to being destroyed in World War II. Just like in Tallinn, there is a House of the Blackheads. This is very ornate. Bright red brick walls, statues around the building which include St George slaying the dragon. White highlights curve around the alcoves, the tops, the curved framing sides like skilled decorative piped icing. Light blue strips tell the outside what they are looking at, the large round clockface with golden dials.

Golden-yellow flowers blossom on the flat top, eternally immortal, with a spaghetti junction of wires that is a weathervane topped with a golden figure riding a horse. All in all, it is impressive, beautiful, intimidating. Opened only, to unmarried men. Inside Gustav tells them it has rich colourful ceiling paintings for which they have to take his word for, as he swiftly moves on down the street. This does leave Eddy to wonder wordlessly, just how a married man has managed to see inside.

Eddy is getting fed up, he wants to enjoy the sights. Not feel he is on a Contiki tour. He motions Lia over.

'See that?' Eddy points to a small stone brick church that tiers into a golden spire. 'I am going in, up. Coming?'

She turns to her father. Her father entices her away with words as he turns his back on the entrance. She then speaks out. Turns to Eddy, they enter. Footsteps echo in the open space of St Peters Church. A sign suggests that they go up to a viewing platform, so Eddy uses this to get away from her father, and enjoy the city from above, rather than speed through it. A sharp left takes them seventy-two metres inside the spires for breath-taking views across the city. They are on the shoulders of the tallest church in Latvia, what better way to view the city.

The wide dark blue Daugava River casts its prominent meandering style through the sprawling, growing city. The city has been built and rebuilt, always in the same style but with the original wood structure, being now metal. The Riga Cathedral is still huge from this viewing position. The curving buildings, that are narrow like books on a shelf, but with many windows look slightly similar to those in Amsterdam. Liv Square seems to be bustling now with entertainers, artists and beggars. Eddy turns to Lia, facing his back to the glittering city.

'What is going on?' Eddy aimed to use eye contact, but cannot help but look down at his feet as he asks the question.

'What? What do you mean?'

'I get it. I get that your father has not seen you, but does he need to be so…' He struggles, not with a word to finish the sentence, but whether he should voice it out loud. Lia asks him to continue without words, just a shrug of the shoulders and a doe-eyed expression. 'Does he need to be so rude. To me. God Damn IT! He, well, he does not know me. At ALL!'

'He is not.' Her voice, her body language tells him that he understands what he is asking but really does not want to admit it. Especially to him, in spite of everything, Gustav is her father. Blood. Nothing like Eddy.

'Something.' Eddy touches her shoulders. 'It is just…' He sighs breathlessly and slow. 'Lia, sorry but, well, he just seems. He does not like me. He is clear with that. He just can NOT be any clearer.'

'I am not going to fight with you. Not today. Not any day.'

'Yes. Nor do I. OK, o-kay we will NOT have a loud listening moment.'

'Latvians are reserved. By nature. You heard what had happened in Estonia. Learnt, sorry. You know that. It is the same here. Well they just don't want to get attracted, attached I mean. They, they do not want to be left open, in case, or, they know you will leave. I won't. I will always be his daughter. Look…I just can't explain it. Please.'

'What are you saying? We are not going to lose the distance. You. You have all decided in a family talk, today, that I am not part of it. The future.'

'Foolish talk. You are being. You are a fool. Of course. What? I DON'T WANT to FIGHT. Get that into your thick skull, EDDY.'

'Calm down.' Using the same tried, tested and failed technique of patting and soothing worries away by means of the knee, Eddy does the same to Lia's shoulders. 'Sorry, my love. You're right, foolish talk.' He does not believe his own deflection in his previous statement.

Eddy moves away. Looks over the city, thinks of Sydney, of home. Is it that he is building things ridiculously in his mind? Are all cities filled with people that avoid eye contact, generally mind their own business and can be construed as being rude, impolite. If you smile at someone in Sydney, would they shy away? Probably. In his head, in his heart, he knows that Lia has won this battle, but there still is a war raging. He still thinks that Gustav, her father, does not want to know him. What was mentioned this morning at the breakfast table has not been able to be let go by Eddy, in his mind, like a dog with a bone, he cannot let go.

'Okay.' Eddy appears to be starting most sentences with okay, as if justifying his next move. 'Okay, here it is. I am sorry, but I am wrong. I guess your dad just wants to spend time with you. I am an unwelcoming distraction.'

'No.'

'Listen. You know it to be true. He wants to be with you, to spend time with you. I am not, I am not part of his planned reunion. Fact. It's okay. I am, I am okay with it.' He takes her hands and kisses both of them. 'You know it to be true.'

They travel without a sound down the dark spiralled narrow passageway into the outside bright light. On one of the numerous benches outside, Gustav has found the only one shaded. He is surrounded by grey pigeons as he tosses torn pieces of bread on the floor around him as he peacefully smokes his pipe. He sees them leave the church, but does not get up to acknowledge their reappearance. When they get closer, he speaks through the pipe smoke to Lia. She laughs. Eddy stares on.

'He thought we had gone out through the toilet window.' She laughs as she pulls her father up by his outstretched arms.

Lia turns translator once again. As Gustav points high above, to a very small limestone carved face in the tall heavenward brick walls of Saint John Lutheran Church, named after St John the Baptist. Lia tells Eddy, through Gustav, that this is a Dominican monk, but so many stories originate from the face looking out. Eddy waits for a story, but nothing comes forth, it is left unelaborated on. Quickly he points to an open fence door. Through to the left, he tells them, this is where the founder of Riga lived, Bishop Albert, in what is now St John's Yard.

After the tribe of Liv elders, who told him to build his bishopric here, Bishop Albert named the city of Riga after the Rīdzenes River. Above the rustic brick archway hangs the ancient seal of Riga. Honestly, Lia and Eddy would have missed it if Gustav had not pointed it out as they were walking the opposite way. Carved in the wall are two roaring, dancing lions clutching onto a crest with a peaked roof gateway with flags blowing in the wind and two keys in an 'X' in between.

Gustav tells a story of two monks that were bricked up into the wall. Then and there, they fed for the rest of their lives through a small window from the outside. On Eddy's query to why, Gustav does not know how to respond, he looks around as if looking for the answer. He suggests, by looking directly at Lia, that he is not sure if anyone really knows the answer to this question.

Beggars are everywhere, but do not seem to bother them. Maybe it is the fluency of the dominating Russian language that is putting them off, making them think of them all as collectively, as locals. They do seem to approach the tourists that speak a foreign language. When these beggars approach these obvious tourists, they want something from them. That is the essential truth. Everywhere in the world it is the same. They are not engaging people for company.

However, Lia felt so safe as not only in the presence of her father, police regularly are seen in patrols of twos, sometimes fours, in very bright fluorescent yellow striped markers on the top of their uniforms. They are nonchalantly strolling, relaxed as if on a break. Not looking for trouble, but more waiting for it to find them. They nod, a nonsmiling acknowledgement to them all as they let them pass the narrow street.

They turn back at Lia's implication that a rest was in order. Overlooked before, next to St Peters Church they stop for a coffee At a café called Golden Coffee. Written in bold golden writing on a plastic sign that looked very out of a place on the façade of the old stone, light grey building. This blazon dreadful logo cast even more astounding perplexing speculations, how on earth did they not see this café before.

Eddy was left to observe his surroundings as Lia and her father nattered. He finished first. He went to pay. What Eddy found interesting, was that the money was placed in a bowl in the centre of the table. The server then took the bowl with the money away and returned the change in the same bowl. Her father states a tradition that instantly bring to light the reason, it is rude to hand money directly to the servers in Latvia.

Rich coming from him, Eddy thought. He still had not warmed to him. Ironic for him to consider anything to be done so it, as not happening to be openly rude or offensive. Yet Eddy felt he was so cold to him.

Unwillingly, they have come to the end of the old town sector of Gustav's walking tour. Lia pleads from behind the back of her father who straightforwardly walks out. She wishes to go around again. He strolls off towards the busy road, unhearing, possibly uncaring what she really wanted. It seems that they are to carry on their walk into the newer part of the city. The dividing line in the ground is the abrupt stop of the beautiful cobblestones to the smooth uncharacteristic pavement. Technology shines in their face with the announcement of traffic lights.

The main difference from Russia and the Baltic states is that the green man actually means it is realistically safe to cross. On the green man becoming visible, Eddy stepped out, he nearly got sideswiped by a slow-moving car that had no intention of stopping. Maybe because he had just gained momentum and feared stopping would be permanent.

'You still need to look!' Lia announces harshly to Eddy. Simultaneously, she jerks his arm back unsympathetically at his scratch by the Grim Reaper's scythe, solely for her to be able to scowl at him. He glares back at Lia, his eyes demonstrating the fact that she insinuates it would have been his fault if he had gotten hit. Granted, for the most part people look intently at the lights at crossings to change before walking. Granted, they look instinctively before crossing any road. Ungranted, they do not expect to get hit when deemed safe.

Whereas, even though it is illegal and Eddy has the fines to prove it, people do tend to cross anywhere in Australia, crossing or no crossing. Streetwise was born rather than taught to Sydneysiders. Nowadays, most roads are one-way, so the situation is now even easier to gamble with an element of low risk.

Gustav does not flinch. There is no screech of tyres, only the commotion of audible grunting from the pair. Eddy ponders that he hoped, perhaps cruelly, that he would have got harvested by the Reaper. On the other side he has crossed the road, he waits while watching the elderly guys play chess in one of the sociable abundant parks that caresses the canal. In front of Lia and Eddy is a dark brown Laima clock tower. She speaks of this being a meeting point for many years. Gustav chimes in to speak of Laima being the pride of Latvian industry. Being a symbol of Latvia, the chocolate factory still produces products today. Eddy comments on the name being similar to hers, Lia.

'SOFIJA!' Her father shouts while looking directly at Eddy.

He then mumbles, with anger etched all over his face. Eddy keeps hearing, thus making out Sofija and Lia coming up several occasions. He is guessing to what could have struck the match of firing ferocity as they go head to head. His guessing is found to be correct, that he verbally spits out that Lia is not her name. Eddy looked at Lia. Her expression told him to let it go. Eddy looked away from Gustav, from Lia. From the direction he looks, Eddy can see the Freedom monument. Poignantly presenting something he was not feeling at the moment. He felt he was a prisoner of conscience.

Well, for the most part, they have had a great morning. They walk for a little bit longer around the winding gravel pathways of the park. Gustav puffing enjoyably on his pipe, whilst cascading huge curls of grey smoke behind him like a steam engine huffing and puffing the soft rolling hills. Occasionally from out of his pockets he casts showers of stale breadcrumbs for the birds, despite the fact that they nervously flitch their heads, the dangers get quickly disregarded as a vast flight of pigeon's flock to the ground to collect his bounty.

Incredibly he walks even slower, to the point that he nearly pauses while watching the chess being played by the Laima Clock Tower as if yearning to be one of the players. They all stroll in silence through the noises of the traffic, people and nature, taking their time to submerge in the pleasant environment. Gustav seems to be content, with encouraging hand moments for them to go on. He looks tired. He turns to buy a newspaper from the dilapidated stall and sits on one of the singular empty benches. Lia mentioned a time to be back. They continue to destinations within the city unknown, uncared for as they explored without a map, without an agenda.

The afternoon comes around fast, possibly too fast. An hour had flown as they return to the bench to see Gustav's open newspaper on his lap rustling in the breeze, where his frail hand gingerly clasps his pipe as he silently snores. A quick photograph by Lia before she softly wakes him. They retire back to the family home.

Her father cannot come in, so leaves them at the front entrance. She pleads unheard wishes which go unreciprocated. She cannot understand his term of 'cannot'. She is noticeable sad, but as they climb the flight of stairs, she is held in esteem with the beaming family members excited to see her. Like the pigeons in the park they flock to her, showering her with lovingly amorously admiration. Talking at the same time to ask about her day, if she was hungry? Thirsty? Tired? Making Eddy feel welcome.

Out of the crowd, a tender arm locking into his as an elderly man, Eddy had forgotten his role in the family tree, guides him to a seat before thrusting a clinking cup of tea under his nose. The glowing white smile of polished dentures spreads over his expression to give a prominent appearance of geniality. A pat on his hand, as if he was made of eggshells as he turns slowly around. He shuffles to the table, arm outstretched ready to grab the brewing teapot, to pour a tea for Lia. Another elderly lady is passing home-made grain oat biscuits around the room. More photographs are shared. Stories told. Laughs. Weeps. Enjoyment remembered. People reminisced. Memories being made.

Bedtime arrived just before midnight. While they were out the families have managed to resurrect two separate beds, in two separate rooms for the young unmarried couple. It seems that last night was strictly a one-off. They honour, respect her family's stringent rules. It is the first time in ages, since they care to remember that they have slept in separate rooms, let alone beds. A kiss of longing and they part for the night.

After what can only be described as a surprising sleep given the circumstances. An extraordinary sleep that was as perfect as perfect could get, Eddy wakes, looking into the eyes of his beloved. Lia has creeped in at the most romantic quintessential moment. Lia leans over as Eddy blinks open his brown eyes. He is startled for a brief second as his eyes focus to who this taste is before kissing back. Yet to only embrace her firmly, with a soft pleasurable groan as she delicately kisses his lips, as she softly murmurs a sexy, seductive tease: 'Welcome to Latvia'.

He grips the back of her head as her hair shields down like a silk veil over their faces. He wants to unleash his animal instincts and pull her into his lair. He wants to savagely make passionate love to her in her motherland. She wants that too. The way her body arcs towards him says that she too wants her own wicked way with Eddy. Lia pulls away from the precipice of desire. Lingers a few seconds, lips pressing hard against one another. Deliberately hovering above Eddy, looking into his eyes, as he looks into hers. This is love. No words. Just connection. Like unseen electricity they have that intensity, that resilient compelling current.

'Let's go for a run!' she announces, completely taking Eddy by devastating bewilderment. She needs to get rid of this pent-up energy. She resentfully tears herself away from his body, his lips. Not quite what Eddy was hoping for. Nevertheless, it seems that this would be a great way, perhaps the only way to burn off the sexual energy. They quickly dress to make a short run. Running away from the old town at more of a jog as the hour is spent talking, sweating, bantering.

In the shower Eddy hears Lia, resisting the urge to join her. It is a strange feeling to have something, that you have, but you cannot have. Over coffee she hatches the plan in which she spoke about with Eddy on the run. She wants to show him a slice of her childhood. He needs no persuasion to take a trip to the place she calls Jūmula.

With the most bizarre looking entourage of shapes, heights and colours her family escort her to the bus stop a few short steps up the road. They arrive, just in time to step aboard straight away. Lia shoos the approach of money from the relatives to pay for the bus, for food.

After a relatively short journey in the peaceful confinement of the very modern, luxurious shiny bright sky-blue bus that sparkles through the green leafed canopy like a river flowing home, they come to a parting in the seemingly curtained trees. Opening up to an isolated beach, twinkling of jewels on the smooth rippling white caps of the unruffled waves. A few undulating sandy dunes entwined with brown, grey gnarly roots, fringed by looming green trees and a grey shingle space where the bus swings round to slowly skid to a stop. The doors swing open, the saltiness in air purifies the stuffy brand-new smell of the bus. The falsetto whistling of bird's wrestle with the disturbing ruckus of human interference.

This is where Lia grew up throughout the summers. She leaps out to immediately head to the beach front. She sinks her knees into the sand, Eddy comes to her side. She paints the picture of a young Lia for Eddy, using the crashing soft waves as the soundtrack. Screens envelope Eddy to recess into her mind of childhood innocence spent playing at the beach, rummaging in the adjacent forest in one of a thousand different childhood games.

All the while that she played, her mother worked. She worked two full days. These were often long, extremely hard days on her feet, her knees, cleaning, scrubbing. Followed by a single day off. Then she started again in a continuous working cycle which lasted throughout the entire summer. That single day off, she cherished her time with Lia.

These were the carefree summers before, before the war really took its deathly grip on Europe. The firm grip coming through expectantly, but still unexpectedly when the political war arrived on Latvia's doorstep. Barging its way, all the way through the door without invitation, no remorse, no guilt. Clenching to take hold of the nation. Compressing to shatter the lives, life's from the bodies of what they knew to be honest work, simple pay and enough money for food, shelter and warmth. To be squeezed to prove the hard life was easy compared to this grapple with an evil adversary.

Instantaneously, the smell of the pine trees wraps an aromatic blanket of fresh comfort around them as they step up from the beach, walk hand in hand through the shelter of the trees keeping the vast stretch of white sands, ice-blue waters and blue clear skies on their left. It is a postcard. It is chilly so the ice-blue colour is probably a good indication to the temperatures. The beach is deserted apart from a scattering of people walking their dogs, or, doing their exercises. It is a perfect day for a walk, but no way hot enough for a swim, although some actually were braving the sub-zero temperatures which were surely more at home for a polar bear.

As Eddy and Lia are made of softer stuff, not the fur of polar bears or meat of walruses, or any other Artic animal, they resist the little-to-no temptation of taking a dip.

Halfway down the brown dry path, sheltered in the shadows of the tall column trunks of the pine trees with green starting midway to create a luscious bushy canopy, is a delightful quaint wooden shack. It is as if they had entered into a fairy-tale land of Brothers Grimm. The shadows flickers across their faces, the silence of the birds, the odd rustle from the undergrowth, the snap of a twig makes them turn and stare at moving leaves. The edge, the nerves, the worrying apprehension. The mind conjuring befalling events of what is going to come to pass.

They have stepped into, stepping further into the beginnings of Little Red Riding Hood in the forest scene where a murder has taken place. An open door shows a rustic muddled of pots and pans hanging on butcher's hooks from thin wooden poles on thick string hanging from the ceiling. The grey, tin plated roof curves, bends as a tall string of spiring smoke from the rickety leaning metal chimney shows life inside. They pause. From the open kitchen door, a swift moving blur passes by.

They catch a glimpse of a scurrying purple stained and red splattered apron of a fast moving, scurrying chef in black trousers and brown, aged shirt. Out of the door, coming invitingly over in the direction of them is wafting intensifying aromas heightening flavour, enhancing insatiable hunger. The chef rushes passed again, he stops in his tracks. Looks at them, as they look at him. A broken, crooked set of nicotine or coffee yellow stained teeth is flashed under the border of his brown, greying bushy beard. He smiles, waves to them, like he knows them. Motions them with a hand gesture, pointing them around to the entrance from his doorway, not stepping down the remaining three wooden steps to the ground.

They have stopped walking, considering walking back, yet an invisible force drags them quite willingly onward. They creep continuingly in their approach, to go towards the enchanted ramshackle cabin. The chef takes this as they are coming in. He spins around, shouts somethings towards the front. They hold close to the shack to reassure themselves that it is in fact real. At the entrance they are greeted by a young lady who silently signals them to sit. They sit down under the eaves of the decked front as water is poured into clear rainbow catching glasses. With a slight uneven lean off the buckling wooden-planked deck the table is propped up by bunches of torn paper, supported by small blocks of wood. From the side they can see the beautiful framed passageway that they have just come from. The sun shines rays through the trees that catch magical beams to highlight the colourful flutter wings of a kaleidoscope of butterflies.

The lady appears with a creased small notepad, the creak in the floorboards gives her presence away as they groan under what can only be her slight weight. Lia orders in Russian, which surprises the lady. She laughs as she expresses that they did not look from around here. They have what Eddy deems a beautiful conversation of hand clasps, gasps, giggles all under bright open eyes and teeth-baring smiles. Eddy notes that nothing was written by the lady as she thrusts it deep into her frilly light pink pinafore with lace trim.

Lia turns to Eddy, and reassuringly taps her hand on his, remarking, 'you will love it'. He assumes she means what she has just ordered. As they wait a song transmits through small crackling speakers, getting softly carried over the pine-scented and beetroot-tainted airwaves. Lia mentions that this was in the charts when she was a child, but different. Not only the lyrics have been changed, the words are now spoken in English, so hence the different translation. She has finished telling her story when Lia's ordered dishes arrive.

A brown clay bowl with orange terracotta rim is filled with a hearty red pool of liquid that is as transcending in its hypnotic colour as its richness. With a pink hue of cabbage and beetroot Borsch. The smells are salivating as the steam escapes in the cold air, penetrating all their senses. Next to the bowl is ripped pieces of crusty bread in a straw basket. Placed between is a brown, clay bowl of pelmeni. Looking like small tortellini's, these pork-filled dumplings that have been lightly fried sided with a small brown clay jug of runny sour cream heavily laced with dill.

Lia explains that she got asked if she wanted boiled or fried. As fried was the way her mother used to do it so that is why she opted for that way. The polite, young waitress, that they both come to the same conclusion, is the chef's daughter. She brings two clean, spare bowls. Lia shares as she explains the pelmeni. With the first mouthful, Eddy gets a sensational burst of flavours that subtly work together and do not compete with each other, but complement each other.

'When I was young,' Lia reminisces out aloud. Pouring her heart out across the table to Eddy, as he clumsily sips, drips and splashes the shared borsch over him, the poor choice of coloured tablecloth and the bowl. Lia does not say anything about the red blemishes that scatter Eddy's side of the small table to form a polka dot style.

'Younger I mean, well anyway, when I was younger, my mother used to give me pelmeni as a packed lunch. She would always have some in the freezer ready to go. When my father went hunting, he would take some. A frozen bag fresh out of the freezer and cooks it during his day.' She giggles into the air, 'It is the Latvian instant noodles.' Eddy is really not sure if she is joking or for real, but laughs along with her giggles.

Lia's mood has noticeably changed since arriving in Latvia. She had been so nervous through the journey to get here, but now having arrived. Getting the first warm embrace by her estranged family that is united once again over continents, hearing the stories, through these she has been lifted. She has been happier than her normal happy self. She has been remarkable. She is remarkable.

After their early lunch, a brunch if you please, they walk out, a different way that they had got to the hidden enthralling cabin. Sheltered by the sun in a canopy of pine trees is a neglected war memorial a few short strides away. Here the sun penetrates like a sieve to cast waves of shadows to shed a charm relaxing aura over the area. Although in need of love, it is not forgotten. An oil lamp burns feebly on the exact spot where an eternal flame once stood. Surrounded by uneven rectangle blocks in neat rows but moved on the bare, grass-patched earth by the effects of the weather. Some yellow flowers have tried to blossom on the barren cracks in the ground with a small fierce persistent patch where seeds are sprouting out in green shoots.

The centrepiece is a grey wall. In the centre are carved profile views of three soldiers' heads and shoulders in a marching pose. With stern, serious black faces facing in the same direction in a cubism style. In the crevasses, weeds are sprouting, on the left soldier the weeds have formed an overgrown mossy moustache. The combination of the natural silence of Mother Nature's breeze playing melodies with the trees, the magical flakes of light that float around, the warm ambient temperatures and the feeling of the lost being forgotten but remembered penetrates their souls with a tinge of regretful soothing.

Lia cannot remember this being here. Then a cloaked secret wind nearly knocks her off her feet as she remembers being here. At this spot. A spot where a creaky swing was. Before the bad. Before the war. At a time before the war this was a place of childhood innocence. She never returned when the war started. The war took her innocence. Her Childhood was taken. Her memories remained good.

Here was a great, summertime memory for which the wave has crashed into her with a wave of sadness. Eddy senses her body shake. He watches from behind the sculpture looking at the bed of magnificent wildflowers showcasing a fantasy of colours and aromas, a stone's throw away from the gentle rhythmical soft collapse of each wave on the bright white sand beach. Lia joins him, they say nothing, they hold hands, they know something happened but do not need to speak about it. The sounds, smells, warmth and sandy grass underfoot that is becoming more sand by each step is appreciated by them both. Lia tells Eddy what happened. His hand grips tighter. No words. Her head rests on his shoulder. Their appreciation for each other is mutual to the surroundings.

As they finally arrive late, a veil of darkness has descended over the city, after a great day. Riga has a few lights but not many colourful glows for which they would associate with a capital city. They walk along the canal. Birds are heard but not seen. The grass banks slope into the canal with groups of people talking loudly, laughing, and up to harmless fun. Lia stops to peer over one of the low-lying metal, arched bridges.

'You know,' Lia observes as she leans over the green metal railings, 'you know, when I was a girl, there was a fine to walk on this very grass. You would have to pay the issued on the spot fine. If this is the same, it is not enforced. Look at the many people. It is a good thing. It must be a thing of the past, the fine that is. Look. Let's go. It must be fine, not a fine now!' She offers a joking flippant play on words which confuses Eddy rather than make him laugh.

Eddy does not see, but is twirled and pulled as Lia yanks his arm away and down the other side of the bank. A cold breeze has stirred up as she chicanes around the romantic leisurely strolls to a large glass teapot. Lia looks up with a smiling question. Eddy nods his head in approval.

Glass windows curve and they can see some cushions free as they are being watched from inside. Riga is seen in a three-hundred-and-sixty-degree view, including the glass teapot lid is a sense of the starry diamond glistening dark skies. They walk in, the heat envelopes them, the sweet, spice aromas entice them through wrapping blankets of good vibes over them. The small counter is a chipper enthusiastic young bearded fellow with a leather apron with golden brass studs. Looking somewhat out of an S and M convention he fits into this hipster scene perfectly, effortlessly with a deep booming raspy voice that holds a tone from a matured well-made instrument.

He engrosses Lia into conversation as Eddy stands in the way, in the doorway as people move in, out, he moves side to side. She sniffs small wooden boxes that he presents under her nose. She screws her face. Nods. Acts indifferent with hand gestures of not being too sure. Eddy continues to be an artic penguin shuffling from one foot to the other to allow people to walk out, in and the door to swing open, shut. Lia orders.

'Finally!' Eddy thinks with a vocal heavy sigh.

With the gracefully fragile touch, the man delicately concocts a brew in a dented, scratched copper saucepan. The steam coils with smells like a cauldron pot with the sorcerer blending together a spell with a frown, a flick of the wrist, a pinch of a herb, snap of a twig, it is a dance of the hands that create the brew for which he carefully pours through a chinois into another pot as if the brew itself was a fragile piece of moving breakable glass.

Lia pays the money to a separate lady beside him as he toils, boils. The brass teapot with a golden cloth handle is placed on a small thin wooden tray. Two dark green saucers, with two teaspoons and two small dark green delicate teacups perched on them. Lia handed this to Eddy. He was at long last becoming useful. They walk upstairs via a creaking, narrow, small planked wood spiral staircase with Eddy trying not to spill the tea, while clinking his way patiently up.

Once upstairs, they find a place. The immediate glass is the walkway for which they both have to slightly lean on to for purchase. Around the middle are colourful large cushions. They settle on one of the marshmallow soft fabric large colourful squares that looks out to Riga through the glass. A small folding table is put up for Eddy to place the tray on. They take their shoes off as Lia instructed and placed with the others near the glass, on a small perch.

The vibe is electrically soothing but so chilled. They are not old, but the youth is the main census. Eddy wonders why they are having tea when if this was Australia it be the pub. Chilled electric music is piped through at a level that it can be heard but perfectly balanced, so they are not shouting. They perch towards each other on the side with legs in a slight arch not overlapping the soft cushion. Eddy pours the tea. They talk about the day. The preeminent ending to a premium day of what they did. Two different eyes seeing the same thing and taking different things from it.

Two different eras pass in Lia's eyes, to see the contrast. To drag the memories up so they can regrow in the untouched soils of the past. The nicest way to end any day. Lia blossoms up memories after memories as the bud's flourish with stories she tells about Jūmula. Never told to anyone before. Eddy focuses on her making images in his mind to what he could not have adequately done if not having visited today. She talks about playing alone. With childhood dreams being her weapon for imagination. They share. They laugh. They cry joyous soft waterless tears that only the eyes feel. They seal the day with a kiss. They feel love hurtling through their bodies.

The family are waiting up to speak to them about their day when all they want to do is go to sleep, together, but end up going to their own separate beds.

In a bizarre twist to what was planned for the next day, Lia's family insist on taking her away, alone. After a cove of clandestine hush-hush secret whispers between the relatives it comes to light to why. Eddy wonders why they whisper in the corners as he cannot understand anyway, but Lia tells Eddy that today they want to take her to the her resting place, her mother's gravestone. She says that he is very much a part of her family, thus theirs and pleads for them to allow him to come as well. She wants him with her. They will not take him with her. She is an irrational quiver of emotions for which the cries and noises escape her. Noises that have never escaped her before. She is a melting pot for which she cannot control her own heat. Not so much of a battle but a declaration the voices were lost, he was not to go.

She is sobbing, trying, failing to keep quiet on Eddy's shoulders as the car outside beeps softly. The relatives encourage her to come by yelling. To follow. She stays a bit longer. BEEP. A little louder and longer this time. She grips him so fiercely. Not wanting to let him go. Then a quick violent fiery squeeze before releasing, reluctantly letting him go. She has to push him away to stop her vice grip returning over him. He stares into her bloodshot, watery puffy eyes surrounded by red. He wipes the tears away with his thumbs. Kisses her forehead. She manages a smile for him. He urges, encourages her to go down the stairs. Go to the car. She wants. But fears.

BEEEEEP. She jumps. She goes. Walks backward. Out the door. Turns. Down the stairs. Eddy is left. Alone. A single house key in his hand. He cannot remember her placing it there. He is a shell of himself. Not sure what to do. Still as a statue. Looking at the open door, down the dark corridor stairs. The latch of the bottom door clicks softly shut. He was alone. He is alone. He cries. Sobs. Uncontrollable weeps heavy tears that he had kept inside until Lia left.

He so, so, so wanted to be with her. He felt empty. He so wanted more than anything to be there by her side for her. He wanted to be the knight in shining chef whites. To be the one that she knew she could rely on. The one that would be there for her. He was not. He was left alone. He was in a crumbled heap on the timber floorboards in a foetal position. Forcefully shaking hard. Ferociously sobbing wildly.

Should he leave? He does not know. He fidgets. Strides long strides as he paces the small living room. He goes for a run. Trying to expel the nervous energy. He comes back. Gets ready. The time drags. The seconds seem to be taunting Eddy as they slowly grind their way around the clock face, lingering on every second. Every car that passes by he rushes to the window. Peeks out. Searching for the dark brown Lada with rusting wheels with no hubcaps.

On more than a dozen occasions, he has returned to the wooden uncomfortable chair in the kitchen. To return yet again to the staring contest with the hideously coloured purple clock on the wall. The ticking gets louder. Like a short bursting staccato construction drill it gets worse. Echoes louder. The grating unwilling procession of the shorter hand, dragging its heels in, to sluggishly move forward at a snail's pace. After the umpteenth time he hears a car. He nearly slips his hand on the edge of the chair as he launches to the window once again. He is anxious. It is the car. It is the brown Lada. Finally!

He is surprised to see beaming smiles spilling out of the car. He is hearing laughter, unforced and natural. He tries to look calm as he goes to the kitchen to make a drink. He resists the urge to open the door. To greet them all. But to be more honest to greet Lia. To see her. He is worried. Lia opens the door first. Calls out to Eddy while turning her head to scan the room. He walks out of the kitchen. She flings towards him. Arms around his neck. Kisses on the cheek. Nearly knocking him off his feet. She pulls him in a weird unconventional wrestling move to wholeheartedly take him away. The other family are not in the apartment as they go into another room. She closes the door. The other family shouts hellos. Eddy shouts back. Lia shouts something, not letting her eyes leave Eddy's. Grips his face and passionately and forcefully kisses his lips.

'You,' she deep-breathlessly moans in an escape of yearning. 'You, Eddy, I so, so wanted you there.' She breathes out between frequent kisses around his mouth.

'Errr…' He pauses. He does not want to interrupt. He does not want to ask the stupid question, however, the moment he stops, he starts again. 'Are you…okay?'

She pushes his chest away, moves her body back. 'Yes.'

In that instant, an argument was brewing. A storm coming fast was approaching. For what was a peaceful moment just a few seconds ago, the tranquillity was metamorphosing to turmoil.

'Yes, Of course. Why? Don't I seem it? What? You think I am not! Not?'

'No, no. Please. You misunderstand.' Eddy was backstepping quicker than a rabbit that had strolled into a pride of lions.

She taps her foot. Eddy approaches, arms wide open. 'It was stupid, yeah I know, but I genuinely, I. Thought. Are you all right?'

'Yes.' The black clouds disappear as quickly as they appeared.

Tenderly, he takes her hands, lifts her head up. 'Sorry,' he mouths.

She looks deeply into his sympathetic expression. Sees the concern in his compassionate eyes. She sees the affection he meant. She moves in. Leans in. A kiss. Slow, gentle. She grips him softly, then intensely. He returns the intimacy.

'So…' they move together towards the bed and perch on the edge as she tells her day. Hands held in her lap she begins with a barely controlled tremor.

'So. It, well, we drive and outside the cemetery gates I was hit. It was so hard. The emotions hit me. I wanted to go in but, I just could not go in. I was, frozen. It was. I don't know, but. Yes, this is going to be stupid, I know, she, mother, mama has gone. But. But…seeing her name etched in the stone would confirm my deepest fears. I had struggled so hard to accept it. I was standing. Thinking if that cut that was loosely healed, would, open. I did not know, know if I was ready for that…hurt. I was being coaxed by, my family, My, Family.'

She paused at that thought. Her family. It has been so long since she has been around her family.

'My family started telling me stories. Times before the war came. Before the evil descended into Latvia. Before the destruction of their lives. My life. Stories of what they had built. Stories of how my mamma and papa met. The news of me, coming into the world, being held for the first time. Seeing my eyes. Stories of mama from the family, my family that knew her. The nearest, dearest, the one's that knew, it, well, just made me smile, walk, take the steps to the gravestone, to say goodbye. Made, this made me sad. I missed my family, so very much. I forgot I had a family. Someone, people that loved me. These. Today, it reminded me that, well, that I do not have that, this in Australia.'

A pang of jealousy, a spear of hurt struck Eddy, erupted through him as devastating as Godzilla let loose on the city. However, it was not his time for him to talk about his emotional state of mind. He crammed his green-eyed monster back into its box, away from her eyes. She was still speaking.

'Something that, that I did not even know I missed, was missing, and, here…it was, all the time…around me, here, in Latvia. I, well, I missed that feeling of, of not being alone. All alone. I was not alone. I said goodbye to mamma. I cried. They left me to cry. I loved them for that, their instinct.'

'Let's get out of here.' Eddy gently motions for her to take a walk with a slight pull of her arm.

Lia is brimming with tears as she tells her family that she is going for a walk. Her teeth are gripping her quivering bottom lip. Her face feels as if tremors in beads of rapid moving, squirming snakes are crawling under her skin. Lurking beneath, ready to burst through at any moment. The emotions she was feeling are something strange, new to her and very unwelcoming for her. She could not explain it adequately to Eddy. So, she chose not to.

They walk in a gentle rhythm, warm hand in warm hand, warm body beside warm body, shielding themselves from the cold strong gusts of wind. Without consciously knowing it, once again just like the previous evening they find themselves at the glass tea shop. They were cold so they go inside for warmth, tea and cuddles. In this enclosed fishbowl Lia spoke more of the stories that her family told about the summer times at Jurmūla Beach, the Riverina of the Baltics. She tells him that her mother got paid peanuts to work there.

Especially once the travelling was taking out, the accommodation on the occasional busy seasons, and her own apparent insistence of having a soup, or a pelmeni. She worked there purely, as she thought it would be good for Lia to be out of the city. She did it solely for Lia, so much for her, without wanting anything from herself, just mutual love. Lia ruefully regretted that she had thought that she had distanced her from her friends, in a personal exile of sorts. She, regretted that she never thanked her, voiced her thoughts. She thought, felt that she pushed her away. She wanted me to stay. She did not want me to go, but she did what was right for her.

Lia rose, her back straight as she straightened her legs and her pale bare delicate feet and softly shouted in barely an audible whisper, towards the dark shadowed buildings of Riga.

'Glasnost,' followed by the whispered 'Perestroika'. Silence followed. Eddy did not know what to say, what she just said.

'In the car back, they told me about Vladimir Ilyich Ulyanov, Lenin and the demonstrations for independence.' Lia takes the lead in explaining her nonsensical words that Eddy has no comprehension to understand. 'Those shouts were made in the safety of the car. Those shouts were made in the demonstration meaning Open, Restructuring.'

Switching faster than a drunk behind a wheel with the same disregarding recklessness of swaying between the wrong and right side of the road, illiterate thinking they change subjects. They continued to speak with erratic discord.

Next on the plucked from thin air list was why Russia, although heavily spoken, was not met with a pleasing tone outside of the cities. That was the way of the walk, the talk. Her family came up so often in their conversations, to the point that Eddy forgot all about his. Politics, what was happening back in Australia, the World, America. Then, family. The nation, then back to family.

Finally, as if Lia needed to get a few trivial facts, information about everything apart from the thing that is really playing on her mind. Lia talks about her past, her relationship with her mother, her recently departed mother, of which time was not a healer. To her, it was always recent. Raw. With her she held her voice, her wisdom, her advice in everything she did. She so tried to see the world like she did, through people's hearts, looking beyond the physical, the mental. To really see what they are trying to do. Not, the effects of what they do, for she looked for the bright, the good, the gold rather than silver lining in everyone in every single situation. It was her mother's gift to her. Even with the war, the brutality, she defended them. Never rose her voice, her fists in anger.

Her father's relationship was strained. It was a parental link, sure, but sometimes even that was thinner than a microscopic thread. This was not to say that Lia did not love him. Lia did, of course, but he was not there when she needed him. When she really needed him. He was not there to listen to his cries. He was not there to call her about his wife, her mother, for he got someone else to tell her. A stranger to tell her the most important human being to her was no longer available to talk to. That world tilting piece of information that changed her view on life forever was made by a strange voice on the other side of a cold phone. Maybe he was feeling the pain. Lia strove to do the same as her mother, look for the light, but, she, she felt, thought, still thinks, that he should have been the one to call. Specially to make that all-important call.

He moved on shortly after her death. A new life, bride. He turned up today for such a short time that Lia thought it was pointless. She felt uncharacteristically angered by his presence. She briefly, oh so briefly met her stepmother today. The situation was not ideal, although pleasant it was quick, very short. Lia felt she was deliberately dismissive in her answers to her questions. She recognised her voice as the voice. That voice that gave her the worst news she had ever, or ever wanted to hear. They both knew, said nothing. They both knew what the other was thinking. Her father did not want to be there, clearly. He just moved on without a word, no goodbye into the distance. Once more, Lia felt abandoned by him.

The welcoming warmth of the family home was silent with a single glow of a small lamp at the top of the stairs left on to guide their way. A message under the lamp, a folded piece of

426

paper scribbled from a relative that her father wanted to spend the day tomorrow with just the two of them, no one else. For once she was not going to be the third, the spare wheel, with the voice of death with them. Eddy senses the fragile shell. Sees the paper quiver in her hands. He wants to spend the night with her, protect her. Nevertheless, in respectfulness of her family decide that the separated approach was for the best. Afterall he could feel the eggshells cracking under his feet.

Lia is excited as she gets up to prepare for the day with her father. She is nervous, but buries that deep, deep down under a disguising smile. She is not entirely sure what she is to expect for today. Her mind is raging like an untamed bonfire with fireworks of disconcertment despite her calm composure. One thing is for sure; a bridge is in dire need of being fixed.

Politely refusing the advances of the rest of Lia's family to spend the day with them, Eddy has decided to be a tourist, get some sightseeing in, his meditation. The truth was, he needed time to contemplate what was going on, or more to the point that charade to what is really going on. They share a lingering kiss on the cracked, uneven pavement as they disperse in separate directions, to different hidden agendas shrouded in thick blankets of mystery. Eddy's purpose is to distract his mind from overthinking, from thinking the worse. He watches her leave in a plume of dark grey smoke and a noise of an unhappy engine of the car wondering if this was the end.

Gustav did not even come out of the car. Through the dusty shine of the window he waved without a slight glimmer of emotion. In fact, as Eddy walks in the opposite direction, he wonders if that wave was intended for Lia, certainly not for him.

After hearing of the effects first-hand of the war from his, now latest heavily extended family, he decides to learn more. He heads to Powder Tower for which the War Museum is located. The cobbled small streets of the old town are brimming with character, in contrast to the dilapidated concrete of rapid urban growth of characteristic mainstream regimented order. After the somewhat less than comfortable first encounter with Lia's family, he feels happier to be here.

He surprises himself that he remembers the location of the beautiful brick cylinder tower. As he gets closer to the sparkling copper point top with the vivid green sprawling ivy slowly covering the small red bricks to present a pleasant contrast in the warm summer sun, he spreads his arms out, as if symbolising that he is taking flight from the families nest. In the soft, caressing breeze the red rectangle cloth with its white narrow middle of the national Latvian flag rustles softly taking many breaks as it hangs down the steel pole. He struts uphill to effortlessly buy a ticket before entering the introductory floor of the three floored museum.

The journey takes him through World War One to World War Two with other wars in between and over. Unfortunately, English is not on display anywhere, but the general jest is apparent, so obvious. The military, the political history in visual form is amazing. Spread over an extensive, impressive display. Originally the name of the building was called the Sand Tower, as it was surrounded by dunes. It was then used to store gunpowder, hence the name that has stuck today on all the maps, local tongues. This is the last remaining structure of the old defensive towers which were in the beginning equalling over twenty similar towers.

Eddy feels a little disappointed as he leaves. The smile evaporates away into his chest, his eyes glaze over with sadness, he slumps his shoulders. Looking down at his feet he shuffles along the smooth cobblestones. He came here to learn more, but with his non-existent Russian or for that matter Latvian vocabulary, he is limited to what he can actually learn from only visual aid, especially on such an intense studying topic. He sees so many propaganda motives in the posters, art and advertisements.

At the end of the exhibition, surrounded by moving classical music is a promise of what the Latvian people can expect in the future. The music still echoes in his mind as he slowly looks down at the neutral coloured stones. Something for them to look forward to is presented. To Eddy it is a collection of high-rise monstrosities that will destroy the character to which he is enjoying. He is on his way to the said eyesores.

Near here is the Swedish Gate, a stone gate built to commemorate Swede's occupation of the city in 1698. Rather simple in design its purpose was to link the residential inside with the barracks outside. The local executioner used to live above here, in the modest brick townhouse with a beautiful orange tiled sloping roof. Legend has it that when he was at work, he used to place a red rose on the windowsill. Eddy scans each of the windows to see. He must be off duty!

One of the most popular buildings is the Three Brothers, a collection of old stone houses, the oldest in Riga. Built in different centuries the size from the oldest on the right in white stone, to the youngest on the left in pale, moss-like green. This noticeable smaller one tells more than the eyes sees, it tells the tale of the tax requirements, price of land and the privacy. The oldest has many smaller windows, with the younger ones a few larger but not as many windows. He is looking around his surroundings once more, doing what a sightseer should be doing, not a moping teenager.

As if all roads lead to Dome Square, he finds himself back in the heart. Eddy turns and heads a different direction away to find himself at stone walls, once part of the city's fortifications, he is looking up at Riga Castle. A collection of dark red and white flags of Latvia blows from the increasingly stronger breeze. Armed soldiers are everywhere to be seen. This was the castle, but now it is the Presidential Palace. Eddy looks at the structure, the magnificence and concludes that if he had a choice, he would choose this as his home as well.

Near St Peters Church on a patch of green, he sees a column of animals on each other's shoulders. Dubbed the Town Musicians of Bremen, it is a story from the Brothers Grimm. The bottom Donkey supports a tower of a dog, a cat and a rooster, who aim to look through a cottage window to save it from robbers. Here it is said that the animals are using it to peer through the iron curtain. Eddy stares at this rather grotesque statue with a leering, amusing tone. An almost mocking tendency evoked in the facial expressions of the statues reflects onto him.

BEEP.

From his chest pocket on his red, black and blue plaid lumberjack shirt, the mobile phone dings a soft single chime. Although not rushed, he gets a message from Lia to meet under the towering pillar in front of the Freedom Memorial. This was a phone given to him from his family in case he got lost or needed it. He was not sure if he should look, but as it had not gone off all day, he sensed it would be important, or at least for him. He was aiming to stroll more and contemplate the animal column.

As if hypnotised by the chime, the pivotal message makes him moves, without intending it he briskly walks on a mission. Chicaning around people like a non-touching pinball in the narrow channels of the old town. He is almost running rather than walking. When he gets there, he is panting noisily. She is nowhere. He sends a message stating he has arrived and if she wanted to do as the locals do, meet at the clichéd Laima Clock tower. This suggestion immediately falls on deaf eyes. He waits.

He looks up at the lady holding the three stars. No time frame was discussed, however something in the message, something that he had felt in the short simple words: MEET ME AT FREEDOM MEMORIAL, made him want to be there for her promptly without her needing to ask. Afterall, being in a relationship is about being there for someone, without that person expecting them. This was without doubt one of those moments.

From across the oddly quiet square, Eddy spots her. She strides in long, deliberate steps. Her pale red scarf that he had never seen her wear before trailing behind her in her wake. She is frowning, hard. As she gets closer, she is nothing short of trailing smoke from her nostrils, her ears. She looks at him. She is face-to-face. In his space. She is fuming. Eddy feels the heat radiating the intensity of her anger. He leans in to give a peck on the cheek. She accepts it. She nestles her lips on the heat of her blood red right cheek.

Inside, as he withdraws, he imaginarily wipes his brow in relief, partly that this latest mood is nothing to do with him, equally that he can bring her back. Instinctively she grabs

428

his hand tightly, draws him towards her and clutches his back in a tight squeezing embrace. Her shoulders shake as she brings the ripples of the tears from waving towards him uncontrolled without inhibition. A few seconds elapse. She slows down her body convulsion. She lessens the grip on his hand. Escorts him just as suddenly to the nearest café with a yank. They sit under one of the enormous square parasols advertising the local alcoholic brew.

They are in Liv Square. So many people are in this small space, but they feel alone. It is a perfectly sunny cold day without an ounce of wind. They feel each other. They feel, see, hear nothing of their surroundings. The waitress attempts to burst their bubble as Eddy orders two coffees in English, without even attempting to lean towards a Russian dialect. It is just after lunch, only a handful of people are around this café. A gust of wind blows one of the hay cushioned wooden chairs that they are also sitting on. It skims behind them into the square narrowly missing an unsuspecting couple of tourists looking up at a particular attractive building taking photographs. Eddy's eyes flick for the briefest minute. He is in the moment.

Lia is pouring her heart out. She has detached her speech in a similar way in which she used to speak about her life in Latvia. She fidgets with her burgundy paper serviette. She focuses into Eddy's eyes. This nervous energy that she is displaying is something that Eddy had not seen from her before. She is unconfident. The barista comes over with the coffees as the waitress pours water from a carafe into small glass tumblers. Eddy smiles a thanks without leaving the power of Lia's fiery compelling eyes.

'He said. He…said that I, IIIIIII!' she screams in teeth-clenched fury. Spittle escaping from the slightest gap in the space between her top and bottom teeth. White knuckles screwing up the serviette. She fights to recompose herself.

'Tell…' Eddy attempts to soothe her worries with a soft stroke of her hand, never losing eye contact.

'My father…' She interrupts. She moves her hand away to a defensive position as she wraps her arms around her chest. 'He, my father. He said I was a…mistake.' With that last word, the dam was lifted on her emotions. Her thoughts. Her feeling ravishing, running, untamed free. 'My mother did not want me. He did not want me. What? Why? The actual fuck?'

Eddy leans forward with his arms and grips her hands. She unchains the shackles of her arms to deliver him her hands. She caresses them as she speaks, yells, screams. He stokes hers with his thumbs. He ponders on the reason she went. He chooses not to voice his thoughts that instead of building bridges, it would seem that her father wanted to burn them down. It seems that her father was blaming her mother on everything, not limited to be the reason for the start of the war.

It was a reckless, appalling act to change the love of someone. To use ridiculous tactics to hurt, name, scar and destroy what should have been a great day. An everlasting memory. Lia was feeling anger. She wanted nothing to do with him. Eddy at last speaks. He endeavours for her not to slam that door shut. He attempts to mediate the story by urging Lia to act with rational thinking, not impulsive rage. That fury of closing that door, nailing it shut would be extreme, it could, it would, be extremely, if not impossible to reopen. The last few minutes of his voice nearly developing the spark needed for the one-sided chat to become an argument. Eddy lets her accumulating fact that he spoke the truth burst out into a ferocious enraged rant.

Over the relationship, he has learnt that she is explosive in her reactions. He has found that if she talks it out, without interruptions, the talking out loud actually helps her to organise her thoughts. Helps her to process. Helps her to come to the correct conclusion in her mind, not necessary the right one, but that's life. You learn a lot more by a mistake, than being right all the time. The important thing is not to regret, but to learn from mistakes.

Her grip is softening up. She is cool, calm and collected. She is breathing fast, breathlessly. She is exhausted. Later she will, they will return to this conversation. She will then be in a better mind to articulate a better thought process. Rational slowly restoring to what Eddy influence charms over her, she smiles. This is for the first time her demeanour has positively improved since Eddy has seen her back at the family home this morning.

They are silently floating around the old town, in a daytime daze strolling through the afternoon. Close, but untouching as they are looking at nothing in particular, going to a destination unknown. Lia is thinking. Eddy lets her reflect on the conversations between her and her father this morning.

The silence is broken. Lia starts telling an occasional story, not from her time in the morning which Eddy expected, but her time in the past as they ring around revolving in the same spot as they turn, twist, return and wind around the cobbled brick paths of this enchanting part of the city. A randomly placed inconspicuous plaque for which Eddy walked straight past catches Lia's eye. She stops in her tracks. Reads the message that states that John F Kennedy, the former American President, one of the most famous, spent a summer here in 1939 as a student. Lia reads it but says nothing.

Eddy can see her mind working, flickering. She turns, moves into the closeness of Eddy to embrace him. She cries.

Eventually, unconsciously unplanned, they find themselves at the river, looking at the glass large teapot. They mutually untie their scarfs from around their neck as they walk towards the light. Gloves are pulled off their hands and are placed in their pockets as the warmth from the amber glow of the opening door captures them like a sci-fi tractor beam. Eddy started the day not that cold so went for brown shorts with a warmer top. He is shivering so this choice of attire is putting him in the early stages of hypothermia. He carried on, said nothing although this warm break was enormously appreciated indeed.

Time is not an issue here. They talk, well Lia talks and Eddy listens. She wants to get out. She needs time out. She is impulsive that she wants to leave tomorrow. She wants to be away from her father, so she can think about want to do about her father.

It is a short walk to the railway station. Eddy cannot make her reconsider. There they buy a ticket, a bus ticket, hence tomorrow they are resolutely going away. It happened so quickly. Eddy wrestled to negotiate a time to think with Lia, that she needed to think about this before buying, before leaving. He lost this battle. And, how? Her mind was made up. He was told in uncertain terms that he either went with her, or she would leave him behind. Until that point in time that she was ready to return, if she ever was.

Justifiably, Eddy was hurt by this accusation. He had been by her side this whole journey, taking her shit. However, this was not a time for him. He could do his own soul-searching, licking of his wounds later. For now, it was Lia's time that he needed to focus on. Yet again, he was giving her feelings precedence above his own personal hurt.

They return to the family home. Lia tells them gently, which escalates into a very heated discussion. They were struggling to understand her decision. In only a way a caring family can do, they accept her reasoning. They, like all families, may not agree, but they have this uncanny way of shifting the thoughts and feelings to make Lia feel supported. Afterall, they have just reconnected with her. It would be foolish for all of them to snip the fragile thin thread this relationship hangs by.

In the dark, moonlit early hours of a contradictory cold, summer's morning, they board a simple dark green bus to Lithuania. Her family have all come to see her off, with one noticeable exception. They wave, imprisoning tears in their eyes waiting for the opportunity to escape, ready to surge forth. Without words, with sad smiles behind a silence that speaks louder than words. Lia sobs in her seat, hands on the windowpane. Sadness consumes her.

If it was not for the fast-moving bus, Eddy wonders if she would have actually moved away, left her family. Eddy makes a comment to change the subject. Lia secretly loves him for that. Once more they travel through into another country. As the sun rises Eddy remarks with the realisation that they have not been asked to produce their passport since leaving Estonia. Eddy and Lia find themselves restlessly sleeping the journey. They surprise themselves at just how tired they are.

When they did stir, they found themselves staring out the window at a land of villages left in a time lock. Where horses are working alongside the farmers. Where old buildings finely made of wood are dotted one after another in the surrounding green, yellow or red landscape of fields with farm animals roaming, eating in the fresher than fresh air. Many of the properties do not have a noticeable separation of a wall, or a hedge, or a line of trees. The view from the bus gives a welcoming, invitingly friendly sense of countryside living in a forever generous community.

This longer, but so much cheaper, bus route did have this incredible charm which is unconceivable in this modern age to view this time of the lost age. It was appealingly charismatically charming that made them smile, wish whimsical thoughts of how life could be easier and then the nodding dog to slumber.

Their luggage is minimal with most left in Latvia which gives the family a certain amount of sanguinity. It has the feeling of travelling through states, rather than countries, with the difference coming only when they depart the bus.

The currency changes, this keeps their mind focused in mathematic equations, divisions and concluding figures so they do not overspend their rather tight budget. A small stop, seemingly on the side of a gravelled road. The change of vehicle is surrounded by different sized crosses on the high ground in the near field in Sauli, this sees them get aboard a local bus, for which they nestled in behind. This rusting bus amazingly is older. The noise stops them from sleeping. The air stuffy. The springs in the seats are protruding through the restraining dark red vinyl covering.

A call bellows from the front of the bus to announce that the uncomfortable six-and-a-half-hour journey is over. That they are soon to be arriving into the capital, Vilnius.

Lithuanian Regroup to Recover

It is strange that somethings just click into place. The easy, seamless change of buses. As their plans were preposterously last minute, they get off the bus with no map, no plan, simply, no idea. Lia asks the driver for assistance. He shakes heavily which Eddy is not sure if it due to his advanced age in years or the effects of the run-down bus. His wrinkling tremoring hand points towards a train station. Eddy feels a little annoyed at his unhelpful manner, if it was not for Lia's reassurance to him that he pointed and croaked, 'tourist office inside'. His frown turns to a smile and he thanks the driver, remorseful for his negative thoughts.

With their life's possessions on their backs for the next chapter, they cross a quiet small road towards a grey block ugly station. Stepping up the grey stone steps they are astounded with the scene that is behind the vile large metal grey doors. Eddy opens the heavy doors for Lia to walk through into a grand theatre-like affair. Glittering lights are suspended on decorative teardrop chandeliers that reflect, bounce and compliment the tall golden shiny pillars, the gold covered statues, the mosaic artwork in the large oval frames that dominate the arched ceilings.

In the middle, in a small hut akin to a white and silver chapel was the promised aforementioned tourist office. One side had a window where an elderly lady was proudly queen of this roost. She points to the side where a heavy door is strenuously yanked open to enter. She comes around from her desk. Considering her fragile demeanour where she is stooped over in her red cardigan and woollen black skirt with thick heavy boots, she greets them with her hand. A surprisingly robust, strong hand grip. She, without asking, pours two cups of black coffee into white flimsy plastic cups as she spills a little when handing them over.

These tasted awful, heavily brewed and warm at best; however, they sip them, thank her and drink the pure mud-like liquid. Without upsetting the tourist officer, they answer her questions about them. She actually seemed genuinely interested to their story. She wanted to know where they had been, where they were going to, and wanted to see, especially here. Some personal questions were asked. They elaborated on some truths, they slightly fabricated on some, gave some white lies to the others.

This was not to be deceitful, but more to be aloof with their want of information from here, not their want to give too much information out. It was almost as if she had been an old mate, or a long-lost relative wanting to retrace the lost threads of time. The energy that she transcends, the information that she has at hand about Vilnius was infectious. Eddy is still groggy from the impromptu bus ride doze, even though she grins high above his tiredness. They joyfully devour her information.

They finally leave, unable to swallow the last mouthfuls of black-brown sludge at the bottom of their cups. Unlike their cups they leave with a clear idea. A clean plan to what to do, where to go and more importantly where to stay. A short walk that she tells them is suggested and is the perfect hostel. A bed, shower and warmth. As promised, it is on the corner, up three flights of steep stairs. The young lady is painting her nails in blood red as she barely acknowledges the door opening, less the people directly in front of her.

'Hello?' they enquire hopefully.

'Reservation, you have?' She is abrupt, borderline rude.

'No, but—'

'No!' she exclaims. She has stepped over that borderline into rude. 'WHY? NOT?' She harshly yells.

'What?' It may be the tiredness, but Eddy is losing his temper. He feels it rising in volcanic rage inside of him ready to erupt. She pushes her feet off the top of her desk. Slams the nail brush down on the table. Turns a page. Smiles and declares, 'Lithuanian joke.'

Eddy looks at Lia to say in a monotonous, sarcastic manner: 'Must remember that one!'

The surly receptionist gives them a room which is not ready yet but said they can leave their bags if they choose. Their meagre possessions are left to the right of the desk, leaning on a dying pot plant as Lia hands over the money, to retrieve the keys and are told a few rules about the place. As they turn and head out, she calls them back, like dogs.

'Hey. HEY!' They turn, they retreat. 'Hey. If you go to park. Be sure not to close eyes. Illegal to sleep. You be fined. Good day.' It was a pleasant warning. They are flabbergasted from her mixed signals. Was she rude or polite, they question. As she returns to do her more pressing concern of doing her nails, they turn to leave once more.

Eddy opens the door for Lia, proving that chivalry is not dead. Lia pauses in the threshold to whisper a mocking statement. She simply states that they can sit in the park. They can sunbathe. They can sit, read, but above all really not completely relax. Is it not ironic to be that serious.

The weather is damp, relatively warmer than Latvia. The hostel is on the outskirts of the old town which is cheaper, and a short walk to the action. They pound the worn old town cobbles for the afternoon before heading back and checking in properly as instructed within the house rules. They then leave as soon as their bags have hit the empty beds in different bunks of an empty tiny room containing three bunkbeds and a scattering of clothes.

It is now eight in the evening. They take a side street off the main road in the old town, a light is glowing on and shimmering on the curved pavements. They stumble into a bar. A tiny, small, low-lying ceilinged bar. The amber, flickering candlelight give the effect of blossoming the promise of warmth. Down a couple of thick stone, steep steps they are into the cramped, crowded bar with brick walls, stone slanted floor, similar to the ones in the street. As if the floor itself has bled in to keep warm. Wooden beams support the uneven roof which they duck under to finish off the cosy character of this magical bar. They find a table towards the back around the cluttering of wooden furniture in various styles but in the same dark mahogany timber. These generate a warmth of their own. They take their coats off immediately, make themselves comfortable.

Eddy leaves Lia to go to the bar. He comes back with what was sold to him as a dark, home-brewed beer for him and a large glass of red wine for her. He asked for her favourite, a Malbec, but is not really sure that what he had asked for is what he had been given. He takes the seat in front of her and tells her that he ordered the special as he was hungry, so assumed she would be. She was delighted that he took the lead. Maybe mispronouncing it, more than likely mispronouncing as she giggled at his naivety. He thinks it is called Kemesky Keptune.

Across the small, rough, rustic table, they grip their hands as they talk about what has been happening to Lia. It was her trip, yes, but Eddy was starting to get annoyed to this being a constant feature. He hid the resentment well. The spotlight was firmly on her. Conversely, he does think it is a testament that they are never lost for words. They talk openly, honestly, without running out of things to share.

It took a while for Lia, but the drawbridge was brought down, the gate open, her heart exposed. Just as she was baring her soul a server came over. Infront of them she placed two large oval wooden plates with a smell that was indescribably mouth-wateringly appetising. The smell alone, made their mouth melt, salivating. Through the aromatic mist they both look through, towards each other, she nods her head in approval at his choice. If it tastes as good as the aroma promises, then this could be some treat.

The first spoonful entering Lia's mouth, the instantaneous open-wide eyes tells Eddy all he needs to know. He concurs her sentiments. It was delightful. A collection of petit flavoursome wild mushrooms similar to chanterelles bursts through first, soothingly followed by the saltness of bacon, the soft cabbage, the earthy starch of potato sided with sour gherkins. It is complementally magnificent.

The server returns with apologies as she knocks Lia's arm to place a plate of sliced dark rye bread, which is apparently called rugine duona according to her. Slightly warm, this comes at the perfect time to be able to wipe their plates clean like a sponge. This was amazing. It matched everything from the service, the atmosphere, price and the company. It was movie made brilliance. What more could they ask for the first day, in a new country. This stopped Lia's thought process centred on her family for which they did not return to for the rest of this evening.

Completely different to the previous day, the next morning did not perform to script. It never really got back on the dreamscape path. It was pouring ice-cold droplets of fast rain. They head for touristic shelter. Unconventionally they head to the former KGB headquarters. These premises house the Museum to the Genocide of the Lithuanian People. A strange subject to entertain them at the present time being a dreadfully dreary, drizzling day but in any case, this was Lia's idea. Eddy wanted to take one of the proposed daytrips out of the city. Her idea left him speechless, however he went along with it without objective hesitation.

On route she tried to attempt to explain without making complete sense, Eddy sensed that she was trying to make sense of it herself, hence the cryptic explanation to why. She stated that she was attempting to understand her youth better. She was wanting to understand what her family sheltered her away from, thus take her out of the situation by sending her away. She was too young to realise what was happening around her. She could feel her purity being contaminated, every second of every day with the vessel becoming full. To the point of being unfilterable from deceitful corruption, all the while she stayed in Latvia. She was pushed away for her own good. All the days that her mother was maintaining her innocence. Around her the borders of a remorseful immoral world that was building up rapidly around them like a virus was starting to suffocate everyone within. She wanted to understand her youth.

The grey large paving stones of the pavement hits the stone wall of the KGB building. The changing of colour and material is instant. The walls were obviously built to house importance. Glossy grey and red stone are in a marble style. A new acquisition of each of the large bricks have a name and a date. Each single brick is a person who died behind these colourful walls. After the first level the flat name after name brick changes back to the original light grey, to an almost blue tainted cubism, in the simplistic architectural building.

Just before the large wooden oak door with large glass windows, which is the entrance, is a bouquet of fresh yellow daffodils with short, clipped green stems. They look down at where they step, so not to stand on them and discover a plaque. The silky-smooth paving stone, out of sync with the other paving slabs inscribes a clear tribute. Here was the spot where a young lady met her grisly end. She jumped from the third floor to end her life rather than the KGB doing it for her. Eddy questions if they should go inside. They are not even inside where they see a wall of memorial for the killed, as well as a memorial plaque for a person who killed herself due to what happened inside.

They pay the lady at the desk to walk through a turnstile into the prison, torture chambers. She strongly suggests that they go to the top floor, the third floor and make their way down. This, they are told gives a real historical of the events that happened from 1940–90 with glass cabinets, documentary materials and papers.

The third floor is the paperwork, photographs, what is really left of what should not have been left, proof of what happened. The second floor takes them onto the offices of the KGB with more paperwork, many booklets supporting portraits of Lenin, Stalin or both on the walls. They are silent. The only noise is their footsteps on the wooden floorboards. They read the script, descriptions and motion the same way through the timeline.

These opening two floors are explaining the worst, softening them for what the ground floor is to offer, the most disturbing floor. The floor for interrogation. The floor of minuscule cells. The brown, leather studded door is a padded cell that is small, dark, cramped. Inside the black cushioned room is an elongated sleeved shirt hanging on a metal spiked hook which barely fits into the bloodstained splattered walls of the room. This also goes to show the small size of the room. The rooms for strong interrogation, or torture as they know it to be called. Also, the execution room where even after giving their truths they were murdered for their own sacrifice.

An exercise yard, which is a sinister joke. Would they really have an exercise yard for the prisoners here when they are trying to extract information. The yard is surrounded by dark green metal fence with six rows of barbed wire at the very top, nothing more than a canopy of violence. An emblem type badge of the single manhole cover in the middle which cannot be taken off without machinery shows that this was no joke.

Back on the ground floor are different walls to the conventional, disturbing walls. Walls of skulls, bones, remnants of human life. It is bizarre, a bizarre piece of art demonstrating what, once, was, here. The actually named torture rooms are cracked filled plaster. If only the walls could talk. A hose is struggling to stay on the plaster leaning away from the bare brick that is exposed. Lia and Eddy look at each other in the cramped conditions of the torture rooms. Each other thinking the same thing. The hose was not used to water the plants, but for cleaning up the mess. Gnarly holes that movies had taught them come from bullets, nothing else, the handyman did not want to test his new drill. Eddy hoped that Lia found answers, for him it was too much to take.

They learn that the Soviets brutally occupied Lithuanian between 1940 and 1991, that was no surprise, but the length was. In that time frame two-hundred and forty-two labour and extermination camps held the people of Lithuania. According to the reports on record here. It is estimated that a colossal figure of over one-hundred and thirty-five thousand Baltic citizens were killed or shipped to death camps in one single year, in 1940. Then, during 1945 until 1949, a further four-hundred and thirty-five thousand Baltic citizens were killed.

Over three thousand Lithuanians were sent to slave labour or extermination camps, and they never returned. These statistics alarm Eddy and Lia. They were silent before. Now they are quieter than the innocent death-marked graves in which they were reading about. They are completely hushed as they processed the disturbing information that was shockingly real. For comparison the Nazis exterminated only, yes 'only', as the text displayed it was written, 'only two-hundred thousand Lithuanian Jews'. As if they were proud not to have done that many!

No photography was allowed inside. This would normally annoy Eddy; nevertheless, he saw this as a positive. On this occasion Eddy saw it as a respectfulness to the people that were imprisoned here, tortured here, interrogated here, transported from here, and, ultimately met their maker here. It was as sacred as a church, as respectful as a cemetery.

As hard as the stone walls surrounding them, the grasping realisation of the coldness suffocates them. The impact that the regime had on the people here hits them equally hard. The gruelling lack of civilised gentleness in the face of blatant brutality and inhumaneness sends shivers down to their core. They look at one another before deciding if they want to walk the stone, chipped-edged steep spiral steps down to the basement. They have wondered if they have seen enough. They do not voice any answers. Nevertheless, they find themselves descending, almost trudging slowly down.

In the fully lit corridor of the basement are two dark rooms, barely bigger than a wardrobe. The light shines in dimly to illuminate the main floor but leaves the corners as dark as the secrets that the rooms contain. These rooms are so small that people could not even sit-down inside. These were the cubicles where the prisoners waited while the papers were being checked. Directly next door was the interrogation room, another bare room with a metal mounted desk in the centre, surrounded by a dirty cream, grey white wall.

Walking in, Eddy almost tripped over. His right foot plummeted about a foot below the threshold. Stumbling forward, he glanced back to see the lip for which the door was mounted on from the hallway entrance. To also see Lia in the entrance way, offering no help at all as she was folded over, clutching her stomach tightly in fits of hysteria. It was as if her pressure value had been freed. Quite inappropriate given the situation but she could not help herself. Eddy attempts to make her quiet by shh-ing her.

She muffles her mouth with her hands, breathes deeply to make an effort to regain her composure. Out of the corner of his eye, Eddy saw a description on the wall explaining the vertical drop. It would seem that this room was actually filled with icy cold water. Lia has carefully joined Eddy inside. Still sniggering shyly, yet reading the description as well. On the written instruction, they look back at the dirty wall to see the depiction, a clear discolouring of lighter grey below a clear line. Just below the back wall was a disc. About an inch long, the metal disc protruded out, like a blade that had been thrown into the wall, consequently embedded. This small shard was the standing point for the prisoners.

Only just enough space on the platform for toes, definitely not enough space for both feet, even a single foot. This room was a torture chamber, no doubt about it, it was nothing more than a shallow tank. The prisoner was stripped naked and locked in this room, this cell. This could be refrigerated, or in the winter simply ventilated to the outside temperatures that can be, well, freezing. To lower the temperature still, below freezing point, salt was added.

The poor prisoner would have to stay awake, stay focused, stay balanced on the small metal disc. Doing so may stop them from freezing to death. Yet, the cruel combination, a cruel game by the guards, the KGB, gave them little hope. The combination of the time in the cell, the sleep deprivation, the extreme cold. The outcome was pretty likely for the unlucky person the moment the individual entered the interrogation room. This might as well be a coffin for the condemned man. Death was patiently following the prisoner the moment he crossed this particular threshold.

They come to the end. Only to have to remind themselves that this was relatively recent. This way of life, or should that be, this way of death, only ended in 1991. All these torture rooms, cells and various artefacts were in full use until this date. This was beyond doubt a place to get a comprehension on the confrontable merciless conditions. A place to get an idea for what it would have been like. It told a brief glimpse of the events that happened in Latvia for Lia, but if half of what she had just learnt was real, the fear. That fear was the fuel the family needed to fund her escape from foreboding changes in times. Changes that were happening back then. Changes that were more-than-likely going to follow one day, very soon, into their private lives. Fear spoke, her family reacted.

From here, they leave the building to a brand-new day. The rain had stopped. The grey clouds dispersed. The skies clear. They head to Gediminas Castle Tower for a promised good view of the city. The colourful red, blue and yellow striped flag of the Lithuanian pride waves in the soundless gentle wind that shows their destination like a pinpoint on a map. It is a struggling, strenuous walk over the rain-soaked worn small pebbles of the pathway that are slippery and treacherous. Along the fringes on the green cut soggy grass are numerous benches that are thoughtfully placed to aid the less abled, exhausted tourists. Like a stunted gnome on a grassy knoll is the small, narrow bricked hexagonal tower watching over the city. With the ground levelling out, the bumpy, unsteady short cobbled climb comes to an end.

This three-tier tower is the only complete structure that remains of the thirteenth century castle which stood here. Standing on this spot for hundreds of years until the Russian occupation in 1655–1661 were almost everything was completely destroyed; this is the only remaining intact structure standing. Small decaying parts of the wall and a dilapidated building remain before they walk through the black, small stooping former gateway and travel up to the top. A standing description plaque explains the full lone, long story.

In a nutshell, the oldest state in the Baltics was founded in 1251 after King Mindaugas united all the tribes of Lithuanian. Grand Duke Gediminas of Lithuania was hunting in the sacred surrounding forests when he started to feel tired. In the crevice of an old large tree he rested. Quickly the short rest, fell into a deep slumber. He dreamt a dream in which he saw a large iron wolf standing atop of the hill, the same hill that he killed a bison earlier. The wolf howls, as loud as a thousand wolves as he raised proudly his head to cry out to the skies.

With the sun casting its shadow over his face, Grand Duke Gediminas of Lithuania wakes. Bearing down on him, seeing if he was alright, he sees a friend, a pagan priest, Lizadeika. He asked him to untangle the wisdom within the dream. Lizadeika states the iron wolf symbolises an insurmountable castle, and a city will be founded by the ruler of the place. That city became the capital of Lithuania. The howling wolf represented the fame of the city that will reach the furthest corners of the world. Thus, with this advice the Grand Duke Gediminas built the capital.

Over the course of history, which expands thousands of years, seven-hundred years of wars and occupations, the first mention of the country was in 1009, with the capital mentioned later in 1323.

Inside a small, modest museum hides archaeological findings from the castles glory days with sketches, paintings and ideas of what the huge complex would have looked like. One of the floors is dedicated to the Baltic Way. This is not what Eddy thought it would be. He was expecting a traditional way of life, a floor of cultures, folk idioms, tales, legends and other things that give a country its character, but he was so far off the line that his mark ended in South America. The Baltic Way was a human chain which began at this tower and stretched until its end in Tallinn, Estonia. He had heard of it in Estonia, but this gave a lot more photographic evidence, history and reason.

It was a peaceful political demonstration that happened on 23 August 1989 with about twenty-three million people linking their hands across three countries, spanning six-hundred and seventy-five kilometres. At the time, these three countries were states of the Soviet Union and hoping for independence. Seven months after this protest, Lithuania declared independence. One more flight of steep stone stairs sees them basking in the sunlight from above. The view is as promised. Beautiful. Chillingly beautiful.

'This is cracking.' Eddy understates the magnificent view around them.

The green, wet glistening trees sparkle as if covered in silver tinsel. The red tiles of the sloping rooftops reflect the chimney stacks, bell towers and clock towers which protrude out in irregular heights. The old town is one of the biggest, in terms of size, that they have seen. In front of them it spreads out like a luxurious vibrant expertly sowed adored blanket. Rolling over green hills to churches with twin clock, bell towers in beige with dark brown onion tops like erect bobbins. It really is a testament to the Lithuanians that have resisted the urge to destroy the history for progress, for a modern city. Like many cities that they have been too. They turn around to see that over the River Vilna that has indeed happened, so they turn back to the beauty with their back to the ugly forms of protest.

In over a hundred years, they might have a generation of children that are looking at the modern world with the adored look that they are sharing with the old town as a different form of architecture, has altered their 'progress' term. This would probably seem archaic, useless or just plain out-of-date. The old remnants of the castle wall, the ancient river, and then the modern world are kept apart. Fusing into the new district by a fence of large, but not large enough bushy trees is the unifying of the city where all dates come together.

They walk down, which actually seems harder on the knees than going up. Although the sun has dried up most of the traces of the rain, thus the slippery risk of falling over has eradicated, it still proves hazardous.

Safely at the bottom, they cross a cement bridge of tarnished steel handrails over the River Vilna to three white crosses. From the top of the tower, Lia had pointed out these to be their next destination. It seemed so close to them from atop the hill, but a little dip down and a much more steeper earthen path walk proved to be hard, if not harder than the previous uphill walk. They pass a cluster of dead brown leaves resting on broken, abandoned eroding, fractured grey stone crosses.

The fir trees have left their mark over them in a cruel broken Christmas tale where stumps continue to grow gracelessly under them with others ready for the upcoming years end. The smell of the pine is so strong and intense that it is inviting as well as overpowering. They look back at the tower and see a tour group has arrived. The top is filled to the rim with a colourful assortment of jumpers and coats. Thankfully the timing was perfect for them.

Nearer the destination crosses, they saw a plaque.

'This is a memorial,' she explains, looking at the Latin marble etched sign in the three erected bright white crosses that loom above them. The middle one holds the mystery of this story in the flat base before giving to a more elaborate, but simply executed three-dimensional cluster of these three crosses.

'A memorial to three monks,' she attempts to translate. 'They were crucified on this hill. In the seventeenth century, then soon after these. Well, those crosses were erected.' She points to the damaged ones that they passed under the pine trees a few metres away. 'But. These ones here. These ones are standing replicas; I think of actual replicas. I am struggling to understand but I think a set of three, for each monk got knocked down. Then during the Soviet times knocked down again and these, yes, these are those crosses on the floor. The original are the ones that were embedded in the earth at the start of the path, the place that the rains, weather has taken them to after many years. These ones…' she looks up, 'were erected again after 1989. Sorry in 1989. My Latin is rusty. Did that make sense. Any sense at all. I'll try again…'

'Honestly mate. I would not have known what these were so, to me job…' Eddy thumbs his right hand as if he had lost the words to finish that simple sentence passably adequately.

They turn to go another way down the hill to see, in the hope that it would be easier. Instantly, this seemed to be a mistake. If anything, harder once again. Too late to turn around, they persevere.

They stroll to the bottom as the lazy ripples of the River Vilna accompanies them. Hearing the soft lapping of water on the stone bank on their side, relaxes them. The larger ripples towards the grass bank on the other, is scattered with solitary people sitting peacefully on the grass verge, trying their luck at a spot of fishing. As they get closer to the suburb Užupio, the river becomes an orchestra of fast-moving water with the birds joining in from the galleries of the treetops, the traffic a distant hum in the background like a set of static—interfered speakers.

Nature has turned on its style. The pine trees caressing the smell and adding green colours of needles to the water that race past them. The bottom of the river seems to be nothing more than chestnut brown mud and dark, dirty green moss-covered rock which blends like a brewing tea to make the clearness of the water a mystery to them.

A magnificent Gothic red brick church with twines, branches and curving pillars like bricked ivy over the structure looked great from the tower but from here something else altogether. Eye-catchingly dazzling. The spectacular black diamond windows in small blocks off the building is a unique feature. This church is as if the plaster facework has been taken off and you can see the artery and veins of the blood-filled life below. It is an ever so slight detour which sees them at the base of St Anne's Church built in 1581. Worth it as this is truly a work of art.

The metal door is gothic with the handle being two snakes that meet at the mouth to form an oval loop. To keep the handle from falling is a smiling horned face of a square-jawed man, like a jester of sorts. They enter inside with immediate surprise as how small the alter is considering its grand promise outside. The thin, small brickwork continues but more modesty to act as a vein work over the arches and down the pillars whereas the rest is in glowing white plaster with colourful shades from the purple, blue and gold stain glass windows. Small black and white squared tiles leave a soft everlasting echo as they step forth.

On the modest rows of dark brown wooden pews is a lone woman dressed in corporate attire of a black and grey pinstriped jacket paying her respects. She is so in the moment that she does not turn at the newcomers into the church as the sound of the large door slamming shut disturbs the silence behind them but faces directly straight ahead. Hands in front of her. Eddy tries to grab the door before the crash as he sees the error of his ways but grasps thin air.

The lady mumbles towards the towering alter of God in a red cloak with hands open in acceptance in the middle showing the Holy Trinity in three separate decorative levels. It is a small colourful scene of silent respect. They walk much more softly as they take a seat with the boom of the metal door returning to its closed state with a slight tremulous clatter before the latch nestles into place once more. They look around them. Happy to get a bit of a rest surrounded by tranquillity.

Back out, they carefully make sure that the door is closed by their hand. They cross the river to their intended next destination. They got recommended to have a visit to this unofficial breakaway, known as the Independent Republic of Užupio, which literally means the other side of the river. The entrance is the townships constitution on shiny copper coloured metal sheets in different languages. They find one in English and proceed to scan the forty-one points. Here they point various points to each other. Such as everyone has a right to die, but this is not an obligation. Such as everyone has the right to appreciate their unimportance, that one sounded a bit melancholy with a side of sorrowful infinite sadness.

The grass path of trodden earth that they had been walking on has turned to cobble stones. A glorious angle balancing on a golden ball playing a bizarre horn-like instrument seems to welcome everyone into the very quaint village-esque place on a towering cylindrical column. The houses line the road in blocks of colour. First, they were pale blue, then mustard seed yellow, then pale green, well you get the idea. Within one of the alcoves in the embarkments perches a bronze mermaid that gazes with a tranquillity, wishful state looking skyward, ready to dive into the river below. Just like a siren she is said to lure travellers in.

Once she has teased them, tormented them with her desires she ensures that those travellers will not be travelling no-more, they will forever stay. The graffiti in bold pink and white is everywhere, however where she sits it stops, not one ounce of paint is around her immediate vicinity. Lia wonders if this is an unwritten respect that got missed off the constitution. As they get closer, she seems to be almost in a trancelike spell of her own.

Other sculptures seem to crop up everywhere. A white marble backpacking Jesus makes them both mutually smile with the same thought. In his cross like pose with the bag as his cross they discuss the relevance. Art seems to be the theme with paintings on the café walls rather than pictures, the backs of the houses covered in artwork. Boats which used to be for the water are restricted to being plant holders, within works of art, or are the works of art never to sail again. It has a Woodstock theme to it as people wear similar attire of the seventies, the sickly smell of cannabis is universally spread and the feel-good vibes after the war, after the nervous times is relaxed, soft-drug induced calm floats on non-violence.

They stop for a coffee while they recharge before heading back. In the city centre at Cathedral Square in the shadows of the dominating white Vilnius Cathedral is the statue of the founder, a modern statue done in a traditional older style. The granite tall plinth has the ancient crests. The Grand Duke Gediminas stands atop in heavy armour in black iron looking across as if conducting a symphony with a sword for his music to be heard. Behind him in battle attire is a horse that waits for him to ride her.

'According to this brochure,' Lia speaks up. Up until this moment she had been reading the tourist booklet that was given to her. 'This, the plinth was made from Ukrainian granite. It is avoided as people fear that is may be contaminated by radiation from Chernobyl.'

'Actually…' Eddy feels the odd time that he can act like a knowledge know-it-all. 'According to my school days. All granite is radioactive. You can tell Mr Gordon, Lia, that I was listening when he shouted at me for staring out the window.'

Lia looks bewildered, not very impressed, but nudges his shoulder as a sympathetic notification. They walk past the bell tower that the Duke is looking towards with the backdrop from the pillared, dome-topped Vilnius Cathedral, which was once part of the original defensive tower. They carry on to walk around the corner to the National Museum. The large paving slabbed area leads them to the only King of Lithuanian, well a statue in any case. On the seven-hundred-and-fifty-year anniversary of his coronation, on 6 July 1253, the stone statue was erected. Crowned King by Papal Bull.

But just ten years later, himself and his heirs were assassinated to go down, literally, as the only Baltic King. The grey stone throne melts, morphs into his body and hands that give the shape rather than any detail in him, bar his coronation spectre and ball in his hands. His small head on the colossal shoulders are a simple plain design of a long-haired King with a simple winged crown and bearded handsome face looking without emotion, head tilting slightly to his left.

Spreading over the clear skies like a looming spaceship, the grey clouds emerge deeper, greatly darker than an eclipse of the sun slowly sending shadows of shade over the city, casting a net of darkness in daylight. They look up, as everyone around them does with this rapid transformation of conditions. In the distance they see what is coming, the unmistakable veil of rain is heading on its way. No time for cover, faster than the four horsemen, the raid ascends.

The noise on metal is deafening. They see it, but cannot, consequently do not respond quick enough. They run to retreat from the onslaught cowering with shoulders hunched over in a feeble attempt to defend themselves. They are back near the old town when the large droplets start falling amazingly heavier as if made of lead, but as fragile as glass. Their shatter on contact with what they strike below. Lia and Eddy jump in and out of establishments doorways along the path of various selling and trading shops up the main street towards the hostel. There is the point where the shops end, the heavens have really open hells fury, thick, fast and with no mercy everything gets saturated quickly. Across the narrow path is a bar. They skip over.

In that short passage, they are drenched. Saturated to the bone. Salvation within the crowded bar, as the door closes which also gives the end of the day for sightseeing. They order two steins of Svytury, a golden lager that is local. The stein is printed in white capitals on a black banner with the name. Above the name is a tower in a yellow badge, surrounded by hops with an eagle ready to soar above. The white froth is shaving foam thick as it trickles down the chilled thick glass.

Within minutes, two large white plates with large rims hold what they ordered. Eddy was not sure, but Lia found Zeppelin's apt choice of dish considering the cloud formations. She had ordered two. Described on the menu as a traditional Lithuanian dish had Eddy sold.

In these thick potato dumplings are meat-stuffed with a lazy gollop of runny sour cream and bits of crispy bacon. These pieces of bacon are strewn thoughtlessly, as if they were thrown from the other side of the kitchen on their way to the barren wooden dimly lit bar, as if they nearly forgot to add the final ingredient. The surrounding decor is as dark as outside, amplified by the doomsday gloom. Dark, moody paintings adorn the wooden walls that cover the stone walls. Dusty dried wildflowers and hops hang from the ceiling on wooden cradles suspended by black hooks.

The bartender, a middle-aged man with a protruding beer belly, has been scrubbing the same glass since they entered, gazing out of the open door, slowly turning the glass in his hand. Eddy thinks that he can kept rubbing the glass, but a genie is not going to be released to give him three wishes. Despite the God-awful presentation, the food was delicate, light and salivating. The young lady server did amazingly well to seal this traditional dish to make them eat her words. She placed it down and told them it was a good choice, a smile and 'don't be fooled by the look'. She was spot on when she left with a parting remark spoken in an almost Yoda-like sentence, 'Regret it you won't.'

The foreboding sinister clouds that quickly came over with the torrent downpour is quickly leaving like a blanket being dragged over a miniature town by a child on his way to bed. They are halfway through their beers as the blue skies return. The clouds change to whispers of white with grey tainted curves. The last of the rain leaves rainbows in different aspects of the skies, the ground, within the puddles as if trapped there for eternity. The bar does not seem as dark now.

The waitress returns to clear the plates. Her English is splendidly pronounced, although somewhat jumbled up in the order. She pours another two steins without them asking, they were too polite to say no, so they drank them but asked for the bill to stop the flow as well as to serve as a subtle hint. She seems to have nothing to do, so she takes the opportunity to practise her English. She talks about some stories of the city as she sits next to Lia, uninvited, but welcomed. They talk about their journey thus far. For which there were still hoping for a happy ending result. The server gives recommendations of things to see while they stay in her city.

A little tipsy they leave the bar to head to one of the servers' recommendations. The archway is large, narrow and flat. Flowers adorn the three black railed balcony sills with golden highlights, above with the middle one the largest. Three windows of which, again the middle is the largest. In pale blue with white pillars. The triarchy has the all-seeing eye in gold with rays of golden lights. Above this is a tiny bell in a small bell tower where a cross holds the figure of a golden Jesus Christ. The recommendation that they stare upon is the Aušros Vartai, the Gates of Dawn.

This is only one of the town's nine gates still intact. It is tall. Walking through the large arched entrance they feel like midgets. The stone stars lead directly to a chapel over the arch. It is fairly cramped. One of Eastern Europe's leading pilgrimage destinations equipped with its own miracle working icon of the virgin that was stolen from the Crimea by Grand Duke Algirdas. Although they call it a souvenir, with which is posh talk for stolen, nothing more, nothing less.

The other side is not so glamourous. A lot simpler in design. A white thin layer of plaster covers the bricks for which a perfectly cut out rectangle show what it underneath. Above the curved arch of the threshold is a fading painting of Jesus. Round open holes like small wheel-barrow grey tyres with the hub as the hole. Above, along the top is a line of grey decorative, flying mythical grey thin griffins holding a crest with a red background. In a white shape is a man riding a horse, his sword drawn for battle.

They wake early. They take a daytrip out of the city, another of the server's suggestions from yesterday. It is just after five in the morning when they leave the hostel to the groaning protesting of their many dormmates at the earliest of their start, even though they were as quiet as church mice. The alarm, the springs of the bed and the general movement could not be unmistakably avoided. They are at the train station by five-thirty to board the train to Trakai. When they got back to the hostel last night and spoke about this place many people recommended the sight as something they should see, hence the peer pressure won through their doubts.

After a smooth, rhythmic train ride in the silence of the carriage. Fighting the sleep away so they do not miss their stop, they arrive. They walk down a corridor of trees to be confronted by one of the three large unspoiled lakes that comprise Trakai, Bernadinu Lukos. Richly painted colourful small wooden painted buoys bobs on the velvety stroking sensations of the dark blue reflective waters. The landscape that they scan over is picturesque. Immediately they are feeling glee to have taken the advice and come here. They see straight away why tourists and locals alike find this a popular destination.

Being only forty minutes away from the city. It is a world away from the traffic, and pollution filled capital. Rolling hills, spellbound forest where fairy tales come from, lakes of endless possibilities. An orange sign shows the direction to Trakai Castle. On route a brilliantly crafted floating bridge goes towards the castle, across one of the other lakes. It is shaky, but safe, with the stumbling feeling of having frogs' legs to walk instead of the biped's legs. Lia calls it the seasick bridge as she stumbles like a drunk staggering over to the other side.

The smell from the tree's envelopes their senses. They feel like Hansel and Gretel, following the orange breadcrumbs to the castle. They look to the left and stop, well rock. The orange castle reflects in the lake. It is a marvellous view as if it was a model toy. On crossing two better bridges that are foundational sound. The last is wide and the first view was great, this was splendid. Stone borderline bases with red tops, peaked towers and no other people. They are alone. The weather is warm, the skies are cloudy but unthreatening.

A small modest island between the two bridges is guarded by a totem pole with a stern king's head carved as the crowning glory. This was the old capital in 1321, also famous for its presence of Karaites. They did not know either what that meant but the sign stated it so forthrightly that they felt they should have known the meaning. A different sign down the gravelled path gives the answer. Karaites is a faith which combines the bases on the Old Testament with Islamic elements.

They have arrived too early; the fairy-tale castle is not yet open. In the perfect frame of the countryside. It is a nice location. Every photograph comes out great as the subject is outstanding. Plaques are in English everywhere which helps them pass the time with information. The description of everything that is seen is amazingly accurate. They look between the plaque to a sentence of description, back to the plaque and back to the writing. They read everything. They take everything in. After lunchtime tour bus, after tour bus starts to arrive with eager camera toting, snapping, light flashing tourist crashing out and into the castle. They were correct in their choice to come early. This starts getting worse by the minute. People are cambering out; this is their cue to leave. They have had a pleasurable time which was well worth the trip.

Going through the Krarime's old town, a delightful town of small squashed houses with tall peaked roofs in colourful hues. Each one is immaculately designed, detailed and kept. Each one has three windows looking out to the curving street and positioned side on. The crusaders came through here and fought here. History are rooted, deeply in the soil. The Karates are a mix of a Judaic and a Hebrew sect that originated from Baghdad. They adhere to the Torah, rejecting the rabbinic Talmud. They speak the Turkic language, also have preserved their traditions since living here from the fourteenth century.

They come to the isolated forlorn train station. A simple but pretty, green painted and red bordered wooden planked shack with a significant characteristic attractiveness together with unique charming aspects make it noticeable, to catch the eye. It was strange that the modern train would arrive here as if it had gone back in time. Through the trees the light strokes perfect affection on the newly painted vivid colours to shine in the shadows. Rather than wait another two hours for the futuristic train in comparison that they arrived here on; they choose unchartered territory.

They see a timetable for a bus route. They decided to buy tickets for the local bus which was going to be here shortly. That decision was immediately regretted as they hold the brown paper torn tickets in their hand and see the local bus bounce into the potholed area of the, apparent, bus depot behind the train station. Plumes of dirty putrid dark smoke fuse with the gravel decelerating skidding to a halting cloud of smog. They stand gawking, frozen in time. Even the foul-smelling waft does not rustle them.

The door noisily creaks open, resisting the advance. This bus was as old as the shack without the love or respect. They board the shaky, rusty covered dented and scratched covered threadbare bus. Lia points out a piece of string to keep the swinging thin metal door from flying open unannounced. It was a near-death experience. The driver negotiated the other cars on the road which became clearly obvious as to why it was in such a bad state.

He must have been a former stockcar driver. The way he was taking over other vehicles with evident disregard for anyone's safety. He must be reminiscing that past life, reliving those blazing glory days. All the time while his passengers were losing their glory days through stress, fear of losing their lives. The blur outside the window was an endeavour to take their mind off the hellish trip, the countryside view looked wonderful from the pure glimpse. The trip could not have been any more dangerous as if the route had been designed by a terrorist group, and the driver a terrorist radical leader.

Back in Lithuania, they pack their bags. Still shaking. Both unsure if it was for the jerky, lack of suspension bus or the sheer fear. They, well, Lia has decided to go back to Australia. So, really, it could be that apprehension in the wonderment if the correct decision was made, or not. A drink in the bar after their trip confirmed this. It was a slow discussion while sucking a few beers. In the chill which Eddy felt and Lia seemed oblivious to, she rang from an exposed telephone box in the elements of the Lithuanian surrounding environments.

Contained in that long telephone call, Lia discusses the options to her family. It is all one-sided as Eddy hears the emotion, but does not feel the connection. They decide that she will pick their stuff up later. When they return, shortly. As she relayed the conversation to Eddy, she was not sure how short, or when exactly the return would be. She was still hurt by her father's words.

The journey back, although the time passes pleasantly, even though they may have done very little, but think, talk, they were not bored. They spoke of the trip, the trip before Latvia. The babushkas came up often. The variety of what they sold from pickled raspberries to home-smoked and probably caught fish. Pancakes with goats' cheese and many other home-cooked products. And the smell. Ohh, the heavenly smell. They wished some of that food, friendly old faces were the air attendants on this plane journey back to Australia.

Home, but Far, Far from Home

The first week back in Australia was busy. They felt like they were starting from scratch. After months in each other's pockets they seemed to be spending less and less time with each other. Things became the norm quickly. Getting back into the same-old routine, blinkers on to what happened in Latvia. They were meeting people. They have had no time to really talk since the aeroplane. Or did they purposely try to avoid the harsh questions?

Eddy did sense that Lia wanted to say something. He sensed that she was keeping something from him. She was finding the words hard to deal with, to take care of. An unescapable feeling of an undertow dragging her down above the rippling surface that was having to cover it all up. Eddy did not want to force the subject, as if that alone would be the driving force to hammer the nails in the coffin called love.

Alas, it came at the most inopportune time. They were in dire need of food shopping.

It was the beginning of July in Sydney with the weather warmer than average. They got a run in together. Everything was normal. They headed to the supermarket. They were not alone, it was packed. They were in two minds whether to turn around but, well, after all they were here so, why not. They head inside the claustrophobic overheated store of angry consumers. They were quick. They got what they needed without missing anything, but they really did not want to have to spend any more time in the hot, overbearing, baby-crying, loud, trolley-raged shoppers within the store. They were in, they were out, in just under an hour.

They were making their way back to the car, across the parking lot with the trolley that wanted to go in any direction but forward. They were talking about nothing, while Eddy wrestled with the wonky wheels of the trolley that he seemed to always get when he came here. He got there and placed the purchased items in the boot of their dusty, dark-blue car. The boot shut with an echo around the cemented underground parking space.

'Ya lyublui vas,' Lia said as she delicately placed a kiss on Eddy's cheek.

'I love you too,' Eddy returned the words with meaning and a kiss of his own on her forehead.

The language people speak has a relation to the language people think. So, just maybe that is why the language of the males and females differ. More to the very point this is why the language of love is vastly different between each gender, heck each person. It is so much bigger than the four-letter word it represents. Although the word was spoken. It seemed just a word, without the real meaning.

'He didn't like that you called him after my mother and not by my name. A name he gave her, a name that should, a name to be used,' Lia spoke as the door slammed shut. Out of the blue, she instantly rued her decision to come up over the surface, to say her worries. Eddy unlatched his fastened seatbelt to turn to her.

'Who's he?' Eddy enquires, confused. Then, lightbulb. The bulb did not go on in the conventional sense, but shattered as if struck by a poisoned arrow.

'Father. Gustav. He wanted you to call me by my name.' She was out now, no point burying her head underneath for a second time.

'What? Where did this come from? Why now do you, do you drop this bombshell?'

'Not a bombshell,' she defended, yet this was escalating fast into an argument.

'It is. He did not like me?'

'He, well, he did not say that.'

'WHAT? He. I bloody knew it. I KNEW it!'

'Look, Eddy, this started the argument with my father. He said he did not like you calling me Laima. He thought it disrespectful. He felt you did not, didn't respect me. I see that look. You do. I know that. I defended it. Protected you. The accusation. At the end of the day, I asked you to call me Lai, Lia. Why are we yelling at each other?'

'We AREN'T! ARE WE?' He contradicted himself as he could not help but speak by shouting.

'OK THEN, why are we having this loud listening session?'

'OK. Yes. We may be. But you just said your father didn't like me. That it caused the argument that ended the relationship between you. And you then say it is not a bombshell. Come on, Lia. COME. ON.'

'Look. I said he was wrong.'

They were stuck in time, going around the same argument when a car from behind beeped to let them know to move. They waved an apology and the conversation, argument was not forgotten but left alone. They got a wave from the other car that was heavily laced in frustration as they reversed to make way.

Unable to drop the subject, Eddy immediately finds a place to pull over. Since arriving back, Lia has been submerged in finding out more about her motherland, before and during the war. Not so much after. It was British author Ethel Snowden who coined the expression The Iron Curtain. Lia had spent many nights talking to Eddy about what she was learning, in turn he was learning too. Nothing was mentioned on the more meaningful deeper level in which was the subject that they should have been studying. In Ethel Snowden's book, *Through Bolshevik Russia*, she spoke about the communism under the Bolshevik regime, as well as the geographical border. However, she is not credited for the reference today. It is no other than Joseph Goebbels. He used it in his journal at the end of the Nazi regime in Germany.

The Nazi Minister of Finance, Lutz Graf Schwerin Von Krosigir, used it in a radio broadcast arguing that the Soviet Army was occupying one country after another in order to commit war crimes without anyone outside the iron curtain seeing. Eddy's commit of 'cloak and dagger' was returned with an unamused look, he then continued, foolishly, 'not to call the kettle black?'

443

When Goebbels used it, he was not the Minister of Propaganda, but in charge of theatres and culture. He used it to describe the events behind the scene not visible by the audience, hence cut off from observations. The geographical iron curtain was the boundary that divided Europe politically and military at the end of World War Two until the end of the Cold War. The Iron curtain was officially lifted on the 27th June 1989. If only Lia's mother had waited a few more years, maybe, just maybe, that lifting would have resulted in a change for the better, for the positive. Although it would not have led Lia to Eddy. Eddy was now inside Lia's Iron Curtain. This was cruelly rewarding, but necessary justified and had to happen.

On each of the telephone conversations that Lia and her mother used to have, she never regretted her heart retching decision to let her baby go. She firmly believes to believe. Refuses to refuse that she did not make the correct move for the love of her daughter. Accepting that she did right. She would not have done anything different. She did it through love, for love. After the heart-to-heart in the car, things were aired but nothing was aired out.

Lia was back working for the same Russian company, as ironic as it seemed. Lia's mother strove to move her from Stalin's policies to gain a better way of life in Australia, but it would seem her love of her land was strong, as she found herself working in her native tongue. Nevertheless, when the Soviet Union fell apart, she was offered a job straight out of college, with no experience. It was strange, but did not seem it. The Australian company got brought out by the Russians who recognised the business opportunities in Russia, but by predominantly working outside of Russia the stigma was diluted.

The company wanted to build a bridge between the two very different countries with different cultures. They needed a young someone who understood the culture, the traditions, not just speak the language. Without knowing it she was being groomed. She was being watched in her education. She was being motioned in her progression that was just right. She was being motioned into her decision; her correct choices were made before she knew that she was making them. Russia was looking to boost the economy. Business practises in the former Communist state scared investment away. That, with the global recession, made this prospect built on shaky, unstable ground.

Lia started with the firm in 1999, on her twentieth birthday. Ten years later, a report, which was conveniently leaked onto the Internet, ranked the countries on their attributes towards foreign investment. The report ranked the Russian Federation one-hundred and twentieth in the World. With no pun intended, Russia struck when the iron was not only hot, but scorching, they attacked. They bought out the Australian company. When the stock market was high, they bought. Yet they did not see the high cost, they saw only the highs that it would ultimately encounter. Murmurs around the watercooler suggested the former Australian company was a smoke screen and nothing more than a name. A pretty logo as mirrors.

With all this confusion and hearsay, Lia took it day by day, stride by stride. To her it was just idle gossip. She did not feel that she had to keep looking over her shoulder for the sacking blow of the knife in her back. She listened. It was hard not to. She did not let the gossip control her feelings. Lia found the opportunity exciting. She continued to graft. To work hard. Harder than most who had resigned to the fact that it was for nothing. Slowly she moved up the ladder. Carefully trying not to upset no-one on each run on her route to the top. Although this was an impossible dream as someone, somewhere, felt that they should have got promoted ahead of her.

Lia had stopped talking about work. Eddy was baffled at her change of direction in the conversations. It was as if each scene had a different dialogue which did not flow. The journey to, the shopping, the car park, the lay-by and now the drive home. It was as if a word salad of sorts was trying to arrange each part of the dish in order, in her mind into neat little rows.

Back at home, the shopping was being put away with the radio softly singing a story about how great life is. Meanwhile, the kettle boiled, and the Single Origin roasted coffee was placed in the percolator. After four minutes, it was plunged and ready. Just in time, with the clearing up being finished. Lia poured two cups of black, dark coffee with citrus undertones as Eddy took the rubbish out to the bin outside.

They returned and sat on the back stone steps looking out to the wooden stained bright orange fence in the chill of the winter sun. Impromptu, nevertheless given the theme of the day this did not shock or surprise Eddy. Lia started opening her locked chest of memories. Floating fiercely to the surface, each bursting bubble was a revelation. Eddy nearly dropped his brown clay cup in his softly gripped hands. It was hard for Eddy to see the images she was portraying after seeing Latvia just over a week earlier. It was harder for Lia to speak of the visions that she was painting in front of Eddy's eyes. Reasonably, this did devastate and awe Eddy's listening ears.

Like most what was being considered the outside world, Eddy had seen photographs. He had been in the Baltic states and seen different photographs. A different point of view, of opinion. He was so confused to what was true. What was real, what was propaganda. Hearing Lia speak in her disconnected demeanour it was apparent to Eddy that what she was speaking was the truth.

Lia spoke of her mother.

Lia spoke of her family, minus her father.

Not one word about her father.

Lia spoke the truth.

She made a vision of her mother in a pair of brown woollen gloved hands, that enveloped her younger own black woollen gloves, which transferred a loving warmth through. Lia was back there, in that contained memory as if it was happening all over again, presently right within that very moment. They queued in the cold, barely daylight streets with other people looking glum, cold. The snow reflected a sparkle of the sun, appearing in the dark blue hue of the skies. The beautiful sunrise was seen.

But no-one in the shivering queue registered the beauty of nature. The people stood huddled in their thick coats, over many layers, but still shivered. Matted scarfs around the necks looking down at the ground. Cold. Hungry. The dirty brown sludge of melted snow and ice. These people were literally grounded by the weight of desperate poverty. Every day they would queue. In the same queue. The queues that seemed to be longer every day. Day by day. Queuing for the daily basics. Sometimes they left empty handed after spending a day freezing themselves to the bone. Pleasantries in this unpleasant world are no longer something that happens.

Barely is a Good Morning uttered, nothing else spoken, they grunt an acknowledgement of recognition at one another. Lia, Mother and Child would walk the twenty-five minutes, briskly trying not to slip on the black mirror-evil ice. They would join the back of the queue and wait, moving as slow as ice. The waiting was the hardest part as they did not know what would be left on the shelves, if anything. When they got to the front it was a risky endeavour of the luck of the draw. Occasionally, they used to walk around to find a shorter queue. This, they quickly realised was nothing more than an urban legend, a mythical unicorn.

From that point after, the fruition was that they would join the same queue, at the same time, every single day with the same hope. The penguin-shuffling queue would come a result. This particular memory they get to the head of the queue and are allowed in. On the wooden shelves, empty produce were displayed as a couple of tins alone, until they walked in. They seized them, leaving the shelves bare of necessities. Lia got given a brown card booklet of paper to pass over the counter. In return the sour faced elderly trembling lady that had wrinkles on wrinkles, with more lines showing the hardships of life, struggles that are etched and scribbled inside and on the face like a readable book, she would scrawl a tick, initial and pass back over the brown card.

From behind, they turned and grabbed a crusty loaf of bread before handling the book, worn at the edges. Passing the bread over the dirty, smeared glass countertop. A store that was once held up in pride of being kept clean and tidy was a shadow of itself. Book in pocket, tins in hands and bread cradled in their arms. A successful journey today as they enter back into the cold, from the cold.

Back on the streets, teenagers, children, some so very young. Too young, as they should not be reduced to this, they scour the streets as they search for jobs like rats searching for food. It is sad. They have dropped into desperation. They are doing things that they should not do to stay alive. They have joined gangs who promise them an escape from this life. They believe in the strength of numbers. They are fearful, breeding fear to hide from their own fear. They dive into bins, legs dangling as they hunt a present-day exploration for the treasure of food.

Others are coming back from cleaning jobs. Dirty, smudged black faces, necks, hands and legs marching in a line of children that are lucky, yes lucky to have a job to come back from. Empty eyes peering into where a soul once was. The smell comes first, then the echo sound of the padding of bare broken feet on the stone pavements. Clothes hanging, rather than fitting them. They were living shadows, walking like zombies, in heavy contrast to the white snow, comparable to their spirits. After long hours in the mines or in dusty warehouses, which they were told, which they did not care and too tired to disbelieve was simply for—The Effort.

Lia took the card in an unconscious protective impulse. She held the brown card tightly in her fingertips as if it was a golden ticket, slightly embedding a crease in the top left corner. Tomorrow this same piece of paper could get them not only bread, but also knobs of butter. Feeling rewarded as they walk back, they look out for the children of this damned, cursed epoch. Temptation makes a thief; desperation makes people act out of character. They were wary of everyone, even family. They cradle, while shielding their bounty. Lia's mum would always whisper the same sentiments.

'We are lucky to get this much. We have to thank God for that.' Lia hears her mother's voice as if she is next to her, whispering directly into her ear.

An accordion, from the trembling cold fragile hands of an ageing lady, with a strong purposeful touch plays down the crumbling street of rundown houses. An old man joins in on his scratched viola. A stray dog, nothing more than a panting weary bag of bones. In former times an unlikely couple, but in these times, nothing was impossible. They do, in essence, share a common goal, a hope for any scraps. The dog has taken residence in her open case behind her, in the worn stained dark blue felt protective lining. A lone song in the lone breeze. She hears it now, as if someone is playing it in front of her.

The memory ended without an ending as Lia trailed off into her own reminiscences. A half smile on her lips. A tear in her eye. Brimming with a sadness of loneliness.

Then the real bolt from the blue collided with their worlds. It was suspected, yet not wanting to give air to it being considered. Let alone believe that it could actually happen. The truth lay discrete, ready to attach and be relinquished to create complete annihilation. Lia had made no secret of her desire to return to Latvia. Recently, she had spoken honestly and openly to Eddy about this yearning.

Up till now, Eddy thought it was just that, a yearn, a want, not, he thought, a calling to perform as well as achieve. Nevertheless, to want to go back soon, maybe next week. As soon as that, without him, well that left a crater in his soul that was more than collateral damage. Could anything fill in the void that would be left behind?

She always said to him that half her heart was left behind when she left the first time, now most of it has been left there. She would never feel completely loved if her heart is incomplete. Eddy would never, never stop her from leaving, from going back.

Unknowingly to Eddy, she put in a transfer at work. She trusted Eddy completely, except she was unsure whether to mention this. She could not fully explain enough to tell him. One sunny winter's day she got offered a transfer to Latvia, particularly Riga. She did not have time to think. More to the point, she did not want time to think.

'Yes! Oh my God! Yes!' she blurted it out to her senior manager, without consultation, without even thinking about Eddy's feelings. She felt 'no' was not in her vocabulary. She wanted this. The yes was doubted with guilt. Lia's secret was ready to be revealed, hence needed to be acknowledged. The yearn was being itched, answered.

That evening they talked about it together. She had not let slip that she had accepted the role. She tried to let him feel that the decision was made together. Unknowing the real truth he was happy for her to pursue her ideology if it meant she would be completely loved. When all was said and done Eddy was a romantic. He wanted not to be loved, but feel loved. Everything else could drift by. That was what he cared for more. That was, he felt, his true meaning in life. To help people be loved so he could feel loved.

Lia wanted to learn about her country while being in her country. She wanted, she longed for her heart to be complete. But, nevertheless, she was confused. She wanted the truth. She had heard her mother's side, the medias view from a heavily western perspective, with the same being said for the historians. She wanted to make her own mind up of what the truth could be. Nevertheless, she wanted to learn from the same words, her native words, while reading on the same soil where it happened. Surely the truth must be embedded in the lines of the soils. Yet, she may never find the truth, the full unconditioned truth anyway. This she accepts, but to get close. Even to get close would be enough. That thought alone brought a smile on top of her smile, to her lips.

The Nazi point of view, with regards to the signing of the Molotov-Ribbentrop Pact was significant then, as it is now. With over eighty years that the Pact which triggered World War Two has passed. Hence the domino effect of detrimental apocalyptic catastrophic proportions. The Pact, that led to the occupation of Poland, then the Baltic States was biased to Western Culture. Lia sought to prove, or to disprove this theory. This historical event. Lia believes the media overlooked the small detail with the Soviet Union's role with its leader Joseph Stalin running the show. Although the Nazi and the Soviet Union wanted different things, different ideologies which caused a conflict. The Soviet Union wanted communism. Through war and violence, death and greed they, together dragged Latvia, and consequently the world into war.

Under the noses of the world, Lia sees the communist ideology is coming back. In an attempt to restore the Union, the Soviet Union glory, elements of Nazism and Russian Czarist Imperialism is growing in the human blood enriched soils. One goal. One dream is used. One ideology. One party. As Lenin famously said, 'The Capitalists will sell us the rope with which we will hang them.'

After all that was said and done, Eddy realises one thing, that he was in a veil of love. That he actually loved Lia, but he was not sure if it was because of her history. He had to ask himself a question, what had he learned in over thirty years of living? When he compared it to the life that Lia had had, is having, his was a page in a book—hers was the whole novel.

Then the flash before his eyes. He had been duped. She had won him over craftier than the slyest fox. He knew that she had already made her mind to go, but wanted the mutual agreement. He let her have it. She knew it too, but also said nothing. Spreading over him was a peculiar feel with apparently no words could explain. A feeling that he had never felt before. Eddy hushed her. A serene unfolded ambience touched them. A calming as silence. A heartfelt embrace. Silent tears.

So, this was the end. She wanted to go alone. She wanted a new chapter for her personal book. She did not want the end, but that was the tearful evening of circumstances that had concluded with the invariable finale. No different passage could get a different ending. This was it, every time. They posed different avenues, they got to the same brick wall ending.

'Do you know…' He sighs over a bottled beer on the pale cream sofa. Lia, who is not a big drinker, is so far from reality that she can barely left her head up, lift her ears to listen. She does not want to speak, but does want to listen.

'Allow me to speak honestly. That, there is some people, in life that you feel a bond with. And…sometimes it's not returned and that's okay. Because…you wanna fix, find, you generally interested in finding who that person is. How they tick? What makes them? Some person, some person you just don't give a shit, but I think that is human. I THINK THAT'S HUMAN! You know, to not care about certain people. But…you care enough to respect them…erm…now.' Eddy sighs again. He knows he is talking to himself, but it feels good to voice his word salad. 'But to actually find out about someone. Find out the layers, you, you don't give a crap about the looks, the appearance, the car, where they live, the money they earn, what they do, what they work, what they were? It's all bullshit. You are generally interested about who that person is. And that is beautiful. It's not returned.'

'It is returned,' Lia stirs a remark. Eddy was not really talking about their relationship, but more a collection of his own mistakes.

'But—'

'You don't think I love you? You don't think that I don't want this to happen?'

'I feel like everyone is looking for something. Some people you will liken to, you just, you just, urgh. I guess it's a form of people. People-ology. That you want a connection. You want…Psychology, people-ology, whatever you want to call it. You want the connection. You want to know what. What makes that person such a…a…bitch, a douchebag, a bully, a nice guy, a funny guy, a person to talk to.'

'Hey, where is this going?'

'It's not about you. Let me finish. But. You only get that by talking to that individual. Go past the conceit, the bravado, the charade, the mask, to use a cliché. But. I am interested in you, Lia. And that's why I want to know. And I can't do it in a non-sexual, creepy I-wanna-make-love-to-you kinda way. I just want to know who you are. Who you were. That is beautiful. I guess… Well, I guess you need to find that too.'

Nothing is said. The sound of the muffled traffic blurs behind them through the frosted window. His mouth moves but he cannot say the words to be freed. Trapped, deep, deeply lodged in her throat. The sound to be released of what she wants to say, and what he wants to say. Sober casts a cloak over her.

She wants to unleash what is in her heart. She wants to be honest. The want to focus on what is going wrong in the relationship that is tearing the love out, leaving nothing, not even friendship. But her voice firstly needs to overcome the obstacles of pain, sadness, disappointment, anger and longing. These are suffocating her. She needs to let them go. He feels what is coming. She needs to let go. They need to let go. He fears the imminent break-up. The ending of the chapter.

I didn't play too much in this scene. I can see the other parts doing it for me through them playing their parts in Lia. It was obvious and profound that Eddy felt something that he had not felt. Never felt anything like this before. It was something that made him. It was not just patience. It was not just love. It was something more. This something made him hold on. Hold on for the ride of his life. Ultimately it was the path of Lia. She, was the one that ended it. Even if, deep down she did not really want to.

Darkness descended. She was, she is his everything, but now nothing. So real but vanishing into the beach cooling breeze like sands across the ocean. She holds her near. Drags a blanket over her shivering shoulders.

He had to push his pride aside, come to terms with the pain. He spoke to mates in a way he had never done before. He was open. He was honest. He was telling them his pain. He was telling them what he was feeling. This was nervous unshaken ground for him, as it was for his mates.

Eddy sits in the departure terminal in Sydney's International Airport. Rustling on the uncomfortable grey steel chair with a thin cushion which questions what the point in it is. They said goodbye. Tears in her eyes as she said so long to her long love. He was in shock. No tears could be shed. He was staring into his minds blank space, with many people rushing around, the noise of children, people, the talon, the announcements but he heard and saw nothing. He stands.

The smell of the nearby café, new plastic and vinyl suitcases whizzing by on small wheels. A person knocks him, right in front of his vision but he did not feel it. He swayed like a buoy, but returned to his zombie state. Many thoughts are entering, re-entering his mind.

He is thinking of the meaning of love. Meaning of life. He is weak, vulnerable and not as strong as he thinks he is.

Sitting in the cold aircon passageway, he doubts his decision. One seed of doubt is blossoming into a tree. He is doubting what he is doing here, when Lia is so close, but travelling so far away. He could change his mind, and buy a ticket. Throw his caution to the wind. To see what could happen. Lia is in the forefront of his mind. He is thinking of her infectious laugh. Her contagious personality which even the darkest corners, areas of the land or in the body would get lit, illuminated, made better for being in contact with her. This was not a feeling, but it actually made it better.

For the first time in a good few minutes, he draws a loud breath in as he takes in his surroundings. He sees smiles, laughter, tears and hears gushes of loved ones saying goodbye, saying hello. Not really knowing if they will see each other again. People around him a-changing. Every smile, every person, sunlit exposing a hidden attractiveness. Sometimes without knowing the beauty is gone. It is never too late to realise, but it seems that Eddy has let her go. The memory will always remain. Eddy mumbles to himself as he somehow finds the strength to wrench his way towards the exit door. He walks in the opposite direction to the doors that Lia walked through. Going in opposite paths. Not for the first time he doubts his actions. No glance back.

'Goodbye. Goodbye. Goodbye, my love,' he mumbles.

Life is that. Life is theirs. Life is to enjoy. Life is sometimes two lives going to two different, but not necessarily better, paths.

'Goodbye. Goodbye. Goodbye, my love,' he repeats.

As he walked out into the open air, a girl gave him a tear and using her index finger placed it in his eye. Eddy did not know her name. Nothing was said to one another. What she did made Eddy smile. What she did made Eddy shed that single tear. She was a stranger. She sensed his turmoil. She patted his shoulder. She reassured him in that simple, fleeting human touch that everything was going to be just fine. Eddy needed, heck, everyone needs a moment like this. The simple act of compassion to tell him that. A soothing connection. A soothing voice to tell him. That it is a beautiful life.

This beautiful ordeal took Eddy a long time to come to terms with. He often contemplated about chasing her. After all it is only natural for a man to pursue a woman. He called her, but it was hard to hang up, as that would mean saying goodbye again. A clean break was needed. It was fair to say that this relation for both of them went above and beyond their own expectations. He said then, he would say later that he would never forget her. He was placed firmly, to remain, as they say, in the friendzone. Her personality affected him profoundly. This made him feel joy. Her love for stopping in midst flow to smell a flower. Lia, although her real name was Sofija, literally made him stop to smell the flowers.

In the darkness, I stand. No-one can see me but my voice echoes around as the triad of love gods discuss the next stage of events. They hover over the vision of Eddy, head in hands, not sure what he is doing, what he has done, what he should be doing.

'So, will you leave him, Himeros?' I ask unannounced, also to break up their idle chatter.

'No. Not yet,' Himeros responds with slight trepidation, an uneasy tremor in his voice that was uncharacteristic for him.

'Good. Good. Make sure you tease him with your hunger, so he keeps feeling the want, to want badly what he can't have.'

'Yes. I will use all my—'

'POWER!'

'No sexual desire to make him wish, know that he made a mistake, but, but will give him nothing to aid his situation. For every time he thinks he can. Anteros will be there, in his thoughts, to show that mutual love is not requited. If it was, she would not have left.'

'I like that,' Eros speaks. The God of Mischievous Love has been causing problems by unleashing his bow of love on couples to make them cheat. Although I cannot get rid of him. As he is the cause of the flame of love in the hearts of the humans as well as the Gods.

'I can help with that, Himeros,' the third and final triad known as Erotes enters the debate. He flutters his wings as he draws closer towards my voice. 'After all, I am the God of sexual longing, I can help.' He bows his head as he knows he has overstepped his jurisdiction.

'Yes. Yes, that. All three can be there for him.'

I laugh as my voice lingers enough to be heard before fading out.

Present Day
You Never Know What You Truly Have...
Then It's Gone

Eddy does not know why he woke up thinking of Lia. To dredge up this bad memory of the split over the many good ones. He went to bed thinking about Beth-Annie, whether he should send that message he had in his drafts. Who's scared of whom? He was scared that he knew what the silence meant. No news was bad news in this case.

Eddy was a guy waiting for execution. He wanted release, to gain a new lease of life. He also wanted her. Maybe these last two memories held more than he would ever put together. They were two different people. Never connected. But... The same, the same burning desire that he wanted it to work. That fuelled his heart. No smoke without desire.

Thirty-Two Years Old
What Just Happened?

Drenched. Pelted by waves. Over. Over again. Each breath. Water follows. Eddy splutters. He rocks. Rolls. He is scared. Out of control. He sees where he was. Now from afar. Tries again. To regain control. Another breath. An involuntary gulp of salty sea water. Compressed under the weight. He is suffocating. Unable to breathe. He is drowning. Where is his anchor? His ship? His safety?

The spray from the stormy wind slaps Eddy around the face with the assistance of each towering wave. He frantically rolls with the storm making the rules. His stomach lost in the air as he plummets down from yet another wave of despair. Swipe. A blow as he hits the bottom of the wave. To be taken up again. On this terrifying life-ending ride.

Moments ago, seconds ago he was sailing the seas of tranquillity. He was at the bow of the ship. He could not see a single ripple on the remarkably flat horizon. The air stroked his skin like a soothing massage. The salt tantalised his mouth, giving him a pleasant accompaniment on his moist lips. The sun, nothing more but a soothing influence to heighten his false feeling of enlightenment.

On the contrary, in a reversal of roles, he is now really drowning. The same sensations are now intense. No question about it, he is struggling to stay afloat in the hostile seas. Struggling for life. Hanging on with all his might, onto a broken plank of wood. The remains of a vast masterpiece. This was part of the bigger thing in front of him. That thing was a ship. A beautiful masterpiece on the ancient oceans, the seven seas. The peaceful sailing of Moses's basket, the belief of eternal bliss, was, perilously floating into the future.

In Noah's Ark, the humanity that was worth saving where invited. Both sexes gave the animal kingdom hope. Thus, re-establishing the breeds. But here, Eddy was. He was cast away. Cast off. Watching the ship of hope sink. He was. He is a survivor. He will hold on. Gripping with white knuckles, sore arms as if his life depended on it. It did. He was not invited to save his own breed. A beast. An oddity.

Around him wreckage was banging, knocking, smashing into him. Attempting to take him out. To end his cursed life.

Let the waves take him. A voice said.

Let the pain stop. Another voice.

Stop the pain.

Stop the hanging on.

Give up.

He did not listen. He did not listen to his voice, in his mind. He wanted to live. Not ready to say goodbye. He gripped tighter to life. Still he is floating, on the relentless topsy-turvy turns of the washing machine. Still floating, to fulfil his soul purpose, to survive. He will never surrender. Parts of the ship remind him of the magnificence of the beauty for which the ship resembled. The loud sound of the wind is unrelenting. What happened? How was he one minute enjoying the ride, to the next second, plummeting, towering, rocking, twisting, turning and striving, to stay alive. Eddy's arms bowed over the slim piece of wreckage to hang on for his life. In part, to the physical being which was the ship in its glory. In part, the conceptual of being part, of, that…glory.

No happy memories remain. It is a simple will to survive. Subconsciously maybe he was always just floating along, alone. A couple, as two united beings.

Crash. Another wave. Gasp. A breath. Wave, goodbye. Crash. No mercy. Just enough time to get enough breath to, crash. Wave. Gasp. Breath. Exertions. Breathe. Effort to live. To not. To die. Eddy grips on to the flimsy resemblance of life. Crash. Wipe out. Not wiped out. Crash.

As if the time were days, the waves appeared to feel like they were becoming less strong. He is getting weaker. Or, is he getting stronger? Surely that is impossible. Improbable, surely, considering how long he has been teetering on the edge of existence. Each wave is, was becoming less frequent. He is getting more tired. Each wave is trying to finish him. He is resilient. He can fully breathe a good salty-water-free breath. The ship is not seen. A crashing wave takes him under.

Suddenly, out of the strength, comes the calm. A calm that Eddy was fearing. Scared as he thought that this would never come. The waves are weaker, less tall, less overpowering. Eddy sees a large, strong, unrelentless wave coming. He finds time to brace the unpreventable impact. Yes, it hurts him, but as he is prepared for each wave, it absorbs the force. The clouds are becoming cream, white to silver. The light is penetrating through. The warmth, coming. The end, near. But, he has survived the tempest.

Breathe in. Breathe out. Take in the pure fresh air. Exhausted yet energetic as life starts anew.

Kymopoleia, the daughter of Poseidon, was losing her strength within her violent storm waves. Aeoulus, the King of the Winds, had locked the storm winds away, back in the hollows of the floating island of Aeolia after I had released them. Eddy was unprepared. I wanted to test him. Kymopoleia's husband, Briareus, God of the Violent Sea Storms, returned to the ocean bed. Penthos remained. Next to Eddy. Tending to Eddy. Specifically to victimise him. He got excited when he cried for loved ones gone. Although he focused on the departed, this level of grief that Eddy was feeling benefitted his desire. Eddy cried. In releasing relief. He could not stop.

Eddy for each wave, a soaking of grief showers saturated him to his inner core. But, amongst the sobbing, the spluttering he is still. Still hanging on to the wreckage. He has generated a want for the wave. It makes him feel. He survives with them. With all the waves that have come, gone, he knows more will follow. These will continue to wash over him, sometimes without warning.

Eddy did not feel that this relationship was on the rocks. She, apparently did. As, as suddenly that the floating, calming sailing was happening, the ship ran aground under tremendous power of the wind, waves. Their relationship broke apart at the seams. However, he snaps. The anchor to which he was tied to. The same anchor of the ship that kept him warm, kept him safe, inspired strength to achieve the impossible. Well, now, Eddy breaks away. Floats aimlessly. Without purpose. Crash. Another wave comes over him. In the largest wave of darkness, a light will find its way through.

Eddy gasps. Pants heavily. Back straight. Doona drenched. Rivers of sweat. Beads of hot dampness perspires over him. Falls in big, heavy drops from his brow. The soaked grey singlet clings to him like a second skin. He is woken as he floats. A dream. Was it? Yes, it was, just a dream? How real it felt.

What just happened? To regain a relationship, you must keep the couple in the ship. The moment Eddy was looking at the ship. He was looking at a relationship, rather than being in a relationship. But, who was he thinking off? He was floating in the end. He was inescapable with no way to minimise the damage that was being done. In the darkness, shadows of the past are evil ghosts imitating lost loves. He did not know who he was thinking off. As clear as a bell when he woke, quickly the memory of the storm evaporates into the air around him, unseen. Lost souls, lost relationships.

Eddy looks at his arm. At the scars. A sign of life lived. They have healed. A reminder remains. Scars are ugly. Nevertheless, each scar hides a story. Each scar holds a memory. Each scar serves a purpose. We are born pure but always leave with scars. We all have broken pieces around us, he is now beginning to understand why. Why he needs to hold onto some pieces, let go of others and burn the rest.

A wave of relief takes his breath away. He did not see that one coming. Under the weight he is suffocating, once again. An invisible anchor ties him to the resemblance of the ship, a lost love, a love lost. He cries in the darkness. Each moment he gets further from the shipwreck. He is still tied to her. Who is her? Irregular waves. He was drowning. He did not let it take him. The oceans of despair, did not, will not take him under.

When he thinks of the shipwreck. His last memories, he sees the ship, floating, sailing. He sees him, happy, a complete piece, on the bow. Eddy cannot help thinking. With a strain, with a whispering quiver in his voice, he speaks out into the darkness, 'What just happened?'

The Hardest Part of Life
Last Year

Eddy smiles at his life. Standing in his rolled-up sleeves of his chef whites looking out over the pass to the unmanned restaurant. Behind him, the sound of boiling sauces with steam bellowing out from the various sized pots escaping clouds of smells. In his profession, most would not know what it is actually like to make a living, working in a kitchen as a professional chef. He is probably arrogant, like most chefs, in this belief. He feels he is superhuman with most not being able to do his job day in, day out. Purely because from the apprentice days he is told that asking for help is a weakness. So, he does not teach anyone his job fully.

Nevertheless, not immortal in a holier-than-thou kinda way, but more for the people who host a dinner party every blue moon to think that they can run a restaurant themselves. The truth is to be a chef, to make it as a chef, you need to find these unknown quantities of a bottomless vault to draw physical and mental strength when you think you have none left. It consumes the world that he lives in. It is not the hours themselves that is the problem. It is the unsociable nature of those hours. Chefs have a unique oxymoron. They are experts in prioritising at work; outside, they are as effective as a new-born baby.

From the humblest beginnings over breakfast. That the short walk rises the superiority that gives the willingness to overpower every single obstacle to conquer every single day a fresh. The never-say-die to get the living shit emotionally beaten out of him, daily. To get the opportunity to handle the raw, fresh produce to create a beautiful creation of art. For which in minutes will be demolished by a guest, but essentially enjoyed all the same. To express himself daily, he is lucky, very lucky to be doing a job he enjoys.

To learn early in his career that weekends, public holidays are a distant dream, which the ordinary folk enjoy. The days that they enjoy are days that he will work. A day off is a Monday where no-one goes out, but on the plus side, everything is open. Where you catch up on personal chores, taking care of oneself. The standard working week for most can fit into two days for a chef at the peak time. In the silly season. Most of this time is standing, where the only seat is when you drop the kids off at the pool.

The brigade of the kitchen is an unbreakable bond of trust, brutal honesty, unflattering reliance and comradery of bad, off colour, black, dark jokes. Sometimes sick jokes. They never apologise for their jokes. Jokes are with the soul understanding that they do not mean what they say, most of the time. It is a way to get through the long day. The faith that Eddy puts in the people around him to do their job is indomitable. Unspoken assurance with more than a hint of loyalty. A brigade will never sink. If one person falls, another will bring that person up, they start as a team, they leave as a team, their own their own mistakes, their celebrate their successes as a team, there are one team.

Mentally is strengthened by the front of house's lack of ability to write a chit, to order a correct meal, to not say no, but to say yes to any guest on every whim. Eddy, of course, is accommodating like the rest of his team to requests, but some just make his blood boil underneath, which occasional comes out in spitting words of fury. He wonders if people are given a menu, or a blank sheet of paper.

Close calls with knifes do not phase Eddy. Burns are daily. Nicks are the territory. He tests the limits of his physical body. When he clutches a hot pan, when a dry cloth is not to be found. He grabs instinctively to save the food. Ignoring the searing heat that scorches the bare palms of his hands. Safely at the destination, he deposits the food on a silver salver, lined with a disposable paper towel. To drain the oil and bring the food to the pass for plating before the food is beyond cooked and overdone, rendering it unservable. Pain forgotten as he starts the next part of the table.

Physically, his agility of a mountain goat on the sloping tiled floors that lean towards the drainage points to give him wickedly cut defining calves. He moves, pivots, stops, jumps, twists, dips and turns around the kitchen avoiding the other chefs that do the same. Lifting from the ovens, sliding over the stoves, checking the sous-vide temperatures. To avoid the overeager kitchen hand that moves on a personal mission with stacks of toppling plates. The sound of the sizzling meats on the coal-fired chargrill. Bubbling oil. Overspilling water that splashes on the backs of the hot metal tops. The cluttering of cutlery being washed for the next service. The sounds of the single words of the range, the narrow passageway.

Not one person will upset the tottering, shaky balance of a kitchen's rhythm. Chefs know teamwork. Eddy knows what the people around him do for him. Like a marriage, a lover's tiff will happen occasionally. The truth is that it is spoken, yelled or screamed out, but, the golden rule is to never leave an argument open. Always close it off before the shift ends. Sometimes to start a new. No argument is laid to rest until it is settled.

From the chirping calls of the first docket just after midday, the melody that becomes the foreground music for the next few hours. Near the end the cleaning begins. The blue flames of the gas lights and dulled to their pilots. Ordering lists are written. Mise-en-Place lists are organised. At the end, they finally clean everything. Everything is taken apart. Chefs balance on hot stoves to clean the walls. Showering in soap suds that run down their arms. Chefs move the equipment to get behind. Everything is cleaned again for a new day.

Adapting to the guests is amazing to negotiate in the split seconds of time. Each chef in the kitchen, each kitchenhand has a piece of their heart on each dish. Eddy may serve hundreds of dishes a day but one mistake, one complaint is something he beats himself up over. He strives to grow, improve, always do better by never accepting the mediocre. One mistake is analysed to what he can improve on. He will return on. Do better. Never to make the same mistake again.

In love, Eddy does the same. Eddy takes everything personally. He takes the stress out of a day by blowing the froth of a few from another bar, a different bar each day. This is ultimately followed by bad decisions. But, when all is said and done, what other job can you express creativity daily. What other job can you do something different with the same results. Eddy gets excited by new ingredients, new suppliers offering new products. Alas is the heat of battle surrounded by noise. Feeling the surge of adrenaline. Having a laugh with the brigade one minute, to wanting to rip their necks off to shit down their necks the next.

A chef's life is not easy. Depression. Alcohol. Drugs. Caffeine. Chefs will fall into one of these addictions. The hours. Poor pay. Heat. Ridicule. Frustrations. Sleep deprived. Chefs will endure this and more. They do have the ability to express a meal, dish that they are proud to serve.

Eddy smiles at his life but is not sure if it is what he wants it to be.

Eddy is getting tired to pick himself up daily, hourly. He feels more and more like he is on trial. Publicly executed. Physically exposed. Mentally and psychologically tested. Eddy feels left to hang. To slowly die. The vultures circle overhead. They wait to peck out the shattered, tired, spent worn-out decomposed eyes of him as he stares vacantly over the dazzling, shining pass with the lights reflecting from the streetlights. The lights off as a battle ends. A new one begins tomorrow. He nurses a heavy head. He made an understandable bad decision last night. He turned up with a foggy, dusty mind that ached. He put on a face of being clean, fresh with clear resolution of mind to work organised. Now, at the end of the day he is beaten. He is weary. He mocks a wry smile but is wondering if his life is what it was all cracked up to be.

For a while he has been trying to focus on himself. He is not going to get frustrated by people around him. These people tell him how to run his kitchen. They arrive late, they leave early, they do not pull their own sleeves up to do work, but point fingers for everyone else.

Fingers and words laced with blame. He leads by example with good old-fashioned elbow grease to get the work done. To gain a respect within his team so that the example is made, the par level, the benchmark is clear. If he will do it, everyone else will. It is in the dim amber glow that he realises that ultimately the only battle that eventually can be won, is the one with himself.

Today, a new day he builds a wall up. He encourages the brigade to joke, talk about the life in Sydney, the world, the rich and the famous but he does not get involved. He is constantly plugged into work. Even if he is not there, his mind is. He thinks works. Dreams work. Will die for work.

He was constantly tired, but today he feels exhausted. A lot more drained than normal. The fuel of coffee was not restoring his vital get-up-and-go. He was trying to fall out of the idea of falling in love. For some reason, this was on his mind. He was working on autopilot in work. Outside of work he was in his head. On a collision course with himself, to destroy himself.

Then just when Eddy was ready to completely lose sight of one of the most important things in life, he got reluctantly dragged out of the dark, ebbing, flowing waves of work. He was not only spending a great deal of time either at work, thinking of work, he was drowning in it. He was consumed by the nature that started to control him. He was depressed. He did not know it. Did not want to recognise it.

He found himself looking up the number for help. This was a motion that surprised him. He was looking at the number on his mobile phone for Lifeline.

'Imagine if a customer wanted John Dory?' His sous chef spoke out of the blue. He was demonstrating a flimsily constructed argument to illustrate his self-destructive pitfalls. 'But,' he continues, 'you told her to order the Cape Grim scotch fillet. What will she be?'

'What are you talking about?' Eddy agitatedly snaps. 'If there is a point? What are you talking about, you shit?'

'Listen. Wait. Think. What would you feel?'

'Okay mate. I will entertain your…fantasy. Tell me what you are getting at?'

'Think. It is frustrating.'

'You are going the right way to get a punch, chef mate.'

'Chef. Look, someone wants something. You are offering something completely different. You want something but are doing something completely different.'

'Who? What? Come on, mate. Fuck off the cryptic shit!'

'If you do not stop letting work consume you, soon you will be lost. The moment you are there, there is no turning back. You are becoming an island. You need something more than work.'

'You…you are impossible.'

'Impossibly right?' He winks as he returns to the blue chopping board to prepare the cooled, cooked Eastern Rock lobsters for lunch.

He slides his mobile phone back in his pocket and returns to his own preparations for service, yet still in silence. His mind thinking of life, rather than death.

Eddy had been flirting with a new waitress. He did not want anything to happen, as this would be the proof that his own relationship had ended. A bad decision, a kiss had given her hope. A flame the size of the smallest lighter was wavering in the strongest gale. A light of hope. He knew that he would not take it any further.

'Forget about her.' He speaks as he returns to pick up his rosewood handled cooks knife as if reading her thoughts as his. Trying to turn Eddy's mindset around, his own mind was having a conversation of its own.

A good hour had passed, and his sous chef was back with a change of tact. A brutally honest, 'do or die' lack of sensitivity. He went for the throat. Harsh. But very fair. Eddy was seeing that he had slipped off the mark. His work was consuming him. He was focussed on work and exercise. He wanted to exhaust himself from thinking so he could fall asleep at night in a heap. He thought of work, before work, during work and after work. He was not ready to let Beth-Annie go. To let her leave her mind. He needed to break the cycle. He was not happy. Not even remotely close to being happy.

It is the sad realisation when Eddy feels lost. He feels abandoned, by no-one in particular. He looks around at couples sharing tender moments and thinks what has he done wrong. Like a book being dropped from the tallest skyscraper that surrounds him, it dawns on him. He has brought it on himself. He has been career focus. Simple. Anything that has been an obstacle where his focus could be distracted, he has dismissed it and left it on the wayside.

He has had opportunities. He has had time when he imagined a life with a person for that which has made him act in idiotic irrational ways. That should be the no judgement stage of a relationship, but it has been the pivotable stage. As he stands looking up at the fast-moving white clouds through the restaurant windows, those stages have ended in the pressure being too high for the said potential love which has ended with him here, almost alone.

He has been guilty of saying things for a reaction. Whether it is to see if he is being heard or just to know that what he has done has had that desired effect. With the essence of silence without any retort, it needles him sharply within his skin. Slowly, painfully burrowing a seed of doubt that leads to the mind. He has a career. A strong career but at what cost? It feels a Pyrrhic Victory, as he has no one to share these accolades with. His rewards. His trophies. Lie in the blackest, recesses of his bedroom bottom drawer. Generating dust.

In time for service, he is back. Game face on. Back in the game. It is a hot bright day where the ray's stream in from the large open skylight offering a slight natural breeze to the heat of the busy kitchen. It is a busy service. He is working hard, sweating harder and getting the work done effectively with a great sense of pride and achievement in every food that leaves the pass. He is not running one-hundred percent, he feels his mind is away. Is this really what he wants, knows he has it.

He is moving the mountain of work with a teaspoon, in an organised, ethical way. No-one can ever question his passion, his work ethic his love of what he does. The produce that comes in fresh from the market. He is encouraged by hearing the story of the farm, field, orchard to be grown for the table. He respects the commodity as it has been treated with respect and a living being has died to create a love outside of death.

The kitchen is a well-oiled machine where chefs dance around each other with a mutterings of 'behind', 'backs', 'corner' while Eddy shouts 'six minutes on table four and fifty-five. Follow that in two minutes with table eleven'. In unison, the loud clear response of 'Oui Chef' comes back from every station within the brigade. He has generated a respectful aura of mutual appreciation for the long-standing hours that these chefs do for him.

It is hard, hot, heavy work with a lot of stress. Whereas most jobs are physically or mentally draining. Being a head chef has the opportune luck of being both, simultaneously. The sad news is the only sit down these chefs get from the minute they wake up to when they go back to that, sometimes different bed, is when they snatch a few minutes to sit on an upturned milkcrate in the corner of the kitchen while hurriedly eating a leftover or mistake from a stainless-steel bowl.

Each dish that get presented onto the pass goes under intense scrutiny. Each brigade brings a different element and then the scurry back when Eddy gives a slight nod of his head. A dish has the great ability to evoke a childhood memory by the appearance, the smell, the taste or texture. For him the smell of ripening rock melons take him back to his grandfather's apartment in France, specifically the larder but that smell of the warm melon sparks a lightning bolt of triggered electric memories that do nothing but bring a smile, an occasional tear and a privileged tug at his heartstrings.

It takes a different character. He must be confrontational at times, brutally honest whereas some would deem him rude. That in-tray of dockets needs to be done in an organised, precise and precision timed manner. Nothing can wait until tomorrow, or later. An error from a single person backs the whole brigade up. He tries to nurture that mistake by the individual. Although he prefers a customer waiting an extra few minutes to get the right food than mediocre food leaving the pass. What they put towards a dish is personal. A piece of their heart goes on every single dish. A negative response is hard to take, but must be taken constructively. It is a personal attack, no doubt what people say.

Nevertheless, that individual must learn, has to bounce back, try and conquer the next thing he is doing. With the mistakes comes education. An error is the greatest way to learn. Eddy uses mistakes as a tool to coach, to teach and to inspire all the chefs around him to grow together, as a team. He has been there. He knows exactly what it is like to be constantly kicked in the guts. He does not do those tactics but uses them to improve the skills of the chefs as a team, never highlighting the wrong in an individual. Of course, they know who it is aimed at.

Chefs are not idiots. But a moral unspoken code is to give banter, to give a joke but when the doors open, game face is firmly on. It stays on. It does, never leaves, until the doors are shut. Then through the clean down is discussions about service. No one leaves mad. No one leaves without saying what is on their mind. For tomorrow starts a new. A clean slate is started.

Undercurrents of moans and groans are heard as they change as a team. They have finished as a team. Volcanic bursts of anger are the musical accomplishment. Some chefs turn up tired, after a night out with a hangover which would cripple most, but they fight through it without signs of a struggle.

He waits until the team has gone. He is the last one to go. He ghosts around the kitchen, making sure everything is off that should be off. Everything is clean. Refrigerators and freezers are shut. Temperatures are recorded. Gas is off. Lights off.

As one day ends, and he changes to walk home, thinking of work, dropping into a random bar to think some more about if everything is done. He thinks of specials. If everything is ordered. What needs to be done in the next few hours. What his team around him need to do.

It is a dark period as he lifts his heavy head up from the bar counter. The sun is shining outside, through the grimy windows cast a shadow over him. Lately Eddy has felt like he has been trying to not crack the shattered remains of the eggshells underneath his feet as he traces his previous steps around the kitchen, the office. He is doing his job under pressure.

He, though, has had enough.

He wants a job that he can get a life to work balance better. In his mind, he has written the resignation many times. In his office a well contrived resignation letter is wrote and worked on.

The line chef's resignation is bizarrely fitting. In the kitchen they tend to shout 'fuck' a hell of a lot, whilst throwing things around. Or, they just never turn up again.

Eddy is ready to quit. But not like that. He is shouting in his head, that echoes around getting louder. He is ready to return to the butcher's shop. The perfect circle. An easier way of life and leave everything that he has struggled, fought and died many times for. He wants to focus on his relationship. He will take a step down from his career, money and success that he has fought to achieve.

His relationships have always taken a back step, a back seat. He needs to apply the same passion to his work that he does outside. It dawned on him as he walked to work after barely five hours sleep. He is struggling. He is struggling to live. To want to live. He is working his way to a lonely grave, where no-on will be mourning him, probably as his mates are chefs and will be more-than-likely working. His sous chef tells him that he should put on his tombstone; 'Here lies blah blah blah…he always knew where a stack of clean T-towels was hidden.'

After no sleep and a fair amount of alcohol, he returns. After a long discussion with the owner trying to persuade him to stay, he reluctantly accepts his resignation. He retorts with when does a dream become an obsession? Eddy says nothing as he slowly closes the manager's door. It is a sombre heart that he decides that this is the end of a long working relationship where he got him, after trying for many years, to lose him in just a few minutes. Truthfully, he saw it coming, however did not want to confront the issue.

In a telephone call, from the dusty busy loading dock he tells Beth-Annie what he has chosen to do. She is not happy; in fact, she is furious. She seems to be hung-up that he resigned, without a consultation with her. She hangs up from the other side of the city where she is working. Eddy walks the steel steps up to the kitchen past the office to work. He has told his sous chef but has taken the choice that he will not tell the rest of his brigade until the end of the week. They need to be focused. They need to be unassuming in his wishes and intentions. Today was not the day to break the news to his chefs. An expected busy day was beckoning.

Over the years, he has been more than a leader. He has been the marriage counsellor to Joe. The birth officer to Liz. The teacher to Tommo. The shoulder to cry on for the homesick Mumood. The plumber to the dishwasher. The mechanic to various other forms of kitchen equipment. He has lived in this place for the past few years. He has generated relationships with suppliers. He has formed connections, bonds, and open, brutally honest communication with everyone. He is to let this down, to whimper without a fight. The truth is he was not protecting his chefs, his friends, his mates, but, he was protecting himself. He wanted, needed to process that he was stepping down to give more to another person. The person that he feels is the right person. He was unquestionably not sure if he was happy with the situation or happy to hell. He was in the tides of depression and needed to save himself.

Later in the evening, as he poured a glass of deep red Malbec, Beth-Annie's favourite, an effort to fan the winds of an argument, Eddy had just finished preparing a meal. A bit like a busman's holiday yet he believed this would cushion the blow. However, as the door opened, the atmosphere froze, the air rushed out of the door as if getting out of the way, retreating. Evidently, Beth-Annie was still not calm. She could not believe that he made the discussion without her guidance, her support.

The drop of money was one of the issues. It was bizarre to think that she was focused on this trivial issue. Her blinding point of view was baffling. She seemed to not care that he chose this radical U-turn to return back to where he started, for her. As if money was the cataract for the downpour of ferocious aggression, this was a feeble dispute. They were not on the breadline, nor where they going to be. He bit his tongue, hard, it was not the money, it was so he did not do something that he could not take back. Sure, she would be making more money, she would be the breadwinner. He would not need it. He would make do, budget with what he was given and still would not lose out.

Through the whole argument, Eddy was having an inner monologue of what he wanted to say in her agitated impassioned dialogue. He did not what to interrupt with a strong plausible awareness of fear. Money. Greed. Of the deadly sins he was already participating in gluttony with his excess of drinking, he was trying not to retaliate wrath, thus kept a firm lip on his boiling emotions. By giving gentle answers he strokes the wrath to turn the vengeful anger away, however, a harsh word from Beth-Annie stirs the pot of anger within him.

Whatever it was, did not come to his mouth, depart his lips. He fruitlessly laid insignificant claims in the argument to show he was listening. Nevertheless, wherever you pigeonhole the cause of the disagreement, the truth was money was painting of the cracks to a much bigger problem. She chose to focus on the money as being the pivotal concern. He chose to focus on his life.

As long as money is being made, it should not be a complaint. Is the love the same? As long as you are in love, is love doing the exact same thing? Love is indeed blind. Eddy would do anything for Beth-Annie. Primarily, he resigned for himself. He did it for her, so he did not have to miss those engagements, the family get-togethers, meaning, consequently not missing out on the life that is happening around him. The more she shouted, the more the cruelly tainted words did not make sense to him. He was thinking if she would have done the same. If she would change anything, the smallest thing for him. Furthermore, it should not be questioned if that is reciprocated, but, here they were, arguing that very point.

He was leaving a job he loved to fix the love that was fracturing. To fix himself from breaking.

The raging argument continued into the evening, but all Eddy could see was good. He made excuses for the bad behaviour. When a relationship goes, starts to go sour, he wants to fight. When the plaster over the cracks crack. When the paint is tarnished. When the cracks become chasms, the bad leaks out. No matter how many excuses that are tried, tested to patch them up they still seep through. Eventually the bad will engulf them. The flame of hope will become the flame of stifling suffocation. The vision will be hazy. A canyon will form spilling out bad excuses.

At this moment, at this time, is when Eddy sees red raging anger. Looking through hate-filled eyes of what should have been a celebration, became a travesty. He will work on the cracks, but wonders if it is worth doing so. He has stopped his lashing torrent of vocal demonstrations with a gestured flick of his lazy hand from his wrist before he knew it. She reacted, completely unaware that he did so to prevent the irreparable. On his snaking tongue are deadly venom words that want to be sprayed out like a barrage of machine-gun fire.

They are not perfect. It would be boring if they were. They do not live in Thomas More's ideal Utopia. They have their cross to bear, but conceal it. If they wear it exposed on their sleeve or in their heart it would be easier. He will not blow blue smoke up her to let her hear the words she wanted to hear. She was his confident through his pinnacle ride to the top. He was tired. It was time for his cross to be revealed. He wrote his story. He only has his self to blame. He gave her the life she wanted at a cost to his life.

The hardest part of life is to give up something you love…For a love.

He collapsed down in a heap on the soft cushions that contrasted his softly stated words with a harsh edge. He forthrightly spoke of his discussion that was fundamentally his. Why he did it. For the first time he was completely honest to the torment that was going on inside of him. He sobbed like a new-born baby as he slid off the sofa to the floor. The was the first time Eddy had exposed himself to anyone. He could not even look up at Beth-Annie.

Eddy exposed his emotions as if he was undressing himself for the first time. He was naked, more willingly than he wanted to be. It was not just himself but his damaged core, his vanishing soul that he spoke off. Between him and her, everything was about him, spread out on the beige tiled floor for her to read. His last few weeks of grief ridden anguish. His story of his own death-marked life that he was balancing on. He spoke of his own destruction. The job was killing him viciously.

She embraced him on the floor. Her body surrounded his trembling form. Apologies were cried out. He was a man in need of fixing. Beth-Annie was not sure if she was the person to fix him for, she did not know how, but she would promise to put him back into shape. She would make an effort.

In the following weeks, this did not improve. Although Eddy was not desperately clinging onto life on the cliff of suicidal temptation. He suspected he was doing it hard, alone. Beth-Annie had taken the route to ignore what had happened. Unawareness was harmony. He had to admit that just speaking about it made a huge difference to him. Eddy did feel happier at work. He actually felt delighted to wake up to go to work. He was the strongest he had felt in a long time since the bad thoughts have proverbially had sex and travelled. Beth-Annie was distant in her emotions, a guard had gone up. Still together as a couple, it seemed for her autopilot was turned on.

In spite of everything, Beth-Annie was pulling away. She had all but moved out, spending more and more time at her place with her ex-roommate. She was blowing off plans. Instigating conversations that only headed down a path of confrontation. If this was it. If this was truly it, was it too much to ask for Eddy to have a clearer ending? For him it was totally normal to want clarity. Banter would appear in text messages, only to vanish as soon as he would ask to meet up for drinks, before or after work. Communication was happening less on the phone but more by text or direct messages, or, another form of contact that was non-verbal.

They had shared similar joys, stresses and memories but over the last few weeks these had been less frequent. It was a case of mirror, mirror on the wall. Who's the fairest of them all? Yet the question was more directly at who was being unfair, or who was looking to much at the other persons reflection to see their own.

It is an eerie quiet Wednesday night. The lone ring on the receiving side of Eddy's mobile goes predictably to voice mail. The woodpecker digital high-pitched chime of the nearby crossroads shrills out for no-one to cross. A light warmth in the breeze carries an odourless smell. Somewhere from an unseen corner a car patiently waits, its car engine idly humming wanting for the red to change to green. A bus pulls up with the soft screech of tyres on the hot tarmac with water from the rebellious unmanaged sprinkler from the park. The city is coming up to midnight. It is quiet. In the park, couples lay out with mouths moving but unheard voices. Rats scurry around from one flowerbed to the other. Possums clamber above the trees. He staggers back from the pub after that all too familiar quick one after work.

What Goes On Inside
Six Months Ago

At the end of the day, does it matter what someone else thinks? Eddy is having one of those days. One of those days, that it does, in fact, matter what someone else thinks. It came unsuspectingly, like rain on a sunny day to drown the good sensations to engulf him in layer upon layer of corrupted negativity. He is surrounded by beauty. The oncoming summer has flirtatiously coaxed out the purple and blue dreamy petals of the jacaranda. Vibrant soft blooms in canopies of wavy linen float in the trees all over the place, rippling through each of the suburbs of the city. The aroma is soft, delicate and comforting in the company of a vibrant sight which energises and stimulates the spirit.

Well, on a normal day, it is a blissfully tranquil experience that brings a smile to locals, as well as tourists. Up until now, it has not had the desired influencing effect that it normally has. Eddy is stuck in his head. The engine is running, traveling as he is working on what would normally be a delightful glorious day. Unfortunately, driving the normal route. A route he has travelled countless days to be able to navigate with minimal concentration. Essentially, though, he is not behind the wheel.

He is overanalysing everything from the past relationships to the barely freestanding present one. This rarely ends well for anyone. Nevertheless, he keeps balancing those plates in his head. Striving to try to understand why one stops twirling to fall, to smash. Whereas others, throughout the fluctuating, he is able to keep spinning just that little bit longer. Running around, spinning, balancing. Until that approaching crash. That always happens, as predictable as each off the stars in the night sky will successively die. To reset, restack and try spinning again with the hope that he can keep them all spinning in unison.

Today's aim is simple. His aim is to finish work. To retreat to the safe haven of his dark, curtain drawn room. Even though his demons have left him, they do inhabit him from time to time to remind him that he is not out of the dark woods yet. Then again, now he can see the glimmering hoping light through the dense forest of vanquishing trees. But, today, he just wants to be alone. To feel the cold dark shroud the length and breadth of his soul. Alone. Single-handedly with no-one else. Alone with his thoughts.

The mischievous devil tongue lashing flickering of the wind is howling at his ashen, strained, unshaven face that blows through the open driver's side window. Licking roughly gruffly like a rant and raging wild blood-thirsty beast. He woke with a sense of unease, nothing compared to his feeling now. As if he was not feeling one hundred percent within himself. The beasts heat on his cheek is felt. The beasts smell of oppression. The beasts savour in conquering Eddy's fears to make him become fearful. Fearful to open himself, ever again. Hard pressed against the stone walls. Unable to move, able to feel. Not a prison as that at least has bars. What can he be to go back to the abyss? For then he has a choice, endure or fall. Plunge deep down without knowing if they would be a way to climb out, on the other hand, he would have escaped, been freed.

Another storm, with intense fury as if in a closed in globe. Sweeping through him like a living bush fire fury-ravaged flame. The light-flickered fragments of his mind are whirling through in the heart of a fire-spiked tornado. No-one sees what is going on through the other side of the windows within his soul. Each delivery is met with a cheery smile as the recipient gets their order, he gets a signature and the gloom comes over him. As soon as the business's threshold is behind him.

Pages of various letters, notes, messages and emails clutter into his conscious acutely aware frame of mind. Intense heat of angered losing love. Even though fastmoving the lines in each sentence are very clear. They continue to find, search and locate him when he thought he had discarded them permanently to the memories of time. Trapped in a chest called loved. They hurt, just as much as they did the first time around. Those scars being ripped open, open to the howling elements of his pain-aching mind. These flimsily tattered pieces strike him, pierce his skin, to embed. What is more, penetrate his soul with a rude polluted impurity.

Of course, he is examining and studying each sentence, the placement of a comma, the subject matter to pick a way that the outcome would be different. It could be. It could not be now. Impossible to say if a comma being deleted would have an overall effect or an affect. Why does he do this to himself. Keep self-torturing himself. Drag up the roots that will never grow to blossom a bond. Not now, no more. He is tormenting himself becoming entrapped in chains of guilt, decision of reopening healed scars, whips of remorse in a lonely cage of regret. Inflicting needless punishment.

He lets the winds of past come to him with each hand written, electronic communication to batter him relentlessly, constantly so he can peel each of the million layers, to question his motives, to reconstruct again the same why's without answering any of the questions except generating many more. To resurge through the strong, gale force winds spiked with javelins of red-hot embers pushing him back, stopping him from walking with any forward momentum to leave the past, as just that, the past. It cannot be unambiguous to be fastened, to be wrapped in a neat, organised parcel and stored forever. However, it needs, nay, requisitioned duty-bound to be ended. Maybe it should be burned, seared, out of Eddy.

Everyone works for the basic necessities that humans have evolved from. Back in the midst of time people hunted for food and built shelter. Nowadays everyone works for these, to put food on the table, a roof over their head. The only difference is extra money is used for play. In play it is time spent around people that share a mutual understanding or interest to put them in the same place to share an emotion. Whether that is a sad movie, a laughing comedian show, a taste and visual spectacle from food and drink or a competition to watch the many avenues of sport. The list can go on depending on the person or couple.

The truth is no-one really goes out to hurt anyone intentionally. They do not wake up with the pretence that they are going to run over an elderly lady crossing a zebra crossing. No-one should. Eddy does not but it happens. It has happened to him, is happening and he has inflicted the same on other people. He has hurt people through lost love, love given and not given back. It seems to be happening to him.

It would seem that Beth-Annie is sitting on the fence. Eddy is chasing in quicksand. He feels that she is showing disrespect to him or devaluing his feelings, yet, he still wants her. Friends have suggested, numerous times, that it would be healthier for everyone to close the book on this non-relationship in the cloak of being in a relationship. Unfortunately, he would continue to pursuit in the game called love. Hunting for that happy ending.

Under his tired, worn brown leather boots he stands on the scattered remains of a trail generated by hurt he has caused, or been the cause off. The trail, the uneven broken hearts underfoot should be behind him, not the progression where he stomps, stamps, jumps and turns his heels into, which just do not do anything to break them. To grind them into dust, so the wind can carry them, far, far, away, to scatter them away from his route.

For it appears to Eddy, each time he leaves this place, they merge, blend to metamorphosise to a stronger bloody-fussing irritation that rise. Intensifying and amplifying like strong vines that rapidly consume his boots, his upturned bottoms of his filthy light blue jeans. To embed themselves under his skin so not only can he feel the pain, the hurt. He has the bonus of being able to think, breathe, feel, bleed that period all over again.

These conversations that he has had. These arguments, whimsical off-the-cuff remarks are dissected to aim for a reason that something that starts with so much promise, ends an implausible far-fetched fantasy, that sometimes never, really begins. Eddy wonders, absurdly, he knows it, but cannot seem to stop himself. Nevertheless, he wonders if he accented a word with the wrong inflection? Maybe, just maybe, he paused too long after a question, in mid-sentence? Causing the silence to say a lot more than a thousand words could ever say.

He was telling himself that he was learning from the mistakes that he had made. He always felt it was his fault. No-one was ever going to convince him differently. Unconsciously, with a hit of consciously, he did not want to change the trail of broken hearts, but, use them to learn. Well, that was what he told himself. The truth was the pain showed him that he still cared. He cannot stop the wind. He cannot stop heartache. But, he can stop the pain.

Because she was so elusive, she hid in the shadows of the gloom. Aletheia, the spirit of truth fought words with Dolos, the spirit of trickery and his colleague Apate, the spirit of deception. The three of them were causing a conflict within Eddy. As if dancing a waltz with three different beats to mortally suggest; approach, torment, death. Neither was winning, but I took a certain amount of pleasure to see that this, although unplanned, was having a more confounded meaningful influencing force than I had initially envisioned.

Eddy looks over his soiled hands through a water-glazed shield. A sprawling dark, grey army of prickly sharp sensations crawl over his dirty hands. He cannot shake them off. He turns his hands over, but they remain hooked onto his skin. Burrowing themselves to cause more pain, on top of the growing empty pain that no medicine, no operation could fix. These were the feelings, the unsaid moments. A smooth touch. A presumably, ostensibly sideways glance. A kiss on the lips, rather than the cheek. Scrutinised. Scrutinised. Scrutinised each one. Each memory. Each moment.

On his knees he combs his fingers through the cremated ashes of the remains of what was, but now, never more. Searching frantically for a single morsel to rescue. A morsel that can be used to change a moment, to change himself, to change the pattern of history that keeps repeating.

Prometheus created false hope, Elpis. When he took away the foresight of his own doom Moros, he replaced it with Elpis. Prometheus believed in doing this he actually saved mankind from misery. People on the mortal coil would argue this fact. The same people that have experienced false hope, which is the entirety of mankind would argue this idealistic campaign. This noble dream. This Utopia that was being made for not only mankind, but by the Gods, Goddesses, Spirits and Daemons, alas, only selfishly for themselves. Utopia was an unattainable object, feeling, being, reality.

The balances of love and hate, joy and grief, harmony and discord. Many lists which undermine the others. Which constantly fight the other. Which is always a positive to a negative. The precarious balance officially results in a tug of war where nothing can conquer the other. One would have the power for a short time, for it to be dragged to another. A balance that was needed for Utopia. This was rarely seen, as the balance was never shared for long. As mentioned before, pain is to know you're alive.

I enjoyed seeing this shifting of balance. The constant rocking of an indecisive mind of worries as fragile as rock-a-bye-baby in the towering windy treetops. I watched with gleeful learning.

Then, in a complete flip of the coin. Another shift of balance. Eddy tells himself to move on. He drags himself up in a slow, awkward nervous-filled movement. He tells himself he can discard the unresolved bullshit. He can move on. Get up. Walk proud. Forward. Looking back, only occasionally, to see the rippling smooth waves of memories. No skies of regrets. No looming clouds of melancholy despondency.

Sounds simple. Too simple. Right? But, oh so right. Eddy knew this, but found himself here. Knee deep in bulldust being tormented by bullshit. He knew this. Eddy knew this analysing of unchangeable past times was getting him nowhere. Literally. Each time he started this unannounced quest within himself, he knew he would not find what he was looking for. He knew he would pick open the healing scars to bleed one more. Twice more. Many times, more. How much pain can the same torment bleed?

Trawling through the wreckage, he is adamant that this will be the last time that he comes to this barren place. This unstable surface of his mind is constantly erupting with different possibilities, which do not help him from living a life. It was a ridiculous, self-harming exercise that only caused pointless pain. As long as he unintentionally does not hurt anyone at the end. Surely, it does not matter what someone, anyone, else thinks.

At the end of the day, it only matters what he thinks. Time to move on across the ashy remains of his fire, burnt land that will be, now, behind him forever.

The Trip to an Opinion that Matters the Most: Happiness
Three Months Ago

In the present relationship. That's a good one! In the present fractured relationship, Eddy asks himself knowingly, if he actually learnt anything in any of the previous long-term relationship. Albeit the shorter ones. For that matter, any? They were all very different people with very, sometimes extremely, different needs. He knows the answer, so he instantly answers it honestly. Eddy actually did not learn a single thing. Anything. It was him? Was it him? At that moment, he regretted not taking this foresight into the current relationship.

He went into this one with an open mind. He thought that he had done this with Lia, and he did, except for this was from the first impression. He did not want the heavy baggage dragging him down. He was so much more open than he had ever been. He exposed his innermost feelings. He was him. He was not trying to be someone he was not. Someone he thought Beth-Annie wanted. He wanted the relationship to be based on truth, and virtue, thus no deception to put on a show so it would grow into an everlasting correlated amorous relationship.

With Beth-Annie, from the opening conversation, he was honest. He started early, hence, to prove to himself that she wanted him, he wanted her, therefore they were not being unrelated superfluous imposters.

Although there were some things of his past, that he purposefully selected to not divulge to her. This was not him being dishonest, just opting not to share at this stage. But. Afterall he was new to this open, honest, let's talk about our feeling's mumbo jumble. Would he though, he means share now? Should he then of discussed what he has not made clear before now?

He was back there, questioning his decisions, explaining some of the reasons he did things the way he did? Would it be too late to change anything? The reasons behind some of his choices? Was it too late? Could it ever be too late? Of course, it could. He has no idea why he is so secretive about certain elements of his past. The only motive was that he did not want to seem vulnerable.

In his familiar working home, away from home is where he feels that he belongs. Eddy was surrounded by the familiar blue-grey plastic bags that hang from the gleaming menacing butchers hooks as sharp as the reminder that he had daggers aiming for his back. Formally in the place of his previous life. A chapter not rewritten but wrote a fresh. The owner accepted him, just like a prodigal son with arms wide open when he arrived back through the white painted wooden back door over a year ago. He was passionate about his job, this job.

The owner taught him, moulded him, so he knew what he was getting. A cup brimming with contagious enthusiasm overflowing with passion. For he was a young boy then. Today he has the lines in his eyes of an older man that reads resolutely comparable to a cynic. Rarely spoken, but the eyes do not lie, they are layered with pessimistic circles that hang in control of the disappointment for all to see. Of a life not planned out the way he thought. That his parents envisioned when he was a baby in arms.

For now, he has no family, no children, no bloodline to hear his stories, to give him insight to the past. But then again, after just a few hours back into his happy working place, he was giving a lift. Each day he was wiping back the layers of regret. Pangs of disappointed guilt that hang by fingernails to his misconceived notion that he is a failure in the eyes of his family. He does not want to be a failure in the eyes of Beth-Annie as well.

A different workforce was present, had changed in the year. A new dawn. He was back and they knew it. He was given an aura of respect. He was given a certain element of favouritism for which they gave him stick for. He loved the banter, revelled in it. He was one of the guys. He was a butcher, with a little responsibility of doing the ordering, but primary he was a butcher, nothing more.

In this environment, the owner was the leader. If he, or anyone else, was not doing their job, he was the one that served as the trial, judge and jury. If truth be told, everyone did their job. Sure, in this place where blokes are constantly living in each other's pockets, friction always happens. A mere lovers' tiff. It is forgotten as if it was never started. A beer at the end. A pat on the back. Or some tough talking along the lines of 'take a spoonful of cement, mate, and toughen the fuck up', or words to that effect. Nothing is ever left unsaid, left to brew, other than sorted before they leave. The unwritten butcher's code.

Eddy started earlier. He opened up for the guys. He finished later, not much later but he had to make sure everything was done for the next shift. It was his Friday. He was getting a rare weekend off, just like normal folk. He was changed in his civvies ready to walk out of the door. He got changed with Cyclopes, a nickname given to Gaz due to his glass eye while they exchanged a few toilet humour-based jokes about a regular customer. In jest but funny all the same. He locked Cyclopes out with a fist pump as the rays of the sun made them both squint. All that remained was the close down.

He moved to the front of the shop and pulled down the thick, black vinyl shards that covered the large front windows. With a soft click they are locked into place and the brass hoop is positioned over the blunt golden hook. The sun shimmers over the metal hooks, the clean steel benches, the blades of various knives that magnetically hang on the strip of metal and black plastic on the white shiny tiled wall. With an uncontainable glimmer of excitement, he seems to float and skip around as he checks that everything that should be off is off, everything is put away and labelled, and everything is on that should be on.

He pulls the black plastic till tray and takes it to the smallest wheel rolling piece of wood that acts as the desk. On the corner is a telephone, which is rarely used these days, a black leather hand over book where he will write the takings and any issues. He does not sit down but leans over like a blue polished egg from his blue cotton singlet. He switches the old metal, gnarly reading lamp on, repositions the head as he draws the black book near with his other hand. Using the blue-ribbon fabric, he opens it to today's date. Moves it over a page and starts to write the start of an ordering list, a mise-en-place list.

He then counts out the float in change, works out the takings cash, cards and writes them all into the book. Monday morning, he will enter these into the computer. Today, it can wait. It balances so he is not worried. A quick text to Jonsey. Around him, the kitchen is starting to relax with a cacophony of electric clicks, switches going on or off and the tinging of metal from the countertops. The heavy clonk of the fridge motions that the defrost mode is over and the fridge fans will soon follow. The silence settles over like a smooth blanket straight out of the dryer. One quick inspection in the walk-in. The plastic large flaps send shivers up his spine. The cold air touches his bare arms. He closes it, satisfied that everything is stored correctly, labelled and in the correct place.

He closes the metal back door to a soft click into place. The silent alarm is set. Outside with a tingling soft breeze, surrounded by yellow, red and green plastic coloured lid bins to one side. A broken brick wall the other. He listens pressed to the cool door. A car passes. A bird squawks. An electronic long, deep toned beep comes from behind the thinly painted white steel door. Eddy moves away, satisfied to be finishing work for a few days, and the alarm engaged. He leaves work on the mat to pick it up when he returns.

Although he changed jobs for a love, he loved not worrying about it when away. A chef's life is a sacrifice which is a killer for their lifestyle. He missed so many occasions as the world plays, not anymore. It is a rationally fear swaying on the edge of irrational to feel like the team will fail without you, that you return having let them down.

All day, Eddy has been floating on a cloud of laughing gas. His elevated mood was infectiously passed on to his co-workers therefore the customers. It was not due to the pending escape from the norm nor the rare weekend off.

That day began like any other. Lethargic in an everything that is ordinary routine. Then mid-morning he received the message. A message that stopped the monotony. Like a warm welcoming heat from a fragrant cindering burning log fire, the smooth smoke surged a radiance of positivity that crept through him reminiscent of the glowing ashes. Only one person presently could make him feel that good. Warm, friendly and comforted. The soft double chime flashed with her name. Beth-Annie had been in touch.

Ignoring the rather impersonal message, as he was not focusing on the negatives. It was a message after too long, that was the positive. A gap that was widening larger than the slow relentless marching seconds, hours, days, weeks. A simple promise that she will call later. He was leaving for, flying to Melbourne tonight. Eddy hoped that the call did not arrive while he was in transit. Foolishly he toyed with the idea to cancel the flight, the trip, the well needed rather than deserved break. But, he craved this with itching desire. It was a contradiction in terms to say he needed time with his mates but, he also needed to stay away from them. Thus, he booked accommodation rather than staying at one of the many places that he could have with any one of his many mates.

For some reasons, the plane rising in altitude through the clouds dusted away his nervous tension. The strained tension that he should have stayed at home to stare at the mobile phone waiting like a dog looking outside for his owner to return from work. Or, was it that necessary evil that he could not turn on, hence not keep constantly checking that was making him feel easily more relaxed. That he did not just turn off his mobile but also his mind. Or, simply that Beth-Annie had made her existence known. Or, lastly, leaving the familiarity of routine, surroundings, the same old same old. The main reason he was actually going. He was going to have a blow out with old mates. Mates that knew him better than anyone. Mates that he did not see often as enough as he wanted.

The grey holding cabin of the aircraft shook as it ventures higher, deeper into the evening skies whispered with fairy floss pink clouds. Eddy looks around at his surroundings. He sees different poses, postures. Several cannot take their eyes off their screens, earphones attached, unconnected to everyone and everything around them. Eddy thinks of the small connections he has made in small talk before flying in his seat. A restaurant recommendation, an event that he did not know was happening to be happening, a friendship made or a shared taxi from the airport. These guys that cannot disconnect are unwittingly losing the human desire to connect. Whereas some are profoundly relaxed as they read the day's crisp Sydney Morning Herald brought with a coffee in the morning.

Others look panic stricken. Eyes wide open, looking straight ahead, trying, failing to look chilled. The white-knuckle grip from their rigid straight arms on the armrests are a huge giveaway to their inner feelings. Their feet firmly rooted on the thin blue carpeted floor. The only thing that moves apart from their booming beating heart are the steady motion of the beads of sweat that heighten as the plane reaches the ultimate level of verticality. Somewhere behind him a baby cries, loud. The shaking continues. Eddy wonders when the shaking will stop, but often thinks that when the plane has pierced through the barrier of thin visible motions of air it will stop. Sometimes it does not. This was one of the times. A speaker comes over calmly that the beverage service has been suspended while the turbulence continues.

Eddy's feelings differ. Sometimes he feels scared, he is not afraid to admit it but often he puts it down to being anxious. Other times calm as if he is lying on a technicoloured deckchair, not of his preference, on a perfect beach scene, which is his preference. The aircraft finally ceases to shake. The rigid middle-aged lady from Perth beside him takes a few more seconds to relax, waiting for the shaking to recommence before enjoying the ride. Coming in separate notions as if the brain wants to relax, the body stubbornly refuses by being unresponsive by fighting against the rational.

Eddy, however, feels like he has the past few weeks, numb. Going with the motions. Unwaveringly indifferent. His mind welcomes the future with a warm embrace. Beth-Annie has been in contact. He will be connecting with mates. He, for the first time in absolutely too long to care to remember he is stress-free.

Eddy is a devoted frequent flyer with Virgin Airlines. Ever since he had the misfortune to be on the receiving end of one of their competitors' cancellations, he has stubbornly refused to fly with that airline or affiliation again. Regardless of cost, he just does not care. He remembers that October day five years ago very well. Still talks about it often. Before that time, he used to check them all. Every single one of the airlines out to see the cheapest, or preferred time schedules. Now, regardless of cost, time or inconvenience he adamantly opts for Virgin. In the last five years only once has he flown another flight. This was due to being booked by his work, thus him not having a say. He hated every moment due to his mind knowing that he was giving money to the opposition rival airline.

That day, five years ago. He was with the same branch of mates that he was going to see today. Before his flight he was having brunch after a great night out at Crown Casino. This was a quick drink in the early rays of the morning to take away the hangover, to top up the night before. A quick one to catch up on before flying out to different destinations. That night earlier had started similar. A drink before checking in that led to the bags being dumped only to be found at the same place in the early hours of said morning. Yet, how often is that the case. No pun intended. When one, turns into more, turns into an absolutely amazing night. The unplanned nights tend to be the greatest, the best nights. Maybe because there are no expectations. That Saturday night was one of those nights.

The morning, five years ago, he wakes up feeling rather sorry for himself, looking at his mobile for the time and seeing a blank screen due to no battery. This time he was staying at mates. So, he kicked off his shoes with the light flooding in from the television and caveman-esque stumped over to the bathroom, knocking into furniture on route. He looked at himself in the mirror as he splashes cold water over himself. He looked like a warmed-up zombie. He smiles. He got ready. In this time, his mate, Jacob, had risen and was ready.

Coming out of the bathroom, he was caught by the smell of fresh coffee. He turned to see Jacob, laughed at the state of him and they grunted to each other as they sipped their hot beverage. This seemed to take the edge of the hungover, so he called the troops to go for breakfast. It was an hour later when they had walked to the Temple, a café that was a central meeting point for them all. Eddy, with his luggage found a plug and preceded to recharge his mobile. They discussed the night before. Like a colourful patchwork quilt they ensued to put together what happened last night. Laughs, shocked amusing giggles and banter commenced as it was a great night, a good as their all remembered.

Jacob reminds Eddy of his forthcoming flight. He reaches down to see his mobile. He still had not turned it on. When it lit up, a cacophony of beeps tells him he has missed the world around him. Out of the many, one message caught his eye. It was a message that was so impersonal but had a very important significance. His flight had been cancelled. If anything, that can immediately slap a good feeling out, it was the present premonition of doom. It was a Sunday. He was feeling incredibly dusty. He needed to get back for work. This was non-negotiable.

As an operational manager where people expected him to be there, it was unavoidable and near-impossible to alter at this short notice. Eating his beer breakfast with one hand as he balanced his mobile phone with another, he dialled and rang the number on the message. An automatic robot voice stating that he was in a queue. Counting down from eight in line he eventually got a young female, human voice. The response was not a great prognostication. He was stuttering questions and pleads as the other side was bluntly uncourteously stating the next flight would be Monday. He needed to get this sorted, so he made his goodbyes hastily to his mates as he hailed a passing cab.

On his way to the airport, he rang again and asked about a sister airline. The same brick wall was encountered with no door. He was going to the airport to get on a flight to Brisbane, to sleep in his own bed to be at work Monday morning. Nothing was going to stop him achieving this aim. As he entered the terminal doors the cool, calm Melbourne environment was a front for these very different chaotic scenes. It was a farce. Obviously, he was not the only one that has had his plans changed. Obviously, he was not the only one that needed to get, or needed to be somewhere else. Not the only one that has their plans altered with no fault of their own.

He joins the back of an impatient queue. People were voicing objections, cursing with an unmistakeable aura of being clearly, visibly agitated, annoyed and evidently frustrated. He was not sure if his desired answer was at the end of this penguin-waddling, pigeon-footing queue. After a long, long wait. Well it actually was not that long, but it felt like a drain of life's energies a waste of life. From this close to the service desk, manned by two people, he could hear the voiced objections, cursing. See the fury in some of the spit-filled sprays of voices. The bargaining of being close to selling their own soul for a seat. He was next.

Eddy got called forward. He walked up and pleaded his case. Infuriatingly, he was not given an explanation which heightened his maddening mind. The next flight was the same as on the phone earlier but with the added bonus of being later now, Monday afternoon. This was not good enough. Stemming the tide of vexingly frustrations, he politely insisted, through an element of gritted teeth, that he get given a scat today. The young man robotically responded with the scripted 'all flights are now full'.

But what really got him. What pushed out the keystone, what made the dam of frustration burst into the ocean of calm was the attitude of this spotty-faced, snot-bellowing child that held his options in his hands, literally at his fingertips. He was close to nailing his coffin of a chance of a flight as he vented. Exploded. The matter of fact way in which he stated, 'you should have gotten here earlier'. As if Eddy would have known that this was going to happen. Followed by the straw that broke the camel's back—'that's why you get insurance'.

Eddy's back was firmly up. This was not coming down anytime soon. Five years on it still hasn't. He demanded a refund. Eventually, he got told that it would be in vouchers received via email, minus administration. So, it cost him to cancel a flight that they cancelled because they offered an alternative. He was steaming. Furious. He stormed over to the empty Virgin desk. They helped him. They gave him what it proudly stated above their heads, customer service. They accommodated him. After explaining the story, they even offered the taxi back to his home to be paid. This was accepted with a golden star placed on their airline.

He got back to Brisbane at cost. He fought for the money over the next few weeks and finally got vouchers which were promised to him. Not prepared to use them but wanted them to pay for the flight that got cancelled. To get the cancellation fee returned. The fact that they said they postponed his flight but did not cancel it was bullshit. He fought. Hard. They buckled as he was not going to let it slide. Eddy did not care if it was fifty cents over, he was not going to lose. The fact of the matter that it cost him more as he got a flight last minute from the airport. However, Virgin saved his skin, essentially his job. He used the vouchers, reluctantly. But since that one flight was used it has been the last that he has done himself. Hence the reason he stubbornly goes for virgin literally at any cost.

Back to the present, he looks around at the reassuring light grey interior of the aeroplane. So many reasons for people to be taking flights around the world today, around Australia. He ponders. Is it for seeing different things? Smelling and tasting different things. He wonders if these people are going to see friends, to go for an event, for work, pleasure, a secret rendezvous, to break away the restraints of normality for which Eddy himself, is doing. Or for another reason for which he cannot think off. Many people are connected to something. He is just looking around without distractions. No phone, no headphones just the light breeze of the overhead air-conditioner and mumbles contained in conversations, oh and the babies cries that has now gone to a dull roar.

With the tyres hitting the speeding runway with a bump, a jerk, it was realised just how much he needed this break. As soon as he got told he could use his mobile he got it switched on. He called Jacob to tell him he had landed. Although truth be said he could have used his mobile at any time, even connect to various chatting portals, but he used it as an exercise of control, to be released from the imagined burdensome shackles.

As agreed in his dark blue Subaru he was outside the terminal waiting. Jacob was a leg heavy guy, by that Eddy means he was all legs, like a giraffe but without the long neck. His body was smaller, nevertheless, for sure, he was taller than most. Make no mistaking that he knows when it is raining before anyone else in Melbourne. So, in this small compact car, it is comical. His legs are pressed to his chest even with the seat as back as far as it will go, he holds a yoga pose of awkward ungainliness.

'Thought you were going to sell this tinned sardine, mate.' Eddy gestures with a wave of his arm as he dumps his bag in front of him as he plonks himself in the passenger's seat, kicking away the empty cups and plastic bottles around his feet.

'Mate,' Jacob stifles a laugh, 'that does not count as a G'day!'

'MATE!' Eddy amusingly exaggerates. 'How you go'in? Better?' He mocks.

'Mate,' he ignores his fist punch, 'good. I'm great.' He then turns to embrace, a smack on the back, a handshake.

From a recent trip to Hawaii, he comments on the name of the car. Jacob always seems to be galivanting somewhere. To envious destinations untrodden by a majority of his mates.

'I decided to keep it because it is a name for a Japanese term for the six stars in the Taurus constellation, Pleiades. That is only seen from Japan, and Hawaii. If you look at the badge, you will see the six stars…well it is also known as the Seven Sisters, due to, even I meant, these stars were once Atlas' daughters. One of the stars is invisible, hence the six stars…'

'Where do you get this shit?'

'Volcanic information centre, where else!' They both laugh.

'Honestly mate, great to see.' Eddy continues, 'How was it then? Hawaii?'

'Rivers of fire, lava fountains, steaming craters. Awesome stuff. Put it on your list.' He swings like a Richter Scale back and forth from home to Hawaii, work to play.

'You couldn't sell it. Could you?' The banter had begun which will be the underscore for the weekend.

Eddy smiles at his passion. Jacob is a great mate. He only remembers when he sees him that he does not see him often enough. Jay as he prefers to be called, travels a lot, for this fact Eddy playfully continues to call him Jacob. He works bloody hard as an electronic engineer on various projects around Australia. He uses them to then go off on long holidays exploring regions, rather than trying to visit as many different countries as possible.

For example, he will hike for ten days in Alaska, go kayaking for a week in New Zealand, before coming back a different route to the starting point. He never rubs salt in the wounds of his mates that he is seeing great places, but does send the occasional photograph on a media feed. He has a keen eye for photography that whets Eddy's appetite for travelporn yearning.

As they drive over the wide, quieter than normal freeway into the city, they account a quick assessment of their lives. Work, drama and living the dream.

With Jacob's eye-catching cramped wacky position already getting people to point and laugh, he edges on the side of caution when driving to get no more uncalled attention. Yet, a testament to how well he knows the roads, or the free-flowing traffic council planning, in no time they were at Eddy's place of stay on the outskirts of the city. He dropped him off so he could go back to his place to drop off the car to meet imminently in the city, which is on both their doorsteps on separate sides of the main grid-like district.

Eddy waves to the bellowing plumes of trailing black smoke. Spluttering a little as he turns towards the reception, up the three wide long stone steps, he checks his phone. No message, no indication of contact. It is not funny. He stands outside looking at the paint-peeling green front door which is more residential than hotel.

A sudden wave of hankering rushes over him on a crest of anger. He was angry that the promised message was not received saying, in his delusion, she missed him, that she wanted to talk about the situation. It was a fantasy in his forever optimistic mind. He looked out with red mist clouding his vision. Taken in deep-breathes he struggles to regain composure before turning to enter the hotel.

He opted for this hotel, more of a quirky bed and breakfast, a short walk away from the main St Kilda tram route into the city. He walked through the door after brushing off the anger as if it was an unwelcoming falling leaf. The owner was way to chipper, with a certain affiliation to, or for, cats, some others would honestly say a rather weird fetish. Cats were everywhere. In different forms. Different poses. Different ornaments. Clocks, draught excluders, paperweights, pictures, paintings, but not a single real, moving furball anywhere to be seen. Anyway, he got his key and walked up the stairs, down the corridor. He threw his black small gym bag on the threadbare pale-yellow bed, with the tight-stretched white linen sheets and locked the door.

Anger subsided, he stepped out. Down the awful creaking stairs, he went by the reception to ask if his key opened the front door in the case he returned late. It was a guarantee, that it would happen. A different woman was behind the desk, a younger one. She must have just started. But seemed to have the preoccupied intentions of what was going on tonight, or on her media feed holding presidency to the person that was standing directly in front of her.

Eddy tapped his keys on the top of the clear plastic protecting sheet that covered the delightfully stained wooden desk to gain her attention. With all the effort of an iron collar around her neck, she lifted her head up slowly, with her eyes looking up first without a word. He asked the simple question that she could easily answer. She answered with a blow of the cheeks, louder than warranted heavy sigh and the thumbed slide of her mobile so she could inconveniently do the job that she was getting paid to do. It seemed to be such an effort for her.

He had not even fully turned away to walk back down the corridor when lightning quick, her mobile was back in her hands. Like the Incredible Hulk, he could sense the anger running through his veins once more, yet rather than burst his clothes in bottled up fury, he wanted to shout. Scream spittle-laced venomous words on the polite line to get her priorities in order. How would she cope? In the real world? Away from her palm-in-her-hand technology? What had she missed in the seconds that she had to be away from the screen? Heaven forbid she missed a photograph of a television dinner. He found himself mumbling words like his father used to do about the youth of today.

What was wrong with Eddy? He had an unnatural anger about him. He wanted to shout at the receptionist for the problems that was going on in his life, but use her unprofessionalism as the fuel. He tried not to vent. He needed to return to his room. Recompose himself again.

For what was described as a studio apartment is laughable. Through the brimming tears of his inability to fully control his emotions he managed to squeeze out a giggle, more of a tittle. He saw the flat-screen television fixed on the dirty, black smudged finger and hand printed wall with the cables trailing like snakes in an untidy mess. Under the small window is a smaller, barely big enough for a plate, square metal table with two grey metal, grey cushioned seated chairs. The assortment looked as ugly as it did uncomfortable.

The kitchen area was a sink, a bar fridge, a microwave and a kettle with enough crockery and cutlery for only one person. The countertops were stained, chipped, filthy with no attention to cleaning, detail or basic hygiene practises. It needed some tender care, he thought to concede with the better option to more like rip out and start again the whole room. The bathroom was an icebox. The open window brought in the chilly wind that was blowing from outside. He closed it firmly, but a draught still came through.

The walls were chipped, stained and a dirty nicotine yellow colour with the shower worse. The shower head was too small for an average person to stand under without crouching down, as if it had been designed for the sole purpose of Danny DeVito. The tiles were chipped with mould residing in the open fissures. The sink was made so low that it could easily have been mistaken for a bidet. He walked back into the bed, sat down to take his shoes off. It was actually a lot more comfortable than it looked. The small window looked out to the busy streets of Melbourne with the curtains offering no privacy. He decided to try and draw the dark grey blinds to get changed.

They did not span the area of the windows. He bowed his head, to shake it from side-to-side with a pfft of resignation. Although the flight was not long, he wanted to shower, get changed to wash the frequent tides of anger away. At that time, he did not know it was going to be as quick as it was. No matter how long he waited, there was no hot water. On enquiring about this to the receptionist, who was seriously lacking customer service, she replied, 'Well, yeah,'—matter-of-factly—'it goes on at four in the morning, until midday.' Like it was a fact that everyone should know. Eddy did not feel the shower had washed the anger as it was penetrating through his pores, heightened by the lack of humanity that his receptionist held, on top of the disappointing room. He felt enraged, disheartened. He needed to get out of the hotel.

In that short time inside hotel hell, the blanket of darkness has descended over the city. The lights where flickering on. The sound, uncannily quiet for a beating city. The air, a cooling breeze that grabbed him like an escort to guide him to the streets he knew exceptionally well.

He knew Melbourne like a loving mate. He has previously come for many reasons, either work or, like today pleasure. He enjoyed visiting, but could never live here. Mainly due to the horizontal rain on the gusts of frosty proportions of Antarctic chills. He adores the vibrant coffee shops, the art that is on every corner, the laneways. The people here seem to have more time for strangers than Sydneysiders, but he is a Sydneysider and he loves his city. That gives him the right that he can talk bad about it, but no-one else can.

Foolishly, against his rational mind, Eddy has devised the perfect whimsical fairy tale endings. Fuelling hazardously idiotically entertained fantasies about things working out with Beth-Annie. Deep down he knew. He was asking so many questions that were shooting like out-of-control fireworks in his head, that landed on more questions to erupt again. Causing more unquestionable fireworks. Striving, straining. Unable to put any of them out. Questions he had already asked.

Those questions he could unquestionably answer, for sure, but he wanted to hear the answers from her. How could she do this? In various, different forms. How could she do this to him? Questions were shouting out loud, in his head, to the universe, to the higher being, a being he did not necessary believe in. Was he cursed? A stupid question. If he was indeed, doomed, would he be living a life of being alone, miserable, isolated from human companionship. That thought stopped him in his tracks. He absentmindedly thought of Romeo and Juliet. Star-crossed lovers, in a bitter feud, that ended in tragedy. He thought of the scenarios that could be offered. That could be made up to what he was feeling.

Recently, Beth-Annie had not had the greatest time in work. Why was he looking for excuses for her behaviour? Nevertheless, he did. She had been flogged, hard. The managers around her were after more of her, more than the pound of flesh that they were already getting. But, unwilling to pay more, or to get any more staff to help with the additional workload. Eddy blamed this situation. Trying to unconvincingly convince himself that this situation had led to the demise, of their relationship. The strains of her work have crept into the strains of their interactions, rather than pulling together pulling further apart. This slowly dragged down the magnificent wall of their relationship. He felt incensed. He was livid. Bizarrely though. Not at her, but her managers. It was ridiculous. He was justifying her by excusing her actions to be someone else's fault.

It was ridiculous that Eddy was reliving the same tired questions, to Beth-Annie's actions. Why was she acting in this, specific way? Towards him and not her managers? This was a clear case of emotional abuse. It was tearing him apart. Inside his guts wrenched by an invisible force that ripped him into bloody useless pieces like a frenzy of piranhas feeding of his body and soul. Unmerciful. And they knew. Each bite was at the maximum demoralising, soul-destroying, heart-breaking destruction to destroy him bit by bit, in stages, unable to defend himself.

From within, he feels like his very core is decaying. Losing more of himself each, and every day. He feels a shell of vulnerability that would break so easily. A tiny tender crack in his mask would make his already susceptible masquerade shatter.

Beth-Annie had already pulled his wings off leaving him unprotected and exposed, not able to escape. Now, she is holding a magnifying glass. She is like a cruel child using his diminishingly inner light to burn away his insides, his, and, slowly…killing him…harshly…unfairly. She is hiding herself away. She is guarding the thoughts that she has. Unfairly stripped, concealed on her chest, like a heavy, homemade bomb strapped tightly, restrictively around her body.

But Beth-Annie does not want to let Eddy know the problem, her issues. She does not want to detonate the bomb. He did not know what it holds. He wondered if she, really knew, wanted to know. If she was scared of the aftermath. She was undeniably scared. He knows her well, better than her friends think she knows her. He likes to think he cares. This is her way of dealing with the mixed emotions. Sensations that she has been feeling. He tells himself; it is this care for him that is stopping her from expressing herself.

'AGHHH!'

He yells. In the middle of the street. Stops and yells out on the way to meet the mates. Towards the shadows shared from the streetlights on the parked cars. Again, excuses are being made for her actions.

'AGHHHHH!'

Another yell of frustration, this one prolonged with a slight crack as it vibrated through the empty residential street. A cat is startled. From above the bright plastic yellow lid of the bin, the cat just stares, poised ready to move. On the verge of fleeing.

She once told a joke that her father calls her sister's boyfriends 'the current one'. He is starting to believe that this was what her father called her current boyfriends.

That last realisation was thunderstruck which saw resentment clouding his already uncertain judgement. This made him think irrational thoughts. This anger. This intense feel of anger he was not used to having outside of the kitchen. He did not want to feel this way towards another human being, another living being. He did not want to feel this way. He was blaming everything, especially him. Then, blaming everything from her. Blaming everything from the situation. Blaming any situation that he could vaguely link to this current epitomise that represented what he was going through.

Eddy does not want his last feelings of Beth-Annie to be this hate-filled emotion. He wants to think, feel, see the good times. The vividness of that smiling image, one of many flicking like the many pages in a gentle breeze, stroking each page that creates a calm within. This image though. This stayed with him. The rage was on his shoulders, a heavy burden of wrath that continued to bear on him, push his shoulders his head his spirit down.

This vision in front of him, as clear as a picture-perfect day, as unseen as a ghost. This was a great memory. it was a nippy winters morning. Walking up a steep hill, in the middle of a quiet road. Hands in pockets, but linked around their arms. They were talking with red noses from the bitter cold wind. They were walking back from the corner coffee shop, their place that their religiously went every Saturday to catch up. Their place to make time for each other. The steep hill rose quickly. A smiling pleasant image. The smell from the sea of salt and seaweed. The smell of the tall fir trees. She pulled out of the chain-linking arms and did a slight innocent skip, followed by a childlike short squeal of glee, as she high-pitched the elongated single word, 'me' at the end of a sentence. A pleading request asking him to stay and talk, rather than go to work.

'Spend the day with MEEEeeeeeee,' he recalls her squealing.

Eddy took that moment then. He took that moment like others before, after for granted. He used them to push down, to bury the anger inside him from rising up. He is not alone in these feelings. He knows that everyone takes these feelings, words, moments for granted. It is these moments that he, she, they feel so damn good. Something so simple that can make one's heart skip a beat, literally. It is so perfect. That you do not even miss it, until it is gone. Then you realise that it is these times that are the best times. For that moment of granted, will never happen again. It is ended.

People, and Eddy was no exception, do not see the future with a dead-end, a sudden stop. They see a long highway, where nothing blocks that forward progression of their relationship that they are in. All of a sudden, suddenly that image changes. That vivid image projects in his mind, on his now closed eyelids, that pang of a motion causes hurt.

He snapped open his eyes wide with a watery glaze, as if he had just gotten punched in his stomach, a nausea feeling rumbled within him. Still standing, waiting for the tram. Missing the many that stopped, paused, went by, with one by just a few seconds as it left him in his thoughts. As he reinstated himself firmly back in the present, after his journey in the past in his personal pages of his own memoire. He leans forward, his arms tightly hugging around his stomach. A glimpse of the past that should be the future. The past was fantastic, now a fantasy. It will not happen again.

The ghost punch aches him back with the awareness that those, and others are lost in the relic times of the past. He saw the problems hidden in the tape of her homemade bomb, tightly wrapped around her chest. The contents of that bomb, on the other hand, he does not know what they could hold. When, if it will ever detonate. The problem is a bomb is armed. The emotional anger is building in him, destroying any good intentions that he has. He has not felt sodden pain like this before. The same questions return, repeat, like a stuck record. His head is now in his hands. A tram comes. He gets on. He rests his head on the blue, plastic feeling seat in front of him. The tram jerks away. His mind progresses, limited progressions, pivotal decisions that have made up his life thus far.

'Today,' Eddy whispers as a promise to himself, but to the hard cushion empty seat beside him. 'Today, I move on. Regardless of what the convocation is. I. Will. Move. On.'

I look happy. I am. I am relishing in the discord in Eddy. I enjoy it like the aftermath of a bloody battle scene, I see the anger within him. Surging, uncontrollable highs, then the depressing sharp terrifying depth of the lows. I have seen the infuriated madden cries of the people on the battlefields through the centuries. Cries which continue with them by the people that have survived. Who have watched loved ones die. Friends die. Mates. Haunted. Death shepherds them like sheep to their own slaughter in mocking attire. That shared laugh. A shared smile, which time, I, have taken away.

All that is left is the open unfixed empty eyes, the open mouth not to laugh again, and, the bodies' position not to moved again. And, the survivor before him, in front of his victim. Touch him, as he is touching him. Being touched by him. Why did he survive when he did not? I will take him. Do Not Worry about that. First, I want him to feel the emotional pain at the highest possible threshold level. I feed off this pain like the lust a vampire has for blood. The bloodshed that shows the pain. This discord, it makes me salivate at the scene. The lost love that binds these, fools. I laugh. For which I have split them apart in the most violent way. I smile as I see this battle happening inside of Eddy. It makes me happy.

To my right is Erais, the daughter of Ares, the Goddess of discord. She is the opposite of Cupid. She accompanies me through the charred human ashes of life before us both on the battlefield as we walk. The other Gods and Goddesses have gone. Smiling, we walk. We absorb through deep breaths the metallic iron smell of blood that caresses our sensations. Hearing the groans of peoples last breaths. Their last hopeful screams of unheard help. To anyone, prayers and bargaining to God. Touched by the destruction of people who can, but choose not to. People that save themselves first, and, last. This race cannot seem to live in peace, although I make sure that never happens. The clattering landscape of blood, bodies, armour, broken bones, has tarnished the fields. This, to us, has never looked so beautiful. I feel elevated by the atmosphere, the perception of carnage. Happy with the, the, unharmony.

Eddy looks on. It was the unnatural fury that he felt rising in him, this surge of hatred was the catalyst that impelled him to make a getaway. It was uncharacteristic of him. The chance to see his long, unseen mates a sign. When he was constantly with her, it seemed to even attempt to make time to see them was near impossible. Getting away to break the normality of his present lifestyle is welcoming. To relish in the waking of a different time, for doing different things. Seeing different sights. Smelling, tasting different things. Honestly, many reasons come into his mind to why people leave a place to start a new. That thought shakes him to look up. He sees his stop as if a spiritual force was flowing through him, telling him that his stop is now.

He goes back to the thought of anew, if only he knew. He was not here to start afresh. He wonders why that thought popped into his mind like a burst balloon pricked by a pin of longing desire. That thought was now escalating, growing into numerous branching possibilities to change his life. Here he stands on the apocalypse precipice. Winds are pushing him to fall down the sheer drop. He nervously edges slightly to the abyss; he leans to look down. He can see the possibilities of diving in, down, into a new life, somewhere new, different.

Eddy will. It will take time, but he is feeling like he will get there, wherever there is! Eddy looks towards New Years as a clichéd new start. Not necessary in his job, or his situ, but more importantly within himself. It is strange what your mind throws up sometimes in the midst of a war. He feels like he has just won a battle in the immeasurable sporadic hostile inner conflict, that no-one will see in full.

Eddy arrives slightly earlier on the fringes of the central business district of Melbourne. He looks at his mobile, still no message. He loudly sighs edged with heavy stains of disappointment as his mobile forcefully gets plunged deeply into the pocket of his jeans in frustration. Jacob had organised the meeting place to be a bar on Flinders Street. This was close to the train station so that it is an easy centre point for many to come. He knew it by name, but could not picture it until he was looking towards the building.

As he stood closer, the noise got louder every time the door opened, happy screams, laughs and clinks of glass. The pop music with a rapping bridge has no chance of competing in this jubilant, carnival of a day off festivities. The scores of people were spilling out of the packed to the rafters open bar.

On opening the large glass doors, he leaves the cold wind behind, with it the outside reality for which he wanted to forget for the day, maybe forever as his earlier oath suggested. Considering his previous daydreaming moments, he is surprised that he is on time. Immediately his eyes scanned around as his ears pin back to listen out towards the tell-tale laugh of Jacob. Like a foghorn, before seeing him he hears him. So, through the crowds he starts walking towards the sound. He beelines like an Australian version of Tai Chi as he manoeuvrers around people, dodging schooners of beers, stubbies, waving hands and stumbling pub goers as he spots the source of the laugh, Jacob.

He got quickly introduced around the rectangle wooden table scattered with drinks half empty, half full and beer-soaked coasters to the various people that will play this scene where nothing else, at this time, is as important to him.

As quickly as the names were being thrown at him amongst the noise, he was trying to juggle them to remember all the faces, but ended up dropping most instantaneously after hearing them. He was shaking hands. With each shake saying the name in his head. This did not work as well as he hoped, well, did not work at all.

There was a place at the end of the table which Jacob gestured him towards, near a gorgeous, infectious smiling Salli. Now he would remember this pretty face. Jacob obviously did not go out as much as he used to, as his dress-up for a night out consisted of his much-cherished Indigenous inspired Melbourne Storm top. He rose to free his seat to get a round in. Eddy mountainously stumbled his words in the presence of this beautiful golden blonde hair lady next to him.

He tried to not stare but looked her up and down and cast into his mind what she was wearing as her poutful pale pink lips narrated a story. Simple, sexy high-heeled leather brown ankle boots, a shiny black miniskirt and a sparkling silver, gold and blue loose-fitting top which hid everything, but seductively clung to her curves as if the fabric had a temptress nature of its own. The glittering top in the soft light aroused the sensory visions of Eddy.

She smelt divine, intoxicating subtle with a floral perfume to torment him further. A safe tendency he went for the clichéd collection of go-to questions as a trigger-happy defence that rolled off his tongue effortlessly to return his calm composure. But, not his still rampantly beating heart. For which made him then instantly felt embarrassed for forgetting her answers. Where she worked? Is she from round here? And, the classic, do you come here often? She giggled as he bowed his head in shame with that dozy statement. It was cringeworthy. He was not trying to chat her up. On the contrary, he was looking for friendship, good laughs.

This early evening had started undeniably right since entering. His mind did not go to his mobile, to even check. Stubbies clinked around the tables. Teeth on show in broad laughs, smiles, jokes. A bartender came over and balanced the empties on a large black circular tray, took it back to the bar with the grace of a dancer, the poise of a model and the refinement of an artist. He was an older man which told Eddy that many days at university learning his trade had brought him back here to earn for his career.

Geez, a college mate of Jay is now a carpenter. Geez trained as an electrician but the more he learnt the less he loved it, so changed as soon as he qualified to become an apprentice. His hands covered the scars, and roughness of laborious hours with a perfect singlet tan complimented by a sunglasses permanent white Zorro like mask around his head. What was so refreshing about this table that Eddy found himself part of was the fact that not one person shared the same job, it was very, very refreshing.

Eddy introduced himself as a butcher, which he actually was very happy with. Salli was a human resource officer for Moët. This went unspoken but it baffled the shit out of Eddy. Did they really need human resources personnel, or human remains department, obviously yes, but really? Ellie was close to Salli and they would giggle as if back in the schoolyards of school frequently. It was clear before they stated it that Ellie and Salli went to school together. They had the friendship that was as close now as it was back then. They met up on most weekends, not normally at the bar, but a keep fit session in the park, a coffee or a date night for mates. they even spent family times together. Ellie was an accountant for Melbourne University but referred it to a shit-kicking job where she constantly robs Peter to feed Paul.

In the corner, but loud enough for everyone to hear, was the overly confident Dan-O. A handsome man, which he knew. A probation officer who was constantly trying to be the main focus point of the group. He strived attention. He worked in the largest prison in Victoria so it would seem his job came into his lifestyle as he could never be nervous, or let his guard down, literally, hence he was constantly overbearing. Next to him, unfortunately placed in his shadow was the cute, timid, but pleasant Caz, a primary school teacher working in Ballarat. Almost librarian in her approach with a mouse-like voice that could not vie with the well of characters on display.

Many more would come and go through the evening, but these people were the nucleus for the fantastic evening to start. As he was in full swing of enjoyment, a feel on his thigh caused him a shock of irritation.

A soft vibration in his left-hand jean pocket makes Eddy take the option of creating a false excuse that he needs the toilet. Through a haze of thick, smelling smoke, he races outside. While still in motion, his mobile is retrieved and answered in a swift flick of the finger so not to miss the call. He cannot hear a thing. He is shouting. His heart elevates as the name flashes on the screen is the name that he hoped to see. He is so excited.

She, on the other hand, is monotonous. Obviously uninterested with this inconvenient errand. A resentment pang of anger rises in him, not for the first time today. It is so close to being released, simmering on the surface. She soothes the boiling turbulence by stating unconvincingly that she wants to meet up. He did not have the strength to ask the reason, for fear of the answer. She wanted to meet in person. It was the fire in his heart, more of a spark that was struggling to stay alight.

Although the news was great, the delivery was poor, but, he still found himself skipping through the noisy bar that was no closer to quieting down with the setting sun. In fact doing the opposite. That quick telephone call seemed to inject a dormant confident Eddy with energy. He returned to the bar and chatted more animatedly. The end of the evening was drawing near. The bar was slightly, ever so slightly quieter, but the noise was louder, much louder. Jacob takes Eddy aside as he orders a round of sambuca shots which always seems a good idea at the end of the night. The cloak of mateship shouldering over him as they motion towards the bar. The conversation earlier on the mobile was spoken about. Jacob has a phenomenal ability for being honest, but compassionate at the same time.

He sees the changes over the night, since he last time they met together. He tells Eddy to turn it in, that he is happy with his present, burning news, but to be cautious. Not to get his hopes up. Especially considering that it looks more likely to be anticipating the prophet of the forthcoming catastrophe of doom, rather than his illusion of joy. Eddy knows. Jacob knows that he knows. Eddy needs this chat. Jacob is in a fresh relationship with Ellie for which he suspected with the hand slaps. It was one of those relationships that were not supposed to happen, but does. He was using his all too recent broken relationship to quell Eddy's optimistic nature. He was making sense. Eddy hated to admit it. Although he did not fully listen. Jacob played one more roll of the dice, Salli.

'You are a man. You will do whatever you want,' Jacob states. 'But mate, be careful. You know what I think of her. I will not lie. You can. Mate, really? You can do better. Salli, eh eh. You will do better. She is emotionally abusing you. Simple as FUCK...'

Jacob pulls away with the black and white sticky shots of sambuca to the table as Eddy gets his change. He follows with the stubbie chasers. Eddy has heard this, and similar speech's like this before. The truth is love is blurring his rational vision, he cannot see himself with anyone else. Sad, but very true. Alcohol is playing a part in his head as the negative, depressive monsters are starting to come out and play. They get some fries to share, to absorb the copious amounts of alcohol. The chat. The lecture. The speech is in repeat. A rant that lasts to the early hours comes in irregular tides. The numbers dwindle to a few, the nucleus.

He, Eddy and Ellie go back to his hotel room. The room is colder inside than out. They have a few bottles and share them over the same conversation about closing the chapter for good. It is stuck on repeat until they pass out.

He wakes up by his pre-set alarm. He stumbles, trips, crawls to get showered to make his flight. Last night was a great night. He wakes Jacob and Ellie who have slept half on the sofa, half off, in a car crash pose that looks more awkward than uncomfortable. He was dusty. He was trying to get his mind straight and he was focused on what they said the night before. They grunt conversations behind fake smiles that they were not in the alcoholic pain zone. The trip was needed, but fruitless. He has been constantly thinking of Beth-Annie since waking up. About the pending rendezvous.

He seemed to leap up the steel aircraft steps. Nursing a magnificent hangover where he was not sure if he was going to vomit or not. He is unfazed by the rocking of the aircraft. He was asleep before the plane had levelled out. Probably snoring but he could not tell. A smile on his gaping open-mouthed filling with drool. A swarm of excited bees are rising in his stomach that lull the nausea that comes with the alcohol poisoning.

The bump on the tarmac wakes him up; he is back in Sydney. A weighty start seemed to shake the cobwebs that held his head together to fall apart to throb with legs to eight corners of his skull. Bright eyes with glazed pupils. He takes a little while but then Beth-Annie seeps into his mind with the next bump on the Sydney tarmac. As the plane taxis he has his mobile turned on and immediately in hand.

Technically, it was not supposed to be turned on yet, nevertheless he wanted the comfort of not having the get-together cancelled. He is not alone as a crescendo of various beeps, tones and chimes echoes around the cabin of the plane as mobiles are restarted, turned on, taken off airplane mode. He sees the message he hopes for. A simple one, as cold as the conversation the night before. Although nothing else was needed.

'ONE PM ADDITION. YES?'

Bless her, Eddy thought as he read the message with an idiotic, goofy smile, rubbing his mouth with the upturned part of his hand to remove the slug-like trail of saliva. She must mean Edition, but as always, she heard a different thing. She was a very intelligent woman but had lapses of common-sense. This example brought a nostalgic pang of sentimental longing. She would often sing wrong words to songs that she thought she heard. She would try and be smarter than she was but end up mixing words up to mean different things to what she was trying to say. It was her unintentional magic trick which never failed to make Eddy laugh.

He knew the café very well. He responded 'yes' straightaway. Eddy found it a bit conceited, but hid it around her. The café was just down the road from him, his favourite. She would speak of it like someone would describe a wine, that it was unassuming, simple with a touch of being a hipster haven without falling for all that bullshit. He liked it for the main reason you should like a café; the coffee was always on point. He can easily get the bus from the airport, dump his bag at home and head straight down without rushing. Perfect. As long as the bay of nausea stays, well at bay.

He arrives early. His head is pounding like a freight train with a locomotion of words, sensations, worries, drink. He has ordered his usual. A batch brew where he opted for a flat white with soy for her. She often changed her order but thought this would be a safe bet, after all he paid for it. She was now late. She was always late. Nevertheless, he was starting to fear the evitable.

BEEP BEEP.

Eddy receives a message. She sends a text.

'I HAVE BEEN THINKING TODAY. IT SEEMS WE HAVE BEEN OUT OF SYNC. I THINK WE NEED TIME AND SPACE TO DECIDE WHAT WE WANT.'

The stinging hot rage of full-blown ferocity reared its head again. As he threw her coffee aside from the outside table to the floor. Splattering an unassuming red car as the lid exploding off, the milky brown coffee spreading around as the paper cup hits the car door which just happened to be parked on the side of this road. He walked off before the cup settles fully. Onlookers look. He did not even finish his coffee. He needs to move. He mutters angry words under his breath.

He hears, or thinks he hears, people commenting on his volatile behaviour. He tries to calm down. He is raging. He could not stomach anything. It was not even two hours when they set this time to meet up. He rang Jacob. Pacing hard in short, small circles in the silent alleyway behind his unit. The more he spoke, the more he shouted, swore and spoke in short sentences of venting savage intensity. Explained the situation in hateful spits of noises that made no sense.

Jacob listened. He resisted the urge to state the obvious, and the I told you so sentiments. He did what a mate should do, listened, was close enough to offer a shoulder, but too far from him to not grab him to shake sense into him. Jacob could not help to feel worried about upsetting him with wrong words so let him rant.

Eddy could not believe that she wanted space. After so much time apart, she wanted more space. Sometimes, most of the time if he is honest, that ship has sailed. He is not in a relationship. Sometimes he maintains the stubbornness that it is. She wants closure. She has truly darkened up his day. This was supposed to be a jubilant celebration of two people uniting. Being adults to talk about their issues.

This turn of events quickly has made him fill up to the peak with mad bubbling blistering lava rage. This was so illiberal. A case of how it would affect her, not, how it will affect him? How Eddy feels? She could not care less. Eddy is a mere him. She is the almighty importance. The argument in his head is steamrolling any positives as he speaks, nay yells on his mobile to Jacob.

Momentum of this magnitude was akin to a heavy, huge piece of natural disasters that can go and destroy everything in his path like a raging bush fire. The beauty that was there is unseen, flattened into the ground. Could it be reborn? Why was she doing this? But, more to the point why was Eddy letting her do this? He was at that stage where he was so angry that he might just hurt himself. Nothing was working to extinguish the flames from growing larger with each thought. Fuelled by memories, destroying the good times in engulfing heat.

Lyssa is in her element. Citing herself with having the grandiose self-proclaimed trademark of being, rather than having, an evident passion for war. She seductively hisses to herself, 'Passionate War', as she watches her annihilation. At the same time, she bows to disappear into the cast played at her role, for it was executed very well done. Her sly smile states arrogantly she knows it.

By means of her role complete, she beams a brazen grin. One of those devil smiles that sees she has done it for her own good to cause pain. One of those bloodthirsty smiles that twinkle in her eyes as they are opened as wide as they can go so as not to miss a piece of the aftermath. She compliments herself for her mind-conflicting turmoil. The pain inflicted on her prey, Eddy. She ruefully smiles at her handiwork, while gleefully rubbing her hands.

Behind her she has had the assistance from Furor, the Goddess of Fury, and Ira, the Goddess of Wrath. With herself being the Goddess of Mad Rage, she has injected anger in snappishness quick bursts of hot, tempered, vexation like escaping spurts of toxic poisonous gasses. In surges of frantic, uncontrolled, hysterical moments of pure dangerous painful yearning, she infiltrated, gored on Eddy's good moods. Being part of the Maniai, she has had a magnificent cast to choose for her support. She chose these two, inasmuch as she had the ability to multiply into her supporting members to act as her host. Although this talent was not explored today, fore she did not know that it was going to be this easy to fill Eddy's mind with her, it was a handy ace to have.

I feared the role. I feared letting her take a stand. I feared that she would surpass her mandate, causing Eddy unreasonable pain for which she would destroy him, rendering him useless to my ultimate grand plan. She has a great talent, this is indisputable. But, with this talent, she was uncontrollable, verging on the brink of insanity.

I knew her parents very well. Where she grew up, for I grew up there too. She is the daughter of Nyx, the Goddess of Black Night. Nyx was an enigma, she was the mother of mysterious inexplicable unpleasantries, such as death, and ghosts. Lyssa's father was Erebus. Together, they lived in the dark regions of the Underworld, which Erebus helped rule. The dead would pass immediately to Erebus, the darkness between Mother Earth and Hades, Pluto. This region of deep, darkness and shadow existed where they raised Lyssa. It was in this barren environment that Lyssa used her wild emotions to experiment her unique ranges. Harnessed them for her control, solely.

She swiftly teamed up and fell into the circle of mates of the evil spirits. United they called themselves the Maniai. Each one she used for her gain, to learn their personal traits. Here she learnt from the spirits of madness, frenzy and insanity. I think the latter is where she got most of her strength. All, of her unpredictability. Lyssa's infernal sisters, the Furies, which where united as the Goddesses of Vengeance and Retribution. There was Alecto, known as the unceasing one, Tisiphone, the avenger of murder and Megaera, the jealous one. As this collective trio they were often referred to as the Kindly Ones. It is safe to say she learnt nothing from them.

I watched her blossom from the Underworld. I handpicked her, as I did them all. Through this whole process Oizys, the Goddess of worry warned me about her irrational tendencies of Lyssa. He was constantly acting out his own talent as his own persona influenced his being. Of course, I feared her, but, I needed Eddy to represent the fear, so I could truly see how he would cope. I scoffed at his inability to control, harness Lyssa. The ease in which she penetrated his bravado. She took over him. Although it lasted a day, Lyssa achieved the correct answer. I smile as I feel I have chosen wisely in Eddy. Certain aspects of this journey have made me listen too much to Oizys. Made me wonder if I had indeed chosen appropriately.

Eddy knows it was all her fault.

He could not bear to admit it.

To…himself.

Pause...for that Moment of Reflection
Ten Weeks Ago

Eddy is here. Contentedly immersed in a stifling divulging peaceful stillness. The dainty echoing noise of the solitary single member of staffs slow moving footsteps graces across the room. A pause, a scuffling of toes followed by the release of air from the black plastic high stool. From behind him he senses her as she picks up her book. A rustling scrape of paper pages tells him his thoughts do not let him down, thenceforth silence returns. She with her book. Him with his empty thoughts.

On a low leather red buttoned pew, he sits within a converted warehouse in a narrow back street between two more prominent streets in Surry Hills. His back, stiffly straight, gives him a view for all the better for his eyes to be direct with the piece of art that has taken his eye today. His favourite quiet place. A diamond in the rough unlit back street, only slightly bigger than an alley. Slightly chilled on this humid Sydney day as the click and silently running whirring of an air conditioner that ever so faintly lowly hums, blends into the background to maintain that controlled temperature of ambient chilliness and tranquillity. This place has become his place for reflection, contemplation for years. Never expressed to no-one. A place for him to get his spirit back. For him, it is Sydney's best kept hidden treasure.

The warehouse is the former home as well as studio of Australian artist Brett Whiteley. He worked here from 1985 until his death in 1992. After that time, it became an art gallery, seemingly left as he left it. Eddy cared for art, yet it was safe to presume that at the same time he never really took time to understand it. A steady appreciation for the craft. Through one of his darker times, he found art as an escape. A way to mull over thoughts to turn them over in his mind, until the clogs of contemplated mechanism construct a settled resolve. This happened many years before now, but he never forgot the feeling that a piece of art was able to conjure up deep surges within him. Art was his epiphany, if you will.

That is why he came here. Also, for another reason, well, like a library, art galleries tend to be quiet, away from technology, no electronic beeps, no louder than necessary conversations that people hear only one way of an odd conversation, hence no idle chatter, inappropriate opinions. Here he is. He is holding nothing. He handed in his black gym bag at the entrance. This has undoubtably seen better days but been part of his own journey. A broken zip that only works one-way, where he placed his keys and mobile phone.

A hole from a knife carried that pierced through his canvas sheet to give a glimpse of the dull life he lives on an ordinary day. A hole that grows larger day by day, combining the true fact that he could escape it if he truly wanted. A smell firmly impregnated with the dirty mash off cooking, stewing a faint rancid whiff that no amount of washing can remove. A white cloudlike stain of a deodorant roll-on that had spilled over, one trip too long ago to remember, too long ago to still be fragrant. He was attached to the memories the bag represented. One day, soon, he will have to replace it.

Cat-like agile with the prowess of a ballerina he relocates, stealth-like to another seat, in the presence of another wall. From above he hears the echo of a few footsteps on the dark brown wooden panels, rather than the exposed floorboards in the other areas. He thought it was just him and the female member of staff. He had not realised that a couple were upstairs, lurking as quiet as church mice. As he is softly perched on the edge of a soft, but firm grey long leather cushioned bench in front of a different piece of art he follows the sound directly above him with his eyes. The tiresome groaning of the open set of steps that under duress lets them descend. As the shoes and ankles come into view, he returns to the painting, yet unseeing what is in front of him.

His eyes are trying to look behind him, a fruitless exercise. That dragging curiosity made him snap like an elastic band to turn around. Being as gracefully subtle as an insensitive sledgehammer he swivelled his head around quickly towards the bottom of the steps as they step from the last wooden rung coming into full view. At that very same moment that he was rubbernecking, they stared directly back at him. Failing in his attempt to act nonchalant, he browsed his eyes over the artwork traversed wall to return to his origin a few seconds earlier. Feeling bashfully ashamed in the act, as well as the impetuous thought: 'Why are they a couple?' Irrationally foolish as it was unpredictably absurd to belittle happiness.

He loosens up. He is leaning backwards with his arms outstretched looking at this one particular painting with interest. He feels the calmness in his chest. Hears the murmur of his heart. His bottom straddles the seat precariously perched on the edge of the silky drop. On the white-washed brick wall in front of him is a trio of works. The one that has his attention is in the centre. 'Walking down a street at Palm Beach thinking about Vincent', 1972. He sees the influences. He likes this.

In the golden-framed painting are swirling colours of yellow, blues and greens flanking the middle of the turning road. Eddy imagines that he is standing looking down the turning road, everything outside of the frame is non-existent, not real anymore. The colours swirl around with a dreamlike essence that takes Eddy on a hypnotic journey. He is sitting in real life but walking and standing immersed within the painting before him. He looks at the bushes on the fringes of the road for any signs of life. Sees nothing. He is alone. Happy. Reflective. His personal calmative zenith.

Seconds pass. A disturbing tremor in the streams of tranquillity. He is hoping, wanting a car to come. A startling revelation in itself. A truck, a road train, something, he did not care what. Something to hurt him physically with force to cause pain. This surprisingly injection of doom hit his chest. Alas he did not flitch from the impact, he felt it all the same. Was it just pain he yearned for, or a way to rid the pain contained inside him.

He does not want to die. Does he? Who, really does? Does anyone? Even the people at the end of their life. When they have planned their exit strategy. Do they regret their life decision. That last moment. That last act in their journey that for them they cannot stop. The perfect schemes of the flawless tick of time, that very moment of backing out is at the last stage, no-way back once the tock comes. Only the climaxing end. Eddy does want to feel pain. This emptiness is not making him feel alive. He comes back to the place to find his epiphany.

He slowly rises. He walks up to the painting. So close that he can see each paint stroke, each bristle of the brush on the plywood. Tries to smell the surroundings on the path, but the leather is strong. The sky is a well, in the centre is a small button of a lightbulb that has been fitted to represent the bright blazing orb of the sun. The white rays of light spread out. His closeness throws shards of threadlike javelin rainbows of colours through his vision. Eddy some days thinks the sun is setting, other days rising. Lately he cannot seem to dictate his waking mood.

More importantly, he cannot seem to change it from the waking up persona. Forlornly, the sun sets more than rises within him surrounded behind his happy-go-lucky manifested appearance. Today, his mental frame of mind is setting. He looks at the weary, heavy branches of the trees that seem to be ready for bed. The sun is agreeing. He is tranced within the rich, vibrant lively artwork. The sun, it seems to be setting, very apt as he takes each piece as tired, each leaf as being spent, each line as ready to end it for the day. Hypnotic in a daze he looks intently to absorb every single second that Whiteley had exhausted over this piece of art.

In the background, a documentary film has started. Being played with a single sounding violin, slow and very deliberate to articulate a sensation. Accompanied by the tinkling of the high notes from a piano like the soft sounds of rain. Eddy came here to think. He loves the sound. Normally feels relaxed by the simplicity. Just not today. The soft rain is like hail on a tin roof. The claustrophobic, softly played documentary of tributes to Brett Whiteley's art surrounds him, lifts him into the swirling colours of the painting in front of him to effectively drown him.

He has to step back in his mind, meditate and relax. Deep within him he absorbs unfathomable and profound questions to answer unanswered, unquestionable, illogical reasons. He is lost. Trying to be found. He is tunnel visioned at the painting. Trying to see the remedies to his loneliness. The clogs are grinding, screeching, deafening a roar of ear-splitting agonising sufferings. Creating not a residue fragment of answering the demons.

He shouts in his mind, to himself:

WHY DOES SHE HAVE A RESPONSE TO HER DISRESPONSIBILITY?
SHE HAS NOT SHOWN REMORSE.
DEMONSTRATED ANY SHAME...
REPENTANCE
SHE WILL NOT...
NEVER...
TESTIFY AS I AM FORCED TO—

He seems to be cutting himself off. An argument with himself. Trying to be nice. To justify her actions to his reactions and to reason an explanation. He is not finding his reflection today.

Although exhibits change, he finds himself to this part of the former home, the area headlined the 'Beach'. On the rare occasion that it gets repositioned, or heaven forbid moved, he finds himself drawn like a riptide towards it. However, at the end of the day, it is the place for him to become calm. To be brushed with soothing strokes of calm influence. The painting often helps. He sees something different.

But. Today, he is struggling to reason an understanding of calm. He rarely goes upstairs to the former living quarters. Yet today he does. Photographs, personal objects, postcards, his personal music collection is being played and unfinished artwork, sketches are shrewd over the floor, left as he left it. Around the walls are graffiti covered quotes, images stuck in reckless abandonment. A stack of reference books, equipment. It is lived in. He slowly walks around. Softly but his footsteps sound heavy, even though he is walking like a burglar, an intruder in a home. He does not find what he is looking for. In truth he did not know what answers he wanted to find.

He turns back to the painting, retraces his imaginary steps. He has used this painting as a form of meditation before, he seems to always get something new from it. Reasons that he has only just thought of doing, he vows to place this painting on his mobile phone as his screensaver. He always tries to make sense of everything while beholding the attraction, an endeavour that he has never been able to complete. Consequently, the sensations that run through him to be in front of the original is indescribable. He wonders if the same can be done on his tiny, *days of your life's* mobile screen.

All the shit out in the real world is forgotten when he immerses himself into this painting. Although it is unusual for him not to get his mojo back straightaway in stepping foot in here. It occurs occasionally, but then again, he has always won the previous fights against the demons from dragging him down in a few torturous lengthy heart-wrenching moments. As if the threshold to the gallery itself holds the unmoved doorway key into his own down-to-earth portal, in not only body, but more essentially his mind. Behind him is forgotten, as he moves through an invisible magical waterfall that makes him step instantly from one realm to another, a vastly extremely altered parallel universe.

This imaginary stroll through the artwork around him is a dream. The waterfall has washed all the weight off his shoulders. This place is his returning. This is his self-meditation. This magnificent displayed artwork, literally, works wonders. Art forms as a haven to his repetitively interrogative mind. He gets taken to memories locked away. Yet, today was a struggle to get to his happy place. Even though not unusual, it was always encountered with unwelcoming receptions. He fought to get, well, happy. His mind was a well-behaved obedient friend one minute. To the next, a ferocious hysterical mixture of chaos and agony. In a flash, his mental state was in a penitent mood. All for him to foolishly welcome back like a prodigal son. For only the knives, the copious array of sharp and blunt knives, to come out and play. Today was different. His mind was distraught, untameable.

His mind raced back. As if trying to piece together the fragmented origins of when he was starting to become a shadow of himself. As if in that moment. That epoch where the threads of his personal story tore heedlessly open. The insignificant, one time healed scarred wound commenced to unravel down a chasm of desolation. Endlessly without any much-needed closure. He remembers a time. Back when he used to enjoy life's pleasures way, way too much. To the maximum extreme. Now, his mind is constantly working. He seems to not be able to shut the voices out. Turn the noise off. To stop. To relax…fully. He remembers a time, years ago. When he enjoyed his life.

Like a fisherman flinging a line out towards the forgotten depths for an, up to that time, neglected catch of the day, his mind has cast a line to such a phase in his own life back when. A pinpoint in his own unique biography that trickled drips out in opposition to the acute gathering tempest from within his inner bleakness. A younger he was on his shared bed. Coming down from a towering high after a great forgettable time out. Slowly spiralling around, helter-skelter descending into a confused throng, coupled with the speedy reckless mosh pit of tornados. His girlfriend at the time was in the same bed, sound asleep, unaware of his plight. Wisely, she did not go out with him.

It was an impromptu drink after work that led to a pub, a club, a casino, a gutter. He came back with barely a couple of hours sleep. He tossed, turned. He was wild in his twitching, waving his arms to fail to push the delighted evil spirited demons elsewhere. Eventually, her sleep was rudely awakened. Arms flailing, they hit her, waking her. Panicking her. He screamed into the unknown. She screamed under the unknown. He shouted out. She got up, watched him thrashing in the sheets, flogging the mattress. He was asking for the voices to stop. She was shocked, unsure what to do. What should she do? To try and stop him, get hit again or let the scene play out?

He was screaming for it to end. Louder with a fearful noise coming from the dying depths of his soul. She thought he was going to say goodbye, with no goodbyes. She reached for the half-empty glass of water on her bedside. Threw it over him. To no prevail. She has to do something. She left the bedroom. She went to prevent his pain by causing an intervention. She got the neighbours to help. She, together with them holding his arms, she wakes him. She told him not to end his time on Earth. He was confused. Wide-eyed, sweating, tense. Baffled to be talked to like he has just come out of an operation surrounded by a face he saw familiar and some he did not. Confused to be told that he was going to end his life. What was he going to do? Slice his wrists with a pillow! He was sleeping. Wasn't he? Later on, as he went from hot to cold, feverish to comatose, dead to the world to alert as she explained what happened over a closely watched vigilance.

As he walked carefully treading the boards with predetermined footsteps, he is focused on his own prologued theatre in himself. Eddy is not sure why his mind spun to this rapid, hurried assessment of a small note in his life. Although in that postscript, as his beginning thinking the whys? Eventually, it did dawn on him. It did clear his mind as he thinks in that moment back then. That point was when the addiction ruled him. This was the first time his mind had conjured up suicidal tendencies. Tendencies that had laid dormant in his mind, forevermore now stirred awakened, ad infinitum. Just maybe this episode was the opening of that single seed, the self-loathing despising sentiments to come out of its shell, to start to blossom maddening ivy like vines in the depths of despair.

For what Eddy's soul did not know back then in those isolated ungodly hours of darkness, but most certainly what he did know for sure after that unblessed night, was his spirit in its entirety was fractured, crying for help, although hampered by the denial for his innermost

486

personal cries to be given permission to voice his bleak expression. That living nightmare, that episode was indeed the slippery high-speeding, head-on collision end of that particular relationship. The truth of the matter was that he was either on alcohol, drugs or both, on a daily basis.

Principally, she did not know how to handle him. His mood, when he was coming off, or starved for one was different. He was always frighteningly different. He was impulsively uncontrolled like a blood-thirsty wolf in the bay of the full moonlight, wildly frenetic. Spit-raged revulsion, to loved up suitor, to womanising Lothario, to hysterical outbursts. No fairground ride had this many ups and downs, certainly not the amusement. Eddy was an unhealthy toxic incitement for her to feel anything close to real love. At first, she had the foolish notion that she could save him. The main problem is that a person must want to be saved. Eddy did not feel he had abandoned hope, or his soul had been forsaken, thus he did not feel he needed saving.

A hole where his heart should have been was fed off other people's human misery, but none would nourish his insatiable lust more than his own. He was using the plentiful variety of poisons to get rid of the pain, yet they made him unhappy, when all he sought was happiness, some kind of bliss. Desperately dangerous to everyone, like he was a contagious suicidal ailment that spread ill-fated abandonment of hope. The buried toxic seed was certainly revealed that night.

No more blanket of mystery lay underneath in his own time. In spite of this, as quick as sunnies could cover his eyes, he would conceal his pell-mell, his hurly-burly personal profoundly secret turmoil. Dishonourably granted to thrive beneath his picture of health.

No-one can replace a fellow human being. When she left, he counteracted that pain the only way he knew how, more drugs and alcohol on top of his already exceedingly higher-than-warranted personally prescribed amount. The essential detail is that not one person being happy works. If one is not responded to change, even attempting to make things healthier within the unity of one, the fragile reasons to hold together the castle of cards together will fall, it has to be of stronger foundations for progression. The ingredient that inhibits a fusion is a direct characteristic chemistry of a unique part that makes, that person whole.

Everyone strives for a connection, but that single connection will bind two people. This is hard to find, for some. Others it is effortlessly slow and frustrating. Why is it? Every civilisation believes the same in different forms, but the essentials are the same. Two people. Two souls. To connect. To Be One. No-one is the same. Not one fingerprint is the same. No one-sided effort without another can form a bridge to bond the harmony of a couple. Unless Eddy faced his demons, it was never going to work. Yet, he felt he had no demons to face, let alone fight.

His cloud-filled hazy mind was preventing him to see clearly. It was hard for him to find the author, even harder for him to admit that it was a book written in himself. The discovery of this, that led to the recognition that it was himself that Eddy needed to drastically transform, hence, to be prepared to even begin the battle of wills, self-control. One of many battles to flatten, crush and beat the sorrowfulness out of him before the war could be, eventually, won.

More's the pity, if he was not successful. If he allowed just the slightest crack for a relapse to occur the malicious ivy will continue to sprout threads after that, to grip as strong as a vice with reprehensible unemotional coils. A strong intensifying reason to exaggerate the desire once more. This would happen, typically when he was at his weakest ebb.

Ultimately, Eddy did find out that he needed saving. Much too late to save the relationship, early enough to save his job. More seriously, decisively as much as necessary to save himself from further harm from himself. It took him to be found, scarcely with any signs of being alive, a rasp of breathing that was choking on his own bodily fluids. Almost as if his body had started to fight back and reject the self-deprecation enduring torture.

After a particularly long session of anything he had to be taken in every which way. An off-duty security guard found him in the gutter, lying in his own filth, covered in his own vomit. An incredibly awful hard night in hospital followed. Shivering, sweating, screaming, a psychotic desperate shell of himself. Skinny, gaunt, pale, he was wasting away in body, as well as mind. A touch-and-go moment where his spirit had had enough but his body wanted to live, to his amazement, for evermore. Drifting in and out of consciousness on the wingless flight, plummeting through the airs of oblivion skirting in the vicinity of his own extinction, he writhed in shaming grief.

Unhappy at the loss of time, life, energy. Unhappy at losing so much, to so little. Unhappy that he hid the misery under another thicker blanket of more misery. Happy a life force was glowing stronger than he had felt since...he does not remember when. Happy with this comfort in the uncomfortable anguish that he had found courage to force life back through his veins. Just, Solely, Happy.

I did feel he needed a shock at this stage. He needed to love living so my plan could take effect. Someone that was dead to the living world was useless to him. I had already decided that if this did not work, I would have to restart my work on a different subject. I was reluctant to recommence again. It was an arduous and laborious chore. A task to find another subject as perfectly posed as Eddy. Mercifully that night in hospital worked. It was the shake-up Eddy needed. Hence to obtain my subject back on the rails that I determine.

In the beeping of the machines. In the shadows of the chilly airs. In the pungent odour of medicine, antiseptic and defeat. Out of the tainted vomit-layered throat he shouted out, gut wrenchingly screeched. He cried; he cried a lot. He could not stop. In a place so full of pain and suffering, he was suffering himself to get rid of the self-conflicted fiends that he had to allow to play to be disciplined.

As tormented in agony by the inner fires of hell, to the angelic soothing of chalk-scratched promise of redemption in outer heaven, he searched for salvation. He got much needed help. It was hard to admit to himself that he needed this help, harder still to then take it. Something in him knew that this was a warning. Next stop may be his last. As he knew going cold turkey was not going to resolve in the long-term, he embraced change.

'How great is that,' he mused. He was getting changed to leave. The paper-thin gown was discarded to the change of clothes that were given to him. As he placed the grey, hideously ugly sweater over his tight skins protruding clear indentations of bones, he hastily discarded the notion. The bearing in mind that these could have been the clothes of an unfortunate person where he stood, another laid for eternity. He allowed this thought to fleetingly pass as he mused once again, without letting the smile that wanted to spread over his face, for he really wanted to shout out.

'How great...how great is it to know. To really, to know that a person. That he does want to live. Live a life worth living.'

Nevertheless, this revelation also acts as a sword, deep within the beaten heart for he feared defeat. All the same he placed the drab heavy large grey sweater over his thin frame, as a knight putting on his armour to take the first nervous steps into a battle where he may see the light of the day, or the light at the end of the tunnel.

Life is hard. Through his numerous sessions, he was told that phrase: Life is Hard. The truth is, which he believed, Living is Harder. No-one lied to him.

Maybe he should have called that girl, to say he was changing. Essentially, every person in the whole world are shining for that single connection to make any person united. The curtain is still up, but slumps down quickly, deteriorating on impact. He has to move on. Leave, without the past.

He thinks about this time. This time that has passed. In this relationship he is a good man. Not always the good man in the past relationships. He knows that now. He improves himself in each one to better the coherence of his way of thinking, and way of behaving to prove that he is that good man he thinks he is. In his mind that he always could become, that now he is.

He leaves the gallery at the closing time of four in the afternoon, never before time if he can help it. He slowly moves, his knees creak and his back demonstrates the movement. His argument has quelled. Today he has travelled years back to the time where and when he was undead. He feels like he has had a genuine reflection on his past that can only help his future.

He has given no ambiguous answers, but he feels relieved that he knows the core for which he can track, like Sherlock Holmes to solve the mysteries of those sought-after uncertainties.

Outside, he pauses, he takes a deep medicative meditative breath in. Lingers the air inside his gaping mouth as if he is tasting a quality wine, before slowly releasing Sydney's city air-seasoned flavour through pursed lips that are in dire need of a drink. He is surrounded by a golden silence. In the near distance a tumbling sound of a screeched surprised cat knocking over a pot plant does nothing to disturb the peace he has. This draws his head to turn into the source of the smooth fragrant sweet secretions of an equally agreeable floral design. A peek between the rotting blue paint shedding wooden fence conveys a living flamboyant multicoloured garden scene.

A picture from a particular meticulous garden exhibit that would proudly line the pages of *Home and Gardens*. A display that shows more than hours of passion, but an enjoyment, a sense of pride in literally keeping the homeowners house in tremendous order. At the same time as he lets the light from the crimson glow of the sun wash his face as he basks with eyes softly shut, he breathes the perfume in. He is sure that he can sleep tonight. His absolute unequivocal questions immediately dissolve in the warm rays of the sun.

He feels the sun's warmth cool. He opens his eyes, glances up to see so many translucent brown bats moving in the same direction across the blue skies. He knows there is a poignant reason for this display of a colony of bats instead of a flock of birds. He keeps his eyes on the black flapping cloud as they eclipse the sun in a paintbrush stroke as they head towards Hyde Park. He watches every single one.

Is this a significant change in Eddy's life, were as the whole of nature seems to be playing in the most impressive bringing together to harmonise in such a perfect pitch. The worlds gone topsy-turvy for a moment to show him even ugly to one, can still be lovely to others. One part of him has recently died, but another has been born. The part of regret singed by the flames of disappointment were no longer needed to poke away a throbbing pain in his conscience. Tragedy is a foreign country where it is hard to know the correct ways to deal with or understand how to communicate properly what the soul wants to allow to go, to liberate the true thing that is manifesting like acid inside him. He left the gallery, leaving regret to depart his life. In turn a new burning has rekindled.

Still overhead, the bats flee from their unknown exodus. Head craned upwards at this spectacular viewing, he wonders if he can truly embrace the new ideas that are unfamiliar to him. To live without regret, so when he is standing at the pearly gates and he is asked that question about regrets, he will indeed have too few to mention. Can he do it alone? Will he be the solitary dot on one side of the dice, or will the universe help and surround him on the other? He does not know what he is, he knows the wings have changed. A spiritual growth is beginning. The worries for today are off his shoulders.

A rogue bat leaves the formation. Looking down. As the creature hovers, staring directly at Eddy, into his soul with a bright, blood red sunsetting chill. Bats are fearful. A shiver comes over him. Is it not one of the forms that Count Dracula used? Thus, akin to this rogue that has taken a particular interest in him striking him with the same forceful strength as Dracula caused a fearful reaction to what he attempted to do. From the weak defenceless point of view, he returns the gaze. Seeing the almost flickering of the red eyes like fire he remains, trying not to break his stare with a blink, a wink or a single bat of an eyelid he looks intently.

If he was not mistaken, he swore he saw in the grotesque creatures eyes a reminder of what he has just come from. In the reflection of each other's eyes, his personal demons in the eyes of the beholder speak to his soul that there is nothing to fear, but fear itself. The eyes of the bat lighten, he flies away in a jerking pitching path where his colony travel to. He turns to get blinded by the disclosed sun, furthermore he is blindly entering some unknown situation on a new path. The last bat is far, far in the distance. Having tried to drain him of self-confidence his head is steadfast on his poised upright back that strides homeward bound. He has misunderstood potential to explore in a locked chamber of his heart in his own untrodden foreign land.

He is still getting used, on most nights, to sleeping on his own. He falls asleep lingering on the bat's strange behaviour. Bats do not enter his sleep, hence no nightmares. For the first time in many weeks, he sleeps soundly.

Even Hope Flees
Two Months Ago

So, it begins again. The rising of hope. Like the crystal-clear droplets of future from the fountain of youth, each one shines with promise to drop and shatter in the slightest of instance. Yet, as luck would not have it, the hope was false hope. Alas, despite all of the previous warnings, Eddy emerged upbeat. In Eddy's heart and mind, he was feeling optimistic again. Love was beginning to grow for a second time. He once again took the fooling fragile step of not doing what he wanted to do in order to make Beth-Annie happy. He felt that, he actually believed that she was worth it.

Afterall, he saw her as a unicorn, one of a kind. A mythical chance of a partnership that dreams were made of. Fairy tales were based on these foundations. Eddy neglected to see that most fairy tales end in tragedy, unless Walt Disney takes control, therefore planting the happy-ever-after spin on it. He wanted that. He wanted her to be happy. What is more he also wanted them to have the happy-ever-after fantasy. And, foolishly, he believed that he was going to get just that.

In his heart, he wanted to ask so many questions. The why she had taken him down that emotional journey of being unwanted, being an outcast like the deformed appearance of the *Hunchback of Notre Dame*. Banished to live a life through other people's points of view.

In spite of everything that had happened, which seemed in the past for now, today they were travelling together to her childhood home, Orange. A short three-and-a-half-hour drive from Sydney, leaving the city skyscrapers behind, to pass through the picturesque Blue Mountains. The quaint small towns that appeared to be only made up of one road, and then, a blink and it has gone in the diminishing image disappearing from vision in the rear-view mirror make it a pleasant change from the incessant hubbub of city life.

A stunning drive through the Australian bush. Besides soaring red stone cliffs that the road goes through, winding around, escalating up and down, rolling like a marble smoothly through the man-made grey tracks, but he had eyes focused only on her answers, not the spectacular scenery. He used the time wisely, to talk.

She held his hand as he drove, talked but looked out of the window disengaged from the blurred khaki hues fleeting by. At her comment about the dryness he sees the barren, yellow, rain-starved countryside that this summer had given this year. He used this as a way of stemming the emotional tides of the conversation. It was a particularly low rainfall this year, this apparent scene shows the repercussions of this. Also, as already they were not enough ineffective feeble friendly fire. He deflected further irrelevant rubber bullets off their not premeditated protective chain mailed ballroom attire. He points out the white arrow pointing far right into the red zone, the high hazard careful danger zone of an imminent bushfire that would only take a spark to ignite.

Altering subjects in a dancefloor chorography of perfectly placed areas under discussed magnifying glasses. Melodic themes from matters of the heart to topical issues at home and abroad. They danced to the different beats, around the more specify pressing issues that needed clarifying afoot. Just like the pending bushfire, the spark of a miscued accent would generate the kind of conditions for a fiery heated conversation. As a not so much an if, but a when it will happen. Comparable to the bushfire, if they catch it early enough, they can have power over the rage. Of course, the big if, if they catch it early enough.

He extends his hand across the gearstick to hold hers. Readily available she opens her hand, locks firmly enough to unite the security of trust. She softly traces her thumb over his hand in the warmness of her lap. It felt good. It felt like no time had passed. They were connecting again. It was a little strange, out of rhythm at first but before they even left Sydney a conversation had started. It was comfortable. The silence was comfortable. Hope was rising high, from the watery flames to erupt into fireworks inside of his inner self, his psyche.

When they had come to the other side of the Blue Mountains, the curving road became flatter once more. They headed into the deep growth of tall trees with rustling crisp orange shades brushed by the shining blonde straw-coloured rising sun. Eddy had seen the café in the distance first, as the childlike Beth-Annie closed her eyes to formally welcome in the day. Shadowed fingers swept across her silky-smooth light brown tanned skin looking for flaws that did not exist. Suddenly Eddy pulled over without a single word causing her heart to get lost in the catching of her own breath.

A sigh of relief as the oblivious Eddy pointed out the sign above the single-storeyed wooden shop. The storefront was as wide as if the doors stretched to fill the space. The windows were placed meticulously to represent a Dalí illusion, a creation of a face as well as a shop front. The doors smiled to greet them below his roof-hat for the self-proclaimed sign proudly roared to be the 'best coffee this side of Italy'.

A remarkable stake to declare. It was a calling for him to sample it. That rather ambitious claim made the thirst accelerate. Eyes fixed, for which his mind pondered the truth in it as he briskly strode the three short steps to the doors. Turning at the top to see Beth-Annie lagging behind. He yells cheerfully back, 'It has to be a tongue-in-cheek claim.' All the time impatiently pacing.

Beth-Annie quickly caught up, nursing her neck. The rather impulsive stop had caused Bethany to snap her head in panic, wanting to ask sharply, 'What is going on!' She said all she wanted to say through the glare of her eyes, the grasp of his hand. He pointed with his free hand at the brown, weather-worn sign. She smiled; she knew. She could not help but find him adorable in his stupid actions. She shuffled her feet, hand over her brow, rubbing her eyes. She knew how some people got hangry. Well, Eddy got cangry. He yearned for coffee like some people yearned for food. Coffee helped stem this foolhardy, outright idiotic flow. In his humble way of apologising, Eddy opens the door to allow Beth-Annie to walk in first.

I have brought back Elpis, Goddess of False Hope. Although she never really left. Eddy lived, unknowingly, with Elpis by his side. She was there as Eddy was born and she will be there when he lives his last moments in an unsuccessful hope of not breathing his last breath.

This Elpis is the hope that Beth-Annie would return. His candle relit with more general expectation that Elpis fanned with hope, and to leave the caressing want of her, Beth-Annie in his life. That false hope that he created a fantasy of dreamlike proportions that it would, genuinely actually happen. Elpis went to Beth-Annie to get her to call him, to spend this weekend away. She initially could not work out why she felt the desire to take this trip with him, but I made it happen.

There was a rumour that she was my daughter, yet she is Nyx's. Elpis seems to find a flower in the bleakest of situations. She holds the colour, the fragrance in her optimistic approach to look forward. Always finding the flower, the bright side. Elpis cannot be a comfort. Hope is a comfort. That is for Spes. Elpis knows that hope is nothing but a bridge to pain, that will sooner or later show its face.

The sheltering form of Oneiroi came along to view. The spirit of dreams actually proved a good source for me. He is split into four aspects of egotistic characterising elements for which have different names. Epiales is the spirit of nightmares, Morpheus the God of the dreams which take the form of humans, Phantasos the spirit of dreams in fantasies who take shapes in inanimate objects and Phobetor, who is the spirit of nightmares in the forms of animals. I use Phantasos to work with Elpis to generate a false dream of something that could possibly happen.

Eddy has taken the hook of hope as sincere, Beth-Annie is not completely under any of them. She still has her free will. A free will that is tugging at her one way to remove herself from this cruel exercise. Unluckily for her, Elpis is using her to attract the delusion of rekindling relationship flames, thus being despicably hypocritically insincere. Against her resolve, her will, her free will, she is two-faced as the pawn in this scene.

Eddy had to laugh at the Crème Brûlée flavoured teabags. He could not help the noise from escaping his mouth. 'So, Vanilla then!' he mused. It was preposterous for this flavour to sell anywhere in the world. He had not seen something so ridiculous in a long time, he had to take a photograph of it. No-one would believe him. This must have been a hard sell here. Even for the city, with the copious amounts of people that want to be different. It would have taken a magnificent marketing campaign headed by the most influential movie star, ever, to sell this mockery.

Hence, by doing as the star did, they actually follow each other's trends. But let alone a small town that did not need, want, or desire to be keeping up with the Joneses. They either liked things because they liked them. Wanted things because they needed, or wanted them. Not for materialistic bonus points at a dinner party. Eddy liked these communities. Hard-working, honest people that work on the land, help the land and appreciate the land. This made this sell, coupled by the inflated price tag even more side-splittingly comical to him.

Having had his nice, black sugarless coffee, although he has had better, he is back in his happy place. They were back on the road for the last leg of the journey. They entered the outskirts of her hometown just before midday. Her back is straightened, proud as she recognises the narrow road, the signs on the mailboxes of the farms. Her mood, with her posture heighten, elevate in recognition of what the home straight represents. Comfort, security.

At the point where the farmlands get more residential is a wooden billboard. Looking a combination of weather-fared, barely enough strength to stay upright and toughened by what looks like bullet holes, it battles to state loud in bold fifties décor:

Welcome to Orange. Banjo Patterson Country

She turned to him with an eager smile, rigidly posed. A smile that muffled her high-pitched words. She spoke fast as she explained that this sign was what she would always remember when she was younger in coming back from trips away. In the holidays spent away, normally on the coast, to being back at home. Coming back to her comfortable bed. Back with schoolmates, friends and familiarity. Sometimes she would be even more excited by this sign, than leaving for the beach.

The sadness that a holiday was over was quickly replaced with an air of happiness in seeing her mates, but more importantly, her beloved horse, Firkin. Of course, Firkin is no longer in Orange now, but she talks of her as if she was. A rich stitch in her tapestry that would never fade. Her beloved horse which when brought was nearly sold again. A beloved horse that was boisterous. A beloved horse that was dangerous to everyone accept her.

They have made this journey before, but she still guides Eddy around the small city centre to the end of the cul-de-sac at the eastern side of town from Ramse Street. He lets her have this moment. It was at the end of Moad Place with her parents two large cars, and a neglected horsebox taken the space in the carport that they park outside. The white metal fence is a modern-day picket fence that keeps the excited childhood grey whippet called Travis from running into the road. Travis barks quickly, loudly and affectionately. Honestly, Eddy is confused to who is more excited to be seeing each other after a long period away, the dog or her.

Beth-Annie rushes out the car, leaving the black door wide open as she opens the gate to Travis who jumps up at her, licks her face. Her eyes are googled at his white piercing wide orbs that show a love unconditional in both of their glares.

He grabs one of the small bags for the short stay to an empty looking house. Two small brick steps lead to a covered veranda with an inviting soft-looking cushioned-sprawled brown wicker double seat swaying chair looking out to the road. A brass horse-head knocker is left untouched as Beth-Annie slides past to push open the door. Travis walks by Eddy's side with Beth-Annie calling out. No-one inside. Her mum is not at home.

As if the moons aligned together, a soft vibration came from her pocket. Her mother had sent a message stating she was still shopping for dinner and running late. The outside makes the inside look larger or the other way round. The door opens to a wood-fire place with a U-shaped sitting amenity with a glass coffee table in the centre of a white woollen rug. Family photographs adorn the walls, in frames on the furniture competing with the china plates, horse trophy's and memorabilia. A small corridor leads to the parent's rooms which is understandable out of bounds.

At the end was her childhood room. A small single bed that seems to be left as she would have left it. A large poster of a horse is above her bed. A bedside table with a light and alarm clock. A dresser decorated with colourful make-up accessories with a small non-dancing, stuck in a twirl tiny dancer which is in need of rewinding. Through a door into the open plan gallery-style kitchen, dining room and television room.

More photographs with a roaring fire welcoming them into this room as Beth-Annie does a hasty whirlwind tour making sure that her father is not asleep somewhere. She points to a closed door and states the bathroom, toilet and laundry is through there. A room off the living area was her brother's room. She states to put the bags here. A double bed fills the room. It is large, tall and very soft as he sits on it with Beth-Annie to share a lingering kiss.

Lastly was a conservatory with a pool table, an office of sorts and another entertaining room. The front garden flows perfectly into the back garden with a small but perfectly sized pool and no less than three sheds. When Eddy enquired, he got the response of 'one for Dad, the other for storage and the other for stuff that we should get rid of, but don't, like my redundant horse-riding gear'.

To the right, in the sun-kissed rockery, wholly cared for lovingly and tenderly is the gravestone and burial place of Firkin. Beth-Annie pauses at the memories that these simple rocks represent as she blinks back into the present.

Admittedly, they were a little earlier than planned, but this did give Beth-Annie more time to play with Travis in the backyard. Eddy was forgotten. He felt a pang of ridiculous jealousy. Veneered timber floorboards are spread throughout the open plan spared of numerous doors to create a spacious impression. Purely brought and impeccably intended rugs and mats are ingeniously positioned around the floors as he softly treads back through. He goes back to the car, shuts the still-open passenger door, grabs her bag out of the boot, leaving her satchel which contains her laptop for work, a needless interference for this weekend.

Crossing through the gate, making sure it is shut, tightly locked and into the manicured garden beds that fringed the perfectly lawned grass. A perfectly trimmed green block hedge the same height of the bright white tall fence acts as the barrier. He closed the mosquito-screen of her home, leaving the air to naturally come forth. He takes their bags into the bedroom. He watches them play from the back-patio doors. Mirroring them, seeing a reflection of him in the glass he also sees a gleeful smile has spread over his face.

The family photographs are scattered in various poses, occasions and growing-up stages taking pride on every spare space on the walls or shelves. Like Beth-Annie and her brother and sister. Like her parents, and their siblings and like their parents before. They were all born and raised in Orange. None have wandered far from their nest. He tries to retrace the progression of the photographs in a chronical order to pass the time, hence, not to disturb Beth-Annie's returning to youth.

Caryll, Beth-Annie's mum hails her arrival from the open doorway. Unknown to her, Travis had already betrayed her and alerted them all to her presence. She sensed Caryll before her call to scamper around the house to her provider, skidding around the corner with a twinkling sound of marbles on ice. She limply pats Travis on his slobbering lips first, before throwing her arms around her daughter, hugging her fiercely on the veranda. Frantically wagging his tail, clearly grinning and moving around, Travis tries to nestle his head, to be part of the embrace.

The triad have a fast conversation of words and barking before Eddy is introduced. For no reason, Beth-Annie sheds a tear. Then they go back to everything from a news report of no elaboration but headlines, to local news in the first steps across of the threshold. Then continuing to touch on everything from the car, to the house, to the job in a matter of seconds as they head towards the kitchen. Eddy picks up the canvas bags of groceries that tumble out their contents onto the wooden deck. Gently pushing Travis's sniffing nose away from the treasures within. He hears the soaring tones of two friends more than a daughter and mother. It is a unique bond that nothing can rival.

Finally, Caryll is given space to gingerly exchange a peck on the cheek to Eddy with the briefest pleasantries of small talk. It was not their first time that they had met, but there is a slight, peculiar uncomfortable feel to their chit-chatting of uneasy words. Eddy is wise to why. He knows the bond they share. He guesses that she would have told her everything, as yet he is unsure in what light the story portrayed him. They have talked more than met over the past three weeks.

It is for that reason he does not know if Caryll knows the full circumstances of their fragmented relationship. He cannot even explain it. A yo-yo relationship that is on and off again more times than an indicator waiting to cross a busy highway in peak traffic. Yet, the way she tenderly rests her hand on his arm. The soft tones of her voice gives him comfort that she possesses, for the most part, the good side, or the impartial point of view. Of course, if the going got tough she would side with her daughter. After the first jerky questions, sporadic spoken answers. This reasonably unreasoned awkwardness passes quickly as they find a regularity.

Surprisingly for them both, perhaps detecting the rockiness in their correlation, Beth-Annie sneaks up behind Eddy into the kitchen to grab his hand in her hand and tenderly, oh so tenderly, places a dry kiss on his arm. Caryll turns her head to notice this fitting together of broken hearts with a look to Eddy that, again irrationally, suggests she wryly sneers rather than shines reverential expression.

Beth-Annie steals a longing look deep into the eyes of Eddy to tell him that it was filled with honest, genuine affection. Seeing Eddy catch her expression, Caryll promptly busies herself in the kitchen to make space for which she graciously points for Eddy to place the bags on the counter with a courteous nod of thanks. He actually forgot he was still carrying them.

Without argument, not that she would have got one, she, without delay makes a light lunch of sliced thin fresh smoked ham and mature cheddar sandwiches on a grain and oat thickly sliced fresh bread. Although not sounding that great by her simple announcement of a 'ham and cheese sanga is on the table.' It was, and it was very filling. They eat with a fresh brewed coffee and chat over the heavily varnished pine table.

The conversation was flowing effortlessly easy as weak as water. Travis was patiently waiting for the meekest hole in their etiquette for one of them to throw him a crust. The struggling to stay alight log fire crackling from the next room filled the house with the aroma of being warm, safe and very homely. A bird sings from outside as the conversation relaxes into an open discussion where topics are finished off with personal opinion, some of them shared, some stand alone but with no judgement, ensuing an argument, or hotly heated debate.

Caryll wanted to show off to Eddy her hometown and insisted on taking them around. It was indeed strange to think that the amount of times the they had been here as a couple, they had not seen the sights that others would have seen, which obviously now, Beth-Annie took for granted.

She drove slowly. Pointed out certain places of interest to her. Where she worked, her former family home, all with stories about specific places. An elevating, winding road fringed with trees, takes them to spot where they can see the whole town below. Beth-Annie whispers that this was a popular make-out spot. Eddy made a joke about not really wanting a mother-daughter threesome. A joke that went firmly south, but made him wink and chuckle to Beth-Annie who after a brief second saw the funny side of the ill-timed joke. He tried to reassert himself by asking if she ever fooled about up here. She stated 'no' way, way too quickly to even sound remotely true.

It was far too swiftly getting late in the evening. The day was beginning to draw to an end. The dark cloak of night was wishing the sun adieu, the silver moon was casting deposits of light in graceful traces of smooth fingers. Lights were flickering on as they headed home from the bright, shivering air-conditioned cold shops with bags full of groceries to cook the evening meal.

The kitchen in every home has the phenomenal ability of connecting people. And this one was only too familiar. The comfy looking set of suites were left to lounge as the wooden chairs around the wooden dining table was the place to be. Over a glass of the regions famous red wine they talk about politics to homelife, to work to sport, to jokes, stories and memories. It was a delightful evening of wine. A steak cooked to perfection with rosemary roasted vegetables and potato's.

The first thing to dry up was the wine, rather than the chatter. So, Caryll did the only thing that civilised people could do in this situation, she went to the drinks cupboard and got the aged whisky. Eddy missed this feel of family life. He, as well as Beth-Annie would never admit this openly, but it was glaringly obvious for all to see. For she missed her family. He missed not having his.

By the end of the evening, their cheekbones ached through the smiling. Their abdominal muscles ached by the incessant continual belly laughs. Their eyes cried all the tears of joy through giggles that they could not hold. Crying is good. In the finest seconds of this occasion, discarding the salty tears purified the soul. Memories made that gives the heart a profound reason to keep beating a drum to adventure for another such time. This night seemed healthy. They all felt suited…as a family.

They cannot remember when they went to bed. They fell asleep in each other's arms. Talking, wanting each other's company, each other's raw attraction rather than physical momentum. To wake, seemingly in the same position. After last night they woke looking into the same doting, caring eyes. A perfect smile. A warm kiss. A tender look. Prising themselves away they got ready. They heard Caryll whistling, the noise of pans on the stove, chopping and sizzling of that unmistakable smell of salivating bacon. They knew they should at least offer to help, but, they held each other behind closed doors. Wondering why they cannot seem to make this work. Saying nothing. Not one of them wanting this feeling to end. Both of them equally wanted it, so why was it so God Damn Hard to achieve the possible.

They joined Caryll to have breakfast outside in the sun while reading the daily newspaper in episodic uncommunicativeness. It was noticeable that Caryll carried herself with an air of fragility. She struggled to swallow the last two mouthfuls of her now-cold coffee. She seemed to brace herself, a self-medicative approach to make certain her whole self was ready to move. Eddy noticed these signs as he indeed was doing the exact same thing.

An understandable mannerism as they all nursed a rather dusty head from a seventy-thirty combination of alcohol and sleep deprivation. The only one acting unaware of their struggles was Travis. He made the gently retreat to doze off in front of the gentle dying embers of the log fire at some point during the evening. The strikingly attractive light grey whippet, with his white markings like war paint on his face sniffed energetically in the flower beds, lounging in his domain of the perfectly trimmed backyard grass while chasing the occasional bird, fly or butterfly that enters his own personal space. He was not so much as a warrior but a protector. Although Beth-Annie's father was not around—as he was in Melbourne on a business conference—he came up in conversation often between the rustling wind-carried leaves of the newspaper.

Caryll has had a lighter breakfast of a single dry piece of toast and not long ago brewed percolated coffee. She politely excuses herself from the table. Tentatively lowering her back as she picks up a small wooden basket by the back door with various gardening tools protruding out, and some well-used gloves hanging off the sides. She is a healthy thin, strong woman in good physical shape that holds her posture by means of having proud grace in herself as well as her homes appearance. She gently kneels in the flowerbed where Travis was only body and legs a few minutes earlier. She proceeds to pick out the weeds. They continue to enjoy the bacon, eggs and homemade grape and apple jam. Occasionally echoing a sentence, phrase or quote from an article. No matter who brought the topic up the other person responded in the same way, an indifferent nod of the head, a pokerfaced smile and an indecipherable meaningless mumble.

Although she was a teacher by trade, her husband was the design for the garden. A retired landscape gardener for the local parks and gardens in, and around Orange that got forced, in preference to his passion, to take an office job for a local insurance firm. Forced by the pregnancy as it would not have supported them. The pay was awful for a gardener; thus, he was placed in that position. Having to make a choice between his family and his job, his love and his passion. Putting a price, quite literally on his family.

As she toiled the flowerbeds, Caryll explained the reason for the flowers while keeping her head bowed firmly looking at the work that she maintained. Eddy eagerly listened as this was the first time he had heard the motives, which no doubt had been hammered into her since they first met, before Beth-Annie was their daughter. However, like anyone that has a borderline infatuation for their craft to someone that adores to hear the intense zeal tones in a speech, Eddy absorbs the information.

She recounts that certain flowers were not only chosen for colour, but location for the most or lease sun, wind or shade. Chillies were used for colour and a deterrent for Travis to wreak havoc. Eddy could not help but think that it was a shame that these yellow and red sunburst tubulars were not for cooking or eating. The garden was a magnificent fragrant jungle of pulsating art. The smells that enveloped their senses as they moved to sit on the swaying wicker seat behind. Combined with the steaming mugs of coffee, the picking out of the teeth of the toasted sour dough with the unusual combination of the jam that worked, Eddy looked over the garden with more detail than before. It was warm enough in light T-shirt and jeans.

They both listened to Caryll speak as she looked down at her efforts, scrupulously working on another flowerbed. Undoubtedly, Eddy was sure that Beth-Annie had heard this speech before, but nursed her coffee mug with her pyjama-covered knees up to her chest with the sweetest of miens, cherishing the shared love of him in his creation being cared by her. A look that Eddy had forgotten she possessed. Innocence.

A short walk down a small hill and they were in the centre of the town. This was a time were the mine was the salt of the earth. The mining town was something that was holding a majority of people here. The streets were laced with gold, as expensive cars would go by, driven by people barely out of nappies but never less brought with their own cash. The money was excellent. For not needing qualifications, many children just left school when they could, to work the mines. The qualifications could be earned there, although many did not as they saw the cash come in, thought about the day and not the time ahead. The money. As well as the status of being able to climb the ladder quickly. Birds sang, Travis barked occasionally, and the country smells, sounds and calmness was only broken by the youngsters in their new, gleaming, custom-fitted cars.

Beth-Annie moves towards the park. She voluntarily lays down, grabs the newspaper out of Eddy's hand. Instinctively gives back the sports pages and starts reading the current news article that she started at the breakfast table. She knowingly distracts Eddy as he tries to read last night's reports to keep looking at her perfect peach activewear, which they were doing something not even close. Her legs bent back, swinging, lazily in her skin tight grey pants that stroked her smooth, pert bottom as if attentively painted on with single bristles of a brush.

It was not an overly erotic scene, but maybe it was the innocence of it that made Eddy want to join her and have his wicked way with her. Right there. In the park. It was the other locals barely a few metres away. Tending to their own park life that prevented that thought progressing into an action. Nevertheless, it was a blissful scene in the absence of all-inclusive relaxation. Beth-Annie catches Eddy stare as he does not even attempt to hide his glare. She crawls, ascends on her knees, leans between his crotch on the bench. He leans down as they meet in the middle. She kisses him and takes his hand. Pulls him as they both get to their feet. Without unlocking her hands, it is time for home.

The pending moment that Eddy was hoping for before heading back was firmly slammed shut as Caryll messages Beth-Annie to meet for coffee. The shrill tones bellowed out for them to go for a stroll back into town. Basking in the numerous cafés that had spilled onto the pavement were many people. The smell of roasting, filtering, brewing coffee enveloped the shoppers in tugs of vapour to bring them through the doors. The bakery, the 'only one' according to Caryll, was too good to resist.

Cheese and ham croissants with cheese within the pastry as well as inside was a revelation. They were not even hungry but were compelled to order, eat and enjoy them. This time away was perfect. It could not have been planned better. A step into a life of harmony that the black and white movies portray so well.

Disappointment after disappointment. Hope followed by hope that got shot out of the air to drop as quickly as it rose. Eddy told himself that he was not going to get carried away in the moment. But. He could not help it. He was falling head-over-heels for her once again. She was teasing him with hope that it was not, in fact, over.

The evening was coming around quickly, the time to head back to Sydney was blowing the sand away quicker than a hurricane. Despite this, they did not rush. The slow amble back to her home, although no longer her permanent home, she still could not escape the tendency to call it home. The walk was filled with the sharing of more childhood memories of the adventures of a younger Beth-Annie. She pointed out many ordinary sights with special particular meanings, for instance pointing out an alley that she ran away from the local storekeeper after being caught trying to steal a fifteen-cent candy bar. With the spilling of tales, they skipped along homeward bound. In an almost childlike way they swung their hands, which, for the most part seemed playfully apt with reference to the very personal sightseeing tour. It was a weekend of never before shared stories from her. A weekend of sharing.

Taking no time to retrieve their belongings and packing them into the car, they said their goodbyes. Suddenly, Beth-Annie exploded out of the car. An astonished Eddy thought she had forgotten something important. Well, it was to her; she had forgotten to kiss Travis goodbye.

In no time, the melancholy chilling dusk brought its lingering touch into the car. The windscreen revealing a few keepsakes that she persuaded her mother to part with. Frequently they appeared in reverse by means of the illuminating amber streetlights that guided them along the highway. The conversation was sad. This was not uncommon, as she always was downhearted after leaving home. He wondered why she did not move back. The whole ride home rode the rhythmical smooth tarmac across the velvetiness dejection moods with joyful reminiscences as they fondled each other's free hand. No mobiles came out to play. Just them. Her head resting on his driving shoulders. That evening saw them back in Sydney, Eddy's home. The candle of hope brightly burned.

Elpis, the essence of false hope, was playing with Eddy like a cat plays with a yarn of wool. Not breaking ranks is Epimetheus, rather foolish but always comes to light after events as the God of Afterthought. His father, however, is invited by Elpis. Prophasis, the God of Excuse, is the string that forms the ball of wool. Yarning strings of fiction in an atypical network of excuses. Layer upon layer, but in being so, it happened that the seed does not fall far from the tree as he is the proverbial fool. His excuses tangle free to unveil threads of dishonest excuses. Elpis laid her cards on the table to prove that the hope, was in fact her doing. A false hope bound by excuses.

Out of the night, no warning, just the sneaking of a thief in the shadows grabbing the mouth to stop an alerting suspicion sound penetrating the darkness. Without forewarning an argument happened. It was over nothing. It was something, that Eddy only would dare to admit to himself, to some degree he felt that Beth-Annie seemed to have premeditated the whole act. Something that she wanted to happen, so she had an excuse for the great weekend to come tearing down in shreds of regret.

She really enjoyed herself. Considering she did not know why the impulse came, she never if truth be told had intentions that it would be fun. She hated the feeling that spread over her. Moreover, to the point that she did want to rekindle the fire. She was strongly considering adding a log to the smouldering ashes. The attraction was lit. She found herself remembering why she loved Eddy, rather than confirming that she was right in her belief to end it. She was confused. She did not want the end; on the other hand, she wanted the end. Her whole thought process was in complete disarray. Eddy was unequally confused. Confused to her actions, her overreactions.

The feeble reason, the ridiculous excuse that started the ever so weak argument begun with him taken a shower first. To exit the bathroom for her turn, to only leave the toilet seat up. In his own apartment! Was it really the end of the world? Really necessary to start World War Three?

Beth-Annie grabbed his car keys from the fruit bowl in the hallway as she stormed out in a huff. Leaving the door wide open she disappeared from view. She drove off into the night. The sound of the screeching of tyres and engines heard in the distance long after the rear red lights had gone out of the frame.

Eddy was at the threshold with the light behind him casting no shadow into the dark empty street. He had no words. Mouth gaping open as he was dumbstruck on what had just happened in a matter of milliseconds. He wondered how, but what is more, that if somehow this messy scene could have been avoided. The hope was torched into trailing wisps of small fragile flowing ashes that transcended ruin. Beth-Annie left, leaving an uncomfortable peace. Leaving Eddy in pieces. It was cruel. He closed the front door. He would try her mobile.

Eddy had scarcely closed the door when he fished his mobile out. He fingered over Beth-Annie. That call will have to wait. She would not pick up. He knew that. She needed to cool down. So, he called Jay. Tried to explain the weekend until that strange moment of nightmarish proportions. Jay listened with only the occasional grunt that he was in true fact paying attention until he was sure that this was his cue to say something.

'Cheer up. Things we, I mean, will get better and you will be laughing again.'

Eddy loved the fact that he did not resort to the clichéd responses that he had heard before.

'Thanks Jay.' He smiled satirically, for the first time since his life came crashing down, once again. Mainly due to Jay hanging on as he placed the situation into a gibberish consortium of words to explain something, he did not know he could verbalise. Jay understood his torment. 'Thanks…Jay, but how can I laugh tomorrow when…when I don't even feel like smiling today?'

Eddy did not listen to the response as he watched a car pass, hoping that it was his car, his lady, Beth-Annie. Only for it to be not only a different car, make, model but no female behind the steering wheel. He thanked Jay yet again, as he turned his mobile off, turned into the darkness as the silent tears started streaming down his face.

As the latch of the bedroom door echoed into the hallway, he paused. That sound resounded within him. That sound was like a barring of their prison cell. Incarcerating the relationship in a miserable life sentence. An emotional way to end four years together. Just like the first night in prison the graveness of the situation will confront him in the death of the night where the only light came through the window. The traumatised remaining pieces of his heart sucking all the air out of the room to feebly attempt to resuscitate his obliterated spiritual core. Only succeeding in suffocating his will to live.

Eddy cannot sleep. His mind was negotiating with Beth-Annie. A conversation where you are having it with someone that is not there. He thrashes the mattress as he gets up. Sits down at his desk he decided to write down what he has rushing around his head. Incidentally, astonishingly he writes in the style of a letter. Carefully he wrote, stating that he did not know why the relationship broke down, but he deserved a second chance, to give her a better experience. He was bargaining. He was asking the powers above, below and around him promising to be a better person. He smirks a sly one through closed lips as he breathes a short breath out of his nose, all awhile he shakes his head at a line, he deems stupid. Inside of writing in his mind, he takes the magnificent notion of actually writing it down with pen and paper.

He then retrieves another piece of paper from the drawer to start another letter. This one is filled with rage. He writes this down with the aim that it will never be seen by anyone else, much more it will never be seen by Beth-Annie. He was hurt, but even in his hurt he did not want him to be the cause of her feeling his pain. In her reading his poisonous words it would undoubtably hurt her. Each letter is gorged, each finished word is almost scratched deeply into the paper with the anger he possesses in his white-knuckled terrifying hand that he grips harder to stop him from shaking.

Fear and anger combine to prevent him to write. Determination with pure teeth-clenched gritting inclination makes him continue. He drools on the freshly laid ink. Leaving pools of blotted marks. He would never want her eyes to meet what he had etched into the paper. As in doing so her eyes meeting these lines would cause more pain than he would ever intend on anyone he loved.

He is starting to feel better. Albeit still suffering. This simple exercise is proving to be therapeutic. Foolishly promising to be the man she wants. But, he really does not know what he actually did wrong, was doing wrong, no, what he actually did wrong. An ironic laugh without the fuel of laughter came across raspy and harsh.

He carried on writing until the morning was breaking. Compact balls of screwed up written pages strew around him, on the ground, the table, some launched to roll to a resting point under the sofa. All night he has been attempting to resolve the old age equation, the complexity of love. Trying to explain the unexplainable scientifically explainable formula to a loving relationship. Trying to figure out why the one he wanted does not want him back. This unreciprocated love. This question that has never been answered since the beginning of time. His mind changes tact to go to great measures to put his insecurities at ease.

'Is she gay? Does she not know? Does she not want to admit it to herself?'

His mind was a frightening place where speedbumps were placed for him to slow down, to eventually stop but he kept driving through them. Each barrier to protect him from himself, he kept exploding right through with another reason to why this was happening.

'Gay!'

This time, he actually speaks the word out loud. He looks at the mirror to his right. Catching sight of his eyes that were bloodshot from tears, dragged heavy from exhaustion and pale from heartache, he blurted out a sardonic giggle. It was his mind laughing out at his look. Fireworks erupting around, igniting the pure unadulterated absurdity as he whispers once, to shout out as he repeats himself:

'I WISH SHE SAID. WOULD HAVE SAID THAT…THAT SHE WAS GAY!'

He was carrying on like a porkchop with no-one to stop him.
He had to be the one to stop him.
He quickly pulled himself together. He was on the brink of going indisputably insane. He headed to the shower to cleanse himself of these irrational outbursts of friction induced concocted fabricated emissions. As the cool water ran down his clothed body, he still stubbornly refused to go along with the truth that it was ending. His head pressed firmly on the white tiled cubicle, eyes closed, allowing the water to flow over him. Fighting his feelings.

Was still standing in a no-man's state of refusal to accept it was actually over. He needed her to say it. Either that she did not love him anymore, or to say it was over.

He also thought about going down the risky, treacherous road of enlisting friends and family to aid him, to talk to her. To help him find out what she is thinking. To find out if she did, in fact think of him, at, all. Talk about him in a positive light. Or, even give him an element of closure by disclosure by disclosing what he actually did.

BEEP BEEP.

His mobile chimes him awake. He was still damp in his clothes lying precariously perched on the edge of the bottom of his bed. He was tired but could not recall falling asleep. He peels himself towards the sound. A message. The message on the banner feed is probably the closest indication to this being the end. Beth-Annie did not have the backbone to say it, so went for the cliché. That gutless approach. That line that says so much as an opposite to the other three words that people find hard to say for the first time. Yet, these were three nails hammered deeply into the three sides of the four-sided coffin:

'I need time.'

Eddy is no fool, so why was he acting like one.

In his heart, Eddy knows that this is it. However, he does not want to recognise the fact. It was a great trip, barely twelve hours ago. Normally, when you are shown such a personal aspect of someone's life, in this instance the family homelife, it means that they want to go on with the loving process. To progress what you, as a couple, are doing. After he wished her good morning with a kiss shared, warm, thoughtful and receptive. This morning, he shared the loneliest of kisses.

Another barrier. Another if. Maybe the last roll of the dice came in the sex. Having sex in her family home did not go to plan. Eddy felt uncomfortable. He always took a long time to climax. Here is what his doctor called, rather playfully as a syndrome called the Delivery Boy. Then professionally explained it as meaning that he wants his partner to fully enjoy the experience first so he can then be validated in having a time of his own. He wanted her to climax many times before he did. He would go above and beyond, literally to give her every aspect of a sexual awakening. He had never encountered a problem with this.

However, Beth-Annie was an exception. She felt that it was her that was not good enough. Eddy explain, rather fruitlessly the reason. He explained that they could enjoy fourplay, messing around without arriving at the station early. This conversation occurred, reoccurred and never really went away. They talked about the white elephant in the room but never solved it. Beth-Annie saw it as a negative. Eddy saw it as a positive. It was not a problem for him. She insisted that he went to the doctors for which he got diagnosed for another diagnosis.

Still the white elephant remained, mockingly. Yet in the family home back in Orange. For the first time though, Eddy could not climax however they tried, as long as they kept on going. It was being in the quiet place, her mother sleeping a few feet away in the home without many doors. He was scared stiff, but unable to relax.

Still he is being shot by reasoned bullets in no-man's land. Standing at a crossroads with several spokes like a wooden cart. Eddy can go forward and forget about her…eventually. He can turn left, right, and one day hope to bump into her. Or, he can go backwards and fight for her right now. Eddy knew what he could do. He also knew what he should do. For reasons unclear he did what he could, his mind argued why, and rather than what his heart should do he went with what he should not do.

I see this at the point that I know I have chosen wisely. Eddy was going to die. Eddy did not know this. He would continue to live his life in a fabrication that it will keep going and he will keep loving. I go to agents of Moirai, fates. They are present at birth. They tell me the length of Eddy's life, with Moros, the Spirit of Doom who personally tells me the moment for which this man will meet his inevitable destruction.

Only one man can choose to save a person from fate—Zeus. It is for this reason that I travel to them under the cloak of stealth so he will not save Eddy on the point that fate will seize them. As fate is determined at his death, the Goddess of Fate becomes the Goddess of Death, Thanatoio. I can see him changing with the pending anticipation of the beckoning end. I tell him to hold tight that it will not happen soon.

For Eddy, it takes a few more days to sink in. He is still bargaining. Left out in the cold, colder than the coldest winter. Like an unwanted Christmas puppy, he is a bleak undesirable outcast. For Eddy it has sunken in. Eddy needs to rise above the waves. He needs, must, needs to make the best of it. Eddy needs to prove himself that he can do it. That he can do it again. Eddy can do it. Eddy will not only swim. Eddy will not only conquer. Eddy will dive up and keep rising his body. Eddy will show himself what he can achieve. His personal mission has been accepted.

New start.

New life.

New Eddy.

A flap of the mailbox. The scratch of metal on metal. The abruptly halting jingle of small pieces of metal on the beige tiled floor. He knows that sound. He throws himself towards the front door to see his car keys on the floor. Urgently pulls the front door open as the scraping of keys demonstrate underneath. He scans everywhere. Sees no-one. Throws himself into the street. Calls out her name like a madman. Not a single sign of life.

Then, it hit…

Depression
Four Weeks Ago

'AGHHHHHH!'

In an unguarded moment, Eddy shouts out with his face tightening around his clenched jaw.

'AGHHHHHH!'

The second time around, his hollow voice squeezes out through more teeth-gritted force, that seemed to project a trembling distress signal. Producing an alien sound extending from the back of the throat to crawl and scratch itself out. A sound he never knew he possessed. A sound, almost as if his body cried out in protest, in need of being rescued.

The warm water cascades down disguising his salty tears that he tastes on his lips. Soapy water drips from his forehead, running down his nose. His hand rests against the brown large tiled walls to prop him up. Veins protruding out as if he is struggling to push the immoveable wall. Head bowed down. The crescendo splashing of the water crashes louder with each reverberation. Each drop more shriller, more piercing. The deafening sound as if he is part of a mighty waterfall is still not drowning out his dooming sensational feelings.

A split second earlier, he was showering normally. Getting ready for work. Unthinkingly lathering himself. Abruptly out of a peaceful scene, an unexpected piercing harpooning presented itself through the mist. That penetrating thought that instantly caused him agony. With the blow he immediately reacted by shouting out, but down to the grey tiled floor. Looking unfocused as if he had been punched, hard, in the gut, he watched a reel of memories that sped past him like he was in a Formula One racer at Bathurst circling the drain, rapidly descending down the rabbit hole.

The pink bar of Imperial Leather soap lazily slips out of his hand as the blow strikes. Falling in slow motion in acrobatic spins to bounce and skid over the floor like a renegade bobsleigh. The shower head continued to fall a stream of water rinsing the lathered soap suds from his body, nonetheless, rinsing nothing else.

He lifts his head away from the falling water to look up towards the heavens. He aches. He feels unclean. He feels cheated. Stained. He feels, alone. Even though he sees the speeding filmstrip in his mind's eye, he is left unthinking. He is not thinking about anything. He is concentrating on the pain. Yet, on the contrary what he sees should fill him with something. This vulnerable event, fills him with nothing, but by some means, drains more of a vacant emptiness of space of which was once overflowing with love. A love that is missing now. Departed. Dead. Decaying. Deceased.

'Aghhhh…'

This time it is barely audible. It is a breathless sigh. He did not know these floods that was covering over him, consuming him. He was in the tight invisible sweeping tide of depression. No lifeguards patrolled this particular beach. For a few days he had been at the beach watching these negative tides splash him. He was tired with the constant threat, having to be strong, having to remain invincible. Up till now, he had won every battle.

Earlier, he woke fatigued. He went to get ready for work but felt weak. Today that beach seemed smaller, he was surrounded. The tides took him, wave after wave, he was being conquered. He went to go with the flow, he did not want to fight anymore. He was exhausted. He surrendered himself to the onslaught. He thought that the place that these tides were taking him would not be worse than where he was at this present moment. Eddy laid down his arms to concede defeat.

He had been unhappy for a while.

Depression.

That is what they call it.

To put depression into words is something that men do not do. Most men do not do, Eddy is most men. It is something that Eddy absolutely without a shadow of a doubt does not do. That most craziness stuff that batters, echoes and pinballs around his head in unimaginable urgencies, notions, irrational states of mind, bordering on rational mental states is his declining downturn. Thoughts that rise, plummet in uncontrollable surges, eruptions, bursts and explosions that implode internally within his head, affecting him without.

Intentions are fed that he wants to do, but does not know how to do. Confused is an understatement. So many emotional questions in a large space. He is surrounded by so many to feel so alone. The gushing tides of scares and fears bursts through a trust broken. That leads him to feel he only has himself. He can only count on himself. He has no-one, but himself to rely on. And, that person, Eddy, was slowly breaking away, crumbling piece by piece in unfixable dust. Today he was a shadow. Tomorrow…what will he be?

The ghost of Arceophon gleefully looks on at Eddy's demise. He knows well the feeling. For he had a love that was forbidden by her father. He took no solace in the fact that Aphrodite's, seeing the way in which he starved himself to die out of hunger was for an unfilled passionate love, as a result was angry.

Arceophon had his hoped dashed by Arsinoe, who did not fight for their love. Arsinoe, the daughter of King Nicocreon of Salamis, did not want the bloodline to be soiled by his Phoenician descent. When Arsinoe leaned out of the window at the funeral of Arceophon. She saw where the fellow citizen grieved while burying him with honours, Aphrodite's, with her anger turned her to flint.

Out of the shadows, comes a Mayan Goddess, Ixtab. He speaks to the flickering presence of Arceophon. He is eager for the thoughts to tie him, to die, and commit him to the acceptable passage to lead directly to paradise. Yet being dead already this was out of both of their hands. However, she was here for another purpose. She had food and drink ready for Eddy under the shade of the World Tree. Ixtab did not see suicide as a bad thing. She would look after them, guide them, protect them. Arceophon shed a dry, dusty tear at her remarks.

I looked on. Although I was studying human behaviour, it turns out that I have much to learn about my kind. Ixtab turns towards me. She slowly comes forth. We both know what she will ask when she speaks to me, but I am not sure of this being the correct way to end Eddy's story.

Eddy shakes enough of himself back to the present. He lingers at the shiny edge of the razor on the clear green glass shelve. He thinks, contemplates the what ifs, followed by that no-one will miss him if he does go. He lingers a little too long to stir fully back to the real world. He needs to finish getting ready for work. The old age saying, '…of things happen for a reason', is the only mantra that is left rebounding around his mind. Getting louder, louder and louder. Trying to penetrate the belief that it is true. He never believes this. Moreover now.

'Enlighten me. PLEASE!' he shouts out to no-one.

Exasperatingly, he has no more tears to cry. Followed by a heavy sigh, to stop the crescendo of words that is becoming a clattering din, like a one-man-band falling down numerous flights of stairs. He wants that anonymous, any-nonymous person to help him out.

'Pl…ease…'

He is on the verge of screaming as he cracks out the last two words of the sentence.

'…Enlighten…ME.' The words are spoken clearly, even though being muffled by a soft probing annoying ache from the depths of his darkening heart. He ties the laces of his runners as he breathes out a repetition of the hope.

'EN-lighten me. Please. As I need, I NEED to see the light again.'

He gets himself upright. Leaves for work. Walking on thin ice he knows for this few hours of a day, when he is at work, he can forget what ails him. There is no-where he would want to be right now. He does not need to be alone. He wants to share his time with no-one but, does not want to be on his own.

On his way, he distracts himself from his coiling, snaking murky descent of the irresponsibility perceivable notion of killing himself, so, he calls Jay. He yearns to see the light of reason to why he should feel like the light of darkness is this bleak. For only seeing what he does not want to see he sees the only finale. He cannot even see a crack in the obscurity of blackness to where any light of hope to fill him with faith would penetrate through.

Jay listened as he spoke of his abandonment. He uttered a soft word every now and again. But when he did speak in length, it was a wisdom that he had never heard him be so opinionated before. The beauty of knowing someone for so long that they, even mates, have the ability of surprising him. This would normally be the catalyst of a propeller to rise him above the ending brooding menacing dark clouds. Although that was not the case. He was grateful to Jay. His words were correct. He acknowledged him, accepted his voice when he stated that he was searching for a unicorn. Someone to give him unconditional love.

Eddy was never going to find it, that was what Jay was convinced about. But Eddy felt that he had it. He was not sure that if he had let it go, or if she was let go. He was distraught that he had been solely responsible for the relationships demise. Jay did not force the latter issue as Eddy's ears were closed off to all rational explanations.

Eddy programmes himself on autopilot over the next few days. He has taken the step of disconnecting himself from his friends, his family, everyone. He has taken a few days sick, where the doctors waiting room had been a different bar. Where his medicine has been the top shelf. For when he can, he locks himself away. Blinds drawn. Darkness is his friend. Constantly on the verge of tears. Has trouble sleeping. Rarely sleeping in the bed they shared.

'I can't get to sleep.'

When he does, he dozes. He feels night chills, nightmares of thoughts, of Beth-Annie. He cuddles a bottle of vodka. He has raging fits of arguments. With no-one but himself. Eats only because he has too. He has no appetite for food, for life. To live. Darkness and Fury are his companions with alcohols negativity to cause eternal fights.

Eddy feels nothing except hopelessness, which takes him down a path which was believed that nothing will ever feel the same. Nothing will return to his level of normal. Before Beth-Annie he had a life. A love for life. Before she came into his life the feelings, he had for everything was special. Somehow, without reason, without knowing, it was gone.

When the love burnt out, it burnt out the surrounding love of hobbies, of life. For what he felt before, nothing will feel, taste, smell the same. Nothing will ever be, or, feel as he was feeling before she came into his life. He will never feel the past. He will never feel different from this moment. Will he never move on. Nothing will ever work out for him. In the past, now, or in the future.

After two weeks in the dark. Two weeks in her shadows. Two weeks of getting nothing back to his messages of all forms available.

He was locked in her shadows of the unknown. Deep in her pockets like a rubber ball, for which she has only ever used when wanting something. Wanting someone to make her feel better. When wanting to play with Eddy's turmoil of emotional feelings. To bring Eddy out of the dark shadows, when he wanted someone to toil with.

What aggravates him. People tell him how he should feel. People should be honest with him. People should be honest with people to how they feel. They should not, they should never play an emotional game of abuse.

A message at eight minutes past ten in the evening after two weeks of unanswered everything's, might just be the greatest line. Great, as in a great abyss of unvoiced screaming unfree falling. The radiating light on his mobile that lights the gloom after the two soft high-pitched dings gave the simple, short line.

'I NEED TIME.'

He was half attached to the real world but reread the message again. Did he read it correctly? Was there more? He opened the full message. That short three-worded sentence was, in fact, the full message. This made him scream out the anger-filled vent.

'WHAT?'

At the top of his lungs, he shrieked, surrounded by a spraying of spit. He tightly gripped the mobile phone in his hand with unconditional hatred. This was the same last time. It had been weeks. Why cannot she just say it, if she wants to say it.

'HOW MUCH FUCKING TIME DOES SHE NEED?
'HOW MUCH FUCKING MORE TIME DOES SHE NEED TO TAKE FROM ME?'

In the darkness, he leaped up like a rocket of pure frenzied ferocity. He had so much energy that required attention. He paced, heavily around his small bedroom. Accompanied with a shake of the head. A slight tremor of a laugh, he asked the question again. After spending two weeks apart she wanted space. It could have been a mere joke, should have been. A cruel, gnarly twisting shredded remains of his sensitive heart lines were rapidly unwinding.

Eddy knew the answer. It was deep inside the pockets of Beth-Annie's already made-up mind. He needed her to be honest with him. Herself. To speak the truth. For once in the past few months all he wanted, he was entitled to surely, was the simple truth to be released.

That night was the usual reckless one. He was up, down, pacing, tossing, turning. Men on death row would have had more sleep. He wanted to respond to her message. He did not. He looked back over the message, all over again. He wrote a message. Deleted it. Rewrote. Deleted it. The night went on like this. Love killed the mind. His mind was dying. He was seriously, for the first time wanting to end the pain. His love-scorched mind was attempting his heart to suicide. Vodka in hand, he swigged until the alcohol had its spellbinding effect.

In the morning, with an all too familiar grainy head that he nursed with a glass of red wine, he wrote a short message down on paper that he wanted Beth-Annie to see. After much deliberation, changing, rewording and correcting, he eventually transposed the words to a text message. Only to idle away more seconds hovering over the arrowed send button. Letting the lights die down before shaking them back on the screen.

He did not want to go with the clichés of whys, followed by the promises that he can change, but wanted to be to the point, honest and open, transparent. Very unlike to how he was being treated. Be that as it may, he took the higher ground. He simply acknowledged her point of view, without fully understanding it. He felt by accepting the situation, giving her the desired space, he was not pushing her further away. Keeping in line with the gap that she actually was dictating by pushing him away. He held the foolish notion that giving her the space would actually make Beth-Annie miss him. Eddy was kidding himself. He held a candle of hope that the love may return. He was delusional.

Beth-Annie, I love you. I will give you the space you need. However long. It seemed so right in Orange but now so wrong in Sydney. I wonder if we can start again. If we can connect like we did at the beginning. Please don't write us off yet. Hope to speak to you sooner rather than later. Take care, take time, Eddy XXX

Sent. The whoosh of the message being sent did not make him feel as good as he expected. He is angry. An idea fringing with a more-than-slight possibility that he needed to ask the questions, demand the answers. He was ready to jump with car keys in hand to the door. Brimming on the verge of bordering, posed, ready to go to her door. Ready to drive to her apartment. He is resisting the urge to act unhinged, with the very strong view of coming across deranged. He is wanting answers. He wants to get the answers.

Slowly, he releases the keys to a soft chink that rest on varied silver and gold coins in the garish green, orange-painted Clarice Cliff-style fruit bowl. He rubs the rim of the bowl. This was an idea he has kept since his college days. When he gave up smoking, he had a lot more shrapnel in his pocket than he had had previously. His mates suggested at the end of the day to place the change he accumulated into a fruit bowl near the door and use this for coffee, a sweet treat. Due to plastic being his choice of money more and more nowadays, the shrapnel allowance has been reduced, but the large bowl has remained. As a testament, always beside the front door. He moves away from his door. In doing so steps away from her door. Giving her, her space.

Time drags its heels into the red earth. The sunsets over another day. His second bottle of red wine shines a shadow over the golden sands that give a slight blood red hue. He looks down as if telling the time of the sundial.

'Time goes fast when you are not imprisoned by it,' he slurs as he dribbles the wine down his chin as if he has just sucked the blood out of the sinking, deflating sun. Tortured by time, he seems to drag himself painfully through each day. She is being knowingly cruel, like a kid playing with ants while searching them out through the sun rays of a magnifying glass.

It has only been a few days since that cursed message; I NEED TIME. At present the lapse of time is causing Eddy to become more confused. Currently, he is getting increasingly upset. She was driving him mad. The more time she was taking, the more time he was brooding, the more reason she was giving him to spiral deeper into depression. Being pushed, closer towards that edge. The drop of no return.

How long is time?

When do you give time?

When is enough time?

If the 'time' is the dictation?

Questions formidably formed cobwebs spraying out in thick threads which were leaving him more mystified. Claustrophobia deprived of escape. Clouding up his vision, disconcerting his weak saddening mind.

He stares through the thick white steam that cascades skywards from his untouched black coffee that he cradles in both his hands. Through the thin wispy veil, he watches couples pass on the promenade of Rushcutters Bay, hand in hand.

'FOOLS,' he mutters under his breath with more breath than coherent sound.

He thinks they all are fools. It is a scenic day on the magnificent beaches of Sydney. He has come to a place that he has not been to, for a long time. A place that he had never frequented with Beth-Annie, hence, here he shares no memories of her. People are beaming smiles as strong as the sun. The mutual laughs are heard everywhere. All around like the grains of the sea in the salty air is affection. Eddy wonders if these couples are in a relationship or, they just think they are or, that one thinks they are when the other is actually pulling out already. That person is leading them along so the break will be easier on that person, not the other. In the warm breeze Eddy glances from the top of his coffee mug. He is feeling salty. He is feeling upset and angry at a result of being embarrassed by Beth-Annie. By her promises.

He takes a walk to clear his mind. Eddy is very melancholy. He has valued every single one of his relationships that he has been in. Well, he thinks he has. He is under the strong belief that the women did not give him a chance. That he was not treated with honesty and transparency. They were, are, after someone better, not him. Mates have tried to console him. He does not let them in. They say that the last girlfriends were not anyone worth sharing the same air space with, after the events have ended. Always after. Although these mates, did not speak of their concerns when they were together. Strange, that now, they have now found a voice.

The cliché of more fish in the sea was wasted, as he had the only fish he wanted. He did not want to go fishing anymore. He wonders why commitment is such a taboo. Past loves have mentioned that they want to settle, but the thought at the time was something he wanted, but also wanted to tick some boxes for himself. When he wanted to settle, he found that other people did not want to at the same time. The final step further down the relationship checklist actually put them off. Rather than being with one person, they do not entertain that they simply want that with him, so they simply walk away, nay flee.

Their mates are unpractical with a logic that makes absolutely no sense to Eddy. He makes the assumption that they do not actually know themselves. The logical response to not commit when they have stated that is what they want is baffling. They will not admit to falling in love. At the end of the day the fall will be hurtful. The risk. To get a heart broken. They do not even open the door to their heart to let love in. They look at other relationships and think the grass is greener. The moment they step on the grass, they run. They cite 'wanting space'.

One even cited to Eddy the reason for ending a relationship was 'distance'. They would not fly a short distance to meet someone they love. When the prospect of Eddy offering to move closer came up, the gate to the heart was shut. Slammed, a moat built, a locked drawbridge, the moat filled with bloodthirsty sharks, followed by snipers on the watch towers. Thou shall not enter. As quick as a snip, all lines of communication were irreversibly severed.

Eddy thought Beth-Annie was different. He thought that he was in a relationship where they shared the same intentions.

No good angel was present. He was aloof. The angel on his left shoulder was constantly pulling his strings like a puppet. He was losing his own sense of control.

Eddy tried to push the depression away by sleeping around. He wanted to feel valued. By not valuing anyone. How incongruous! He was obtaining relief in a hook-up, without the breakup. He was not proud of bed hopping by pure sexual attraction. Getting laid for Eddy was as easy as getting drunk. These short minutes of hedonism made him feel great. It was short, sweet. The great feeling ended quickly, before he had even unfastened his condom. The temporary fulfilment that he cherished for a short time was enough time for Eddy to make a decision. Eddy really liked Beth-Annie, loved her. He easily fell in love with her.

His coffee is quenched dry, bar a few drops. He sits back down on the café chair. He has spent the duration watching, thinking. Watching the unobtainable. Thinking a question which was still not forming correctly. Why are relationships so hard to find? Harder to stay in? Harder to keep? Eddy has failed in all his loves. He told himself that Beth-Annie was going to be different. He was letting her go for her space that she wished for, but he is fighting, still fighting. He wants her to fight, so she will come back to stay. Each passing day he is forgetting what love was. What love felt like. The devil in his mood was taunting his angel that strove to convince him that love was not forgotten.

Losing love. It was gone. Had gone. Not coming back. Love lost.

The other women were let go before love could grow. Beth-Annie was a quitter. She wanted it easy. She was not prepared to invest herself for what she feels, she could do better. The other women were not prepared to make a single sacrifice, whereas he made them on a daily basis. He believed in them. He could not help thinking that she was probably smiling, laughing in the basking glow of the sun safe in the bosom of heat. He was in the cold, ground crumbling unstable heap of sharp ashes that remain.

Beth-Annie did say that she hated his excitement. A quenchable thirst for doing thrilling experiences, for those first-time memories. She wanted the adventure but did not want to jeopardise her fragile perfect balance. She never wanted to leave her comfort zone in any aspect. She did not have the patience to want to have a relationship as that was, just, too hard. It meant changing her routine, habits and upsetting her equilibrium. Too much of a pleasure to risk gaining from her own selfishly poised comfort zone.

She wanted it handed to her on a plate. She wanted the end result, without the thrill and excitement of putting her heart out there in dangers way. She wanted the maturity of a relationship, without putting in the hard yards, years. She wanted that emotional connection, without spending the best, worse and silent times together. Apparently, she wanted a connection without building a connection. Not taking the time and patience to find out if Eddy was that, mythical one that she craved. It was not worth her time, her risk, her patience, her love, to find out if Eddy was, in fact, the one.

To snap Beth-Annie out of his circling train of thoughts to Noanswerville, his mobile chimed, twice. He looked at the message that appeared on the screen. He had arranged to meet a mate later on today, here, but he had just cancelled. He turned it off, placed his mobile back in his jean pocket and smiled a half smile. Technology was evil. He hated the presence on him. He wanted nothing more but to rid of the technology that he needed. The small silver box was the only way of contacting and being contacted. That thought made him fish his mobile back out and turn it on vibrate mode. He could not even succumb to completely turning it off.

He thought of her again. Because of Beth-Annie, he took all the other women off his feed. Out of his media sites, so she would not get jealous. Although at the time he did not realise that she did not do the same. It was a comical response in hindsight. She, as many people do, look for gratification in what they do. Looking for validation that they are good, strong, committed. Whether that is an accomplishment, in a career or a small molehill that they urge to make a huge mountain. She would spend time and patience with hundreds of people at the same time. She could do that, but still not respond to Eddy.

To say she was social, was a tag she gave herself. The funny thing is she was not, online, for sure. But from the couch, a lone café table, her safety cushion. She was as social as a hermit. The notification that a message had been seen, liked, commented on, made her feel worthful rather than worthless. She would watch his moves on every media snap on. She lingered in his life without being active. She was constantly orbiting Eddy, in spite of that she carried on ghosting him in real-life.

Although credit where credit is due. Technology did bring people closer to people. You could chat to people over the other side of the world as if they are in the same room. You can send a message, so they receive it while you sleep. It was amazing.

Yet, the speed was also causing the English language to slowly die. Bethany would constantly text people, snapchat, and respond with an emoji, a one-word answer. Conversations were dying. Then basic grammar was starting to fade, replaced firstly by numbers and letters, shortened and abbreviated. To now, to simple symbols, pictures. Soon there would be nothing to talk about as people would only use pictures, no words, just like the Ancient Egyptians. It is a brave new world of stupidity, that is just around the corner.

Eddy's past loves have conquered the world, but not felt a single emotion along the way. He was a little cynical. A touch of bitterness. The most primitive emotion he thinks that they did not see, feel. Love. The most rewarding thing you can receive, if you risk it by giving it out. Technology is evolution, but what is it when it goes backwards. Eddy has front row seats to the tickets to the end of the world. For this he tries not to let his mobile phone dictate his life. With all the thousands that are staring blankly in front of his scene at the mobile phones in front of them that shine the only light that some would ever see. A thousand more are getting lost in the space between nothingness.

'A brave new world. WORLD,' Eddy murmurs to himself. Then with more gusto he performs a line to no-one in particular: 'more like a faint-hearted, hated, fault-filled world of oblivion.'

His chair squeaks on the pale blue sea reflecting tiles as he pushes back. He needs to stop thinking too much. He thinks of the other women. The other women are not worth the brain power to think about. Anymore. As abruptly as Eddy stands, he is already in motion. Discarding a red twenty-dollar bill under the peppershaker he discards his thoughts. He has split his brain of blood and left the remains at the table behind him. Left behind in his shadows of his past. He is walking to a pub, any pub. Drinking is going to fuel his sleep tonight.

He sees his destination and proceeds to cross the road to it. Orders a drink in the dark room towards the back of the brightly open, glass window covered entrance. The barman tells him that it is better to love, than not to love at all. What a croak of shit. He is getting numb with drink. The alcohol is fuelling his veins, flowing through to dilute his senses. He is happier to not feel anything, than to feel anything at all.

Eddy sits on a tall stool, looking to the back of the bar, through the optics he can see the entrance. Outside the bubble of the world continues to go on around him. Eddy does not care. Each sip of the craft beer he is filling up with lifeless deadness of endless, unquenchable empty hopelessness. Eddy cannot see through the darkness of negativity. He cannot escape his bubble. His bubble that separates him from the rest of the outside world. A bubble that burst apart at the seams.

Beth-Annie walks on amidst the carnage with an air of intolerance. He cannot help for her to come into his mind. How can he stop this? He thinks that she has the emotions, the reasons strapped to her chest like a homemade bomb. She is shielding her thoughts away from Eddy. Why does she need space when she is not giving him a trickle of her thoughts. It is frustrating.

He is slumped over the wooden bar. His arms sprawled in front of him like a ragdoll. He is one of a few, so the barman lets him be. He is not causing trouble. His back is curved. He swallows a mouthful of beer. He brushes a spillage from the corner of his mouth with his thumb. The barman returns. He does that thing where he seems to be searching Eddy's face to form the right question by turning his mind inside out with his eyes.

'With my job comes the confidence. You can tell me?' he softly states talking to Eddy's heart. The funny thing is he is a huge man-mountain of a guy. Riddled in tattoos that have been faded by the sun, covered by the wiry black hairs of his arms. He shaven head tinged with dustings of grey. A tight black T-shirt advertising a craft beer that is tightly snug around his boulder biceps tense from hurling kegs all-day. Eddy thought he would have a husky, growl to his voice. He was wrong. His slightly high voice was almost feminine. Each sentence was finished with a high-pitched accent as if he was repetitively asking a question was getting damn-right annoying.

'Beer me.'

'Look. You will not find the answers at the bottom.'

'Beer…please.'

He pours. He searches. He leans in close as he places the overspilling beer on a new plain black coaster. Very much interfering with Eddy's own personal space, he simply states, matter-of-factly, 'An almost love is not worth it!' He turns and leaves to tend to another person.

Eddy did not appreciate his question, statement or whatever it was. He was not a mate of his. He had no right to ask that. This was not the first time he had heard this. It was the first time he had felt it. For that is all it was. He is rattled by maybe it was an almost love. He did not believe that, but wanted to. Was that all it was anyway? Was it a potential to love for Beth-Annie. For Eddy, it was a love. A love for which he had never felt before.

He is spiralling down the endless helter-skelter to which the end is to end the pain, to end life. The intimate bond that he had has ruptured. The aftermath of discarded emotions are strewn over the ground, broken, fractured, scarred. These pieces are ruined. None of these singed remains can return a heartbeat. He has lost his existence by isolating himself to exacerbate his mental pain. His very real physical pain. He cannot contain his feelings, ironically, he also cannot release to anyone his own feelings.

In his pits of depression, he was looking up and wondering if it was an almost love. Was Beth-Annie an infatuation rather than the real thing.

People have started to come into the bar. To the point that he feels surrounded by them, but still cannot shake the feeling of loneliness. He knows that no-one here understands what he is going through. He looks around at the connection that these strangers are making with a bitter taste of aversion towards him as he scoffs. Repulsed at the sound of the annoying laughter. The echoes of laughter in the surrounding amusement is playing havoc, he thinks the high-pitched squealing is taunting him. Spitefully provoking. Laughing at his expense. Anger is rising.

An almost love.

The thought comes back like a reoccurring nightmare. He ponders. It was not an almost love. It was a love. Her hand on his. Her eyes connecting through the space so intensively that the strength in them could, would overpower every and anyone. Hasty words spoken over the course of a lazy Sunday afternoon while she read the newspaper. Beth-Annie became part of him. But her silence is making him sad, feel lonely. Trembling hands lift the lightly iced amber beer to his lips. He is mourning the sense of togetherness. He misses Beth-Annie. He misses the relationship. He misses the company. He misses someone to do things with.

Eddy tries to climb out of the narrow pit of depression but keeps falling back in on a loose handhold. He is climbing but escalating the sense of fear. He is staring down at the empty glass with the clinging remains of froth through grainy focused eyes. He hails a new one, like a taxicab by a wave of his hand, no eye contact. The barman speaks again as he takes the coloured plastic notes from under the empty glass. He might as well be speaking underwater as he just hears a gurgling nonsensical human sound coming from his pencil-thin lips.

The prospect of being single again, possibly for a longer time than he wants, or even the fear of being single forever. He is rocking from fear, anger and pervading soaking cold sweats of guilt. In the shadows of the dark well, on the bottom guilt is covering him, saturating him over his perception of failures to not have made a single one of his relationships work. The beer is accompanied by a dimpled lightly iced clear glass of a brown whisky. The change is put aside for the beer, with the words 'on the house.'

It could be the alcohol; it could be the unfolding patterns of predictable motions from the depths of his internal murkiness of claustrophobic high walls. He is numb.

ALMOST LOVE. ALMOST LOVE. All most love. Or must love.

The greatest line. The greatest untruth.

Beth-Annie will not risk giving her all. Hence, Eddy is crippled by her lack of risk to potentially risk a would be love. A love, from almost. For him, he was open and placed his secret self in her hands. She cast him away. She extinguished the flames of love to leave the smoke of despair. He was no doubt depressed.

Eddy slowly emotionally digests the nature of his encumbering depression. His grief will never go away. It will become irrelevant. It will be something that happened a footnote in his past.

He starts to grieve his loss. Eddy wants to find the right person. He does feel worried that he would misconstrue love if the slightest sign of interest was shown towards him. He is vulnerable that he will fall into a false love. Happy in the company. Being with someone. Someone that apparently wants him. The sad thing is that someone probably wants him more than he wants them. Yet, as she will not be her Mrs Right. It will end.

At the end of any given day, the truth is if he fakes a love. If he believes that a love will materialise, he has learnt nothing. Overall, he wants to be with someone because he loves her. She would love him. Not because they needed company, companionship, mateship. He can get company from his rejected friends that he has isolated. Family that he has disconnected himself from. A pet dog. He will only settle with someone that actually loves him.

Eddy finds himself gravitating towards a manifest of a lingering sadness that is causing him a hint of peace at the impending loss. The grief will not leave him like his shadow. The depression will come in smaller waves. The sun was rising up over a horizon of acceptance. He is letting go of the relationship while moving forwards with his new life. A new chapter starts here. He leaves the bar with a prominent stagger. He drags his heels as he looks down but up in his heart.

He is thinking a pinball of scenarios that he can climb out of the depression. It will be no time limit, but he cannot sulk about it any longer. Rushing the process by leaping out will be his vehicle to fall back down. Thus, the climb is never going to be easy. But then again, he will do it. Rise, once, again. Rise out of this depression.

Old Flame Burns Out
Ten Days Ago

Eddy was being aloof. Cavalier in his approach. He was drinking too much. Taking anything, everything to get him away from reality while sleeping with anything in a skirt. He did not care. Well, he told himself this. In the quiet moment when he was alone, he was lonely. It was in his tornado alcohol and drug fuelled evening that he bumped into an ex. This was many years ago but seeing her for the first time filled him up with an embarrassment that he had never experienced before.

It was something that should not have been. But, of course it happened. Years before they met. Two people that society dictates is a taboo. That they should not be together, gets together. Although nothing has bothered Eddy about, what he deems a ridiculous exercise of discussion. This leads penultimately to money. And, after an increasingly tedious affair becomes legit. This exercise comes true, but never affected him. The, this taboo does,

This relationship came to part by an older man taken her away. If anything can give more unseen harm to a man, it must be this. Although people do not like it, the person on the receiving end can eventually find some understanding in the methods which caused the split. If Eddy was traded for a man with more money, larger ambitions, greater interests or younger it be acceptable. But older! That was a blow to the gut. The heart is the size of a small fist, but this heart was being gripped hard. To render Eddy crippled in an emotional heap on the floor.

The conflict starts with damn right honest envy and inadequacy. The latter he has never voiced. Never felt he had to. The first is voiced. In the forms of opinions about unknowns. Did she go for him for the money, the status, the ladder climbing potential? What should be apparent is the other person knew that it was not right. Sara wanted him for him. She did not want Eddy. Hence, she broke the chain with a ludicrous excuse, hoping to make a band aid peel off, ridding the direct hit off rejection. The lie, or as she still uses to this day, the excuse was correct in being used to protect him.

The excuse actually does nothing to help; the reverse, in fact. The truth would have been favourable. Honesty would win. However, he started to heal when he found out the real reason which acted as a double blow. Sara wanted this older man over Eddy for no other reason than she felt she loved him more. That was a tough pill to swallow. Something that really baffled him then, now, he moved on. At the time he resorted to childlike, playground essences of innuendo with irrational espionage. He became a stalker until he found out the truth.

Through the dark, flashing coloured lights of the Oxford Street bar he saw her first. He was not sure if it was her at first as years had passed, she had changed her hair, so Eddy stared as if trying to work out a magic eye puzzle. She saw him stare. Instantly recognised him. Smiled and ran over so fast, through the bar and into his arms. He caught her in the midst of the dancefloor to grip tightly. They kissed. It was naturally odd but strangely right. No more drink was needed, the glass abandoned on the ledge.

They enjoyed themselves in the back alley. Amongst the drug takers, the people who had drunk too much, the homeless. In this putrid environment they gave into life's best attributes. It was reckless with no expectations. No holds barred. It was great. No mistake it opened questions with Eddy thinking if Sara and Kev were still together.

After the raw explosion of reassurance of sexual healing they headed to another bar. They talked. Kev and Sara lasted over five years. Eddy had so many questions. For once he did not hold back. Like a reporter with the first taste of Dracula fuelled blood for a story he asked everything. He, has to admit some of the answers were not nice to hear, but with no emotional baggage. No love between them. No hurt that could be done. It was easy to ask, it was easier to hear.

She was his last. His last sexual encounter. His last meaningful conversation with a girl. He did not need to see anyone to drink his alcohol. It was as if that moment. In that soul moment, hearing Sara go through similar experiences to him shook him awake. Hearing him answer honestly, for the first time, he did not kid himself. Have a connection to the past which was then discarded that night. This night took his libido away. For good…

So Long, So Wrong
Seven Days

A wonderful yet windy early morning in Sydney had turned colder, greyer and darker by the afternoon. It was not just the weather that changed. Eddy's elated mood had been swept aside, escalating dust which cast a dirty veil towards the future rendering it unseen, signing off the present with a premature valedictory farewell. Taking into consideration it was barely past five in the afternoon the dark, brooding clouds had ascended quickly, clearing all the blue skies, blocking the sun. The streets where plummeted into a twilight with the streetlights flickering as if confused whether they should be on or off.

This morning, Eddy had a skip in his step. He woke, reborn. He felt, he had turned the corner. Took all his alcoholic bottles and straightforwardly poured its contents down the kitchen sink. Each bottle into the recycling and straight outside for collection. However later into the afternoon he turned back, into himself. In that moment he knew. He knew deep, deep, very deep down, inside that he had turned the last corner. The cycle of grief had ended. He had found himself once again. Finally. He was relieved. Except he still felt broken.

Although no streamers of multi-coloured trajectory filled the air. No cheers. No woops, whoops and hastily overwrought, abundantly enthusiastically clapping could be heard. No joyful brass music, with a fast-steady beat of a side bass drum. No smells of excitement. No carnival. No smiling faces. No, No. No, this was not a day he thought it would be like. He was not in a celebratory mood. He wanted nothing more than the sadness to go away. Like an unwanted house guest, the pain in his heart had gone, but not without leaving a gaping wound. Yes, it was true that Eddy was at the end of the cycle. But. Eddy felt like he was back in denial. Denying that it has, truly ended.

Eddy is in his dark blue metallic car that reflects his mood. The car was in desperate need of a thorough wash, as was his soul. He felt a few drops of rain as he got into the driver's seat. He needed time to well, reflect. He drove the short distance to his personal quiet space to mull over his next move. A move for a change that will be as important to his future, as it is right now, at his present. He smoothly inserts his car between the tight, thick white lines. He drove as smooth as a cloud, as he dreamily parked in the deserted carpark.

Here, he pauses on the high point of the harbour cliff, just above Gordons Bay. The rumble of the mechanic ting, ting, ting, to a silent murmur of the fan belt slowly turning, swirling to a halt. The engine is off. The lights are clicked off. The doors are tapped to be locked in a unison of switching catches. He reclines back in the black leather driver's seat briefly, before bending, launching himself forward. His dark red T-shirt falls tightly over his taught supporting shoulders. His arms rest over the black steering wheel. He is slightly slumped over. This causes his head to bow down a touch.

In spite of this, his gaze still looks through the windscreen wiper smeared glass. His gaze is unfocused. Into a future unacknowledged. Over the high dark towering waves, he looks out. They thunderously crash over the concrete walkway with a sound of impending destruction. Cracks of light that fork through the skies flash the sign of the imminent tempest. The commotion in the atmosphere send currents of dread. Of hope.

The lightning flashes Eddy's stress-ravaged face. Displaying each scar of pain, in burning parading white light flares. Each line of a story that he thinks may happen. Each tale still not written. Each yarn unravelled. He does not blink with the deafening boom that echoes off the grey hued cliffs. He does not jolt with the staccato clapping of demi-quaver deafening blasts of thunder. Abruptly. With an opening of a shower tap, water dynamically falls. Swiftly the vigorous rain forms puddles, lakes, rivers. The deluge streams down the windscreen. Torrents rush down the pitched channel on the way to the large grated storm drain as if in a race.

Devoid of logical thought. Eddy opens the door of his immaculately shining Toyota Yarras that has a film of rippling silk draped over it. He steps out into the surging flow of the flood spilling down the curve of the road. His hand grips the top of the cold door. In front of him is a black moving curtain view of the darkness concealed. The edges of the carpark are like fast-flowing dark armed tributaries filled with mystery. Dark matter. As his right foot sinks into the barrage. The water spills over his grey and red Brooks runners.

The gush of water must find another way, nevertheless, spills over this obstacle. It surges over his runners, instantly saturating his, until that time, pristine white Bond socks. The rippling muddy brown waters lick his light blue jeans. Yet, he does not react to the icy cold dirty water that has entered his personal space. Yet, he still does not flicker with the illuminating light. Yet, he seems statuesque in his absence of sensation. The radiant glow shows the gnarly trees being bent over by the strong roaring force of the wind. Straining at breaking point to be barely holding resilience. The smell of mud reasserts itself into the air. The rain pounds down to soften the earth, making a soft thud, leaving a terrain of tiny moulds converted to look like blackened brown pin cushions. Leaving a continuously changing small craterous planet landscape.

Eddy thinks for a few seconds. Oblivious to the harsh surroundings.

He stands in the storm. Looking towards the advancement of the storm. Embracing the cold storm, warmly. The rain hitting him like small glass icicles on his exposed flesh. Penetrating within his skin. The wind trying to move him. He stands firm like a durable sculpture. The noise of the hard-fast rain. The rushing floods of water. The loud claps of thunder. The invisible wind, with great force is seen. Mother Nature's four horseman descend to an apocalypse of Sydney's personal magnificence, proceeding onward with a band of its own wild orchestra.

It could be the ferocious storm. It could be the negative electricity in the atmosphere. It could be the harsh conditions. Resembling the weather, mirroring his feelings. Stirring inside, outside, in a visual symphony of sensations that he cannot possibly sort to understand. Comprehend what is happening. Something is rousing inside him. But What?

Earlier, a few short hours ago, he woke. A normal routine day. The predictive warm, wonderful day. Now, the doom, the gloom. He was not only feeling this sensation, but it was imitated around him.

BOOM!

Echoing around him, until it reverberates inside him to then ricochet within him, painfully vibrating. With that definite striking assault of the earth-shaking.

BOOM!

He was lurched into realisation. He had an empathy. He finally felt that he understood. He knew what he was to do. His grey skies where crystal river mountain clear.

He needed to let go. He felt the emotions surge through him to one place. Building inside him. Ready to explode like the anger of the Incredible Hulk. It needed to be released. The feelings cannot be contained within him any longer. They were destroying him from the core. With an ascending crescendo of almighty noise. The sound that continued to rumble after the initial loud clap. The tremors around him, made him feels connected.

The rousing inside him was not anger. It was him accepting. It was him letting go of the pain. He had managed to negotiate himself through the battlefield. The coincidental meeting with Sara. The honest and frank chat that he had not had for weeks. The cloak of deceit, the mask of lies, the chains of anguish had been cast down. He had awoken himself to be free.

With the rain pushing into his face. Dripping down his nose, his forehead. Sticking his hair to his skin, he closes his eyes. He lets the storm rinse him. He wants to be pure, to be clean. In that moment. In this time, with everything circling him he thinks, 'maybe he can turn this around'. Although not with just the thought, but armed with that actual belief. He believed he could move on. He could move forward. He could rise, leap, crush and trample anything that got in his way. He could, he would get to the end of this vicious cycle of grief. He would come through to break this life-threatening disparaging chain of failing disillusionment, to be cured. To be rid of the infectious disease.

Nevertheless, in all honesty, he knew he could not close the door on Beth-Annie completely. He hated that he was not ready to rid her. He was not ready to wash her out of his life, his soul, his spirit, as easy as she had done.

Hell.

Eddy did not want it anymore. He did not want the pain. He did not want the confusion. In his eye, he is a man on the edge. Surrounded by the storm he is enveloping in the mixture of rejection's, denunciation's that he has been experiencing in the past few months.

He saw no light, just like this afternoon.

No positives, just like his life.

No doors open to a different route, just like his journey.

No…hope. For. Him. Unless, he let her go.

He slips on the muddy grass slightly with his left foot and walks towards the edge of the concrete promenade. The frothy sea waves spray him with coldness that for the first time makes him sense this outside world evidently visible. He soldiers on. He carries on struggling to force himself forward. Then, close to the edge. Where the muddy grass drips the storm water. He carries on. He launches himself off. Eyes squeezed shut. Body taut. Features creased in his face with pain. Tears being crushed back into his eyes.

He falls, plummets down, deep down into the dark marching high seas. The wind blows onto his face. The rain that is falling hits him on the way down, it feels like mini pebbles thrown by angry villages. Each drop is a javelin of pain against his exposed skin. He is the monster of this piece. He does not know why.

SMACK!

A policeman slams his window with the palm of his hand, causing Eddy to wake up with a jump.

'No camping,' he barks through the window as he marches on.

Eddy abruptly opens his eyes. He checks himself. Hits himself to feel dryness. The day is beautiful. He is in his car. He is where he was. Never left. Where did he go? Where? Why? Then it struck him. Like he was actually hitting the unmerciful surf below. He was accepting the circumstances that he found himself in. He was accepting that it was over. He was starting to be able to grieve the loss. As he had admitted to himself that he wanted and was willing to progress, to make headway. He actually was.

It seemed almost in the plot of a totally unplanned storyline that the storm would coincide with his emotion. The matching similarities were uncanny. But through the large windscreen, he basks in the sunlight as a cloud covers the sun for a few seconds. Enough time to cast a long second of a shadow over his determined growing newfound perspective. A glow of his inner wall represented so well in his façade, was shining through.

He returns to the daydream of the coldness that he feels inside. Still he remembers yet, relishes the soothing warmth and heat of the outside world penetrating his inner world. He shivers and feels the cold and feels unloved. He feels acceptance. He wraps his arms around his body. He accepts that this will be the only contact that he will receive for a while. As he accepts the feeling of being alone, once, again.

His emotions were the sky that he could not see beyond the blue. A projection of his feelings displayed for everyone that wants to see, to see. Though not everyone saw what they were truly seeing. As the passage of a beautiful day was what they saw. Only outlived by the storm that sulked in, refusing to pass without some destruction.

Against his better judgement, Eddy keyed in a message, already anticipating the silence from her side.

The key to this conversation was firmly in her fingers and the lock, well, she held with her want. A want that she did not want. She did not want to answer. She did not want to explain. She did not want to mature. She did not want to play adult.

After a while he appreciates that his mates have not moved on. They were silent, but had never left his side. He opens the door to them; they are still behind the closed, now open door. The same was said about his family. He reconnects, slowly. He enters each call, message and visit with a sense of trepidation. Obviously, he has nothing to worry about. Each one talks like no time has passed. Each mate, each family member portrays mateship on a level which makes Eddy embarrassed that he felt that he had to leave them alone. He had to travel on a personal journey to a deserted island, to be with himself. He travelled on his own, but he sees that they were always there. By his side, helping him to walk.

Although he did hope that they left the same clichés at the front doorstep. At the end of the day they had plenty of time to think of new sayings, rather than the same old, same said, unimaginative Hallmark proverbs similar to: 'there are plenty more fish in the sea'.

Even though he swore blind that he had washed his hands with Beth-Annie, he did not want any other fish, he wanted her, Beth-Annie. His white whale was an obsession, no doubt. He wanted Beth-Annie, but the more he caught up with her, the more she pushed further, further away.

Eddy was petrified to enter the world ex-free. It was only now that he was facing that very real feeling. That the imagination was soon, to become a reality. He has conclusively acknowledged to not search for the answer. The answers to why, how or when the break-up started? To the climax of the end? For which he was undoubtably facing. These can only be answered by Beth-Annie. The insatiable force of the ex. In letting go of the try, and will, to understand the 'why', he feels he has not turned the corner, but bolted around it to keep on running in a vicious cycle to dig a moat where he is now climbing out off. Freedom is no longer FREEDOOM.

Acceptance takes many forms and Eddy believes he has found his.

The Recommendation
Five Days Ago

Eddy's mate, Jay, is on a brief working related trip to Sydney. The timing could not have been more perfect. Possibly things were really starting to benefit Eddy. They are looking out to the golden sands that are being stroked by the shimmering diamond encrusted rolls of the ripping waves, caressed by the warm sea breeze with the coconut traces of sunscreen lotion in the air. The rustic coloured wooden benches which deposits the tiniest glittering paint peels off on to their clothes as they stand, to fall to the floor as they go to order.

The unusual décor adds to the charm. The rusty copper-brown bicycle hangs above the entrance with also serves as the o's in the name to spell COOL Café. After years of coming here, he had finally found out that instead of being a hip way of using the bicycle wheels in cool, it actually is an acronym for Coffee Of Origin Lifecycle. He particularly liked the way lifecycle was used in the name to mean evolution, to tie in fantastically well with the cycle logo.

They are mopping up the last remains of their breakfast of sous-vide poached eggs with avocado flavoured with lime, sea salt and olive oil, the mandatory add on of bacon that had been threatened by the stove rather than heated as they place the last crust of the soaked up sour dough toast into their mouths. The bacon was the way they like it, still oinking, still raw. Eddy does not have to ask anymore as when they see him, they know. They do not come for the view, or the food. Both are brilliant to behold. Yet it is the perfect cup of coffee. That is the thing that makes them want to return, time after time again. This is the main reason that they have travelled to this place, past numerous cafés. The coffee is always on point every single time.

The barista, Emerson, knows his job very well. If they did not see him from behind the gleaming mirrored coffee machine with red cups, they would have kept on walking to another one of their favourites. Steam rises in fits and bursts as person after person continues the revolving steady stream of customers. The sound of the milk heating. The clink of spoons on china. The magical way his arms operate to control as if he has more than one pair of arms as his body stands firm. He is an act to feast your eyes on.

Emerson is tall with a dusting of a light brown beard. His grey steel-eyes are focused in concentration as his arms and hands move in synchronised movements, his head looking down acutely at the art he is making. His smile is there, but hidden by the longer, trimmed stringy hairs, for which he insists is the hipster style. One of those faces and builds that to some extent, Eddy can recognise why some of his female friends think he is cute. Other times, he just looks adorably gangly.

He is the young co-owner with his mother, Kaz, who works behind the scenes in the small, cupboard sized kitchen. They share the exact same characteristics and features, not the beard or moustache though. Emerson, the rather unusual name, is after the progressive rock band E.L.P, where his dad was an enormous fan. When he passed, they decided to use the money they inherited to buy this place. They put his bike above the door as a tribute to his hobby, as well as a link to him.

Emerson's younger brother is Lake. There was no Palmer. In his own words Lake jokes that his parents stopped after him as they had accomplished perfection. It was a tongue-in-cheek joke that was tried, tested and consigned to flawless excellence. It brought a smile to everyone that knew him, as the ironic thing was that he was the most modest, humble and down-to-earth person that walked Sydney. His cocky and smug comment just did not prove true to who he really was in anyway. It was an egotistical saying, that was arrogant, when he was not even close to touching that stage in his own character. Lake helped clear the tables, cash up the till, wash-up while balancing a law degree at university. It was a family affair. It was Emerson and Kaz predominately, but Lake did not mind helping where he could. It felt cosy, friendly.

Eddy and Jay had caught up on the trivial things that all people talk about after meeting for the first time in a long time. The same repeated line: What has been going on? Along with other stuff for which they both unknowingly know how they can even fill the airspace with answers, let alone actually, really be able to talk about such mundane topics. These topics, these such unimportant subjects, that they are instantly, as forgetful as the breath that comes out with them. That they can scarcely believe that they even find ways to talk about them.

After their breakfast, when they had ordered another couple of coffee's they really get down to the nitty-gritty. Eddy leans forward over his cleaner than clear thick cream plates to make it known that he was going to be serious for a minute. The coffee comes over just as Eddy starts to open his mouth. They thank Emerson, they clink their second coffee as Lake takes the plates smoothly like a magician trick from under their noses.

Eddy's body is closed but his attitude is open. He laughed out loud. Smiles, showing the lost treasures of his white teeth. Jay sees a transformation to why he became mates with him back in the day. Here was the friend that made him laugh, that laughed with him, and, laughed at him. He talked about his daytime nightmare that was the pivotal point of his awareness that he needed to change. The nightmare was easier for him to share than he thought it would be. Once he started the words flowed out of him.

'Welcome back, mate.' The brown and grey terracotta coffee mugs clink a dull thud as they met across the light brown wooden folding table, that shows signs of once being pillar box red. With humour being the essential ingredient, Eddy tells Jay of his decision, a way to end the chapter. Emerson has placed they coffee in personal mugs, rather than the generic red that the other customers receive.

They are laughing over the pure stupidity of Eddy's explanation from the night before. His day did not end in the car, parked on the cliffs of Sydney.

Later that night, Eddy was half watching television in a comatose state. More watching the flashing figures, colours on the screen with the dialogue being just white noise. Being disturbing flickers in front of him that where very much in the background of the room, in front of him. He was planning a new course to his journey. His attention, firstly, was to come back into reality. By all things, a fictitious advert stirred him into the night. Spoke to him like a sharp slap, hard, across his face.

Once gained, he focused on the glowing lights of the television screen. An Australian sun-kissed bronze-skinned female Myrrha, with golden sand-coloured hair in conservative beachwear slowly walks towards a kitchen. In the sink of soapy suds flowing over was a male Adonis with obvious muscles bulging under his blue checked shirt, angular Roman statue cheekbones of a faultless, textbook exquisiteness of the perfect male. The flawless couple were replaying in a clean kitchen. He is drying his hands, she is putting away the last dried fork, in the raptures of the perfect score of love soon to be played.

Eddy looks at it as something he will miss. He sees the washing-up liquid come to the forefront of the screen. He sees them embrace in a hazy blur from behind the main image. He gets pierced with sadness. Not a single tear leaves his eyes, but a flood on Noah biblical proportions. He rocks on the brown leather couch telling himself out loud that he will be okay. That this is normal. The pinprick of the advert had burst his hard-built poignant-defending wall to let a flood flow. His world tilted in that moment. His earlier daydream was accepted but, this moment it was trusted with a higher level of faith. He was getting back to the old Eddy.

When he was telling Jay this story, he was sniggering like a schoolboy. He could not believe how stupid it sounded when voiced out loud. When Jay could not conceal anymore.

He started roaring with his louder than loud laugh, as well as struggling to speak. Astonished that an advert for washing-up liquid had been the catalyst. They were on the verge of having hysteric fits. Their laughter brought smiles, giggles, whispers of appreciation from around, happiness was contagious. A little boy asked his hand-holding father, 'What they were laughing at?'

He just responded, 'They are mates, it is what mates do!'

'What the fuck, the actual fuck has my life turned into?' Eddy howls.

Once again, the normally stiff-lipped Eddy, who typically kept everything personal under wraps, was resorted to sharing in engulfing tears of joy. This time laughing, teeming with delightful ecstasy. Eddy had no idea how long it had been since he had really belly laughed until this moment. It did not feel good, but fan-tas-tic. So, so long overdue.

Once the laughs had subsided. They finished their coffee with the affirmation that Eddy would in fact move on and Jay would support him.

After saying their goodbyes for another long break. Jay to the airport via a taxi, Eddy drops into the local library. Jay spoke about a book that he thought of straight away after listening to Eddy speak his soul. But he wanted to make sure he was out of the woods before recommending it. Jay was an avid reader. He always had been. To Jay, television was an alien concept that he watched sport and occasionally news, with but little to nothing else. When he got into the taxi, he passed a line ripped piece of paper through the crack of the window. Scribbled in his barely legible scrawl was the title and the author of the book for him to either hire or buy. He did not care, but he had been persistent that he had to read it.

After a little help, he eventually walked out the heritage-listed former Town Hall painted custard yellow building, with the 1969 book. The smell that only books can conjure up transports him back to his school days. That musty, damp, pleasant smell of anticipation. The pages of this book were frayed at the edges as he flicked through, worn by years of loving use, scuffed corners held by many different hands and that feel of paper pages in his hand rather than a flick of a finger on cold plastic.

He had always preferred the feel of paper books in his hands. The feel of turning the pages. The bookmark being placed closer to the end of the book each time you read a little bit more. The matured well literary treat was in his, by comparison, new hands. When Jay suggested this book, he needed to write it down as he would never have remembered it. For him, as he had never heard of the author, let alone the book. Also, the doors of a library have an uncanny knack of dousing him in a forgetful shower. For as he is walking to the library, he remembers what he is looking for only to step inside the walls and instantly forget.

Now, thanks to Jay writing the information on a rather scrappy piece of paper that he had evidently been holding onto for a while, he is holding, under his arm, the book. Written by Elisabeth Kübler-Ross was this 'famous', according to Jay, book—*On Death and Dying*. Unsurprisingly, he was not born in the year this book was released. He cannot recall the book being taught at school. He wondered how Jay would have come across it. Still, after Jay explained the pretext of the book, Eddy voiced that this book may not be appropriate. Jay insisted on him giving it a try, Eddy half-promised. He surprised himself when he followed through straight away on his word by making a beeline detour on his route to the library on the hill in Paddington, opposite the Reservoir. Being a somewhat obscure written piece, he assumed that they would not have it anyway.

Jay explained the book in the way that he knew precisely the content of the book, without revealing the author or the book by name. Jay's passion made it sound interesting. He had the ability to sell ice to Eskimo's if he was passionate about a subject. He should have been an English teacher. He had a thirst for knowledge. A love for the knowledge. An appreciation for a writer, an author, a piece of work.

Jay was looking away from the main scene when he explained this book to Eddy though. He explained to Eddy that this was the book that could explain better what he had gone through. They were both waiting for the taxi. He had been bottling up his view. In this extraordinary book, a pioneering forerunner on this untravelled subject, Kübler-Rose outlines the phases of grieving for the first time. The stages of five, for which people go through when dealing with grief.

Just when Eddy thought that Jay was actually trying to nail the final lid on the coffin that he was in fact dead, he came to the point of the recommendation. People have likened the stages of grief to the aftermath of being out of a relationship. It was here that Eddy saw sense in Jay's bizarre route to understand. It was his fervent impassioned drive that convinced Eddy to search the book out. It was Jay's glowing recommendation that made him go straight to the library to check out the book.

Now, en route home, he was ready to explore what lay beneath the plain covers.

Over a glass of watered down deep red Malbec wine, he read, skimmed and finished his way through this inspirational, but very intense book. He was drinking because he wanted, not because he needed yet he was still on that slippery slope so watered it down to get the taste. By the end of that very evening, in the silence, the only light from his reading lamp he skipped around the back through various pages. Some made sense. Some was evidently not for him. He had to admit it was dated but, the overall core of the information was on point. It revelated within him. Vibrated his own spirit. He finds a ray of white teethed to smile through the mist towards the future, of nothing but blue skied day.

It was a look at death. It all made perfect sense. He was grieving, then. He was grieving, now. The loss of Beth-Annie out of his life was as if it was a death. But he was alive. He needed to act alive.

Love Inseverable
Three Days Ago

'What just happened?
   'What was I doing?
   'Why did I believe that this was right?
   'How could I be so foolish?
   'I was close, wasn't I?
   '…close to seeing…being…better?
   'How could I be falling into this?
   'Again?'

Eddy thought a machine gun of questions as he gripped the hot black leather steering wheel. It was slippery with a greasy film of sweat. He had to grip harder. Under his firmly gripped fists at eleven and two he drove. He was furious with himself. His idiotic tendencies had led the anger flood through his veins. He was driving too fast around the small backstreets of Sydney. In his mind he was trying to be quicker to get to his destination. However, the recent roadwork around the city has caused him to stop, start, reverse, return. His plan was heavily flawed. Fuelled on the pure essence of fury. These diversions were adding much more flames to the intense wrath. He was incensed.

A destination that he knew, oh too well. He was following her. He was telling himself that he was protecting her. But, by following her. On, when, advancing on the edge of madness.

'Was he making the right decision?' Again, more thoughts.
   'Should he pull over?
   'Relax.'

He tried to convince himself that he was following her for protection. Not stalking her in peril.

Minutes earlier.

His mind's washing machine had been opened mid cycle. Out flowed the thoughts, the collusion of events that had got him on this hectic, wretchedness-filled speeding highway to suffering.

Barely a few minutes earlier.

Eddy had just shared the same warm bed with Beth-Annie.

'How did this happen? Happen to go so wrong?'

A few minutes earlier, they had shared the ruffled sheets of his bed. Over which a few photographs had been scattered. A bottle of wine. Nostalgia. Shared memories. Shared moments. Reminisces. All to the conclusion. A shared argument. Like a bat out of hell it came from nowhere. No time to stop the ferocity. It was such a pleasant evening. She stormed out. The door slamming, vibrating in the lock, shaking within the hinges.

He felt sick to his stomach. She was angry. If he was driving on rage. She was also driving home on rage. She had not called since leaving. Why would she? She was driving. But, rational thinking was not on his top level of his irrational sensible list. He was sick to the stomach. He was predicting an accident. He expected the worse. He expected her to have a kangaroo drop in front of her. The alcohol surely would be inhibiting her reactions.

A rapidly moving car, driven in rage, through blurred weeping tears. It would, inevitably, looming faster than her tyres were rotating cause her to horrifically crash. On the last lonely stretch of road from the highway to her house. At the darkest moment of the night, she would be alone. How long would she lay there dying? That sickness. That feeling of helplessness would only go away when he heard the key in the lock.

Then, and only then, he would sigh. A long heavy sigh as if he had been holding his breath from the last shout out, the slam of the front door. Until that moment he hears her breath, he can then sigh in relief. Despite that time, he was chasing her. To see the red lights of her car. To see that she made it home safely. Not necessary knock on the door, but seeing the car parked outside, the lights on inside, would mean she was safe.

'All that matters is a beautiful life with or without her.'

Then, that moment of doubt to where she was going. Not, certainly sure, she was going home, to her place. She was not coming back to Eddy's home, that he was sure. She wanted nothing to do with him. He carried on in his pursuit.

On the highway now. That lone last stretch. Trying to rush, but not speed, but speed he did. Trying to catch up, without aggravating the hostile situation. His eyes frenziedly switch, twitch. Up, down. He feverishly peeks between the speedometer, to the road, to the hiding waiting policeman with a speed gun. His mind casts back to the day that is happening. That has happened.

That day. When Eddy had arrived back, he cast his belongings from his pockets, missing his fruit bowl entirely. He had had a horrendous day at work. He did not want to talk about it. He was angry, mad at the surroundings that certain planets, stars and moons had coincided and aligned to make his day a momentous immeasurable fuck up. As if God was looking down at him. God was bored and used him as a voodoo doll of sorts, to play with to make himself laugh. That bloody day.

Then. That time after work was a magical experience of Disney proportions. It was a precious moment. It was a cherished moment to come in. He walked across the threshold, from the sidewalk to the home that they had made together where only one remained. Surprised to see Beth-Annie there, yet instantly jubilant. Smiling, oblivious to what had happened. Concerned that she did not reply to a single message from him. However, he did not want to trudge that foul matter of things up in fear of introducing a barrage of animosity. If she was feeling any anxiety, she hid it well from behind her smile, her perfect stance.

He had a cloud of thunder that covered him, drenched him to the core. He could not shake it. Overjoyed that she was there, even this did not fully shake his mood for the simple reason that he had to know her reasons for being here.

She embraced him with a warmth of welcoming after he had made the last of the five steep steps up to the veranda. He returned her hug with equally warm sentiments. Awkwardly fluid for Eddy, she opened the door and walked into his home. He emptied his pockets onto the floor. Letting each coin, safety pin and his bunch of keys scatter, which at the same time, as he clumsily kneeled to stop the calamity, apologising as he said he was aiming for the bowl. She cutely winked at his innocent debacle. She right away knew that he was not throwing his toys out of his pockets in a childish tantrum, but genuinely having a rather unlucky moment.

He sat on the high stool on the kitchen island looking at the kitchen. Rosy red cheeks to reveal his embarrassment. Remaining eye-contactless to display his awkwardness. After a few seconds he had recomposed himself to look up. She was opposite, hands under her chin in a cherub posture of angelic deportment. She brought two cups of coffee over, with one under her triangle, and the other one nestled between the space of her and Eddy. The whispering steams from the black mug the only separation between their faces as he talked. He had a lot to say.

He also wondered intermediately about the coffee being so quick, wondering if she let herself in first to brew the percolator. That thought did not matter. Concerning yes, but not significant in this moment of time. He continued talking. She listened. She would know what he wanted without a voice but let him vent. Eddy did not say everything that he had kept bottled up. He allowed the objectives to fizz, to air. His anger from his bloody day was still bubbling like boiling molten rock under the surface. This made his tone; his points seem edgier. He was speaking with a newfound honest demeanour.

He finishes with a short question that he had been wondering since seeing her. It was there and he wondered how he could phrase it in a nice way. He thoughts went up in smoke as he blurted out, 'So. Why are you here?'

He could not believe how curtly the words rang out. He swivelled on his chair. Swung his legs out. Within a few short steps he was outside, onto the balcony. Looking over the flickering lights, hearing the barking of dogs, the incessant squawking of the cockatoos.

Beth-Annie did not need to say anything for Eddy could feel her behind him. She slid over a stubbie on the silver-metal rail. He grabbed it without looking away from the houses gleaming with orange glowing lights. She sat behind him on one of the wooden deck chairs, long legs towards him. She sat close enough to be close but not close enough to be overbearing. Eddy did not want to talk. It was her turn.

'How was your day?' she, almost lovingly, enquired.

However, somehow, she made him open up…again. Within seconds of the softest of touches on the back of his knees, he bared his soul. He collapsed in the seat next to her. He laid out in exquisite detail what happened in his day. How the day unfolded into a chaotic mess of confusion that the lines of optimism were tangled with no possible way of untangling them to get a clear view of what needed to happen to clear the situation.

Within a few seconds, he was letting the shouldering rock that was his burden be lifted by Beth-Annie. He hated her for making it so easy for him to be so comfortable around her. The moody cloud over his head was turning grey, drying his core. Instantly over the rooftops the darkness was turning the moon whiter than white like a melting milk chocolate orb that would easily disappear in the warmth of the night. Before he knew it, he was laughing. He was smiling at the ridiculousness of the small things that had made his day a huge headache.

Beth-Annie spoke the littlest of little parts in Eddy's monologue, but mainly listened in silence. It was a precious moment to be able to talk when you do not want to. It was a glorious, precious moment to share something so simple. So pure and, so enchanting that his mood evaporated. His vision was clear. He knew what he should do to make the situation clearer. Was this what love was about? He could not let her go.

She was back. Damn. At that moment he did not know if he loved, hated or loved to hate her. She was here though. Possibly. Back for good. Yet, she still had not answered his burning question.

'Your turn.' Simultaneously turning his head to the side to look at Beth-Annie.

'For what?' Turning her head to look at him as the moon cast a shadow over his features to portray a person that was trusted, that was loveable.

'You never answered. Why did you come here? Surely not to listen about my day. Surely the latest splurging cooking, dating or whatever shit that is on television was not worse than hearing about my day!'

'Let's not—'

'Your…turn.'

'I wanted to see you…OK.'

The night started to nip its coldness. They retired indoors. They talked. Frighteningly enough like old times. They went to bed together. Frankly he was not convinced with her answer, but he had to admit it did feel good to be wanted once more.

Eddy loved the twilight shine of the moonlight that was flooding through the window when she fell asleep, slightly curled with her back to him. She had a peaceful smile. He wondered what she was dreaming about. She was a sight to behold. She was his.

Was. That bloody unendurable day. If only it had ended there. Them both fully clothed asleep until the morning.

Regrettably, they woke. A shoebox of photographs from under the bed evoked topics to pursue. Recommencing their talking, sharing, discussing, debating and even light-hearted arguing. All these were moments that he enjoyed. He did enjoy sex, but this bond was what he truly missed. He loved that she had a point of view. That she did not agree to disagree. That she felt passionate to argue a point. If she felt she needed to be heard, she would be.

Her highway of her mind was a network of roads that never seemed to unexpectedly surprise him. She would come out with the most stupid thing, sometimes, which made him giggle with astonishment. The most intelligent thing, that made him think. The most bizarre thing, that made him confused. The most complex thing, that made him bewildered. She was complex. That was true. The logic that is Beth-Annie, is flawless. This was something she wanted Eddy to believe, but she knew when she was beaten. She would never admit it. Sorry, she rarely admitted it. They were in love? They could not live with each other. They could not live without each other. They were in love.

Was.

Beth-Annie turned him on. She did not have to do anything. She just had to be the person that she was. She did not have to try. She lifted him up. She was his all. His nothing. She followed him. He followed her. They led each other. The dream survived in them. A fire burning. They felt so alive around each other. They were alive around each other.

Was.

All that matters is a beautiful death without her.

A chime in the dark of night. She reached over to the nightstand. Felt her mobile. Looked at the shining screen. Not her mobile. A message. They had the same mobile. His mobile. She picked up his mobile. The banner feed for him, not her. The light fuelled an ignition to a blazing inferno.

The argument. Over nothing. A message from a girl at Eddy's work. Taken wrong. She put a simple 'X' at the end. So showed the full message.

HEY BABE, SOZ BOUT 2DAY. B OK 2MORROW. X

It meant nothing to Eddy. Everything to Beth-Annie. Why would he do something that would jeopardise this thing he wanted? Instead of talking she rose to a level of anger that erupted with volcanic passionate blazing red mist fury. Spittle corroding accusations. Thunderously, leaving the bedroom with a deafening slam of the door. Shouting finger pointing allegation of him having been sleeping around. Screaming as she went to undermine and quash his protestations, his protesting clarifications. Throwing objects towards the pursuing Eddy that dogged and cowered the airborne raid. She slammed the front door with all her might as the walls seemed to shake. Then the car door. A screech of tyres. High revs. Gone.

Eddy was left dazed. Unsure of his next move. He picked his keys from the floor where he accidently discarded them. Beth-Annie became the hunted. Not in a predatory way.

Thoughts were confounding in his brain. He was growing madder, if that was possible. He was wondering if he should break down the walls of his brain to the outside world. Did he want to venture out? He did. But the real question was if he was ready to. It was a question that needed no answer. His mates were supporting him. They did not say the right things. They were great mates. They did not say what they should say, to make a mate better. They told the truth. Even if that said truth, hurt, they did not care, so to speak, they wanted to give it to him straight. They were Eddy's mates and he deserved to know exactly what they thought. Great mates. Eddy was very lucky to have this base. Although he did not listen to them over Beth-Annie. They said he should 'cut her loose'. He could not. It was strange that his mind flickered to his mates. Would he wait for her to come back, would she come back.

Eddy wanted to be there. Wanted to be with her. Wanted to be next to Beth-Annie. He wanted to love her like no-one else could. Beth-Annie blamed him. Eddy was not sure what for. His mates told him she was not a nice person to conflict the emotional guilt unto him. To cover him in emotional suicidal tendencies. The emotions were guarded around her chest like a home-made bomb that lingered in the shadows waiting to come out and, BOOM. Surprise him with another devastating blow. Just like tonight.

She was not on the highway. He had managed to drive slower to see if she had come off the road. At the junction to leave he was relieved that she, if in fact she was going home, had made it this far without injury.

He was not prepared to be a rubber ball in her dark corners of her pocket. A ball which she would bring out, bounce, play with. Then, to stuff back inside when she had played enough. He was fed up of being a plaything, her plaything. Her brush that would stroke her ego. She wanted something that she thought he could not give. He wanted to be there. She wanted Eddy to be anywhere but there.

He did not understand how he became a victim. She was the one that took. He became touched by her. Although he did not fake anything in her presence, it seemed she did. Eddy's mate told her that he did not need her when, he was yearning for her. Eddy's mates were right. Eddy would see this, but it will take a lot of time in his eyes, before he could see this through the dust of his foundations as they crumbled around him.

A heavy sigh exploded from him. He felt his chest reduce, the quivering of his lips. Poorly parked, but parked nevertheless was her car. Peering from beneath the roof of his car he leered towards her apartment. Lights were on. He could see a silhouette, an outline of a sole petite figure. It had to be her. He was glad she had made it home. Thankful and free from worry. His mate's words rang through him. Should he finally take his mates advice and finally server the ties. Let her go. Leave. Drive. Drive away for good. He turned the lights off to watch the lights of her apartment dance on and off. The engine lay idle.

Was that love?

What was he going to do now that the love had gone?

Beth-Annie said goodbye.

Don't say goodbye.

Please.

Begging.

Sobbing.

Don't say goodbye.

Say you love me.

Say you want me.

Need me.

Goodbye?

Huh!

Bad bye.

Is there such a thing as Bad Bye?

Yes.

Was that love?

Was?

Love.

What is love?

Who knows?

Was?

Was that it?

Is that it?

What is it?

?

This is Eddy going out of his mind. Thought after thought ricocheting around his head like explosive rapid pinball bursts from unknown, surprise attacking personal conflicting bombs.

For a few long minutes, he was staking out her house. Looking for a second time, but this time more intently at the car for any mark. Without the slightest scratch, dent, dink on the side closest to him he was rest assured. He saw the lights in the house go off as she walked room-to-room. He lingered. In the shadows. When the last light was off. With that reassurance that she would not be going anywhere else tonight he turns his lights on and drove off. Calm. Relaxed. Another sigh escaped him.

This bloody awful day.

Eventually, he started to see her in another way. He kept to the speed limits and drove with caution. He saw her as a past memory. As an object in his rear-view mirror, behind him. Eddy did not need Beth-Annie. Ultimately, he had accepted the ending.

He is heartbroken.

It would be.

Weeping through glazed eyes as he now drove slowly back.

His car door was closed. Finally slammed shut. He closed his front door. Chapter closed on the battle after battle of the war that has finally ended.

Goodnight and Bad Bye, Beth-Annie.

Love Lost.

Love Let Go.

Love Insufferable.

Time for Change
Early Last Week

Eddy needed a new outlook and a different prospect. For this reason, he decided to go away. Once again, he felt today was the climaxing right stage where the powerful urge was too much to resist. This time on his own, seeing no one. This was not an impulsive thing, although the timing was. This was something that he had been thinking about for a few days. If he was honest though, it was more like as long as a few weeks. He kept coming up with the notion of escaping everything in his immediate life, to wipe the slate clean and reset his soul, restart his life.

Nevertheless, recently, over the past few hours of the present day, it had gained momentum. Rattling harder and harder around his head so he could not ignore the ceaseless screech any longer. He had decided for this to become an action. He just needed, needs space. His space. To clear the rattling from inside his head. This time with no distractions. This time away from anything that remotely reminds him of his former, his existing life. Somewhere unfamiliar. A place that has no connections to his past. Where though?

One small obstacle. He must clear the days with his boss first. He calls his boss at home. It is after work. Later in the day but not long since he had left. Rather than waiting he wanted an answer this evening. When his boss picked up, he proceeded to ask for the next week off. It was very short notice, being a couple of days away. So, he cannot really be surprised at the outcome. The rejection. The going around the houses approach for saying 'no'.

Although his boss is a great one. Just when he thought that his hopes were to be dashed, he offered a compromise. His boss hated saying no with a passion. Hated to disappoint anyone that he saw as being a loyal, trustworthy member of staff to him. Rather than being the bad guy he offered an alternative. Thus, in this scenario he offered up a solution. Also, he had a slightly different agenda, he was motivated to help Eddy out.

It did not take a rocket scientist to figure out that he was not himself. That he needed to get away from it all. To come back more focused. To return better understanding and complete in himself. Heck, his boss was honest when he would settle for a little more focus. In his eyes, negotiating an arrangement would be a huge help in promoting his wellbeing, thus bringing Eddy back to his productive self. Therefore, they agreed for him to have a long weekend that involved this Friday, tomorrow, and the following Monday and Tuesday, thus being back at work for the busier Wednesday to Saturday preparation days. Eddy was in no position to argue, so he joyfully approved his terms. He accepted and smiled at the screen of his mobile as it faded to black.

In his own way, Eddy tried to move on over the subsequent few hours. He talked to mates. Went around for beers. Played footy in the park. Having a drunken experience over that ill-fated 'quick one after work'. For which he really enjoyed for the record. His disconnected members of his social network had seen him come out of his cocoon.

After a few slow events that he did not attend more than attended or even promised to be attending. He was an unsociable caterpillar. A lone small outwardly insignificant person. Then to be a complete recluse, an essential hermit when with Beth-Annie. And now, he was changing. He was a social butterfly. The life was back flowing within him, contagious to all around by colour, humour, news and sport.

Back at his place, slightly tipsy but not drunk he went home to pack. That afternoon bridging into the evening he cleaned his apartment from top to bottom. After that, over the course of an hour he had touched base with everyone. Whether by speaking or flicking a message. He was back, as were his mates and family members. These things over the past small amount of days assisted him in moving on. They never actually left him, but walked beside him as he kept social distancing.

He was in bed by the granddaddy hour of eight-thirty in the evening to aim to wake refreshed. He drifted into a deep sleep fast, in barely a few seconds. Yet, just as quickly, his mind started to have uncertainties. That night was long even though he knew he was doing the right thing. A restless sleep. The mind seemed to wait until his head hit the pillow to start asking every question, wondering every issue, doubting every decision, pondering about every single thing. This is where the slight ticking pain in the back of his head vibrated through him. Too many photographs around.

He swore that he could still smell her fragrance. Occasionally when doing his washing a long, silky fine hair that was from her would come out of his jeans, shorts, briefs. His mind conjured up random, somewhat ludicrous memories and attachments. Yet he was smiling. The weight of that decision was lifted. It was warranted. He needed to be completely alone.

Even though he accepted the end. Albeit he knew that he did not want to go back even if she presented herself, he did not quite believe himself. He still needed to feel the acceptance fully from within, an inner peace of tranquillity. Harmony on the seas of reconciliation from the war that continually raged. Eddy thought, felt, that being alone would help. In actual fact, he was adamant that it would. Being in a different space. A place where he could actually feel for the first time in many years that feeling he yearned. The realistic feel of truthfully being alone. What that would actually feel like. And, that harbouring fear of being alone, was not something to fear. The reality was. It was good to be alone. That is what he was after. Closure. Nevertheless, there in it laid the fear. He needed to do it to regain his self. His self-control to return. Basically, just 'to toughen up, Princess' and 'Man-up'.

The early morning dragged like a stubborn horse at the start line. Horseshoe feet pressing down into the brown soiled racetrack, adamantly refusing to follow the others around the short course, to let him sleep. The shrill tone emanating from his mobile rudely altered him to a new day. Why was it without an alarm he could not sleep, with an alarm he felt that he could have slept, needed to sleep longer. The sun had just started to rise, creeping across his doona from the unblinded window. Sending shadows of light like piercing needles that hurt his eyes as he adjusted from the darkness. Birds were having a squawking war outside. The reversing beeping of a garbage truck followed by the heavy, clumpy roll of the large wheel bins to curb side.

Traffic noise let him know it was a Friday. Finally, though, when he thought that the clock was teasing him in going slower than possible the night was officially done, the morning had arisen. Dusting off the lack of sleep with a vigour as if he had the best night sleep that he could have possibly devoured. The week for Eddy finished. Ended. It was time to get going. The weekend was starting.

The smell of burnt toast accompanied by chatter from the unit opposite gave him the extra push to rise for himself. He went through the motions, eyes half open. Coffee on as he cleaned his bedroom. A juddering irritating scrape of chairs, short and curt made him look up to where the sound resounded to tut in disapproval. He was an autopilot driven comatose zombie that felt unattractive as he psychosomatically thoughtlessly ticked each box of his mental checklist in his rehearsed mind. The noise from above, although not loud, was interrupting his process. In spite of that, this was not his first rodeo. He could have done it with his eyes closed. He basically did.

He carefully, methodically, packed his black sports bag taking all the essentials for a short trip. This was the first time he had not packed any cables, or for that matter any electronic devices, not even his old, worn, broken screened iPod. A sentimental item that he often got laughed out when he brought it out but had the songs, the only songs he really needed to listen to. That iPod on shuffle gave him a mix of music that took him over a wealth of different eras, memories and people.

He was tired without actually knowing. Mentally exhausted his head ached, quite the reverse of a headache, but a throbbing want, desire to have a break and calm down. Physically, if he wanted, he could run a marathon, he will not, of course, but he has the strength to, just not the time.

Over a microwaved leftover lasagne dinner, he nearly ended pig like into his food as he chewed on his meal as if this was the marathon race. His appetite was better, but still not up to much. He ate half of the remains for breakfast before throwing the rest in the single bin with everything, so no rubbish remained inside of his place. He cleaned up, showered. Last-minute doubts were pushed aside.

The strangest thing on this particular day was that he was not feeling. He was numb. He should have been feeling great, surely. No work. No plans. But. But, having made this life-changing decision after such a procrastinated duration of long-suffering he was feeling emotionless. His impassive demeanour was not what he was expecting. Despite the fact that he had put his mind at ease. He had unlocked his body from the chains that tied him by the invisible force of Beth-Annie, wherever she was. He said he did not care, but he did, secretly.

The door closed gradually behind him, feeling like the opening of a new part of his life rather than a closing of another. The freshness of the air, the warmth of the sun, the glow of the fire through the trees, the sound of nature combined with urban living was the sustenance he required. He breathed in. Inhaled the smells around him with eyes tightly shut. Released, deliberately slowly, with determination. His thoughts ran clear like a mountain spring. He was completely liberated. Unshackled and released from the murderous love that killed his mind, he thought back to the preceding moments. He should have skipped out of bed. Sung in the shower. Danced while drying himself.

The realistic truth was different. He felt strange. He did not know how he felt. He never thought of how he would have handled this unknown territory other than being relieved. Again, the realistic means were that he was not as pleased as he imagined this scene transpiring. He could not put his finger on it. If someone put a gun to his head to explain what emotion he was expressing, he would have been shot. As he could muster no words. Find not a single sentence that could describe this numbness that bordered on being quite unhappily happy.

The last month, he had regressed to a small vulnerable toddler. The last month before, he was a moody teenager. The normally confident Eddy was replaced by an unsure, bewildered toddler.

He was finding that the more time he now possessed was a burden. He was cursed with the time that was burning him with red-hot ambiguity pokers of questioning uncertainties. Each new day was a reminder. He was experiencing everything new again. Buying a coffee, he still asked for his long black and Beth-Annie's skinny flatty, as a false of habit. He was open to see everything as a new person. This break from the normal comfort zone was taking some getting used to. A new perspective was beginning.

'AGHHH!'

He bellowed in pure frustration as he put his runners on. He roared from the back of his throat through gritted teeth at his incapability in being a man. His flawed struggle in being, what they call, a proper masculine man. He was never really sure what that truly meant. He assumed it embodied braveness with a bold confidence combined with dominant traits that did not crumble. As in the collapsing of his self-worth, his character would prove that he was weak, that he was dolefully tragic.

More than once, he had let himself and others down. He was, thought, with a personal pride and honour that he was reappearing after being dormant. Yet he was angry at himself. His own personal imperfections, his own weaknesses. All the same, he was striving towards being a person, he was emerging to be that whole man that had his life completely in order, together. Not this fragile Fabergé shell that painted an image of everything was fine and dandy in the world outside, but inside the slightest knock would see him shatter into pieces. That even all the Kings horses and all the Kings men in the entire world could not put him back together.

He regrouped. He was on the correct path now. Only he was the sole one that could place any barricades in front of him. He did possess the complete mental strength to force his way through, smashing and shoving each one aside to press on.

After a brief meditation of exhales and inhales from the veranda. Hearing with eyes shut the world of traffic. The everyday noise of the outside civilisation that did not have any idea of his ordeal in his inner torment. He opened wide his eyes, to slightly squint from the rising golden sun. One more deep breath in. As he released the air slowly and controlled, he took his first step as a man. Behind him, he left his home couped up with his past. The memories that were already beginning to scatter, to not be put back together. To dissolve, to never be a hardened reality ever again.

Descending down the steep concrete steps with the small carry bag in his right hand, that gently bumped the back of his right knee with each lurching step, he silently ticked off a mental checklist to make sure that he had not forgotten anything. In his other hand he gripped lightly his keys and mobile. With each new concrete step his foot rested on, the restrictive shackles faded away, he felt the weight lifted, unclenching its hold around his legs and arms. He was feeling like a prisoner getting ready to inhale that free air once again. That mixed anticipation of dread and excitement.

Just as the front gate was drawing shut, he cursed. Dropped his bag and skipped up the steps. In the blink of an eye opening the front door one last time. Through the tiniest of gaps, so not to get drawn back in, he gently threw his mobile on to the dark wooden table. In one fell swoop he felt the lock of the door click into place, to simultaneously hear a clinking thud of the table with a hushed slide of the mobile on the wood, to rest with a slight clink of glass at the fruit bowl. He honestly, really, did not care if it slid off. He was not needing it. He was not going to cross that threshold even if he heard his mobile hit the panelled floor.

He had no aspirations to take anything as a portal to the world he desired to escape. No distractions for him to threaten his own self-repair. In one of the sleepless split seconds early, in the darkness of this morning, he had decided to go through the whole self-imposed rehabilitation with an unplugging philosophy. He had decided earlier, but it was natural to leave with keys, wallet and mobile. Now it was uncanny to leave without his mobile. This time it seems strange as if he has forgotten something, he feels slightly naked. He shakes it off. This was the last chain that needed to be left here. He drops the last step, as he bends down to retrieve his bag. He potently strides forth, the gate jingles for a brief moment as it rests into its rusting latch.

He debarked from his comfort zone, to feel a little uncomfortable. Yet, that was the idea. He did not need his mobile. A practiced tradition saw him do it instinctively, with a degree of dependency. The slammed shut object made him on purposely consciously aware that he had nothing to keep in contact, or with whom to keep contact with. Or, more to the point, nothing for him to use for contact. This simple act of doing made an out coil of that overbearing invisible tight, boa constrictive chain fall from his weary shoulders.

He grinned. He experienced a pleasant rise of exhilarating happiness. The confident strides in his march, his head held high. His presence spoke a fresh take within that was materialising out.

As he walked down, under the fire escape metal stairs above the shortcut to the bustling outside world he was contemplating if he needed to go away for this. Instead, did he just need to see something that reminded him of nothing from anything that went before. With him being lost in thought he knocked into a random stranger as he walked left, his mind went right. Mumbled apologies as he realises he was walking mindlessly to work. He does the exact same route that he does every day to arrive at work.

But today, instead of leaning right down to the Quay, he moves up the small hill to the left. He is heading to Central train station. His destination on this journey was undetermined.

His destination to what he would find there was clear, himself. It will do him good. Afterall the age-old cliché of a change is as good as a holiday surely will be beneficial. He is toying with the idea of not coming back. That is one of a cluster of weird thoughts that burst in his thought-provoking fluid mind.

He had hoped. He did anticipate that he would be on a train by now, rather than marching the streets of Sydney still. However, due to the slightest error he needs to get a later train after nine in the morning, once he had been to the bank. The reason was the Smart ATM that he wanted to use to place some money in his account decided not to be that smart late last night.

Unquestionably proving that one of his close mates was the salt of the earth, when he asked him for a small amount of cash, he got some, but then decided that he did not want to take all the money as cash. He was worried in case he was caught napping. An opportunist would take his money out of his pocket while in slumber. So, he decided to deposit half. Not risking the modern technology to get it right. He in person wanted to hand the human teller the money and receive a receipt that his wishes were carried out.

He waits outside, in the faintly blustery street with roasted coffee beans being carried up on the breeze. Droplets of dust sparkle in the long rays of the morning sun as the busy network of commuters hurry unconnectedly to their surroundings to get to work. He picks up his ears at the noise of the city, hence ignoring it as he fishes for his mobile. Then realises his comfort blanket was left on the table.

As a result, he replays Jay with the quick call from last night to pass the time. In spite of this being an off the cuff call to Jay, as he had already bothered him a lot through the past week, he did not sound annoyed, but genuinely happy to be Eddy's confidant. On the other side of the phone, Jay was breathless. He recalls wondering if he caught him at a time that was personal. Before having to ask that awkward question, Jay assures him that he is rushing to get ready for a business dinner.

Regardless of his preoccupied mind, he still manages to drop a boulder of knowledge in Eddy's pool of educated learning. Back then it brought what it is doing now. This feeling of mateship brings a splashing tear to Eddy's eye. Jay, who is never backwards about going forwards, tells him in brutally honest truth that no relationship is easy. Eddy is well aware of this.

Jay, though, mentions the vices, attitudes and the things that make a relationship is the acceptance of these things. To make the unrealistic aim that Eddy would like everything about Beth-Annie is a unicorn-like preposterous dream. The same claim is vice versa. There is no such thing. Jay trounces in the boulder. Jay insists that to live happily ever after is nothing more than a pure fairy-tale. To find someone that loves your flaws, as well as your strengths is out there. Somewhere. He tells Eddy to not stop fishing. He needs to cast his line in for his one true fish. To grow up, is to learn. Everyone will break Eddy's heart. Even the person they believed was not going to let them down, probably will. To love. To Live. Taxes. Death. That are the four certain guarantees of this wonderful life.

With Eddy on the verge of blubbering on hearing Jay's earnest tones on record as the banking staff emerge to unlock the doors. They say their goodbyes. Even with this conversation in his head, Eddy finds himself mouthing a 'goodbye'. He wishes that he could just hear his voice, to tell him in proud earnestness, 'Thank you'. Eddy is going to be one of the first into the bank. He positions his feet to be able to move quickly to be near the head of the queue. Close enough to see through the pristine glass door a trio of eager tellers smiling their coffee-stained teeth for the start of day.

Eddy slows his gait, almost to a mortified shuffle as he looks down at his boyish feet, while he shakes his head. It is in this instant that it occurs to him. When saying goodbye to Jay last night he said more. He wonders why, after he said to Jay 'Goodbye', he followed it with, 'love you'. Jay brushed it off on the phone, but he now wonders two things. One, if he meant it. Two, if he heard it. Then continues to mull over if it was what they called a bromance. One thing was certain, he did appreciate that he had a trustworthy, honest mate. Just maybe it is in actual fact a brotherly love.

The large heavy looking glass doors effortlessly, electronically slide sideways. To part like a silent glimmering mirrored curtain to let him walk in. Eddy enters the National Australia Bank, which is now simply called NAB in the heart beating pulsing centre of Sydney. The glass floor to ceiling ground floor, for which the bank is situated within the heritage listed two-tiered building is as clinical as an operating theatre. To see the ornate décor of the exterior on the sandstone walls it gives the impression that from stepping out of the pavement into the shop, he appeared to effectively step from 1920s Sydney, accelerative plunging one-hundred years into the present.

If it was not for the black, red star and white nab logo he would feel he was here for a medical procedure. It was a wide-open floor. A smell of nothing, just the very vague hint of pine disinfectant from the recently mopped false marble-etched floor. Each counter was a block of matt whitewash where no cables, screens or distasteful untidiness was seen from the customers point of view. Large advertisements clumsily draped on weighty canvas sheets, used for their latest hard sell and promotion, hung from silky thin wires that reflect the sunlight in glittering shines. Much the same way as a spiderweb would sparkle after a light rain. They are positioned in such a strategic way that no matter why anyone had to come into the bank, they could not miss the message being delivered.

Today was a home loan, by the looks of it state unrealistic exceptional rates where alarm bells would ring to read all the terms and conditions thoroughly before accepting this devil's bargain. Each of the staff wore the exact same colour code in slightly different instances depending on genre. Name tags on the right breast are perfectly horizontal and shining.

He sees his teller is called 'Joy', smiles as he introduces himself with identity cards at the ready. All the same, he does not address her by her displayed name. Very polite and very to the point, he explains what he would like today. Against everything that he was going to do, he, not for the first time in this still very early day, he proceeds on impulse. He spontaneously closes all his accounts. It could be that, after all, he has come in for that medical procedure he feels in the impersonality of the room.

The teller perseveres to implement an account autopsy. He takes every last cent of his money out. Maybe, just maybe he had subconsciously decided not to come back. Or at least for the time being. He fought back the strangeness of his undertakings that he did not want to carry too much money for security reason and now he was taking all his money. He did not even know his motives. Even if he had any. Yet, he consciously continued to answer the security questions that Joy was robotically asking. All the while having the, what now appeared insincere smile never leaving her lips. The engaging initial spark in her eyes, of a candle in the darkness, withering down to detach and become as one with the interior design. Joy was undoubtedly professional, but deferentially disengaged from her namesake.

He is incredibly surprised by just how easy it was to walk in, to then subsequently walk out with all his cash. Certainly, astounded by the rapid nature it transpired to close all his account fully, to thenceforth take all that he struggled to build after losing so much. A proof of identification here, his pin there, his signature in the ridiculously small thick black-lined box, along with a routinely short question to 'why?'. He paused mid-signature. He had no answer to that simple question. He mumbled a jerking response with words to the assumption of wanting cash on the hip, so to speak.

Apparently, it seemed to not make a difference what he said. As he looked up while sliding the piece of paper over, he very much doubted that Joy was even listening to the answer. Her head was down. Her straw-like strawberry blonde hair that was in a neat bun at the back of her head had let slip some locks, swung like a ticking clock to the front of her bowed face.

He felt alone. A single chilly bead of sweat escaped his armpit and quickly ran down his ribcage. It struck him viewing the polished fingernails stroke his hard-earned cash through the artificial unbreakable glass what his life had amassed to. It was in the colourful notes being counted before him that he realised that when a relationship broke down, he was broke.

Eddy was fully committed to this past one. Wherein he gave much more into it than just himself.

The added cost of re-buying things had burned a hole in his wallet. The things that were shared had mounted. He just left them with Beth-Annie. When they lived together, they shared everything. Eddy got rid of a lot of his everyday things such as doonas, pots, pans, blankets and other run-of-the-mill things that everyone needs in their home. This is not to mention the larger electrical equipment like fridges, the basic virtually fundamental need for a bed. Before he knew it, six months had passed. He was nursing a broken wallet, bleeding from the various incisions. Barely a small crack to his chasm gulfing broken heart ruptured as the loss of rational thinking. Love was not only blind, but foolish and careless it would appear.

As the last of the small columns of money was counted, she looked up. Each colour was separated, rather than the expected nominations of tens. She slowly counted each note as she spoke loud enough for him to hear the wealth, or in this case the non-existent wealth he possessed. He did not want to believe it was so little, regrettably he had no choice but to accept his poverty. His savings had dwindled from a rather tidy nest egg to a deconstructed disfigured egg. All this evidently in a seductive tempestuous wink of Beth-Annie's eye.

This is the burden of Eddy. He always puts himself in a relationship. He throws himself in; he fully commits himself. It is not him being flashy. If he needs to travel, change plans at expense or do things that mean the money may be dearer he does. He never tells the person involved, as he hopes that participating in him doing a little more in his book, will show just how hopelessly devoted and dedicated he is. His cavalier approach to money in building the steel bridge of relationships did not matter to him. He moved obstacles to be with someone.

He changed his plans around that someone, always at his cost. It was always him that flew, drove or used another means of transport to be with that someone. He paid for the meals, gas, accommodation. He never came out up on the deal, yet, he did not care. He never minded doing this. When he was in a relationship, he was looking long-term, never at the short. For him it was never a fling. If he was after that he would not outlay any cost. He went the extraordinary tactic with stating his case clear, simple beforehand, when he felt that something was becoming nurtured, thus important to him.

With his preoccupied mind, the thoughts blowing around like paper in a tornado confronting him with questions, notes, comments and still images. He left the NAB absentmindedly with the pen still in his hand, while his other protectively grasps his healthy-looking black leather wallet of plastic bank notes peering out as he holds it firmly in his clenched fist hidden deep inside his pocket.

On the sensation of a rather small, cylindrical object in what should have been his free hand he looks down to see the unintentionally stolen black NAB pen. It is too late to go back and return it. He thinks to himself, acknowledging the truth. He honestly cannot be bothered to go backwards and waste more time in getting to the station. He can only think that he took the pen as a subconscious reaction to needing the feel of something in his hand. The way a former smoker trying to quit will bring something to their lips. For him it was not a cigarette, but his mobile.

As he gained momentum in his weaving gait through the onrushing stream of people, he inadvertently by mistake grazed people with his bumping bag. He kept smacking his pocket with his right hand. Left-hand pocket wallet, as it was, always has been, he constantly needs to confirm that he has not dropped his lifeline. Right hand, keys jingle in an irritating regular pulse. He nervously twirls the black pen up and over his fingers.

He briskly negotiates the individuals with all the light-footed majestic fleetness of all the invisible waves of horses. Arion continues to guide him with soothing words. The streets are busy. The Sydney streets are seldom quiet. He dodges and weaves his way through like a stray dog around the busy suits. No-one notices him. No-one acknowledges him. He is the one avoiding people in a daze. He is consciously aware of them all while he keeps an internal monologue with Arion. His destination is the train station, but he has no idea why he is rushing. Afterall, it is not as if he has a timetable to keep too.

The twisted gnarly trees are the people in their grey, charcoal, black and brown suits. The dark cemetery rich smelling soil, the pavement. The looming grey clouds of a brewing storm, are in fact the perfectly white fairy floss clouds in a pale blue sky. The impending doom is the metallic traffic fumes. The riotous noise of crashing, crushing, clattering and drilling from behind the bright coloured visible safety net is the busy hive of construction work. Footsteps merge into a cacophony.

Eddy is a rib-displaying stray dog that people would knock. Well, to be honest would actually rather kick away with the assumption that it is carrying an infectious disease than give it a bath, shelter and an essential good feed. He was turning into a ghost. He was vanishing on his way to disappear. He was still not fully out of the woods of melancholia. A nice way of verbalising the negatively endorsed sigma filled term of depression, yet he is on the fringes. He is one step into the daylight or one step back into the dark. Purely his choice.

Then a thought flashed across his mind out of the blue. Then stayed as the single bolt spread, without reason making him think of a Shakespearian play that he studied many, many years ago at school. He cannot fathom why this spontaneous memory comes to him out of nowhere. In a hushed tone even more abruptly he finds himself muttering the lines, as he negotiates the flashing torrent of people. He got some wrong but recites this memory as best as he can remember:

'All the World's a stage,
And all the men and women are merely players.
They have their exits and their entrances
And each man plays his own part.
At first, the baby mulling and puking in his mother's arms
The second…
The third…'

He knows he gets the words wrong, or in the wrong order, or the story line incorrect, but he goes on marching the words to the rhythm of each step as he makes his way forward.

Up till now he has been progressing forward in a steady momentum. Yet the closer he got; a fear spread over him. As he approached through the cluttered, narrow streets of the surrounding areas of Surry Hills and Chippendale the contrast is apparent to the uniformed grand station before him. For which Eddy has always insisted is one of the best, grandeur stations in the world. Of course, he is biased. A born and bred Sydneysider that he is. He is very passionate about his hometown, and for that matter his country. He gets abnormally defensive when people from another town talk badly about HIS home.

As he sauntered forward, Eddy's feet were getting heavier. His gait turned into a resisted augmented jerking action with these invisible tides fighting in opposition to impede him. It was as if the tarmac was melting around him. People around him were walking like Jesus on water. He was sinking like the Titanic. Heavier, faster and unexplained. The pavement was turning into a wet, dark grey quicksand. Slowly, as he gets closer, he is knee deep. Edging through, bit-by-bit, he moves uninhibited with power and might. His legs ache with each slow trudged step in his advance. His thighs push aside the viscous dark volcanic cool lava. He will progress.

As if it was with a mind of its own, the molten rock formed a tight hard slab of stone, which, pulled his legs. Pulling his body. Holding him back like a chained dog to his own backyard. Yet, he fought on. Leaving his comfort zone. He wanted it more. He wanted to turn the page. Start afresh. He wanted the end to be…here.

It is a lethal game of chance to try and cross Elizabeth Street in the city with its many lanes. The cars, motorbikes and riders spin around given it a sense of Sydney's own Russian Roulette. The New South Wales centre for road safety is trying to kerb the fatalities that are rising steadily with on average, sixteen lives lost a day. The serious injuries would show far inflated figures. They have introduced heavy fines for jaywalking, for which Eddy has been caught.

Mobile phone apps to display the heavy, dangerous points as well as introducing more crossings. Despite all of this, people, like Eddy, take their chances. Everyone is on their own personal mission for which it seems life is a chance for which they are willing to take to get to that destination quicker. He manages it across the busy hectic frenetic rush-hour traffic to find himself in another tide. The surging sailing tide of people that all seem to be coming towards him. He is in the opposite direction fighting his way through. His legs still heavy that substantially affect his momentum.

The light hits the correct places of the beautiful beige seventy-five metre tower that looms magnificently over the whole 1906 Central Station to add to Eddy's appreciating grandeur. Eddy though is gritting his teeth to get closer. Through his peripheral vision, on the sloping banks of the downtrodden verges in Belmore Park he sees the clutter of mess left by the unfortunate homeless. This green patch of grass was a wonder when he was growing up. He used to play cricket here. He used to meet up with mates before going out here. It seems that the local council cannot do anything about this advancing problem that makes the place unsightly. In turn this gives a rather nervous, unsafe persona to the showcase. An image that should present a safe haven. A beautiful park should be for what visitors see upon exiting. Suits to walk their walk. People to enjoy. Instead they hurry through as if the slightest pause would be a fatal infectious mistake.

Trudging into the shadows under the sandstone, through the hideously ugly electronic door. A disappointingly blot of modern monstrosity which is an unnecessary immorality. Are people in that much of a rush that they cannot pull or push a hand-carved wooden door? Eddy steps into his belief of the grandest of grand building.

He is a fighter. Not a single person can ever take that away from him. Through his life he has been knocked, tripped, pushed and slapped, who hasn't, but he forever progressed through it. When the supernatural tough, taut threads loop around his body to drag him back he has powered on. When his heartstrings have been threatened with all they can take to breaking point, he has driven on. Forever resilient.

As he enters the hall, he dusts his jacket off like he has just come in from an unexpected downpour. He checks his left-hand pocket again. He removed the illusory burdensome chains with a few hastily shrugs of his shoulders. He wipes his feet on the rough brown doormat. He looks around him. In awe-inspired recognition for the craftsman before him he smiles. The outstanding concourse runs the length of fifteen stud-ended platforms.

He has stepped into a featured, characteristic building of elegance and taste. This preservation of past-time accomplishment is a testament to people that appreciate the new. At the same time would like one foot in tribute to the past. The modern, sprawling skyward growing modern city surrounds this sparkling jewel. The state-of-the-art designs of the clinical foyers. The plain plastic imitation marble décor. The impersonal hideous characteristic cutting-edge of the face of the future is behind him as he stands seeing the true marvel of skill, workmanship and craft.

High above him, the green-painted arches of steel hold the roof to let the sunlight flood in. The large shining golden hanging orbs perfectly light the composition of this man-made structure. In the centre, a large unpretentiously sophisticated white clock with black hands, hangs down. Almost forgotten by the busy network of people below. A graceful reminder of the norm, only a few decades ago. This clock, high above in the rafters, has calmly whispered the ticked seconds away as below millions have passed in various scurrying directions on the shiny pink and white tiled floor below.

This clock face has seen the frustrations of numerous people. Some are seen as being unambiguously exasperated with head in hands, mutters of annoyance. Some hopelessly watch the back end of the train that they hoped to catch slowly, but gaining impetus as it accelerates away from leaving the platform. Others have been seen to breathe an exhaled breath of triumph as they punch the air in exhilaration as they barely catch one at the last possible second.

From this established time-honoured architecture, the unmistakable signs. The growing virus of the modern age creeping in. Slowly penetrating its unfortunately unnecessary evil upon the scene. Before the metal fence that divides the paid train customers to the platforms is a shield of blue electronic vertical screens that flicker times, tables and platforms. To the left is the inner city departures. To the right is the rest of the country. A yellow digital clock sits in the middle. Loudly clicking above the blue screens.

A collection of colourful mass demographics stands transfixed at the blue monitors waiting for their orders. Some have carry-ons, satchels, briefcases, handbags and bizarrely enough, surfboards. While others have backpacks, wheeled cases and large duffle bags. Eddy is in the majority with his meagre possessions of clothes and toiletries in his small black sports bag. He joins the flock and immediately impersonates their craned neck tilting forward to the glowing blue.

He looks around at the craned necks. Then looks around his area for nothing in particular, with no particular place to go, he has a moment of uncertainty. A shiny black marble plinth catches his eye, that draws him in with curiosity. This is not his first rodeo. This is not the first time he has been here, near this very spot. He has been here more times that he cares to count. Yet, this is the first time he has seen this. He weaves through the eye of the needle hemmed in by the gathering crowds to the chubby, smartly dressed bust that is proudly mounted on the plinth.

A polished reflecting golden plaque states he is the 'Father of the NSW Railway. John Whitton'. In this quiet alcove he looks on, just like the clock above. A detailed description tells all that care to read his work. The engineers-in-chief did a vast thing during his tenure. A map of the state of New South Wales within the golden plaque shows the growth of track from a mere thirty-seven kilometres to an abundant three-thousand, five-hundred- and thirty-eight-kilometre web of rail spreading over the state. Connecting places easier, better and more efficiently.

He removes himself from looking for a destination. For the first time in a while that has been too long, he surveys his environment. he takes note of the ornate sandstone, the beauty within. The carvings, the crests, the decorative exquisite splendour of Central Station. It is as if he knows he will not see it again, or at least for a longer while.

He watches one of the squashed flat-nosed yellow and grey electric train depart one of the platforms. They are virtually soundless, but for a genteel hum. Some other trains pull into a soft thud as they gently impact the buffers at the end of the track. Electronic signs show where they have been or where they are set to go on the backs, front and sides of the train in yellow electronic lights illuminated like a Christmas Tree. Eddy is in no hurry. He has no need to place the presents under the tree before sunrise. He still needs a destination. He looks at the large list of departures, the map sprawling through towns he had never heard off. More's the pity with no breath-taking revelation.

He goes to a nearby bench to take a load off. He places his bag between his feet, to squeeze it in with his calves. He stretches his arms over the dark, green metal bench. Followed by his legs that are hovering above the floor for a few seconds before returning to grip his bag. Coincidentally he rests on the perfect vantage point. He can clearly see the blue timetable through his dark brown Oakley sunnies. He is waiting for that imaginary lightning to strike. A place name to resound within him. Either by the screen, or by the list of destinations of stops over the loud, static-less talon speakers that musically chime out at irregular intervals. He tearfully absorbs, without shedding a tear, the black capital sign of 'CENTRAL'. Its appearance is old, but newly painted to be looking prominent on the fresh, white background. Very retro. He watches people. Still though, no-one notices him.

He looks through the tiles below his feet to imagine the same atmosphere as he leans forward. Underneath him are a further ten platforms that form the subway portion of Central Station. The forever popular City Circle and Bondi Junction depart from the earth below.

Tiled stairwells. Tiled tunnels. Murals with paintings of the birth of New South Wales railways. The evolution with technology, people's needs. Some stations have closed. Others opened. Plans for the future. The re-immergence of the tramways. Buskers give different music to the echo of the footsteps. Most is pleasant and great to hear as a pleasurable collaboration with the rumbling hubbub. A very small portion of them should be refined a hell of a lot more in their noise-proof garages before unleashing their shrill on the public.

Where he sits, and where others tread, was a site of Devonshire Street Cemetery in 1901. When this site was finally chosen after numerous proposals, the bodies were exhumed and reburied around the other city cemeteries. Some believe that the ghosts remain, living in their original resting point, searching for their bodies. Two platforms are unused, not finished at all. The government at the time run out of money to continue the building of these lines. They abruptly stop as quickly as the dried-up empty coffers did. These would have connected Bondi Beach and the Eastern suburbs a lot better. Something that the city still is sincerely lacking. If only they found the money, they could be saving a lot more now. It would have been better for all, for sure.

Eddy looks up. Repositioning his back against the bench he shuns the modern electronic clock on glaring display in favour of the old-time clock face above him. The ornate pointed black hands tell travellers to relax, rush or swear in annoyance, twinged with disappointment in their inability to manage time, the fire in which we all burn.

After watching him, it is now me who silently, imperceptibly and undetectably takes my place next to him.

Eddy feels a change in the air. He sees nothing. He puts it down to a draught from outside. He then shivers. He reaches out to feel nothing beside him. His spine tingles like a thousand spiders have fleetfooted run down each bone. He feels the atmosphere change, lighten. The chill rising up through his body. Despite these chilly feelings he actually relaxes more. He would think he instinctively curls in himself to retain warmth. But he slumps slightly. The cold air lifts the weight off his shoulders. He feels at peace. Fully relaxed. The world tilted. Tilting.

I have watched him over many years. Although I had a moment of contemplation to whether the end will happen my decision has not been rethought. I do not wonder if I should change my mind. I am adamant that I have followed my instructions. I have learnt the deserved lesson. I will complete my mandate. Eddy is fully relaxed. I pat his right leg as I adopt my position to fully engage in the final undertaking. It is unmistakeable that this is the end of suffering life. Although at the same time, it is clearly identifiable to be no more the end than the beginning of Eddy's edification life.

Eddy softly closes his eyes.

The Rite Passage

Casting over him like a free-falling fisherman's net without escaping the invisible sense of moral blindness, the undetectable shawl cascades over Eddy. Not a deity, but the spirit. A spirit which is Atë. He sympathetically soothes any delusion that Eddy holds of his body living through this. That human instinct that he can fight this, with the foolish belief that he can in fact triumph. The aura of infatuation is causing a carefree mellow sensation vibrating through him. He is agreeable with the hushed mute that he cannot rebuild the ruin he is leaving behind.

The sense of natural values within Eddy are being painlessly erased as Atë draws in the net. Eddy is emotionally strong, but the tense hard pull of Atë is overpowering. As his own body willingly surrenders, his own soul is a consoling surprise to him. Antagonising is his mind. The reluctant want to let go of his memories are not as nearly upsetting as his final thoughts.

The pen drops in slower than slow motion. In the air it seems to hover gracefully down, in the vein of which a floating feather would. Zeus's daughter had quickly been summoned to execute her, his and my final act. Being as attune to her role, she naturally completed the deed before the black pen had come to hit the dirty, worn tiled floor.

Click.

The pen makes a hollow sound which no-one can hear over the ever-revolving world.

Astraea sooths the panic-stricken Eddy. He now knows what is coming. He knows, without knowing that this is the end. His thoughts disturb him. He has no idea how he could possibly know something that he has not been taught. He is filled with dread, the fear of unknowing. How he knows something that has not ever been explained or shown is perplexing to him. He cannot prepare himself for the end, yet, he instinctively knows it is here.

He feels a liberating sensation, akin to relief spread over him. Astraea was the last of the immortals to live with the humans. That gives her a certain kith and kin to them, henceforth to him. She feels his flustered frighten grow and sooths them as a mother would stroke the pain from a young child's hair. Eddy was not immune to the fearful emotional states that were within him. Yet outwardly showed none. Astraea's spiritualistic ethereal touch soothed him. He was open and supportive of the changes inside him. He was not as worried about this end as he ought to be. That thought feared him.

As quick as she had come, on its second bounce she had gone.

Click.

Eddy has not moved. He was still slumped on the bench. The only thing that happened was a sharp draw of breath that was unheard amongst the commotion around him. As the split second of the end was played in front of him, he was seeing a different sight.

In an over-slowed motion highlight reel, he was shown his life in a flash. The golden light zipped in front of his eyes as slow as a destructive cannonball. In his mind's eye he saw his life. He played and lived every moment for the second time, exactly the same as the first. Seeing mistakes, feeling the emotions from the conversations. Understanding the wishes, the unresolved dreams and the unexpressed fantasies. Some fulfilled, others left empty. He saw so many styles of haircuts, of clothes. He could not believe that, of all the thoughts that entered his mind first, it was his fashion choices that lingered. Why would he focus on this bizarre irrelevance, and not the glaringly importance of this reel.

If the doctors could retrieve the last dialogue from his mind it would be this. This afterthought, of the downright ridiculous thought. His inexplicable notion of him to think clear, with a certain clarity as he cursed himself with torment to what he decided to focus on, his haircut. For he was shouting loud enough, devoid of his lips moving, deprived of a sound coming from his body. A sound that no-one could hear, nor even he could feel.

Then…a curtain came down of stillness.

Then… the coherent harmony of reason.

'That relationship has ruined me.'

'I will be alone forever.'

'I won't ever love.'

'I won't ever be loved.'

'Cruel World.'

'Cruel Heart.'

'Cruel Love.'

Then a smile. He changed his thought. Eddy's final thought was of his unique unicorn. His vanished dodo bird representing his non-existent love. Beth-Annie. A love he felt that was not reciprocated. That moment is now gone. What is it?

Click.

The stolen NAB pen fell for the last time. Rested. This is it. Eddy at the end does not need to figure what, it, actually means for he knows, for him, well he thinks that this is it.

As Eddy breathed out his last short breath on Earth. He knew this was very much the end.

I felt him go. I caught him before the gates of the darkness to present him a different path. His path. His unique path built only for him to tread. Surrounded in me are his torments of a spirit that did not want to leave, but a body that had given up. Feeling the warmth of the spirit, I knew that I was justified in my taking. It was right. Eddy was at accordance to what was happening. He will be at acceptance door soon.

Eddy's heart not only broke, but it shattered into pieces. It stopped with a devastating, fragmenting of countless cracks that spread in an instant around in conjunction through his failing heart, to ultimately die. His small fist-shaped heart that held enough splintering implosions punched an everlasting last moment for Eddy. Each crack would heal but leave a scar. Never rebuilt though. Eddy was a fighter, but he was not a miracle worker.

The veracity was that the moment he met Beth-Annie his heart started beating for the very first time. He felt it as the sight of her made him literally skip a beat. He felt the regurgitations of the restart. He felt it then. He did not feel the last beat. From the moment that they stopped being a unity he felt his heart collapse, crumble in the love ashes of what was dying. He felt a pang of pain on the last beat. That first beat was an aching deep, inside his chest, behind his ribcage. A two tone thuddingly soft beat that spoke to her. He felt alive. Eddy felt the cuddle hormone known as oxytocin surge through his body as a relaxing and soothing drive of control washed over him. He did not, any longer feel. Anything. Anyone. Not anything.

Later, out of earshot for Eddy, the doctors would misdiagnose his death as a heart attack. The truth of the matter it was a lot more complex. He died of takotsubo cardiomyopathy. The surge of stress hormones were just too much for Eddy's heart. It was rare to die of this, but it does happen. It did happen. The results are similar, death, hence the misdiagnosing. Dramatic changes in rhythm and blood substances. But unlike a heart attack there is no evidence of blocked heart arteries. The doctor missed this, or, did not even look. For the doctor it was an open-shut case. He died of a broken heart.

Eddy is in nothingness. He feels nothing. He is floating in a clear white space that seems to be cylindrical. Large, looking directly at Eddy's form is this figure. He whispers into a form that appears to hover in the presence of him. The figure shouts over the wind, but the gushing wind drowns the sound.

'These are your thoughts?'

The figure was referring to the sound around the tubular space that was growing louder. He spoke in a question so Eddy's spirit would acknowledge.

'Cut off your thoughts.'

Tremendously forceful in his command.

'You must cut off your thoughts for the silence to even to begin to stop. To silence is to have no thoughts in this space.'

The figures legs are whispered tales that float in front of Eddy. Eddy feels scared. Eddy is terrified. He does as the unidentified figure asks, as he really has no other option. Eddy tries hard, as to disconnect his mind does not come naturally to him.

The large, approaching floating ghostly form that seems to have the answers, stealthily approaches closer. It is hard to cut off thoughts when he has so very many questions. Harder than he thinks, this is his first struggle. His first problem that needs to be solved. His mind is like a screeching alarm with questions that will not stop. Fear is breeding interrogating demands to get answers. He needs to concentrate. He must meditate to clear his mind. He concentrates on nothing but one thing.

For some reason he has chosen a red rubber ball. He thinks only of that ball. The shape, colour, feel. Eddy eventually clears his mind to solely see and focus on the imaginary ball. The noise reduces to a murmured rush of currents of inaudibly indistinctive voices. He recognises his own voice. This springs hope that he can do this first struggle. Then, with only the ball to contend with, he imagines the red ball growing smaller. To the size of a marble now. A grain of red sand from the heart of Australia. A single speck of dust that he barely even sees. At that point... Nothing. Then and there is only silence. Peace. Absolute nothingness. Oblivion.

'So.' The voice is soothing, comforting. 'Who am I?'

His face does not move, other than his power of speech telepathically speaks clear and precise to Eddy. The figure rhetorically asks as he comes closer to Eddy's form. Close enough to touch. Eddy listens intensively. Somewhat scared to speak, to move. Not even sure if he actually can make a sound, let alone move a fluid apparitional muscle.

'Who am I? Well, I am that spirit. The spirit that watches over you. I have so much power in one hand, but so little in the other. You are in, more to the element you are the other. I can guide you, tell you and sometimes give you the route I choose as your only option, but you have freewill. You have the ability to make, think and act in your own mind. You hold that power, I hold the strings. I will decide if you love to love again. I am your swan song ending.'

Eddy tries to speak. In doing so will unleash the thoughts once again. A raspy escape of breathless air comes out as he tries in vain to form the words of a coherent sentence. Yet, surprisingly for him his mouth does not move, his mind speaks. Or at least tries. It is as if he is compelled, suppressed to listen to the ghostlike spirit that explains where he is, what he is, and what he is to do.

'I am death. Your death.'

'MY...DEATH.'

Two words that ricochet painfully, at the same time painlessly to resonant long after the words have left the ghost, that calls himself Death. Death's voice rings. I cannot be dead. He fights the knowing fight of awareness. That single two-word sentence makes him take notice.

He looked shocked. Feels empty. He did not know until that moment that he was actually dead. He thought he was. He was still fighting the fantasy that this was a warped sci-fi dream. The form smiles a lip forming curve that he knows that he had hit the spot.

'I am the cruel twist of fate. I am the spirit, talking to your spirit. I have the power to unite. I had the power over your life. Of others. If I decided that you would live, I would have given you more options to meet a new partner. You would not have felt the same as you did for the one they named Beth-Annie, but you would have loved her, a different one, anew. Today is the first day that you do not feel love again, but only an unaccustomed loss.'

Eddy, confrontational with Death. He takes a moment to comprehend what he has just been told.

'I take a moment to reflect on this part. I let you do the same. This is where people beg, plead and bargain. They want to live again. This is why, I choose to mute them. For clarity. It is unassuming to think that this is negotiable. This is why you cannot answer. You cannot bargain with me, with death. I control your ability to even try.'

Eddy is not an exception to this new rule that started thousands of earth years ago. Remarkably, he shows acceptance. This is a rarity when a spirit does indeed not want to go on. It is here that Eddy realises that he had, in fact, given up on earth.

Journey's End

Eddy is directed through the building where no other buildings exist, more like a glowingly illuminated passageway. They glide pass a series of rooms without doors. Above him, without a roof are seen so many countless galaxies of stars. Most are pure vibrant white, in the company of ruby red, emerald green and sapphire blue orbs of different size, each one sparkling individualistically. This magnificence makes the surrounding passageway light now seem to be diminished weaker. To now appear to glow dusk-like when compared to this delicate glittering orchestra overhead.

An air tightly shields them which makes them float leisurelier, nevertheless comfortable. The smell of nothingness. As if this is what the ozone smells like. Eddy is pleasurably touched with the peaceable sensation of being alone, but reassuringly not feeling alone. The light sound of movement that resembles a soft, brushing touch of fabric stroking in a smooth breeze that gently plays with the hanging linen in a countryside-setting. They glide through. Eddy is not sure of where to, but unconcernedly detached. He is at peace.

Although in the service of King Hades, I have asked his permission to use Charon to aid me in escorting Eddy. Charon is a repulsive figure. He knows this. That is why he hides in the shadow of his deep, blood red cyclonical hat revealing nothing of his face. Walking always two steps behind. Eddy knows someone is close remaining distancing at the rear but is made unaware of who this presence is.

Charon's overgrown dishevelled and unkempt wiry beard is many hues of speckled grey and white. The whiskers make a gateway for his tusked sharp mouth which is barely visible. His hands are holding together in a prayer fashion in front of him, concealed by the sleeves of his red tunic showing only the slightest ribbon of his blue grey human-scaled skin.

As a rite of passage, Eddy got guided by Psykhopompos for his soul to travel to the place of dead. Eddy makes out his figure in the lead, but his view is distorted by a moving air, similar to looking through the thinnest curtain of a flowing waterfall. They all come to an opening. A barren riverbank to the dark-rivered shimmering star-studded flecks of fogginess blues that drift the length and breadth of the running water. Where the only light is from above, and behind.

Psykhopompos, the spiritual guide of the living person's soul, gathers together other spirits from the riverbank, like a shepherd his flock of souls, the shades of the dead are confused. Invisible bars keep them from moving too far as they linger around the shores of Acheron, the River of Pain, in a state of absolute bewilderment. Here is where Charon reveals himself to step towards the banks, to patiently take a fee from each spirit. His clothes are equally as filthy with dirt as it is unkempt with snagged holes. On his right hand is a worn, long pole slightly resembling an oar but not as flat at the end but pointed to a sharp needle like the arrow of a spear. With his left hand he guides people onto the boat.

Eddy cannot stare at him for long as when their eyes meet, his gaze is fierce with blue-red eyes that drills in a cold, empty sensation penetrating distressing fear. As Eddy averts his eyes, he sees around his waist a worn, dirty rope where hangs a smudged hourglass in an antique wooden case, steadily pouring grains of sand.

No sound is present. This foreign unsettling silence is nowhere near as soothing as the passageway for which Eddy has just left. Before him is a long, narrow boat that is neither wood nor metal. It seems to be crawling with black shining lice, reddish-purple earth worms and other bugs as if it is in fact alive. Intermingled together with soft clay of moist soil bound together by the embodiment of the branches of dead trees. In spite of the grotesque appearance it does seem sturdy with smooth outlines, although these do frequently move.

Inside are simple chairs of the same matter. More to the back than the centre of the boat is a leaning T-shaped black as night mast. Almost hidden from view in the bleak backdrop barrenness endures the fluttering squalid foul black sails that hang underneath. Exposed barely by the encrusted greasy film of reflective condensation which grips in extended strands over the torn perforations that mirror the murkiness surrounding them.

As they draw closer, Eddy notices the insects and bugs are considerably more present. A dominance of owning this boat by crawling in, out and around the bones of many different animals and humans that jut out of the side of the boat with the dying scrubland inorganic walls.

The most ornate article is the diamond-cut, egg-shaped lantern secured in position from the bow. The clenched dark ring on the top of the bow is positioned by the mouth of a mysterious Panthera skull. An abnormally large sabre-tooth rises from a stretched out bottom jaw over which the ring of the lantern rests. Tightly grasped by the shortened top jaw with a large parting forehead coupled with monocular eyes. The base of the lantern is held by a grotesque misshapen skeleton of what once was human hands. Broken knuckles, bent fingers and embedded sinews of the wrist cradle the oval lantern to present the displaying light to shine outward, ahead.

Eddy watched Psykhopompos carefully instruct each shade of the dead to enter a unique chair especially for them on the moored boat. Although the chair is in keeping with a rather basic design, each one holds great complex details specifically for the parting shade within its simple design. As for once the shade of the dead, one after the other, are rested on the chair, the design initiates. Magically secretes the mysteries on the brink of their own purpose, ready to be divulged.

A rainbow of colours flickers over them as if a curtain has suddenly soared from the chair legs, up through the mist into the starry night. Disappearing as quickly as hot steam. The shades of the dead look directly into their past, transfixed as if unable to move. They keep eyes on an image solely for them that starts immediately after the flickering rainbow vanishes. They stare with blank expressions mesmerised by the explanation. The unique design in the chair is transformed to a personal message for them. Galvanising to a climaxing portal, an ultimate explanation of why they find themselves here. On the way to arrive at that human unsolved mystery of the meaning of life. Charon seems to be guarding with his eyes one chair in particular. A chair near the bow of the boat.

At this Underworld river, the ferryman, Charon, waits to transport them over the River Styx to Hades. His fee is a single obolus coin that is placed in the mouth of the departing on burial. He stands at the short, seemingly organic gangplank that metamorphoses from the bank out of gnarly dark roots, dying leaves of red, oranges and browns and foliage from beneath the inhospitable riverbank.

Of course, Eddy did not receive such traditional treatment as to be buried. He was here before burial. So, for these souls that were gathered he waits his turn. Without a fee, these shades of the dead are given the torturous moment of uncertainty for all eternity. They are customarily left at the Earthly shores, as the boat leaves them behind. Subsequently for having no home to go and no unknown reason to what has happened, they haunt the world as ghosts. Evermore wondering if they are dreaming, alive or even really dead. Given no indication, without any answers in this mystifying no-man's zone of perpetual unrest between the worlds of the living and the dead, all they can do is drift. The worst gravest fate for all mortals. It is unsurprisingly that this adverse distressing fate leads sooner or later for all ghosts to go mad with troubled thoughts.

SLAM, BANG, SMASH.

A rolling crash of thunderous noise unexpectedly cracks the emptiness that hung in the air since arriving on the shores. Seemingly the noise happens overhead, but then again all around the darkness aids the seriousness of the striking tone. However, as soon as the profound crash explodes, silence immediately implodes to dissipate any change. As if the crash was sucked immediately into a vacuum. All around him in this barren place Eddy sees that no change has occurred. The only thing is the rigid form of Charon. He seems to be glowing.

Charon's shoulders slowly move up and down, as if concentrating on his breathing, keeping control of his simmering mood. The breathing gives way to a tremor that trembles over his figure. Gradually Charon's raises his head. His hood of his hat lifts up from being hung over his bowed head with this meticulous rising as his slow breathing remains strictly controlled. His eyes come into view. No sound, the look alone sends a stark warning forth. His eyes are all red now, flames etched with a wild ferocity that burns a warning for the shade of dead to retreat the gangplank. Peeking from under his hat perfectly cast to the shade of dead. No movement from the shade.

At this point, Charon's eyes are level with the accused, he uses his oar as a weapon. He lifts it, twirls the stick around in a self-assured spin so the sharp point is at the chest of the accused one shade of dead. His crimson eyes ignite even brighter, to emit a second warning. He pushes the shade of dead. It would appear that this shade has not got the money needed to take the trip. When feeling pain was seemingly impossible here, it would seem that the soul felt something, as the way he reacted proved. Jerking his phantasm spirit as if an electric shock had passed through him.

He recoiled in a wrenching motion that sent him flying backwards into the air to fall cripplingly to the ground. All the while sputtering within the being and not being, the seen to not be seen. This spluttering stops as his form becomes the cold shade of dead once again. In an upright position the shade looks back at Charon.

'What try you?' Charon's anger is shrill as he points a bony, elongated index finger covered in snake-like blue grey human-scales towards the accused. His face is still concealed under his hat, but his fire-spitting eyes and his gritted tusked teeth are shown through the wild forest of his beard. As he speaks in impatient hostility, he displays a frightening set of thin razor serrated teeth that line his mouth inside to clench perfectly together as a hunter would gaze upon its prey before the kill. 'I ought to teach your disdain with a glass from the fatal river.'

Sensibly, the shade of dead did not try to enter the gangplank again. It was at that moment that he was nothing more than a lost soul. Confused to where to go, what to do, he continued in his same state of aimless wandering along the shores that was proceeding before Charon arrived.

Eddy was not sure what would happen to him. If he could feel, he would undoubtably be feeling nervous, not so much on the border of fear but more entombed, leaping off into the concentrated chasm of panicking terror. He was one of the last. He had not the fee. Charon's gaze met his. He beckoned Eddy forward with a flicker of his three-pronged serpents' tongue around his lips as if challenging him. Eddy makes slow steps forward. Charon's repulsive threatening face is revealed more with each step.

'You hold us.' He spits out every word with identical venomous irritation. 'Come.'

Eddy has no coin, nothing. Charon's smile's a cold, merciless glower, with his eyes shining an unconcealed excitement show of pleasure. Eddy feels he is so close to having the treatment brought on some of the other shade of dead.

Then and now, he did not know just how close he was, numerous times, for me to start a new project, for him to come here earlier than planned. However, I stuck with my investment. After leaving him on the bench immediately after his mortal death in Central, I went to the riverbanks of the River Styx. He has to go through the passageway as a rite. I wait for him, at the shores. Charon knows that he is my soul. Nevertheless he enjoys this cruel game where he plays with Eddy as if a captured beleaguered victim of suffocating prey on the verge of extinction.

Here is where I finally intercept to make my presence known. This is where I let Eddy see me. From behind Eddy, I place the coin in Charon's left hand not allowing Eddy to see who his saviour is. Charon's eyes immediately simmer to resemble two pink moons, his smile remains as disturbingly evil as always. Once Charon has performed his duties, when everyone is in their unique chair, he escorts Eddy last to the waiting reserved chair near the bow.

I position myself at the immediate front standing ahead of Eddy, with Charon following slightly off centre, behind and to the left. The lantern turns on to a slight wave of his hand. A narrow beam pierces through the dense fog, reflecting the black as tar waters. The gangplank metamorphoses back into the undergrowth as if made of pliable material.

Without rope or reins, he pulls, pushes the now vertically floating spirits including Eddy's along the canal on the River Styx. The dark canopy of branches and leafless trees form a hallway to the Destination Chamber. Using his long, pointed oar he punts into the black tar river causing no ripples, no waves. As if on an invisible stationary bed, they all feel nothing of the sticky river crossing. The only one without an explanation is Eddy. His eyes twitch at the net of black shadowy branches above him.

Still standing, I summon Eddy to pivot up to a near sitting position, so he faces the back of me. As I begin to speak, he focuses straight on the back of my head. Unlike the others, his message will be given by me personally.

'I want to tell you a story, the story. Your story.' I keep looking forward. My voice resonates slightly through the fragile walls that surround us all as we float on, seemingly to an endlessly destination envisioned by the beam of the lantern over this sunless realm. I tell Eddy the complex story of what had happened in simple terms. I tell him who we are. Why the fall of our polytheism happened, but never left. The belief in us as more than one God.

Eddy catches the apparition of himself in the reflection of the waters. He is startled at how at ease he seems. Although consciously aware that he does not control his movements he does look extremely calm. The gushing void in his head has started again as thoughts keep entering his mind. He needs to get rid of the distortion to grasp what is profoundly taking place.

'Once upon a time, how all good fairy tales start but…this was no fairy tale, this was a great story…it is…Your Story.' I turn to look at Eddy as I sense his attention is wavering. He is trying to get rid of his thoughts. Giving my face something to focus on he succeeds in ceasing his distractions. He concentrates resolutely to pay attention once more to what I am teaching.

'In the beginning, there was Chaos. Chaos is the origin of everything. Everything you know, will ever know. Everything you have seen, felt, tasted. It is a direct influence of Chaos. The whole universe came from Chaos. Chaos was a sun with many arms that created around him everything.'

I was silent for a while. The walls lit up as if wanting to evolve and involve themselves into the story to give a visualisation of dreamlike proportions to my narrative. I allow them to show a visual in the confidence that Eddy would identify with my voice this knowledge better.

'Out of the gap came Erebus, darkness with Nyx, the night. Nyx gave birth to terrors, old age, famine, wars as well as killings, quarrels, falsehood, blames and infallible unerring nemesis. This is where death dwelled between Erebus and Nyx. All else was silent, deathly quiet, endlessly dark. Love was born for procreation which was born the bringing of order. From Eros, Love. Gaia, the Earth, Tartarus the Underworld followed. Using Eros's gift, Erebus slept with Nyx to give birth to Ether, heavenly light and Hemera Earthly light.

'They started to birth more reasons. Nyx along created Doom, Fate, Death, Sleep, Dreams, Nemesis and all that dwelled in the darkest of corners to haunt mankind. Gaia give birth to Uranus, the sky. Chaos give Uranus the birds with Hemera, the day. While Gaia gave the land animals while Thalassa of the Sea gave the animals in the sea. Chaos visited Gaia frequently as the visible mist, fog or gloom on the lower atmosphere. She would travel over the world she created.'

After the briefest of pauses, I take up again the wisdom. This pause was to let Eddy absorb all the information that I was bequeathing on him. This would not be the last. I wanted to be sure that he understood, to appreciate why I was narrating to him with such, great detail. It was a lot of new people to understand and with doing so had to relearn everything he thought was to be true.

'The children of the first Gods were called the Titans. These included Oceanus, Tethys, Hyperion, Theia, Coeus, Phoebe, Cronus, Rhea, Mnemosyne, Themis, Crius and Lapetus that brought different reasons for their own existence. Their leader, Cronus. He overthrew his father Uranus to take the throne. He feared that one of his children would do the same so ate them at birth. One child escaped, Zeus had managed to grow up covertly. When Zeus was matured, he came to defeat Cronus. Cronus had prophesied correctly, although the two reasons did differ to why they wanted to be the ruler. Cronus and the Titans fought to retain power against Zeus.

'He led his group called the Olympians. With Zeus leading the Olympians, Atlas leading the Titans, they battled into war. This grew into the war that is known as the Titanomachy. Zeus was eventually victorious. He exiled the Titans to Tartarus. All except one, Atlas, for whom he punished with holding the universe up on his shoulders. Zeus punished Arke, the fraternal twin sister of Iris who betrayed the Olympians by being a spy for the Titans as a messenger.

'Her colourful iridescent wings were taken as she was cast into Tartarus. Zeus gave them to Peleus and Thets as a wedding gift that later gave them to their son Achilles. Arke's twin sister, Iris is the rainbow messenger. In the sky she would have been the first rainbow. If a second rainbow is seen, that is Arke, not to be trusted. Iris is our messenger. She is the pathway to the mortals and the divines.'

Eddy is keeping his eyes on me, but also behind me as the hallucinations explain my words like a movie. I was explaining the beginning and the start of the world in which he walked but not with the understanding he was taught. I knew he would take some time to grasp. I asked others for the best way for me to teach this knowledge and wisdom. No-one knew. All said to overstate the facts, to act like a drill. When all is said and done to give it to him straight. Then to lean back, observe and recognise. If he accepts this reality, then the choice I made was approved, more importantly accepted. I can go forth with further expansions of wisdom. If he rejects, I will be told to dispose of him, and that I need to keep on searching.

'Zeus had with him Horae, the hours of the day. This was the first time that the embodiments of the right moments happened. The rightness of order. Stability with the first generation. Auxo as the grower, Carpo as the fruit-bringer and Thallo as the plant-raiser.'

I need to go on, time is of the essence. I essentially have the time until we reach the other side.

'Zeus is ruler of the Olympians and God of the Sky with the help of major Gods under his rule. Twelve in all. There is Hera, Zeus' wife and Supreme Goddess. She is the protector of married women, marriage and childbirth. Poseidon, God of the Sea. Demeter, Goddess of corn, grain and the harvest. Athena, born fully clad ready for war from Zeus's forehead, she is the Goddess of reason.

'Apollo, God of music and healing. He gave science to humankind to create medicine. Artemis is the Goddess of Chasity, virginity and the natural environment. Ares is the God of War. Aphrodite, Goddess of love, desire and beauty. Hephaestus is the craftsman. He is the God of blacksmiths, he sculptors fire and volcanos. Hermes the God of Commence. He was swift in being a messenger between the Gods and the mortals to the Olympians. Finally, Dionysus the God of Fertility and Wine. They reside on Mount Olympus, the highest point on Gaia, hence their collective name.

'The immortals gave birth to humankind, a race that was similar to them without their gifts that could inhabit the Gaia. Zeus ordered the two sons of Lapetus, Prometheus and Epimetheus to give these mortals, you, various gifts in that hope that you would give us amusement. Epimetheus gave various gist to the animals such as agility, strength, speed. This selfishness left the mortals with nothing, so Prometheus stole off the gods. He took reason from Athena. He took fire from the gates of Hephaestus. All the while sharing his knowledge with them all.

'Off all this treachery, Zeus was angered by fire. This was solely preserved for the Gods. He did not want the mortals to resemble the Gods this much. Zeus punished Prometheus with an eagle that would eat his liver, every day at the edge of the world, Caucasus. At the end of each day Prometheus's liver would grow back so he would have to endure the suffering all over again.

'Then came the second generation. This brought more structure. Dike as justice, with Eirene peace and Eunomia the order of law. Then came the Morias who rose from the strings of Okeanos, the encircling world ocean.

'Gods then started having children with you mortals to produce a breed of demi-gods. From Chaos, everything happened for the right reasons. I am talking to you in the names that you on the mortal coil give us. Our names are the gifts we bear, or the regions we rule. Zeus is still our ruler. Under him is his brother Hades who rules the Underworld. Running wild is Dionysus who had an affectious drunken zest for life for which festivals derived from. He encouraged the arts in plays, in acting. He was a reckless God, without being evil. He is a loveable rogue who did nothing but by being, quite literally the soul of the party, any party. We have been around for over eighteen-thousand years on your mortal coil since you discovered us.'

I cannot help but snigger at that word discovered. As quickly as they discovered us, they dropped us. That is still a debate here, many think fear, others think opportunity. Fully composed again, I continue.

'I do find it strange that for a short time, Poseidon was considered the ruler of us by you at the start. We were worshipped everywhere that the Greeks touched. After many years playing in the rich fabric of the people's lives to be recognised for our efforts was splendid. The Romans adopted some of us after the Greeks but changed our names. We concur that the Christianity religion that you have come about as some of the world wanted to not be part of the Greek or Roman trend.

'After all, they were building roads, houses and applying security, jobs and medical care. For a reason that we did not design you for, you have a tendency to be destructive. The mortals see the bad in the good. They make their own religion. You fight using religion as the accused. It is a virus that spreads in each of you.

'It was at the Battle of Milvian Bridge on 28 October 312 that Constantine claimed to see a sign. He claimed that he saw a cross in the sky. At this battle Constantine, the co-emperor of Rome fought against the rival ruler Maxentius. After seeing the cross, he saw it as a symbol. He encouraged all the Roman soldiers to draw the cross on their shield. He was a victor. He became the sole ruler of Rome. Again, people in power have a thirst to make a change to hallmark their own brand. It is this reason that he grasped Christianity.'

Eddy listened. He watched the flickering images on the walls as he floated passed. He could not explain the feeling of nothingness. It was as if Charon was controlling him like a child does playing his first game. Accept the chair was his shackled instrument where he could not move from. Keeping him steady and focussed nevertheless, it was required. He understood what was being shared. As yet it was not making sense, but he was open-minded to a change. The change.

'So, we were being forgotten in the east,' I go on. 'Not overnight but slowly, the fabric of who we represent was returned to the place we were for the years before the Greeks recognised us. The similarities between the Christianity and the Greek Philosophy aided in their being no bloodshed. For another thing, religion is blamed for everything a lot of the time on Gaia. But, I will leave that for another epoch. The unsung hero is Plato. Plato's revival of his view. For it was of his philosophy with Neoplatonism that helped build the bridge rather than burn it completely.

'The eastern side of the Greek Empire was where we were still fundamentally the main religion. The academy that Plato opened nearly eight-hundred years prior was opened back

549

up in 410AD. The academy was the centre for Neoplatonism. A boiling pot for Greek Philosophical thought. We survived in your minds for another one-hundred and nineteen years. Then Justinian closed it, for good, in favour of Christianity. The area that survived was quickly shrinking. Being split into pockets. Then we vanished. Our statues destroyed. In your minds. To be seen. We were gone. We remained here. We always remained. It is a lot to absorb…'

I am interrupted by Charon. We are outside the open threshold which enters a rocky cave. Charon passes over with a gesture of his hand to me. I receive it and bow in a nod of thanks as he turns and leaves Eddy and I. The place that we are left disconnects from the main boat with a slight lapping noise. The front of the boat immediately rebuilds in exactly the same image. We are in a smaller, but exact replica of Charon's boat.

Everything that Eddy thought was true, right with no reason to question was now illogical, false, wrong. Eddy looks confused as if he is processing all the information.

In a single moment we are through the cave and at a water's edge. A dim casting light glows a walkway as if the non-existent moonlight shines where to go in the darkness. As I motion with a hand to Eddy, he positions himself horizontally. He is standing. He has his own freewill. He cannot run, but that rising was done on his own thoughts. Since coming here, this was the first motion unassisted.

His mind was like a washing machine churning with memories, of ideas, logical understandings being turned upside down, over, over, over again.

They turn through an open, doorless arch from the water's edge into the large circular room following the moonlit oval stones. He turns behind him to see Charon and his shades of dead are nowhere to be seen. Why was he going this way when they were going another? How was it he still did not have his explanation of him? Why the explanation of the realism, the truth was being given to him? Did the other shade of dead get this intended arduous moulded knowledge?

Together, I aid him to glide effortlessly to the centre of the Destination Chamber, leaving the boat behind. As soon as they leave the boat, a similar metamorphosis happens, which was seen to the gangplank. The boat became one to the rock-strewn embankment. Eddy is being gently escorted by me but has no reason to feel fear. It has taken a narrative of thousands of years to get to this time in the present.

The Destination. The Chamber

If steps were trod, the echoes would be forceful. They would resonate with importance to everyone that steps in the Destination Chamber. Above him, through the large domed glass cupola is only sky. Eddy looks up at Uranus, the star-speckled sky. She swirls a twinkling lit masterpiece, in her starry dark crushed concerto with the velvet blue curtain backdrop of night. Her rains impregnated Gaia to give birth to the Titans. This is not merely only sky. Through the glass, pearls glitter.

Each sparkling star is of a different life that lives. A different person. The emotions heighten or dim the light depending on the mood of that person. A bright, fleetingly quick comet blitzes through, on course touching many different stars which show an impact of connection. The comets are a spirit aiding a life decision. When a star light fails, that person has fallen, departed, died. Swirling clusters of stars group resemble the rushing of lives lifetime passages.

He is watching the lives of others without understanding the meaning of the lights, colours, sparkling, growing, thriving, living and dying of the stars. The comets that quickly enter, touching a life to give a slight alteration. The colours that shine different hues fading in and out of some, sometimes changing colour completely in others. It is a hypnotic viewing pleasure.

Eddy listened and is here, not of his own accord. Yet he may have just fought it to not be alone, but on the same path as the other shade of dead heading further down the river. In spite of that, now being here he is glad that the choice, the freewill was taken away from him. Being here, knowing where he would be, he would not have fought it. He does not feel fear anymore. He was not even aware that the sensation was refocussed to the requisite peace of mind, the good sense of being open to the new understands with an absence of any confusion. He has no reason to feel fear as he is subconsciously growing wiser.

From the other side to which he stands, high in the crystal cupola is a large clean-shaven face looking down. Still Eddy glides nearer the centre of the chamber. The matured wrinkled face peers down, watching. He is not saying anything but looking with an expression of interest at what could be happening soon. Learning from this impromptu, unrehearsed turn of events that is going to quickly unfold before his eyes.

'Behold the respectful King of us,' I introduce the clean-shaven face, the all-seeing eye. Eddy looks intently at the wide-open eyes. There is a distorted face, but it is not seen, the focus is on the eyes that seemingly merge into one. A watchful single eye looks down from the centre of the cupola. 'King of Gods. God of the sky. The weather, lightning, law, order and justice. He is the all-powerful without a name, but a title for which you have given him. the title, the name of Zeus. As if naming something makes it easier to understand. The truth is it gives you the illusion. He is the all-powerful. Hard but fair, ruler for all of us.'

Eddy hovers now in the centre. He pivots to be upright, as if on trial in the centre of the chamber as his peers look down. He is perfectly still, standing trial waiting to be judged. With an assuming jury of no-advice but with full confidence around him that the judgement will be sentenced. Above him Zeus looks from the dome as if looking down the lens of a microscope carefully examining him for which Eddy is a speck on a pewter dish.

The crystal palace is supported by clean white marble pillars with indications that meander up in soothing waves to the cupola. In the marble eaves of the reflecting clear, natural lighted dome are many people that are filling the space between the pillars of the glass cupola.

Each place is a ledge, where stands a different person. Around the domes base is a face of a familiar person. Eddy has encountered before each of these nest of faces swarming around the inner ring. If it was a short conversation. A work meeting. A hello. A goodbye. If it was something, someone for whom he connected with on earth that persons face was on that single one level, he saw all the faces supporting the roof.

Once he had felt this experience, but cannot remember when. A dream maybe? He looks past the level of faces and back to the space between the pillar and the glass. In between each pillar is a person on the ledge. Each one is adorned in a burgundy light red silk cloak that glitters and sheens as if a rainbow in all the hues of red are captured inside the material. He has felt the presence but now has a face to the strange sensations that he had experienced.

During his stay on earth, the mortal coil, he had no explanations for what he is seeing but in his mind a bridge has been linked to connect the question to the answer. Each person is linked to his former living. The black silk undergarments under the red cloak hold up different faces that lean down to look at Eddy. Not one of the people have visible legs. Their bodies fade to nothing, but they are all the same height. Each is an imposing moving statue with a different emblem, held together by thick golden string in the centre of their chest clipped by a bold golden copper-esque ring. Eddy slowly spins around to rotate to see each character in his life. In a clear blur he looks around at the many different faces. Each image tells a story of him.

I am standing next to Eddy. I laugh to myself at the way people try to get back to the world of the living, however Eddy is not bargaining. He is accepting his fate with little to no retaliation. I scoff at those fools. The human fools. The fools who think that they can negotiate with me. If I have decided that the end is coming. If the fate is written. If that date, time has come, came, I will not be waivered. The position of their existence will be called loudly into question. I will be asking them a unique question. This could be the last room before the journey over the Styx. I am the quintessential final curtain.

No-one sees me until their curtain comes down. Even then, if then, it is only if I have invested my time in learning their life. If I have learnt through them. Otherwise, it is only a glimpse of me as their soul's and shades of dead travel through. Through this chamber and on like the other shade of dead before Eddy. I am like the wind through their lives. I place fear in the trembling leaves of time. As they hang on to their family connections I see where they are, always. Even, for some, at the end people will not meet me, for I am not their maker. I am the hand that guides them through life. I am the hand that stops them in life.

Within the rich stitch of a colourful tapestry that designs a person's life are so many ghosts, spirits, unseen, unknown parts that join that life together. On the immortal coil of the place that they call Earth, the scientists try to figure out our rich design of the human body. Via deoxyribonucleic acid, DNA, they try to unravel the mystery. To then piece the enigma that lies within. It is a pursuit for which they will never grasp. Never fully appreciate. Will very remotely understand.

It is simple. A person's life is designed, written. It is not encoded in the deoxyribonucleic acid. The scientist that think that life can be disentangled to be solved to find the answer to life are naïve in their approach. Even more naïve is the notion that they can replicate life. For a sophisticated set of minds I, and my companions laugh at the simpleminded nature of the mortal mind to be able to remotely understand the complexity of the immortal soul. A body can be built, fixed, made, but a soul. A soul is unmakeable.

In the soul, the spirit is the feelings of a person. Off course I may change it with the help of my supporting cast, but the essence will always remain the same. Unchangeable. Fixed. Unalterable.

During my walking ever-present shadow through Eddy's life, he has charmed me like a snake coming out of the Indian charmer's basket. Going through his first relationship, I have allowed the delivery of other spirits. They have enabled me to learn further the impulses of a mortal. The ripple of an unassuming variation to shift the slightest tilt of a person to effectively affect another person is, actually true. These are the comets for which any life can send. It is not an enigma. The cliché that the mortals use that everything happens for a reason, or every action has a consequence. Yes, they have freewill, but they are never free to choose their consequences. Which enables me to see other lives and to see what, how it can affect them to affect a difference in the long-term ending.

Has Eddy ever wondered if his dreams were just dreams? Dreaming fantasies or, if there were actually realities. I would talk into his mind through his relaxed night-time ritual. The life passage is full of failures, but it is the learning that stems from the happiness, growth, heartbreak, failure, courage and adventures of the highway of bumps, troughs and breakdowns that a person's soul acquires learnings.

I have been Eddy's walking shadow, always there, never far away. Although I really came into providence at the start of his first relationship. Mainly because this is an area for my personal improvement. During his mortal life I allowed the liberation of other, spirits, to enable me to see other consequences of, what some might construe as ruthless, to see the mortal's reactions. Always under my administration, but to see how he reacts with the effects of them to affect the difference to the path in which he had been travelling. Or to take a person out of the same path he was travelling on. For me, this was fascinating to observe the significance of one, sometimes two moments. Instants to affect the outcome was a startling discovery for me. An educated journey.

I used the term spirit, but really refer to them as Daemons. Each one has been given a trait. These abstract personifications start with emotions in Eddy's state of mind but then come out in voice, the loudest silence, the power of his body. Words just get unleashed with a poisoned smothered tongue, after that an action. Then the aftermath. The product of the Daemons. The love hate, harmony discord, joy and grief patterns do seem to be the basic urges that expressively come out of the psychologically internal battle that is raging in his classified fragile egg shelled confides of his most intimate thoughts.

The simple human conditions of birth death, pleasure pain and fate to opportunity. The qualities that define a Daemon whether in their strength or beauty is what gives Eddy the expressive sentiment to feel their trait through Eddy. It is art, a living masterpiece. Morality is laid for all to see. It is in the reaction that I see the decency of Eddy. The standards that he has. He surprises me on a constant pleasing level that makes me, surprisingly question my own ethics. However, I believe that I have the simple mercy to respect him enough to be allowed to see his integrity. His open honest virtue.

The nature of the hidden voice in his head, his dreams, were so important. This is the very important vehicle that we constantly use for our message to be delivered. We send hints. We persuaded and enticed his mind. We pried open Eddy's mind as easy as novelty plastic handcuffs to unleash these baits of temptations to draw and lure out the corollary. We tried not to use force, but sometimes we had to labour a more assertive incentive.

Finally, in the state of their society, through justice to injustice, peace to war. Not many Daemons have the gift of all seven like I have, so I do assist them in their gifts. I am a full divinity. The others are minors. I, but I have a cult status, still after all this time.

The soft ripples of life is the colourful rolling tapestry. So many weaves. So many threads. Essentialities of each loop, pull and push to tie a life together. For the journey of Eddy's life. Forever expanding and continuous with no end in clear sight. Eddy does not know it. But his tapestry links with others. People bring him up in conversation with him not around, not in the space, the country. These get looped onto his as they tell a story of a warm affection, a glowing hellish anger, a raw bleeding pain or a roaring, belly-rolling laugh.

His remarks, thought of other people, also join in, overlapping. It is a sight to behold. This is the deoxyribonucleic acid that the mortals could never conceivably understand. This complex multifaceted layer of a developing human spirit and soul is unattainable to be able to imagine. Each colour, dropped stitch, peak, trough tells a story of that intricate person. But not only in body, but thoughts from others, memories and wishes. Unconceivable, astonishing beauty that will be nothing short of an extraordinary mind-blowing finishing article. A…beauty.

For Eddy, I was given my next stage of education. I have been around for, oh-so-many years, I knew my culture, yet, I was absorbing the knowledge of the mortals for which I would never be. Of course, I had encountered the reason and the logic through the human's illogical relationships with each other. The impulsive reactions continued to fascinate me. Whether they are, or were lovers, friends or enemies, the interactions seen astounded me.

There is no logical explanations for their actions, subsequent reactions that there consequences presented. I had never witnessed it first-hand, only from afar. It was in Eddy that I saw my chance. I expressed an interest in this powerful life connection to Moigagettes, the God of Fate. I devised a plan, an order of merit.

Moigagettes rules over the three Goddesses of Fate which, collectively are called the Moirai. Each has a purpose. They give the mortals personification and inescapable destiny of life. Thus, the Moirai independently direct their fate. Each person born onto Earth passes through the Moirai. Klotho, with her spindle, The Book of Ate, spins the thread of every persons' lifeline. Lakhesis measures, portions a person's life. Atropos, the last of the Goddesses' cuts the line. She cuts life, short. When Moigagettes is happy. With a mere nod of the head, he allows a mortal to enter the world with a loud deafening scream to announce his or her arrival.

'I saw your thread, Eddy,' I was now addressing Eddy who immediately snapped his head towards me. He had seen me, but I had yet to properly address him. I took him away from the hypnotic crushed jewels above to speak to him exclusively.

'Who—' Eddy was going to ask first, listen later. But I disrupted his questioning. The time was not now.

'Due time that will be answered. The time is not here. I saw your lifeline, your thread as we call it.' I went on explaining, seeing that Eddy was listening. 'As you lived. You lived without interference while you learned to walk, talk, understand and go through the baby, toddler phases. This is when your brain forms the mortal connection. Before your brain wanted you to find a mate, a love. I saw your thread form, change, evolve into this magnum opus. This great work of a life force that you made captivated me. At first, well, I was confused to why you? Your thread showed so much promise, but we were to cut it short before that potential would be reached.'

'I did not fully understand then, honestly ever. But then I asked, "Why him, Moigagettes?" The God of Fate responded with words surrounded by an evident smile, "All relationships end in heartache." This confused me further. To be truthful, I had no idea what he meant then. Now I do. He saw my bewilderment with uncertainty brewing raising clouds that quickly tainted my understandings. I naïvely thought I knew the answer to relationships.

'Moigagettes was quick to flatten my perceptive misguided insight. Moigagettes continued, "Relationships do not have to be love. They could be a collapse of a friendship, family member or of course love but it will result in the mortal's heart aching. The person left behind that did not see it happen will grieve. Eddy will grieve in different ways to what you think you have learnt. It is in the growing with Eddy that you will grow."

'He convinced me that you had the answers I sought. I concede now that that was true. With watching you, I saw the colourful explosions of bursts, eruptions and floods of outbreaking reactions to your sensational inner cries of passion. The peaks, the down dull pale depressions of earthshattering despair that it seems were unrepairable. It was in the first relationship that this abrupt show happened, your show. Your show. Your thread, Eddy. Bravo.'

Eddy soaks up the pails of vast information that he is given. His mind was open to the possibility of everything he was being told before being a lie. He could see the reasons that were spread before him in open transparency. It was subsequently real in the surreal. Worlds colliding except not ending, but in its place joining together.

He looks around with his eye fleetingly, rapidly taking everything in around his new environment. In front of him, to his right side, his left, behind him were these figures. He knew that these were his life puppeteers, formerly. Important figures in his past life as in his understanding of his life now. Essentially these figures pulled the strings that played every scene of his early life, for which that stage is accomplished, gone, not forgotten.

He was a puppet, a pawn in the mortal chessboard for which he would stumble over without a fight when he got told that it was the end, after the ending. Each one of the figures was a stranger in his eyes, but, in his mind-eye he knew each one by name. Startling enough while he examined in a speeding flicker of his dancing glancing eyes each face, he only saw an unrecognisable stranger, yet knew the unseen purpose of who they were. What their role in his lifework achievements, or lack of them, was played by each of the figures, strangers.

His eyes seemed to be an instant facial recognition laser that scanned the contours of the face for his mind, which, immediately flashed the information of who they are, for the role they played in his previous life. No name, no voice, no mannerisms were needed. No introduction was needed but bizarrely, within the enigmatic mysteriously unexplainable extraordinary scene that he was peculiarity part off, he knew them all. A form of déjà vu for which he knew he had contact with them before, not sure when or how though. This was a moment where he did not know how it was possible to possibly know.

Yet, not for the first time in the last few swiftly moments of his duration of time, his mind had patched a jigsaw piece in the understanding puzzle, of what he never thought of before. The impending unrolling of the realistic accurate carpet of an impossible paradox been a uniquely plausible existence of the continuation. The way of life.

The unexplainable was unfurled, expanded, explained. Laid, openly and honestly in front of his very eyes. Everything he had been taught from a baby mewling and puking in his mother's arms had been torpedoed out of the water, through the window. He was covered in the ice-cold water of shocking refreshing realisation. He stared in front of him. Fixed. Open-eyed with the cusp of overflowing knowledge in front of him. He was appreciating, thus craving the reason. An enlightenment.

I could feel the sensation of understanding acceptance running through Eddy. For that I started to give him more details. I gesture for a figure to come down from one of the ledges that surrounds us. From Eddy's left, a figure sprouts large glistening fragile cobweb wings that are as strong as lace that glisten with a touch of morning dew. Gracefully and smoothly down the figure floats and descends to be perfectly positioned in front of Eddy. Eddy takes stock of what he sees. A face. The flickering portrait that metamorphosizes between two faces.

Now, face-to-face, Eddy can see three faces. The lips change as the figures speaks a male's voice. The timber voice remains the same. Eddy attempts to speak. More to show that he knows who he is. To reassure himself, to demonstrate that he does have the power, the will, the strength to firmly place a reassurance of himself to confidently announce who he is by telling him who he is. This is thwarted. Before he can muster a sound. Before he even opens his mouth, the flickering trio portrait speaks.

'I…' The figure tenderly speaks with a slight awkward, half smile. As a youthful secure voice comes from a muddled distorted face the balance is obtained on the ground and he continues, 'As you know…I-I am Erotes. You are man. On Earth, as you call it. The men, women are chess pieces. We are the players. You have your exit. You had your entrance. This is your new entrance.'

The youthfulness of the voice surprises Eddy as his eyes react. The aura of innocence that surrounds his affirmative reassurances with the softness puts Eddy's edgy weariness to rest in a soothing stroke of his musical voice. There is a reason he is the first to address him. In that smooth, hushed melodic tone, he continues with a slight grittiness, 'I appear to you as three. Where you have walked. Where I used to be no stranger. Where people speak to me as a solitary figure. Others, a twin. I have three faces that show different personas. I, have a specific aim. I am love. I am love reciprocated for which you see in the face of Anteros. I am the love wanted in desire hence Himeros. Combined I gave the final face of love. A combination of the two will make it easier for you to accept. I will stick with the face of both, the name of the combined. For I am Erotes.'

With the end of the sentence, the flickering stopped on one face. A sun-stroked soft face of a forty-year look of life that had been seen, been lived. Prominent cheek bones with a strong, hard angular jaw line. His figure became a body. The appearance of a torso that was strong, toned, statuesque. Erotes smiled. He then winked. 'I am profound. I am the intense attraction between two people. I am feared, I should be. For love can break, build and destroy everything you feel that was right. I have been with you for a long, long time.'

'Yes, you shot me.' Eddy does not recognise his own voice. It sounded fragile. It was brittle with a gasping for breath. A frailness that exhales out of his body, rather than resonates. Regardless he persists with his voice becoming his own, his new, his defining identity. 'You kept shooting my heart. Each time I felt love to be floating above it all, you shot my bubble, so I came crashing down. So many times.

'The last time I shattered like a mirror. The mirror of me was unfixable. The last time I could not recognise the shards of jagged remains to the person I once was. You. You were focused on fulfilling someone else's dream. Not mine. I should have anger for you. I don't. You knew my destination. You saw me floating in the wrong direction. You shot me down to put me back on track. It seems I have found my station. I am back. Love is still in me, but I know that I have no need to give it out rather than keep it.'

Erotes shuts his eyes as he slowly bows his head. Eddy has understood his lovingly cruel ways of showing him that he has got so much more to give. Furthermore, Eddy has paused. It was apparent that Eddy did not know. The writing was on the wall. It could not have been larger. Could not have been more in his face if it was written in one-hundred-foot flashing neon lights in a one-hundred-foot room. Eddy could not see that this was it. Eddy was definitely too blind to see. Though, in spite of this, with that silent bow of the head. The slow close of the eyes. That lid shutting, slamming shut was the curtain coming down. It hit Eddy. Around him, the one-hundred-foot lights have collapsed on him.

Eddy, for the first time, realises.

Realises that he is dead.

Dead!

A term that for him meant the end.

He is in the gushing time warp of air escaping him. Love was not in him. He had no love to give. No love to keep. In the midst of his awareness, he nearly misses Erotes speaking. '…too many of the Earth Spirits. You are lucky. In that you are privileged enough to have some explanation for their demise. And you will live, just not as you know it.' Eddy's mind continues to resonate the echo that he is dead. He has died. His ears chime in as he finishes his passage, his last final phrase.

'…you should be so fortunate. I was there at your birth. Surrounded with your family's love. I was present at the birth of Aphrodite's as well. With the same as many others your story is love. That is one, one of the many meanings of life. Everyone's. It is to find that person that you can mutually be with. Be with, without harbouring a fear. A fear that the love will not be given back, just taken.'

Eddy had died with his greatest fear. No one was with him. No one in his life was left to mourn his passing. Celebrate his life. No one to call his love. He had died alone.

Truthfully. It was not as bad as he thought. This shocked him.

That the fear that he feared, was not as fearful as he actually feared.

After Everything Else
Now

The large antique clock above the stone-cold shell of Eddy clicks on as it has done for years. The motion and commotion below of people on their own separate missions make the tick-tocking unheard. The black elongated hands were positioned at precisely eighteen minutes past ten. Eddy's shade of dead had departed from Central a few minutes ago. Eddy had just realised this. No-one else had. For Eddy's body was still here.

Copious amounts of people have passed him in the minutes that have passed away. Some, unbelievably, have even sat next to him for the briefest moment, unaware of his condition as they thoughtlessly waited for a train, a friend, a mate, a lover or the commencement of their own journey. Remarkably enough, some have even made small talk with him. Obviously uncaring in any response, as he was deceased, unable to hear, let alone speak.

Seemingly out of the vast brick pillars that form one of the entrance archways of Central Station, a highly visible security guard comes over. After watching his nonmovement on one of the all-seeing fisheye cameras, he decided it was time to act. In his smart clean shiny, orange fluorescent vest, for which he was still dragging over his shoulders that forms part of his mandatory uniform he sighs at this part of the job. To him, the fluorescent vest was not needed. He was almost out of the door of the cramped security room, which they called the bunker, when his superior chucked it at him. Really? It was not as if he was going to get hit by a moving truck or train at any moment soon. A routine 'move on' procedure did not really necessitate such an eye-catching attire. Reluctantly, the vest finds its resting place covering his entire front and back of his body.

Exhaling an exasperated deep breath, he pauses at the bench where Eddy rests. Apprehensively he slides over to him to nonsensically blend in to not cause any undesirable attention to himself. The security guards took this bothersome part in turns. This happened many more times in the day than they cared to count anymore. However, now in the vicinity, he approached with caution, he had been in these similar routine situations before.

Learning from his, and also hearing from other staff members mistakes, he is fearful of this stranger's response. So many homeless people come in when the station has opened for shelter and warmth, that his duties appeared to mainly involve moving people on. He was used to being ignored. Sometimes, even sworn at, verbally demonstrated as being uncaring or being racist. Remarks that were spiked heavily with venom, sometimes spit and gurgled phlegm. And, although it was rare, on the odd occasion physically assaulted, in general just harmless threatening obscenities.

Therefore, as he is taking all these points into consideration, it is with an air of hesitancy that he nudges the stranger in the arm to wake him up. He is not sure if he was drunk, or just asleep, but he was as sure as hell that he was not welcome to stay there. It was not the first time that he had to wake someone, but each case was treated as the first so not to breed complacency. He jumped to the assumption that he had had too much of a liquid breakfast, as that was generally the norm at this time of the early sun kissed spreading day.

In a way that was brief, but assertive, he prodded him once again, to immediately recoil in expectation of a flailing weak fist-steered arm.

The security guard was a slight man, but the padding of the dark blue puffer jacket beneath the reflective vest gave him an appearance of being a lot bulkier, more muscled than he really was beneath the padded clothes. Maybe it was the designed requirement? Maybe it was the personal aim to appear bigger than one actually was? Whatever the reason, the way he looked was intimidating. The overall effect worked well with his perfectly squared head placed on a man-mountain. He looked in proportion that not only made him look powerful, but also satisfactorily threatening; people would think twice before attacking him. With the most recent prod, Eddy did not respond. Of course, he could not for he had crossed over.

Losing his patience, the security guard assumed he was being blatantly ignored, so he at once made his mind up to speak, to get this over and done with and back to his freshly brewed still piping hot coffee back in the bunker. He bent down as much as his clothes would allow, positioned his mouth close to Eddy's ear. On his haunches ready to spring from his black polished shiny leather-covering heels he leaned in. Startlingly from his stature, he conveyed an unexpectedly high-pitched tone, all the same he used his chimes to order an emphatic command for him to move on. With his words he accompanied another poke with a strong rigid finger, this one was firmer, edging boldly towards an insistent shove.

Eddy moved. More his body lost balance. He slumped over, forward. He nearly fell completely over to the floor. The security guard had to react quickly for Eddy not to fall off his last seat. It was then, with the feel of his ice-cold skin of Eddy's left cheek on his warm living cheek, that the penny dropped for the African-born security guard. The unpleasantly cold flashing feeling detection that this stranger, this guy was not moving on his own freewill. For this young guard that was now in front of Eddy, this security guard that was looking into the unfocused, unseeing eyes of Eddy, this guy had never seen a dead person before. Eddy's eyes looked without seeing his discoverer.

The security guard was not sure what to do. He took a few seconds to understand the gravity of the situation that was bearing down on his shoulders. He positioned Eddy gently, but had to insert some hesitant force to crumple him back into the seat, into the best form of a seating position that he could muster. He was surprised at how heavy he was as he wrestled him back onto the seat.

He then reached for his radio buckled on his black leather belt, getting ready to place that nervous call while his hand rested on Eddy's unmoving chest, making sure that he stayed in position. He felt small beads of sweat hit the top of his calves at the back of his knee behind his dark blue denim jeans. A cold shock that made him slash away with his radio-gripped claw at the folding creases as if it was a crawling insect that laid within. He welcomed any excuse, the briefest of pauses to allow himself an agonised moment of sanity to once again try to take in this uninvited situation.

'He…is dead!'

His lack of voice surprised him. No answer on the radio waves. He repeats, and once again. Even though he was shouting in his mind, the voice that reappeared was no less louder. His voice remained very hushed, very breathless, very weak.

'He'shhhh dead!' he exclaims in a squeak. Then, the initial thought through his saliva-laden mouth was clouded by uncertainty. The immediately following second thought was that he had not actually checked. 'I think. I think he is dead.'

For some unknown reason, this second thought freed his voice up to speak.

'What?' came the reply over the radio in a fuzzy clouded noise. Protocol had been disregarded and a silent question disoriented expression came over the radio. So silent, as if not English but spoken under water the sounds immersed. As the security guard turned up his radio and moved it to his ear, he began hearing one-worded questions such as 'How?', 'Who?' and 'Explain.'

He had instinctively let his hand leave Eddy's chest. He was not holding Eddy down, but mercifully gravity was. He was checking for a pulse. Finding himself clear the clouds around his feelings he was starting to speak normally, although with no less quavering fear betraying his emotional mental state. Yet, still trying to compose himself, he briefly put in as much detail as he processes.

He nervously explains that he has just found a dead body. Inside, he is freaking out, his voice, his quivering breathing exposes that he is not coping particularly well with this uncommon development. He thought for the shortest moment that he was gaining self-control, alas that strength was flowing out quicker than it entered him. If anything, he was on the edge of losing control.

His hands tremble uncontrollably as he tries in vain to find a pulse on the wrist of Eddy. He thought he may get a faint sign, this time. As he does so he listens for breath around his mouth. Trying to feel the slightest sign of life escaping Eddy's wrist, nose or mouth. Nothing. He was as sure as ever that he was in the company of a dead man. The accompanying radio had now changed voice with another person asking where he was exactly in a relaxed demeanour. Conducting also in adamant pleading tones for him to remain controlled, but most of all subtle so not to attract unwanted attention.

The young security guard was flicking his head like a meercat on sentry. For that last pleading request was a little late. He is wearing a bright beacon in a sea of drab, dull working suits, dresses and skirts that bring attention to him amongst the lacklustre fashion attire. He might as well be a lighthouse guiding people towards the destruction rather than away. People had noticed him, noticing the lack of movement in the stranger slouched over. A smell unrecognisable.

He also had a worried look in his white wide eyes, a startled pair of headlights in his expression with the collapsing shocked crumbling of his face as his mouth gawped out in the open for everyone to see that something was not quite right. His jerking head that looked around in every direction for some form of help, a colleague, even a reason. His body language was agitated, nervous with the accurate notion of not sure what he should be doing. He was not coping with this unaccustomed abnormality that his normal dull routine has thrown his way. He was trembling his hands as if he was cold. He was looking around for help as if someone with a cape could rescue him.

He has to keep hope alive and not surrender to the despair that engulfs him. The thing with grief is that it does not change you, it reveals who you are. For the security guard he was exposed as being a false self-assured person. He was trying to stand in optimism after hearing the pleading tones, but he was surrendering to his own sensations that were releasing in radiated mannerisms of awkwardness lit by the uncertainty of how someone should react in these situations.

Even within a stranger, death was wretched. He thought of his family in civil war-torn Africa, a large family that he left with his small family for a better life. Ironically away from death. But death was life. Goodbyes were never easy whether alive or dead. He mumbled a prayer to the stranger, to himself.

He had done his induction a few months prior. His first aid, rescue and emergency training was all up-to-date. If the regular ordinary prepared for but abnormal events had not sent an avalanche of kerb balls he thinks, he believes, that he would have had an inkling of a clue of what to do. But, this? This was not planned. This was not something he had thought of asking on one of the three full-day introduction courses. What else does he do? What should he do?

He looks up at the arched roof, the clock high in the eaves. Asking for a step for him to take his next step in the way of a flashing light of divine intuition. Nothing. Panic was starting to filter through to the outside of his body. He perspires intensely. A gleam that shines from his flawless skin. He sheds a single tear. Not for the loss that he did not know, but for the loss of losing control. As luck would have it this single tear is smothered by his rivers of beading sweat. His breathing was getting quicker, rampant. His fear was breeding him to lose his nerve. he was on the edge of panicking.

A tap on his shoulder startles him. A breath is drawn quickly as his shoulders tenses up. He turns. He launches a hug around the older security guard as the barrier of tears breaks through. This involuntary action was not only unprofessional but unintentionally idiotic. The single one or two that had noticed something did not stop their stride. They rubbernecked a glance as they slowed before moving on with their own life. However, this odd response. This sobbing drew people's attention. A small crowd had started to gather, all sensing that this was not a normal day unfolding. The older security guard quickly reassured the younger as he handed a balled-up roll of toilet paper for his sweat and tears. The older one maintained a calmness that he tried to spread over the small cluster of emerging Sydneysiders.

The younger had managed to maintain himself. Under the instruction of the older he swiftly returned with some cleaning signs to set up a perimeter. The two security guards could not understand this behaviour from strangers to balloon around them in a swell of increasing curiosity. What were they going to do? Watch, apparently. Or, something to tell someone later on in the coming afternoon, the evening over a roadie, or a staffie. Some people have no respect. Some brazenly, boldly show so disrespectfulness to actually take their mobiles out to snapchat, video or take a photograph of this tragic event. A fear of not remembering this awful turn of events on what would have been a rather normal, boring day.

The African expresses regret as he apologises in a stuttering nonsensical ramble as he hugs his caped crusader again. He urgently unlocks his arm from him to whisper in his ear that an ambulance is on its way. They try, in vain with the wave of discouraging futile hope to distract the gathering crown. However human nature can be studied, but not fully learnt and never understood. When one person stops to look, another will, followed by another. It is strange that as individual people that cry out for independence that they still do the same as people do around them.

As the older security guard attempts to keep people from coming too close, a recently read study came to his mind. He was a retired professor of human physiology so continued to read the journals that came through his email. A study was done with paid actors in different office blocks around the world. On different floors the study centred on a lift. The paid actors walked in, uncustomary to what people normally do in turning to look in the direction of the exiting door, they turned their backs to the door, sometimes even to the side wall in the centre of the lift.

With no understanding of why, the other people eventually followed this trend. When asked at the end of the lifts journey, they had no real explanation to why they had followed the bizarre trend. The conclusion was inconclusive is a response to human behaviour acting as others acted. He thought of that as this case raised similar attributes. Not everyone knew what they were observing. Yet people that walked by, stopped to join in, the crowd grew. They peered. Some stayed. Others took a shameless memento on their mobile to continue their own personal route.

The very small majority hastily moved on once seeing the morbid scene, afraid to associate a small portion of themselves as if a contagious disease would land transmitted in sharing the unblinking glaze of this slumped stranger, surrounded by the colourful unconfident vest-wearing security guards as a mental image that could not be shifted.

It was then that the older security guard noticed the pungent smell that was growing more revoltingly intense. He looked and spotted the floor. He jerked the jacket of the African to stop him from walking backwards into it. Eddy was in a pool of his own bodily functions. As his body stopped, he stopped. His body released the toxins within. His body had let go as his hand had of the pen, his heart had of life, his soul had of person. It was only then that the security guards in unison smelt the foul stench and recognised it as human waste. How did they not notice it before? The smell of brewing coffee from the close, but back facing shack was covering the odour with roasting coffee beans, as well as his clothes concealing the image. Nevertheless, it was penetrating. Yet, no-one noticed. It was pooling close. From the doors, the flashing red and blue lights rebounded, reflected off the walls.

The ambulance men showed up with no sirens. No rush. No bags. They knew why they were here and professionally did their own job, which they were no strangers to. The police arrived shortly after to disburse the crowd. The security guards were led away.

Eddy was born alone. He had died alone. He was taken away. He was lonesome and forlorn as if nothing. His body abandoned. He was in death as in life. Alone.

To Reawaken in Labrys

While strangers were coming to terms with Eddy's passing, his shade of dead was learning newfound knowledge of his reasons for being in that authoritarian world. Not so much the meaning of life, but the meaning of living.

Despite the fact that many characters have played many parts in Eddy's life, I introduce them all, one by one. I am careful to use the names that he would have undoubtedly heard before. Hence aiming to make it simpler for him to accept this weird and wonderful developing truth.

Although not all characters remain here, some have places that they must be. I thusly inform them with a visual representation of whom they are. I have enlightened Eddy of the will to know what there purpose was, for which is the way we identify them, I also give the names that they, back on the mortal coil would have nicknamed them, if indeed they were not completely forgotten.

I personally enjoy this personal touch, when nothing will remain personal for Eddy ever again. It is in this moment that he will not need personal touch as he knows it. He will need personal growth, personal sensations to feel the education of knowledge. The primitive being that he was, has, straggled through his old life with is to be transcended onto a larger, broaden scape of boundless ability to enhance a magnificent aptitude of intellectual capacity. It would be exciting for me to see this expansion where improvement is an expanse that holds no bounds. It should be exciting for him.

With each name, it is like I am a host of an old game show as I introduce them all to come running down through a clap, cheer and cries of enthusiasm down to the floor. Of course in this universe, they gracefully glide down to be hovering infront of Eddy. Then in forming a curved triangle-ring around him and myself. They then explain in precise meticulous detail their purpose in life, but specifically within Eddy's life.

Of course, Erotes started. As in the end this small circle of outsiders above him that are acquaint one by one will be forever in his own, most inner circle. As strangers no more but as a supporting network of non-physical spiritual comrades. The first act of many more acts to follow. Eddy seems to relax with each explanation. Eddy feels at ease in this newfound situation. Eddy is accepting this newfound reality. The past life, was a simple unassuming stepping stone to this own personal utopia. With his suffering drawn to a close, he was being enlightened in nibbana.

A tall, lean spirit floats down off a frighteningly statuesque man. Elegantly descending in a simmering veil as the deep burgundy red cloak waves behind him like a trailing flag. His thick dense ginger beard makes him look like the image of a Norse warrior, just like a Viking. Contrarywise this athletic facial appearance is placed on a body of a white African marathon runner. Skinny, gangly awkward arms hang leanly correspondingly muscularly by his side. He nods as he hits the same level as Eddy. A simple gesture of friendship. Eddy responds with nothing.

I go to introduce him, as I have before, but the strong mouth opens with the ginger bristles just showing the pearly whites beyond.

'I am Hedylogos,' He booms.

Four people stand around Eddy. They are all the same height. For some reason, height is seemingly not an issue. Everyone is of the same height. Treated on the same level. No-one is taller, with the exception of Zeus. No-one appears stronger or measured by physical appearance. The heads are designed differently as they are hand moulded by the banes of Mother Earth, Gaia, so negligently unpretentiously developing to allow similar blights to which the mortals possess. But the bodies are different. But not measured. Never determined by appearance.

No-one cares. No-one needs to care. They may look different by face value, but they are beyond doubt truthfully the same worth. The only difference, is the gift they be laid unequivocally with. With this gift is no jealousy. They are simply appreciated for it. They are honoured. They are encouraged as a team, embodied to inspire. They are emboldened as they do not share the same gifts. They are unique in this, and only this way. A weakness by some is a strength by others. All as one they own a bonding of strength. It is together they are brilliantly strong. All the same, yet, on their own they are weak, they are useless.

Imagine going for a walk without shoes. Not on a smooth surface but on glass. The need, well it is nothing more than the ability to walk to a destination. The strong certainty that pain will be felt. This will come along instantly without prior knowledge. So, something else is needed, protection. Therefore a form of some shielding feet coverings is absolutely considered necessary, whether in the fashion of thongs, sandels, shoes, runners.

Then, fuel is needed in food and drink. This will keep on going in the fundamental necessarily compelling need. Together they are as strong as the one before. As each, as a singularity, they are weaker. After protection, food, water, will come an abundant requirement of other things such as shelter, clothes, warmth. Together they are unified, formidable. One without the other will plainly be the weakened demise.

Here, Hedylogos has stopped moving down from his elevated ledge. He is hovering ahead of Eddy. Moving closer to his image, edging face to face. Way too close for Eddy but he cannot move away. He can see the hairs in his nostrils. Feel the breath of his talk on his skin. The smell of nothing but an aura of straightforward honestly.

'I…' His voice is powerful, commanding but with a musical deep melody that makes the former not as intimidating. 'I behold the gift of giving you sweet talk. To be able to get a conversation with a potential mate. I find the words for you to aid in the term that you purely call flattery.'

Eddy is extremely baffled as to why that is a gift. Equally questioning his condescending obtained voice as not being sweet, more laced in terror. Eddy understands the need, but could it really be considered a gift. Although, as quick as the words leave him, another floats down as Hedylogos glides backwards to assumes his position to the left of Erotes.

'Behold, Menoetius,' I announce with a wave of my right hand and arm.

As he comes closer, Eddy sees a scar running down his right cheek as raw as if it was done a few hours ago. He ponders what, how he had gotten this weeping scar. By the stroke of a knife in battle or by shaving with garden shears? Freckles act as a mask under his eyes and over the bridge of his impishly perk white nose. Bright red flowing ginger hair shines on top of his head like a ramshackle messy cut of turmeric fairy floss in a distressed just woken-up look.

'HE…HE…HE…' Memoetius speaks in a stuttering shrill voice. That timbre holds a high-pitched tone that is boyish which aptly suits his youthful face. His voice penetrates to vibrate inside Eddy with each syllable. With dynamism, Memoetius raises his right limb up with the whispering, wave of unearthly clothes-like rags loosly falling down his arm. He continues to raise his arm to rigidly firmly point skyward, up to the face that watches down through the crystal glass. He obviously has a keen way of adding theatrical poise to his performance. For added emphasis, he repeats the first word again, this time with more prominence.

'HE…HE….HE kill-ed ME…ME…ME.' The anger was passionate. In the shrill staccato sentence the voice came from a deep chasm of bitterness. 'I am back, as I…I…I do serve a pur…pur…purpose here. Everywhere. I served one th…th…then. And, now. Despite my librarian bu…but…but…butter-would-not-melt-in-my-mouth look I…I…I am the one that strikes violent an…anger. I…I…I… invoke rash actions in… you. I am your sim…sim…sim…your simmering pot of rage that is always inside you, be…be…because of me—'

'As you see, you can see…' I interrupt the proceedings of Memoetius. He is fierce but his voice is annoying. He does, for the most part all of his undertakings, fortuitously, by act rather than voice. Memoetius knows his time is over as he sulks back to the arc that is forming the start of a ring next to Hedylogos.

'It is a lot to absorb.' I return to look directly at Eddy. 'These Gods that talk are in no particular order. They are the ones that are here. As well as additional Gods that are excepted as on another mission at this particular time. Eventually you will get to meet the majority. You are here for the next two entirety immortal loops. This is not the time to explain about our time measures. This is not a time to explain the whole repercussions of your mortal life.'

I take a moment to assess if the information is too much. I can say more than Eddy knows. He cannot say more that he knows. He will soon change his name. I will give him the option to see his passing back as a glimpse on his previous life. I would recommend he does not as that can cause more pain than a knife can ever inflict. I will let him know that he will still be thought off. It is the same that a person does continue to live on in memories. People will still learn from that person that has left even in death what they had said, done or been. They will continue to affect someone along the shape of the path for which he existed and influenced. His own tapestry will continue to grow, albeit slow but sure, as whom he touched will keep him alive.

'Unfortunatly, the large portion of time in which we have been generous in giving to you will still not be enough to meet everyone,' I say the latter proclamation as a disclaimer. Because in the function I am required to fulfil, I endeavour to make sure he meets everyone so I can continue my lesson. 'Considering that I mentioned on the way here that we have always been here. Surely, if nothing else, you can see that now. The Greeks named us. The Romans confused us. And then, your time misperceived to take no heed to us. By your failings to differentiate each one of us, you merged us, you disorganised us. Each one of us is different, diverse with a different committed allegiance. A duty of our own. Sometimes subtle.

'In this time, these two entirety loops, you will learn our names by purpose, not by the names you think you know. More have come along. You,will be one. Each one of your measures of time gives a new God, or Goddess. We evolve with your capability in grasping what can be done. We are not just keeping to our traditional ways. But, evolving to your modern world. To adapt, to use your electronics, your technology in a way that aids you and is a strong advantage to us. We have always had Hermes for silent communication from a far. He is athletic, strong and forever youthful. The son of Zeus and Maia, Hermes is the messenger for us. He gave birth to Ilektronikus through the river of the underworld, recognised as Phlegethon, the river of fire.

'Forged by none other than Hephaestus, a crippled bearded man with hammer, tongs and anvil. Despite his grotesque hands he created a devastatingly nimble elegant lady. She is a great addition to your world that is still evolving. She is for your ability to not speak to each other as often as possible. As often as you can. Technology for you has advanced quicker than your connections. This is sad. It makes me sad. As it is nessesary for you to need sleep, but it seems that you misuse this to talk through electronic devises. These are some of your acts.'

On cue, I prompt Ilektronikus to approach from above. She is clear, bright and translucent like a valiant lightning bolt. She is slim, extraordinarily beautiful with a cold-glaze of mistrust, unconvinced mystery and a coldness for which no one can ever get close to. Yet her eyes are immaculate pure clear river green-blue that could sail you away to pleasures of pain. A stimulating appearance combined with an unreceptive attraction. After the slightest glimmer she flickers whilst lingering infront of Eddy. Steel-eyed piercing fixed focus as if measuring her quarry she looks him up and down, then penetrates him with her blue haunting eyes for a second that seemed more like a day. She says nothing. She positions to the left of the developing ring.

'Ahhhhh…'

For the first time, I recognise a question from Eddy. He has asked many for which I have ignored to let him know I am giving him the answers in the order I see fit, also I am in control. No words were said, none were needed. Telepathically he spoke to me, as he had done unaware that I was reading every thought that he thought. Communicating with his fearful steel-eyed stare, I see a question. A question in dire need of a response.

'That is worthy of an answer,' I acknowledge. 'You ask where have we come from. I assume you're talking about the human beings?'

Eddy nods his head as a single leaf shakes off the branches of a wind-moving tree from outside the crystal cupola. The first time he has seen vegetation, it flutters to a rest before Eddy. This tree is him, a sign of his becoming. This lime green leaf will form a laurel of peace, a symbol to represent his powers to be.

He wants the answer. At the same time, his nervous quiver fears the answer. He has a sense of insatiable thirst for knowledge.

'You have Deucalion to thank for your exsistence, your creation,' I inform Eddy. 'He is not here, but his wife is. Pyrrha.'

Pyrrha comes from behind Eddy in a twirling spiral infront of him with the grace of a ballerina. A golden mane of silk wavy hair trails down her face like a parted golden-haired waterfall. Fringing a face that shows the murmured undercurrents of time for which she is proud off. Her voice is hauntingly enticing with a musky husky sweet maternal melody of protection.

'I am Pyrrha.' Her tongue seems to roll arout the rr's as if purring her own name. 'I was the first born of a mortal mother. I am fire. My husband, Deucalion is the son of Prometheus. Your kind insulted his memory by changing his name and true purpose. You called him Noah. NOAH! Our God Zeus was far from being happy with this…betrayal is what he felt, we felt. He was disgusted by the behaviour of King Lynceus of Arcadia. The reason is something we do not discuss. At this time at least.

'The King offered humans as sacrifices. The furious Zeus turned him along with his family into wolves as he returned to Olympus to plan the rebuilding of the human race. Prometheus heard on the wind and warned his son, my husband. At this time, we ruled the Kingdom of Phthia. He built an ark. Instead of animals, he stocked it with food. When stocked, The Deluge started. Rain began falling, hard, fast, relentless. Stopping only nine days later. Only when we could see the very tops of the highest mountains. We were the only survivors of the Great Deluge. We offered sacrifices to Zeus on top of our resting place on Parnassus. With no answer emerging.

'We sought Themis, the Goddess of Order. One of the, if not the original Gods. She, the daughter of Gaia. We waited, prayed at the shrine of Themis. Finally we were answered by her appearance in person. She instructed us to re-people the Earth. We had to use the bones of their mother, her mother, which we would sow by casting over our shoulders.'

Pyrrha laughs as if a rainbow has obtained a voice. A sniggering diminuendo with tightly pursed lips. 'We were confused. Then, after pondering this strange cryptic information, we understood. The stones of our Mother were the bones. The soil stones were the bones of Mother Earth, Gaia. We did as instructed. For Deucalion cast the new race of men. I cast the new race of women. I, am, daughter of Epimetheus and Pandora.'

'Gaia,' I intervene once again, 'was born of Chaos. Gaia is both Mother and Mate of the sky, Uranus, and the Mother of the Seas. She is Mother of the Titans, the Cyclops and the Hecatoncheries. The Hecatoncheries are remarkable thundred-handed working giants that are called Cottus the Furious, Briareus the Vigorous and Gyes the Big Limbed. She is always aware of what happens on her. For what you call Earth. What you called Earth. Your former home. She is a being.'

'May I…' the bold, ancient voice came from the right of Eddy. His eye flicked in the direction of the voice. His face turned. I beckoned him forward.

An elderly, white-haired man with pale wrinkled skin with each crease telling a courageous strong chronicle as dramatic as any masterpiece of art. His arms waved as he spoke. He told his story with a fresh glitter in his eyes.

'Hesiod, a mortal like you, called me Theogony. The name stuck.' An animated voice that did not suit his appearance. Spreading across his face was a perfect grin of white teeth that brought a kindness to his aura. In turn making a scared-stiff Eddy relax in his calming contagious atmosphere. He had now positioned himself ahead of Eddy.

'Whowl,' Theogony smirked, 'you have many questions. Relax. These can wait. Relax. I believe no-one has welcomed you to Labrys, House of the Double Axe. This was built by Daedalus for King Minos. Be aware when you wander the corridors. These are filled with pleasure, filled with pain, with torture. Originally built to conceal the Minotaur. But, to give him freedom, but no escape. That is the floor below us. On the other hand, as indeed mentioned, we have grown. We are a world of our own. We are many worlds above your Earth. For you will see.'

He spoke in pictures full of colour and animation. 'When Asterion, the King of Crete and Europa died he was the disputed successor. He built an altar to Poseidon on the sea shore. There he prayed for a bull to sacrifice to prove he was a worthy ruler. Poseidon sent a glorious white bull. However Minos could not bear to sacrifice such a magnificent creature. He turned it loose amongst the Royal herds. This made Poseidon very, very angry. He took cruel revenge by having Mino's wife, Queen Pasiphae to acquire an overpowering lust for the bull.

'After fleeing from Athenes the great craftman and artificer, Daedalus arrived to Crete. He reached Crete in fear of retribution in Athenes after murdering his apprentice. Which also was his nephew Talos. It was becoming commonly known that Talos was improving better, becoming increasingly greater than Daedalus. Although Daedalus had nothing to worry about. Yet, he feared these developments, these rumours, these allegations. Daedalus was the inventer of the plumb-line, the axe and the saw. When he discovered glue he became the first man to understand the value of salis. The value of masts. His statues were so skilfully fashioned that they moved like the living creatures he created. Again…enough of your questions. Hush. I am getting there. I will tell you why he is relevant to this story. Wait. Hold your questions.'

Theogony brushes the soft whiskers of his beard as he waits for silence. Like a conductor before he starts a symphony, he patiently delays his speech. He hears quietness. He slowly raises his gaze to that of Eddy's. Pauses to have not only an effect but the reassurance that he will remain quiet before restarting,

'Daedalus worked at the Palace. Queen Pasiphae hired him. Then asked him a favour. She asked for a false cow in which she could conceal herself inside. To go unnoticed. He was the only one that could have made such a entity successful. To be unconceivable to notice the difference between a born, and a made. The overpowering lust. The fortunate love made her plan work. She was with the bull. However, taken unawares she was mounted by the bull. She gave birth to a half-man, half-bull. Born was the Minotaur.

'King Minos ordered Daedalus to build the place below. The place for the Minotaur to be unseen, but too live happily. Like the River Maeander, this edifice with numerous passageways, turnings and openings with closings and twistings would eventually come back on itself. His work went with punishment. He and his son, Icarus, were imprisoned in his made labyrinth.

'In confinement, he constructed two pairs of wings to escape. He wanted to return to Crete. He needed the wings as King Minos controlled the seas. Once created they set off with their wings. Through a facet of tears, Daedalus pleaded for his son, Icarus not to get too close to Helios, the Sun God. But, Icarus did not listen. He flew too close. The heat melted the wax which held the feathers in place. He plummeted to the sea. King Minos took him. Drowned him. Daedalus tried to save him. He changed route. He flew to safely on land in Sicily.

'Minos was not only delighted with capturing Icarus, he wanted him as well. He went after him. King Minos wanted to capture him quickly so set out in immediate pursuit. On his journey he brought a triton shell. King Minos was cunning, he was wise. He was smart and very resourceful. He offered a rich reward for anyone who could pass a linen thread through the whole shell. He went to see King Cocalus. He knew that the King of Sicily knew the man. King Minos knew that the only person who had the gift to be able to do such a task, an impossible task was one man, Daedalus.

'Daedalus did not see the trick. He wanted to show King Cocalus that he was the gifted man to be hired by the island. Hence saved. Daedalus bore a tiny hole in the shell. He then proceeded to attach the linen thread to an ant. Smeared the entrance with honey. From the otherside he let the ant free. The busy ant ran through the spirals to the sweetness. As a result, after a short while, the ant came out the otherside with the delicate linen. He took this back to King Cocalus.

'He was so excited and so willing to show off what his Kingdom could become with his help. King Minos saw the answer he craved. He demanded the surrender of the craftman. This upset his host. King Cocalus reminded King Minos for where he stood. That he unwillingly exploited him to plot the murder of one of his guests, his new member of staff. Also, that, he not only unwillingly exploited him to plot the murder of his guest, but on his soil, within his own palace, his home.

'The insulted King Cocalus protected Daedalus who asked him to murder King Minos in retaliation. This was granted. Therefore Daedalus installed a duct in the ceiling of the palace bath. King Cocalus offered King Minos a bath before he voyaged back to Crete. While King Minos was using the luxuriating steamy warmth of the palace bath the duct opened up unexpectedly. Boiling water gushed out, down, over King Minos. He was suffocated. Killed. His body was solemnly conveyed back to Crete as a result of a tragic accident. Daedalus returned as well, back to Crete. He built more of this palace. This house, our homes, your new home.'

'Now listen, and listen good,' I direct Eddy with the startling understanding that he needs right now. Theogony leaves his side to merge into the background. Eddy's mind has been constantly throwing up many questions. The same two being particularly persistent. Sounding like a gas-boiled kettle that is whistling to broadcast a pure racket it needs to be taken off. This grating shrill is to me now becoming increasingly irritating for me to listen to any further. In need of an answer, I give it to him.

'I hear you constantly ask the same question.' I say without hiding my irritation in him not listening fully as he is focused on this mortal question. 'Is this heaven or hell? The truth of the matter is that no hell exsists. That was something that the mortals made up. You have your good book, The Bible. Where is the bad book? None. So why? It baffles me. Why do you insist on the hell? On there being a hell? It…baffles me.' My frustration was boiling over so I needed to pause. I needed to collect myself and explain rationally.

'This is not hell, as you call it. This is not heaven. We do not believe in hell, or an evil the same way as you do. We all believe that man commit evil, just as they do good. This is down to himself. The mortals do not need a prompting from a good or evil force, they do it on their own free will. We have given you all free will. That is not to say that we do not punish the bad deeds. Anyone that is foolish enough to offend us were punnished, still are, by the Gods. The King, the Lord of the other Worlds having nothing to do with your good and bad reactions but we do give you actions, more or less.

'Let me explain. There are five Rivers of Hades. I collected you from the River of Hatred, the Styx. Nearby is the River of Unmindfulness, Lethe. The Lethe flows around the poppy covered entrance of the Cave of Hypnos, God of Sleep, where no light or sound are to ever enter. Following the river would have taken you through to the Underworld. If I let you go through your cause, this is the place where you would have had a choice here. If you chose to drink from the river, you would have forgotten everything from your past.

'Souls that longed to be returned would drink from here, to be reincarnated. The other choice, for which is normally chosen, is to remember everything. All the knowledge, all the experiences ferried over to live a life of happeness. You would pass the fields of glittering armour through a murky mist. This is Elysium, the paradise for the heroes that would live in their immortal life of happiness. Trojan warriors mix with Kosovo fighters. Grecian warriors mix with Afghanistan soldiers. No-one is less of a hero. They fought for what they believed.

'Here, they live together in peaceful friendship. The Germans and Allies laugh on that Christmas Day when they played football together only to go back shooting one another hours later.

'Another segment of the story of us, coincidentally you. I showed you a glimpsed of this on the way. In spite of this I get the impression that I need to colour in the drawings for you to understand fully. At the beginning, I told you Uranus is a form of Heaven for us if you like. Gaia, who we established is Earth. Together, they gave birth to Cronus. Cronus and his brothers and sisters were collectively called the Titans. You never worshipped them, but you call sporting teams after them. Again…this baffles me! Nevertheless, they are the birth of us, the birth of us all.

'Uranus, well, he was jealous of them. He confined the Titans in the body of Gaia. Gaia struggled with the burden. Intimidated and unsettled she sought help from her bravest son, Cronus to put an end to her suffering. She gave Cronus, a harvester, a new sickle. When it came to it only Cronus was willing to do the dirty deed. The next time Uranus approached Cronus he was ready. Gaia had laid a trap, Cronus was a part of the bait. Cronus castrated Uranus. From the blood that fell on Gaia came the Furies, The Kindly Ones and the Hecatoncheires, the Giant Gods of coilent storms and hurricanes.

'From the genitals, for which Cronus threw into the sea, was born Aphrodites. Uranus was defeated. He left Gaia to the Titans. Cronus, with his sister Rhea, an unwilling consort became rulers. On leaving, Uranus warned his victorious son that, just like him, he would be overthrown by one of his own sons. One day.

'Cronus feared this. To protect himself, he swallowed his children as soon as Rhea gave birth to them. One by one, they were swallowed. At first Hestia, Demeter, Hera, Hades and Poseidon. Rhea wanted to bring a person into the world and see them grow, she sorted Gaia for advise. Gaia told Rhea to give a stone to Cronus the next time a child was born to deceive him. This was done. The son was hid away in a cave on Mount Ida in Crete. He was raised by a goat named Amalthea.

'A company of Kouretes, armoured male dancers were instructed to sing, dance and clap to make as much noise as possible to mute the infants cries. They danced, shouted, sung, clapped their hands and stomped their feet to successfully mask the noise of Cronus's youngest son. That son was Zeus. I am repeating myself to add colour to the drawings. When Zeus was mature, Rhea persuaded Cronus to forget his fears and bring up the children. He did, beginning with the stone, swallowed, in the place of Zeus. His brothers and sisters followed.

'Zeus and his siblings fought Cronus for ten years for what he did to them. Cronus had the Titans. However, Zeus and his brothers had the Cyclops and the Hecatoncheires. After ten years they were victorious. With the victor, Uranus's prophecy was also proved correct.

'Zeus remains our undisputed ruler. He imprisoned his defeated kinsmen in Tartarus, in the underworld. He entered the Kingdom ruling from Mt Olympus. His brother ruled with him, together. Hades, for which you met along the River of Woeful pain, Archeron, took you to the Judges of the Dead.

'Three former mortal men of former time make up the Judges of the Dead. The aforementioned King Minos, the former King of Crete who is the Judge of the Final Vote. Rhadamanthys, the former lawmaker is the Judge of the Men of Asia. Lastly, Aiakos, the former King of Aegina is the guardian of the Keys of Hades and the Judge of the Men of Europe. They judge you and make the decision of where you belong.

'The Judges judged. A very few were sent to the Islands of the Blest. Surrounded by Elysium, where in the two places they would be in a blessfully happy life, not oblivion. Cronus is the King of the Island of Blest. He is held on a very tight leash by Zeus. Thus, let us not forget that afteral he is his father. He wanted him to serve a purpose, hence this appointment. This is where you stand within. Within that area, but in this palace. Your life will continue. Your body will not, has not. The other is the place for which if you have offended us you go with the punishment already decreed, Tartarus.

'Don't. DO NOT CONFUSE TARTARUS WITH HELL! Hades was the place for the dead where as Tartarus was a prison. Once the shade of dead got off Charon's ferry and stepped onto Hades they were given a reminiscent association of themselves. They were recognisable, with personalities and memories, but no more substance than a reflection on the water or the feel of smoke. They enjoyed no pleasures of senses. No hunger, thirst, conversation or reflection of anger.

'They lived in the inactive realm of darkness. There is not a hell. That is the human word I will not use to describe it. Tartarus is where the rivals of the Gods went after war. Where the criminals ended up. Where the ferocious monsters stayed. Where the punishments happened.

'To be condemned, you would be tossed in great winds for a full year, then would have to fall for ten days from the bronze doors to reach the stony pit from Hades to Tartarus. Here, you would see Sisypjus who tried to cheat death. He forever pushes a boulder of salvation up a hill for it to get close and roll back down for him to do it again, again and again but never getting the boulder to the top. Tantalus, who tried to steal the Gods' food, Ambrosia, to give to the mortals. Then he tried to feed his own son, Pelops, in a stew to the Gods. He succumbed to eternal thirst and hunger. He is in a pool of water to his chin, but when he bows his head to drink, the water recedes. Over his head are the trees of fruit-laden branches; when he tries to grasp at them, the wind blows them out of reach.

'So, in conclusion. Each shade of dead is judged its own fate. The dead were punished or rewarded for their behaviour while alive. As a soul, you are given the choice to remember or to forget. With that, you will remain here, or be reincarnated.'

Eddy was still mystified. He understood it clearer, well, thought he understood it better at least. But the principles, that was were he was having trouble coming to terms with and accepting. Not understanding the reason for not having a hell, but a heaven that was seemingly everywhere. He liked the idea. If the truth was to be told he liked the philosophy. Yet he could not fully grasp it. It was like when he was back in school and explained long division. He could understand it, but when an exam came up he could not put it into the working-out column. Even though he could get the answer, that was always correct. He could not explain how he knew.

He was also still wrestling with the notion that he is no longer going to be able to walk, run. The notion that he will not be able to see Jay, his mates, continue his life. Live his life. That was a shattering realisation. He was young. He questioned the love he lost. Even with the clarification of his new home. He still wrestled in the struggling grips that were not being prised open to reveal the true conception of the reality he was in. Other figures came down to introduce themselves. To then make the circle around them bigger.

Hypnos, the God of Sleep, aided me in Eddy's design when it was the time to bring him here. His twin brother, Thanatos, the spirit of death with his iron heart along with a spirit that is just as cold, tried in vain for me to use him as well. They both have a gentle touch. Still Hypnos would be a non-violent death, whereas Thanatos…

If I used Thanatos, it would mean the chance that Eddy being in a single piece and here would be extremely slim. If I unleashed him, he would make it that Eddy would never wake up again into this part of his life. Moreover, Eddy may have to go down the dying route of exceptional pain. Lurking in the shadows with him came the Keres. I had to fend off the Keres, the blood-craving sisters, on numerous occasions. They had, always had, a violent death in store for everyone, markedly Eddy. They loved to be part of slaughter and disease. They craved it like an obsessive addiction.

'You have your religions.' I sense and hear his inner torment. I try to offer a pool of clarity for his thoughts. I give it one more attempt for him to understand. To toss the mortal learnings aside and embrace this genuine truthful reality. For this reason, I call him by his birth name. 'Eddy. Although you do not believe in us anymore. We are a meagre footnote of study for those that want to know. Many people ignore us as a…fairytale. Our Gods, Goddesses, Spirits, Daemons. These beings that are beings, that the Romans, the Greeks so heavily believe in, are in the smallest section in Greek mythology in the bookstore under the fantasy section.

'Ironically, we are the ones that truly define who you are. Poignantly, we are what you are. What you do. For, why you do things. Since, or for the reason that we are not in the forefront of your mind does not mean we are not the cogs, the wheels, the chains in your life. It does not mean that we are fact, not your fiction. We are here. Everywhere. We…are…just…not…there. There in your life to be seen all of the time.

'Life is a mortal coil of emotions Eddy. Spirits are with you. Aiding you. We are the actions to reactions that can change an action. A word syllabled into accents can change the outcome. We are around. We are still very much around. While as other religions compete against, and with each other, we are around and through them. It is us, not in them, that we were born from.

'We all are the wirings within your personality. The lines in your play. The doings that proceed your life. Ultimately, at the end of your mortal journey, we are here. You see what you are. We explain the meaning of your unique lives. We are here for you. So you have the tools to start anew.'

This seems to have rung true. I can see the acceptance brewing. I need to hammer in the point now. I point to a handsome, chiselled strong body with a patch of dark curly hair on his chest, a short-trimmed stubble of a casting shadow of a dark beard on the moulded masculine strong jawline. With a smile, his high cheekbones bounce as Pothos is satisfied in the gratefulness that it is finally his turn to address the beginner. Comically small light grey wings that flash as if made of a substance as weak as water bring him stylishly down.

'I am one of the love Gods known as the Erotes, but I am Pothos.' His quivering tones were beautifully awe-inspiring. In merely a few words he had developed a sexual yearning for everyone around him. As if his voice vibrates from an elaborate soundbox envisaged by a bravura hallowed mind of an architect that triumphed in creating this unimpeachable sound. 'I came down at the start but as I was such a presence in your life I returned to my other form. It was a pleasure to share love with, through you. From the establishment of you, throughout your mortal life and subsequently to the end. I gave you the meaning of life. The meaning of your life is—'

'ENOUGH!' I bellow while casting a muting spell on Pothos. Just before he reveals that earth-shattering revelation that no-one needs to know…yet. Of course, Eddy will learn it, but this is not the place. Certainly not the time. Not when so much has been explained to him. He needs to understand that, before the multifarious complex idea of the simple answer that everyone craves on Earth. Eddy will learn it.

'But—' Pothos tries to speak, or defend. I am not sure, but I also am not risking him dropping the meteoric destructive boulder of knowledge. Releasing that now would be a spectacular tremendous derailment on Eddy's future path.

'E…NOUGH,' my word reverberates around the chamber, crashing from one pillar to the other.

'But…' Pothos pleads, 'but, but. What is the point, as it will not harm him now?'

I do not answer. Pothos had a point, a strong point. However, he must digest that he is dead, that he is a shade of dead. That the information he has learnt for the past several years has been a lie.

I motion Pothos to join the curved bordering wall as I introduce the remaining few left. Each descend down creating a finished bordering wall. In front of the centring well of Eddy is a rippling well of bodies to the real faces.

Pothos, the God of Passionate Longing, is sombre. He is sulking with his head bowed as his big introduction is cut short. Epione, the Goddess of the soothing of pain, patronises

Pothos as he comes down to nestle next to him. I take up a position hovering beside Eddy. I turn with Eddy at the well of faces before I face him once more.

'Alas, I hail you your new name. Eddy, you will be taught how to accept turmoil. You will become the God of Understanding Mayhem. From now on, you are Maelstromialis. Greetings.' A brief cheer floods the house. 'That only really leaves me.'

A theatrical pause silences the room. For I have never given my name this soon in a prologue.

'I am Cupid's opposite, an accomplice of death. The last beat of your broken heart.' Another pause. The sword of Themis to cut fact from fiction would be useful to cut the tension in the air that had risen, surrounding them.

Maelstromialis, formally Eddy, and I are in the increasingly shrinking well of figures as we face each other in the centre.

'Deimos, please lift your spirit of fear, dread and terror off Maelstromialis.' This was done instantly with Maelstromialis feeling tranquil completely, for the first time since that long forgotten time on the bench at Central Station. He could not taste or smell, as these had to be relearned, but he could feel without touching, speak without a voice and hear with detecting.

'No one told you that grief would feel like fear. I say an unhappy man wants distractions. A means for him to be taken out of himself, his own feelings. You have never sort that. Honourable. You only wanted to give love, not essentially obligatory that you want. That you want to receive love in return. A noble act that brings you here. Self-sacrificing.

I am here not to give you suffering
I am here so you can understand
I am here to show you life's brilliance from all eyes

You are here to seek pleasure
You are here to seek what you desire through fear
You are here to seek enlightenment

We are here to care for you
We are here as mirrors for you to see yourself
We are here to see ourselves in you

Together we will learn why you suffered
Together we will hold others to support them, to let them grow
Together we will envelope in the basking education of light

Here we are not judged
Here we never wonder the meanings of specific words or actions
Here we will teach, be taught, learn

I am Death, but not as you know it.'

His fear ebbs and flows to a termination. More figures flow into the chamber as if greeting a friend rather than a stranger. They talk in hushed tones. Maelstromialis feels nothing. He knows this is it. At the end of his mortal tale is the start of his new. He is in a rightful kingdom. His home. This end of the tail is not the end of his life. The start of a new awaits him.

For this is the meaning of life. To live. To love. To die.

'Is this it?' is what Eddy's old self really asks, rather than: 'This is it?'

Maelstromialis speaks out loud for the first time.

'This is it!'

His voice appears to sound the same. He was expecting it to be different, it does have a slight chamber acoustic melody in the tone. He talks with unmoving lips. His mouth does not move, his voice reverberates as if answering itself. On the return, he does not recognise his voice. It has changed to be less body and more spirit.

'This is it!' he repeats as if to confirm his own voice. 'So, this is not it, but more accurately, this is the start, the beginning over again, distinctively, that was not it.'

Eddy has gone. His body has gone. He remains.

He is now onto the meaning of spirit.